Bestsellers in Nineteenth-Century America

Bestsellers in Nineteenth-Century America
An Anthology

Edited by
Paul C. Gutjahr

ANTHEM PRESS

Anthem Press
An imprint of Wimbledon Publishing Company
www.anthempress.com

This edition first published in UK and USA 2019
by ANTHEM PRESS
75–76 Blackfriars Road, London SE1 8HA, UK
or PO Box 9779, London SW19 7ZG, UK
and
244 Madison Ave #116, New York, NY 10016, USA

First published in the UK and USA by Anthem Press 2016

British Library Cataloguing-in-Publication Data
A catalogue record for this book is available from the British Library.

ISBN-13: 978-1-78527-191-5 (Pbk)
ISBN-10: 1-78527-191-1 (Pbk)

This title is also available as an e-book.

For Bob, Jim and David
and
Norman and Aletta (*in memoriam*)
extended, and treasured, family.

No act of kindness, no matter how small, is ever wasted.
Aesop

CONTENTS

CONTENTS   ix

LIST OF FIGURES

PREFACE

One of the wonders of printed material is its persuasive power. It can threaten, promise, cajole, and insinuate ideas of lasting influence. Such influence manifests itself in a number of ways, but perhaps one of the most obvious is found in the development of national mythologies. For example, consider the story of George Washington cutting down a cherry tree, a deed he then nobly confesses with the now-immortal words, "I can't tell a lie." It is a story that has become synonymous with George Washington, yet it was a fable created by Parson Weems in his tremendously popular biography of the first president.

True or not, such stories reveal a great deal about a culture's thought and life. This volume gathers popular stories that tap into a wide range of nineteenth-century American self-perceptions, fears, dreams and longings. The nineteenth century is particularly important for such stories because it was a period when these tales increasingly reached their audience in printed forms, as the highly oral culture of the eighteenth century was giving way to a more print-bound culture. This change meant that ever-wider audiences could gain access to, and be influenced by, the same information. In the nineteenth century, the world of American citizens was increasingly formed, framed and fractured by the power of print.

Behind the growing print culture found in the nineteenth-century United States stood the fact that American publishing came of age in this century. Whereas printed material had been relatively scarce at the close of the eighteenth century, with most families owning perhaps a Bible and an almanac, by the time of the Civil War thousands of tracts, novels, self-help books, tour guides, magazines and newspapers were littering American parlors. Publishers at the turn of the nineteenth century rarely produced print runs over two thousand copies. By mid-century, American publishing had so radically changed that editions of 30,000, 75,000 or even 100,000 copies were common. The forty newspapers published during the American Revolution gave way by the 1860s to more than two thousand daily and weekly papers. By the end of the century, books and other forms of published material were reaching the remotest parts of the country as an evermore advanced transportation network, an increasingly efficient mail system and an army of some fifty thousand door-to-door book salesmen offered an unprecedented range of printed literature to American readers.

The amazing growth of America's publishing enterprises did not happen in a vacuum. These enterprises grew proportionately with rising American literacy rates and multiplying motivations for the consumption of printed matter. As the century wore on, a number of factors propelled American reading habits, including the desire for economic gain, social distinction, political involvement and entertainment.

Reading offered people an opportunity for greater social mobility. Those who could read were better able to adapt to the changing employment market of the nineteenth century, in which literacy skills were increasingly prized for the better-paying, more-prestigious jobs. The massive numbers of self-help books and reform literature that circulated among Americans in the nineteenth century also helped people know how to think and act in ways that distinguished them as socially refined. Such social distinction could also be attained by studying the Greek and Roman classics, an oft-used marker of gentility and good social breeding.

Americans also read so that they might gain the information they needed to participate in their local and national governments. From an early age, Americans were taught that democracy demanded participation, and meaningful participation demanded accurate information. Thus the political interests of nineteenth-century readers helped fuel a tremendous rise in newspaper circulation and the appearance of a host of printed matter such as political biographies and verbatim reproductions of countless legislative speeches and debates.

And Americans read because it was fun. There was great pleasure to be found in learning new things and entering new worlds. The genres of history, travel and adventure enjoyed enormous popularity. The astounding appeal of Lew Wallace's *Ben-Hur* can be attributed, at least in part, to the way in which this work incorporated all three of these genres. Reading also changed from a largely oral activity, in which a father might read aloud the Bible or Bunyan's *Pilgrim's Progress* to his family, to a much more individualized practice. This change opened the door for readers to enjoy a wider, often more illicit, range of material. Once shunned as corrupting, reading novels became a central avenue toward entertainment before the end of the century.

The present collection was conceived with the desire to capture some of the excitement and diversity of the print culture that was so influential in nineteenth-century American thought and society. It gives a special emphasis to those works that sold astoundingly well when they first appeared. Herman Melville's *Moby-Dick* may be extremely well known and widely read today, but when it first appeared it sold so poorly that its publication almost bankrupted the author. In contrast to *Moby-Dick*, the works in this collection sold extremely well when they first appeared, attracting huge readerships and often inspiring other works, such as plays and sequels, which made them all the more popular. Two other factors influenced the choice of texts: a preference for depth over breadth, and an interest in presenting works standing in dialogue with one another. The rationale here is simple. Reading entire works and longer excerpts gives one a fuller appreciation of an author's intellectual design and enables one to examine narrative arcs and developed lines of argument. Reading works speaking to—and against—other works recreates something of the dynamic of the vital cultural conversations taking place in this period. (The list on pages xvii–xix identifies some of the essential thematic intersections among the texts in this collection.)

This collection makes no claim to cover all, or even most, of the important facets of nineteenth-century popular literature. But it does open a modest window into the vast array of literature avidly produced and just as avidly consumed during this period. Through this window, it is hoped that readers will catch informative glimpses that will entice them into further explorations of the splendidly diverse and always amazing print culture that influenced every aspect of nineteenth-century American life.

ACKNOWLEDGMENTS

One incurs many debts in publishing a book, and in that spirit I would like to extend my sincere gratitude to the many individuals who helped bring this book to completion. My editors at Anthem, Tej Sood and Brian Stone, were incredibly supportive and efficient in helping this work along. I also had an amazing editorial assistant in Richard Higgins, who did much of the heavy lifting in terms of making sure the text was formatted and proofread correctly. Kerilyn Harkaway-Krieger was also of help in preparing the manuscript. And Christoph Irmscher, whose encyclopedic intellectual breadth keeps me ever in awe of him, was incredibly generous in helping me figure out this or that obscure reference—I owe many a footnote to Christoph's expertise. I also wish to say that, although I had a great deal of help in preparing this book for publication, I alone am responsible for any errors that may appear in its pages.

I continue to owe much to friends such as Bob Brown and Alex Van Riesen, who just keep me sane in my life journey through their friendship and their ability to make me laugh. They constantly shine a bit of light into the dark corners of my own often overfull and overanxious life.

I have a family that continues to enable me to do the work I love. I thank my wife, Cathy, and my sons, Isaac and Jeremiah, for putting up with my absences—both physical and emotional—as I struggled to finish what became a rather mammoth undertaking. As always, my father, mother and sister, Karen, stand as the absolute gold standard of generosity and support. My family has always been there for me in countless ways as I negotiate the varied demands of my career.

Finally, I dedicate this book to my Uncle Norman and Aunt Aletta Cole and their sons, Bob, Jim and David. I have been immensely blessed to have both a wonderful immediate and a wonderful extended family. The Coles have always modeled for me a kind of reflexive, unselfish and often understated kindness that embodies Aesop's famous moral that "no act of kindness, no matter how small, is ever wasted." Whether it was Norman showing me magic tricks, Aletta sewing me my own special quilt, Bob letting me be his whist partner when I was hardly even old enough to fan the cards in my hand, Jim making me laugh or David taking me to movies, I have always benefitted in profound, and all-too-often unacknowledged, ways from their constant acts of kindness. I do not exaggerate when I say that the Coles have shown me great love over the years, and words fail me here as I wish to express my gratitude to them.

THEMATIC CONNECTIONS

Singleness and Marriage
Charlotte Temple
Awful Disclosures
The Quaker City
Evangeline
Reveries of a Bachelor
Uncle Tom's Cabin
Malaeska
Little Women
The Hidden Hand
In His Steps

Care and Education of the Young
Life of Washington
"To Mothers"
"Murderers of Fathers, and Murderers of Mothers"
Awful Disclosures
Treatise on Domestic Economy
Uncle Tom's Cabin
Ten Nights in a Bar-Room
Malaeska
Ragged Dick
Little Women
The Gates Ajar
"The Luck of Roaring Camp"
The Hidden Hand
Ben-Hur

Proper Conduct
Life of Washington
"The Forgiving African"
"Murderers of Fathers, and Murderers of Mothers"
"To Mothers"
"Novel Reading"

Awful Disclosures
Treatise on Domestic Economy
Self-Instructor in Phrenology
The Quaker City
Ten Nights in a Bar-Room
Ragged Dick
Little Women
"The Luck of Roaring Camp"
The Gates Ajar
In His Steps

Temperance
"Murderers of Fathers, and Murderers of Mothers"
The Quaker City
Ten Nights in a Bar-Room
The Hidden Hand
In His Steps

Slavery
"The Forgiving African"
Uncle Tom's Cabin
The Hidden Hand

Novel Reading
"Novel Reading"
Reveries of a Bachelor
Little Women
The Gates Ajar
In His Steps

Rural Life
Charlotte Temple
Evangeline
Uncle Tom's Cabin
Reveries of a Bachelor

Ten Nights in a Bar-Room
The Hidden Hand

The South
Evangeline
Uncle Tom's Cabin
The Hidden Hand

Business
Treatise on Domestic Economy
The Quaker City
Ten Nights in a Bar-Room
Uncle Tom's Cabin
Ragged Dick
Ben-Hur
In His Steps

Domesticity and Gender Roles
Charlotte Temple
Awful Disclosures
Treatise on Domestic Economy
"To Mothers"
The Quaker City
Evangeline
Reveries of a Bachelor
Uncle Tom's Cabin
Ten Nights in a Bar-Room
Malaeska
Ragged Dick
"The Luck of Roaring Camp"
Little Women
The Gates Ajar
Ben-Hur
The Hidden Hand
In His Steps

Masculinity
Life of Washington
"Murderers of Fathers, and Murderers of Mothers"
Awful Disclosures
Self-Instructor in Phrenology
The Quaker City

Reveries of a Bachelor
Uncle Tom's Cabin
Ten Nights in a Bar-Room
"The Luck of Roaring Camp"
Ben-Hur

Social Reform
Life of Washington
"To Mothers"
"Murderers of Fathers, and Murderers of Mothers"
"Novel Reading"
The Quaker City
Uncle Tom's Cabin
Ten Nights in a Bar-Room
"John Jenkins"
In His Steps

Religion
Life of Washington
"To Mothers"
"Murderers of Fathers, and Murderers of Mothers"
"Novel Reading"
Awful Disclosures
Treatise on Domestic Economy
Evangeline
The Quaker City
Reveries of a Bachelor
"John Jenkins"
"The Luck of Roaring Camp"
The Gates Ajar
Little Women
Ragged Dick
Uncle Tom's Cabin
Malaeska
Ben-Hur
In His Steps

Urban Life
"Murderers of Fathers, and Murderers of Mothers"
Awful Disclosures

The Quaker City
Malaeska
Ben-Hur
Ten Nights in a Bar-Room
In His Steps

The West
Evangeline
Malaeska
The Gates Ajar
"The Luck of Roaring Camp"
In His Steps

Race
Self-Instructor in Phrenology
The Quaker City
Uncle Tom's Cabin
Malaeska
Ben-Hur

Published in 1868
Ragged Dick
Little Women
The Gates Ajar
The Hidden Hand (second appearance)
"The Luck of Roaring Camp"

Chapter One

SUSANNA HASWELL ROWSON

(1762–1824)

Susanna Haswell Rowson was born in England and emigrated to the American colonies in 1766. She traveled back to England in 1778, but five years later once again returned to America, where she would remain. While still young, she married William Rowson, a poor choice because it turned out he was both an alcoholic and a man incapable of holding a job. Thus, Susanna Rowson was forced to become the provider for the family, a duty that demanded she undertake a number of professions, including actress, teacher and author.

Rowson eventually found success, not only as a teacher of the daughters of some of Massachusetts's most socially prominent families, but also as a writer of plays, poems, short stories and novels. In 1791, she published *Charlotte, A Tale of Truth* (later retitled *Charlotte Temple*), widely considered the first best-selling novel in America. For more than a century, *Charlotte Temple* enjoyed astounding popularity on both sides of the Atlantic. Endlessly imitated, dramatized and translated into various languages, the novel appeared in over 150 editions during the nineteenth century.

Charlotte Temple is an early example of the already-popular didactic genre of seduction novels. It tells the story of a young English girl who rashly allows her lover to take her to America, forsaking her honorable parents for a less-honorable future. The tragic figure of Charlotte so captured the American imagination that an actual grave site was established in New York City in the early nineteenth century, and countless readers over the years visited her supposed burial plot to place on her grave locks of hair, burned love letters and other tokens of esteem and commiseration. The book stands as a vivid meditation on personal responsibility, as Charlotte and a number of her fellow characters become exemplars of how poor decisions inevitably lead to unfortunate and sometimes even devastating consequences.

CHARLOTTE TEMPLE

CHARLOTTE.

A TALE OF TRUTH.

_By_ Mrs. ROWSON,

OF THE NEW THEATRE, PHILADELPHIA;
AUTHOR OF _VICTORIA, THE INQUISITOR,_
FILLE DE CHAMBRE, &c.

IN TWO VOLUMES.

She was her parent's only joy :
They had but one—one darling child.
ROMEO AND JULIET.

Her form was faultlefs, and her mind,
Untainted yet by art,
Was noble, juft, humane, and kind,
And virtue warm'd her heart.
But ah ! the cruel fpoiler came——

VOL. I.

PHILADELPHIA:
PRINTED BY D. HUMPHREYS,
FOR M. CAREY, No. 118, MARKET-STREET.
M.DCC.XCIV.

Title page from the 1794 edition of _Charlotte Temple_ brought out by the famous Philadelphia publisher Mathew Carey (Courtesy Lilly Library, Bloomington, IN).

This text is reprinted from the first American edition published in 1794 by Mathew Carey of Philadelphia under the title, _Charlotte, A Tale of Truth._ For his third edition of 1797, Carey changed the title to _Charlotte Temple,_ a title that is used in most subsequent editions of the book.

Preface

FOR the perusal of the young and thoughtless of the fair sex, this Tale of Truth is designed; and I could wish my fair readers to consider it as not merely the effusion of Fancy, but as a reality. The circumstances on which I have founded this novel were related to me some little time since by an old lady who had personally known Charlotte, though she concealed the real names of the characters, and likewise the place where the unfortunate scenes were acted: yet as it was impossible to offer a relation to the public in such an imperfect state, I have thrown over the whole a slight veil of fiction, and substituted names and places according to my own fancy. The principal characters in this little tale are now consigned to the silent tomb: it can therefore hurt the feelings of no one; and may, I flatter myself, be of service to some who are so unfortunate as to have neither friends to advise, or understanding to direct them, through the various and unexpected evils that attend a young and unprotected woman in her first entrance into life.

While the tear of compassion still trembled in my eye for the fate of the unhappy Charlotte, I may have children of my own, said I, to whom this recital may be of use, and if to your own children, said Benevolence, why not to the many daughters of Misfortune who, deprived of natural friends, or spoilt by a mistaken education, are thrown on an unfeeling world without the least power to defend themselves from the snares not only of the other sex, but from the more dangerous arts of the profligate of their own.

Sensible as I am that a novel writer, at a time when such a variety of works are ushered into the world under that name, stands but a poor chance for fame in the annals of literature, but conscious that I wrote with a mind anxious for the happiness of that sex whose morals and conduct have so powerful an influence on mankind in general; and convinced that I have not wrote a line that conveys a wrong idea to the head or a corrupt wish to the heart, I shall rest satisfied in the purity of my own intentions, and if I merit not applause, I feel that I dread not censure.

If the following tale should save one hapless fair one from the errors which ruined poor Charlotte, or rescue from impending misery the heart of one anxious parent, I shall feel a much higher gratification in reflecting on this trifling performance, than could possibly result from the applause which might attend the most elegant finished piece of literature whose tendency might deprave the heart or mislead the understanding.

Charlotte Temple, Volume I

Chapter I

A Boarding School

"ARE you for a walk," said Montraville to his companion, as they arose from table; "are you for a walk? or shall we order the chaise and proceed to Portsmouth?" Belcour preferred the former; and they sauntered out to view the town, and to make remarks on the inhabitants, as they returned from church.

Montraville was a Lieutenant in the army: Belcour was his brother officer: they had been to take leave of their friends previous to their departure for America, and were now returning to Portsmouth, where the troops waited orders for embarkation. They had stopped at Chichester to dine; and knowing they had sufficient time to reach the place of destination before dark, and yet allow them a walk, had resolved, it being Sunday afternoon, to take a survey of the Chichester ladies as they returned from their devotions.

They had gratified their curiosity, and were preparing to return to the inn without honouring any of the belles with particular notice, when Madame Du Pont, at the head of her school, descended from the church. Such an assemblage of youth and innocence naturally attracted the young soldiers: they stopped; and, as the little cavalcade passed, almost involuntarily pulled off their hats. A tall, elegant girl looked at Montraville and blushed: he instantly recollected the features of Charlotte Temple, whom he had once seen and danced with at a ball at Portsmouth. At that time he thought on her only as a very lovely child, she being then only thirteen; but the improvement two years had made in her person, and the blush of recollection which suffused her cheeks as she passed, awakened in his bosom new and pleasing ideas. Vanity led him to think that pleasure at again beholding him might have occasioned the emotion he had witnessed, and the same vanity led him to wish to see her again.

"She is the sweetest girl in the world," said he, as he entered the inn. Belcour stared. "Did you not notice her?" continued Montraville: "she had on a blue bonnet, and with a pair of lovely eyes of the same colour, has contrived to make me feel devilish odd about the heart."

"Pho," said Belcour, "a musket ball from our friends, the Americans, may in less than two months make you feel worse."

"I never think of the future," replied Montraville; "but am determined to make the most of the present, and would willingly compound with any kind Familiar who would inform me who the girl is, and how I might be likely to obtain an interview."

But no kind Familiar at that time appearing, and the chaise which they had ordered, driving up to the door, Montraville and his companion were obliged to take leave of Chichester and its fair inhabitant, and proceed on their journey.

But Charlotte had made too great an impression on his mind to be easily eradicated: having therefore spent three whole days in thinking on her and in endeavouring to form some plan for seeing her, he determined to set off for Chichester, and trust to chance either to favour or frustrate his designs. Arriving at the verge of the town, he dismounted, and sending the servant forward with the horses, proceeded toward the place, where, in the midst of an extensive pleasure ground, stood the mansion which contained the lovely Charlotte Temple. Montraville leaned on a broken gate, and looked earnestly at the house. The wall which surrounded it was high, and perhaps the Argus's who guarded the Hesperian fruit[1] within, were more watchful than those famed of old.

"'Tis a romantic attempt," said he; "and should I even succeed in seeing and conversing with her, it can be productive of no good: I must of necessity leave England in a few days, and probably may never return; why then should I endeavour to engage the affections of this lovely girl, only to leave her a prey to a thousand inquietudes, of which at present she has no idea? I will return to Portsmouth and think no more about her."

The evening now was closed; a serene stillness reigned; and the chaste Queen of Night with her silver crescent faintly illuminated the hemisphere. The mind of Montraville was hushed into composure by the serenity of the surrounding objects. "I will think on her no more," said he, and turned with an intention to leave the place; but as he turned, he saw the gate which led to the pleasure grounds open, and two women come out, who walked arm-in-arm across the field.

---

1 Ancient kings of Greece who kept watch over their country.

"I will at least see who these are," said he. He overtook them, and giving them the compliments of the evening, begged leave to see them into the more frequented parts of the town: but how was he delighted, when, waiting for an answer, he discovered, under the concealment of a large bonnet, the face of Charlotte Temple.

He soon found means to ingratiate himself with her companion, who was a French teacher at the school, and, at parting, slipped a letter he had purposely written, into Charlotte's hand, and five guineas into that of Mademoiselle, who promised she would endeavour to bring her young charge into the field again the next evening.

Chapter II

Domestic Concerns

MR. Temple was the youngest son of a nobleman whose fortune was by no means adequate to the antiquity, grandeur, and I may add, pride of the family. He saw his elder brother made completely wretched by marrying a disagreeable woman, whose fortune helped to prop the sinking dignity of the house; and he beheld his sisters legally prostituted to old, decrepid men, whose titles gave them consequence in the eyes of the world, and whose affluence rendered them splendidly miserable. "I will not sacrifice internal happiness for outward shew," said he: "I will seek Content; and, if I find her in a cottage, will embrace her with as much cordiality as I should if seated on a throne."

Mr. Temple possessed a small estate of about five hundred pounds a year; and with that he resolved to preserve independence, to marry where the feelings of his heart should direct him, and to confine his expenses within the limits of his income. He had a heart open to every generous feeling of humanity, and a hand ready to dispense to those who wanted part of the blessings he enjoyed himself.

As he was universally known to be the friend of the unfortunate, his advice and bounty was frequently solicited; nor was it seldom that he sought out indigent merit, and raised it from obscurity, confining his own expenses within a very narrow compass.

"You are a benevolent fellow," said a young officer to him one day; "and I have a great mind to give you a fine subject to exercise the goodness of your heart upon."

"You cannot oblige me more," said Temple, "than to point out any way by which I can be serviceable to my fellow creatures."

"Come along then," said the young man, "we will go and visit a man who is not in so good a lodging as he deserves; and, were it not that he has an angel with him, who comforts and supports him, he must long since have sunk under his misfortunes." The young man's heart was too full to proceed; and Temple, unwilling to irritate his feelings by making further enquiries, followed him in silence, til they arrived at the Fleet prison.

The officer enquired for Captain Eldridge: a person led them up several pair of dirty stairs, and pointing to a door which led to a miserable, small apartment, said that was the Captain's room, and retired.

The officer, whose name was Blakeney, tapped at the door, and was bid to enter by a voice melodiously soft. He opened the door, and discovered to Temple a scene which rivetted him to the spot with astonishment.

The apartment, though small, and bearing strong marks of poverty, was neat in the extreme. In an arm-chair, his head reclined upon his hand, his eyes fixed on a book which lay open before him, sat an aged man in a Lieutenant's uniform, which, though threadbare, would sooner call a blush of shame into the face of those who could neglect real merit, than cause the hectic of confusion to glow on the cheeks of him who wore it.

Beside him sat a lovely creature busied in painting a fan mount. She was fair as the lily, but sorrow had nipped the rose in her cheek before it was half blown. Her eyes were blue; and her hair, which was light brown, was slightly confined under a plain muslin cap, tied round with a black ribbon; a white linen gown and plain lawn handkerchief composed the remainder of her dress; and in this simple attire, she was more irresistibly charming to such a heart as Temple's, than she would have been, if adorned with all the splendor of a courtly belle.

When they entered, the old man arose from his seat, and shaking Blakeney by the hand with great cordiality, offered Temple his chair; and there being but three in the room, seated himself on the side of his little bed with evident composure.

"This is a strange place," said he to Temple, "to receive visitors of distinction in; but we must fit our feelings to our station. While I am not ashamed to own the cause which brought me here, why should I blush at my situation? Our misfortunes are not our faults; and were it not for that poor girl –"

Here the philosopher was lost in the father. He rose hastily from his seat, and walking toward the window, wiped off a tear which he was afraid would tarnish the cheek of a sailor.

Temple cast his eye on Miss Eldridge: a pellucid drop had stolen from her eyes, and fallen upon a rose she was painting. It blotted and discoloured the flower. "'Tis emblematic," said he mentally: "the rose of youth and health soon fades when watered by the tear of affliction."

"My friend Blakeney," said he, addressing the old man, "told me I could be of service to you: be so kind then, dear Sir, as to point out some way in which I can relieve the anxiety of your heart and increase the pleasures of my own."

"My good young man," said Eldridge, "you know not what you offer. While deprived of my liberty I cannot be free from anxiety on my own account; but that is a trifling concern; my anxious thoughts extend to one more dear a thousand times than life: I am a poor weak old man, and must expect in a few years to sink into silence and oblivion; but when I am gone, who will protect that fair bud of innocence from the blasts of adversity, or from the cruel hand of insult and dishonour."

"Oh, my father!" cried Miss Eldridge, tenderly taking his hand, "be not anxious on that account; for daily are my prayers offered to heaven that our lives may terminate at the same instant, and one grave receive us both; for why should I live when deprived of my only friend."

Temple was moved even to tears. "You will both live many years," said he, "and I hope see much happiness. Cheerly, my friend, cheerly; these passing clouds of adversity will serve only to make the sunshine of prosperity more pleasing. But we are losing time: you might ere this have told me who were your creditors, what were their demands, and other particulars necessary to your liberation."

"My story is short," said Mr. Eldridge, "but there are some particulars which will wring my heart barely to remember; yet to one whose offers of friendship appear so open and disinterested, I will relate every circumstance that led to my present, painful situation. But my child," continued he, addressing his daughter, "let me prevail on you to take this opportunity, while my friends are with me, to enjoy the benefit of air and exercise. Go, my love; leave me now; to-morrow at your usual hour I will expect you."

Miss Eldridge impressed on his cheek the kiss of filial affection, and obeyed.

Chapter III

Unexpected Misfortunes

"My Life," said Mr. Eldridge, "till within these few years was marked by no particular circumstance deserving notice. I early embraced the life of a sailor, and have served my King with unremitted ardour for many years. At the age of twenty-five I married an amiable woman; one son, and the girl who just now left us, were the fruits of our union. My boy had genius and spirit. I straitened my little income to give him a liberal education, but the rapid progress he made in his studies amply compensated for the inconvenience. At the academy where he received his education he commenced an acquaintance with a Mr. Lewis, a young man of affluent fortune: as they grew up their intimacy ripened into friendship, and they became almost inseparable companions.

"George chose the profession of a soldier. I had neither friends or money to procure him a commission, and had wished him to embrace a nautical life: but this was repugnant to his wishes, and I ceased to urge him on the subject.

"The friendship subsisting between Lewis and my son was of such a nature as gave him free access to our family; and so specious was his manner that we hesitated not to state to him all our little difficulties in regard to George's future views. He listened to us with attention, and offered to advance any sum necessary for his first setting out.

"I embraced the offer, and gave him my note for the payment of it, but he would not suffer me to mention any stipulated time, as he said I might do it whenever most convenient to myself. About this time my dear Lucy returned from school, and I soon began to imagine Lewis looked at her with eyes of affection. I gave my child a caution to beware of him, and to look on her mother as her friend. She was unaffectedly artless; and when, as I suspected, Lewis made professions of love, she confided in her parents, and assured us her heart was perfectly unbiassed in his favour, and she would chearfully submit to our direction.

"I took an early opportunity of questioning him concerning his intentions towards my child: he gave an equivocal answer, and I forbade him the house.

"The next day he sent and demanded payment of his money. It was not in my power to comply with the demand. I requested three days to endeavour to raise it, determining in that time to mortgage my half pay, and live on a small annuity which my wife possessed, rather than be under an obligation to so worthless a man: but this short time was not allowed me; for that evening, as I was sitting down to supper, unsuspicious of danger, an officer entered, and tore me from the embraces of my family.

"My wife had been for some time in a declining state of health: ruin at once so unexpected and inevitable was a stroke she was not prepared to bear, and I saw her faint into the arms of our servant, as I left my own habitation for the comfortless walls of a prison. My poor Lucy, distracted with her fears for us both, sunk on the floor and endeavoured to detain me by her feeble efforts; but in vain; they forced open her arms; she shrieked, and fell prostrate. But pardon me. The horrors of that night unman me. I cannot proceed."

He rose from his seat, and walked several times across the room: at length, attaining more composure, he cried—"What a mere infant I am! Why, Sir, I never felt thus in the day of battle."

"No," said Temple; "but the truly brave soul is tremblingly alive to the feelings of humanity."

"True," replied the old man, (something like satisfaction darting across his features) "and painful as these feelings are, I would not exchange them for that torpor which the stoic mistakes for philosophy. How many exquisite delights should I have passed by unnoticed, but for these keen sensations, this quick sense of happiness or misery? Then let us, my friend, take the cup of life as it is presented to us, tempered by the hand of a wise Providence; be thankful for the good, be patient under the evil, and presume not to enquire why the latter predominates."

"This is true philosophy," said Temple.

"'Tis the only way to reconcile ourselves to the cross events of life," replied he. "But I forget myself. I will not longer intrude on your patience, but proceed in my melancholy tale.

"The very evening that I was taken to prison, my son arrived from Ireland, where he had been some time with his regiment. From the distracted expressions of his mother and sister, he learnt by whom I had been arrested; and, late as it was, flew on the wings of wounded affection, to the house of his false friend, and earnestly enquired the cause of this cruel conduct. With all the calmness of a cool deliberate villain, he avowed his passion for Lucy; declared her situation in life would not permit him to marry her; but offered to release me immediately, and make any settlement on her, if George would persuade her to live, as he impiously termed it, a life of honour.

"Fired at the insult offered to a man and a soldier, my boy struck the villain, and a challenge ensued. He then went to a coffee-house in the neighbourhood and wrote a long affectionate letter to me, blaming himself severely for having introduced Lewis into the family, or permitted him to confer an obligation, which had brought inevitable ruin on us all. He begged me, whatever might be the event of the ensuing morning, not to suffer regret or unavailing sorrow for his fate, to encrease the anguish of my heart, which he greatly feared was already insupportable.

"This letter was delivered to me early in the morning. It would be vain to attempt describing my feelings on the perusal of it; suffice it to say, that a merciful Providence interposed, and I was for three weeks insensible to miseries almost beyond the strength of human nature to support.

"A fever and strong delirium seized me, and my life was despaired of. At length, nature, overpowered with fatigue, gave way to the salutary power of rest, and a quiet slumber of some hours restored me to reason, though the extreme weakness of my frame prevented my feeling my distress so acutely as I otherways should.

"The first object that struck me on awaking, was Lucy sitting by my bedside; her pale countenance and sable dress prevented my enquiries for poor George: for the letter I had received from him, was the first thing that occurred to my memory. By degrees the rest returned: I recollected being arrested, but could no ways account for being in this apartment, whither they had conveyed me during my illness.

"I was so weak as to be almost unable to speak. I pressed Lucy's hand, and looked earnestly round the apartment in search of another dear object.

"Where is your mother?" said I, faintly.

"The poor girl could not answer: she shook her head in expressive silence; and throwing herself on the bed, folded her arms about me, and burst into tears.

"What! both gone?" said I.

"Both, she replied, endeavouring to restrain her emotions: "but they are happy, no doubt."

Here Mr. Eldridge paused: the recollection of the scene was too painful to permit him to proceed.

Chapter IV

Change of Fortune

"IT was some days," continued Mr. Eldridge, recovering himself, "before I could venture to enquire the particulars of what had happened during my illness: at length I assumed courage to ask my dear girl how long her mother and brother had been dead: she told me, that the morning after my arrest, George came home early to enquire after his mother's health, staid with them but a few minutes, seemed greatly agitated at parting, but gave them strict charge to keep up their spirits, and hope every thing would turn out for the best. In about two hours after, as they were sitting at breakfast, and endeavouring to strike out some plan to attain my liberty, they heard a loud rap at the door, which Lucy running to open, she met the bleeding body of her brother, borne in by two men who had lifted him from a litter, on which they had brought him from the place where he fought. Her poor mother, weakened by illness and the struggles of the preceding night, was not able to support this shock; gasping for breath, her looks wild and haggard, she reached the apartment where they had carried her dying son. She knelt by the bed side; and taking his cold hand, 'my poor boy,' said she, 'I will not be parted from thee: husband! son! both at once lost. Father of mercies, spare me!' She fell into a strong convulsion, and expired in about two hours. In the mean time, a surgeon had dressed George's wounds; but they were in such a situation as to bar the smallest hopes of recovery. He never was sensible from the time he was brought home, and died that evening in the arms of his sister.

"Late as it was when this event took place, my affectionate Lucy insisted on coming to me. 'What must he feel,' said she, 'at our apparent neglect, and how shall I inform him of the afflictions with which it has pleased heaven to visit us?'

"She left the care of the dear departed ones to some neighbours who had kindly come in to comfort and assist her; and on entering the house where I was confined, found me in the situation I have mentioned.

"How she supported herself in these trying moments, I know not: heaven, no doubt, was with her; and her anxiety to preserve the life of one parent in some measure abated her affliction for the loss of the other.

"My circumstances were greatly embarrassed, my acquaintance few, and those few utterly unable to assist me. When my wife and son were committed to their kindred earth, my creditors seized my house and furniture, which not being sufficient to discharge all their demands, detainers were lodged against me. No friend stepped forward to my relief; from the grave of her mother, my beloved Lucy followed an almost dying father to this melancholy place.

"Here we have been nearly a year and a half. My half-pay I have given up to satisfy my creditors, and my child supports me by her industry: sometimes by fine needlework, sometimes by painting. She leaves me every night, and goes to a lodging near the bridge; but returns in the morning, to chear me with her smiles, and bless me by her duteous affection. A lady once offered her an asylum in her family; but she would not leave me. 'We are all the world to each other,' said she. 'I thank God, I have health and spirits to improve the talents with which nature has endowed me; and I trust if I employ them in the support of a beloved parent, I shall not be thought an unprofitable servant. While he lives, I pray for strength to pursue my employment; and when it pleases heaven to take one of us, may it give the survivor resignation to bear the separation as we ought: till then I will never leave him.'

"But where is this inhuman persecutor?" said Temple.

"He has been abroad ever since," replied the old man; "but he has left orders with his lawyer never to give up the note till the utmost farthing is paid."

"And how much is the amount of your debts in all?" said Temple.

"Five hundred pounds," he replied.

Temple started: it was more than he expected. "But something must be done," said he: "that sweet maid must not wear out her life in a prison. I will see you again to-morrow, my friend," said he, shaking Eldridge's hand: "keep up your spirits: light and shade are not more happily blended than are the pleasures and pains of life; and the horrors of the one serve only to increase the splendor of the other."

"You never lost a wife and son," said Eldridge.

"No," replied he, "but I can feel for those that have." Eldridge pressed his hand as they went toward the door, and they parted in silence.

When they got without the walls of the prison, Temple thanked his friend Blakeney for introducing him to so worthy a character; and telling him he had a particular engagement in the city, wished him a good evening.

"And what is to be done for this distressed man," said Temple, as he walked up Ludgate Hill. "Would to heaven I had a fortune that would enable me instantly to discharge his debt: what exquisite transport, to see the expressive eyes of Lucy beaming at once with pleasure for her father's deliverance, and gratitude for her deliverer: but is not my fortune affluence," continued he, "nay superfluous wealth, when compared to the extreme indigence of Eldridge; and what have I done to deserve ease and plenty, while a brave worthy officer starves in a prison? Three hundred a year is surely sufficient for all my wants and wishes: at any rate Eldridge must be relieved."

When the heart has will, the hands can soon find means to execute a good action.

Temple was a young man, his feelings warm and impetuous; unacquainted with the world, his heart had not been rendered callous by being convinced of its fraud and hypocrisy. He pitied their sufferings, overlooked their faults, thought every bosom as generous as his own, and would chearfully have divided his last guinea with an unfortunate fellow creature.

No wonder, then, that such a man (without waiting a moment for the interference of Madam Prudence) should resolve to raise money sufficient for the relief of Eldridge, by mortgaging part of his fortune.

We will not enquire too minutely into the cause which might actuate him in this instance: suffice it to say, he immediately put the plan in execution; and in three days from the time he first saw the unfortunate Lieutenant, he had the superlative felicity of seeing him at liberty, and receiving an ample reward in the tearful eye and half articulated thanks of the grateful Lucy.

"And pray, young man," said his father to him one morning, "what are your designs in visiting thus constantly that old man and his daughter?"

Temple was at a loss for a reply: he had never asked himself the question: he hesitated; and his father continued—

"It was not till within these few days that I heard in what manner your acquaintance first commenced, and cannot suppose any thing but attachment to the daughter could carry you such imprudent lengths for the father: it certainly must be her art that drew you in to mortgage part of your fortune."

"Art, Sir!" cried Temple eagerly. "Lucy Eldridge is as free from art as she is from every other error: she is —"

"Everything that is amiable and lovely," said his father, interrupting him ironically: "no doubt in your opinion she is a pattern of excellence for all her sex to follow; but come, Sir, pray tell me what are your designs towards this paragon. I hope you do not intend to complete your folly by marrying her."

"Were my fortune such as would support her according to her merit, I don't know a woman more formed to insure happiness in the married state."

"Then prithee, my dear lad," said his father, "since your rank and fortune are so much beneath what your *Princess* might expect, be so kind as to turn your eyes on Miss Weatherby; who, having only an estate of three thousand a year, is more upon a level with you, and whose father yesterday solicited the mighty honour of your alliance. I shall leave you to consider on this offer; and pray remember, that your union with Miss Weatherby will put it in your power to be more liberally the friend of Lucy Eldridge."

The old gentleman walked in a stately manner out of the room; and Temple stood almost petrified with astonishment, contempt, and rage.

Chapter V

Such Things Are

MISS Weatherby was the only child of a wealthy man, almost idolized by her parents, flattered by her dependants, and never contradicted even by those who called themselves her friends: I cannot give a better description than by the following lines.

> The lovely maid whose form and face
> Nature has deck'd with ev'ry grace,
> But in whose breast no virtues glow,
> Whose heart ne'er felt another's woe,
> Whose hand ne'er smooth'd the bed of pain,
> Or eas'd the captive's galling chain;
> But like the tulip caught the eye,
> Born just to be admir'd and die;
> When gone, no one regrets its loss,
> Or scarce remembers that it was.

Such was Miss Weatherby: her form lovely as nature could make it, but her mind uncultivated, her heart unfeeling, her passions impetuous, and her brain almost turned with flattery, dissipation, and pleasure; and such was the girl, whom a partial grandfather left independent mistress of the fortune before mentioned.

She had seen Temple frequently; and fancying she could never be happy without him, nor once imagining he could refuse a girl of her beauty and fortune, she prevailed on her fond father to offer the alliance to the old Earl of D—,[2] Mr. Temple's father.

The Earl had received the offer courteously: he thought it a great match for Henry; and was too fashionable a man to suppose a wife could be any impediment to the friendship he professed for Eldridge and his daughter.

---

2 A member of Britain's nobility, an earl ranks below a duke and marquess and above a viscount. The feminine equivalent of an earl is a countess.

Unfortunately for Temple, he thought quite otherwise: the conversation he had just had with his father, discovered to him the situation of his heart; and he found that the most affluent fortune would bring no increase of happiness unless Lucy Eldridge shared it with him; and the knowledge of the purity of her sentiments, and the integrity of his own heart, made him shudder at the idea his father had started, of marrying a woman for no other reason than because the affluence of her fortune would enable him to injure her by maintaining in splendor the woman to whom his heart was devoted: he therefore resolved to refuse Miss Weatherby, and be the event what it might, offer his heart and hand to Lucy Eldridge.

Full of this determination, he fought his father, declared his resolution, and was commanded never more to appear in his presence. Temple bowed; his heart was too full to permit him to speak; he left the house precipitately, and hastened to relate the cause of his sorrows to his good old friend and his amiable daughter.

In the mean time, the Earl, vexed to the soul that such a fortune should be lost, determined to offer himself a candidate for Miss Weatherby's favour.

What wonderful changes are wrought by that reigning power, ambition! the love-sick girl, when first she heard of Temple's refusal, wept, raved, tore her hair, and vowed to found a protestant nunnery with her fortune; and by commencing abbess, shut herself up from the sight of cruel ungrateful man for ever.

Her father was a man of the world: he suffered this first transport to subside, and then very deliberately unfolded to her the offers of the old Earl, expatiated on the many benefits arising from an elevated title, painted in glowing colours the surprise and vexation of Temple when he should see her figuring as a Countess and his mother-in-law, and begged her to consider well before she made any rash vows.

The *distressed* fair one dried her tears, listened patiently, and at length declared she believed the surest method to revenge the slight put on her by the son, would be to accept the father: so said so done, and in a few days she became the Countess D—.

Temple heard the news with emotion: he had lost his father's favour by avowing his passion for Lucy, and he saw now there was no hope of regaining it: "but he shall not make me miserable," said he. "Lucy and I have no ambitious notions: we can live on three hundred a year for some little time, till the mortgage is paid off, and then we shall have sufficient not only for the comforts but many of the little elegancies of life. We will purchase a little cottage, my Lucy," said he, "and thither with your reverend father we will retire; we will forget there are such things as splendor, profusion, and dissipation: we will have some cows, and you shall be queen of the dairy; in a morning, while I look after my garden, you shall take a basket on your arm, and sally forth to feed your poultry; and as they flutter round you in token of humble gratitude, your father shall smoke his pipe in a woodbine alcove, and viewing the serenity of your countenance, feel such real pleasure dilate his own heart, as shall make him forget he had ever been unhappy."

Lucy smiled; and Temple saw it was a smile of approbation. He sought and found a cottage suited to his taste; thither, attended by Love and Hymen, the happy trio retired; where, during many years of uninterrupted felicity, they cast not a wish beyond the little boundaries of their own tenement. Plenty, and her handmaid, Prudence, presided at their board, Hospitality stood at their gate, Peace smiled on each face, Content reigned in each heart, and Love and Health strewed roses on their pillows.

Such were the parents of Charlotte Temple, who was the only pledge of their mutual love, and who, at the earnest entreaty of a particular friend, was permitted to finish the education her mother had begun, at Madame Du Pont's school, where we first introduced her to the acquaintance of the reader.

Chapter VI

An Intriguing Teacher

MADAME Du Pont was a woman every way calculated to take the care of young ladies, had that care entirely devolved on herself; but it was impossible to attend the education of a numerous school without proper assistants; and those assistants were not always the kind of people whose conversation and morals were exactly such as parents of delicacy and refinement would wish a daughter to copy. Among the teachers at Madame Du Pont's school, was Mademoiselle La Rue, who added to a pleasing person and insinuating address, a liberal education and the manners of a gentlewoman. She was recommended to the school by a lady whose humanity overstepped the bounds of discretion: for though she knew Miss La Rue had eloped from a convent with a young officer, and, on coming to England, had lived with several different men in open defiance of all moral and religious duties; yet, finding her reduced to the most abject want, and believing the penitence which she professed to be sincere, she took her into her own family, and from thence recommended her to Madame Du Pont, as thinking the situation more suitable for a woman of her abilities. But Mademoiselle possessed too much of the spirit of intrigue to remain long without adventures. At church, where she constantly appeared, her person attracted the attention of a young man who was upon a visit at a gentleman's seat in the neighbourhood: she had met him several times clandestinely; and being invited to come out that evening, and eat some fruit and pastry in a summer-house belonging to the gentleman he was visiting, and requested to bring some of the ladies with her, Charlotte being her favourite, was fixed on to accompany her.

The mind of youth eagerly catches at promised pleasure: pure and innocent by nature, it thinks not of the dangers lurking beneath those pleasures, till too late to avoid them: when Mademoiselle asked Charlotte to go with her, she mentioned the gentleman as a relation, and spoke in such high terms of the elegance of his gardens, the sprightliness of his conversation, and the liberality with which he ever entertained his guests, that Charlotte thought only of the pleasure she should enjoy in the visit,—not on the imprudence of going without her governess's knowledge, or of the danger to which she exposed herself in visiting the house of a gay young man of fashion.

Madame Du Pont was gone out for the evening, and the rest of the ladies retired to rest, when Charlotte and the teacher stole out at the back gate, and in crossing the field, were accosted by Montraville, as mentioned in the first chapter.

Charlotte was disappointed in the pleasure she had promised herself from this visit. The levity of the gentlemen and the freedom of their conversation disgusted her. She was astonished at the liberties Mademoiselle permitted them to take; grew thoughtful and uneasy, and heartily wished herself at home again in her own chamber.

Perhaps one cause of that wish might be, an earnest desire to see the contents of the letter which had been put into her hand by Montraville.

Any reader who has the least knowledge of the world, will easily imagine the letter was made up of encomiums on her beauty, and vows of everlasting love and constancy; nor will he be surprised that a heart open to every gentle, generous sentiment, should feel itself warmed by gratitude for a man who professed to feel so much for her; nor is it improbable but her mind might revert to the agreeable person and martial appearance of Montraville.

In affairs of love, a young heart is never in more danger than when attempted by a handsome young soldier. A man of an indifferent appearance, will, when arrayed in a military habit, shew to advantage; but when beauty of person, elegance of manner, and an easy method of paying compliments, are united to the scarlet coat, smart cockade, and military sash, ah! well-a-day for the poor girl who gazes on him: she is in imminent danger; but if she listens to him with pleasure, 'tis all over with her, and from that moment she has neither eyes nor ears for any other object.

Now, my dear sober matron, (if a sober matron should deign to turn over these pages, before she trusts them to the eye of a darling daughter,) let me intreat you not to put on a grave face, and throw down the book in a passion and declare 'tis enough to turn the heads of half the girls in England; I do solemnly protest, my dear madam, I mean no more by what I have here advanced, than to ridicule those romantic girls, who foolishly imagine a red coat and silver epaulet constitute the fine gentleman; and should that fine gentleman make half a dozen fine speeches to them, they will imagine themselves so much in love as to fancy it a meritorious action to jump out of a two pair of stairs window, abandon their friends, and trust entirely to the honour of a man, who perhaps hardly knows the meaning of the word, and if he does, will be too much the modern man of refinement, to practice it in their favour.

Gracious heaven! when I think on the miseries that must rend the heart of a doating parent, when he sees the darling of his age at first seduced from his protection, and afterwards abandoned, by the very wretch whose promises of love decoyed her from the paternal roof—when he sees her poor and wretched, her bosom torn between remorse for her crime and love for her vile betrayer—when fancy paints to me the good old man stooping to raise the weeping penitent, while every tear from her eye is numbered by drops from his bleeding heart, my bosom glows with honest indignation, and I wish for power to extirpate those monsters of seduction from the earth.

Oh my dear girls—for to such only am I writing—listen not to the voice of love, unless sanctioned by paternal approbation: be assured, it is now past the days of romance: no woman can be run away with contrary to her own inclination: then kneel down each morning, and request kind heaven to keep you free from temptation, or, should it please to suffer you to be tried, pray for fortitude to resist the impulse of inclination when it runs counter to the precepts of religion and virtue.

Chapter VII

Natural Sense of Propriety Inherent in the Female Bosom

"I CANNOT think we have done exactly right in going out this evening, Mademoiselle," said Charlotte, seating herself when she entered her apartment: "nay, I am sure it was not right; for I expected to be very happy, but was sadly disappointed."

"It was your own fault, then," replied Mademoiselle: "for I am sure my cousin omitted nothing that could serve to render the evening agreeable."

"True," said Charlotte: "but I thought the gentlemen were very free in their manner: I wonder you would suffer them to behave as they did."

"Prithee, don't be such a foolish little prude," said the artful woman, affecting anger: "I invited you to go in hopes it would divert you, and be an agreeable change of scene;

however, if your delicacy was hurt by the behaviour of the gentlemen, you need not go again; so there let it rest."

"I do not intend to go again," said Charlotte, gravely taking off her bonnet, and beginning to prepare for bed: "I am sure, if Madame Du Pont knew we had been out to-night, she would be very angry; and it is ten to one but she hears of it by some means or other."

"Nay, Miss," said La Rue, "perhaps your mighty sense of propriety may lead you to tell her yourself: and in order to avoid the censure you would incur, should she hear of it by accident, throw the blame on me: but I confess I deserve it: it will be a very kind return for that partiality which led me to prefer you before any of the rest of the ladies; but perhaps it will give you pleasure," continued she, letting fall some hypocritical tears, "to see me deprived of bread, and for an action which by the most rigid could only be esteemed an inadvertency, lose my place and character, and be driven again into the world, where I have already suffered all the evils attendant on poverty."

This was touching Charlotte in the most vulnerable part: she rose from her seat, and taking Mademoiselle's hand—"You know, my dear La Rue," said she, "I love you too well, to do anything that would injure you in my governess's opinion: I am only sorry we went out this evening."

"I don't believe it, Charlotte," said she, assuming a little vivacity; "for if you had not gone out, you would not have seen the gentleman who met us crossing the field; and I rather think you were pleased with his conversation."

"I had seen him once before," replied Charlotte, "and thought him an agreeable man; and you know one is always pleased to see a person with whom one has passed several chearful hours. "But," said she pausing, and drawing the letter from her pocket, while a gentle suffusion of vermillion tinged her neck and face, "he gave me this letter; what shall I do with it?"

"Read it, to be sure," returned Mademoiselle.

"I am afraid I ought not," said Charlotte: "my mother has often told me, I should never read a letter given by a young man, without first giving it to her."

"Lord bless you, my dear girl," cried the teacher smiling, "have you a mind to be in leading strings all your life time. Prithee open the letter, read it, and judge for yourself; if you show it your mother, the consequence will be, you will be taken from school, and a strict guard kept over you; so you will stand no chance of ever seeing the smart young officer again."

"I should not like to leave school yet," replied Charlotte, "till I have attained a greater proficiency in my Italian and music. But you can, if you please, Mademoiselle, take the letter back to Montraville, and tell him I wish him well, but cannot, with any propriety, enter into a clandestine correspondence with him." She laid the letter on the table, and began to undress herself.

"Well," said La Rue, "I vow you are an unaccountable girl: have you no curiosity to see the inside now? for my part I could no more let a letter addressed to me lie unopened so long, than I could work miracles: he writes a good hand," continued she, turning the letter, to look at the superscription.

"'Tis well enough," said Charlotte, drawing it towards her.

"He is a genteel young fellow," said La Rue carelessly, folding up her apron at the same time; "but I think he is marked with the small pox."

"Oh you are greatly mistaken," said Charlotte eagerly; "he has a remarkable clear skin and fine complexion."

"His eyes, if I could judge by what I saw," said La Rue, "are grey and want expression."
"By no means," replied Charlotte; "they are the most expressive eyes I ever saw."
"Well, child, whether they are grey or black is of no consequence: you have determined not to read his letter; so it is likely you will never either see or hear from him again."
Charlotte took up the letter, and Mademoiselle continued—

"He is most probably going to America; and if ever you should hear any account of him, it may possibly be that he is killed; and though he loved you ever so fervently, though his last breath should be spent in a prayer for your happiness, it can be nothing to you: you can feel nothing for the fate of the man, whose letters you will not open, and whose sufferings you will not alleviate, by permitting him to think you would remember him when absent, and pray for his safety."

Charlotte still held the letter in her hand: her heart swelled at the conclusion of Mademoiselle's speech, and a tear dropped upon the wafer that closed it.

"The wafer is not dry yet," said she, "and sure there can be no great harm –" She hesitated. La Rue was silent. "I may read it, Mademoiselle, and return it afterwards."

"Certainly," replied Mademoiselle.

"At any rate I am determined not to answer it," continued Charlotte, as she opened the letter.

Here let me stop to make one remark, and trust me my very heart aches while I write it; but certain I am, that when once a woman has stifled the sense of shame in her own bosom, when once she has lost sight of the basis on which reputation, honour, every thing that should be dear to the female heart, rests, she grows hardened in guilt, and will spare no pains to bring down innocence and beauty to the shocking level with herself: and this proceeds from that diabolical spirit of envy, which repines at seeing another in the full possession of that respect and esteem which she can no longer hope to enjoy.

Mademoiselle eyed the unsuspecting Charlotte, as she perused the letter, with a malignant pleasure. She saw, that the contents had awakened new emotions in her youthful bosom: she encouraged her hopes, calmed her fears, and before they parted for the night, it was determined that she should meet Montraville the ensuing evening.

Chapter VIII

Domestic Pleasures Planned

"I THINK, my dear," said Mrs. Temple, laying her hand on her husband's arm as they were walking together in the garden, "I think next Wednesday is Charlotte's birth day: now I have formed a little scheme in my own mind, to give her an agreeable surprise; and if you have no objection, we will send for her home on that day." Temple pressed his wife's hand in token of approbation, and she proceeded.—"You know the little alcove at the bottom of the garden, of which Charlotte is so fond? I have an inclination to deck this out in a fanciful manner, and invite all her little friends to partake of a collation of fruit, sweetmeats, and other things suitable to the general taste of young guests; and to make it more pleasing to Charlotte, she shall be mistress of the feast, and entertain her visitors in this alcove. I know she will be delighted; and to complete all, they shall have some music, and finish with a dance."

"A very fine plan, indeed," said Temple, smiling; "and you really suppose I will wink at your indulging the girl in this manner? You will quite spoil her, Lucy; indeed you will."

"She is the only child we have," said Mrs. Temple, the whole tenderness of a mother adding animation to her fine countenance; but it was withal tempered so sweetly with the meek affection and submissive duty of the wife, that as she paused expecting her husband's answer, he gazed at her tenderly, and found he was unable to refuse her request.

"She is a good girl," said Temple.

"She is, indeed," replied the fond mother exultingly, "a grateful, affectionate girl; and I am sure will never lose sight of the duty she owes her parents."

"If she does," said he, "she must forget the example set her by the best of mothers."

Mrs. Temple could not reply; but the delightful sensation that dilated her heart sparkled in her intelligent eyes and heightened the vermillion on her cheeks.

Of all the pleasures of which the human mind is sensible, there is none equal to that which warms and expands the bosom, when listening to commendations bestowed on us by a beloved object, and are conscious of having deserved them.

Ye giddy flutterers in the fantastic round of dissipation, who eagerly seek pleasure in the lofty dome, rich treat, and midnight revel—tell me, ye thoughtless daughters of folly, have ye ever found the phantom you have so long sought with such unremitted assiduity? Has she not always eluded your grasp, and when you have reached your hand to take the cup she extends to her deluded votaries, have you not found the long-expected draught strongly tinctured with the bitter dregs of disappointment? I know you have: I see it in the wan cheek, sunk eye, and air of chagrin, which ever mark the children of dissipation. Pleasure is a vain illusion; she draws you on to a thousand follies, errors, and I may say vices, and then leaves you to deplore your thoughtless credulity.

Look, my dear friends, at yonder lovely Virgin, arrayed in a white robe devoid of ornament; behold the meekness of her countenance, the modesty of her gait; her handmaids are *Humility, Filial Piety, Conjugal Affection, Industry,* and *Benevolence;* her name is *Content;* she holds in her hand the cup of true felicity, and when once you have formed an intimate acquaintance with these her attendants, nay you must admit them as your bosom friends and chief counsellors, then, whatever may be your situation in life, the meek eyed Virgin will immediately take up her abode with you.

Is poverty your portion?—she will lighten your labours, preside at your frugal board, and watch your quiet slumbers.

Is your state mediocrity?—she will heighten every blessing you enjoy, by informing you how grateful you should be to that bountiful Providence who might have placed you in the most abject situation; and, by teaching you to weigh your blessings against your deserts, show you how much more you receive than you have a right to expect.

Are you possessed of affluence?—what an inexhaustible fund of happiness will she lay before you! To relieve the distressed, redress the injured, in short, to perform all the good works of peace and mercy.

Content, my dear friends, will blunt even the arrows of adversity, so that they cannot materially harm you. She will dwell in the humblest cottage; she will attend you even to a prison. Her parent is Religion; her sisters, Patience and Hope. She will pass with you through life, smoothing the rough paths, and tread to earth those thorns which every one must meet with as they journey onward to the appointed goal. She will soften the pains of sickness, continue with you even in the cold gloomy hour of death, and, chearing you with the smiles of her heaven-born sister, Hope, lead you triumphant to a blissfull eternity.

I confess I have rambled strangely from my story: but what of that? if I have been so lucky as to find the road to happiness, why should I be such a niggard as to omit so good an opportunity of pointing out the way to others. The very basis of true peace of mind is a benevolent wish to see all the world as happy as one's self; and from my soul do I pity the selfish churl, who, remembering the little bickerings of anger, envy, and fifty other disagreeables to which frail mortality is subject; would wish to revenge the affront which pride whispers him he has received. For my own part, I can safely declare, there is not a human being in the universe, whose prosperity I should not rejoice in, and to whose happiness I would not contribute to the utmost limit of my power: and may my offences be no more remembered in the day of general retribution, than as from my soul I forgive every offence or injury received from a fellow creature.

Merciful heaven! who would exchange the rapture of such a reflexion for all the gaudy tinsel which the world calls pleasure!

But to return.—Content dwelt in Mrs. Temple's bosom, and spread a charming animation over her countenance, as her husband led her in, to lay the plan she had formed (for the celebration of Charlotte's birth day,) before Mr. Eldridge.

Chapter IX

We Know Not What a Day May Bring Forth

VARIOUS were the sensations which agitated the mind of Charlotte, during the day preceding the evening in which she was to meet Montraville. Several times did she almost resolve to go to her governess, show her the letter, and be guided by her advice: but Charlotte had taken one step in the ways of imprudence; and when that is once done, there are always innumerable obstacles to prevent the erring person returning to the path of rectitude: yet these obstacles, however forcible they may appear in general, exist chiefly in imagination.

Charlotte feared the anger of her governess: she loved her mother, and the very idea of incurring her displeasure, gave her the greatest uneasiness: but there was a more forcible reason still remaining: should she show the letter to Madame Du Pont, she must confess the means by which it came into her possession; and what would be the consequence? Mademoiselle would be turned out of doors.

"I must not be ungrateful," said she. "La Rue is very kind to me; besides I can, when I see Montraville, inform him of the impropriety of our continuing to see or correspond with each other, and request him to come no more to Chichester."

However prudent Charlotte might be in these resolutions, she certainly did not take a proper method to confirm herself in them. Several times in the course of the day, she indulged herself in reading over the letter, and each time she read it, the contents sunk deeper in her heart. As evening drew near, she caught herself frequently consulting her watch. "I wish this foolish meeting was over," said she, by way of apology to her own heart, "I wish it was over; for when I have seen him, and convinced him my resolution is not to be shaken, I shall feel my mind much easier."

The appointed hour arrived. Charlotte and Mademoiselle eluded the eye of vigilance; and Montraville, who had waited their coming with impatience, received them with rapturous and unbounded acknowledgments for their condescension: he had wisely brought Belcour with him to entertain Mademoiselle, while he enjoyed an uninterrupted conversation with Charlotte.

Belcour was a man whose character might be comprised in a few words; and as he will make some figure in the ensuing pages, I shall here describe him. He possessed a genteel fortune, and had a liberal education; dissipated, thoughtless, and capricious, he paid little regard to the moral duties, and less to religious ones: eager in the pursuit of pleasure, he minded not the miseries he inflicted on others, provided his own wishes, however extravagant, were gratified. Self, darling self, was the idol he worshipped, and to that he would have sacrificed the interest and happiness of all mankind. Such was the friend of Montraville: will not the reader be ready to imagine, that the man who could regard such a character, must be actuated by the same feelings, follow the same pursuits, and be equally unworthy with the person to whom he thus gave his confidence?

But Montraville was a different character: generous in his disposition, liberal in his opinions, and good-natured almost to a fault; yet eager and impetuous in the pursuit of a favorite object, he staid not to reflect on the consequence which might follow the attainment of his wishes; with a mind ever open to conviction, had he been so fortunate as to possess a friend who would have pointed out the cruelty of endeavouring to gain the heart of an innocent artless girl, when he knew it was utterly impossible for him to marry her, and when the gratification of his passion would be unavoidable infamy and misery to her, and a cause of never-ceasing remorse to himself: had these dreadful consequences been placed before him in a proper light, the humanity of his nature would have urged him to give up the pursuit: but Belcour was not this friend; he rather encouraged the growing passion of Montraville; and being pleased with the vivacity of Mademoiselle, resolved to leave no argument untried, which he thought might prevail on her to be the companion of their intended voyage; and he made no doubt but her example, added to the rhetoric of Montraville, would persuade Charlotte to go with them.

Charlotte had, when she went out to meet Montraville, flattered herself that her resolution was not to be shaken, and that, conscious of the impropriety of her conduct in having a clandestine intercourse with a stranger, she would never repeat the indiscretion.

But alas! poor Charlotte, she knew not the deceitfulness of her own heart, or she would have avoided the trial of her stability.

Montraville was tender, eloquent, ardent, and yet respectful. "Shall I not see you once more," said he, "before I leave England? will you not bless me by an assurance, that when we are divided by a vast expanse of sea I shall not be forgotten?"

Charlotte sighed.

"Why that sigh, my dear Charlotte? could I flatter myself that a fear for my safety, or a wish for my welfare occasioned it, how happy would it make me."

"I shall ever wish you well, Montraville," said she; "but we must meet no more."

"Oh say not so, my lovely girl: reflect, that when I leave my native land, perhaps a few short weeks may terminate my existence; the perils of the ocean—the dangers of war —"

"I can hear no more," said Charlotte in a tremulous voice. "I must leave you."

"Say you will see me once again."

"I dare not," said she.

"Only for one half hour to-morrow evening: 'tis my last request. I shall never trouble you again, Charlotte."

"I know not what to say," cried Charlotte, struggling to draw her hands from him: "let me leave you now."

"And you will come to-morrow," said Montraville.

"Perhaps I may," said she.

"Adieu then. I will live upon that hope till we meet again."

He kissed her hand. She sighed an adieu, and catching hold of Mademoiselle's arm, hastily entered the garden gate.

Chapter X

When We Have Excited Curiosity, It Is but an Act of Good Nature to Gratify It

MONTRAVILLE was the youngest son of a gentleman of fortune, whose family being numerous, he was obliged to bring up his sons to genteel professions, by the exercise of which they might hope to raise themselves into notice.

"My daughters," said he, "have been educated like gentlewomen; and should I die before they are settled, they must have some provision made, to place them above the snares and temptations which vice ever holds out to the elegant, accomplished female, when oppressed by the frowns of poverty and the sting of dependance: my boys, with only moderate incomes, when placed in the church, at the bar, or in the field, may exert their talents, make themselves friends, and raise their fortunes on the basis of merit."

When Montraville chose the profession of arms, his father presented him with a commission, and made him a handsome provision for his private purse. "Now, my boy," said he, "go! seek glory in the field of battle. You have received from me all I shall ever have it in my power to bestow: it is certain I have interest to gain you promotion; but be assured that interest shall never be exerted, unless by your future conduct you deserve it. Remember, therefore, your success in life depends entirely on yourself. There is one thing I think it my duty to caution you against; the precipitancy with which young men frequently rush into matrimonial engagements, and by their thoughtlessness draw many a deserving woman into scenes of poverty and distress. A soldier has no business to think of a wife till his rank is such as to place him above the fear of bringing into the world a train of helpless innocents, heirs only to penury and affliction. If, indeed, a woman, "whose fortune is sufficient to preserve you in that state of independence I would teach you to prize, should generously bestow herself on a young soldier, whose chief hope of future prosperity depended on his success in the field—if such a woman should offer—every barrier is removed, and I should rejoice in an union which would promise so much felicity. But mark me, boy, if, on the contrary, you rush into a precipitate union with a girl of little or no fortune, take the poor creature from a comfortable home and kind friends, and plunge her into all the evils a narrow income and increasing family can inflict, I will leave you to enjoy the blessed fruits of your rashness; for by all that is sacred, neither my interest or fortune shall ever be exerted in your favour. I am serious," continued he, "therefore imprint this conversation on your memory, and let it influence your future conduct. Your happiness will always be dear to me; and I wish to warn you of a rock on which the peace of many an honest fellow has been wrecked; for believe me, the difficulties and dangers of the longest winter campaign are much easier to be borne, than the pangs that would seize your heart, when you beheld the woman of your choice, the children of your affection, involved in penury and distress, and reflected that it was your own folly and precipitancy had been the prime cause of their sufferings."

As this conversation passed but a few hours before Montraville took leave of his father, it was deeply impressed on his mind: when, therefore, Belcour came with him to the place of assignation with Charlotte, he directed him to enquire of the French woman what were Miss Temple's expectations in regard to fortune.

Mademoiselle informed him, that though Charlotte's father possessed a genteel independence, it was by no means probable that he could give his daughter more than a thousand pounds; and in case she did not marry to his liking, it was possible he might not give her a single *sous*; nor did it appear the least likely, that Mr. Temple would agree to her union with a young man on the point of embarking for the feat of war.

Montraville therefore concluded it was impossible he should ever marry Charlotte Temple; and what end he proposed to himself by continuing the acquaintance he had commenced with her, he did not at that moment give himself time to enquire.

Chapter **XI**

Conflict of Love and Duty

ALMOST a week was now gone, and Charlotte continued every evening to meet Montraville, and in her heart every meeting was resolved to be the last; but alas! when Montraville at parting would earnestly intreat one more interview, that treacherous heart betrayed her; and, forgetful of its resolution, pleaded the cause of the enemy so powerfully, that Charlotte was unable to resist. Another and another meeting succeeded; and so well did Montraville improve each opportunity, that the heedless girl at length confessed no idea could be so painful to her as that of never seeing him again.

"Then we will never be parted," said he.

"Ah, Montraville," replied Charlotte, forcing a smile, "how can it be avoided? My parents would never consent to our union; and even could they be brought to approve it, how should I bear to be separated from my kind, my beloved mother?"

"Then you love your parents more than you do me, Charlotte?"

"I hope I do," said she, blushing and looking down, "I hope my affection for them will ever keep me from infringing the laws of filial duty."

"Well, Charlotte," said Montraville gravely, and letting go her hand, "since that is the case, I find I have deceived myself with fallacious hopes. I had flattered my fond heart, that I was dearer to Charlotte than any thing in the world beside. I thought that you would for my sake have braved the dangers of the ocean, that you would, by your affection and smiles, have softened the hardships of war, and, had it been my fate to fall, that your tenderness would chear the hour of death, and smooth my passage to another world. But farewel, Charlotte! I see you never loved me. I shall now welcome the friendly ball that deprives me of the sense of my misery."

"Oh stay, unkind Montraville," cried she, catching hold of his arm, as he pretended to leave her, "stay, and to calm your fears, I will here protest that was it not for the fear of giving pain to the best of parents, and returning their kindness with ingratitude, I would follow you through every danger, and, in studying to promote your happiness, insure my own. But I cannot break my mother's heart, Montraville; I must not bring the grey hairs of my doating grand-father with sorrow to the grave, or make my beloved father perhaps curse the hour that gave me birth." She covered her face with her hands, and burst into tears.

"All these distressing scenes, my dear Charlotte," cried Montraville, "are merely the chimeras of a disturbed fancy. Your parents might perhaps grieve at first; but when they heard from your own hand that you was with a man of honour, and that it was to insure your felicity by an union with him, to which you feared they would never have given their assent, that you left their protection, they will, be assured, forgive an error which love alone occasioned, and when we return from America, receive you with open arms and tears of joy."

Belcour and Mademoiselle heard this last speech, and conceiving it a proper time to throw in their advice and persuasions, approached Charlotte, and so well seconded the entreaties of Montraville, that finding Mademoiselle intended going with Belcour, and feeling her own treacherous heart too much inclined to accompany them, the hapless Charlotte, in an evil hour, consented that the next evening they should bring a chaise[3] to the end of the town, and that she would leave her friends, and throw herself entirely on the protection of Montraville. "But should you," said she, looking earnestly at him, her eyes full of tears, "should you, forgetful of your promises, and repenting the engagements you here voluntarily enter into, forsake and leave me on a foreign shore –"

"Judge not so meanly of me," said he. "The moment we reach our place of destination, Hymen shall sanctify our love; and when I shall forget your goodness, may heaven forget me."

"Ah," said Charlotte, leaning on Mademoiselle's arm as they walked up the garden together, "I have forgot all that I ought to have remembered, in consenting to this intended elopement."

"You are a strange girl," said Mademoiselle: "you never know your own mind two minutes at a time. Just now you declared Montraville's happiness was what you prized most in the world; and now I suppose you repent having insured that happiness by agreeing to accompany him abroad."

"Indeed I do repent," replied Charlotte, "from my soul: but while discretion points out the impropriety of my conduct, inclination urges me on to ruin."

"Ruin! fiddlestick!" said Mademoiselle; "am I not going with you? and do I feel any of these qualms?"

"You do not renounce a tender father and mother," said Charlotte.

"But I hazard my dear reputation," replied Mademoiselle, bridling.

"True," replied Charlotte, "but you do not feel what I do." She then bade her good night: but sleep was a stranger to her eyes, and the tear of anguish watered her pillow.

Chapter XII

Nature's last, best gift:
Creature in whom excell'd, whatever could
To sight or thought be nam'd!
Holy, divine! good, amiable, and sweet!
How thou art fall'n!—

WHEN Charlotte left her restless bed, her languid eye and pale cheek discovered to Madame Du Pont the little repose she had tasted.

"My dear child," said the affectionate governess, "what is the cause of the languor so apparent in your frame? Are you not well?"

"Yes, my dear Madam, very well," replied Charlotte, attempting to smile, "but I know not how it was; I could not sleep last night, and my spirits are depressed this morning."

"Come chear up, my love," said the governess; "I believe I have brought a cordial to revive them. I have just received a letter from your good mama, and here is one for yourself."

---

3 A light, open-air carriage, often drawn by a single horse.

Charlotte hastily took the letter: it contained these words—

"As to-morrow is the anniversary of the happy day that gave my beloved girl to the anxious wishes of a maternal heart, I have requested your governess to let you come home and spend it with us; and as I know you to be a good affectionate child, and make it your study to improve in those branches of education which you know will give most pleasure to your delighted parents, as a reward for your diligence and attention I have prepared an agreeable surprise for your reception. Your grand-father, eager to embrace the darling of his aged heart, will come in the chaise for you; so hold yourself in readiness to attend him by nine o'clock. Your dear father joins in every tender wish for your health and future felicity, which warms the heart of my dear Charlotte's affectionate mother,

L. Temple."

"Gracious heaven!" cried Charlotte, forgetting where she was, and raising her streaming eyes as in earnest supplication.

Madame Du Pont was surprised. "Why these tears, my love?" said she. "Why this seeming agitation? I thought the letter would have rejoiced, instead of distressing you."

"It does rejoice me," replied Charlotte, endeavouring at composure, "but I was praying for merit to deserve the unremitted attentions of the best of parents."

"You do right," said Madame Du Pont, "to ask the assistance of heaven that you may continue to deserve their love. Continue, my dear Charlotte, in the course you have ever pursued, and you will insure at once their happiness and your own."

"Oh!" cried Charlotte, as her governess left her, "I have forfeited both for ever! Yet let me reflect:—the irrevocable step is not yet taken: it is not too late to recede from the brink of a precipice, from which I can only behold the dark abyss of ruin, shame, and remorse!"

She arose from her seat, and flew to the apartment of La Rue. "Oh Mademoiselle!" said she, "I am snatched by a miracle from destruction! This letter has saved me: it has opened my eyes to the folly I was so near committing. I will not go, Mademoiselle; I will not wound the hearts of those dear parents who make my happiness the whole study of their lives."

"Well," said Mademoiselle, "do as you please, Miss; but pray understand that my resolution is taken, and it is not in your power to alter it. I shall meet the gentlemen at the appointed hour, and shall not be surprized at any outrage which Montraville may commit, when he finds himself disappointed. Indeed I should not be astonished, was he to come immediately here, and reproach you for your instability in the hearing of the whole school: and what will be the consequence? you will bear the odium of having formed the resolution of eloping, and every girl of spirit will laugh at your want of fortitude to put it in execution, while prudes and fools will load you with reproach and contempt. You will have lost the confidence of your parents, incurred their anger, and the scoffs of the world; and what fruit do you expect to reap from this piece of heroism, (for such no doubt you think it is?) you will have the pleasure to reflect, that you have deceived the man who adores you, and whom in your heart you prefer to all other men, and that you are separated from him for ever."

This eloquent harangue was given with such volubility, that Charlotte could not find an opportunity to interrupt her, or to offer a single word till the whole was finished, and then found her ideas so confused, that she knew not what to say.

At length she determined that she would go with Mademoiselle to the place of assig-nation, convince Montraville of the necessity of adhering to the resolution of remaining behind; assure him of her affection, and bid him adieu.

Charlotte formed this plan in her mind, and exulted in the certainty of its success. "How shall I rejoice," said she, "in this triumph of reason over inclination, and, when in the arms of my affectionate parents, lift up my soul in gratitude to heaven as I look back on the dangers I have escaped!"

The hour of assignation arrived: Mademoiselle put what money and valuables she pos-sessed in her pocket, and advised Charlotte to do the same; but she refused; "my resolution is fixed," said she; "I will sacrifice love to duty."

Mademoiselle smiled internally; and they proceeded softly down the back stairs and out of the garden gate. Montraville and Belcour were ready to receive them.

"Now," said Montraville, taking Charlotte in his arms, "you are mine for ever."

"No," said she, withdrawing from his embrace, "I am come to take an everlasting farewel."

It would be useless to repeat the conversation that here ensued; suffice it to say, that Montraville used every argument that had formerly been successful, Charlotte's resolution began to waver, and he drew her almost imperceptibly towards the chaise.

"I cannot go," said she: "cease, dear Montraville, to persuade. I must not: religion, duty, forbid."

"Cruel Charlotte," said he, "if you disappoint my ardent hopes, by all that is sacred, this hand shall put a period to my existence. I cannot—will not live without you."

"Alas! my torn heart!" said Charlotte, "how shall I act?"

"Let me direct you," said Montraville, lifting her into the chaise.

"Oh! my dear forsaken parents!" cried Charlotte.

The chaise drove off. She shrieked, and fainted into the arms of her betrayer.

Chapter XIII

Cruel Disappointment

"WHAT pleasure," cried Mr. Eldridge, as he stepped into the chaise to go for his grand-daughter, "what pleasure expands the heart of an old man when he beholds the progeny of a beloved child growing up in every virtue that adorned the minds of her parents. I foolishly thought, some few years since, that every sense of joy was buried in the graves of my dear partner and my son; but my Lucy, by her filial affection, soothed my soul to peace, and this dear Charlotte has twined herself round my heart, and opened such new scenes of delight to my view, that I almost forget I have ever been unhappy."

When the chaise stopped, he alighted with the alacrity of youth; so much do the emo-tions of the soul influence the body.

It was half past eight o'clock; the ladies were assembled in the school room, and Madame Du Pont was preparing to offer the morning sacrifice of prayer and praise, when it was discovered, that Mademoiselle and Charlotte were missing.

"She is busy, no doubt," said the governess, "in preparing Charlotte for her little excur-sion; but pleasure should never make us forget our duty to our Creator. Go, one of you, and bid them both attend prayers."

The lady who went to summon them, soon returned, and informed the governess, that the room was locked, and that she had knocked repeatedly, but obtained no answer. "Good heaven!" cried Madame Du Pont, "this is very strange:" and turning pale with terror, she went hastily to the door, and ordered it to be forced open. The apartment instantly discovered, that no person had been in it the preceding night, the beds appearing as though just made. The house was instantly a scene of confusion: the garden, the pleasure grounds were searched to no purpose, every apartment rang with the names of Miss Temple and Mademoiselle; but they were too distant to hear; and every face wore the marks of disappointment.

Mr. Eldridge was sitting in the parlour, eagerly expecting his grand-daughter to descend, ready equipped for her journey: he heard the confusion that reigned in the house; he heard the name of Charlotte frequently repeated. "What can be the matter?" said he, rising and opening the door: "I fear some accident has befallen my dear girl."

The governess entered. The visible agitation of her countenance discovered that something extraordinary had happened.

"Where is Charlotte?" said he, "Why does not my child come to welcome her doating parent?"

"Be composed, my dear Sir," said Madame Du Pont, "do not frighten yourself unnecessarily. She is not in the house at present; but as Mademoiselle is undoubtedly with her, she will speedily return in safety; and I hope they will both be able to account for this unseasonable absence in such a manner as shall remove our present uneasiness."

"Madam," cried the old man, with an angry look, "has my child been accustomed to go out without leave, with no other company or protector than that French woman. Pardon me, Madam, I mean no reflections on your country, but I never did like Mademoiselle La Rue; I think she was a very improper person to be entrusted with the care of such a girl as Charlotte Temple, or to be suffered to take her from under your immediate protection."

"You wrong me, Mr. Eldridge," replied she, "if you suppose I have ever permitted your grand-daughter to go out unless with the other ladies. I would to heaven I could form any probable conjecture concerning her absence this morning, but it is a mystery which her return can alone unravel."

Servants were now dispatched to every place where there was the least hope of hearing any tidings of the fugitives, but in vain. Dreadful were the hours of horrid suspense which Mr. Eldridge passed till twelve o'clock, when that suspense was reduced to a shocking certainty, and every spark of hope which till then they had indulged, was in a moment extinguished.

Mr. Eldridge was preparing, with a heavy heart, to return to his anxiously-expecting children, when Madame Du Pont received the following note without either name or date.

"Miss Temple is well, and wishes to relieve the anxiety of her parents, by letting them know she has voluntarily put herself under the protection of a man whose future study shall be to make her happy. Pursuit is needless; the measures taken to avoid discovery are too effectual to be eluded. When she thinks her friends are reconciled to this precipitate step, they may perhaps be informed of her place of residence. Mademoiselle is with her."

As Madame Du Pont read these cruel lines, she turned pale as ashes, her limbs trembled, and she was forced to call for a glass of water. She loved Charlotte truly; and when she reflected on the innocence and gentleness of her disposition, she concluded that it must have been the advice and machinations of La Rue, which led her to this imprudent action;

she recollected her agitation at the receipt of her mother's letter, and saw in it the conflict of her mind.

"Does that letter relate to Charlotte?" said Mr. Eldridge, having waited some time in expectation of Madame Du Pont's speaking.

"It does," said she. "Charlotte is well, but cannot return today."

"Not return, Madam? where is she? who will detain her from her fond, expecting parents?"

"You distract me with these questions, Mr. Eldridge. Indeed I know not where she is, or who has seduced her from her duty."

The whole truth now rushed at once upon Mr. Eldridge's mind. "She has eloped then," said he. "My child is betrayed; the darling, the comfort of my aged heart, is lost. Oh would to heaven I had died but yesterday."

A violent gush of grief in some measure relieved him, and, after several vain attempts, he at length assumed sufficient composure to read the note.

"And how shall I return to my children?" said he: "how approach that mansion, so late the habitation of peace? Alas! my dear Lucy, how will you support these heart-rending tidings? or how shall I be enabled to console you, who need so much consolation myself?"

The old man returned to the chaise, but the light step and chearful countenance were no more; sorrow filled his heart, and guided his motions; he seated himself in the chaise, his venerable head reclined upon his bosom, his hands were folded, his eye fixed on vacancy, and the large drops of sorrow rolled silently down his cheeks. There was a mixture of anguish and resignation depicted in his countenance, as if he would say, henceforth who shall dare to boast his happiness, or even in idea contemplate his treasure, lest, in the very moment his heart is exulting in its own felicity, the object which constitutes that felicity should be torn from him.

Chapter XIV

Maternal Sorrow

SLOW and heavy passed the time while the carriage was conveying Mr. Eldridge home; and yet when he came in sight of the house, he wished a longer reprieve from the dreadful task of informing Mr. and Mrs. Temple of their daughter's elopement.

It is easy to judge the anxiety of these affectionate parents, when they found the return of their father delayed so much beyond the expected time. They were now met in the dining parlour, and several of the young people who had been invited were already arrived. Each different part of the company was employed in the same manner, looking out at the windows which faced the road. At length the long-expected chaise appeared. Mrs. Temple ran out to receive and welcome her darling: her young companions flocked round the door, each one eager to give her joy on the return of her birth-day. The door of the chaise was opened: Charlotte was not there. "Where is my child?" cried Mrs. Temple, in breathless agitation.

Mr. Eldridge could not answer: he took hold of his daughter's hand and led her into the house; and sinking on the first chair he came to, burst into tears, and sobbed aloud.

"She is dead," cried Mrs. Temple. "Oh my dear Charlotte!" and clasping her hands in an agony of distress, fell into strong hysterics.

Mr. Temple, who had stood speechless with surprize and fear, now ventured to enquire if indeed his Charlotte was no more. Mr. Eldridge led him into another apartment; and putting the fatal note into his hand, cried—"Bear it like a Christian," and turned from him, endeavouring to suppress his own too visible emotions.

It would be vain to attempt describing what Mr. Temple felt whilst he hastily ran over the dreadful lines: when he had finished, the paper dropt from his unnerved hand. "Gracious heaven!" said he, "could Charlotte act thus?" Neither tear nor sigh escaped him; and he sat the image of mute sorrow, till roused from his stupor by the repeated shrieks of Mrs. Temple. He rose hastily, and rushing into the apartment where she was, folded his arms about her, and saying—"Let us be patient, my dear Lucy," nature relieved his almost bursting heart by a friendly gush of tears.

Should any one, presuming on his own philosophic temper, look with an eye of contempt on the man who could indulge a woman's weakness, let him remember that man was a father, and he will then pity the misery which wrung those drops from a noble, generous heart.

Mrs. Temple beginning to be a little more composed, but still imagining her child was dead, her husband, gently taking her hand, cried—"You are mistaken, my love. Charlotte is not dead."

"Then she is very ill, else why did she not come? But I will go to her: the chaise is still at the door: let me go instantly to the dear girl. If I was ill, she would fly to attend me, to alleviate my sufferings, and chear me with her love."

"Be calm, my dearest Lucy, and I will tell you all," said Mr. Temple. "You must not go, indeed you must not; it will be of no use."

"Temple," said she, assuming a look of firmness and composure, "tell me the truth I beseech you. I cannot bear this dreadful suspense. What misfortune has befallen my child? Let me know the worst, and I will endeavour to bear it as I ought."

"Lucy," replied Mr. Temple, "imagine your daughter alive, and in no danger of death: what misfortune would you then dread?"

"There is one misfortune which is worse than death. But I know my child too well to suspect—"

"Be not too confident, Lucy."

"Oh heavens!" said she, "what horrid images do you start: is it possible she should forget—"

"She has forgot us all, my love; she has preferred the love of a stranger to the affectionate protection of her friends."

"Not eloped?" cried she eagerly.

Mr. Temple was silent.

"You cannot contradict it," said she. "I see my fate in those tearful eyes. Oh Charlotte! Charlotte! how ill have you requited our tenderness! But, Father of Mercies," continued she, sinking on her knees, and raising her streaming eyes and clasped hands to heaven, "this once vouchsafe to hear a fond, a distracted mother's prayer. Oh let thy bounteous Providence watch over and protect the dear thoughtless girl, save her from the miseries which I fear will be her portion, and oh! of thine infinite mercy, make her not a mother, lest she should one day feel what I now suffer."

The last words faultered on her tongue, and she fell fainting into the arms of her husband, who had involuntarily dropped on his knees beside her.

A mother's anguish, when disappointed in her tenderest hopes, none but a mother can conceive. Yet, my dear young readers, I would have you read this scene with attention, and reflect that you may yourselves one day be mothers. Oh my friends, as you value your eternal happiness, wound not, by thoughtless ingratitude, the peace of the mother who bore you: remember the tenderness, the care, the unremitting anxiety with which she has attended to all your wants and wishes from earliest infancy to the present day; behold the mild ray of affectionate applause that beams from her eye on the performance of your duty: listen to her reproofs with silent attention; they proceed from a heart anxious for your future felicity: you must love her; nature, all-powerful nature, has planted the seeds of filial affection in your bosoms.

Then once more read over the sorrows of poor Mrs. Temple, and remember, the mother whom you so dearly love and venerate will feel the same, when you, forgetful of the respect due to your maker and yourself, forsake the paths of virtue for those of vice and folly.

Chapter XV

Embarkation

IT was with the utmost difficulty that the united efforts of Mademoiselle and Montraville could support Charlotte's spirits during their short ride from Chichester to Portsmouth, where a boat waited to take them immediately on board the ship in which they were to embark for America.

As soon as she became tolerably composed, she entreated pen and ink to write to her parents. This she did in the most affecting, artless manner, entreating their pardon and blessing, and describing the dreadful situation of her mind, the conflict she suffered in endeavouring to conquer this unfortunate attachment, and concluded with saying, her only hope of future comfort consisted in the (perhaps delusive) idea she indulged, of being once more folded in their protecting arms, and hearing the words of peace and pardon from their lips.

The tears streamed incessantly while she was writing, and she was frequently obliged to lay down her pen: but when the task was completed, and she had committed the letter to the care of Montraville to be sent to the post office, she became more calm, and indulging the delightful hope of soon receiving an answer that would seal her pardon, she in some measure assumed her usual chearfulness.

But Montraville knew too well the consequences that must unavoidably ensue, should this letter reach Mr. Temple: he therefore wisely resolved to walk on the deck, tear it in pieces, and commit the fragments to the care of Neptune, who might or might not, as it suited his convenience, convey them on shore.

All Charlotte's hopes and wishes were now concentred in one, namely that the fleet might be detained at Spithead till she could receive a letter from her friends: but in this she was disappointed, for the second morning after she went on board, the signal was made, the fleet weighed anchor, and in a few hours (the wind being favourable) they bid adieu to the white cliffs of Albion.

In the mean time every enquiry that could be thought of was made by Mr. and Mrs. Temple; for many days did they indulge the fond hope that she was merely gone off to be married, and that when the indissoluble knot was once tied, she would return with the partner she had chosen, and entreat their blessing and forgiveness.

"And shall we not forgive her?" said Mr. Temple.

"Forgive her!" exclaimed the mother. "Oh yes, whatever be our errors, is she not our child? and though bowed to the earth even with shame and remorse, is it not our duty to raise the poor penitent, and whisper peace and comfort to her desponding soul? would she but return, with rapture would I fold her to my heart, and bury every remembrance of her faults in the dear embrace."

But still day after day passed on, and Charlotte did not appear, nor were any tidings to be heard of her: yet each rising morning was welcomed by some new hope—the evening brought with it disappointment. At length hope was no more; despair usurped her place; and the mansion which was once the mansion of peace, became the habitation of pale, dejected melancholy.

The chearful smile that was wont to adorn the face of Mrs. Temple was fled, and had it not been for the support of unaffected piety, and a consciousness of having ever set before her child the fairest example, she must have sunk under this heavy affliction.

"Since," said she, "the severest scrutiny cannot charge me with any breach of duty to have deserved this severe chastisement, I will bow before the power who inflicts it with humble resignation to his will; nor shall the duty of a wife be totally absorbed in the feelings of the mother; I will endeavour to appear more chearful, and by appearing in some measure to have conquered my own sorrow, alleviate the sufferings of my husband, and rouse him from that torpor into which this misfortune has plunged him. My father too demands my care and attention: I must not, by a selfish indulgence of my own grief, forget the interest those two dear objects take in my happiness or misery: I will wear a smile on my face, though the thorn rankles in my heart; and if by so doing, I in the smallest degree contribute to restore their peace of mind, I shall be amply rewarded for the pain the concealment of my own feelings may occasion.

Thus argued this excellent woman: and in the execution of so laudable a resolution we shall leave her, to follow the fortunes of the hapless victim of imprudence and evil counsellors.

Chapter XVI

Necessary Digression

ON board of the ship in which Charlotte and Mademoiselle were embarked, was an officer of large unincumbered fortune and elevated rank, and whom I shall call Crayton.

He was one of those men, who, having travelled in their youth, pretend to have contracted a peculiar fondness for every thing foreign, and to hold in contempt the productions of their own country; and this affected partiality extended even to the women.

With him therefore the blushing modesty and unaffected simplicity of Charlotte passed unnoticed; but the forward pertness of La Rue, the freedom of her conversation, the elegance of her person, mixed with a certain engaging *je ne sais quoi,* perfectly enchanted him.

The reader no doubt has already developed the character of La Rue: designing, artful, and selfish, she had accepted the devoirs of Belcour because she was heartily weary of the retired life she led at the school, wished to be released from what she deemed a slavery, and to return to that vortex of folly and dissipation which had once plunged her into the deepest misery; but her plan she flattered herself was now better formed: she resolved to put herself under the protection of no man till she had first secured a settlement; but the clandestine manner in which she left Madame Du Pont's prevented her putting this plan in execution, though Belcour solemnly protested he would make her a handsome settlement the moment they arrived at Portsmouth. This he afterwards contrived to evade by a pretended hurry of business; La Rue readily conceiving he never meant to fulfil his promise, determined to change her battery, and attack the heart of Colonel Crayton. She soon discovered the partiality he entertained for her nation; and having imposed on him a feigned tale of distress, representing Belcour as a villain who had seduced her from her friends under promise of marriage, and afterwards betrayed her, pretending great remorse for the errors she had committed, and declaring whatever her affection for Belcour might have been, it was now entirely extinguished, and she wished for nothing more than an opportunity to leave a course of life which her soul abhorred; but she had no friends to apply to, they had all renounced her, and guilt and misery would undoubtedly be her future portion through life.

Crayton was possessed of many amiable qualities, though the peculiar trait in his character, which we have already mentioned, in a great measure threw a shade over them. He was beloved for his humanity and benevolence by all who knew him, but he was easy and unsuspicious himself, and became a dupe to the artifice of others.

He was, when very young, united to an amiable Parisian lady, and perhaps it was his affection for her that laid the foundation for the partiality he ever retained for the whole nation. He had by her one daughter, who entered into the world but a few hours before her mother left it. This lady was universally beloved and admired, being endowed with all the virtues of her mother, without the weakness of the father: she was married to Major Beauchamp, and was at this time in the same fleet with her father, attending her husband to New-York.

Crayton was melted by the affected contrition and distress of La Rue: he would converse with her for hours, read to her, play cards with her, listen to all her complaints, and promise to protect her to the utmost of his power. La Rue easily saw his character; her sole aim was to awaken a passion in his bosom that might turn out to her advantage, and in this aim she was but too successful, for before the voyage was finished, the infatuated Colonel gave her from under his hand a promise of marriage on their arrival at New-York, under forfeiture of five thousand pounds.

And how did our poor Charlotte pass her time during a tedious and tempestuous passage? naturally delicate, the fatigue and sickness which she endured rendered her so weak as to be almost entirely confined to her bed: yet the kindness and attention of Montraville in some measure contributed to alleviate her sufferings, and the hope of hearing from her friends soon after her arrival, kept up her spirits, and cheered many a gloomy hour.

But during the voyage a great revolution took place not only in the fortune of La Rue but in the bosom of Belcour: whilst in pursuit of his amour with Mademoiselle, he had attended little to the interesting, inobtrusive charms of Charlotte, but when, cloyed by possession, and disgusted with the art and dissimulation of one, he beheld the simplicity and gentleness of the other, the contrast became too striking not to fill him at once with surprise and admiration. He frequently conversed with Charlotte; he found her sensible, well informed, but diffident and unassuming. The languor which the fatigue of her body and perturbation of her mind spread over her delicate features, served only in his opinion to render her more lovely: he knew that Montraville did not design to marry her, and he formed a resolution to endeavour to gain her himself whenever Montraville should leave her.

Let not the reader imagine Belcour's designs were honourable. Alas! when once a woman has forgot the respect due to herself, by yielding to the solicitations of illicit love, they lose all their consequence, even in the eyes of the man whose art has betrayed them, and for whose sake they have sacrificed every valuable consideration.

The heedless Fair, who stoops to guilty joys,
A man may pity—but he must despise.

Nay, every libertine will think he has a right to insult her with his licentious passion; and should the unhappy creature shrink from the insolent overture, he will sneeringly taunt her with pretence of modesty.

Chapter XVII

A Wedding

ON the day before their arrival at New-York, after dinner, Crayton arose from his seat, and placing himself by Mademoiselle, thus addressed the company—

"As we are now nearly arrived at our destined port, I think it but my duty to inform you, my friends, that this lady," (taking her hand,) "has placed herself under my protection. I have seen and severely felt the anguish of her heart, and through every shade which cruelty or malice may throw over her, can discover the most amiable qualities. I thought it but necessary to mention my esteem for her before our disembarkation, as it is my fixed resolution, the morning after we land, to give her an undoubted title to my favour and protection by honourably uniting my fate to hers. I would wish every gentleman here therefore to remember that her honour henceforth is mine, and," continued he, looking at Belcour, "should any man presume to speak in the least disrespectfully of her, I shall not hesitate to pronounce him a scoundrel."

Belcour cast at him a smile of contempt, and bowing profoundly low, wished Mademoiselle much joy in the proposed union; and assuring the Colonel that he need not be in the least apprehensive of any one throwing the least odium on the character of his lady, shook him by the hand with ridiculous gravity, and left the cabin.

The truth was, he was glad to be rid of La Rue, and so he was but freed from her, he cared not who fell a victim to her infamous arts.

The inexperienced Charlotte was astonished at what she heard. She thought La Rue had, like herself, only been urged by the force of her attachment to Belcour, to quit her friends, and follow him to the feat of war: how wonderful then, that she should resolve to marry another man. It was certainly extremely wrong. It was indelicate. She mentioned her thoughts to Montraville. He laughed at her simplicity, called her a little ideot, and patting her on the cheek, said she knew nothing of the world. "If the world sanctifies such things, 'tis a very bad world I think," said Charlotte. "Why I always understood they were to have been married when they arrived at New-York. I am sure Mademoiselle told me Belcour promised to marry her."

"Well, and suppose he did?"

"Why, he should be obliged to keep his word I think."

"Well, but I suppose he has changed his mind," said Montraville, "and then you know the case is altered."

Charlotte looked at him attentively for a moment. A full sense of her own situation rushed upon her mind. She burst into tears, and remained silent. Montraville too well understood the cause of her tears. He kissed her cheek, and bidding her not make herself uneasy, unable to bear the silent but keen remonstrance, hastily left her.

The next morning by sun-rise they found themselves at anchor before the city of New-York. A boat was ordered to convey the ladies on shore. Crayton accompanied them;

and they were shewn to a house of public entertainment. Scarcely were they seated when the door opened, and the Colonel found himself in the arms of his daughter, who had landed a few minutes before him. The first transport of meeting subsided, Crayton introduced his daughter to Mademoiselle La Rue, as an old friend of her mother's, (for the artful French woman had really made it appear to the credulous Colonel that she was in the same convent with his first wife, and, though much younger, had received many tokens of her esteem and regard.)

"If, Mademoiselle," said Mrs. Beauchamp, "you were the friend of my mother, you must be worthy the esteem of all good hearts."

"Mademoiselle will soon honour our family," said Crayton, "by supplying the place that valuable woman filled: and as you are married, my dear, I think you will not blame—"

"Hush, my dear Sir," replied Mrs. Beauchamp: "I know my duty too well to scrutinize your conduct. Be assured, my dear father, your happiness is mine. I shall rejoice in it, and sincerely love the person who contributes to it. But tell me," continued she, turning to Charlotte, "who is this lovely girl? Is she your sister, Mademoiselle?"

A blush, deep as the glow of the carnation, suffused the cheeks of Charlotte.

"It is a young lady," replied the Colonel, "who came in the same vessel with us from England." He then drew his daughter aside, and told her in a whisper, Charlotte was the mistress of Montraville.

"What a pity!" said Mrs. Beauchamp softly, (casting a most compassionate glance at her.) "But surely her mind is not depraved. The goodness of her heart is depicted in her ingenuous countenance."

"Charlotte caught the word pity. "And am I already fallen so low?" said she. A sigh escaped her, and a tear was ready to start, but Montraville appeared, and she checked the rising emotion. Mademoiselle went with the Colonel and his daughter to another apartment. Charlotte remained with Montraville and Belcour. The next morning the Colonel performed his promise, and La Rue became in due form Mrs. Crayton, exulted in her own good fortune, and dared to look with an eye of contempt on the unfortunate but far less guilty Charlotte.

END OF THE FIRST VOLUME.

Charlotte Temple, Volume II

Chapter XVIII

Reflections

"AND am I indeed fallen so low," said Charlotte, "as to be only pitied? Will the voice of approbation no more meet my ear? and shall I never again possess a friend, whose face will wear a smile of joy whenever I approach? Alas! how thoughtless, how dreadfully imprudent have I been! I know not which is most painful to endure, the sneer of contempt, or the glance of compassion, which is depicted in the various countenances of my own sex: they are both equally humiliating. Ah! my dear parents, could you now see the child of your affections, the daughter whom you so dearly loved, a poor solitary being, without society, here wearing out her heavy hours in deep regret and anguish of heart, no kind friend of her own sex to whom she can unbosom her griefs, no beloved mother, no woman of character will appear in my company, and low as your Charlotte is fallen, she cannot associate with infamy."

These were the painful reflections which occupied the mind of Charlotte. Montraville had placed her in a small house a few miles from New-York: he gave her one female attendant, and supplied her with what money she wanted; but business and pleasure so entirely occupied his time, that he had little to devote to the woman, whom he had brought from all her connections, and robbed of innocence. Sometimes, indeed, he would steal out at the close of evening, and pass a few hours with her; and then so much was she attached to him, that all her sorrows were forgotten while blest with his society: she would enjoy a walk by moonlight, or sit by him in a little arbour at the bottom of the garden, and play on the harp, accompanying it with her plaintive, harmonious voice. But often, very often, did he promise to renew his visits, and, forgetful of his promise, leave her to mourn her disappointment. What painful hours of expectation would she pass! She would sit at a window which looked toward a field he used to cross, counting the minutes, and straining her eyes to catch the first glimpse of his person, till blinded with tears of disappointment, she would lean her head on her hands, and give free vent to her sorrows: then catching at some new hope, she would again renew her watchful position, till the shades of evening enveloped every object in a dusky cloud: she would then renew her complaints, and, with a heart bursting with disappointed love and wounded sensibility, retire to a bed which remorse had strewed with thorns, and court in vain that comforter of weary nature (who seldom visits the unhappy) to come and steep her senses in oblivion.

Who can form an adequate idea of the sorrow that preyed upon the mind of Charlotte? The wife, whose breast glows with affection to her husband, and who in return meets only indifference, can but faintly conceive her anguish. Dreadfully painful is the situation of such a woman, but she has many comforts of which our poor Charlotte was deprived. The duteous, faithful wife, though treated with indifference, has one solid pleasure within her own bosom, she can reflect that she has not deserved neglect—that she has ever fulfilled the duties of her station with the strictest exactness; she may hope, by constant assiduity and unremitted attention, to recall her wanderer, and be doubly happy in his returning affection; she knows he cannot leave her to unite himself to another: he cannot cast her out to poverty and contempt; she looks around her, and sees the smile of friendly welcome, or the tear of affectionate consolation, on the face of every person whom she favours with her esteem; and from all these circumstances she gathers comfort: but the poor girl by thoughtless passion led astray, who, in parting with her honour, has forfeited the esteem of the very man to whom she has sacrificed every thing dear and valuable in life, feels his indifference in the fruit of her own folly, and laments her want of power to recall his lost affection; she knows there is no tie but honour, and that, in a man who has been guilty of seduction, is but very feeble: he may leave her in a moment to shame and want; he may marry and forsake her for ever; and should he, she has no redress, no friendly, soothing companion to pour into her wounded mind the balm of consolation, no benevolent hand to lead her back to the path of rectitude; she has disgraced her friends, forfeited the good opinion of the world, and undone herself; she feels herself a poor solitary being in the midst of surrounding multitudes; shame bows her to the earth, remorse tears her distracted mind, and guilt, poverty, and disease close the dreadful scene: she sinks unnoticed to oblivion. The finger of contempt may point out to some passing daughter of youthful mirth, the humble bed where lies this frail sister of mortality; and will she, in the unbounded gaiety of her heart, exult in her own unblemished fame, and triumph over the silent ashes of the dead? Oh no! has she a heart of sensibility, she will stop, and thus address the unhappy victim of folly—

"Thou had'st thy faults, but sure thy sufferings have expiated them: thy errors brought thee to an early grave; but thou wert a fellow-creature—thou hast been unhappy—then be those errors forgotten."

Then, as she stoops to pluck the noxious weed from off the sod, a tear will fall, and consecrate the spot to Charity.

For ever honoured be the sacred drop of humanity; the angel of mercy shall record its source, and the soul from whence it sprang shall be immortal.

My dear Madam, contract not your brow into a frown of disapprobation. I mean not to extenuate the faults of those unhappy women who fall victims to guilt and folly; but surely, when we reflect how many errors we are ourselves subject to, how many secret faults lie hid in the recesses of our hearts, which we should blush to have brought into open day (and yet those faults require the lenity and pity of a benevolent judge, or awful would be our prospect of futurity) I say, my dear Madam, when we consider this, we surely may pity the faults of others.

Believe me, many an unfortunate female, who has once strayed into the thorny paths of vice, would gladly return to virtue, was any generous friend to endeavour to raise and re-assure her; but alas! it cannot be, you say; the world would deride and scoff. Then let me tell you, Madam, 'tis a very unfeeling world, and does not deserve half the blessings which a bountiful Providence showers upon it.

Oh, thou benevolent giver of all good! how shall we erring mortals dare to look up to thy mercy in the great day of retribution, if we now uncharitably refuse to overlook the errors, or alleviate the miseries, of our fellow-creatures.

Chapter XIX

A Mistake Discovered

JULIA Franklin was the only child of a man of large property, who, at the age of eighteen, left her independent mistress of an unincumbered income of seven hundred a year; she was a girl of a lively disposition, and humane, susceptible heart: she resided in New-York with an uncle, who loved her too well, and had too high an opinion of her prudence, to scrutinize her actions so much as would have been necessary with many young ladies, who were not blest with her discretion: she was, at the time Montraville arrived at New-York, the life of society, and the universal toast. Montraville was introduced to her by the following accident.

One night when he was upon guard, a dreadful fire broke out near Mr. Franklin's house, which, in a few hours, reduced that and several others to ashes; fortunately no lives were lost, and, by the assiduity of the soldiers, much valuable property was saved from the flames. In the midst of the confusion an old gentleman came up to Montraville, and, putting a small box into his hands, cried—"Keep it, my good Sir, till I come to you again;" and then rushing again into the thickest of the croud, Montraville saw him no more. He waited till the fire was quite extinguished and the mob dispersed; but in vain: the old gentleman did not appear to claim his property; and Montraville, fearing to make any enquiry, lest he should meet with impostors who might lay claim, without any legal right, to the box, carried it to his lodgings, and locked it up: he naturally imagined, that the person who committed it to his care knew him, and would, in a day or two, reclaim it; but several weeks, passed on, and no enquiry being made, he began to be uneasy, and resolved to examine the contents of the box, and if they were, as he supposed, valuable, to spare no pains to discover, and restore them to the owner. Upon opening it, he found it contained jewels to a large amount, about two hundred pounds in money, and a miniature picture set for a bracelet. On examining the picture, he thought he had somewhere seen features very like it, but could not recollect where. A few days after, being at a public assembly, he saw Miss Franklin, and the likeness was too evident to be mistaken: he enquired among his brother officers if any of them knew her, and found one who was upon terms of intimacy in the family: "then introduce me to her immediately," said he, "for I am certain I can inform her of something which will give her peculiar pleasure."

He was immediately introduced, found she was the owner of the jewels, and was invited to breakfast the next morning in order to their restoration. This whole evening Montraville was honoured with Julia's hand; the lively sallies of her wit, the elegance of her manner, powerfully charmed him: he forgot Charlotte, and indulged himself in saying every thing that was polite and tender to Julia. But on retiring, recollection returned. "What am I about?" said he: "though I cannot marry Charlotte, I cannot be villain enough to forsake her, nor must I dare to trifle with the heart of Julia Franklin. I will return this box," said he, "which has been the source of so much uneasiness already, and in the evening pay a visit to my poor melancholy Charlotte, and endeavour to forget this fascinating Julia."

He arose, dressed himself, and taking the picture out, "I will reserve this from the rest," said he, "and by presenting it to her when she thinks it is lost, enhance the value of the obligation." He repaired to Mr. Franklin's, and found Julia in the breakfast parlour alone.

"How happy am I, Madam," said he, "that being the fortunate instrument of saving these jewels has been the means of procuring me the acquaintance of so amiable a lady. There are the jewels and money all safe."

"But where is the picture, Sir?" said Julia.

"Here, Madam. I would not willingly part with it."

"It is the portrait of my mother," said she, taking it from him: "'tis all that remains." She pressed it to her lips, and a tear trembled in her eyes. Montraville glanced his eye on her grey night gown and black ribbon, and his own feelings prevented a reply.

Julia Franklin was the very reverse of Charlotte Temple: she was tall, elegantly shaped, and possessed much of the air and manner of a woman of fashion; her complexion was a clear brown, enlivened with the glow of health, her eyes, full, black, and sparkling, darted their intelligent glances through long silken lashes; her hair was shining brown, and her features regular and striking; there was an air of innocent gaiety that played about her countenance, where good humour sat triumphant.

"I have been mistaken," said Montraville. "I imagined I loved Charlotte: but alas! I am now too late convinced my attachment to her was merely the impulse of the moment. I fear I have not only entailed lasting misery on that poor girl, but also thrown a barrier in the way of my own happiness, which it will be impossible to surmount. I feel I love Julia Franklin with ardour and sincerity; yet, when in her presence, I am sensible of my own inability to offer a heart worthy her acceptance, and remain silent."

Full of these painful thoughts, Montraville walked out to see Charlotte: she saw him approach, and ran out to meet him: she banished from her countenance the air of discontent which ever appeared when he was absent, and met him with a smile of joy.

"I thought you had forgot me, Montraville," said she, "and was very unhappy."

"I shall never forget you, Charlotte," he replied, pressing her hand.

The uncommon gravity of his countenance, and the brevity of his reply, alarmed her.

"You are not well," said she; "your hand is hot; your eyes are heavy; you are very ill."

"I am a villain," said he mentally, as he turned from her to hide his emotions.

"But come," continued she tenderly, "you shall go to bed, and I will sit by, and watch you; you will be better when you have slept."

Montraville was glad to retire, and by pretending sleep, hide the agitation of his mind from her penetrating eye. Charlotte watched by him till a late hour, and then, lying softly down by his side, sunk into a profound sleep, from whence she awoke not till late the next morning.

Chapter XX

Virtue never appears so amiable as when reaching forth
her hand to raise a fallen sister.

Chapter of Accidents.

WHEN Charlotte awoke, she missed Montraville; but thinking he might have arisen early to enjoy the beauties of the morning, she was preparing to follow him, when casting her eye on the table, she saw a note, and opening it hastily, found these words—

"My dear Charlotte must not be surprised, if she does not see me again for some time: unavoidable business will prevent me that pleasure: be assured I am quite well this morning; and what your fond imagination magnified into illness, was nothing more than fatigue, which a few hours rest has entirely removed. Make yourself happy, and be certain of the unalterable friendship of

"MONTRAVILLE."

"Friendship!" said Charlotte emphatically, as she finished the note, "is it come to this at last? Alas! poor, forsaken Charlotte, thy doom is now but too apparent. Montraville is no longer interested in thy happiness; and shame, remorse, and disappointed love will henceforth be thy only attendants."

Though these were the ideas that involuntarily rushed upon the mind of Charlotte as she perused the fatal note, yet after a few hours had elapsed, the syren[4] Hope again took possession of her bosom, and she flattered herself she could, on a second perusal, discover an air of tenderness in the few lines he had left, which at first had escaped her notice.

"He certainly cannot be so base as to leave me," said she, "and in stiling himself my friend does he not promise to protect me. I will not torment myself with these causeless fears; I will place a confidence in his honour; and sure he will not be so unjust as to abuse it."

Just as she had by this manner of reasoning brought her mind to some tolerable degree of composure, she was surprised by a visit from Belcour. The dejection visible in Charlotte's countenance, her swoln eyes and neglected attire, at once told him she was unhappy: he made no doubt but Montraville had, by his coldness, alarmed her suspicions, and was resolved, if possible, to rouse her to jealousy, urge her to reproach him, and by that means occasion a breach between them. "If I can once convince her that she has a rival," said he, "she will listen to my passion if it is only to revenge his slights." Belcour knew but little of the female heart; and what he did know was only of those of loose and dissolute lives.

---

4 Syrens (also spelled "sirens") were mythical figures in ancient Greece who would lure sailors to their death by enchanting them with their beautiful voices.

He had no idea that a woman might fall a victim to imprudence, and yet retain so strong a sense of honour, as to reject with horror and contempt every solicitation to a second fault. He never imagined that a gentle, generous female heart, once tenderly attached, when treated with unkindness might break, but would never harbour a thought of revenge.

His visit was not long, but before he went he fixed a scorpion in the heart of Charlotte, whose venom embittered every future hour of her life.

We will now return for a moment to Colonel Crayton. He had been three months married, and in that little time had discovered that the conduct of his lady was not so prudent as it ought to have been: but remonstrance was vain; her temper was violent; and to the Colonel's great misfortune he had conceived a sincere affection for her: she saw her own power, and, with the art of a Circe,[5] made every action appear to him in what light she pleased: his acquaintance laughed at his blindness, his friends pitied his infatuation, his amiable daughter, Mrs. Beauchamp, in secret deplored the loss of her father's affection, and grieved that he should be so entirely swayed by an artful, and, she much feared, infamous woman.

Mrs. Beauchamp was mild and engaging; she loved not the hurry and bustle of a city, and had prevailed on her husband to take a house a few miles from New-York. Chance led her into the same neighbourhood with Charlotte; their houses stood within a short space of each other, and their gardens joined: she had not been long in her new habitation before the figure of Charlotte struck her; she recollected her interesting features; she saw the melancholy so conspicuous in her countenance, and her heart bled at the reflection, that perhaps deprived of honour, friends, all that was valuable in life, she was doomed to linger out a wretched existence in a strange land, and sink brokenhearted into an untimely grave. "Would to heaven I could snatch her from so hard a fate," said she; "but the merciless world has barred the doors of compassion against a poor weak girl, who, perhaps, had she one kind friend to raise and reassure her, would gladly return to peace and virtue; nay, even the woman who dares to pity, and endeavour to recall a wandering sister, incurs the sneer of contempt and ridicule, for an action in which even angels are said to rejoice."

The longer Mrs. Beauchamp was a witness to the solitary life Charlotte led, the more she wished to speak to her, and often as she saw her cheeks wet with the tears of anguish, she would say—"Dear sufferer, how gladly would I pour into your heart the balm of consolation, were it not for the fear of derision."

But an accident soon happened which made her resolve to brave even the scoffs of the world, rather than not enjoy the heavenly satisfaction of comforting a desponding fellow-creature.

Mrs. Beauchamp was an early riser. She was one morning walking in the garden, leaning on her husband's arm, when the sound of a harp attracted their notice: they listened attentively, and heard a soft melodious voice distinctly sing the following stanzas:

Thou glorious orb, supremely bright,
    Just rising from the sea,
To chear all nature with thy light,
    What are thy beams to me?

---

5 In Greek mythology, Circe was a goddess of magic and transformation, able to manipulate those around her by using herbal potions.

In vain thy glories bid me rise,
    To hail the new-born day,
Alas! my morning sacrifice
    Is still to weep and pray.
For what are nature's charms combin'd,
    To one, whose weary breast
Can neither peace nor comfort find,
    Nor friend whereon to rest?
Oh! never! never! whilst I live
    Can my heart's anguish cease:
Come, friendly death, thy mandate give,
    And let me be at peace.

"'Tis poor Charlotte!" said Mrs. Beauchamp, the pellucid drop of humanity stealing down her cheek.

Captain Beauchamp was alarmed at her emotion. "What Charlotte?" said he; "do you know her?"

In the accent of a pitying angel did she disclose to her husband Charlotte's unhappy situation, and the frequent wish she had formed of being serviceable to her. "I fear," continued she, "the poor girl has been basely betrayed; and if I thought you would not blame me, I would pay her a visit, offer her my friendship, and endeavour to restore to her heart that peace she seems to have lost, and so pathetically laments. Who knows, my dear," laying her hand affectionately on his arm, "who knows but she has left some kind, affectionate parents to lament her errors, and would she return, they might with rapture receive the poor penitent, and wash away her faults in tears of joy. Oh! what a glorious reflexion would it be for me could I be the happy instrument of restoring her. Her heart may not be depraved, Beauchamp."

"Exalted woman!" cried Beauchamp, embracing her, "how dost thou rise every moment in my esteem. Follow the impulse of thy generous heart, my Emily. Let prudes and fools censure if they dare, and blame a sensibility they never felt; I will exultingly tell them that the heart that is truly virtuous is ever inclined to pity and forgive the errors of its fellow-creatures."

A beam of exulting joy played round the animated countenance of Mrs. Beauchamp, at these encomiums bestowed on her by a beloved husband, the most delightful sensations pervaded her heart, and, having breakfasted, she prepared to visit Charlotte.

Chapter XXI

Teach me to feel another's woe,
To hide the fault I see,
That mercy I to others show,
That mercy show to me.   *Pope.*[6]

WHEN Mrs. Beauchamp was dressed, she began to feel embarrassed at the thought of beginning an acquaintance with Charlotte, and was distressed how to make the first visit.

---

6 From the poem "The Universal Prayer" by Alexander Pope (1738).

"I cannot go without some introduction," said she, "it will look so like impertinent curiosity." At length recollecting herself, she stepped into the garden, and gathering a few fine cucumbers, took them in her hand by way of apology for her visit.

A glow of conscious shame vermillioned Charlotte's face as Mrs. Beauchamp entered. "You will pardon me, Madam," said she, "for not having before paid my respects to so amiable a neighbour; but we English people always keep up that reserve which is the characteristic of our nation wherever we go. I have taken the liberty to bring you a few cucumbers, for I observed you had none in your garden."

Charlotte, though naturally polite and well-bred, was so confused she could hardly speak. Her kind visitor endeavoured to relieve her by not noticing her embarrassment. "I am come, Madam," continued she, "to request you will spend the day with me. I shall be alone; and, as we are both strangers in this country, we may hereafter be extremely happy in each other's friendship."

"Your friendship, Madam," said Charlotte blushing, "is an honour to all who are favoured with it. Little as I have seen of this part of the world, I am no stranger to Mrs. Beauchamp's goodness of heart and known humanity: but my friendship—" She paused, glanced her eye upon her own visible situation, and, spite of her endeavours to suppress them, burst into tears.

Mrs. Beauchamp guessed the source from whence those tears flowed. "You seem unhappy, Madam," said she: "shall I be thought worthy your confidence? will you entrust me with the cause of your sorrow, and rest on my assurances to exert my utmost power to serve you." Charlotte returned a look of gratitude, but could not speak, and Mrs. Beauchamp continued— "My heart was interested in your behalf the first moment I saw you, and I only lament I had not made earlier overtures towards an acquaintance; but I flatter myself you will henceforth consider me as your friend."

"Oh Madam!" cried Charlotte, "I have forfeited the good opinion of all my friends; I have forsaken them, and undone myself."

"Come, come, my dear," said Mrs. Beauchamp, "you must not indulge these gloomy thoughts: you are not I hope so miserable as you imagine yourself: endeavour to be composed, and let me be favoured with your company at dinner, when, if you can bring yourself to think me your friend, and repose a confidence in me, I am ready to convince you it shall not be abused." She then arose, and bade her good morning.

At the dining hour Charlotte repaired to Mrs. Beauchamp's, and during dinner assumed as composed an aspect as possible; but when the cloth was removed, she summoned all her resolution and determined to make Mrs. Beauchamp acquainted with every circumstance preceding her unfortunate elopement, and the earnest desire she had to quit a way of life so repugnant to her feelings.

With the benignant aspect of an angel of mercy did Mrs. Beauchamp listen to the artless tale: she was shocked to the soul to find how large a share La Rue had in the seduction of this amiable girl, and a tear fell, when she reflected so vile a woman was now the wife of her father. When Charlotte had finished, she gave her a little time to collect her scattered spirits, and then asked her if she had never written to her friends. "Oh yes, Madam," said she, "frequently: but I have broke their hearts: they are either dead or have cast me off for ever, for I have never received a single line from them."

"I rather suspect," said Mrs. Beauchamp, "they have never had your letters: but suppose you were to hear from them, and they were willing to receive you, would you then leave this cruel Montraville, and return to them?"

"Would I!" said Charlotte, clasping her hands; "would not the poor sailor, tost on a tempestuous ocean, threatened every moment with death, gladly return to the shore he had left to trust to its deceitful calmness? Oh, my dear Madam, I would return, though to do it I were obliged to walk barefoot over a burning desart, and beg a scanty pittance of each traveller to support my existence. I would endure it all chearfully, could I but once more see my dear, blessed mother, hear her pronounce my pardon, and bless me before I died; but alas! I shall never see her more; she has blotted the ungrateful Charlotte from her remembrance, and I shall sink to the grave loaded with her's and my father's curse."

Mrs. Beauchamp endeavoured to sooth her. "You shall write to them again," said she, "and I will see that the letter is sent by the first packet that sails for England; in the mean time keep up your spirits, and hope every thing, by daring to deserve it."

She then turned the conversation, and Charlotte having taken a cup of tea, wished her benevolent friend a good evening.

Chapter XXII

Sorrows of the Heart

WHEN Charlotte got home she endeavoured to collect her thoughts, and took up a pen in order to address those dear parents, whom, spite of her errors, she still loved with the utmost tenderness, but vain was every effort to write with the least coherence; her tears fell so fast they almost blinded her; and as she proceeded to describe her unhappy situation, she became so agitated that she was obliged to give over the attempt and retire to bed, where, overcome with the fatigue her mind had undergone, she fell into a slumber which greatly refreshed her, and she arose in the morning with spirits more adequate to the painful task she had to perform, and, after several attempts, at length concluded the following letter to her mother—

To MRS. TEMPLE.
New-York.

"Will my once kind, my ever beloved mother, deign to receive a letter from her guilty, but repentant child? or has she, justly incensed at my ingratitude, driven the unhappy Charlotte from her remembrance? Alas! thou much injured mother! shouldst thou even disown me, I dare not complain, because I know I have deserved it: but yet, believe me, guilty as I am, and cruelly as I have disappointed the hopes of the fondest parents, that ever girl had, even in the moment when, forgetful of my duty, I fled from you and happiness, even then I loved you most, and my heart bled at the thought of what you would suffer. Oh! never, never! whilst I have existence, will the agony of that moment be erased from my memory. It seemed like the separation of soul and body. What can I plead in excuse for my conduct? alas! nothing! That I loved my seducer is but too true! yet powerful as that passion is when operating in a young heart glowing with sensibility, it never would have conquered my affection to you, my beloved parents, had I not been encouraged, nay, urged to take the fatally imprudent step, by one of my own sex, who, under the mask of friendship, drew me on to ruin. Yet think not your Charlotte was so lost as to voluntarily rush into a life of infamy; no, my dear mother, deceived by the specious appearance of my betrayer, and every suspicion lulled asleep by the most solemn promises of marriage, I thought not those promises would so easily be forgotten. I never once reflected that the man who could stoop to seduction, would not hesitate to forsake the wretched object of his passion, whenever his capricious heart grew weary of her tenderness. When we arrived at this place, I vainly expected him to fulfil his engagements, but was at last fatally convinced he had never intended to make me his wife, or if he had once thought of it, his mind was now altered. I scorned to claim from his humanity what I could not obtain from his love: I was conscious of having forfeited the only gem that could render me respectable in the eye of the world. I locked my sorrows in my own bosom, and bore my injuries in silence. But how shall I proceed? This man, this cruel Montraville, for whom I sacrificed honour, happiness, and the love of my friends, no longer looks on me with affection, but scorns the credulous girl whom his art has made miserable. Could you see me, my dear parents, without society, without friends, stung with remorse, and (I feel the burning blush of shame die my cheeks while I write it) tortured with the pangs of disappointed love; cut to the soul by the indifference of him, who, having deprived me of every other comfort, no longer thinks it worth his while to sooth the heart where he has planted the thorn of never-ceasing regret. My daily employment is to think of you and weep, to pray for your happiness and deplore my own folly: my nights are scarce more happy, for if by chance I close my weary eyes, and hope some small forgetfulness of sorrow, some little time to pass in sweet oblivion, fancy, still waking, wafts me home to you: I see your beloved forms, I kneel and hear the blessed words of peace and pardon. Extatic joy pervades my soul; I reach my arms to catch your dear embraces; the motion chases the illusive dream; I wake to real misery. At other times I see my father angry and frowning, point to horrid caves, where, on the cold damp ground, in the agonies of death, I see my dear mother and my revered grand-father. I strive to raise you; you push me from you, and shrieking cry—"Charlotte, thou hast murdered me!" Horror and despair tear every tortured nerve; I start, and leave my restless bed, weary and unrefreshed.

"Shocking as these reflexions are, I have yet one more dreadful than the rest. Mother, my dear mother! do not let me quite break your heart when I tell you, in a few months I shall bring into the world an innocent witness of my guilt. Oh my bleeding heart, I shall bring a poor little helpless creature, heir to infamy and shame.

"This alone has urged me once more to address you, to interest you in behalf of this poor unborn, and beg you to extend your protection to the child of your lost Charlotte; for my own part I have wrote so often, so frequently have pleaded for forgiveness, and entreated to be received once more beneath the paternal roof, that having received no answer, not even one line, I much fear you have cast me from you for ever.

"But sure you cannot refuse to protect my innocent infant: it partakes not of its mother's guilt. Oh my father, oh beloved mother, now do I feel the anguish I inflicted on your hearts recoiling with double force upon my own.

"If my child should be a girl (which heaven forbid) tell her the unhappy fate of her mother, and teach her to avoid my errors; if a boy, teach him to lament my miseries, but tell him not who inflicted them, lest in wishing to revenge his mother's injuries, he should wound the peace of his father.

"And now, dear friends of my soul, kind guardians of my infancy, farewell. I feel I never more must hope to see you; the anguish of my heart strikes at the strings of life, and in a short time I shall be at rest. Oh could I but receive your blessing and forgiveness before I died, it would smooth my passage to the peaceful grave, and be a blessed foretaste of a happy eternity. I beseech you, curse me not, my adored parents, but let a tear of pity and pardon fall to the memory of your lost   CHARLOTTE.

Chapter XXIII

A Man May Smile, and Smile, and Be a Villain[7]

WHILE Charlotte was enjoying some small degree of comfort in the consoling friendship of Mrs. Beauchamp, Montraville was advancing rapidly in his affection towards Miss Franklin. Julia was an amiable girl; she saw only the fair side of his character; she possessed an independent fortune, and resolved to be happy with the man of her heart, though his rank and fortune were by no means so exalted as she had a right to expect; she saw the passion which Montraville struggled to conceal; she wondered at his timidity, but imagined the distance fortune had placed between them occasioned his backwardness, and made every advance which strict prudence and a becoming modesty would permit. Montraville saw with pleasure he was not indifferent to her, but a spark of honour which animated his bosom would not suffer him to take advantage of her partiality. He was well acquainted with Charlotte's situation, and he thought there would be a double cruelty in forsaking her at such a time; and to marry Miss Franklin, while honour, humanity, every sacred law, obliged him still to protect and support Charlotte, was a baseness which his soul shuddered at.

He communicated his uneasiness to Belcour: it was the very thing this pretended friend had wished. "And do you really," said he, laughing, "hesitate at marrying the lovely Julia, and becoming master of her fortune, because a little foolish, fond girl chose to leave her friends, and run away with you to America. Dear Montraville, act more like a man of sense; this whining, pining Charlotte, who occasions you so much uneasiness, would have eloped with somebody else if she had not with you."

"Would to heaven," said Montraville, "I had never seen her; my regard for her was but the momentary passion of desire, but I feel I shall love and revere Julia Franklin as long as I live; yet to leave poor Charlotte in her present situation would be cruel beyond description."

"Oh my good sentimental friend," said Belcour, "do you imagine no body has a right to provide for the brat but yourself."

Montraville started. "Sure," said he, "you cannot mean to insinuate that Charlotte is false."

"I don't insinuate it," said Belcour, "I know it."

Montraville turned pale as ashes. "Then there is no faith in woman," said he.

"While I thought you attached to her," said Belcour with an air of indifference, "I never wished to make you uneasy by mentioning her perfidy, but as I know you love and are beloved by Miss Franklin, I was determined not to let these foolish scruples of honour step between you and happiness, or your tenderness for the peace of a perfidious girl prevent your uniting yourself to a woman of honour."

"Good heavens!" said Montraville, "what poignant reflections does a man endure who sees a lovely woman plunged in infamy, and is conscious he was her first seducer; but are you certain of what you say, Belcour?"

"So far," replied he, "that I myself have received advances from her which I would not take advantage of out of regard to you: but hang it, think no more about her. I dined at Franklin's to-day, and Julia bid me seek and bring you to tea: so come along, my lad, make good use of opportunity, and seize the gifts of fortune while they are within your reach."

---

7 William Shakespeare, *Hamlet*, act 1, scene 5.

Montraville was too much agitated to pass a happy evening even in the company of Julia Franklin: he determined to visit Charlotte early the next morning, tax her with her falsehood, and take an everlasting leave of her; but when the morning came, he was commanded on duty, and for six weeks was prevented from putting his design in execution. At length he found an hour to spare, and walked out to spend it with Charlotte: it was near four o'clock in the afternoon when he arrived at her cottage; she was not in the parlour, and without calling the servant he walked up stairs, thinking to find her in her bed room. He opened the door, and the first object that met his eyes was Charlotte asleep on the bed, and Belcour by her side.

"Death and distraction," said he, stamping, "this is too much. Rise, villain, and defend yourself." Belcour sprang from the bed. The noise awoke Charlotte; terrified at the furious appearance of Montraville, and seeing Belcour with him in the chamber, she caught hold of his arm as he stood by the bed-side, and eagerly asked what was the matter.

"Treacherous, infamous girl," said he, "can you ask? How came he here?" pointing to Belcour.

"As heaven is my witness," replied she weeping, "I do not know. I have not seen him for these three weeks."

"Then you confess he sometimes visits you?"

"He came sometimes by your desire."

"'Tis false; I never desired him to come, and you know I did not: but mark me, Charlotte, from this instant our connexion is at an end. Let Belcour, or any other of your favoured lovers, take you and provide for you; I have done with you for ever."

He was then going to leave her; but starting wildly from the bed, she threw herself on her knees before him, protesting her innocence and entreating him not to leave her. "Oh Montraville," said she, "kill me, for pity's sake kill me, but do not doubt my fidelity. Do not leave me in this horrid situation; for the sake of your unborn child, oh! spurn not the wretched mother from you."

"Charlotte," said he, with a firm voice, "I shall take care that neither you nor your child want any thing in the approaching painful hour; but we meet no more." He then endeavoured to raise her from the ground; but in vain; she clung about his knees, entreating him to believe her innocent, and conjuring Belcour to clear up the dreadful mystery.

Belcour cast on Montraville a smile of contempt: it irritated him almost to madness; he broke from the feeble arms of the distressed girl; she shrieked and fell prostrate on the floor. Montraville instantly left the house and returned hastily to the city.

Chapter XXIV

Mystery Developed

UNFORTUNATELY for Charlotte, about three weeks before this unhappy rencontre, Captain Beauchamp, being ordered to Rhode-Island, his lady had accompanied him, so that Charlotte was deprived of her friendly advice and consoling society. The afternoon on which Montraville had visited her she had found herself languid and fatigued, and after making a very slight dinner had lain down to endeavour to recruit her exhausted spirits, and, contrary to her expectations, had fallen asleep. She had not long been lain down, when Belcour arrived, for he took every opportunity of visiting her, and striving to awaken her resentment against Montraville. He enquired of the servant where her mistress was, and being told she was asleep, took up a book to amuse himself: having sat a few minutes, he by chance cast his eyes towards the road, and saw Montraville approaching; he instantly conceived the diabolical scheme of ruining the unhappy Charlotte in his opinion for ever; he therefore stole softly up stairs, and laying himself by her side with the greatest precaution, for fear she should awake, was in that situation discovered by his credulous friend.

When Montraville spurned the weeping Charlotte from him, and left her almost distracted with terror and despair, Belcour raised her from the floor, and leading her down stairs, assumed the part of a tender, consoling friend; she listened to the arguments he advanced with apparent composure; but this was only the calm of a moment: the remembrance of Montraville's recent cruelty again rushed upon her mind: she pushed him from her with some violence, and crying—"Leave me, Sir, I beseech you leave me, for much I fear you have been the cause of my fidelity being suspected; go, leave me to the accumulated miseries my own imprudence has brought upon me."

She then left him with precipitation, and retiring to her own apartment, threw herself on the bed, and gave vent to an agony of grief which it is impossible to describe.

It now occurred to Belcour that she might possibly write to Montraville, and endeavour to convince him of her innocence: he was well aware of her pathetic remonstrances, and, sensible of the tenderness of Montraville's heart, resolved to prevent any letters ever reaching him: he therefore called the servant, and, by the powerful persuasion of a bribe, prevailed with her to promise whatever letters her mistress might write should be sent to him. He then left a polite, tender note for Charlotte, and returned to New-York. His first business was to seek Montraville, and endeavour to convince him that what had happened would ultimately tend to his happiness: he found him in his apartment, solitary, pensive, and wrapped in disagreeable reflections.

"Why how now, whining, pining lover?" said he, clapping him on the shoulder. Montraville started; a momentary flush of resentment crossed his cheek, but instantly gave place to a death-like paleness, occasioned by painful remembrance—remembrance awakened by that monitor, whom, though we may in vain endeavour, we can never entirely silence.

"Belcour," said he, "you have injured me in a tender point."

"Prithee, Jack," replied Belcour, "do not make a serious matter of it: how could I refuse the girl's advances? and thank heaven she is not your wife."

"True," said Montraville; "but she was innocent when I first knew her. It was I seduced her, Belcour. Had it not been for me, she had still been virtuous and happy in the affection and protection of her family."

"Pshaw," replied Belcour, laughing, "if you had not taken advantage of her easy nature, some other would, and where is the difference, pray?"

"I wish I had never seen her," cried he passionately, and starting from his seat. "Oh that cursed French woman," added he with vehemence, "had it not been for her, I might have been happy—" He paused.

"With Julia Franklin," said Belcour. The name, like a sudden spark of electric fire, seemed for a moment to suspend his faculties—for a moment he was transfixed; but recovering, he caught Belcour's hand, and cried—"Stop! stop! I beseech you, name not the lovely Julia and the wretched Montraville in the same breath. I am a seducer, a mean, ungenerous seducer of unsuspecting innocence. I dare not hope that purity like her's would stoop to unite itself with black, premeditated guilt: yet by heavens I swear, Belcour, I thought I loved the lost, abandoned Charlotte till I saw Julia—I thought I never could forsake her; but the heart is deceitful, and I now can plainly discriminate between the impulse of a youthful passion, and the pure flame of disinterested affection."

At that instant Julia Franklin passed the window, leaning on her uncle's arm. She curtseyed as she passed, and, with the bewitching smile of modest chearfulness, cried— "Do you bury yourselves in the house this fine evening, gents?" There was something in the voice! the manner! the look! that was altogether irresistible. "Perhaps she wishes my company," said Montraville mentally, as he snatched up his hat: "if I thought she loved me, I would confess my errors, and trust to her generosity to pity and pardon me." He soon overtook her, and offering her his arm, they sauntered to pleasant but unfrequented walks. Belcour drew Mr. Franklin on one side and entered into a political discourse: they walked faster than the young people, and Belcour by some means contrived entirely to lose sight of them. It was a fine evening in the beginning of autumn; the last remains of day-light faintly streaked the western sky, while the moon, with pale and virgin lustre in the room of gorgeous gold and purple, ornamented the canopy of heaven with silver, fleecy clouds, which now and then half hid her lovely face, and, by partly concealing, heightened every beauty; the zephyrs whispered softly through the trees, which now began to shed their leafy honours; a solemn silence reigned: and to a happy mind an evening such as this would give serenity, and calm, unruffled pleasure; but to Montraville, while it soothed the turbulence of his passions, it brought increase of melancholy reflections. Julia was leaning on his arm: he took her hand in his, and pressing it tenderly, sighed deeply, but continued silent. Julia was embarrassed; she wished to break a silence so unaccountable, but was unable; she loved Montraville, she saw he was unhappy, and wished to know the cause of his uneasiness, but that innate modesty, which nature has implanted in the female breast, prevented her enquiring. "I am bad company, Miss Franklin," said he, at last recollecting himself; "but I have met with something to-day that has greatly distressed me, and I cannot shake off the disagreeable impression it has made on my mind."

"I am sorry," she replied, "that you have any cause of inquietude. I am sure if you were as happy as you deserve, and as all your friends wish you—" She hesitated. "And might I," replied he with some animation, "presume to rank the amiable Julia in that number?"

"Certainly," said she, "the service you have rendered me, the knowledge of your worth, all combine to make me esteem you."

"Esteem, my lovely Julia," said he passionately, "is but a poor cold word. I would if I dared, if I thought I merited your attention—but no, I must not—honour forbids. I am beneath your notice, Julia, I am miserable and cannot hope to be otherwise."

"Alas!" said Julia, "I pity you."

"Oh thou condescending charmer," said he, "how that sweet word chears my sad heart. Indeed if you knew all, you would pity; but at the same time I fear you would despise me."

Just then they were again joined by Mr. Franklin and Belcour. It had interrupted an interesting discourse. They found it impossible to converse on indifferent subjects, and proceeded home in silence. At Mr. Franklin's door Montraville again pressed Julia's hand, and faintly articulating "good night," retired to his lodgings dispirited and wretched, from a consciousness that he deserved not the affection, with which he plainly saw he was honoured.

Chapter XXV

Reception of a Letter

"AND where now is our poor Charlotte?" said Mr. Temple one evening, as the cold blasts of autumn whistled rudely over the heath, and the yellow appearance of the distant wood, spoke the near approach of winter. In vain the chearful fire blazed on the hearth, in vain was he surrounded by all the comforts of life; the parent was still alive in his heart, and when he thought that perhaps his once darling child was ere this exposed to all the miseries of want in a distant land, without a friend to sooth and comfort her, without the benignant look of compassion to chear, or the angelic voice of pity to pour the balm of consolation on her wounded heart; when he thought of this, his whole soul dissolved in tenderness; and while he wiped the tear of anguish from the eye of his patient, uncomplaining Lucy, he struggled to suppress the sympathizing drop that started in his own.

"Oh, my poor girl," said Mrs. Temple, "how must she be altered, else surely she would have relieved our agonizing minds by one line to say she lived—to say she had not quite forgot the parents who almost idolized her."

"Gracious heaven," said Mr. Temple, starting from his seat, "who would wish to be a father, to experience the agonizing pangs inflicted on a parent's heart by the ingratitude of a child?" Mrs. Temple wept: her father took her hand; he would have said, "be comforted my child," but the words died on his tongue. The sad silence that ensued was interrupted by a loud rap at the door. In a moment a servant entered with a letter in his hand.

Mrs. Temple took it from him: she cast her eyes upon the superscription; she knew the writing. "'Tis Charlotte," said she, eagerly breaking the seal, "she has not quite forgot us." But before she had half gone through the contents, a sudden sickness seized her; she grew cold and giddy, and putting it into her husband's hand, she cried—"Read it: I cannot." Mr. Temple attempted to read it aloud, but frequently paused to give vent to his tears. "My poor deluded child," said he, when he had finished.

"Oh, shall we not forgive the dear penitent?" said Mrs. Temple. "We must, we will, my love; she is willing to return, and 'tis our duty to receive her."

"Father of mercy," said Mr. Eldridge, raising his clasped hands, "let me but live once more to see the dear wanderer restored to her afflicted parents, and take me from this world of sorrow whenever it seemeth best to thy wisdom."

"Yes, we will receive her," said Mr. Temple; "we will endeavour to heal her wounded spirit, and speak peace and comfort to her agitated soul. I will write to her to return immediately."

"Oh!" said Mrs. Temple, "I would if possible fly to her, support and chear the dear sufferer in the approaching hour of distress, and tell her how nearly penitence is allied to virtue. Cannot we go and conduct her home, my love?" continued she, laying her hand on his arm. "My father will surely forgive our absence if we go to bring home his darling."

"You cannot go, my Lucy," said Mr. Temple: "the delicacy of your frame would but poorly sustain the fatigue of a long voyage; but I will go and bring the gentle penitent to your arms: we may still see many years of happiness."

The struggle in the bosom of Mrs. Temple between maternal and conjugal tenderness was long and painful. At length the former triumphed, and she consented that her husband should set forward to New-York by the first opportunity: she wrote to her Charlotte in the tenderest, most consoling manner, and looked forward to the happy hour, when she should again embrace her, with the most animated hope.

Chapter XXVI

What Might Be Expected

IN the mean time the passion Montraville had conceived for Julia Franklin daily increased, and he saw evidently how much he was beloved by that amiable girl: he was likewise strongly prepossessed with an idea of Charlotte's perfidy. What wonder then if he gave himself up to the delightful sensation which pervaded his bosom; and finding no obstacle arise to oppose his happiness, he solicited and obtained the hand of Julia. A few days before his marriage he thus addressed Belcour:

"Though Charlotte, by her abandoned conduct, has thrown herself from my protection, I still hold myself bound to support her till relieved from her present condition, and also to provide for the child. I do not intend to see her again, but I will place a sum of money in your hands, which will amply supply her with every convenience; but should she require more, let her have it, and I will see it repaid. I wish I could prevail on the poor deluded girl to return to her friends: she was an only child, and I make no doubt but that they would joyfully receive her; it would shock me greatly to see her henceforth leading a life of infamy, as I should always accuse myself of being the primary cause of all her errors. If she should chuse to remain under your protection, be kind to her, Belcour, I conjure you. Let not satiety prompt you to treat her in such a manner, as may drive her to actions which necessity might urge her to, while her better reason disapproved them: she shall never want a friend while I live, but I never more desire to behold her; her presence would be always painful to me, and a glance from her eye would call the blush of conscious guilt into my cheek.

"I will write a letter to her, which you may deliver when I am gone, as I shall go to St. Eustatia[8] the day after my union with Julia, who will accompany me."

Belcour promised to fulfil the request of his friend, though nothing was farther from his intentions, than the least design of delivering the letter, or making Charlotte acquainted with the provision Montraville had made for her; he was bent on the complete ruin of the unhappy girl, and supposed, by reducing her to an entire dependance on him, to bring her by degrees to consent to gratify his ungenerous passion.

The evening before the day appointed for the nuptials of Montraville and Julia, the former retired early to his apartment; and ruminating on the past scenes of his life, suffered the keenest remorse in the remembrance of Charlotte's seduction. "Poor girl," said he, "I will at least write and bid her adieu; I will too endeavour to awaken that love of virtue in her bosom which her unfortunate attachment to me has extinguished." He took up the pen and began to write, but words were denied him. How could he address the woman whom he had seduced, and whom, though he thought unworthy his tenderness, he was about to bid adieu for ever? How should he tell her that he was going to abjure her, to enter into the most indissoluble ties with another, and that he could not even own the infant which she bore as his child? Several letters were begun and destroyed: at length he completed the following:

To Charlotte

"Though I have taken up my pen to address you, my poor injured girl, I feel I am inadequate to the task; yet, however painful the endeavour, I could not resolve upon

---

8 St. Eustatia is a small island in the Caribbean.

leaving you for ever without one kind line to bid you adieu, to tell you how my heart bleeds at the remembrance of what you was, before you saw the hated Montraville. Even now imagination paints the scene, when, torn by contending passions, when, struggling between love and duty, you fainted in my arms, and I lifted you into the chaise: I see the agony of your mind, when, recovering, you found yourself on the road to Portsmouth: but how, my gentle girl, how could you, when so justly impressed with the value of virtue, how could you, when loving as I thought you loved me, yield to the solicitations of Belcour?

"Oh Charlotte, conscience tells me it was I, villain that I am, who first taught you the allurements of guilty pleasure; it was I who dragged you from the calm repose which innocence and virtue ever enjoy; and can I, dare I tell you, it was not love prompted to the horrid deed? No, thou dear, fallen angel, believe your repentant Montraville, when he tells you the man who truly loves will never betray the object of his affection. Adieu, Charlotte: could you still find charms in a life of unoffending innocence, return to your parents; you shall never want the means of support both for yourself and child. Oh! gracious heaven! may that child be entirely free from the vices of its father and the weakness of its mother.

"To-morrow—but no, I cannot tell you what to-morrow will produce; Belcour will inform you: he also has cash for you, which I beg you will ask for whenever you may want it. Once more adieu: believe me could I hear you was returned to your friends, and enjoying that tranquillity of which I have robbed you, I should be as completely happy as even you, in your fondest hours, could wish me, but till then a gloom will obscure the brightest prospects of Montraville."

After he had sealed this letter he threw himself on the bed, and enjoyed a few hours repose. Early in the morning Belcour tapped at his door: he arose hastily, and prepared to meet his Julia at the altar.

"This is the letter to Charlotte," said he, giving it to Belcour: "take it to her when we are gone to Eustatia; and I conjure you, my dear friend, not to use any sophistical arguments to prevent her return to virtue; but should she incline that way, encourage her in the thought, and assist her to put her design in execution.

Chapter XXVII

Pensive she mourn'd, and hung her languid head,
Like a fair lily overcharg'd with dew.

CHARLOTTE had now been left almost three months a prey to her own melancholy reflexions—sad companions indeed; nor did any one break in upon her solitude but Belcour, who once or twice called to enquire after her health, and tell her he had in vain endeavoured to bring Montraville to hear reason; and once, but only once, was her mind cheared by the receipt of an affectionate letter from Mrs. Beauchamp. Often had she wrote to her perfidious seducer, and with the most persuasive eloquence endeavoured to convince him of her innocence; but these letters were never suffered to reach the hands of Montraville, or they must, though on the very eve of marriage, have prevented his deserting the wretched girl. Real anguish of heart had in a great measure faded her charms, her cheeks were pale from want of rest, and her eyes, by frequent, indeed almost continued weeping, were sunk and heavy. Sometimes a gleam of hope would play about her heart when she thought of her parents—"They cannot surely," she would say, "refuse to forgive me; or should they deny their pardon to me, they will not hate my innocent infant on account of its mother's errors." How often did the poor mourner wish for the consoling presence of the benevolent Mrs. Beauchamp.

"If she were here," she would cry, "she would certainly comfort me, and sooth the distraction of my soul."

She was sitting one afternoon, wrapped in these melancholy reflexions, when she was interrupted by the entrance of Belcour. Great as the alteration was which incessant sorrow had made on her person, she was still interesting, still charming; and the unhallowed flame, which had urged Belcour to plant dissension between her and Montraville, still raged in his bosom: he was determined, if possible, to make her his mistress; nay, he had even conceived the diabolical scheme of taking her to New-York, and making her appear in every public place where it was likely she should meet Montraville, that he might be a witness to his unmanly triumph.

When he entered the room where Charlotte was sitting, he assumed the look of tender, consolatory friendship. "And how does my lovely Charlotte?" said he, taking her hand: "I fear you are not so well as I could wish."

"I am not well, Mr. Belcour," said she, "very far from it; but the pains and infirmities of the body I could easily bear, nay, submit to them with patience, were they not aggravated by the most insupportable anguish of my mind."

"You are not happy, Charlotte," said he, with a look of well- dissembled sorrow.

"Alas!" replied she mournfully, shaking her head, "how can I be happy, deserted and forsaken as I am, without a friend of my own sex to whom I can unburthen my full heart, nay, my fidelity suspected by the very man for whom I have sacrificed every thing valuable in life, for whom I have made myself a poor despised creature, an outcast from society, an object only of contempt and pity."

"You think too meanly of yourself, Miss Temple: there is no one who would dare to treat you with contempt: all who have the pleasure of knowing you must admire and esteem. You are lonely here, my dear girl; give me leave to conduct you to New-York, where the agreeable society of some ladies, to whom I will introduce you, will dispel these sad thoughts, and I shall again see returning chearfulness animate those lovely features."

"Oh never! never!" cried Charlotte, emphatically: "the virtuous part of my sex will scorn me, and I will never associate with infamy. No, Belcour, here let me hide my shame and sorrow, here let me spend my few remaining days in obscurity, unknown and unpitied, here let me die unlamented, and my name sink to oblivion." Here her tears stopped her utterance. Belcour was awed to silence: he dared not interrupt her; and after a moment's pause she proceeded—"I once had conceived the thought of going to New-York to seek out the still dear, though cruel, ungenerous Montraville, to throw myself at his feet, and entreat his compassion; heaven knows, not for myself; if I am no longer beloved, I will not be indebted to his pity to redress my injuries, but I would have knelt and entreated him not to forsake my poor unborn—" She could say no more; a crimson glow rushed over her cheeks, and covering her face with her hands, she sobbed aloud.

Something like humanity was awakened in Belcour's breast by this pathetic speech: he arose and walked towards the window; but the selfish passion which had taken possession of his heart, soon stifled these finer emotions; and he thought if Charlotte was once convinced she had no longer any dependance on Montraville, she would more readily, throw herself on his protection. Determined, therefore, to inform her of all that had happened, he again resumed his seat; and finding she began to be more composed, enquired if she had ever heard from Montraville since the unfortunate recontre[9] in her bed chamber.

"Ah no," said she. "I fear I shall never hear from him again."

"I am greatly of your opinion," said Belcour, "for he has been for some time past greatly attached—"

At the word "attached" a death-like paleness overspread the countenance of Charlotte, but she applied to some hartshorn which stood beside her, and Belcour proceeded.

"He has been for some time past greatly attached to one Miss Franklin, a pleasing lively girl, with a large fortune."

"She may be richer, may be handsomer," cried Charlotte, "but cannot love him so well. Oh may she beware of his art, and not trust him too far as I have done."

"He addresses her publicly," said he, "and it was rumoured they were to be married before he sailed for Eustatia, whither his company is ordered."

"Belcour," said Charlotte, seizing his hand, and gazing at him earnestly, while her pale lips trembled with convulsive agony, "tell me, and tell me truly, I beseech you, do you think he can be such a villain as to marry another woman, and leave me to die with want and misery in a strange land: tell me what you think; I can bear it very well; I will not shrink from this heaviest stroke of fate; I have deserved my afflictions, and I will endeavour to bear them as I ought."

"I fear," said Belcour, "he can be that villain."

"Perhaps," cried she, eagerly interrupting him, "perhaps he is married already: come, let me know the worst," continued she with an affected look of composure: "you need not be afraid, I shall not send the fortunate lady a bowl of poison."

"Well then, my dear girl," said he, deceived by her appearance, "they were married on Thursday, and yesterday morning they sailed for Eustatia."

"Married—gone—say you?" cried she in a distracted accent, "what without a last farewell, without one thought on my unhappy situation! Oh Montraville, may God forgive your perfidy." She shrieked, and Belcour sprang forward just in time to prevent her falling to the floor.

Alarming faintings now succeeded each other, and she was conveyed to her bed, from whence she earnestly prayed she might never more arise. Belcour staid with her that night, and in the morning found her in a high fever. The fits she had been seized with had greatly terrified him; and confined as she now was to a bed of sickness, she was no longer an object of desire: it is true for several days he went constantly to see her, but her pale, emaciated appearance disgusted him: his visits became less frequent; he forgot the solemn charge given him by Montraville; he even forgot the money entrusted to his care; and, the burning blush of indignation and shame tinges my cheek while I write it, this disgrace to humanity and manhood at length forgot even the injured Charlotte; and, attracted by the blooming health of a farmer's daughter, whom he had seen in his frequent excursions to the country, he left the unhappy girl to sink unnoticed to the grave, a prey to sickness, grief, and penury; while he, having triumphed over the virtue of the artless cottager, rioted in all the intemperance of luxury and lawless pleasure.

---

9 Encounter.

Chapter XXVIII

A Trifling Retrospect

"BLESS my heart," cries my young, volatile reader, "I shall never have patience to get through these volumes, there are so many ahs! and ohs! so much fainting, tears, and distress, I am sick to death of the subject." My dear, chearful, innocent girl, for innocent I will suppose you to be, or you would acutely feel the woes of Charlotte, did conscience say, thus might it have been with me, had not Providence interposed to snatch me from destruction: therefore, my lively, innocent girl, I must request your patience: I am writing a tale of truth: I mean to write it to the heart: but if perchance the heart is rendered impenetrable by unbounded prosperity, or a continuance in vice, I expect not my tale to please, nay, I even expect it will be thrown by with disgust. But softly, gentle fair one; I pray you throw it not aside till you have perused the whole; mayhap you may find something therein to repay you for the trouble. Methinks I see a sarcastic smile sit on your countenance.—"And what," cry you, "does the conceited author suppose we can glean from these pages, if Charlotte is held up as an object of terror, to prevent us from falling into guilty errors? does not La Rue triumph in her shame, and by adding art to guilt, obtain the affection of a worthy man, and rise to a station where she is beheld with respect, and chearfully received into all companies. What then is the moral you would inculcate? Would you wish us to think that a deviation from virtue, if covered by art and hypocrisy, is not an object of detestation, but on the contrary shall raise us to fame and honour? while the hapless girl who falls a victim to her too great sensibility, shall be loaded with ignominy and shame?" No, my fair querist, I mean no such thing. Remember the endeavours of the wicked are often suffered to prosper, that in the end their fall may be attended with more bitterness of heart; while the cup of affliction is poured out for wise and salutary ends, and they who are compelled to drain it even to the bitter dregs, often find comfort at the bottom; the tear of penitence blots their offences from the book of fate, and they rise from the heavy, painful trial, purified and fit for a mansion in the kingdom of eternity.

Yes, my young friends, the tear of compassion shall fall for the fate of Charlotte, while the name of La Rue shall be detested and despised. For Charlotte, the soul melts with sympathy; for La Rue, it feels nothing but horror and contempt. But perhaps your gay hearts would rather follow the fortunate Mrs. Crayton through the scenes of pleasure and dissipation in which she was engaged, than listen to the complaints and miseries of Charlotte. I will for once oblige you; I will for once follow her to midnight revels, balls, and scenes of gaiety, for in such was she constantly engaged.

I have said her person was lovely; let us add that she was surrounded by splendor and affluence, and he must know but little of the world who can wonder, (however faulty such a woman's conduct,) at her being followed by the men, and her company courted by the women: in short Mrs. Crayton was the universal favourite: she set the fashions, she was toasted by all the gentlemen, and copied by all the ladies.

Colonel Crayton was a domestic man. Could he be happy with such a woman? impossible! Remonstrance was vain: he might as well have preached to the winds, as endeavour to persuade her from any action, however ridiculous, on which she had set her mind: in short, after a little ineffectual struggle, he gave up the attempt, and left her to follow the bent of her own inclinations: what those were, I think the reader must have seen enough of her character to form a just idea. Among the number who paid their devotions at her shrine, she singled one, a young Ensign of mean birth, indifferent education, and weak intellects.

How such a man came into the army, we hardly know to account for, and how he afterwards rose to posts of honour is likewise strange and wonderful. But fortune is blind, and so are those too frequently who have the power of dispensing her favours: else why do we see fools and knaves at the very top of the wheel, while patient merit sinks to the extreme of the opposite abyss. But we may form a thousand conjectures on this subject, and yet never hit on the right. Let us therefore endeavour to deserve her smiles, and whether we succeed or not, we shall feel more innate satisfaction, than thousands of those who bask in the sunshine of her favour unworthily. But to return to Mrs. Crayton: this young man, whom I shall distinguish by the name of Corydon, was the reigning favourite of her heart. He escorted her to the play, danced with her at every ball, and when indisposition prevented her going out, it was he alone who was permitted to chear the gloomy solitude to which she was obliged to confine herself. Did she ever think of poor Charlotte?—if she did, my dear Miss, it was only to laugh at the poor girl's want of spirit in consenting to be moped up in the country, while Montraville was enjoying all the pleasures of a gay, dissipated city. When she heard of his marriage, she smiling said, so there's an end of Madam Charlotte's hopes. I wonder who will take her now, or what will become of the little affected prude?

But as you have lead to the subject, I think we may as well return to the distressed Charlotte, and not, like the unfeeling Mrs. Crayton, shut our hearts to the call of humanity.

Chapter XXIX

We Go Forward Again

THE strength of Charlotte's constitution combatted against her disorder, and she began slowly to recover, though she still laboured under a violent depression of spirits: how must that depression be encreased, when, upon examining her little store, she found herself reduced to one solitary guinea, and that during her illness the attendance of an apothecary and nurse, together with many other unavoidable expences, had involved her in debt, from which she saw no method of extricating herself. As to the faint hope which she had entertained of hearing from and being relieved by her parents; it now entirely forsook her, for it was above four months since her letter was dispatched, and she had received no answer: she therefore imagined that her conduct had either entirely alienated their affection from her, or broken their hearts, and she must never more hope to receive their blessing.

Never did any human being wish for death with greater fervency or with juster cause; yet she had too just a sense of the duties of the Christian religion to attempt to put a period to her own existence. "I have but to be patient a little longer," she would cry, "and nature, fatigued and fainting, will throw off this heavy load of mortality, and I shall be released from all my sufferings."

It was one cold stormy day in the latter end of December, as Charlotte sat by a handful of fire, the low state of her finances not allowing her to replenish her stock of fuel, and prudence teaching her to be careful of what she had, when she was surprised by the entrance of a farmer's wife, who, without much ceremony, seated herself, and began this curious harangue.

"I'm come to see if as how you can pay your rent, because as how we hear Captain Montable is gone away, and it's fifty to one if he b'ant killed afore he comes back again; an then, Miss, or Ma'am, or whatever you may be, as I was saying to my husband, where are we to look for our money."

This was a stroke altogether unexpected by Charlotte: she knew so little of the ways of the world that she had never bestowed a thought on the payment for the rent of the house; she knew indeed that she owed a good deal, but this was never reckoned among the others: she was thunder-struck; she hardly knew what answer to make, yet it was absolutely necessary that she should say something; and judging of the gentleness of every female disposition by her own, she thought the best way to interest the woman in her favour would be to tell her candidly to what a situation she was reduced, and how little probability there was of her ever paying any body.

Alas poor Charlotte, how confined was her knowledge of human nature, or she would have been convinced that the only way to insure the friendship and assistance of your surrounding acquaintance is to convince them you do not require it, for when once the petrifying aspect of distress and penury appear, whose qualities, like Medusa's head,[10] can change to stone all that look upon it; when once this Gorgon claims acquaintance with us, the phantom of friendship, that before courted our notice, will vanish into unsubstantial air, and the whole world before us appear a barren waste. Pardon me, ye dear spirits of benevolence, whose benign smiles and chearful-giving hand have strewed sweet flowers on many a thorny path through which my wayward fate forced me to pass; think not, that, in condemning the unfeeling texture of the human heart, I forget the spring from whence flow all the comforts I enjoy: oh no! I look up to you as to bright constellations, gathering new splendours from the surrounding darkness; but ah! whilst I adore the benignant rays that cheared and illumined my heart, I mourn that their influence cannot extend to all the sons and daughters of affliction.

"Indeed, Madam," said poor Charlotte in a tremulous accent, "I am at a loss what to do. Montraville placed me here, and promised to defray all my expenses: but he has forgot his promise, he has forsaken me, and I have no friend who has either power or will to relieve me. Let me hope, as you see my unhappy situation, your charity—"

"Charity," cried the woman impatiently interrupting her, "charity indeed: why, Mistress, charity begins at home, and I have seven children at home, *honest, lawful* children, and it is my duty to keep them; and do you think I will give away my property to a nasty, impudent hussey, to maintain her and her bastard; an I was saying to my husband the other day what will this world come to; honest women are nothing now-a-days, while the harlotings are set up for fine ladies, and look upon us no more nor the dirt they walk upon: but let me tell you, my fine spoken Ma'am, I must have my money; so seeing as how you can't pay it, why you must troop, and leave all your fine gimcracks and fal der ralls behind you. I don't ask for no more nor my right, and nobody shall dare for to go for to hinder me of it."

"Oh heavens," cried Charlotte, clasping her hands, "what will become of me?"

"Come on ye!" retorted the unfeeling wretch: "why go to the barracks and work for a morsel of bread; wash and mend the soldiers cloaths, an cook their victuals, and not expect to live in idleness on honest people's means. Oh I wish I could see the day when all such cattle were obliged to work hard and eat little; it's only what they deserve."

"Father of mercy," cried Charlotte, "I acknowledge thy correction just; but prepare me, I beseech thee, for the portion of misery thou may'st please to lay upon me."

---

10 In ancient Greek mythology, Medusa was a Gorgon (a female monster) with the body of a woman but hair composed of snakes. Those who gazed directly into her eyes were turned to stone.

"Well," said the woman, "I shall go an tell my husband as how you can't pay; and so d'ye see, Ma'am, get ready to be packing away this very night, for you should not stay another night in this house, though I was sure you would lay in the street."

Charlotte bowed her head in silence; but the anguish of her heart was too great to permit her to articulate a single word.

Chapter XXX

And what is friendship but a name,
A charm that lulls to sleep,
A shade that follows wealth and fame,
But leaves the wretch to weep.

WHEN Charlotte was left to herself, she began to think what course she must take, or to whom she could apply, to prevent her perishing for want, or perhaps that very night falling a victim to the inclemency of the season. After many perplexed thoughts, she at last determined to set out for New-York, and enquire out Mrs. Crayton, from whom she had no doubt but she should obtain immediate relief as soon as her distress was made known; she had no sooner formed this resolution than she resolved immediately to put it in execution: she therefore wrote the following little billet to Mrs. Crayton, thinking if she should have company with her it would be better to send it in than to request to see her.

To MRS. CRAYTON.
"MADAM,

"When we left our native land, that dear, happy land which now contains all that is dear to the wretched Charlotte, our prospects were the same; we both, pardon me, Madam, if I say, we both too easily followed the impulse of our treacherous hearts, and trusted our happiness on a tempestuous ocean, where mine has been wrecked and lost for ever; you have been more fortunate—you are united to a man of honour and humanity, united by the most sacred ties, respected, esteemed, and admired, and surrounded by innumerable blessings of which I am bereaved, enjoying those pleasures which have fled my bosom never to return; alas! sorrow and deep regret have taken their place. Behold me, Madam, a poor forsaken wanderer, who has no where to lay her weary head, wherewith to supply the wants of nature, or to shield her from the inclemency of the weather. To you I sue, to you I look for pity and relief. I ask not to be received as an intimate or an equal; only for charity's sweet sake receive me into your hospitable mansion, allot me the meanest apartment in it, and let me breath out my soul in prayers for your happiness; I cannot, I feel I cannot long bear up under the accumulated woes that pour in upon me; but oh! my dear Madam, for the love of heaven suffer me not to expire in the street; and when I am at peace, as soon I shall be, extend your compassion to my helpless offspring, should it please heaven that it should survive its unhappy mother. A gleam of joy breaks in on my benighted soul while I reflect that you cannot, will not refuse your protection to the heart-broken.   CHARLOTTE."

When Charlotte had finished this letter, late as it was in the afternoon, and though the snow began to fall very fast, she tied up a few necessaries which she had prepared against her expected confinement, and terrified lest she should be again exposed to the insults of her barbarous landlady, more dreadful to her wounded spirit than either storm or darkness, she set forward for New-York.

It may be asked by those, who, in a work of this kind, love to cavil at every trifling omission, whether Charlotte did not possess any valuable of which she could have disposed, and by that means have supported herself till Mrs. Beauchamp's return, when she would have been certain of receiving every tender attention which compassion and friendship could dictate: but let me entreat these wise, penetrating gentlemen to reflect, that when Charlotte left England, it was in such haste that there was no time to purchase any thing more than what was wanted for immediate use on the voyage, and after her arrival at New-York, Montraville's affection soon began to decline, so that her whole wardrobe consisted of only necessaries, and as to baubles, with which fond lovers often load their mistresses, she possessed not one, except a plain gold locket of small value, which contained a lock of her mother's hair, and which the greatest extremity of want could not have forced her to part with.

I hope, Sir, your prejudices are now removed in regard to the probability of my story? Oh they are. Well then, with your leave, I will proceed.

The distance from the house which our suffering heroine occupied, to New-York, was not very great, yet the snow fell so fast, and the cold so intense, that, being unable from her situation to walk quick, she found herself almost sinking with cold and fatigue before she reached the town; her garments, which were merely suitable to the summer season, being an undress robe of plain white muslin, were wet through, and a thin black cloak and bonnet, very improper habiliments for such a climate, but poorly defended her from the cold. In this situation she reached the city, and enquired of a foot soldier whom she met, the way to Colonel Crayton's.

"Bless you; my sweet lady," said the soldier with a voice and look of compassion, "I will shew you the way with all my heart; but if you are going to make a petition to Madam Crayton it is all to no purpose I assure you: if you please I will conduct you to Mr. Franklin's; though Miss Julia is married and gone now, yet the old gentleman is very good."

"Julia Franklin," said Charlotte; "is she not married to Montraville?"

"Yes," replied the soldier, "and may God bless them, for a better officer never lived, he is so good to us all; and as to Miss Julia, all the poor folk almost worshipped her."

"Gracious heaven," cried Charlotte, "is Montraville unjust then to none but me."

The soldier now shewed her Colonel Crayton's door, and, with a beating heart, she knocked for admission.

Chapter XXXI

Subject Continued

WHEN the door was opened, Charlotte, in a voice rendered scarcely articulate, through cold and the extreme agitation of her mind, demanded whether Mrs. Crayton was at home. The servant hesitated: he knew that his lady was engaged at a game of picquet with her dear Corydon, nor could he think she would like to be disturbed by a person whose appearance spoke her of so little consequence as Charlotte; yet there was something in her countenance that rather interested him in her favour, and he said his lady was engaged, but if she had any particular message he would deliver it.

"Take up this letter," said Charlotte: "tell her the unhappy writer of it waits in her hall for an answer."

The tremulous accent, the tearful eye, must have moved any heart not composed of adamant. The man took the letter from the poor suppliant, and hastily ascended the stair case.

"A letter, Madam," said he, presenting it to his lady: "an immediate answer is required."

Mrs. Crayton glanced her eye carelessly over the contents. "What stuff is this;" cried she haughtily; "have not I told you a thousand times that I will not be plagued with beggars, and petitions from people one knows nothing about? Go tell the woman I can't do any thing in it. I'm sorry, but one can't relieve every body."

The servant bowed, and heavily returned with this chilling message to Charlotte.

"Surely," said she, "Mrs. Crayton has not read my letter. Go, my good friend, pray go back to her; tell her it is Charlotte Temple who requests beneath her hospitable roof to find shelter from the inclemency of the season."

"Prithee, don't plague me, man," cried Mrs. Crayton impatiently, as the servant advanced something in behalf of the unhappy girl. "I tell you I don't know her."

"Not know me," cried Charlotte, rushing into the room, (for she had followed the man up stairs) "not know me, not remember the ruined Charlotte Temple, who, but for you, perhaps might still have been innocent, still have been happy. Oh! La Rue, this is beyond every thing I could have believed possible."

"Upon my honour, Miss," replied the unfeeling woman with the utmost effrontery, "this is a most unaccountable address: it is beyond my comprehension. John," continued she, turning to the servant, "the young woman is certainly out of her senses: do pray take her away, she terrifies me to death."

"Oh God," cried Charlotte, clasping her hands in an agony, "this is too much; what will become of me? but I will not leave you; they shall not tear me from you; here on my knees I conjure you to save me from perishing in the streets; if you really have forgot me, oh for charity's sweet sake this night let me be sheltered from the winter's piercing cold."

The kneeling figure of Charlotte in her affecting situation might have moved the heart of a stoic to compassion; but Mrs. Crayton remained inflexible. In vain did Charlotte recount the time they had known each other at Chichester, in vain mention their being in the same ship, in vain were the names of Montraville and Belcour mentioned. Mrs. Crayton could only say she was sorry for her imprudence, but could not think of having her own reputation endangered by encouraging a woman of that kind in her own house, besides she did not know what trouble and expense she might bring upon her husband by giving shelter to a woman in her situation.

"I can at least die here," said Charlotte, "I feel I cannot long survive this dreadful conflict. Father of mercy, here let me finish my existence." Her agonizing sensations overpowered her, and she fell senseless on the floor.

"Take her away," said Mrs. Crayton, "she will really frighten me into hysterics; take her away I say this instant."

"And where must I take the poor creature?" said the servant with a voice and look of compassion.

"Any where," cried she hastily, "only don't let me ever see her again. I declare she has flurried me so I shan't be myself again this fortnight."

John, assisted by his fellow-servant, raised and carried her down stairs. "Poor soul," said he, "you shall not lay in the street this night. I have a bed and a poor little hovel, where my wife and her little ones rest them, but they shall watch to night, and you shall be sheltered from danger." They placed her in a chair; and the benevolent man, assisted by one of his comrades, carried her to the place where his wife and children lived. A surgeon was sent for: he bled her, she gave signs of returning life, and before the dawn gave birth to a female infant. After this event she lay for some hours in a kind of stupor; and if at any time she spoke, it was with a quickness and incoherence that plainly evinced the total deprivation of her reason.

Chapter XXXII

Reasons Why and Wherefore

THE reader of sensibility may perhaps be astonished to find Mrs. Crayton could so positively deny any knowledge of Charlotte; it is therefore but just that her conduct should in some measure be accounted for. She had ever been fully sensible of the superiority of Charlotte's sense and virtue; she was conscious that she had never swerved from rectitude, had it not been for her bad precepts and worse example. These were things as yet unknown to her husband, and she wished not to have that part of her conduct exposed to him, as she had great reason to fear she had already lost considerable part of that power she once maintained over him. She trembled whilst Charlotte was in the house, lest the Colonel should return; she perfectly well remembered how much he seemed interested in her favour whilst on their passage from England, and made no doubt, but, should he see her in her present distress, he would offer her an asylum, and protect her to the utmost of his power. In that case she feared the unguarded nature of Charlotte might discover to the Colonel the part she had taken in the unhappy girl's elopement, and she well knew the contrast between her own and Charlotte's conduct would make the former appear in no very respectable light. Had she reflected properly, she would have afforded the poor girl protection; and by enjoining her silence, ensured it by acts of repeated kindness; but vice in general blinds its votaries, and they discover their real characters to the world when they are most studious to preserve appearances.

Just so it happened with Mrs. Crayton: her servants made no scruple of mentioning the cruel conduct of their lady to a poor distressed lunatic who claimed her protection; every one joined in reprobating her inhumanity; nay even Corydon thought she might at least have ordered her to be taken care of, but he dare not even hint it to her, for he lived but in her smiles, and drew from her lavish fondness large sums to support an extravagance to which the state of his own finances was very inadequate; it cannot therefore be supposed that he wished Mrs. Crayton to be very liberal in her bounty to the afflicted suppliant; yet vice had not so entirely seared over his heart, but the sorrows of Charlotte could find a vulnerable part.

Charlotte had now been three days with her humane preservers, but she was totally insensible of every thing: she raved incessantly for Montraville and her father: she was not conscious of being a mother, nor took the least notice of her child except to ask whose it was, and why it was not carried to its parents.

"Oh," said she one day, starting up on hearing the infant cry, "why, why will you keep that child here; I am sure you would not if you knew how hard it was for a mother to be parted from her infant: it is like tearing the cords of life asunder. Oh could you see the horrid sight which I now behold—there—there stands my dear mother, her poor bosom bleeding at every vein, her gentle, affectionate heart torn in a thousand pieces, and all for the loss of a ruined, ungrateful child. Save me—save me—from her frown. I dare not—indeed I dare not speak to her."

Such were the dreadful images that haunted her distracted mind, and nature was sinking fast under the dreadful malady which medicine had no power to remove. The surgeon who attended her was a humane man; he exerted his utmost abilities to save her, but he saw she was in want of many necessaries and comforts, which the poverty of her hospitable host rendered him unable to provide: he therefore determined to make her situation known to some of the officers' ladies, and endeavour to make a collection for her relief.

When he returned home, after making this resolution, he found a message from Mrs. Beauchamp, who had just arrived from Rhode-Island, requesting he would call and see one of her children, who was very unwell. "I do not know," said he, as he was hastening to obey the summons, "I do not know a woman to whom I could apply with more hope of success than Mrs. Beauchamp. I will endeavour to interest her in this poor girl's behalf; she wants the soothing balm of friendly consolation: we may perhaps save her; we will try at least."

"And where is she," cried Mrs. Beauchamp when he had prescribed something for the child, and told his little pathetic tale, "where is she, Sir? we will go to her immediately. Heaven forbid that I should be deaf to the calls of humanity. Come we will go this instant." Then seizing the doctor's arm, they sought the habitation that contained the dying Charlotte.

Chapter XXXIII

Which People Void of Feeling Need Not Read

WHEN Mrs. Beauchamp entered the apartment of the poor sufferer, she started back with horror. On a wretched bed, without hangings and but poorly supplied with covering, lay the emaciated figure of what still retained the semblance of a lovely woman, though sickness had so altered her features that Mrs. Beauchamp had not the least recollection of her person. In one corner of the room stood a woman washing, and, shivering over a small fire, two healthy but half naked children; the infant was asleep beside its mother, and, on a chair by the bed side, stood a porrenger[11] and wooden spoon, containing a little gruel, and a tea-cup with about two spoonfulls of wine in it. Mrs. Beauchamp had never before beheld such a scene of poverty; she shuddered involuntarily, and exclaiming—"heaven preserve us!" leaned on the back of a chair ready to sink to the earth. The doctor repented having so precipitately brought her into this affecting scene; but there was no time for apologies: Charlotte caught the sound of her voice, and starting almost out of bed, exclaimed—"Angel of peace and mercy, art thou come to deliver me? Oh, I know you are, for whenever you was near me I felt eased of half my sorrows; but you don't know me, nor can I, with all the recollection I am mistress of, remember your name just now, but I know that benevolent countenance, and the softness of that voice which has so often comforted the wretched Charlotte."

Mrs. Beauchamp had, during the time Charlotte was speaking, seated herself on the bed and taken one of her hands; she looked at her attentively, and at the name of Charlotte she perfectly conceived the whole shocking affair. A faint sickness came over her. "Gracious heaven," said she, "is this possible?" and bursting into tears, she reclined the burning head of Charlotte on her own bosom; and folding her arms about her, wept over her in silence. "Oh," said Charlotte, "you are very good to weep thus for me: it is a long time since I shed a tear for myself: my head and heart are both on fire, but these tears of your's seem to cool and refresh it. Oh now I remember you said you would send a letter

---

11 Soup bowl.

o my poor father: do you think he ever received it? or perhaps you have brought me an answer: why don't you speak, Madam? Does he say I may go home? Well he is very good; I shall soon be ready."

She then made an effort to get out of bed; but being prevented, her frenzy again returned, and she raved with the greatest wildness and incoherence. Mrs. Beauchamp, finding it was impossible for her to be removed, contented herself with ordering the apartment to be made more comfortable, and procuring a proper nurse for both mother and child; and having learnt the particulars of Charlotte's fruitless application to Mrs. Crayton from honest John, she amply rewarded him for his benevolence, and returned home with a heart oppressed with many painful sensations, but yet rendered easy by the reflexion that she had performed her duty towards a distressed fellow-creature.

Early the next morning she again visited Charlotte, and found her tolerably composed; she called her by name, thanked her for her goodness, and when her child was brought to her, pressed it in her arms, wept over it, and called it the offspring of disobedience. Mrs. Beauchamp was delighted to see her so much amended, and began to hope she might recover, and, spite of her former errors, become an useful and respectable member of society; but the arrival of the doctor put an end to these delusive hopes: he said nature was making her last effort, and a few hours would most probably consign the unhappy girl to her kindred dust.

Being asked how she found herself, she replied—"Why better, much better, doctor. I hope now I have but little more to suffer. I had last night a few hours sleep, and when I awoke recovered the full power of recollection. I am quite sensible of my weakness; I feel I have but little longer to combat with the shafts of affliction. I have an humble confidence in the mercy of him who died to save the world, and trust that my sufferings in this state of mortality, joined to my unfeigned repentance, through his mercy, have blotted my offences from the sight of my offended maker. I have but one care—my poor infant! Father of mercy," continued she, raising her eyes, "of thy infinite goodness, grant that the sins of the parent be not visited on the unoffending child. May those who taught me to despise thy laws be forgiven; lay not my offences to their charge, I beseech thee; and oh! shower the choicest of thy blessings on those whose pity has soothed the afflicted heart, and made easy even the bed of pain and sickness."

She was exhausted by this fervent address to the throne of mercy, and though her lips still moved her voice became inarticulate: she lay for some time as it were in a doze, and then recovering, faintly pressed Mrs, Beauchamp's hand, and requested that a clergyman might be sent for.

On his arrival she joined fervently in the pious office, frequently mentioning her ingratitude to her parents as what lay most heavy at her heart. When she had performed the last solemn duty, and was preparing to lie down, a little bustle on the outside door occasioned Mrs. Beauchamp to open it, and enquire the cause. A man in appearance about forty, presented himself, and asked for Mrs. Beauchamp.

"That is my name, Sir," said she.

"Oh then, my dear Madam," cried he, "tell me where I may find my poor, ruined, but repentant child."

Mrs. Beauchamp was surprised and affected; she knew not what to say; she foresaw the agony this interview would occasion Mr. Temple, who had just arrived in search of his Charlotte, and yet was sensible that the pardon and blessing of her father would soften even the agonies of death to the daughter.

She hesitated. "Tell me, Madam," cried he wildly, "tell me, I beseech thee, does she live? shall I see my darling once again? Perhaps she is in this house. Lead, lead me to her, that I may bless her, and then lie down and die."

The ardent manner in which he uttered these words occasioned him to raise his voice. It caught the ear of Charlotte: she knew the beloved sound: and uttering a loud shriek, she sprang forward as Mr. Temple entered the room. "My adored father." "My long lost child." Nature could support no more, and they both sunk lifeless into the arms of the attendants.

Charlotte was again put into bed, and a few moments restored Mr. Temple: but to describe the agony of his sufferings is past the power of any one, who, though they may readily conceive, cannot delineate the dreadful scene. Every eye gave testimony of what each heart felt—but all were silent.

When Charlotte recovered, she found herself supported in her father's arms. She cast on him a most expressive look, but was unable to speak. A reviving cordial was administered. She then asked, in a low voice, for her child: it was brought to her: she put it in her father's arms. "Protect her," said she, "and bless your dying—"

Unable to finish the sentence, she sunk back on her pillow: her countenance was serenely composed; she regarded her father as he pressed the infant to his breast with a steadfast look; a sudden beam of joy passed across her languid features, she raised her eyes to heaven—and then closed them for ever.

Chapter XXXIV

Retribution

IN the mean time Montraville having received orders to return to New-York, arrived, and having still some remains of compassionate tenderness for the woman whom he regarded as brought to shame by himself, he went out in search of Belcour, to enquire whether she was safe, and whether the child lived. He found him immersed in dissipation, and could gain no other intelligence than that Charlotte had left him, and that he knew not what was become of her.

"I cannot believe it possible," said Montraville, "that a mind once so pure as Charlotte Temple's, should so suddenly become the mansion of vice. Beware, Belcour," continued he, "beware if you have dared to behave either unjust or dishonourably to that poor girl, your life shall pay the forfeit:—I will revenge her cause."

He immediately went into the country, to the house where he had left Charlotte. It was desolate. After much enquiry he at length found the servant girl who had lived with her. From her he learnt the misery Charlotte had endured from the complicated evils of illness, poverty, and a broken heart, and that she had set out on foot for New-York, on a cold winter's evening; but she could inform him no further.

Tortured almost to madness by this shocking account, he returned to the city, but, before he reached it, the evening was drawing to a close. In entering the town he was obliged to pass several little huts, the residence of poor women who supported themselves by washing the cloaths of the officers and soldiers. It was nearly dark: he heard from a neighbouring steeple a solemn toll that seemed to say some poor mortal was going to their last mansion: the sound struck on the heart of Montraville, and he involuntarily stopped, when, from one of the houses, he saw the appearance of a funeral. Almost unknowing what he did, he followed at a small distance; and as they let the coffin into the grave, he enquired of a soldier who stood by, and had just brushed off a tear that did honour to his heart, who it was that was just buried. "An please your honour," said the man, "'tis a poor girl that was brought from her friends by a cruel man, who left her when she was big with child, and married another." Montraville stood motionless, and the man proceeded— "I met her myself not a fortnight since one night all wet and cold in the streets; she went to Madam Crayton's, but she would not take her in, and so the poor thing went raving mad." Montraville could bear no more; he struck his hands against his forehead with violence; and exclaiming "poor murdered Charlotte!" ran with precipitation towards the place where they were heaping the earth on her remains. "Hold, hold, one moment," said he. "Close not the grave of the injured Charlotte Temple till I have taken vengeance on her murderer."

"Rash young man," said Mr. Temple, "who art thou that thus disturbest the last mournful rites of the dead, and rudely breakest in upon the grief of an afflicted father."

"If thou art the father of Charlotte Temple," said he, gazing at him with mingled horror and amazement—"if thou art her father—I am Montraville." Then falling on his knees, he continued—"Here is my bosom. I bare it to receive the stroke I merit. Strike—strike now, and save me from the misery of reflexion."

"Alas!" said Mr. Temple, "if thou wert the seducer of my child, thy own reflexions be thy punishment. I wrest not the power from the hand of omnipotence. Look on that little heap of earth, there hast thou buried the only joy of a fond father. Look at it often; and may thy heart feel such true sorrow as shall merit the mercy of heaven." He turned from him; and Montraville starting up from the ground, where he had thrown himself, and at that instant remembering the perfidy of Belcour, flew like lightning to his lodgings. Belcour was intoxicated; Montraville impetuous: they fought, and the sword of the latter entered the heart of his adversary. He fell, and expired almost instantly. Montraville had received a slight wound; and overcome with the agitation of his mind and loss of blood, was carried in a state of insensibility to his distracted wife. A dangerous illness and obstinate delirium ensued, during which he raved incessantly for Charlotte: but a strong constitution, and the tender assiduities of Julia, in time overcame the disorder. He recovered; but to the end of his life was subject to severe fits of melancholy, and while he remained at New-York frequently retired to the church-yard, where he would weep over the grave, and regret the untimely fate of the lovely Charlotte Temple.

Chapter XXXV

Conclusion

SHORTLY after the interment of his daughter, Mr. Temple, with his dear little charge and her nurse, set forward for England. It would be impossible to do justice to the meeting scene between him, his Lucy, and her aged father. Every heart of sensibility can easily conceive their feelings. After the first tumult of grief was subsided, Mrs. Temple gave up the chief of her time to her grand-child, and as she grew up and improved, began to almost fancy she again possessed her Charlotte.

It was about ten years after these painful events, that Mr. and Mrs. Temple, having buried their father, were obliged to come to London on particular business, and brought the little Lucy with them. They had been walking one evening, when on their return they found a poor wretch sitting on the steps of the door. She attempted to rise as they approached, but from extreme weakness was unable, and after several fruitless efforts fell back in a fit. Mr. Temple was not one of those men who stand to consider whether by assisting an object in distress they shall not inconvenience themselves, but instigated by the impulse of a noble feeling heart, immediately ordered her to be carried into the house, and proper restoratives applied.

She soon recovered; and fixing her eyes on Mrs. Temple, cried— "You know not, Madam, what you do; you know not whom you are relieving, or you would curse me in the bitterness of your heart. Come not near me, Madam, I shall contaminate you. I am the viper that stung your peace. I am the woman who turned the poor Charlotte out to perish in the street. Heaven have mercy! I see her now," continued she looking at Lucy; "such, such was the fair bud of innocence that my vile arts blasted ere it was half blown."

It was in vain that Mr. and Mrs. Temple intreated her to be composed and to take some refreshment. She only drank half a glass of wine; and then told them that she had been separated from her husband seven years, the chief of which she had passed in riot, dissipation, and vice, till, overtaken by poverty and sickness, she had been reduced to part with every valuable, and thought only of ending her life in a prison; when a benevolent friend paid her debts and released her; but that her illness encreasing, she had no possible means of supporting herself, and her friends were weary of relieving her. "I have fasted," said she, "two days, and last night lay my aching head on the cold pavement: indeed it was but just that I should experience those miseries myself which I had unfeelingly inflicted on others."

Greatly as Mr. Temple had reason to detest Mrs. Crayton, he could not behold her in this distress without some emotions of pity. He gave her shelter that night beneath his hospitable roof, and the next day got her admission into an hospital; where having lingered a few weeks, she died, a striking example that vice, however prosperous in the beginning, in the end leads only to misery and shame.

FINIS.

Chapter Two

MASON LOCKE WEEMS
(1759–1825)

Mason Locke Weems was arguably one of early America's most impor-
tant traveling book salesmen. He was also an Episcopal priest and spent
much of his life moralizing in either spoken or written forms. Ordained
in 1784, Weems spent little of his life as a traditional rector. He left the
parish ministry in 1792 and began his long affiliation with America's nas-
cent book trade. He began by reprinting books, trying his own hand at
writing, and in 1794 joined forces with Philadelphia publisher Mathew
Carey. For nearly three decades, Weems traveled up and down the East
Coast selling books, sometimes Carey's, sometimes the works of other publishers, and
sometimes his own.

In 1800, Weems wrote the first of the many semifactual biographies he would produce,
A History of the Life and Death, Virtues and Exploits of General George Washington. He wrote this
book knowing full well that he could capitalize on the outpouring of grief over Washington's
recent death on December 14, 1799. Weems's knowledge of the American book-buying
public proved sound; the slender volume sold extremely well. Weems revised his book on
Washington several times, substantially enlarging it in 1808, when he renamed the work
*The Life of Washington; with Curious Anecdotes, Equally Honourable to Himself and Exemplary to His
Young Countrymen.* As this change in title indicates, his life of Washington was a moral tale.
Weems did not only tell his readers Washington's story, but he made that story a kind of
sermon, full of information on what made Washington a saint and how others might attain
the same sort of moral perfection.

Weems's moralizing biography of Washington highlights a tension found throughout
nineteenth-century popular literature. While edification was clearly a value, Weems's years
of bookselling experience told him that for edifying tales to sell, they also needed to entertain. Consequently, in his writing he blurred the lines between fact and fiction, didacticism
and diversion.

THE LIFE OF WASHINGTON; WITH CURIOUS ANECDOTES, EQUALLY HONORABLE TO HIMSELF AND EXEMPLARY TO HIS YOUNG COUNTRYMEN

Frontispiece portrait of George Washington from a second improved edition of the biography reprinted for Weems by the Philadelphia printer John Bioren in 1800 (Courtesy Lilly Library, Bloomington, IN).

Mason Locke Weems, *The Life of Washington: with Curious Anecdotes, Equally Honorable to Himself and Exemplary to His Young Countrymen*, 9th edition. Philadelphia: Mathew Carey, 1809.

Chapter I

Oh! as along the stream of time thy name
Expanded flies, and gathers all its fame;
May then these lines to future days descend,
And prove thy country's good thine *only end!*

"Ah, *gentlemen!*"—exclaimed Bonaparte[1]—'twas just as he was about to embark for Egypt
… some young Americans happening at Toulon, and anxious to see the mighty Corsican,
had obtained the honour of an introduction to him. Scarcely were past the customary salutations, when he eagerly asked, *"how fares your countryman, the great* WASHINGTON?" "He
was very well," replied the youths, brightening at the thought that they were the countrymen of Washington; "he was very well, general, when we left America."—*"Ah, gentlemen!"*
rejoined he, *"Washington can never be otherwise than well:—The measure of his fame is full—Posterity
shall talk of him with reverence as the founder of a great empire, when my name shall be lost in the vortex
of Revolutions!"*
 Who then that has a spark of virtuous curiosity, but must wish to know the history of
him whose name could thus awaken the sigh even of Bonaparte? But is not his history
already known? Have not a thousand orators spread his fame abroad, bright as his own
Potomac, when he reflects the morning sun, and flames like a sea of liquid gold, the wonder
and delight of all the neighbouring shores? Yes, they have indeed spread his fame abroad
… his fame as Generalissimo of the armies, and first President of the councils of his nation.
But this is not *half his* fame… True, he is there seen in *greatness,* but it is only the greatness
of public character, which is no evidence of *true greatness;* for a public character is often an
artificial one. At the head of an army or nation, where gold and glory are at stake, and
where a man feels himself the *burning focus* of unnumbered eyes; he must be a paltry fellow
indeed, who does not play his part pretty handsomely … even the common passions of
pride, avarice, or ambition, will put him up to his metal, and call forth his best and bravest
doings. But let all this heat and blaze of public situation and incitement be withdrawn; let
him be thrust back into the shade of private life, and you shall see how soon, like a forced
plant robbed of its hot-bed, he will drop his false foliage and fruit, and stand forth confessed
in native stickweed sterility and worthlessness… There was Benedict Arnold[2]—while strut-
ting a brigadier general on the public stage, he could play you the *great man,* on a handsome
scale … he out-marched Hannibal,[3] and outfought Burgoyne[4] … he chaced the British like
curlews, or cooped them up like chickens! and yet in the *private walks of life,* in Philadelphia,
he could swindle rum from the commissary's stores, and, with the aid of loose women, retail

---

1 Napoleon Bonaparte (1769–1821) became ruler of France soon after the French Revolution. He
 kept Europe in an almost constant state of war for more than a decade, and he was a student of
 the military tactics George Washington used during the American Revolution. In 1798, Napoleon
 invaded Egypt to threaten England's trade route with India.
2 Benedict Arnold (1741–1801) was a brilliant American general who shifted his allegiance to the
 British in the middle of the American Revolution.
3 Hannibal (247–183 BCE) was one of the most successful Carthaginian generals during the Punic
 Wars. One of his many amazing military feats was crossing the Alps with elephants to march
 on Rome.
4 A British general, John Burgoyne (1722–1792) became famous when he captured Fort Ticonderoga
 during the American Revolution.

it by the gill!! ... And there was the great duke of Marlborough[5] too—his public character a thunderbolt in war! Britain's boast, and terror of the French! But his private character what? Why a *swindler* to whom not *Arnold's* self could hold a candle; a perfect nondescript of baseness; a shaver of farthings from the poor sixpenny pay of his own brave soldiers!!!

It is not then in the glare of *public*, but in the shade *of private life*, that we are to look for the man. Private life is always *real* life. Behind the curtain, where the eyes of the million are not upon him, and where a man can have no motive but *inclination*, no excitement but *honest nature*, there he will always be sure to act *himself*; consequently, if he act greatly, he must be great indeed. Hence it has been justly said, that, "our *private deeds*, if *noble*, are noblest of our lives."

Of these private deeds of Washington very little has been said. In most of the elegant orations pronounced to his praise, you see nothing of Washington below *the clouds*—nothing of Washington the *dutiful son*—the affectionate brother—the cheerful schoolboy—the diligent surveyor—the neat draftsman—the laborious farmer—and widow's husband—the orphan's father—the poor man's friend. No! this is not the Washington you see; 'tis only Washington the HERO, and the Demigod.... Washington the *sun beam* in council, or the *storm* in war.

And in all the ensigns of character, amidst which he is generally drawn, you see none that represent him what he really was, "*the Jupiter Conservator*,"[6] *the friend and benefactor of men*. Where's his bright ploughshare that he loved—or his wheat-crowned fields, waving in yellow ridges before the wanton breeze—or his hills whitened over with flocks—or his clover-covered pastures spread with innumerous herds—or his neat-clad servants, with songs rolling the heavy harvest before them? Such were the scenes of *peace, plenty*, and *happiness*, in which Washington delighted. But his eulogists have denied him *these*, the only scenes which belong to man the great, and have trick'd him up in the vile drapery of man the *little*. See! there he stands! with the port of Mars "*the destroyer*," dark frowning over the fields of war ... the lightning of Potter's blade is by his side—the deep-mouthed cannon is before him, disgorging its flesh-mangling balls— his war-horse paws with impatience to bear him, a speedy thunderbolt, against the pale and bleeding ranks of Britain!—These are the drawings usually given of Washington; drawings masterly no doubt, and perhaps justly descriptive of him in some scenes of his life; but scenes they were, which I am sure his soul *abhorred*, and in which at any rate, you see nothing of his *private virtues*. These old fashioned commodities are generally thrown into the back ground of the picture, and treated, as the grandees at the London and Paris routs, treat their good old *aunts* and *grandmothers*, huddling them together into the *back rooms*, there to wheeze and cough by themselves, and not depress the fine laudanum-raised spirits of the *young sparklers*. And yet it was to those *old-fashioned virtues* that our hero owed every thing. For they in fact were the food of the great actions of him, whom men call Washington. It was they that enabled him, first to triumph over *himself*, then over the *British*, and uniformly to set such bright examples of *human perfectibility* and *true greatness*, that compared therewith, the history of his capturing Cornwallis and Tarleton,[7] with

---

5 The Duke of Marlborough (1650–1722), one of Britain's greatest generals, led successful British campaigns against the French.

6 Jupiter was the most powerful and highest-ranking Roman god. He used thunderbolts as his weapon and was also known as the "Light-Bringer." Jupiter was especially interested in upholding oaths and served as the chief divine protector of the Roman Republic.

7 Charles Cornwallis (1738–1805) and Banastre Tarleton (1754–1833) were both high-ranking British officers who were defeated in Revolutionary War battles. Ironically, Cornwallis was one

their buccaneering legions, sounds almost as *small* as the story of old General Putnam's[8] catching his wolf and her lamb-killing whelps.

Since then it is the private virtues that lay the foundation of all human excellence—since it was these that exalted Washington to be *"Columbia's[9] first* and *greatest Son,"* be it our first care to present these, in all their lustre, before the admiring eyes of our *children.* To *them* his private character is *every thing;* his public, hardly *any thing.* For how glorious soever it may have been in Washington to have undertaken the emancipation of his country; to have stemmed the long tide of adversity; to have baffled every effort of a wealthy and warlike nation; to have obtained for his countrymen the completest victory, and for himself the most unbounded power; and then to have returned that power, accompanied with all the weight of his own great character and advice to establish a government that should immortalize the blessings of liberty … however glorious, I say, all this may have been to himself, or instructive to future generals and presidents, yet does it but *little* concern our *children.* For who among us can hope that his son shall ever be called, like Washington, to direct the storm of war, or to ravish the ears of deeply listening Senates? To be constantly placing him then, before our children, in this high character, what is it but like springing in the clouds a golden Phoenix,[10] which no mortal calibre can ever hope to reach? Or like setting pictures of the Mammoth before the *mice* whom "not all the manna of Heaven" can ever raise to equality? Oh no! give us his *private virtues!* In *these,* every youth is interested, because in these every youth may become a Washington—a Washington in piety and patriotism,—in industry and honour—and consequently a Washington, in what alone deserves the name, SELF ESTEEM and UNIVERSAL RESPECT.

Chapter II

Birth and Education

Children like tender osiers take the bow;
And as they first are form'd for ever grow.

To this day numbers of good Christians can hardly find faith to believe that Washington was, bona fide, *a Virginian! "What! a buckskin!"* say they with a smile, *"George Washington a buckskin! pshaw! impossible! he was certainly an European: So great a man could never have been born in America."*

So *great a man could never have been born in America!*—Why that's the very *prince of reasons* why he should have been born here! Nature, we know, is fond of *harmonies;* and *paria paribus,* that is, *great things to great,* is the rule she delights to work by. Where, for example, do we look for the *whale* "the biggest born of nature?" not, I trow, in a *millpond,* but in the main ocean; *"there go the great ships,"* and there are the spoutings of whales amidst their boiling foam.

---

of the best British generals of the war, yet in 1781 he suffered a major defeat at Yorktown, Virginia, deciding the war in America's favor.

8 Rufus Putnam (1738–1824), a general during the American Revolution, later used his name and resources to help settle the vast frontier regions of Ohio.

9 Columbia is another name for the United States.

10 The phoenix is a legendary bird known for its remarkable beauty and ability to cheat death by rising from the funeral pyre that supposedly had consumed it.

By the same rule, where shall we look for Washington, the greatest among men, but in *America?* That greatest Continent, which, rising from beneath the frozen pole, stretches far and wide to the south, running almost *"whole the length of this vast terrene,"* and sustaining on her ample sides the roaring shock of half the watery globe. And equal to its size, is the furniture of this vast continent, where the Almighty has reared his cloud-capt mountains, and spread his sea-like lakes, and poured his mighty rivers, and hurled down his thundering cataracts in a style of the *sublime,* so far superior to any thing of the kind in the other continents, that we may fairly conclude that great men and great deeds are designed for America.

This seems to be the verdict of honest analogy; and accordingly we find America the honoured cradle of Washington, who was born on Pope's creek, in Westmoreland county, Virginia, the 22d of February, 1732. His father, whose name was Augustin Washington, was also a Virginian, but his grandfather (John) was an Englishman, who came over and settled in Virginia in 1657.

His father fully persuaded that a marriage of virtuous love comes nearest to angelic life, early stepped up to the *altar* with glowing cheeks and joy sparkling eyes, while by his side, with soft warm hand, sweetly trembling in his, stood the angel form of the lovely Miss Dandridge.

After several years of great domestic happiness, Mr. Washington was separated, by death, from this excellent woman, who left him and two children to lament her early fate.

Fully persuaded still, that *"it is not good for man to be alone,"* he renewed, for the second time, the chaste delights of matrimonial love. His consort was Miss Mary Ball, a young lady of fortune, and descended from one of the best families in Virginia.

From his intermarriage with this charming girl, it would appear that our Hero's father must have possessed either a very pleasing person, or highly polished manners, or perhaps *both; for,* from what I can learn, he was at that time at least 40 years old! while she, on the other hand, was universally toasted as the belle of the Northern Neck, and in the full bloom and freshness of love-inspiring sixteen. This I have from one who tells me that he has carried down many a sett dance with her; I mean that amiable and pleasant old gentleman, John Fitzhugh, Esq. of Stafford, *who* was, all his life, a neighbour and intimate of the Washington family. By his first wife, Mr. Washington had two children, both sons—Lawrence and Augustin. By his second wife, he had five children, four sons and a daughter—George, Samuel, John, Charles, and Elizabeth. Those *over delicate* ones, who are ready to faint at thought of a second marriage, might do well to remember, that the greatest man that ever lived was the son of this second marriage!

Little George had scarcely attained his fifth year, when his father left Pope's creek, and came up to a plantation which he had in Stafford, opposite to Fredericksburg. The house in which he lived is still to be seen. It lifts its low and modest front of faded red, over the turbid waters of Rappahannock; whither, to this day, numbers of people repair, and, with emotions unutterable, looking at the weatherbeaten mansion, exclaim, *"Here's the house where the Great Washington was born!"*

But it is all a mistake; for he was born, as I said, at Pope's creek, in Westmoreland county, near the margin of his own roaring Potomac.

The first place of education to which George was ever sent, was a little *"old field school,"* kept by one of his father's tenants, named Hobby; an honest, poor old man, who acted in the double character of sexton and schoolmaster. On his skill as a gravedigger, tradition is silent; but for a teacher of youth, his qualifications were certainly of the humbler sort;

making what is generally called an A. B. C. schoolmaster. Such was the preceptor who first taught Washington the knowledge of letters! Hobby lived to see his young pupil in all his glory, and rejoiced exceedingly. In his cups—for, though a *sexton*, he would sometimes drink, particularly on the General's birth-days—he used to boast, that "'*twas he, who, between his knees, had laid the foundation of George Washington's greatness.*"

But though George was early sent to a schoolmaster, yet he was not on that account neglected by his father. Deeply sensible of the *loveliness* and *worth* of which human nature is capable, through the *virtues* and *graces* early implanted in the heart, he never for a moment, lost sight of George in those all-important respects.

To assist his son to overcome that selfish spirit which too often leads children to fret and fight about trifles, was a notable care of Mr. Washington. For this purpose, of all the presents, such as cakes, fruit, &c. he received, he was always desired to give a liberal part to his play-mates. To enable him to do this with more alacrity, his father would remind him of the love which he would hereby gain, and the frequent presents which would in return be made *to him;* and also would tell of that great and good God, who delights above all things to see children love one another, and will assuredly reward them for acting so amiable a part.

Some idea of Mr. Washington's plan of education in this respect, may be collected from the following anecdote, related to me twenty years ago by an aged lady, who was a distant relative, and when a girl spent much of her time in the family.

"*On a fine morning,*" said she, "*in the fall of 1737, Mr. Washington, having little George by the hand, came to the door and asked my cousin Washington and myself to walk with him to the orchard, promising he would show us a fine sight. On arriving at the orchard, we were presented with a fine sight indeed. The whole earth, as far as we could see, was strewed with fruit: and yet the trees were bending under the weight of apples, which hung in clusters like grapes, and vainly strove to hide their blushing cheeks behind the green leaves. Now, George, said his father, look here, my son! don't you remember when this good cousin of yours brought you that fine large apple last spring, how hardly I could prevail on you to divide with your brothers and sisters; though I promised you that if you would but do it, God Almighty would give you plenty of apples this fall. Poor George could not say a word; but hanging down his head, looked quite confused, while with his little naked toes he scratched in the soft ground. Now look up, my son, continued his father, look up, George! and see there how richly the blessed God has made good my promise to you. Wherever you turn your eyes, you see the trees loaded with fine fruit; many of them indeed breaking down, while the ground is covered with mellow apples more than you could ever eat, my son, in all your life time.*"

George looked in silence on the wide wilderness of fruit; he marked the busy humming bees, and heard the gay notes of birds, then lifting his eyes filled with shining moisture, to his father, he softly said, "*Well, Pa, only forgive me this time; see if I ever be so stingy any more.*"

Some, when they look up to the oak whose giant arms throw a darkening shade over distant acres, or whose single trunk lays the keel of a man of war, cannot bear to hear of the time when this mighty plant was but an acorn, which a pig could have demolished: but others, who know their value, like to learn the soil and situation which best produces such noble trees. Thus, parents that are *wise* will listen well pleased, while I relate how moved the steps of the youthful Washington, whose single worth far outweighs all the oaks of Bashan and the red spicy cedars of Lebanon. Yes, they will listen delighted while I tell of their Washington in the days of his youth, when his little feet were swift towards the nests of birds; or when, wearied in the chace of the butterfly, he laid him down on his grassy couch and slept, while ministering spirits, with their roseate wings, fanned his glowing cheeks, and kissed his lips of innocence with that fervent love which makes *the Heaven!*

Never did the wise Ulysses[11] take more pains with his beloved Telemachus, than did Mr. Washington with George, to inspire him with an *early love of truth.* "Truth, George," (said he) "is the loveliest quality of youth. I would ride fifty miles, my son, to see the little boy whose heart is so *honest,* and his lips so *pure,* that we may depend on every word he says. O how lovely does such a child appear in the eyes of every body! His parents dote on him; his relations glory in him; they are constantly praising him to their children, whom they beg to imitate him. They are often sending for him, to visit them; and receive him, when he comes, with as much joy as if he were a little angel, come to set pretty examples to their children.

"But, Oh! how different, George, is the case with the boy who is so given to lying, that nobody can believe a word he says! He is looked at with aversion wherever he goes, and parents dread to see him come among their children. Oh, George! my son! rather than see you come to this pass, dear as you are to my heart, gladly would I assist to nail you up in your little coffin, and follow you to your grave. Hard, indeed, would it be to me to give up my son, whose little feet are always so ready to run about with me, and whose fondly looking eyes and sweet prattle make so large a part of my happiness: but still I would give him up, rather than see him a common liar.

"Pa, (said George very seriously) do I ever tell lies?"

"No, George, I *thank God* you do not, my son; and I rejoice in the hope you never will. At least, you shall never, from me, have cause to be guilty of so shameful a thing. Many parents, indeed, even compel their children to this vile practice, by barbarously beating them for every little fault; hence, on the next offence, the little terrified creature slips out a *lie!* just to escape the rod. But as to yourself, George, you know I have *always* told you, and now tell you again, that, whenever by accident you do any thing wrong, which must often be the case, as you are but a poor little boy yet, without *experience* or *knowledge,* never tell a falsehood to conceal it; but come *bravely* up, my son, like a *little man,* and tell me of it: and instead of beating you, George, I will but the more honour and love you for it, my dear."

This, you'll say, was sowing good seed!—Yes, it was: and the crop, thank God, was, as I believe it ever will be, where a man acts the true parent, that is, the *Guardian Angel,* by his child.

The following anecdote is a *case in point.* It is too valuable to be lost, and too true to be doubted; for it was communicated to me by the same excellent lady to whom I am indebted for the last.

"When George," said she, "was about six years old, he was made the wealthy master of a *hatchet!* of which, like most little boys, he was immoderately fond, and was constantly going about chopping every thing that came in his way. One day, in the garden, where he often amused himself hacking his mother's pea-sticks, he unluckily tried the edge of his hatchet on the body of a beautiful young English cherry-tree, which he barked so terribly, that I don't believe the tree ever got the better of it. The next morning the old gentleman finding out what had befallen his tree, which, by the by, was a great favourite, came into the house, and with much warmth asked for the mischievous author, declaring at the same time, that he would not have taken five guineas for his tree. Nobody could tell him any thing about it. Presently George and his hatchet made their appearance. *George,* said his father, *do you know who killed that beautiful little cherry-tree yonder in the garden?* This was a *tough question;* and George staggered under it for a moment; but quickly recovered himself: and looking at his father, with the sweet face of youth brightened with the inexpressible charm

---

11 Ulysses, hero of Homer's epic poem, *The Odyssey,* had a son named Telemachus.

of all-conquering truth, he bravely cried out, "*I can't tell a lie, Pa; you know I can't tell a lie. I did cut it with my hatchet.*"—*Run to my arms, you dearest boy,* cried his father in transports, *run to my arms; glad am I, George, that you killed my tree; for you have paid me for it a thousand fold. Such an act of heroism in my son, is more worth than a thousand trees, though blossomed with silver, and their fruits of purest gold.*

It was in this way, by interesting at once both his *heart* and *head,* that Mr. Washington conducted George with great ease and pleasure along the happy paths of virtue. But well knowing that his beloved charge, soon to be a man, would be left exposed to numberless temptations, both from himself and from others, his heart throbbed with the tenderest anxiety to make him acquainted with that great being, whom to know and love, is to possess the surest defence against vice, and the best of all motives to virtue and happiness. To startle George into a lively sense of his Maker, he fell upon the following very curious but impressive expedient:

One day he went into the garden, and prepared a little bed of finely pulverized earth, on which he wrote George's name at full, in large letters—then strewing in plenty of cabbage seed, he covered them up and smoothed all over nicely with the roller. This bed he purposely prepared close along side of a gooseberry walk, which happening at this time to be well hung with ripe fruit, he knew would be honoured with George's visits pretty regularly every day. Not many mornings had passed away before in came George, with eyes wild rolling, and his little cheeks ready to burst with *great news.*

"O Pa! come here! come here!"

"What's the matter, my son, what's the matter?"

"O come here, I tell you, Pa, come here! and I'll show you such a sight as you never saw in all your life time."

The old gentleman suspecting what George would be at, gave him his hand, which he seized with great eagerness, and tugging him along through the garden, led him up point blank to the bed whereon was inscribed, in large letters, and in all the freshness of newly sprung plants, the full name of

GEORGE WASHINGTON

"There, Pa!" said George, quite in an ecstasy of astonishment, "did you ever see such a sight in all your life time?"

"Why it seems like a curious affair, sure enough, George!"

"But, Pa, who did make it there, who did make it there?"

"It grew there by *chance,* I suppose my son."

"By *chance,* Pa! O no! no! it never did grow there by *chance,* Pa; indeed that it never did!"

"High! why not, my son?"

"Why, Pa, did you ever see any body's name in a plant bed before?"

"Well, but George, such a thing might happen, though you never saw it before!"

"Yes, Pa, but I did never see the little plants grow up so as to make *one single* letter of my name before. Now, how could they grow up so as to make *all* the letters of my name! and then standing one after another, to spell *my name so exactly!*—and all so neat and even too, at top and bottom!! O Pa, you must not say *chance* did all this. Indeed *somebody* did it; and I dare say now, Pa, *you* did do it just to scare *me,* because I am your little boy."

His father smiled, and said, "Well George, you have guessed right—I indeed *did* it; but not to *scare* you, my son; but to learn you a great thing which I wish you to understand. I want, my son, to introduce you to your *true* Father."

"High, Pa, an't *you* my *true* father, that has loved me, and been so good to me always?"

"Yes, George, I am your father as the world calls it: and I love you very dearly too. But yet with all my love for you, George, I am but a poor good-for-nothing sort of a father in comparison of one you have."

"Aye! I know, well enough whom you mean, Pa. You mean God Almighty, don't you?"

"Yes, my son, I mean him indeed. *He is* your *true* Father, George."

"But, Pa, where is God Almighty? I did never *see* him yet."

"True, my son; but though you never *saw* him, yet he is always with you. You did not see me when ten days ago I made this little plant bed, where you see your name in such beauti-ful green letters; but though you did not *see* me here, yet you know I was here!!"

"Yes, Pa, that I do—I know you was here."

"Well then, and as my son could not believe that *chance* had made and put together so exactly the *letters* of his name, (though only sixteen) then how can he believe that *chance* could have made and put together all those millions and millions of things that are now so exactly fitted to his good? That my son may look at every thing around him, see! what fine eyes he has got! and a little pug nose to smell the sweet flowers! and pretty ears to hear sweet sound! and a lovely mouth for his bread and butter! and O, the little ivory teeth to cut it for him! and the dear little tongue to prattle with his father! and precious little hands and fingers to hold his playthings! and beautiful little feet for him to run about upon! and when my little rogue of a son is tired with running about, then the still night comes for him to lie down, and his mother sings, and the little crickets chirp him to sleep! and as soon as he has slept enough, and jumps up fresh and strong as a little buck, there the sweet golden light is ready for him! When he looks down into the water, there he sees the beautiful silver fishes for him! and up in the *trees* there are the apples, and peaches, and *thousands* of sweet fruits for him! and *all, all around* him, wherever my dear boy looks, he sees every thing just to his *wants and wishes;*—the bubbling springs with cool sweet water for him to drink! and the wood to make him sparkling fires when he is cold! and beautiful horses for him to ride! and strong oxen to work for him! and the *good* cows to give him milk! and bees to make sweet honey for his sweeter mouth! and the little lambs, with snowy wool, for beautiful clothes for him! Now, these and all the *ten thousand thousand other good things* more than my son can ever think of, and all so exactly fitted to his use and *delight*... Now how could chance ever have done all this for my little son? Oh George! ..."

He would have gone on, but George, who had hung upon his father's words with looks and eyes of all-devouring attention, here broke out—

"Oh Pa, that's enough! that's enough! It can't be chance, indeed, it can't be chance, that made and gave me all these things."

"What was it then, do you think, my son?"

"Indeed, Pa, I don't know, unless it was *God Almighty!*"

"Yes, George, he it was, my son, and nobody else."

"Well, but Pa, (continued George) does God Almighty give me *every thing?* Don't you give me *some things*, Pa?"

"I give *you* something, indeed! Oh! how can 1 give you any thing, George! I, who have nothing on earth that I can call my own, no, not even the breath I draw!"

"High, Pa! isn't that great big house your house, and this garden, and the horses yonder, and oxen, and sheep, and trees, and every thing, isn't all yours, Pa?"

"Oh no! my son! no! Why you make me shrink into nothing, George, when you talk of all these belonging to *me*, who can't even make *a grain of sand!* Oh, how could I, my son, have given life to those great oxen and horses, when I can't give life even to a fly?— no! for if the poorest fly were killed, it is not your father, George, nor all the men in the world, that could ever make him alive again!"

At this, George fell into a profound silence, while his pensive looks showed that his youthful soul was labouring with some idea never felt before. Perhaps it was at that moment, that the good Spirit of God ingrafted on his heart that germ of *piety*, which filled his after life with so many of the precious fruits of *morality*.

Chapter III

George's father dies—his education continued by his mother—
his behaviour under school-master Williams

Thus pleasantly, on wings of down, passed away the few short years of little George's and his father's *earthly* acquaintance. Sweetly ruled by the sceptre of REASON, George almost adored his father; and thus sweetly *obeyed* with all the cheerfulness of Love, his father doted on George... And though very different in their years, yet parental and filial love rendered them so mutually dear, that the old gentleman was often heard to regret, that *the school took his little companion so much from him*—while George, on the other hand, would often quit his playmates to run home and converse with his more beloved father.

But George was not long to enjoy the pleasure or the profit of such a companion; for scarcely had he attained his tenth year, before his father was seized with the gout in the stomach, which carried him off in a few days. George was not at home when his father was taken ill. He was on a visit to some of his cousins in Chotank, about twenty miles off; and his father, unwilling to interrupt his pleasures, for it was but seldom that he visited, would not at first allow him to be sent for. But finding that he was going very fast, he begged that they would send for him in all haste ... he often asked if he was come, and said how happy he should be, once more to see his little son, and give him his blessing before he died. But alas! he never enjoyed that last mournful pleasure; for George did not reach home until a few hours before his father's death, and then he was speechless! The moment he alighted, he ran into the chamber where he lay. But oh! what were his feelings when he saw the sad change that had passed upon him! when he beheld those eyes, late so *bright* and *fond*, now reft of all their lustre, faintly looking on him from their hollow sockets, and through swelling tears, in mute but melting language, bidding him a LAST, LAST FAREWELL! ... Rushing with sobs and cries, he fell upon his father's neck ... he kissed him a thousand and a thousand times, and bathed his clay-cold face with scalding tears.

O happiest youth! Happiest in that love, which thus, to its enamoured soul strained an aged an[d] expiring sire. O! worthiest to be the founder of a JUST and EQUAL GOVERNMENT, lasting as thy own deathless name! And O! happiest old man! thus luxuriously expiring in the arms of such a child! O! well requited for teaching him that LOVE OF HIS GOD *(the only fountain of every virtuous love)* in return for which he gave thee ('twas all he had) *himself*—his *fondest company*—his *sweetest looks and prattle*. He now gives thee his little strong embraces, with artless sighs and tears; faithful to thee still, his feet will follow thee to thy grave: and when thy beloved corse is let down to the stones of the pit, with streaming eyes he will rush to the brink, to take *one more* look, while his bursting heart will give thee its last trembling cry... *O my father! my father!*

But, though he had lost his best of friends, yet he never lost those divine sentiments which that friend had so carefully inculcated. On the contrary, interwoven with the fibres of his heart, they seemed to "grow with his growth, and to strengthen with his strength." The *memory* of his father, often bathed with *a tear*— the memory of his father now sleeping in his grave, was felt to impose a more sacred obligation to do what, 'twas known, would rejoice his departed shade. This was very happily displayed, in every part of his deportment, from the moment of his earliest intercourse with mankind.

Soon after the death of his father, his mother sent him down to Westmoreland, the place of his nativity, where he lived with his half-brother Augustin, and went to school to a Mr. Williams, an excellent teacher in that neighbourhood. He carried with him his virtues, *his zeal for unblemished character, his love of truth, and detestation of whatever was false and base.* A gilt chariot with richest robes and liveried servants, could not half so substantially have befriended him; for in a very short time, so completely had his virtues secured the love and confidence of the boys, his *word* was just as current among them as a *law*. A very aged gentleman, formerly a school-mate of his, has often assured me, (while pleasing recollection brightened his furrowed cheeks,) that nothing was more common, when the boys were in high dispute about a question of fact, than for some little shaver among the mimic heroes, to call out *"well boys! George Washington was there; George Washington was there; he knows all about it; and if he don't say it was so, then we will give it up,"*—*"done,"* said the adverse party. Then away they would trot to hunt for George. Soon as his verdict was heard, the party favoured would begin to crow, and then all hands would return to play again.

About five years after the death of his father, he quitted school for ever, leaving the boys in tears for his departure: for he had ever lived among them, in the spirit of a brother. He was never guilty of so brutish a practice as that of fighting them himself, nor would he, when able to prevent it, allow them to fight one another. If he could not disarm their savage passions by his arguments, he would instantly go to the master, and inform him of their barbarous intentions.

"The boys," said the same good old gentleman, "were often angry with George for this"—But he used to say, "angry or not angry, you shall never, boys, have my consent to a practice so shocking! shocking even in *slaves* and *dogs;* then how utterly scandalous in little boys at school, who ought to look on one another as brothers. And what must be the feelings of our tender parents, when, instead of seeing us come home smiling and lovely, as the JOYS OF THEIR HEARTS! they see us creeping in like young *blackguards*, with our heads *bound up, black eyes*, and *bloody clothes!* And what is all this for? Why, that we *may get praise!!* But the truth is, a quarrelsome boy was never sincerely praised! Big boys, of the *vulgar sort*, indeed may praise him; but it is only as they would a silly game cock, that fights for their *pastime*—and the little boys are sure to praise him, but it is only as they would a bull dog—to keep him from tearing them!!"

Some of his historians have said, and many believe, that Washington was a *Latin scholar!* But 'tis an error. He never learned a syllable of Latin. His second and last teacher, Mr. Williams, was indeed a capital hand—but not at Latin; for of that he understood perhaps as little as Balaam's ass[12]—but at *reading, spelling, English grammar, arithmetic, surveying, book-keeping and geography*, he was indeed famous. And in these useful arts, 'tis said, he often boasted that he had made *young George Washington as great a scholar as himself.*

---

12 Balaam was an Old Testament prophet (Num. 22–24) whose donkey, although it was only a beast of burden, recognized an angel of the Lord.

Born to be a soldier, Washington early discovered symptoms of nature's intentions towards him. In his 11th year, while at school under old Mr. Hobby, he used to divide his play-mates into two parties, *or armies*. One of these, for distinction sake, was called *French*, the other *American*. A big boy at the school, named William Bustle, commanded the former, George commanded the latter. And every day, at play-time, with corn-stalks for muskets, and calabashes for drums, the two armies would turn out, and march, and counter-march, and file off or fight their mimic battles, with great fury. This was fine sport for George, whose passion for active exercise was so strong, that at play-time no weather could keep him within doors. His *fair cousins*, who visited at his mother's, used to complain, that *"George was not fond of their company, like other boys; but soon as he had got his task, would run out to play."* But such trifling play as marbles and tops he could never abide. They did not afford him exercise enough. His delight was in that of the manliest sort, which, by stringing the limbs and swelling the muscles, promotes the kindliest flow of blood and spirits. At jumping with a long pole, or heaving heavy weights, for his years he hardly had an equal. And as to running, the swift-footed Achilles could scarcely have matched his speed.

"Egad! he ran wonderfully," said my amiable and aged friend, John Fitzhugh, esq. who knew him well. *"We had nobody here-abouts, that could come near him. There was young Langhorn Dade, of Westmoreland, a confounded clean made, tight young fellow, and a mighty swift runner too ... but then he was no match for George: Langy, indeed, did not like to give it up; and would brag that he had sometimes brought George to a tie. But I believe he was mistaken: for I have seen them run together many a time; and George always beat him easy enough."*

Col. Lewis Willis, his play-mate and kinsman, has been heard to say, that he has often seen him throw a stone across Rappahannock, at the lower ferry of Fredericksburg. It would be no easy matter to find a man, now-a-days, who could do it.

Indeed, his father before him was a man of extraordinary strength. His gun, which to this day is called *Washington's fowling-piece*, and now the property of Mr. Harry Fitzhugh, of Chotank, is of such enormous weight, that not one man in a hundred can fire it without a rest. And yet throughout that country it is said, that he made nothing of holding it off at arms length, and blazing away at the swans on Potomac; of which he has been known to kill *rank* and *file*, seven or eight at a shot.

But to return to George... It appears that from the start he was a boy of an uncommonly warm and noble heart; insomuch that Lawrence, though but his *half-brother*, took such a liking to him, even above his *own* brother Augustin, that he would always have George with him when he could get him; and often pressed him to come and live with him. But, as if led by some secret impulse, George declined the offer, and went up, as we have seen, to work, in the back-woods, as Lord Fairfax's surveyor! However, when Lawrence was taken with the consumption, and advised by his physicians to make a trip to Bermuda, George could not resist any longer, but hastened down to his brother at Mount Vernon, and went with him to Bermuda. It was at Bermuda that George took the small-pox, which marked him rather agreeably than otherwise. Lawrence never recovered, but returned to Virginia, where he died just after his brother George had fought his hard battle against the French and Indians, at Fort Necessity, as the reader will presently learn.

Lawrence did not live to see George after that; but he lived to hear of his fame; for as the French and Indians were at that time a great public terror, the people could not help being very loud in their praise of a youth, who with so slender a force had dared to meet them in their own country, and had given them such a check.

And when Lawrence heard of his favourite young brother, that he had fought so gallantly for his country, and that the whole land was filled with his praise, he *wept* for joy. And such is the victory of love over nature, that though fast sinking under the fever and cough of a consumption in its extreme stage, he did not seem to mind it, but spent his last moments in fondly talking of his brother George, who, he said, *"he had always believed, would one day or other be a great man!"*

On opening his will, it was found that George had lost nothing by his dutiful and affectionate behaviour to his brother Lawrence. For having now no issue, (his only child, a little daughter, lately dying) he left to George all his rich lands in Berkley, together with his great estate on Potomac, called MOUNT VERNON,[13] in honour of old Admiral Vernon, by whom he had been treated with great politeness, while a volunteer with him at the unfortunate siege of Carthagena, in 1741.

Chapter XIII

Character of Washington

> Let the poor witling argue all he can,
> It is Religion still that makes the man.

When the children of the years to come, hearing his great name re-echoed from every lip, shall say to their fathers, *"what was it that raised Washington to such height of glory?"* let them be told that it was HIS GREAT TALENTS, CONSTANTLY GUIDED AND GUARDED BY RELIGION. For how shall man, *frail man*, prone to inglorious ease and pleasure, ever ascend the arduous steps of virtue, unless animated by the *mighty hopes* of religion? Or what shall stop him in his swift descent to infamy and vice, if unawed by that dread power which proclaims to the guilty that their secret crimes are seen, and shall not go unpunished? Hence the wise, in all ages, have pronounced, that *"there never was a truly great man without religion."*

There have, indeed, been *courageous generals*, and *cunning statesmen*, without religion, but mere courage or cunning, however paramount, never yet made a man great.

> Admit that this can conquer, that can cheat!
> 'Tis phrase absurd to call a villain *great!*
> Who wickedly is wise, or madly brave,
> Is but the more a fool, the more a knave.

No! To be truly great, a man must have not only great talents, but those talents must be constantly exerted on great, i.e. good actions—*and perseveringly* too—for if he should turn aside to vice—farewell to his heroism. Hence, when Epaminondas was asked which was the greatest man, himself or Pelopidas?[14] he replied, *"wait till we are dead:["]* meaning that the all of heroism depends on *perseverance* in great good actions. But, sensual and grovelling as man is, what can incline and elevate him to those things like religion, that divine power, to

---

13 George Washington inherited this 5,000-acre estate (in Virginia) from his elder half brother, Lawrence. It was named for Admiral Edward Vernon, with whom Lawrence had served in the Caribbean. After his father's death, George spent part of his youth at Mount Vernon with Lawrence.

14 The Theban leaders Epaminondas and Pelopidas worked together to break the military dominance of Sparta and raise Thebes to become the central power in ancient Greece for a short period (371–62 BCE).

whom alone it belongs to present those vast and eternal *goods* and *ills* which best alarm our fears, enrapture our hopes, inflame the worthiest loves, rouse the truest avarice, and in short touch every spring and passion of our souls in favour of virtue and noble actions.

Did SHAME restrain Alcibiades from a base action in the presence of Socrates?[15] *"Behold,"* says religion, "a *greater than Socrates is here!"*

Did LOVE embolden Jacob[16] to brave fourteen years of slavery for an earthly beauty? Religion springs that eternal love, for whose sake good men can even glory in laborious duties.

Did the ambition of a civic crown animate Scipio[17] to heroic deeds? Religion holds a crown, at the sight of which the laurels of a Caesar[18] droop to weeds.

Did avarice urge Cortez[19] through a thousand toils and dangers for wealth? Religion points to those treasures in heaven, compared to which all diamond beds and mines of massy gold are but trash.

Did good Aurelius[20] study the happiness of his subjects for this world's glory? Religion displays that world of glory, where those who have laboured to make others happy, shall *"shine like stars for ever and ever."*

Does the fear of death deter man from horrid crimes? Religion adds infinite horrors to that fear—it warns them of a death both of soul and body in hell.

In short, what motives under heaven can restrain men from vices and crimes, and urge them on, full stretch, after individual and national happiness, like those of religion? For lack of these motives, alas! how many who once dazzled the world with the glare of their exploits, are now eclipsed and set to rise no more!

There was Arnold, who, in courage and military talents, glittered in the same firmament with Washington, and, for a while, his face shone like the star of the morning; but alas! for lack of Washington's religion, he soon fell, like Lucifer, from a heaven of glory, into an abyss of never-ending infamy.

And there was general Charles Lee,[21] too, confessedly a great wit, a great scholar, a great soldier, but, after all, not a great man. For, through lack of that magnanimous benevolence which religion inspires, he fell into the vile state of *envy*, and, on the plains of Monmouth, rather than fight to immortalize Washington, he chose to retreat and disgrace himself.

There was the gallant general Hamilton[22] also—a gigantic genius—*a statesman* fit to rule the mightiest monarchy—a soldier *"fit to stand by Washington, and give command."* But alas! for

---

15 Alcibiades (450–404 BCE) was an early student and ally of the great Greek philosopher Socrates (470–399 BCE), but later abandoned Socrates's teachings for political power and its rewards.

16 Jacob waited 14 years to marry Rachel (Gen. 29).

17 Name of two Roman generals, both renowned for their brilliant strategies in the wars between Rome and Carthage.

18 Julius Caesar (100–14 BCE) was a great Roman general and politician who played a pivotal role in turning the Roman Republic into the Roman Empire. His military exploits often were rewarded with the much-coveted victory crown of laurel leaves.

19 Hernán Cortés (1485–1547) was an early explorer of Central America who was driven by a thirst for the riches and fame that accompanied the conquest of new lands for Spain.

20 Marcus Aurelius (121–180) was both a Roman emperor and a distinguished stoic philosopher who wrote extensively on how to best pursue contentment amid life's tribulations.

21 At the Revolutionary War battle of Monmouth in 1778, Charles Lee ordered a retreat that cost General Washington a victory. He was later court-martialed for this act.

22 Not known for his commitment to religion, Alexander Hamilton (1755–1804) was an immensely pragmatic and gifted leader, both during and after the Revolution. His career was cut short when he was killed in a duel by Aaron Burr.

lack of religion, see how all was lost! preferring the praise of man to that praise *"which cometh from God,"* and pursuing the phantom honour up to the pistol's mouth, he is cut off at once from life and greatness, and leaves his family and country to mourn his hapless fate.

And there was the fascinating colonel Burr.[23] A man born to be *great*—brave as Caesar, polished as Chesterfield,[24] eloquent as Cicero,[25] and, lifted by the strong arm of his country, he rose fast, and bade fair soon to fill the place where Washington had sat. But, alas! lacking religion, he could not wait the spontaneous fall of the rich honours ripening over his head, but in evil hour stretched forth his hand to the forbidden fruit, and by that fatal act was cast out from the Eden of our republic, and amerced of greatness for ever.

But why should I summon the Arnolds and Lees, the Hamiltons and Burrs of the earth to give sad evidence, that no valour, no genius alone can make men great? do we not daily meet with instances, of youth amiable and promising as their fond parents' wishes, who yet, merely for lack of religion, soon make shipwreck of every precious hope, sacrificing their gold to gamblers, their health to harlots, and their glory to grog—making conscience their curse, this life a purgatory, and the next a hell!! In fact, a young man, though of the finest talents and education, without religion, is but like a gorgeous ship without ballast. Highly painted and with flowing canvas, she launches out on the deep; and, during a smooth sea and gentle breeze, she moves along stately as the pride of ocean; but, as soon as the stormy winds descend, and the blackening billows begin to roll, suddenly she is overset, and disappears for ever. But who is this coming, thus gloriously along, with masts towering to heaven, and his sails white, looming like the mountain of snows? Who is it but *"Columbia's first and greatest son!"* whose talents, like the sails of a mighty ship spread far and wide, catching the gales of heaven, while his capacious soul, stored with the rich ballast of religion, remains firm and unshaken as the ponderous rock. The warm zephyrs of prosperity breathe meltingly upon him—the rough storms of adversity descend—the big billows of affliction dash, but nothing can move him; his eye is fixed on God! the *present joys* of an approving conscience, and the hope of that glory which fadeth not away; these comfort and support him.

"There exists," says Washington, *"in the economy of nature, an inseparable connexion between duty and advantage."*—The whole life of this great man bears glorious witness to the truth of this his favourite aphorism. At the giddy age of fourteen, when the spirits of youth are all on tiptoe for freedom and adventures, he felt a strong desire to go to sea; but, very opposite to his wishes, his mother declared that she could not bear to part with him. His trial must have been very severe; for I have been told that a midshipman's commission was actually in his pocket—his trunk of clothes on board the ship—his honour in some sort pledged—his young companions importunate with him to go—and his whole soul panting for the promised pleasures of the voyage; but religion whispered *"honour thy mother, and grieve not the spirit of her who bore thee."*

---

23 Aaron Burr (1756–1836) attained important posts, including vice president under Thomas Jefferson, but is remembered chiefly for the duel in which he killed Alexander Hamilton. His reputation and career never fully recovered after Hamilton's death.

24 Philip Dromer Stanhope (1694–1773), the 4th Earl of Chesterfield, was a famous British statesman and diplomat. His *Letters to His Son* and *Letters to His Godson* became tremendously popular guides on manners.

25 Along with the Athenian, Demosthenes (384–322 BCE), the Roman, Marcus Tullius Cicero, (106–43 BCE) was widely considered one of the two greatest orators of the ancient Western world.

Instantly the glorious boy sacrificed inclination to duty—dropt all thoughts of the voyage, and gave tears of joy to his widowed mother, in clasping to her bosom a dear child who could deny himself to make her happy.

'Tis said, that, when he saw the last boat going on board, with several of his youthful friends in it—when he saw the flash and heard the report of the signal gun for sailing, and the ship in all her pride of canvas rounding off for sea, he could not bear it, but turned away, and, half choaked with grief, went into the room where his mother sat. *"George, my dear!"* said she, *"have you already repented that you made your mother so happy just now?"* Upon this, falling on her bosom, with his arms round her neck, and a gush of tears, he said, *"my dear mother, I must not deny that I am sorry; but, indeed, I feel that I should be much more sorry, were I on board the ship, and knew that you were unhappy."*

"Well," replied she embracing him tenderly, *"God, I hope, will reward my dear boy for this, some day or other."* Now see here, young reader, and learn that he who prescribes our duty, is able to reward it. Had George left his fond mother to a broken heart, and gone off to sea, 'tis next to certain that he would never have taken that active part in the French and Indian war, which, by securing to him the hearts of his countrymen, paved the way for all his future greatness.

Now for another instance of the wonderful effect of religion on Washington's fortune. Shortly after returning from the war of Cuba, Lawrence (his *half* brother) was taken with the consumption, which made him so excessively fretful, that his *own* brother, Augustin, would seldom come near him. But George, whose heart was early under the softening and sweetening influences of religion, felt such a tenderness for his poor sick brother, that he not only put up with his peevishness, but seemed, from what I have been told, never so happy as when he was with him. He accompanied him to the island of Bermuda, in quest of health—and, after their return to Mount Vernon, often as his duty to lord Fairfax permitted, he would come down from the back woods to see him. And while with him he was always contriving or doing something to cheer and comfort his brother. Sometimes with his gun he would go out in quest of partridges and snipes, and other fine flavoured game, to tempt his brother's sickly appetite, and gain him strength. At other times he would sit for hours and read to him some entertaining book—and, when his cough came on, he would support his drooping head, and wipe the cold dew from his forehead, or the phlegm from his lips, and give him his medicine, or smooth his pillow; and all with such alacrity and artless tenderness as proved the sweetest cordial to his brother's spirits. For he was often heard to say to the Fairfax family, into which he married, that *"he should think nothing of his sickness, if he could but always have his brother George with him."* Well, what was the consequence? Why, when Lawrence came to die, he left almost the whole of his large estate to George, which served as another noble step to his future greatness.

For further proof of *"the inseparable connexion between duty and advantage,"* let us look at Washington's conduct through the French and Indian war.[26] To a man of his uncommon military mind, and skill in the arts of Indian warfare, the pride and precipitance of general Braddock[27] must have been excessively disgusting and disheartening. But we hear nothing of his *threatening* either to leave or supplant Braddock. On the contrary, he nobly brooked

---

26 The French and Indian War was a nine-year conflict (1754–63) in which Britain defeated France for control of North America.

27 Edward Braddock (1695–1755), best known as an unsuccessful British commander in the French and Indian War, died of wounds sustained in battle.

his rude manners, gallantly obeyed his rash orders, and, as far as in him lay, endeavoured to correct their fatal tendencies.

And, after the death of Braddock, and the desertion of Dunbar,[28] that weak old man, governor Dinwiddie,[29] added infinitely to his hardships and hazards, by appointing him to the defence of the frontiers, and yet withholding the necessary forces and supplies. But though by that means, the western country was continually overrun by the enemy, and cruelly deluged in blood—though much wearied in body by marchings and watchings, and worse tortured in soul, by the murders and desolations of the inhabitants, he shrinks not from *duty*—still seeking the smiles of conscience as his greatest good; and as the sorest evil, dreading its frowns, he bravely maintained his ground, and, after three years of unequalled dangers and difficulties, succeeded.

Well, what was the consequence? why it drew upon him, from his admiring country-men, such an unbounded confidence in his principles and patriotism, as secured to him the command of the *American armies*, in the revolutionary war!

And there again the connexion between *"duty and advantage"* was as gloriously displayed. For though congress was, in legal and political knowledge an enlightened body, and for patriotism equal to the senators of Republican Rome, yet certainly in military matters they were no more to be compared to him, than those others were to Hannibal. But still, though they were constantly thwarting his counsels, and in place of good soldiers sending him raw militia, thus compelling inactivity, or ensuring defeat—dragging out the war—dispiriting the nation—and disgracing him, yet we hear from him no gusts of passion; no dark intrigues to supplant congress, and, with the help of an idolizing nation and army, to snatch the power from their hands, and make himself king. On the contrary, he continues to treat congress as a virtuous son his respected parents. He points out wiser measures, but in defect of their adoption, makes the best use of those they give him, and at length, through the mighty blessing of God, established the independence of his country, and then went back to his plough.

Well, what was the consequence? why, these noble acts so completely filled up the meas-ure of his country's love for him, as to give him that first of all felicities, the felicity to be the guardian angel of his country, and able by the magic of his name, to scatter every cloud of danger that gathered over her head.

For example, at the close of the war, when the army, about to be disbanded with-out their wages, was wrought up to such a pitch of discontent and rage, as seriously to threaten *civil war*, see the wonderful influence which their love for him gave him over themselves! In the height of their passion, and that a very natural passion too, he but makes a short speech to them, and the storm is laid! the tumult subsides! and the soldiers, after all their hardships, consent to ground their arms, and return home without a penny in their pockets!!!

---

28 Thomas Dunbar (? −1767) served alongside Washington under Braddock during the French and Indian War. After Braddock was killed along with many of his troops, Dunbar withdrew with his command to the safety of Philadelphia, leaving much of Virginia unprotected from the French and Indians.

29 Robert Dinwiddie (1690? −1770) was governor of Virginia during the French and Indian War. After Braddock's death, he made Washington responsible for defending the Virginia frontier. Washington constantly sought more supplies and troops from Dinwiddie, who was slow to provide them.

Also, in that very alarming dispute between Vermont and Pennsylvania, where the furious parties, in spite of all the efforts of congress and their governors, had actually shouldered their guns, and were dragging on their cannon for a bloody fight—Washington only dropt them a few lines of his advice, and instantly they faced about for their homes, and laying by their weapons, seized their ploughs again, like dutiful children, on whose kindling passions a beloved father had shaken his hoary locks!!

And, in the western counties of Pennsylvania, where certain blind patriots, affecting to strain at the gnat of a small excise, but ready enough to swallow the hellish camel of rebellion, had kindled the flames of civil war,[30] and thrown the whole nation into a tremor, Washington had just to send around a circular to the people of the union, stating the infinite importance of maintaining the SACRED REIGN OF THE LAWS, and instantly twenty thousand well-armed volunteers dashed out among the insurgents, and without shedding a drop of blood, extinguished the insurrection!

In short, it were endless to enumerate the many horrid insurrections and bloody wars which were saved to this country by Washington, and all through the divine force of *early religion!* for it was this that enabled him inflexibly to do his duty, by imitating God in his glorious works of wisdom and benevolence; and all the rest followed as naturally as light follows the sun.

We have seen at page 15 of this little work,[31] with what pleasure the youthful Washington hung upon his father's lips, while descanting on the adorable wisdom and benevolent designs of God in all parts of this beautiful and harmonious creation. By such lessons in the book of nature, this virtuous youth was easily prepared for the far higher and surer lectures of revelation, I mean that blessed gospel which contains the MORAL philosophy of heaven. There he learnt, that *"God is love"*—and that all that he desires, with respect to men, is to glorify himself in their happiness—and since virtue is indispensable to that happiness, the infinite and eternal weight of God's attributes must be for virtue, and against vice; and consequently that God will sooner or later gloriously reward the one and punish the other. This was the creed of Washington. And looking on it as the only basis of human virtue and happiness, he very cordially embraced it himself, and wished for nothing so much as to see all others embrace it.

I have often been told by colonel Ben Temple, (of King William county, Virginia), who was one of his aids in the French and Indian war, that he has frequently known Washington, on the sabbath, read the scriptures and pray with his regiment, in the absence of the chaplain; and also that, on sudden and unexpected visits into his marquee, he has, more than once, found him on his knees at his devotions.

The Reverend Mr. Lee Massey, long a rector of Washington's parish, and from early life his intimate, has assured me a thousand times, that "he never knew so constant a churchman as Washington. And his behaviour in the house of God," added my reverend friend, "was so deeply reverential, that it produced the happiest effects on my congregation, and greatly assisted me in my moralizing labours. No company ever kept him from church. I have been many a time at Mount Vernon on the sabbath morning, when his

---

30 In the years immediately following the American Revolution, the United States was threatened by civil war. Everything from state borders to taxation was in dispute, with no central power to adjudicate matters. Washington attempted to defuse these problems by working to establish a strong, centralized federal government.

31 See p. 74 of this anthology.

breakfast table was filled with guests. But to him they furnished no pretext for neglecting his God, and losing the satisfaction of setting a good example. For instead of staying at home out of a false complaisance to them, he used constantly to invite them to accompany him."

His secretary, judge Harrison, has frequently been heard to say, that, "whenever the general would be spared from camp on the sabbath, he never failed riding out to some neighbouring church, to join those who were publicly worshipping the Great Creator."

And while he resided at Philadelphia, as president of the United States, his constant and cheerful attendance on divine service was such as to convince every reflecting mind that he deemed no levee so honourable as that of his Almighty Maker; no pleasures equal to those of devotion; and no business a sufficient excuse for neglecting his supreme benefactor.

In the winter of '77, while Washington, with the American army lay encamped at Valley Forge, a certain good old friend, of the respectable family and name of Potts, if I mistake not, had occasion to pass through the woods near head-quarters. Treading his way along the venerable grove, suddenly he heard the sound of a human voice, which as he advanced increased on his ear, and at length became like the voice of one speaking much in earnest. As he approached the spot with a cautious step, whom should he behold, in a dark natural bower of ancient oaks, but the commander in chief of the American armies on his knees at prayer! Motionless with surprise, friend Potts continued on the place till the general, having ended his devotions, arose, and, with a countenance of angel serenity, retired to headquarters: friend Potts then went home, and on entering his parlour called out to his wife, "Sarah, my dear! Sarah! All's well! all's well! George Washington will yet prevail!"

"What's the matter, Isaac?" replied she; "thee seems moved."

"Well, if I seem moved, 'tis no more than what I am. I have this day seen what I never expected. Thee knows that I always thought the sword and the gospel utterly inconsistent; and that no man could be a soldier and a christian at the same time. But George Washington has this day convinced me of my mistake."

He then related what he had seen, and concluded with this prophetical remark—"If George Washington be not a man of God, I am greatly deceived—and still more shall I be deceived if God do not, through him, work out a great salvation for America."

When he was told that the British troops at Lexington, on the memorable 19th of April, 1775, had fired on and killed several of the Americans, he replied, "I *grieve for the death of my countrymen, but rejoice that the British are still so determined to keep God on our side,*" alluding to that noble sentiment which he has since so happily expressed; viz. "*The smiles of Heaven can never be expected on a nation that disregards the eternal rules of order and right, which Heaven itself has ordained.*"

When called by his country in 1775, to lead her free-born sons against the arms of Britain, what charming modesty, what noble self-distrust, what pious confidence in Heaven, appeared in all his answers. "*My diffidence in my own abilities, says he, was superseded by a confidence in the rectitude of our cause and the patronage of Heaven.*"

And when called to the presidency by the unanimous voice of the nation, thanking him for his great services past, with anticipations of equally great to come, his answer deserves approbation.

"*When I contemplate the interposition of providence, as it was visibly manifested in guiding us through the revolution, in preparing us for the reception of a general government, and in conciliating the good will of the people of America towards one another after its adoption; I feel myself oppressed and almost overwhelmed with a sense of the divine munificence. I feel that nothing is due to my personal agency in all those complicated and wonderful events, except what can simply be attributed to the exertions of an honest zeal for the good of my country.*"

And when he presented himself for the first time before that august body, the congress of the U. States, April 30th, 1789—when he saw before him the pride of Columbia in her chosen sons, assembled to consult how best to strengthen the chain of love between the states—to preserve friendship and harmony with foreign powers—to secure the blessings of civil and religious liberty—and to build up our young republic a great and happy people among the nations of the earth—never patriot entered on such important business with fairer hopes, whether we consider the unanimity and confidence of the citizens, or his own and the abilities and virtues of his fellow-counsellors.

But all this would not do; nothing short of the *divine friendship* could satisfy Washington. Feeling the magnitude, difficulty, and danger of managing such an assemblage of communities and interests; dreading the machinations of bad men, and well knowing the insufficiency of all second causes, even the *best;* he piously reminds congress of the wisdom of imploring the benediction of the *great first Cause*, without which he knew that his beloved country could never prosper.

"It would," says he, "be peculiarly improper to omit, in this first official act, my fervent supplications to that Almighty Being who rules over the universe; who presides in the councils of nations; and whose providential aids can supply every human defect, that his benediction may consecrate to the liberties and happiness of the people of the United States, a government instituted by themselves for these essential purposes, and may enable every instrument employed in its administration to execute with success the functions allotted to his charge. In tendering this homage to the great Author of every public and private good, I assure myself that it expresses your sentiments not less than my own; nor those of my fellow-citizens at large less than either. No people can be bound to acknowledge and adore the invisible hand which conducts the affairs of men, more than the people of the United States. Every step, by which they have advanced to the character of an independent nation, seems to have been distinguished by some token of providential agency. These reflections, arising out of the present crisis, have forced themselves too strongly on my mind to be suppressed. You will join with me, I trust, in thinking, that there are none, under the influence of which the proceedings of a new and free government can more auspiciously commence."

And after having come near to the close of this the most sensible and virtuous speech ever made to a sensible and virtuous representation of a free people, he adds—"I shall take my present leave: but not without resorting *once more* to the benign Parent of the human race in humble supplication, that, since he has been pleased to favour the American people with opportunities for deliberating with perfect tranquillity, and dispositions for deciding with unparalleled unanimity, on a form of government for the security of their union, and the advancement of their happiness; so his divine blessings may be equally conspicuous in the enlarged views, the temperate consultations, and the wise measures, on which the success of this government must depend."

In this constant disposition to look for national happiness only in national morals, flowing from the *sublime* affections and blessed hopes of religion, Washington agreed with those great legislators of nations, Moses, Lycurgus, and Numa.[32] "*I ask not gold for Spartans,*" said Lycurgus. "*Virtue is better than all gold.*" The event showed his wisdom. The Spartans were invincible all the days of their own virtue, even 500 years.

"I ask not wealth for Israel," cried Moses.—"But O that they were wise!—that they did but fear God and keep his commandments! the Lord himself would be their sun and

---

32 All famous lawmakers of the ancient world: Moses for the Israelites, Lycurgus for the Spartans and Numa for the Romans.

shield." The event proved Moses a true prophet. For while they were religious they were unconquerable. "United as brothers, swift as eagles, stronger than lions, one could chase a thousand, and two put ten thousand to flight."

"Of all the dispositions and habits which lead to the prosperity of a nation," says Washington, "religion is the indispensable support. Volumes could not trace all its connexions with private and public happiness. Let it simply be asked, where is the security for property, for reputation, for life itself, if there be no fear of God on the minds of those who give their oaths in courts of justice!"

But some will tell us, that *human laws* are sufficient for the purpose!

Human laws!—Human nonsense! For how often, even where the cries and screams of the wretched called aloud for lightning-speeded vengeance, have we not seen the sword of human law loiter in its coward scabbard, afraid of angry royalty? Did not that vile queen Jezebel,[33] having a mind to compliment her husband with a vineyard belonging to poor Naboth, suborn a couple of villains to take a false oath against him, and then cause him to be dragged out with his little motherless, crying babes, and barbarously stoned to death?

Great God! what bloody tragedies have been acted on the poor ones of the earth, by kings and great men, who were *above* the laws, and had no sense of religion to keep them in awe! And if men be not above the laws, yet what horrid crimes! what ruinous robberies! what wide-wasting flames! what cruel murders may they not commit in *secret*, if they be not withheld by the sacred arm of religion! "In vain, therefore," says Washington, "would that man claim the tribute of patriotism, who should do any thing to discountenance religion and morality, those great pillars of human happiness, those firmest props of the duties of men and citizens. The mere politician, equally with the pious man, ought to respect and cherish them."

But others have said, and with a serious face too, that a *sense of honour*, is sufficient to preserve men from base actions! O blasphemy to sense! Do we not daily hear of *men of honour*, by dice and cards, draining their fellow-citizens of the last cent, reducing them to a dung-hill, or driving them to a pistol? Do we not daily hear *of men of honour* corrupting their neighbours' wives and daughters, and then murdering their husbands and brothers in duels? Bind such selfish, such inhuman beings, by a sense of honour!! Why not bind roaring lions with cob-webs? "No," exclaims Washington, "whatever a sense of honour may do on men of refined education, and on minds of a peculiar structure, reason and experience both forbid us to expect that national morality can prevail, in exclusion of religious principles."

And truly Washington had abundant reason, from his own *happy experience*, to recommend religion so heartily to others.

For besides all those inestimable favours which he received from her at the hands of her celestial daughters, the *Virtues;* she threw over him her own magic mantle of *Character.* And it was this that immortalized Washington. By inspiring his countrymen with the profoundest veneration for him as the *best of men*, it naturally smoothed his way to supreme command; so that when War, that monster of hell, came on roaring against America, with all his death's heads and garments rolled in blood, the nation unanimously placed Washington at the head of their armies, from a natural persuasion that so good a man must be the peculiar favourite of Heaven, and the fastest friend of his country. How far this precious instinct in favour of goodness was corrected, or how far Washington's conduct was honourable to religion and glorious to himself and country, bright ages to come, and happy millions yet unborn, will, we hope, declare.

---

33 Jezebel was King Ahab's queen in the Old Testament (1 Kings 17–21). She has become synonymous with the wicked, treacherous woman who stops at nothing to get her way.

Chapter Three

AMERICAN TRACT SOCIETY

(1825–Present)

With the disestablishment of religion by the early nineteenth century, American Protestants began to turn to a number of benevolent societies in order to help ensure the virtue and Christian character of the nation. Many of these societies were involved in publishing. Organizations such as the American Bible Society (1816), the American Sunday School Union (1824) and the American Tract Society (1825) spearheaded a print revolution in the United States as they used the latest publishing technology to flood the nation with Christian literature.

By the late 1820s, the American Tract Society was distributing five million pages of printed material annually, making its material among the most widely circulated and familiar literature of the country's antebellum period. The majority of tracts from the Society were four to sixteen pages in length, but the Society also printed longer works, such as editions of the New Testament, Richard Baxter's *Call to the Unconverted* and annual releases of its immensely popular *Christian Almanac*. The Society used a vast system of volunteers and colporteurs—paid traveling agents—to distribute its literature.

The first article of the American Tract Society's Constitution stated that the Society's goal was "to diffuse a knowledge of our Lord Jesus Christ as the redeemer of sinners, and to promote the interests of vital godliness and sound morality, by the circulation of Religious Tracts, calculated to receive the approbation of all Evangelical Christians." In order to obtain this Evangelical approbation, the Society attempted to avoid all sectarianism, whether it be theological or political. For example, before the Civil War the Society took pains to avoid publishing inflammatory literature on slavery. The Society constantly worked to produce material that would encourage the participation of the broadest possible Protestant coalition. Thus, while much of its material came from British authors, the literature of the American Tract Society offers a revealing look into the mainstream intellectual currents of nineteenth-century American Protestantism. And, although in its early years it stood against the novel, the millions of moral tales that it distributed in tract form, such as "The Forgiving African," helped set the stage for the popularity of religious fiction in the United States.

Tract No. 92

The Forgiving African

An Authentic Narrative

Journeying on business through the western part of the state of New-York, in the summer of 1816, I stopped at an inn on Saturday evening, in a thinly settled part of the country, and put up for the Sabbath. Upon inquiry, I was informed that there was no place of public worship within a number of miles. The thought of spending the Lord's day in such a situation spread a gloom over my mind. But how often is God better to us than our fears! Being weary with my journey, and having committed myself to the Keeper of Israel, I retired to rest, under an affecting sense of the goodness of God. The morning dawned upon me in a composed frame of spirit; and every thing seemed to conspire to produce in me wonder, adoration, and love. As I cast my eyes over the rich scenery of nature's works, I could not but exclaim, raising my thoughts to the Maker of them all, These "thus wondrous fair, Thyself how wondrous then!" The day did not pass without some lively tokens of the divine presence. The pages of the written word were open before me, and I was enabled to see the beauty of its doctrines, and to taste the sweetness of its promises.

Towards the close of the day, being disturbed by the noisy and profane conversation of some persons who had called at the inn, I "went out in the field to meditate at eventide." I directed my steps towards the wood, in a path which led through beautiful fields richly laden with the bounties of Providence. I had but just penetrated the border of the forest, when the sound of a voice fell upon my ear. I paused; the tone seemed to be that of supplication. Approaching the place whence it proceeded, I perceived, beside a large oak, a negro woman, apparently advanced in life, upon her knees, with her hands clasped together, and her eyes steadfastly fixed upon heaven. I listened, and was struck with astonishment, to hear one of the sable daughters of Ethiopia, in the most importunate manner, raising her prayer to God. Never before did I witness such simplicity, such fervor, such engagedness. Like a true daughter of Jacob, she seemed to have power with the Angel of God. That part of her prayer which I distinctly heard, was confined to herself and her master.

"O Lord, bless my master. When he calls upon thee to damn his soul, do not hear him, do not hear him, but hear me—save him—make him know he is wicked, and he will pray to thee. I am afraid, O Lord, I have wished him bad wishes in my heart—keep me from wishing him bad—though he whips me and beats me sore, tell me of my sins, and make me pray more to thee—make me more glad for what thou hast done for me, a poor negro."

As she arose from her kneeling posture, her eye glanced upon me. Ingenuous confusion overspread her countenance on being thus discovered. She was preparing hastily to retreat, when I called to her in a mild tone, bade her not to be alarmed, and told her I was pleased to find her so well employed. Encouraged by the mildness of my address, she came towards me. I inquired into her situation and circumstances, and she seemed very happy of the opportunity of making them known. I asked her why she came to this place to pray? She answered that her master was a very wicked man, and would not, if he knew it, allow her to pray at all. The reason of her coming there at this time to pray, was, that her master had been beating her that day, and she was afraid she had not felt right towards him, and that she had done wrong also by not submitting with more resignation to her unhappy lot.

I asked her how she came to think it was her duty to pray? She said she had once heard a woman pray in a barn—that the woman prayed for the whole world—said they were all sinners, and going the road to hell—and that after she heard this woman's prayer, she thought it was her duty to pray too. But for a long time she felt that she was so bad that she could not pray. After a while she found that she could pray, and that she loved to pray. It seemed to do her good, she said, after her master had been beating her, to go away into the fields or woods and pray to the Lord. I found she had never enjoyed the means of any kind of instruction—she could not read—had never heard a sermon, nor been to a place of worship. Nor had she ever communicated her feelings to any person before. She was once surprised and detected by her mistress at prayer, who coming to call her in haste one morning, found her on her knees, and withdrew.

I inquired of her whether there were no religious people in the place. She mentioned as the only one, the woman before spoken of, whom she had heard pray a number of times; but she had never conversed with her. I then told her that there were many people in the world who had similar sentiments with her's respecting God and prayer. Her eyes sparkled on hearing this intelligence; she listened with eagerness while I entered into some particulars respecting the new birth and the way of salvation through a crucified Redeemer. The truths of the Gospel were to her as cold water to a thirsty soul. Her countenance, now glowing with wonder, now suffused with tears, now lighted up with joy, is still present to my imagination. She appeared very anxious to be instructed herself: but this was not all: she entreated me to go and converse and pray with her master; and to pray for him when alone. When I was about leaving her, never expecting to see her again in this world, I exhorted her to continue in the exercise of a submissive and forgiving spirit towards her master, and to commit herself into the hands of Him who judgeth righteously; encouraging her with the prospect of a speedy release from all her sufferings, and that, in due season, if she persevered in well doing, she would, through grace, reap a rich reward in the kingdom of glory.

Never was I so fully convinced that the religion of Christ consists very much in *the spirit of love and forgiveness*. The native pride of the human heart is quick-sighted in discerning ill treatment: violent and unrelenting in its resentments. Too many, alas! even of those who bear the Christian name, and profess an assured hope of pardon from their final Judge, know not how to forget or forgive an offence of a fellow worm. Such a professor may appear to be planted in the vineyard of the Lord; but his fruits are the grapes of Sodom and the clusters of Gomorrah.

This poor woman, often cruelly treated by the hands of an unkind and unfeeling master, showed nothing like anger or revenge. While smarting under the wounds inflicted by his cruelty, she would retire beyond the sight and hearing of mortals, to pray for his welfare. When speaking of the conduct of her master, she did not dwell upon his faults with seeming pleasure and delight. The ingenuousness of her love and compassion manifested itself in a very different manner. Her love to God showed itself in secret, persevering, and importunate prayer for her master; in earnestly requesting me to go and converse and pray with him; and in entreating me, with a countenance visibly marked with sincerity and love, to pray for him when I was alone. Nothing did she appear to desire more than her master's eternal welfare. Such a spirit as this must be religion; it is the very spirit of Christ; and if so, nothing short of such a temper can be religion. It is an easy thing to talk and pray—words are light and airy things—but to love our enemy, to do all in our power to promote his present and future wellbeing—this requires grace indeed.

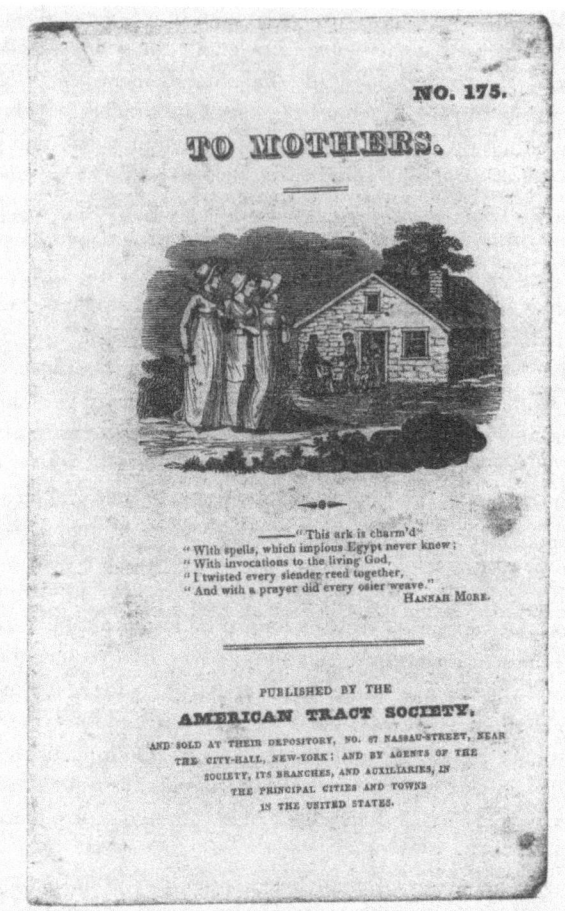

"To Mothers," Tract No. 175 (New York: American Tract Society, n.d.) This cover is representative of those found on the shorter tracts distributed by this society.

Reader, have you from the heart forgiven all who have injured you? If not, can you hope God will forgive you? Think of your offences against him, in thought, in word, and conduct. Think of the love of Christ in dying for his enemies, that all who believe in him may be saved. Go to him, confessing your sins and trusting in his mercy. Henceforward let love to God and love to man reign in your heart, that, when weighted in the balance of eternal truth, you may not be found wanting the meek and holy temper of this poor slave.

Tract No. 175

To Mothers

In the vicinity of P—— there was a pious mother, who had the happiness of seeing her children, in very early life, brought to the knowledge of the truth, walking in the fear of the Lord, and ornaments in the Christian Church. A clergyman, who was travelling, heard this circumstance respecting this mother, and wished very much to see her, thinking that there might be *something* peculiar in her mode of giving religious instruction, which rendered it so effectual. He accordingly visited her, and inquired respecting the manner in which she discharged the duties of a mother, in educating her children.

The woman replied, that she did not know as she had been more faithful than any Christian mother would be, in the religious instruction of her children. After a little conversation, however, she said:

"While my children were infants on my lap, as I washed them, I raised my heart to God, that he would wash them in that blood which cleanseth from sin. As I clothed them in the morning, I asked my Heavenly Father to clothe them with the robe of Christ's righteousness. As I provided them food, I prayed that God would feed their souls with the bread of heaven, and give them to drink the water of life. When I have prepared them for the house of God, I have plead that their bodies might be fit temples for the Holy Ghost to dwell in. When they left me for the week-day school, I followed their infant footsteps with a prayer, that their path through life might be like that of the just, which shineth more and more unto the perfect day. And as I committed them to the rest of the night, the silent breathing of my soul has been, that their Heavenly Father would take them to his embrace, and fold them in his paternal arms."

Here is the influence of the *silent, unseen* exertions of a mother: an influence which will be felt, when those external accomplishments, and fleeting enjoyments which many labour to give their children, shall be forgotten, or remembered only as the means of facilitating a rapid descent to the world of sorrow. In this little story two things strike our attention: these efforts were made *early*, and with a *reliance on the divine blessing*. This mother *felt* that she received her children from God, and was accountable to him for the manner in which she trained them up. She knew that her labours would be vain, unless God should in mercy grant her the aid of his Spirit, to sanctify and save the soul; therefore, through *all* the duties of the day, and all the interesting periods of childhood, she looked up to a God who is ever near to those who will call upon him, and who will listen to their cries. How happy must be that household whose God is the Lord; what heavenly joy beams from every countenance, and with what glorious hopes do they look beyond the grave to that mansion provided for them in their Father's house; and thrice happy must be that *mother*, who, in the fear of God, and in reference to eternity, has thus performed her duty.

There are feelings in a *mother's* bosom, which are known only by a mother: the tie which binds her to her children, is one compared with which all other ties are feeble. It is to these feelings that the fact just stated will speak a language which must be understood; and it must strike a note on this chord that will vibrate through every fibre of the soul. While appeals are often made to him who has lived long in sin, that fall like the sound of the empty wind upon his ear; and the voice of warning thunders in its truths to hearts of adamant; the appeal now made, is to an ear which is not deaf, to a heart which can feel.

The noise and tumult of the active world often drown the "still small voice"[1] of the Gospel, which sounds in the ears of the man of business; and worldly wisdom and strict calculation sometimes lead men to neglect the question, "What will it profit a man, if he gain the whole world, and lose his soul?"[2] But this Tract is designed for a different situation

1 Kings 19:12.
2 Matt. 16:26; Mark 8:36.

in life; for those who do not mingle in the bustle and hurry of the world; who are retired to a more quiet, though not to an unimportant sphere. In some hour of silent meditation this may fall into the hands of a *mother;* and the duties it recommends can be performed even while engaged in the common business of the family.

It is no fiction of poetry that,
"Just as the twig is bent, the tree's inclined."

When the mind begins to open, and the attention is first arrested by the objects that surround us, much depends upon her, who, in that tender period, shall make the *first* impressions upon that mind, and first direct its attention.

It is *then* that the mother has an access and an influence which cannot be attained at any other period. The first inquiries of the little infant must be answered by her who gave it birth. As he gazes upon those twinkling stars that glitter in the evening sky, and asks, "Who made those shining things?" it is a mother's duty to tell the little prattler of that great and good being who dwells in the heavens, and who is the Father of all our mercies.

And as the mind enlarges, the mother tells the little listener of that Jesus who lay in a manger, and died on the cross. And when she softens its pillow for its nightly slumbers, and watches its closing eyes, it is her privilege to hear it lisp, "*Our Father,*" and direct it to love that Father whose name it so early speaks. Let this golden opportunity pass, these days of childhood roll away, and the mind be filled only with fabled stories, or sportive songs, and the precious immortal is trained for some other state than the paradise above. Do you say that you are *ignorant,* and are not capable of giving instruction? As your child clings to your bosom and directs his inquiring countenance to you for some interesting story, you know enough to tell him of some hero or king; and can you not tell him of the King of Zion, the Prince of Peace? And what more could the learned philosopher tell this infant mind?

You are *unknown* and *obscure,* did you say? But you are known to your child, and your influence with your child is greater than that of a Legislator or General. "Say not, I, who am obscure, may act without restraint, especially when secluded from the world, in the retirement of my family. *Obscure! You* are *immortal.* You must go to the *judgment;* and every whisper of your life will be exhibited, before an assembled universe! *Secluded!*—What if the eye of the world does not follow you into the domestic circle? Is it not restraint enough that your *child* is there? That child has a *soul,* worth more than a million globes of gold. That child, too, may become a legislator, or a judge, or a pastor in a church. Take care, you who are a mother! You act under a dreadful responsibility. You cannot *stir,* without touching some string that will vibrate after your head is laid in the dust. One word of pious counsel, or one word of sinful levity or passion, uttered in the hearing of your child, may produce an effect on your children's children. Nay, its influence may be felt on the other side of the globe, and may extend into eternity." Your words are received with confidence, and "*My mother told me so,*" is an argument of sufficient weight to convince the child of the most important truths.

Here you have an influence which no other creature can have, and can exert it in circumstances the most favourable. It is not to open to a son the stores of science, that may qualify him to rank among the learned and the wise of the world: it is not to adorn a daughter with those accomplishments which shall attract the attention of those who crowd the hall of pleasure, or move in the circle of refinement and fashion.

But the object is far more *noble,* more worthy the undivided attention of those who live for immortality. That child who now prattles on your knee, or sports around your dwelling, may yet tell some perishing heathen of Jesus of Nazareth; may yet be an able soldier in the army of Immanuel, and may plant the standard of the cross on the shores of Greenland, or under the burning sun of Africa. *Look at facts.* What first led the pious and eminently useful John Newton[3] to the knowledge of the truth? The instructions of his mother, given at the early period of *four years,* fastened upon his conscience, and led him to a Saviour.

Can you estimate the effect of his labours? Not till you can compute the usefulness of Buchanan and Scott, who were converted by his instrumentality—till you can see the full blaze of that light which the former carried into the heart of heathen India; and witness the domestic comfort and brightening hopes occasioned by the labours of the latter. Who taught young Timothy, an early labourer in the vineyard of Jesus Christ, the first lessons of religious truth? Who led Samuel, a prophet and a judge in Israel, while he was yet *young,* to the house of the Lord, and dedicated him to the service of the God of heaven?[4] *A praying mother.*

Though the seed thus sown in childhood may not spring up and bring forth fruit while under the maternal eye, yet we must not conclude that it is lost. A clergyman recently met a seaman in the street of a neighbouring city, and pressed upon him the duty of attending to the concerns of his soul. The hardy mariner burst into tears, and exclaimed, *"Stop, stop, don't talk to me so; it is just as my mother talked to me when I was a boy."* A mother's counsel had followed him through all his wanderings, and still the words of her who prayed for him retained their hold on his conscience. The time has come when it is esteemed a greater honour to be the mother of a Brainerd or a Martyn,[5] than of a Cæsar or Napoleon. And suppose the mothers of these men, whose characters, though so widely different, are so universally known, should, from their unchanging state, look upon those sons whom they have nourished; what would be the view presented to them? Who would not choose to have given birth to the Christian heroes? It is not for this short state of existence only that you are to train your children. The little group that now cluster around you are destined for immortality. When the world on which they stand shall have passed away, and its pleasures and its honours shall be forgotten, then they whom you have introduced to this state of being will but begin to live. Their characters are now forming for *eternity,* and you are aiding to form them.

Though you may not design it, though you may quiet yourself, that if you can do them no good, you will not do them injury; yet you exert an influence which *is* felt, and will be felt when your head is laid in the dust. Let, then, this appeal to a mother's feelings be heard, let it come to your own bosom, and ponder it in your heart.

Do you know the way to a throne of mercy; and can you kneel before it, and forget the children of your love? Can you watch their closing eyes, and not commit them to your God? Can you labour that they may enjoy the good things of this fleeting world, and not *pray* that God would prepare them for that upon which they will soon enter? You see them growing

---

3 John Newton (1725–1807) was an English slave trader who converted to Christianity. He then enjoyed an active ministry that included writing the hymn "Amazing Grace."

4 1 Sam. 1–2.

5 David Brainerd (1718–1747) and Henry Martyn (1781–1812) were both Protestant missionaries who spent their lives winning souls, not wars.

up around you without hope and without God in the world: though you may be unable to do more, can you refuse to *pray*, that he who in a peculiar manner extends the arms of mercy to those in the morning of life, would take them to his embrace, and prepare them for his kingdom?

You have seen the hand of disease fasten upon them, and have passed days of anxious toil and nights of sleepless solicitude to arrest their malady; and have cried from a bursting heart, "Oh, spare my child!" You have seen the object of your tenderest affection sinking in the arms of death, and with a heart rent with anguish have said with the nobleman, "Come down ere my child die." And when the last duties of parental affection were performed, and the grave had closed over the child of your bosom, you have perhaps looked back to the time when it was under your care, and mourned that you thought no more of its immortal part, that you prayed no more for its precious soul.

If you have passed through scenes like these; if you have thus felt; then remember those now in life and health, and improve the opportunity now given you.

The time for your exertion is very *short*. Soon your children will arrive at that period of life when a mother's influence will be very feebly felt, unless it has been *early* exerted. Would you find in them a rich source of consolation when your head shall become white with years, and your body be bending to the grave; then you will *now* commit them to him who can sanctify and save the soul. Should you go down to the grave and leave these objects of your love in a cold, unfeeling world, what better can you do for them than to secure the friendship of one who sticketh closer than a brother, and whose love is stronger than death.

The tender tie which now binds you to them will soon be dissolved; you cannot resist the stroke which shall tear them from your bosom. You may have felt the pang—your heart may have been filled with sorrow. O then, if you ever pray, if your soul ever went out to *your* Father and *your* God, in humble petitions; tell him of your children who know him not: when you know what it is to wrestle in secret with the God of Jacob, give him back in faith your *children*.[6] Then you may hope, through grace, to say, in that other world to which you are going, "Lord, here am I, and the children thou hast given me."

Should this paper fall into the hands of a mother who never *prayed* even for herself; she *must*, she *cannot but* pray for those to whom she has given life. *Prayerless mother! spare*, oh, *spare* your child; stop where you now are, on the threshold of eternity, and remember, as you gaze on that countenance which smiles in your bosom, that you have *never prayed* for its soul, which will live for ever. Have you a mother's feelings, and can you still neglect it?

Oh! give me poverty, give me pain; leave me friendless and forsaken by the world—but leave me not to the embrace of a *prayerless mother*—leave not my soul to the care of one who never raised her weeping eyes to heaven, to implore its blessings on my head.

Are you a *mother*, and can you close your eyes upon the scenes of earth, and remember that you never raised, even in your silent breathings, the desires of your heart to heaven for a child, perhaps your only darling?

In some lonely hour, when the labours of the day are ended, and you have performed the last act of kindness for your sleeping babes; kneel, if you never have before, kneel before Him who seeth your heart in that silent hour, and utter one short prayer, one broken petition of penitence, faith, and love to the Saviour of sinners, for your dear children.

---

6 Gen. 32:24–32.

Tract No. 512

Murderers of Fathers, and Murderers of Mothers[7]

BY REV. EDWARD HITCHCOCK, D.D.

PRESIDENT OF AMHERST COLLEGE

In the Scriptures, as well as in common language, murder does not always mean the destruction of natural life by an act of violence. "Whosoever hateth his brother," says John, "is a murderer;" that is, he has the essential spirit of a murderer. We say, also, that he is a murderer who unnecessarily pursues a course of conduct by which the reputation or happiness of another is destroyed, and his life shortened. In this sense, then, murder is a common crime, committed by multitudes who never imagine that they are guilty—committed sometimes upon those who are truly beloved by the murderer, and are his best friends. And strange as it may seem, this crime is more common among the young than any other class, and their parents are the victims. I shall not charge any of my youthful readers with being murderers of fathers, and murderers of mothers; but as I point out some of the principal modes in which they may become such, let them honestly inquire, whether they have not already commenced the fearful work.[8]

1. The young man may become the murderer of his father and his mother *by making the idle and the immoral, the unprincipled or the irreligious, his chosen companions.*

The principles on which the remarks I am about to make are founded, apply equally to youth of either sex. But for the sake of brevity, I shall speak only of young men. From his earliest days, it is the strong desire and effort of Christian parents to preserve the mind of their son free from the impurities and fascinations of vice; and until they find him associating with the idle, the unprincipled, and the immoral, they imagine their efforts to be successful. But his choice of companions reveals the plague-spot on his heart. He would not associate with the wicked, if he did not relish their society; and he would not relish it, if the contagion of vice had not invaded his purity of principle and feeling. With the love of sin in his heart, what now shall prevent the inexperienced youth from the lawless indulgence of his passions, with reckless companions to lead the way? How feeble will be the warning voice of parental affection to resist the strong current of sinful inclination. As yet he knows not from experience the bitter consequences of a sinful course. But parents know that *"the wages of sin is death"*[9]—death to all true peace of mind—death to all hopes of usefulness and reputation—death temporal, and death eternal. The son, however, imagines no danger from his associates. He sees in them honorable feelings and noble purposes, and only occasionally do they show their aversion to what they call bigotry and intolerance in religion, and unreasonable strictness of morality. And what danger in such society to him, who has so much respect for religion, and who knows how to take care of himself? Alas, his parents realize that his danger is more imminent than if he consorted with the openly profligate, because he feels in no danger, and drinks in the poison without knowing it. The dreadful anticipation of having their child ruined for this world and another, fills their hearts with such anguish as a parent only can know. It brings upon them early gray hairs, ploughs deep

---

7 1 Timothy 1:9.
8 1 John 3:15.
9 Rom. 6:23.

furrows upon their foreheads, and urges them prematurely towards the grave. It is in fact slow, but in many cases, certain murder. Yet how easy for you, O young man, by abandoning those companions, to save your parents, and to save yourself!

2. The young man may murder his father and his mother *by immoral and ungrateful conduct*.

Fearful as parents are, when their son shows a fondness for idle or immoral companions, that he will soon become like them in practice, they cannot give up the fond hope that God's restraining grace and parental admonition may save him from actual dissipation and profligacy. But when they find that the fear of God and the warnings of conscience are so overcome that habitual wickedness is committed, it is as if a deep murderer's stab had been aimed at their hearts. Can it be, that their darling boy, whom they had successfully taught to be industrious and economical, has become a reckless, idle spendthrift; not merely of money, but of time and opportunities far more valuable than money? Can it be, that one lately so obedient to parental authority, and so tenderly alive to his parents' happiness, now tramples on their authority, and is indifferent to their feelings? Can it be, that one instructed so carefully to regard the Sabbath as holy time, now devotes that day to the perusal of secular newspapers or novels, to wandering about the streets, to rides of pleasure, and to the society of irreligious companions? Once he rarely ventured far, by day or by night, without parental advice and permission; and he failed not to kneel, at an early hour of the evening, at the family altar of devotion, as a delightful preparation for early and sweet repose. But he has learnt to trust his own feelings when and where to go, and what company to keep; and often is he, when the hour of evening prayer arrives, at the convivial board, joining in the lascivious song and the Bacchanalian[10] shout, instead of supplication and praise to Jehovah. Parental admonition and entreaty awaken only disgust and insolence, and his father and mother perceive that they have lost their hold upon the conscience of their son. Such a transformation of a frank, open-hearted child, into a reckless, unfeeling profligate, changes parental anxiety into agony. And yet their feelings must be in a great measure concealed from him who causes their anguish, lest his hard heart should lead him to add to his other crimes, mockery and insult towards those who gave him birth. Therefore must they bear the trial in silence, and let it prey upon their spirits, until they sigh for a release from a world that is to them only a scene of hopelessness and suffering.

It is in the way pointed out under this head, that is, by immoral and ungrateful conduct, that very many become murderers of fathers, and murderers of mothers. Therefore let me dwell longer upon this point, and refer to some specific examples.

The time has come when the youth must quit the paternal roof, to become, it may be, an apprentice in some handicraft, or to engage in mercantile or agricultural pursuits. Going to some country town reputed as moral and religious, his parents feel less solicitude for his safety. But when hints reach them of his prodigal habits, irregular hours, profane language, and neglect of business, their hearts begin to writhe with torturing anticipations. By letter and personal address, they lift loud the note of warning. But in his haggard countenance and reckless conduct, they read the broad marks of dissipation. Out of the reach of watchful and controlling parents, evil companionship has led to evil actions; and now it will require little short of a miracle to save him from ruin. Instead of rising to respectability

---

10 Sharing the characteristics of the orgy-like Roman festival of Bacchus, the deity of wine.

and distinction, as his fond parents had hoped, he will grovel along through the years of manhood, useless and known only for his vices, seeking only low pleasures and low society, with a broken constitution, and a mind ignorant and degraded, until an early grave opens to receive him. But often he will drag down his broken-hearted parents to the same narrow house; and there will they lie, the murderer and the murdered, side by side, till they go up together to the final judgment.

It may be, that the youth, on leaving home, is sent to the city, and for a time is aware that dangers of almost every name will meet him there. But vice soon becomes familiar to his observation: fascinating companions, graceful in manners, and generous in professions, introduce him to the social circle, where a magic influence comes over him to dispel every fear of danger. The same companions lead him to the theatre, a place where he finds much to amuse and delight, and little apparently to injure; and hence he infers that its dangers have been exaggerated by his parents, and he ventures again and again to the brilliant and enchanting spot. The snare is well laid and baited, and the bird falls into it and is taken. But this is only the gilded entrance to the dark labyrinth of iniquity. With his passions excited by the scenes of the theatre, the youth is easily lured by cunning companions into the gaming-house, and the place of the midnight carousal. Maddened there by the alcoholic bowl, he soon becomes as bold and reckless as his most unprincipled companions. The next step is to enter her house whose "steps take hold on hell." There the last trace of moral and religious principle in his bosom is blotted out; the voice of conscience is effectually smothered; and when his purse becomes empty by his dissipation, he is prepared to replenish it from the coffers of his employer. Deeper and deeper does he dip his hand into the forbidden treasure, until detection follows, and the brand of infamy is publicly stamped upon his character. If he escapes the penitentiary, it is only to be looked upon with scorn by the world, and with pity by the Christian; and after herding for a time with the dregs of society, to be thrown into the drunkard's and the felon's grave, unnoticed and unlamented. But what a terrible termination of a parent's fond hopes! What a dreadful metamorphosis of a beloved son, whom they sent forth untarnished, and with lofty expectations, from their Christian home! How much worse to bear than the assassin's dagger, was each successive development of his depravity; and how terribly must the final result have completed a father's and a mother's immolation!

Perhaps the youth leaves home for the college, or the academy; and for one, it may be, where there are many influences and strong, in favor of religion and morality. But the purest of them has its dangers; and some of these dangers are peculiar, and assail the young man unawares, and he falls an easy prey to the wiles of the wicked. At home he had been taught, that a man could not be placed in any circumstances where he could be released from obligations to obey the laws of religion and morality, or might connive at wickedness in others, and omit to bear testimony against it. But in the literary institution to which he attaches himself, he finds that he must modify these so-called puritanical notions. *Certain rules of honor*, instead of strict moral and religious principle, must regulate all his conduct towards his companions. He cannot find any one who can tell him exactly what these rules are; but he is distinctly informed, that they require him to close his eyes and ears as much as possible against the wickedness of his fellow-students, and to wink at immoral conduct in them, which he would feel bound to expose in any other member of the community. At any rate, he must suffer undeserved punishment himself, rather than expose the evil deeds of a classmate; and always be ready to vindicate the honor and reputation of his fellows. At first, his rigid views of duty are shocked by such requisitions; but finding that compliance or persecution awaits him, many a young man has not moral courage enough to take his firm stand on the platform of the Bible. He submits to the trammels imposed upon him and thus sacrifices his independence; for this is only the beginning of his degradation.

Those who have driven him to abandon one important point, well know that he can be made to yield others. The next step is to draw him into the society of the idle and the reckless: and alas, what literary institution does not contain some such? There for a time he meets with little to shock his moral sensibilities, except perhaps an occasional joke upon religion, an inuendo against bigotry and intolerance, and possibly a little profaneness. His companions are indeed jovial, but they are amiable and gentlemanly; and their society occasionally seems almost essential to relieve the monotony and cheerlessness of college life. Ere long, however, the oath becomes more frequent, the mirth more boisterous, and the card-table and the wine-cup are introduced. To escape detection, these convivial entertainments must be deferred till the midnight hour, and of course the subsequent day be devoted to recovery from the debauch. The youth's literary standing soon sinks; he loses his habits of study, and falls under censure; but instead of reforming, he is irritated by expostulation and warning. Detection serves only to lead him to adopt more effectual measures to avoid it in future.

In short, he has become almost irreclaimably dissipated before his parents are aware that he has turned aside at all from the right path. They had supposed him possessed of superior talents; and with virtuous principles, that he would be proof against temptation. The intimation of his deviations, therefore, comes upon them with the suddenness and severity of the assassin's stab. With the earnestness of parental affection, they immediately appeal to every principle in their son which they suppose capable of being called into action. They cannot believe that he has so soon abandoned his bright hopes of future distinction, nor lost his respect for parental authority, or his filial attachments, nor become insensible to the sanctions of religion. They, therefore, press upon him all these considerations; and that is usually the crisis in the young man's history. If parental authority and affection triumph, and he relents, and breaks off his bad habits, abandons his evil companions, he will be saved from utter ruin. But if his proud heart spurns a parent's counsel and exhortation, the last hold upon him is gone, and it will be but a short time before he reaches the bottom of the gulf of infamy. If he should be smuggled through college, it will be only to tantalize a little longer his parents' hopes, and to throw himself upon the community as a useless weight. Those parents must see him still grovelling with the idle and the dissipated; and thankful should they be, if his broken constitution should carry him prematurely to the grave by natural disease, before his depravity has outraged society so that he must expiate his crimes in the dungeon for life, or upon the scaffold. But how much easier for his wretched parents to fall by the literal murderer's assault, than thus to be suspended on the rack of uncertainty year after year, and at last to feel life and hope expire together. Alas, how many parents are at this moment stretched upon that rack, and destined to the same extinction of life and hope.

In all the examples that I have now given, and indeed as a general fact, the beginning and chief agent of ruin to the inexperienced youth, is the secret convivial frolic with jovial and unprincipled companions. And in fact, in no other place will his religious principles sooner yield, or parental lessons be forgotten, or the fear of God and man be cast off, and his low appetites and passions triumph over reason and conscience. For there the lewd and ribald song soon salutes his ears; low, vulgar wit takes the place of reason; the sober and the religious are made the butt of ridicule; and there, sometimes at least, the cup of intoxication goes round, and the youth, perhaps almost for the first time, "looks upon the wine when it is red, when it giveth its color in the cup, when it moveth itself aright," until his firmest temperance principles are overcome, and the fatal cup is lifted to his mouth; and with that first draught he swallows scorpions and daggers. True, he may have no suspicion of the dangers that await him there; nay, he may suppose that by entering that circle he is only preparing himself for the circles of gentility and fashion, and that unless he does there learn to sip the alcoholic bowl with politeness, he can never be admitted to the society of the wealthy and influential. But his father and mother know, every experienced man knows, because again and again have they seen the fatal process carried through, that the young man, however firm he may suppose his principles and yet uncorrupt his practice, who enters these convivial circles, has placed one foot within the purlieus[11] of hell. He has entered a moral Maelstrom, and begun those fatal gyrations, which, without miraculous deliverance, will become swifter and swifter, narrower and narrower, until he goes down like lightning into the central vortex, and disappears for ever. O terrible delusion! To what multitudes of talented and amiable, yet inexperienced young men, has the convivial frolic proved fatal for this world and another. "Can a man take fire in his bosom, and his clothes not be burnt? Can one go upon hot coals, and his feet not be burnt?"

But parents are not thus deceived; and as one development after another comes out, as wicked actions succeed to wicked companionship, they see and know the fatal end to which he is hastening. Though his path be crooked, they know how slippery and downward it is, and how difficult for one who has entered upon it to thread his way back to virtue and to heaven. For one who has thus returned, they have seen a thousand buried beneath the waves of everlasting infamy and despair. Each successive act of wickedness, therefore, of which their son is guilty, makes a deeper and a deeper murderer's stab into their hearts. They know that idleness and duplicity, intemperance, profaneness, and licentiousness, are sins that not only paralyze the conscience, but rot out the heart and the intellect, and leave the miserable victim to sink down early, a loathsome mass of corruption, into hell.

One other mode of murdering fathers and mothers I ought to describe under this head, because it approaches nearer to literal murder than any which has been named. As the father approaches the dotage of old age, he is apt to repose an overweening confidence in a favorite son, and in an unguarded hour, *transfers to him his property.* And it would indeed seem that a father might be sure of an ample support and kind treatment from an own son, whom he had treated thus generously; for to that father he was indebted for existence, for support in infancy, for an education, and now for an estate earned by a life of labor. But alas, melancholy facts show that there are some so devoid of natural affection, as well as of all honorable feeling and religious principle, as to feel their parents to be a burden, so soon as they have obtained their property; and who will treat them unkindly for the very purpose of shortening their days. It is base enough for a child to refuse to sustain his aged and feeble parents because they have been unable to bequeath him any property. But when they have actually done this, it becomes barbarous and detestable in the extreme; and if there be any sin which will provoke God to punish it in a special manner, it is this. But why do I enlarge? For he who has become so dead to every sentiment of nature and religion as to abuse an aged parent, has a conscience too deeply enveloped by the callous folds of selfishness and meanness to be reached by any words of mine.

---

11 Purlieus are the outskirts or surroundings of an area.

3. The young man may murder his father and his mother *by embracing dangerous religious error.*

Men embrace errors in religion, either because they lead unholy lives, or cherish a self-righteous, unsubmissive spirit. The more wicked a man's life, the more reckless must he be in his opinions, in order to quiet his conscience. Self-righteousness and pride require a system of error more refined, and more capable of literary embellishment; and the nearer it approaches in appearance to the true Gospel, the more acceptable will it be, because conscience, that stern advocate for evangelical piety in the heart, will be thus more easily satisfied. But it is essential, that such a system be wanting in all that is vital in the Gospel, or it will not quiet the fears of one who expects to enter heaven without a new heart. The particular form of error embraced is of little consequence in the view of the parent, provided it leave his son to rest easy without a new heart. He may fancy that he differs so little from his father that it is of small importance; while yet it is as mysterious to him as it was to Nicodemus, how a man can be born again. Ignorant of this doctrine, his parents know that he differs enough from them to shut him out of heaven as certainly as if with the fool he had said, "There is no God"; for, "*Except a man be born again, he cannot see the kingdom of God.*"[12]

It is the loss of his soul, not a bigoted attachment to a particular creed, that makes these parents so anxious. They well know how easy it is for the advocates of almost any error, even of Atheism itself, to array a list of names distinguished in literature and science as its supporters; and they know, too, how fascinating to the youthful mind, is a reputation for talents and learning. Whatever religious opinions such men embrace, the young are ready to suppose safe and true; although, in fact, such men are probably of all others most apt to embrace error, because they usually give less serious attention to the subject, have more pride of opinion, and are usually more stubborn in their prejudices. Besides, when a man has once adopted some plausible and popular system of error, and thrown around it the drapery of literature and philosophy, he is the most unlikely of all men to see his lost condition, and flee to that only name under heaven whereby he can be saved. Therefore it is that these parents are so distressed when they find their son reposing quietly upon the gilded and downy couch of error, where he is most likely to be "given up to strong delusions to believe a lie, that he might be damned."

4. The young man may murder his father and his mother *by neglecting personal religion.*

The grand object of all their toils and prayers for their child, is his conversion. Until this great change pass over him, they feel as if the grand business of life, for which chiefly he was created, had been neglected. For, without a new heart, they know he must be lost; and yet he, like others, is liable at any moment to be summoned into eternity. Hence, though he be moral and amiable, a respecter of religion, and even distinguished among men, they look with comparative indifference and dissatisfaction upon all his acquisitions which leave him destitute of a new heart. Can it be, that they have brought up a child only to endure everlasting misery? From his earliest days they consecrated him in prayer and faith to God; and as he grew up, every opportunity was seized upon to store his mind with the truths of religion, and to impress his conscience with his guilt and danger. Sometimes his heart seemed to relent, and the tear of anxiety was seen in his eye. But

---

12 John 3:3.

these signs proved only the morning cloud and early dew; and though the years of his minority are almost or quite gone, he still remains unconverted; and every year the work is delayed, only deepens parental anxiety, because the hope of his salvation so rapidly diminishes.

During the childhood and youth of most persons, there are certain memorable events, each of which forms a sort of crisis in their history. One of these is sickness. At such a time, when the youth needs the supports of religion, he finds that he has none on which he dare rest. His morality, his kind feelings towards others, his upright and honorable conduct, and even his attention to the outward forms of religion, he finds will not form a resting-place for his soul, in that dark valley he seems about to enter. Oh, had he listened to parental instruction and entreaty while in health, he might now have had a rock to stand upon, amid the surging billows. If he should recover, surely he cannot longer neglect the great salvation. So feels the youth, and so feel his parents. He does recover; but his former stupor creeps over him again, and his agonized parents have every reason to expect that his next sickness will find him, like the last, entirely unprepared to die.

It may be that the youth is called to severe affliction, in the sudden departure of a brother, a sister, or chosen companion. A dying friend sounds in his ears a piercing note of warning. It falls upon him like a sudden peal of thunder, and awakens him from his deep spiritual slumbers. Strong hope that the hour of his conversion has come, springs up in the bosom of his affectionate parents. But the cup of happiness, which with a trembling hand they are lifting to their lips, is destined to be dashed upon the ground, leaving only the dregs of disappointment for them to taste. Their son's religious impressions gradually wear away, and he sinks into a deeper sleep than ever, while they awake to keener suffering.

Another season of deep solicitude and strong hope to Christian parents, is a revival of religion. If their son be not awakened and converted then, they know how faint is the probability that he will turn to God during the season of general indifference that too often follows a time of special religious interest. Nay, they fear, that having resisted the special influences of such a season, his heart will be so hardened that no future means will avail to subdue it. Intense, therefore, is the anxiety which Christian parents feel for their unconverted and unawakened son, during such a work. They have long beheld him twisted and crushed in the folds of the hydra-headed monster sin, and now they see approaching a more than Herculean Deliverer,[13] ready to set the dying captive free. Alas, must they see their child spurn the only power that can deliver him, and permit the monster to wind another coil around his heart? He does not, indeed, see how bitter is the anguish of disappointment in their souls, when the special work of God draws to a close, and he remains unconverted. But their closets, the midnight hour, the stars of heaven, and the God of heaven witness their deep distress, when, from a bleeding heart, the parent exclaims, "Is Ephraim my dear son? Is he a pleasant child?" "How can I give thee up, Ephraim? How can I deliver thee, Israel?" Ah, they must give him up; but it will break their hearts. They will go down to an early grave, murdered by a beloved son.

In view of this subject, thus presented, let the young man who reads these pages honestly inquire, whether he is not really, though perhaps unconsciously, among the murderers of fathers, and the murderers of mothers. Is he not the child of pious parents, and yet wedded

---

13 The Hydra was a nine-headed gigantic monster. As one head was cut off, two grew back in its place. Hercules eventually found a way to kill the monster.

to a companionship with those whom he knows to be idle, or unprincipled, or immoral, or irreligious? Nay, is he not conscious of indulging in some immoral practices? Has he not fortified himself in the belief of principles which effectually shield him from conviction of sin, and keep the slumbers of spiritual death unbroken? At least, does he not, from year to year, neglect personal religion, even under the loudest calls and the most urgent appeals, and the rebukes of conscience, and the strivings of the Spirit? If such be your character, in any of these respects, little do you know what a bitter cup you are compelling your father and mother to drink. It is known, that certain poisons may be administered in so small doses as to be unnoticed at the time, but great enough, by repetition, to insure the death of the victim. That fatal act you are practising upon your dearest earthly friends, who would gladly endure suffering and death, could they ward them off from you.

This charge you may think extravagant and untrue. The smile of affection meets you under the paternal roof, and the tenderest solicitude is manifested for your welfare. Ah, natural affection will glow in those parents' hearts till they are cold in the grave; nor will the hope of your conversion entirely abandon them, while you live and they can pray. But knowing as they do, how dangerous are the companions with whom you associate, or the evil habits you indulge, or the religious errors you have embraced or your long-continued indifference and stupidity respecting your own salvation, their hearts sink with discouragement; they tremble lest you are given over to blindness of mind and hardness of heart, and their faith falters when they pray for your conversion. Though concealed from your eye, a secret anguish on your account is preying upon their life. The mother who bore you—she whose tears fell often upon your infant cheek, as over your cradle she agonized in prayer for your early conversion—she who has often grown pale with midnight watchings by your sick-bed—she who first taught your infant lips the language of prayer—she who has followed you with her prayers, and tears, and counsels, in all your wanderings—that mother's heart you are now filling with deep distress, if indeed that distress and her toils for you have not already carried her down to an early grave. That father, too, who has cheerfully foregone a thousand pleasures, and made a thousand sacrifices, and submitted to multiplied cares and toils, for your support and education—whose hopes have been centred in you, and who has long felt as if death would be welcome, could it secure your conversion—O, what desolation reigns in that father's heart, as he sees you, after all his prayers and labors, still moving unconcernedly on the road to death. Or it may be, that his early grey hairs ere now have been brought down with sorrow to the grave. Oh, you are the murderer of those parents, whether you realize it or not, as really as if you had stolen to their bed at midnight, and buried the fatal steel in their bosoms; and for that deed you must answer at the final day of trial, when the wounds you have inflicted will be exposed to the view of the universe.

But after all, though there is a solemn reality in these representations, I am fully aware that most of those who are thus the murderers of fathers, and the murderers of mothers, are totally unconscious of the influence they are exerting upon their parents' happiness. Nay, though they must know that every wrong course they take, and even their continued neglect of religion, cannot but thwart the strongest desires of those parents' hearts, still they cling to them with strong attachment. For filial affection is a chord in the human heart that retains its sensibility when sin has paralyzed every thing besides; and even the desperate criminal, who has set heaven and earth at defiance, melts and weeps at the name of father or mother. Would to God I could make that chord vibrate, till it should rouse you, O ye unconverted young men, from the stupor of sin, and convert you, from the murderers, into the temporal saviors of your parents. Should you see that father and mother in the hands of the literal assassin, and their blood were streaming, and their death-cry came into your ears for help, how would you rush to their rescue, though a hundred swords were drawn to oppose you. Ah, they *are* in the assassin's hands—but *thou*, unconverted youth, art the man. They *are* covered with wounds, and their lifeblood is flowing out like water. But your sins, your unbelief and stupidity, are the sword that has cloven their hearts asunder. They *are* crying for help: but it is to God for your conversion. The language of Christ for his murderers is theirs: "Father, forgive them, for they know not what they do."[14] But can you be forgiven, if you persist in destroying the peace and happiness of those who gave you being, and commit suicide, also, upon your own most precious soul? Never! Yet if you will be persuaded to yield your heart to the claims of the Lord Jesus Christ, forgiveness, free, and full, and everlasting, will be lavished upon you. The wounds you have inflicted upon your earthly parents will be healed as if by miraculous touch; and your father on earth, and your Father in heaven, will joyfully exclaim, "Bring forth the best robe, and put it on him; and put a ring on his hand, and shoes on his feet. For this my son was dead, and is alive again, he was lost, and is found."[15]

Tract No. 515

Novel-Reading

Few persons suspect how many novels are written, and printed, and sold. There are about five thousand five hundred offered for sale in this country. If a man were to read one a week for seventy-five years, he would not be through the list. There are, of course, many novel-readers. Something on a great scale will be the result. What will it be; good or evil? Let us see.

It is natural to inquire, Who write novels? A few pious persons have written works which are sometimes called novels. But they are too serious for the gay, and too gay for the serious. So they are seldom read. Others are written by moral persons, who really seem anxious to teach some truth in an easy way. But nearly or quite all such are thought dull; and so they lie, covered with dust, on the shelves of the bookseller, are sent to auction, and used as waste paper. The popular novels of our day are, to a great extent, written by men who are known to be lax in principle, and loose in life. England and France contain no men who are more free from the restraints of sound morality, than their leading novelists. They are literal and "literary debauchees."

But do not novels contain many good things, which cannot be learned elsewhere? I answer, they do not. It is confessed that they never teach science. It is no less true, that they pervert history, or supplant it by fiction. This is throughout true of Walter Scott,[16] who has excelled all modern novelists in the charms of style. The literature of novels is commonly poor, and that of the best cannot compare with the standard English and French classics. Even Scott's best tales are intended to ridicule the best men, and to excuse or extol the worst men of their age. Like Hume,[17] he was an apologist of tyrants, whose crimes ought to have taken away both their crowns and their lives. I beseech you not to read novels. I will give my reasons.

1. Their *general tendency* is to evil. They present vice and virtue in false colors. They dress up vice in gayety, mirth, and long success. They put virtue and piety in some odious or ridiculous posture. Suspicion, jealousy, pride, revenge, vanity, rivalries, resistance of the

---

14 Luke 23:34.
15 Reference to Jesus's story of the return of the prodigal son, Luke 15:11–32.
16 Sir Walter Scott (1771–1832) was an immensely popular Scottish novelist and considered by many to be the greatest British writer of historical novels.
17 David Hume (1711–1776) was a Scottish philosopher who wrote important works on epistemology and religious skepticism.

laws, rebellion against parents, theft, murder, suicide, and even piracy are so represented in novels as to diminish, if not to take away the horror which all the virtuous feel against these sins and crimes. Almost all that is shocking in vice is combined with some noble qual- ity, so as to make the hero on the whole an attractive character. The thief, the pirate, and especially the rake, are often presented as successful, elegant, and happy. Novels abound in immodest and profane allusions or expressions. Wantonness, pride, anger, and unholy love are the elements of most of them. They are full of exaggerations of men and things. They fill the mind with false estimates of human life. In them the romantic prevails over the real. A book of this sort is very dangerous to the young, for in them the imagination is already too powerful for the judgment.

2. Novels beget *a vain turn of mind*. So true is this, that not one in a hundred of novel- readers is suspected, or is willing to be suspected of being devout. Who by reading a novel of the present day was ever inclined to prayer or praise? Novel-reading is most unhappy in its effects on the female mind. It so unfits it for devotion, that even in the house of God levity or tedium commonly rules it. Thus practical atheism is engendered. The duties of life are serious and weighty. They whose trade it is to trifle and to nourish vanity, cannot be expected to be-well-informed, or well-disposed respecting serious things. However much novel-readers may weep over fictitious misery, it is found that they generally have little or no sympathy with real suffering. Did you never know a mother to send away a sick child, or a daughter to neglect a sick mother, for the purpose of finishing a novel? If irreligion and impiety do not flourish under such influences, effects cannot be traced to causes.

3. The price of these books is often low, yet the *cost* of them in a lifetime is very great. Miss W. borrowed some books, yet she paid seventy dollars in one year for novels alone. Doing this for fifteen years, she would spend one thousand and fifty dollars. Yet her neph- ews and nieces were growing up without an education. Mrs. L. stinted her family in groceri- ies, that she might have a new novel every month. Mr. C. pleaded want of means to aid to orphan asylum, yet he paid more than sixty dollars a year for novels for his daughters. Novels have, in the last five years, cost the people of the United States from twelve to fifteen millions of dollars. For one, they have paid thirty thousand dollars. This waste is wanton. No good is received in return.

4. Novel-reading is a great *waste of time*—time,

That stuff that life is made of,
And which, when lost, is never lost alone,
Because it carries souls upon its wings.

Nothing is so valuable as that which is of great use, yet cannot be bought with any thing else. We must have time to think calmly and maturely of a thousand things, to improve our minds, to acquire the knowledge of God, and to perform many pressing duties. The business of life is to act well our part here, and prepare for that solemn exchange of worlds which awaits us. He whose time is spent without economy and wasted on trifles, will awake and find himself undone, and will "mourn at the last, when his flesh and his body are con- sumed, and say, How have I hated instruction, and my heart despised reproof!"

5. The effects of novel-reading on *morals* are disastrous. Many young offenders are made so by the wretched tales which now abound. In one city, in less than three months, three youths were convicted of crimes committed in imitation of the hero of a novel. Here is a court of justice in session. Blood has been shed. Men are on trial for their lives. All the

parties involved are intelligent and wealthy. The community is excited. Crowds throng the court-room from day to day. The papers are filled with the letters which led to the tragical end of one, and the misery of many. The whole scene is painful in the highest degree. Among the witnesses is one of manly form, polished manners, and hoary locks. Even the stranger does him reverence. His country has honored him. He must testify, and so sure as he does, he will tell the truth; for he has honor, and blood is concerned. He says, The husband of my daughter was "kind, honorable, and affectionate," and "if my daughter has been in an unhappy state of mind, I attribute it to the impure works of Eugene Sue and Bulwer."[18] All these cases have been judicially investigated and published to the world. They have filled many a virtuous mind with horror, and every judicious parent with concern.

Nor is novel-reading a wholesome recreation. It is not a recreation at all. It is an ensnaring and engrossing occupation. Once begin a novel, and husband, children, prayer, filial duties, are esteemed trifles until it is finished. The end of the story is the charm. Who reads a novel a second time?

Some say, Others do it, and so may we. But others are no law to us. The prevalence of an evil renders it the more binding on us to resist the current.

Novel-reading makes none wiser, or better, or happier. In life it helps none. In death it soothes none, but fills many with poignant regrets. At the bar of God, no man will doubt that madness was in his heart, when he could thus kill time and vitiate his principles. I add,

1. Parents, know what books your children read. If there were not a novel on earth, you still should select their reading. Leave not such a matter to chance, to giddiness, or vice. Give your children good books. A bad book is poison. If you love misery, furnish novels to your children.

2. Young people, be warned in time. Many, as unsuspecting as you, have been ruined. Be not rebellious, to your own undoing. Listen to the voice of kindness, which says, Beware, beware of novels.

3. Pastors, see that you do all in your power to break up a practice which will ruin your young people, and render your ministry fruitless. I was shocked when I heard of one of you recommending a novel which exposed the arts of the Jesuits. The Jesuits are indeed bad, but not worse than Sue.

4. Booksellers, let me say a word. A young man, with a hurried manner, entered a druggist's shop and asked for an ounce of laudanum. It was refused. He went to another and got it, and next morning was a corpse. Which of these druggists acted right? You sell poison when you sell novels. They kill souls. You sell for gain. "Woe to him that coveteth an evil covetousness to his house, that he may set his nest on high, that he may be delivered from the power of evil! Thou hast consulted shame to thy house by cutting off many people, and hast sinned against thy soul. For the stone shall cry out of the wall, and the beam out of the timber shall answer it."[19] You may make money by depraving the public morals, but for all these things God will bring you into judgment.

---

18 Eugene Sue (1804–1857) and Edward George Earle Bulwer-Lytton (1803–1873) were prolific novelists who wrote sensational, entertaining stories.

19 Hab. 2:11.

Chapter Four

MARIA MONK
(1816–1849?)

American Protestantism has long had a virulent anti-Catholic strain that, in the years leading up to the Civil War, manifested itself with particular ferocity. Believing that Catholics disdained the Holy Bible, gave divine status to the Virgin Mary and traded precious democracy for monarchy led by the pope, nineteenth-century Protestants put immense amounts of time and energy into attempting to convert Catholics to Protestantism.

As German and Irish Catholics immigrated to the United States in ever-increasing numbers in the 1820s and 1830s, Protestants unleashed a massive array of anti-Catholic propaganda with the hopes of mobilizing ever-greater resources against the insidious Catholic menace. No piece of antebellum anti-Catholic literature enjoyed greater popularity than *Awful Disclosures, by Maria Monk, of the Hotel Dieu Nunnery of Montreal*, a convent-captivity narrative supposedly written by Maria Monk. A treatise that purportedly chronicled the lascivious and murderous nature of Catholic convent life, Maria Monk told a tale of her life as a former nun and how she eventually escaped convent life, giving birth to a son in 1835.

In the first 25 years of publication, *Awful Disclosures* would sell more than 300,000 copies, an absolutely staggering figure in that period. It would also prove to be the catalyst behind the appearance of a host of other Catholic and anti-Catholic material. Almost upon its release in book form, questions were raised about the authenticity of Maria Monk's background as a nun and about the contents of the book. Sides were taken energetically, and a massive amount of material appeared proving and disproving Monk's claims. The truth of the issue initially remained obscure, but later it became increasingly clear that Maria Monk was mentally unstable and that her tale was a fantastic fabrication. Such revelations, however, did not stop thousands of Americans from continuing to view *Awful Disclosures* as a completely trustworthy exposé of Catholicism.

The book itself is a fascinating window into early nineteenth-century religious tensions, as well as a commentary on the role of motherhood in the young republic. In *Awful Disclosures*, the malevolent influence of Catholicism threatens the very ideals and form of American motherhood, as mothers (whether they be mother superiors, mothers who give up their daughters to the convent or pregnant nuns) all come to misdirect their energies to destroy that which they have been entrusted to nurture.

AWFUL DISCLOSURES, BY MARIA MONK, OF THE HOTEL DIEU NUNNERY OF MONTREAL

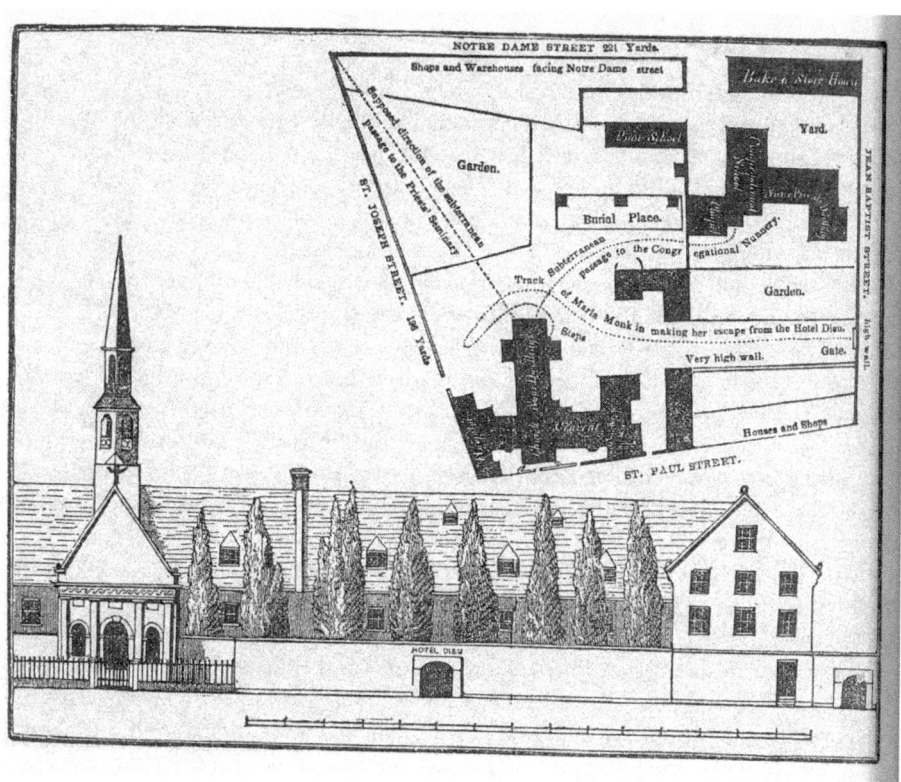

Two foldout maps were included in many early editions of Maria Monk's *Awful Disclosures*. This map shows the exterior picture of the nunnery along with the route Monk took to escape (*Awful Disclosures*, Revised, New York: Published by Maria Monk, 1836). The second map can be found on page 121 of this anthology.

These selections follow an edition that appeared in the first year of the work's release: *Awful Disclosures, by Maria Monk, of the Hotel Dieu Nunnery of Montreal.* New York: Published by Maria Monk, 1836.

Preface

This volume embraces the contents of the first editions of my "Awful Disclosures," together with the Sequel of my Narrative, giving an account of events after my escape from the Nunnery, and of my return to Montreal to procure a legal investigation of my charges. It also furnishes all the testimony that has been published against me, of every description, as well as that which has been given in confirmation of my story. At the close, will be found a Review of the whole Subject, furnished by a gentleman well qualified for the purpose; and, finally, a short Supplement, giving further particulars interesting to the public.

I present this volume to the reader, with feelings which, I trust, will be in some degree appreciated when it has been read and reflected upon. A hasty perusal, and an imperfect apprehension of its contents, can never produce such impressions as it has been my design to make by the statements I have laid before the world. I know that misapprehensions exist in the minds of some virtuous people. I am not disposed to condemn their motives, for it does not seem wonderful, that in a pure state of society, and in the midst of Christian families, there should be persons who regard the crimes I have mentioned as too monstrous to be believed. It certainly is creditable to American manners and character, that the people are inclined, at the first sight, to turn from my story with horror.

There is also an excuse for those, who, having received only a general impression concerning the nature of my Disclosures, question the propriety of publishing such immorality to the world. They fear that the minds of the young at least may be polluted. To such I have to say, that this objection was examined, and set aside, long before they had an opportunity to make it. I solemnly believe it is necessary to inform parents at least, that the ruin from which I have barely escaped, lies in the way of their children even if delicacy must be in some degree wounded by revealing the fact. I understand the case, alas! from too bitter experience. Many an innocent girl may this year be exposed to the dangers of which I was ignorant. I am resolved, that so far as depends on me, not one more victim shall fall into the hands of those enemies in whose power I so lately have been. I know what it is to be under the domination of Nuns and Priests; and I maintain that it is a far greater offence against virtue and decency to conceal, than to proclaim their crimes. Ah! had a single warning voice even whispered to me a word of caution, had even a gentle note of alarm been sounded to me, it might have turned back my foot from the Convent when it was upon the threshold! If, therefore, there is any one now bending a step that way, whom I have not yet alarmed, I will cry *beware!*

But the virtuous reader need not fear, in the following pages, to meet with vice presented in any dress but her own deformity. No one can accuse me of giving a single attraction to crime. On the contrary, I intend my book shall be a warning to those who may hereafter be tempted by vice; and with the confidence that such it will prove to be, I commend it to the careful examination of virtuous parents, and am willing to abide by their unbiased opinion, with regard both to my truth, my motives, and the interest which the public have in the developments it contains.

I would now appeal to the world, and ask, whether I have not done all that could have been expected of me, and all that lay in my power, to bring to an investigation the charges I have brought against the priests and nuns of Canada. Although it was necessary to the cause of truth, that I should, in some degree, implicate myself, I have not hesitated to appear as a voluntary self-accuser before the world. While there was a hope that the authorities in Canada might be prevailed upon to bring the subject to a legal investigation,

I travelled to Montreal, in a feeble state of health, and with an infant in my arms only three weeks old. In the face of many threats and dangers, I spent nearly a month in that city, in vain attempts to bring my cause to a trial. When all prospect of success in this undertaking had disappeared, and not till then, I determined to make my accusations through the press and, although misrepresentations and scandals, flattery and fear, have been resorted to, to nullify or to suppress my testimony, I have persevered, although, as many of my friends have thought, at the risk of abduction or death.

I have, I think, afforded every opportunity that could be reasonably expected, to judge of my credibility. I have appealed to the existence of things in the Hotel Dieu Nunnery, as the great criterion of the truth of my story. I have described the apartments, and now, in this volume, have added many further particulars, with such a draft of them as my memory has enabled me to make. I have offered, in case I should be proved an impostor, to submit to any punishment which may be proposed—even to a redelivery into the hands of my bitterest enemies, to suffer what they may please to inflict.

Now, in these circumstances, I would ask the people of the United States, whether my duty has not been discharged? Have I not done what I ought, to inform and to alarm them? I would also solemnly appeal to the Government of Great Britain, under whose guardianship is the province oppressed by the gloomy institution from which I have escaped, and ask, whether such atrocities ought to be tolerated, and even protected, by an enlightened and Christian power? I trust the hour is near, when the dens of the Hotel Dieu will be laid open, when the tyrants who have polluted it will be brought out, with the wretched victims of their oppression and crimes.

Chapter I

Early Recollections

Early Life—Religious Education neglected—First Schools—Entrance into the School of the Congregational Nunnery—Brief Account of the Nunneries in Montreal— The Congregational Nunnery—The Black Nunnery—The Grey Nunnery—Public Respect for these Institutions—Instruction Received—The Catechism—The Bible.

My parents were both from Scotland, but had been resident in Lower Canada some time before their marriage, which took place in Montreal; and in that city I have spent most of my life. I was born at St. John's, where they lived for a short time. My father was an officer under the British government, and my mother has enjoyed a pension on that account ever since his death.

According to my earliest recollections, he was attentive to his family; and a particular passage from the Bible, which often occurred to my mind in after life, I may very probably have been taught by him, as after his death I do not recollect to have received any religious instruction at home; and was not even brought up to read the scriptures: my mother, although nominally a Protestant, not being accustomed to pay attention to her children in this respect. She was rather inclined to think well of the Catholics, and often attended their churches. To my want of religious instruction at home, and the ignorance of my Creator, and my duty, which was its natural effect, I think I can trace my introduction to Convents, and the scenes which I am to describe in this narrative.

When about six or seven years of age, I went to school to a Mr. Workman, a Protestant, who taught in Sacrament-street, and remained several months. There I learned to read and write, and arithmetic as far as division. All the progress I ever made in those branches was gained in that school, as I have never improved in any of them since.

A number of girls of my acquaintance went to school to the nuns of the Congregational Nunnery, or Sisters of Charity, as they are sometimes called. The schools taught by them are perhaps more numerous than some of my readers may imagine. Nuns are sent out from that Convent to many of the towns and villages of Canada to teach small schools; and some of them are established as instructresses in different parts of the United States. When I was about ten years old, my mother asked me one day if I should not like to learn to read and write French; and I then began to think seriously of attending the school in the Congregational Nunnery. I had already some acquaintance with that language, sufficient to speak it a little, as I heard it every day, and my mother knew something of it.

I have a distinct recollection of my first entrance into the Nunnery; and the day was an important one in my life, as on it commenced my acquaintance with a Convent. I was conducted by some of my young friends along Nôtre Dame-street, till we reached the gate. Entering that, we walked some distance along the side of a building towards the chapel, until we reached a door, stopped, and rung a bell. This was soon opened, and entering, we proceeded through a long covered passage till we took a short turn to the left, soon after which we reached the door of the school-room. On my entrance, the Superior met me, and told me first of all, that I must always dip my fingers into the holy water at her door, cross myself, and say a short prayer; and this she told me was always required of Protestant as well as Catholic children.

There were about fifty girls in the school, and the nuns professed to teach something of reading, writing, arithmetic, and geography. The methods however were very imperfect, and little attention was devoted to them, the time being in a great degree engrossed with lessons in needle-work, which was performed with much skill. The nuns had no very regular parts assigned them in the management of the schools. They were rather rough and unpolished in their manners, often exclaiming, "c'est un menti," (that's a lie,) and "mon Dieu," (my God,) on the most trivial occasions. Their writing was quite poor, and it was not uncommon for them to put a capital letter in the middle of a word. The only book on geography which we studied, was a catechism of geography, from which we learnt by heart a few questions and answers. We were sometimes referred to a map, but it was only to point out Montreal or Quebec, or some other prominent name, while we had no instruction beyond.

It may be necessary for the information of some of my readers, to mention that there are three distinct Convents in Montreal, all of different kinds; that is, founded on different plans, and governed by different rules. Their names are as follows:—

1st. The Congregational Nunnery.
2d. The Black Nunnery, or Convent of Sister Bourgeoise.
3d. The Grey Nunnery.

The first of these professes to be devoted entirely to the education of girls. It would require however only a proper examination to prove that, with the exception of needle-work, hardly any thing is taught excepting prayers and the catechism; the instruction in reading, writing &c., in fact, amounting to very little, and often to nothing. This Convent is adjacent to that next to be spoken of, being separated from it only by a wall. The second professes to be a charitable institution for the care of the sick, and the supply of bread and medicines for the poor; and something is done in these departments of charity, although but an insignificant amount, compared with the size of the buildings, and the number of the inmates.

The Grey Nunnery, which is situated in a distant part of the city, is also a large edifice, containing departments for the care of insane persons and foundlings. With this, however, I have less personal acquaintance than with either of the others. I have often seen two of the Grey nuns, and know that their rules, as well as those of the Congregational Nunnery, do not confine them always within their walls, like those of the Black Nunnery. These two Convents have their common names (Black and Grey) from the colours of the dresses worn by their inmates.

In all these three Convents, there are certain apartments into which strangers can gain admittance, but others from which they are always excluded. In all, large quantities of various ornaments are made by the nuns, which are exposed for sale in the *Ornament* Rooms, and afford large pecuniary receipts every year, which contribute much to their incomes. In these rooms visiters often purchase such things as please them from some of the old[1] and confidential nuns who have the charge of them.

From all that appears to the public eye, the nuns of these Convents are devoted to the charitable objects appropriate to each, the labour of making different articles, known to be manufactured by them, and the religious observances, which occupy a large portion of their time. They are regarded with much respect by the people at large; and now and then when a novice takes the veil,[2] she is supposed to retire from the temptations and troubles of this world into a state of holy seclusion, where, by prayer, self-mortification, and good deeds, she prepares herself for heaven. Sometimes the Superior of a Convent obtains the character of working miracles; and when such a one dies, it is published through the country, and crowds throng the Convent, who think indulgences are to be derived from bits of her clothes or other things she has possessed; and many have sent articles to be touched to her bed or chair, in which a degree of virtue is thought to remain. I used to participate in such ideas and feelings, and began by degrees to look upon a nun as the happiest of women, and a Convent as the most peaceful, holy, and delightful place of abode. It is true, some pains were taken to impress such views upon me. Some of the priests of the Seminary often visited the Congregational Nunnery, and both catechised and talked with us on religion. The Superior of the Black Nunnery adjoining, also, occasionally came into the School, enlarged on the advantages we enjoyed in having such teachers, and dropped something now and then relating to her own Convent, calculated to make us entertain the highest ideas of it, and to make us sometimes think of the possibility of getting into it.

Among the instructions given us by the priests, some of the most pointed were those directed against the Protestant Bible. They often enlarged upon the evil tendency of that book, and told us that but for it many a soul now condemned to hell, and suffering eternal punishment, might have been in happiness. They could not say any thing in its favour: for that would be speaking against religion and against God. They warned us against it, and represented it as a thing very dangerous to our souls. In confirmation of this, they would repeat some of the answers taught us at catechism, a few of which I will here give. We

---

1 [Author's Original Note] The term "old nun," does not always indicate superior age.
2 A novice is a candidate for admission to a religious order. A novice becomes an official member of the convent upon taking certain vows and going through a ceremony known as *taking the veil*, which symbolically represents marriage to Christ.

had little catechisms ("Le Petit Catechism") put into our hands to study but the priests soon began to teach us a new set of answers, which were not to be found in our books, from some of which I received new ideas, and got, as I thought, important light on religious subjects, which confirmed me more and more in my belief in the Roman Catholic doctrines. These questions and answers I can still recall with tolerable accuracy, and some of them I will add here. I never have read them, as we were taught them only by word of mouth.

Question. "Pourquoi le bon Dieu n'a pas fait tous les commandemens?

Réponse. "Parce que l'homme n'est pas si fort qu'il peut garder tous ses commandemens.

Q. "Why did not God make all the commandments?

A. "Because man is not strong enough to keep them.

And another. *Q.* "Pourquoi l'homme ne lit pas l'Evangile?

R. "Parce que l'esprit de l'homme est trop borné et trop faîble pour comprendre qu'est ce que Dieu a écrit.

Q. "Why are men not to read the New Testament?"

A. "Because the mind of man is too limited and weak to understand what God has written."

These questions and answers are not to be found in the common catechisms in use in Montreal and other places where I have been, but all the children in the Congregational Nunnery were taught them, and many more not found in these books.

Chapter II

Congregational Nunnery

Story told by a fellow Pupil against a Priest—Other Stories—Pretty Mary—Confess to Father Richards—My subsequent Confessions—Left the Congregational Nunnery.

There was a girl thirteen years old whom I knew in the School, who resided in the neighbourhood of my mother, and with whom I had been familiar. She told me one day at school of the conduct of a priest with her at confession, at which I was astonished. It was of so criminal and shameful a nature, I could hardly believe it, and yet I had so much confidence that she spoke the truth, that I could not discredit it.

She was partly persuaded by the priest to believe he could not sin, because he was a priest, and that any thing he did to her would sanctify her; and yet she seemed somewhat doubtful how she should act. A priest, she had been told by him, is a holy man, and appointed to a holy office, and therefore what would be wicked in other men, could not be so in him. She told me that she had informed her mother of it, who expressed no anger nor disapprobation, but only enjoined it upon her not to speak of it; and remarked to her, that as priests were not like other men, but holy, and sent to instruct and save us, whatever they did was right.

I afterward confessed to the priest that I had heard the story, and had a penance to perform for indulging a sinful curiosity in making inquiries; and the girl had another for communicating it. I afterward learned that other children had been treated in the same manner, and also of similar proceedings in other places.

Indeed, it was not long before such language was used to me, and I well remember how my views of right and wrong were shaken by it. Another girl at the School, from a place above Montreal, called the Lac, told me the following story of what had occurred recently in that vicinity. A young squaw, called la Belle Marie, (pretty Mary,) had been seen going to confession at the house of the priest, who lived a little out of the village. La Belle Marie was afterward missed, and her murdered body was found in the river. A knife was also found covered with blood, bearing the priest's name. Great indignation was excited among the Indians, and the priest immediately absconded, and was never heard from again. A note was found on his table addressed to him, telling him to fly if he was guilty.

It was supposed that the priest was fearful that his conduct might be betrayed by this young female; and he undertook to clear himself by killing her.

These stories struck me with surprise at first, but I gradually began to feel differently, even supposing them true, and to look upon the priests as men incapable of sin; besides, when I first went to confession, which I did to Father Richards, in the old French church, (since taken down,) I heard nothing improper; and it was not until I had been several times, that the priests became more and more bold, and were at length indecent in their questions and even in their conduct when I confessed to them in the Sacristie.[3] This subject I believe is not understood nor suspected among Protestants; and it is not my intention to speak of it very particularly, because it is impossible to do so without saying things both shameful and demoralizing.

I will only say here, that when quite a child, I had from the mouths of the priests at confession what I cannot repeat, with treatment corresponding; and several females in Canada have recently assured me, that they have repeatedly, and indeed regularly, been required to answer the same and other like questions, many of which present to the mind deeds which the most iniquitous and corrupt heart could hardly invent.

There was a frequent change of teachers in the School of the Nunnery; and no regular system was pursued in our instruction. There were many nuns who came and went while I was there, being frequently called in and out without any perceptible reason. They supply school teachers to many of the country towns, usually two for each of the towns with which I was acquainted, besides sending Sisters of Charity to different parts of the United States. Among those whom I saw most, was Saint Patrick, an old woman for a nun, (that is, about forty,) very ignorant, and gross in her manners, with quite a beard on her face, and very cross and disagreeable. She was sometimes our teacher in sewing, and was appointed to keep order among us. We were allowed to enter only a few of the rooms in the Congregational Nunnery, although it was not considered one of the secluded Convents.

In the Black Nunnery, which is very near the Congregational, is an hospital for sick people from the city; and sometimes some of our boarders, such as were indisposed, were sent there to be cured. I was once taken ill myself and sent there, where I remained a few days.

There were beds enough for a considerable number more. A physician attended it daily; and there are a number of the veiled nuns of that Convent who spend most of their time there.

These would also sometimes read lectures and repeat prayers to us.

After I had been in the Congregational Nunnery about two years, I left it, and attended several different schools for a short time; but I soon became dissatisfied, having many and severe

---

3 A room where sacred vessels and vestments are kept, and where clergy dress in preparation for services.

rials to endure at home, which my feelings will not allow me to describe; and as my Catholic acquaintances had often spoken to me in favour of their faith, I was inclined to believe it true, although, as I before said, I knew little of any religion. While out of the nunnery, I saw nothing of religion. If I had, I believe I should never have thought of becoming a nun.

Chapter VI

Taking the Veil

Taking the Veil—Interview afterward with the Superior—Surprise and horror at her Disclosures—Resolution to Submit.

I was introduced into the Superior's room on the evening preceding the day on which I was to take the veil, to have an interview with the Bishop. The Superior was present, and the interview lasted about half an hour. The Bishop on this as on other occasions appeared to me habitually rough in his manners. His address was by no means prepossessing.

Before I took the veil, I was ornamented for the ceremony, and was clothed in a rich dress belonging to the Convent, which was used on such occasions; and placed not far from the altar in the chapel, in the view of a number of spectators who had assembled, perhaps about forty. Taking the veil is an affair which occurs so frequently in Montreal, that it has long ceased to be regarded as a novelty; and, although notice had been given in the French parish church as usual, only a small audience had assembled, as I have mentioned.

Being well prepared with a long training, and frequent rehearsals, for what I was to perform, I stood waiting in my large flowing dress for the appearance of the Bishop. He soon presented himself, entering by the door behind the altar; I then threw myself at his feet, and asked him to confer upon me the veil. He expressed his consent, and threw it over my head, saying, "Receive the veil, O thou spouse of Jesus Christ;" and then turning to the Superior, I threw myself prostrate at her feet, according to my instructions, repeating what I had before done at rehearsals, and made a movement as if to kiss her feet. This she prevented, or appeared to prevent, catching me by a sudden motion of her hand, and granted my request. I then kneeled before the Holy Sacrament, that is, a very large round wafer held by the Bishop between his fore-finger and thumb, and made my vows.

This wafer I had been taught to regard with the utmost veneration, as the real body of Jesus Christ, the presence of which made the vows uttered before it binding in the most solemn manner.

After taking the vows, I proceeded to a small apartment behind the altar, accompanied by four nuns, where was a coffin prepared with my nun name engraven upon it:

"Saint Eustace"[4]

My companions lifted it by four handles attached to it, while I threw off my dress, and put on that of a nun of Soeur Bourgeoise; and then we all returned to the chapel. I proceeded first, and was followed by the four nuns; the Bishop naming a number of worldly pleasures

---

4 Saint Eustace (second century) was the most famous of the early Christian martyrs. Refusing to sacrifice to the Roman gods, he was roasted to death inside a brass bull.

in rapid succession, in reply to which I as rapidly repeated—"Je renonce, je renonce, je renonce"—[I renounce, I renounce, I renounce.]

The coffin was then placed in front of the altar, and I advanced to lay myself in it. This coffin was to be deposited, after the ceremony, in an outhouse, to be preserved until my death, when it was to receive my corpse. There were reflections which I naturally made at the time, but I stepped in, extended myself, and lay still. A pillow had been placed at the head of the coffin, to support my head in a comfortable position. A large, thick black cloth was then spread over me, and the chanting of Latin hymns immediately commenced. My thoughts were not the most pleasing during the time I lay in that situation. The pall, or Drap Mortel, as the cloth is called, had a strong smell of incense, which was always disagreeable to me, and then proved almost suffocating. I recollected also a story I had heard of a novice, who, in taking the veil, lay down in her coffin like me, and was covered in the same manner, but on the removal of the covering was found dead.

When I was uncovered, I rose, stepped out of my coffin, and kneeled. The Bishop then addressed these words to the Superior, "Take care and keep pure and spotless this young virgin, whom Christ has consecrated to himself this day." After which the music commenced, and here the whole was finished. I then proceeded from the chapel, and returned to the Superior's room, followed by the other nuns, who walked two by two, in their customary manner, with their hands folded on their breasts, and their eyes cast down upon the floor. The nun who was to be my companion in future, then walked at the end of the procession. On reaching the Superior's door, they all left me, and I entered alone, and found her with the Bishop and two priests.

The Superior now informed me, that having taken the black veil, it only remained that I should swear the three oaths customary on becoming a nun; and that some explanations would be necessary from her. I was now, she told me, to have access to every part of the edifice, even to the cellar, where two of the sisters were imprisoned for causes which she did not mention. I must be informed, that one of my great duties was, to obey the priests in all things; and this I soon learnt, to my utter astonishment and horror, was to live in the practice of criminal intercourse with them. I expressed some of the feelings which this announcement excited in me, which came upon me like a flash of lightning but the only effect was to set her arguing with me, in favour of the crime, representing it as a virtue acceptable to God, and honourable to me. The priests, she said, were not situated like other men, being forbidden to marry; while they lived secluded, laborious, and self-denying lives for our salvation. They might, indeed, be considered our saviours, as without their services we could not obtain the pardon of sin, and must go to hell. Now, it was our solemn duty, on withdrawing from the world, to consecrate our lives to religion, to practise every species of self-denial. We could not become too humble, nor mortify our feelings too far; this was to be done by opposing them, and acting contrary to them; and what she proposed was, therefore, pleasing in the sight of God. I now felt how foolish I had been to place myself in the power of such persons as were around me.

From what she said I could draw no other conclusion, but that I was required to act like the most abandoned of beings, and that all my future associates were habitually guilty of the most heinous and detestable crimes. When I repeated my expressions of surprise and horror, she told me that such feelings were very common at first, and that many other nuns had expressed themselves as I did, who had long since changed their minds. She even said, that on her entrance into the nunnery, she had felt like me.

Doubts, she declared, were among our greatest enemies. They would lead us to question every point of duty, and induce us to waver at every step. They arose only from remaining imperfection, and were always evidence of sin. Our only way was to dismiss them immediately, repent, and confess them. They were deadly sins, and would condemn us to hell, if we should die without confessing them. Priests, she insisted, could not sin. It was a thing impossible. Every thing that they did, and wished, was of course right. She hoped I would see the reasonableness and duty of the oaths I was to take, and be faithful to them.

She gave me another piece of information which excited other feelings in me, scarcely less dreadful. Infants were sometimes born in the convent: but they were always baptized and immediately strangled! This secured their everlasting happiness; for the baptism purified them from all sinfulness, and being sent out of the world before they had time to do any thing wrong, they were at once admitted into heaven. How happy, she exclaimed, are those who secure immortal happiness to such little beings! Their little souls would thank those who kill their bodies, if they had it in their power!

Into what a place and among what society had I been admitted! How differently did a Convent now appear from what I had supposed it to be! The holy women I had always fancied the nuns to be, the venerable Lady Superior, what were they? And the priests of the Seminary adjoining, some of whom indeed I had had reason to think were base and profligate men, what were they all? I now learnt they were often admitted into the nunnery, and allowed to indulge in the greatest crimes, which they and others called virtues.

After having listened for some time to the Superior alone, a number of the nuns were admitted, and took a free part in the conversation. They concurred in every thing which she had told me, and repeated, without any signs of shame or compunction, things which criminated themselves. I must acknowledge the truth, and declare that all this had an effect upon my mind. I questioned whether I might not be in the wrong, and felt as if their reasoning might have some just foundation. I had been several years under the tuition of Catholics, and was ignorant of the Scriptures, and unaccustomed to the society, example, and conversation of Protestants; had not heard any appeal to the Bible as authority, but had been taught, both by precept and example, to receive as truth every thing said by the priests. I had not heard their authority questioned, nor any thing said of any other standard of faith but their declarations. I had long been familiar with the corrupt and licentious expressions which some of them use at confessions, and believed that other women were also. I had no standard of duty to refer to, and no judgment of my own which I knew how to use, or thought of using.

All around me insisted that my doubts proved only my own ignorance and sinfulness; that they knew by experience they would soon give place to true knowledge, and an advance in religion; and I felt something like indecision.

Still, there was so much that disgusted me in the discovery I had now made, of the debased characters around me, that I would most gladly have escaped from the nunnery, and never returned. But that was a thing not to be thought of. I was in their power, and this I deeply felt, while I thought there was not one among the whole number of nuns to whom I could look for kindness. There was one, however, who began to speak to me at length in a tone that gained something of my confidence,—the nun whom I have mentioned before as distinguished by her oddity, Jane Ray,[5] who made us so much amusement when I was a

---

5 Introduced earlier, Jane Ray is an older nun (some thirty years of age) who is of an independent and ungovernable nature. Upon receiving the veil, she did not take a new name, but kept her own.

novice. Although, as I have remarked, there was nothing in her face, form, or manners, to give me any pleasure, she addressed me with apparent friendliness; and while she seemed to concur with some things spoken by them, took an opportunity to whisper a few words in my ear, unheard by them, intimating that I had better comply with every thing the Superior desired, if I would save my life. I was somewhat alarmed before, but I now became much more so, and determined to make no further resistance. The Superior then made me repeat the three oaths; and when I had sworn them, I was shown into one of the community rooms, and remained some time with the nuns, who were released from their usual employments, and enjoying a recreation day, on account of the admission of a new sister. My feelings during the remainder of that day, I shall not attempt to describe; but pass on to mention the ceremonies which took place at dinner. This description may give an idea of the manner in which we always took our meals; although there were some points in which the breakfast and supper were different.

At 11 o'clock the bell rung for dinner, and the nuns all took their places in a double row, in the same order as that in which they left the chapel in the morning, except that my companion and myself were stationed at the end of the line. Standing thus for a moment with our hands placed one on the other over the breast, and hidden in our large cuffs, with our heads bent forward, and eyes fixed on the floor; an old nun who stood at the door, clapped her hands as a signal for us to proceed, and the procession moved on, while we all commenced the repetition of litanies. We walked on in this order, repeating all the way, until we reached the door of the dining-room, where we were divided into two lines; those on the right passing down one side of the long table, and those on the left the other, till all were in, and each stopped in her place. The plates were all ranged, each with a knife, fork, and spoon, rolled up in a napkin, and tied round with a linen band marked with the owner's name. My own plate, knife, fork, &c., were prepared like the rest, and on the band around them I found my new name written:— "Saint Eustace."

There we stood till all had concluded the litany; when the old nun who had taken her place at the head of the table next to the door, said the prayer before meat, beginning "Benedicite,"[6] and we sat down. I do not remember of what our dinner consisted, but we usually had soup and some plain dish of meat, the remains of which were occasionally served up at supper as a fricassee. One of the nuns who had been appointed to read that day, rose and began a lecture from a book put into her hands by the Superior, while the rest of us ate in perfect silence. The nun who reads during dinner, stays afterward to dine. As fast as we finished our meals, each rolled up her knife, fork, and spoon in her napkin, and bound them together with the band, and set with hands folded. The old nun then said a short prayer, rose, stepped a little aside, clapped her hands, and we marched towards the door, bowing as we passed before a little chapel or glass box, containing a wax image of the infant Jesus.

Nothing important occurred until late in the afternoon, when as I was sitting in the community room, Father Dufrèsne called me out, saying he wished to speak with me. I feared what was his intention; but I dared not disobey. In a private apartment he treated me in a brutal manner; and from two other priests, I afterward received similar usage that evening.

Monk tells the reader that "her irregularities were found to be numerous, and penances were of so little use in governing her, that she was pitied by some, who thought her partially insane. She was therefore commonly spoken of as mad Jane Ray. […]"

6 "Bless you"; a blessing asked at meals.

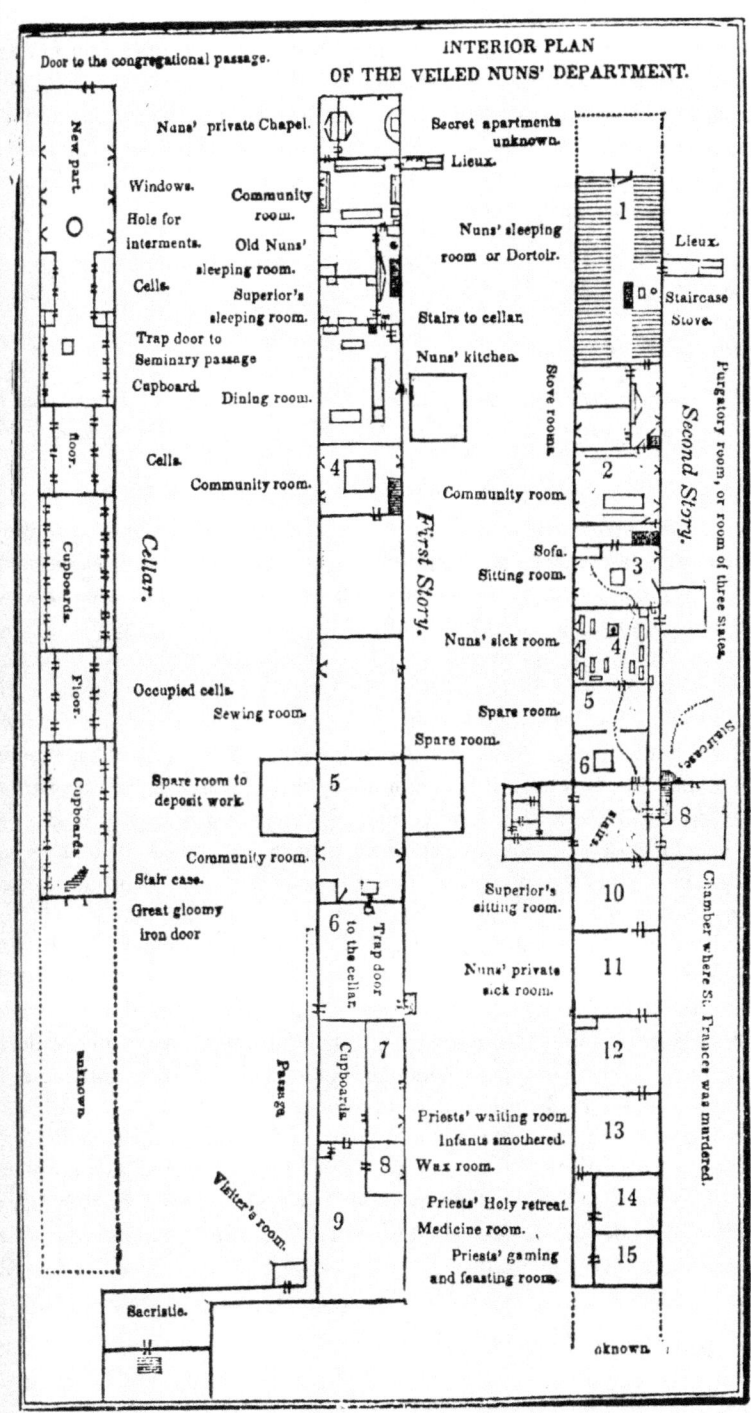

The second map offers a layout of the nunnery's interior rooms. Note the location of trapdoors and the identification of the room where infants were killed (*Awful Disclosures*, Revised, New York: Published by Maria Monk, 1836).

Father Dufrèsne afterward appeared again; and I was compelled to remain in company with him until morning.

I am assured that the conduct of priests in our Convent has never been exposed, and is not imagined by the people of the United States. This induces me to say what I do, notwithstanding the strong reasons I have to let it remain unknown. Still, I cannot force myself to speak on such subjects except in the most brief manner.

Chapter VIII

Description of Apartments

Description of Apartments in the Black Nunnery, in order.—1st Floor—2d Floor— The Founder—Superior's Management with the Friends of Novices— Religious Lies—Criminality of concealing Sins at Confession.

I will now give from memory, a general description of the interior of the Convent of Black nuns, except the few apartments which I never saw. I may be inaccurate in some things, as the apartments and passages of that spacious building are numerous and various; but I am willing to risk my credit for truth and sincerity on the general correspondence, between my description and things as they are. And this would, perhaps, be as good a case as any by which to test the truth of my statements, were it possible to obtain access to the interior. It is well known, that none but veiled nuns, the bishop, and priests, are ever admitted; and, of course, that I cannot have seen what I profess to describe, if I have not been a Black nun.[7] The priests who read this book, will acknowledge to themselves the truth of my description; but will, of course, deny it to the world, and probably exert themselves to destroy my credit. I offer to every reader the following description, knowing that time may possibly throw open those secret recesses, and allow the entrance of those who can satisfy themselves, with their own eyes, of its truth. Some of my declarations may be thought deficient in evidence; and this they must of necessity be in the present state of things. But here is a kind of evidence on which I rely, as I see how unquestionable and satisfactory it must prove, whenever it shall be obtained.

If the interior of the Black Nunnery, whenever it shall be examined, is materially different from the following description, then I can claim no confidence of my readers. If it resembles it, they will, I presume, place confidence in some of those declarations, on which I may never be corroborated by true and living witnesses.

I am sensible that great changes may be made in the furniture of apartments; that new walls may be constructed or old ones removed; and I have been credibly informed, that masons have been employed in the nunnery since I left it. I well know, however, that entire changes cannot be made; and that enough must remain as it was to substantiate my description, whenever the truth shall be known.

The First Story

Beginning at the extremity of the right wing of the Convent, towards Notre Dame-street, on the first story, there is—

---

7 [Author's Original Note] I ought to have made an exception here, which I may enlarge upon in future. Certain other persons are sometimes admitted.

1st. The nuns' private chapel, adjoining which is a passage to a small projection of the building, extending from the upper story to the ground, with very small windows. Into the passage we were sometimes required to bring wood from the yard, and pile it up for use.

2d. A large community-room, with plain benches fixed against the wall to sit, and lower ones in front to place our feet upon. There is a fountain in the passage near the chimney at the farther end, for washing the hands and face, with a green curtain sliding on a rod before it. This passage leads to the old nuns' sleeping-room on the right, and the Superior's sleeping-room, just beyond it, as well as to a staircase which conducts to the nuns' sleeping-room, or dortoir, above. At the end of the passage is a door opening into—

3d. The dining-room; this is larger than the community-room, and has three long tables for eating, and a chapelle, or collection of little pictures, a crucifix, and a small image of the infant Saviour in a glass case. This apartment has four doors, by the first of which we are supposed to have entered, while one opens to a pantry, and the third and fourth to the two next apartments.

4th. A large community-room, with tables for sewing, and a staircase on the opposite left-hand corner.

5th. A community-room for prayer, used by both nuns and novices. In the farther right-hand corner is a small room partitioned off, called the room for the examination of conscience, which I had visited while a novice by permission of the Superior, and where nuns and novices occasionally resorted to reflect on their character, usually in preparation for the sacrament, or when they had transgressed some of the rules. This little room was hardly large enough to contain half a dozen persons at a time.

6th. Next beyond is a large community-room for Sundays. A door leads to the yard, and thence to a gate in the wall on the cross street.

7th. Adjoining this is a sitting room, fronting on the cross street, with two windows, and a storeroom on the side opposite them. There is but little furniture, and that very plain.

8th. From this room a door leads into what I may call the wax-room, as it contains many figures in wax, not intended for sale. There we sometimes used to pray, or meditate on the Saviour's passion. This room projects from the main building; leaving it, you enter a long passage, with cupboards on the right, in which are stored crockery-ware, knives and forks, and other articles of table furniture, to replace those worn out or broken—all of the plainest description; also, shovels, tongs, &c. This passage leads to—

9th. A corner room, with a few benches, &c. and a door leading to a gate on the street. Here some of the medicines were kept, and persons were often admitted on business, or to obtain medicines with tickets from the priests; and waited till the Superior or an old nun could be sent for. Beyond this room we were never allowed to go; and I cannot speak from personal knowledge of what came next.

The Second Story

Beginning, as before, at the western extremity of the same wing, but on the second story, the farthest apartment in that direction which I ever entered was—

1st. The nuns' sleeping-room, or dormitory, which I have already described. Here is an access to the projection mentioned in speaking of the first story. The stairs by which we came up to bed are at the farther end of the room; and near them a crucifix and font of holy water. A door at the end of the room opens into a passage, with two small rooms, and closets between them, containing bedclothes. Next you enter—

2d. A small community-room, beyond which is a passage with a narrow staircase, seldom used, which leads into the fourth community-room, in the first story. Following the passage just mentioned, you enter by a door—

3d. A little sitting-room, furnished in the following manner: with chairs, a sofa, on the north side, covered with a red-figured cover and fringe, a table in the middle, commonly bearing one or two books, an inkstand, pens, &c. At one corner is a little projection into the room, caused by a staircase leading from above to the floor below, without any communication with the second story. This room has a door opening upon a staircase leading down to the yard, on the opposite side of which is a gate opening into the cross street. By this way the physician is admitted, except when he comes later than usual. When he comes in, he usually sits a little while, until a nun goes into the adjoining nuns' sick-room, to see if all is ready, and returns to admit him. After prescribing for the patients he goes no farther, but returns by the way he enters; and these two are the only rooms into which he is ever admitted, except the public hospital.

4th. The nuns' sick-room adjoins the little sitting-room on the east, and has, I think, four windows towards the north, with beds ranged in two rows from end to end, and a few more between them, near the opposite extremity. The door from the sitting-room swings to the left, and behind it is a table, while a glass case, to the right, contains a wax figure of the infant Saviour, with several sheep. Near the northeastern corner of this room are two doors, one of which opens into a long and narrow passage leading to the head of the great staircase that conducts to the cross street. By this passage the physician sometimes finds his way to the sick-room, when he comes later than usual. He rings the bell at the gate, which I was told had a concealed pull, known only to him and the priests, proceeds up-stairs and through the passage, rapping three times at the door of the sick-room, which is opened by a nun in attendance, after she has given one rap in reply. When he has visited his patients, and prescribed for them, he returns by the same way.

5th. Next beyond this sick-room, is a large unoccupied apartment, half divided by two partial partitions, which leave an open space in the middle. Here some of the old nuns commonly sit in the daytime.

6th. A door from this apartment opens into another, not appropriated to any particular use, but containing a table, where medicines are sometimes prepared by an old nun, who is usually found there. Passing through this room, you enter a passage, with doors on its four sides: that on the left, which is kept fastened on the inside, leads to the staircase and gate; that in front, to private sick-rooms, soon to be described.

7th. That on the right leads to another, appropriated to nuns suffering with the most loathsome disease. There were usually a number of straw mattresses in that room, as I well knew, having helped to carry them in after the yard-man had filled them. A door beyond enters into a storeroom, which extends also beyond this apartment. On the right, another door opens into another passage, crossing which, you enter by a door—

8th. A room with a bed and screen in one corner, on which nuns were laid to be examined before their introduction into the sick-room last mentioned. Another door, opposite the former, opens into a passage, in which is a staircase leading down.

9th. Beyond this is a spare-room, sometimes used to store apples, boxes of different things, &c.

10th. Returning now to the passage which opens on one side upon the stairs to the gate, we enter the only remaining door, which leads into an apartment usually occupied by some of the old nuns, and frequently by the Superior.

11th, and 12th. Beyond this are two more sick-rooms, in one of which those nuns stay who are waiting their accouchement,[8] and in the other, those who have passed it.

13th. The next is a small sitting-room, where a priest waits to baptize the infants previous to their murder. A passage leads from this room, on the left, by the doors of two succeeding apartments, neither of which have I ever entered.

14th. The first of them is the "holy retreat," or room occupied by the priests, while suffering the penalty of their licentiousness.

15th. The other is a sitting-room, to which they have access. Beyond these the passage leads to two rooms, containing closets for the storage of various articles, and two others where persons are received who come on business.

The public hospitals succeed, and extend a considerable distance, I believe, to the extremity of the building. By a public entrance in that part, priests often come into the nunnery; and I have often seen some of them thereabouts, who must have entered by that way. Indeed, priests often get into the "holy retreat" without exposing themselves to the view of persons in other parts of the Convent, and have been first known to be there, by the yard-man being sent to the Seminary for their clothes.

The Congregational Nunnery was founded by a nun called Sister Bourgeoise. She taught a school in Montreal, and left property for the foundation of a Convent. Her body is buried, and her heart is kept, under the nunnery, in an iron chest, which has been shown to me, with the assurance that it continues in perfect preservation, although she has been dead more than one hundred and fifty years. In the chapel is the following inscription: "Sœur Bourgeoise, Fondatrice du Convent"—Sister Bourgeoise, Founder of the Convent.

Nothing was more common than for the Superior to step hastily into our community-rooms, while numbers of us were assembled there, and hastily communicate her wishes in words like these:—

"Here are the parents of such a novice: come with me, and bear me out in this story."

She would then mention the outlines of a tissue of falsehoods, she had just invented, that we might be prepared to fabricate circumstances, and throw in whatever else might favour the deception. This was justified, and indeed most highly commended, by the system of faith in which we were instructed.

It was a common remark made at the initiation of a new nun into the Black nun department, that is, to receive the black veil, that the introduction of another novice into the Convent as a veiled nun, caused the introduction of a veiled nun into heaven as a saint, which was on account of the singular disappearance of some of the older nuns at the entrance of new ones!

To witness the scenes which often occurred between us and strangers, would have struck a person very powerfully, if he had known how truth was set at naught. The Superior, with a serious and dignified air, and a pleasant voice and aspect, would commence a recital of things most favourable to the character of the absent novice, and representing her as equally fond of her situation, and beloved by the other inmates. The tale told by the Superior, whatever it was, however unheard before might have been any of her statements,

---

8 Accouchement refers to the preparation for or process of giving birth.

was then attested by us, who, in every way we could think of, endeavoured to confirm her declarations, beyond the reach of doubt.

Sometimes the Superior would intrust the management of such a case to some of the nuns, whether to habituate us to the practice in which she was so highly accomplished, or to relieve herself of what would have been a serious burden to most other persons, or to ascertain whether she could depend upon us, or all together, I cannot tell. Often, however, have I seen her throw open a door, and, say, in a hurried manner, "Who can tell the best story?"

One point, on which we received frequent and particular instructions was, the nature of falsehoods. On this subject I have heard many a speech, I had almost said many a sermon; and I was led to believe that it was one of great importance, one on which it was a duty to be well informed, as well as to act. "What!" exclaimed a priest one day—"what, a nun of your age, and not know the difference between a wicked and a religious lie!"

He then went on, as had been done many times previously in my hearing, to show the essential difference between the two different kinds of falsehoods. A lie told merely for the injury of another, for our own interest alone, or for no object at all, he painted as a sin worthy of penance. But a lie told for the good of the church or Convent, was meritorious, and of course the telling of it a duty. And of this class of lies there were many varieties and shades. This doctrine has been inculcated on me and my companions in the nunnery, more times than I can enumerate; and to say that it was generally received, would be to tell a part of the truth. We often saw the practice of it, and were frequently made to take part in it. Whenever any thing which the Superior thought important, could be most conveniently accomplished by falsehood, she resorted to it without scruple.

There was a class of cases in which she more frequently relied on deception than any other.

The friends of novices frequently applied at the Convent to see them, or at least to inquire after their welfare. It was common for them to be politely refused an interview, on some account or other, generally a mere pretext; and then the Superior usually sought to make as favourable an impression as possible on the visitors. Sometimes she would make up a story on the spot, and tell the strangers; requiring some of us to confirm it, in the most convincing way we could.

At other times she would prefer to make over to us the task of deceiving, and we were commended in proportion to our ingenuity and success.

Some nun usually showed her submission, by immediately stepping forward. She would then add, perhaps, that the parents of such a novice, whom she named, were in waiting, and it was necessary that they should be told such, and such, and such things. To perform so difficult a task well, was considered a difficult duty, and it was one of the most certain ways to gain the favour of the Superior. Whoever volunteered to make a story on the spot, was sent immediately to tell it, and the other nuns present were hurried off with her under strict injunctions to uphold her in every thing she might state. The Superior, as there was every reason to believe, on all such occasions, when she did not herself appear, hastened to the apartment adjoining that in which the nuns were going, there to listen through the thin partition, to hear whether all performed their parts aright. It was not uncommon for her to go rather further, when she wanted time to give such explanations as she could have desired. She would then enter abruptly, ask, "Who can tell a good story this morning?" and hurry us off without a moment's delay, to do our best at a venture, without waiting for instructions. It would be curious, could a stranger from "the wicked world" outside the Convent witness such a scene. One of the nuns, who felt in a favourable humour to undertake the proposed task, would step promptly forward, and signify her readiness in the usual way: by a knowing wink of one eye, and a slight toss of the head.

"Well, go and do the best you can," the Superior would say; "and all the rest of you must mind and swear to it." The latter part of the order, at least, was always performed for in every such case, all the nuns present appeared as unanimous witnesses of every thing that was uttered by the spokesman of the day.

We were constantly hearing it repeated, that we must never again look upon ourselves as our own; but must remember, that we were solemnly and irrevocably devoted to God. Whatever was required of us, we were called upon to yield under the most solemn considerations. I cannot speak on every particular with equal freedom; but I wish my readers clearly to understand the condition in which we were placed, and the means used to reduce us to what we had to submit to. Not only were we required to perform the several tasks imposed upon us at work, prayers, and penances, under the idea that we were performing solemn duties to our Maker, but every thing else which was required of us, we were constantly told, was something indispensable in his sight. The priests, we admitted, were the servants of God, specially appointed by his authority, to teach us our duty, to absolve us from sin, and to lead us to heaven. Without their assistance, we had allowed we could never enjoy the favour of God: unless they administered the sacraments to us, we could not enjoy everlasting happiness. Having consented to acknowledge all this, we had no objection to urge against admitting any other demand that might be made for or by them. If we thought an act ever so criminal, the Superior would tell us, that the priests acted under the direct sanction of God, and *could not sin.* Of course, then, it could not be wrong to comply with any of their requests, because they could not demand any thing but what was right. On the contrary, to refuse to do any thing they asked, would necessarily be sinful. Such doctrines admitted, and such practices performed, it will not seem wonderful when I mention that we often felt something of their preposterous character.

Sometimes we took pleasure in ridiculing some of the favourite themes of our teachers; and I recollect one subject particularly, which at one period afforded us repeated merriment. It may seem irreverent in me to give the account, but I do it to show how things of a solemn nature were sometimes treated in the Convent, by women bearing the title of saints. A Canadian Novice, who spoke very broken English, one day remarked that she was performing some duty "for the God." This peculiar expression had something ridiculous to the ears of some of us; and it was soon repeated again and again, in application to various ceremonies which we had to perform. Mad Jane Ray seized upon it with avidity, and with her aid it soon took the place of a by-word in conversation, so that we were constantly reminding each other, that we were doing this and that thing, how trifling and unmeaning soever, "for the God." Nor did we stop here: when the Superior called upon us to bear witness to one of her religious lies, or to fabricate the most spurious one the time would admit; to save her the trouble, we were sure to be reminded, on our way to the stranger's room, that we were doing it "for the God." And so it was when other things were mentioned—every thing which belonged to our condition, was spoken of in similar terms.

I have hardly detained the reader long enough on the subject, to give him a just impression of the stress laid on confession. It is one of the great points to which our attention was constantly directed. We were directed to keep a strict and constant watch over our thoughts; to have continually before our minds the rules of the Convent, to compare the one with the other, remember every devotion, and tell all, even the smallest, at confession, either to the Superior, or to the priest. My mind was thus kept in a continual state of activity, which proved very wearisome; and it required the constant exertion of our teachers, to keep us up to the practice they inculcated.

Another tale recurs to me, of those which were frequently told us to make us feel the importance of unreserved confession.

A nun of our Convent, who had hidden some sin from her confessor, died suddenly, and without any one to confess her. Her sisters assembled to pray for the peace of her soul, when she appeared, and informed them, that it would be of no use, but rather troublesome to her, as her pardon was impossible.[9] The doctrine is, that prayers made for souls guilty of unconfessed sin, do but sink them deeper in hell; and this is the reason I have heard given for not praying for Protestants.

The authority of the priests in every thing, and the enormity of every act which opposes it, were also impressed upon our minds, in various ways, by our teachers. A "Father" told us the following story one day at catechism.

A man once died who had failed to pay some money which the priest had asked of him; he was condemned to be burnt in purgatory until he should pay it, but had permission to come back to this world, and take a human body to work in. He made his appearance therefore again on earth, and hired himself to a rich man as a labourer. He worked all day with the fire burning in him, unseen by other people; but while he was in bed that night, a girl in an adjoining room, perceiving the smell of brimstone, looked through a crack in the wall, and saw him covered with flames. She informed his master, who questioned him the next morning, and found that his hired man was secretly suffering the pains of purgatory, for neglecting to pay a certain sum of money to the priest. He, therefore, furnished him the amount due; it was paid, and the servant went off immediately to heaven. The priest cannot forgive any debt due unto him, because it is the Lord's estate.

While at confession, I was urged to hide nothing from the priest, and have been told by them, that they already knew what was in my heart, but would not tell, because it was necessary for me to confess it. I really believed that the priests were acquainted with my thoughts; and often stood in great awe of them. They often told me they had power to strike me dead at any moment.

Chapter XVII

Treatment of Young Infants

Treatment of young Infants in the Convent—Talking in Sleep—Amusements— Ceremonies at the public interment of deceased Nuns—Sudden disappearance of the Old Superior—Introduction of the new one—Superstition—Alarm of a Nun— Difficulty of Communication with other Nuns.

It will be recollected, that I was informed immediately after receiving the veil, that infants were occasionally murdered in the Convent. I was one day in the nuns' private sick-room, when I had an opportunity, unsought for, of witnessing deeds of such a nature. It was, perhaps, a month after the death of Saint Francis. Two little twin babes, the children of Saint

---

9 [Author's Original Note] Since the first edition, I have found this tale related in a Romish book, as one of very ancient date. It was told to us as having taken place in our Convent.

Catharine, were brought to a priest, who was in the room, for baptism. I was present while the ceremony was performed, with the Superior and several of the old nuns, whose names I never knew, they being called Ma tante, Aunt.

The priests took turns in attending to confession and catechism in the Convent, usually three months at a time, though sometimes longer periods. The priest then on duty was Father Larkin. He is a good-looking European, and has a brother who is a professor in the college. He baptized and then put oil upon the heads of the infants, as is the custom after baptism. They were then taken, one after another, by one of the old nuns, in the presence of us all. She pressed her hand upon the mouth and nose of the first, so tight that it could not breathe, and in a few minutes, when the hand was removed, it was dead. She then took the other, and treated it in the same way. No sound was heard, and both the children were corpses. The greatest indifference was shown by all present during this operation; for all, as I well knew, were long accustomed to such scenes. The little bodies were then taken into the cellar, thrown into the pit[10] I have mentioned, and covered with a quantity of lime.

I afterward saw another new-born infant treated in the same manner, in the same place: but the actors in the scene I choose not to name, nor the circumstances, as every thing connected with it is of a peculiarly trying and painful nature to my own feelings.

These were the only instances of infanticide I witnessed; and it seemed to be merely owing to accident that I was then present. So far as I know, there were no pains taken to preserve secrecy on this subject; that is, I saw no attempt made to keep any of the inmates of the Convent in ignorance of the murder of children. On the contrary, others were told, as well as myself, on their first admission as veiled nuns, that all infants born in the place were baptized and killed, without loss of time; and I had been called to witness the murder of the three just mentioned, only because I happened to be in the room at the time.

That others were killed in the same manner during my stay in the nunnery, I am well assured.

How many there were I cannot tell, and having taken no account of those I heard of, I cannot speak with precision; I believe, however, that I learnt through nuns, that at least eighteen or twenty infants were smothered, and secretly buried in the cellar, while I was a nun.

One of the effects of the weariness of our bodies and minds, was our proneness to talk in our sleep. It was both ludicrous and painful to hear the nuns repeat their prayers in the course of the night, as they frequently did in their dreams. Required to keep our minds continually on the stretch, both in watching our conduct, in remembering the rules and our prayers, under the fear of the consequences of any neglect, when we closed our eyes in sleep, we often went over again the scenes of the day; and it was no uncommon thing for me to hear a nun repeat one or two of our long exercises in the dead of night. Sometimes, by the time she had finished, another, in a different part of the room, would happen to take a similar turn, and commence a similar recitation; and I have known cases in which several such unconscious exercises were performed, all within an hour or two.

---

10 Earlier in her account, Maria Monk is sent to the convent's cellar for coal, where she discovers several cells with imprisoned nuns, and "a hole dug so deep into the earth that I could perceive no bottom [...] and unprotected by any kind of curb, so that one might easily have walked into it, in the dark."

We had now and then a recreation-day, when we were relieved from our customary labour, and from all prayers except those for morning and evening, and the short ones said at every striking of the clock. The greater part of our time was then occupied with different games, particularly backgammon and drafts, and in such conversation as did not relate to our past lives, and the outside of the Convent. Sometimes, however, our sports would be interrupted on such days by the entrance of one of the priests, who would come in and propose that his fête, the birthday of his patron saint, should be kept by "the saints." We saints!

Several nuns died at different times while I was in the Convent; how many I cannot say, but there was a considerable number: I might rather say, many in proportion to the number in the nunnery. The proportion of deaths I am sure was very large. There were always some in the nuns' sick-rooms, and several interments took place in the chapel.

When a Black nun is dead, the corpse is dressed as if living, and placed in the chapel in a sitting posture, within the railing round the altar, with a book in the hand, as if reading. Persons are then freely admitted from the street, and some of them kneel and pray before it. No particular notoriety is given, I believe, to this exhibition out of the Convent; but such a case usually excites some attention.

The living nuns are required to say prayers for the delivery of their deceased sister from purgatory, being informed, as in all other such cases that if she is not there, and has no need of our intercession, our prayers are in no danger of being thrown away, as they will be set down to the account of some of our departed friends, or at least to that of the souls which have no acquaintances to pray for them.

It was customary for us occasionally to kneel before a dead nun thus seated in the chapel, and I have often performed that task. It was always painful, for the ghastly countenance being seen whenever I raised my eyes, and the feeling that the position and dress were entirely opposed to every idea of propriety in such a case, always made me melancholy.

The Superior sometimes left the Convent, and was absent for an hour, or several hours, at a time, but we never knew of it until she had returned, and were not informed where she had been. I one day had reason to presume that she had recently paid a visit to the priests' farm, though I had not direct evidence that such was the fact. The priests' farm is a fine tract of land belonging to the Seminary, a little distance from the city, near the Lachine road with a large old-fashioned edifice upon it. I happened to be in the Superior's room on the day alluded to, when she made some remark on the plainness and poverty of her furniture. I replied, that she was not proud, and could not be dissatisfied on that account; she answered—

"No; but if I was, how much superior is the furniture at the priests' farm! the poorest room there is furnished better than the best of mine."

I was one day mending the fire in the Superior's room, when a priest was conversing with her on the scarcity of money; and I heard him say, that very little money was received by the priests for prayers, but that the principal part came with penances and absolutions.

One of the most remarkable and unaccountable things that happened in the Convent, was the disappearance of the old Superior. She had performed her customary part during the day, and had acted and appeared just as usual. She had shown no symptoms of ill health, met with no particular difficulty in conducting business, and no agitation, anxiety, or gloom, had been noticed in her conduct. We had no reason to suppose that during that day she had expected any thing particular to occur, any more than the rest of us. After the close of our customary labours and evening lecture, she dismissed us to retire to bed, exactly in her usual manner. The next morning the bell rang, we sprang from our bed, hurried on our clothes as usual, and proceeded to the community-room in double line, to commence the morning exercises. There, to our surprise, we found Bishop Lartigue; but the Superior was nowhere to be seen. The Bishop soon addressed us, instead of her, and informed us, that a lady near him, whom he presented to us, was now the Superior of the Convent, and enjoined upon us the same respect and obedience which we had paid to her predecessor.

The lady he introduced to us was one of our oldest nuns, Saint Du****, a very large, fleshy woman, with swelled limbs, which rendered her very slow in walking, and often gave her great distress. Not a word was dropped from which we could conjecture the cause of this change, nor of the fate of the old Superior. I took the first opportunity to inquire of one of the nuns, whom I dared talk to, what had become of her; but I found them as ignorant as myself, though suspicious that she had been murdered by the orders of the Bishop. Never did I obtain any light on her mysterious disappearance. I am confident, however, that if the Bishop wished to get rid of her privately and by foul means, he had ample opportunities and power at his command. Jane Ray, as usual, could not allow such an occurrence to pass by without intimating her own suspicions more plainly than any other of the nuns would have dared to do. She spoke out one day, in the community-room, and said, "I'm going to have a hunt in the cellar for my old Superior."

"Hush, Jane Ray!" exclaimed some of the nuns, "you'll be punished."

"My mother used to tell me," replied Jane, "never to be afraid of the face of man."

It cannot be thought strange that we were superstitious. Some were more easily terrified than others, by unaccountable sights and sounds: but all of us believed in the power and occasional appearance of spirits, and were ready to look for them at almost any time. I have seen several instances of alarm caused by such superstition, and have experienced it myself more than once. I was one day sitting mending aprons, beside one of the old nuns, in a community-room, while the litanies were repeating; as I was very easy to laugh, Saint Ignace, or Agnes, came in, walked up to her with much agitation, and began to whisper in her ear. She usually talked but little, and that made me more curious to know what was the matter with her. I overheard her say to the old nun, in much alarm, that in the cellar, from which she had just returned, she had heard the most dreadful groans that ever came from any being. This was enough to give me uneasiness. I could not account for the appearance of an evil spirit in any part of the Convent, for I had been assured that the only one ever known there, was that of the nun who had died with an unconfessed sin, and that others were kept at a distance by the holy water that was rather profusely used in different parts of the nunnery. Still, I presumed that the sounds heard by Saint Ignace must have proceeded from some devil, and I felt great dread at the thought of visiting the cellar again. I determined to seek further information of the terrified nun; but when I addressed her on the subject, at recreation-time, the first opportunity I could find, she replied, that I was always trying to make her break silence, and walked off to another group in the room, so that I could obtain no satisfaction.

It is remarkable that in our nunnery, we were almost entirely cut off from the means of knowing any thing, even of each other. There were many nuns whom I know nothing of to this day, after having been in the same rooms with them every day and night for many months. There was a nun, whom I supposed to be in the Convent, and whom I was anxious to learn something about from the time of my entrance as a novice; but I never was able to learn any thing concerning her, not even whether she was in the nunnery or not, whether alive or dead. She was the daughter of a rich family, residing at Point aux Trembles, of whom I had heard my mother speak before I entered the Convent. The name of her family I think was Lafayette, and she was thought to be from Europe. She was known to have taken the black veil; but as I was not acquainted with the name of the Saint she had assumed, and I could not describe her in "the world," all my inquiries and observations proved entirely in vain.

I had heard before my entrance into the Convent, that one of the nuns had made her escape from it during the last war, and once inquired about her of the Superior. She admitted that such was the fact; but I was never able to learn any particulars concerning her name, origin, or manner of escape.

Chapter XIX

The Priests of the District

The Priests of the District of Montreal have free access to the Black Nunnery—Crimes committed and required by them—The Pope's Command to commit indecent Crimes— Characters of the Old and New Superiors— The timidity of the latter—I began to be employed in the Hospitals—Some account of them—Warning given me by a sick Nun—Penance by Hanging.

I have mentioned before, that the country, as far down as Three Rivers, is furnished with priests by the Seminary of Montreal; and that these hundred and fifty men are liable to be occasionally transferred from one station to another. Numbers of them are often to be seen in the streets of Montreal, as they may find a home in the Seminary.

They are considered as having an equal right to enter the Black Nunnery whenever they please; and then, according to our oaths, they have complete control over the nuns. To name all the works of shame of which they are guilty in that retreat, would require much time and space, neither would it be necessary to the accomplishment of my object, which is, the publication of but some of their criminality to the world, and the development, in general terms, of scenes thus far carried on in secret within the walls of that Convent, where I was so long an inmate.

Secure against detection by the world, they never believed that an eyewitness would ever escape to tell of their crimes, and declare some of their names before the world; but the time has come, and some of their deeds of darkness must come to the day. I have seen in the nunnery, the priests from more, I presume, than a hundred country places, admitted for shameful and criminal purposes: from St. Charles, St. Denis, St. Mark's, St. Antoine, Chambly, Bertier, St. John's, &c. &c.

How unexpected to them will be the disclosures I make! Shut up in a place from which there has been thought to be but one way of egress, and that the passage to the grave, they considered themselves safe in perpetrating crimes in our presence, and in making us share in their criminality as often as they chose, and conducted more shamelessly than even the brutes. These debauchees would come in without ceremony, concealing their names, both by night and by day, where the cries and pains of the injured innocence of their victims could never reach the world, for relief or redress for their wrongs; without remorse or shame, they would glory in torturing, in the most barbarous manner, the feelings of those under their power; telling us, at the same time, that this mortifying the flesh was religion, and pleasing to God.

We were sometimes invited to put ourselves to voluntary sufferings in a variety of ways, not for a penance, but to show our devotion to God. A priest would sometimes say to us—

"Now, which of you have love enough for Jesus Christ to stick a pin through your cheeks?"

Some of us would signify our readiness, and immediately thrust one through up to the head. Sometimes he would propose that we should repeat the operation several times on the spot; and the cheeks of a number of nuns would be bloody.

There were other acts occasionally proposed and consented to, which I cannot name | in a book. Such the Superior would sometimes command us to perform; many of them things not only useless and unheard of, but loathsome and indecent in the highest possible degree. How they could ever have been invented I never could conceive. Things were done worse than the entire exposure of the person, though this was occasionally required of several at once, in the presence of priests.

The Superior of the Seminary would sometimes come and inform us, that he had received orders from the Pope, to request that those nuns who possessed the greatest devotion and faith, should be requested to perform some particular deeds, which he named or described in our presence, but of which no decent or moral person could ever endure to speak. I cannot repeat what would injure any ear, not debased to the lowest possible degree. I am bound by a regard to truth, however, to confess, that deluded women were found among us, who would comply with those requests.

There was a great difference between the characters of our old and new Superior, which soon became obvious. The former used to say she liked to walk, because it would prevent her from becoming corpulent. She was, therefore, very active, and constantly going about from one part of the nunnery to another, overseeing us at our various employments. I never saw in her any appearance of timidity: she seemed, on the contrary, bold and mas-culine, and sometimes much more than that, cruel and cold-blooded, in scenes calculated to overcome any common person. Such a character she had particularly exhibited at the murder of Saint Francis.[11]

The new Superior, on the other hand, was so heavy and lame, that she walked with much difficulty, and consequently exercised a less vigilant oversight of the nuns. She was also of a timid disposition, or else had been overcome by some great fright in her past life; for she was apt to become alarmed in the night, and never liked to be alone in the dark. She had long performed the part of an old nun, which is that of a spy upon the younger ones, and was well known to us in that character, under the name of Ste. Margarite. Soon after her promotion to the station of Superior, she appointed me to sleep in her apartment, and assigned me a sofa to lie upon. One night, while I was asleep, she suddenly threw herself upon me, and exclaimed in great alarm, "Oh! mon Dieu! mon Dieu! Qu'est que ça?" Oh, my God! my God! What is that? I jumped up and looked about the room, but saw noth-ing, and endeavoured to convince her that there was nothing extraordinary there. But she insisted that a ghost had come and held her bed-curtain, so that she could not draw it.

---

11 Earlier in the narrative, Maria tells of the convent trial of Saint Francis, in which the bishop and four other priests condemn her to death because she would not kill infants, obey orders from superiors to do immoral acts and wished to escape the convent.

I examined it, and found that the curtain had been caught by a pin in the valance, which had held it back; but it was impossible to tranquillize her for some time. She insisted on my sleeping with her the rest of the night, and I stretched myself across the foot of her bed, and slept there till morning.

During the last part of my stay in the Convent, I was often employed in attending in the hospitals. There are, as I have before mentioned, several apartments devoted to the sick, and there is a physician of Montreal, who attends as physician to the Convent. It must not be supposed, however, that he knows anything concerning the private hospitals. It is a fact of great importance to be distinctly understood, and constantly borne in mind, that he is never, under any circumstances, admitted into the private hospital-rooms. Of those he sees nothing more than any stranger whatever. He is limited to the care of those patients who are admitted from the city into the public hospital, and one of the nuns' hospitals, and these he visits every day. Sick poor are received for charity by the institution, attended by some of the nuns, and often go away with the highest ideas of their charitable characters and holy lives. The physician himself might perhaps in some cases share in the delusion.

I frequently followed Dr. Nelson through the public hospital, at the direction of the Superior, with pen, ink, and paper in my hands, and wrote down the prescriptions which he ordered for the different patients. These were afterward prepared and administered by the attendants. About a year before I left the Convent, I was first appointed to attend the private sick-rooms, and was frequently employed in that duty up to the day of my departure. Of course, I had opportunities to observe the number and classes of patients treated there: and in what I am to say on the subject, I appeal with perfect confidence to any true and competent witness to confirm my words, whenever such a witness may appear.

It would be vain for anybody who has merely visited the Convent from curiosity, or resided in it as a novice, to question my declarations. Such a person must necessarily be ignorant of even the existence of the private rooms, unless informed by some one else. Such rooms, however, there are, and I could relate many things which have passed there during the hours I was employed in them, as I have stated.

One night I was called to sit up with an old nun, named Saint Clare, who, in going downstairs, had dislocated a limb, and lay in a sick-room adjoining an hospital. She seemed to be a little out of her head a part of the time, but appeared to be quite in possession of her reason most of the night. It was easy to pretend that she was delirious, but I considered her as speaking the truth, though I felt reluctant to repeat what I heard her say, and excused myself from mentioning it even at confession, on the ground that the Superior thought her deranged.

What led her to some of the most remarkable parts of her conversation, was a motion I made, in the course of the night, to take the light out of her little room into the adjoining apartment, to look once more at the sick persons there. She begged me not to leave her a moment in the dark, for she could not bear it. "I have witnessed so many horrid scenes," said she, "in this Convent, that I want somebody near me constantly, and must always have a light burning in my room. I cannot tell you," she added, "what things I remember, for they would frighten you too much. What you have seen are nothing to them. Many a murder have I witnessed; many a nice young creature has been killed in this nunnery. I advise you to be very cautious—keep every thing to yourself—there are many here ready to betray you."

What it was that induced the old nun to express so much kindness to me I could not tell, unless she was frightened at the recollection of her own crimes, and those of others, and elt grateful for the care I took of her. She had been one of the night-watches, and never before showed me any particular kindness. She did not indeed go into detail concerning the transactions to which she alluded, but told me that some nuns had been murdered under great aggravations of cruelty, by being gagged, and left to starve in the cells, or having their flesh burnt off their bones with red-hot irons.

It was uncommon to find compunction expressed by any of the nuns. Habit renders us insensible to the sufferings of others, and careless about our own sins. I had become so hardened myself, that I find it difficult to rid myself of many of my former false principles and views of right and wrong.

I was one day set to wash some of the empty bottles from the cellar, which had contained the liquid that was poured into the cemetery there. A number of these had been brought from the corner where so many of them were always to be seen, and placed at the head of the cellar stairs, and there we were required to take them and wash them out. We poured in water and rinsed them; a few drops, which got upon our clothes, soon made holes in them. I think the liquid was called vitriol, or some such name; and I heard some persons say, that it would soon destroy the flesh, and even the bones of the dead. At another time, we were furnished with a little of the liquid, which was mixed with a quantity of water, and used in dying some cloth black, which was wanted at funerals, in the chapels. Our hands were turned very black by being dipped in it, but a few drops of some other liquid were mixed with fresh water and given us to wash in, which left our skin of a bright red.

The bottles of which I spoke were made of very thick, dark coloured glass, large at the bottom, and from recollection, I should say held something less than a gallon.

I was once much shocked, on entering the room for the examination of conscience, at seeing a nun hanging by a cord from a ring in the ceiling, with her head downward. Her clothes had been tied round with a leathern strap, to keep them in their place, and then she had been fastened in that situation, with her head some distance from the floor. Her face had a very unpleasant appearance, being dark-coloured and swollen by the rushing in of the blood; her hands were tied, and her mouth stopped with a large gag. This nun proved to be no other than Jane Ray, who for some fault had been condemned to this punishment.

This was not, however, a solitary case; I heard of numbers who were "hung," as it was called, at different times; and I saw Saint Hypolite and Saint Luke undergoing it. This was considered a most distressing punishment; and it was the only one which Jane Ray could not endure, of all she had tried.

Some of the nuns would allude to it in her presence, but it usually made her angry. It was probably practised in the same place while I was a novice; but I never heard or thought of such a thing in those days. Whenever we wished to enter the room for the examination of conscience, we had to ask leave; and after some delay were permitted to go, but always under a strict charge to bend the head forward, and keep the eyes fixed upon the floor.

Chapter XX

More Visits

More visits to the imprisoned Nuns—Their fears—Others temporarily put into the Cells— Reliques—The Agnus Dei—The Priests' private Hospital, or Holy Retreat—Secret Rooms in the Eastern Wing—Reports of Murders in the Convent—The Superior's private Records—Number of Nuns in the Convent—Desire of Escape—Urgent reason for it— Plan—Deliberation—Attempt—Success.

I often seized an opportunity, when I safely could, to speak a cheering or friendly word to one of the poor prisoners, in passing their cells, on my errands in the cellars. For a time I supposed them to be sisters; but I afterward discovered that this was not the case. I found that they were always under the fear of suffering some punishment, in case they should be found talking with a person not commissioned to attend them. They would often ask, "Is not somebody coming?"

I could easily believe what I heard affirmed by others, that fear was the severest of their sufferings. Confined in the dark, in so gloomy a place, with the long and spacious arched cellar stretching off this way and that, visited only now and then by a solitary nun, with whom they were afraid to speak their feelings, and with only the miserable society of each other; how gloomy thus to spend day after day, months, and even years, without any prospect of liberation, and liable every moment to any other fate to which the Bishop or Superior might condemn them! But these poor creatures must have known something of the horrors perpetrated in other parts of the building, and could not have been ignorant of the hole in the cellar, which was not far from their cells, and the use to which it was devoted. One of them told me, in confidence, she wished they could get out. They must also have been often disturbed in their sleep, if they ever did sleep, by the numerous priests who passed through the trapdoor at no great distance. To be subject to such trials for a single day would be dreadful; but these nuns had them to endure for years.

I often felt much compassion for them, and wished to see them released; but at other times, yielding to the doctrine perpetually taught us in the Convent, that our future happiness would be proportioned to the sufferings we had to undergo in this world, I would rest satisfied that their imprisonment was a real blessing to them. Others, I presume, participated with me in such feelings. One Sunday afternoon, after we had performed all our ceremonies, and were engaged as usual, at that time, with backgammon and other amusements, one of the young nuns exclaimed, "Oh, how headstrong are those wretches in the cells—they are as bad as the day they were first put in!"

This exclamation was made, as I supposed, in consequence of some recent conversation with them, as I knew her to be particularly acquainted with the older one.

Some of the vacant cells were occasionally used for temporary imprisonment. Three nuns were confined in them, to my knowledge, for disobedience to the Superior, as she called it. They did not join the rest in singing in the evening, being exhausted by the various exertions of the day. The Superior ordered them to sing, and as they did not comply, after her command had been twice repeated, she ordered them away to the cells.

They were immediately taken down into the cellar, placed in separate dungeons, and the doors shut and barred upon them. There they remained through that night, the following day, and second night, but were released in time to attend mass on the second morning.

The Superior used occasionally to show something in a glass box, which we were required to regard with the highest degree of reverence. It was made of wax, and called an Agnus Dei.[12] She used to exhibit it to us when we were in a state of grace: that is, after confession and before sacrament. She said it had been blessed *in the very dish in which our Saviour*

---

12 A cake of wax, blessed by the Pope, stamped with a figure of a lamb bearing a cross and flag.

had eaten. It was brought from Rome. Every time we kissed it, or even looked at it, we were told it gave a hundred days release from purgatory to ourselves, or if we did not need it, to our next of kin in purgatory, if not a Protestant. If we had no such kinsman, the benefit was to go to the souls in purgatory not prayed for.

Jane Ray would sometimes say to me, "Let's kiss it—some of our friends will thank us for it."

I have been repeatedly employed in carrying dainties of different kinds to the little private room I have mentioned, next beyond the Superior's sitting-room, in the second story, which the priests made their *"Holy Retreat."* That room I never was allowed to enter. I could only go to the door with a waiter of refreshments, set it down upon a little stand near it, give three raps on the door, and then retire to a distance to await orders. When any thing was to be taken away, it was placed on the stand by the Superior, who then gave three raps for me, and closed the door.

The Bishop I saw at least once when he appeared worse for wine, or something of the kind. After partaking of refreshments in the Convent, he sent for all the nuns, and, on our appearance, gave us his blessing, and put a piece of poundcake on the shoulder of each of us, in a manner which appeared singular and foolish.

There are three rooms in the Black Nunnery which I never entered. I had enjoyed much liberty, and had seen, as I supposed, all parts of the building, when one day I observed an old nun go to a corner of an apartment near the northern end of the western wing, push the end of her scissors into a crack in the panelled wall, and pull out a door. I was much surprised, because I never had conjectured that any door was there; and it appeared, when I afterward examined the place, that no indication of it could be discovered on the closest scrutiny. I stepped forward to see what was within, and saw three rooms opening into each other; but the nun refused to admit me within the door, which she said led to rooms kept as depositories.

She herself entered and closed the door, so that I could not satisfy my curiosity; and no occasion presented itself. I always had a strong desire to know the use of these apartments: for I am sure they must have been designed for some purpose of which I was intentionally kept ignorant, otherwise they would never have remained unknown to me so long. Besides, the old nun evidently had some strong reasons for denying me admission, though she endeavoured to quiet my curiosity.

The Superior, after my admission into the Convent, had told me that I had access to every room in the building; and I had seen places which bore witness to the cruelties and the crimes committed under her commands or sanction; but here was a succession of rooms which had been concealed from me, and so constructed as if designed to be unknown to all but a few. I am sure that any person, who might be able to examine the wall in that place, would pronounce that secret door a surprising piece of work. I never saw any thing of the kind which appeared to me so ingenious and skilfully made. I told Jane Ray what I had seen, and she said, at once, "We will get in and see what is there," But I suppose she never found an opportunity.

I naturally felt a good deal of curiosity to learn whether such scenes, as I had witnessed in the death of Saint Francis, were common or rare, and took an opportunity to inquire of Jane Ray. Her reply was—

"Oh, yes; and there were many murdered while you was a novice, whom you heard nothing about."

This was all I ever learnt on the subject; but although I was told nothing of the manner in which they were killed, I supposed it to be the same which I had seen practised, viz. by smothering.

I went into the Superior's parlour one day for something, and found Jane Ray there alone, looking into a book with an appearance of interest. I asked her what it was, but she made some trifling answer, and laid it by, as if unwilling to let me take it. There are two bookcases in the room; one on the right as you enter the door, and the other opposite, near the window and the sofa. The former contains the lecture-books and other printed volumes, the latter seemed to be filled with note and account books. I have often seen the keys in the bookcases while I have been dusting the furniture, and sometimes observed letters stuck up in the room; although I never looked into one, or thought of doing so, as we were under strict orders not to touch any of them, and the idea of sins and penances was always present with me.

Some time after the occasion mentioned, I was sent into the Superior's room, with Jane, to arrange it; and as the same book was lying out of the case, she said, "Come, let us look into it." I immediately consented, and we opened it, and turned over several leaves. It was about a foot and a half long, as nearly as I can remember, a foot wide, and about two inches thick, though I cannot speak with particular precision, as Jane frightened me almost as soon as I touched it, by exclaiming. "There, you have looked into it, and if you tell of me, I will of you."

The thought of being subjected to a severe penance, which I had reason to apprehend, fluttered me very much; and although I tried to overcome my fears, I did not succeed very well. I reflected, however, that the sin was already committed, and that it would not be increased if I examined the book. I, therefore, looked a little at several pages, though I still felt a good deal of agitation. I saw, at once, that the volume was a record of the entrance of nuns and novices into the Convent, and of the births that had taken place in the Convent. Entries of the last description were made in a brief manner, on the following plan: I do not give the names or dates as real, but only to show the form of entering them.

Saint Mary delivered of a son, March 16, 1834.

Saint Clarice delivered of a daughter, April 2, 1834.

Saint Matilda delivered of a daughter, April 30, 1834.

No mention was made in the book of the death of the children, though I well knew not one of them could be living at that time.

Now I presume that the period the book embraced, was about two years, as several names near the beginning I knew, but I can form only a rough conjecture of the number of infants born, and murdered of course, records of which it contained. I suppose the book contained at least one hundred pages, that one fourth were written upon, and that each page contained fifteen distinct records. Several pages were devoted to the list of births. On this supposition there must have been a large number, which I can easily believe to have been born there in the course of two years.

What were the contents of the other books belonging to the same case with that which I looked into, I have no idea having never dared to touch one of them; I believe, however, that Jane Ray was well acquainted with them, knowing, as I do, her intelligence and prying disposition. If she could be brought to give her testimony, she would doubtless unfold many curious particulars now unknown.

I am able, in consequence of a circumstances which appeared accidental, to state with confidence the exact number of persons in the Convent one day of the week in which I left it. This may be a point of some interest, as several secret deaths had occurred since my taking the veil, and many burials had been openly made in the chapel.

I was appointed, at the time mentioned, to lay out the covers for all the inmates of the Convent, including the nuns in the cells. These covers, as I have said before, were linen bands, to be bound around the knives, forks, spoons, and napkins, for eating. These were for all the nuns and novices, and amounted to two hundred and ten. As the number of novices was then about thirty, I know that there must have been at that time about one hundred and eighty veiled nuns.

I was occasionally troubled with a desire of escaping from the nunnery, and was much distressed whenever I felt so evil an imagination rise in my mind. I believed that it was a sin, a great sin, and did not fail to confess at every opportunity, that I felt discontent. My confessors informed me that I was beset by an evil spirit, and urged me to pray against it. Still, however, every now and then, I would think, "Oh, if I could get out!"

At length one of the priests, to whom I had confessed this sin, informed me, for my comfort, that he had begun to pray to Saint Anthony, and hoped his intercession would, by-and-by, drive away the evil spirit. My desire of escape was partly excited by the fear of bringing an infant to the murderous hands of my companions, or of taking a potion whose violent effects I too well knew.

One evening, however, I found myself more filled with the desire of escape than ever and what exertions I made to dismiss the thought, proved entirely unavailing. During evening prayers, I became quite occupied with it; and when the time for meditation arrived, instead of falling into a doze as I often did, although I was a good deal fatigued, I found no difficulty in keeping awake. When this exercise was over, and the other nuns were about to retire to the sleeping room, my station being in the private sick-room for the night, I withdrew to my post, which was the little sitting-room adjoining it.

Here, then, I threw myself upon the sofa, and, being alone, reflected a few moments on the manner of escaping which had occurred to me. The physician had arrived a little before, at half-past eight; and I had now to accompany him, as usual, from bed to bed, with pen, ink, and paper, to write down his prescriptions for the direction of the old nun, who was to see them administered. What I wrote that evening, I cannot now recollect, as my mind was uncommonly agitated; but my customary way was to note down briefly his orders in this manner:

1 d salts, St. Matilde.

1 blister, St. Genevieve, &c. &c.

I remember that I wrote three such orders that evening, and then, having finished the rounds, I returned for a few minutes to the sitting-room.

There were two ways of access to the street from those rooms: first, the more direct, from the passage adjoining the sick-room, down-stairs, through a door, into the nunnery-yard, and through a wicket-gate; that is the way by which the physician usually enters at night, and he is provided with a key for that purpose.

It would have been unsafe, however, for me to pass out that way, because a man is kept continually in the yard, near the gate, who sleeps at night in a small hut near the door, to escape whose observation would be impossible. My only hope, therefore, was, that I might gain my passage through the other way, to do which I must pass through the sick-room, then through a passage, or small room, usually occupied by an old nun; another passage and staircase leading down to the yard, and a large gate opening into the cross street. I had no liberty ever to go beyond the sick-room, and knew that several of the doors might be fastened. Still, I determined to try; although I have often since been astonished at my boldness in undertaking what would expose me to so many hazards of failure, and to severe punishment if found out.

It seemed as if I acted under some extraordinary impulse, which encouraged me to do what I should hardly at any other moment have thought of undertaking. I had set but a short time upon the sofa, however, before I rose, with a desperate determination to make the experiment. I therefore walked hastily across the sick-room, passed into the nun's room, walked by her in a great hurry, and almost without giving her time to speak or think, said,— "A message!" and in an instant was through the door, and in the next passage. I think there was another nun with her at the moment; and it is probable that my hurried manner, and prompt intimation that I was sent on a pressing mission to the Superior, prevented them from entertaining any suspicion of my intention. Besides, I had the written orders of the physician in my hand, which may have tended to mislead them; and it was well known to some of the nuns, that I had twice left the Convent and returned from choice; so that I was probably more likely to be trusted to remain than many of the others.

The passage which I had now reached had several doors, with all which I was acquainted; that on the opposite side opened into a community-room, where I should probably have found some of the old nuns at that hour, and they would certainly have stopped me. On the left, however, was a large door, both locked and barred; but I gave the door a sudden swing, that it might creak as little as possible, being of iron. Down the stairs I hurried, and making my way through the door into the yard, stepped across it, unbarred the great gate, and was at liberty!

Chapter Five

ORSON SQUIRE FOWLER (1809–1887) AND LORENZO NILES FOWLER (1811–1896)

Phrenology, a science centered on discovering and exploiting correlations between the shape of a person's head and that person's personality and intellect, enjoyed incredible popularity among Americans throughout the nineteenth century. Franz Joseph Gall (1758–1828), a Viennese physician, created what others would later call this "science of the mind." Gall argued that the brain could be separated into 37 different "organs," all of which corresponded to a different mental faculty, such as "spirituality," "self-esteem," "hope" and "destructiveness." He believed that one could identify every person's strong and weak organs by the shape of his or her head and then move to improve areas that were underdeveloped and take advantage of a person's natural gifts. It was a highly optimistic system that promised tremendous self-improvement based on rigorous self-examination and discipline.

Orson Fowler   Lorenzo Fowler

By the 1830s, more than forty phrenological societies had been established in the United States, and by the 1850s even the smallest American towns had been touched by a frenzied interest in the possibilities of phrenology. "Bump doctors" traveled the countryside lecturing, selling phrenological books and tracts and analyzing the heads of all willing to pay their fees. Countless Americans applied phrenology to the most practical matters of their lives, from choosing a mate to picking a career.

The most successful popularizers and educators of phrenology in America were members of the Fowler family: Orson, Lorenzo, Charlotte, and Charlotte's husband, Samuel Wells. Among the earliest traveling phrenologists, Orson and Lorenzo crisscrossed the country, promoting phrenology through their writings, lectures, and consultations. Among the more famous heads they analyzed were those of John Brown, Horace Greeley, Walt Whitman, Mark Twain and Clara Barton. They eventually stopped traveling to establish the American Phrenological Institute in New York City, edit the country's first phrenological magazine, *American Phrenological Journal*, and work on a host of other phrenological projects and writings. One of their most famous works was *The Illustrated Self-Instructor in Phrenology and Physiology*. First published in 1840, it proved to be one of the century's most popular self-instruction manuals, going through more than twenty editions in the next fifty years.

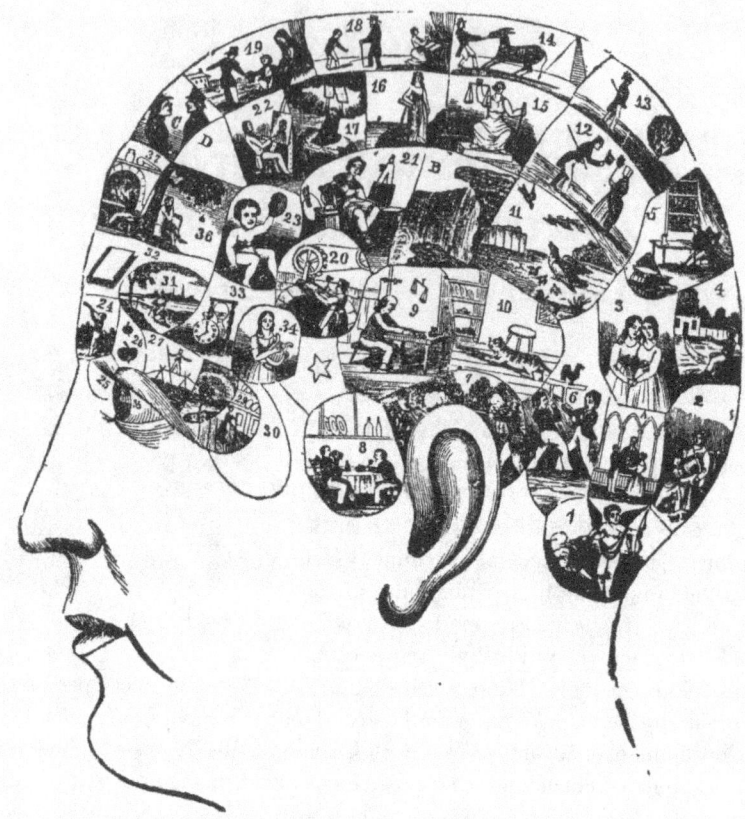

NUMBERING AND DEFINITION OF THE ORGANS.

1. AMATIVENESS, Sexual and connubial love.
2. PHILOPROGENITIVENESS, Parental love.
3. ADHESIVENESS, Friendship—sociability.
4. UNION FOR LIFE, Love of one only.
5. INHABITIVENESS, Love of home.
6. CONTINUITY, One thing at a time.
7. COMBATIVENESS, Resistance—defence.
8. DESTRUCTIVENESS, Executiveness—force.
9. ALIMENTIVENESS, Appetite, hunger.
10. ACQUISITIVENESS, Accumulation.
11. SECRETIVENESS, Policy—management.
12. CAUTIOUSNESS, Prudence, provision.
13. APPROBATIVENESS, Ambition—display.
14. SELF-ESTEEM, Self-respect—dignity.
15. FIRMNESS, Decision—perseverance.
16. CONSCIENTIOUSNESS, Justice—equity
17. HOPE, Expectation—enterprise
18. SPIRITUALITY, Intuition--spiritual revery.
19. VENERATION, Devotion—respect.
20. BENEVOLENCE, Kindness—goodness.
21. CONSTRUCTIVNESS, Mechanical ingenuity

21. IDEALITY, Refinement—taste—purity.
B. SUBLIMITY, Love of grandeur.
22. IMITATION, Copying—patterning.
23. MIRTHFULNESS, Jocoseness—wit—fun.
24. INDIVIDUALITY, Observation.
25. FORM, Recollection of shape.
26. SIZE, Measuring by the eye.
27. WEIGHT, Balancing—climbing.
28. COLOR, Judgment of colors.
29. ORDER, Method—system--arrangement
30. CALCULATION, Mental arithmetic.
31. LOCALITY. Recollection of places.
32. EVENTUALITY, Memory of facts.
33. TIME, Cognizance of duration.
34. TUNE, Music—melody by ear.
35. LANGUAGE, Expression of ideas.
36. CAUSALITY, Applying causes to effects.
37. COMPARISON, inductive reasoning.
C. HUMAN NATURE, perception of motives
D. AGREEABLENESS, Pleasantness—suavity

Frontispiece Illustration, "Symbolical Head," from an 1854 edition of Fowlers' *The Illustrated Self-Instructor* (New York: Fowler and Wells).

O. S. and L. N. Fowler, *The Illustrated Self-Instructor in Phrenology and Physiology with One Hundred Engravings, and a Chart of the Character.* New York: Fowler and Wells Publishers, 1854.

The Illustrated Self-Instructor In Phrenology and Physiology With One Hundred Engravings, and A Chart of the Character

Section I

Physiological Conditions as Affecting and Indicating Character

1.—Value of Self-Knowledge

"KNOWLEDGE is power"—to accomplish, to enjoy—and these are the only ends for which man was created. ALL knowledge confers this power. Thus, how incalculably, and in how many ways, have recent discoveries in chemistry enhanced human happiness, of which the lucifer match furnishes a *home* example. Increasing knowledge in agriculture is doubling the means of human sustenance. How immeasurably have modern mechanical improvements multiplied, and cheapened all the comforts of life. How greatly have steamboats and railroads added to the former stock of human success and pleasures. Similar remarks apply to all other kinds of knowledge, and as it increases from age to age will it proportionally multiply all forms of human happiness. In fact, its inherent *nature* and legitimate effect is to promote every species of enjoyment and success. Other things being equal, those who know most, by a law of things, can both accomplish and enjoy most; while ignorance instead of being bliss, is the greatest cause of human weakness, wickedness, and woe. Hence, to ENLIGHTEN man, is *the* way to reform and perfect him.

But self-knowledge is, of all its other kinds, both the most useful and promotive of personal and universal happiness and success. "Know thyself" was written, in golden capitals, upon the splendid temple of Delphos,[1] as the most important maxim the wise men of Greece could transmit to unborn generations; and the Scriptures wisely command us to "search our own hearts."[2] Since all happiness flows from obeying, and all pain from violating, the LAWS OF OUR BEINGS, to know our own selves is to know these laws, and becomes the first step in the road of their obedience, which is life. Self-knowledge, by teaching the laws and conditions of life and health, becomes the most efficacious means of prolonging the former and increasing the latter—both of which are *paramount* conditions of enjoying and accomplishing. It also shows us our natural talents, capabilities, virtues, vices, strong and weak points, liabilities to err, etc., and thereby points out, unmistakably, those occupations and spheres in which we can and cannot succeed and shine; and develops the laws and conditions of human and personal virtue and moral perfection, as well as of vice, and how to avoid it. It is, therefore, the quintessence of all knowledge; places its possessor upon the very acme of enjoyment and perfection; and bestows the highest powers and richest treasures mortals can possess. In short, to know ourselves perfectly, is to know every law of our being, every condition of happiness, and every cause of suffering; and to *practice* such knowledge, is to render ourselves as perfectly happy, throughout every department of our being, as we can possibly be and live. And since nothing in nature stands alone, but each is reciprocally related to all, and all, collectively, form one magnificent whole—since all stars and worlds mutually act and react upon each other, to cause day and

---

1 Ancient Greek temple dedicated to Apollo. It housed a famous oracle capable of offering an inquirer supernatural knowledge about past, present and future.
2 Scriptural paraphrase, closely resembling Ps. 139:23.

night, summer and winter, sun and rain, blossom and fruit; since every genus, species, and individual throughout nature is second or sixteenth cousin to every other; and since man is the epitome of universal nature, the embodiment of all her functions, the focus of all her light, and representative of all her perfections—of course to understand *him* thoroughly is to know *all* things. Nor can nature be studied advantageously without him for a text-book, nor he without her.

Moreover, since man is composed of mind *and* body, both reciprocally and most intimately related to each other—since his mentality is manifested only by bodily organs, and the latter depends wholly upon the former, of course his mind can be studied only through its ORGANIC relations. If it were manifested independently of his physiology, it might be studied separately, but since all his organic conditions modify his mentality, the two must be studied TOGETHER. Heretofore humanity has been studied by piecemeal. Anatomists have investigated only his organic structure, and there stopped; and mental philosophers have studied him metaphysically, wholly regardless of all his physiological relations; while theologians have theorized upon his moral faculties alone; and hence their utter barrenness, from Aristotle[3] down. As if one should study nothing but the trunk a tree, another only its roots, a third its leaves, or fruit, without compounding their researches, of what value is such piecemeal study? If the physical man constituted one whole being, and the mental another, their separate study might be useful; but since all we know of mind, and can do with it, is manifested and done wholly by means of physical instruments—especially since every possible condition and change of the physiology correspondingly affects the mentality—of course their MUTUAL relations, and the laws of their RECIPROCAL action, must be investigated *collectively*. Besides, every mental philosopher has deduced his system from his own closet cogitations, and hence their babel-like confusion. But within the last half century, a new star, or rather sun, has arisen upon the horizon of mind—a sun which puts the finger of SCIENTIFIC CERTAINTY upon every mental faculty, and discloses those *physiological* conditions which affect, increase or diminish, purify or corrupt, or in any other way modify, either the mind itself, or its products—thought, feeling, and character—and thereby reduces mental study to that same *tangible* basis of *proportion* in which all science consists; leaving nothing dark or doubtful, but developing the true SCIENCE OF MIND, and the laws of its action. Of this, the greatest of all discoveries, Gall was the author, and Phrenology and Physiology the instruments which conjointly embrace whatever appertains to mind, and to man, in all his organic relations, show how to perfect the former by improving the latter, and disclose specific SIGNS OF CHARACTER, by which we may know ourselves and our fellow-men with certainty—a species of knowledge most delightful in acquisition, and valuable in application.

2.—Structure Corresponds with Character

Throughout universal nature, the structure of all things is powerful or weak, hard or soft, coarse or fine, etc., in accordance with its functions; and in this there is a philosophical fitness or adaptation. What immense power of function trees put forth, to rear and sustain aloft, at such great mechanical disadvantage, their ponderous load and vast canvas

---

3 Along with Plato, Aristotle (384–322 BCE) is considered one of the two greatest intellects produced by ancient Greece. He is best known for his work in philosophy and science.

of leaves, limbs, and fruit or seeds, spread out to all the surgings of tempestuous winds and storms; and the *texture* of wood is as compact and firm as its functional power is prodigious. Hence its value as timber. But tender vegetables, grains, etc., require little power, and accordingly are fragile in structure. Lions, tigers, hyenas, and all powerfully strong beasts, have a correspondingly powerful organic structure. The muscular strength of lions is so extraordinary, that seizing wild cattle by the neck, they dash through thicket, marsh, and ravine, for hours together, as a cat would drag a squirrel, and their roar is most terrific; and so powerful is their structure, that it took Drs. McClintock, Allen, myself, and two experienced "resurrectionists," FOUR HOURS, though we worked with might and main, just to cut off a magnificent Numidian[4] lion's head. So hard and tough were the muscles and tendons of his neck, that cutting them seemed like severing wire, and after slitting all we could, we were finally obliged to employ a powerful purchase to start them. It took over three hard days' work to remove his skin. So compact are the skins of the elephant, rhinoceros, alligator, and some other animals of great muscular might, that rifle-balls, shot against them, flatten and fall at their feet—their structure being as dense as their strength is mighty—while feeble animals have a correspondingly soft structure. In like manner, the flesh of strong persons is dense and most elastic, while those of weakly ones are flabby, and yield to pressure.

Moreover, fineness of texture manifests exquisiteness of sensibility, as seen by contrasting human organism and feelings with brutes, or fine-haired persons with coarse-haired. Of course, a similar relation and adaptation exist between all other organic characteristics and their functions. In short, it is a law as philosophical as universal, that the structure of all beings, and of each of their organs, corresponds perfectly with their functions—a LAW based in the very nature and fitness of things, and governing all shades and diversities of organization and manifestation. Accordingly those who are coarse-skinned are coarse in feeling, and coarse-grained throughout; while those finely organized are fine-minded, and thus of all other textures of hair, skin, etc.

3.— Shape Corresponds with Character

Matter, in its primeval state, was "without form, and void,"[5] or gaseous, but slowly condensing, it solidified or CRYSTALLIZED into minerals and rocks—and all rocks and minerals are crystalline—which, decomposed by sun and air, form soil, and finally assume organic, or animal and vegetable forms. All crystals assume *angular* forms, and all vegetables and animals those more or less *spherical*, as seeds, fruits, etc., in proportion as they are lower or higher in the creative scale; though other conditions sometimes modify this result.

Nature also manifests certain types of character in and by corresponding types of form. Thus all trees bear a general resemblance to all other trees in growth and general character, and also in shape; and those most nearly allied in character approximate in shape, as pine, hemlock, firs, etc., while every tree of a given kind is shaped like all others of that kind, in bark, limb, leaf, and fruit. So all grains, grasses, fruits, and every bear, horse, elephant, and human being bear a close resemblance to all others

---

4 Ancient reference to North Africa.
5 Gen. 1:2.

of its kind, both in character and configuration, and on this resemblance all scientific classification is based. And, since this general correspondence exists between all the divisions and subdivisions into classes, genera, and species of nature's works, of course the resemblance is perfect between *all the details* of outward forms and inward mental characteristics; for this law, seen to govern nature in the outline, must of course govern her in all her minutest details; so that every existing outward shape is but the mirrored reflection of its inner likeness. Moreover, since nature always clothes like mentalities in like shapes, as oak, pine, apple, and other trees, and all lions, sheep, fish, etc., in other general types of form, of course the more nearly any two beings approximate to each other in mental disposition, do they resemble each other in shape. Thus, not only do tiger form and character always accompany each other, but leopards, panthers, cats, and all feline species resemble this tiger shape more or less closely, according as their dispositions approach or depart from his; and monkeys approach nearer to the human shape, and also mentality, than any other animal except orang-outangs, which are still more human both in shape and character, and form the connecting link between man and brute. How absolute and universal, therefore, the correspondence, both in general outline and minute detail, between shape and character. Hence the shape of all things becomes a sure index of its mentality.

4.—Resemblance between Human and Animal Physiognomy and Character

Moreover, some men closely resemble one or another of the animal species, in both looks and character; that is, have the eagle, or bull-dog, or lion, or baboon expression of face, and when they do, have the corresponding characteristics. Thus the lion's head and face are broad and stout built, with a heavy beard and mane, and a mouth rendered square by small front and large eye teeth, and its corners slightly turning downward; and that human "Lion of the North"—who takes hold only of some great undertaking, which he pursues with indomitable energy, rarely pounces on his prey, but when he does, so roars that a nation quakes; demolishes his victim; and is an intellectual king among men—bears no slight physiognomical resemblance in his stout form, square face and mouth, large nose, and open countenance, to the king of beasts.

TRISTAM BURGESS, called in Congress the "Bald Eagle," from his having the aquiline or eagle-bill nose, a projection in the upper lip, falling into an indentation in the lower, his eagle-shaped eyes and eyebrows, as seen in the accompanying engraving, eagle-like in character, was the most sarcastic, tearing, and soaring man of his day, John Randolph[6] excepted. And whoever has a long, hooked, hawk-bill, or common nose, wide mouth, spare form, prominence at the lower and middle part of the forehead, is very fierce when assailed, high tempered, vindictive, efficient, and aspiring, and will fly higher and farther than others.

---

6 John Randolph (1773–1833) was an American politician best remembered for his aggressive debating style and attachment to the doctrine of states' rights.

The Lion Face

No.1. Daniel Webster[7]

The Eagle Face

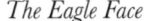

No. 2. Tristam Burgess[8]

---

7 Daniel Webster (1782–1852) was a forceful lawyer and politician, considered to be one of the best orators of his day.
8 Tristam Burgess (1770–1853) was a US congressman from Rhode Island.

TIGERS are always spare, muscular, long, full over the eyes, large-mouthed, and have eyes slanting downward from their outer to inner angles; and human beings thus physiog-nomically characterized, are fierce, domineering, revengeful, most enterprising, not over humane, a terror to enemies, and conspicuous somewhere.

BULL-DOGS, generally fleshy, square-mouthed—because their tusks project and front teeth retire—broad-headed, indolent unless roused, but then terribly fierce, have their cor-respondent men and women, whose growling, coarse, heavy voices, full habit, logy yet powerful motions, square face, down-turned corners of mouth, and general physiognomi-cal cast betoken their second-cousin relationship to this growling, biting race, of which the old line-tender at the Newburgh dock[9] is a sample.

SWINE—fat, logy, lazy, good-dispositioned, flat and hollow-nosed—have their cous-ins in large-abdomened, pud-nosed, double-chinned, talkative, story-enjoying, beer-loving, good-feeling, yes, yes, humans, who love some easy business, and hate HARD work.

Horses, oxen, sheep, owls, doves, snakes, and even frogs, etc., also have their men and women cousins, together with their accompanying characters.

These resemblances are more difficult to describe than to recognize; but the forms of mouth, nose, and chin, and sound of voice, are the best basis of observation.

5.—Beautiful, Homely, and Other Forms

In accordance with this general law, that shape is as character, well-proportioned per-sons have harmony of features, and well-balanced minds; whereas those, some of whose features stick right out, and others fall far in, have uneven, ill-balanced characters, so that homely, disjointed exteriors indicate corresponding interiors, while evenly-balanced and exquisitely formed men and women have well-balanced and susceptible mentalities. Hence, women, more beautiful than men, have finer feelings, and greater perfection of character, yet are less powerful—and the more beautifully formed the woman the more exquisite and perfect her mentality. True, some handsome women often make the greatest scolds, just as the sweetest things, when soured, become correspondingly sour. The finest things, when perverted, become the worst. These two extremes are the worst tempered— those naturally beautiful and fine skinned, become so exquisitely organized, that when perverted they are proportionally bad, and those naturally ugly-formed, become ugly by nature.

Yet ordinary-looking persons are often excellent dispositioned, benevolent, talented, etc., because they have a few POWERFUL traits, and also features—the very thing we are explaining; that is, they have EXTREMES alike of face and character. Thus it is that every diversity of character has its correspondence in both the organic texture and physiognomi-cal form. To elucidate this subject fully we must explain another law, that of

6.—Homogeneousness, or Oneness of Structure

Every part of every thing bears an exact correspondence to that thing AS A WHOLE. Thus, tall-bodied trees have long branches and leaves, and short-bodied trees, short branches

---

9 Guard dog commonly found on the docks of Newburgh, a city in southeastern New York on the west bank of the Hudson River.

and roots; while creeping vines, as the grape, honey-suckle, etc., have long, slim roots that run under ground as extensively as their tops do above. The Rhode Island greening is a large, well-proportioned apple and its tree is large in trunk, limb, leaf, and root, and symmetrical, while the gillifleur is conical and its tree long limbed and even high to a peak at the top, while flat and broad-topped trees bear wide, flat, sunken-eyed apples. Very thrifty growing trees, as the Baldwin, fall pippin, Bartlet, black Tartarian, etc., generally bear large fruit, while small fruit, as the seckle pear, lady apple, bell de choisa cherry, grow slowly, and have many small twigs and branches. Beautiful trees that bear red fruit, as the Baldwin, etc., have red inner bark; while yellow and green-colored fruits grow on trees the inner mind of whose limbs is yellow or green. Peach-trees, that bear early peaches, have deeply-notched leaves, and the converse of late ones; so that, by these and other physiognomical signs, experienced nurserymen can tell what a given tree is at first sight.

In accordance with this law of unity of structure, long-handed persons have long fingers, toes, arms, legs, bodies, heads, and phrenological organs; while short and broad-shouldered persons are short and broad-handed and fingered, faced, nosed, and limbed, and wide and low bodied. When the bones on the hand are prominent, all the bones, nose included, are generally so, and thus of all other characteristics of the hand and any other part of the body. Hence, let a hand be thrust through a hole, and I will tell the general character of its owner, because if it is large or small, hard or soft, strong or weak, firm or flabby, coarse-grained or fine-textured, even or prominent, rough or smooth, small-boned or large-boned, or whatever else, his whole body is built upon the same principle, with which his brain and mentality also correspond. Hence small-nosed persons have little soul, and large-nosed a great deal of character of some kind; large nostrils indicate powerful lungs and bodies; while narrow nostrils indicate weak ones. Flat noses indicate flat minds, and prominent noses strong points of character; sharp noses, keen, clear intellects and intense feelings; blunt noses, obtuse minds; long noses, long heads; hollow noses, tame characters; finely-formed noses, well-proportioned character, etc.; and thus of every part of the body. And it is meet philosophical, accordant with the principles of adaptation, that this should be thus; and renders observations on character easy and correct. In general, too, tall persons have high heads, and are more aspiring, aim high, and seek conspicuosity, while short ones have flat heads, and seek worldly pleasures. Tall persons are rarely mean, though often grasping; but very penurious persons are often broad built. Small persons generally have exquisite mentalities, yet less power; while great men are rarely dwarfs, though great size often co-exists with sluggishness. To particularize—there are four leading forms which indicate generic characteristics, all existing in every one yet in different DEGREES. They are these:

7.—*The Broad, or Vital Structure*

Thus, Indian ponies are broad built or thick set, and accordingly very tough, hardy, enduring of labor, and tenacious of life, yet less active and nimble. Bull-dogs, elephants, and all round-favored animals and men, also illustrate this law. Rotundity, with a moderate-sized head, indicates ancestral longevity; and, unless health has been abused, renders it possessor strong constitutioned, slow to ripen, or better as they grow older; full of animal life; self-caring; money-making; fond of animal pleasures; good feeling, yet spirited when roused; impulsive; more given to physical than mental action; better adapted to business than study, and talking than writing; more eloquent than argumentative; wide rather than high or long headed; more glowing than cool in feeling; and more enthusiastic than logical or deep. The preceding likeness represents this class, and his ancestors exceeded 100. He has never been sick; can endure any thing, and can never sit much in doors.

The Vital, or Animal Temperament

No. 3. Hall

8.—The Muscular, or Powerful Temperament

Gives projecting features, bones, noses, eyebrows, etc., with distinctness of muscle; and renders its possessors strong; tough; thorough going; forcible; easy, yet powerful of motion; perhaps slow, but very stout; strongly marked, if not idiosyncratic; determined; and impressive both physically and mentally, who stamp their character on all they touch, of whom Alexander Campbell[10] is a good example.

---

10 Alexander Campbell (1788–1866) was an important religious leader who helped found the immensely popular Disciples of Christ denomination.

Prominent, or Powerful

No. 4. Alexander Campbell

9.—The Long, or Active Form

Gives ACTIVITY. Thus the gazelle; deer greyhound, weasel, and all long and slim animals, are sprightly, light-motioned, agile, quick, nimble, and full of action; and those persons thus formed are restless, wide awake, always doing, eager, uncommonly quick to think and feel, sprightly in conversation, versatile in talent, flexible, suggestive, abounding in idea, apt at most things; exposed to consumption, because their action exceeds their strength, early ripe, brilliant, and liable to premature exhaustion and disease, because the mentality predominates over the vitality; of which Captain Knight, of the ship "New World," who has a world-wide reputation for activity, enterprise, daring, impetuousness, promptness, judgment, earnestness of execution, affability, and sprightliness, furnishes a good example.

Long, or Active

No. 5. Capt. Knight

10.—The Sharp and Angular, or Mental Organization

Have ardent desires; intense feelings; keen susceptibilities; enjoy and suffer in the extreme; are whole-souled; sensitive; positive in likes and dislikes: cordial; enthusiastic; impulsive; have their hobbies; abound in good feeling, yet are quick-tempered; excitable; liable to extremes; too much creatures of feeling, and have a great deal of what we call soul, or passion, or warmth of feeling. This temperament prevails in BRILLIANT writers or speakers, who are too refined and sensitive for the mass of mankind. They gleam in their career of genius, and are liable to burn out their vital powers on the altar of nervous excitability, and like Pollok, H. K. White, McDonald Clarke, or Leggett, fall victims to premature death. Early attention to the physical training of children, would spare to the world the lives and usefulness of some of the brightest stars in the firmament of science.

Sharp and Angular, or Excitable

No. 6. Voltaire[11]

11.—Combinations of Temperament

These shapes, or structures, called temperaments, however, never exist separately; yet since all may be strong, or all weak, or either predominant or deficient, of course their COMBI-NATIONS with each other and with the Phrenology exert potent influences over character, and put the observer in possession of both the outline and the inner temple of character.

---

11 Voltaire (1694–1778) was a famous French writer who had a pronounced influence in the French Enlightenment.

Breadth of organization gives endurance, animal power, and animal feelings; and sharpness gives intensity of action, along with mind as mind and the two united give both that rapidity and clearness of mind and that intense glow of feeling which make the orator. Accordingly, all truly eloquent men will be found to be broad built, round-shouldered, portly, and fleshy, and yet rather sharp-featured. Of these, Sidney Smith[12] furnishes a sample.

His nose indicates the sharpness of the mental temperament, and his fullness of face the breadth of the animal—the blending of which gives that condensation of fervor and intellectuality which make him Sidney Smith. Intensity of feeling is the leading element of good speaking, for this excites feeling, and moves the masses. Wirt had this temperament. It predominates in Preston, and in every man noted for eloquence.

The Excitable, Oratorical, or Mental Vital

No. 7. Sidney Smith

The sharp and broad, combined with smallness of stature, is still more susceptible, yet lacks strength. Such will be extremely happy, or most miserable, or both, and are liable to die young, because their action is too great for their endurance.

The vital mental, or broad and sharp, gives great power of constitution, excellent lungs and stomach, strong enjoying susceptibilities intense love of pleasure, a happy, ease-loving cast of body and mind; powerful passions, most intense feelings, and a story and song-loving disposition; and, with large Tune, superior singing powers. This is, PAR EXCELLENCE,

---

12 Sidney Smith (1764–1840) was a British admiral who distinguished himself against Napoleon's navy.

the singing temperament. It also loves poetry and eloquence, and often executes them. Of this organism, its accompanying character, Dempster,[13] furnishes an excellent example.

Sound Sharp Organization

No. 8. Dempster

Vital Motive

No. 9. Phineas Stevens[14]

---

13 Possibly George Dempster (1736?–1818), a noted Scottish agriculturalist who also served as a member of Parliament for 29 years.
14 Phineas Stevens (1706–1756) was a noted hunter, tracker, and soldier. He became a hero during the French and Indian War, in which he successfully defended a fort with only thirty men against more than four-hundred French soldiers.

THE VITAL MOTIVE APPARATUS, or powerful and animal temperament, is indicated by the broad and prominent in shape, and renders its possessor of good size and height, if not large; well-proportioned; broad-shouldered; muscular, nose and cheek-bones prominent; visage strongly marked; features often coarse and homely; countenance stern and harsh: face red; hair red or sandy, if not coarse; and movements strong, but often awkward, and seldom polished. He will be best adapted to some laborious occupation, and enjoy hard work more than books or literary pursuits; have great power of feeling, and thus require much self-government; possess more talent than he exhibits to others, manifest his mind more in his business, in creating resources and managing matters, than in literary pursuits or mind as such; and improve with age, growing better and more intellectual as he grows older; and manufactures as much animal steam as he can work off, even if he works all the time hard. Such men ACCOMPLISH; are strong-minded; sensible; hard to beat; indomitable; often impulsive; and strong in passion when once aroused; as well as often excellent men. Yet this temperament is capable of being depraved, especially if the subject drinks. Sailors usually have this temperament, because fresh air and hard work induce it.

THE MOTIVE MENTAL TEMPERAMENT, or the prominent and sharp in structure, with the motive predominant, and the vital average or full, is of good size; rather tall and slim; lean and raw-boned, if not homely and awkward; poor in flesh; bones and features prominent, particularly the nose; a firm and distinct muscle, and a good physical organization; a keen, piercing, penetrating eye; the front upper teeth rather large and projecting; the hands, fingers, and limbs all long; a long face, and often a high forehead; a firm, rapid, energetic walk; and great ease and efficiency of action, accompanied with little fatigue.

Prominent and Sharp

No. 10. Dr. Caldwell[15]

He will have strong desires, and much energy of character; will take hold of projects with both hands, and drive forward in spite of obstacles, and hence is calculated to accomplish a great deal; is not idle or lazy, but generally prefers to wait upon himself; will move, walk, etc.

---

15 Charles Caldwell (1772–1853) was a noted physician and a founder of what would become the University of Louisville School of Medicine.

in a decided, forcible, and straightforward manner; have strong passions; a tough and wiry brain and body; a strong and vigorous mind; good judgment; a clear head, and talents more solid than brilliant; be long-headed; bold; cool; calculating; fond of deep reasoning and philosophizing, of hard thinking, and the graver and more solid branches of learning. This is the thorough-going temperament; imparts business powers; predisposes to hard work, and is indispensable to those who engage in great undertakings, or who would rise to eminence.

One having the mental temperament predominant, the motive full or large, and the vital average to full, will differ in build from the preceding description only in his being smaller, taller in proportion, and more spare. He will have a reflective, thinking, planning, discriminating cast of mind; a great fondness for literature, science, and intellectual pursuits of the deeper graver kind; be inclined to choose a professional or mental occupation; to exercise his body much, but his mind more; will have a high forehead; good moral faculties; and the brain developed more from the root of the nose, over to Philoprogenitiveness,[16] than around the ears. In character, also, the moral and intellectual faculties will predominate. This temperament is seldom connected with depravity, but generally with talent, and a manifestation, not only of superior talents, but of the solid, metaphysical, reasoning, investigating intellect; a fondness for natural philosophy, the natural sciences, etc. It is also the temperament for authorship and clear-headed, labored productions. It predominates in Revs. Jonathan Edwards, Wilbur Fiske, N. Taylor, E. A. Parke, Leonard Bacon, Albert Barnes, Oberlin, and Pres. Day; Drs. Parish and Rush; in Hitchcock, Jas. Brown, the grammarian, ex-U. S. Attorney-General Butler, Hugh L. White, Wise, Asher Robbins, Walter Jones, Esq., of Washington, D. C., Franklin, Alex. Hamilton, Chief-Justice Marshall,

The Mental Motive Temperament

No. 11. William Cullen Bryant

---

16 Character of a loving parent.

Calhoun, John Q. Adams, Percival, Noah Webster, Geo. Combe, Lucretia Mott, Catherine Waterman, Mrs. Sigourney, and nearly every distinguished author and scholar.[17] The accompanying engraving of William Cullen Bryant[18] furnishes as excellent an illustration of the shape that accompanies this temperament, as his character does of its accompanying mentality.

THE LONG AND SHARP combine the highest order of action and energy with promptness, clearness, and untiring assiduity, and considerable power. Such are best fitted for some light, active business, requiring more brightness and quickness than power, such as merchants.

THE ORGANS THAT ACCOMPANY GIVEN TEMPERAMENTS.—Not only do certain outlines of character and drifts of talent go along with certain kinds of organizations, but certain phrenological developments accompany certain temperaments. As the pepper secretes the smarting, the sugar-cane sweetness, castor-beans and whales, oil, etc., throughout nature, so certain temperaments secrete more brain than others; and some, brain in particular regions of the head; and others, brain in other regions of the head—but all form most of those organs best adapted to carry out those characteristics already shown to accompany the several temperaments. Thus, the vital or animal temperament secretes brain in the neighborhood of the ears, so that along with breadth of body goes that width of head which gives that full development of the animal organs which is required by the animal temperament. Thus, breadth of form, width of head, and animality of temperament and character, all go together.

PROMINENCE of organization, or the motive or powerful temperament, gives force of character, and secretes brain in the crown of the head, and over the eyes, along with Combativeness, Destructiveness, Appetite, and Acquisitiveness. These are the very organs required by this temperament; for they complete that force which embodies the leading element of this organization. I never saw this temperament unaccompanied with prodigious Firmness, and great Combativeness and perceptives.

THE MENTAL VITAL.—The finest and most exquisite organization is that which unites the mental in predominance with the animal, the prominent retiring. In this case, the person is rather short, the form light, the face and person full, and the hair brown or auburn, or between the two. It will sometimes be found in men, but much oftener in women. It is the feeling, sentimental, exalted, angelic temperament; and always imparts purity, sweetness, devotion, exquisiteness, susceptibility, loveliness, and great moral worth.

---

17 The Fowlers produce a veritable "who's who" list here of famous eighteenth- and nineteenth-century theologians, writers, politicians, lawyers and educators to prove their point.

18 William Cullen Bryant (1794–1878) was a noted early American nature poet and editor of New York's *Evening Post*.

Mental Vital

No. 12. Fanny Forrester[19]

The phrenological organs which accompany this temperament, are smaller Firmness, deficient Self-Esteem, large or very large Approbativeness, smaller Destructiveness, Appetite not large, Adhesiveness and Philoprogenitiveness very large, Amativeness fair; the head wide, not directly round the ears, but at the upper part of the sides, including Ideality, Mirthfulness, Sublimity, and Cautiousness; and a fine top head, rising at Benevolence quite as much as at Firmness, and being wide on the top, whereas the motive temperament gives perhaps a ridge in the middle of the head, but not breadth on the top, and leaves the head much higher at the back part than at Benevolence. Benevolence, however, often accompanies the animal temperament, and especially that quiet goodness which grants favors because the donor is too pliable, or too easy, to refuse them. But for tenderness of sympathy, and whole-souled interest for mankind, no temperament is equal to the vital mental. The motive mental, however, is the one most common in reformers. The reason is this. The mentality imparted by this temperament sees the miseries of mankind, and weeps over them; and the force of character imparted by it pushes vigorously plans for their amelioration. The outer portion of Causality, which plans, often accompanies the animal temperament; the inner, which reasons, the motive mental and mental.

   The more perfect these organic conditions, the better. Greater breadth than sharpness, or more vitality than action, causes sluggishness, dullness of feeling, and inertness, while too great action for strength, wears out its possessor prematurely. More prominence than sharpness, leaves talents latent, or undeveloped, while predominant sharpness and breadth, give such exquisite sensibilities, as that many things harrow up all the finer sensibilities of keen-feeling souls. But when all are powerful and EQUALLY BALANCED, they combine all the conditions of power, activity, and susceptibility; allow neither icy coldness, nor passion's burning heat, but unite cool judgment, intense but well-governed feelings, great force of both character and intellect, and perfect consistency and discretion with extraordinary energy; sound common sense, and far-seeing sagacity, with brilliancy; and bestow

---

19 Fanny Forrester was the pen name for Emily Chubbock (1817–1854), a missionary wife and the writer of numerous popular novels for children and young people.

the highest order of Physiology and Phrenology. Such an organization and character were those of WASHINGTON.

Besides these prominent signs of character, there are many others, among which,

A Well-Balanced Organ

No. 13. Washington

12.—The Laugh Corresponds with the Character

Those who laugh very heartily, have much cordiality and whole-souledness of character, except that those who laugh heartily at trifles, have much feeling, yet little sense. Those whose giggles are rapid, but light, have much intensity of feeling, yet lack power; whereas those who combine rapidity with force in laughing, combine them in character. One of the greatest workers I ever employed, I hired just because he laughed heartily, and he worked just as he laughed. But a colored domestic who laughed very rapidly, but lightly, took a great many steps to do almost nothing, and though she worked fast, accomplished little. Vulgar persons always laugh vulgarly, and refined persons show refinement in their laugh. Those who ha, ha, right out, unreservedly, have no cunning, and are open-hearted in every thing; while those who suppress laughter, and try to control their countenances in it, are more or less secretive. Those who laugh with their mouth closed, are non-committal; while those who throw it wide open, are unguarded and unequivocal in character. Those who, suppressing laughter for a while, burst forth volcano-like, have strong characteristics, but are well governed, yet violent when they give way to their feelings. Then there is the intellectual laugh, the love laugh, the horse laugh, the Philoprogenitive laugh, the friendly laugh, and many other kinds of laugh, each indicative of corresponding mental developments.

13.—The Walk as Indicating Character

As already shown, texture corresponds to character, and motion to texture, and therefore to character. Those whose motions are awkward, yet easy, possess much efficiency and positiveness of character, yet lack polish; and just in proportion as they become refined in mind will their mode of carriage be correspondingly improved. A short and quick step, indicates a brisk and active, but rather contracted mind, whereas those who take long steps, generally have long heads; yet if their stop be slow, they will make comparatively little progress, while those whose step is LONG AND QUICK, will accomplish proportionately much, and pass most of their competitors on the highway of life. Their heads and plans, too, will partake of the same far-reaching character evinced in their carriage. Those who sluff or drag their heels, drag and drawl in every thing; while those who walk with a springing, bounding step, abound in mental snap and spring. Those whose walk is mincing, affected, and artificial, rarely, if ever, accomplish much; whereas those who walk carelessly, that is naturally, are just what they appear to he, and put on nothing for outside show. Those who, in walking, roll from side to side, lack directness of character, and side every way, according to circumstances; whereas, those who take a bee line—that is, whose body moves neither to the right nor left, but straight forward—have a corresponding directness of purpose, and oneness of character. Those also who tetter up and down when they walk, rising an inch or two every step, will have many corresponding ups and downs in life, because of their irregularity of character and feeling. Those, too, who make a great ado in walking, will make much needless parade in every thing else, and hence spend a great amount of useless steam in all they undertake, yet accomplish little; whereas those who walk easily, or expend little strength in walking, will accomplish great results with a little strength, both mentally and physically. In short, every individual has his own peculiar mode of moving, which exactly accords with his mental character; so that, as far as you can see such modes, you can decipher such outlines of character.

To DANCING, these principles apply equally. Dr. Wieting, the celebrated lecturer on physiology, once asked where he could find something on the temperaments, and was answered, "Nowhere; but if I can ever see you among men, I will give you a PRACTICAL lesson upon it." Accordingly, afterward, chance threw us together in a hotel, in which was a dancing-school that evening. Insisting on the fulfillment of our promise, we accompanied him into the dancing saloon, and pointed out, first, a small, delicately moulded, fine skinned, pocket-Venus, whose motions were light, easy, waving, and rather characterless, who put forth but little strength in dancing. We remarked—"She is very exquisite in feelings, but rather light in the upper story, lacking sense, thought, and strength of mind." Of a large, raw-boned, bouncing Betty, who threw herself far up, and came down good and solid, when she danced, we remarked—"She is one of your strong, powerful, determined characters, well suited to do up rough work, but utterly destitute of polish, though possessed of great force." Others came in for their share of criticism—some being all dandy, others all business, yet none all intellect.

14.—The Mode of Shaking Hands

Also expresses character. Thus those who give a tame and loose hand, and shake lightly, have a cold, if not heartless and selfish disposition, rarely sacrificing much for others— probably conservatives, and lack warmth of soul. But those who grasp firmly, and shake heartily, have a corresponding whole-souledness of character, are hospitable, and will sacrifice business to friends; while those who bow low when they shake hands, add deference to friendship, and are easily led, for good or bad, by friends.

15.—The Mouth and Eyes Peculiarly Expressive of Character

Every mouth differs from every other, and indicates a coincident character. Large mouths express a corresponding quantity of mentality, while small ones indicate a lesser amount of mentality. A coarsely formed mouth indicates power of character, while one finely formed indicates exquisite susceptibilities. Hence small, delicately-formed mouths, indicate only common minds, but very fine feelings, with much perfection of character. Whenever the muscles about the mouth are distinct the character is correspondingly positive, and the reverse. Those who open their mouths wide and frequently, thereby evince an open soul, while closed mouths, unless to hide deformed teeth, are proportionately secretive.

And thus of the eyes. In travelling west, in 1842, we examined a man who made great pretension to religion, but was destitute of Conscience, whom we afterward ascertained to be an impostor. While attending the Farmers' Club, in New York, this scamp came in, and besides keeping his eyes half closed half the time, frequently shut them so as to peep out upon those present, but opened them barely enough to secure vision. Those who keep their eyes half shut, are peekaboos and eaves-droppers, and those who use squinting glasses are no better, unless they merely copy a foolish fashion. The use of quizzing glasses indicates either defective sight or defective mentalities, but are rarely if ever employed except as a fashionable appendage.

Those, too, who keep their coats buttoned up, fancy high-necked and closed dresses, etc., are equally non-communicative, but those who like open, free, flowing garments, are equally open-hearted and communicative.

16.—Intonations as Expressive of Character

Whatever makes a noise, from the deafening roar of sea, cataract, and whirlwind's mighty crash, through all forms of animal life, to the sweet and gentle voice of woman, makes a sound which agrees perfectly with its character. Thus the terrific roar of the lion, and the soft cooing of the dove, correspond exactly with their respective dispositions; while the rough and powerful bellow of the bull, the fierce yell of the tiger, the coarse guttural moan of the hyena, and the swinish grunt, the sweet warblings of birds, in contrast with the raven's croak, and owl's hoot, each corresponds perfectly with their respective characteristics. And this law holds equally true of man—that the human intonations are as superior to brutal as human character exceeds animal. Accordingly, the peculiarities of every human being are expressed in his voice, and mode of speaking. Coarse-grained and powerfully animal organizations have a coarse, harsh, and grating voice, while in exact proportion as persons become refined, and elevated mentally, will their tones of voice become correspondingly refined and perfected. We little realize how much of character we infer from this source. Thus, some female friends are visiting me transiently. A male friend, staying with me, enters the room, is seen by my female company, and his walks, dress, manners, etc., closely scrutinized, yet says nothing, and retires, leaving a comparatively indistinct impression as to his character upon my female visitors, whereas, if he simply said yes or no, the mere SOUNDS of his voice communicates to their minds most of his character, and serves to fix distinctly upon their minds clear and correct general ideas of his mentality.

The barbarous races use the guttural sounds, more than the civilized. Thus Indians talk more down the throat than white men, and thus of those men who are lower or higher in the human scale. Those whose voices are clear and distinct have clear minds, while those who only half form their words, or are heard indistinctly, say by deaf persons, are mentally obtuse. Those who have sharp, shrill intonations have correspondingly intense feelings, and equal sharpness both of anger and kindness, as is exemplified by every scold in the world; whereas those with smooth, or sweet voices have corresponding evenness and goodness of character. Yet contradictory as it may seem, these same persons not unfrequently combine both sharpness and softness of voice, and such always combine them in character. There is also the intellectual, the moral, the animal, the selfish, the benignant, the mirthful, the devout, the love, and many other intonations, each accompanying corresponding peculiarities of characters. In short, every individual is compelled, by every word he utters, to manifest something of his true character—a sign of character as diversified as it is correct.

17.—Hair, Skin, Etc., as Indicating Character

Coarseness of texture indicates a coarseness of function; while a fine organization indicates a corresponding fineness of mentality. And since when one part is coarse or fine, all are equally so, so, therefore, coarseness of skin and hair indicate a coarse-grained brain, and coarseness of mind; yet since coarseness indicates power, such persons usually possess a great deal of character of some kind. Hence dark-skinned nations are behind light-haired in all the improvements of the age, and the higher finer manifestations of humanity. So, too, dark-haired persons, like Webster are frequently possessed of great power, yet lack the finer and more delicate shadings of sensibility and purity. Coarse black hair and skin, or coarse red hair and face, indicate powerful animal propensities, together with corresponding strength of character; while fine and light hair indicate quick susceptibilities, together with purity, refinement, and good taste. Fine dark or brown hair, indicates a combination of exquisite susceptibilities with great strength of character; while auburn-colored hair, and a florid countenance, indicate the highest order of exquisiteness and intensity of feeling, yet with corresponding purity of character and love of virtue, together with the highest susceptibilities of enjoyment and suffering. And the intermediate colors and textures indicate intermediate mentalities. Coarse-haired persons should never turn dentists or clerks, but should seek some out-door employment; and would be hotter contented with rough, hard work than a light or sedentary occupation, although mental and sprightly occupations would serve to refine and improve them; while dark and fine-haired persons may choose purely intellectual occupations, and become lecturers or writers with fair prospects of success. Red-haired persons should seek out-door employment, for they require a great amount of air and exercise; while those who have light, fine hair, should choose occupations involving taste and mental acumen, yet take bodily exercise enough to tone and vigorate their system.

Generally, whenever skin, hair, or features are fine or coarse, the others are equally so. Yet some inherit fineness from one parent, and coarseness from the other, while the color of the eye generally corresponds with that of the skin, and expresses character. Light eyes indicate warmth of feeling, and dark eyes power. The mere expression of eye conveys precise ideas of the existing and predominant states of the mentality and physiology. As long as the constitution remains unimpaired, the eye is clear and bright, but becomes languid and soulless in proportion as the brain has been enfeebled. Wild, erratic persons, have a half-crazed expression of eye, while calmness, benignancy, intelligence, purity, sweetness, love, lasciviousness, anger, and all the other mental affections, express themselves quite as distinctly in the eye as voice, or any other mode.

18.—Physiognomy

Jackson Davis well remarked that, in the spirit land, conversation is carried on mainly, not by words, but by EXPRESSION AND COUNTENANCE—that spirits look their thoughts and motions, rather than talk them. Certain it is that the countenance discloses a greater amount of thought and feeling, together with their nicer shades and phases, than words can possibly communicate. Whether we will or no, we cannot HELP revealing the innermost recesses of our souls in our faces. By what means is this effected? Clairvoyants say by magnetic centres, called poles; each physical and mental organ has its pole stationed in a given part of the face, so that, when such organ becomes active, it influences such poles, and contracts facial muscles, which express the corresponding emotions. That there exists an intimate relation between the stomach and one part of the face, the lungs and another, etc., is proved by the fact that consumptive patients always have a hectic flush on the cheek, just externally from the lower portion of the nose, while inactive lungs cause paleness, and healthy ones give the rosy cheek; and that dyspeptic patients are always lank and thin opposite the double teeth, while those whose digestion is good, are full between the corners of the mouth and lower portion of the ears. Since, therefore, some of the states of some of the internal organs express themselves in the face, of course every organ of the body must do the same—the magnetic pole of the heart beginning in the chin. Those whose circulation is vigorous, have broad and rather prominent chins; while those who are small and narrow-chinned have feeble hearts; and thus all the other internal organs have their magnetic poles in various parts of the face.

In like manner have all the PHRENOLOGICAL organs. In 1841, Dr. Sherwood, La Roy Sunderland, and O. S. Fowler, aided by a magnetic subject, located the poles of most of the phrenological and physiological organs, some of which were as follows: Acquisitiveness on each side of the middle portion of the nose, at its junction with the check, causing breadth of nose in proportion to the money-grasping instincts, while a narrow nose indicated a want of the speculative turn. Firmness is in the upper lip, midway between its edge and the nose, giving length, prominence, and a compression of the upper lip. Hence, when we would exhort to determined perseverance, we say, "Keep a stiff upper lip." Self-Esteem has its pole externally from that of Firmness, and between the outer portion of the nose and the mouth, causing a fullness, as if a quid of tobacco were under the upper lip. The affections were described as having their poles in the edges of the lips, and hence the philosophy of kissing. The pole of Mirthfulness is located externally, and above the outer corners of the mouth, and hence the drawing up of these corners in laughter. Approbativeness has its pole directly outward from these corners, and hence the approbative laugh does not turn the corners of the month upward, but draws them straight back, or outwardly. Like locations were assigned to nearly all the other organs. That physiognomy has its science—that fixed and absolute relations exist between the phrenological organs and given portions of the face is not a matter of question. The natural language of the organs, as seen in the attitudes of the head, indicate not only the presence of large and active organs, but also the signs of their deficiency. Self-Esteem throws the head upward and backward toward the seat of its organ; Approbativeness, back and toward the side; Philoprogenitiveness, directly back, but not upward; Firmness draws the head up, in a stiff, perpendicular position; Individuality thrusts the head forward toward its organ and gives the man a staring, gazing aspect; small Self-Esteem lets the head droop forward. Man was made both to disclose his own character, and to read that of others. Than this form of knowledge, none is more inviting or useful. Hence God has caused the inherent character of every living being and thing to gush out through every organ of the body, and every avenue of the soul; and also created in both brute and man a character-reading faculty, to take intuitive cognizance of the mental operations. Nor will she let any one lie, any more than lie herself, but compels all to carry the flag of their character at their mast-heads, so that all acquainted with the signs may see and read. If we attempt deception, the very effort convicts us. If all nature's signs of character were fully understood, all could read not only all the main characters of all they see, but even most thoughts and feelings passing in the mind for the time being—a gift worth more than Astor's millions.[20]

19.—Redness and Paleness of Face

Thus far our remarks have appertained to the constant colors of the face, yet those colors are often diversified or changed for the time being.

Thus, at one time, the whole countenance will be pale, at another, very red; each of which indicates the existing states of body and mind. Or thus; when the system is in a perfectly healthy state, the whole face will be suffused with the glow of health and beauty, and have a red, but never an inflamed aspect; yet any permanent injury of health, which prostrates the bodily energies, will change this florid complexion into dullness of countenance indicating that but little blood comes to the surface or flows to the head and a corresponding stagnation of the physical and mental powers. Yet, after a time, this dullness frequently gives way to a fiery redness; not the floridness of health, but the redness of inflammation and false excitement, which indicates a corresponding depreciation of the mental faculties. Very red-faced persons, so far from being the most healthy, are frequently the most diseased, and are correspondingly more animal and sensual in character; because physiological inflammation irritates the propensities more, relatively, than the moral and intellectual faculties, though it may, for the time being, increase the latter also. When the moral and intellectual faculties greatly predominate over the animal, such redness of the face may not cause coarse animality, because while it heightens the animal nature, it also increases the intellectual and moral, which, being the larger, hold them in check, but when the animal about equals the moral and intellectual, this inflammation evinces a greater increase of animality than intellectuality and morality. Gross sensualists, and depraved sinners, generally have a fiery, red countenance. Stand aloof from them, for their passions are

---

20 John Jacob Astor (1763–1848), through his involvement in the fur business, founded a dynastic business family of immense wealth.

all on fire, ready to ignite and explode on provocations so slight that a healthy physiology would scarcely notice them. This point can hardly be more fully intelligible; but let readers note the difference between a healthy floridness of face, and the fiery redness of drunkards, debauchees, meat-eaters, etc. Nor does an inflamed physiology merely increase the animal nature, but gives a far more *depraved*, and sensual cast to it, thus doubly increasing the tendency to depravity.

20.—Health and Disease as Affecting Mentality

Health and disease affects the mind as much as body. Virtue, goodness, etc., are only the healthy or normal exercise of our various faculties, while depravity and sin are only the sickly exercise of these same organs. Holiness and moral excellence, as well as badness, depend far less upon the relative SIZE of the phrenological organs, than upon their direction or tone and character, and this depends upon the STATE OF THE BODY. Or thus; a healthy physiology tends to produce a healthy action of the phrenological organs, which is virtue and happiness; while an unhealthy physiology produces that sickly exercise of the mental faculties, especially of the animal propensities, which constitutes depravity and produces misery. Hence those phrenologists who look exclusively to the predominant SIZE of the animal organs, for vicious manifestations, and regard their average size as indicative of virtue, have this great lesson to learn, that health of body produces health of mind and purity of feelings, while all forms of bodily disease, in the very nature of things, tend to corrupt the feelings and deprave the soul. While, therefore, phrenologists should scrutinize the size of organs closely, they should observe the STATE OF HEALTH much more minutely, for most of their errors are explainable on this ground: that the organs described produced vicious inclinations, not because they were so large but because they were physically SICK, and hence take on a morally DEFORMED mode of action. Phrenologists, look ye well to these points, more fully explained in our other phrenological works.

Section II

Phrenological Conditions as Indicating Character

21.—Definition and Proof

PHRENOLOGY points out those relations established by nature between given developments and conditions of brain and corresponding manifestations of MIND. Its simple yet comprehensive definition is this: every faculty of the mind is manifested by means of particular portions of the BRAIN called its organs, the size of which, other things being equal, is proportionate to its power of function. For example: it teaches that parental love is manifested by one organ, or portion of the brain; appetite by another, reason by a third, etc., which are large the stronger these corresponding mental powers.

Are, then, particular portions of the brain larger or smaller in proportion as particular mental characteristics are stronger or weaker? Our short-hand answer is illustrated by the following anecdote. A Mr. Juror was once summoned to attend court, but died before its sitting. It therefore devolved upon Mr. Simple to state to the court the reason of his nonappearance. Accordingly, when Mr. Juror's name was called, Mr. Simple responded, "May

it please the court, I have twenty-one reasons why Mr. Juror is not in attendance. The firs
is, he is DEAD. The second is—" "That ONE will answer," responded the judge. "One
such reason is amply sufficient." But few of the many proofs that Phrenology is true wil
here be stated, yet those few are DECISIVE.

First. THE BRAIN IS THE ORGAN OF THE MIND. This is assumed, because too
universally admitted to require proof.

Secondly. Is the brain, then, a SINGLE organ, or is it a bundle of organs? Does the
WHOLE brain think, remember, love, hate, etc.; or does one portion reason, anothe
worship, another love money, etc.? This is the determining point. To decide it affirm-
atively, establishes Phrenology; negatively, overthrows it. It is proved by the following facts.

THE EXERCISE OF DIFFERENT FUNCTIONS SIMULTANEOUSLY.—We can
walk, think, talk, remember, love, and many other things all TOGETHER,—the mind
being, in this respect, like a stringed instrument, with several strings vibrating at a time,
instead of like a flute which stops the preceding sound when it commences succeeding
ones; whereas, if it were a single organ, it must stop thinking the instant it began to talk,
could not love a friend and express that love at the same time, and could do but one thing
at once.

MONOMANIA.—Since mental derangement is caused only by cerebral disorder, if
the brain were a single organ, the WHOLE mind must be sane or insane together; whereas
most insane persons are deranged only on one or two points, a conclusive proof of the
plurality of the brain and mental faculties.

DIVERSITY OF TALENT, or the fact that some are remarkable for sense, but poor
in memory, or the reverse; some forgetting names, but remembering faces; some great
mechanics, but poor speakers, or the reverse; others splendid natural singers, but no
mechanics, etc., etc., conducts us to a similar conclusion.

INJURIES OF THE BRAIN furnish still more demonstrative proof. If Phrenology
be true, to wound and inflame Tune, for example, would create a singing disposition;
Veneration, a praying desire; Cautiousness, groundless fears; and so of all the other organs.
And thus it is. Nor can this class of facts be evaded. They abound in all phrenological
works, especially periodicals, and drive and clench the nail of proof.

COMPARATIVE PHRENOLOGY, or the perfect coincidence existing between the
developments and characters of animals, constitutes the highest proof of all. Since man
and brute are fashioned upon one great model, those same great optical laws governing the
vision of both, that same principle of muscular contraction which enables the eagle to soar
aloft beyond our vision, and the whale to furrow and foam the vasty deep, and enabling
man to walk forth in the conscious pride of his strength, and thus of all their other common
functions; of course, if man is created in accordance with phrenological laws, brutes must
also be; and the reverse. If, then, this science is true of either, it must be true of both; must
pervade all forms of organization. What, then, are the facts?

Phrenology locates the animal propensities at the SIDES of the head, between and around
the ears; the social affections in its BACK and LOWER portion; the aspiring faculties in
its CROWN; the moral on its TOP; and the intellectual on the FOREHEAD; the perceptives,
which, related to matter, OVER THE EYES; and the reflectives in the UPPER part of the
forehead. (See cut No. 14.)

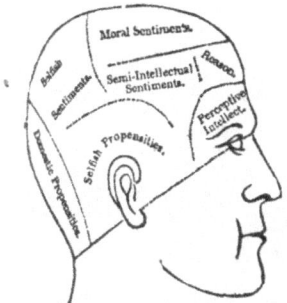

No. 14. Grouping of Organs

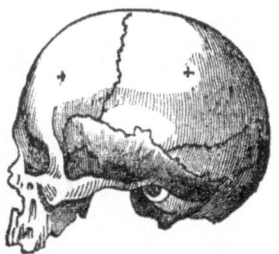

No. 15. Human Skull

No. 16. Snake

No. 17. Turtle

Now since brutes possess at least only weak moral and reflective faculties, they should, if Phrenology were true, have little top head, and thus it is. Not one of all the following drawings of animals, have much brain in either the reflective or moral region. Almost all their mentality consists of the ANIMAL PROPENSITIES, and nearly all their brain is BETWEEN and AROUND THEIR EARS, just where, according to Phrenology, it should be. Yet the skulls of all human beings rise high above the eyes and ears, and are long on top, that is, have intellectual and moral ORGANS, as we know they possess these mental ELEMENTS. Comparing the accompanying human skull with those of brutes, thus those of snakes, frogs, turtles, alligators, etc., slope straight back from the nose; that is, have almost no moral or intellectual organs; tigers, dogs, lions, etc., have a little more, yet how insignificant compared with man, while monkeys are between them in these organs and their faculties. Here, then, is INDUCTIVE proof of Phrenology as extensive as the whole brute creation on the one hand, contrasted with the entire human family on the other.

Again, Destructiveness is located by Phrenology over the ears, so as to render the head wide in proportion as this organ is developed. Accordingly, all carnivorous animals should be wide-headed at the ears, all herbivorous, narrow. And thus they are, as seen in tigers, hyenas, bears, cats, foxes, ichneumons,[21] etc., compared with rabbits, sheep etc. (Cuts 18, 19, 20, 21, 22, 23, 24, 25, 26, 27, 28, 29, and 30).

---

21 Mongooses.

Destructive Large

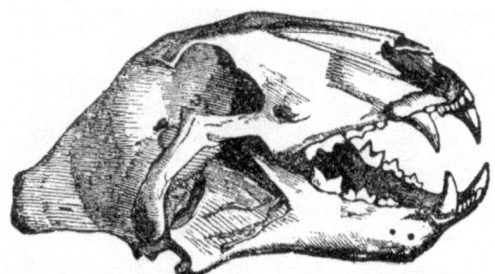

No. 18. Tiger—Side View

No. 19. Hyena—Side View

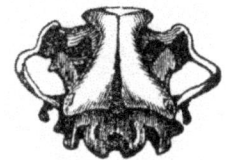

No. 20. Hyena—Back View

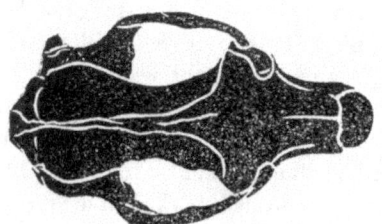

No. 21. Bear—Top View

No. 22. Bear—Back View

Destructive Small

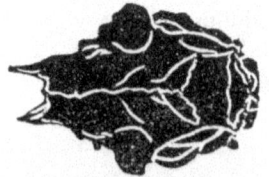

No. 23. Sheep—Top View

No. 24. Rabbit—Side View

To large Destructiveness, in cats, foxes, ichneumons, etc., add large SECRETIVNESS, both in character and head.

Secretiveness and Destructiveness Both Large

No. 25.
Fox—Side View

No. 26.
Ichneumon—Side View

No. 27.
Ichneumon—Back View

No. 28.
Cat—Back View

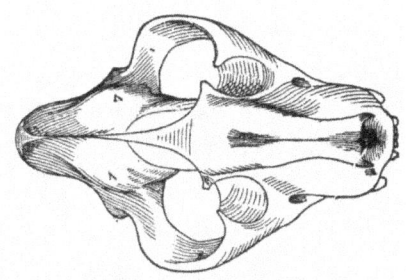

No. 29.
Cat—Side View

No. 30. Lion—Top View

Fowls, in like manner, correspond perfectly in head and character. Thus, owls, hawks, eagles, etc., have very wide heads, and ferocious dispositions; while hens, turkeys, etc., have narrow heads, and little Destructiveness in character (cuts 31, 32, and 33).

Destructiveness Large and Small

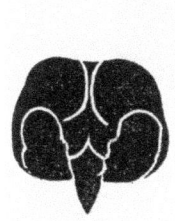

No. 31.
Owl—Top View

No. 32.
Hawk—Top View

No. 33.
Hen—Top View

The crow (cut 34) has very large Secretiveness and Cautiousness in the head, as he is known to have in character.

Secretiveness and Cautiousness Large

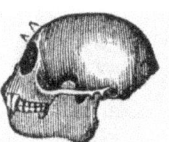

No. 34.
Crow

No. 35.
Intelligent
Monkey

No. 36.
Intelligent Monkey—
Side View

Monkeys, too, bear additional testimony to the truth of phrenological science. They possess, in character, strong perceptive powers, but weak reflectives, and powerful propensities, with feeble moral elements. Accordingly they are full over the eyes, but slope straight back at the reasoning and moral faculties, while the propensities engross most of their brain.

Some Moral and Reflective Brain

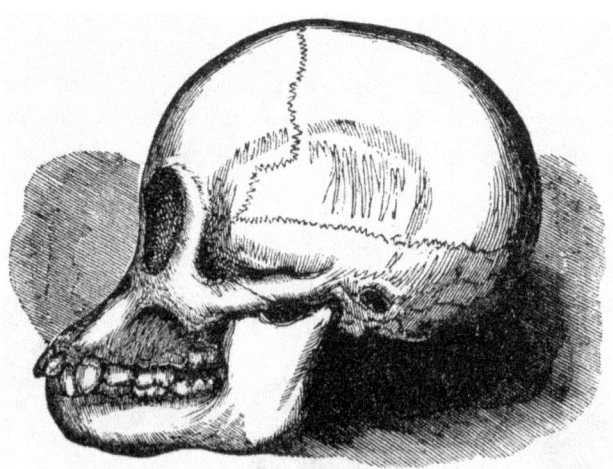

No. 37. The Orang-Outang

The ORANG-OUTANG has more forehead than any other animal, both perceptive and reflective, with some moral sentiments, and accordingly is called the "half-reasoning man," its Phrenology corresponding perfectly with its character.

Perceptives Larger than Reflectives

No. 38. African Head

No. 39. Indian Chief

The various races also accord with phrenological science. Thus, Africans generally have full perceptives, and large Tune and Language but retiring Causality, and accordingly are deficient in reasoning capacity, yet have excellent memories and lingual and musical powers.

Large and Small Intellects

No. 43. Bacon

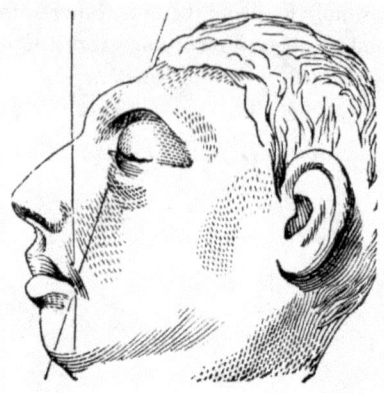

No. 44. Idiot

Indians possess extraordinary strength of the propensities and perceptives, yet have not great moral or inventive power; and, hence, have very wide, round, conical, and rather low heads.

Indian skulls can always be selected from Caucasian, just by these developments; while the Caucasian race is superior in reasoning power and moral elevation to all the other races, and, accordingly, have higher and bolder foreheads, and more elevated and elongated top heads.

Finally, contrast the massive foreheads of all giant-minded men—Bacons, Franklins, Miltons,[22] etc., with idiotic heads.

In short, every human, every brutal head, is constructed throughout strictly on phrenological principles. Ransack air, earth, and water and not one palpable exception ever has been, ever can be adduced. This WHOLE-SOUL view of this science precludes the possibility of mistake. Phrenology is therefore a PART AND PARCEL OF NATURE—A UNIVERSAL FACT.

The Philosophy of Phrenology

All truth bears upon its front unmistakable evidence of its divine origin, in its philosophical consistency, fitness, and beauty, whereas all untruth is grossly and palpably deformed. All truth, also, harmonizes with all other truth, and conflicts with all error, so that to ascertain what is true, and detect what is false, is perfectly easy. Apply this test, intellectual reader to one after another of the doctrines, as presented in this science. But enough on this point of proofs. Let us proceed to its illustration.

22.—Phrenological Signs of Character

The brain is not only the organ of the mind, the dome of thought, the palace of the soul, but is equally the organ of the *body*, over which it exerts an all-potent influence for good or

---

22 Francis Bacon (1561–1626), Benjamin Franklin (1706–1790) and John Milton (1608–1674) were leading intellectuals of their times. Each distinguished himself by contributing to several fields of intellectual inquiry during his lifetime.

ill, to weaken or stimulate, to kill or make alive. In short, the brain is the organ of the body in general, and of all its organs in particular. It sends forth those nerves which keep muscles, liver, bowels, and all the other bodily organs in a high or low state of action; and, more than all other causes, invites or repels disease, prolongs or shortens life, and treats the body as its galley-slave. Hence, healthy cerebral action is indispensable to bodily health. Hence, too, we walk or work so much more easily and efficiently when we take an *interest* in what we do. Therefore those who would be happy or talented must first and mainly keep their BRAIN vigorous and healthy.

The brain is subdivided into two hemispheres, the right and left, by the falciform process of the dura mater, a membrane which dips down one to two inches into the brain, and runs from the root of the nose over to the nape of the neck. This arrangement renders all the phrenological organs DOUBLE. Thus, as there are two eyes, ears, etc., that when one is diseased, the other can carry forward the functions, so there are two lobes to each phreno-logical organ, one on each side. The brain is divided thus: the feelings occupy that portion commonly covered by the hair, while the forehead is occupied by the intellectual organs. These greater divisions are subdivided into the animal brain, located between and around the ears; the aspiring faculties, which occupy the crown of the head; the moral and religious sentiments, which occupy the top; the physico-perceptives, located over the eyes; and the reflectives, in the upper portion of the forehead. The predominance of these respective groups produces both particular shapes, and corresponding traits of character. Thus, when the head projects far back behind the ears, hanging over and downward in the occipital region, it indicates very strong domestic ties and social affections, a love of home, its rela-tions and endearments, and a corresponding high capacity of being happy in the family, and of making the family happy. Very wide and round heads, on the contrary, indicate strong animal and selfish propensities, while thin, narrow heads, indicate a corresponding want of selfishness and animality. A head projecting far up at the crown, indicates an aspiring, self-elevating disposition, proudness of character, and a desire to be and to do something great; while the flattened crown indicates a want of ambition, energy, and aspiration. A head high, long, and wide upon the top, but narrow between the ears, indicates Causality, moral virtue, much practical goodness, and a corresponding elevation of character; while a low or narrow top head indicates a corresponding deficiency of these humane and religious susceptibilities. A head wide at the upper part of the temples, indicates a corresponding desire for personal perfection, together with a love of the beautiful and refined, while narrowness in this region evinces a want of taste, with much coarseness of feeling. Fullness over the eyes indicates excellent practical judgment of matters and things appertaining to property, science, and nature in general; while narrow, straight eyebrows, indicate poor practical judgment of mat-ter, its quality, relations, and uses. Fullness from the root of the nose upward, indicates great practical talent, love of knowledge, desire to see, and ability to do to advantage, together with sprightliness of mind; while a hollow in the middle of the forehead indicates want of memory and inability to show off to advantage. A bold, high forehead, indicates strong rea-soning capabilities, while a retiring forehead indicates less soundness, but more availability of talent.

23.—The Natural Language of the Faculties

Phrenology shows that every faculty, when active, throws head and body in the direction of that faculty. Thus, intellect, in the fore part of the head, throws it directly forward, and

No. 40. Washington Irving

produces a forward hanging motion of the head. Hence intellectual men never carry their heads backward and upward, but always forward; and logical speakers move their heads in a straight line, usually forward, toward their audience; while vain speakers carry their heads backward. Perceptive intellect, when active, throws out the chin and lower portions of the face; while reflective intellect causes the upper portion of the forehead to hang forward, and draws in the chin, as in the engravings of Franklin, Webster, and other great thinkers. Benevolence throws the head and body slightly forward, leaning toward the object which excites its sympathy; while Veneration causes a low bow, which, the world over, is a token of respect; yet, when Veneration is exercised toward the Deity, as in devout prayer, it throws the head UPWARD; and, as we use intellect at the same time, the head is generally directed forward. Ideality throws the head slightly forward, and to one side, as in Washington Irving,[23] a man as gifted in taste and imagination as almost any living writer; and, in his portraits, his finger rests upon this faculty; while in Sterne, the finger rests upon Mirthlfulness. Very firm men stand straight up and down, inclining not a hair's breadth forward or backward, or to the right or left; hence the expression, "He is an up-and-down man." And this organ is located exactly on a line with the body. Self-Esteem, located in the back and upper portion of the head, throws the head and body upward and backward. Large feeling, pompous persons, always walk in a very dignified, majestic posture, and always throw their heads in the direction of Self-Esteem; whilst approbative persons throw their heads backward, but to the one side or both. The difference between these two organs being comparatively slight, only the practical Phrenologist's eye can perfectly distinguish them.

---

23 Washington Irving (1783–1859) was an American author of extreme popularity and international reputation in the early nineteenth century.

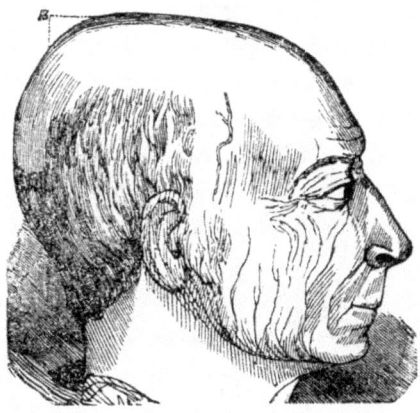

No. 45. A Conceited Simpleton

There is, moreover, a natural language of money-loving, and that is a leaning forward and turning of the head to one side, as if in ardent pursuit of something, and ready to grasp it with outstreteched arms; while Alimentiveness, situated lower down, hugs itself down to the dainty dish with the greediness of an epicure, better seen than described. The shake of the head is the natural language of Combativeness, and means no, or I resist you. Those who are combating earnestly upon politics, or any other subject, shake the head more or less violently, according to the power of the combative feeling, but always shake it slightly inclining *backwards*; while Destructiveness, inclining forward, causes a shaking of the head slightly forward, and turning to one side. When a person who threatens you shakes his head violently, and holds it partially backward, and to one side, never fear—he is only barking; but whenever he inclines his head to one side, and shakes it violently, that dog will bite, whether possessed of two legs or four. The social affections are located in the *back* part of the head; and, accordingly, woman being more loving than man, when not under the influence of the other faculties, usually inclines her head backward toward the neck; and when she kisses children, and those whom she loves, always turns the head directly backward, and rolls it from side to side, on the back of the neck. Thus it is that all the various postures assumed by it individually, are expressive of the present or the permanent activity of their respective faculties.

24.—Organic Tone or Quality of Brain

This condition modifies character more than any other. It is, indeed, the summing up of all. It consists of two kinds, original and acquired. The former, inherited from parents, embraces the pristine vigor and power with which the life principle was started, and gives what we will call SNAP; while the latter embraces the *existing* states of the organism as affected by health or debility, artificial habits—such as dyspeptic and other affections, caused by injurious qualities and quantities of food, by artificial stimulants, as tea, coffee, tobacco, or alcoholic drinks—the deranged or healthy states of the nervous system; too much or too little exercise, abor, sleep, breath, etc., etc.; and whatever other conditions are embraced in health and disease, or in any way affect them. Of course, the parental may

No. 44. Jonathan Edwards[24]

be good, but acquired poor, or the reverse, according as the subject is strengthening or enfeebling, building up or breaking down his physical constitution, by correct or erroneous physiological habits. Yet, in most persons, the parental is many hundred per cent, better than the acquired.

PARENTAL GOOD, OR VERY GOOD, gives corresponding innate vigor and energy, or that heart and bottom which wears like iron, and bends, willow-like, without breaking, and performs more with a given size, than greater size, and less inherent "snap;" and gives thoroughness and edge to the mentality, just as good steel, well tempered, does to the tool.

PARENTAL FAIR gives a good share of the presiding qualities, yet nothing remarkable; with acquired good, endures and accomplishes much; without it, soon breaks down.

PARENTAL POOR leaves its subject poorly organized, bodily and mentally, and proportionally low in the creative scale.

ACQUIRED GOOD enables whatever of life power there is, to perform all of which it is capable; with parental good, furnishes a full supply of vital power, and that activity which works it all up in mental or physical labor. With parental very good, puts forth a most astonishing amount of effort, and endures wonders without injury; possesses remarkable clearness and wholeness of mind; thinks and feels directly to the purpose; gives point and cogency to every thing; and confers a superior amount of healthy intellectuality, morality, and mentality, in general.

ACQUIRED FAIR, with parental average, gives fair natural talents, and mental and physical vigor, yet nothing remarkable; will lead a common-place life, and possess an everyday character, memory, etc.; will not set the world on fire, nor be insignificant, but, with cultivation, will do well.

ACQUIRED POOR will be unable to put forth its inherent power; is weak and inefficient, though desirous of doing something; with parental good, may take hold resolutely, but soon tires, and finds it impossible to sustain that powerful action with which it naturally commences.

---

24 Jonathan Edwards (1703–1758) was perhaps the premier theologian of eighteenth-century American Puritanism.

No. 45. Emerson, an Idiot

25.—States of the Nervous System

A good nervous condition enables its possessor to put forth sound and healthy mental and physical efforts; gives a calm, quiet, happy, contented frame of mind, and a strong tendency to enjoy every thing—even the bad; makes the most of life's joys, and the least of its sorrows; confers full possession of all its innate powers; and predisposes to a right exercise of all the faculties.

Disordered nerves produce an irritated, craving, dissatisfied state of mind, and a tendency to depravity in some of its forms, with a half paralyzed, lax, inefficient state of mind and body.

26.—Size of Head as Influencing Character

SIZE of head and organs, other things being equal, is the great phrenological condition. Though tape measurements, taken around the head, from Individuality to Philoprogenitiveness, give some idea of the size of brain, the fact that some heads are round, others long, some low, and others high, so modifies these measurements that they do not convey any very correct idea of the actual quantity of brain. Yet these measurements range somewhat as follows. Least size of adults compatible with fair talents, 20 ¼; 20 ¾ to 21 ¼, moderate; 21 ¼ to 22, average; 22 to 22 ¾ full; 22 ¾ to 23 ¾, large; above 23 ¾, very large. Female heads, ½ to ¾ below these averages.

LARGE.—One having a large sized brain, with activity *average*, will *possess* considerable energy of intellect and feeling, yet seldom manifest it, unless it is brought out by some powerful stimulus, and will be rather too indolent to exert, especially his *intellect*: with activity *full*, will be endowed with an uncommon amount of the mental power, and be capable of doing a good deal, yet require considerable to awaken him to that vigorous effort of mind of which he is capable; if his powers are not called out by circumstances, and his organs of practical intellect are only average or full, he may pass through life without attracting notice, or manifesting more than an ordinary share of talent: but if the perceptive faculties are strong, or very strong, and his natural powers put in vigorous requisition, he will manifest a vigor and energy of intellect and feeling quite above mediocrity; be adequate to undertakings which demand originality of mind and force of character, yet, after all, be rather indolent: with activity *great, or very great,* will combine great *power* of mind with great activity; exercise a commanding influence over those minds with which he comes in contact; when he enjoys, will enjoy intensely, and when he suffers, suffer equally so; be susceptible of strong excitement, and, with the organs of the propelling powers, and of practical intellect, large or very large, will possess all the mental capabilities for conducting a large business; for rising to eminence, if not to preeminence; and discover great force of character and power of intellect and feeling: with activity *moderate,* when powerfully excited, will evince considerable energy of intellect and feeling, yet be too indolent and too sluggish to do much; lack clearness and force of idea, and intenseness of feeling; unless literally driven to it, will not be likely to be much or to do much, and yet actually *possess* more vigor of mind, and energy of feeling, than he will manifest; with activity small, or very small, will border upon idiocy.

VERY LARGE.—One having a very large head, with activity *average* or *full,* on great occasions, or when his powers are thoroughly roused, will be truly great; but upon ordinary occasions, will seldom manifest any remarkable amount of mind or feeling, and perhaps pass through life with the credit of being a person of good natural abilities and judgment, yet nothing more; with *great* activity and strength, and large intellectual organs, will be a natural genius, endowed with very superior powers of mind and vigor of intellect; and, even though deprived of the advantages of education, his natural talents will surmount all obstacles, and make him truly talented; with activity *very great,* and the organs of practical intellect and of the propelling powers large, or very large, will possess the first order of natural abilities; manifest a clearness and force of intellect which will astonish the world, and a power of feeling which will carry all before him; and, with proper cultivation, enable him to become a bright star in the firmament of intellectual greatness, upon which coming ages may gaze with delight and astonishment. His mental enjoyment will be most exquisite, and his sufferings equally keen.

FULL.—One having a full-sized brain, with activity *great, or very great,* and the organs of practical intellect and of the propelling powers large, or very large, although will not possess *greatness* of intellect, nor a deep, strong mind, will be very clever; have considerable talent, and that so distributed that it will show to be *more* than it really is; is capable of being a good scholar, doing a fine business, and, with advantages and application, of distinguishing himself somewhat; yet he is inadequate to a great undertaking; cannot sway an extensive influence, nor be really great; with activity *full, or average,* will do only tolerably well, and manifest only a common share of talent; with activity *moderate, or small,* will neither be nor do much worthy of notice.

AVERAGE, with activity great, manifests a quick, clear, sprightly mind and off-hand talents; and is capable of doing a fair business, especially if the stamina is good; with activity *very great,* and the organs of the propelling powers and of practical intellect large, or very large, is capable of doing a good business, and may pass for a man of fair talent, yet will not be original or profound; will be quick of perception; have a good practical understanding; will do well *in his sphere,* yet never manifest greatness, and out of his sphere, be common-place; with activity only *average,* will discover only an ordinary amount of intellect; be inadequate to any important undertaking; yet, in a small sphere, or one that requires only a mechanical routine of business, may do well; with *moderate or small* activity, will hardly have common sense.

MODERATE.—One with a head of only moderate size, combined with *great* or *very great activity,* and the organs of the propelling powers and of practical intellect large, will possess a tolerable share of intellect, yet be more showy than sound; with others to plan for and direct him, will execute to advantage, yet be unable to do much alone; will have a very active mind, and be quick of perception, yet, after all, have, a contracted intellect; possess only a small mental calibre, and lack momentum, both of mind and character; with activity only *average, or fair*, will have but a moderate *amount* of intellect, and even this scanty allowance will be too sluggish for action, so that he will neither suffer nor enjoy much; with activity *moderate or small*, will be idiotic.

SMALL OR VERY SMALL.—One with a small or very small head, no matter what may be the activity of his mind, will be incapable of much intellectual effort; of comprehending even easy subjects; or of experiencing much pain or pleasure; in short, will be mentally imbecile.

47.—*Size of Brain as Affecting Mentality*

Most great men have great heads. Webster's head measures over 24 inches, and Clay's[25] considerably above 23; and this is about Van Buren's[26] size; Chief Justice Gibson's, the greatest jurist in Pennsylvania, 24 ¼; Napoleon's[27] reached nearly or quite to 24, his hat passing easily over the head of one of his officers, which measured 23 ½; and Hamilton's[28] hat passed over the head of a man whose head measured 23 ½. Burke's[29] head was immense, so was Jefferson's;[30] while Franklin's hat passed over the ears of a 24-inch head. Small and average sized heads often astonish us by their brilliancy and learning, and, perhaps, eloquence, yet they fail in that commanding greatness which impresses and sways mind. The phrenological law is, that size, other things being equal, is a measure of power; yet these other conditions, such as activity, power of motive, wealth, physiological habits, etc., increase or diminish the mentality, even more than size.

---

25 Henry Clay (1777–1852) was an American senator of such diplomatic and political skill that he came to be known as "The Great Compromiser."

26 Martin Van Buren (1782–1862) was the eighth president of the United States.

27 Napoleon Bonaparte (1769–1821) became ruler of France soon after the French Revolution. He is considered one of the greatest military strategists of the nineteenth century.

28 Alexander Hamilton (1755?–1804) was one of the premier political theorists of the early United States. He championed a strong central government.

29 Edmund Burke (1729–1797) was an important eighteenth-century British politician and political philosopher.

30 Thomas Jefferson (1743–1826) led the committee that wrote the Declaration of Independence and was the third president of the United States.

Chapter Six

CATHARINE ESTHER BEECHER
(1800–1878)

Catharine Beecher was the eldest daughter of Lyman Beecher, making her part of one of the most famous and distinguished families in nineteenth-century America. She had as siblings the noted author Harriet Beecher Stowe and preacher Henry Ward Beecher. Losing her fiancé in a shipwreck early in her life, she never married. Instead, she dedicated herself to helping her extended family and tirelessly working for the cause of women's education.

In 1823 Beecher established the first of several rigorous academies she founded for women. Her educational philosophy was driven by the conviction that women played a key role in the development and well-being of the country as a whole, and thus they needed to be educated in earnest, not simply taught to paint, sew and play the piano.

Although she wrote constantly on the cause of women's education, her most famous and enduring work was *A Treatise on Domestic Economy*, which first appeared in 1841. It proved so popular and influential that it was reprinted annually for the next 15 years. In it, Beecher combined her views on women's role in society with the immensely popular literary genres of self-help and etiquette books. Beecher instructed women on everything from the unique social status of American women to how to wash feathers and trim wicks.

A Treatise on Domestic Economy would become most famous for how it clearly articulated a view of two spheres of influence: the male sphere outside the home and the female sphere within the home. Within this twin-sphere ideology, Beecher championed what would later become known as "domestic feminism," the view that, while women were still responsible for the domestic world of the home, their every action influenced the world at large. Whether educating their children to be good citizens or creating a safe place for a weary husband to rejuvenate himself, women were pivotal agents of influence entrusted with duties essential to cultivating the virtuous character necessary for the survival of democracy in the United States.

Catharine E. Beecher, *A Treatise on Domestic Economy for the Use of Young Ladies at Home and at School.* Boston: Marsh, Capen, Lyon and Webb, 1841.

A TREATISE ON DOMESTIC ECONOMY FOR THE USE OF YOUNG LADIES AT HOME AND AT SCHOOL

Chapter I

The Peculiar Responsibilities of American Women

American Women should feel a peculiar interest in Democratic Institutions. The maxim of our Civil Institutions. Its identity with the main principle of Christianity. Relations involving subordination; why they are needful. Examples. How these relations are decided in a Democracy. What decides the Equity of any Law or Institution. The principle of Aristocracy. The tendency of Democracy in respect to the interests of Women. Illustrated in the United States. Testimony of De Tocqueville. In what respects are Women subordinate? and why? Wherein are they equal or superior in influence? and how are they placed by courtesy? How can American Women rectify any real disadvantages involved in our Civil Institutions? Opinion of De Tocqueville as to the influence and example of American Democracy. Responsibilities involved in this view, especially those of American Women.

There are some reasons why American women should feel an interest in the support of the democratic institutions of their Country, which it is important that they should consider. The great maxim, which is the basis of all our civil and political institutions, is, that "all men are created equal," and that they are equally entitled to "life, liberty, and the pursuit of happiness."[1]

But it can readily be seen, that this is only another mode of expressing the fundamental principle which the Great Ruler of the Universe has established, as the law of His eternal government. "Thou shalt love thy neighbor as thyself;"[2] and "Whatsoever ye would that men should do to you, do ye even so to them."[3] These are the Scripture forms, by which the Supreme Lawgiver requires that each individual of our race shall regard the happiness of others, as of the same value as his own; and which forbids any institution, in private or civil life, which secures advantages to one class, by sacrificing the interests of another.

The principles of democracy, then, are identical with the principles of Christianity.

But, in order that each individual may pursue and secure the highest degree of happiness within his reach, unimpeded by the selfish interests of others, a system of laws must be established, which sustain certain relations and dependencies in social and civil life. What these relations and their attending obligations shall be, are to be determined, not with reference to the wishes and interests of a few, but solely with reference to the general good of all; so that each individual shall have his own interest, as much as the public benefit, secured by them.

For this purpose, it is needful that certain relations be sustained, that involve the duties of subordination. There must be the magistrate and the subject, one of whom is the

---

1 Both of these quotations are from the Declaration of Independence.
2 Matt. 19:19.
3 Matt. 7:12.

superior, and the other the inferior. There must be the relations of husband and wife, parent and child, teacher and pupil, employer and employed, each involving the relative duties of subordination. The superior in certain particulars is to direct, and the inferior is to yield obedience. Society could never go forward, harmoniously, nor could any craft or profession be successfully pursued, unless these superior and subordinate relations be instituted and sustained.

But who shall take the higher, and who the subordinate, stations in social and civil life? This matter, in the case of parents and children, is decided by the Creator. He has given children to the control of parents, as their superiors, and to them they remain subordinate, to a certain age, or so long as they are members of their household. And parents can delegate such a portion of their authority to teachers and employers, as the interests of their children require.

In most other cases, in a truly democratic state, each individual is allowed to choose for himself, who shall take the position of his superior. No woman is forced to obey any husband but the one she chooses for herself; nor is she obliged to take a husband, if she prefers to remain single. So every domestic, and every artisan or laborer, after passing from parental control, can choose the employer to whom he is to accord obedience, or, if he prefers to relinquish certain advantages, he can remain without taking a subordinate place to any employer.

Each subject, also, has equal power with every other, to decide who shall be his superior as a ruler. The weakest, the poorest, the most illiterate, has the same opportunity to determine this question, as the richest, the most learned, and the most exalted.

And the various privileges that wealth secures, are equally open to all classes. Every man may aim at riches, unimpeded by any law or institution that secures peculiar privileges to a favored class at the expense of another. Every law, and every institution, is tested by examining whether it secures equal advantages to all; and if the people become convinced that any regulation sacrifices the good of the majority to the interests of the smaller number, they have power to abolish it.

The institutions of monarchical and aristocratic nations are based on precisely opposite principles. They secure, to certain small and favored classes, advantages which can be maintained, only by sacrificing the interests of the great mass of the people. Thus, the throne and aristocracy of England are supported by laws and customs, that burden the lower classes with taxes, so enormous, as to deprive them of all the luxuries, and of most of the comforts, of life. Poor dwellings, scanty food, unhealthy employments, excessive labor, and entire destitution of the means and time for education, are appointed for the lower classes, that a few may live in palaces, and riot in every indulgence.

The tendencies of democratic institutions, in reference to the rights and interests of the female sex, have been fully developed in the United States; and it is in this aspect, that the subject is one of peculiar interest to American women. In this Country, it is established, both by opinion and by practice, that women have an equal interest in all social and civil concerns; and that no domestic, civil, or political, institution, is right that sacrifices her interest to promote that of the other sex. But in order to secure her the more firmly in all these privileges, it is decided, that, in the domestic relation, she take a subordinate station, and that, in civil and political concerns, her interests be intrusted to the other sex, without her taking any part in voting, or in making and administering laws. The result of this order of things has been fairly tested, and is thus portrayed by M. De Tocqueville,[4] a writer, who for intelligence, fidelity, and ability, ranks second to none.[5]

The following extracts present his views.

"There are people in Europe, who, confounding together the different characteristics of the sexes, would make of man and woman, beings not only equal, but alike. They would give to both the same functions, impose on both the same duties, and grant to both the same rights. They would mix them in all things,—their business, their occupations, their pleasures. It may readily be conceived, that, by *thus* attempting to make one sex equal to the other, both are degraded; and from so preposterous a medley of the works of Nature, nothing could ever result, but weak men and disorderly women.

"It is not thus that the Americans understand the species of democratic equality, which may be established between the sexes. They admit, that, as Nature has appointed such wide differences between the physical and moral constitutions of man and woman, her manifest design was, to give a distinct employment to their various faculties; and they hold, that improvement does not consist in making beings so dissimilar do pretty nearly the same things, but in getting each of them to fulfil their respective tasks, in the best possible manner. The Americans have applied to the sexes the great principle of political economy, which governs the manufactories of our age, by carefully dividing the duties of man from those of woman, in order that the great work of society may be the better carried on.

"In no country has such constant care been taken, as in America, to trace two clearly distinct lines of action for the two sexes, and to make them keep pace one with the other, but in two pathways which are always different. American women never manage the outward concerns of the family, or conduct a business, or take a part in political life; nor are they, on the other hand, ever compelled to perform the rough labor of the fields, or to make any of those laborious exertions, which demand the exertion of physical strength. No families are so poor, as to form an exception to this rule.

"If, on the one hand, an American woman cannot escape from the quiet circle of domestic employments, on the other hand, she is never forced to go beyond it. Hence it is, that the women of America, who often exhibit a masculine strength of understanding, and a manly energy, generally preserve great delicacy of personal appearance, and always retain the manners of women, although they sometimes show that they have the hearts and minds of men.

---

4 Alexis de Tocqueville (1805–1859) was a French political scientist and historian who visited the United States and wrote *Democracy in America* (1835–1840), an insightful commentary on the country's social and political system.

5 [Author's Original Note] The work of [Tocqueville], entitled "Democracy in America," secured for him a prize from the National Academy, at Paris. The following extract expresses an opinion, in which most of the best qualified judges would coincide.

"The manner of conducting the inquiry which the Author has instituted; the intimate acquaintance with all our institutions and relations, every where evinced; the careful and profound thought; and, above all, the spirit of truth, which animates and pervades the whole work, will not only commend it to the present generation, but render it a monument of the age in which it is produced."

"In Europe, it has already taken its stand with Montesquieu, Bacon, Milton, and Locke. In America, it will be regarded, not only as a classic philosophical treatise of the highest order, but as indispensable in the education of every statesman, and of every citizen who desires thoroughly to comprehend the institutions of his Country."

"Nor have the Americans ever supposed, that one consequence of democratic principles, is, the subversion of marital power, or the confusion of the natural authorities in families. They hold, that every association must have a head, in order to accomplish its object; and that the natural head of the conjugal association is man. They do not, therefore, deny him the right of directing his partner; and they maintain, that, in the smaller association of husband and wife, as well as in the great social community, the object of democracy is, to regulate and legalize the powers which are necessary, not to subvert all power.

"This opinion is not peculiar to one sex, and contested by the other. I never observed, that the women of America considered conjugal authority as a fortunate usurpation of their rights, nor that they thought themselves degraded by submitting to it. It appears to me, on the contrary, that they attach a sort of pride to the voluntary surrender of their own will, and make it their boast to bend themselves to the yoke, not to shake it off. Such, at least, is the feeling expressed by the most virtuous of their sex; the others are silent; and in the United States, it is not the practice for a guilty wife to clamor for the rights of woman, while she is trampling on her holiest duties.

"Although the travellers, who have visited North America, differ on a great number of points, they agree in remarking, that morals are far more strict, there, than elsewhere. It is evident that, on this point, the Americans are very superior to their progenitors, the English." "In England, as in all other countries of Europe, public malice is constantly attacking the frailties of women. Philosophers and statesmen are heard to deplore, that morals are not sufficiently strict; and the literary productions of the country constantly lead one to suppose so. In America, all books, novels not excepted, suppose women to be chaste; and no one thinks of relating affairs of gallantry.

"It has often been remarked, that, in Europe, a certain degree of contempt lurks, even in the flattery which men lavish upon women. Although a European frequently affects to be the slave of woman, it may be seen, that he never sincerely thinks her his equal. In the United States, men seldom compliment women, but they daily show how much they esteem them. They constantly display an entire confidence in the understanding of a wife, and a profound respect for her freedom. They have decided that her mind is just as fitted as that of a man to discover the plain truth, and her heart as firm to embrace it, and they have never sought to place her virtue, any more than his, under the shelter of prejudice, ignorance, and fear.

"It would seem, that in Europe, where man so easily submits to the despotic sway of woman, they are nevertheless curtailed of some of the greatest qualities of the human species, and considered as seductive, but imperfect beings, and (what may well provoke astonishment) women ultimately look upon themselves in the same light, and almost consider it as a privilege that they are entitled to show themselves futile, feeble, and timid. The women of America claim no such privileges.

"It is true, that the Americans rarely lavish upon women those eager attentions which are commonly paid them in Europe. But their conduct to women always implies, that they suppose them to be virtuous and refined; and such is the respect entertained for the moral freedom of the sex, that, in presence of a woman, the most guarded language is used, lest her ear should be offended by an expression. In America, a young unmarried woman may, alone, and without fear, undertake a long journey.

"Thus the Americans do not think that man and woman have either the duty, or the right, to perform the same offices, but they show an equal regard for both their respective parts; and, though their lot is different, they consider both of them, as beings of equal value. They do not give to the courage of woman the same form, or the same direction as to that of man; but they never doubt her courage: and if they hold that man and his partner ought not always to exercise their intellect and understanding in the same manner, they at least believe the understanding of the one to be as sound as that of the other and her intellect to be as clear. Thus, then, while they have allowed the social inferiority of woman to subsist, they have done all they could to raise her, morally and intellectually, to the level of man; and, in this respect, they appear to me to have excellently understood the true principle of democratic improvement.

"As for myself, I do not hesitate to avow, that, although the women of the United States are confined within the narrow circle of domestic life, and their situation is, in some respects, one of extreme dependence. I have nowhere seen women occupying a loftier position; and if I were asked, now that I am drawing to the close of this work, in which I have spoken of so many important things done by the Americans, to what the singular prosperity and growing strength of that people ought mainly to be attributed, I should reply,—*to the superiority of their women.*"

This testimony of a foreigner, who has had abundant opportunities of making a comparison, is sanctioned by the assent of all candid and intelligent men, who have enjoyed similar opportunities.

It appears, then, that it is in America, alone, that women are raised to an equality with the other sex; and that, both in theory and practice, their interests are regarded as of equal value. They are made subordinate in station, only where a regard to their best interests demands it, while, as if in compensation for this, by custom and courtesy, they are always treated as superiors. Universally, in this Country, through every class of society, precedence is given to woman, in all the comforts, conveniences, and courtesies, of life.

In civil and political affairs, American women take no interest or concern, except so far as they sympathize with their family and personal friends; but in all cases, in which they do feel a concern, their opinions and feelings have a consideration, equal, or even superior, to that of the other sex.

In matters pertaining to the education of their children, in the selection and support of a clergyman, in all benevolent enterprises, and in all questions relating to morals or manners, they have a superior influence. In all such concerns, it would be impossible to carry a point, contrary to their judgement and feelings; while an enterprise, sustained by them, will seldom fail of success.

If those who are bewailing themselves over the fancied wrongs and injuries of women in this Nation, could only see things as they are, they would know, that, whatever remnants of a barbarous or aristocratic age may remain in our civil institutions, in reference to the interests of women, it is only because they are ignorant of it, or do not use their influence to have them rectified; for it is very certain that there is nothing reasonable which American women would unite in asking, that would not readily be bestowed.

The preceding remarks, then, illustrate the position, that the democratic institutions of this Country are in reality no other than the principles of Christianity carried into operation, and that they tend to place woman in her true position in society, as having equal rights with the other sex; and that, in fact, they have secured to American women a lofty and fortunate position, which, as yet, has been attained by the women of no other nation.

There is another topic, presented in the work of the above author, which demands the profound attention of American women.

The following is taken from that part of the Introduction to the work, illustrating the position, that, for ages, there has been a constant progress, in all civilized nations, towards the democratic equality attained in this country.

"The various occurrences of national existence have every where turned to the advantage of democracy; all men have aided it by their exertions; those who have intentionally labored in its cause, and those who have served it unwittingly; those who have fought for it, and those who have declared themselves its opponents, have all been driven along in the same track, have all labored to one end;" "all have been blind instruments in the hands of God."

"The gradual development of the equality of conditions, is, therefore, a Providential fact; and it possesses all the characteristics of a Divine decree: it is universal, it is durable, it constantly eludes all human interference, and all events, as well as all men, contribute to its progress."

"The whole book, which is here offered to the public, has been written under the impression of a kind of religious dread, produced in the Author's mind, by the contemplation of so irresistible a revolution, which has advanced for centuries, in spite of such amazing obstacles, and which is still proceeding in the midst of the ruins it has made.

"It is not necessary that God Himself should speak, in order to disclose to us the unquestionable signs of His will. We can discern them in the habitual course of Nature, and in the invariable tendency of events."

"If the men of our time were led, by attentive observation, and by sincere reflection, to acknowledge that the gradual and progressive development of social equality is at once the past and future of their history, this solitary truth would confer the sacred character of a Divine decree upon the change. To attempt to check democracy, would be, in that case, to resist the will of God; and the nations would then be constrained to make the best of the social lot awarded to them by Providence."

"It is not, then, merely to satisfy a legitimate curiosity, that I have examined America; my wish has been to find instruction by which we may ourselves profit." "I have not even affected to discuss whether the social revolution, which I believe to be irresistible, is advantageous or prejudicial to mankind. I have acknowledged this revolution, as a fact already accomplished, or on the eve of its accomplishment; and I have selected the nation, from among those which have undergone it, in which its development has been the most peaceful and the most complete, in order to discern its natural consequences, and, if it be possible, to distinguish the means by which it may be rendered profitable. I confess, that in America I saw more than America; I sought the image of democracy itself, with its inclinations, its character, its prejudices, and its passions, in order to learn what we have to fear, or to hope, from its progress."

It thus appears, that the sublime and elevating anticipations which have filled the mind and heart of the religious world, have become so far developed, that philosophers and statesmen perceive the signs of its approach and are predicting the same grand consummation. There is a day advancing, "by seers predicted, and by poets sung," when the curse of selfishness shall be removed; when "scenes surpassing fable, and yet true,"[6] shall be

---

6 From *The Task: A Poem* (1785), a book-length work by poet William Cowper (1731–1800). This line comes from Book VI, "The Winter Walk at Noon."

realized; when all nations shall rejoice and be made blessed, under those benevolent influences which the Messiah came to establish on earth.

And this is the nation, which the Disposer of events designs shall go forth as the cynosure[7] of nations, to guide them to the light and blessedness of that day. To us is committed the grand, the responsible privilege, of exhibiting to the world, the beneficent influences of Christianity, when carried into every social, civil, and political institution, and though we have, as yet, made such imperfect advances, already the light is streaming into the dark prison-house of despotic lands, while startled kings and sages, philosophers and statesmen, are watching us with that interest which a career so illustrious, and so involving their own destiny, is calculated to excite. They are studying our institutions scrutinizing our experience, and watching for our mistakes, that they may learn whether "a social revolution, so irresistible, be advantageous or prejudicial to mankind."

There are persons, who regard these interesting truths merely as food for national vanity; but every reflecting and Christian mind, must consider it as an occasion for solemn and anxious reflection. Are we, then, a spectacle to the world? Has the Eternal Lawgiver appointed us to work out a problem involving the destiny of the whole earth? Are such momentous interests to be advanced or retarded, just in proportion as we are faithful to our high trust? "What manner of persons, then, ought we to be," in attempting to sustain so solemn, so glorious a responsibility?

But the part to be enacted by American women, in this great moral enterprise, is the point to which special attention should here be directed.

The success of democratic institutions, as is conceded by all, depends upon the intellectual and moral character of the mass of the people. If they are intelligent and virtuous, democracy is a blessing; but if they are ignorant and wicked, it is only a curse, and as much more dreadful than any other form of civil government, as a thousand tyrants are more to be dreaded than one. It is equally conceded, that the formation of the moral and intellectual character of the young is committed mainly to the female hand. The mother writes the character of the future man; the sister bends the fibres that hereafter are the forest tree; the wife sways the heart, whose energies may turn for good or for evil the destinies of a nation. Let the women of a country be made virtuous and intelligent, and the men will certainly be the same. The proper education of a man decides the welfare of an individual; but educate a woman, and the interests of a whole family are secured.

If this be so, as none will deny, then to American women, more than to any others on earth, is committed the exalted privilege of extending over the world those blessed influences, that are to renovate degraded man, and "clothe all climes with beauty."[8]

No American woman, then, has any occasion for feeling that hers is an humble or insignificant lot. The value of what an individual accomplishes, is to be estimated by the importance of the enterprise achieved, and not by the particular position of the laborer. The drops of heaven that freshen the earth are each of equal value, whether they fall in the lowland meadow, or the princely parterre.[9] The builders of a temple are of equal importance, whether they labor on the foundations, or toil upon the dome.

Thus, also, with those labors that are to be made effectual in the regeneration of the Earth. The woman who is rearing a family of children; the woman who labors in the

---

7 Director.
8 A line from William Cowper's *The Task: A Poem*, Book VI, "The Winter Walk at Noon."
9 An ornamental garden bed.

schoolroom; the woman who, in her retired chamber, earns, with her needle, the mite to contribute for the intellectual and moral elevation of her country; even the humble domestic, whose example and influence may be moulding and forming young minds, while her faithful services sustain a prosperous domestic state;—each and all may be cheered by the consciousness, that they are agents in accomplishing the greatest work that ever was committed to human responsibility. It is the building of a glorious temple, whose base shall be coextensive with the bounds of the earth, whose summit shall pierce the skies, whose splendor shall beam on all lands, and those who hew the lowliest stone, as much as those who carve the highest capital, will be equally honored when its top-stone shall be laid, with new rejoicings of the morning stars, and shoutings of the sons of God.

Chapter XII

On Domestic Manners

What are Good-manners. Defect in American Manners. Coldness and Reserve of the Descendants of the Puritans accounted for. Cause of the Want of Courtesy in American Manners. Want of Discrimination. Difference of Principles regulating Aristocratic and Democratic Manners. Rules for regulating the Courtesies founded on Precedence of Age, Office, and Station, in a Democracy. Manners appropriate to Superiors and Subordinates. Peculiar Defect of Americans in this Respect. This to be remedied in the Domestic Circle, alone. Rules of Precedence to be enforced in the Family. Manners and tones towards Superiors to be regulated in the Family. Treatment of grown Brothers and Sisters by Young Children. Acknowledgement of Favors by Children to be required. Children to ask leave or apologize in certain cases. Rules for avoiding Remarks that would the Feelings of Others. Rules of Hospitality. Conventional Rules. Rules for Table Manners. Caution as to teaching these Rules to Children. Caution as to Allowances to be made for those deficient in Good-manners. Comparison of English and American Manners. America may hope to excel all Nations in Refinement, Taste, and Good-breeding; and why. Effects of Wealth and Equalisation of Labor. Allusion to the Manners of Courts in the past Century.

Good-manners are the expressions of benevolence in personal intercourse, by which we endeavor to promote the comfort and enjoyment of others, and to avoid all that gives needless pain. It is the exterior exhibition of the Divine precept which requires us to do to others as we would that they should do to us. It is saying, by our deportment, to all around, that we consider their feelings, tastes, and convenience, as equal in value to our own.

Good-manners lead us to avoid all practices that offend the taste of others; all violations of the conventional rules of propriety; all rude and disrespectful language and deportment; and all remarks that would tend to wound the feelings of another.

There is a defect in the manners of the American people, especially in the free States, which is a serious one, and which can never be efficiently remedied, except in the domestic circle, and in early life. It is a deficiency in the free expression of kindly feelings and sympathetic emotions, and a want of courtesy in deportment. The causes, which have led to this result, may easily be traced.

The forefathers of this Nation, to a wide extent, were men who were driven from their native land, by laws and customs which they believed to be opposed both to civil and religious freedom. The sufferings they were called to endure, the subduing of those gentler feelings which bind us to country, kindred, and home, and the constant subordination of the passions to stern principle, induced characters of great firmness and self-control.

They gave up the comforts and refinements of a civilized country, and came as pilgrims to a hard soil, a cold clime, and a heathen shore. They were constantly called to encounter danger, privations, sickness, loneliness, and death; and all these, their religion taught them to meet with calmness, fortitude, and submission. And thus it became the custom and habit of the whole mass, to repress, rather than to encourage, the expression of feeling.

Persons who are called to constant and protracted suffering and privation, are forced to subdue and conceal emotion; for the free expression of it would double their own suffering, and increase the sufferings of others. Those, only, who are free from care and anxiety, and whose minds are mainly occupied by cheerful emotions, are at full liberty to unveil their feelings.

It was under such stern and rigorous discipline, that the first children in New England were reared; and the manners and habits of parents are usually, to a great extent, transmitted to children. Thus it comes about, that the descendants of the Puritans, now scattered over every part of the Nation, are predisposed to conceal the gentler emotions, while their manners are calm, decided, and cold, rather than free and impulsive. Of course, there are very many exceptions to these predominating results.

The causes, to which we may attribute a general want of courtesy in manners, are certain incidental results of our democratic institutions. Our ancestors, and their descendants, have constantly been combating the aristocratic principle, which would exalt one class of men at the expense of another. They have had to contend with this principle, not only in civil, but in social, life. Almost every American, in his own person, as well as in behalf of his class, has had to assume and defend the main principle of democracy,—that every man's feelings and interests are equal in value to those of every other man. But, in doing this, there has been some want of clear discrimination. Because claims founded on distinctions of mere birth and position were found to be injurious, many have gone to the extreme of inferring that all distinctions, involving subordination, are useless. Such would regard children as equals to parents, pupils to teachers, domestics to their employers, and subjects to magistrates; and that, too, in all respects.

The fact, that certain grades of superiority and subordination are needful, both for individual and for public benefit, has not been clearly discerned; and there has been a gradual tendency to an extreme, which has sensibly affected our manners. All the proprieties and courtesies which depend on the recognition of the relative duties of superior and subordinate, have been warred upon, and thus we see, to an increasing extent, disrespectful treatment of parents from children, of teachers from pupils, of employers from domestics, and of the aged from the young. Children too often address their parents in the same style and manner as they do their companions. Domestics address their employers, and the visiters of the family, as they do their associates; while, in all classes and circles, there is a gradual decay in courtesy of address.

In cases, too, where kindness is rendered, it is often accompanied with a cold unsympathizing manner, which greatly lessens its value, while kindness or politeness is received in a similar style of *nonchalance,* as if it were but the payment of a just due.

It is owing to these causes, that the American people, especially the inhabitants of New England, do not do themselves justice. For, while those, who are near enough to learn their real character and feelings, can discern the most generous impulses, and the most kindly sympathies, they are so veiled, in a composed and indifferent demeanor, as to be almost entirely concealed from strangers.

These defects in our national manners, it especially falls to the care of mothers, and all who have charge of the young, to rectify; and if they seriously undertake the matter, and wisely adapt means to ends, these defects will be remedied. With reference to this object, the following ideas are suggested.

The law of Christianity and of democracy, which teaches that all men are born equal, and that their interests and feelings should be regarded as of equal value, seems to be adopted in aristocratic circles, with exclusive reference to the class in which the individual moves. The courtly gentleman addresses all of his own class with politeness and respect, and in all his actions seems to allow that the feelings and convenience of others are to be regarded the same as his own. But his demeanor to those of inferior station is not based on the same rule.

Among those who make up aristocratic circles, such as are above them, are deemed of superior, and such as are below, of inferior, value. Thus, if a young, ignorant, and vicious coxcomb, happens to be born a lord, the aged, the virtuous, the learned, and the well-bred of another class must give his convenience the precedence, and must address him in terms of respect. So when a man of noble birth is thrown among the lower classes, he demeans himself in a style, which, to persons of his own class, would be deemed the height of assumption and rudeness.

Now the principles of democracy require, that the same courtesy, which we accord our own circle, shall be extended to every class and condition; and that distinctions of superiority and subordination shall depend, not on accidents of birth, fortune, or occupation, but solely on those relations, which the good of all classes equally require. The distinctions demanded in a democratic state, are simply those, which result from relations that are common to every class, and which are for the benefit of all.

It is for the benefit of all, that children be subordinate to parents, pupils to teachers, the employed to their employers, and subjects to magistrates. In addition to this, it is for the general wellbeing, that the comfort and convenience of the delicate and feeble should be preferred to that of the strong and healthy, who would suffer less by any deprivation.

It is on these principles, that the rules of good-breeding, in a democratic state, must be founded. It is, indeed, assumed, that the value of the happiness of each individual is the same as that of every other; but as there always must be occasions, where there are advantages which all cannot enjoy, there must be general rules for regulating a selection Otherwise, there would be constant scrambling among those of equal claims, and brute force must be the final resort, in which case the strongest would have the best of everything. The democratic rule, then, is, that superiors in age, station, or office, have precedence of subordinates; and that age and feebleness have precedence of youth and strength.

It is on this principle, that the feebler sex has precedence of more vigorous man, while the young and healthy give precedence to age or feebleness.

There is, also, a style of deportment and address, which is appropriate to these different relations. It is suitable for a superior to secure compliance with his wishes from those subordinate to him, by commands; but a subordinate must secure compliance with his wishes, from a superior, by requests. It is suitable for a parent, teacher, or employer, to admonish for neglect of duty; it is not suitable for an inferior to take such a course to a superior. It is suitable for a superior to take precedence of a subordinate, without any remark; but in such cases, an inferior should ask leave, or offer an apology. It is proper for a superior to use the language and manners of freedom and familiarity which would be improper from a subordinate to a superior.

It is a want of proper regard to these proprieties, which occasions the chief defect in American manners. It is very common to see children talking to their parents in a style proper only between equals; so, also, the young address their elders, and those employed their employers, in a style which is inappropriate to their relative positions. It is not merely towards superiors that a respectful address is required; every person likes to be treated with courtesy and respect, and therefore the law of benevolence demands such demeanor towards all whom we meet in the social intercourse of life. "Be ye courteous,"[10] is the direction of the Apostle, in reference to our treatment of *all*.

It is in early life, and in the domestic circle, alone, that good-manners can be successfully cultivated. There is nothing that so much depends on *habit*, as the constantly recurring proprieties of good-breeding; and if a child grows up without forming such habits, it is very rarely the case that they can be formed at a later period. The feeling that it is of little consequence how we behave at home, if we conduct properly abroad, is a very fallacious one. Persons who are careless and illbred at home, may imagine that they can assume good-manners abroad; but they mistake. Fixed habits of tone, manner, language, and movements, cannot be suddenly altered; and those who are illbred at home, even when they try to hide their bad habits, are sure to violate many of the obvious rules of propriety, and yet be unconscious of it.

And there is nothing which would so effectually remove prejudice against our democratic institutions, as the general cultivation of good-breeding in the domestic circle. Good-manners are the exterior of benevolence, the minute and often recurring exhibitions of "peace and good-will;" and the nation, as well as the individual, which most excels in the exterior, as well as the internal principle, will be most respected and beloved.

The following are the leading points, which claim attention from those who have the care of the young.

In the first place, in the family, there should be required a strict attention to the rules of precedence, and those modes of address appropriate to the various relations to be sustained. Children should always be required to offer their superiors, in age or station, precedence in all comforts and conveniences, and always address them in a respectful tone and manner. The custom of adding "Sir," or "Ma'am," to "Yes," or "No," is a valuable practice, as a perpetual indication of a respectful recognition of superiority. It is now going out of fashion, even among the most wellbred people; probably from want of consideration of its importance. Every remnant of courtesy in address, in our customs, should be carefully cherished, by all who feel a value for the proprieties of good-breeding.

If parents allow their children to talk to them, and to the grown persons in the family, in the same style in which they address each other, it will be vain to hope for the courtesy of manner and tone, which good-breeding demands in the general intercourse of society. In a large family, where the elder children are grown up and the younger are small, it is important to require the latter to treat the elder as superiors. There are none so ready as young children to assume airs of equality; and if they are allowed to treat one class of superiors in age and character disrespectfully, they will soon use the privilege universally. This is the reason why the youngest children of a family are most apt to be pert, forward, and unmannerly.

Another point to be aimed at, is, to require children always to acknowledge every act of kindness and attention, either by words or manner. If they are trained always to make

---

10 Eph. 4:32.

grateful acknowledgements, when receiving favors, one of the objectionable features in American manners will be avoided.

Again, children should be required to ask leave, whenever they wish to gratify curiosity, or use an article which belongs to another. And if cases occur, when they cannot comply with the rules of good-breeding, as, for instance, when they must step between a person and the fire, or take the chair of an older person, they should be required either to ask leave, or offer an apology.

There is another point of good-breeding, which cannot, in all cases, be applied by children, in its widest extent. It is that which requires us to avoid all remarks which tend to embarrass, vex, mortify, or in any way wound the feelings, of another. To notice personal defects; to allude to others' faults, or the faults of their friends; to speak disparagingly of the sect or party to which a person belongs; to be inattentive, when addressed in conversation; to contradict flatly; to speak in contemptuous tones of opinions expressed by another;— all these are violations of the rules of good-breeding, which children should be taught to regard. Under this head, comes the practice of whispering, and staring about, when a teacher, or lecturer, or clergyman, is addressing a class or audience. Such inattention is practically saying that what the person is uttering is not worth attending to, and persons of real good-breeding always avoid it. Loud talking and laughing, in a large assembly, even when no exercises are going on; yawning and gaping in company; and not looking in the face a person who is addressing you, are deemed marks of ill-breeding.

Another branch of good-manners, relates to the duties of hospitality. Politeness requires us to welcome visiters with cordiality; to offer them the best accommodations; to address conversation to them; and to express, by tone and manner, kindness and respect. Offering the hand to all visiters, at one's own house, is a courteous and hospitable custom; and a cordial shake of the hand, when friends meet, would abate much of the coldness of manner ascribed to Americans.

The last point of good-breeding to be noticed, refers to the conventional rules of propriety and good taste. Of these, the first class relates to the avoidance of all disgusting or offensive personal habits, such as fingering the hair; cleaning the teeth or nails; picking the nose; spitting on carpets; snuffing, instead of using a handkerchief, or using the article in an offensive manner; lifting up the boots or shoes, as some men do, to tend them on the knee, or to finger them;—all these tricks, either at table or in society, children should be taught to avoid.

Another branch under this head, may be called *table manners.* To persons of good-breeding, nothing is more annoying, than violating the conventional proprieties of the table. Reaching over another person's plate; standing up to reach distant articles, instead of asking to have them passed; using one's own knife, and spoon, for butter, salt, or sugar, when it is the custom of the family to provide separate utensils for the purpose; setting cups, with tea dripping from them, on the table-cloth, instead of the mats or small plates provided for the purpose; using the table-cloth instead of the napkins provided; eating fast and in a noisy manner; putting large pieces in the mouth; looking and eating as if very hungry, or as if anxious to get at certain dishes; sitting at too great a distance from the table, and dropping food; laying the knife and fork on the table-cloth, instead of on the bread, or the edge of the plate;—all these particulars children should be taught to avoid. It is always desirable, too, to require children, when at table with grown persons, to be silent, except when addressed by others; or else their chattering will interrupt the conversation and comfort of their elders. They should always be required, too, to wait *in silence,* till all the older persons are helped.

All these things should be taught to children, gradually, and with great patience and gentleness. Some parents, who make good-manners a great object, are in danger of making their children perpetually uncomfortable, by suddenly surrounding them with so many rules, that they must inevitably violate some one or other a great part of the time. It is much better to begin with a few rules, and be steady and persevering with these till a habit is formed, and then take a few more, thus making the process easy and gradual. Otherwise, the temper of children will be injured; or, hopeless of fulfilling so many requisitions, they will become reckless and indifferent to all.

But in reference to those who have enjoyed advantages for the cultivation of good-manners, and who duly estimate its importance, one caution is important. Those who never have had such habits formed in youth, are under disadvantages, which no benevolence of temper can remedy. They may often violate the taste and feelings of others, not from a want of proper regard for them, but from ignorance of custom, or want of habit, or abstraction of mind, or from other causes, which demand forbearance and sympathy, rather than displeasure. An ability to bear patiently with defects in manners, and to make candid and considerate allowance for a want of advantages, or for peculiarities in mental habits, is one mark of the benevolence of real good-breeding.

The advocates of monarchical and aristocratic institutions have always had great plausibility given to their views, by the seeming tendencies of our institutions to insubordination and bad-manners. And it has been too indiscriminately conceded, by the defenders of our institutions, that such are these tendencies, and that the offensive points in American manners, are the necessary result of democratic principles.

But it is believed that both facts and reasonings are in opposition to this opinion. The following extract from the work of De Tocqueville exhibits the opinion of an impartial observer, when comparing American manners with those of the English, who are confessedly the most aristocratic of all people.

He previously remarks on the tendency of aristocracy to make men more sympathizing with persons of their own peculiar class, and less so towards those of lower degree; which he illustrates by the deportment of nobles to their boors,[11] and slaveholders towards slaves. And he claims that the progress in equality of conditions has always been attended with a corresponding refinement of manners and humanity of feeling. "While the English," says he, "retain the bloody traces of the dark ages in their penal legislation, the Americans have almost expunged capital punishments from their codes. North America is, I think, the only country upon earth, in which the life of no one citizen has been taken for political offence in the course of the last fifty years."

He then contrasts American manners with the English, claiming that the Americans are much the most affable, mild, and social. "In America, where the privileges of birth never existed, and where riches confer no peculiar rights on their possessors, men acquainted with each other are very ready to frequent the same places, and find neither peril nor advantage in the free interchange of their thoughts. If they meet by accident, they neither seek nor avoid intercourse; their manner is therefore natural, frank, and open." "If their demeanor is often cold and serious, it is never haughty or constrained." But an "aristocratic pride is still extremely great among the English; and as the limits of aristocracy are ill-defined, every body lives in constant dread, lest advantage should be taken of his familiarity. Unable to judge at once of the social position of those he meets, an Englishman prudently avoids all contact with them. Men are afraid lest some slight service rendered should draw them

---

11 Peasants.

into an unsuitable acquaintance; they dread civilities, and they avoid the obtrusive gratitude of a stranger as much as his hatred."

Thus *facts* seem to show that when the most aristocratic nation in the world is compared,
as to manners, with the most democratic, the judgement of strangers is in favor of the latter.

And if good-manners are the outward exhibition of the democratic fundamental principle of impartial benevolence and equal rights, surely the nation that adopts this rule,
both in social and civil life, is the most likely to secure the desirable exterior. The aristocrat,
by his principles, extends the exterior of impartial benevolence to his own class only; the
democratic principle requires it to be extended *to all*.

There is reason, therefore, to hope and expect more refined and polished manners in
America, than in any other land; while all the developments of taste and refinement, such
as poetry, music, painting, sculpture, and architecture, it may be expected, will come to a
higher state of perfection, here, than in any other nation.

If this Country increases in virtue and intelligence, as it may, there is no end to the
wealth that will pour in as the result of our resources of climate, soil, and navigation, and
the skill, industry, energy, and enterprise, of our countrymen. This wealth, if used as intelligence and virtue will dictate, will furnish the means for a superior education to all and all
the facilities for the refinement of taste, intellect, and feeling.

Moreover, in this Country, labor is ceasing to be the badge of a lower class; so that
already it is disreputable for a man to be "a lazy gentleman." And this feeling will increase,
till there will be such an equalisation of labor, as will afford all the time needful for every
class to improve the many advantages offered to them. Already, in Boston, through the
munificence of some of her citizens, there are literary and scientific advantages offered to
all classes of the citizens, rarely enjoyed elsewhere. In Cincinnati, too, the advantages of
education, now offered to the poorest classes, without charge, surpass what, a few years ago,
most wealthy men could purchase, for any price. And it is believed, that a time will come,
when the poorest boy in America can secure advantages which will equal what the heir of
the proudest peerage can now command.

The records of the courts of France and Germany, (as detailed by the Duchess of
Orleans,[12]) in and succeeding the brilliant reign of Louis the Fourteenth,—a period which
was deemed the acme of elegance and refinement,—exhibit a grossness, a vulgarity, and a
coarseness, not to be found among the lowest of our respectable poor. And the biography
of Beau Nash,[13] who attempted to reform the manners of the gentry in the times of Queen
Anne,[14] exhibits violations of the rules of decency, which the commonest yeoman of this
Land would feel disgraced in perpetrating.

This shows that our lowest classes, at this period, are more refined than were the highest
in aristocratic lands, a hundred years ago; and another century may show the lowest classes,
in wealth, in this Country, attaining as high a polish, as adorns those who now are leaders
of good-manners in the courts of kings.

---

12 Anne-Marie-Louie Motpensier (1627–1693), duchess of Orleans, was a princess of the royal
house of France and writer of short novels and literary portraits.

13 Englishman Richard "Beau" Nash (1674–1762) made himself into an important judge and
standard of proper etiquette and fashion in the eighteenth century.

14 Anne (1675–1714) was an English queen who reigned from 1702 to 1714.

Chapter Seven

GEORGE LIPPARD
(1822–1854)

After studying first to become a Methodist minister and then a lawyer, George Lippard turned to writing as a career. He began with satirical newspaper pieces in the early 1840s, but in 1844 he began to serialize what would become one of the best-selling novels in antebellum America: *The Quaker City; or, The Monks of Monk-Hall*. Representative of a popular nineteenth-century literary genre scholars have come to call city-mysteries novels, *The Quaker City* flew off booksellers' shelves, selling 60,000 copies in its first year and then 10,000 copies annually for the next decade.

Lippard based *The Quaker City* on a much-publicized 1843 Philadelphia murder case that resulted from the abduction and seduction of a respectable woman on the false promise of marriage. Lippard added countless elements to this story, which created tremendous interest in Philadelphia as local readers attempted to separate fact from fiction. The book itself is an odd mixture of elements, including: anti-Catholicism, anti-Protestantism, secret societies, domesticity gone awry, the gothic, popular science, seduction and rape, economic injustice, necrophilia, prostitution, temperance work and adultery.

Lippard was a dedicated social reformer who used his writing to disseminate his views on American social evils and how they might be cured. His own philosophy was on the radical end of the spectrum for its day, concentrating on equality in terms of both class and gender. At the core of *The Quaker City* stands Lippard's belief in humanity's boundless capacity for evil and hypocrisy, and an equally strong conviction that it is only in confronting the darkest elements of the human heart that a better society might be created.

THE QUAKER CITY

Or, The Monks of Monk Hall
A Romance of Philadelphia Life, Mystery, and Crime

Title Page (Philadelphia: T.B. Peterson, 1876, Courtesy Lilly Library, Bloomington, IN).

George Lippard, *The Quaker City; or, The Monks of Monk Hall, a Romance of Philadelphia Life, Mystery, and Crime*. Philadelphia: Leary, Stuart, 1876.

Preface to This Edition

My Publishers ask me to write a Preface for this new Edition of the Quaker City. What shall I say? Shall I at this time enter into a full explanation of the motives which induced me to write this Work? Shall I tell how it has been praised—how abused—how it has on the one hand been cited as a Work of great merit, and on the other, how it has been denounced as the most immoral work of the age?

The reader will spare me the task. The Quaker City has passed through many Editions in America, as well as in London. It has also been translated and numerous editions of it have been published in Germany, and a beautiful edition in four volumes, is now before me, bearing the imprint of Otto Wigand, Leipsic, as Publisher, and the name of Frederick Gerstaker, as the Author.

Taking all these facts into consideration, it seems but just that I should say a word for myself on this occasion.

The motive which impelled me to write this Work may be stated in a few words.

I was the only Protector of an Orphan Sister. I was fearful that I might be taken away by death, leaving her alone in the world. I knew too well that law of society which makes a virtue of the dishonor of a poor girl, while it justly holds the seduction of a rich man's child as an infamous crime. These thoughts impressed me deeply. I determined to write a book, founded upon the following idea:

That the seduction of a poor and innocent girl, is a deed altogether as criminal as deliberate murder. It is worse than the murder of the body, for it is the assassination of the soul. If the murderer deserves death by the gallows, then the assassin of chastity and maidenhood is worthy of death by the hands of any man, and in any place.

This was the first idea of the Work. It embodies a sophism, but it is a sophism that errs on the right side. But as I progressed in my task, other ideas were added to the original thought. Secluded in my room, having no familiarity with the vices of a large city, save from my studentship in the office of an Attorney-General—the Confessional of our Protestant communities—I determined to write a book which should describe all the phases of a corrupt social system, as manifested in the city of Philadelphia. The results of my labors was this book, which has been more attacked, and more read, than any work of American fiction ever published.

And now, I can say with truth, that whatever faults may be discovered in this Work, that my motive in its composition was honest, was pure, was as destitute of any idea of sensualism, as certain of the persons who have attacked it without reading a single page, are of candor, of a moral life, or a heart capable of generous emotions.

To the young man and young woman who may read this book when I am dead, I have a word to say:

Would to God that the evils recorded in these pages, were not based upon facts. Would to God that the experience of my life had not impressed me so vividly with the colossal vices and the terrible deformities, presented in the social system of this Large City, in the Nineteenth Century. You will read this work when the hand which pens this line is dust. If you discover one word in its pages, that has a tendency to develop one impure thought, I beseech you reject that word. If you discover a chapter, a page, or a line, that conflicts with the great idea of Human Brotherhood, promulgated by the Redeemer, I ask you with all my soul, reject that chapter, that passage, that line. At the same time remember the idea which impelled me to produce the book. Remember the my life from the age of sixteen up to twenty-five was one perpetual battle with hardship and difficulty, such as do not often fall to the lot of a young man—such as rarely is recorded in the experience of childhood or manhood. Take the book with all its faults and all its virtues. Judge it as you yourself would wish to be judged. Do not wrest a line from these pages, for the encouragement of a bad thought or a bad deed.

George Lippard.
[1849 Edition]

Inscribed to the Memory of Charles Brockden Brown

The Origin and Object of This Book

One winter night I was called to the bedside of a dying friend. I found him sitting up in his death-couch, pale and trembling yet unawed by the gathering shadows of the tomb. His white hairs fell over his clammy brow, his dark grey eye, glared with the unnatural light, which, heralds the approach of death. Old K—— had been a singular man. He had been a profound lawyer, without fame or judgeship. In quiet he pursued his dreamy way, deriving sufficient from his profession, to support him in decency and honor. In a city, where no man has a friend, that has not money to back him, the good old lawyer had been my friend. He was one of those old-fashioned lawyers who delight to bury themselves among their books, who love the law for its theory, and not for its trick and craft and despicable chicanery. Old K—— had been my friend, and now I sat by his bedside in his last hour.

"Death is coming," he said with a calm smile, "but I dread him not. My accounts with God are settled; my face is clammy with the death-sweat, but I have no fear. When I am gone, you will find in yonder desk, a large pacquet, inscribed with your name. This pacquet, contains the records of my experience as a private councillor and a lawyer, for the last thirty years. You are young and friendless, but you have a pen, which will prove your best friend. I bequeath these Papers to you; they may be made serviceable to yourself and to the world—"

In a faint voice, I asked the good old lawyer, concerning the nature of these records.

"They contain a full and terrible developement of the Secret Life of Philadelphia. In that pacquet, you will find, records of crimes, that never came to trial, murders that have never been divulged; there you will discover the results of secret examinations, held by official personages, in relation to atrocities almost too horrible for belief—"

"Then," said I, "Philadelphia is not so pure as it looks?"

"Alas, alas, that I should have to say it," said the old man with an expression of deep sorrow, "But whenever I behold its regular streets and formal look, I think of The Whited Sepulchre,[1] without all purity, within, all rottenness and dead men's bones. Have you courage, to write a book from those papers?"

"Courage?"

"Aye, courage, for the day has come, when a man dare not speak a plain truth, without all the pitiful things of this world, rising up against him, with adder's tongues and

---

1 Matt. 23:77.

treacherous hands. Write a book, with all your heart bent on some good object, and for every word you write, you will find a low-bred calumniator, eager to befoul you with his slanders. Have you courage, to write a book from the materials, which I leave you, which shall be devoted to these objects. To defend the sanctity of female honor; to show how miserable and corrupt is that Pseudo-Christianity which tramples on every principle ever preached or practised by the Saviour Jesus; to lay bare vice in high places, and strip gilded crimes of their tinsel. Have you courage for this?"

I could only take the old man's hand, within my own, and murmur faintly, "I'll try!"

"Have you courage, to lift the cover from the Whited Sepulchre, and while the world is crying honor to its outward purity, to show the festering corruption that rankles in its depths? Then those records are yours!"

I sat beside the deathbed of the old man all night long. His last hours were past in calm converse, full of hope and trust in God. Near the break of day, he died. God bless him! He was my friend, when I had nothing but an orphan's gratitude, to tender in return for his friendship. He was a lawyer, and *honest;* a Christian and yet no bigot; a philosopher and yet no sceptic.

After his funeral, I received the pacquet of papers, inscribed with my name, and endorsed, REVELATIONS OF THE SECRET LIFE OF PHILADELPHIA, *being the records of thirty years practice as a councillor,* by * * * K——.

The present book is founded upon those portions of the Revelations, more intimately connected with the present day.

With the same sincerity with which I have written this Book of the Quaker City, I now give it to my countrymen, as an illustration of the life, mystery and crime of Philadelphia.

Book the First

The First Night

Mary, the Merchant's Daughter

Chapter First

The Wager in the Oyster-Cellar

"I say, gentlemen, shall we make a night of it? That's the question gents. Shall we elevate the—the devil along Chesnut street, or shall we subside quietly to our homes? Let's toss up for it—which shall have the night—brandy and oysters, or quilts and featherbeds?" And as he spoke, the little man broke loose from the grasp of his friends, and retiring to the shelter of an awning-post, flung his cloak over his shoulder with a vast deal of drunken dignity, while his vacant eyes were fixed upon the convivial group scattered along the pavement.

"Brandy"—cried a gentleman distinguished by a very pursy figure, enveloped in a snow-white overcoat, and a very round face, illuminated by a pear-shaped nose—"Brandy is a gentleman—a per—perfect gentleman. He leaves no head-ache next morning by way of a card. Champagne's a sucker—a hypocritical scoundrel, who first goes down your throat, smooth as oil, and then—a—a—very much so—how d——d irregular these bricks are—puts a powder-mill in your head and blows it up—dam 'im!— Mem:—Byrnewood—d'ye hear? write to the corporation to-morrow, about these curst mountainous pavements—" And having thus said, the pursy gentleman retreated to the shelter of another awning-post, leaving the two remaining members of the convival party, in full possession of the pavement, which they laid out in any given number of garden-plots without delay.

"Byrnewood—d'ye hear?" exclaimed the tallest gentleman of the twain, gathering his frogged overcoat closer around him, while his mustachioed lip was wreathed in a drunken smile—"Look yonder at the statehouse—sing—singular phenomenon! There's the original steeple and a duplicate. Two steeples, by Jupiter! Remarkable effect of moonlight! Very— Doesn't it strike you, Byrnewood, that yonder watch-box is walking across the street, to black the lamp-post's eyes—for—for—making a face at him?"

The gentleman thus addressed, instead of replying to the sagacious query of his friend, occupied a small portion of his leisure time in performing an irregular Spanish dance along the pavement, terminating in a pleasant combination of the cachuca, with a genuine New Jersey double-shuffle. This accomplished, he drew his well proportioned figure to its full height, cast back his cloak from his shoulders, and turned his face to the moonlit sky. As he gazed upon the heavens, clear, cold, and serene as death, the moonlight falling over his features, disclosed a handsome tho' pallid face, relieved by long curling locks of jet black hair. For a moment he seemed intensely absorbed amid the intricacies of a philosophical reverie, for he frequently put his thumb to his nose, and described circles in the air with his outspread fingers. At last tottering to a seat on a fireplug, he delivered himself of this remarkable expression of opinion—

"Miller[2] the Prophet's right! Right I say! The world—d——n the plug, how it shakes— the world is coming to an end for certain—for, d'ye see boys—there's *two* moons shining up yonder this blessed night sure as fate—"

The scene would have furnished a tolerable good subject for an effective convivial picture.

There, seated on the door-way step of a four storied dwelling, his arms crossed over his muscular chest, his right hand grasping a massive gold-headed cane, Mr. Gustavus Lorrimer, commonly styled the handsome Gus Lorrimer, in especial reference to his well-known favor among the ladies, presented to the full glare of the moonbeams, a fine manly countenance, marked by a brilliant dark eye, a nose slightly aquiline, a firm lip clothed with a mustache, while his hat tossed slightly to one side, disclosed a bold and prominent forehead, relieved by thick clusters of rich brown hair. His dark eye at all times full of fire, shone with a glance of unmistakeable humor, as he regarded his friend seated on the fire-plug directly opposite the doorway steps.

This friend—Mr. Byrnewood, as he had been introduced to Lorrimer—was engaged in performing an extemporaneous musical entertainment on the top of the fire-plug with his fingers, while his legs were entwined around it, as though the gentleman was urging a first-rate courser at the top of his speed.

His cloak thrown back from his shoulders, his slight though well-proportioned and muscular form, was revealed to the eye, enveloped in a closely fitting black frock-coat. His face

---

2 William Miller (1782–1849) founded an American religious movement known as Millerism. Miller prophesied that Christ would return in 1843 (later adjusted to October 22, 1844). At one point, Miller estimated that between fifty and one hundred thousand Americans believed in his views.

was very pale, and his long hair, which swept in thick ringlets to his shoulders, was dark as a raven's wing, yet his forehead was high and massive, his features regular, and his jet-black eye, bright as a flame-coal. His lips, now wreathing in the very silly smile peculiar to all worshippers of the bottle-god, were, it is true, somewhat slight and thin, and when in repose inclining to severity in expression; yet the general effect of his countenance was highly interesting, and his figure manly and graceful in its outlines, although not so tall by half-a-head as the magnificent Gus Lorrimer.

While he is beating a tattoo on the fire-plug, let us not forget our other friends, Col. Mutchins, in his snow-white overcoat and shiny hat; and Mr. Sylvester J. Petriken, in his glazed cap and long cloak, as leaning against opposite awning posts, they gaze in each others faces and afford a beautiful contrast for the pencil of our friend Darley.

Col. Mutchins' face, you will observe, is very much like a picture of a dissipated full-moon, with a large red pear stuck in the centre for a nose, while two small black beads, placed in corresponding circles of crimson tape, supply the place of eyes. The Colonel's figure is short, thick-set, and corpulent; he is very broad across the shoulders, broader across the waist, and very well developed in the region of the hands and boots. The gentleman, clinging nervously to the opposite awning post, is remarkable for three things—smallness of stature, slightness of figure, and slimness of legs. His head is very large, his face remarkable for its pallor, is long and square—looking as though it had been laid out with a rule and compass—with a straight formal nose, placed some distance above a wide mouth marked by two parallel lines, in the way of lips. His protuberant brow, faintly relieved by irregular locks of mole-skin colored hair, surmounted by a high glazed cap, overarches two large, oyster-like eyes, that roll about in their orbits with the regularity of machinery. These eyes remind you of nothing more, than those glassy things which, in obedience to a wire, give animation to the expressive face of a Dresden wax-doll.

And over this scene of quadruple convivialism, shone the midnight moon, her full glory beaming from a serene winter sky, upon the roofs and steeples of the Quaker City. The long shadows of the houses on the opposite side of the way, fell darkly along the street, while in the distance, terminating the dim perspective, arose the State-House buildings, with the steeple shooting upward into the clear blue sky.

"That champagne—" hiccuped Mr. Petriken, clinging to the awning-post, under a painful impression that it was endeavoring to throw him down—"That champagne was very strong—and the oysters—Oh my—"

"As mortal beings we are subject to sud—sudden sickness—" observed the sententious Mutchins, gathering his awning-post in a fonder embrace.

"I say, Byrnewood—how shall we terminate the night? Did I understand you that the d—l was to be raised? If so, let's start. Think how many bells are to be pulled, how many watch-boxes to be attacked, how many—curse the thing, I believe I'm toddied—watchmen to be licked. Come on boys?"

"Hist! Gus! You'll scare the fire-plug. He's trying to run off with me—the scoundrel. Wait till I put the spurs to him, I say!"

"Come on boys. Let's go round to Smokey Chiffin's oyster cellar and have a cozy supper. Come on I say. Take my arm, Byrnewood—there, steady—here Petriken, never mind the awning-post, take this other arm—now Mutchins hook Silly's arm and let's travel—"

But Mutchins—who, by the way, had been out in a buffaloe hunt the year before—was now engaged in an imaginary, though desperate fight with a Sioux warrior, whom he belabored with terrific shrieks and yells.

"D——n the fool—he'll have us all in the watch house—" exclaimed Lorrimer, who appeared to be the soberest of the party by several bottles—"Fun is fun, but this thing of cutting up shines in Chesnut street, after twelve, when it—keep steady Silly—amounts to yelling like a devil in harness is—un-un-der-stand me, no fun. Come along, Mutchy my boy!"

And arm in arm, linked four abreast, like horses very tastelessly matched, the boon companions tottered along Chesnut street, toward Smokey Chiffin's oyster cellar, where they arrived, with but a single interruption.

"Hao-pao-twel-o-glor-a-a-damuley-mor!"

This mysterious combination of sounds emanated from a stout gentleman in a slouching hat, and four or five overcoats, who, with a small piece of cord-wood in his hand met our party breast to breast, as they were speeding onward in full career.

"I say stranger—do that over again—will yo'?" shrieked Petriken, turning his square face over his shoulder and gazing at the retreating figure with the cord-stick and the overcoats—"Jist do that again if you please. Let me go I tell you. Gus. Don't you see, this is some—dis-distinguished vocal-ist from London? What a pathos there is in his voice-—so deep—so full—why Brough is nothing to him! Knock Wood, and Seg- Seguin—and Shrival—and a dozen more into a musical cocked-hat, and they can't equal our mys-mysterious friend—"

"I say you'd better tortle on my coveys—" cried he of the great coats and cord stick, in a subterranean voice—"Or p'r'aps, my fellers, ye'd like to tend Mayor Scott's tea-party—would ye?"

"Thank you kindly—" exclaimed Gus Lorrimer in an insinuating tone, "otherwise engaged. But my friend—if you will allow me to ask—what *do* you mean by that infernal noise you produced just now? Let us into the lark?"

The gentleman of the cord stick and overcoats, was however beyond hearing by this time, and our friends moved on their way. Byrnewood observing in an under tone, somewhat roughened by hiccups, that on his soul, he believed that queer old cove, in the slouched hat, meant by his mysterious noise to impart the important truth that *it was half-past twelve o'clock and a moonlight morning.*

Descending into Smokey Chiffin's subterranean retreat, our friends were waited upon by a very small man, with a sharp face and a white apron, and a figure so lank and slender, that the idea involuntarily arose to the spectators mind, of whole days and nights of severe training, having been bestowed upon a human frame, in order to reduce it to a degree of thinness quite visionary.

"Come my 'Virginia abstraction'—" exclaimed Lorrimer—"Show us into a private room, and tell us what you've got for supper—"

"This way sir—this way gents—" cried Smokey Chiffin, as the thin gentleman was rather familiarly styled—"What got for supper? Woodcock sir? excellent sir. Venison sir; excellent sir. Oysters sir, stewed, sir, fried sir, roasted sir, or in the shell sir. Excellent sir. Some right fresh, fed on corn-meal sir. What have sir? Excellent sir. This way gents—"

And as he thus delivered his bill of fare, the host, attended by his customers, disappeared from the refectory proper, through an obscure door into the private room.

There may be some of our readers who have never been within the confines of one of those oyster-caverns which abound in the Quaker City. For their especial benefit, we will endeavor to pencil forth a few of the most prominent characteristics of the "Oyster Saloon by Mr. Samuel Chiffin."

Lighted by flaring gas-pipes, it was divided into two sections by a blazing hot coal stove. The section beyond the stove, wrapt in comparative obscurity, was occupied by two opposing rows of 'boxes,' looking very much like conventual stalls, ranged side by side, for the accommodation of the brothers of some old-time monastery. The other section, all light, and glitter, and show, was ornamented at its extreme end, by a tremendous mirror, in which a toper might look, time after time, in order to note the various degrees of drunkenness through which he passed. An oyster-box, embellished by a glorious display of tin signs with gilt letters, holding out inviting manifestations of "oysters stewed fried or in the shell," occupied one entire side of this section, gazing directly in the face of the liquor bar placed opposite, garnished with an imposing array of decanters, paint gilding and glasses.

And the company gathered here? Not very select you may be sure. Four or five gentlemen with seedy coats and efflorescent noses were warming themselves around the stove, and discussing the leading questions of the day; two individuals whose visits to the bar had been rather frequent, were kneeling in one corner, swearing at a very ragged dog, whom they could'nt persuade to try a glass of 'Imperial Elevator,' and seated astride of a chair, silent and alone, a young man whose rakish look and ruffled attire betrayed the medical student on his first 'spree' was endeavouring to hold himself steady, and look uncommonly sober; which endeavour always produces, as every body knows, the most ridiculous phase of drunkenness.

These Oyster Cellers are queer things. Like the caverns of old story, in which the Giants,[3] those ante-diluvian rowdies, used to sit all day long, and use the most disreputable arts to inveigle lonely travellers into their clutches, so these modern dens, are occupied by a jolly old Giant of a decanter, who too often lures the unsuspecting into his embrace. A strange tale might be told, could the stairway leading down into the Oyster Celler be gifted with the power of speech. Here Youth has gone down laughing merrily and here Youth has come up, his ruddy cheek wrinkled and his voice quavering with premature age. Here Wealth has gone down, and kept going down until at last he came up with his empty pocket, turned inside out, and the gripe of grim starvation on his shoulder. Here Hope, so young, so gay, so light-hearted has gone down, and came up transformed into a very devil with sunken cheeks, bleared eyes, and a cankered heart. Oh merry cavern of the Oyster Celler, nestling under the ground so close to Independence Hall, how great the wonders, how mighty the doings, how surprising the changes accomplished in your pleasant den, by your jolly old Giant of a Decanter!

It is here in this Oyster Celler, that we open the fearful tragedy which it is the painful object of our narrative, to tell. Here amid paint, and glitter and gilding, amid the clink of glasses and the roar of drinking songs, occurred a scene, which trifling and insipid as it may appear to the casual observer, was but the initial letter to a long and dreary alphabet of crime, mystery and bloodshed.

In a room, small and comfortable, lighted by gas and warmed by a cheerful coal-fire, around a table furnished with various luxuries, and garnished with an array of long necked bottles, we find our friends of the convivial party. Their revel had swelled to the highest, glass clinked against glass, bottle after bottle had been exhausted, voices began to mingle

---

3 In Greek mythology, the Giants lost a titanic struggle with the Olympians. After most of them were slain, they were buried or retreated under mountains, where they still cause problems by doing such things as luring people into caves or causing volcanic explosions.

together, the drinking song and the prurient story began to pass from lip to lip, while our sedate friend, Smokey Chiffin, sate silently on the sofa, regarding the drunken bout with a glance of quiet satisfaction.

"Let me see—let me see"—he murmured quietly to himself—"Four bottles o'Cham. at two dollars a bottle—four times two is eight. Hum—hum. They'll drink six more. Let's call it twelve altogether. Say twenty-four shiners for supper and all. Hum—hum—Gus pays for all. That fellow Petriken's a sponge. Wonder when Col. Mutchins will call for the cards? Don't know who this fellow Byrnewood is? New face—may be he's a *roper*[4] too? We'll see—we'll see."

"Give us your hand, Gus"—cried Byrnewood, rising from his seat and flinging his hand unsteadily across the table—"Damme, I like you old fellow. Never—never—knew until to-night—met you at Mutchin's room—wish I'd known you all my life—Give us your hand, my boy!"

Calm and magnificent, Gustavus extended his hand, and exclaimed, in a voice, which champagne could not deprive of its sweetness, that it gave him pleasure to know such a regular bird as Mister Byrnewood; great pleasure; extraordinary pleasure.

"You see, fellows, I believe I'll take a spree for three days—wont go home, or to the store in Front street. Mean to keep it up until after Christmas. Wants three days o'Christmas—mean to jolly—ha—ha—how the room reels."

"Gentle-men—I don't know what is the matter with me—" observed Petriken, who rested his elbows helplessly on the table, as he looked around with his square face, length-ened into a vacant stare—"There's somethin' queer a-goin' on with my eyes. I seem to see spiders—lots o' 'em—playin' corner-ball with roaches. See anything o' the kind, Mutchins?"

"Why—why—" replied that sentential gentleman as his red round face was over-spread by a commiserating smile—"Why the fact is—Silly—you've been drinkin'. By the bye does'nt it strike you that there's something queer going on with that gas light. I say, Smokey, is'nt there a beetle tryin' to mash his brains out against that gas-pipe?"

"Gentlemen—I will give you a toast!" exclaimed Lorrimer, as he stood erect, the bold outline of his manly form, his handsome face, the high forehead relieved by thick masses of brown hair, the aquiline nose, the rounded chin, and the curving lip darkened by a mustache, all shown to advantage in the glowing light—"Gentlemen fill your glasses—no heeltaps! WOMAN!"

"WOMAN!" shrieked the other three, springing unsteadily to their feet, and raising their glasses on high—"WOMAN! Three times three—hip-hip-hurrah!"

"Women!" muttered Sylvester Petriken—"Women for ever! when we're babies she nusses us, when we're boys she lathers us, when we're men she bedevils and bewitches us!"

"Woman—" muttered Colonel Mutchins—"without her what 'ud life be? A dickey without a 'plete,' a collar without starch!"

"We can't help it if we fascinate 'em?" exclaimed Byrnewood—"Can we Gus?"

"All fate, my boy—all fate. By the bye—set down boys. I've got a nice little adventure of my own to tell. Smokey—bring us some soda to sober off with—"

---

4 [Author's Original Note] This genteel term is applied to a well-dressed edition of the vulgar stool-pigeon, used by gamblers to decoy the unwary into their dens. The stool-pigeon is the loafer decoy, the roper is very aristocratic, prevails in the large hotel and is called a—gentleman.

Gentlemen—" cried Petriken, sinking heavily in his chair—"Did any of you see the last number of my magazine? 'The Ladies' Western Hemisphere and Continental Organ.' Offers the following inducements to sub—subscribers—one fashion-plate and two steel engravings per number—48 pages, octavo—Sylvester J. Petriken, Editor and Proprietor, office 209 Drayman's alley, up stairs. Damme, Mutchins, what's your idea of fleas?"

There was not, it is true, the most visible connexion between the Ladies Continental Organ and the peculiar insect, so troublesome to young puppies and very small kittens, yet as Mr. Petriken was not exactly sober, and Col. Mutchins very far from the temperance pledge, the idea seemed to tickle them both immensely and they joined in a hearty laugh, which terminated in another glass from a fresh bottle of champagne.

"Let's have your story, Gus!" shouted Byrnewood—"Let's have your story! Damme—life's but a porcelain cup—to-day we have it, tomorrow we hav'nt—why not fill it with sweetness?"

As he said this, in tones indistinct with liquor he flung his long curling hair back from his brow, and tossed his glass unsteadily on high.

Life a porcelain cup, why not fill it with sweetness? Great God of Mercy! Could the terrible future, which was to break, in a few brief hours, with all its horrors, on the head of this young man, who now sat unconsciously at the drinking board, have at that moment assumed a tangible form, it would have stood like an incarnate devil at his shoulder, its outstretched hand, pouring the very gall of despair into the cup of his life, crowding it to the brim with the wormwood of death.

"Well boys for my story. It's a story of a sweet girl, my boys—a sweet girl about sixteen, with a large blue eye, a cheek like a ripe peach, and a lip like a rose-bud cleft in two—"

"Honor bright Gus. Damme, that's a quotation from my last Ladies' Western Hem. Damme Gus—"

"Byrnewood do hold poor Silly down. There's this material difference, boys, between a ripe peach or a cleft rose-bud, and a dear little woman's lips or cheek. A ripe peach won't throb and grow warm if you lay your cheek against it, and I never yet heard of a rose-bud that kissed back again. She's as lovely a girl as ever trod the streets of the Quaker City. Noble bust—slender waist—small feet and delicate hands. Her hair? damme, Byrnewood, you'd give your eyes for the privilege of twining your hands through the rich locks of her dark brown hair—"

"Well, well, go on. Who is this girl; uncover the mystery!"

"Patience, my boy, patience. A little of that soda if you please. Now, gentlemen, I want you to listen attentively, for let me tell you, you don't hear a story like mine every day in the year."

Half sobered by the combined influences of the soda water and the interest of Lorrimer's story, Byrnewood leaned forward, fixing his full dark eyes intently upon the face of Gus, who was seated opposite; while Col. Mutchins straightened himself in his chair, and even Petriken's vacant face glowed with a momentary aspect of sobriety.

"I see, boys, that you expect something nice. (Smokey put some more coal on the fire.) Well Byrnewood, you must know I'm a devil of a fellow among the girls—and—and—d——n the thing, I don't know how to get at it. Well, here goes. About two weeks ago I was strolling along Chesnut street towards evening, with Boney (that's my big wolf dog, you know?) at my heels. I was just wondering where I should spend the evening; whether

I should go to see Forrest at the Walnut,[5] or take a turn round town; when who should I see walking ahead of me, but one of the prettiest figures in the world, in a black silk mantilla, with one of these saucy kiss-me-if-you-dare bonnets on her head. The walk of the creature, and a little glimpse of her ankle excited my curiosity, and I pushed ahead to get a view of her face. By Jupiter, you never saw such a face! so soft, so melting, and—damme—so innocent. She looked positively bewitching in that saucy bonnet, with her hair parted over her forehead, and resting each cheek in a mass of the richest curls, that ever hung from the brow of mortal woman—"

"Well, Gus, we'll imagine all this. She was beautiful as a houri,[6] and priceless as the philosopher's stone[7] —"

"Byrnewood you are too impatient. A pretty woman in a black silk mantilla, with a lovely face peeping from a provoking bonnet, may seem nothing to you, but the strangest part of the adventure is yet to come. As I looked in the face of this lovely girl, she, to my utter astonishment addressed me in the softest voice in the world, and—"

"Called you by name?"

"No. Not precisely. It seems she mistook me for some gentleman whom she had seen at a country boarding-school. I took advantage of her mistake, walked by her side for some squares along Chesnut street, and—"

"Became thoroughly acquainted with her, I suppose?" suggested Byrnewood.

"Well, you may judge so, when I mention one trifling fact for your consideration. This night, at three o'clock, this innocent girl, the flower of one of the first families in the city, forsaking home and friends, and all that these sweet girls are wont to hold dear, will seek repose in my arms—"

"She can't be *much*—" exclaimed Byrnewood, over whose face a look of scornful incredulity had been gathering for some few moments past—"Pass that champagne, Petriken my boy. Gus, I don't mean to offend you, but I rather think you've been hum-bugged by some 'slewer?' "[8]

A frown darkened over Lorrimer's brow, and even as he sate, you might see his chest heave and his form dilate.

"Do you mean to doubt my word—*Sir?*"

"Not at all, not at all. But you must confess, the thing looks rather improbable. (Will you smoke, Col.?) May I ask whether there was any one in company with the lady when first you met her?"

"A Miss something or other—I forget her name. A very passable beauty of twenty and upwards, and I may add, a very convenient one, for she carried my letters, and otherwise favored my cause with the sweet girl."

"And this 'sweet girl' is the flower of one of the first families in the city?" asked Byrnewood with a half formed sneer on his upper lip.

"She is—" answered Lorrimer, lighting a cigar.

---

5 Edwin Forrest (1806–1872) was one of the nineteenth-century's most famous and controversial actors. He often performed at the Walnut Street Theatre in Philadelphia.

6 In Muslim belief, a houri is one of the beautiful maidens who live in paradise with the blessed.

7 Stone capable of turning base metals into gold.

8 [Author's Original Note] A cant term used by profligates for female servants of indifferent character.

"And this girl, to-night, leaves home and friends for you, and three hours hence will repose in your arms?"

"She will—" and Lorrimer vacantly eyed a column of smoke winding upward to the ceiling.

"You will not marry her?"

"Ha-ha-ha! You're ahead of me now. Only a pretended marriage, my boy. As for this 'life interest' in a woman, it don't suite my taste. A nice little sham marriage, my boy, is better than ten real ones—"

"You would be a d——d fool to marry a woman who flung herself in your power in this manner. How do you know she is respectable? Did you ever visit her at her father's house? What is her name? Do enlighten us a little—"

"You're 'cute, my boy, mighty 'cute, as the Yankees says, but not so 'cute as you think. Her name? D'ye think I'm so particularly verdant as to tell it? I know her name, could tell you the figure of her father's wealth, but have never been inside of the threshold of her home. Secret meetings, secret walks and even an assumed name, are oftentimes wonderfully convenient."

"Gus, here is a hundred dollar bill on the Bank of North America. I am, as you see, somewhat interested in your story. I will stake this hundred dollars that the girl who seeks your arms to-night, is not respectable, is not connected with one of the first families in the city, and more than all has never been any better than a common lady of the sidewalk—"

"Book that bet, Mutchins. You heard it, Silly. And now, Byrnewood, here is another hundred, which I will deposit with yours in Mutchins' hands until the bet is decided. Come with me and I'll prove to you that you've lost. You shall witness the wedding—ha, ha—and to your own sense of honor will I confide the secret of the lady's name and position—"

"The bet is booked and the money is safe"—murmured the sententious Mutchins, enclosing the notes in the leaves of his pocket-book—"I've heard of many rum go's but *this is* the rummest go of all."

"If I may be allowed to use the expression, this question involves a mystery. A decided mystery. For instance, what's the lady's name? There is a point from which Hypothesis may derive some labor. 'What's in a name'—as Shakespeare says. I say, gents, let's pick out a dozen names, and toss up which shall have it?"

This rather profound remark of Mr. Petriken's was received with unanimous neglect.

It was observable that during this conversation, both Lorrimer and Byrnewood had been gradually recovering from the effects of their debauch. Lorrimer seemed somewhat offended at the distrust manifested by Byrnewood; who, in his turn, appeared to believe the adventure just related with very many doubts and modifications.

Lorrimer leaned over the table and whispered in Sylvester's ear.

"Damme—damme my fellow"—murmured Sylvester, apparently in reply to the whispered remark of his friend—"It cannot be done. Why man it's a penitentiary offence."

Lorrimer again hissed a meaning whisper in the ear of the little man.

"Well, well, as it is your wish I'll do it. A cool fifty, did you say? You think a devlish sight of the girl—do you then? I must provide myself with a gown and prayer book? I flatter myself I'll rather become them—three o'clock, did you say?"

"Aye—aye—" answered Lorrimer, turning to the rubicund face of Col. Mutchins and whispering hurriedly in his ear.

A pleasant smile overspread the face of the benevolent man, and his pear-shaped nose seemed to grow expressive for a single moment.

"D——d good idea? I'll be your too-confiding uncle? Eh? Stern but relenting? I'll bless the union with my benediction—*I'll give the bride away?*"

"Come along Byrnewood. Here Smokey is the money for our supper. Mark you gentlemen, Mr. Petriken and Col. Mutchins—the hour is three o'clock. Don't fail me, if the d——l himself stands in the way. Take my arm Byrnewood and let's travel—"

"Then 'hey for the wedding.' Daylight will tell who wins!"

And as they left the room arm in arm, bound on the adventure so suddenly undertaken, and so full of interest and romance, Petriken looked vacantly in Mutchins' face, and Mutchins returned the look with a steady gaze that seemed to say—"How much did he give you, old boy?"

Whether Sylvester translated the look in this manner, it is difficult to tell, but certain it is, that as he poured a bumper from a fresh bottle of champagne, he motioned the Colonel to do the same, and murmured in an absent manner, or perhaps by way of a sentiment, the remarkable words—

"Fifty dollars! Egad that 'ill buy two steel engravings and three fashion plates for the next number of the Ladies' Western Hemisphere. 'Economy is wealth,' and the best way to learn to fly is to creep—creep very low, remarkably low, d——d low—*always creep!*"

Chapter Second

Mary, the Merchant's Daughter

Leaning gently forward, her shawl falling carelessly from her shoulders, and her bonnet thrown back from her brow, the fair girl impressed a kiss on the cheek of her father, while the glossy ringlets of her hair mingled their luxuriant brown with the white locks of the kind old man.

The father seated on the sofa, his hands clasping her slight and delicate fingers, looked up into her beaming face with a look of unspeakable affection, while a warm glow of feeling flushed over the pale face of the mother, a fine matronly dame of some forty-five, who stood gazing on her daughter, with one hand resting on the husband's shoulder.

The mild beams of an astral lamp diffused a softened and pleasing light through the Parlor. The large mirror glittering over the mantle, the curtains of crimson silk depending along the windows, the sofa on which the old man was seated, the carpet of the finest texture, the costly chairs, the paintings that hung along the walls, and in fine all the appointments of the parlor, designated the abode of luxury and affluence.

The father, who sate on the sofa gazing in the face of his child, was a man of some sixty years, with a fine venerable countenance, wrinkled by care and time, with thin locks of snow-white hair falling along his high pale forehead. In his calm blue eye, looking forth from the shadow of a thick grey eyebrow, and in the general contour of his face, you might trace as forcible a resemblance to his daughter, as ever was witnessed between an old man just passing away from life, and a fair young girl, blooming and blushing on the very threshold of womanhood. The old man was clad in glossy black, and his entire appearance, marked the respectable merchant, who, retiring from active business, sought in the quietude of his own home, all the joys, that life, wealth or affection united and linked in blessings, have in their power to bestow.

The mother, who stood resting her hand on her husband's shoulder, was, we have said, a fine matronly dame of forty-five. A mild pale face, a deep black eye, and masses of raven hair, slightly sprinkled with the silver threads of age, parted over a calm forehead, and tastefully disposed beneath a plain cap of lace, gave the mother an appearance of sweetness and dignity combined, that was eminently effective in winning the respect and love of all who looked upon her.

"Mary—my child—how lovely you have grown!" exclaimed the Merchant, in a deep quiet tone, as he pressed her fair hands within his own, and looked up in her face.

"Nonsense! You will make the child vain—" whispered the wife playfully, yet her face flushed with affection, and her eyes shone an answer to her husband's praise.

The girl was indeed beautiful.

As she stood there, in that quiet parlor, gazing in her father's face, she looked like a breathing picture of youth, girlhood and innocence, painted by the finger of God. Her face was very beautiful. The small bonnet thrown back from her forehead, suffered the rich curls of her brown hair to escape, and they fell twining and glossy along each swelling cheek, as though they loved to rest upon the velvet skin. The features were regular, her lips were full red and ripe, her round chin varied by a bewitching dimple, and her eyes were large, blue and eloquent, with long and trembling lashes. You looked in those eyes, and felt that all the sunlight of a woman's soul was shining on you. The face was lovely, most lovely, the skin, soft, velvety, blooming and transparent, the eyes full of soul, the lips sweet with the ripeness of maidenhood, and the brow calm and white as alabaster, yet was there no remarkable manifestation of thought, or mind, or intellect visible in the lines of that fair countenance. It was the face of a woman formed to lean, to cling, to love, and never to lean on but one arm, never to cling but to one bosom, never to love but once, and that till death and forever.

The fair round neck, and well-developed bust, shown to advantage in the close fitting dress of black silk, the slender waist, and the ripening proportions of her figure, terminated by slight ankles and delicate feet, all gave you the idea of a bud breaking into bloom, a blossom ripening into fruit, or what is higher and holier, a pure and happy soul manifesting itself to the world, through the rounded outlines of a woman's form.

"Come, come father, you must not detain me any longer—" exclaimed the daughter in a sweet and low-toned voice—"You know aunt Emily has been teasing me these two weeks, ever since I returned from boarding-school, to come and stay with her all night. You know I was always a favorite with the dear old soul. She wants to contrive some agreeable surprise for my birth-day, I believe. I'm sixteen next Christmas, and that is three days off. Do let me go, that's a good father—"

"Had'nt you better put on your cloak, my love?" interrupted the Mother, regarding the daughter with a look of fond affection—"The night is very cold, and you may suffer from exposure to the winter air—"

"Oh no, no, no mother—" replied the fair girl, laughingly—"I *do* so hate these cloaks—they're so bungling and so heavy! I'll just fling my shawl across my shoulders, and run all the way to Aunt Emily's. You know it's only two squares distant in Third Street—"

"And then old Lewey will see you safe to the door?" exclaimed the Mother—"Well, well, go along my dear child, take good care of yourself, and give my love to your Aunt—"

"These old maids are queer things"—said the Merchant with a smile—"Take care Mary or Aunt Emily will find out all your secrets—"

And the old man smiled pleasantly to himself, for the idea of a girl, so young, so innocent, having any secrets to be found out, was too amusing to be entertained without a smile.

A shade fell over the daughters face so sudden and melancholy that her parents started with surprise.

"Why do you look so sad, my child!" exclaimed the Father, looking up in his daughter's face. "What is there in the world to sadden *you*, my Mary?"

"Nothing, father, nothing—" murmured Mary, flinging her form on her father's bosom and twining her arms round his neck as she kissed him again and again—"Only I was thinking—just thinking of Christmas, and——"

The fair girl rose suddenly from her father's bosom, and flung her arms hurriedly around her mother's neck, imprinting kiss after kiss on her lips.

"Good bye mother—I'll be back—I'll be back—to-morrow."

And in an instant she glided hastily to the door and left the room.

"Lewey is'nt it very cold to night!" she asked as she observed the white-haired negro-servant waiting in the hall, wrapped up in an enormous overcoat, with a comforter around his neck and a close fur cap surmounting his grey wool and chubby round face—"I'm sorry to take you out in the cold, Lewey."

"Bress de baby's soul—" murmured the old negro opening the door—"Habbent I nuss you in dese arms when you warnt so high? Lewey take cold? Debbil a cold dis nigger take for no price when a-waitin' on missa Mary—"

Mary stood upon the threshold of her home looking out into the cold starlit night. Her face was for a moment overshadowed by an expression of the deepest melancholy, and her small foot trembled as it stepped over the threshold. She looked hurriedly along gloomy street, then cast her glance backwards into the entry, and then with a wild bound she retraced her steps, and stood beside her father and her mother.

Again she kissed them, again flung her arms round their necks, and again bounded along the entry crying laughingly to her parents—"Good night—good night—I'll be back to-morrow."

Again she stood upon the threshold, but all traces of laughter had vanished from her face. She was sad and silent, and there were tears in her eyes. At least the old negro said so afterwards, and also that her tiny foot, when resting on the door-sill, trembled like any leaf.

Why should her eye grow dim with tears and her foot tremble? Would not that tiny foot, when next it crossed the threshold, bound forward with a gladsome movement, as the bride sprung to meet her father and her mother once again? Would not that calm blue eye, now filled with tears, grow bright with a joy before unknown, when it glanced over the husband's form, as for the first time he stood in the father's presence? Would not Christmas Eve be a merry night for the bride and all her friends as they went shouting merrily through the luxuriantly furnished chambers of her father's mansion? Why should *she* fear to cross the threshold of her home, when her coming back was to be heralded with blessings and crowned with love?

How will the future answer these trembling questions of that stainless heart?

She crossed the threshold, and not daring to look back, hurried along the gloomy street. It was clear, cold, starlight, and the pathways were comparatively deserted. The keen winter wind nipped her cheek, and chilled her form, but above her, the stars seemed smiling her "onward," and she fancied the good angels, that ever watch over woman's first and world-trusting love, looking kindly upon her from the skies.

After traversing Third street for some two squares, she stood before an ancient three-storied dwelling, at the corner of Third and —— streets, with the name of 'Miss. E. Graham,' on the door plate.

"Lewey you need'nt wait—" she said kindly—yet not without a deeper motive than kindness—to the aged Negro who had attended her thus far—"I'll ring the bell myself. You had better hurry home and warm yourself—and remember, Lewey, tell father and mother that they need not expect me home before to-morrow at noon. Good night, Lewey."

"Good night, Missa Mary, Lor' Moses lub your soul—" muttered the honest old Negro, as, pulling his fur cap over his eyes, he strode homeward—"Dat ar babby's a angel, dat is widout de wings. De Lor grant when dis here ole nigger gets to yander firmey-ment—dat is if niggers gets dar at all—he may be 'pinted to one ob de benches near Missa Mary, so he can wait on her, handy as nuffin—dats all. She's a angel, and dis here night, is a leetle colder dan any night in de memory ob dat genel'man de Fine Col'ector nebber finds—de berry oldest inhabitant."

Thus murmuring, Lewey trudged on his way, leaving Mary standing in front of Aunt Emily's door. Did she pull the bell? I trow not, for no sooner was the negro out of sight, than the tall figure of a woman, dressed in black, with a long veil drooping over her face, glided round the corner and stood by her side.

"Oh—Bessie—is that you?" cried Mary, in a trembling voice—"I'm so frightened I don't know what to do—Oh Bessie—Bessie don't you think I had better turn back—"

"*He* waits for you—" said the strange woman, in a husky voice.

Mary hurriedly laid her hand on the stranger's arm. Her face was overspread with a sudden expression of feeling, like a gleam of sunshine, seen through a broken cloud on a stormy day, and in a moment, they were speeding down Third street toward the southern districts of the Quaker City. Another moment, and the eye might look for them in vain.

And as they disappeared the State House clock rung out the hour of nine. This, as the reader will perceive, was just four hours previous to the time when Byrnewood and Lorrimer closed their wager in the subterranean establishment along Chesnut street. To the wager and its result we now turn our attention and the reader's interest.

Chapter Third

Byrnewood and Lorrimer

The harsh sound of their footsteps, resounding along the frozen pavement, awoke the echoes of the State House buildings, as linked arm in arm, Byrnewood and Lorrimer hurried along Chesnut street, their figures thrown in lengthened shadow by the beams of the setting moon.

The tall, manly and muscular figure of Lorrimer, attired in a close-fitting black overcoat, presented a fine contrast to the slight yet well-proportioned form of Byrnewood, which now and then became visible as the wind flung his voluminous cloak back from his shoulders. The firm and measured stride of Lorrimer, the light and agile footsteps of Byrnewood, the glowing countenance of the magnificent Gus, the pale solemn face of the young Merchant, the rich brown hair which hung in clustering masses around the brow of the first, and the long dark hair which fell sweeping to the very shoulders of his companion, all furnished the details of a vivid contrast, worthy the effective portraiture of a master in our sister-art.

"Almost as cold as charity, Byrnewood my boy—" exclaimed Lorrimer, as he gathered Byrnewood's arm more closely within his own—"Do you know, my fellow, that I believe vastly in faces?"

"How so?"

"I can tell a man's character from his face, the moment I clap my eye on him. I like or dislike at first sight. Now there's Silly Petriken's face—how do you translate it?"

"The fact is, Lorrimer, I know very little about him. I was introduced to him, for the first time, at a party, where he was enrapturing some sentimental old maids, with a few quires of sonnets on every thing in general. Since that occasion I have never met him, until tonight, when he hailed me in Chesnut street, and forced me into Mutchin's room at the United States Hotel. You know the rest—"

"Well, well, with regard to Petriken, a single word. Clever fellow, clever, but like Mutchins, he sells for a reasonable price. I buy them both. By Jupiter! the town swarms with such fellows, who will sell themselves to any master for a trifle. Petriken—poor fellow—his face indicates his character—a solemn pimp, a sententious parasite. Mutchins is just the other way—an agreeable jolly old-dog of a pander. They hire themselves to me for the season—I use and, of course, despise them—"

"Your remarks are truly flattering to these worthy gentlemen!" said Byrnewood, drily.

"And now my fellow, you may think me insincere, but I tell you frankly, that the moment I first saw your face, I liked you, and resolved you should be my friend. For your sake I am about to do a thing which I would do for no living man, and possible no dead one—"

"And that is —" interrupted Byrnewood.

"Just listen my fellow. Did you ever hear any rumors of a queer old house down town, kept by a reputable old lady, and supported by the purses of goodly citizens, whose names you never hear without the addition of 'respectable,' 'celebrated,' or —ha—ha—'pious'— *most* 'pious?' A queer old house my good fellow, where, during the long hours of the winter nights, your husband, so kind and good, forgets his wife, your merchant his ledger, your lawyer his quibbles, your parson his prayers? A queer old house, my good fellow, where wine and women mingle their attractions, where at once you sip the honey from a red-lip, and a sparkling bubble from the champagne? Where luxuriantly-furnished chambers resound all night long with the rustling of cards, or the clink of glasses, or—it may be—the gentle ripple of voices, murmuring in a kiss? A queer old house, my dear fellow, in short, where the very devil is played under a cloak, and sin grows fat within the shelter of quiet rooms and impenetrable walls—"

"Ha—ha—Lorrimer you are eloquent! Faith, I've heard some rumors of such a queer old house, but always deemed them fabulous—"

"The old house is a fact, my boy, a fact. Within its walls this night I will wed my pretty bride, and within its walls, my fellow, despite the pains and penalties of our Club you shall enter—"

"I should like it of all things in the world. How is your club styled?"

"All in good time, my friend. Each member, you see, once a week, has the privilege of introducing a friend. The same friend must never enter the Club House twice. Now I have rather overstepped the rules of the Club in other respects—it will require all my tact to pass you in to-night. It shall be done, however—and mark me—you will obtain a few fresh ideas of the nature of the *secret life* of this good Quaker City—"

"Why Lorrimer—" exclaimed Byrnewood, as they approached the corner of Eighth and Chesnut—"You seem to have a pretty good idea of life in general—"

"Life?" echoed the magnificent Gus, in that tone of enthusiasm peculiar to the convivialist when recovering from the first excitement of the bottle—"Life? What is it? As brilliant and as brief as a champagne bubble! To day a jolly carouse in an oyster cellar, to-morrow a nice little picnic party in a grave-yard. One moment you gather the apple, the next it is ashes. Every thing fleeting and nothing stable, every thing shifting and changing, and nothing substantial! A bundle of hopes and fears, deceits and confidences, joys and miseries, strapped to a fellow's back like Pedlar's wares—"

"Huzza! Bravo—the *Reverend* Gus Lorrimer preaches. And what moral does your reverence deduce from all this!"

"One word, my fellow—Enjoy! Enjoy till the last nerve loses its delicacy of sense; enjoy till the last sinew is unstrung; enjoy till the eye flings out its last glance, till the voice cracks and the blood stagnates; *enjoy,* always *enjoy,* and at last—"

"Aye, aye—that terrible *at last*—"

"At last, when you can enjoy no longer, creep into a nice cozy house, some eight feet deep, by six long and two wide, wrap yourself up in a comfortable quilt of white, and tell the worms—those jolly gleaners of the scraps of the feast of life—that they may fall to and be d——d to 'em—"

"Ha—ha—Lorrimer! Who would have thought this of you?"

"Tell me, my fellow, what business do you follow?"

"Rather an abrupt question. However, I'm the junior partner in the importing house of Livingston, Harvey, & Co., along Front street—"

"And I—" replied Gustavus slowly and with deliberation—"And I am junior and senior partner in a snug little wholesale business of my own. The firm is Lorrimer, & Co.—the place of business is everywhere about town—and the business itself is enjoyment, nothing but enjoyment; wine and woman forever! And as for the capital—I've an unassuming sum of one hundred thousand dollars, am independent of all relations, and bid fair to live at least a score of years longer. Now my fellow, you know me—come, spice us up a few of your own secrets. Have you no interesting little *amour* for my private ear?"

"By Heaven, I'd forgotten all about it!" cried Byrnewood starting aside from his companion as they stood in the full glare of the gas-lamp at the corner of Eighth and Chesnut street—"I'd forgotten all about the letter!"

"The letter? What letter?"

"Why just before Petriken hailed me in Chesnut street this evening—or rather *last* evening—a letter was placed in my hands, which I neglected to read. I know the handwriting on the direction, however. It's from a dear little love of a girl, who, some six months ago, was a servant in my father's house. A sweet girl, Lorrimer—and—you know how these things work—she was lovely, innocent and too confiding, and I was but a—man—"

"And she a 'slewer.' Rather a low walk of business for *you,* my boy. However, let's read the letter by lamplight—"

"Here it is—'Dear Byrnewood—I would like very much to see you to-night. I am in great distress. Meet me at the corner of Fourth and Chesnut streets at nine o'clock or you will regret it to the day of your death. Oh for God's sake do meet me—Annie.' What a pretty hand she writes—Eh! Lorrimer! That 'for God's sake' is rather cramped—and—egad! there's the stain of a tear—"

"These things are quite customary. These letters and these tears. The dear little women can only use these arguments when they yield too much to our persuasions—"

"And yet—d——n the thing—how unfortunate for the girl my acquaintance has proved! She had to leave my father's house on account of—of—the *circumstance* becoming too apparent, and her parents are very poor. I should have liked to have seen her to-night. However, it will do in the morning. And now, Lorrimer, which way?"

"To the 'queer old house' down town. By the bye, there goes the State House—one o'clock, by Jupiter! We've two good hours yet to decide the wager. Let's spend half an hour in a visit to a certain friend of mine. Here, Byrnewood, let me instruct you in the mysteries of the 'lark'—"

And, leaning aside, the magnificent Gus whispered in the ear of his friend, with as great an appearance of mystery as the most profound secret might be supposed to demand.

"Do you take, my fellow?"

"Capital, capital—" replied Byrnewood, crushing the letter into his pocket—"We shall crowd this night with adventures—that's certain!"

The dawn of daylight—it is true—closed the accounts of a night somewhat crowded with incidents. Did these merry gentlemen who stood laughing so cheerily at the corner of Eighth and Chesnut streets, at the hour of one, their faces glowing in the light of the midnight moon, did they guess the nature of the incidents which five o'clock in the morning could disclose? God of Heaven—might no angel of mercy drop from the skies and warn them back in their career?

No warning came, no omen scared them back. Passing down Eighth street, they turned up Walnut, which they left at Thirteenth. Turning down Thirteenth they presently stood before a small old fashioned two storied building, with a green door and a bull window, that occupied nearly the entire width of the front, protruding in the light. A tin placed between the door and window, bore the inscription, "*. *****, ASTROLOGER."

"Wonder if the old cove's in bed—" exclaimed Lorrimer, and as he spoke the green door opened, as if in answer to his question, and the figure of a man, muffled up in the thick folds of a cloak with his hat drawn over his eyes, glided out of the Astrologer's house, and hurried down Thirteenth street.

"Ha—ha—devilish cunning, but not so cunning as he thinks!" laughed Byrnewood—"I saw his face—it's old Grab-and-Snatch, the President of the —— Bank, which every body says is on the eve of a grand blow-up!"

"The respectable old gentleman has been consulting the stars with regard to the prospects of his bank—ha—ha! However, my boy, the door is open—let's enter! Let's consult this familiar of the fates, this intimate acquaintance of the Future!"

Chapter Fourth

The Astrologer

In a small room, remarkable for the air of comfort imparted by the combined effects of the neatly white-washed walls, the floor, plainly carpeted, and the snug little wood-stove roaring in front of the hearth, sat a man of some forty-five winters, bending over the table in the corner, covered with strange-looking books and loose manuscripts.

The light of the iron lamp which stood in the centre of the table, resting on a copy of Cornelius Agrippa, fell full and strongly over the face and form of the Astrologer, disclosing every line of his countenance, and illumining the corner where he sat, while the more distant parts of the room were comparatively dim and shadowy.

As he sat in the large old-fashioned arm-chair, bending down earnestly over a massive manuscript, covered with strange characters and crossed by intricate lines, the lamp-beams disclosed a face, which somewhat plain and unmeaning in repose, was now agitated by an expression of the deepest interest. The brow, neither very high nor very low, shaded by tangled locks of thin brown hair, was corrugated with deep furrows, the eyebrows were firmly set together, the nostrils dilated, and the lips tightly compressed, while the full grey eyes, staring vacantly on the manuscript, indicated by the glassy film spread over each pupil, that the mind of the Astrologer, instead of being occupied with outward objects, was buried within itself, in the contemplation of some intricate subject of thought.

There was nothing in the dress of the man, or in the appearance of his room, that might realize the ideas commonly attached to the Astrologer and his den. Here were no melo-dramatic curtains swinging solemnly to and fro, brilliant and terrible with the emblazoned death's-head and cross-bones. Here were no blue lights imparting a lurid radiance to a row of grinning skeletons, here were no ghostly forms standing pale and erect, their glassy eyes freezing the spectator's blood with horror, here was neither goblin, devil, or mischievous ape, which, as every romance reader knows, have been the companions of the Astrologer from time immemorial; here was nothing but a plain man, seated in an old-fashioned arm chair, within the walls of a comfortable room, warmed by a roaring little stove.

No cap of sable relieved the Astrologer's brow, no gown of black velvet, tricked out with mysterious emblems in gold and precious stones, fell in sweeping folds around the outlines of his spare figure. A plain white overcoat, much worn and out at the elbows, a striped vest not remarkable for its shape or fashion, a cross-barred neckerchief, and a simple linen shirt collar completed the attire of the astrologer who sat reading at the table.

The walls of the room were hung with the Horoscopes of illustrious men, Washington, Byron, and Napoleon, delineated on large sheets of paper, and surrounded by plain frames of black wood; the table was piled with the works of Sibly, Lilly, Cornelius Agrippa and other masters in the mystic art; while at the feet of the Astrologer nestled a fine black cat, whose large whiskers and glossy fur, would seem to afford no arguments in favor of the supposition entertained by the neighbors, that she was a devil in disguise, a sort of familiar spirit on leave of absence from the infernal regions.

"I'm but a poor man—" said the Astrologer, turning one of the leaves of the massive volume in manuscript which he held in his hand—"I'm but a poor man, and the lawyer, and the doctor, and the parson all despise me, and yet—" his lip wreathed with a sneer-ing smile—"this little room has seen them all within its walls, begging from the humble man some knowledge of the future! Here they come—one and all—the fools, pretend-ing to despise my science, and yet willing to place themselves in my power, while they affect to doubt. Ha-ha—here are their Nativities one and all—That" he continued, turning over a leaf—"is the Horoscope of a clergyman—Holy man of God!—He wanted to know whether he could ruin an innocent girl in his congregation without discovery. And that is the Horoscope of a lawyer, who takes fees from both sides. His desire is to know, whether he can perjure himself in a case now in court without detection. Noble counsellor! This Doctor—" and he turned over another leaf—"told me that he had a delicate case in hand. A pretty girl had been ruined and so on—the seducer wants to destroy the fruit of his crime and desires the doctor to undertake the job. Doctor wants to know what moment will be auspicious—ha-ha!"

And thus turning from page to page, he disclosed the remarkable fact, that the great, the good, and the wise of the Quaker City, who met the mere name of astrology, when uttered in public, with a most withering sneer, still under the cover of night, were happy to steal to the astrologer's room, and obtain some glimpses of their future destiny through the oracle of the stars.

"A black-eyed woman—lusty and amorous—wants to know whether she can present her husband with a pair of horns on a certain night? I warned her not to proceed in her course of guilt. She does proceed—and will be exposed to her husband's hate and public scorn—" And thus murmuring, the Astrologer turned to another leaf.

"The Horoscope of a puppy-faced editor! A spaniel, a snake, and an ape—he is a combination of the three. Wants to know when he can run off with a lady of the *ballet* at the theatre, without being caught by his creditors? Also, whether next Thursday is an auspicious day for a little piece of roguery he has in view? The penitentiary looms darkly in the distance—let the editor of the 'DAILY BLACK MAIL' beware—"

Another leaf inscribed with a distinguished name, arrested the Astrologer's attention. "Ha—ha! This fellow is a man of fashion, a buck of Chesnut street, and—and a Colonel! He lives—*I* know *how*—the fashionables who follow in his wake don't *dream* of his means of livelihood. He has committed a crime—an astounding crime—wants to know whether his associate will betray him! I told him *he* would. The Colonel laughed at me, although he paid for the knowledge. In a week the fine, sweet, perfumed gentle man will be lodged at public expense—"

The Astrologer laid down the volume, and in a moment seemed to have fallen into the same train of thought, marked by the corrugated brow and glassy eye, that occupied his mind at the commencement of this scene. His lips moved tremulously, and his hands ever and anon were pressed against his wrinkled brow. Every moment his eye grew more glassy, and his mouth more fixedly compressed, and at last, leaning his elbows on the table with his hands nervously clasped, his gaze was fixed on the blank wall opposite, in a wild and vacant stare that betrayed the painful abstraction of his mind from all visible objects.

And as he sat there enwrapt in thought, a footstep, inaudible to his ear, creaked on the stairway that ascended into the Astrologer's chamber from the room below, and in a moment, silent and unperceived, Gus Lorrimer stood behind his chair, looking over his head, his very breath hushed and his hands upraised.

"In all my history I remember nothing half so strange. All is full of light except one point of the future, and that is dark as death!" Thus ran the murmured soliloquy of the Astrologer—"And yet they will be here to-night—here—here both of them, or there's no truth in the stars. Lorrimer must beware—"

"Ha—ha—ha—" laughed a bold and manly voice—"An old stage trick, that. You didn't hear my footsteps on the stairs—did you? Oh no—oh no. Of course you didn't. Come—come, my old boy, that claptrap mention of my name, is rather too stale, even for a three-fipenny-bit melo-drama—"

The sudden start which the Astrologer gave, the unaffected look of surprise which flashed over his features at the sight of the gentleman of pleasure, convinced Lorrimer that he had done him rank injustice.

"Sit down, sir—I have much to say to you—" said the Astrologer, in a voice strikingly contrasted with his usual tone, it was so deep, so full and so calmly deliberate—"Last Thursday morning at this hour you gave me the day and hour of your birth. You wished me to cast your horoscope. You wished to know whether you would be successful in an enterprise which you mediated. Am I correct in this?"

"You are, my old humbug[9]—that is my *friend*—" replied Lorrimer, flinging himself into a seat.

"Humbug?" cried the other with a quiet sneer—"You may alter your opinion after awhile, my young friend. Since last Thursday morning I have given the most careful attention to your horoscope. It is one of the most startling that ever I beheld. You were born under one of the most favorable aspects of the heavens, born, it would seem, but to succeed in all your wishes; and yet your future fate is wrapt in some terrible mystery—"

"Like a kitten in a wet blanket, for instance?" said Lorrimer, in the vain endeavor, to shake off a strange feeling of awe, produced by the manner of the Astrologer.

---

9 An imposter, deceiver.

"This night I was occupied with your horoscope when a strange circumstance attracted my attention. Even while I was examining book after book, in the effort to see more clearly into your future, I discovered that you were making a new acquaintance at some festival, some wine-drinking or other affair of the kind. This new acquaintance is a man with a pale face, long dark hair and dark eyes. So the stars tell me. Your fate and the fate of this young man are linked together till death. So the heavens tell me, and the heavens never lie."

"Yes—yes—my friend, very good—" replied Gustavus with a smile—"Very good, my dear sir. Your conclusions are perfect—your prophetic gift without reproach. But you forget one slight circumstance:—I have made no new acquaintance to-night! I have been at no wine-drinking! I have seen no interesting young man with a pale face and long dark hair—"

"Then my science is a lie!" exclaimed the Astrologer, with a puzzled look—"The stars declare that this very night, you first came in contact with the man, whose fate henceforth is linked with your own. The future has a doom in store for one of ye. The stars do not tell me which shall feel the terror of the doom, but that it will be inflicted by one of ye upon the other, is certain—"

"Well, let us suppose, for the sake of argument, that I did meet this mysterious young man with long black hair. What follows?"

"Three days ago, a young man, whose appearance corresponds with the indication given by the stars of the new acquaintance you were to make this very night, came to me and desired me to cast his horoscope. The future of this young man, is as like yours as night is to-night. He too is threatened with a doom—either to be suffered or inflicted. This doom will lower over his head within three days. At the hour of sunset on next Saturday—Christmas Eve—a terrible calamity will overtake him. At the same hour, and in the same manner, a terrible calamity will blacken your life forever. The same doubt prevails in both cases—whether you will endure this calamity in your own person, or be the means of inflicting its horrors on some other man, doomed and fated by the stars—"

"What connection has this young man with the 'new acquaintance' which you say I have formed to-night?"

"I suspect that this young man and your new acquaintance are *one*. If so, I warn you, by your soul, beware of him—this stranger to you!"

"And why *beware of me?*" said a calm and quiet voice at the shoulder of the Astrologer.

As though a shell had burst in the centre of that quiet room, he started, he trembled, arose to his feet. Byrnewood, the young merchant, calm and silent, stood beside him.

"I warn ye." He shrieked in a tone of wild excitement, with his grey eyes dilating and flashing beneath the woven eyebrows—"I warn ye both—beware of each other! Let this meeting at my house be your last on earth, and ye are saved! Meet again, or pursue any adventure together, and ye are lost and lost forever! I tell ye, scornful men that ye are, that ask my science to aid you, and then mock its lessons, I tell ye, by the Living God who writes his will, in letters of fire on the wide scroll of the firmament, that in the hand of the dim Future is a Goblet steeped in the bitterness of death, and that goblet one or the other must drink, within three little days!"

And striding wildly along the room, while Byrnewood stood awed, and the even cheek of Lorrimer grew pale, he gave free impulse to one of those wild deliriums excitement peculiar to his long habits of abstraction and thought. The full truth, the terrible truth, seemed crowding on his brain, arrayed in various images of horror, and he shrieked forth his interpretation of the future, in wild and broken sentences.

"Young man, three days ago you sought to know the future. You had never spoken to the man who sits in yonder chair. I cast your horoscope—I found your destiny like the destiny of this man who affects to sneer at my science. My art availed me no further I could not identify you with the man who first met Lorrimer this night, amid revelry and wine. Now I can supply the broken chain. You and his new-formed acquaintance are one. And now the light of the stars breaks more plainly on me—*within three days, one of you will die by the other's hand*—"

Lorrimer slowly arose to his feet, as though the effort gave him pain. His cheek was pale, and beaded drops of sweat stood on his brow. His parted lips, his upraised hands and flashing eyes attested his interest in the astrologer's words. Meanwhile, starting suddenly aside, Byrnewood veiled his face in his hands, as his breast swelled and quivered with sudden emotion.

Stern and erect, in his plain white overcoat, untricked with gold or gems, stood the Astrologer, his tangled brown hair flung back from his brow, while, with his outstretched hand and flashing eye, he spoke forth the fierce images of his brain.

"Three days from this, as the sun goes down, on Christmas eve, one of you will die by the other's hand. As sure as there is a God in Heaven, his stars have spoken, and it will be so!"

"What will be the manner of *the death?*" exclaimed Lorrimer, in a low-tuned voice, as he endeavored to subdue the sudden agitation inspired by the Astrologer's words, while Byrnewood raised his head and awaited the answer with evident interest.

"There is the cloud and the mystery—" exclaimed the Astrologer, fixing his eye on vacancy, while his outstretched hand trembled like a leaf in the wind—"The death will overtake the doomed man on a river, and yet it will not be by water; it will kill him by means of fire and yet he will not perish in the midst of flames—"

There was a dead pause for a single instant. There stood the Astrologer, his features working as with a convulsive spasm, the light falling boldly over his slight figure and homely attire, and there at his side, gazing in his face, stood Byrnewood, the young merchant, silent as if a spell had fallen on him, while on the other side, Gustavus Lorrimer, half recoiling, his brow woven in a frown, and his dark eyes flashing with a strange glance, seemed making a fearful effect to command his emotion, and dispel the gloom which the weird prophecy had flung over his soul.

"Pah! What fools we are! To stand here listening to the ravings of a madman or a knave—" cried Byrnewood, with a forced laugh, as he shook off the spell that seemed to bind him—"What does he know of the future—more than we? Eh? Lorrimer? Perhaps, sir, since you are so familiar with fate, destiny and all that, you can tell us the nature of the adventure on which Lorrimer is bound to-night?"

The Astrologer turned and looked upon him. There was something so calmly scornful in his glance, that Byrnewood averted his eyes.

"The adventure is connected with the honor of an innocent woman—" said the Astrologer—"More than this I know not, save that a foul outrage will be done this very night. And—hark ye sir—either the heavens are false, or your future destiny hangs upon this adventure. Give up the adventure at once, go back in your course, part from one another, part this moment never to meet again, and you will be saved. Advance and you are lost!"

Lorrimer stood silent, thoughtful and pale as death. It becomes me not to look beyond the veil that hangs between the Visible and the Invisible, but it may be, that in the silent pause of thought which the libertine's face manifested, his soul received some indications of the future from the very throne of God. Men call these sudden shadows, presentiments; to the eyes of angels they may be, but messages of warning spoken to the soul, in the spirit-tongues of those awful beings whose habitation is beyond the threshold of time. What did Lorrimer behold that he stood so silent, so pale, so thoughtful? Did Christmas Eve, and the River, and the Death, come terrible and shadow-like to his soul?

"Pshaw! Lorrimer you are not frightened by the preachings of this fortune-teller?" cried Byrnewood with a laugh and a sneer—"You will not give up the girl? Ha—ha— scared by an owl! Ha—ha—What would Petriken say? Imagine the rich laugh of Mutchins—ha—ha—Gus Lorrimer scared by an owl!"

"Give up the girl?" cried Lorrimer, with a blasphemous oath, that profaned the name of the Saviour—"Give up the girl? Never! She shall repose in my arms before daylight! Heaven nor hell shall scare me back! There's your money Mister Fortune Teller—your croaking deserves the silver, the d——l knows! Come on Byrnewood—let us away."

"Wait till I pay the gentleman for our coffins—" laughed Byrnewood, flinging some silver on the table—"See that they're ready by Saturday night, old boy? D'ye mind? You are hand-in-glove with some respectable undertaker—no doubt—and can give him our measure. Good bye—old fellow—good bye! Now, Lorrimer, away—"

"Away, away to Monk-hall!"

And in a moment they had disappeared down the stairway, and were passing through the lower room toward the street.

"On Christmas Eve, at the hour of sunset—" shrieked the Astrologer, his features convulsed with anger, and his voice wild and piercing in its tones—"One of you will die by the other's hand! The winding sheet[10] is woven, and the coffin made—you are rushing madly on your doom!"

Chapter Fifth

Dora Livingstone

It was a nice cozy place, that old counting-house room, with its smoky walls, its cheerful coal-fire burning in the rusty grate, and its stained and blackened floor. A snug little room, illuminated by a gaslight, subdued to a shadowy and sleepy brilliancy, with the Merchant's Almanac and four or five old pictures scattered along the walls, an old oaken desk with immense legs, all carved and curled into a thousand shapes, standing in one corner, and a massive door, whose glass window opened a mysterious view into the regions of the warehouse, where casks of old cogniac lay, side by side, in lengthened rows, like jolly old fellows at a party, as they whisper quietly to one another on the leading questions of the day.

Seated in front of the coal fire, his legs elevated above his head, resting on the mantel-piece, a gentleman, of some twenty-five years, with his arms crossed and a pipe in his mouth, seemed engaged in an earnest endeavour to wrap himself up in a cloak of tobacco smoke, in order to prepare for a journey into the land of Nod, while the tumbler of punch standing on the small table at his elbow, showed that he was by no means opposed to that orthodox principle which recognizes the triple marriage of brandy, lemon and sugar as a

---

10 A sheet used to wrap a corpse before burial.

highly necessary addition to the creature comforts of the human being, in no way to be despised or neglected by thinking men.

You would not have called this gentleman well-proportioned, and yet his figure was long and slender, you could not have styled his dress eminently fashionable, and yet his frock coat was shaped of the finest black cloth, you would not have looked upon his face as the most handsome in the world, and yet it was a finely-marked countenance, with a decided, if not highly intellectual, expression. If the truth must be told, his coat, though fashioned of the finest cloth, was made a little too full in one place, a little too scant in another, and buttoned up somewhat too high in the throat, for a gentleman whose ambition it was to flourish on the southern side of Chesnut street, amid the animated cloths and silks of a fashionable promenade. And then the large black stock, encircling his neck, with the crumpled, though snow-white, shirt collar, gave a harsh relief to his countenance, while the carelessly-disposed wristbands, crushed back over the upturned cuffs of his coat, designated the man who went in for comfort, and flung fashion to the haberdashers and dry goods clerks.

As for his face, whenever the curtain of tobacco smoke rolled aside, you beheld, as I have said, a finely-marked countenance, with rather lank cheeks, a sharp aquiline nose, thin lips, biting and sarcastic in expression, a full square chin, and eyes of the peculiar class, intensely dark and piercing in their glance, that remind you of a flame without heat, cold, glittering and snake-like. His forehead was high and bold, with long and lanky black hair falling back from its outlines, and resting, without love-lock or curl, in straight masses behind each ear.

"Queer world this!" began our comfortable friend, falling into one of those broken soliloquies, generated by the pipe and the bowl, in which the stops are supplied by puffs of smoke, and the paragraph terminated by a sip of the punch—"Don't know much about other worlds, but it strikes me that if a prize were offered somewhere by somebody, for the queerest world a-going, this world of ours might be rigged up nice, and sent in like a bit of show beef, as the premium queer world. No man smokes a cigar that ever tried a pipe, but an ass. I was a small boy once—ragged little devil *that* Luke Harvey, who used to run about old Livingstone's importing warehouse. Indelicate little fellow: wore his ruffles out behind. Kicked and cuffed because he was poor—served him right— dammim. Old Liv. died—young Albert took the store—capital, cool one hundred thousand. Luke Harvey rose to a clerkship. Began to be a fine fellow—well-dressed, and of course virtuous. D——d queer fellow, Luke. Last year taken into partnership along with young fellow whose daddy's worth at least one hun. thousand. Firm now—Livingstone, Harvey, & Co. Clever punch, that. Little too much lemon—d——d it, the sugar's out.

"Queer thing, that! Some weeks ago respectable old gentleman in white cravat and hump-back, came to counting house. Old fellow hailed from Charleston. Had rather a Jewish twang on his tongue. Presented Livingstone a letter of credit drawn by a Charleston house on our firm. Letter from Grayson, Ballenger, & Co., for a cool hundred thousand. Old white cravat got it. D——n that rat in the partition—why can't he eat his victuals in quiet? Two weeks since, news came that G. B. & Co. never gave such letter— a forgery, a complete swindle. Comfortable, that. Hot coals on one's bare skull, quite pleasant in comparison. Livingstone in New York—been trying for a week to track up the villain. Must get new pipe to-morrow. Mem. get one with Judas Iscariot[11] painted on the bowl. Honest

---

11 The disciple who betrayed Jesus.

rogue, that. Went and hanged himself after he sold his master. Wonder how full the town would be if all who have sold their God for gold would hang themselves? Hooks in market house would rise. Bear queer fruit—eh? D——d good tobacco. By the bye—must go home. Another sip of the punch and I'm off. Ha—ha—good idea that of the handsome Colonel! Great buck, man of fashion and long-haired Apollo.[12] Called here this evening to see me— smelt like a civet cat.[13] Must flourish his pocket- book before my eyes by way of a genteel brag. Dropped a letter from a bundle of notes. Valuable letter that. Wouldn't part with it for a cool thousand—rather think it will raise the devil—let me see—"

And laying down his pipe, Mr. Luke Harvey drew a neatly-folded billetdoux[14] from an inside pocket of his coat, and holding it in the glare of the light perused its direction, which was written in a fair and delicate woman's hand.

"'Col. Fitz-Cowles—United States Hotel'" —he murmured—"good idea, Colonel, to drop *such* a letter out of your pocket-book. Won't trouble you none? 'Spose not—ha, ha, ha—d——d good idea!"

The idea appeared to tickle him immensely, for he chuckled in a deep, self-satisfied tone as he drew on his bearskin overcoat, and even while he extinguished the gas-light, and covered up the fire, his chuckle grew into a laugh, which deepened into a hearty guffaw, as striding through the dark warehouse, he gained the front door, and looked out into the deserted street.

"Ha-ha-ha—to drop such a dear creature's letter!"—he laughed, locking the door of the warehouse—"Wonder if it won't raise h——l? I loved a woman once. Luke, you were a d——d fool *that* time. Jilted—yes jilted. That's the word I believe? Maybe I won't have my revenge? Perhaps not—very likely not—"

With this momentous letter, so carelessly dropped by the insinuating millionaire, Colonel Fitz-Cowles resting on his mind, and stirring his features with frequent spasmodic attacks of laughter, our friend, Mr. Harvey, pursued his way along Front street, and turning up Chesnut street, arrived at the corner of Third, where he halted for a few moments in order to ascertain the difference in time, between his gold-repeater and the State House clock, which had just struck one.

While thus engaged, intently perusing the face of his watch by the light of the moon, a stout middle-aged gentleman, wrapped up in a thick overcoat, with a carpet bag in his hand, came striding rapidly across the street, and for a moment stood silent and unper-ceived at his shoulder.

"Well Luke—is the repeater right and the State House wrong?" said a hearty cheerful voice, and the middle-aged gentleman laid his hand on Mr. Harvey's shoulder.

"Ah-ha! Mr. Livingstone! Is that you?" cried Luke, suddenly wheeling round and gazing into the frank and manly countenance of the new-comer—"When did you get back from New York?"

"Just this moment arrived. I did not expect to return within a week from this time, and therefore come upon you by a little surprise. I wrote to Mrs. L. yesterday, telling her I would not be in town until the Christmas holidays were over. She'll be rather surprised to see me, I suppose?"

"Rather!" echoed Luke, drily.

---

12 The Greek and Roman god of sunlight, prophecy, and music.
13 Skunk.
14 A love letter.

"Come Luke, take my arm, and let's walk up toward my house. I have much to say to you. In the first place have you any thing new?"

While Mr. Harvey is imparting his budget of news to the senior partner of the firm of Livingstone, Harvey & Co., as they stroll slowly along Chesnut street, we will make some few notes of his present appearance.

Stout, muscular, and large-boned, with a figure slightly inclining towards corpulence, Mr. Livingstone strode along the pavement with a firm and measured step, that attested all the matured strength and vigor peculiar to robust middle age. He was six feet high, with broad shoulders and muscular chest. His face was full, bold, and massive, rather bronzed in hue, and bearing some slight traces of the ravages of small-pox. Once or twice as he walked along, he lifted his hat from his face, and his forehead, rendered more conspicuous by some slight baldness, was exposed to view. It was high, and wide, and massive, bulging outward prominently in the region of the reflective organs, and faintly relieved by his short brown hair. His eyes, bold and large, of a calm clear blue, were rendered strangely expressive by the contrast of the jet-black eyebrows. His nose was firm and Roman in contour, his mouth marked by full and determined lips, his chin square and prominent, while the lengthened outline of the lower jaw, from the chin to the ear, gave his countenance an expression of inflexible resolution. In short, it was the face of a man, whose mind, great in resources, had only found room for the display of its tamest powers, in enlarged mercantile operations, while its dark and desperate elements, from the want of adversity, revenge or hate to rouse them into action, had lain still and dormant for some twenty long years of active life. He never dreamed himself that he carried a hidden hell within his soul.

Had this man been born poor, it is probable that in his attempt to rise, the grim hand of want would have dragged from their lurking-places, these dark and fearful elements of his being. But wealth had lapped him at his birth, smiled on him in his youth, walked by him through life, and the moment for the trial of all his powers had never happened. He was a fine man, a noble merchant, and a good citizen—we but repeat the stereotyped phrases of the town—and yet, quiet and close, near the heart of this cheerful-faced man, lay a sleeping devil, who had been dozing away there all his life, and only waiting the call of destiny to spring into terrible action, and rend that manly bosom with his fangs.

"Have you heard any news of the—forger?" asked Luke Harvey, when he had delivered his budget of news—"Any intelligence of the respectable gentleman in the white cravat and hump-back?"

"He played the same game in New York that he played in our city. Wherever I went, I heard nothing but 'Mr. Ellis Mortimer, of Charleston, bought goods to a large amount here, on the strength of a letter of credit, drawn on your house by Grayson, Ballenger, & Co.,' or that 'Mr. Mortimer bought goods to a large amount in such-and-such a-store, backed by the same letter of credit—' No less than twelve wholesale houses gave him credit to an almost unlimited extent. In all cases the goods were despatched to the various auctions and sold at half-cost, while Mr. Ellis Mortimer pocketed the cash—"

"And you have no traces of this prince of swindlers?"

"None! all the police in New York have been raising heaven-and-earth to catch him for this week past, but without success. At last I have come to the conclusion that he is lurking about this city, with the respectable sum of two hundred thousand dollars in his possession. I am half-inclined to believe that he is not alone in this business—there may be a combination of scoundrels concerned in the affair. To-morrow the police shall ransack every hiding-hole and cranny in the city. My friend, Col. Fitz-Cowles gave me some valuable suggestions before I left for New York—I will ask his advice, in regard to the matter, the first thing in the morning—"

"Very fine man, that Col. Fitz-Cowles—" observed Luke, as they turned down Fourth street—"Splendid fellow. Dresses well—gives capital terrapin suppers at the United States—inoculates all the bucks about town with his style of hat. Capital fellow—Son of an English Earl—ain't he, Mr. Livingstone?"

"So I have understood—" replied Mr. Livingstone, not exactly liking the quiet sneer which lurked under the innocent manner of his partner—"at least so it is rumored—"

"Got lots of money—a millionaire—no end to his wealth. By the bye, where the d——l did he come from? isn't he a Southern planter with acres of niggers and prairies cotton?"

"Luke, that's a very strange question to ask me. You just now asked me, whether he was the son of an English Earl—did'nt you?"

"Believe I did. To tell the truth, I've heard both stories about him, and some dozen more. An heir-apparent to an English Earldom, a rich planter from the South, the son of a Boston *magnifique*,[15] the only child of a rich Mexican—these things you will see, don't mix well. Who the devil is our long-haired friend, anyhow?"

"Tut-tut—Luke this is all folly. You know that Col. Fitz-Cowles is received in the best society, mingles with the *ton*[16] of the Quaker City, is 'squired about by our judges and lawyers, and can always find scores of friends to help him spend his fortune—"

"Fine man, that Col. Fitz-Cowles. Very," said the other in his dry and biting tone.

"Do you know, Luke, that I think the married men the happiest in the world?" said Livingstone, drawing the arm of his partner closely within his own—"Now look at my case for instance. A year ago I was a miserable bachelor. The loss of one hundred thousand dollars then, would have driven me frantic. Now I have a sweet young wife to cheer me, her smile welcomes me home; the first tone of her voice, and my loss is forgotten!"

The Merchant paused. His eye glistened with a tear, and he felt his heart grow warm, in his bosom, as the vision of his sweet young wife, now so calmly sleeping on her solitary bed rose before him. He imagined her smile of welcome as she beheld him suddenly appear by her bedside; he felt her arms so full and round twining fondly round his neck and he tried to fancy—but the attempt was vain—the luxury of a kiss from her red ripe lips.

"You may think me uxorious, Luke—" he resumed in his deep manly voice—"But I do think that God never made a nobler woman than my Dora! Look at the sacrifice she made for my sake? Young, blooming, and but twenty summers old, she forgot the disparity of my years, and consented to share my bachelor's-home—"

"She *is* a noble woman—" observed Luke, and then he looked at the moon and whistled an air from the very select operatic spectacle of 'Bone Squash.'

"Noble in heart and soul!" exclaimed Livingstone—"confess, Luke that we married men live more in an hour than you dull bachelors in a year—"

"Oh—yes—certainly! You may well talk when you have such a handsome wife! Egad— if I was'nt afraid it would make you jealous—I would say that Mrs. Livingstone has the most splendid form I ever beheld—"

There was a slight contortion of Mr. Harvey's upper lip as he spoke, which looked very much like a sneer.

---

15 An admirable person.
16 Fashionable element.

"And then her heart, Luke, her heart! So noble, so good, so affectionate! I wish you could have seen her, where first I beheld her—in a small and meanly furnished apartment, at the bed-side of a dying mother! They were in reduced circumstances, for her father had died insolvent. He had been my father's friend, and I thought it my duty to visit the widowed mother and the orphan daughter. By-the-bye, Luke, I now remember that I saw you at their house in Wood street once—did you know the family?"

"Miss Dora's father had been kind to me—" said Luke in a quiet tone. There was a strange light in his dark eye as he spoke, and a remarkable tremor on his lip.

"Well, well, Luke—here's my house—" exclaimed Mr. Livingstone, as they arrived in front of a lofty four storied mansion, situated in the aristocratic square, as it is called, along south Fourth street. "It is lucky I have my dead-latch key. I can enter without disturbing the servants. Come up stairs, into the front parlor with me, Luke; I want to have a few more words with you about the forgery—"

They entered the door of the mansion, passed along a wide and roomy entry, ascended a richly carpeted staircase, and, traversing the entry in the second story, in a moment stood in the centre of the spacious parlor, fronting the street on the second floor. In another moment, Mr. Livingstone, by the aid of some Lucifer matches which he found on the mantle, lighted a small bed-lamp, standing amid the glittering volumes that were piled on the centre table. The dim light of the lamp flickering around the room, revealed the various characteristics of an apartment furnished in a style of lavish magnificence. Above the mantle flashed an enormous mirror, on one side of the parlor was an inviting sofa, on the other, a piano; two splendid ottomans stood in front of the fireless hearth, and, curtains of splendid silk hung drooping heavily along the three lofty windows that looked into the street. In fine, the parlor was all that the upholsterer and cabinet maker combined could make it, a depository of luxurious appointments and costly furniture.

"Draw your seat near the centre table, Luke—" cried Mr. Livingstone, as he flung himself into a comfortable rocking chair, and gazed around the room with an expression of quiet satisfaction—"Don't speak too loud, Luke, for Dora is sleeping in the next room. You know I want to take her by a little surprise—eh, Luke? She doesn't expect me from New York for a week yet—I am the last person in the world she thinks to see tonight. Clearly so—ha—ha!"

And the merchant chuckled gaily, rubbed his hands together, glanced at the folding doors that opened into the bed-chamber, where slept his blooming wife, and then turning round, looked in the face of Luke Harvey with a smile, that seemed to say—'I can't help it if you bachelors are miserable—pity you, but can't help it.'

"It *would* be a pity to awaken Mrs. Livingstone—" said Luke fixing his brilliant dark eye on the face of the senior partner, with a look so meaning and yet mysterious, that Mr. Livingstone involuntarily averted his gaze—"A very great pity. By the bye, with regard to the forgery—"

"Let me recapitulate the facts. Some weeks ago we received a letter from the respectable house of Grayson, Ballenger, & Co., Charleston, stating that they had made a large purchase in cotton from a rich planter—Mr. Ellis Mortimer, who, in a week or so, would visit Philadelphia, with a letter of credit on our house for one hundred thousand dollars. They gave us this intimation in order that we might be prepared to cash the letter of credit at right. Well, in a week a gentleman of respectable exterior appeared, stated that he was Mr. Ellis Mortimer, presented his letter of credit; it was cashed and we wrote to Grayson, Ballenger, & Co., announcing the fact—"

"They returned the agreeable answer that Mr. Ellis Mortimer had not yet left Charleston for Philadelphia, but had altered his intention and was about to sail for London. That the gentleman in the white cravat and hump-back was an imposter, and the letter of credit a—forgery. There was considerable mystery in the affair; for instance, how did the imposter gain all the necessary information with regard to Mr. Mortimer's visit, how did he acquire a knowledge of the signature of the Charleston house?"

"Listen and I will tell you. Last week, in New York, I received a letter from the Charleston house announcing these additional facts. It appears that in the beginning of fall they received a letter from a Mr. Albert Hazelton Munroe, representing himself as a rich planter in Wainbridge, South Carolina. He had a large amount of cotton to sell, and would like to procure advances on it from the Charleston house. They wrote him an answer to his letter, asking the quality of the cotton, and so forth, and soliciting an interview with Mr. Munroe when he visited Charleston. In the beginning of November Mr. Munroe, a dark-complexioned man, dressed like a careless country squire, entered their store for the first time, and commenced a series of negotiations about his cotton, which had resulted in nothing, when another planter, Mr. Ellis Mortimer, appeared in the scene, sold his cotton and requested the letter of credit on our house. Mr. Munroe was in the store every day— was a jolly unpretending fellow—familiar with all the clerks—and on intimate terms with Messrs. Grayson, Ballenger, & Co. The letter written to our house, intimating the intended visit of Mr. Mortimer to this city, had been very carelessly left open for a few moments on the counting house desk, and Mr. Munroe was observed glancing over its contents by one of the clerks. The day after that letter had been despatched to Philadelphia, Mr. Albert H. Munroe suddenly disappeared, and had not been heard of since. The Charleston house suspect him of the whole forgery in all its details—"

"Very likely. He saw the letter on the counter—forged the letter of credit—and despatched his accomplice to Philadelphia without delay—"

"Now for the consequences of this forgery. On Monday morning next we have an engagement of one hundred thousand dollars to meet, which, under present circumstances, may plunge our house into the vortex of bankruptcy. Unless this imposter is discovered, unless his connection with this Munroe is clearly ascertained before next Monday, I must look forward to that day as one of the greatest danger to our house. You see our position, Luke?"

"Yes, yes—" answered Luke, as he arose, and, advancing, gazed fixedly into the face of Mr. Livingstone—"I see *our* position, and I see *your* position in more respects than one—"

"Confound the thing, man, how you stare in my face. Do you see anything peculiar about my countenance, that you peruse it so attentively?"

"Ha—ha—" cried Luke, with a hysterical laugh—"Ha—ha! Nothing but—horns. Horns, sir, I say—horns. A fine branching pair! Ha—ha—Why damn it, Livingstone, you won't be able to enter the church door, next Sunday, without stooping—*those* horns are so d——d large!"

Livingstone looked at him with a face of blank wonder. He evidently supposed that Luke had been seized with sudden madness. To see a man who is your familiar friend and partner, abruptly break off a conversation on matters of the most importance, and stare vacantly in your face as he compliments you on some fancied resemblance which you bear to a full-grown stag, is, it must be confessed, a spectacle somewhat unfrequent in this world of ours, and rather adapted to excite a feeling of astonishment whenever it happens.

"Mr. Harvey—are—you—mad?" asked Livingstone, in a calm deliberate tone.

Harvey slowly leaned forward and brought his face so near Livingstone's that the latter could feel his breath on his cheek. He applied his mouth to the ear of the senior partner, and whispered a single word.

When a soldier, in battle, receives a bullet directly in the heart, he springs in the air with one convulsive spasm, flings his arms aloft and utters a groan that thrills the man who hears it with a horror never to be forgotten. With that same convulsive movement, with that same deep groan of horror and anguish Livingstone, the merchant, sprang to his feet, and confronted the utterer of that single word.

"Harvey—" he said, in a low tone, and with white and trembling lips, while his calm blue eye flashed with that deep glance of excitement, most terrible when visible in a calm blue eye—"Harvey, you had better never been born, than utter that word again. To trifle with a thing of this kind is worse than death. Harvey, I advise you to leave me—I am losing all command of myself—there is a voice within me tempting me to murder you—for God's sake quit my sight—"

Harvey looked in his face, fearless and undaunted, though his snake-like eye blazed like a coal of fire, and his thin lips quivered as with the death spasm.

"*Cuckold!*"[17] he shrieked in a hissing voice, with a wild hysterical laugh.

Livingstone started back aghast. The purple veins stood out like cords on his bronzed forehead, and his right hand trembled like a leaf as it was thrust within the breast of his coat. His blue eye—great God! how glassy it had grown—was fixed upon the form of Luke Harvey as if meditating where to strike.

"To the bedchamber—" shrieked Luke. "If *she* is there, I am a liar and a dog, and deserve to die. *Cuckold*, I say, and will prove it—to the bedchamber!"

And to the bedchamber with an even stride, though his massive form quivered like an oak shaken by the hurricane, strode the merchant. The folding door slid back—he had disappeared into the bedchamber.

There was silence for a single instant, like the silence in the graveyard, between the last word of the prayer, and the first rattling sound of the clods upon the coffin.

In a moment Livingstone again strode into the parlor. His face was the hue of ashes. You could see that the struggle at work within his heart was like the agony of the strong man wrestling with death. *This* struggle was tenfold more terrible than death—death in its vilest form. It forced the big beaded drops of sweat out from the corded veins on his brow, it drove the blood from his face, leaving a black and discolored streak beneath each eye.

"She is not there—" he said, taking Luke by the hand, which he wrung with an iron grasp, and murmured again—"She is not there—"

"False to her husband's bed and honor—" exclaimed Luke, the agitation which had convulsed his face, subsiding into a look of heart-wrung compassion, as he looked upon the terrible results of his disclosure—"False as hell, and vile as false!"

An object on the centre table, half concealed by the bed-lamp arrested the husband's attention. He thrust aside the lamp and beheld a note, addressed to himself, in Mrs. Livingstone's hand.

With a trembling hand the merchant tore the note open, and while Luke stood fixedly regarding him, perused its contents.

And as he read, the blood came back to his cheeks, the glance to his eyes, and his brow reddened over with one burning flush of indignation.

---

17 The husband of an unfaithful wife.

"Liar and dog!" he shouted, in tones hoarse with rage, as he grasped Luke Harvey by the throat with a sudden movement—"Your lie was well coined, but look here! Ha—ha—" and he shook Luke to and fro like a broken reed—"Here is my wife's letter. Here, sir, look at it, and I'll force you to eat your own foul words. Here, expecting that I might suddenly return from New York, my wife has written down that she would be absent from home to-night. A sick friend, a school-day companion, now reduced to widowhood penury, solicited her company by her dying bed, and my wife could not refuse. Read, sir—oh read!"

"Take your hand from my throat or I'll do you a mischief—" murmured Luke, in a choking voice as he grew black in the face. "I will, by God—"

"Read—sir—oh read!" shouted Livingstone, as he forced Luke into a chair and thrust the letter into his hands—"Read, sir, and then crawl from this room like a vile dog as you are. To-morrow I will settle with you—"

Luke sank in the chair, took the letter, and with a pale face, varied by a crimson spot on each cheek, he began to read, while Livingstone, towering and erect, stood regarding him with a look of incarnate scorn.

It was observable that while Luke perused the letter, his head dropped slowly down as though in the endeavor to see more clearly, and his unoccupied hand was suddenly thrust within the breast of his overcoat.

"That is a very good letter. Well written, and she minds her stops—" exclaimed Luke calmly, as he handed the letter back to Mr. Livingstone—"Quite an effort of composition. I didn't think Dora had so much tact—"

The merchant was thunderstruck with the composure exhibited by the slanderer and the liar. He glanced over Luke's features with a quick nervous glance, and then looked at the letter which he held in his hand.

"Ha! This is not the same letter!" he shouted, in tones of mingled rage and wonder—"This letter is addressed to Col. 'Fitz-Cowles'—"

"It was dropped in the counting house by the Colonel this evening—" said Luke with the air of a man who was prepared for any hazard—"The Colonel is a very fine man. A favorite with the fair sex. Read it—*Oh* read—"

With a look of wonder Mr. Livingstone opened the letter. There was a quivering start in his whole frame, when he first observed the handwriting.

But as he went on, drinking in word after word, his countenance, so full of meaning and expression, was like a mirror, in which different faces are seen, one after another, by sudden transition. At first his face grew crimson, then it was pale as death in an instant. Then his lips dropped apart, and his eyes were covered with a glassy film. Then a deep wrinkle shot upward between his brows, and then, black and ghastly, the circles of discolored flesh were visible beneath each eye. The quivering nostrils—the trembling hands—the heaving chest—did man ever die with a struggle terrible as this?

He sank heavily into a chair, and crushing the letter between his fingers, buried his face in his hands.

"Oh my God—" he groaned—"Oh my God—and I loved her so!"

And then between the very fingers convulsively clutching the fatal letter, there fell large and scalding tears, drop by drop, pouring heavily, like the first tokens of a coming thunder-bolt, on a summer day.

Luke Harvey arose, and strode hurriedly along the floor. The sight was too much for him to bear. And yet as he turned away he heard the groans of the strong man in his agony, and the heart-wrung words came, like the voice of the dying, to his ear—

"Oh my God, oh my God, and I loved her so!"

When Luke again turned and gazed upon the betrayed husband, he beheld a sight that filled him with unutterable horror.

There, as he sat, his face buried in his hands, his head bowed on his breast, his brow was partly exposed to the glare of the lamp-beams, and all around that brow, amid the locks of his dark brown hair, were streaks of hoary white. The hair of the merchant had withered at the root. The blow was so sudden, so blighting, and so terrible, that even his strong mind reeled, his brain tottered, and in the effort to command his reason, his hair grew white with agony.[18]

"Would to God I had not told him—" murmured Luke—"I knew not that he loved her so—I knew not—and yet—ha, ha, *I* loved her once—"

"Luke—my friend—" said Livingstone in a tremulous voice as he raised his face— "Know you anything of *the place*—named in—the letter?"

"I do—and will lead you there—" answered Luke, his face resuming its original expression of agitation—"Come!" he cried, in a husky voice, as olden-time memories seemed striving at his heart—"Come!"

"Can you gain me access to the house—to *the*—*the* room?"

"Did I not track them thither last night? *Come!*"

The merchant slowly rose and took a pair of pistols from his carpet bag. They were small and convenient travelling pistols, mounted in silver, with those noiseless 'patent' triggers that emit no clicking sound by way of warning. He inspected the percussion caps, and sounded each pistol barrel.

"Silent and sure—" muttered Luke—"They are each loaded with a single ball."

"Which way do you lead? To the southern part of the city?"

"To Southwark—" answered Luke, leading the way from the parlor—"To the rookery, to the den, to the pest-house—"

In a moment they stood upon the door step of the merchant's princely mansion, the vivid light of the December moon, imparting a ghastly hue to Livingstone's face, with the glassy eyes, rendered more fearful by the discolored circles of flesh beneath, the furrowed brow, and the white lips, all fixed in an expression stern and resolute as death.

Luke flung his hand to the south, and his dark impenetrable eyes shone with meaning. The merchant placed his partner's arm within his own, and they hurried down Fourth street with a single word from Luke— "To Monk-hall!"

Chapter Sixth

Monk-Hall[19]

Strange traditions have come down to our time, in relation to a massive edifice, which, long before the Revolution, stood in the centre of an extensive garden, surrounded by a brick wall, and encircled by a deep grove of horse-chesnut and beechen trees. This edifice was located on the out-skirts of the southern part of the city, and the garden overspread some acres, occupying a space full as large as a modern square.

---

18 [Author's Original Note] This is a fact, established by the evidence of a medical gentleman of the first reputation.

19 [Author's Original Note] No reader who wishes to understand this story in all its details will fail to peruse this chapter.

This mansion, but rarely seen by intrusive eyes, had been originally erected by a wealthy foreigner, sometime previous to the Revolution. Who this foreigner was, his name or his history, has not been recorded by tradition; but his mansion, in its general construction and details, indicate a mind rendered whimsical and capricious by excessive wealth.

The front of the mansion, one plain mass of black and red brick, disposed like the alternate colors of a chessboard, looked towards the south. A massive hall-door, defended by heavy pillars, and surmounted by an intricate cornice, all carved and sculptured into hideous satyr-faces; three ranges of deep square windows, with cumbrous sash frames and small panes of glass; a deep and sloping roof, elaborate with ornaments of painted wood along the eaves, and rising into a gabled peak directly over the hall-door, while its outlines were varied by rows of substantial chimneys, fashioned into strange and uncouth shapes,—all combined, produced a general impression of ease and grandeur that was highly effective in awing the spirits of any of the simple citizens who might obtain a casual glance of the house through the long avenue of trees extending from the garden gate.

This impression of awe was somewhat deepened by various rumors that obtained through the southern part of the Quaker City. It was said that the wealthy proprietor, not satisfied with building a fine house with three stories above ground, had also constructed three stories of spacious chambers below the level of the earth. This was calculated to stir the curiosity and perhaps the scandal of the town, and as a matter of course strange rumors began to prevail about midnight orgies held by the godless proprietor in his subterranean apartments, where wine was drunken without stint, and beauty ruined without remorse. Veiled figures had been seen passing through the garden gate after night, and men were not wanting to swear that these figures, in dark robes and sweeping veils, were pretty damsels with neat ankles and soft eyes.

As time passed on, the rumors grew and the mystery deepened. The neatly-constructed stable at the end of the garden was said to be connected with the house, some hundred yards distant, by a subterranean passage. The two wings, branching out at either extremity of the rear of the mansion, looked down upon a courtyard, separated by a light wicket fence from the garden walks. The court-yard, overarched by an awning in summer time, was said to be the scene of splendid festivals to which the grandees of the city were invited. From the western wing of the mansion arose a square lantern-like structure, which the gossips called a tower, and hinted sagely of witchcraft and devildom whenever it was named. They called the proprietor, a libertine, a gourmand, an astrologer and a wizard. He feasted in the day and he consulted his friend, the Devil, at night. He drank wine at all times, and betrayed innocence on every occasion. In short the seclusion of the mansion, its singular structure, its wall of brick and its grove of impenetrable trees, gave rise to all sorts of stories, and the proprietor has come down to our time with a decidedly bad character, although it is more than likely that he was nothing but a wealthy Englishman, whimsical and eccentric, the boon-companion and friend of Governor Evans, the rollicking Chief Magistrate of the Province.

Although tradition has not preserved the name of the mysterious individual yet the title of his singular mansion, is still on record.

It was called—Monk-hall.

There are conflicting traditions which assert that this title owed its origin to other sources. A Catholic Priest occupied the mansion after the original proprietor went home to his native land, or slid into his grave; it was occupied as a Nunnery, as a Monastery, or as a resort for the Sisters of Charity; the mass had been said within its walls, its subterranean chambers converted into cells, its tower transformed into an oratory of prayer— such are the dim legends which were rife some forty years ago, concerning Monk-hall, long after the city, in its southern march, had cut down the trees, overturned the wall, levelled the garden into building lots and divided it by streets and alleys into a dozen triangles and squares.

Some of these legends, so vague and so conflicting, are still preserved in the memories of aged men and white-haired matrons, who will sit by the hour and describe the gradual change which time and improvement, those twin desolators of the beautiful, had accomplished with Monk-hall.

Soon after the Revolution, fine brick buildings began to spring up along the streets which surrounded the garden, while the alleys traversing its area, grew lively with long lines of frame houses, variously fashioned and painted, whose denizens awoke the echoes of the place with the sound of the hammer and the grating of the saw. Time passed on, and the distinctive features of the old mansion and garden were utterly changed. Could the old proprietor have risen from his grave, and desired to pay another visit to his friend, the Devil, in the subterranean chambers of his former home, he would have had, to say the least of it, a devil of a time in finding the way. Where the old brick wall had stood he would have found long rows of dwelling houses, some four storied, some three or one, some brick, some frame, a few pebble-dashed, and all alive with inhabitants.

In his attempt to find the Hall, he would have had to wind up a narrow alley, turn down a court, strike up an avenue, which it would take some knowledge of municipal geography to navigate. At last, emerging into a narrow street where four alleys crossed, he would behold his magnificent mansion of Monk-hall with a printing office on one side and a stereotype foundry on the other, while on the opposite side of the way, a mass of miserable frame houses seemed about to commit suicide and fling themselves madly into the gutter, and in the distance a long line of dwellings, offices, and factories, looming in broken perspective, looked as if they wanted to shake hands across the narrow street. The southern front of the house—alas, how changed—alone is visible. The shutters on one side of the hall-door are nailed up and hermetically closed, while, on the other, shutters within the glasses bar out the light of day. The semi-circular window in the centre of the gabled-peak has been built up with brick, yet our good friend would find the tower on the western wing in tolerable good preservation. The stable one hundred yards distant from Monk-hall—what has become of it? Perhaps it is pulled down, or it may be that a splendid dwelling towers in its place? It is still in existence, standing amid the edifices of a busy street, its walls old and tottering, its ancient stable-floor turned into a bulk window, surmounted by the golden balls of a Pawnbroker, while within its Precincts, rooms furnished for household use supply the place of the stalls of the olden-time. Does the subterranean passage still exist? Future pages of our story may possibly answer that question.

Could our ancient and ghostly proprietor, glide into the tenements adjoining Monk-hall, and ask the mechanic or his wife, the printer or the factory man to tell him the story of the strange old building, he would find that the most remarkable ignorance prevailed regard to the structure, its origin and history. One man might tell him that it had been factory, or a convent, or the Lord knows what, another might intimate that it had been a church, a third (and he belonged to the most numerous class) would reply in a surly tone that he knew nothing about the old brick nuisance, while in the breasts of one or two aged men and matrons, yet living in Southwark, would be discovered the only chronicles of the ancient structure now extant, the only records of its history or name. Did our spirit friend glide over the threshold and enter the chambers of his home, his eye would, perhaps, behold scenes that rivalled, in vice and magnificence, anything that legend chronicled of the olden-time of Monk-hall, although its exterior was so desolate, and its outside-door of green blinds varied by a big brass plate, bore the respectable and saintly name of "ABIJAH K. JONES," in immense letters, half indistinct with dirt and rust.

Who this Abijah K. Jones was, no one knew, although the owner of the house a good christian, who had a pew in ——church, where he took the sacrament at least once a month, might have been able to tell with very little research. Yet what of that? Abijah K. Jones might have nightly entertained the infernal regions in his house, and not a word been said about it; because, as the pious landlord would observe, when cramming Abijah's rent-money into the same pocket-book that contained some tract-society receipts,—"Good tenant that!—pays his rent with the regularity of clockwork!"

Chapter Seventh

The Monks of Monk Hall

The moon was shining brightly over the face of the old mansion, while the opposite side of the alley lay in dim and heavy shadow. The light brown hue of the closed shutters afforded a vivid contrast to the surface of the front, which had the strikingly gloomy effect always produced by the intermixture of black and red brick, disposed like the colors of a chessboard, in the structure of a mansion. The massive cornice above the hall- door, the heavy eaves of the roof, the gabled peak rising in the centre, and the cumbrous frames of the many windows,—all stood out boldly in the moonlight, from the dismal relief of the building's front.

The numerous chimneys with their fantastic shapes rose grimly in the moonlight, like a strange band of goblin sentinels, perched of the roof to watch the mansion. The general effect was that of an ancient structure falling to decay, deserted by all inhabitants save the rats that gnawed the wainscot along the thick old walls. The door-plate that glittered on the faded door, half covered as it was with rust and verdigris, with its saintly name afforded the only signs of the actual occupation of Monk-hall by human beings: in all other respects it looked so desolate, so time-worn, so like a mausoleum for old furniture, and crumbling tapestry, for high-backed mahogany chairs, gigantic bedsteads, and strange looking mirrors, veiled in the thick folds of the spider's web.

Dim and indistinct, like the booming of a distant cannon, the sound of the State-House bell, thrilled along the intricate maze of streets and alleys. It struck the hour of two. The murmur of the last stroke of the bell, so dim and indistinct, was mingled with the echo of approaching footsteps, and in a moment two figures turned the corner of an alley that wound among the tangled labyrinth of avenues, and came hastening on toward the lonely mansion; lonely even amid tenements and houses, gathered as thickly together as the cells in a bee-hive.

"I say, Gus, what a devil of a way you've led me!" cried one of the strangers, with a thick cloak wrapped round his limbs—"up one alley and down another, around one street and through another, backwards and forwards, round this way and round that—damme if I can tell which is north or south except by the moon!"

"Hist! my fellow—don't mention names—cardinal doctrine that on an affair of this kind—" answered the tall figure, whose towering form was enveloped in a frogged overcoat—"Remember, you pass in as *my friend*. Wait a moment—we'll see whether old Devil-Bug is awake."

Ascending the granite steps of the mansion, he gave three distinct raps with his gold-headed cane, on the surface of the brass-plate. In a moment the rattling of a heavy chain, and the sound of a bolt, slowly withdrawn, was heard within, and the door of the mansion, beyond the outside door of green blinds, receded about the width of an inch.

"Who's there, a disturbin' honest folks this hour o' the night—" said a voice, that came grumbling through the blinds of the green door, like the sound of a grindstone that hasn't been oiled for some years—"What the devil you want? Go about your business—or I'll call the watch—"

"I say, Devil-Bug, what hour o' th' night is it?" exclaimed Lorrimer in a whispered tone.

"'Dinner time'—" replied the grindstone voice slightly oiled—"Come in sir. Did'nt know 'twas you. How the devil should I? Come in—"

As the voice grunted this invitation, Lorrimer seized Byrnewood by the arm, and glided through the opened door.

Byrnewood looked around in wonder, as he discovered that the front door opened into a small closet or room, some ten feet square, the floor bare and uncarpeted, the ceiling darkened by smoke, while a large coal fire, burning in a rusty grate, afforded both light and heat to the apartment.

The heat was close and stifling, while the light, but dim and flickering, disclosed the form of the door-keeper of Monk-hall, as he stood directly in front of the grate, surrounded by the details of his den.

"This is *my friend*—" said Lorrimer in a meaning tone—"You understand, Devil-Bug?"

"Yes—" grunted the grindstone voice—"I understand. O'course. But my name is Bijah K. Jones, *if* you please, my pertikler friend. I never know'd sich a individooal as Devil-Bug—"

It requires no great stretch of fancy to imagine that his Satanic majesty, once on a time, in a merry mood, created a huge insect, in order to test his inventive powers. Certainly that insect—which it was quite natural to designate by the name of Devil-Bug—stood in the full light of the grate, gazing steadfastly in Byrnewood's face. It was a strange thickset specimen of flesh and blood, with a short body, marked by immensely broad shoulders, long arms and thin distorted legs. The head of the creature was ludicrously large in proportion to the body. Long masses of stiff black hair fell tangled and matted over a forehead, protuberent to deformity. A flat nose with wide nostrils shooting out into each cheek like the smaller wings of an insect, an immense mouth whose heavy lips disclosed two long rows of bristling teeth, a pointed chin, blackened by a heavy beard, and massive eyebrows meeting over the nose, all furnished the details of a countenance, not exactly calculated to inspire the most pleasant feelings in the world. One eye, small black and shapen like a bead, stared steadily in Byrnewood's face, while the other socket was empty, shrivelled and orbless. The eyelids of the vacant socket were joined together like the opposing edges of a curtain, while the other eye gained additional brilliancy and effect from the loss of its fellow member.

The shoulders of the Devil-Bug, protruding in unsightly knobs, the wide chest, and the long arms with talon-like fingers, so vividly contrasted with the thin and distorted legs, all attested that the remarkable strength of the man was located in the upper part of his body.

"Well, Abijah, are you satisfied?" asked Lorrimer, as he perceived Byrnewood shrink back with disgust from the door-keeper's gaze—"*This* gentleman, I say, is *my* friend?"

"So I s'pose," grunted Abijah—"Here, Musquito, mark this man—here, Glow-worm, mark him, I say. This is Monk Gusty's friend. Can't you move quicker, you ugly devils?"

From either side of the fire-place, as he spoke, emerged a tall Herculean negro, with a form of strength and sinews of iron. Moving slowly along the floor, from the darkness which had enshrouded their massive outlines, they stood silent and motionless gazing with look of stolid indifference upon the face of the new-comer. Byrnewood had started aside in disgust from the Devil-Bug, as he was styled in the slang of Monk-hall, but certainly these additional insects, nestling in the den of the other, were rather singular specimens of the glow-worm and musquito. Their attire was plain and simple. Each negro was dressed in coarse corduroy trowsers, and a flaring red flannel shirt. The face of Glow-worm was marked by a hideous flat nose, a receding forehead, and a wide mouth with immense lips that buried all traces of a chin and disclosed two rows of teeth protruding like the tusks of a wild boar. Musquito had the same flat nose, the same receding forehead, but his thick lips, tightly compressed, were drawn down on either side towards his jaw, presenting an outline something like the two sides of a triangle, while his sharp and pointed chin was in direct contrast to the long chinless jaw of the other. Their eyes, large, rolling and vacant, stared from bulging eyelids, that protruded beyond the outline of the brows. Altogether, each negro presented as hideous a picture of mere brute strength, linked with a form scarcely human, as the imagination of man might well conceive.

"This is Monk Gusty's friend—" muttered Abijah, or Devil-Bug, as the reader likes—"Mark him, Musquito—Mark him, Glow-worm, I say. Mind ye now—this man don't leave the house except with Gusty? D'ye hear, ye black devils?"

Each negro growled assent.

"Queer specimens of a Musquito and a Glow-worm, I say—" laughed Byrnewood in the effort to smother his disgust—"Eh? Lorrimer?"

"This way, my fellow—" answered the magnificent Gus, gently leading his friend through a small door, which led from the doorkeeper's closet—"This way. Now for the club—and then for the wager!"

Looking around in wonder, Byrnewood discovered that they had passed into the hall of an old-time mansion, with the beams of the moon, falling from a skylight in the roof far above, down over the windings of a massive staircase.

"This is rather a strange place—eh? Gus?" whispered Byrnewood, as he gazed around the hall, and marked the ancient look of the place—"why the d——l don't *they* have a light—those *insects*—ha-ha—whom we have just left?"

"Secrecy—my fellow—secrecy! Those are the 'police' of Monk-Hall, certain to be at hand in case of a row. You see, the entire arrangements of this place may be explained in one word—it is easy enough for a stranger—that's you, my boy—to find his way *in*, but it would puzzle him like the devil to find his way *out*. That is, without assistance. Take my arm Byrnewood—we must descend to the club room"

"*Descend?*"

"Yes my fellow. *Descend*, for we hold our meetings one story under ground. Its likely all the fellows—or Monks, to speak in the slang of the club—are now most royally drunk, so I can slide you in among them, without much notice. You can remain there while I go and prepare the bride—ha—ha—ha! the *bride* for your visit—"

Meanwhile, grasping Byrnewood by the arm, he had led the way along the hall, beyond the staircase, into the thick darkness, which rested upon this part of the place, unillumined by a ray of light.

"Hold my arm, as tight as you can—" he whispered—"There is a staircase somewhere here. Softly—softly—now I have it. Tread with care, Byrnewood—In a moment we will be in the midst of the Monks of Monk-Hall—"

And as they descended the subterranean stairway, surrounded by the darkness of midnight, Byrnewood found it difficult to subdue a feeling of awe which began to spread like a shadow over his soul. This feeling it was not easy to analyze. It may have been a combination of feelings; the consideration of the darkness and loneliness of the place, his almost entire ignorance of the handsome libertine who was now leading him—he knew not where; or perhaps the earnest words of the Astrologer, fraught with doom and death, came home to his soul like a vivid presentiment, in that moment of uncertainty and gloom.

"Don't you hear their shouts, my boy—" whispered Lorrimer—"Faith, they must be *drunk* as judges, every man of them! Why Byrnewood, you're as still as death—"

"To tell you the truth, Lorrimer, this place looks like the den of some old wizard—it's so d——d gloomy—"

Here we are at the door: Now mark me, Byrnewood—you must walk in the club-room, Monk's room as they call it, directly at my back. While I salute the Monks of Monk-hall, you will slide into a vacant seat at the table, and mingle in the revelry of the place until I return—"

Stooping through a narrow door, whose receding panels flung a blaze of light along the darkness of the passage, Lorrimer, with Byrnewood at his back, descended three wooden steps, that led from the door-sill to the floor, and in a moment, stood amid the revellers of Monk-hall.

In a long, narrow room, lighted by the blaze of a large chandelier, with a low ceiling and a wide floor, covered with a double-range of carpets, around a table spread with the relics of their feast, were grouped the Monks of Monk-hall.

They hailed Lorrimer with a shout, and as they rose to greet him, Byrnewood glided into a vacant arm-chair near the head of the table, and in a moment his companion had disappeared.

"I'll be with you in a moment, Monks of Monk-hall—" he shouted as he glided through the narrow door—"A little affair to settle up stairs—you know me—nice little girl—ha-ha-ha—"

"Ha-ha-ha—" echoed the band of revellers, raising their glasses merrily on high, Byrnewood glanced hurriedly around. The room, long and spacious as it was the floor covered with the most gorgeous carpeting, and the low ceiling, embellished with a faded painting in fresco, still wore an antiquated, not to say, dark and gloomy appearance. The walls were concealed by huge panels of wainscot, intricate with uncouth sculpturings of fawns and satyrs,[20] and other hideous creations of classic mythology. At one end of the room, reaching from floor to ceiling, glared an immense mirror, framed in massive walnut, its glittering surface, reflecting the long festal board, with its encircling band of revellers. Inserted in the corresponding panels of the wainscot, on either side of the small door, at the opposite end of the room, two large pictures, evidently the work of a master hand,

---

20 Fawns are young deer, and this appears to be a misspelling of the mythological faun, a lustful rural figure with goat's horns; satyrs in Greek mythology were forest deities often associated with lechery.

indicated the mingled worship of the devotees of Monk-hall. In the picture on the right of the door, Bacchus, the jolly god of mirth and wine, was represented rising from a festal-board, his brow wreathed in clustering grapes, while his hand swung aloft, a goblet filled with the purple blood of the grape. In the other painting, along a couch as dark as night, with a softened radiance falling over her uncovered form, lay a sleeping Venus, her full arms, twining above her head, while her lips were dropped apart, as though she murmured in her slumber. Straight and erect, behind the chair of the President or Abbot of the board, arose the effigy of a monk, whose long black robes fell drooping to the floor, while his cowl hung heavily over his brow, and his right hand raised on high a goblet of gold. From beneath the shadow of the falling cowl, glared a fleshless skeleton head, with the orbless eye-sockets, the cavity of the nose, and the long rows of grinning teeth, turned to a faint and ghastly crimson by the lampbeams. The hand that held the goblet on high, was a grisly skeleton hand; the long and thin fingers of bone, twining firmly around the glittering bowl.

And over this scene, over the paintings and the mirror, over the gloomy wainscot along the walls, and over the faces of the revellers with the Skeleton-Monk, grinning derision at their scene of bestial enjoyment, shone the red beams of the massive chandelier, the body and limbs of which were fashioned into the form of a grim Satyr, with a light flaring from his skull, a flame emerging from each eye, while his extended hands flung streams of fire on either side, and his knees were huddled up against his breast. The design was like a nightmare dream, so grotesque and terrible, and it completed the strange and ghostly appearance of the room.

Around the long and narrow board, strown with the relics of the feast, which had evidently been some hours in progress, sate the Monks of Monk-hall, some thirty in number, flinging their glasses on high, while the room echoed with their oaths and drunken shouts. Some lay with their heads thrown helplessly on the table, others were gazing round in sleepy drunkenness, others had fallen to the floor in a state of unconscious intoxication, while a few there were who still kept up the spirit of the feast, although their incoherent words and heavy eyes proclaimed that they too were fast advancing to that state of brutal inebriety, when strange-looking stars shine in the place of the lamps, when the bottles dance and even tables perform the cracovienne, while all sorts of beehives create a buzzing murmur in the air.

And the Monks of Monk-hall—who are they?

Grim-faced personages in long black robes and drooping cowls? Stern old men with beads around their necks and crucifix in hand? Blood-thirsty characters, perhaps, or black-browed ruffians, or wanfaced outcasts of society?

Ah no, ah no! From the eloquent, the learned, and—don't you laugh—from the pious of the Quaker City, the old Skeleton-Monk had selected the members of his band. Here were lawyers from the court, doctors from the school, and judges[21] from the bench. Here too, ruddy and round faced, sate a demure parson, whose white hands and soft words, had made him the idol of his wealthy congregation. Here was a puffy-faced Editor side by side with a Magazine Proprietor; here were sleek-visaged tradesmen, with round faces and gouty hands, whose voices, now shouting the drinking song had re-echoed the prayer and the psalm in the aristocratic church, not longer than a Sunday ago; here were solemn-faced merchants, whose names were wont to figure largely in the records of 'Bible Societies,' 'Tract Societies' and 'Send Flannel-to-the-South-Sea-Islanders Societies;' here

---

21 [Author's Original Note] This of course alludes to judges of distant country courts.

were reputable married men, with grown up children at college, and trustful wives sleeping quietly in their dreamless beds at home; here were hopeful sons, clerks in wholesale stores, who raised the wine-glass on high with hands which, not three hours since, had been busy with the cash-book of the employer, here in fine were men of all classes,—poets, authors, lawyers, judges, doctors, merchants, gamblers, and—this is no libel I hope—*one* parson, a fine red-faced parson, whose glowing face would have warmed a poor man on a cold day. Moderately drunk, or deeply drunk, or vilely drunk, all the members of the board who still maintained their arm-chairs, kept up a running fire of oaths, disjointed remarks, mingled with small talk very much broken, and snatches of bacchanalian songs, slightly improved by a peculiar chorus of hiccups.

While Byrnewood, with a sleeping man on either side of him, gazed around in sober wonder, this was the fashion of the conversation among the Monks of Monk-hall.

"Judge—I say, judge—that last Charge o' yours was capital—" hiccupped a round-faced lawyer, leaning over the table—"Touched on the vices of the day—ha—ha! 'Dens of iniquity and holes of wickedness'—its very words!—'exist in city, which want the strong arm of the law to uproot and ex-ex—d———n the hard words—exterminate them!'"

"Good—my—very—words—" replied the Judge, who sat gazing around with a smile of imbecile fatuity—"Yet, Bellamy, not quite so good as your words, when your wife—how this d———d room swims—found out your *liaison* with the Actress! Ha—ha, gents—too d———d good that—"

"Ha—ha—ha—" laughed some dozen of the company—"let's hear it—let's hear it—"

"Why—you—see—" replied the Judge—"Bellamy is *so* d———d fat, (just keep them bottles from dancing about the table!) so *very* fat, that the i-i-idea of his writing a love-letter is rath-rather improbable. Nevertheless—he did—to a pretty actress, Madame De Flum— and left it on his office table. His wife found it—oh Lord—what a scene! ranted—raved— tore her hair. 'My dear—' said our fat friend, 'do be calm—this is the copy of a letter in a breach of promise case, on which I am about to bring suit for a—lady—client. The mistake of the names is the fault of my clerk. Do—oh—*do* be calm.' His wife swallowed the story— clever story for a fat man—very!"

"Friends and Brethren, what shall ye do to be saved?" shouted the beefy-faced parson, in the long-drawn nasal tones peculiar to his pulpit or lecture-room—"When we con-consider the wickedness of the age, when we reflect tha-that there are thousands da-i-ly and hou-r-ly going down to per-per-dition, should we not cry from the depths of our souls, like Jonah from the depths of the sea—I say, give us the brandy, Mutchins!"

"Gentlemen, allow me to read you a poem—" muttered a personage, whose cheeks blushed from habitual kisses of the bottle, as he staggered from his chair, and endeavoured to stand erect—"It's a—poem—on (what an unsteady floor this is—hold it, Petriken, I say)—on the Ten Commandments. I've dedicated it to our Rev-Reverend friend yonder. There's a touch in it, gentlemen—if I may use the expression—above ordinary butter-milk. A sweetness, a path-pathos, a mildness, a-a-vein, gentlemen, of the strictest mo-ral-i-ty. I will read sonnet one—'Thou shalt not take the co-eternal name'— eh? Dammit! This is *a bill!*—I've left the sonnet at home—"

"Curse it—how I'll cut this fellow up in my next Black-Mail!" murmured the puffy-faced editor, in a tone which he deemed inaudible to the poet—"Unless he comes down handsome—I'll give him a stinger, a real scorcher—"

"Will you, though?" shouted the poet, turning round with a drunken stare, and aiming a blow at the half-stupid face of the editor—"Take that you fungus—you abortion—you d———d gleaner of a common sewer—you———"

"Gentlemen, I con-consider myself grossly insulted—" muttered the editor, as the poet's blow took effect on his wig and sent it spinning to the other end of the table—"Is the *Daily Black Mail* come to this?"

Here he made a lunge at the author of the 'Ten Commandments, a Series of Sonnets,' and, joined in a fond embrace, they fell insensible to the floor.

"Take that wig out of my plate—" shouted a deep voice from the head of the table— "Wigs, as a general thing, are not very nice with oysters, but that fellow's wig—ugh! Faugh!"

Attracted by the sound of the voice, Byrnewood glanced towards the head of the table. There, straight and erect, sate the Abbot of the night, a gentleman elected by the fraternity to preside over their feasts. He was a man of some thirty odd years, dressed in a suit of glossy black, with a form remarkable for its combination of strength with symmetry. His face, long and dusky, lighted by the gleam of a dark eye, indicating the man whose whole life had been one series of plot, scheme, and intrigue, was relieved by heavy masses of long black hair—resembling, in its texture, the mane of a horse—which fell in curling locks to his shoulders. It needed not a second glance to inform Byrnewood that he beheld the hero of Chesnut street, the distinguished millionaire, Col. Fitz-Cowles. The elegant cut of his dark vest, which gathered over his prominent chest and around his slender waist, with the nicety of a glove, the plain black scarf, fastened by a breast-pin of solid gold, the glossy black of his dress-coat, shapen of the best French cloth, all disclosed the idol of the tailors, the dream of the fashionable belles, the envy of the dry goods clerks, Algernon Fitz-Cowles. He seemed, by far, the most sober man in the company. Every now and then Byrnewood beheld him glance anxiously toward the door as though he wished to escape from the room. And after every glance, as he beheld one Monk after another kissing the carpet, bottle in hand, the interesting Colonel would join heartily in the drunken bout, raising his voice with the loudest, and emptying his glass with the most drunken. Yet, to the eye of Byrnewood, this looked more like a mere counterfeit of a drunkard's manner than the thing itself. It was evident that the handsome millionaire emptied his glass under the table.

The revel now grew wild and furious. As bottle after bottle was consumed, so the actors in the scene began to appear, more and more, in their true characters. At last all disguise seemed thrown aside, and each voice, joining in the chorus of disjointed remarks, indicated that its owner imagined himself amid the scenes of his daily life.

"Gentlemen—allow—me—to read you a tale—a tale from the German on *Transcendental Essences*—" cried Petriken, rising, for he too was there, forgetful, like Mutchins, of his promise to Lorrimer—"This, gents, is a tale for my next Western Hem.:" here his oyster-like eyes rolled ghastily—"The Ladies Western Hem., forty-eight pages—monthly—offers following inducements—two dollars—" at this point of his handbill the gentleman staggered wofully—"Office No. 209 Drayman's Alley—hurrah Mutchins what's your idea of soft crabs?"

Here the literary gentleman fell heavily to the floor, mingled in the same heap that contained the poet and the wigless editor. In a moment he rose heavily to his feet, and staggered slowly to Mutchin's side.

"Gentlemen of the jury, I charge you—" began the Judge.

"Your honor, I beg leave to open this case—" interrupted the lawyer.

"My friends and brethren," cried the parson—"what shall ye do to be saved— oh—"

"Hand us the brandy—" shouted Mutchins.

"Mutchy—Mutchy—I say—" hiccupped Petriken—"Rem-Rem-em-ber the gown and the prayer book—"

"Silly—we must take a wash-off—" cried Mutchins, starting suddenly from his seat—
"The thing—had slipped my memory—this way, my parson—ha, ha, ha—"

And taking Silly by the arm, he staggered from the room in company with the tow-haired gentleman.

"Lord look down upon these thy children, and—" continued the parson, who, like the others, appeared unconscious of the retreat of Petriken and his comrade.

"Hand the oysters this way—" remarked a mercantile gentleman, with a nose decorated by yellowish streaks from a mustard bottle.

"Boys I tell you the fire's up this alley—" cried another merchant—rather an amateur in fires when sober—"Here's the plug—now then—"

"Gentlemen of the Grand Jury, I beg leave to tell you that the amount of sin committed in this place in your very eyesight, cannot be tolerated by the court any longer. Dens of iniquity must be uprooted—who the h———ll flung that celery stalk in my eye?"

"Who soaked my cigar in champagne?"

"Somebody's lit another chandelier—"

"Hand us the brandy—"

"Did you say I didn't put down my name for 'one hundred,' to the Tract Society?"

"No I didn't, but I do now—"

"Say it again, and I'll tie you up in a meal bag—"

"My friends—" said the reverend gentleman, staggering to his feet—"What is this I see—confusion and drunkenness? Is this a scene for the house of God?" He glanced around with a look of sober reproof, and then suddenly exclaimed—"No heeltaps but show your bottoms—ha-ha-ha!"

There was another person who regarded this scene of bestial mirth with the same cool glance as Byrnewood. He was a young man with a massive face, and a deep piercing brown eye. His figure was somewhat stout, his attire careless, and his entire appearance disclosed the young Philadelphia lawyer. Changing his seat to Byrnewood's vicinity, he entered into conversation with the young merchant, and after making some pointed remarks in regard to the various members of the company, he stated that he had been lured thither by Mutchins, who had fancied he might cheat him out of a snug sum at the roulette table, or the farobank in the course of the night.

"Roulette-table—faro-bank?" muttered Byrnewood, incredulously.

"Why, my friend—" cried the young lawyer, who gave his name as Boyd Merivale—"Don't you know that this is one of the vilest rookeries in the world? It unites in all its details the house-of-ill-fame, the clubhouse, and the gambling hell. Egad! I well remember the first time I set my foot within its doors! What I beheld then, I can never forget—"

"You have been here before, then?"

"Yes have I! As I perceive you are unacquainted with the place, I will tell you my experience of

A NIGHT IN MONK-HALL[22]

Six years ago, in 1836, on a foggy night in spring, at the hour of one o'clock, I found myself reposing in one of the chambers of this mansion, on an old-fashioned bed, side by side with a

22 [Author's Original Note] The reader will remember, that Merivale entered Monk-Hall *for no licentious object, but with the distinct purpose of discovering the retreat of Western.* This story, told in Merivale's own words, is strictly true.

girl, who, before her seduction, had resided in my native village. It was one o'clock when I was aroused by a hushed sound, like the noise of a distant struggle. I awoke, started up in bed, and looked round. The room was entirely without light, save from the fire-place, where a few pieces of half-burned wood, emitted a dim and uncertain flame. Now it flashed up brightly, giving a strange lustre to the old furniture of the room, the high-backed mahogany chairs, the antiquated bureau, and the low ceiling, with heavy cornices around the walls. Again the flame died away and all was darkness. I listened intently. I could hear no sound, save the breathing of the girl who slept by my side. And as I listened, a sudden awe came over me. True, I heard no noise, but that my sleep had been broken by a most appaling sound, I could not doubt. And the stories I had heard of Monk-hall came over me. Years before, in my native village, a wild rollicking fellow, Paul Western, Cashier of the County Bank, had indulged my fancy with strange stories of a brothel, situated in the outskirts of Philadelphia. Paul was a wild fellow, rather good looking, and went often to the city on business. He spoke of Monk-hall as a place hard to find, abounding in mysteries, and darkened by hideous crimes committed within its walls. It had three stories of chambers beneath the earth, as well as above. Each of these chambers was supplied with trapdoors, through which the unsuspecting man might be flung by his murderer, without a moment's warning. There was but one range of rooms above the ground, where these trap-doors existed. From the garret to the first story, all in the same line, like the hatchways in a storehouse, sank this range of trapdoors, all carefully concealed by the manner in which the carpets were fixed. A secret spring in the wall of any one of these chambers, communicated with the spring hidden beneath the carpet. The spring in the wall might be so arranged, that a single footstep pressed on the spring, under the carpet, would open the trap-door, and plunge the victim headlong through the aperture. In such cases no man could stride across the floor without peril of his life. Beneath the ground another range of trap-doors were placed in the same manner, in the floors of three stories of the subterranean chambers. They plunged the victim—God knows where! With such arrangements for murder above and beneath the earth, might there not exist hideous pits or deep wells, far below the third story under ground, where the body of the victim would rot in darkness forever? As I remembered these details, the connection between Paul Western, the cheerful bachelor, and Emily Walraven, the woman who was sleeping at my side, flashed over my mind. The child of one of the first men of B——, educated without regard to expense by the doating father, with a mind singularly masculine, and a tall queenly form, a face distinguished for its beauty and a manner remarkable for its ladylike elegance, poor Emily had been seduced, some three years before, and soon after disappeared from the town. Her seducer no one knew, though from some hints dropped casually by my friend Paul, I judged that he at least could tell. Rumors came to the place, from time to time in relation to the beautiful but fallen girl. One rumor stated that she was now living as the mistress of a wealthy planter, who made his residence at times in Philadelphia. Another declared that she had become a common creature of the town, and this—great God, how terrible!—killed her poor father. The rumor flew round the village to-day—next Sunday old Walraven was dead and buried. They say that in his dying hour he charged Paul Western with his daughter's shame, and shrieked a father's curse upon his head. He left no property, for his troubles had preyed on his mind until he neglected his affairs, and he died insolvent.

Well two years passed on, and no one heard a word more of poor Emily. Suddenly in the spring of 1836, when this town as well as the whole Union was convulsed with the fever of speculation, Paul Western, after a visit to Philadelphia, with some funds of the Bank, amounting to near thirty thousand dollars, in his possession, suddenly disappeared, no one knew whither. My father was largely interested in the bank. He despatched me to town, in order that I might make a desperate effort to track up the footsteps of Western. Some items in the papers stated that the Cashier had fled to Texas, others that he had been drowned by accident, others that he had been spirited away. I alone possessed a clue to the place of his concealment—thus ran my thoughts at all events—and that clue was locked in the bosom of Emily Walraven, the betrayed and deeply-injured girl. Sometime before his disappearance, and after the death of old Walraven, Paul disclosed to me, under a solemn pledge of secresy, the fact that Emily was living in Philadelphia, under his protection, supported by his money. He stated that he had furnished rooms at the brothel called Monk-hall. With this fact resting on my mind, I had hurried to Philadelphia. For days my search for Emily Walraven was in vain. One night, when about giving up the chase as hopeless, I strolled to the Chesnut Street Theatre. Forrest was playing Richelieu—there was a row in the third tier—a bully had offered violence to one of the ladies of the town. Attracted by the noise, I joined the throng rushing up stairs, and beheld the girl who had been stricken, standing pale and erect, a small poignard in her upraised hand, while her eyes flashed with rage as she dared the drunken 'buffer' to strike her again. I stood thunderstruck as I recognized Emily Walraven in the degraded yet beautiful woman who stood before me. Springing forward, with one blow I felled the bully to the floor, and in another moment, seizing Emily by the arm, I hurried down stairs, evaded the constables, who were about to arrest her, and gained the street. It was yet early in the evening—there were no cabs in the street—so I had to walk home with her.

All this I remembered well, as I sat listening in the lonely room.

I remembered the big tears that started from her eyes when she recognized me, her wild exclamations when I spoke of her course of life. "Don't talk to me—" she had almost shrieked as we hurried along the street—"it's too late for me to change now. For God's sake let me be happy in my degradation."

I remembered the warm flush of indignation that reddened over her face, as pointing carelessly to a figure which I observed through the fog, some distance ahead, I exclaimed— "Is not that Paul Western yonder?" Her voice was very deep and not at all natural in its tone as she replied, with assumed unconcern—"I know nothing about the man." At last, after threading a labyrinth of streets, compared to which the puzzling garden was a mere frolic, we had gained Monk-hall, the place celebrated by the wonderful stories of my friend Western. Egad! As we neared the door I could have sworn that I beheld Western himself disappear in the door but this doubtless, I reasoned, had been a mere fancy.

Silence still prevailed in the room, still I heard but the sound of Emily breathing in her sleep, and yet my mind grew more and more heavy, with some unknown feeling of awe. I remembered with painful distinctness the hang-dog aspect of the door-keeper who had let us in, and the cut-throat visages of his two attendants seemed staring me visibly in the face. I grew quite nervous. Dark ideas of murder and the devil knows what, began to chill my very soul. I bitterly remembered that I had no arms. The only thing I carried with me was a slight cane, which had been lent me by the Landlord of the——Hotel. It was a mere switch of a thing.

As these things came stealing over me, the strange connexion between the fate of Western and that of the beautiful woman who lay beside me, the sudden disappearance of the former, the mysterious character of Monk-hall, the startling sounds which had aroused me, the lonely appearance of the room, fitfully lighted by the glare on the hearth, all combined, deepened the impression of awe, which had gradually gained possession of my faculties. I feared to stir. You may have felt this feeling—this strange and incomprehensible feeling—but if you have not, just imagine a man seized with the night-mare when wide awake.

I was sitting upright in bed, chilled to the very heart, afraid to move an inch, almost afraid to breathe, when, far, far down through the chambers of the old mansion, I heard a faint hushed sound, like a man endeavouring to cry out when attacked by night-mare, and then—great God how distinct!—I heard the cry of 'Murder, murder, murder!' far, far, far below me.

The cry aroused Emily from her sleep. She started up in bed and whispered, in a voice without tremor—"What is the matter Boyd—"

"Listen—" I cried with chattering teeth, and again, up from the depths of the mansion welled that awful sound, *Murder!* Murder! Murder! growing louder every time. Then far, far, far down I could hear a gurgling sound. It grew fainter every moment. Fainter, fainter, fainter. All was still as death.

"What does this mean?" I whispered almost fiercely, turning to Emily by my side— "What does this mean?" And a dark suspicion flashed over my mind.

The flame shot upward in the fireplace, and revealed every line of her intellectual countenance.

Her dark eyes looked firmly in my face as she answered, "In God's name I know not!"

The manner of the answer satisfied me as to her firmness, if it did not convince me of her innocence. I sat silent and sullen, conjuring over the incidents of the night.

"Come, Boyd—" she cried, as she arose from the bed—"You must leave the house. I never entertain visitors after this hour. It is my custom. I thank you for your protection at the theatre, but you must go home—"

Her manner was calm and self-possessed. I turned to her in perfect amazement.

"I will not leave the house—" I said, as a dim vision of being attacked by assassins on the stairway, arose to my mind.

"There is Devil-Bug and his cut-throat negroes—" thought I—"nothing so easy as to give me a 'cliff' with a knife from some dark corner; nothing so secret as my burial-place in some dark hole in the cellar—"

"I won't go home—" said I, aloud.

Emily looked at me in perfect wonder. It may have been affected, and it may have been real.

"Well then, I must go down stairs to get something to eat—" she said, in the most natural manner in the world—"I usually eat something about this hour—"

"You may eat old Devil-Bug and his niggers, if you like—" I replied laughing—"But out of this house my father's son don't stir till broad daylight."

With a careless laugh, she wound her night gown around her, opened the door, and disappeared in the dark. Down, down, down, I could hear her go, her footsteps echoing along the stairway of the old mansion, down, down, down. In a few moments all was still.

Here I was, in a pretty 'fix.' In a lonely room at midnight, ignorant of the passages of the wizard's den, without arms, and with the pleasant prospect of the young lady coming back with Devil-Bug and his niggers to despatch me. I had heard the cry of 'Murder'—so ran my reasoning—they, that is the murderers—would suspect that I was a witness to their guilt, and, of course, would send me down some d——d trap-door on an especial message to the devil.

This was decidedly a bad case. I began to look around the room for some chance of escape, some arms to defend myself, or, perhaps from a motive of laudible curiosity, to know something more about the place where my death was to happen.

One moment, regular as the ticking of a clock, the room would be illuminated by a flash of red light from the fire-place, the next it would be dark as a grave. Seizing the opportunity afforded by the flash, I observed some of the details of the room. On the right side of the fireplace there was a closet: the door fastened to the post by a very singular button, shaped like a diamond; about as long as your little finger and twice as thick. On the other side of the fire-place, near the ceiling, was a small oblong window, about as large as two half sheets of writing paper, pasted together at the ends. Here let me explain the use of this window. The back part of Monk-hall is utterly destitute of windows. Light, faint and dim you may be sure, is admitted from the front by small windows, placed in the wall of each room. How many rooms there are on a floor, I know not, but, be they five or ten, or twenty, they are all lighted in this way.

Well, as I looked at this window, I perceived one corner of the curtain on the other side was turned up. This gave me very unpleasant ideas. I almost fancied I beheld a human face pressed against the glass, looking at me. Then the flash on the hearth died away, and all was dark. I heard a faint creaking noise—the light from the hearth again lighted the place— could I believe my eyes—the button on the closet-door turned slowly round!

Slowly—slowly—slowly it turned, making a slight grating noise. This circumstance, slight as it may appear to you, filled me with horror. What could turn the button, but a human hand? Slowly, slowly it turned, and the door sprung open with a whizzing sound. All was dark again. The cold sweat stood out on my forehead. Was my armed murderer waiting to spring at my throat? I passed a moment of intense horror. At last, springing hastily forward, I swung the door shut, and fastened the button. I can swear that I fastened it as tight as ever button was fastened. Regaining the bed I silently awaited the result. Another flash of light—Great God!—I could swear there was a face pressed against the oblong window! Another moment and it is darkness—creak, creak, creak—is that the sound of the button again? It was light again, and there, before my very eyes, the button moved slowly round! Slowly, slowly, slowly!

The door flew open again. I sat still as a statue. I felt it difficult to breathe. Was my enemy playing with me, like the cat ere she destroys her game!

I absently extended my hand. It touched the small black stick given me by the Landlord of the——Hotel in the beginning of the evening. I drew it to me, like a friend. Grasping it with both hands, I calculated the amount of service it might do me. And as I grasped it, the top seemed parting from the lower portion of the cane. Great God! It was a sword cane! Ha-ha! I could at least strike *one* blow! My murderers should not despatch me without an effort of resistance. You see my arm is none of the puniest in the world; I may say that there are worse men than Boyd Merivale for a fight.

Clutching the sword-cane, I rushed forward, and standing on the threshold of the opened door, I made a lunge with all my strength through the darkness of the recess. Though I extended my arm to its full length, and the sword was not less than eighteen inches long, yet to my utter astonishment, I struck but the empty air! Another lunge and the same result!

Things began to grow rather queer. I was decidedly beat out as they say. I shut the closet door again, retreated to the bed, sword in hand, and awaited the result. I heard a sound, but it was the footstep of poor Emily, who that moment returned with a bed-lamp in one hand, and a small waiter, supplied with a boiled chicken and a bottle of wine in the other.

There was nothing remarkable in her look, her face was calm, and her boiled chicken and bottle of wine, decidedly common place.

"Great God—" she cried as she gazed in my countenance—"What is the matter with you? Your face is quite livid—and your eyes are fairly starting from their sockets—"

"Good reason—" said I, as I *felt* that my lips were clammy and white—"That d———d button has been going round ever since you left, and that d———d door has been springing open every time it was shut—"

"Ha-ha-ha—" she laughed—"Would it have sprung open if you had not shut it?"

This was a very clear question and easy to answer; but—

"Mark you, my lady—" said I—"Here am I in a lonely house, under peculiar circumstances. I am waked up by the cry of 'Murder'—a door springs open without a hand being visible—a face peers at me through a window. As a matter of course I suspect there has been foul work done here to-night. And through every room of this house, Emily you must lead the way, while I follow, this good sword in hand. If the light goes out, or if you blow it out, you are to be pitied, for in either case, I swear by Living God, I will run you through with this sword—"

"Ha-ha-ha—" she fairly screamed with laughter as she sprung to the closet-door— "Behold the mystery—"

And with her fair fingers she pointed to the socket of the button, and to the centre of the door. The door has been 'sprung,' as it is termed, by the weather. That is, the centre bulged inward, leaving the edge toward the door-post to press the contrary direction. The socket of the button, by continual wear, had been increased to twice its original size. Whenever the door was first buttoned, the head of the screw pressed against one of the edges of the socket. In a moment the pressure of the edge of the door, which you will remember was directed outward, dislodged the head of the screw and it sank, well-nigh half an inch into the worn socket of the button. Then the button, removed *farther* from the door than at first, would slowly turn, and the door spring open. All this was plain enough, and I smiled at my recent fright.

"Very good, Emily—" I laughed—"But the mystery of this sword—what of that? I made a lunge in the closet and it touched nothing—"

"You are suspicious, Boyd—" she answered with a laugh—"But the fact is, the closet is rather a deep one—"

"Rather—" said I—"and so are you, my dear—"

There may have been something very meaning in my manner, but certainly, though her full black eyes looked fixedly on me, yet I thought her face grew a shade paler as I spoke.

"And my dear—" I continued—"What do you make of the face peeping through the window:—"

"All fancy—all fancy—" she replied, but as she spoke I saw her eye glance hurriedly toward the very window. Did she *too* fear that she might behold a face?

"We will search the closet—" I remarked, throwing open the door—"What have we here? Nothing but an old cloak hanging to a hook—let's try it with my sword!"

Again I made a lunge with my sword: again I thrust at the empty air.

"Emily, there is a room beyond this cloak—you will enter first if you please. Remember my warning about the light if you please—"

"Oh now that I remember, this closet *does* open into the next room—" she said gaily, although her cheek—so it struck me—grew a little paler and her lip trembled slightly—"I had quite forgotten the circumstance—"

"Enter Emily, and don't forget the light—"

She flung the door aside and passed on with the light in her hand. I followed her. We stood in a small room, lighted like the other by an oblong window. There was no other window, no door, no outlet of any sort. Even a chimney-place was wanting. In one corner stood a massive bed—the quilt was unruffled. Two or three old fashioned chairs were scattered round the room, and from the spot where I stood looking over the foot of the bed, I could see the top of another chair, and nothing more, between the bed and the wall.

A trifling fact in Emily's behaviour may be remarked. The moment the light of the lamp which she held in her hand flashed round the room, she turned to me with a smile, and leading the way round the corner of the foot of the bed, asked me in a pleasant voice "Did I see any thing remarkable there?"

She shaded her eyes from the lamp as she spoke, and toyed me playfully under the chin. You will bear in mind that at this moment, I had turned my face toward the closet by which we had entered. My back was therefore toward the part of the room most remote from the closet. It was a trifling fact, but I may as well tell you, that the manner in which Emily held the light, threw that portion of the room, between the foot of the bed and the wall in complete shadow, while the rest of the chamber was bright as day.

Smilingly Emily toyed me under the chin, and at that moment I thought she looked extremely beautiful.

By Jove! I wish you could have seen her eyes shine, and her cheek—Lord bless you—a full blown rose wasn't a circumstance to it. She looked so beautiful, in fact, as she came sideling up to me, that I stepped backward in order to have a full view of her before I pressed a kiss on her pouting lips. I did step back, and did kiss her. It wasn't singular, perhaps, but her lips were hot as a coal. Again she advanced to me, again chucked me under the chin. Again I stepped back to look at her, again I wished to taste her lips so pouting, but rather warm, when—

To tell you the truth, stranger, even at this late day the remembrance makes my blood run cold!

——When I heard a sound like the sweeping of a tree-limb against a closed shutter, it was so faint and distant, and a stream of cold air came rushing up my back.

I turned around carelessly to ascertain the cause. I took but a single glance, and then— by G——d—I sprung at least ten feet from the place. There, at my very back, between the bed and the wall, opposite its foot, I beheld a carpeted space some three feet square, sinking slowly down, and separating itself from the floor. I had stepped my foot upon the spring— made ready for me, to be sure—and the trap-door sank below me.

You may suppose my feelings were somewhat excited. In truth, my heart, for a moment, felt as though it was turning to a ball of ice. First I looked at the trap-door and then at Emily. Her face was pale as ashes, and she leaned, trembling, against the bedpost. Advancing, sword in hand, I gazed down the trap-door. Great God! how dark and gloomy the pit looked! From room to room, from floor to floor, a succession of traps had fallen— far below—it looked like a mile, although that was but an exaggeration natural to a highly excited mind—far, far below gleamed a light, and a buzzing murmur came up this hatchway of death.

Stooping slowly down, sword in hand, my eye on the alert for Miss Emily, I disengaged a piece of linen, from a nail, near the edge of the trap-door. Where the linen—it was a shirt wristband—had been fastened, the carpet was slightly torn, as though a man in falling had grasped it with his finger ends.

The wristband was, in more correct language, a ruffle for the wrist. It came to my mind, in this moment, that I had often ridiculed Paul Western for his queer old bachelor ways. Among other odd notions, he had worn ruffles at his wrist. As I gathered this little piece of linen in my grasp, the trap-door slowly rose. I turned to look for Miss Emily, she had changed her position, and stood pressing her hand against the opposite wall.

"Now, Miss Emily, my dear—" I cried, advancing toward her—"Give me a plain answer to a plain question—and tell me—what in the devil do you think of yourself?"

Perfectly white in the face, she glided across the room and stood at the foot of the bed, in her former position leaning against the post for support. You will observe that her form concealed the chair, whose top I had only seen across the bed.

"Step aside, Miss Emily, my dear—" I said, in as quiet a tone as I could command—"Or you see, my lady, I'll have to use a little necessary force—"

Instead of stepping aside, as a peaceable woman would have done, she sits right down in the chair, fixing those full black eyes of her's on my face, with a glance that looked very much like madness.

Extending my hand, I raised her from the seat. She rested like a dead weight in my arms. She had fainted. Wrapped in her night-gown, I laid her on the bed, and then examined the chair in the corner. Something about this chair attracted my attention. A coat hung over the round—a blue coat with metal buttons. A buff vest hung under this coat; and a high stock, with a shirt collar.

I knew these things at once. They belonged to my friend, Paul Western.

"And so, my lady—" I cried, forgetting that she had fainted; "Mr. Western came home, from the theatre, to his rooms, arrived just before us, took off his coat and vest, and stock and collar—maybe was just about to take off his boots—when he stepped on the spring and in a moment was in—in h——ll—"

Taking the light in one hand, I dragged or carried her, into the other room and laid her on the bed. After half an hour or so, she came to her senses.

"You see—you see—" were her first words uttered, with her eyes flashing like live-coals, and her lips white as marble—"You see, I could not help it, for my father's curse was upon him!"

She laughed wildly, and lay in my arms a maniac.

Stranger, I'll make a short story of the thing now. How I watched her all night till broad day, how I escaped from the house—for Mr. Devil-Bug, it seems, didn't suspect I knew anything—how I returned home without any news of Paul Western, are matters easy to conceive as tell.

Why didn't I institute a search? Fiddle-faddle! Blazon my name to the world as a visiter to a Bagnio?[23] Sensible thing, that! And then, although I was sure in my own soul, that the clothes which I had discovered belonged to Paul Western, it would have been most difficult to establish this fact in Court. One word more and I have done.

Never since that night has Paul Western been heard of by living man. Never since that night has Emily Walraven been seen in this breathing world. You start. Let me whisper a word in your ear. Suppose Emily joined in Western's murder from motives of revenge, what then were Devil-Bug's? *(He* of course was the real murderer.) Why the money to be sure. Why he troubled with Emily as a witness of his guilt, or a sharer of his money? This is rather a—a *dark house,* and it's my opinion, stranger, that *he murdered her too!*

---

23 A brothel.

Ha-ha—why here's all the room to ourselves! All the club have either disappeared, or lie drunk on the floor! I saw Fitz-Cowles—I know him—sneak off a few moments since—I could tell by his eye that he is after some devils-trick! The parson has gone, and the judge has gone, the lawyer has fallen among the slain, and so, wishing you good night, stranger, I'll vanish! Beware of the Monks of Monk-hall!"

Byrnewood was alone.

His head was depressed, his arms were folded, and his eye, gazing vacantly on the table, shone and glistened with the internal agitation of his brain. He sate there, silent, motionless, awed to the very soul. The story of the stranger had thrilled him to the heart, had aroused a strange train of thought, and now rested like an oppressive weight upon his brain.

Byrnewood gazed around. With a sudden effort he shook off the spell of absence which mingled with an incomprehensible feeling of awe, had enchained his faculties. He looked around the room. He was, indeed, alone. Above him, the hideous Satyr chandelier, still flared its red light over the table, over the mirror, and along the gloomy wainscot of the walls. Around the table, grouped in various attitudes of unconscious drunkenness, lay the members of the drinking party, the merry Monks of Monk-hall. There lay the poet, with his sanguine face shining redly in the light, while his hand rested on the bare scalp of the wigless editor, there snored some dozen merchants, all doubled up together, like the slain in battle, and there, a solitary doctor, who had fallen asleep on his knees, was dozing away with one eye wide open, while his right hand brushed away a solitary fly from his pimpled nose.

The scene was not calculated to produce the most serious feelings in the world. There was inebriety—as the refined phrase it—in every shape, inebriety on its face, inebriety with its mouth wide open, inebriety on its knees brushing a fly from its nose, inebriety groaning, grunting, or snoring, inebriety doubled up—mingled in a mass of limbs, heads and bodies, woven together—or flat inebriety simply straightened out on its back with its nose performing a select overture of snores. To be brief, there, scattered over the floor, lay drunkenness—as the vulgar will style it—in every shape, moddled after various patterns, and taken by that ingenious artist, the Bottle, fresh from real life.

Raising his eyes from the prostrate members of the club, Byrnewood started with involuntary surprise as he beheld, standing at the tables-head, the black-robed figure of the Skeleton-Monk, with his hand of bone flinging aloft the goblet, while his fleshless brow glared in the light, from the shadow of the falling cowl. As the light flickered to and fro, it gave the grinning teeth of the Skeleton the appearance of life and animation for a single moment. Byrnewood thought he beheld the teeth move in a ghastly smile; he even fancied that the orbless sockets, gleaming beneath the white brow, flashed with the glance of life, and gazed sneeringly in his face.

He started with involuntary horror, and then sate silent as before. And as you can feel cold or heat steal over you by slow degrees, so he felt that same strange feeling of awe, which he had known that night for the first time in his life, come slowly over him moving like a shadow over his soul, and stealing like a paralysis through his every limb. He sate like a man suddenly frozen.

"My God!" he murmured—and the sound of his voice frightened him—"How strange I feel! Can this be the first attack of some terrible disease—or—is it, but the effect of the horrible story related by the stranger? I have read in books that a feeling like this steals over a man, just before some terrible calamity breaks over his head—this is fearful as death itself!"

He was silent again, and then the exclamation broke from his lips— "Lorrimer—why does he not return? He has been absent full an hour—what does it mean? Can the words of that—pshaw! that fortune teller have any truth in them? How can Lorrimer injure me— how can I injure him? Three days hence—Christmas—ha, ha—I believe I'm going mad— there's cold sweat on my forehead—"

As he spoke he raised his left hand to his brow, and in the action, the gleam of a plain ring on his finger met his eye. He kissed it suddenly, and kissed it again and again? Was it the gift of his ladye-love?

"God bless her—God bless her! Wo to the man who shall do *her* wrong—and yet poor Annie—"

He rose suddenly from his seat and strode towards the door.

"I know not why it is, but I feel as though an invisible hand, was urging me onward through the rooms of this house! And onward I will go, until I discover Lorrimer or solve the mystery of this den. God knows, I feel—pshaw! I'm only nervous—as though I was walking to my death."

Passing through the narrow door-way, he cautiously ascended the dark staircase, and a moment stood on the first floor. The moon was still shining through the distant skylight, down over the windings of the massive stairway. All was silent as death within the mansion. Not a sound, not even the murmur of a voice or the hushed tread of a foot-step could be heard. Winding his cloak tightly around his limbs, Byrnewood rushed up the stair- case, tra- versing two steps at a time, and treading softly, for fear of discovery. He reached the second floor. Still the place was silent and dismal, still the column of moonlight pouring through the skylight, over the windings of the staircase only rendered the surrounding darkness more gloomy and indistinct. Up the winding staircase he again resumed his way and in a moment stood upon the landing or hall of the third floor. This was an oblong space, with the doors of many rooms fashioned in its walls. Another stairway led upward from the floor, but the attention of Byrnewood was arrested by a single ray of light, that for a moment flickered along the thick darkness of the southern end of the hall. Stepping forward hast- ily, Byrnewood found all progress arrested by the opposing front of a solid wall. He gazed toward his left—it was so dark, that he could not see his hand before his eyes. Turning his glance to the right, as his vision became more accustomed to the darkness, he beheld the dim walls of a long corridor, at whose entrance he stood, and whose farther extreme was illumined by a light, that to all appearance, flashed from an open door. Without a moment's thought he strode along the thickly carpeted passage of the corridor; he stood in the full glow of the light flashing from the open door.

Looking through the doorway, he beheld a large chamber furnished in a style of lavish magnificence, and lighted by a splendid chandelier. It was silent and deserted. From the ceiling to the floor, along the wall opposite the doorway, hung a curtain of damask silk, trailing in heavy folds, along the gorgeous carpet. Impelled by the strange impulse that had urged him thus far, Byrnewood entered the chamber, and without pausing to admire its gorgeous appointments, strode forward to the damask curtain.

He swung one of its hangings aside, expecting to behold the extreme wall of the cham- ber. To his entire wonder, another chamber, as spacious as the one in which he stood, lay open to his gaze. The walls were all one gorgeous picture, evidently painted by a master- hand. Blue skies, deep green forests, dashing waterfalls and a cool calm lake, in which fair women were laving their limbs, broke on the eyes of the intruder, as he turned his gaze from wall to wall. A curtain of azure, sprinkled with a border of golden leaves, hung along the farther extremity of the room. In one corner stood a massive bed, whose snow-white counterpane, fell smoothly and unruffled to the very floor, mingling with the long curtains, which pure and stainless as the counterpane, hung around the couch in graceful festoons, like the wings of a bird guarding its resting place.

"The bridal-bed!" murmured Byrnewood, as he flung the curtains of gold and azure, hurriedly aside.

A murmur of surprise, mingled with admiration, escaped from his lips, as he beheld the small closet, for it could scarcely be called a room, which the undrawn curtaining threw open to his gaze.

It was indeed a small and elegant room, lined along its four sides with drooping curtains of faint-hued crimson silk. The ceiling itself was but a continuation of these curtains, or hangings, for they were gathered in the centre, by a single star of gold. The carpet on the floor was of the same faint-crimson color, and the large sofa, placed along one side of the apartment, was covered with velvet, that harmonized in hue, with both carpet and hangings. On the snow-white cloth, of a small table placed in the centre of the room, stood a large wax candle, burning in a candlestick of silver, and flinging a subdued and mellow light around the plate. There was a neat little couch, standing in the corner, with a *toilette* at its foot. The quilt on the couch was ruffled, as though some one had lately risen from it, and the equipage of the *toilette* looked as though it had been recently used.

The faint light falling over the hangings, whose hue resembled the first flush of day, the luxurious sofa, the neat though diminutive couch, the small table in the centre, the carpet whose colors were in elegant harmony with the hue of the curtains, all combined, gave the place an air of splendid comfort—if we may join these incongruous words—that indicated the sleeping chamber of a lovely woman.

"This has been the resting place of the *bride*—" murmured Byrnewood, gazing in admiration around the room—"It looks elegant it is true, but if she is the innocent thing Lorrimer would have me believe, then better for her, to have slept in the foulest gutter of the streets, than to have lain for an instant in this woman-trap—"

There was a woman's dress—a frock of plain black silk—flung over one of the rounds of the sofa. Anxious to gather some idea of the form of the bride—oh foul prostitution of the name!—from the shape of the dress, Byrnewood raised the frock and examined its details. As he did this, the sound of voices came hushed and murmuring to his ear from a room, opposite the chamber which he had but a moment left. Half occupied in listening to these voices, Byrnewood glanced at the dress which he held in his hand, and as he took in its various details of style and shape, the pupil of his full black eye dilated, and his cheek became colorless as death.

Then the room seemed to swim around him, and he pressed his hand forcibly against his brow, as if to assure himself, that he was not entangled in the mazes of some hideous dream.

Then, letting his own cloak and the black silk dress fall on the floor at once, he walked with a measured step toward that side of the room opposite the Painted Chamber.

The voices grew louder in the next room. Byrnewood listened in silence. His face was even paler than before, and you could see how desperate was the effort which he made to suppress an involuntary cry of horror, that came rising to his lips. Extending his hand, he pushed the curtain slightly aside, and looked into the next room.

The extended hand fell like a dead weight to his side.

Over his entire countenance flashed a mingled expression of surprise, and horror, and woe, that convulsed every feature with a spasmodic movement, and forced his large black eyes from their very sockets. For a moment he looked as if about to fall lifeless on the floor, and then it was evident that he exerted all his energies to control this most fearful agitation. He pressed both hands nervously against his forehead, as though his brain was tortured by internal flame. Then he reared his form proudly erect, and stood apparently firm and self possessed, although his countenance looked more like the face of a corpse than the face of a living man.

And as he stood there, silent and firm, although his very reason tottered to its ruin, there glided to his back, like an omen of death, pursuing the footsteps of life, the distorted form of the Door-keeper of Monk-hall, his huge bony arms upraised, his hideous face convulsed in a loathsome grin, while his solitary eye glared out from its sunken socket, a flame lighted in a skull, grotesque yet terrible.

In vain was the momentary firmness which Byrnewood had aroused to his aid! In vain was the effort that suppressed his breath, that clenched his hands, that forced the clammy sweat from his brow! He felt the awful agony that convulsed his soul rising to his lips—he would have given the world to stifle it—but in vain, in vain were all his superhuman efforts!

One terrific howl, like the yell of a man flung suddenly over a cataract, broke from his lips. He thrust aside the curtain, and strode madly through its folds into the next room.

Chapter Eighth

Mother Nancy and Long-Haired Bess

"So ye have lured the pretty dove into the cage, at last—" said the old lady, with a pleasant smile, as she poised a nice morsel of buttered toast between her fingers—"This tea is most too weak—a little more out of the caddy, Bessie, dear. Lord! who'd a-thought you'd a-caught the baby-face so easy! Does the kettle boil, my dear? I put it on the fire before you left, and you've been away near an hour, so it ought to be hissing hot by this time. Caught her at last! Hah-hah—hey? Bessie? You're a reg'lar keen one, I must say!"

And with the mild words the old lady arranged the tea things on the small table, covered with a neat white cloth, and pouring out a cup of 'Gunpowder,' chuckled pleasantly to herself, as though she and the buttered toast had a quiet little joke together.

"Spankin' cold night, I tell ye, Mother Nancy—" exclaimed the young lady in black as she flung herself in a chair, and tossed her bonnet on the old sofa—"Precious time I've had with that little chit of a thing! Up one street and down another, I've been racing for this blessed hour! And the regular white and black 'uns I've been forced to tell! Oh crickey—don't mention 'em, I beg—"

"Sit down, Bess—sit down, Bessie, that's a dove—" said the delighted old lady, crunching the toast between her toothless gums—"and tell us all about it from the first! These things are quite refreshin' to us old stagers."

"What a perfect old d——l—" muttered Bessie, as she drew her seat near the supper table—"These oysters are quite delightful—stewed to a turn, I do declare—" she continued, aloud—"Got a little drop o' the 'lively'—hey, Mother?"

"Yes, dovey—here's the key of the closet. Get the bottle, my dear. A leetle—jist a *leetle*—don't go ugly with one's tea—"

While the tall and queenly Bessie is engaged in securing a drop of the lively, we will take a passing glance at Mother Perkins, the respectable Lady Abbess of Monk-hall.

As she sate in that formal arm-chair, straight and erect, her portly form clad in sombre black, with a plain white collar around her neck and a bunch of keys at her girdle, Mother Nancy looked, for all the world, like a quiet old body, whose only delight was to scatter blessings around her, give large alms to the poor, and bestow unlimited amounts of tracts among the vicious. A good, dear, old body, was Mother Nancy, although her face was decidedly prepossessing. A low forehead, surmounted by a perfect tower-of-Babel of a cap, a little sharp nose looking out from two cheeks disposed in immense collops of yellowish flesh, two small grey eyes encircled by a wilderness of wrinkles, a deep indentation where a mouth should have been, and a sharp chin, ornamented with a slight 'imperial' of stiff grey beard; such were the details of a countenance, on which seventy years had showered their sins, and cares, and crimes, without making the dear old lady, for a moment, pause in her career.

And such a career! God of Heaven! did womanhood, which in its dawn, or bloom, or full maturity, is so beautiful, which even in its decline is lovely, which in trembling old age is venerable, did womanhood ever sink so low as this? How many of the graves in an hundred churchyards, graves of the fair and beautiful, had been dug by the gouty hands of the vile old hag, who sate chuckling in her quiet arm-chair? How many of the betrayed maidens, found rotting on the rivers waves, dangling from the garret rafter, starving in the streets, or resting, vile and loathsome, in the Greenhouse;[24] how many of these will, at the last day when the accounts of this lovely earth will be closed forever, rise up and curse the old hag with their ruin, with their shame, with their unwept death?

The details of the old lady's room by no means indicated her disposition, or the course of her life. It was a fine old room with walls neatly papered, all full of nooks and corners, and warmed by a cheerful wood fire blazing on the spacious hearth. One whole side of the room seemed to have been attacked with some strange eruptive disease, and broken out into an erysipelas of cupboards and closets. An old desk that might have told a world of wonders of Noah's Ark from its own personal experience, could it have spoken, stood in one corner, and a large side-board, on whose top a fat fellow of a decanter seemed drilling some raw recruits of bottles and glasses into military order, occupied one entire side of the room, or cell, of the Lady Abbess.

There are few persons in the world who have not a favourite of some kind, either a baby, or a parrot, or a canary, or a cat, or, in desperate cases, a pig. Mother Nancy had her favourite as well as less reputable people. A huge bull dog, with sore eyes and a ragged tail—that seemed to have been purchased at a second-had store during the hard times—lay nestling at the old lady's feet, looking very much like the candidate whom all the old and surly dogs would choose for Alderman, in case the canine race had the privilege of electing an officer of that honorable class, among themselves. This dog, so old bachelor-like and aldermanic in appearance, the old lady was wont to call by the name of 'Dolph,' being the short for 'Dolphin,' of which remarkable fish the animal was supposed to be a decided copy.

"Here's the 'lively,' Mother Nancy—" observed Miss Bessie, as she resumed her seat at the supper table—"It's the real hot stuff and *no* mistake. The oysters, if you please—a little o' that pepper. Any mustard there? Now then, Mother, let's be comfortable—"

---

24 The house for the unknown dead.

"But" observed the old lady pouring a glass of the 'Lively' from a decanter labelled 'Brandy'—"But Bessie my love, I'm a-waitin' to hear all about this little dove whom you trapped to night—"

It may be as well to remark that Bessie, was a tall queenly girl of some twenty-five, with a form that had once been beautiful beyond description, and even now in its ruins, was lovely to look upon, while her faded face, marked by a high brow and raven-black hair, was still enlivened by the glance of two large dark eyes, that were susceptable of any expression, love or hate, revenge or jealousy; anything but fear. Her complexion was a very faint brown with a deep rose-tint on each cheek. She was still beautiful, although a long career of dissipation had given a faded look to the outlines of her face, indenting a slight wrinkle between her arching brows, and slightly discoloring the flesh beneath each eye.

This here "Lively" is first rate, after the tramp I've had—" said Bessie as her eyes grew brighter with the 'lively' effects of the bottle—"You know Mother Nancy its three weeks since Gus mentioned the *thing* to me—"

"What thing, my dear?"

"Why that he'd like to have a little dove for himself—something above the common run. Something from the aristocracy of the Quaker City—you know?"

"Yes my dear. Here Dolph—here Dolph-ee—here's a nice bit for Dolph—"

"Gus agreed to give me something handsome if I could manage it for him, so I undertook the thing. The bread if you please, Mother. You know I'm rather expert in such matters?"

"There ain't you beat my dear. Be quiet Dolph—that's a nice Dolph-ee—"

"For a week all my efforts were in vain. I could'nt discover anything that was likely to suit the taste of Gus—At last he put me on the right track himself—"

"He did, did he? Ah deary me, but Gus is a regular lark. You can't perduce his ekle—"

"One day strolling up Third Street, Gus was attracted by the sight of a pretty girl, sitting at the window of a wealthy merchant, who has just retired from business. You've heard of old Arlington? Try the 'Lively' Mother. Gus made some enquiries; found that the young lady had just returned, from the Moravian boarding school at Bethlehem. She was innocent, inexperienced, and all that. Suited Lorrimer's taste. He swore he'd have her."

"So you undertook to catch her, did ye? Butter my dear?"

"That did I. The way I managed it was a caution. Dressing myself in solemn black, I strolled along Third street, one mild winter evening, some two weeks since. Mary—that's her name—was standing at the front door, gazing carelessly down the street. I tripped up the steps and asked in my most winning tone——"

"You can act the lady when you like, Bess. That's a fact.—"

"Whether Mr. Elmwood lived there? Of course she answered 'No.' But in making an apology for my intrusion, I managed to state that Mr. Elmwood was my uncle, that I had just come to the city on a visit, and had left my aunt's in Spruce street, but a few moments ago, thinking to pay a nice little call on my dear old relative—"

"Just like you Bessie! So you scraped acquaintance with her?"

"Fresh from boarding school, as ignorant of the world as the babe unborn, the girl was interested in me, I suppose, and swallowed the white'uns I told her, without a single suspicion, The next day about noon, I met her as she was hurrying to see an old aunt, who lived two or three Squares below her father's house. She was all in a glow, for she had been hurrying along rather fast, anxious to reach her aunt's house, as soon as possible. I spoke to her—proposed a walk—she assented with a smile of pleasure. I told her a long story of my sorrows; how I had been engaged to be married, how my lover had died of consumption but a month ago; that he was such a nice young man, with curly hair, and hazel eyes, and that I was in black for his death. I put peach fur over her eyes, by whole hand's full I tell you. The girl was interested, and like all young girls, she was delighted to become the *confidante* of an amiable young lady, who had a little love-romance of real life, to disclose. Oysters, Mother Nancy—"

"The long and short of it was, that you wormed yourself into her confidence? That it my dear? Keep still Dolph or Dolph's mommy would drop little bit of hot tea on Dolph's head—"

"We walked out together for three days, just toward dark in the evening. You can fancy Mother, how I wound myself into the heart of this young girl. Closer and closer every day I tightened the cords that bound us, and on the third evening I believe she would have died for me.—"

"Well, well child, when did Gusty first speak to her? A little more of the "Gunpowder" my dear—"

"One evening I persuaded her to take a stroll along Chesnut Street with me. Gus was at our heels you may be sure. He passed on a little-a-head determining to speak to her, at all hazards. She saved him the trouble. Lord love you Mother Nancy, she spoke to him first—"

"Be still Dolph—be still Dolph-ee! Now Bessie that's a leetle too strong! Not the tea, but the story. She so innocent and baby-like speak first to a strange man? Ask me to believe in tea made out of turnip tops will ye?—"

"She mistook him for a Mr. Belmont whom she had seen at Bethlehem. He did not undeceive her, until she was completely in his power. He walked by her side that evening up and down Chesnut Street, for nearly an hour. I saw at once, that her girlish fancy was caught by his smooth tongue, and handsome form. The next night he met us again, and the next, and the next—Lord pity her—the poor child was *now* entirely at his mercy—"

"Ha—ha—Gusty is sich a devil. Put the kettle on the fire my dear. Let's try a little of the 'Lively.' And how did she—this baby-faced doll—keep these walks secret from the eyes of her folks? Eh? Bessie?"

"Easy as *that*—" replied Bessie gracefully snapping her fingers—"Every time she went out, she told father and mother' that she went to see her old Aunt. I hinted at first, that our friendship would be more romantic, if concealed from all intrusive eyes. The girl took the hint. Lorrimer with his smooth tongue, told her a long story about his eccentric uncle who had sworn he should not marry, for years to come; and therefore he was obliged to keep his attentions to her, hidden from both of their families. Gusty was dependent on this old uncle—you know? Once married, the old uncle would relent as he beheld the beauty and innocence of the young—*wife!* So Gusty made her believe. You can imagine the whole trap. We had her in our power. Last night she consented to leave her home for Lorrimer's *family* mansion. He was to marry her, the approval of his uncle—that imaginary old Gentleman—was to be obtained, and on Christmas Eve, Mr. and—ha, ha, ha—*Mistress* Lorrimer, were to rush into old Middleton's house, fall on their knees, invoke the old man's blessing; be forgiven and be happy! Hand us the toast Mother Nancy—"

"And to night the girl *did* leave the old folk's house? Entered the door of Monk-hall, thinking it was Lorrimer's *family* Mansion, and to-morrow morning at three o'clock will be married—eh? Bess?"

"Married, pshaw! *Over the left.* Lorrimer said he would get that fellow Petriken to person-ate the Parson—Mutchins the gambler, acts the old uncle; you, Mother Nancy must, dress up for the kind and amiable grandma—suit you to a T? Lorrimer pays high for his rooms you know?"

" 'Spose it must be done. It's now after ten o'clock. You left the baby-face sleeping, eh? At half-past two you'll have to rouse her, to dress. Be quiet Dolph or I'll scald its head— that's a dear. Now Bessie tell me the truth, did you never regret that you had undertaken the job? The girl you say is so innocent?"

"Regret?" cried Bess with a flashing eye—"Why should I regret? Have I not as good a right to the comforts of a home, to the smile of a father, the love of a mother, as she? Have I not been robbed of all these? Of all that is most sacred to woman? Is this innocent Mary, a whit better than I *was* when the devil in human shape first dragged me from my home? I feel happy—aye happy—when I can drag another woman, into the same foul pit, where I am doomed to lie and rot—"

"Yet this thing was *so* innocent—" cried the good old lady patting Dolph on the head— "I confess I laugh at all qualms—all petty scruples, but you were so different when first I knew you—you *Emily*, you—"

"*Emily*—" shrieked the other as she sprung suddenly to her feet—"You hag of the devil—call me by that name again, and as God will judge at the last day, I'll throttle you!" She shook her clenched hand across the table, and her eyes were bloodshot with sudden rage—" '*Emily!*' Your mother called you by that name when a little child—" She cried with a burst of feeling, most fearful to behold in one so fallen—"Your father blessed you by that name, the night before you fled from his roof!"

" 'Emily!' Aye, *he*, the foul betrayer, whispered that name with a smile as he entered the Chamber, from which he never came forth again—You remember it old hell-cat, do ye?—"

"Not so loud, Good G——d, not so loud—" cried the astonished Mother Nancy— "Abuse me Bessie dear—but not so loud; down Dolph don't mind the girl, she's mad—not so loud, I say—"

"I can see him now!" cried the fallen girl, as with her tall form raised to its full height, she fixed her flashing eye on vacancy—"He enters the room—that room with the—the trap-door you know? 'Good night, Emily,' he said, and smiled—'*Emily,*' and—my father had cursed him! I laid me down and rested by another man's side. *He* thought I slept. Slept! ha, ha! When, with my entire soul, I listened to the foot-steps in the next room—ha, ha—when I heard the creaking sound of the falling trap, when I drank in the cry of agony, when I heard that name 'Emily, oh Emily,' come shrieking up the pit of death! My father had cursed him, and he died! 'Emily'—oh my God—" and she wrung her hands in very agony—"Roll back the years of my life, blot out the foul record of my sins, let me, oh God—you are all powerful and can do it—let me be a child again, a little child, and though I crawl through life in the rags of a beggar, I will never cease to bless—oh God—to bless your name—"

She fell heavily to her seat, and, covering her face with her hands, wept the scalding tears of guilt and shame.

" 'Gal's been a-takin' opium—" said the old lady, calmly—"And the fit's come on her. 'Sarves her right. 'Told her never to mix her brandy with opium—"

"Did I regret having undertaken the ruin of the girl—" said Bess, in a whisper, that made even the old lady start with surprise—"Regret? I tell ye, old hell-dame as you are, that my very heart strings seemed breaking within me to-night, as I led her from her home—"

"What the d——l did you do it for, then? Here's a nice Dolph—eat a piece o' buttered toast—that's a good Dolph-ee—"

"When the seducer first assailed me—" continued Bess, in an absent tone—"He assailed a woman, with a mind stored with knowledge of the world's ways, a soul full as crafty as his own, a wit sharp and keen as ever dropped poison or sweetness from a woman's tongue! But this girl, so child-like, so unsuspecting, so innocent! my God! how it wrung my heart, when I first discovered that she *loved* Lorrimer, loved him without one shade of gross feeling, loved him without a doubt, warmly, devotedly, with all the trustfulness of an angel-soul, fresh from the hands of God! Never a bird fell more helplessly into the yawning jaws of the snake, that had charmed it to ruin, than poor Mary fell into the accursed wiles of Lorrimer! And yet I, *I* aided him—"

"So you did. The more shame for you to harm sich a dove. Go up stairs, my dear, and let her loose. We'll consent, won't we? Ha-ha! Why Bess, I thought you had more sense than to go on this way. What *will* become of you?"

"I suppose that I will die in the same ditch where the souls of so many of my vile sisterhood have crept forth from their leprous bodies? Eh, Mother Nance? Die in a ditch? '*Emily*' die in a ditch? And then in the next world—ha, ha, ha—I see a big lake of fire, on which souls are dancing like moths in a candle—ha, ha, ha!"

"Reely, gal, you must leave off that opium. Gus promised you some five or six hundred if you caught this gal, and you can't go back now—"

"Yes, I know it! I know it! *Forward's* the word if the next stop plunges me in hell—"

And the girl buried her face in her hands, and was silent again. Let not the reader wonder at the mass of contradictions, heaped together in the character of this miserable wreck of a woman. One moment conversing in the slang of a brothel, like a thing lapped from her birth in pollution; the next, whispering forth her ravings in language indicative of the educated woman of her purer days; one instant glorying in her shame, the next recoiling in horror as she viewed the dark path which she had trodden, the darker path which she was yet to tread—these paradoxes are things of every day occurrence, only to be explained, when the mass of good and evil, found in every human heart, is divided into distinct parts, no more to mingle in one, no more to occasion an eternal contest in the self-warring heart of man.

"Well, well, Bessie—go to bed and sleep a little—that's a dear—" said the old lady, with a pleasing smile—"Opium isn't good for you, and you know it. A leetle nap 'ill do you good. Sleep a bit, and then you'll be right fresh for the wedding. Three o'clock you know—Come along, Dolph, mommy must go 'tend to some little things about the house—Come along, *Dolph-ee*—Sleep a leetle, Bessie, that's a dear!"

Chapter Ninth

The Bride

A chapter in which every woman may find some leaves of her own heart,
read with the eyes of a high and holy love

"Mary!"

Oh sweetest name of woman! name by which some of us may hail a wife, or a sister in heaven; name so soft, and rippling, and musical; name of the mother of Jesus, made holy by poetry and religion!—how foully were you profaned by the lips that whispered your sound of gentleness in the sleeper's ear!

"Mary!"

The fair girl stirred in her sleep, and her lips dropped gently apart as she whispered a single word—

"Lorraine!"

"The assumed name of Lorrimer—" exclaimed the woman, who stood by the bedside—"Gus has some taste, even in his vilest loves! But, with this girl—this child—good Heavens: how refined! He shrunk at the very idea of *her* voice whispering the name which had been shouted by his devil mates at a drinking bout! So he told the girl to call him—not Gusty, no, no, but something musical—*Lorraine!*"

And, stooping over the couch, the queenly woman, with her proud form arrayed in a dress of snow white silk, and her raven-black hair gathered in thick tresses along her neck, so full and round, applied her lips to the ear of the sleeper and whispered in a softened tone—

"Mary! Awake—it is your wedding night!"

The room was still as death. Not a sound save the faint breathing of the sleeper; all hushed and still. The light of the wax candle standing on the table in the centre of the Rose Chamber—as it was called—fell mild and softened over the hangings of faint crimson, with the effect of evening twilight.

The maiden—pure and without stain—lay sleeping on the small couch that occupied one corner of the closet. Her fair limbs were enshrouded in the light folds of a night-robe, and she lay in an attitude of perfect repose, one glowing cheek resting upon her uncovered arm, while over the other, waved the loosened curls of her glossy hair. The parting lips disclosed her teeth, white as ivory, while her youthful bosom came heaving up from the folds of her night-robe, like a billow that trembles for a moment in the moonlight, and then is suddenly lost to view. She lay there in all the ripening beauty of maidenhood, the light falling gently over her young limbs, their outlines marked by the easy folds of her robe, resembling in their roundness and richness of proportion, the swelling fulness of the rosebud that needs but another beam of light, to open it into its perfect bloom.

The arching eyebrows, the closed lids, with the long lashes resting on the cheek, the parted lips, and the round chin, with its smiling dimple, all these were beautiful, but oh how fair and beautiful the maiden's dreams. Rosier than her cheeks, sweeter than her breath, lovelier than her kiss—lovely as her own stainless soul, on whose leaves was written but one motto of simple meaning—"*Love in life, in death, and for ever.*"

And in all her dreams she beheld but one form, heard the whisper of but one voice, shared the sympathies of but one heart! *He* was her dream, her life, her *God*—him had she trusted with her all, in earth or heaven, him did she love with the uncalculating abandonment of self, that marks the first passion of an innocent woman!

[25] And was there aught of *earth* in this love? Did the fever of sensual passion throb in the pulses of her virgin blood? Did she love Lorrimer because his eyes was bright, his form magnificent, his countenance full of healthy manliness? No, no, no! Shame on the fools of either sex, who read the first love of a stainless woman, with the eyes of Sense. She loved Lorrimer for a something which he did not possess, which vile worldlings of his class never will possess. For the magic with which her fancy had enshrouded his face and form, she loved him, for the wierd fascination which *her own soul* had flung around his very existence,

---

25 [Author's Original Note] The reader who desires to understand, thoroughly, the pure love of an innocent girl for a corrupt libertine, will not fail to peruse this passage.

for a dream of which *he* was the idol, for a waking trance in which *he* walked as her good Angel, for imagination, for fancy, for any thing but *sense,* she loved him.

It was her first love.

She knew not that this fluttering fascination, which bound her to his slightest look or tone—like the charmed bird to the lulling music which the snake is said to murmur, as he ensnares his prey—she knew not that this fluttering fascination, was but the blind admiration of the moth, as it floats in the light of the flame, which will at last consume it.

She knew not that in her own organization, were hidden the sympathies of an animal as well as of an intellectual nature, that the blood in her veins only waited an opportunity to betray her, that in the very atmosphere of the holiest love of woman, crouched a sleeping fiend, who at the first whisperings of her Wronger, would arise with hot breath and blood shot eyes, to wreak eternal ruin on her, woman's-honor.

For this is the doctrine we deem it right to hold in regard to woman. Like man she is a combination of an animal, with an intellectual nature. Unlike man her animal nature is a *passive* thing, that must be roused ere it will develope itself in action. Let the intellectual nature of woman, be the only object of man's influence, and woman will love him most holily. But let him play with her animal nature as you would toy with the machinery of a watch, let him rouse the treacherous blood, let him fan the pulse into quick, feverish throbbings, let him warm the heart with convulsive beatings, and the woman becomes like himself, but a mere animal. *Sense* rises like a vapor, and utterly darkens *Soul.*

And shall we heap shame on woman, because man, neglecting her holiest nature, may devote all the energies which God has given him, to rouse her gross and earthy powers into action? On whose head is the shame, or whose the wrong? Oh, would man but learn the solemn truth—that no angel around God's throne is purer than Woman when her intellectual nature alone is stirred into development, that no devil crouching in the flames of hell is fouler than Woman, when her animal nature alone is roused into action— would man but learn and revere this fearful truth, would woman but treasure it in her inmost soul, then would never a shriek arise to heaven, heaping curses on the betrayer's head, then would never a wrong done to maiden virtue, give the suicide's grave its victim, then in truth, would woman walk the earth, the spirit of light that the holiest Lover ever deemed her!

And the maiden lay dreaming of her lover, while the form of the tall and stately woman, stood by the bedside, like her Evil Angel, as with a mingled smile and sneer, she bade the girl arise, for it was her wedding night. *Her wedding night!*

Mary! Awake—it is your wedding night!"

Mary murmured in her sleep, and then opened her large blue eyes, and arose in the couch.

"Has—*he* come?" were the first words she murmured in her musical tones, that came low and softened to the listeners ear—"Has *he* come?"

"Not yet—not yet—my dear—" said long-haired Bess, assisting the young to rise from the couch, with all imaginable tenderness of manner—"You see Mary love, it's half-past two o'clock and over, and of course, high time for you to dress. Throw back your night-gown my love, and let me arrange your hair. How soft and silky—it needs but little aid from my hands, to render each tress a perfect charm—"

"Is it not very strange Bessie—" said Mary opening her large blue eyes with bewildered glance as she spoke.

"What is strange? I see nothing strange except the remarkable beauty of these curls—"

"That I should first meet him, in such a singular manner, that he should love me, that for his sake I should fly to his uncle's mansion and that you Bessie—my dear good friend—should consent from mere friendship to leave your home and bear me company. All this is very strange—how like the stories we read in a book! And his stern old uncle you say has relented?"

"Perfectly resigned to the match my dear. That's the way with all these relations—is not that curl perfect?—when they've made all the mischief they can, and find it amounts to nothing, at the last moment they roll up their eyes, and declare with a sigh—that they're *resigned* to the match. And his dear old grand-ma—She lives here you know? There that is right—your curls should fall in a shower over your snow-white neck—The dear old lady is in a perfect fever to see you! She helped me to get everything ready for the wedding—"

"Oh Bessie—Is it not most sad?" said Mary as her blue eyes shone with a glance of deep feeling—"To think that Albert and you should love one another, so fondly, and after all, that he should die, leaving you alone in this cheerless world! How terrible! *If* Lorraine should die—"

A deep shade of feeling passed over Mary's face, and her lip trembled. Bessie held her head down, for a moment, as her fair fingers, ran twining among the tresses of the Bride. Was it to conceal a tear, or a—smile?

"Alas! *He* is in his grave! Yet it is the *memory* of his love, that makes me take such a warm interest in your union with Lorraine. This plain fillet of silver, with its diamond star—how well it becomes your brow! You never yet found a woman, who knew what it was to love, that would not fight for two true-hearted lovers, against the world! Do you think Mary dear, that I could have sanctioned your flight to this house, if my very soul had not been interested in your happiness? Not I—not I. Now slip off your night-gown my dear—Have you seen the wedding dress?"

"It seems to me—" said Mary, whose thoughts dwelt solely on her love for Lorrimer—"That there is something deeply touching in a wedding that is held at this hour of the night! Every thing is calm and tranquil; the earth lies sleeping, while Heaven itself watches over the union of two hearts that are all in all to each other—"

The words look plain and simple, but the tone in which she spoke was one of the deepest feeling. Her very soul was in her words. Her blue eyes dilated with a sudden enthusiasm, and the color went and came along her glowing cheek, until it resembled a fair flower, one moment resting in the shade, the next bathing in the sunlight.

"Let me assist you to put on this wedding dress. Is it not beautiful? That boddice of white silk was Lorrimer's taste. To be sure I gave the dress-maker a few hints. Is it not perfect? How gently the folds of the skirt rest on your figure! It is a perfect fit, I do declare! Why Mary you are *too* beautiful! Well, well, handsome as he is, Lorrimer ought to be half crazy with vanity, when such a Bride is hanging on his arm!"

A few moments sufficed to array the maiden for the bridal.—

Mary stood erect on the floor, blush after blush coursing over her cheek, as she surveyed the folds of her gorgeous wedding dress.

It was in truth a dress most worthy of her face and form. From the shoulders to the waist her figure was enveloped in a boddice of snow-white satin, that gathered over her swelling bosom, with such gracefulness of shape that every beauty of her form,—the width of the shoulders, and the gradual falling off, of the outline of the waist,—was clearly perceptible.

Fitting closely around the bust, it gave to view her fair round neck, half-concealed by the drooping curls of glossy hair, and a glimpse of each shoulder, so delicate and white, swelling away into the fullness of the virgin bosom, that rose heaving above the border of lace. From the waist downward, in many a fold, but with perfect adaptation to her form, the gorgeous skirt of satin, fell sweeping to the floor, leaving one small and tiny foot, enclosed in a neat slipper, that clung to it as though it had grown there, exposed to the eye.

The softened light falling over the rose-hued hangings of the room, threw the figure of the maiden out from the dim back-ground, in gentle and effective prominence. Her brown tresses showering down over each cheek, and falling along her neck and shoulders, waved gently to and fro, and caught a glossy richness from the light. Her fair shoulders, her full bosom, her long but not too slender waist, the downward proportions of her figure, swelling with the full outlines of ripening maidenhood; all arrayed in the graceful dress of snow-white satin, stood out in the dim light, relieved most effectively by the rose-hued hangings, in the background.

As yet her arms, unhidden by sleeve or robe, gave their clear, transparent skin, their fullness of outline, their perfect loveliness of shape, all freely to the light.

"Is it not a gorgeous dress?" said long-haired Bess, as she gazed with unfeigned admiration upon the face and form of the beautiful maiden—"As gorgeous, dear Mary, as you are beautiful!"

"Oh it will be such a happy time!" cried Mary, in a tone that scarcely rose above a whisper, while her blue eyes flashed with a glance of deep emotion—"There will sit my father and there my mother, in the cheerful parlor on Christmas Eve! My father's grey hairs and my mother's kindly face, will be lighted up by the same glow of light. And their eyes will be heavy with tears—with weeping for me, Bessie, their 'lost child,' as they will call me. When behold! the door opens, Lorraine enters with me, his wife, yes, yes *his wife* by his side. We fling ourselves at the feet of our father and mother—for they will be *ours*, then! We crave their forgiveness! Lorraine calls me his wife—we beg their forgiveness and their blessing in the same breath! Oh it will be such a happy time! And my brother he will be there too—*he* will like Lorraine, for he has a noble heart! Don't you see the picture, Bessie? I see it as plainly as though it was this moment before me, and—my father—oh how he will weep when again he clasps his daughter in his arms!"

There she stood, her fair hands clasped trembling together, her eyes flashing in ecstacy, while her heart, throbbing and throbbing like some wild bird, endeavoring to burst the bars of its cage, sent her bosom heaving into view.

Bessie made no reply. True she attempted some common-place phrase, but the words died in her throat. She turned her head away, and—thank God, she was not *yet* fallen to the lowest deep of woman's degradation—a tear, big and scalding, came rolling down her cheek.

And while Mary stood with her eyes gazing on the vacant air, with the manner of one entranced, while Bess—poor and fallen woman!—turned away her face to hide the falling tear, the curtains that concealed the entrance to the Painted Chamber were suddenly thrust aside, and the figure of a man came stealing along with a noiseless footstep.

Gus Lorrimer, silent and unperceived, in all the splendor of his manly beauty, stood gazing upon the form of his victim, with a glance of deep and soul-felt admiration.

His tall form was shown to the utmost advantage, by a plain suit of black cloth. A dress coat of the most exquisite shape, black pantaloons that fitted neatly around his well-formed limbs, a vest of plain white Marseilles,[26] gathering easily across the outlines of his massive

---

26 A firm cotton fabric.

chest, a snow-white shirt front, and a falling collar, confined by a simple black cravat; such were the brief details of his neat but effective costume. His manly face was all in a glow with health and excitement. Clustering curls of dark brown hair fell carelessly along his open brow. His clear, dark-hazel eye, gave forth a flashing glance, that failed to reveal anything but the frank and manly qualities of a generous heart. You did not read the villain, in his glance. The aquiline nose, the rounded chin, the curving lip, darkened by a graceful moustache, the arching eyebrows, which gave additional effect to the dark eyes; all formed the details of a countenance that ever struck the beholder with its beaming expression of health, soul, and manliness, combined.

And as Gus Lorrimer stood gazing in silent admiration upon his victim, few of his boon companions would have recognized, in his thoughtful countenance, the careless though handsome face of the reveller, who gave life and spirit to their drinking scenes.

The truth is, there were *two* Lorrimers in *one*. There was a careless, dashing, handsome fellow who could kill a basket of champagne with any body, drive the neatest 'turn out' in the way of horse flesh that the town ever saw, carry a 'frolic' so far that the watchman would feel bound to take it up and carry it a little farther—This was the magnificent Gus Lorrimer.

And then there was a tall, handsome man, with a thoughtful countenance, and a deep, dark hazel eye, who would sit down by the side of an innocent woman, and whisper in her ear, in a low-toned voice for hours together, with an earnestness of manner and an intensity of gaze, that failed in its effect, not once in a hundred times. Without any remarkable knowledge derived from education, this man knew every leaf of woman's many-leaved heart, and knew how to apply the revealings, which the fair book opened to his gaze. His gaze, in some cases, in itself was fascination; his low-toned voice, in too many instances, whispered its sentences of passion to ears, that heard it to their eternal sorrow. This man threw his whole soul, in his every passion. He plead with a woman, like a man under sentence of death pleading for his life. Is it a wonder that he was but rarely unsuccessful? This man, so deeply read in woman's heart, was the 'inner man' of the handsome fellow, with the dashing exterior. Assuming a name, never spoken to his ear, save in the soft whispers of one of his many victims, he styled himself Lorraine Lorrimer.

"Oh, Bessie, is not this Love—a strange mystery?" exclaimed Mary, as though communing with her own heart—"Before I loved, my soul was calm and quiet. I had no thought beyond my school-books—no deeper mystery than my embroidery-frame. *Now*—the very air is changed. The atmosphere in which I breathe is no longer the same. Wherever I move *his* face is before me. Whatever may be my thoughts, the thought of *him* is never absent for a moment. In my dreams I see him smile. When awake, his eyes, so deep, so burning in their gaze—even when he is absent—seem forever looking into mine. Oh, Bessie—tell me, tell me—is it given to man to adore his God? Is it not also given to woman to adore the *one* she loves? Woman's *religion* is her *love*—"

And as the beautiful enthusiast, *whose mind had been developed in utter seclusion from the world*, gave forth these revelations of her heart, in broken and abrupt sentences, Lorrimer drew a step nearer, and gazed upon her with a look in which passion rose predominant, even above admiration.

"Oh, Bessie, can it be that his love will ever grow cold? Will his voice ever lose its tones of gentleness, will his gaze ever cease to bind me to him, as it enchains me now?"

"Mary!" whispered a strange voice in a low and softened murmur.

She turned hastily round, she beheld the arms outspread to receive her, she saw the manly face of him she loved all a-glow with rapture, her fair blue eyes returned his gaze, "Lorraine," she murmured, in a faint whisper, and then her head rested upon his bosom, while her form trembled in his embrace.

"Oh, Lorraine—" she again murmured, as, with one fair hand resting upon each arm of her lover, she gazed upward in his face, while her blue eyes shone with all the feeling of her inmost soul. "Oh—Lorraine—will you love me ever?"

"Mary—" he answered, gazing down upon her blushing face, as he uttered her name in a prolonged whisper, that gave all its melody of sound to her ear—"Mary can you doubt me?"

And as there he stood gazing upon that youthful face, now flushed over with an expression of all-trusting love, as he drank in the glance of her large blue eyes, and felt her trembling form resting gently in his arms, the foul purpose of his heart was, for a moment, forgotten, for a moment his heart rose swelling within him, and the thought flashed over his soul, that for the fair creature, who hung fascinated on his every look, his life he could willingly lay down.

"Ha-ha—" muttered Bess, who stood regarding the pair with a glance of doubtful meaning—"I really believe that Lorrimer is quite as much in love, as the poor child! Good idea, that! A man, whose heart has been the highway of a thousand loves—a man like this, to fall in love with a mere baby-face! Mary, dear—" she continued aloud, too happy to break the reverie which enchained the seducer and his victim—"Mary, dear, hadn't I better help you to put on your wedding robe?"

Lorrimer turned and looked at her with a sudden scowl of anger. In a moment his face resumed its smile—

"Mary—" he cried, laughingly—"let me be your costumer, for once. My hands must help you on with the wedding robe. Nay, nay, you must not deny me. Hand me the dress, Bessie—"

It was a splendid robe of the same satin, as the other part of her dress. Gathering tightly around her form, it was designed to remain open in front, while the skirt fell trailing along the floor. Falling aside from the bust, where outlines were so gracefully developed by the tight-fitting boddice of white satin, its opposite sides were connected by interlacing threads of silvercord, crossed and recrossed over the heaving bosom. Long and drooping sleeves, edged with silver lace, were designed to give bewitching glimpses of the maiden's full and rounded arms. In fine, the whole dress was in the style of some sixty years since, such as our grand-dames designated by the euphonious name of 'a gown and curricle.'

"How well the dress becomes you Mary!" exclaimed Lorrimer with a smile as he flung the robe over her shoulders—"How elegant the fall of that sleeve! Ha—ha—Mary you *must* allow me to lace these silver cords in front. I'm afraid I would make but an awkward lady's-maid. What say you Bessie? Mary, your arms seem to love the light embrace of these drooping sleeves. You must forgive me, Mary, but I thought the style of the dress would please you, so I asked our good friend Bessie here to have it made. By my soul, you give additional beauty to the wedding dress. Is she not beautiful Bessie?"

"Most beautiful—" exclaimed Bess, as for the moment, her gaze of unfeigned admiration was fixed upon the Bride, arrayed in the full splendor of her wedding robes—"Most beautiful!"

"Mary, your hand—" whispered Lorrimer to the fair girl, who stood blushing at his side.

With a heaving bosom, and a flashing eye, Mary slowly reached forth her fair and delicate right hand. Lorrimer grasped the trembling fingers within his own, and winding his unoccupied arm around her waist he suffered her head, with all its shower of glossy tresses, to fall gently on his shoulders. A blush, warm and sudden, came over her face. He impressed one long and lingering kiss upon her lips. They returned the pressure, and clung to his lips as though they had grown there.

"Mary, my own sweet love—" he murmured in a low tone, that thrilled to her very heart—"Now I kiss you as the dearest thing to me in the wide world. Another moment, and from those same lips will I snatch the first kiss of my lovely bride! To the Wedding Room my love!"

Fair and blushing as the dawn, stainless as the new-fallen snow, loving as one of God's own cherubim, he led her gently from the place, motioning onward with his hand as again and again he whispered "To the Wedding Room my love, to the Wedding Room!"

"To the Wedding Room—" echoed Bess who followed in her Brides-maid robes—"To the Wedding Room—ha, ha, ha, say rather to h——ll!"

There was something most solemn, not to say thoughtful and melancholy, in the appearance of that lonely room. It was wide and spacious, and warmed by invisible means, with heated air. Huge panels of wainscotting covered the lofty walls, and even the ceiling was concealed by massive slabs of dark walnut. The floor was all one polished surface of mahogany, destitute of carpet or covering of any kind. A few high-backed mahogany chairs, standing along the walls, were the only furniture of the place. The entrance to the Rose Chamber, was concealed by a dark curtain, and in the western, and northern walls, were fashioned two massive doors, formed like the wainscotting, of dark and gloomy walnut.

In the centre of the glittering mahogany floor, arose a small table or altar, covered with a drooping cloth, white and stainless as the driven snow. Two massive wax candles, placed in candlesticks of silver, stood on the white cloth of the altar, imparting a dim and dusky light to the room. In that dim light the sombre panelling of the walls and the ceiling, the burnished floor of mahogany as dark as the walnut-wood that concealed the ceiling and the walls, looked heavy and gloomy, as though the place was a vault of death, instead of a cheerful Wedding Room.

As yet the place was silent and solitary. The light flickered dimly along the walls, and over the mahogany floor, which shone like a rippling lake in the moonlight. As you gazed upon the desolate appearance of that place, with the solitary wax lights burning like two watching souls, in the centre, you would have given the world, to have seen the room tenanted by living beings; in its present stillness and solitude, it looked so much like, one of those chambers in olden story, where the ghosts of a departed family, were wont to assemble once a year, in order to revive the memories of their lives on earth.

It might have been three o'clock, or even half an hour later, when the western door swung slowly open, and the Clergyman, who was to solemnize this marriage, came striding somewhat unsteadily along the floor. Clad in robes of flowing white—he had borrowed them from the Theatre—with a Prayer Book in his hand, Petriken as he glanced uneasily around the room, did not look at all unlike a Minister of a particular class. His long, square, lugubrious face, slightly varied by red streaks around each eye, was tortured into an expression of the deepest solemnity. He took his position in silence, near the Altar.

Then came the relenting Uncle, striding heavily at the parson's heels—He was clad in a light blue coat with metal buttons, a buff vest, striped trowsers, and an enormous scarf, whose mingled colors of blue and gold, gathered closely around his short fat neck. His full-moon face—looking very much like the face of a relenting uncle, who is willing to bestow mercy upon a wild young dog of a nephew, to almost any extent—afforded a pleasing relief to his pear-shaped nose, which stood out in the light, like a piece of carved work from a crimson wall. Silently the relenting Uncle, took his position beside the venerable Clergyman.

Then dressed in solemn black, the respected Grand-ma of the Bridegroom, who was in such a fever to see the Bride, came stepping mincingly along the floor, glancing from side to side with an amiable look that ruffled the yellowish flesh of her colloped cheeks.

The 'imperial' on her chin had been softened down, and with the aid of a glossy dress of black silk, and a tower of Babel cap, she looked quite venerable. Had it not been a certain twinkle in her eyes, you could have fallen in her arms and kissed her; she looked so much like one of those dear old souls, who make mischief in families and distribute tracts and cold victuals to the poor. The Grand-ma took her position on the left of the Clergyman.

And in this position, gathered around the Altar, they stood for some five minutes silently awaiting the appearance of the Bridegroom and the Bride.

Chapter Tenth

The Bridal

"I say Mutchy, my boy—" said Petriken, in a tone that indicated some lingering effects of his late debauch—"How *do* I do it? Clever—hey? D'ye like this face? Good—*is* it? If my magazine fails, I think I'll enter the ministry for good. Why not start a Church of my own? When a man's fit for nothin' else, he can always find fools enough to build him a church, and glorify him into a saint—"

"Do you think I *do* the Uncle well?" whispered Mutchins, drawing his shirt collar up from the depths of his scarf, into which it had fallen—"Devilish lucky you gave me the hint in time. 'Been the d——l to pay if we'd a-disappointed Gus. What am I to say, Silly. 'Is *she* not *beautiful!*' in a sort of an *aside* tone, and then fall on her neck and kiss her? Eh, Silly?'

"That'll be coming it a little *too* strong—" said Petriken, smoothing back his tow-colored hair—"You're merely to take her by the fingertips, and start as if her beauty overcame you, then exclaim 'God bless you my love, God bless you—' as though your feelings were too strong for utterance—"

" 'God bless you, my love—' " echoed Mutchins—" 'God bless you'—that will do—hey, Silly? I feel quite an interest in her already. Now Aunty, my dear and kind-hearted old relative, what in the d——l are *you* to do?"

"Maybe I'll get up a convulsion or two—" said the dear old lady, as her colloped cheeks waggled heavily with a smile—her enemies would have called it a hideous grin—"Maybe I'll do a hysteric or so. Maybe I won't? Dear me, I'm in sich a fever to see my little pet of a grand-daughter! Ain't I?"

"Hist!" whispered Petriken—"There they are in the next room. I think I heard a kiss. Hush! Here they come—d——n it, I can't find the marriage ceremony—"

No sooner had the words passed his lips, than Lorrimer appeared in the small doorway opening into the Rose Chamber, and stepped softly along the floor of the Walnut Room. Mary in all her beauty hung on his arm. Her robe of satin wound round her limbs, and trailed along the floor as she walked. At her side came Long-haired Bess, glancing in the faces of the wedding guests with a meaning smile.

"Nephew, I forgive you. God bless you, my dear—I approve my nephew's choice—God bless you, my dear—"

And, as though his feelings overcame him, Mutchins veiled his face in a large red handkerchief; beneath whose capacious shelter he covertly supplied his mouth with a fresh morsel of tobacco.

"And is *this* 'my grandchild?' Is this the dear pet? How shall I love her? Shan't I, grandson? Oh my precious, how do you *do?*"

The clergyman saluted the bride with a low bow.

A deep blush came mantling over Mary's face as she received these words of affection and tokens of kindness from the Minister and the relatives of her husband, while a slight, yet meaning, expression of disgust flashed over Lorrimer's features, as he observed the manner in which his minions and panders performed their parts.

With a glance of fire, Lorrimer motioned the clergyman to proceed with the ceremony. This was the manner of the marriage.

Hand joined in hand, Lorrimer and Mary stood before the altar. The bridesmaid stood near the trembling bride, whispering slight sentences of consolation in her ear. On the right hand of the clergyman, stood Mutchins, his red round face, subdued into an expression of the deepest solemnity; on the other side, the vile hag of Monk-hall, with folded arms, and grinning lips, calmly surveyed the face of the fair young bride.

In a deep-toned voice, Petriken began the sublime marriage ceremony of the Protestant Episcopal Church. There was no hope for the bride now. Trapped, decoyed, betrayed, she was about to be offered up, a terrible sacrifice, on that unhallowed altar. Her trembling tones, joined with the deep voice of Lorrimer in every response, and the marriage ceremony, drew near its completion. "There is no hope for her *now*"—muttered Bess, as her face shone with a glance of momentary compassion—"She is sold into the arms of shame!"

And at that moment, as the bride stood in all her beauty before the altar, her eyes downcast, her long hair showering down over her shoulders, her face warming with blush after blush, while her voice in low tones murmured each trembling response of the fatal ceremony, at the very moment when Lorrimer gazing upon her face with a look of the deepest satisfaction, fancied the fulfilment of the maiden's dishonour, there shrieked from the next chamber, a yell of such superhuman agony and horror, that the wedding guests were frozen with a sudden awe, and transfixed like figures of marble to the floor.

The book fell from Petriken's trembling hands; Mutchins turned pale, and the old hag started backward with sudden horror, while Bess stood as though stricken with the touch of death. Mary, poor Mary, grew white as the grave-cloth, in the face; her hand dropped stiffly to her side, and she felt her heart grow icy within her bosom.

Lorrimer alone, fearless and undaunted, turned in the direction from whence that fearful yell had shrieked, and as he turned he started back with evident surprise, mingled with some feelings of horror and alarm.

There, striding along the floor, came the figure of a young man, whose footsteps trembled as he walked, whose face was livid as the face of a corpse, whose long black hair waved wild and tangled, back from his pale forehead. His eye—Great God!—it shone as with a gleam from the flames of hell.

He moved his trembling lips, as he came striding on—for a moment the word, he essayed to speak, struck in his throat.

At last with a wild movement of his arms, he shouted in a voice whose tones of horror, mingled with heart-rendering pathos, no man would like to hear twice in a life time, he shouted a single word—

"MARY!"

The bride turned slowly round. Her face was pale as death, and her blue eyes grew glassy as she turned. She beheld the form of the intruder. One glance was enough.

"MY BROTHER!" she shrieked, and started forward as though about to spring in the strangers arms; but suddenly recoiling she fell heavily upon the breast of Lorrimer.

There was a moment of silence—all was hushed as the grave.

The stranger stood silent and motionless, regarding the awe-stricken bridal party, with one settled and burning gaze. One and all, they shrank back as if blasted by his look. Even Lorrimer turned his head aside and held his breath, for very awe.

The stranger advanced another step, and stood gazing in Lorrimer's face.

"*My Sister!*" he cried in a husky voice, and then as if all further words died in his throat, his face was convulsed by a spasmodic movement, and he shook his clenched hand madly in the seducer's face.

"Your name—" cried Lorrimer, as he laid the fainting form of the Bride in the arms of Long-haired Bess—"Your name is Byrnewood. This lady is named Mary Arlington. There is some mistake here. The lady is no sister of yours—"

"My name—" said the other, with a ghastly smile—"Ask this palefaced craven what is my name! He introduced me to you, this night by my full name. You at once forgot, all but my first name. My name, sir, is *Byrnewood Arlington*. A name, sir, you will have cause to remember in this world and—devil that you are!—in the next if you harm the slightest hair on the head of this innocent girl—"

Lorrimer started back aghast. The full horror of his mistake rushed upon him. And in that moment, while the fainting girl lay insensible in Bessie's arms; while Petriken and Mutchins, and the haggard old Abbess of the den, stood stricken dumb with astonishment, quailing beneath the glance of the stranger; a long and bony arm was thrust from behind the back of Byrnewood Arlington, the grim face Devil-Bug shone for a moment in the light, and then a massive hand with talon-fingers, fell like a weight upon the wick of each candle, and the room was wrapt in midnight blackness.

Then there was a trampling of feet to and fro, a gleam of light flashed for a moment, through the passage, opening into the Rose Chamber, and then all was dark again.

"They are bearing my sister away!" was the thought that flashed over the mind of the Brother, as he rushed toward the passage of the Rose Chamber—"I will rescue her from their grasp at the peril of my life!"

He rushed along, in the darkness, toward the curtain that concealed the entrance into the Rose Chamber. He attempted to pass beyond the curtain, but he was received in the embrace of two muscular arms, that raised him from his feet as though he had been a mere child, and then dashed him to the floor, with the impulse of a giant's strength.

"Ha-ha-ha!—" laughed a hoarse voice—"You don't pass here, Mister. Not while 'Bijah's about! No you don't, my feller—ha, ha, ha!"

"A light, Devil-Bug—" exclaimed a voice, that sounded from the centre of the darkened room.

In a moment a light, grasped in the talon-fingers of the Doorkeeper of Monk-Hall, flashed around the place. Silent and alone Gus Lorrimer, stood in the centre of the room, his arms folded across his breast, while the dark frown on his brow was the only outward manifestation of the violence of the struggle that had convulsed his very soul, during that solitary moment of utter darkness. Calling all the resources of his mind to his aid, he had resolved upon his course of action.

"It is a fearful remedy, but a sure one—" he muttered as he again faced Byrnewood, who had just risen from the floor, where he had been thrown by Mr. Abijah K. Jones—"Begone Devil-Bug—" he continued aloud—"But wait without and see that Glowworm and Musquito are at hand," He added in a meaning whisper. "Now Sir, I have a word to say to *you*—" And as he spoke he confronted the Brother of the girl, whose ruin he had contrived with the ingenuity of an accomplished libertine, mingled with all the craft of an incarnate fiend.

Aching in every limb from his recent fall, Byrnewood stood pale and silent, regarding the libertine with a settled gaze. In the effort to command his feelings, he pressed his teeth against his lower lip, until a thin line of blood trickled down to his chin.

"You will allow that this, is a most peculiar case—" he exclaimed with a calm gaze, as he confronted Byrnewood—"One in fact, that demands some painful thought. Will you favor me with ten minutes private conversation?"

"You are very polite—" exclaimed Byrnewood with a withering sneer—"Here is a man, who commits a wrong for which h——ll itself has no name, and then—instead of shrinking from the sight of the man he has injured, beyond the power of words to tell—he cooly demands ten minutes private conversation!"

"It is your interest to grant my request—" replied Lorrimer, with a manner as collected as though he had merely said 'Pass the bottle, Byrnewood!'

"I presume I must submit—" replied Byrnewood—"But after the ten minutes are past—remember—that there is not a fiend in hell whom I would not sooner hug to my bosom, than grant one moment's conversation to—a—a—man—ha, ha—a *man* like you. My sister's honor may be in your power. But remember—that as surely as you wrong her, so surely you will pay for that wrong, with your life—"

"You then, grant me ten minutes conversation? You give me your word that during this period, you will keep your seat, and listen patiently to all, that I may have to say? You nod assent. Follow me, then. A footstep or so this way, will lead us to a pleasant room, the last of this range, where we can talk the matter over—"

He flung open the western door of the Walnut room, and led the way along a narrow entry, up a stairway with some five steps, and in a moment stood before a small doorway, closing the passage at the head of the stairs. At every footstep of the way, he held the light extended at arms length, and regarded Byrnewood with the cautious glance of a man who is not certain at what moment, a concealed enemy may strike him in the back.

"My Library Sir—" exclaimed Lorrimer as pushing open the door, he entered a small oblong room, some twenty-feet in length and about half that extent in width. "A quiet little place where I sometimes amuse myself with a book. There is a chair Sir— please be seated—"

Seating himself upon a small stool, that stood near the wall of the room, furthest from the door, Byrnewood with a single glance, took in all the details of the place. It was a small unpretending room, oblong in form, with rows of shelves along its longest walls, facing each other, supplied with books of all classes, and of every description, from the pondrous history to the trashy novel. The other walls at either end, were concealed by plain and neat paper, of a modern pattern, which by no means harmonized with the ancient style of the carpet, whose half-faded colors glowed dimly in the light. Along the wall of the chamber opposite Byrnewood, extended an old-fashioned sofa, wide and roomy as a small sleeping couch; and from the centre of the place, arose a massive table, fashioned like a chest, with substantial sides of carved oak, supplying the place of legs. To all appearance it was fixed and jointed, into the floor of the room.

Altogether the entire room, as its details were dimly revealed by the beams of the flickering lamp, wore a cheerless and desolate look, increased by the absence of windows from the walls, and the ancient and worn-out appearance which characterized the stool, the sofa and the table; the only furniture of the place. There was no visible hearth, and no sign of fire, while the air cold and chilling had a musty and unwholesome taint, as though the room had not been visited or opened for years.

Placing the lamp on the solitary table, Lorrimer flung himself carelessly on the sofa and motioned Byrnewood, to draw his seat nearer to the light. As Byrnewood seated himself beside the chest-like table, with his cheek resting on his hand, the full details of his countenance, so pale, so colorless, so corpse-like, were disclosed to the keen gaze of Lorrimer. The face of the Brother, was perfectly calm, although the large black eyes dilated with a glance that revealed the Soul, turning madly on itself and gnawing its own life, in very madness of thought, while from the lips tightly compressed, there still trickled down, the same thin line of blood, rendered even more crimson and distinct, by the extreme pallor of the countenance.

"You will at least admit, that *I have won the wager*—" said Lorrimer, in a meaning tone, as he fixed his gaze upon the death-like countenance of Byrnewood Arlington.

Byrnewood started, raised his hands suddenly, as if about to grasp the libertine by the throat, and then folding his arms tightly over his chest, he exclaimed in a voice marked by unatural calmness—

"For ten minutes, sir, I have promised to listen to all—*all* you may have to say. Go on, sir. But do not, I beseech you, tempt me too far—"

"Exactly half-past three by my repeater—" cooly replied Lorrimer, looking at his watch—"At twenty minutes of four, our conversations ends. Very good. Now, sir, listen to my proposition. Give me your word of honor, and your oath, that when you leave this house, you will preserve the most positive secrecy with regard to—to—*everything*—you may have witnessed within its walls; promise me this, under your word of honor and your solemn oath, and I will give you my word of honor, my oath, that, in one hour from daybreak, your sister shall be taken to her home, pure and stainless, as when first she left her father's threshold. Do you agree to this?"

"Do you see this hand?" answered Byrnewood, with a nervous tremour of his lips, that imparted an almost savage sneer to his countenance—"Do you see this flame? Sooner than agree to leave these walls, without—my—my—without Mary, pure and stainless, mark ye, I would hold this good right hand in the blaze of this lamp, until the flesh fell blackened and festering from the very bone. Are you answered?"

"Excuse me, sir—I was not speaking of any *anatomical experiments;* however interesting such little efforts in the surgical line, may be to you. I wished to make a compromise—"

"A *compromise!*" echoed Byrnewood.

"Yes, a compromise. That melodramatic sneer becomes you well, but it would suit the pantomimist at the Walnut street Theatre much better. What have I done with the girl, that you, or any other young blood about town, would *not do*, under similar circumstances. Who was it, that entered so heartily into the joke of the *sham* marriage, when it was named in the Oyster Cellar? Who was it called the astrologer a knave—a fortune teller—a catch-penny cheat, when he—simple man!—advised me to give up the girl? I perceive, sir, you are touched. I am glad to observe, that you appreciate the graphic truth of my remarks. You will not sneer at the word '*compromise*' again, will you?"

"Oh, Mary! oh, Mary!"—whispered Byrnewood, drawing his arms yet more closely over his breast, as though in the effort to command his agitation—"Mary! Was I placing your honor in the dice-box, when I made the wager with yonder—*man?* Was it your ruin the astrologer foretold, when he urged this *devil*—to turn back in his career? Was it my *voice* that cheered *him* onward in his work of infamy? Oh Mary, was it for *this*, for *this*, that I loved you as brother never loved sister? Was it for this, that I wound you close to my inmost heart, since first I could think or feel? Was it for *this*, that in the holiest of all my memories, all my hopes, your name was enshrined? Was it for this, that I pictured, again and again, every hour in the day, every moment of the night, the unclouded prospects of your future life? Oh Mary, oh Mary, I may be wrong, I may be vile, I may be sunken as low as the *man* before me, yet my love for you, has been without spot, and without limit! And now Mary—oh *now*—"

He paused. There was a husky sound in his throat, and the blood trickled faster from his tortured lip.

Lorrimer looked at him silently for a moment, and then, taking a small pen-knife from his pocket, began to pare his nails, with a quiet and absent air, as though he did'nt exactly know what to do with himself. He wore the careless and easy look of a gentleman, who having just dined, is wondering where in the deuce he shall spend the afternoon.

"I say, Byrnie my boy—" he cried suddenly, with his eyes fixed on the operations of the knife—"Devilish odd, ain't it? That little affair of yours, with *Annie?* Wonder if she has any *brother?* Keen cut *that*—"

Had Mr. Lorrimer intended the allusion, about the keenness of the 'cut,' for Byrnewood instead of his nail-paring knife, the remark would, perhaps, have been equally applicable. Byrnewood shivered at the name of Annie, as though an ague-fit had passed suddenly over him. The 'cut' was rather keen, and somewhat deep. This careless kind of intellectual surgery, sometimes makes ghastly wounds in the soul, which it so pleasantly dissects.

"May I ask what will be your course, in case you leave this place, without the lady? You are silent. I suppose there will be a suit instituted for '*abduction*,' and a thousand legal et ceteras? This place will be ransacked for the girl, and your humble servant will be threatened with the Penitentiary? A pleasant prospect, truly. Why do you look so earnestly at that hand?"

"You have your pleasant prospects—I have mine—" exclaimed Byrnewood with a convulsive smile—"You see that right hand, do you? I was just thinking, how long it might be, ere that hand would be reddened with your heart's blood—"

"Poh! poh! Such talk is d——d boyish. D'ye agree to my proposition? Yes or no?"

"You have had my answer—"

"In case I surrender the girl to you, will you then promise unbroken secrecy, with regard to the events of this night?"

"I will make no terms whatever with a *scoundrel* and a *coward!*" hissed Byrnewood, between his clenched teeth.

"Pshaw! It is high time this mask should be cast aside—" exclaimed Lorrimer, as his eye flashed with an expression of triumph, mingled with anger and scorn—"And do you suppose that on any condition, or for any consideration, I would leave this fair prize slip from my grasp? Why, innocent that you are, you might have piled oath on oath, until your very breath grew husky in the effort, and still—still—despite of all your oaths, the girl would remain mine!

"Know me as I am! Not the mere man-about-town, not the wine-drinking companion, not the fashionable addle-head you think me, but the *Man of Pleasure!* You will please observe, how much lies concealed in that title. You have talents—these talents have been from childhood, devoted to books, or mercantile pursuits. I have some talent—I flatter myself—and that talent, aided and strengthened in all its efforts, by wealth from very boyhood, has been devoted to Pleasure, which, in plain English, means—Woman.

"Woman—the means of securing her affection, of compassing her ruin, of enjoying her beauty, has been my book, my study, my science, nay my *profession* from boyhood. And am I, to be foiled in one of the most intricate of all my adventures, by such a child—a mere boy like you? Are you to frighten me, to scare me back in the path I have chosen; to wrest this flower, to obtain which I have perilled so much, are *you* to wrest this flower from *my* grasp? You are *so* strong, *so* mighty, you talk of reddening your hand in my heart's blood—and all such silly vaporing, that would be hissed by the pit-boy's, if they but heard it, spouted forth by a fifth-rate hero of the green-room—and yet with all this—*you are my prisoner—*"

"*Your prisoner?*" echoed Byrnewood slowly rising to his feet.

"Keep cool Sir—" cried Lorrimer with a glance of scorn—"Two minutes of the ten, yet remain. I have your word of honor, you will remember. Yes—*my prisoner!* Why do you suppose for a moment, that I would let you go forth from this house, when you have it in your power to raise the whole city on my head? You know that I have placed myself under the ban of the laws by this adventure. You know that the Penitentiary would open its doors to enclose me, in case I was to be tried for this affair. You know that popular indignation, poverty and disgrace, stare me in the very eyes, the moment this adventure is published to the world, and yet—ha, ha, ha—you still think me, the egregious ass, to open the doors of Monk-Hall to you, and pleasantly bid you go forth, and ruin me forever! Sir, you are my prisoner."

"Ha—ha—ha! I will be even with you—" laughed Byrnewood—"You may murder me, in the act but I still have the power to arouse the neighbourhood. I can shriek for help. I can yell out the cry of Murder, from this foul den, until your doors are flung open by the police, and the secrets of your rookery laid bare to the public gaze—"

"Scream, yell, cry out, until your throat cracks! Who will hear you? Do you know how many feet, you are standing, above the level of the earth? Do you know the thickness of these walls? Do you know that you stand in the Tower-Room of Monk-Hall? Try your voice—by all means—I should like to hear you cry Murder or Fire, or even hurra for some political candidate, if the humor takes you—"

Byrnewood sank slowly in his seat, and rested his cheek upon his hand. His face was even paler than before—the consciousness that he was in the power of this libertine, for life or death, or any act of outrage, came stealing round his heart, like the probings of a surgeon's knife.

"Go on Sir—" he muttered biting his nether lip, until the blood once more came trickling down to his chin—"The hour is yours. *Mine will come—*"

"At my bidding; not a moment sooner—" laughed Lorrimer rising his feet—"Why man, death surrounds you in a thousand forms, and you know it not. You may walk on Death, you may breathe it, you may drink it, you may draw it to you with a fingers-touch, and yet be as unconscious of its presence, as a blind man is of a shadow in the night—"

Byrnewood slowly rose from his seat. He clasped his hands nervously together, and his lips muttered an incoherent sound as he endeavoured to speak.

"Do what you will with me—" he cried, in a husky voice—"But oh, for the sake of God, *do not wrong my sister!*"

"She is in *my* power!" whispered Lorrimer, with a smile, as he gazed upon the agitated countenance of the brother—"She is in *my* power!"

"Then by the eternal God, you are in mine!" shrieked Byrnewood, as with one wild bound, he sprung at the tall form of Lorrimer, and fixed both hands around his throat, with a grasp like that of the tigress when she fights for her young—"You are in my power! You cannot unloose my grasp! Ha—ha—you grow black in the face! Struggle!—struggle!— With all your strength you cannot tear my hands from your throat—you shall die like a felon, by the eternal God!"

Lorrimer was taken by complete surprise. The wild bound of Byrnewood had been so sudden, the grasp of his hands, was so much like the terrific clutch with which the drowning man makes a last struggle for life, that for a single moment, the handsome Gus Lorrimer reeled to and fro like a drunken man, while his manly features darkened over with a hue of livid blackness, as ghastly as it was instantaneous. The struggle lasted but a single moment. With the convulsive grasp tightening around his throat, Lorrimer sank suddenly on one knee, dragging his antagonist with him, and as he sank, extending his arm, with an effort as desperate as that which fixed the clinched fingers around his throat, he struck Byrnewood a violent blow with his fist, directly behind the ear. Byrnewood sank senseless to the floor, his fingers unclosing their grasp of Lorrimer's throat, as slowly and stiffly as though they were seized with a sudden cramp.

"Pretty devilish and d——d hasty!" muttered Lorrimer, arranging his cravat and vest— "Left the marks of his fingers on my throat, I'll be bound! Hallo—Musquito! Hallo, Glow-worm—here's work for you!"

The door of the room swung suddenly open, and the herculean negroes stood in the doorway, their sable faces, agitated by the same hideous grin, while the sleeves of the red flannel shirts, which formed their common costume, rolled up to the shoulders disclosed the iron-sinews of their jet-black arms.

"Mark this man, I say—"

"Yes—Massa—I doo-es—" chuckled Musquito, as his loathsome lips, inclining suddenly downward toward the jaw, on either side of his face, were convulsed by a brutal grin—"Dis nigger nebber mark a man yet, but dat *somefin'* cum ob it—"

"Massa Gusty no want de critter to go out ob dis 'ere door?" exclaimed Glow-worm, as the long rows of his teeth, bristling from his thick lips, shone in the light like the fangs of some strange beast—" 'Spose he go out ob dat door? 'Spose de nigger no mash him head, *bad?* Ain't Glow-worm got fist? Hah-hah! 'Sketo did you ebber see dis chile (child) knock an ox down? Hah-hah!"

"You are to watch outside the door all night—" exclaimed Lorrimer, as he stood upon the threshold—"Let him not leave the room on the peril of your lives. D'ye mark me, fellows?"

And as he spoke, motioning the negroes from the room, he closed the door and disappeared.

He had not gone a moment when Byrnewood, recovering from the stunning effect of the blow which had saved Lorrimer's life, slowly staggered to his feet, and gazing around with a bewildered glance.

" '*On Christmas Eve*—' " he murmured wildly, as though repeating words whispered to his ear in a dream—" '*On Christmas Eve, at the hour of sundown, one of ye will die by the other's hand—the winding sheet is woven and the coffin made!*' "

Chapter Eleventh

Devil-Bug

"It don't skeer me, I tell ye! For six long years, day and night, it has laid by my side, with its jaw broke and its tongue stickin' out, and yet I ain't a bit skeered! There it is now—on my left side, ye mind—in the light of the fire. Ain't it an ugly corpse? Hey? A reel nasty christian, I tell ye! Jist look at the knees, drawed up to the chin, jist look at the eyes, hanging out on the cheeks, jist look at the jaw all smashed and broke—look at the big, black tongue, stickin' from between the teeth— say it ain't an ugly corpse, will ye?

"Sometimes I can hear him groan—*only* sometimes! I've always noticed when anything bad is a-goin to come across me, that critter groans and groans! Jist as I struck him down, he lays afore me now. Whiz—wh-i-z he came down the hatchway—three stories, every bit of it! Curse it, why hadn't I the last trap-door open? He fell on the floor, pretty much mashed up, but—but he wasn't dead—

"He riz on his feet. Just as he lays on the floor—in his shirt sleeves, with his jaw broke and his tongue out —he riz on his feet. Didn't he groan? I put him down, I tell ye! Down— down! Ha! What was a sledge hammer to this fist, in that pertikler minnit? Crack, crack went the spring of the last trap-door—and the body fell—the devil knows where—I don't. I put it out o' my sight, and yet it came back to me, and crouched down at my side, the next minnit. It's been there ever since. If I sleep, or if I'm wide awake, it's there—*there*—always on my left side, where I hain't got no eye to see it, and yet I do—I *do* see it. What a cussed fool I was arter all! To kill him, and he not got a cent in his pockets! Bah! Whenever I think of it I grow feverish. And there he is now—With his d——d ugly jaw. How he lolls his tongue out—and his eyes! *Ugh!* But I ain't a bit skeered. No. Not me. I can bear wuss things than that 'are—"

The light from the blazing coal-fire, streamed around the Door-keeper's den. Seated close by the grate, in a crouching attitude, his feet drawn together, his big hands grasping each knee with a convulsive clutch, his head lowered on his breast, and his face, warmed to a crimson red by the glare of the flame, moistened with thick drops of perspiration; Devil-Bug turned the orbless eye-socket to the floor at his left side, as though it was gifted with full powers of sight, while his solitary eye, grew larger and more burning in its fixed gaze, until at last, it seemed to stand out, from his overhanging brow, like a separate flame.

The agitation of the man was at once singular and fearful. Oozing from his swarthy brow, the thick drops of sweat fell trickling over his hideous face, moistening his matted hair, until it hung, damp and heavy over his eyebrows. The lips of his wide mouth receding to his flat nose and pointed chin, disclosed the long rows of bristling teeth, fixed as closely together, as though the man, had been suddenly seized with lock-jaw. His face was all one loathsome grimace, as with his blazing eye, fixed upon the fire, he seemed gazing upon the floor at his left, with the shrunken and eyeless socket, of the other side of his face.

This creature, who sate crouching in the light of the fire, muttering words of strange meaning to himself, presented a fearful study for the Christian and Philanthropist. His Soul was like his body, a mass of hideous and distorted energy.

Born in a brothel, the offspring of foulest sin and pollution, he had grown from very childhood, in full and continual sight of scenes of vice, wretchedness and squalor.

From his very birth, he had breathed an atmosphere of infamy.

To him, there was no such thing as *good* in the world.

His world— his place of birth, his home in infancy, childhood and manhood, his only theatre of action— had been the common house of ill-fame. No mother had ever spoken words of kindness to him; no father had ever held him in his arms. Sister, brother, friends; he had none of these. He had come into the world without a name; his present one, being the standing designation of the successive Doorkeepers of Monk-hall, which he in vain endeavoured to assume, leaving the slang title bestowed on him in childhood, to die in forgetfulness.

Abijah K. Jones he might call himself, but he was Devil-Bug still.

His loathsome look, his distorted form, and hideous soul, all seemed to crowd on his memory, at the same moment, when the word "Devil-Bug"—rang on his ear. That word uttered, and he stood apart from the human race; that word spoken, and he seemed to feel, that he was something distinct from the mass of men, a wild beast, a snake, a reptile, or a devil incarnate—any thing but a—man.

The same instinctive pleasure that other men, may feel in acts of benevolence, of compassion or love, warmed the breast of Devil-Bug, when enjoyed in any deed, marked by especial *cruelty*. This word will scarcely express the instinctive impulse of his soul. He loved not so much to kill, as to observe the blood of his victim, fall drop by drop, as to note the convulsive look of death, as to hear the last throttling rattle in the throat of the dying.

For years and years, the instinctive impulse, had worked in his own bosom, without vent. The murder which had dyed his hands, with human blood for the first time, some six years ago, opened wide to his soul, the pathway of crime, which it was his doom and his delight to tread. Ever since the night of the Murder, his victim, hideous and repulsive, had lain beside him, crushed and mangled, as he fell through the death-trap. The corpse was never absent from his fancy; which in this instance had assumed the place of eyesight. Did he sit—it was at his left side. Did he walk—crushed and mangled as it was, it glided with him. Did he sleep—it still was at his side, ever present with him, always staring him in the face, with all its loathsome details of horror and bloodshed.

Since the night of the Murder, a longing desire had grown up, within this creature, to lay another corpse beside his solitary victim. Were there he thought, two corpses, ever at this side, the terrible details of the mangled form and crushed countenance of the first, would lose half their horror, all their distinctness. He longed to surround himself with the Phantoms of new victims. In the *number* of his crimes, he even anticipated pleasure.

It was this man, this deplorable moral monstrosity, who knew no God, who feared no devil, whose existence was one instinctive impulse of cruelty and bloodshed, it was this Outlaw of heaven and earth and hell, who held the life of Byrnewood Arlington in his grasp.

"It's near about mornin' and that ere boy ought to have somethin' to eat. A leetle to drink—per'aps? Now *sup*-pose, I should take him up, a biled chicken and a bottle o' wine. He sits down by the table o' course to eat—I fix his plate on a pertikler side. As he planks down into the cheer, his foot touches a spring. What is the consekence? He git's a fall and hurts hisself. *Sup*-pose he drinks the wine? Three stories down the hatchway— reether an ugly tumble. He git's crazy, and wont know nothin' for days. Very pecooliar wine—got it from the Doctor who used to come here—dint kill a man, only makes him mad-like. The Man with th' Poker is n't nothin' to this stuff—Hallo! Who's there?"

"Only me, Bijah—" cried a woman's voice, and the queenly form of Long Haired Bess with a dark shawl thrown over her bridesmaid's dress advanced toward the light—"I've just left Lorrimer. He's with the girl you know? He sent me down here, to tell you to keep close watch on that young fellow—"

"Jist as if I couldn't do it mesself—" grunted Abijah in his grind-stone voice—"Always a-orderin' a feller about? That's his way. Spose you cant make yourself useful? Kin you? Then take some biled chicken—and a bottle o' wine up to the younk chap. Guess he's most starved—"

"Shall I get the chicken and the wine?" asked Bess gazing steadily in Abijah's face.

"What the thunder you look in my face that way fur? No you shant git 'em. Git 'em mes-self. Wait here till I come back. Do'nt let any one in without the pass word—'What hour of the night—' and the answer 'Dinner time—' you know?"

And as Devil-Bug strode heavily from the den, and was heard going down into the cel-lars of the mansion, Bess stood silent and erect before the fire, her face, shadowed by an expression of painful thought, while her dark eyes, shot a wild glance from beneath her arching brows, suddenly compressed in a frown.

"Some mischief at work I suppose—" she whispered in a hissing voice—"I've sold myself to shame, but not to Murder!"

A low knock resounded from the front door.

Suddenly undrawing the bolt and flinging the chain aside, Bess gazed through a crevice of the opened door, upon the new-comers, who stood beyond the out-side door of green blinds.

"Who's there?" she said in a low voice.

"Ha—ha—" laughed one of the strangers—"It's bonny Bess. 'What hour of the night' is it, my dear?"

" 'Dinner time', you fool—" replied the young lady opening the outside door—"Come in Luke! Ha! There is a stranger with you! *Your friend* Luke?"

"Aye, aye, Bessie my love,—" answered Luke as he entered the den, with the stranger at his side—"Did ye hear the Devil-Bug say, whether there was fire in my room? all right—hey? And *cards* you know Bess—*cards?* This gentleman and I, want to amuse ourselves with a little game. Bye-the-bye—where's Fitz-Cowles? I should like him to join us. Seen him to night my dear?"

"Up stairs you know Luke—" answered Bess with a meaning smile—" *'Veiled figure,'* Luke you know? That's a game above your fancy I should suppose?"

And as she said this with an expressive glance of her dark eye, Bess observed that the stranger who accompanied Luke, was a very tall, stout man, wrapped up in a thick over-coat, whose upraised collar, concealed his face to the very eyes. His eyes were visible for a single moment, however as half-hidden by the shadow of Luke's figure, the stranger strode swiftly across the floor of the den. Bess started, with a feeling of terror, akin to the awe one experiences in the presence of a madman, as those eyes, so calm and yet so burning in their fixed gaze, flashed for a moment in the red light.

"Luke, I am—ready—" said the Stranger in a smothered voice—"To *the room* Luke— to *the Room!*"

Without a word Luke led the way from the den, and in a moment Bess heard the half-hushed sound of their footsteps, as they ascended the staircase of the mansion.

"That's a strange eye for a man who's only *a-goin'* to play cards—" muttered Bess as she stood by the fireplace—"Now it's more like the eye of a man, who's been playin' all night, and lost his very soul in a game with the D——l! Lord!—But that's a wicked eye for a dark night!"

"Here's the biled chicken and the wine—" grated the harsh voice of Devil-Bug, who approached the fire, with a large 'waiter' in his arms—"Take it up to the feller, Bess. He's hungry praps? And d'ye mind gal—set his plate on the side of the table, furthest from the door?"

"Any particular reason for that, 'Bijah?"

"Cuss it gal, cant you do it, without axeing questions? It's only a whim o' mine. That bottle is worth its weight in red goold. Don't taste such Madeery every day I tell you. Poor fellow—guess he's a-most starved—"

"Well, well, I'll take him the chicken and the wine—" exclaimed Bess pleasantly as she took possession of the 'waiter' with its cold chicken and luscious wine—"Hang it though, when I come to think o' it, why couldn't you have taken it up yourself? 'Bijah you're growin' lazy— "

"Mind gal—" grunted Devil-Bug as the girl disappeared through the door—"Set his plate on the side of the table furthest from the door. D'ye hear? It's a whim o' mine— furthest from the door—d'ye hear"

"'Furthest from the door'—" echoed Bess, and in a moment her foot-steps resounded with a low pattering noise along the massive staircase.

"The *Spring*—and the *bottle*—" muttered Devil-Bug as he resumed his seat beside the fire—"It seems to me, I should like to creep up stairs, and listen at his door to see how them things work. The niggers is there: but no matter. May be he'll howl—or groan—or do all sorts of ravin's? Gusty did not exactly tell me to do all this—but I guess he'll grin as wide as any body, *when the thing is done*. It seems to me I should like, to see how them things works. It'ud be nice to listen a bit at his door. Wonder if that gal suspicions anything?"

He rubbed his hands earnestly together, as a man is want to do, under the influence of some pleasing idea, and his solitary eye, dilated and sparkled, with a glance of the most remarkable satisfaction. A slight chuckle shook his distorted frame, and his lips performed a succession of vivid spasms which an ignorant observer might have confounded under the general name of laughter.

"Poor feller—guess he's cold without a fire—" said complacent Devil-Bug as he rubbed his hands cheerfully together—"I might build him a little fire. I might—I might—ha! ha! ha!" he arose slowly to his feet, and laughed so loud, that the echoes of his voice resounded from the den, along the hall, and up the staircase of the mansion—"I might try *that*'—he cried with a hideous glow of exultation—"Wonder *how that* would *work?*"

Opening the door of a closet on one side of the fire-place, he drew from its depths, a small furnace of iron; such as housewives use for domestic purposes. He placed the furnace in the full light of the fire, surveyed it closely, rubbed his hands pleasantly together yet once more, while a deep chuckle shook his form, from head to foot. His face wore an expression of extreme good humor—the visage of a drunken loafer, as he flings a penny to a ragged sweep, was nothing in comparison.

"A leetle kindlin' wood—" he muttered, drawing to the fire an old sack that had lain concealed in the darkness—"And a leetle charcoal! Makes a *rougeing* hot fire! Fat pine and charcoal—ha, ha, ha! Rather guess the poor fellow's cold! Now for a light—Cuss it how the fat pin blazes!"

He waited but a single moment for the wood and charcoal to ignite. It flared up at first in a smoky blaze, and then subsided into a clear and brilliant flame. Seizing the iron handle of the furnace Devil-Bug suddenly raised it from the floor, and rushed from the den, and up the staircase of the mansion, as though his very life hung on his speed. And as he ascended the stairway, the light of the furnace gradually increasing to a vivid flame, was thrown upward over his hideous face, turning the beetling brow, the flat nose and the wide mouth with its bristling teeth, to a hue of dusky red. One moment as he swung the furnace from side to side, you beheld his face and form in a glow of blood red light, and the next it was suddenly lost to view, while the vessel of iron, with its burning coals, seemed gliding up the stairway, impelled by a single swarthy hand, with fingers like talons and sinews starting out from the skin like knotted cords.

"Halloo! I didn't know Monk Luke was in his room—" he muttered, as he paused for a moment before a massive door, opening into the hall, which extended along the mansion, above the first stairway—"There's a streak of light from the keyhole of his door! And voices inside the room—but no matter! The charcoal's a-burnin'—and—wonder how *that'll work?*"

And up the staircase of the mansion he pursued his way, flinging the blazing furnace from side to side, while his face, grew like the visage of a very devil, as again the words rose to his lips—

"The charcoal's a-burnin'— wonder how *that'll* work?"

The light still flickered through the keyhole of the massive door.

Within the sombre panels, it shone over the rich furniture of an apartment, long and wide, with high ceiling and wainscotted walls. There was a gorgeous carpet on the floor, a thickly curtained bed in one corner, a comfortable fire burning in the grate, and a large table standing near the center of the room, on which a plain lamp, darkened by a heavy shade, was burning. The shade flung the light of the lamp down over the table—it was covered with books, cards, and wine glasses—and around the carpet, for the space of a yard or more, while the other portions of the apartment, were enveloped in faint twilight.

And in that dim light, near the fire, stood two men, steadfastly regarding each other in the face. The snake-like eye of the tall and slender man, was fixed in keen gaze upon the bronzed face of his companion, whose stout and imposing form seemed yet more large and commanding in its proportions, as occasional flashes from the fireplace lighted up the dim twilight. It was a strange thing, to see those large blue eyes, gleaming from the bronzed face, with such a calm and yet burning lustre.

"Luke—to the—the—*room*—" whispered a voice, husky with suppressed agitation.

"He is calm—" muttered Luke to himself—"I led him a d——l of a way in order to give him time to command his feelings. He is calm now—and it's *too late to go back.*"

Extending his hand he reached a small dark lanthern from the mantel-piece, and walked softly across the floor. Opening the door of a wide closet, he motioned Livingstone to approach.

"You see, this is rather a spacious closet—" Luke whispered, as silently drawing Livingstone within the recess, he closed the door, leaving them enveloped in thick darkness—"The back wall of the closet, is nothing less than a portion of the wainscotting of the next room. Give me your hand—it is firm, by G——d!—Do you feel that bolt? It's a little one, but once withdrawn, the panelling swings away from the closet like a door, and—egad!—the next room lays before you!"

While Livingstone stood in the thick darkness of the closet, silent as death, Luke slowly drew the bolt. Another touch, and the door would swing open into the next room. Luke could hear the hard breathing of the Merchant, and the hand which he touched suddenly became cold as ice.

As though by mere accident, in that moment of suspense, when their joined fingers touched the bolt, Harvey allowed the door of the dark lanthern, to spring suddenly open. The face of Livingstone, every line and feature, was disclosed in the light, with appaling distinctness. Luke was prepared for a sight of some interest, but no sooner did the light fall on the Merchant's face, than he gave a start of involuntary horror. It was as though the face of a corpse, suddenly recalled to life, had risen before him. White and livid and ghastly, with the discolored circles of flesh deepening beneath each eye, and with the large blue eyes, steadily glaring from the dark eyebrows, it was a countenance to strike the very heart with fear and horror. The firm lips wore a blueish hue, as though the man had been dead for days, and corruption was eating its way through his vitals. Around his high and massive brow, hung his hair, in slight masses; fearful streaks of white resting like scattered ashes, among the locks of dark brown.

"Well, Luke—you see—I am calm—" whispered Livingstone, smiling, with his lips still compressed—"I—am—calm—"

Luke slowly withdrew the bolt, and closed the door of the lanthern. The secret door, of the wainscotting swung open with a faint noise.

"Listen!" he whispered to Livingstone, as the dark room lay before them—"Listen!"

And with his very breath hushed, Livingstone silently listened. A low sound like a woman breathing in her sleep, came faintly to his ear. Luke felt the Merchant start as though he was reeling beneath a sudden blow.

"Give me the dark lanthern—" whispered Livingstone—"*The pistols I have!*" he continued, hissing the words through his clinched teeth—"The room is dark, but I can discern the outlines of the bed—"

He pressed Luke by the hand with a firm grasp, took the lanthern, carefully closing its door, and strode with a noiseless footstep, into the dark room.

Luke remained in the closet, listening with hushed breath.

There was a pause for a moment. It seemed an age to the listener. Not a sound, not a footstep, not even the rustling of the bed-curtains. All was silent as the grave-vault, which has not been disturbed for years.

Luke listened. He leaned from the closet and gazed into the dark room. It was indeed dark. Not the outline of a chair, or a sofa, or the slightest piece of furniture could he discern. True, near the centre of the place, arose a towering object, whose outlines seemed a shade lighter than the rest of the room. This might be the bed, thought Luke, and again holding his breath, he listened for the slightest sound.

All was dark and still.

Presently Luke heard a low gurgling noise, like the sound produced by a drowning man. Then all was silent as before.

In a moment the gurgling noise was heard again, and a sudden blaze of light streamed around the room.

Chapter Twelfth

The Tower Room

"My sister is in his power, for any act of wrong, for any deed of outrage! And I cannot strike a blow in her defence! A solitary wall may separate us—in one room the sister pleads with the villain for mercy—in the other, trapped and imprisoned, the brother hears her cry of agony, and cannot—cannot raise a finger in her behalf! Ha! The door is fast—I hear the hushed breathing of negroes on the other side. I have read many legends of a place of torment in the other world, but what devil could contrive a hell like this?"

He flung himself on the sofa, and covered his face with his hands. The lamp burning dimly on the solitary table, flung a faint and dusky light around the walls of the Tower Room.

Byrnewood lay in dim shadow, with his limbs thrown carelessly along the sofa, his outspread hands covering his face, while the long curls of his raven-black hair, fell wild and tangled over his forehead. As he lay there, with his dress disordered and his form resting on the sofa, in an attitude which, careless as it was, resembled the crouching position of one who suffers from the cold chill succeeding fever, you might have taken him for an inanimate effigy, instead of a living and breathing man.

No heaving of the chest, no quick and gasping respiration, no convulsive movements of the fingers, indicated the agitation which shook his soul to its centre. He lay quiet and motionless, his white hands, concealing his livid face, while a single glimpse of his forehead was visible between the tangled locks of his raven hair.

The silence of the room was broken by the creaking of the door, as it swung slowly open.

Bess silently entered the room, holding the waiter with the cold chicken and bottle of Madeira in her hands. She hurriedly closed the door and advanced to the solitary table. Her face was very pale, and her long dark hair, hung in disordered tresses around her full voluptuous neck. The dark shawl which she had thrown over her bridesmaid's dress, had fallen from her shoulders and hung loosely from her arms as she walked. Her entire appearance betrayed agitation and haste.

"He sleeps!" she murmured, arranging the refreshments—provided by Devil-Bug—along the surface of the chest-like table—"'Fix his plate on the side of the table furthest from the door'—what could the monster mean? Ha! There may be a secret spring on that side of the table, which the foot of the victim is designed to touch. I'll warn him of his danger—and then, the *bottle*— "

She said she would warn Byrnewood of his danger, and yet she lingered about the small table, her confused and hurried manner betraying her irresolution and changeability of purpose. Byrnewood still lay silent and motionless on the sofa. As far from slumber as the victim writhing on the rack, he was still unconscious of the presence of Longhaired Bess. His mind was utterly absorbed in the harrowing details of the mental struggle, that shook his soul to its foundations.

At first, arranging the knife and plate on one side of the table, and then on the other, now placing the bottle in one position and again in another, it was evident that Long-haired Bess was absent, confused and deeply agitated. The side-long glance, which every other instant, she threw over her shoulder at the reclining form of Byrnewood, was fraught with deep and painful meaning. At last, with a hurried footstep, she approached the sofa, and glancing cautiously at the door, which hung slightly ajar, she laid her hand lightly on Byrnewood's shoulder.

"I come to warn you of your danger—" she whispered in his ear.

Byrnewood looked up in wonder and then an expression of intolerable disgust impressed every line of his countenance.

"Your touch is pollution—" he said, shaking her hand from his shoulder—"You were one of the minions of the villain. You plotted my sister's dishonor— "

"I come to warn you of your danger!" whispered Bess, with a flashing eye—"You behold refreshments spread for you on yonder table. You see the bottle o' wine. On peril of your life don't drink anything— "

"But rale good brandy—" grated a harsh voice at her shoulder—"Liqu-ood hell-fire for ever! That's the stuff, my feller! Ha! ha! ha!"

With the same start of surprise, Byrnewood sprang to his feet, and Bess turned hurriedly around, while their eyes were fixed upon the face of the new-comer.

Devil-Bug, hideous and grinning, with the furnace of burning coals in his hand, stood before them. His solitary eye rested upon the face of Long-haired Bess with a meaning look, and his visage passed through the series of spasmodic contortions peculiar to his expressive features, as he stood swinging the furnace from side to side.

"You can go, Bessie, my duck—" he said, with a pleasant way of speaking, original with himself. "This 'ere party don't want you no more. You see, my feller citizen—" he continued, turning to Byrnewood— "yer humble servant thought you might be hungry, so he sent you suffin' to eat. Thought you might be cold; so he brung you some coals to warm yesself. You can *re*-tire, Bessie—"

He gently led her to the door, fixing his eye upon her face, with a look, as full of venom as a spiders sting.

"You'd a-spilt it all—would yo'?" he hissed the whisper in her ear as he pushed her from the room—"Good night my dear—" he continued aloud—"You better go home."

Your mammy's a waitin' tea for you. Now I'll make you a little bit o' fire, Mister, if you please—"

"Fire?" echoed Byrnewood— "I see no fire-place—"

"That's all you know about it"—answered Devil-Bug swinging the furnace from side to side—"You think them 'are's books do you? Look a little closer, next time. The walls are only painted like books and shelves—false book-cases you see. And then there's glass doors, jist like real book-cases. They did it in the old times—them queer old chaps as used to keep house here, all alone to themselves. Nice fire-place—aint it?"

He opened two folding leaves of the false book-case near the centre of the wall opposite the door, and a small fire-place neatly white-washed and free from ashes or the remains of any former fire, became visible. Stooping on his knees, Devil-Bug proceeded to arrange the furnace in the hearth, while the half-closed folding leaves of the bookcase, well-nigh concealed him from view.

"A false bookcase on either side of the room! Ha! Books of all classes, painted on the pannels, within the sashes, with inimitable skill! They deceived me, in the dim light of yonder lamp. What can this mean? By my life, I shrewdly suspect, that these bookcases, conceal secret passages, leading from this den— "

Byrnewood flung himself on the sofa, and again covered his face with his hands.

"Blazes up quite comfortable—" muttered Devil-Bug, as half concealed by the folding doors of the central part of the bookcase, he stooped over the furnace of blazing coal, warming his hands in the flame. "A nice fire, and a nice fire-place. But I'll have to discharge my bricklayer for one thing. Got him to fix up this harth not long ago. Scoundrel walled up the chimbley. Did ye ever hear of sich rascality? Konsekence is, this young gentleman will be rather uncomfortable a cause, the charcoal smoke wont find no vent. If I should happen to shut the door right tight he might die. He might so. Things jist as bad have happened afore now. He *might* die. Ha— ha—ha—" he chuckled as he retired from the fire-place, screening the blazing furnace, with the half-closed doors of the book-case—"Wonder how *that* 'ill work!"

He approached the side of Byrnewood, with that same hideous grin distorting his features, but had not advanced two steps, when he started backward with a moment of involuntary horror.

"Look here you sir—" he whispered grasping Byrnewood by the arm—"Jist look here a minnit. You see the floor at my left side—do you? Now tell us the truth, aint there a dead man layin' there? His jaw broke and his tongue out? Not that I'm afeered, but I wants to satisfy my mind. Jist take a good look while I hold still—"

"I see nothing but the carpet—" answered Byrnewood with a look of loathing, as he observed this strange being, standing before him, motionless as a statue, while his left hand pointed to the floor—"I see nothing but the carpet."

"Don't see a dead man, with his knees drawed up to his breast, and his tongue stickin' out? Well that's queer. I'd take my book oath, that the feller was a layin' there, nasty as a snake— Hows'ever re-fresh yourself young man. There's plenty to eat and drink and—" he pointed to the hearth as he spoke—"There's a nice comfortable fire. Good charcoal— and—I wonder's how *that* 'ill *work*—"

Closing the door, he stood in the small recess, at the head of the stairs, leading to the Tower-Room. The huge forms of the negroes, Musquito and Glow-worm, were flung along the floor, while their hard breathing indicated that they slumbered on their watch. Listening intently for a single moment, at the door of the Tower-Room, Devil-Bug slowly turned the key in the lock, and then withdrawing it from the keyhole placed it in his pocket. He stepped carefully over the forms of the sleeping negroes, and passed his hands slowly along the panelling of the recess, opposite the door.

"The spring—ha, ha—I've found it—" he muttered in the darkness.—"The bookcases dont conceal no passage between the walls of this 'ere Tower, and the room itself—do they? O'course they do not. Quiet little places where a feller can say his prayers and eat ground-nuts. Ha! Ha! Ha! I must see how *that* 'ill work."

The panelling slid back as he touched the spring and Devil-Bug disappeared into the secret recess or passage, between the false bookcases and the massive walls of the Tower; as the solitary chamber, rising from the western wing of Monk-Hall, was termed in the legends of the place.

Meanwhile within the Tower-Room. Byrnewood Arlington paced slowly up and down the floor, his arms folded, and his face, impressed with a fixed expression, that forced his lips tightly together, darkened his brows in a settled frown and drove the blood from his entire visage, until it wore the livid hues of death.

"My sister in his power! Last night she was pure and stainless—to morrow morning dawns and she will be a thing stained with pollution, dishonored by a hideous crime! No lapse of time, no prayers to Heaven, no bitter tears of repentance can ever wash out the foul stains of her dishonor. And I am a prisoner, while she shrieks for help and shrieks in vain—"

As Byrnewood spoke, striding rapidly along the floor, a grateful warmth began to steal around the room, dispelling the chill and damp, which seemed to infect the very air, with an unwholesome taint.

"And we have been children together! I have held her in these arms, when she was but a babe—a smiling babe, with golden hair and laughing cheeks! And then when she left home for school, how it wrung my soul to part with her! So young, so lighthearted, so innocent! Three years pass—she returns grown up into a lovely girl—whose pure soul, a very devil would not dare to tarnish—she return to bless the sight of her father—her mother, with her laughing face and she is—*dishonored!* I never knew the meaning of the word till now— *dishonored* by a villain— "

He flung himself on the sofa, and covered his face with his hands.

"And yet I, I, wronged an innocent girl, because she was my father's servant! Great God! Can she, have a brother to feel for her ruin? My punishment is just, but Mary—Oh! whom did she ever harm, whom *could* she ever wrong?"

He was silent again. And while his brain was tortured by the fierce struggles of thought, while the memories of earlier days came thronging over his soul—the image of his sister, present in every thought, and shining brightest in each old-time memory—he could feel, the grateful heat which pervaded the atmosphere of the room, restoring warmth and comfort to his limbs, while his blood flowed more freely in his veins.

There was a long pause, in which his very soul was absorbed in a delirium of thought. It may have been the effect of internal agitation, or the result of his half-crazed intellect acting on his physical system, but after the lapse of some few minutes, he was aroused from his reverie, by a painful throbbing around his temples, which for a single moment destroyed all consciousness, and just as suddenly restored him to a keen and terrible sense of his appaling situation. Now his brain seemed to swim in a wild delirium and in a single instant as the throbbing around his temples grew more violent, his mental vision, seemed clearer and more vigorous than ever.

"I can scarcely breathe!" he muttered, as he fell back on the sofa, after a vain attempt to rise—There is a hand grasping me by the throat—I feel the fingers clutching the veins with the grasp of a demon. My heart—ah!—it is turning to ice—to ice—and now it is fire! My heart is a ball of flame—the blood boils in my veins—"

He sprung to his feet, with a wild bound and his hands clutched madly at his throat, as though he would free the veins from the grasp of the invisible fingers, which were pressing through the very skin.

He staggered to and fro along the floor, with his arms flung overhead as if to ward off the attacks of some invisible foe.

His face was ghastly pale, one moment; the next it flushed with the hues of a crimson flame. His large black eyes dilated in their glance, and stood out from the lids as though they were about to fall from their sockets. His mouth distended with a convulsive grimace, while his teeth were firmly clenched together. One instant his brain would be perfectly conscious in all its operations, the next his senses would swim in a fearful delirium.

"My God—My God!" he shouted in one of those momentary intervals of consciousness, as he staggered wildly along the floor—"I am dying—I am dying! My breath comes thick and gaspingly—my veins are chilled—ha, ha—they are turned to fire again—"

Even in his delirium he was conscious of a singular circumstance. A portion of the panelling of the false bookcase, along the wall opposite the fire, receded suddenly, within the sash of the central glass-door, leaving a space of black and vacant darkness. The aperture was in the top of the bookcase, near the ceiling of the room.

Turning toward the hearth, Byrnewood endeavoured to regain the sofa, but the room seemed swimming around him, and with a wild movement, he again staggered toward the bookcase opposite the fire.

He started backward as a new horror met his gaze.

A hideous face glared upon him, from the aperture of the book-case, like some picture of a fiend's visage, suddenly thrust against the glass-door of the book-case.

A hideous face, with a single burning eye, with a wide mouth distending in a loathsome grin, with long rows of fang-like teeth, and a protuberant brow, overhung by thick masses of matted hair. This face alone was visible, surrounded by the darkness which marked the square outline of the aperture. It was, indeed, like a hideous picture framed in ebony, although you could see the muscles of the face in motion, while the flat nose was pressed against the glass of the book-case, and the thick lips were now tightly closed, and again distending in hideous grin.

"Ho! ho! ho!" a laugh like the shout of a devil, came echoing through the glass, faint and subdued, yet wild and terrible to hear—"The charcoal— the charcoal! Wonder how *that'll work!*"

Byrnewood stood silent and erect, while the throbbing of his temples, the gasping of his breath, and the deadening sensation around his heart, subsided for a single moment.

The full horror of his situation rushed upon him. He was dying by the gas escaping from charcoal, in a room, rendered impervious to the air; closed and sealed for the purpose of this horrible death.

A brilliant idea flashed across his brain.

"I will overturn the furnace—" he muttered, rushing toward the hearth—"I will extinguish the flame!"

With a sudden bound he sprang forward, but in the very action, fell to the floor, like a drunken man.

His breath came in thick convulsive gasps, his heart grew like a mass of fire, while his brain was tortured by one intense and agonizing throb of pain, as though some invisible hand had wound a red hot wire round his forehead. He lay on the floor, with his outspread hands grasping the air in the effort to rise.

"It works, it works!" shouted the voice of Devil-Bug, as his loath-some countenance was pressed against the glass-door of the book-case—"Ha! ha! ha! He is on the floor—he cannot rise—he is in the clutch of death. How the poor feller kicks and scuffles!"

A wild, wild shriek echoing from a distant room came faintly to Byrnewood's ear. That sound of a woman's voice, shrieking for help, in an emphasis of despair, aroused the dying man from the spell which began to deaden his senses.

"It is my sister's voice!" he exclaimed, springing to his feet with a last effort of strength— "She is in the hands of the villain! I will save her— I will save her—"

"The sister outraged! The brother murdered!" shouted Devil-Bug, through the glass-door—"I wonder how *that'll work!*"

Byrnewood rushed towards the door; it was locked and secured. All hope was in vain. He must die. Die, while his sister's shriek for aid rang on his ears, die, with the loathsome face of his murderer pressed against the glass, while his blazing eye feasted on his last convulsive agonies, die, with youth on his brow, with health in his heart! Die, with all purposed vengeance on his sister's wronger unfulfilled; die, by no sudden blow, by no dagger thrust, by no pistol shot, but by the most loathsome of all deaths, by suffocation.

"Ha! ha!" the thought flashed over his brain—"The hangman's rope were a priceless luxury to me in this dread hour!"

Staggering slowly along the floor, with footsteps as heavy as though he had leaden weights attached to his feet, he approached the chest-like table, and with a faint effort to recover his balance, sunk down on the floor, in a crouching position, while his outspread hands clutched faintly at the air.

In a moment he rolled slowly from side to side, and lay on his back with his face to the ceiling, and his arms extended on either side. His eyes were suddenly covered with a glassy film, his lower jaw separated from the upper, leaving his mouth wide open, while room grew warmer, the air more dense and suffocating.

"Help— help!" murmured Byrnewood, in a smothered voice, like the sound produced by a man throttled by nightmare—"Help! help!"

" 'By-a-baby, go to sleep'—that's a good feller—" the voice of Devil-Bug came like a faint echo through the glass—"A drop from the bottle 'ud do you good, and—jist reach your right hand a leetle bit further! There ain't no spring there, I *sup*-pose? Ain't there? Ho-ho-ho!"

And Byrnewood could feel a delicious languor stealing over his frame, as he lay there on the floor, helpless and motionless, while the voice of Devil-Bug rang in his ears The throbbing of his temples had subsided, he no more experienced the quick gasping struggle for breath, his heart no more passed through the quick transitions from cold to heat, from ice to fire, his veins no more felt like streams of molten lead. He was sinking quietly in a soft and pleasing slumber. The film grew more glassy in each eye, his jaws hung further apart, and the heaving of his chest subsided, until a faint and tremulous motion, was the only indication that life had not yet fled from his frame. His outspread arms seemed to grow stiffened and dead as he rested on the floor, while the joints of the fingers moved faintly to and fro, with a fluttering motion, that afforded a strange contrast to the complete repose of his body and limbs. His feet were pointed upward, like the feet of a corpse, arrayed for burial.

The dim light burning on the chest-like table, afforded a faint light to the ghastly scene. There were the untouched refreshments, the cold chicken and the bottle of wine, giving the place the air of a quiet supper-room, there were the false book cases, indicating a resort for meditation and study, there was the cheerful furnace, its glowing flame flashing through the half-closed doors, speaking a pleasant tale of fireside joys and comforts, and there, along the carpet, stiffening and ghastly lay the form of Byrnewood Arlington, slowly and quietly yielding to the slumber of death, while a hideous face peered through the glass-door, all distorted by a sickening grimace, and a solitary eye, that gleamed like a live coal, drank in the tremulous agonies of the dying man.

"Reach his hand a leetle bit further—that's a good feller. Won't have no tumble down three stories, nor nothin', if his fingers touch the spring? Ho-ho! Quiet now, I guess. Jist look how his fingers tremble—He! he! he! Hallo! He's on his feet agin!"

With the last involuntary struggle of a strong man wrestling for his life, Byrnewood Arlington sprang to his feet, and reaching forth his hand with the same mechanical impulse that had raised him from the floor, he seized the bottle of wine; he raised it to his lips, and the wine poured gurgling down his throat.

"Hain't got no opium in, I *sup*-pose? Not the least mossel. Cuss it, how he staggers! Believe my soul he's comin' to life agin'—"

Byrnewood glanced around with a look of momentary consciousness. The drugged wine, for a single moment, created a violent reaction in his system, and he became fully sensible of the awful death that awaited him. He could feel the hot air, warming his cheek, he could see the visage of Devil-Bug peering at him thro' the glass-door, and the danger which menaced his sister, came home like some horrible phantom to his soul. He felt in his very soul that but a single moment more of consciousness, would be permitted him, for action. That moment past, and the death by charcoal, would be quietly and surely accomplished.

"Keep me, oh Heaven!" he whispered as his mind ran over various expedients for escape—"Aid me, in this, my last effort, that I may live to avenge my sister's dishonor!"

It was his design to make one sudden and desperate spring toward the glass-door, through which the hideous visage of Devil-Bug, glared in his face and as he madly dashed his hands through the glass, the room would be filled with a current of fresh air.

This was his resolve, but it came too late. As he turned, to make this desperate spring, his heel pressed against an object, rising from the floor, near a corner of the chest-like table. It was but a small object, resembling a nail or spike, which has not been driven to the head, in the planking of a floor, but suffered to remain half-exposed and open to the view.

And yet the very moment Byrnewood's heel, pressed against the trifling object, the floor on which he stood gave way beneath him, with a low rustling sound, half of the Chamber was changed into one black and yawning chasm, and the lamp standing on the table suddenly disappeared, leaving the place wrapt in thick darkness.

Another moment passed, and while Byrnewood reeled in the darkness, on the verge of the sunken trap-door, a hushed and distant sound, echoed far below as from the depths of some deep and dismal well. The lamp had fallen in the chasm, and the faint sound heard far, far below was the only indication that it had reached the bottom of the gloomy void, sinking down like a well into the cellars of Monk-hall.

Byrnewood tottered on the verge of the chasm, while a current of cold air came sweeping upward from its depths. The foul atmosphere of the Tower Room, lost half its deadly qualities, in a single moment, as the cool air, came rushing from the chasm.

Byrnewood felt the effects of the charcoal rapidly passing from his system, and his mind regained its full consciousness as his hot brow, received the freshning blast of winter air, pouring over the parched and heated skin.

But the current of pure air, came too late for his salvation. Tottering in the darkness on the very verge of the sunken trap-door, he made one desperate struggle to preserve his balance, but in vain. For a moment his form swung to and fro, and then his feet slid from under him; and then with a maddening shriek, he fell.

"God save poor Mary!"

How that last cry of the doomed man shrieked around the panelled walls of the Tower Room!

"Wonder how *that'ill work!*" the hoarse voice of Devil-Bug, shrieked through the darkness—"Down— down—*down!* Ah-ha! Three stories—down—down—down! I wonders how that 'ill work!"

Separated from the Tower Room by the glass-door, Devil-Bug pressed his ear against the glass, and listened for the death-groans of the doomed man.

A low moaning sound, like the groan of a man, who trembles under the operations of a surgeon's knife, came faintly to his ear. In a moment, Devil-Bug, thought he heard a sound like a door suddenly opened, and then, the murmur of voices, whispering some quick and hurried words, resounded along the Tower Room. Then there was a subdued noise, like a man struggling on the brink of the chasm, and then a hushed sound, that might have been taken for the tread of a footstep mingled with the closing of a door, came faintly through the glass of the book-case.

Gliding silently from the secret recess, behind the panelling of the Tower Room, Devil-Bug stepped over the forms of the slumbering negroes and descended the stairway leading to the Walnut Room. The scene of the wedding was wrapt in midnight darkness. Passing softly along the floor, Devil-Bug, reached the entrance to the Rose Chamber, and flung the hangings aside, with a cautious movement of his talon-like fingers.

"I merely wanted a light—" exclaimed Devil-Bug, as he stood gazing into the Rose chamber—"But here's a candle, and a purty sight into the bargain!"

He disappeared through the doorway, and after the lapse of a few moments, again emerged into the Walnut Room, holding a lighted candle in his hand.

"Amazin' circumstance, *that*—" he chuckled, as he strode across the glittering floor— "The brother *fell* in that 'are room, and the sister *fell* in *that*; about the same time. They *fell* in different ways though. Strange world, this. Let's see what become of the brother— Charcoal and opium—ho! ho! ho!"

Before another moment had elapsed, he stood before the door of Tower Room. Musquito and Glow-worm still slumbered on their watch, their huge forms and hideous faces, dimly developed in the beams of the light, which the Doorkeeper carried in his hand. Devil-Bug listened intently for a single moment, but not the slightest sound disturbed the silence of the Tower room.

He opened the door, he strode along the carpet, he stood on the verge of the chasm produced by the falling of the death-trap.

"Down—down! Three stories, and the pit below! Ha! Let me hold the light, a leetle nearer! Every trap-door is open—he is safe enough! Think I see suffin' white a-flutterin' a-way down there! Hollered pretty loud as he fell—devilish ugly tumble! Guess it 'ill work quite nice for Lorrimer!"

Stooping on his knees with the light extended in his right hand, he again gazed down the hatchway, his solitary eye flashing with excitement, as he endeavoured to pierce the gloom of the dark void beneath.

"He's gone to see his friends below! Sartin sure! No sound—no groan—not even a holler!"

Arising from his kneeling position, Devil-Bug approached the recess of the fireplace. On either side, a plain panell of oak, concealed the secret nook behind the false book-case. Placing his hand cautiously along the panell to the right, Devil-Bug examined the details of the carving in each corner, and along its side, with a careful eye.

"Hasn't been opened to-night—" he murmured—"Leads to the Walnut Room, by a round-a-bout way. Convenient little passage, if that fool had only knowed on it!"

In an instant he stood outside of the Tower Room door, holding the key in one hand, and the candlestick in the other.

"Git up you lazy d——l's!" he shouted, bestowing a few pointed kicks upon the carcases of the sleeping negroes—"Git up and mind your eyes, or else I'll pick 'em out o' your head to play marbles with—"

Glow-worm arose slowly from the floor, and Musquito, opening his eyes with a sleepy yawn, stared vacantly in the Doorkeeper's face.

"D'ye hear me? Watch this feller and see that he don't escape? He's a sleepin' now, but there's no knowin'—Watch! I say watch!"

He shuffled slowly along the narrow passage, looking over his shoulder at the grinning negroes, as he passed along, while his face wore its usual pleasant smile, as he again muttered in his hoarse tones—"Watch him ye dogs—I say watch him!"

Another moment, and he stood before the entrance of the Rose Chamber, holding the curtaining aside, while his eye blazed up with an expression of malignant joy. He raised the light on high, and stood gazing silently through the doorway, as though his eyes beheld a spectacle of strange and peculiar interest.

And while he stood there, chuckling pleasantly to himself, with the full light of the candle, flashing over his loathsome face, two figures, stood crouching in the darkness, along the opposite side of the room, and the eastern door hung slightly ajar, as though they had entered the place but a moment before.

Once or twice Devil-Bug turned, as though the sound of suppressed breathing struck his ear, but every time, the shadow of the candle fell along the opposite side of the room, and the crouching figures were concealed from view.

"Quite a pictur'—" chuckled Devil-Bug as he again gazed through the doorway of the Rose Chamber—"A nice little gal and a handsome feller! Ha! Ha! Ha!"

He disappeared through the curtaining, while his pleasant chuckle came echoing through the doorway, with a sound of continued glee, as though the gentleman was highly amused by the spectacle that broke on his gaze.

The silence of the Rose Chamber was broken by the tread of a footstep and the figure of a man, came stealing through the darkness, with the form of a queenly woman by his side.

"Advance—and save your sister's honor—" the deep-toned whisper broke thrillingly on the air.

The man advanced with a hurried step, flung the curtain hastily aside, and gazed within the Rose Chamber.

The horror of that silent gaze, would be ill-repayed by an Eternity of joy.

Chapter Thirteenth

The Crime without a Name

"My brother consents? Oh joy, Lorraine—he consents!"

"Your brother consents to our wedding, my love—"

"How did he first discover, that the wedding was to take place to night?"

"It seems that for several days, he has noticed you walking out with Bess. You see, Mary, this excited his suspicions. He watched you with all a brother's care, and to night, tracked Bess and you, to the doors of this mansion. He was not certain however, that it was *you*, whom he seen, enter my uncle's house—"

"And so he watched all night around the building? Oh Lorraine, *he* is a noble brother!"

"At last, grown feverish with his suspicions, he rung the bell, aroused the servant, and when the door was opened, rushed madly up stairs, and reached the Wedding Room. You know the rest. After the matter was explained to him, he consented to keep our marriage secret until Christmas Eve. He has left the house, satisfied that you are in the care of those who love you. To morrow, Mary, when you have recovered from the effects of the surprise,—which your brother's sudden entrance occasioned—to-morrow we will be married!"

"And on Christmas Eve, hand linked in hand, we will kneel before *our* father, and ask his blessing—"

"One kiss, Mary love, one kiss, and I will leave you for the night—"

And leaning fondly over the fair girl, who was seated on the sofa, her form enveloped in a flowing night-robe, Lorrimer wound his right arm gently around her neck, bending her head slowly backward in the action, and suffering her rich curls to fall showering on her shoulders, while her upturned face, all radiant with affection lay open to his burning gaze, and her ripe lips, dropped slightly apart, disclosing the ivory teeth, seemed to woo and invite the pressure of his kiss.

One kiss, silent and long, and the Lover and the fair girl, seemed to have grown to each others lips.

The wax-light standing on the small table of the Rose Chamber, fell mild and dimly over this living picture of youth and passion.

The tall form of Lorrimer, clad in solemn black, contrasting forcibly with the snow-white robes of the Maiden, his arm flung gently around her neck, her upturned face half-hidden by the falling locks of his dark brown hair, their lips joined and their eyes mingling in the same deep glance of passion, while her bosom rose heaving against his breast, and her arms half-upraised seemed about to entwine his form in their embrace—it was a moment of pure and hallowed love on the part of the fair girl, and even the libertine, for an instant forgot the vileness of his purpose, in that long and silent kiss of stainless passion.

"Mary!" cried Lorrimer, his handsome face flushing over with transport, as silently gliding from his standing position, he assumed his seat at her side—"Oh! would that you were mine! We would flee together from the heartless world—in some silent and shadowy valley, we would forget all, but the love which made us one."

"We would seek a home, quiet and peaceful, as that which this book describes—" whispered Mary laying her hand on Bulwer's play of Claude Mellnotte[27]—"I found the volume on the table, and was reading it, when you came in. Oh, it is all beauty and feeling. You have read it Lorraine?"

"Again and again and have seen it played a hundred times.—'The home, to which love could fulfil its prayers, this hand would lead thee'—" he murmured repeating the first lines of the celebrated description of the Lake of Como—"And yet Mary this is mere romance. A creation of the poet's brain. A fiction as beautiful as a ray of light; and as fleeting. I might tell you a story of a real valley and a real lake,—which I beheld last summer—where love might dwell forever, and dwell in eternal youth and freshness.—"

"Oh tell me—tell me—" cried Mary, gazing in his face with a look of interest.

"Beyond the fair valley of Wyoming,[28] of which so much has been said and sung, there is a high and extensive range of mountains, covered with thick and gloomy forests. One day last September when the summer was yet in its freshness and bloom, toward the hour of sunset, I found myself wandering through a thick wood, that covered the summit of one of the highest of these mountains. I had been engaged in a deer-hunt all day—had strayed from my comrades—and now as night was coming on, was wandering, along a winding path, that led to the top of the mountain—"

Lorrimer paused for a single instant, and gazed intently in Mary's face. Every feature was animated with sudden interest and a warm flush, hung freshly on each cheek.

And as Lorrimer gazed upon the animated face of the innocent girl, marking its rounded outlines, its hues of youth and loveliness, its large blue eyes beaming so gladly upon his countenance, the settled purpose of his soul, came to him, like a sudden shadow darkening over a landscape, after a single gleam of sunlight.

It was the purpose of this libertine to dishonor the stainless girl, before he left her presence.

Before day break she would be a polluted thing, whose name and virtue and soul, would be blasted forever.

In that silent gaze, which drank in the beauty of the maiden's face, Lorrimer arranged his plan of action. The book which he had left open upon the table, the story which he was about to tell, were the first intimations of his atrocious design. While enchaining the mind of the Maiden, with a story full of Romance, it was his intention to wake her animal nature into full action. And when her veins were all alive with fiery pulsations, when her heart grew animate with sensual life, when her eyes swam in the humid moisture of passion, then she would sink helplessly into his arms, and—like the bird to the snake,—flutter to her ruin.

" 'Force'—'violence!' These are but the tools of grown-up children, who know nothing of the mystery of woman's heart—" the thought flashed over Lorrimer's brain, as his lip, wore a very slight but meaning smile—"I have deeper means, than these! I employ neither force, nor threats, nor fraud, nor violence! My victim is the instrument of her own ruin— without one rude grasp from my hand, without one threatening word, she swims willingly to my arms!"

---

27 Claude Mellnotte is the hero of Edward George Bulwer-Lytton's (1803–1873) play *Lady of Lyons*. Claude Mellnotte was a well-known character who became a type for the fiercely romantic restless, brilliant young man.

28 A region in northeastern Pennsylvania along the Susquehanna River.

He took the hand of the fair girl within his own, and looking her steadily in the eye, with a deep gaze which every instant grew more vivid and burning, he went on with his story—and his design.

"The wood grew very dark. Around me, were massive trees with thick branches, and gnarled trunks, bearing witness of the storms of an hundred years. My way led over a path covered with soft forest-moss, and now and then, red gleams of sunlight shot like arrows of gold, between the overhanging leaves. Darker and darker, the twilight sank down upon the forest. At last missing the path, I knew not which way to tread. All was dark and indistinct. Now falling over a crumbling limb, which had been thrown down by a storm long before, now entangled by the wild vines, that overspread portions of the ground, and now missing my foothold in some hidden crevice of the earth, I wandered wearily on. At last climbing up a sudden elevation of the mountain, I stood upon a vast rock, that hung over the depths below, like an immense platform. On all sides, but one, this rock was encircled by a waving wall of forest-leaves. Green shrubs swept circling around, enclosing it like a fairy bower, while the eastern side, lay open to the beams of the moon, which now rose grandly in the vast horizon. Far over wood, far over mountain, far over ravine and dell, this platform-rock, commanded a distant view of the valley of Wyoming.

"The moon was in the sky, Mary: the sky was one vast sheet of blue, undimmed by a single cloud; and beneath the moonbeams lay a sea of forest-leaves, while in the dim distance—like the shore of this leafy ocean—arose the roofs and steeples of a quiet town, with a broad river, rolling along the dark valley, like a banner of silver, flung over a sable-pall—"

"How beautiful!"

And as the murmur escaped Mary's lips, the hand of Lorrimer grew closer in its pressure, while his left arm, wound gently around her waist.

"I stood entranced by the sight. A cool breeze came up the mountain side, imparting a grateful freshness to my cheek. The view was indeed beautiful, but I suddenly remembered that I was without resting-place or shelter. Ignorant of the mountain paths, afar from any farm-house or village, I had still a faint of hope, of discovering the temporary habitation of some hunter, who had encamped in these forest-wilds.

"I turned from the magnificent prospect—I brushed aside the wall of leaves, I looked to the western sky. I shall never forget the view—which like a dream of fairyland—burst on my sight, as pushing the shrubbery aside, I gazed from the western limits of the platform-rock.

"There, below me, imbedded in the very summit of the mountain, lay a calm lake whose crystal-waters, gave back the reflection of forest and sky, like an immense mirror. It was but a mile in length, and half that distance in width. On all sides, sudden and steep, arose the encircling wall of forest trees. Like wine in a goblet, that calm sheet of water, lay in the embrace of the surrounding wall of foliage. The waters were clear, so tranquil, that I could see, down, down, far, far beneath, as if another world, was hidden in their depths. And then from the heights, the luxuriant foliage, as yet untouched by autumn, sank in waves of verdure to the very brink of the lake, the trembling leaves, dipping in the clear, cold waters, with a gentle motion. It was very beautiful Mary and—"

"Oh, most beautiful!"

The left hand of Lorrimer, gently stealing round her form, rested with a faint pressure upon the folds of the night-robe, over her bosom, which now came heaving tremulously into light.

"I looked upon this lovely lake with a keen delight. I gazed upon the tranquil waters, upon the steeps crowned with forest-trees—one side in heavy shadow, the other, gleaming in the advancing moonbeams—I seemed to inhale the quietness, the solitude of the place, as a holy influence, mingling with the very air, I breathed, and a wild transport aroused my soul into an outburst of enthusiasm.

"Here—I cried—is the home for Love! Love, pure and stainless, flying from the crowded city, here can repose, beneath the shadow of quiet rocks, beside the gleam of tranquil waters, within the solitudes of endless forests. Yon sky, so clear, so cloudless, has never beheld a sight of human misery or wo. Yon lake, sweeping beneath me, like another sky, has never been crimsoned by human blood. This quiet valley, hidden from the world now, as it has been hidden since the creation, is but another world where two hearts that love, that mingle in one, that throb but for each other's joy, can dwell forever, in the calm silence of unalloyed affection—"

"A home for love such as angels feel—"

Closer and more close, the hand of Lorrimer pressed against the heaving bosom, with but the slight folds of the night-robe between.

"Here, beside this calm lake, whenever the love of a true woman shall be mine, here, afar from the cares and realities of life, will I dwell! Here, with the means which the accident of fortune has bestowed, will I build, not a temple, not a mansion, not a palace! But a cottage, a quiet home, whose roof shall arise—like a dear hope in the wilderness—from amid the green leaves of embowering trees—"

"You spoke thus, Lorraine? Do I not love you as a true woman should love? Is not your love calm and stainless as the waters of the mountain lake? We will dwell there, Lorraine! Oh, how like romance will be the plain reality of our life!"

"Oh! Mary, my own true love, in that moment as I stood gazing upon the world-hidden lake, my heart all throbbing with strange impulses, my very soul steeped in a holy calm, your form seemed to glide between my eyes and the moonlight! The thought rushed like a prophecy over my soul, that one day, amid the barren wilderness of hearts, which crowd the world, I should fine *one*, *one* heart, whose impulses should be stainless, whose affection should be undying, whose love should be mine! Oh, Mary, in that moment, I felt that my life would, one day, be illumined by your love—"

"And then you knew me not? Oh, Lorraine, is there not a strange mystery in this affection, which makes the heart long for the love, which it shall one day experience, even before the eye has seen the beloved one?"

Brighter grew the glow on her cheek, closer pressed the hand on her bosom, warmer and higher arose that bosom in the light.

"And there, Mary, in that quiet mountain valley, we will seek a home, when we are married. As soon as summer comes, when the trees are green, and the flowers burst from among the moss along the wood-path, we will hasten to the mountain lake, and dwell within the walls of our quiet home. For a home shall be reared for us, Mary, on a green glade that slopes down to the water's brink, with the tall trees sweeping away on either side.

"A quiet little cottage, Mary, with a sloping roof and small windows, all fragrant with wild flowers and forest vines! A garden before the door, Mary, where, in the calm summer morning, you can inhale the sweetness of the flowers, as they breath forth in untamed luxuriance. And then, anchored by the shore, Mary, a light sail-boat will be ready for us ever; to bear us over the clear lake in the early dawn, when the mist winds up in fleecy columns to the sky, or in the twilight, when the red sun flings his last ray over the waters, or in the silent night, when the moon is up, and the stars look kindly on us from the cloudless sky—"

"Alas! Lorraine! Clouds may come and storms, and winter—"

"What care we for winter, when eternal spring is in our hearts! Let winter come with its chill, and its ice and its snows! Beside our cheerful fire, Mary, with our hands clasping some book, whose theme is the trials of two hearts that loved on through difficulty and danger or death, we will sit silently, our hearts throbbing with one delight, while the long hours of the winter evening glide quietly on. Do you see the fire, Mary? How cheerily its beams light our faces as we sit in its kindly light! My arm is round your waist, Mary, my cheek is laid next to yours, our hands are locked together and your heart, Mary, oh how softly its throbbings fall on my ear!"

"Oh, Lorraine! Why is there any care in the world, when two hearts can make such a heaven on earth, with the holy lessons of an all-trusting love—"

"Or it may be, Mary—" and his gaze grew deeper, while his voice sank to a low and thrilling whisper—"Or it may be, Mary, that while we sit beside our winter fire—a fair babe—do not blush, *my wife*—a fair babe will rest smiling on your bosom—"

"Oh, Lorraine—" she murmured, and hid her face upon his breast, her long brown tresses, covering her neck and shoulders like a veil, while Lorraine wound his arms closely round her form, and looked around with a glance full of meaning.

There was triumph in that glance. The libertine felt her heart throbbing against his breast as he held her in his arms, he felt her bosom panting and heaving, and quivering with a quick fluttering pulsation and as he swept the clustering curls aside from her half-hidden face, he saw that her cheek glowed like a new-lighted flame.

"She is mine!" he thought, and a smile of triumph gave a dark aspect to his handsome face.

In a moment Mary raised her glowing countenance from his breast. She gazed around, with a timid, frightened look. Her breath came thick and gaspingly. Her cheeks were all a-glow, her blue eyes swam in a hazy dimness. She felt as though she was about to fall swooning on the floor. For a moment all consciousness seemed to have failed her, while a delirious langor came stealing over her senses. Lorrimer's form seemed to swim in the air before her, and the dim light of the room gave place to a flood of radiance, which seemed all at once to pour on her eyesight from some invisible source. Soft murmurs, like voices heard in a pleasant dream, fell gently on her ears, the langor came deeper and more mellow over her limbs; her bosom rose no longer quick and gaspingly, but in long pulsations, that urged the full globes in all their virgin beauty, softly and slowly into view. Like billows they rose above the folds of the night robe, while the flush grew warmer on her cheek, and her parted lips deepened into a rich vermillion tint.

"She is mine!" and the same dark smile flushed over Lorraine's face. Silent and motionless he sat, regarding his victim with a steadfast glance.

"Oh, Lorraine—" she cried, in a gasping voice, as she felt a strange unconsciousness stealing over her senses—"Oh, Lorraine—save me—save me!"

She arose, tottering on her feet, flinging her hands aloft, as though she stood on the brink of some frightful steep, without the power to retreat from its crumbling edge.

"There is no danger for you, my Mary—" whispered Lorrimer, as he received her falling form in his outspread arms—"There is no danger for you, my Mary—"

He played with the glossy curls of her dark brown hair as he spoke, while his arms gathered her half-swooning form full against his heart.

"She is mine! Her blood is a-flame—her senses swim in a delirium of passion! While the story fell from my lips, I aroused her slumbering woman's nature. Talk of force—ha, ha—She rests on my bosom as though she would grow there—"

As these thoughts half escaped from his lips, in a muttered whisper, his face shone with the glow of sensual passion, while his hazel eye dilated, with a glance, whose intense lustre had but one meaning; dark and atrocious.

She lay on his breast, her senses wrapt in a feverish swoon, that laid her powerless in his arms, while it left her mind vividly sensible of the approaching danger.

"Mary, my love—no danger threatens you—" he whispered playing with her glossy curls—"Look up, my love—*I* am with you, and will shield you from harm!"

Gathering her form in his left arm, secure of his victim, he raised her from his breast, and fixing his gaze upon her blue eyes, humid with moisture, he slowly flung back the night robe from her shoulders. Her bosom, in all its richness of outline, heaving and throbbing with that long pulsation, which urged it upward like a billow, lay open to his gaze.

And at the very moment, that her fair breast was thrown open to his sensual gaze, she sprang from his embrace, with a wild shriek, and instinctively gathered her robe over her bosom, with a trembling movement of her fair white hands. The touch of the seducer's hand, polluting her stainless bosom, had restored her to sudden consciousness.

"Lorraine! Lorraine!" she shrieked, retreating to the farthest corner of the room—"Oh, save me—save me—"

"No danger threatens you, my Mary—"

He advanced, as he spoke, towards the trembling girl, who had shrunk into a corner of the room, crouching closely to the rose-hued hangings, while her head turned over her shoulder and her hands clasped across her bosom, she gazed around with a glance full of terror and alarm.

Lorrimer advanced toward the crouching girl. He had been sure of his victim; he did not dream of any sudden outburst of terror from the half swooning maiden as she lay, helpless on his breast. As he advanced, a change came over his appearance. His face grew purple, and the veins of his eyes filled with thick red blood. He trembled as he walked across the floor, and his chest heaved and throbbed beneath his white vest, as though he found it difficult to breathe.

God save poor Mary, now!

Looking over her shoulder, she caught a gleam of his blood-shot eye, and read her ruin there.

"Mary, there is no danger—" he muttered, in a husky voice, as she shrunk back from his touch—"Let me raise you from the floor—"

"Save me, oh Lorraine—Save me!" she cried, in a voice of terror, crouching closer to the hangings along the wall.

"From what shall I save you?" he whispered, in a voice unnaturally soft and gentle, as though he endeavoured to hide the rising anger which began to gleam from his eye, when he found himself foiled in the very moment of triumph—"From what shall I save you—"

"From yourself—" she shrieked, in a frightened tone—"Oh, Lorraine, you love me. You will not harm me. Oh, save me, save me from yourself!"

Playing with the animal nature of the stainless girl, Lorrimer had aroused the sensual volcano of his own base heart. While he pressed her hand, while he gazed in her eyes, while he wound his embrace around her form, he had anticipated a certain and grateful conquest. He had not dreamed that the humid eye, the heaving bosom, the burning cheek of Mary Arlington, were aught but the signs of his coming triumph. Resistance? Prayers?

Tears? He had not anticipated these. The fiend was up in his soul. The libertine had gone too far to recede.

He stood before the crouching girl, a fearful picture of incarnate lust. Sudden as the shadow after the light this change had passed over his soul. His form arose towering and erect, his chest throbbed with sensual excitement, his hands hung, madly clinched, by his side while his curling hair fell wild and disordered over his brows, darkening in a hideous frown, and his mustachioed lip wore the expression of his fixed and unalterable purpose. His blood-shot eyes, flashed with the unholy light of passion, as he stood sternly surveying the form of his victim. There was something wild and brutal in their savage glare.

"This is all folly—" he said, in that low toned and husky voice—"Rise from the floor, Mary. You don't think I'd harm you?"

He stooped to raise her from the floor, but she shrank from his extended hands as though there was pollution in his slightest touch.

"Mary, I wish you to rise from the floor!"

His clenched hands trembled as he spoke, and the flush of mingled anger and sensual feeling, deepened over his face.

"Oh, Lorraine!" she cried, flinging herself on her knees before him—"Oh, Lorraine— you will not harm *me?* This is not *you*, Lorraine; it cannot be *you*. You would not look darkly on me, your voice would not grow harsh as it whispered my name—It is not Lorraine that I see—it is an evil spirit—"

It was an evil spirit, she said, and yet looked up into his blood-shot eyes for a gleam of mercy as she spoke, and with her trembling fingers, wrung his clinched right hand, and clasped it wildly to her bosom.

Pure, stainless, innocent, her heart a heaven of love, her mind childlike in its knowledge of the World, she knew not what she feared. She did not fear the shame which the good world would heap upon her, she did not fear the Dishonor, because it would be followed by such pollution that, no man in honor might call her—Wife—no child in innocence might whisper her name as—Mother—she did not fear the foul Wrong, as society with its million tongues and eyes, fears it, and holds it in abhorence, ever visiting the guilt of the man upon the head of his trembling victim.

Mary feared the Dishonor, because her soul, with some strange consciousness of approaching evil, deemed it, a foul Spirit, who had arisen, not so much to visit her with wrong as to destroy the Love, she felt for Lorrimer. Not for herself, but for *his* sake, she feared that nameless crime, which already glared upon her from the blood-shot eyes of her Lover. Her *Lover!*

"Oh, Lorraine, you will not harm me! For the sake of God, save me—save me!"

She clasped his hand with a closer grasp and gathered it tremblingly to her bosom, while her eyes dilating with a glance of terror, were fixed upon his face.

"Mary—this is madness—nothing but madness—" he said in that voice, grown hoarse with passion, and rudely tore his hand from her grasp.

Another instant, and stooping suddenly, he caught her form in his arms, and raised her struggling from her very feet.

"Mary—you—are—mine!" he hissed the whisper in her ear, and gathered her quivering form more closely to his heart.

There was a low-toned and hideous laugh, muttering or growling through the air as he spoke, and the form of Devil-Bug, stole with a hushed footstep from the entrance of the

Walnut Chamber, and seizing the light in his talon-fingers, glided from the room, with the same hyena laugh which had announced his appearance.

"The trap—the bottle—the fire, for the *brother*—" he muttered as his solitary eye, glanced upon the Libertine and his struggling victim, neither of whom had marked his entrance—"For the *Sister*—ha! ha! ha! The '*handsome*' Devil-Bug—Monk Gusty— 'tends to her! 'Bijah did'nt listen for nothin'—ha, ha! this beats the *charcoal*, quite hollow!"

He disappeared, and the Rose Chamber was wrapt in midnight darkness.

Darkness! There was a struggle, and a shriek and a prayer. Darkness! There was an oath and a groan, mingling in chorus. Darkness! A wild cry for mercy, a name madly shrieked, and a fierce execration. Darkness! Another struggle, a low moaning sound, and a stillness like that of the grave. Now darkness and silence mingle together and all is still.

In some old book of mysticism and superstition, I have read this wild legend, which mingling as it does the terrible with the grotesque, has still its meaning and its moral.

In the sky, far, far above the earth—so the legend runs—there hangs an Awful Bell, invisible to mortal eye, which angel hands alone may toll, which is never tolled save when the Unpardonable Sin is committed on earth, and then its judgment peal rings out like the blast of the archangel's trumpet, breaking on the ear of the Criminal, and on his ear alone, with a sound that freezes his blood with horror. The peal of the Bell, hung in the azure depths of space, announces to the Guilty one, that he is an outcast from God's mercy for ever, that his Crime can never be pardoned, while the throne of the Eternal endures; that in the hour of Death, his soul will be darkened by the hopeless prospect of an eternity of wo; wo without limit, despair without hope; the torture of the never-dying worm, and the unquenchable flame, forever and forever.

Reader! Did the sound of the Judgment Bell, pealing with one awful toll, from the invisible air, break over the soul of the Libertine, as in darkness and in silence, he stood shuddering over the victim of his Crime?

If in the books of the Last Day, there shall be found written down, but *One unpardonable* crime, that crime will be known as the foul wrong, accomplished in the gaudy Rose Chamber of Monk-hall, by the wretch, who now stood trembling in the darkness of the place, while his victim lay senseless at his feet.

There was darkness and silence for a few brief moments, and then a stream of light flashed around the Rose Chamber.

Like a fiend, returned to witness some appalling scene of guilt, which he had but a moment left, Devil-Bug stood in the doorway of the Walnut Chamber. He grimly smiled, as he surveyed the scene.

And then with a hurried gesture, a pallid face and blood-shot eyes, as though some Phantom tracked his footsteps, Lorrimer rushed madly by him, and disappeared into the Painted Chamber. At the very moment of his disappearance, Devil Bug raised the light on high, and started backward with a sudden impulse of surprise.

"*Dead—Dead* and come to life!" he shrieked, and then the gaze of his solitary eye as fixed upon the entrance to the Walnut Room. With a mechanical gesture, he placed the light upon the table and fled madly from the chamber, while the curtains opening into the Walnut Room rustled to and fro, for a single instant, and then a ghastly face, with livid cheeks and burning eyes, appeared between the crimson folds, gazing silently around the place, with a glance, that no living man would choose to encounter, for his weight in gold— it was so like the look of one arisen from the dead.

Chapter Fourteenth

The Guilty Wife

The light of the dark-lanthern streamed around the spot, where the Merchant stood.

Behind him, all was darkness, while the lanthern, held extended in his left hand, flung a ruddy blaze of light, over the outlines of the massive bed. Long silk curtains, of rich azure, fell drooping in voluminous folds, to the very floor, concealing the bed from view, while from within the gorgeous curtaining, that low softened sound, like a woman breathing in her sleep, came faintly to the Merchant's ear.

Livingstone advanced. The manner in which he held the lanthern flung his face in shadow, but you could see that his form quivered with a tremulous motion, and in the attempt to smother a groan which arose to his lips, a thick gurgling sound like the death-rattle, was heard in his throat.

Gazing from the shadow that enveloped his face, Livingstone, with an involuntary glance took in the details of the gorgeous couch—the rich curtaining of light azure satin, closely drawn around the bed; the canopy overhead surmounted by a circle of glittering stars, arranged like a coronet; and the voluptuous shapes, assumed by the folds, as they fell drooping to the floor, all burst like a picture on his eye.

Beside the bed stood a small table—resembling a lady's work stand—covered with a plain white cloth. The silver sheath of a large Bowie knife, resting on the white cloth, shone glittering in the light, and attracted the Merchant's attention.

He laid the pistol which he held at his right side, upon the table and raised the Bowie knife to the light. The sheath was of massive silver, and the blade of the keenest steel. The handle fashioned like the sheath, of massive silver, bore a single name, engraved in large letters near the hilt. *Algernon Fitz-Cowles,* and on the blade of polished steel, amid a wreath of flowers glittered the motto in the expressive slang of southern braggarts—'Stranger avoid a snag.'

Silently Livingstone examined the blade of the murderous weapon. It was sharp as a razor, with the glittering point inclining from the edge, like a Turkish dagger. The merchant grasped the handle of this knife in his right hand, and holding the lanthern on high, advanced to the bedside.

"His own knife—" muttered Livingstone—"shall find its way to his cankered heart—"

With the point of the knife, he silently parted the hangings of the bed, and the red glare of the lanthern flashed within the azure folds, revealing a small portion of the sleeping couch.

A moment passed, and Livingstone seemed afraid to gaze within the hangings, for he turned his head aside, more than once, and the thick gurgling noise again was heard in his throat. At last, raising the lanthern gently overhead, so that its beams would fall along a small space of the couch, while the rest was left in darkness, and grasping the knife with a firmer hold he gazed upon the spectacle disclosed to his view.

Her head deep sunken in a downy pillow, a beautiful woman, lay wrapt in slumber. By the manner in which the silken folds of the coverlid were disposed, you might see that her form was full, large and voluptuous. Thick masses of jet-black hair fell, glossy and luxuri-ant, over her round neck and along her uncovered bosom, which swelling with the full ripeness of womanhood, rose gently in the light. She lay on her side, with her head resting easily on one large, round arm, half hidden by the masses of black hair, streaming over the snow white pillow, while the other arm was flung carelessly along her form, the light falling softly over the clear transparent skin, the full roundness of its shape, and the small and delicate hand, resting gently on the coverlid.

Her face, appearing amid the tresses of her jet-black hair, like a fair picture half-hidden in sable drapery, was marked by a perfect regularity of feature, a high forehead, arching eyebrows and long dark lashes, resting on the velvet skin of each glowing cheek. Her mouth was opened slightly as she slept, the ivory whiteness of her teeth, gleaming through the rich vermillion of her parted lips.

She lay on that gorgeous couch, in an attitude of voluptuous ease; a perfect incarnation of the Sensual Woman, who combines the beauty of a mere animal, with an intellect strong and resolute in its every purpose.

And over that full bosom, which rose and fell with the gentle impulse of slumber, over that womanly bosom, which should have been the home of pure thoughts and wifely affections, was laid a small and swarthy hand, whose fingers, heavy with rings, pressed against the ivory skin, all streaked with veins of delicate azure, and clung twiningly among the dark tresses that hung drooping over the breast, as its globes rose heaving into view, like worlds of purity and womanhood.

It was a strange sight for a man to see, whose only joy, in earth or heaven, was locked within that snowy bosom, and yet Livingstone, the husband, stood firm and silent, as he gazed upon that strange hand, half hidden by the drooping curls.

It required but a slight motion of his hand, and the glare of the light flashed over the other side of the couch. The flash of the lanthern, among the shadows of the bed, was but for a moment, and yet Livingstone beheld the face of a dark-hued man, whose long dark hair mingled its heavy curls with the glossy tresses of his wife, while his hand reaching over her shoulder, rested, like a thing of foul pollution upon her bosom.

They slumbered together, slumbered in their guilt, and the Avenger stood gazing upon their faces while their hearts were as unconscious of his glance, as they were of the death which glittered over them in the upraised knife.

"Wife of mine—your slumber shall be deep and long—"

And as the whisper hissed from between the clenched teeth of the husband, he raised the dagger suddenly aloft, and then brought it slowly down until its point quivered within a finger's width of the heaving bosom, while the light of the lanthern held above his head, streamed over his livid face, and over the blooming countenance of his fair young wife.

The dagger glittered over her bosom; lower and lower it sank until a deeper respiration, a single heartdrawn sigh, might have forced the silken skin upon the glittering point, when the guilty woman murmured in her sleep.

"Algernon—a coronet—wealth and power—" were the broken words that escaped from her lips.

Again the husband raised the knife but it was with the hand clenched, and the sinews stiffened for the work of death.

"Seek your Algernon in the grave—" he whispered, with a convulsive smile, as his blue eyes, all alive with a glance, like a madman's gaze, surveyed the guilty wife—"Let the coronet be hung around your fleshless skull—let your wealth be a coffin, and—ha! ha!—your power—corruption and decay—"

It may have been that some feeling of the olden-time, when the image of that fair young wife dwelt in the holiest temple of his heart, came suddenly to the mind of the avenger, in that moment of fearful suspense, for his hand trembled for an instant and he turned his gaze aside, while a single scalding tear rolled down his livid cheek.

"Algernon—" murmured the wife—"We will seek a home—"

"In the grave!"

And the dagger rose, and gleamed like a stream of flame overhead, and then sank down with a whirring sound.

Is the bosom red with the stain of blood?

Has the keen knife severed the veins and pierced the heart?

The blow of a strong arm, stricken over Livingstone's shoulder, dashed his hand suddenly aside, and the knife sank to the very hilt in the pillow, within a hair's breadth of Dora's face. The knife touched the side of her cheek, and a long and glossy curl, severed from her head by the blow, lay resting on the pillow.

Livingstone turned suddenly round, with a deep muttered oath, while his massive form rose towering to its full height. Luke Harvey stood before him, his cold and glittering eye, fixed upon his face, with an expression of the deepest agitation.

"Stand back Sir—" muttered Livingstone with a quivering lip—"This spot is sacred to me! I want no witness to my wrong—nor to my vengeance!"

"Ha—ha!" sneered Luke bending forward until his eyes glared fixedly in the face of the Husband—"Is this a vengeance for a man like you?"

"Luke—again I warn you—leave me to my shame, and its punishment—"

"'Shame' 'Punishment!' Ha—ha! You have been wronged in secret, slowly and quietly wronged, and yet would punish that wrong, by a blow that brings but a single pang!"

"Luke—you are right—" whispered Livingstone, his agitated manner subsiding into a look of calm and fearful determination—"The wrong has been secret, long in progress, horrible in result. So let the punishment be. She shall see *the* Death—" and his eyes flashed with a maniac wildness—"She shall see the Death as it slowly approaches, she shall feel it as it winds its very fangs into her very heart, she shall know that all hope is in vain, while my voice will whisper in her freezing ear—'Dora, it is by my will that you die! Shriek—Dora— shriek for aid! Death is cold and icy—I can save you! I your—husband! I can save you, but will not! Die—Adultress—die—'"

"Algernon—" murmured Dora half-awakened from her sleep—"There is a cold hand laid against my cheek—"

"She wakes!" whispered Luke—"The dagger—the lanthern—"

It required but a single moment for Livingstone to draw the knife, from the pillow, where it rested against the blooming cheek of the wife, while Luke, with a sudden moment grasped the lanthern, and closed its door, leaving the Chamber wrapt in midnight darkness.

The husband stood motionless as a stone, and Luke held his very breath, as the voice of Dora broke on their ears, in tones of alarm and terror.

"Algernon—" she whispered, as she started from her slumber—"Awake—Do you not hear the sound of voices, by the bedside? Hist! Could it have been *the* dream? Algernon—"

"Deuced uncomfortable to be waked-up this way—" murmured a sleepy voice— "What's the matter Dora? What about a dream?"

"I was awakened just now from my sleep by the sound of voices.— I thought a blaze of light flashed round the room, while my hus—that is, Livingstone stood at the bedstead. And then I felt a cold hand laid against my cheek—"

"Ha—ha! Rather good, *that!* D'ye know Dora that I had a dream too? I dreamt that I was in the front parlor, second story you know, in your house on Fourth street, when the old fellow came in, and read your note on the table. Ha—ha—and then—are you listening?—I thought that the old gentleman while he was reading, turned to a bright pea-green in the face, and—"

"Hist! Do you not hear some one breathing in the room?"

"Pshaw, Dora, you're nervous! Go to sleep my love. Don't loose your rest for all the dreams in the world. Good night, Dora!"

"A little touch of farce with our tragedy—" half-muttered Luke, as a quiet chuckle shook his frame—"Egad! If they talk in this strain much longer, I'll have to guffaw! It's rather too much for my risibles; this is! A husband standing in the dark by the bedside, while his wife and her paramour are telling their pleasant dreams, in which he figures as the hero—"

Whether a smile passed over Livingstone's face, or a frown, Luke could not tell, for the room was dark as a starlit night, yet the quick gasping sound of a man struggling for breath, heard through the darkness, seem to indicate any thing but the pleasant laugh or the jovial chuckle.

"They sleep again!" muttered Luke—"She has sunken into slumber while Death watches at the bedside. Curse it—how that fellow snores!"

There was a long pause of darkness and silence. No word escaped the Husband's lips, no groan convulsed his chest, no half-muttered cry of agony, indicated the struggle which was silently rending his soul, as with a viper's fangs.

"Livingstone—" whispered Luke after a long pause—"Where are you? Confound it man, I can't hear you breathe. I'm afraid to uncover the light—it may awaken them again. I say Livingstone—hadn't we better leave these quarters—"

"I could have borne expressions of remorse from her lips—I could have listened to sudden outpourings of horror wrung from her soul by the very blackness of her guilt, but grovelling familiarity with vice!"

Matter-of-fact pollution, as you might observe—" whispered Luke.

"Luke, I tell you, the cup is full to overflowing—but I will drain it to the dregs!"

"Now's your time—" whispered Luke, as, swinging the curtain aside, he suffered the light of the lanthern to fall over the bed—"Dora looks quite pretty. Fitz-Cowles decidedly interesting—"

"And on that bosom have I slept!" exclaimed Livingstone, in a voice of agony, as he gazed upon his slumbering wife—"Those arms have clung round my neck—and *now!* Ha! Luke you may think me mad, but I tell ye man, that there is the spirit of a slow and silent revenge creeping through my veins. *She* has *dishonored* me! Do you read anything like *forgiveness* in my face?"

"Not much o' it I assure you. But come, Livingstone—let's be going. This is not the time nor place for your revenge. Let's travel."

Livingstone laid down the bowie knife, and with a smile of bitter mockery, seized a small pair of scissors from the work-basket which stood on the table.

"You smile, Luke?" he whispered, as, leaning over the bedside, he laid his hand upon the jet-black hair of the slumbering Fitz-Cowles;—"Ha-ha! I will leave the place, but d'ye see, Luke, I must take some slight keepsake, to remind me of the gallant Colonel. A lock of his hair, you know, Luke?"

"Egad! Livingstone, I believe you're going mad! A lock of his hair? Pshaw! You'll want a straight jacket soon—"

"And a lock of my Dora's hair—" whispered Livingstone, as his blue eyes flashed from beneath his dark eyebrows, while his lips wore that same mocking smile—"But you see the knife saved me all trouble. Here is a glossy tress severed by the Colonel's dagger. Now let me wind them together, Luke, let me lay them next to my heart, Luke—yes, smile my fellow—Ha! ha! ha!"

"Hist! Your wife stirs in her sleep—you will awaken them again."

"D'ye know, Luke—" cried Livingstone, drawing his partner close to his side, and looking in his face, with a vacant glance, that indicated a temporary derangement of intellect— "D'ye know, Luke, that I didn't do that, o' my own will? Hist! Luke—closer—closer—I'll tell you. The Devil was at the bedside, Luke; he whispered it in my ear, he bade me take these keepsakes—ha, ha, ha—what a jolly set of fellows we are! And then, Luke—" his voice sank to a thrilling whisper—"He pointed with his iron hand to *the last scene,* in which my vengeance shall be complete. She shall beg for mercy, Luke; aye, on her knees, but—ha, ha, ha—*kill—kill—kill!* is written in letters of blood before my eyes, every where, Luke, every where. Don't you see it?"

He pointed vacantly at the air as he spoke, and seized Luke by the shoulder, as though he would command his attention to the blood-red letters.

Luke was conscious that he stood in the presence of a madman.

Inflexible as he was in his own secret purpose of revenge, upon the woman who had trampled on his very heart, Luke still regarded the Merchant with a feeling akin to brotherhood. As the fearful fact impressed itself on his soul, that Livingstone stood before him, deprived of reason, an expression of the deepest feeling shadowed the countenance of Luke, and his voice was broken in its tones as he endeavoured to persuade the madman, to leave the scene of his dishonor and shame.

"Come! Livingstone! let us go—" said Luke, taking his partner by the arm, and leading him gently toward the closet.

"But I've got the keepsakes safe, Luke—" whispered Livingstone, as that wild light flashed from his large blue eyes—"D'ye see the words in the air, Luke? Now they change to her name—Dora, Dora, Dora! All in blood-red letters. I say Luke, let's have a quiet whist party—there's four of us—Dora and I; you and Fitz-Cowles—"

"I'm willing—" exclaimed Luke, as with a quick movement he seized the pistol—left by Livingstone on the table, and concealed it within the breast of his greatcoat—"Suppose we step into the next room, and get every thing ready for the party—"

"You're keen, Luke, keen, but I'm even with you—" whispered Livingstone as his livid face lighted up with a sudden gleam of intelligence—"Here we stand on the threshold of this closet—we are about to leave my wife's bed-room. You think I'm mad. Do I look like a madman? I know there is no whist-party to be held this night, I know that— Hist. Luke. Don't you see it, all pictured forth in the air? The scene of my vengeance? In colors of blood, painted by the Devil's hand? Yonder Luke—yonder! How red it grows—and then in letters of fire, every where, every where, is written—Dora—Dora— Dora—"

It was a fearful spectacle to see that strong man, with his imposing figure, raised to its full stature and his thoughtful brow, lit up with an expression of idiotic wonder, as standing on the verge of the secret door, he pointed wildly at the blood-red picture which his fancy had drawn in the vacant air while his blue eyes dilated with a maniac glance, and his face grew yet more livid and ghastly.

"Come, Livingstone—" cried Luke gently leading him through the closet—"You had better leave this place—"

"And yet Dora, is sleeping here? My young wife? 'The mother of my children?' Do'ye think Luke, that I'd have believed you last Thursday morning, if you had then told me this?

'Livingstone, this day-week, you will leave a chamber in a brothel, and leave your young wife, sleeping in another man's arms.' But never mind Luke—it will all be right. For I tell ye, it is there, there before me in colors of blood! That last scene of my vengeance! And there—there—in letters of flame—Dora!—Dora! Dora!"

And while the fair young wife slept quietly in the bed of guilt and shame, Luke led the Merchant from the room and from the house.

MARY, BYRNEWOOD, AND LORRIMER.—Page 126.

Frontispiece from 1876 edition (Philadelphia: T. B. Peterson, Courtesy Lilly Library, Bloomington, IN).

Chapter Fifteenth

The Dishonor

All was silent within the Rose Chamber. For a single moment that pale visage glared from the crimson hangings, concealing the entrance to the Walnut Room, and then with a measured footstep, Byrnewood Arlington advanced along the floor, his countenance ghastly as the face of Lazarus, at the very instant, when in obedience to the words of the Incarnate, life struggled with corruption and death, over his check and brow.

Bring home to your mind the scene, when Lazarus lay prostrate in the grave, a stiffened corse, his face all clammy with corruption, the closed eyes surrounded by loathsome circles of decay, the cheeks sunken, and the lips fallen in: let the words of Jesus ring in your ears, "Lazarus, come forth!"[29] And then as the blue eyelids slowly unclose, as the gleam of life shoots forth from the glassy eye, as the flush of health struggles with the yellowish hue of decay along each cheek, as life and death mingling in that face for a single moment, maintain a fearful combat for the mastery; then I pray you, gaze upon the visage of Byrnewood Arlington, and mark how like it is to the face of one arisen from the dead; a ghastly face, on whose fixed outline the finger-traces of corruption are yet visible, from whose eyes the film of the grave is not yet passed away.

The gaze of Byrnewood, as he strode from the entrance of the Walnut Chamber, was riveted to the floor. Had the eyes of the rattlesnake gleamed from the carpet, slowly drawing his victim to his ruin, Byrnewood could not have fixed his gaze upon the object in the centre of the floor, with a more fearful and absorbing intensity.

There, thrown prostrate on the gaudy carpet, insensible and motionless, the form of Mary Arlington lay at the brother's feet.

He sank silently on his knees.

He took her small white hand—now cold as marble—within his own, he swept the unbound tresses back from her palid brow. Her eyes were closed as in death, her lips hung apart, the lower one trembling with a scarcely perceptible movement, her cheek was pale as ashes, with a deep red tint in the centre.

Byrnewood uttered no sound, nor shrieked forth any wild exclamation of revenge, or wo, or despair. He silently drew the folds of the night-robe round her form, and veiled her bosom—but a moment agone warmed into a glow by the heart's fires, now paled by the fingers of the ravisher—he veiled her fair young bosom from the light.

It was a sad sight to look upon. That face, so fair and blooming, but a moment past, now pale as death, with spot of burning red on the centre of each cheek: that bosom, a moment since, heaving with passion, now still and motionless; those delicate hands with tiny fingers, which had bravely fought for honor, for virtue, for purity, an instant ago, now resting cold and stiffened by her side.

Thick tresses of dark brown hair, hung round her neck. With that same careful movement of his hand, Byrnewood swept them aside. Along the smooth surface of that fair neck like some noisome reptile, trailing over a lovely flower, a large vein, black and distorted, shot upward, darkening the glossy skin, while it told the story of the maiden's dishonor and shame.

"My sister!" was the solitary exclamation that broke from Byrnewood's lips as he gazed upon the form of the unconscious girl, and his large dark eye, dilating as he spoke, glanced around with an expression of strange meaning.

---

29 John 11:43.

He raised her form in his arms, and kissed her cold lips again and again. No tear trickled from his eyelids; no sigh heaved his bosom; no deep muttered execration manifested the agitation of his soul.

"My sister!" he again whispered, and gathered her more close to his heart.

A slight flush deepening over her cheek, even while he spoke, gave signs of returning consciousness.

Mary slowly unclosed her eyes, and gazed with a wandering glance around the room. An instant passed ere she discovered that she lay in Byrnewood's arms.

"Oh, brother—" she exclaimed, not with a wild shriek, but in a low-toned voice, whose slightest accent quivered with an emphasis of despair—"Oh, brother! Leave me—leave me. I am not worthy of your touch. I am vile, brother, oh, most vile! Leave me—Leave me, for I am lost!"

"Mary!" whispered Byrnewood, resisting her attempt to unwind his arms from her form, while the blood, filling the veins of his throat, produced an effect like strangulation—"Mary! Do not—do not speak thus—I—I—"

He could say no more, but his face dropped on her cold bosom, and the tears, which he had silently prayed for, came at last.

He wept, while that low choaking noise, sounding in his throat, that involuntary heaving of the chest, that nervous quivering of the lip, all betokened the strong man wrestling with his agony.

"Do not weep for me, brother—" she said, in the same low-toned voice—"I am polluted, brother, and am not worthy of the slightest tear you shed for me. Unwind your arms—brother, do not resist me—for the strength of despair is in these hands—unwind your arms, and let me no longer pollute you by my touch—"

There was something fearful in the expression of her face as she spoke. She was no longer the trembling child whose young face, marked the inexperience of her stainless heart. A new world had broken upon her soul, not a world of green trees, silver streams and pleasant flowers, but a chaos of ashes, and mouldering flame; a lurid sky above, a blasted soil below, and one immense horizon of leaden clouds, hemming in the universe of desolation.

She had sprung from the maiden into the woman, but a blight was on her soul forever. The crime had not only stained her person with dishonor, but, like the sickening warmth of the hot-house, it had forced the flower of her soul, into sudden and unnatural maturity. It was the maturity of precocious experience. In her inmost soul, she felt that she was a dishonored thing, whose very touch was pollution, whose presence, among the pure and stainless, would be a bitter mockery and foul reproach. The guilt was not hers, but the Ruin blasted her purity forever.

"Unwind your arms, my brother—" she exclaimed, tearing herself from his embrace, with all a maniac's strength—"I am polluted. You are pure. Oh do not touch me—do not touch me. Leave me to my shame—oh, leave me—"

She unwound her form from his embrace, and sank crouching into a corner of the Rose Chamber, extending her hands with a frightened gesture, as though she feared his slightest touch.

'Mary" shrieked Byrnewood, flinging his arms on high, with a movement of sudden agitation—"Oh, do not look upon me thus! Come to me—oh, Mary—come to me, for I am your brother."

The words, the look and the trembling movement of his outspread arms, all combined, acted like a spell upon the intellect of the ruined girl. She rose wildly to her feet, as though impelled by some invisible influence, and fell tremblingly into her brother's arms.

While one dark and horrible thought, was working its way through the avenues of his soul, he gathered her to his breast again and again.

And in that moment of silence and unutterable thought, the curtains leading into the Painted Chamber were slowly thrust aside, and Lorrimer again appeared upon the scene. Stricken with remorse, he had fled with a madman's haste from the scene of his crime, and while his bosom was torn by a thousand opposing thoughts, he had endeavored to drown the voice within him, and crush the memory of the nameless wrong. It was all in vain. Impelled by an irresistible desire, to look again upon the victim of his crime, he reentered the Rose Chamber. It was a strange sight, to see the Brother kneeling on the floor, as he gathered his sister's form in his arms, and yet the Seducer, gave no sign nor indication of surprise.

A fearful agitation was passing over the Libertine's soul, as unobserved by the brother or sister, he stood gazing upon them with a wandering glance. His face, so lately flushed with passion, in its vilest hues, was now palest and livid. His white lips, trembled with a nervous moment, and his hands, extended on either side, clutched vacantly at the air, as though he wrestled with an unseen foe.

While the thought of horror, was slowly darkening over Byrnewood's soul, a thought as dark and horrible gathered like a Phantom over the mind of Lorrimer.

A single word of explanation, will make the subsequent scene, clear and intelligible to the reader.

From generation to generation, the family of the Lorrimer's, had been subject to an aberration of intellect, as sudden as it was terrible; always resulting from any peculiar agitation of mind, which might convulse the soul, with an emotion remarkable for its power or energy. It was a hallucination, a temporary madness, a sudden derangement of intellect. It always succeeded an uncontrollable outburst of anger, or grief, or joy. From father to son, since the family had first come over to Pennsylvania, with the Proprietor and Peace-Maker William Penn,[30] this temporary derangement of intellect, had descended as a fearful heritage.

Lorrimer had been subject to this madness, but once in his life, when his father's corse lay stiffened before his eyes. And now, as he stood gazing upon the form of the brother and sister, Lorrimer, felt this temporary madness stealing over his soul, in the form of a strange hallucination, while he became conscious, that in a single moment, the horror which shook his frame, would rise to his lips in words of agony and fear.

"Raise your hands with mine, to Heaven, Mary—" exclaimed Byrnewood as the Thought which had been working over his soul, manifested its intensity in words—"Raise your hands with mine, and curse the author of your ruin! Lift your voice with mine, up to the God, who beheld the wrong—who will visit the wronger with a doom meet, for his crime—lift your voice with mine, and curse him—"

"Oh Byrnewood, do not, do not curse *him*. The wrong has been done but do not, I beseech you, visit his head with a curse—"

"Hear me, oh God, before whom, I now raise my hands, in the vow of justice! In life I will be to this wretch, as a Fate, a Doom, a Curse!

---

30 Lorrimer's family is an ancient one in Pennsylvania, having come over with William Penn (1644–1718), the man who oversaw the founding of the Commonwealth of Pennsylvania in 1682. William Penn helped plan the initial design of the city of Philadelphia.

"I am vile—oh God—steeped in the same vices, which blacken the heart of this man, cankered by the same corruption. But the office, which I now take on myself, raising this right hand to thee, in witness of my fixed purpose, would sanctify the darkest fiend in hell! I am the avenger of my sister's wrong! She was innocent, she was pure, she trusted and was betrayed! I will avenge her! Before thee, I swear to visit her wrong, upon the head of her betrayer, with a doom never to be forgotten in the memory of man. This right hand I dedicate to this solemn purpose—come what will, come what may, let danger threaten or death stand in my path, through sickness and health, through riches or poverty, I now swear, to hold my steady pathway onward, my only object in life—the avengement of my sister's wrong! He *shall* die by this hand—oh God—I swear it by thy name—I swear it by my soul—I swear it by the Fiend who impelled the villain to this deed of crime—"

As he whispered forth this oath, in a voice which speaking from the depths of his chest, had a hollow and sepulchral sound, the fair girl flung herself on his breast, and with a wild shriek essayed to delay the utterance of the curse, by gathering his face, to her bosom.

For a moment her efforts were successful. Lorrimer had stood silent and pale, while the deep-toned voice of Byrnewood Arlington, breaking in accents of doom upon his ear, had aided and strengthened the strange hallucination which was slowly gathering over his brain like a mighty spell.

"There is a wide river before me, its broad waves tinged with the last red rays of a winter sunset—" such were the words he murmured, extending his hand, as though pointing to the scene, which dawned upon his soul—"A wide river with its waves surging against the wharves of a mighty city. Afar I behold steeples and roofs and towers, all glowing in the beams of the setting sun. And as I gaze, the waves turn to blood, red and ghastly blood— and now the sky is a-flame, and the clouds sweep slowly past, bathed in the same crimson hue. All is blood—the river rushes before me, and the sky and the city—all pictured in colors of blood.

"An invisible hand is leading me to my doom. There is Death for me, in yonder river, and I know it, yet down, down to the rivers banks, down, down into the red waters, I must go. Ha! ha! 'Tis a merry death! The blood-red waves rise above me—higher, higher, higher! Yonder is the city, yonder the last rays of the setting sun, glitter on the roof and steeple, yonder is the blood-red sky—and ah! I tell ye I will not die—you shall not sink me beneath these gory waves! Devil! Is not your vengeance satisfied—must you feast your eyes with the sight of my closing agonies—must your hand grasp me by the throat, and your foot trample me beneath the waves? I tell you I will not, will not die—"

"Ha—ha—ha! Here's purty going's on—" laughed the hoarse voice of Devil-Bug, as his hideous form appeared in the doorway of the Walnut Chamber, with his attendant negroes at his back—"Seems the gal helped him off. There he sits—the ornery feller, with his sister in his arms—while Gusty, is a-doin' some ravin's on his own individooal hook. Come here Glow-worm—here Musquito—come here my pets, and 'tend to this leetle family party—"

In another instant the Rose Chamber became the scene of a strange picture.

Byrnewood had arisen to his feet, while Lorrimer stood spell-bound by the hallucination which possessed his brain. The handsome Libertine stood in the centre of the room, his form dilating to its full stature, his face the hue of ashes, while with his hazel eyes, glaring on vacancy, he clutched wildly at the air, starting backward at the same moment, as though some invisible hand, was silently impelling him to the brink of the blood-red river, which rolled tumultuously at his feet, which slowly gathered around him, which began to heave upward to his very lips.

On one side, in a half-kneeling position, crouched Mary Arlington, her large blue eyes, starting from her pallid face, as with her upraised hands, crossed over her bosom, she gazed upon the agitated countenance of the seducer, with a glance of mingled awe and wonder; while, on the other side, stern and erect, Byrnewood, with his pale visage darkening in a settled frown, with one foot advanced and his hand upraised, seemed about to strike the libertine to the floor.

In the background, rendered yet more hideous by the dimness of the scene, Devil-Bug stood grinning in derisive triumph as he motioned his attendants, the Herculean negroes, to advance and secure their prey.

There was silence for a single moment. Lorrimer still stood clutching at the vacant air, Mary still gazed upon this face in awe, Byrnewood yet paused in his meditated blow, while Devil-Bug, with Musquito and Glow-worm at his back, seemed quietly enjoying the entire scene, as he glanced from side to side with his solitary eye.

"Unhand me—I will not die—" shrieked Lorrimer, as he fancied that phantom hand, gathering tightly round his throat, while the red waters swept surging to his very lips—"I will not die—I defy—ah! ah! You strangle me—"

"The hour of your death has come! You have said it—and it shall be so!" whispered Byrnewood, advancing a single step, as his dark eye was fixed upon the face of Lorrimer— "While your own guilty heart spreads a blood-red river before your eyes, this hand—no phantom hand—shall work your death!"

He sprang forward, while a shriek arose from Mary's lips, he sprang forward with his eyes blazing with excitement, and his outspread hand ready for the work of vengeance, but as he sprang, the laugh of Devil-Bug echoed at his back, and the sinewy arms of the negroes gathered suddenly round his form and flung him as suddenly to the floor.

"Here's fine goin's on—" exclaimed Devil-Bug, as he glanced from face to face—"A feller who's been a leetle too kind to a gal, stands a-makin' speeches at nothin'. The gal kneels on the carpet as though she were a gettin' up a leetle prayer on her own account; and this 'ere onery feller—git a good grip o' him you bull-dogs—sets up a small shop o' cussin' and sells his cusses for nothin'! Here's a tea party for ye—"

"What does all this mean, Devil-Bug—" exclaimed Lorrimer, in his usual voice, as the hallucination passed from him like a dream, leaving him utterly unconscious of the strange vision which had a moment since absorbed his very soul—"What does all this mean? Ha! Byrnewood and Mary—I remember? *You* are *her* brother—are you not?"

"I am her avenger—" said Byrnewood, with a ghastly smile, as he endeavoured to free himself from the grasp of the negroes—"And your executioner! Within three days you shall die by this hand!"

"Ha-ha-ha!" laughed Devil-Bug—"There's more than one genelman as has got a say in that leetle matter! How d'ye feel, young man? Did you ever take opium afore? You won't go to sleep nor nothin'? We can't do what we like with you? Kin we? Ho-ho-ho! *I vonders how that'ill vork!*"

*   *   *

Editor's Note

Quaker City: The End of the Story

Lippard wrote this book in serial fashion, and a host of new characters are introduced to fill out a volume that will run to nearly six hundred pages when it is published in book form. The characters introduced in "Book the First" are intimately related to the final chapters of the book.

Lorrimer refuses to marry Mary and is killed by Byrnewood, fulfilling the astrologer's prophecy. A group of characters then move to live in a cottage in western Pennsylvania's vale of Wyoming. This group includes: Mary Arlington, Lorrimer's mother and sister and Byrnewood and his wife, Annie (the servant girl he had seduced). Mary never really recovers from her rape and sham marriage; the book ends with her crying out the name: "Lorraine."

There is some ambiguity as to whether or not Devil-Bug is killed at the end of the novel. Fitz-Cowles escapes death for his many crimes, but not prison. The merchant Livingstone is burned to death at his country estate after revealing to his wife Dora that he is of royal blood and could have offered her a true coronet from the English aristocracy. He kills Dora by poisoning her before the fire engulfs the house and kills him.

Bess is repentant for her deeds against Mary and tries to help her escape Lorrimer and Monk-Hall. Mary eventually does escape with the help of Bess. Bess is later found dead near her father's grave. Luke marries a woman named Mabel (an important character later in the book), and they live happily ever after. If there is a character who is positioned as a hero at the end of the book, it is Luke. Oddly enough, it turns out that Mabel is the stunningly beautiful and virtuous daughter of Devil-Bug, who was separated from him at her birth. Finding out that he has a daughter significantly changes the character of Devil-Bug, who is not nearly as evil at the end of the book as he is when we meet him in "Book the First."

Chapter Eight

HENRY WADSWORTH LONGFELLOW
(1807–1882)

Poetry was an immensely popular and prevalent literary form throughout nineteenth-century America, and there was no more popular or widely read poet than Henry Wadsworth Longfellow. Longfellow was born in Portland, Maine, and attended Bowdoin College, where he graduated in 1825 in the same class as Nathaniel Hawthorne. Although Longfellow was originally intent on pursuing a law career, Bowdoin offered him a job as a professor of modern languages, which required him to study in Europe before assuming his teaching position at the college. He studied successfully in Germany, France, Spain and Italy and then took up his duties at Bowdoin only to transfer to a similar teaching position at Harvard a few years later. He taught at Harvard until 1854, when he retired to pursue his literary career full time.

Longfellow began to publish poetry while still teaching, and the popularity of his poetry in the ensuing decades eventually earned him national and international acclaim. He was granted honorary degrees from both Oxford and Cambridge in England. The genesis of his national reputation is found in the publication of what would become his most popular poem, *Evangeline* (1847). The concept of the poem germinated in Longfellow's mind after hearing a tale of lost love in Acadia (a region that included Nova Scotia, Canada, inhabited by settlers of French descent) from his friend Hawthorne.

Longfellow wrote *Evangeline* in dactylic hexameter, a poetic style used by Homer in his *Iliad* and Virgil in his *Aeneid*, and one that thus invoked the great classical epic. The poem tells the story of Evangeline, a girl exiled from her Acadian home, who spends her life searching for her lost love, Gabriel. It is a poem ultimately about a love that can never be realized, and thus it becomes a meditation on a range of themes, including: sacrifice, longing, ethnicity, hope, religious and romantic devotion and the nature of true happiness.

A poetic note on dactylic hexameter:

• A dactyl is a three-syllable poetic foot with the stress pattern: long, short, short
• A spondee is a two-syllable poetic foot with the stress pattern: long, long
• A trochee is a two-syllable poetic foot with the stress pattern: long, short
• A hexameter is a line of poetry that includes six feet

In the strictest sense, the dactylic hexameter includes six dactyl feet, but classical meter allows for the substitution of a spondee (and far less frequently, a trochee) in one foot per hexameter.

Example of dactylic hexameter:

‒ ˇ ˇ   ‒ ˇ ˇ   ‒ ˇ ˇ   ‒ ˇ ˇ   ‒ ˇ ˇ   ‒ ‒

This is the | forest pri | meval. The | murmuring | pines and the | hemlocks

EVANGELINE.

Frontispiece from *Evangeline, A Tale of Acadie*, Minnehaha Edition (Chicago: Thompson & Thomas, 1895).

This text is reprinted from *The Complete Writings of Henry Wadsworth Longfellow*. Boston: Houghton, Mifflin, & Co., 1904. "Acadie" is a French name for "Acadia," a French colony that included what is now Nova Scotia, Canada. The British forcibly displaced French settlers from this area after victory in the French and Indian War (1763).

EVANGELINE

A Tale Of Acadie

This is the forest primeval. The murmuring pines and the hemlocks,
Bearded with moss, and in garments green, indistinct in the twilight,
Stand like Druids[1] of eld, with voices sad and prophetic,
Stand like harpers hoar, with beards that rest on their bosoms.
Loud from its rocky caverns, the deep-voiced neighboring ocean
Speaks, and in accents disconsolate answers the wail of the forest.

This is the forest primeval; but where are the hearts that beneath it
Leaped like the roe, when he hears in the woodland the voice of the huntsman?
Where is the thatch-roofed village, the home of Acadian farmers,—
Men whose lives glided on like rivers that water the woodlands,
Darkened by shadows of earth, but reflecting an image of heaven?
Waste are those pleasant farms, and the farmers forever departed!
Scattered like dust and leaves, when the mighty blasts of October
Seize them, and whirl them aloft, and sprinkle them far o'er the ocean.
Naught but tradition remains of the beautiful village of Grand-Pré.

Ye who believe in affection that hopes, and endures, and is patient,
Ye who believe in the beauty and strength of woman's devotion,
List to the mournful tradition, still sung by the pines of the forest;
List to a Tale of Love in Acadie, home of the happy.

PART THE FIRST

I

In the Acadian land, on the shores of the Basin of Minas,
Distant, secluded, still the little village of Grand-Pré[2]
Lay in the fruitful valley. Vast meadows stretched to the eastward,
Giving the village its name, and pasture to flocks without number.
Dikes, that the hands of farmers had raised with labor incessant,
Shut out the turbulent tides; but at stated seasons the flood-gates
Opened, and welcomed the sea to wander at will o'er the meadows.
West and south there were fields of flax, and orchards and cornfields
Spreading afar and unfenced o'er the plain; and away to the northward
Blomidon rose, and the forests old, and aloft on the mountains
Sea-fogs pitched their tents, and mists from the mighty Atlantic
Looked on the happy valley, but ne'er from their station descended.
There, in the midst of its farms, reposed the Acadian village.

---

1 Celtic religious leaders in ancient Ireland, often associated with the worship of nature and the
veneration of trees.
2 A rural community in Nova Scotia. The name means "Great Meadow." Founded in 1680, it
became the most important settlement in Acadia because of its rich farmland.

Strongly built were the houses, with frames of oak and of hemlock,
Such as the peasants of Normandy built in the reign of the Henries.
Thatched were the roofs, with dormer-windows; and gables projecting
Over the basement below protected and shaded the doorway.
There in the tranquil evenings of summer, when brightly the sunset
Lighted the village street, and gilded the vanes on the chimneys,
Matrons and maidens sat in snow-white caps and in kirtles
Scarlet and blue and green, with distaffs spinning the golden
Flax for the gossiping looms, whose noisy shuttles within doors
Mingled their sounds with the whir of the wheels and the songs of the maidens.
Solemnly down the street came the parish priest, and the children
Paused in their play to kiss the hand he extended to bless them.
Reverend walked he among them; and up rose matrons and maidens,
Hailing his slow approach with words of affectionate welcome.
Then came the laborers home from the field, and serenely the sun sank
Down to his rest, and twilight prevailed. Anon from the belfry
Softly the Angelus[3] sounded, and over the roofs of the village
Columns of pale blue smoke, like clouds of incense ascending,
Rose from a hundred hearths, the home of peace and contentment.
Thus dwelt together in love these simple Acadian farmers, —
Dwelt in the love of God and of man. Alike were they free from
Fear, that reigns with the tyrant, and envy, the vice of republics.
Neither locks had they to their doors, nor bars to their windows;
But their dwellings were open as day and the hearts of the owners;
There the richest was poor, and the poorest lived in abundance.

     Somewhat apart from the village, and nearer the Basin of Minas,
Benedict Bellefontaine, the wealthiest farmer of Grand-Pré,
Dwelt on his goodly acres; and with him, directing his household,
Gentle Evangeline lived, his child, and the pride of the village.
Stalworth and stately in form was the man of seventy winters;
Hearty and hale was he, an oak that is covered with snow-flakes;
White as the snow were his locks, and his cheeks as brown as the oak-leaves.
Fair was she to behold, that maiden of seventeen summers.
Black were her eyes as the berry that grows on the thorn by the wayside,
Black, yet how softly they gleamed beneath the brown shade of her tresses!
Sweet was her breath as the breath of kine that feed in the meadows.
When in the harvest heat she bore to the reapers at noontide
Flagons of home-brewed ale, ah! fair in sooth was the maiden.
Fairer was she when, on Sunday morn, while the bell from its turret
Sprinkled with holy sounds the air, as the priest with his hyssop
Sprinkles the congregation, and scatters blessings upon them,
Down the long street she passed, with her chaplet of beads and her missal,
Wearing her Norman cap, and her kirtle of blue, and the ear-rings,
Brought in the olden time from France, and since, as an heirloom,

---

3 A Catholic call to prayer, often announced with the ringing of a bell.

Handed down from mother to child, through long generations.
But a celestial brightness—a more ethereal beauty—
Shone on her face and encircled her form, when, after confession,
Homeward serenely she walked with God's benediction upon her.
When she had passed, it seemed like the ceasing of exquisite music.

Firmly builded with rafters of oak, the house of the farmer
Stood on the side of a hill commanding the sea; and a shady
Sycamore grew by the door, with a woodbine wreathing around it.
Rudely carved was the porch, with seats beneath; and a footpath
Led through an orchard wide, and disappeared in the meadow.
Under the sycamore-tree were hives overhung by a penthouse,
Such as the traveller sees in regions remote by the roadside,
Built o'er a box for the poor, or the blessed image of Mary.
Farther down, on the slope of the hill, was the well with its moss-grown
Bucket, fastened with iron, and near it a trough for the horses.
Shielding the house from storms, on the north, were the barns and the farmyard.
There stood the broad-wheeled wains and the antique ploughs and the harrows;
There were the folds for the sheep; and there, in his feathered seraglio,
Strutted the lordly turkey, and crowed the cock, with the selfsame
Voice that in ages of old had startled the penitent Peter.[4]
Bursting with hay were the barns, themselves a village. In each one
Far o'er the gable projected a roof of thatch; and a staircase,
Under the sheltering eaves, led up to the odorous corn-loft.
There too the dove-cot stood, with its meek and innocent inmates
Murmuring ever of love; while above it the variant breezes
Numberless noisy weathercocks rattled and sang of mutation.

Thus, at peace with God and the world, the farmer of Grand-Pré
Lived on his sunny farm, and Evangeline governed his household.
Many a youth, as he knelt in church and opened his missal,
Fixed his eyes upon her as the saint of his deepest devotion;
Happy was he who might touch her hand or the hem of her garment!
Many a suitor came to her door, by the darkness befriended,
And, as he knocked and waited to hear the sound of her footsteps,
Knew not which beat the louder, his heart or the knocker of iron;
Or at the joyous feast of the Patron Saint of the village,
Bolder grew, and pressed her hand in the dance as he whispered
Hurried words of love, that seemed a part of the music.
But, among all who came, young Gabriel only was welcome;
Gabriel Lajeunesse, the son of Basil the blacksmith,
Who was a mighty man in the village, and honored of all men;
For, since the birth of time, throughout all ages and nations,
Has the craft of the smith been held in repute by the people.

---

4 Jesus's disciple, Peter, who denied Jesus three times before the cock crowed in the days before
  Christ's crucifixion.

Basil was Benedict's friend. Their children from earliest childhood
Grew up together as brother and sister; and Father Felician,
Priest and pedagogue both in the village, had taught them their letters
Out of the selfsame book, with the hymns of the church and the plain-song.
But when the hymn was sung, and the daily lesson completed,
Swiftly they hurried away to the forge of Basil the blacksmith.
There at the door they stood, with wondering eyes to behold him
Take in his leathern lap the hoof of the horse as a plaything,
Nailing the shoe in its place; while near him the tire of the cart-wheel
Lay like a fiery snake, coiled round in a circle of cinders.
Oft on autumnal eves, when without in the gathering darkness
Bursting with light seemed the smithy, through every cranny and crevice,
Warm by the forge within they watched the laboring bellows,
And as its panting ceased, and the sparks expired in the ashes,
Merrily laughed, and said they were nuns going into the chapel.
Oft on sledges in winter, as swift as the swoop of the eagle,
Down the hillside bounding, they glided away o'er the meadow.
Oft in the barns they climbed to the populous nests on the rafters,
Seeking with eager eyes that wondrous stone, which the swallow
Brings from the shore of the sea to restore the sight of its fledglings;
Lucky was he who found that stone in the nest of the swallow!
Thus passed a few swift years, and they no longer were children.
He was a valiant youth, and his face, like the face of the morning,
Gladdened the earth with its light, and ripened thought into action.
She was a woman now, with the heart and hopes of a woman.
"Sunshine of Saint Eulalie"[5] was she called; for that was the sunshine
Which, as the farmers believed, would load their orchards with apples;
She, too, would bring to her husband's house delight and abundance,
Filling it with love and the ruddy faces of children.

II

Now had the season returned, when the nights grow colder and longer,
And the retreating sun the sign of the Scorpion enters.
Birds of passage sailed through the leaden air, from the ice-bound,
Desolate northern bays to the shores of tropical islands
Harvests were gathered in; and wild with the winds of September
Wrestled the trees of the forest, as Jacob of old with the angel.[6]
All the signs foretold a winter long and inclement.
Bees, with prophetic instinct of want, had hoarded their honey
Till the hives overflowed; and the Indian hunters asserted
Cold would the winter be, for thick was the fur of the foxes.

---

5 Saint Eulalia was a Spanish martyr who resisted the Roman emperor. She survived being burned
   at the stake, only to be beheaded. After her death, her great love enabled her to ascend to Heaven
   in the form of a dove.
6 Genesis 32:24–32.

Such was the advent of autumn. Then followed that beautiful season,
Called by the pious Acadian peasants the Summer of All-Saints!
Filled was the air with a dreamy and magical light; and the landscape
Lay as if new-created in all the freshness of childhood.
Peace seemed to reign upon the earth, and the restless heart of the ocean
Was for a moment consoled. All sounds were in harmony blended.
Voices of children at play, the crowing of cocks in the farmyards,
Whir of wings in the drowsy air, and the cooing of pigeons,
All were subdued and low as the murmurs of love, and the great sun
Looked with the eye of love through the golden vapors around him;
While arrayed in its robes of russet and scarlet and yellow,
Bright with the sheen of the dew, each glittering tree of the forest
Flashed like the plane-tree the Persian[7] adorned with mantles and jewels.

Now recommenced the reign of rest and affection and stillness.
Day with its burden and heat had departed, and twilight descending
Brought back the evening star to the sky, and the herds to the homestead.
Pawing the ground they came, and resting their necks on each other,
And with their nostrils distended inhaling the freshness of evening.
Foremost, bearing the bell, Evangeline's beautiful heifer,
Proud of her snow-white hide, and the ribbon that waved from her collar,
Quietly paced and slow, as if conscious of human affection.
Then came the shepherd back with his bleating flocks from the seaside,
Where was their favorite pasture. Behind them followed the watch-dog,
Patient, full of importance, and grand in the pride of his instinct,
Walking from side to side with a lordly air, and superbly
Waving his bushy tail, and urging forward the stragglers;
Regent of flocks was he when the shepherd slept; their protector,
When from the forest at night, through the starry silence the wolves howled.
Late, with the rising moon, returned the wains from the marshes,
Laden with briny hay, that filled the air with its odor.
Cheerily neighed the steeds, with dew on their manes and their fetlocks,
While aloft on their shoulders the wooden and ponderous saddles,
Painted with brilliant dyes, and adorned with tassels of crimson,
Nodded in bright array, like hollyhocks heavy with blossoms.
Patiently stood the cows meanwhile, and yielded their udders
Unto the milkmaid's hand; whilst loud and in regular cadence
Into the sounding pails the foaming streamlets descended.
Lowing of cattle and peals of laughter were heard in the farmyard,
Echoed back by the barns. Anon they sank into stillness;
Heavily closed, with a jarring sound, the valves of the barn-doors,
Rattled the wooden bars, and all for a season was silent.

---

7 Referring to the ancient King Darius, who was given a tree made of gold by one of his allies, the
immensely wealthy Pythius. Herodotus, *The History of Herodotus*, Book VII.

Indoors, warm by the wide-mouthed fireplace, idly the farmer
Sat in his elbow-chair and watched how the flames and the smoke-wreaths
Struggled together like foes in a burning city. Behind him,
Nodding and mocking along the wall, with gestures fantastic,
Darted his own huge shadow, and vanished away into darkness.
Faces, clumsily carved in oak, on the back of his armchair
Laughed in the flickering light; and the pewter plates on the dresser
Caught and reflected the flame, as shields of armies the sunshine.
Fragments of song the old man sang, and carols of Christmas,
Such as at home, in the olden time, his fathers before him
Sang in their Norman orchards and bright Burgundian vineyards.
Close at her father's side was the gentle Evangeline seated,
Spinning flax for the loom, that stood in the corner behind her,
Silent awhile were its treadles, at rest was its diligent shuttle,
While the monotonous drone of the wheel, like the drone of a bagpipe,
Followed the old man's song and united the fragments together.
As in a church, when the chant of the choir at intervals ceases,
Footfalls are heard in the aisles, or words of the priest at the altar,
So, in each pause of the song, with measured motion the clock clicked.

Thus as they sat, there were footsteps heard, and, suddenly lifted,
Sounded the wooden latch, and the door swung back on its hinges.
Benedict knew by the hob-nailed shoes it was Basil the blacksmith,
And by her beating heart Evangeline knew who was with him.
"Welcome!" the farmer exclaimed, as their footsteps paused on the threshold,
"Welcome, Basil, my friend! Come, take thy place on the settle
Close by the chimney-side, which is always empty without thee;
Take from the shelf overhead thy pipe and the box of tobacco;
Never so much thyself art thou as when through the curling
Smoke of the pipe or the forge thy friendly and jovial face gleams
Round and red as the harvest moon through the mist of the marshes."
Then, with a smile of content, thus answered Basil the blacksmith,
Taking with easy air the accustomed seat by the fireside:
"Benedict Bellefontaine, thou hast ever thy jest and thy ballad!
Ever in cheerfullest mood art thou, when others are filled with
Gloomy forebodings of ill, and see only ruin before them.
Happy art thou, as if every day thou hadst picked up a horseshoe."
Pausing a moment, to take the pipe that Evangeline brought him,
And with a coal from the embers had lighted, he slowly continued:
"Four days now are passed since the English ships at their anchors
Ride in the Gaspereau's mouth, with their cannon pointed against us.
What their design may be is unknown; but all are commanded
On the morrow to meet in the church, where his Majesty's mandate
Will be proclaimed as law in the land. Alas! in the meantime
Many surmises of evil alarm the hearts of the people."
Then made answer the farmer: "Perhaps some friendlier purpose

Brings these ships to our shores. Perhaps the harvests in England
By untimely rains or untimelier heat have been blighted,
And from our bursting barns they would feed their cattle and children."
"Not so thinketh the folk in the village," said, warmly, the blacksmith,
Shaking his head, as in doubt; then, heaving a sigh, he continued:
"Louisburg is not forgotten, nor Beau Séjour, nor Port Royal.[8]
Many already have fled to the forest, and lurk on its outskirts,
Waiting with anxious hearts the dubious fate of to-morrow.
Arms have been taken from us, and warlike weapons of all kinds;
Nothing is left but the blacksmith's sledge and the scythe of the mower."
Then with a pleasant smile made answer the jovial farmer:
"Safer are we unarmed, in the midst of our flocks and our cornfields,
Safer within these peaceful dikes, besieged by the ocean,
Than our fathers in forts, besieged by the enemy's cannon.
Fear no evil, my friend, and to-night may no shadow of sorrow
Fall on this house and hearth; for this is the night of the contract.
Built are the house and the barn. The merry lads of the village
Strongly have built them and well; and, breaking the glebe round about them,
Filled the barn with hay, and the house with food for a twelvemonth.
René Leblanc will be here anon, with his papers and inkhorn.
Shall we not then be glad, and rejoice in the joy of our children?"
As apart by the window she stood, with her hand in her lover's,
Blushing Evangeline heard the words that her father had spoken,
And, as they died on his lips, the worthy notary entered.

III

Bent like a laboring oar, that toils in the surf of the ocean,
Bent, but not broken, by age was the form of the notary public;
Shocks of yellow hair, like the silken floss of the maize, hung
Over his shoulders; his forehead was high; and glasses with horn bows
Sat astride on his nose, with a look of wisdom supernal.
Father of twenty children was he, and more than a hundred
Children's children rode on his knee, and heard his great watch tick.
Four long years in the time of the war had he languished a captive,
Suffering much in an old French fort as the friend of the English.
Now, though warier grown, without all guile or suspicion,
Ripe in wisdom was he, but patient, and simple, and childlike.
He was beloved by all, and most of all by the children;
For he told them tales of the Loup-garou[9] in the forest,
And of the goblin that came in the night to water the horses,
And of the white Létiche, the ghost of a child who unchristened

---

8 Battles between the French and British during the French and Indian War (1754–63).
9 Werewolf.

Died, and was doomed to haunt unseen the chambers of children;
And how on Christmas Eve the oxen talked in the stable,
And how the fever was cured by a spider shut up in a nutshell,
And of the marvellous powers of four-leaved clover and horseshoes,
With whatsoever else was writ in the lore of the village.
Then up rose from his seat by the fireside Basil the blacksmith,
Knocked from his pipe the ashes, and slowly extending his right hand,
"Father Leblanc," he exclaimed, "thou hast heard the talk in the village,
And, perchance, canst tell us some news of these ships and their errand."
Then with modest demeanor made answer the notary public,
"Gossip enough have I heard, in sooth, yet am never the wiser;
And what their errand may be I know not better than others.
Yet am I not of those who imagine some evil intention
Brings them here, for we are at peace; and why then molest us?"
"God's name!" shouted the hasty and somewhat irascible blacksmith;
"Must we in all things look for the how, and the why, and the wherefore?
Daily injustice is done, and might is the right of the strongest!"
But without heeding his warmth, continued the notary public,
"Man is unjust, but God is just; and finally justice
Triumphs; and well I remember a story, that often consoled me,
When as a captive I lay in the old French fort at Port Royal."
This was the old man's favorite tale, and he loved to repeat it
When his neighbors complained that any injustice was done them.
"Once in an ancient city, whose name I no longer remember,
Raised aloft on a column, a brazen statue of Justice
Stood in the public square, upholding the scales in its left hand,
And in its right a sword, as an emblem that justice presided
Over the laws of the land, and the hearts and homes of the people.
Even the birds had built their nests in the scales of the balance,
Having no fear of the sword that flashed in the sunshine above them.
But in the course of time the laws of the land were corrupted;
Might took the place of right, and the weak were oppressed, and the mighty
Ruled with an iron rod. Then it chanced in a nobleman's palace
That a necklace of pearls was lost, and ere long a suspicion
Fell on an orphan girl who lived as a maid in the household.
She, after form of trial condemned to die on the scaffold,
Patiently met her doom at the foot of the statue of Justice.
As to her Father in heaven her innocent spirit ascended,
Lo! o'er the city a tempest rose; and the bolts of the thunder
Smote the statue of bronze, and hurled in wrath from its left hand
Down on the pavement below the clattering scales of the balance,
And in the hollow thereof was found the nest of a magpie,
Into whose clay-built walls the necklace of pearls was inwoven."
Silenced, but not convinced, when the story was ended, the blacksmith
Stood like a man who fain would speak, but findeth no language;
All his thoughts were congealed into lines on his face, as the vapors
Freeze in fantastic shapes on the window-panes in the winter.

Then Evangeline lighted the brazen lamp on the table,
Filled, till it overflowed, the pewter tankard with home-brewed
Nut-brown ale, that was famed for its strength in the village of Grand-Pré;
While from his pocket the notary drew his papers and inkhorn,
Wrote with a steady hand the date and the age of the parties,
Naming the dower of the bride in flocks of sheep and in cattle.
Orderly all things proceeded, and duly and well were completed,
And the great seal of the law was set like a sun on the margin.
Then from his leathern pouch the farmer threw on the table
Three times the old man's fee in solid pieces of silver;
And the notary rising, and blessing the bride and the bridegroom,
Lifted aloft the tankard of ale and drank to their welfare.
Wiping the foam from his lip, he solemnly bowed and departed,
While in silence the others sat and mused by the fireside,
Till Evangeline brought the draught-board out of its corner.
Soon was the game begun. In friendly contention the old men
Laughed at each lucky hit, or unsuccessful manœuvre,
Laughed when a man was crowned, or a breach was made in the king-row.
Meanwhile apart, in the twilight gloom of a window's embrasure,
Sat the lovers, and whispered together, beholding the moon rise
Over the pallid sea, and the silvery mists of the meadows.
Silently one by one, in the infinite meadows of heaven,
Blossomed the lovely stars, the forget-me-nots of the angels.

Thus was the evening passed. Anon the bell from the belfry
Rang out the hour of nine, the village curfew, and straightaway
Rose the guests and departed; and silence reigned in the household.
Many a farewell word and sweet good-night on the door-step
Lingered long in Evangeline's heart, and filled it with gladness.
Carefully then were covered the embers that glowed on the hearth-stone,
And on the oaken stairs resounded the tread of the farmer.
Soon with a soundless step the foot of Evangeline followed.
Up the staircase moved a luminous space in the darkness,
Lighted less by the lamp than the shining face of the maiden.
Silent she passed the hall, and entered the door of her chamber.
Simple that chamber was, with its curtains of white, and its clothes-press
Ample and high, on whose spacious shelves were carefully folded
Linen and woollen stuffs by the hand of Evangeline woven.
This was the precious dower she would bring to her husband in marriage,
Better than flocks and herds, being proofs of her skill as a housewife.
Soon she extinguished her lamp, for the mellow and radiant moonlight
Streamed through the windows, and lighted the room, till the heart of the maiden
Swelled and obeyed its power, like the tremulous tides of the ocean.
Ah! she was fair, exceeding fair to behold, as she stood with
Naked snow-white feet on the gleaming floor of her chamber!
Little she dreamed that below, among the trees of the orchard,
Waited her lover and watched for the gleam of her lamp and her shadow.

Yet were her thoughts of him, and at times a feeling of sadness
Passed o'er her soul, as the sailing shade of clouds in the moonlight
Flitted across the floor and darkened the room for a moment.
And, as she gazed from the window, she saw serenely the moon pass
Forth from the folds of a cloud, and one star follow her footsteps,
As out of Abraham's tent young Ishmael wandered with Hagar![10]

IV

Pleasantly rose next morn the sun on the village of Grand-Pré.
Pleasantly gleamed in the soft, sweet air the Basin of Minas,
Where the ships, with their wavering shadows, were riding at anchor.
Life had long been astir in the village, and clamorous labor
Knocked with its hundred hands at the golden gates of the morning.
Now from the country around, from the farms and neighboring hamlets,
Came in their holiday dresses the blithe Acadian peasants.
Many a glad good-morrow and jocund laugh from the young folk
Made the bright air brighter, as up from the numerous meadows,
Where no path could be seen but the track of wheels in the greensward,
Group after group appeared, and joined, or passed on the highway.
Long ere noon, in the village all sounds of labor were silenced.
Thronged were the streets with people; and noisy groups at the house-doors
Sat in the cheerful sun, and rejoiced and gossiped together.
Every house was an inn, where all were welcomed and feasted;
For with this simple people, who lived like brothers together,
All things were held in common, and what one had was another's.
Yet under Benedict's roof hospitality seemed more abundant:
For Evangeline stood among the guests of her father;
Bright was her face with smiles, and words of welcome and gladness
Fell from her beautiful lips, and blessed the cup as she gave it.

Under the open sky, in the odorous air of the orchard,
Stript of its golden fruit, was spread the feast of betrothal.
There in the shade of the porch were the priest and the notary seated;
There good Benedict sat, and sturdy Basil the blacksmith.
Not far withdrawn from these, by the cider-press and the beehives,
Michael the fiddler was placed, with the gayest of hearts and of waistcoats.
Shadow and light from the leaves alternately played on his snow-white
Hair, as it waved in the wind; and the jolly face of the fiddler
Glowed like a living coal when the ashes are blown from the embers.
Gayly the old man sang to the vibrant sound of his fiddle,
Tous les Bourgeois de Chartres, and *Le Carillon de Dunquerque,*
And anon with his wooden shoes beat time to the music.

---

10 Genesis 21:9–21. Abraham expelled his concubine Hagar and Ishmael, the son he had with
her, to wander in the desert.

Merrily, merrily whirled the wheels of the dizzying dances
Under the orchard-trees and down the path to the meadows;
Old folk and young together, and children mingled among them.
Fairest of all the maids was Evangeline, Benedict's daughter!
Noblest of all the youths was Gabriel, son of the blacksmith!

So passed the morning away. And lo! with a summons sonorous
Sounded the bell from its tower, and over the meadows a drum beat.
Thronged ere long was the church with men. Without, in the churchyard,
Waited the women. They stood by the graves, and hung on the headstones
Garlands of autumn-leaves and evergreens fresh from the forest.
Then came the guard from the ships, and marching proudly among them
Entered the sacred portal. With loud and dissonant clangor
Echoed the sound of their brazen drums from ceiling and casement,—
Echoed a moment only, and slowly the ponderous portal
Closed, and in silence the crowd awaited the will of the soldiers.
Then uprose their commander, and spake from the steps of the altar,
Holding aloft in his hands, with its seals, the royal commission.
"You are convened this day," he said, "by his Majesty's orders.
Clement and kind has he been; but how you have answered his kindness,
Let our own hearts reply! To my natural make and my temper
Painful the task is I do, which to you I know must be grievous.
Yet must I bow and obey, and deliver the will of our monarch;
Namely, that all your lands, and dwellings, and cattle of all kinds
Forfeited be to the crown; and that you yourselves from this province
Be transported to other lands. God grant you may dwell there
Ever as faithful subjects, a happy and peaceable people!
Prisoners now I declare you; for such is his Majesty's pleasure!"
As, when the air is serene in sultry solstice of summer,
Suddenly gathers a storm, and the deadly sling of the hailstones
Beats down the farmer's corn in the field and shatters his windows,
Hiding the sun, and strewing the ground with thatch from the house-roofs,
Bellowing fly the herds, and seek to break their enclosures;
So on the hearts of the people descended the words of the speaker.
Silent a moment they stood in speechless wonder, and then arose
Louder and ever louder a wail of sorrow and anger,
And, by one impulse moved, they madly rushed to the doorway.
Vain was the hope of escape; and cries and fierce imprecations
Rang through the house of prayer; and high o'er the heads of the others
Rose, with his arms uplifted, the figure of Basil the blacksmith,
As, on a stormy sea, a spar is tossed by the billows.
Flushed was his face and distorted with passion; and wildly he shouted,
"Down with the tyrants of England! We never have sworn them allegiance!
Death to these foreign soldiers, who seize on our homes and our harvests!"
More he fain would have said, but the merciless hand of a soldier
Smote him upon the mouth, and dragged him down to the pavement.

In the midst of the strife and tumult of angry contention,
Lo! the door of the chancel opened, and Father Felician
Entered, with serious mien, and ascended the steps of the altar.
Raising his reverend hand, with a gesture he awed into silence
All that clamorous throng; and thus he spake to his people;
Deep were his tones and solemn; in accents measured and mournful
Spake he, as, after the tocsin's alarum, distinctly the clock strikes.
"What is this that ye do, my children? what madness has seized you?
Forty years of my life have I labored among you, and taught you,
Not in word alone, but in deed, to love one another!
Is this the fruit of my toils, of my vigils and prayers and privations?
Have you so soon forgotten all lessons of love and forgiveness?
This is the house of the Prince of Peace,[11] and would you profane it
Thus with violent deeds and hearts overflowing with hatred?
Lo! where the crucified Christ from his cross is gazing upon you!
See! in those sorrowful eyes what meekness and holy compassion!
Hark! how those lips still repeat the prayer, 'O Father, forgive them!'[12]
Let us repeat that prayer in the hour when the wicked assail us,
Let us repeat it now, and say, 'O Father, forgive them!'"
Few were his words of rebuke, but deep in the hearts of his people
Sank they, and sobs of contrition succeeded the passionate outbreak,
While they repeated his prayer, and said, "O Father, forgive them!"

Then came the evening service. The tapers gleamed from the altar.
Fervent and deep was the voice of the priest, and the people responded,
Not with their lips alone, but their hearts; and the Ave Maria[13]
Sang they, and fell on their knees, and their souls, with devotion translated,
Rose on the ardor of prayer, like Elijah ascending to heaven.

Meanwhile had spread in the village the tidings of ill, and on all sides
Wandered, wailing, from house to house the women and children.
Long at her father's door Evangeline stood, with her right hand
Shielding her eyes from the level rays of the sun, that, descending,
Lighted the village street with mysterious splendor, and roofed each
Peasant's cottage with golden thatch, and emblazoned its windows.
Long within had been spread the snow-white cloth on the table;
There stood the wheaten loaf, and the honey fragrant with wild-flowers;
There stood the tankard of ale, and the cheese fresh brought from the dairy,
And, at the head of the board, the great armchair of the farmer.
Thus did Evangeline wait at her father's door, as the sunset
Threw the long shadows of trees o'er the broad ambrosial meadows.
Ah! on her spirit within a deeper shadow had fallen,
And from the fields of her soul a fragrance celestial ascended,—
Charity, meekness, love, and hope, and forgiveness, and patience!

---

11 Jesus Christ.
12 Luke 23:34.
13 Traditional Catholic prayer asking for the Virgin Mary's help.

Then, all-forgetful of self, she wandered into the village,
Cheering with looks and words the mournful hearts of the women,
As o'er the darkening fields with lingering steps they departed,
Urged by their household cares, and the weary feet of their children.
Down sank the great red sun, and in golden, glimmering vapors
Veiled the light of his face, like the Prophet descending from Sinai.
Sweetly over the village the bell of the Angelus sounded.

Meanwhile, amid the gloom, by the church Evangeline lingered.
All was silent within; and in vain at the door and the windows
Stood she, and listened and looked, till, overcome by emotion,
"Gabriel!" cried she aloud with tremulous voice; but no answer
Came from the graves of the dead, nor the gloomier grave of the living.
Slowly at length she returned to the tenantless house of her father.
Smouldered the fire on the hearth, on the board was the supper untasted,
Empty and drear was each room, and haunted with phantoms of terror.
Sadly echoed her step on the stair and the floor of her chamber.
In the dead of the night she heard the disconsolate rain fall
Loud on the withered leaves of the sycamore-tree by the window.
Keenly the lightning flashed; and the voice of the echoing thunder
Told her that God was in heaven, and governed the world he created!
Then she remembered the tale she had heard of the justice of Heaven;
Soothed was her troubled soul, and she peacefully slumbered till morning.

V

Four times the sun had risen and set; and now on the fifth day
Cheerily called the cock to the sleeping maids of the farmhouse.
Soon o'er the yellow fields, in silent and mournful procession,
Came from the neighboring hamlets and farms the Acadian women,
Driving in ponderous wains [14]their household goods to the seashore,
Pausing and looking back to gaze once more on their dwellings,
Ere they were shut from sight by the winding road and the woodland.
Close at their sides their children ran, and urged on the oxen,
While in their little hands they clasped some fragments of playthings.

Thus to the Gaspereau's mouth they hurried; and there on the sea-beach
Piled in confusion lay the household goods of the peasants.
All day long between the shore and the ships did the boats ply;
All day long the wains came laboring down from the village.
Late in the afternoon, when the sun was near to his setting,
Echoed far o'er the fields came the roll of drums from the churchyard.
Thither the women and children thronged. On a sudden the church-doors
Opened, and forth came the guard, and marching in gloomy procession
Followed the long-imprisoned, but patient, Acadian farmers.

---

14 Farm wagons.

Even as pilgrims, who journey afar from their homes and their country,
Sing as they go, and in singing forget they are weary and wayworn,
So with songs on their lips the Acadian peasants descended
Down from the church to the shore, amid their wives and their daughters.
Foremost the young men came; and, raising together their voices,
Sang with tremulous lips a chant of the Catholic Missions:
"Sacred heart of the Savior! O inexhaustible fountain!
Fill our hearts this day with strength and submission and patience!"
Then the old men, as they marched, and the women that stood by the wayside
Joined in the sacred psalm, and the birds in the sunshine above them
Mingled their notes therewith, like voices of spirits departed.

Halfway down to the shore Evangeline waited in silence,
Not overcome with grief, but strong in the hour of affliction,—
Calmly and sadly she waited, until the procession approached her,
And she beheld the face of Gabriel pale with emotion.
Tears then filled her eyes, and eagerly running to meet him,
Clasped she his hands, and laid her head on his shoulder, and whispered,
"Gabriel! be of good cheer! for if we love one another
Nothing, in truth, can harm us, whatever mischances may happen!"
Smiling she spake these words; then suddenly paused, for her father
Saw she slowly advancing. Alas! how changed was his aspect!
Gone was the glow from his cheek, and the fire from his eye, and his footstep
Heavier seemed with the weight of the heavy heart in his bosom.
But with a smile and a sigh, she clasped his neck and embraced him,
Speaking words of endearment where words of comfort availed not.
Thus to the Gaspereau's mouth moved on that mournful procession.

There disorder prevailed, and the tumult and stir of embarking.
Busily plied the freighted boats; and in the confusion
Wives were torn from their husbands, and mothers, too late, saw their children
Left on the land, extending their arms, with wildest entreaties.
So unto separate ships were Basil and Gabriel carried,
While in despair on the shore Evangeline stood with her father.
Half the task was not done when the sun went down, and the twilight
Deepened and darkened around; and in haste the refluent ocean
Fled away from the shore, and left the line of the sand-beach
Covered with waifs of the tide, with kelp and the slippery seaweed.
Farther back in the midst of the household goods and the wagons,
Like to a gypsy camp, or a leaguer after a battle,
All escape cut off by the sea, and the sentinels near them,
Lay encamped for the night the houseless Acadian farmers.
Back to its nethermost caves retreated the bellowing ocean,
Dragging adown the beach the rattling pebbles, and leaving
Inland and far up the shore the stranded boats of the sailors.
Then, as the night descended, the herds returned from their pastures;
Sweet was the moist still air with the odor of milk from their udders;

Lowing they waited, and long, at the well-known bars of the farmyard,—
Waited and looked in vain for the voice and the hand of the milkmaid.
Silence reigned in the streets; from the church no Angelus sounded,
Rose no smoke from the roofs, and gleamed no lights from the windows.

But on the shores meanwhile the evening fires had been kindled,
Built of the drift-wood thrown on the sands from wrecks in the tempest.
Round them shapes of gloom and sorrowful faces were gathered,
Voices of women were heard, and of men, and the crying of children.
Onward from fire to fire, as from hearth to hearth in his parish,
Wandered the faithful priest, consoling and blessing and cheering,
Like unto shipwrecked Paul on Melita's desolate seashore.[15]
Thus he approached the place where Evangeline sat with her father,
And in the flickering light beheld the face of the old man,
Haggard and hollow and wan, and without either thought or emotion,
E'en as the face of a clock from which the hands have been taken.
Vainly Evangeline strove with words and caresses to cheer him,
Vainly offered him food; yet he moved not, he looked not, he spake not,
But, with a vacant stare, ever gazed at the flickering firelight.
"*Benedicite!*"[16] murmured the priest, in tones of compassion.
More he fain would have said, but his heart was full, and his accents
Faltered and paused on his lips, as the feet of a child on the threshold,
Hushed by the scene he beholds, and the awful presence of sorrow.
Silently, therefore, he laid his hand on the head of the maiden,
Raising his tearful eyes to the silent stars that above them
Moved on their way, unperturbed by the wrongs and sorrows of mortals.
Then sat he down at her side, and they wept together in silence.

Suddenly rose from the south a light, as in autumn the blood-red
Moon climbs the crystal walls of heaven, and o'er the horizon
Titan-like stretches its hundred hands upon the mountain and meadow,
Seizing the rocks and the rivers, and piling huge shadows together.
Broader and ever broader it gleamed on the roofs of the village,
Gleamed on the sky and sea, and the ships that lay in the roadstead.
Columns of shining smoke uprose, and flashes of flame were
Thrust through their folds and withdrawn, like the quivering hands of a martyr.
Then as the wind seized the gleeds[17] and the burning thatch, and, uplifting,
Whirled them aloft through the air, at once from a hundred house-tops
Started the sheeted smoke with flashes of flame intermingled.

These things beheld in dismay the crowd on the shore and on shipboard.
Speechless at first they stood, then cried aloud in their anguish,
"We shall behold no more our homes in the village of Grand-Pré!"

---

15 Acts 28:1–10.
16 Bless you!
17 Glowing coals.

Loud on a sudden the cocks began to crow in the farmyards,
Thinking the day had dawned; and anon the lowing of cattle
Came on the evening breeze, by the barking of dogs interrupted.
Then rose a sound of dread, such as startles the sleeping encampments
Far in the Western prairies of forests that skirt the Nebraska,
When the wild horses affrighted sweep by with the speed of the whirlwind,
Or the loud bellowing herds of buffaloes rush to the river.
Such was the sound that arose on the night, as the herds and the horses
Broke through their folds and fences, and madly rushed o'er the meadows.

Overwhelmed with the sight, yet speechless, the priest and the maiden
Gazed on the scene of terror that reddened and widened before them;
And as they turned at length to speak to their silent companion,
Lo! from his seat he had fallen, and stretched abroad on the seashore
Motionless lay his form, from which the soul had departed.
Slowly the priest uplifted the lifeless head, and the maiden
Knelt at her father's side, and wailed aloud in her terror.
Then in a swoon she sank, and lay with her head on his bosom.
Through the long night she lay in deep, oblivious slumber;
And when she awoke from the trance, she beheld a multitude near her.
Faces of friends she beheld, that were mournfully gazing upon her,
Pallid, with tearful eyes, and looks of saddest compassion.
Still the blaze of the burning village illumined the landscape,
Reddened the sky overhead, and gleamed on the faces around her,
And like the day of doom it seemed to her wavering senses.
Then a familiar voice she heard, as it said to the people,
"Let us bury him here by the sea. When a happier season
Brings us again to our home from the unknown land of our exile,
Then shall his sacred dust be piously laid in the churchyard."
Such were the words of the priest. And there in haste by the seaside,
Having the glare of the burning village for funeral torches,
But without bell or book, they buried the farmer of Grand-Pré.
And as the voice of the priest repeated the service of sorrow,
Lo! with a mournful sound, like the voice of a vast congregation,
Solemnly answered the sea, and mingled its roar with the dirges.
'Twas the returning tide, that afar from the waste of the ocean,
With the first dawn of the day, came heaving and hurrying landward.
Then recommenced once more the stir and noise of embarking;
And with the ebb of the tide the ships sailed out of the harbor,
Leaving behind them the dead on the shore, and the village in ruins.

PART THE SECOND

I

Many a weary year had passed since the burning of Grand-Pré,
When on the falling tide the freighted vessels departed,

Bearing a nation, with all its household gods, into exile,
Exile without an end, and without an example in story.
Far asunder, on separate coasts, the Acadians landed;
Scattered were they, like flakes of snow, when the wind from the northeast
Strikes aslant through the fogs that darken the Banks of Newfoundland.
Friendless, homeless, hopeless, they wandered from city to city,
From the cold lakes of the North to sultry Southern savannas,—
From the bleak shores of the sea to the lands where the Father of Waters
Seizes the hills in his hands, and drags them down to the ocean,
Deep in their sands to bury the scattered bones of the mammoth.
Friends they sought and homes; and many, despairing, heart-broken,
Asked of the earth but a grave, and no longer a friend nor a fireside.
Written their history stands on tablets of stone in the churchyards.
Long among them was seen a maiden who waited and wandered,
Lowly and meek in spirit, and patiently suffering all things.
Fair was she and young: but alas! before her extended,
Dreary and vast and silent, the desert of life, with its pathway
Marked by the graves of those who had sorrowed and suffered before her,
Passions long extinguished, and hopes long dead and abandoned,
As the emigrant's way o'er the Western desert is marked by
Camp-fires long consumed, and bones that bleach in the sunshine.
Something there was in her life incomplete, imperfect, unfinished;
As if a morning of June, with all its music and sunshine,
Suddenly paused in the sky, and, fading, slowly descended
Into the east again, from whence it late had arisen.
Sometimes she lingered in towns, till, urged by the fever within her,
Urged by a restless longing, the hunger and thirst of the spirit,
She would commence again her endless search and endeavor;
Sometimes in churchyards strayed, and gazed on the crosses and tombstones,
Sat by some nameless grave, and thought that perhaps in its bosom
He was already at rest, and she longed to slumber beside him.
Sometimes a rumor, a hearsay, an inarticulate whisper,
Came with its airy hand to point and beckon her forward.
Sometimes she spake with those who had seen her beloved and
      known him,
But it was long ago, in some far-off place or forgotten.
"Gabriel Lajeunesse!" they said; "oh, yes! we have seen him.
He was with Basil the blacksmith, and both have gone to the prairies;
Coureurs-des-Bois are they, and famous hunters and trappers."
"Gabriel Lajeunesse!" said others; "oh yes! we have seen him.
He is a Voyageur in the lowlands of Louisiana."
Then would they say, "Dear child! why dream and wait for him longer?
Are there not other youths as fair as Gabriel? others
Who have hearts as tender and true; and spirits as loyal?
Here is Baptiste Leblanc, the notary's son, who has loved thee
Many a tedious year; come, give him thy hand and be happy!

Thou art too fair to be left to braid St. Catherine's tresses."[18]
Then would Evangeline answer, serenely but sadly, "I cannot!
Whither my heart has gone, there follows my hand, and not elsewhere.
For when the heart goes before, like a lamp, and illumines the pathway,
Many things are made clear, that else lie hidden in darkness."
Thereupon the priest, her friend and father-confessor,
Said, with a smile, "O daughter! thy God thus speaketh within thee!
Talk not of wasted affection, affection never was wasted;
If it enrich not the heart of another, its waters, returning
Back to their springs, like the rain, shall fill them full of refreshment;
That which the fountain sends forth returns again to the fountain.
Patience; acccomplish thy labor; accomplish thy work of affection!
Sorrow and silence arc strong, and patient endurance is godlike.
Therefore accomplish thy labor of love, till the heart is made godlike,
Purified, strengthened, perfected, and rendered more worthy of heaven!"
Cheered by the good man's words, Evangeline labored and waited.
Still in her heart she heard the funeral dirge of the ocean,
But with its sound there was mingled a voice that whispered, "Despair not!"
Thus did that poor soul wander in want and cheerless discomfort,
Bleeding, barefooted, over the shards and thorns of existence.
Let me essay, O Muse! to follow the wanderer's footsteps;—
Not through each devious path, each changeful year of existence,
But as a traveller follows a streamlet's course through the valley:
Far from its margin at times, and seeing the gleam of its water
Here and there, in some open space, and at intervals only;
Then drawing nearer its banks, through sylvan glooms that conceal it,
Though he behold it not, he can hear its continuous murmur;
Happy, at length, if he find the spot where it reaches an outlet.

II

It was the month of May. Far down the Beautiful River,
Past the Ohio shore and past the mouth of the Wabash,
Into the golden stream of the broad and swift Mississippi,
Floated a cumbrous boat, that was rowed by Acadian boatmen.
It was a band of exiles: a raft, as it were, from the shipwrecked
Nation, scattered along the coast, now floating together,
Bound by the bonds of a common belief and a common misfortune;
Men and women and children, who, guided by hope or by hearsay,
Sought for their kith and their kin among the few-acred farmers
On the Acadian coast, and the prairies of fair Opelousas.[19]
With them Evangeline went, and her guide, the Father Felician.
Onward o'er sunken sands, through a wilderness sombre with forests,

---

18 A Norman saying that refers to women who do not marry.
19 A town in south-central Louisiana.

Day after day they glided adown the turbulent river;
Night after night, by their blazing fires, encamped on its borders.
Now through rushing chutes, among green islands, where plumelike
Cotton-trees nodded their shadowy crests, they swept with the current,
Then emerged into broad lagoons, where silvery sandbars
Lay in the stream, and along the wimpling waves of their margin,
Shining with snow-white plumes, large flocks of pelicans waded.
Level the landscape grew, and along the shores of the river,
Shaded by china-trees, in the midst of luxuriant gardens,
Stood the houses of planters, with negro-cabins and dove-cots.
They were approaching the region where reigns perpetual summer,
Where through the Golden Coast, and groves of orange and citron,
Sweeps with majestic curve the river away to the eastward.
They, too, swerved from their course; and, entering the Bayou of Plaquemine,[20]
Soon were lost in a maze of sluggish and devious waters,
Which, like a network of steel, extended in every direction.
Over their heads the towering and tenebrous boughs of the cypress
Met in a dusky arch, and trailing mosses in mid-air
Waved like banners that hang on the walls of ancient cathedrals.
Deathlike the silence seemed, and unbroken, save by the herons
Home to their roosts in the cedar-trees returning at sunset,
Or by the owl, as he greeted the moon with demoniac laughter.
Lovely the moonlight was as it glanced and gleamed on the water,
Gleamed on the columns of cypress and cedar sustaining the arches,
Down through whose broken vaults it fell as through chinks in a ruin.
Dreamlike, and indistinct, and strange were all things around them;
And o'er their spirits there came a feeling of wonder and sadness,—
Strange forebodings of ill, unseen and that cannot be compassed.
As, at the tramp of a horse's hoof on the turf of the prairies,
Far in advance are closed the leaves of the shrinking mimosa,
So, at the hoof-beats of fate, with sad forebodings of evil,
Shrinks and closes the heart, ere the stroke of doom had attained it.
But Evangeline's heart was sustained by a vision, that faintly
Floated before her eyes, and beckoned her on through the moonlight.
It was the thought of her brain that assumed the shape of a phantom.
Through those shadowy aisles had Gabriel wandered before her,
And every stroke of the oar now brought him nearer and nearer.

Then in his place, at the prow of the boat, rose one of the oarsmen,
And, as a signal sound, if others like them peradventure
Sailed on those gloomy and midnight streams, blew a blast on his bugle.
Wild through the dark colonnades and corridors leafy the blast rang,
Breaking the seal of silence, and giving tongues to the forest.
Soundless above them the banners of moss just stirred to the music.
Multitudinous echoes awoke and died in the distance,

---

20 A series of navigable waterways on the southern coast of Louisiana.

Over the watery floor, and beneath the reverberant branches;
But not a voice replied; no answer came from the darkness;
And, when the echoes had ceased, like a sense of pain was the silence.
Then Evangeline slept; but the boatmen rowed through the midnight,
Silent at times, then singing familiar Canadian boat-songs,
Such as they sang of old on their own Acadian rivers,
While through the night were heard the mysterious sounds of the desert,
Far off,—indistinct,—as of wave or wind in the forest,
Mixed with the whoop of the crane and the roar of the grim alligator.

Thus ere another noon they emerged from the shades; and before them
Lay, in the golden sun, the lakes of the Atchafalaya.[21]
Water-lilies in myriads rocked on the slight undulations
Made by the passing oars, and, resplendent in beauty, the lotus
Lifted her golden crown above the heads of the boatmen.
Faint was the air with the odorous breath of magnolia blossoms,
And with the heat of noon; and numberless sylvan islands,
Fragrant and thickly embowered with blossoming hedges of roses,
Near to whose shores they glided along, invited to slumber.
Soon by the fairest of these their weary oars were suspended.
Under the boughs of Wachita willows, that grew by the margin,
Safely their boat was moored; and scattered about on the greensward,
Tired with their midnight toil, the weary travellers slumbered.
Over them vast and high extended the cope of a cedar.
Swinging from its great arms, the trumpet-flower and the grapevine
Hung their ladder of ropes aloft like the ladder of Jacob,[22]
On whose pendulous stairs the angels ascending, descending,
Were the swift humming-birds, that flitted from blossom to blossom.
Such was the vision Evangeline saw as she slumbered beneath it.
Filled was her heart with love, and the dawn of an opening heaven
Lighted her soul in sleep with the glory of regions celestial.

Nearer, and ever nearer, among the numberless islands,
Darted a light, swift boat, that sped away o'er the water,
Urged on its course by the sinewy arms of hunters and trappers.
Northward its prow was turned, to the land of the bison and beaver.
At the helm sat a youth, with countenance thoughtful and careworn.
Dark and neglected locks overshadowed his brow, and a sadness
Somewhat beyond his years on his face was legibly written.
Gabriel was it, who, weary with waiting, unhappy and restless,
Sought in the Western wilds oblivion of self and of sorrow.
Swiftly they glided along, close under the lee of the island,
But by the opposite bank, and behind a screen of palmettos,

---

21 The largest wetlands area in the United States, located in southern Louisiana, where the
    Atchafalaya River meets the Gulf of Mexico.
22 Genesis 28:12. Jacob dreamed of a ladder to heaven, full of angels going up and down its rungs.

So they saw not the boat, where it lay concealed in the willows;
All undisturbed by the dash of their oars, and unseen, were the sleepers.
Angel of God was there none to awaken the slumbering maiden.
Swiftly they glided away, like the shade of a cloud on the prairie.
After the sound of their oars on the tholes had died in the distance,
As from a magic trance the sleepers awoke, and the maiden
Said with a sigh to the friendly priest, "O Father Felician!
Something says in my heart that near me Gabriel wanders.
Is it a foolish dream, an idle and vague superstition?
Or has an angel passed, and revealed the truth to my spirit?"
Then, with a blush, she added, "Alas for my credulous fancy!
Unto ears like thine such words as these have no meaning."
But made answer the reverend man, and he smiled as he answered,
"Daughter, thy words are not idle; nor are they to me without meaning.
Feeling is deep and still; and the word that floats on the surface
Is as the tossing buoy, that betrays where the anchor is hidden.
Therefore trust to thy heart, and to what the world calls illusions.
Gabriel truly is near thee; for not far away to the southward,
On the banks of the Têche,[23] are the towns of St. Maur and St. Martin.
There the long-wandering bride shall be given again to her bridegroom,
There the long-absent pastor regain his flock and his sheepfold.
Beautiful is the land, with its prairies and forests of fruit-trees;
Under the feet a garden of flowers, and the bluest of heavens
Bending above, and resting its dome on the walls of the forest.
They who dwell there have named it the Eden of Louisiana!"

   With these words of cheer they arose and continued their journey.
Softly the evening came. The sun from the western horizon
Like a magician extended his golden wand o'er the landscape;
Twinkling vapors arose; and sky and water and forest
Seemed all on fire at the touch, and melted and mingled together.
Hanging between two skies, a cloud with edges of silver,
Floated the boat, with its dripping oars, on the motionless water.
Filled was Evangeline's heart with inexpressible sweetness.
Touched by the magic spell, the sacred fountains of feeling
Glowed with the light of love, as the skies and waters around her.
Then from a neighboring thicket the mocking-bird, wildest of singers,
Swinging aloft on a willow spray that hung o'er the water,
Shook from his little throat such floods of delirious music,
That the whole air and the woods and the waves seemed silent to listen.
Plaintive at first were the tones and sad; then soaring to madness
Seemed they to follow or guide the revel of frenzied Bacchantes.[24]
Single notes were then heard, in sorrowful, low lamentation;
Till, having gathered them all, he flung them abroad in derision,

---

23 A major river that flows southward to connect with the Atchafalaya River.
24 Priests of the god Bacchus, the ancient Greek god of wine and revelry.

As when, after a storm, a gust of wind through the tree-tops
Shakes down the rattling rain in a crystal shower on the branches.
With such a prelude as this, and hearts that throbbed with emotion,
Slowly they entered the Têche, where it flows through the green Opelousas,
And, through the amber air, above the crest of the woodland,
Saw the column of smoke that rose from a neighboring dwelling;—
Sounds of a horn they heard, and the distant lowing of cattle.

III

Near to the bank of the river, o'ershadowed by oaks, from whose branches
Garlands of Spanish moss and of mystic mistletoe flaunted,
Such as the Druids cut down with golden hatchets at Yule-tide,
Stood, secluded and still, the house of the herdsman. A garden
Girded it round about with a belt of luxuriant blossoms,
Filling the air with fragrance. The house itself was of timbers.
Hewn from the cypress-tree, and carefully fitted together.
Large and low was the roof; and on slender columns supported,
Rose-wreathed, vine-encircled, a broad and spacious veranda,
Haunt of the humming-bird and the bee, extended around it.
At each end of the house, amid the flowers of the garden,
Stationed the dove-cots were, as love's perpetual symbol,
Scenes of endless wooing, and endless contentions of rivals.
Silence reigned o'er the place. The line of shadow and sunshine
Ran near the tops of the trees; but the house itself was in shadow,
And from its chimney-top, ascending and slowly expanding
Into the evening air, a thin blue column of smoke rose.
In the rear of the house, from the garden gate, ran a pathway
Through the great groves of oak to the skirts of the limitless prairie,
Into whose sea of flowers the sun was slowly descending.
Full in his track of light, like ships with shadowy canvas
Hanging loose from their spars in a motionless calm in the tropics,
Stood a cluster of trees, with tangled cordage of grapevines.

Just where the woodlands met the flowery surf of the prairie,
Mounted upon his horse, with Spanish saddle and stirrups,
Sat a herdsman, arrayed in gaiters and doublet of deerskin.
Broad and brown was the face that from under the Spanish sombrero
Gazed on the peaceful scene, with the lordly look of its master.
Round about him were numberless herds of kine,[25] that were grazing
Quietly in the meadows, and breathing the vapory freshness
That uprose from the river, and spread itself over the landscape.
Slowly lifting the horn that hung at his side, and expanding
Fully his broad, deep chest, he blew a blast, that resounded
Wildly and sweet and far, through the still damp air of the evening.

---

25 Cows.

Suddenly out of the grass the long white horns of the cattle
Rose like flakes of foam on the adverse currents of ocean.
Silent a moment they gazed, then bellowing rushed o'er the prairie,
And the whole mass became a cloud, a shade in the distance.
Then, as the herdsman turned to the house, through the gate of the garden
Saw he the forms of the priest and the maiden advancing to meet him.
Suddenly down from his horse he sprang in amazement, and forward
Rushed with extended arms and exclamations of wonder;
When they beheld his face, they recognized Basil the blacksmith.
Hearty his welcome was, as he led his guests to the garden.
There in an arbor of roses with endless question and answer
Gave they vent to their hearts, and renewed their friendly embraces,
Laughing and weeping by turns, or sitting silent and thoughtful.
Thoughtful, for Gabriel came not; and now dark doubts and misgivings
Stole o'er the maiden's heart; and Basil, somewhat embarrassed,
Broke the silence and said, "If you came by the Atchafalaya,
How have you nowhere encountered my Gabriel's boat on the bayous?"
Over Evangeline's face at the words of Basil a shade passed.
Tears came into her eyes, and she said, with a tremulous accent,
"Gone? is Gabriel gone?" and, concealing her face on his shoulder,
All her o'er burdened heart gave way, and she wept and lamented.
Then the good Basil said,—and his voice grew blithe as he said it,—
"Be of good cheer, my child; it is only to-day he departed.
Foolish boy! he has left me alone with my herds and my horses.
Moody and restless grown, and tried and troubled, his spirit
Could no longer endure the calm of this quiet existence.
Thinking ever of thee, uncertain and sorrowful ever,
Ever silent, or speaking only of thee and his troubles,
He at length had become so tedious to men and to maidens,
Tedious even to me, that at length I bethought me, and sent him
Unto the town of Adayes[26] to trade for mules with the Spaniards.
Thence he will follow the Indian trails to the Ozark Mountains,[27]
Hunting for furs in the forests, on rivers trapping the beaver.
Therefore be of good cheer; we will follow the fugitive lover;
He is not far on his way, and the Fates and the streams are against him.
Up and away to-morrow, and through the red dew of the morning
We will follow him fast, and bring him back to his prison."

Then glad voices were heard, and up from the banks of the river,
Borne aloft on his comrades' arms, came Michael the fiddler.
Long under Basil's roof had he lived like a god on Olympus,
Having no other care than dispensing music to mortals.
Far renowned was he for his silver locks and his fiddle.
"Long live Michael," they cried, "our brave Arcadian minstrel!"

---

26 Important religious and economic center in Natchitoches region of north central Louisiana.
27 Mountain range largely in Missouri and Arkansas.

As they bore him aloft in triumphal procession; and straightway
Father Felician advanced with Evangeline, greeting the old man
Kindly and oft, and recalling the past, while Basil, enraptured,
Hailed with hilarious joy his old companions and gossips,
Laughing loud and long, and embracing mothers and daughters.
Much they marvelled to see the wealth of the ci-devant blacksmith,
All his domains and his herds, and his patriarchal demeanor;
Much they marvelled to hear his tales of the soil and the climate,
And of the prairies, whose numberless herds were his who would take them;
Each one thought in his heart, that he, too, would go and do likewise.
Thus they ascended the steps, and crossing the breezy veranda,
Entered the hall of the house, where already the supper of Basil
Waited his late return; and they rested and feasted together.

Over the joyous feast the sudden darkness descended.
All was silent without, and, illuming the landscape with silver,
Fair rose the dewy moon and the myriad stars; but within doors,
Brighter than these, shone the faces of friends in the glimmering lamplight.
Then from his station aloft, at the head of the table, the herdsman
Poured forth his heart and his wine together in endless profusion.
Lighting his pipe, that was filled with sweet Natchitoches tobacco,
Thus he spake to his guests, who listened, and smiled as they listened:
"Welcome once more, my friends, who long have been friendless and homeless,
Welcome once more to a home, that is better perchance than the old one!
Here no hungry winter congeals our blood like the rivers;
Here no stony ground provokes the wrath of the farmer.
Smoothly the ploughshare runs through the soil, as a keel through the water.
All the year round the orange-groves are in blossom; and grass grows
More in a single night than a whole Canadian summer.
Here, too, numberless herds run wild and unclaimed in the prairies;
Here, too, lands may be had for the asking, and forests of timber
With a few blows of the axe are hewn and framed into houses.
After your houses are built, and your fields are yellow with harvests,
No King George of England shall drive you away from your homesteads,
Burning your dwellings and barns, and stealing your farms and your cattle."
Speaking these words, he blew a wrathful cloud from his nostrils,
While his huge, brown hand came thundering down on the table,
So that the guests all started; and Father Felician, astounded,
Suddenly paused, with a pinch of snuff halfway to his nostrils.
But the brave Basil resumed, and his words were milder and gayer:
"Only beware of the fever, my friends, beware of the fever!
For it is not like that of our cold Acadian climate,
Cured by wearing a spider hung round one's neck in a nutshell!"
Then there were voices heard at the door, and footsteps approaching
Sounded upon the stairs and the floor of the breezy veranda,
It was the neighboring Creoles and small Acadian planters,
Who had been summoned all to the house of Basil the herdsman.

Merry the meeting was of ancient comrades and neighbors:
Friend clasped friend in his arms; and they who before were as strangers,
Meeting in exile, became straightway as friends to each other,
Drawn by the gentle bond of a common country together.
But in the neighboring hall a strain of music, proceeding
From the accordant strings of Michael's melodious fiddle,
Broke up all further speech. Away, like children delighted,
All things forgotten beside, they gave themselves to the maddening
Whirl of the giddy dance, as it swept and swayed to the music,
Dreamlike, with beaming eyes and the rush of fluttering garments.

Meanwhile, apart, at the head of the hall, the priest and the herdsman
Sat, conversing together of past and present and future;
While Evangeline stood like one entranced, for within her
Olden memories rose, and loud in the midst of the music
Heard she the sound of the sea, and an irrepressible sadness
Came o'er her heart, and unseen she stole forth into the garden.
Beautiful was the night. Behind the black wall of the forest,
Tipping its summit with silver, arose the moon. On the river
Fell here and there through the branches a tremulous gleam of the moonlight,
Like the sweet thoughts of love on a darkened and devious spirit.
Nearer and round about her, the manifold flowers of the garden
Poured out their souls in odors, that were their prayers and confessions
Unto the night, as it went its way, like a silent Carthusian.[28]
Fuller of fragrance than they, and as heavy with shadows and night-dews,
Hung the heart of the maiden. The calm and the magical moonlight
Seemed to inundate her soul with indefinable longings,
As, through the garden gate, and beneath the shade of the oak-trees,
Passed she along the path to the edge of the measureless prairie.
Silent it lay, with a silvery haze upon it, and fireflies
Gleamed and floated away in mingled and infinite numbers.
Over her head the stars, the thoughts of God in the heavens,
Shone on the eyes of man, who had ceased to marvel and worship,
Save when a blazing comet was seen on the walls of that temple,
As if a hand had appeared and written upon them, "Upharsin."[29]
And the soul of the maiden, between the stars and the fireflies,
Wandered alone, and she cried, "O Gabriel! O my beloved!
Art thou so near unto me, and yet I cannot behold thee?
Art thou so near unto me, and yet thy voice does not reach me?
Ah! how often thy feet have trod this path to the prairie!
Ah! how often thine eyes have looked on the woodlands around me!
Ah! how often beneath this oak, returning from labor,
Thou hast lain down to rest, and to dream of me in thy slumbers!

---

28 A member of a Catholic monastic order.
29 Daniel 5:24–28. The final word in the mysterious writing found on King Belshazzar's wall,
    translated "you have been weighed in the balance and found wanting."

When shall these eyes behold, these arms be folded about thee?"
Loud and sudden and near the notes of a whippoorwill sounded
Like a flute in the woods; and anon, through the neighboring thickets,
Farther and farther away it floated and dropped into silence.
"Patience!" whispered the oaks from oracular caverns of darkness:
And, from the moonlit meadow, a sigh responded, "To-morrow!"

Bright rose the sun next day; and all the flowers of the garden
Bathed his shining feet with their tears, and anointed his tresses
With the delicious balm that they bore in their vases of crystal.
"Farewell!" said the priest, as he stood at the shadowy threshold;
"See that you bring us the Prodigal Son[30] from his fasting and famine,
And, too, the Foolish Virgin,[31] who slept when the bridegroom was coming."
"Farewell!" answered the maiden, and, smiling, with Basil descended
Down to the river's brink, where the boatmen already were waiting.
Thus beginning their journey with morning, and sunshine, and gladness,
Swiftly they followed the flight of him who was speeding before them,
Blown by the blast of fate like a dead leaf over the desert.
Not that day, nor the next, nor yet the day that succeeded,
Found they the trace of his course, in lake or forest or river,
Nor, after many days, had they found him; but vague and uncertain
Rumors alone were their guides through a wild and desolate country;
Till, at the little inn of the Spanish town of Adayes,
Weary and worn, they alighted, and learned from the garrulous landlord,
That on the day before, with horses and guides and companions,
Gabriel left the village, and took the road of the prairies.

IV

Far in the West there lies a desert land, where the mountains
Lift, through perpetual snows, their lofty and luminous summits.
Down from their jagged, deep ravines, where the gorge, like a gateway,
Opens a passage rude to the wheels of the emigrant's wagon,
Westward the Oregon flows and the Walleway and Owyhee.[32]
Eastward, with devious course, among the Windriver Mountains,
Through the Sweet-water Valley precipitate leaps the Nebraska;
And to the south, from Fontaine-qui-bout and the Spanish sierras,
Fretted with sands and rocks, and swept by the wind of the desert,
Numberless torrents, with ceaseless sound, descend to the ocean,
Like the great chords of a harp, in loud and solemn vibrations.
Spreading between these streams are the wondrous, beautiful prairies;
Billowy bays of grass ever rolling in shadow and sunshine,

---

30 Luke 15:11–32. The story of a son who left his father's house to find his own way in the world.
31 Matthew 25:1–13. The story of wise and foolish virgins. The foolish ones fell asleep and missed the coming of the bridegroom.
32 Rivers in Oregon and northern Nevada.

Bright with luxuriant clusters of roses and purple amorphas.
Over them wandered the buffalo herds, and the elk and the roebuck,
Over them wandered the wolves, and herds of riderless horses;
Fires that blast and blight, and winds that are weary with travel;
Over them wander the scattered tribes of Ishmael's children,
Staining the desert with blood; and above their terrible war-trails
Circles and sails aloft, on pinions majestic, the vulture,
Like the implacable soul of a chieftain slaughtered in battle,
By invisible stairs ascending and scaling the heavens.
Here and there rise smokes from the camps of these savage marauders;
Here and there rise groves from the margins of swift-running rivers;
And the grim, taciturn bear, the anchorite monk of the desert,
Climbs down their dark ravines to dig for roots by the brookside,
And over all is the sky, the clear and crystalline heaven,
Like the protecting hand of God inverted above them.

Into this wonderful land, at the base of the Ozark Mountains,
Gabriel far had entered, with hunters and trappers behind him.
Day after day, with their Indian guides, the maiden and Basil
Followed his flying steps, and thought each day to o'ertake him.
Sometimes they saw, or thought they saw, the smoke of his camp-fire
Rise in the morning air from the distant plain; but at nightfall,
When they had reached the place, they found only embers and ashes.
And, though their hearts were sad at times and their bodies were weary,
Hope still guided them on, as the magic Fata Morgana[33]
Showed them her lakes of light, that retreated and vanished before them.

Once, as they sat by their evening fire, there silently entered
Into their little camp an Indian woman, whose features
Wore deep traces of sorrow, and patience as great as her sorrow.
She was a Shawnee woman returning home to her people,
From the far-off hunting-grounds of the cruel Camanches,
Where her Canadian husband, a Coureur-des-Bois, had been murdered.
Touched were their hearts at her story, and warmest and friendliest welcome
Gave they, with words of cheer, and she sat and feasted among them
On the buffalo-meat and the venison cooked on the embers.
But when their meal was done, and Basil and all his companions,
Worn with the long day's march and the chase of the deer and the bison,
Stretched themselves on the ground, and slept where the quivering firelight
Flashed on their swarthy cheeks, and their forms wrapped up in their blankets,
Then at the door of Evangeline's tent she sat and repeated
Slowly, with soft, low voice, and the charm of her Indian accent,
All the tale of her love, with its pleasures, and pains, and reverses.
Much Evangeline wept at the tale, and to know that another
Hapless heart like her own had loved and had been disappointed.

---

33 Mirages of narrow bands of light that hover right above the horizon.

Moved to the depths of her soul by pity and woman's compassion,
Yet in her sorrow pleased that one who had suffered was near her,
She in turn related her love and all its disasters.
Mute with wonder the Shawnee sat, and when she had ended
Still was mute; but at length, as if a mysterious horror
Passed through her brain, she spake, and repeated the tale of the Mowis;
Mowis, the bridegroom of snow, who won and wedded a maiden,
But, when the morning came, arose and passed from the wigwam,
Fading and melting away and dissolving into the sunshine,
Till she beheld him no more, though she followed far into the forest.
Then, in those sweet, low tones, that seemed like a weird incantation,
Told she the tale of the fair Lilinau, who was wooed by a phantom,
That through the pines o'er her father's lodge, in the hush of the twilight,
Breathed like the evening wind, and whispered love to the maiden,
Till she followed his green and waving plume through the forest,
And nevermore returned, nor was seen again by her people.
Silent with wonder and strange surprise, Evangeline listened
To the soft flow of her magical words, till the region around her
Seemed like enchanted ground, and her swarthy guest the enchantress.
Slowly over the tops of the Ozark Mountains the moon rose,
Lighting the little tent, and with a mysterious splendor
Touching the sombre leaves, and embracing and filling the woodland.
With a delicious sound the brook rushed by, and the branches
Swayed and sighed overhead in scarcely audible whispers.
Filled with the thoughts of love was Evangeline's heart, but a secret,
Subtile sense crept in of pain and indefinite terror,
As the cold, poisonous snake creeps into the nest of the swallow.
It was no earthly fear. A breath from the region of spirits
Seemed to float in the air of night; and she felt for a moment
That, like the Indian maid, she, too, was pursuing a phantom.
With this thought she slept, and the fear and the phantom had vanished.

Early upon the morrow the march was resumed; and the Shawnee
Said, as they journeyed along, "On the western slope of these mountains
Dwells in his little village the Black Robe chief[34] of the Mission.
Much he teaches the people, and tells them of Mary and Jesus.
Loud laugh their hearts with joy, and weep with pain, as they hear him."
Then, with a sudden and secret emotion, Evangeline answered,
"Let us go to the Mission, for there good tidings await us!"
Thither they turned their steeds; and behind a spur of the mountains,
Just as the sound went down, they heard a murmur of voices,
And in a meadow green and broad, by the bank of a river,
Saw the tents of the Christians, the tents of the Jesuit Mission.
Under a towering oak, that stood in the midst of the village,

---

34 A Roman Catholic Jesuit priest.

Knelt the Black Robe chief with his children. A crucifix fastened
High on the trunk of the tree, and overshadowed by grapevines,
Looked with its agonized face on the multitude kneeling beneath it.
This was their rural chapel. Aloft, through the intricate arches
Of its aërial roof, arose the chant of their vespers,
Mingling its notes with soft susurrus and sighs of the branches.
Silent, with heads uncovered, the travellers, nearer approaching,
Knelt on the swarded floor, and joined in the evening devotions.
But when the service was done, and the benediction had fallen
Forth from the hands of the priest, like seed from the hands of the sower,
Slowly the reverend man advanced to the strangers, and bade them
Welcome; and when they replied, he smiled with benignant expression,
Hearing the homelike sounds of his mother tongue in the forest,
And, with words of kindness, conducted them into his wigwam.
There upon mats and skins they reposed, and on cakes of the maize-ear
Feasted, and slaked their thirst from the water-gourd of the teacher.
Soon was their story told; and the priest with solemnity answered:
"Not six suns have risen and set since Gabriel, seated
On this mat by my side, where now the maiden reposes,
Told me this same sad tale; then arose and continued his journey!"
Soft was the voice of the priest, and he spake with an accent of kindness;
But on Evangeline's heart fell his words as in winter the snow-flakes
Fall into some lone nest from which the birds have departed.
"Far to the north he has gone," continued the priest; "but in autumn,
When the chase is done, will return again to the Mission."
Then Evangeline said, and her voice was meek and submissive,
"Let me remain with thee, for my soul is sad and afflicted."
So seemed it wise and well unto all; and betimes on the morrow,
Mounting his Mexican steed, with his Indian guides and companions,
Homeward Basil returned, and Evangeline stayed at the Mission.

Slowly, slowly, slowly the days succeeded each other,—
Days and weeks and months; and the fields of maize that were springing
Green from the ground when a stranger she came, now waving above her,
Lifted their slender shafts, with leaves interlacing, and forming
Cloisters for mendicant crows and granaries pillaged by squirrels.
Then in the golden weather the maize was husked, and the maidens
Blushed at each blood-red ear, for that betokened a lover,
But at the crooked laughed, and called it a thief in the cornfield.
Even the blood-red ear to Evangeline brought not her lover.
"Patience!" the priest would say; "have faith, and thy prayer will be answered!
Look at this vigorous plant that lifts its head from the meadow,
See how its leaves are turned to the north, as true as the magnet;
This is the compass-flower, that the finger of God has planted
Here in the houseless wild, to direct the traveller's journey
Over the sea-like, pathless, limitless waste of the desert.
Such in the soul of man is faith. The blossoms of passion,

Gay and luxuriant flowers, are brighter and fuller of fragrance,
But they beguile us, and lead us astray, and their odor is deadly.
Only this humble plant can guide us here, and hereafter
Crown us with asphodel flowers, that are wet with the dews of nepenthe."[35]

So came the autumn, and passed, and the winter,— yet Gabriel came not;
Blossomed the opening spring, and the notes of the robin and bluebird
Sounded sweet upon wold and in wood, yet Gabriel came not.
But on the breath of the summer winds a rumor was wafted,
Sweeter than song of bird, or hue or odor of blossom.
Far to the north and east, it said, in the Michigan forests,
Gabriel had his lodge by the banks of the Saginaw River.
And, with returning guides, that sought the lakes of St. Lawrence,
Saying a sad farewell, Evangeline went from the Mission.
When over weary ways, by long and perilous marches,
She had attained at length the depths of the Michigan forests,
Found she the hunter's lodge deserted and fallen to ruin!

Thus did the long sad years glide on, and in seasons and places
Divers and distant far was seen the wandering maiden;—
Now in the Tents of Grace of the meek Moravian Missions,
Now in the noisy camps and the battle-fields of the army,
Now in secluded hamlets, in towns and populous cities.
Like a phantom she came, and passed away unremembered.
Fair was she and young, when in hope began the long journey;
Faded was she and old, when in disappointment it ended.
Each succeeding year stole something away from her beauty,
Leaving behind it, broader and deeper, the gloom and the shadow.
Then there appeared and spread faint streaks of gray o'er her forehead,
Dawn of another life, that broke o'er her earthly horizon,
As in the eastern sky the first faint streaks of the morning.

V

In that delightful land which is washed by the Delaware's waters,
Guarding in sylvan shades the name of Penn the apostle,
Stands on the banks of its beautiful stream the city he founded.
There all the air is balm, and the peach is the emblem of beauty,
And the streets still reëcho the names of the trees of the forest,
As if they fain would appease the Dryads[36] whose haunts they molested.
There from the troubled sea had Evangeline landed, an exile,
Finding among the children of Penn a home and a country.
There old René Leblanc had died; and when he departed,

---

35   A medicine thought to drive away sorrow.
36   Tree nymphs.

Saw at his side only one of all his hundred descendants.
Something at least there was in the friendly streets of the city,
Something that spake to her heart, and made her no longer a stranger;
And her ear was pleased with the Thee and Thou of the Quakers,
For it recalled the past, the old Acadian country,
Where all men were equal, and all were brothers and sisters.
So, when the fruitless search, the disappointed endeavor,
Ended, to recommence no more upon earth, uncomplaining,
Thither, as leaves to the light, were turned her thoughts and her footsteps.
As from the mountain's top the rainy mists of the morning
Roll away, and afar we behold the landscape below us,
Sun-illumined, with shining rivers and cities and hamlets,
So fell the mists from her mind, and she saw the world far below her,
Dark no longer, but all illumined with love; and the pathway
Which she had climbed so far, lying smooth and fair in the distance.
Gabriel was not forgotten. Within her heart was his image,
Clothed in the beauty of love and youth, at last she beheld him,
Only more beautiful made by this death-like silence and absence.
Into her thoughts of him time entered not, for it was not.
Over him years had no power; he was not changed, but transfigured;
He had become to her heart as one who is dead, and not absent;
Patience and abnegation of self, and devotion to others,
This was the lesson a life of trial and sorrow had taught her.
So was her love diffused, but, like to some odorous spices,
Suffered no waste nor loss, though filling the air with aroma.
Other hope had she none, nor wish in life, but to follow
Meekly, with reverent steps, the sacred feet of her Saviour.
Thus many years she lived as a Sister of Mercy; frequenting
Lonely and wretched roofs in the crowded lanes of the city,
Where distress and want concealed themselves from the sunlight,
Where disease and sorrow in garrets languished neglected.
Night after night, when the world was asleep, as the watchman repeated
Loud, through the gusty streets, that all was well in the city,
High at some lonely window he saw the light of her taper.
Day after day, in the gray of the dawn, as slow through the suburbs
Plodded the German farmer, with flowers and fruits for the market,
Met he that meek, pale face, returning home from its watchings.

    Then it came to pass that a pestilence fell on the city,
Presaged by wondrous signs, and mostly by flocks of wild pigeons,
Darkening the sun in their flight, with naught in their craws but an acorn.
And, as the tides of the sea arise in the month of September,
Flooding some silver stream, till it spreads to a lake in the meadow,
So death flooded life, and, o'erflowing its natural margin,
Spread to a brackish lake the silver stream of existence.
Wealth had no power to bribe, nor beauty to charm, the oppressor;
But all perished alike beneath the scourge of his anger;—

Only, alas! the poor, who had neither friends nor attendants,
Crept away to die in the almshouse, home of the homeless.
Then in the suburbs it stood, in the midst of meadows and woodlands;—
Now the city surrounds it; but still, with its gateway and wicket
Meek, in the midst of splendor, its humble walls seem to echo
Softly the words of the Lord: "The poor ye always have with you."
Thither, by night and by day, came the Sister of Mercy. The dying,
Looked up into her face, and thought, indeed, to behold there
Gleams of celestial light encircle her forehead with splendor,
Such as the artist paints o'er the brows of the saints and apostles,
Or such as hangs by night o'er a city seen at a distance.
Unto their eyes it seemed the lamps of the city celestial,
Into whose shining gates ere long their spirits would enter.

Thus, on a Sabbath morn, through the streets, deserted and silent,
Wending her quiet way, she entered the door of the almshouse.
Sweet on the summer air was the odor of flowers in the garden;
And she paused on her way to gather the fairest among them,
That the dying once more might rejoice in their fragrance and beauty.
Then, as she mounted the stairs to the corridors, cooled by the east-wind,
Distant and soft on her ear fell the chimes from the belfry of Christ Church,
While, intermingled with these, across the meadows were wafted
Sounds of psalms, that were sung by the Swedes in their church at Wicaco.
Soft as descending wings fell the calm of the hour on her spirit:
Something within her said, "At length thy trials are ended;"
And, with light in her looks, she entered the chambers of sickness.
Noiselessly moved about the assiduous, careful attendants,
Moistening the feverish lip, and the aching brow, and in silence
Closing the sightless eyes of the dead, and concealing their faces,
Where on their pallets they lay, like drifts of snow by the roadside.
Many a languid head, upraised as Evangeline entered,
Turned on its pillow of pain to gaze while she passed, for her presence
Fell on their hearts like a ray of the sun on the walls of a prison.
And, as she looked around, she saw how Death, the consoler,
Laying his hand upon many a heart, had healed it forever.
Many familiar forms had disappeared in the nighttime;
Vacant their places were, or, filled already by strangers.

Suddenly, as if arrested by fear or a feeling of wonder,
Still she stood, with her colorless lips apart, while a shudder
Ran through her frame, and, forgotten, the flowerets dropped from her fingers,
And from her eyes and cheeks the light and bloom of the morning.
Then there escaped from her lips a cry of such terrible anguish,
That the dying heard it, and started up from their pillows.
On the pallet before her was stretched the form of an old man.
Long, and thin, and gray were the locks that shaded his temples;
But, as he lay in the morning light, his face for a moment

Seemed to assume once more the forms of its earlier manhood;
So are wont to be changed the faces of those who are dying.
Hot and red on his lips still burned the flush of the fever,
As if life, like the Hebrew, with blood had besprinkled its portals,
That the Angel of Death might see the sign, and pass over.[37]
Motionless, senseless, dying, he lay, and his spirit exhausted
Seemed to be sinking down through infinite depths in the darkness,
Darkness of slumber and death, forever sinking and sinking.
Then through those realms of shade, in multiplied reverberations,
Heard he that cry of pain, and through the hush that succeeded
Whispered a gentle voice, in accents tender and saint-like,
"Gabriel! O my beloved!" and died away into silence.
Then he beheld, in a dream, once more the home of his childhood;
Green Acadian meadows, with sylvan rivers among them,
Village, and mountain, and woodlands; and, walking under their shadow,
As in the days of her youth, Evangeline rose in his vision.
Tears came into his eyes; and as slowly he lifted his eyelids,
Vanished the vision away, but Evangeline knelt by his bedside.
Vainly he strove to whisper her name, for the accents unuttered
Died on his lips, and their motion revealed what his tongue would have spoken.
Vainly he strove to rise; and Evangeline, kneeling beside him,
Kissed his dying lips, and laid his head on her bosom.
Sweet was the light of his eyes; but it suddenly sank into darkness,
As when a lamp is blown out by a gust of wind at a casement.

All was ended now, the hope, and the fear, and the sorrow,
All the aching of heart, the restless, unsatisfied longing,
All the dull, deep pain, and constant anguish of patience!
And, as she pressed once more the lifeless head to her bosom,
Meekly she bowed her own, and murmured, "Father, I thank thee!"

Still stands the forest primeval; but far away from its shadow,
Side by side, in their nameless graves, the lovers arc sleeping.
Under the humble walls of the little Catholic churchyard,
In the heart of the city, they lie, unknown and unnoticed.
Daily the tides of life go ebbing and flowing beside them,
Thousands of throbbing hearts, where theirs are at rest and forever,
Thousands of aching brains, where theirs no longer are busy,
Thousands of toiling hands, where theirs have ceased from their labors,
Thousands of weary feet, where theirs have completed their journey!

Still stands the forest primeval; but under the shade of its branches
Dwells another race, with other customs and language.

---

37 Exodus 12:1–13. During the plagues that beset Egypt, God promised Moses that His Angel of
Death would pass over any Hebrew household that had spread the blood of a sacrificial lamb
on its doorposts.

Only along the shore of the mournful and misty Atlantic
Linger a few Acadian peasants, whose fathers from exile
Wandered back to their native land to die in its bosom.
In the fisherman's cot the wheel and the loom are still busy;
Maidens still wear their Norman caps and their kirtles of homespun,
And by the evening fire repeat Evangeline's story,
While from its rocky caverns the deep-voiced, neighboring ocean
Speaks, and in accents disconsolate answers the wail of the forest.

Chapter Nine

DONALD GRANT MITCHELL (IK MARVEL)
(1822–1908)

While women were writing what later scholars would term "sentimental fiction" (stories that encouraged virtue through empathy) by the bucketful throughout the nineteenth century, certain male writers were also writing fiction focused on touching and changing the heart. No male writer had greater success in this vein than Donald Grant Mitchell, who often wrote under the pen name Ik Marvel.

In 1850, Mitchell published *Reveries of a Bachelor*, a story with the telling subtitle A *Book of the Heart*. Based on a short sketch that originally appeared in the *Southern Literary Messenger*, *Reveries of a Bachelor* would sell more than a million copies by the end of the century. Both male and female readers flocked to the book and its musings on the complicated and conflicted nature of bachelorhood.

Mitchell himself had just crossed the threshold into marital bliss in 1850, almost certainly providing him insights as he wrote his extended rumination on American men and marriage. *Reveries of a Bachelor* presents different angles on the struggle over the choice to marry: either a man will subject himself to the domesticating and wholesome influences of a wife, or he will not.

This simplicity of options, however, belies the complexity of intriguing subtexts found throughout the work. Mitchell's *Reveries* is full of dangers. While the married state poses its own threats to independence and individuality, the harmful influences outside marriage are just as real and imminent. The dangers have both personal and national implications. The bachelor risks far more than simply living a life of regret if he does not marry. To refuse to marry is to hobble the family, the foundational social unit of American life, as well as to open oneself up to the darker sides of sexuality, including everything from masturbation to consorting with prostitutes. Marriage becomes the normative state that will ensure both the health of the bachelor and the health of the nation as sexual drive is harnessed for the positive procreation of a still-young nation.

REVERIES OF A BACHELOR
OR, A BOOK OF THE HEART

It is worth the labor—saith Plotinus—to consider well of Love, whether it be a God, or a divell, or passion of the minde, or partly God, partly divell, partly passion.

BURTON'S ANATOMY[1]

Title page (New York: Baker and Scribner, ninth edition, 1851).

Donald Grant Mitchell, *Reveries of a Bachelor: or A Book of the Heart*, 9th edition. New York: Baker and Scribner, 1851.

1 Robert Burton (1577–1640), *Anatomy of Melancholy* (1621), Part III, i.

Preface

THIS book is neither more, nor less than it pretends to be; it is a collection of those floating Reveries which have, from time to time, drifted across my brain. I never yet met with a bachelor who had not his share of just such floating visions; and the only difference between us lies in the fact, that I have tossed them from me in the shape of a Book.

If they had been worked over with more unity of design, I dare say I might have made a respectable novel; as it is, I have chosen the honester way of setting them down as they came seething from my thought, with all their crudities and contrasts, uncovered

As for the truth that is in them, the world may believe what it likes; for having written to humor the world, it would be hard, if I should curtail any of its privileges of judgment. I should think there was as much truth in them, as in most Reveries.

The first story of the book has already had some publicity; and the criticisms upon it. have amused, and pleased me. One honest journalist avows that it could never have been written by a bachelor. I thank him for thinking so well of me; and heartily wish that his thought were as true, as it is kind.

Yet I am inclined to think that bachelors are the only safe, and secure observers of all the phases of married life. The rest of the world have their hobbies; and by law, as well as by immemorial custom are reckoned unfair witnesses in everything relating to their matrimonial affairs.

Perhaps I ought however to make an exception in favor of spinsters, who like us, are independent spectators, and possess just that kind of indifference to the marital state, which makes them intrepid in their observations, and very desirable for—authorities.

As for the style of the book, I have nothing to say for it, except to refer to my title. These are not sermons, nor essays, nor criticisms;—they are only Reveries. And if the reader should stumble upon occasional magniloquence, or be worried with a little too much of sentiment, pray, let him remember,—that I am dreaming.

But while I say this, in the hope of nicking off the wiry edge of my reader's judgment, I shall yet stand up boldly for the general tone, and character of the book. If there is bad feeling in it, or insincerity, or shallow sentiment, or any foolish depth of affection betrayed,—I am responsible; and the critics may expose it to their hearts' content.

I have moreover a kindly feeling for these Reveries, from their very private character; they consist mainly of just such whimseys, and reflections, as a great many brother bachelors are apt to indulge in, but which they are too cautious, or too prudent to lay before the world. As I have in this matter, shown a frankness, and *naiveté* which are unusual, I shall ask a corresponding frankness in my reader; and I can assure him safely that this is eminently one of those books which were 'never intended for publication.'

In the hope that this plain avowal may quicken the reader's charity, and screen me from cruel judgment,

I remain, with sincere good wishes,
Ik Marvel
New York, Nov., 1850.

First Reverie

Smoke, Flame and Ashes

Over a Wood Fire

I have got a quiet farmhouse in the country; a very humble place to be sure, tenanted by a worthy enough man, of the old New-England stamp, where I sometimes go for a day or two in the winter, to look over the farm-accounts, and to see how the stock is thriving on the winter's keep.

One side the door, as you enter from the porch, is a little parlor, scarce twelve feet by ten, with a cosy looking fire-place—a heavy oak floor—a couple of arm chairs and a brown table with carved lions' feet Out of this room opens a little cabinet, only big enough for a broad bachelor bedstead, where I sleep upon feathers, and wake in the morning, with my eye upon a saucy colored, lithographic print[2] of some fancy "Bessy."

It happens to he the only house in the world, of which I am *bona-fide*[3] owner; and I take a vast deal of comfort in treating it just as I choose. I manage to break some article of furniture, almost every time I pay it a visit; and if I cannot open the window readily of a morning, to breathe the fresh air, I knock out a pane or two of glass with my boot. I lean against the walls in a very old arm-chair there is on the promises, and scarce ever fail to worry such a hole in the plastering, as would set me down for a round charge for damages in town, or make a prim housewife fret herself into a raging fever. I laugh out loud with myself, in my big arm-chair, when I think that I am neither afraid of one, nor the other.

As for the fire, I keep the little hearth so hot, as to warm half the cellar below, and the whole space between the jams, roars for hours together, with white flame. To be sure, the windows are not very tight, between broken panes, and bad joints, so that the fire, large as it is, is by no means an extravagant comfort.

As night approaches, I have a huge pile of oak and hickory placed beside the hearth; I put out the tallow candle on the mantel, (using the family snuffers, with one log broke,)—then, drawing my chair directly in front of the blazing wood, and setting one foot on each of the old iron fire-dogs, (until they grow too warm,) I dispose myself for an evening of such sober, and thoughtful quietude, as I believe, on my soul, that very few of my fellow-men have the good fortune to enjoy.

My tenant meantime, in the other room, I can hear now and then,—though there is a thick stone chimney, and broad entry between,—multiplying contrivances with his wife, to put two babies to sleep. This occupies them, I should say, usually an hour; though my only measure of time, (for I never carry a watch into the country,) is the blaze of my fire. By ten, or thereabouts, my stock of wood is nearly exhausted; I pile upon the hot coals what remains, and sit watching how it kindles, and blazes, and goes out,—even like our joys!—and then, slip by the light of the embers into my bed, where I luxuriate in such sound, and healthful slumber, as only such rattling window frames, and country air, can supply.

But to return: the other evening—it happened to be on my last visit to my farm-house— when I had exhausted all the ordinary rural topics of thought, had formed all sorts of

---

2   Popular means of printing in the period, capable of making fine, often colored illustrations in both book and poster formats.
3   Genuine.

conjectures as to the income of the year; had planned a new wall around one lot, and the clearing up of another, now covered with patriarchal wood; and wondered if the little ricketty house would not be after all a snug enough box, to live and to die in—I fell on a sudden into such an unprecedented line of thought, which took such deep hold of my sympathies—sometimes even starting tears—that I determined, the next day, to set as much of it as I could recal, on paper.

Something—it may have been the home-looking blaze, (I am a bachelor of—say six and twenty,) or possibly a plaintive cry of the baby in my tenant's room, had suggested to me the thought of—Marriage.

I piled upon the heated fire-dogs, the last arm-full of my wood; and now, said I, bracing myself courageously between the arms of my chair,—I'll not flinch;—I'll pursue the thought wherever it leads, though it lead me to the d——(I am apt to be hasty,) —at least—continued I, softening,—until my fire is out.

The wood was green, and at first showed no disposition to blaze. It smoked furiously. Smoke, thought I, always goes before blaze; and so does doubt go before decision: and my Reverie, from that very starting point, slipped into this shape:—

I

Smoke—Signifying Doubt

A wife?—thought I;—yes, a wife!

And why?

And pray, my dear sir, why not—why? Why not doubt; why not hesitate; why not: tremble?

Does a man buy a ticket in a lottery—a poor man, whose whole earnings go in to secure the ticket,—without trembling, hesitating, and doubting?

Can a man stake his bachelor respectability, his independence, and comfort, upon the die of absorbing, unchanging, relentless marriage, without trembling at the venture?

Shall a man who has been free to chase his fancies over the wide-world, without lett[4] or hindrance, shut himself up to marriage-ship, within four walls called Home, that are to claim him, his time, his trouble, and his tears, thenceforward forever more, without doubts thick, and thick-coming as Smoke?

Shall he who has been hitherto a mere observer of other men's cares, and business—moving off where they made him sick of heart, approaching whenever and wherever they made him gleeful—shall he now undertake administration of just such cares and business, without qualms? Shall he, whose whole life has been but a nimble succession of escapes from trifling difficulties, now broach without doubtings—that Matrimony, where if difficulty beset him, there is no escape? Shall this brain of mine, careless-working, never tired with idleness, feeding on long vagaries, and high, gigantic castles, dreaming out beatitudes hour by hour—turn itself at length to such dull task-work, as thinking out a livelihood for wife and children?

Where thenceforward will be those sunny dreams, in which I have warmed my fancies, and my heart, and lighted my eye with crystal? This very marriage, which a brilliant working imagination has invested time and again with brightness, and delight, can serve no

---

4 Obstruction.

longer as a mine for teeming fancy: all, alas, will be gone —reduced to the dull standard of the actual! No more room for intrepid forays of imagination—no more gorgeous realm-making—all will be over!

Why not, I thought, go on dreaming?

Can any wife be prettier than an after dinner fancy, idle and yet vivid, can paint for you? Can any children make less noise, than the little rosy-cheeked ones, who have no existence, except in the *omnium gatherum*[5] of your own brain? Can any housewife be more unexceptionable, than she who goes sweeping daintily the cobwebs that gather in your dreams? Can any domestic larder be better stocked, than the private larder of your head dozing on a cushioned chair-back at Delmonico's? Can any family purse be better filled than the exceeding plump one, you dream of, after reading such pleasant books as Munchausen, or Typee?

But if, after all, it must be—duty, or what-not, making provocation—what then? And I clapped my feet hard against the fire-dogs, and leaned back, and turned my face to the ceiling, as much as to say; —And where on earth, then, shall a poor devil look for a wife?

Somebody says, Lyttleton[6] or Shaftesbury[7] I think, that "marriages would be happier if they were all arranged by the Lord Chancellor." Unfortunately, we have no Lord Chancellor to make this commutation of our misery.

Shall a man then scour the country on a mule's back, like Honest Gil Blas[8] of Santillane; or shall he make application to some such intervening providence as Madame St. Mare, who, as I see by the Presse, manages these matters to one's hand, for some five per cent. on the fortunes of the parties?

I have trouted, when the brook was so low, and the sky so hot, that I might as well have thrown my fly upon the turnpike; and I have hunted hare at noon, and wood-cock in snow-time,—never despairing, scarce doubting; but for a poor hunter of his kind, without traps or snares, or any aid of police or constabulary, to traverse the world, where are swarming, on a moderate computation, some three hundred and odd millions of unmarried women, for a single capture—irremediable, unchangeable—and yet a capture which by strange metonymy, not laid down in the books, is very apt to turn captor into captive, and make game of hunter—all this, surely, surely may make a man shrug with doubt!

Then—again,—there are the plaguey wife's-relations. Who knows how many third, fourth, or fifth cousins, will appear at careless complimentary intervals, long after you had settled into the placid belief that all congratulatory visits were at an end? How many twisted headed brothers will be putting in their advice, as a friend to Peggy?

How many maiden aunts will come to spend a month or two with their "dear Peggy," and want to know every tea-time, "if she isn't a dear love of a wife?" Then, dear father-in-law, will beg, (taking dear Peggy's hand in his,) to give a little wholesome counsel; and will be very sure to advise just the contrary of what you had determined to undertake. And dear mamma-in-law, must set her nose into Peggy's cupboard, and insist upon having the key to your own private locker in the wainscot.

Then, perhaps, there is a little bevy of dirty-nosed nephews who come to spend the holydays, and eat up your East India sweetmeats; and who are forever tramping over your

---

5 A gathering of all sorts.

6 Thomas Littleton (1422–1481) wrote the first important English legal text.

7 Anthony Ashley Cooper Shaftesbury (1671–1713) was a famous English politician and philosopher, who wrote extensively on the moral nature of humanity.

8 The roving, adventuresome young hero of a novel by the same name written by the French author Alain-René Lesage (1668–1747).

head, or raising the Old Harry below, while you are busy with your clients. Last, and worst, is some fidgety old uncle, forever too cold or too hot, who vexes you with his patronizing airs, and impudently kisses his little Peggy!

——That could be borne, however: for perhaps he has promised his fortune to Peggy. Peggy, then, will be rich:—(and the thought made me rub my shins, which were now getting comfortably warm upon the fire-dogs.) Then, she will be forever talking of *her* fortune; and pleasantly reminding you on occasion of a favorite purchase,—how lucky that *she* had the means; and dropping hints about economy; and buying very extravagant Paisleys.[9]

She will annoy you by looking over the stock-list at breakfast time; and mention quite carelessly to your clients, that she is interested in *such*, or such a speculation.

She will be provokingly silent when you hint to a tradesman, that you have not the money by you, for his small bill;—in short, she will tear the life out of you, making you pay in righteous retribution of annoyance, grief, vexation, shame, and sickness of heart, for the superlative folly of "marrying rich."

——But if not rich, then poor. Bah! the thought made me stir the coals; but there was still no blaze. The paltry earnings you are able to wring out of clients by the sweat of your brow, will now be all *our* income; you will be pestered for pin-money, and pestered with your poor wife's-relations. Ten to one, she will stickle about taste—"Sir Visto's"—and want to make this so pretty, and that so charming, if she *only* had the means; and is sure Paul (a kiss) can't deny his little Peggy such a trifling sum, and all for the common benefit.

Then she, for one, means that *her* children shan't go a begging for clothes,—and another pull at the purse. Trust a poor mother to dress her children in finery!

Perhaps she is ugly;—not noticeable at first; but growing on her, and (what is worse) growing faster on you. You wonder why you did'nt see that vulgar nose long ago: and that lip—it is very strange, you think, that you ever thought it pretty. And then,—to come to breakfast, with her hair looking as it does, and you, not so much as daring to say— "Peggy, *do* brush your hair!" Her foot too—not very bad when decently *chaussée*[10]—but now since she's married, she does wear such infernal slippers! And yet for all this, to be prigging up for an hour, when any of my old chums come to dine with me!

"Bless your kind hearts! my dear fellows," said I, thrusting the tongs into the coals, and speaking out loud, as if my voice could reach from Virginia to Paris— "not married yet!"

Perhaps Peggy is pretty enough—only shrewish.

——No matter for cold coffee;—you should have been up before.

What sad, thin, poorly cooked chops, to eat with your rolls!

——She thinks they are very good, and wonders how you can set such an example to your children.

The butter is nauseating.

——She has no other, and hopes you'll not raise a storm about butter a little turned.—I think I see myself—ruminated I—sitting meekly at table, scarce daring to lift up my eyes, utterly fagged out with some quarrel of yesterday, choking down detestably sour muffins, that my wife thinks are "delicious"—slipping in dried mouthfuls of burnt ham off the side of my fork tines,—slipping off my chair side-ways at the end, and slipping out with my hat between my knees, to business, and never feeling myself a competent, sound-minded man, till the oak door is between me and Peggy!

---

9 Shawls with curving designs.
10 Adorned.

——"Ha, ha,—not yet!" said I; and in so earnest a tone, that my dog started to his feet—cocked his eye to have a good look into my face—met my smile of triumph with an amiable wag of the tail, and curled up again in the corner.

Again, Peggy is rich enough, well enough, mild enough, only she doesn't care a fig for you. She has married you because father, or grandfather thought the match eligible, and because she didn't wish to disoblige them. Besides, she didn't positively hate you, and thought you were a respectable enough person;—she has told you so repeatedly at dinner. She wonders you like to read poetry; she wishes you would buy her a good cook-book; and insists upon your making your will at the birth of the first baby.

She thinks Captain So-and-So a splendid looking fellow, and wishes you would trim up a little, were it only for appearance' sake.

You need not hurry up from the office so early at night:—she, bless her dear heart!—does not feel lonely. You read to her a love tale; she interrupts the pathetic parts with directions to her seamstress. You read of marriages: she sighs, and asks if Captain So and So has left town? She hates to be mewed up in a cottage, or between brick walls; she does *so* love the Springs!

But, again, Peggy loves you;—at least she swears it, with her hand on the Sorrows of Werter.[11] She has pin-money which she spends for the Literary World, and the Friends in Council. She is not bad-looking, save a bit too much of forehead; nor is she sluttish, unless a *negligé* till three o'clock, and an ink stain on the fore finger be sluttish;—but then she is such a sad blue!

You never fancied when you saw her buried in a three volume novel, that it was anything more than a girlish vagary; and when she quoted Latin, you thought innocently, that she had a capital memory for her samplers.

But to be bored eternally about Divine Danté[12] and funny Goldoni,[13] is too bad. Your copy of Tasso,[14] a treasure print of 1680, is all bethumbed and dogs-eared, and spotted with baby gruel. Even your Seneca[15]—an Elzevir[16]—is all sweaty with handling. She adores La Fontaine,[17] reads Balzac[18] with a kind of artist-scowl, and will not let Greek alone.

You hint at broken rest and an aching head at breakfast, and she will fling you a scrap of Anthology —in lieu of the camphor bottle—or chant the αἰαῖ αἰαῖ, of tragic chorus.[19]

——The nurse is getting dinner; you are holding the baby; Peggy is reading Bruyère.[20]

---

11 *The Sorrows of Young Werther* is a novel of unrequited love by Johann Wolfgang von Goethe (1792–1854).

12 Dante Alighieri (1265–1321) was a renowned Italian poet, writer, and moral philosopher. His most famous work is the *Divine Comedy*.

13 Carlo Goldoni (1707–1793) was an Italian dramatist famous for his comedies.

14 Torquato Tasso (1544–1595) was an Italian poet most famous for his epic poem, *Jerusalem Liberated*, which dealt with the Christian capture of Jerusalem during the First Crusade.

15 Lucius Annaeus Seneca (4 BCE–65 CE) was a leading Roman philosopher and statesman.

16 Famous Dutch publishing family (1587–1681) best known for its editions of Greek and Roman classics.

17 Jean de La Fontaine (1621–1695) was a master French poet.

18 Honoré de Balzac (1799–1850) was a French writer considered by many to be one of the greatest writers of all time.

19 Common phrase of lament in Greek tragedies.

20 Jean de La Bruyère (1645–1696) was a French writer of satires.

The fire smoked thick as pitch, and puffed out little clouds over the chimney piece. I gave the fore-stick a kick, at thought of Peggy, baby, and Bruyère.

——Suddenly the flame flickered bluely athwart the smoke—caught at a twig below—rolled round the mossy oak-stick—twined among the crackling tree-limbs—mounted—lit up the whole body of smoke, and blazed out cheerily and bright. Doubt vanished with Smoke, and Hope began with Flame.

II

Blaze—Signifying Cheer

I pushed my chair back; drew up another stretched out my feet cosily upon it, rested my elbows on the chair arms, leaned my head on one hand and looked straight into the leaping, and dancing flame.

——Love is a flame—ruminated I; and (glancing round the room) how a flame brightens up a man's habitation.

"Carlo," said I, calling up my dog into the light, "good fellow, Carlo!" and I patted him kindly, and he wagged his tail, and laid his nose across my knee, and looked wistfully up in my face; then strode away,—turned to look again, and lay down to sleep.

"Pho, the brute!" said I, "it is not enough after all, to like a dog."

——If now in that chair yonder, not the one your feet lie upon, but the other, beside you—closer yet—were seated a sweet-faced girl, with a pretty little foot lying out upon the hearth—a bit of lace running round the swelling throat—the hair parted to a charm over a forehead fair as any of your dreams;—and if you could reach an arm around that chair back, without fear of giving offence, and suffer your fingers to play idly with those curls that escape down the neck; and if you could clasp with your other hand those little white, taper fingers of hers, which lie so temptingly within reach,—and so, talk softly and low in presence of the blaze, while the hours slip without knowledge, and the winter winds whistle uncared for;—if, in short, you were no bachelor, but the husband of some such sweet image—(dream, call it rather,) would it not be far pleasanter than this cold single night-sitting—counting the sticks—reckoning the length of the blaze, and the height of the falling snow?

And if, some or all of those wild vagaries that grow on your fancy at such an hour, you could whisper into listening, because loving ears—ears not tired with listening, because it is you who whisper—ears ever indulgent because eager to praise;—and if your darkest fancies were lit up, not merely with bright wood fire, but with a ringing laugh of that sweet face turned up in fond rebuke—how far better, than to be waxing black, and sour, over pestilential humors—alone—your very dog asleep!

And if when a glowing thought comes into your brain, quick and sudden, you could tell it over as to a second self, to that sweet creature, who is not away, because she loves to be there; and if you could watch the thought catching that girlish mind, illuming that fair brow, sparkling in those pleasantest of eyes—how far better than to feel it slumbering, and going out, heavy, lifeless, and dead, in your own selfish fancy. And if a generous emotion steals over you—coming, you know not whither, would there not be a richer charm in lavishing it in caress, or endearing word, upon that fondest, and most dear one, than in patting your glossy coated dog, or sinking lonely to smiling slumbers?

How would not benevolence ripen with such monitor to task it! How would not selfishness grow faint and dull, leaning ever to that second self, which is the loved one! How would not guile shiver, and grow weak, before that girl-brow, and eye of innocence How would not all that boyhood prized of enthusiasm, and quick blood, and life, renew itself in such presence!

The fire was getting hotter, and I moved into the middle of the room. The shadows the flames made, were playing like fairy forms over floor, and wall, and ceiling.

My fancy would surely quicken, thought I, if such being were in attendance. Surely, imagination would be stronger, and purer, if it could have the playful fancies of dawning womanhood to delight it. All toil would be torn from mind-labor, if but another heart grew into this present soul, quickening it, warming it, cheering it, bidding it ever,—God speed!

Her face would make a halo, rich as a rainbow, atop of all such noisome things, as we lonely souls call trouble. Her smile would illumine the blackest of crowding cares; and darkness that now seats you despondent, in your solitary chair for days together, weaving bitter fancies, dreaming bitter dreams, would grow light and thin, and spread, and float away,—chased by that beloved smile.

Your friend—poor fellow!—dies:—never mind, that gentle clasp of *her* fingers, as she steals behind you, telling you not to weep—it is worth ten friends!

Your sister, sweet one, is dead—buried. The worms are busy with all her fairness. How it makes you think earth nothing but a spot to dig graves upon!

——It is more: *she*, she says, will be a sister; and the waving curls as she leans upon your shoulder, touch your cheek, and your wet eye turns to meet those other eyes—God has sent his angel, surely!

Your mother, alas for it, she is gone! Is there any bitterness to a youth, alone and home-less, like this?

But you are not homeless; you are not alone: *she* is there;—her tears softening yours, her smile lighting yours, her grief killing yours; and you live again, to assuage that kind sorrow of hers.

Then—those children, rosy, fair-haired; no, they do not disturb you with their prattle now—they are yours! Toss away there on the green-sward—never mind the hyacinths, the snowdrops, the violets, if so be any are there; the perfume of their healthful lips is worth all the flowers of the world. No need now to gather wild bouquets to love, and cherish: flower, tree, gun, are all dead things; things livelier hold your soul.

And she, the mother, sweetest and fairest of all, watching, tending, caressing, loving, till your own heart grows pained with tenderest jealousy, and cures itself with loving.

You have no need now of any cold lecture to teach thankfulness: your heart is full of it. No need now, as once, of bursting blossoms, of trees taking leaf, and greenness, to turn thought kindly, and thankfully; for ever, beside you, there is bloom, and ever beside you there is fruit,—for which eye, heart, and soul are full of unknown, and unspoken, because unspeakable, thank-offering.

And if sickness catches you, binds you, lays you down—no lonely moanings, and wicked curses at careless stepping nurses. *The* step is noiseless, and yet distinct beside you. The white curtains are drawn, or withdrawn by the magic of that other presence; and the soft, cool hand is upon your brow.

No cold comfortings of friend-watchers, merely come in to steal a word away from that outer world which is pulling at their skirts; but, ever, the sad, shaded brow of her, whose lightest sorrow for your sake is your greatest grief,—if it were not a greater joy.

The blaze was leaping light and high, and the wood falling under the growing heat.

——So, continued I, this heart would be at length itself;—striving with every thing gross, even now as it clings to grossness. Love would make its strength native and progressive. Earth's cares would fly. Joys would double. Susceptibilities be quickened; Love master self; and having made the mastery, stretch onward, and upward toward Infinitude.

And, if the end came, and sickness brought that follower—Great Follower—which sooner or later is sure to come after, then the heart, and the hand of Love, ever near, are giving to your tired soul, daily and hourly, lessons of that love which consoles, which triumphs, which circleth all, and centereth in all—Love Infinite, and Divine!

Kind hands—none but *hers*—will smooth the hair upon your brow as the chill grows damp, and heavy on it; and her fingers—none but hers—will lie in yours as the wasted flesh stiffens, and hardens for the ground. *Her* tears,—you could feel no others, if oceans fell—will warm your drooping features once more to life; once more your eye lighted in joyous triumph, kindle in her smile, and then—

The fire fell upon the hearth; the blaze gave a last leap—a flicker—then another—caught a little remaining twig—blazed up—wavered—went out.

There was nothing but a bed of glowing embers, over which the white ashes gathered fast. I was alone, with only my dog for company.

III

Ashes—Signifying Desolation

After all, thought I, ashes follow blaze, inevitably as Death follows Life. Misery treads on the heels of Joy; Anguish rides swift after Pleasure.

"Come to me again, Carlo," said I, to my dog; and I patted him fondly once more, but now only by the light of the dying embers.

It is very little pleasure one takes in fondling brute favorites; but it is a pleasure that when it passes, leaves no void. It is only a little alleviating redundance in your solitary heart-life, which if lost, another can be supplied.

But if your heart, not solitary—not quieting its humors with mere love of chase, or dog—not repressing year after year, its earnest yearnings after something better, and more spiritual,—has fairly linked itself by bonds strong as life, to another heart—is the casting off easy, then?

Is it then only a little heart-redundancy cut off, which the next bright sunset will fill up?

And my fancy, as it had painted doubt under the smoke, and cheer under warmth of the blaze, so now it began under the faint light of the smouldering embers, to picture heart-desolation.

—What kind congratulatory letters, hosts of them, coming from old and half-forgotten friends, now that your happiness is a year, or two years old!

"Beautiful."

——Aye, to be sure beautiful!

"Rich."

——Pho, the dawdler! how little he knows of heart-treasure, who speaks of wealth to a man who loves his wife, as a wife should only be loved!

"Young."

——Young indeed; guileless as infancy; charming as the morning.

Ah, these letters bear a sting: they bring to mind, with new, and newer freshness, if it be possible, the value of that, which you tremble lest you lose.

How anxiously you watch that step—if it lose not its buoyancy; How you study the colour on that cheek, if it grow not fainter; How you tremble at the lustre in those eyes, if it be not the lustre of Death; How you totter under the weight of that muslin sleeve—a phantom weight! How you fear to do it, and yet press forward, to note if that breathing be quickened, as you ascend the home-heights, to look off on sunset lighting the plain.

Is your sleep, quiet sleep, after that she has whispered to you her fears, and in the same breath—soft as a sigh, sharp as an arrow—bid you bear it bravely?

Perhaps,—the embers were now glowing fresher, a little kindling, before the ashes—she triumphs over disease.

But, Poverty, the world's almoner, has come to you with ready, spare hand.

Alone, with your dog living on bones, and you, on hope—kindling each morning, dying slowly each night,—this could be borne. Philosophy would bring home its stores to the lone-man. Money is not in his hand, but Knowledge is in his brain! and from that brain he draws out faster, as he draws slower from his pocket. He remembers: and on remembrance he can live for days, and weeks. The garret, if a garret covers him, is rich in fancies. The rain if it pelts, pelts only him used to rain-peltings. And his dog crouches not in dread, but in companionship. His crust he divides with him, and laughs. He crowns himself with glorious memories of Cervantes,[21] though he begs: if he nights it under the stars, he dreams heaven-sent dreams of the prisoned, and homeless Gallileo.[22]

He hums old sonnets, and snatches of poor Jonson's[23] plays. He chants Dryden's[24] odes, and dwells on Otway's rhyme. He reasons with Bolingbroke[25] or Diogenes,[26] as the humor takes him; and laughs at the world: for the world, thank Heaven, has left him alone!

Keep your money, old misers, and your palaces, old princes,—the world is mine!

> I care not, Fortune, what you me deny,—
> You cannot rob me of free nature's grace,
>   You cannot shut the windows of the sky;
> You cannot bar my constant feet to trace
>   The woods and lawns, by living streams, at eve,
> Let health, my nerves and finer fibres brace,
>   And I, their toys, to the great children, leave,
> Of Fancy, Reason, Virtue, naught can me bereave!

---

21 Miguel de Cervantes Saavedra (1547–1616) stands as one of Spain's most famous novelists, his crowning work being *Don Quixote.*

22 Galileo (1564–1642) was an Italian astronomer imprisoned for his scientific challenges to religious orthodoxy.

23 Ben Jonson (1572–1637) was a famous English dramatist and poet.

24 John Dryden (1631–1700) was an English poet and playwright who enjoyed immense fame in his day.

25 Henry St. John Bolingbroke (1678–1751), first viscount, was an English statesman and philosopher.

26 Diogenes (412?–323 BCE) was an ancient Greek figure famous for his advocacy of self-sufficiency and rejection of luxury.

But—if not alone?

If *she* is clinging to you for support, for consolation, for home, for life—she, reared in luxury perhaps, is faint for bread?

Then, the iron enters the soul; then the nights darken under any sky light. Then the days grow long, even in the solstice of winter.

She may not complain; what then?

Will your heart grow strong, if the strength of her love can dam up the fountains of tears, and the tied tongue not tell of bereavement? Will it solace you to find her parting the poor treasure of food you have stolen for her, with begging, foodless children?

But this ill, strong hands, and Heaven's help, will put down. Wealth again; Flowers again; Patrimonial acres again; Brightness again. But your little Bessy, your favorite child is pining.

Would to God! you say in agony, that wealth could bring fulness again into that blanched cheek, or round those little thin lips once more; but it cannot. Thinner and thinner they grow; plaintive and more plaintive her sweet voice.

"Dear Bessy"—and your tones tremble; you feel that she is on the edge of the grave. Can you pluck her back? Can endearments stay her? Business is heavy, away from the loved child; home, you go, to fondle while yet time is left—but *this* time you are too late. She is gone. She cannot hear you: she cannot thank you for the violets you put within her stiff white hand.

And then—the grassy mound—the cold shadow of head-stone!

The wind, growing with the night, is rattling at the window panes, and whistles dismally. I wipe a tear, and in the interval of my Reverie, thank God, that I am no such mourner.

But gaiety, snail-footed, creeps back to the household. All is bright again;

——the violet bed's not sweeter
Than the delicious breath marriage sends forth.

Her lip is rich and full; her cheek delicate as a flower. Her frailty doubles your love.

And the little one she clasps—frail too—too frail; the boy you had set your hopes and heart on. You have watched him growing, ever prettier, ever winning more and more upon your soul. The love you bore to him when he first lisped names—your name and hers—has doubled in strength now that he asks innocently to be taught of this, or that, and promises you by that quick curiosity that flashes in his eye, a mind full of intelligence.

And some hair-breadth escape by sea, or flood, that he perhaps may have had—which unstrung your soul to such tears, as you pray God may be spared you again—has endeared the little fellow to your heart, a thousand fold.

And, now with his pale sister in the grave, all *that* love has come away from the mound, where worms feast, and centers on the boy.

How you watch the storms lest they harm him! How often you steal to his bed late at night, and lay your hand lightly upon the brow, where the curls cluster thick, rising and falling with the throbbing temples, and watch, for minutes together, the little lips half parted, and listen—your ear close to them—if the breathing be regular and sweet!

But the day comes—the night rather—when you can catch no breathing.

Aye, put your hair away,—compose yourself—listen again.

No, there is nothing!

Put your hand now to his brow,—damp indeed—but not with healthful night-sleep; it is not your hand, no, do not deceive yourself—it is your loved boy's forehead that is so cold; and your loved boy will never speak to you again—never play again—he is dead!

Oh, the tears—the tears; what blessed things are tears! Never fear now to let them fall on his forehead, or his lip, lest you waken him!—Clasp him—clasp him harder—you cannot hurt, you cannot waken him! Lay him down, gently or not, it is the same; he is stiff; he is stark and cold.

But courage is elastic; it is our pride. It recovers itself easier, thought I, than these embers will get into blaze again.

But courage, and patience, and faith, and hope have their limit. Blessed be the man who escapes such trial as will determine limit!

To a lone man it comes not near; for how can trial take hold where there is nothing by which to try?

A funeral? You reason with philosophy. A grave yard? You read Hervey[27] and muse upon the wall. A friend dies? You sigh, you pat your dog,—it is over. Losses? You retrench— you light your pipe—it is forgotten. Calumny? You laugh—you sleep.

But with that childless wife clinging to you in love and sorrow—what then?

Can you take down Seneca now, and coolly blow the dust from the leaf-tops? Can you crimp your lip with Voltaire?[28] Can you smoke idly, your feet dangling with the ivies, your thoughts all waving fancies upon a church-yard wall—a wall that borders the grave of your boy?

Can you amuse yourself by turning stinging Martial[29] into rhyme? Can you pat your dog, and seeing him wakeful and kind, say, "it is enough?" Can you sneer at calumny, and sit by your fire dozing?

Blessed, thought I again, is the man who escapes such trial as will measure the limit of patience and the limit of courage!

But the trial comes:—colder and colder were growing the embers.

That wife, over whom your love broods, is fading. Not beauty fading;—that, now that your heart is wrapped in her being, would be nothing.

She sees with quick eye your dawning apprehension, and she tries hard to make that step of hers elastic.

Your trials and your loves together have centered your affections. They are not now as when you were a lone man, wide spread and superficial. They have caught from domestic attachments a finer tone and touch. They cannot shoot out tendrils into barren world-soil and suck up thence strengthening nutriment. They have grown under the forcing-glass of home-roof, they will not now bear exposure.

You do not now look men in the face as if a heart-bond was linking you—as if a community of feeling lay between. There is a heart-bond that absorbs all others; there is a community that monopolizes your feeling. When the heart lay wide open, before it had grown upon, and closed around particular objects, it could take strength and cheer, from a hundred connections that now seem colder than ice

---

27 James Hervey (1714–1758) was an Anglican clergyman in England who wrote the popular *Meditations among the Tombs* (1746).

28 Voltaire (1694–1778) was a French satirist who wrote biting commentaries on a wide range of social and religious issues.

29 Martial (38?–103) was a Roman poet most famous for his Latin epigrams.

And now those particular objects—alas for you!—are failing.

What anxiety pursues you! How you struggle to fancy—there is no danger; how she struggles to persuade you—there is no danger!

How it grates now on your ear—the toil and turmoil of the city! It was music when you were alone; it was pleasant even, when from the din you were elaborating comforts for the cherished objects;—when you had such sweet escape as evening drew on.

Now it maddens you to see the world careless while you are steeped in care. They hustle you in the street; they smile at you across the table; they bow carelessly over the way; they do not know what canker is at your heart.

The undertaker comes with his bill for the dead boy's funeral. He knows your grief; he is respectful. You bless him in your soul. You wish the laughing street-goers were all undertakers.

Your eye follows the physician as he leaves your house: is he wise, you ask yourself; is he prudent? is he the best? Did he never fail—is he never forgetful?

And now the hand that touches yours, is it no thinner—no whiter than yesterday? Sunny days come when she revives; colour comes back; she breathes freer; she picks flowers; she meets you with a smile: hope lives again.

But the next day of storm she is fallen. She cannot talk even; she presses your hand.

You hurry away from business before your time. What matter for clients—who is to reap the rewards? What matter for fame—whose eye will it brighten? What matter for riches—whose is the inheritance?

You find her propped with pillows; she is looking over a little picture-book bethumbed by the dear boy she has lost. She hides it in her chair; she has pity on you.

——Another day of revival, when the spring sun shines, and flowers open out of doors; she leans on your arm, and strolls into the garden where the first birds are singing. Listen to them with her;—what memories are in bird-songs! You need not shudder at her tears—they are tears of Thanksgiving. Press the hand that lies light upon your arm, and you, too, thank God, while yet you may!

You are early home—mid-afternoon. Your step is not light; it is heavy, terrible.

They have sent for you.

She is lying down; her eyes half closed; her breathing long and interrupted.

She hears you; her eye opens; you put your hand in hers; yours trembles;—hers does not. Her lips move; it is your name.

"Be strong", she says, "God will help you!'

She presses harder your hand:— "Adieu!"

A long breath—another;—you are alone again. No tears now; poor man! You cannot find them!

——Again home early. There is a smell of varnish in your house. A coffin is there; they have clothed the body in decent grave clothes, and the undertaker is screwing down the lid, slipping round on tip-toe. Does he fear to waken her?

He asks you a simple question about the inscription upon the plate, rubbing it with his coat cuff. You look him straight in the eye; you motion to the door; you dare not speak.

He takes up his hat and glides out stealthful as a cat.

The man has done his work well for all. It is a nice coffin—a very nice coffin! Pass your hand over it—how smooth!

Some sprigs of mignionette are lying carelessly in a little gilt-edged saucer. She loved mignionette.

It is a good staunch table the coffin rests on;—it is your table; you are a housekeeper—a man of family!

Aye, of family!—keep clown outcry, or the nurse will be in. Look over at the pinched features; is this all that is left of her? And where is your heart now? No, don't thrust your nails into your hands, nor mangle your lip, nor grate your teeth together. If you could only weep!

——Another day. The coffin is gone out. The stupid mourners have wept—what idle tears! She, with your crushed heart, has gone out!

Will you have pleasant evenings at your home now.

Go into your parlor that your prim housekeeper has made comfortable with clean hearth and blaze of sticks.

Sit down in your chair; there is another velvet-cushioned one, over against yours—empty. You press your fingers on your eye-balls, as if you would press out something that hurt the brain; but you cannot. Your head leans upon your hand; your eyes rest upon the flashing blaze.

Ashes always come after blaze.

Go now into the room where she was sick—softly, lest the prim housekeeper come after. They have put new dimity upon her chair; they have hung new curtains over the bed. They have removed from the stand its phials, and silver bell; they have put a little vase of flowers in their place; the perfume will not offend the sick sense now. They have half opened the window, that the room so long closed may have air. It will not be too cold.

She is not there.

——Oh, God!—thou who dost temper the wind to the shorn lamb—be kind!

The embers were dark; I stirred them; there was no sign of life. My dog was asleep. The clock in my tenant's chamber had struck one.

I dashed a tear or two from my eyes;—how they came there I know not. I half ejaculated a prayer of thanks, that such desolation had not yet come nigh me; and a prayer of hope—that it might never come.

In a half hour more, I was sleeping soundly. My reverie was ended.

Second Reverie

Sea Coal and Anthracite[30]

By a City Grate

Blessed be letters!—they are the monitors, they are also the comforters, and they are the only true heart-talkers! Your speech and their speeches, are conventional; they are moulded by circumstance; they are suggested by the observation, remark, and influence of the parties to whom the speaking is addressed, or by whom it may be overheard.

Your truest thought is modified half through its utterance by a look, a sign, a smile, or a sneer. It is not individual; it is not integral: it is social and mixed,—half of you, and half of others. It bends, it sways, it multiplies, it retires, and it advances, as the talk of others presses, relaxes, or quickens.

But it is not so of Letters:—there you are, with only the soulless pen, and the snow-white, virgin paper. Your soul is measuring itself by itself, and saying its own sayings: there

---

30 A hard coal that burns cleanly.

are no sneers to modify its utterance,—no scowl to scare,—nothing is present, but you, and your thought.

Utter it then freely—write it down—stamp it—burn it in the ink!—There it is, a true soul-print!

Oh, the glory, the freedom, the passion of a letter! It is worth all the lip-talk in the world. Do you say, it is studied, made up, acted, rehearsed, contrived, artistic?

Let me see it then; let me run it over; tell me age, sex, circumstance, and I will tell you if it be studied or real;—if it be the merest lip-slang put into words, or heart-talk blazing on the paper.

I have a little pacquet, not very large, tied up with narrow crimson ribbon, now soiled with frequent handling, which far into some winter's night, I take down from its nook upon my shelf, and untie, and open, and run over, with such sorrow, and such joy,—such tears and such smiles, as I am sure make me for weeks after, a kinder, and holier man.

There are in this little pacquet, letters in the familiar hand of a mother—what gentle admonition;—what tender affection!—God have mercy on him who outlives the tears that such admonitions, and such affection call up to the eye! There are others in the budget, in the delicate, and unformed hand of a loved, and lost sister;—written when she, and you were full of glee, and the best mirth of youthfulness; does it harm you to recall that mirth-fulness? or to trace again, for the hundredth time, that scrawling postscript at the bottom, with its *i*'s so carefully dotted, and its gigantic *t*'s so carefully crossed, by the childish hand of a little brother?

I have added latterly to that pacquet of letters; I almost need a new and longer ribbon; the old one is getting too short. Not a few of these new, and cherished letters, a former Reverie[31] has brought to me; not letters of cold praise, saying it was well done, artfully executed, prettily imagined—no such thing: but letters of sympathy—of sympathy which means sympathy—the παθήμί and the συν.[32]

It would be cold, and dastardly work to copy them; I am too selfish for that. It is enough to say that they, the kind writers, have seen a heart in the Reverie—have felt that it was real, true. They know it; a secret influence has told it. What matters it pray, if literally, there was no wife, and no dead child, and no coffin in the house? Is not feeling, feeling; and heart, heart? Are not these fancies thronging on my brain, bringing tears to my eyes, bringing joy to my soul, as living, as anything human can be living? What if they have no mate-rial type—no objective form? All that is crude,—a mere reduction of ideality to sense,—a transformation of the spiritual to the earthy,—a leveling of soul to matter.

Are we not creatures of thought and passion? Is any thing about us more earnest than that same thought and passion? Is there any thing more real,—more characteristic of that great and dim destiny to which we are born, and which may be written down in that ter-rible word—Forever?

Let those who will then, sneer at what in their wisdom they call untruth—at what is false, because it has no material presence: this does not create falsity; would to Heaven that it did!

And yet, if there was actual, material truth superadded to Reverie, would such objec-tors sympathize the more? No!—a thousand times, no; the heart that has no sympathy with

---

31 [Author's Original Note] The first Reverie—Smoke, Flame, and Ashes, was published some
    months previous to this, in the *Southern Literary Messenger*.
32 The "suffering" and the "with."

thoughts and feelings that scorch the soul, is dead also—whatever its mocking tears, and gestures may say—to a coffin, or a grave!

Let them pass, and we will come back to these cherished letters.

A mother, who has lost a child, has, she says, shed a tear—not one, but many—over the dead boy's coldness. And another, who has not lost, but who trembles lest she lose, has found the words failing as she read, and a dim, sorrow-borne mist, spreading over the page.

Another, yet rejoicing in all those family ties, that make life a charm, has listened nervously to careful reading, until the husband is called home, and the coffin is in the house.— "Stop!"—she says; and a gush of tears tells the rest.

Yet the cold critic will say—"it was artfully done." A curse on him!—it was not art: it was nature.

Another, a young, fresh, healthful girl-mind, has seen something in the love-picture— albeit so weak—of truth; and has kindly believed that it must be earnest. Aye, indeed is it, fair, and generous one,—earnest as life and hope! Who indeed with a heart at all, that has not yet slipped away irreparably, and forever from the shores of youth—from that fairy land which young enthusiasm creates, and over which bright dreams hover—but knows it to be real? And so such things will be real, till hopes are dashed, and Death is come.

Another, a father, has laid down the book in tears.

——God bless them all! How far better this, than the cold praise of newspaper paragraphs, or the critically contrived approval of colder friends!

Let me gather up these letters, carefully,—to be read when the heart is faint, and sick of all that there is unreal, and selfish in the world. Let me tie them together, with a new, and longer bit of ribbon—not by a love knot, that is too hard—but by an easy slipping knot, that so I may get at them the better. And now, they are all together, a snug pacquet, and we will label them, not sentimentally, (I pity the one who thinks it!) but earnestly, and in the best meaning of the term—SOUVENIRES DU CŒUR.[33]

Thanks to my first Reverie, which has added to such a treasure!

——And now to my SECOND REVERIE.

I am no longer in the country. The fields, the trees, the brooks are far away from me, and yet they are very present. A letter from my tenant—how different from those other letters!—lies upon my table, telling me what fields he has broken up for the autumn grain, and how many beeves he is fattening, and how the potatoes are turning out.

But I am in a garret of the city. From my window I look over a mass of crowded housetops—moralizing often upon the scene, but in a strain too long, and sombre to be set down here. In place of the wide country chimney, with its iron five-dogs, is a snug grate, where the maid makes me a fire in the morning, and rekindles it in the afternoon.

I am usually fairly seated in my chair—a cozily stuffed office chair—by five or six o'clock of the evening. The fire has been newly made, perhaps an hour before: first, the maid drops a withe of paper in the bottom of the grate, then a stick or two of pine-wood, and after it a hod of Liverpool coal; so that by the time I am seated for the evening, the sea-coal is fairly in a blaze.

When this has sunk to a level with the second bar of the grate, the maid replenishes it with a hod of Anthracite; and I sit musing and reading, while the new coal warms and kindles—not leaving my place, until it has sunk to the third bar of the grate, which marks my bed-time.

---

33 Mementos of the heart.

I love these accidental measures of the hours, which belong to you, and your life, and not to the world. A watch is no more the measure of your time, than of the time of your neighbors; a church clock is as public, and vulgar as a church-warden. I would as soon think of hiring the parish sexton to make my bed, as to regulate my time by the parish clock.

A shadow that the sun casts upon your carpet, or a streak of light on a slated roof yonder, or the burning of your fire, are pleasant time-keepers,—full of presence, full of companionship, and full of the warning—time is passing!

In the summer season I have even measured my reading, and my night-watch, by the burning of a taper; and I have scratched upon the handle to the little bronze taper-holder, that meaning passage of the New Testament,—Νὺξ γαρ ερχεται—the night cometh!

But I must get upon my Reverie:—it was a drizzly evening; I had worked hard during the day, and had drawn my boots—thrust my feet into slippers—thrown on a Turkish loose dress, and Greek cap—souvenirs to me of other times, and other places—and sat watching the lively, uncertain, yellow play of the bituminous flame.

I

Sea-Coal

It is like a flirt—mused I;—lively, uncertain, bright-colored, waving here and there, melting the coal into black shapeless mass, making foul, sooty smoke, and pasty, trashy residuum! Yet withal,—pleasantly sparkling, dancing, prettily waving, and leaping like a roebuck from point to point.

How like a flirt! And yet is not this tossing caprice of girlhood, to which I liken my sea-coal flame, a native play of life, and belonging by nature to the play-time of life? Is it not a sort of essential fire-kindling to the weightier and truer passions—even as Jenny puts the soft coal first, the better to kindle the anthracite? Is it not a sort of necessary consumption of young vapors, which float in the soul, and which is left thereafter the purer? Is there not a stage somewhere in every man's youth, for just such waving, idle heart-blaze, which means nothing, yet which must be got over?

Lamartine[34] says somewhere, very prettily, that there is more of quick running sap, and floating shade in a young tree; but more of fire in the heart of a sturdy oak:—*Il y a plus de séve folle et d'ombre flottante dans les jeunes plants de la forêt; il y a plus de feu dans le vieux cœur du chêne.*

Is Lamartine playing off his prettiness of expression, dressing up with his poetry,—making a good conscience against the ghost of some accusing Graziella,[35] or is there truth in the matter?

A man who has seen sixty years, whether widower or bachelor, may well put such sentiment into words: it feeds his wasted heart with hope; it renews the exultation of youth by the pleasantest of equivocation, and the most charming of self-confidence. But after all, is it not true? Is not the heart like new blossoming field-plants, whose first flowers are half

---

34 Alphonse de Lamartine (1790–1869) was a French poet and statesman who played a key role in the French Romantic literary movement.

35 Graziella is a Lamartine character (in a story by the same name) based on a young working girl with whom Lamartine had fallen in love.

formed, one-sided perhaps, but by-and-by, in maturity of season, putting out wholesome, well-formed blossoms, that will hold their leaves long and bravely?

Bulwer[36] in his story of the Caxtons, has counted first heart-flights mere fancy-passages— a dalliance with the breezes of love—which pass, and leave healthful heart appetite. Half the reading world has read the story of Trevanion and Pisistratus.[37] But Bulwer is—past; his heart-life is used up—*épuisé*.[38] Such a man can very safely rant about the cool judgment of after years.

Where does Shakspeare put the unripe heart-age?—All of it before the ambition, that alone makes the hero-soul. The Shakspeare man 'sighs like a furnace,' before he stretches his arm to achieve the 'bauble, reputation.'

Yet Shakspeare has meted a soul-love, mature and ripe, without any young furnace sighs to Desdemona and Othello. Cordelia, the sweetest of his play creations, loves without any of the mawkish matter, which makes the whining love of a Juliet. And Florizel in the Winter's Tale, says to Perdita,[39] in the true spirit of a most sound heart—

> My desires
> Run not before mine honor, nor my wishes
> Burn hotter than my faith.

How is it with Hector and Andromache?[40]—no sea-coal blaze, but one that is constant, enduring, pervading: a pair of hearts full of esteem, and best love,—good, honest, and sound.

Look now at Adam and Eve, in God's presence, with Milton for showman. Shall we quote by this sparkling blaze, a gem from the Paradise Lost? We will hum it to ourselves— what Raphael sings to Adam—a classic song.

> ——Him, serve and fear!
> Of other creatures, as Him pleases best
> Wherever placed, let Him dispose; joy thou
> In what he gives to thee, this Paradise
> And thy fair Eve!

And again:

> ——Love refines
> The thoughts, and heart enlarges: hath his seat
> In reason, and is judicious: is the scale
> By which to Heavenly love thou mays't ascend!

---

36 Edward George Bulwer-Lytton (1803–1873) was a popular English novelist best known for his works of historical fiction.
37 Bulwer-Lytton's historical novels included such figures as Trevanion and Pisistratus. Pisistratus was a famous tyrant in ancient Greece.
38 Exhausted.
39 Desdemona, Othello, Cordelia, Juliet, Florizel and Perdita are all characters in Shakespeare's plays who represent different facets of familial and romantic love.
40 Hector is the Trojan hero most celebrated in Homer's *Iliad*. Hector was married to Andromache.

None of the playing sparkle in this love, which belongs to the flame of my sea-coal fire, that is now dancing, lively as a cricket. But on looking about my garret chamber, I can see nothing that resembles the archangel Raphael, or 'thy fair Eve.'

There is a degree of moisture about the sea-coal flame, which with the most earnest of my musing, I find it impossible to attach to that idea of a waving, sparkling heart which my fire suggests. A damp heart must be a foul thing to be sure! But whoever heard of one? Wordsworth[41] somewhere in the Excursion, says:—.

> The good die first,
> And they whose hearts are *dry* as summer dust
> Burn to the socket!

What, in the name of Rydal Mount,[42] is a dry heart? A dusty one, I can conceive of: a bachelor's heart must be somewhat dusty, as he nears the sixtieth summer of his pilgrimage;—and hung over with cobwebs, in which sit such watchful gray old spiders as Avarice, and Selfishness, forever on the look out for such bottle-green flies as Lust.

"I will never"—said I—griping at the elbows of my chair,—"live a bachelor till sixty:—never, so surely as there is hope in man, or charity in woman, or faith in both!"

And with that thought, my heart leaped about in playful coruscations,[43] even like the flame of the sea-coal;—rising, and wrapping round old and tender memories, and images that were present to me,—trying to cling, and yet no sooner fastened, than off—dancing again, riotous in its exultation—a succession of heart-sparkles, blazing, and going out!

——And is there not—mused I,—a portion of this world, forever blazing in just such lively sparkles, waving here and there as the air-currents fan them?

Take for instance your heart of sentiment, and quick sensibility, a weak, warm-working heart, flying off in tangents of unhappy influence, unguided by prudence, and perhaps virtue. There is a paper by Mackenzie[44] in the Mirror for April, 1780, which sets this untoward sensibility in a strong light.

And the more it is indulged, the more strong and binding such a habit of sensibility becomes. Poor Mackenzie himself must have suffered thus; you cannot read his books without feeling it; your eye, in spite of you, runs over with his sensitive griefs, while you are half-ashamed of his success at picture-making. It is a terrible inheritance; and one that a strong man or woman will study to subdue: it is a vain sea-coal sparkling, which will count no good. The world is made of much hard, flinty substance, against which your better, and holier thoughts will be striking fire;—see to it, that the sparks do not burn you!

But what a happy, careless life belongs to this Bachelorhood, in which you may strike out boldly right and left! Your heart is not bound to another which may be full of only sickly vapors of feeling; nor is it frozen to a cold, man's heart under a silk boddice—knowing nothing of tenderness but the name, to prate of; and nothing of soul-confidence, but clumsy confession. And if in your careless out-goings of feeling, you get here, only a little lip vapidity in return; be sure that you will find, elsewhere, a true heart utterance. This last

---

41 William Wordsworth (1770–1850) was an important English Romantic poet. One of his major volumes of poems, *The Excursion*, appeared in 1814.
42 Home of the Wordsworth family.
43 Sparkles.
44 Henry Mackenzie (1745–1831) was a Scottish novelist, poet and playwright best known for his novel, *The Man of Feeling* (1771).

you will cherish in your inner soul—a nucleus for a new group of affections; and the other will pass with a whiff of your cigar.

Or if your feelings are touched, struck, hurt, who is the wiser, or the worse, but you only? And have you not the whole skein of your heart-life in your own fingers to wind, or unwind, in what shape you please? Shake it or twine it, or tangle it, by the light of your fire, as you fancy best. He is a weak man who cannot twist and weave the threads of his feeling—however fine, however tangled, however strained, or however strong—into the great cable of Purpose, by which he lies moored to his life of Action.

Reading is a great, and happy disentangler of all those knotted snarls—those extravagant vagaries, which belong to a heart sparkling with sensibility; but the reading must be cautiously directed. There is old, placid Burton[45] when your soul is weak, and its digestion of life's humors is bad; there is Cowper[46] when your spirit runs into kindly, half-sad, religious musing; there is Crabbe[47] when you would shake off vagary, by a little handling of sharp actualities. There is Voltaire, a homeopathic doctor, whom you can read when you want to make a play of life, and crack jokes at Nature, and be witty with Destiny; there is Rousseau,[48] when you want to lose yourself in a mental dream-land, and be beguiled by the harmony of soul-music and soul-culture.

And when you would shake off this, and be sturdiest among the battlers for hard, world-success, and be forewarned of rocks against which you must surely smite—read Bolingbroke;—run over the letters of Lyttleton; read, and think of what you read, in the cracking lines of Rochefoucauld.[49] How he sums us up in his stinging words!—how he puts the scalpel between the nerves—yet he never hurts; for he is dissecting dead matter.

If you are in a genial careless mood, who is better than such extemporizers of feeling and nature—good-hearted fellows—as Sterne and Fielding?[50]

And then again, there are Milton and Isaiah,[51] to lift up one's soul until it touches cloud-land, and you wander with their guidance, on swift feet, to the very gates of Heaven.

But this sparkling sensibility to one struggling under infirmity, or with grief or poverty, is very dreadful. The soul is too nicely and keenly hinged to be wrenched without mischief. How it shrinks, like a hurt child, from all that is vulgar, harsh, and crude! Alas, for such a man!—he will be buffeted, from beginning to end; his life will be a sea of troubles. The poor victim of his own quick spirit he wanders with a great shield of doubt hung before him, so that none, not even friends can see the goodness of such kindly qualities as belong

---

45 Robert Burton (1577–1640) was an English writer and Anglican clergyman who wrote *Anatomy of Melancholy* (1621), much praised for its style and wealth of philosophical and psychological information.

46 William Cowper (1731–1800) was a tremendously popular English nature poet.

47 George Crabbe (1754–1832) was an English poet who distinguished himself with his commitment to portraying realistic details of everyday life.

48 Jean-Jacques Rousseau (1712–1778) was an immensely influential French philosopher and political theorist who wrote extensively on a number of topics ranging from nature to education.

49 François de la Rochefoucauld (1613–1680) was a French writer and adventurer known for his moral and philosophical maxims.

50 Laurence Sterne (1713–1768) and Henry Fielding (1707–1754) were famous and influential early English novelists renowned for their humor and wit.

51 John Milton (1608–1674) and the Old Testament prophet Isaiah were both recognized for their treatments of the importance of the Messiah in Judeo-Christian thought.

to him. Poverty, if it comes upon him, he wrestles with in secret, with strong, frenzied struggles. He wraps his scant clothes about him to keep him from the cold; and eyes the world, as if every creature in it was breathing chill blasts at him, from every opened mouth. He threads the crowded ways of the city, proud in his griefs, vain in his weakness, not stopping to do good. Bulwer, in the New Timon, has painted in a pair of stinging Pope-like lines, this feeling in a woman:—

Her vengeful pride, a kind of madness grown,
She hugged her wrongs, her sorrow was her throne!

Cold picture! yet the heart was sparkling under it, like my sea-coal fire; lifting and blazing, and lighting and falling,—but with no object; and only such little heat as begins and ends within.

Those fine sensibilities, ever active, are chasing and observing all; they catch a hue from what the dull and callous pass by unnoticed,—because unknown. They blunder at the great variety of the world's opinions; they see tokens of belief, where others see none. That delicate organization is a curse to a man; and yet poor fool, he does not see where his cure lies; he wonders at his griefs, and has never reckoned with himself their source. He studies others, without studying himself. He eats the leaves that sicken, and never plucks up the root that will cure.

With a woman it is worse; with her, this delicate susceptibility is like a frail flower, that quivers at every rough blast of heaven; her own delicacy wounds her; her highest charm is perverted to a curse.

She listens with fear; she reads with trembling; she looks with dread. Her sympathies give a tone, like the harp of Æolus,[52] to the slightest breath. Her sensibility lights up, and quivers and falls, like the flame of a sea-coal fire.

If she loves—(and may not a Bachelor reason on this daintiest of topics)—her love is a gushing, wavy flame, lit up with hope, that has only a little kindling matter to light it; and this soon burns out. Yet intense sensibility will persuade her that the flame still scorches. She will mistake the annoyance of affection unrequited for the sting of a passion, that she fancies still burns. She does not look deep enough to see that the passion is gone, and the shocked sensitiveness emits only faint, yellowish sparkles in its place; her high-wrought organization makes those sparks seem a veritable flame.

With her, judgment, prudence, and discretion are cold measured terms, which have no meaning, except as they attach to the actions of others. Of her own acts, she never predicates them; feeling is much too high, to allow her to submit to any such obtrusive guides of conduct. She needs disappointment to teach her truth;—to teach that all is not gold that glitters—to teach that all warmth does not blaze. But let her beware how she sinks under any fancied disappointments: she who sinks under real disappointment, lacks philosophy; but she who sinks under a fancied one, lacks purpose. Let her flee as the plague, such brooding thoughts as she will love to cherish; let her spurn dark fancies as the visitants of hell; let the soul rise with the blaze of new-kindled, active, and world-wide emotions, and so brighten into steady and constant flame. Let her abjure such poets as Cowper, or Byron,[53]

---

52 Stringed musical instrument played by the wind.
53 George Gordon Byron (1788–1824) was a popular English poet best remembered for his portrayal of the dark, brooding hero in *Don Juan* (1819–1824).

or even Wordsworth; and if she must poetize, let her lay her mind to such manly verse as Pope's,[54] or to such sound and ringing organry as Comus.[55]

My fire was getting dull, and I thrust in the poker: it started up on the instant into a hundred little angry tongues of flame.

——Just so—thought I—the over-sensitive heart once cruelly disturbed, will fling out a score of flaming passions, darting here, and darting there,—half-smoke, half-flame—love and hate—canker and joy—wild in its madness, not knowing whither its sparks are flying. Once break roughly upon the affections, or even the fancied affections of such a soul, and you breed a tornado of maddened action—a whirlwind of fire that hisses, and sends out jets of wild, impulsive combustion, that make the bystanders,—even those most friendly— stand aloof, until the storm is past.

But this is not all that the dashing flame of my sea-coal suggests.

——How like a flirt!—mused I again, recurring to my first thought—so lively, yet uncertain; so bright, yet so flickering! Your true flirt plays with sparkles; her heart, much as there is of it, spends itself in sparkles; she measures it to sparkle, and habit grows into nature, so that anon, it can only sparkle. How carefully she cramps it, if the flames show too great a heat; how dexterously she flings its blaze here and there; how coyly she subdues it; how winningly she lights it!

All this is the entire reverse of the unpremeditated dartings of the soul at which I have been looking; sensibility scorns heart-curbings, and heart-teachings; sensibility enquires not—how much? but only—where?

Your true flirt has a coarse-grained soul; well modulated and well tutored, but there is no fineness in it. All its native fineness is made coarse, by coarse efforts of the will. True feeling is a rustic vulgarity, the flirt does not tolerate; she counts its healthiest and most honest manifestation, all sentiment. Yet she will play you off a pretty string of sentiment, which she has gathered from the poets; she adjusts it prettily as a Ghobelin[56] weaver adjusts the colors in his *tapis*.[57] She shades it off delightfully; there are no bold contrasts, but a most artistic mellow of *nuances*.[58]

She smiles like a wizzard, and jingles it with a laugh, such as tolled the poor home-bound Ulysses to the Circean bower.[59] She has a cast of the head, apt and artful as the most dexterous cast of the best trout-killing rod. Her words sparkle, and flow hurriedly, and with the prettiest doubleness of meaning. Naturalness she copies, and she scorns. She accuses herself of a single expression or regard, which nature prompts. She prides herself on her schooling. She measures her wit by the triumphs of her art; she chuckles over her own falsity to herself. And if by chance her soul—such germ as is left of it—betrays her into untoward confidence, she condemns herself, as if she had committed crime.

She is always gay, because she has no depth of feeling to be stirred. The brook that runs shallow over a hard pebbly bottom always rustles. She is light-hearted, because her heart

---

54 Alexander Pope (1688–1744) was an English poet famous for his satires.

55 *Comus* (1637) was a masque (play) written by John Milton. It highlights the harmonious bliss of heaven and the distressing conflicts of life on earth.

56 The Gobelins were a world-famous French family of weavers and cloth-makers who specialized in tapestries.

57 Cloth full of artistic and colorful designs.

58 Subtle distinctions.

59 Ulysses, the hero of Homer's *Odyssey*, must free himself from the enchantress Circe to continue his voyage home.

floats in sparkles—like my sea-coal fire. She counts on marriage, not as the great absorbent of a heart's-love, and life, but as a happy, feasible, and orderly conventionality, to be played with, and kept at distance, and finally to be accepted as a cover for the faint and tawdry sparkles of an old and cherished heartlessness.

She will not pine under any regrets, because she has no appreciation of any loss: she will not chafe at indifference, because it is her art; she will not be worried with jealousies, because she is ignorant of love. With no conception of the soul in its strength and fulness, she sees no lack of its demands. A thrill, she does not know; a passion, she cannot imagine; joy is a name; grief is another; and Life with its crowding scenes of love, and bitterness, is a play upon the stage.

I think it is Madame Dudevant[60] who says, in something like the same connection:—*Les hiboux ne connaissant pas le chemin par où les aigles vont au soleil.*[61]

——Poor Ned!—mused I, looking at the play of the fire—was a victim and a conqueror. He was a man of a full, strong nature—not a little impulsive—with action too full of earnestness for most of men to see its drift. He had known little of what is called the world; he was fresh in feeling and high of hope; he had been encircled always by friends who loved him, and who, may be, flattered him. Scarce had he entered upon the tangled life of the city, before he met with a sparkling face and an airy step, that stirred something in poor Ned, that he had never felt before. With him, to feel was to act. He was not one to be despised; for notwithstanding he wore a country air, and the awkwardness of a man who has yet the *bien-sèance*[62] of social life before him, he had the soul, the courage, and the talent of a strong man. Little gifted in the knowledge of face-play, he easily mistook those coy manœuvres of a sparkling heart, for something kindred to his own true emotions.

She was proud of the attentions of a man who carried a mind in his brain; and flattered poor Ned almost into servility. Ned had no friends to counsel him; or if he had them, his impulses would have blinded him. Never was dodger more artful at the Olympic Games than the Peggy of Ned's heart-affection. He was charmed, beguiled, entranced.

When Ned spoke of love, she staved it off with the prettiest of sly looks that only bewildered him the more. A charming creature to be sure; coy as a dove!

So he went on, poor fool, until one day—he told me of it with the blood mounting to his temples, and his eye shooting flame—he suffered his feelings to run out in passionate avowal,—entreaty,—everything. She gave a pleasant, noisy laugh, and manifested—such pretty surprise!

He was looking for the intense glow of passion; and lo, there was nothing but the shifting sparkle of a sea-coal flame.

I wrote him a letter of condolence—for I was his senior by a year;—"my dear fellow," said I, "diet yourself; you can find greens at the up-town market; eat a little fish with your dinner; abstain from heating drinks: don't put too much butter to your cauliflower; read one of Jeremy Taylor's[63] sermons, and translate all the quotations at sight; run carefully over that exquisite picture of Geo. Dandin in your Molière,[64] and my word for it, in a week you will be a sound man."

---

60 Amandine Dudevant is the real name of the French novelist George Sand (1804–1876).
61 Owls do not soar as high as eagles.
62 Wonderful stage.
63 Jeremy Taylor (1613–1667) was an Anglican clergyman who distinguished himself as a prolific writer of devotionals.
64 Enjoy that wonderful illustration in your copy of Molière's (1622–1673) play *George Dandin* (1668).

He was too angry to reply; but eighteen months thereafter I got a thick, three-sheeted letter, with a dove upon the seal, telling me that he was as happy as a king: he said he had married a good-hearted, domestic, loving wife, who was as lovely as a Juno day, and that their baby, not three months old, was as bright as a spot of June day sunshine on the grass.

——What a tender, delicate, loving wife—mused I—such flashing, flaming flirt must in the end make;—the prostitute of fashion; the bauble of fifty hearts idle as hers; the shifting make-piece of a stage scene; the actress, now in peasant, and now in princely petticoats! How it would cheer an honest soul to call her—his! What a culmination of his heart-life; what a rich dream-land to be realized!

——Bah! and I thrust the poker into the clotted mass of fading coal—-just such, and so worthless is the used heart of a city flirt; just so the incessant sparkle of her life, and frittering passions, fuses all that is sound and combustible, into black, sooty, shapeless residuum.

When I marry a flirt, I will buy second-hand clothes of the Jews.

——Still—mused I—as the flame danced again—there is a distinction between coquetry and flirtation.

A coquette sparkles, but it is more the sparkle of a harmless and pretty vanity, than of calculation. It is the play of humors in the blood, and not the play of purpose at the heart. It will flicker around a true soul like the blaze around an *omelette au rhum*,[65] leaving the kernel sounder and warmer.

Coquetry, with all its pranks and teasings, makes the spice to your dinner—the mulled wine to your supper. It will drive you to desperation, only to bring you back hotter to the fray. Who would boast a victory that cost no strategy, and no careful disposition of the forces? Who would bulletin such success as my Uncle Toby's, in a back-garden, with only the Corporal Trim for assailant? But let a man be very sure that the city is worth the siege!

Coquetry whets the appetite; flirtation depraves it. Coquetry is the thorn that guards the rose—easily trimmed off when once plucked. Flirtation is like the slime on water-plants, making them hard to handle, and when caught, only to be cherished in slimy waters.

And so, with my eye clinging to the flickering blaze, I see in my reverie, a bright one dancing before me, with sparkling, coquettish smile, teasing me with the prettiest graces in the world;—and I grow maddened between hope and fear, and still watch with my whole soul in my eyes; and see her features by and by relax to pity, as a gleam of sensibility comes stealing over her spirit;—and then to a kindly, feeling regard: presently she approaches,—a coy and doubtful approach—and throws back the ringlets that lie over her cheek, and lays her hand—a little bit of white hand—timidly upon my strong fingers,—and turns her head daintily to one side,—and looks up in my eyes, as they rest on the playing blaze; and my fingers close fast and passionately over that little hand, like a swift night-cloud shrouding the pale tips of Dian;[66]—and my eyes draw nearer and nearer to those blue, laughing, pitying, teasing eyes, and my arm clasps round that shadowy form,—and my lips feel a warm breath—growing warmer and warmer——

Just here the maid comes in, and throws upon the fire a pan-ful of Anthracite, and my sparkling sea-coal reverie is ended.

---

65 Rum omelet.
66 The pale hand of Diana, the elusive goddess of virginity and the hunt.

II

Anthracite

It does not burn freely, so I put on the blower. Quaint and good-natured Xavier de Maistre[67] would have made, I dare say, a pretty epilogue about a sheet-iron blower; but I cannot.

I try to bring back the image that belonged to the lingering bituminous flame, but with my eyes on that dark blower,—how can I?

It is the black curtain of destiny which drops down before our brightest dreams. How often the phantoms of joy regale us, and dance before us—golden-winged, angel-faced, heart-warming, and make an Elysium[68] in which the dreaming soul bathes, and feels translated to another existence; and then—sudden as night, or a cloud—a word, a step, a thought, a memory will chase them away, like scared deer vanishing over a gray horizon of moor-land!

I know not justly, if it be a weakness or a sin to create these phantoms that we love, and to group them into a paradise—soul-created. But if it is a sin, it is a sweet and enchanting sin; and if it is a weakness, it is a strong and stirring weakness. If this heart is sick of the falsities that meet it at every hand, and is eager to spend that power which nature has ribbed it with, on some object worthy of its fulness and depth,—shall it not feel a rich relief,—nay more, an exercise in keeping with its end, if it flow out—strong as a tempest, wild as a rushing river, upon those ideal creations, which imagination invents, and which are tempered by our best sense of beauty, purity, and grace?

——Useless, do you say? Aye, it is as useless as the pleasure of looking hour upon hour, over bright landscapes; it is as useless as the rapt enjoyment of listening with heart full and eyes brimming, to such music as the Miserere[69] at Rome; it is as useless as the ecstacy of kindling your soul into fervor and love, and madness, over pages that reek with genius.

There are indeed base-moulded souls who know nothing of this; they laugh; they sneer; they even affect to pity. Just so the Huns under the avenging Attila,[70] who had been used to foul cookery and steaks stewed under their saddles, laughed brutally at the spiced banquets of an Apicius![71]

——No, this phantom-making is no sin; or if it be, it is sinning with a soul so full, so earnest, that it can cry to Heaven cheerily, and sure of a gracious hearing—*peccavi*— *misericorde!*[72]

But my fire is in a glow, a pleasant glow, throwing a tranquil, steady light to the farthest corner of my garret. How unlike it is, to the flashing play of the sea-coal!—unlike as an unsteady, uncertain-working heart to the true and earnest constancy of one cheerful and right.

After all, thought I, give me such a heart; not bent on vanities, not blazing too sharp with sensibility, not throwing out coquettish jets of flame, not wavering, and meaningless with pretended warmth, but open, glowing and strong. Its dark shades and angles it may

---

67 [Author's Original Note] Voyage autour de Ma Chambre.
68 In Greek mythology, the home of the blessed after their deaths.
69 Catholic mass based on Ps. 51:3 sung the week before Easter.
70 Attila the Hun (406?–453) was one of the most feared leaders of the "barbaric" Eastern European tribes who, like the Germanic tribes, marched against the Roman Empire.
71 Apicius was a legendary ancient Roman gourmand.
72 I have sinned—mercy!

have; for what is a soul worth that does not take a slaty tinge from those griefs that chill the blood? Yet still the fire is gleaming; you see it in the crevices; and anon it will give radiance to the whole mass.

——It hurts the eyes, this fire; and I draw up a screen painted over with rough, but graceful figures.

The true heart wears always the veil of modesty—(not of prudery, which is a dingy, iron, repulsive screen.) It will not allow itself to be looked on too near—it might scorch; but through the veil you feel the warmth; and through the pretty figures that modesty will robe itself in, you can see all the while the golden outlines, and by that token, you *know* that it is glowing and burning with a pure and steady flame.

With such a heart the mind fuses naturally—a holy and heated fusion; they work together like twins-born. With such a heart, as Raphael says to Adam,

Love hath his seat
In reason, and is judicious.

But let me distinguish this heart from your clay-cold, luke-warm, half-hearted soul;—considerate, because ignorant; judicious, because possessed of no latent fires that need a curb; prudish, because with no warm blood to tempt. This sort of soul may pass scatheless through the fiery furnace of life; strong, only in its weakness; pure, because of its failings; and good, only by negation. It may triumph over love, and sin, and death; but it will be a triumph of the beast, which has neither passions to subdue, or energy to attack, or hope to quench.

Let us come back to the steady and earnest heart, glowing like my anthracite coal.

I fancy I see such a one now:—the eye is deep and reaches back to the spirit; it is not the trading eye, weighing your purse; it is not the worldly eye, weighing position; it is not the beastly eye, weighing your appearance; it is the heart's eye, weighing your soul!

It is full of deep, tender, and earnest feeling. It is an eye, which looked on once, you long to look on again; it is an eye which will haunt your dreams,—an eye which will give a colour, in spite of you, to all your reveries. It is an eye which lies before you in your future, like a star in the mariner's heaven; by it, unconsciously, and from force of deep soul-habit, you take all your observations. It is meek and quiet; but it is full, as a spring that gushes in flood; an Aphrodite and a Mercury—a Vauclause and a Clitumnus![73]

The face is an angel face; no matter for curious lines of beauty; no matter for popular talk of prettiness; no matter for its angles, or its proportions; no matter for its colour or its form—the soul is there, illuminating every feature, burnishing every point, hallowing every surface. It tells of honesty, sincerity and worth; it tells of truth and virtue;—and you clasp the image to your heart, as the received ideal of your fondest dreams.

The figure may be this or that, it may be tall or short, it matters nothing,—the heart is there. The talk may be soft or low, serious or piquant—a free and honest soul is warming and softening it all. As you speak, it speaks back again; as you think, it thinks again—(not in conjunction, but in the same sign of the Zodiac;) as you love it loves in return.

——It is the heart for a sister, and happy is the man who can claim such! The warmth that lies in it is not only generous, but religious, genial, devotional, tender, self-sacrificing, and looking heavenward.

A man without some sort of religion, is at best a poor reprobate, the foot-ball of destiny, with no tie linking him to infinity, and the wondrous eternity that is begun with him; but a

---

73　These are famous mythological figures and rivers associated with fertility, abundance and speed.

woman without it, is even worse—a flame without heat, a rainbow without colour, a flower without perfume!

A man may in some sort tie his frail hopes and honors, with weak, shifting ground-tackle to business, or to the world; but a woman without that anchor which they call Faith, is adrift, and a-wreck! A man may clumsily contrive a kind of moral responsibility, out of his relations to mankind; but a woman in her comparatively isolated sphere, where affection and not purpose is the controlling motive, can find no basis for any system of right action, but that of spiritual faith. A man may craze his thought, and his brain, to trustfulness in such poor harborage as Fame and Reputation may stretch before him; but a woman— where can she put her hope in storms, if not in Heaven?

And that sweet trustfulness—that abiding love—that enduring hope, mellowing every page and scene of life, lighting them with pleasantest radiance, when the world-storms break like an army with smoking cannon—what can bestow it all, but a holy soul-tie to what is above the storms, and to what is stronger than an army with cannon? Who that has enjoyed the counsel and the love of a Christian mother, but will echo the thought with energy, and hallow it with a tear?——*et moi, je pleurs.*[74]

My fire is now a mass of red-hot coal. The whole atmosphere of my room is warm. The heart that with its glow can light up, and warm a garret with loose casements and shattered roof, is capable of the best love—domestic love. I draw farther off, and the images upon the screen change. The warmth, the hour, the quiet, create a home feeling; and that feeling, quick as lightning, has stolen from the world of fancy (a Promethean theft,)[75] a home object, about which my musings go on to drape themselves in luxurious reverie.

——There she sits, by the corner of the fire, in a neat home dress, of sober, yet most adorning colour. A little bit of lace ruffle is gathered about the neck, by a blue ribbon; and the ends of the ribbon are crossed under the dimpling chin, and are fastened neatly by a simple, unpretending brooch—your gift. The arm, a pretty taper arm, lies over the carved elbow of the oaken chair; the hand, white and delicate, sustains a little home volume that hangs from her fingers. The forefinger is between the leaves, and the others lie in relief upon the dark embossed cover. She repeats in a silver voice, a line that has attracted her fancy; and you listen—or at any rate, you seem to listen—with your eyes now on the lips, now on the forehead, and now on the finger, where glitters like a star, the marriage ring— little gold band, at which she does not chafe, that tells you,—she is yours!

——Weak testimonial, if that were all that told it! The eye, the voice, the look, the heart, tells you stronger and better, that she is yours. And a feeling within, where it lies you know not, and whence it comes you know not, but sweeping over heart and brain, like a fire-flood, tells you too, that you are hers! Irremediably bound as Massinger's[76] Hortensio:

I am subject to another's will, and can
Nor speak, nor do, without permission from her!

The fire is warm as ever; what length of heat in this hard burning anthracite! It has scarce sunk yet to the second bar of the grate, though the clock upon the church-tower has tolled eleven.

---

74 And I cry.
75 In Greek legend, Prometheus stole fire from the gods in order to give it to humanity.
76 Philip Massinger (1583–1639?) was an English playwright famous for his comedies and satires.

——Aye,—mused I, gaily—such heart does not grow faint, it does not spend itself in idle puffs of blaze, it does not become chilly with the passing years; but it gains and grows in strength, and heat, until the fire of life, is covered over with the ashes of death. Strong or hot as it may be at the first, it loses nothing. It may not indeed, as time advances, throw out, like the coal-fire, when new-lit, jets of blue sparkling flame; it may not continue to bubble, and gush like a fountain at its source, but it will become a strong river of flowing charities.

Clitumnus[77] breaks from under the Tuscan mountains, almost a flood; on a glorious spring day I leaned down and tasted the water, as it boiled from its sources;—the little temple of white marble,—the mountain sides gray with olive orchards,—the white streak of road,—the tall poplars of the river margin were glistening in the bright Italian sunlight, around me. Later, I saw it when it had become a river,—still clear and strong, flowing serenely between its prairie banks, on which the white cattle of the valley browsed; and still farther down, I welcomed it, where it joins the Arno,—flowing slowly under wooded shores, skirting the fair Florence, and the bounteous fields of the bright Cascino;—gathering strength and volume, till between Pisa and Leghorn,—in sight of the wondrous Leaning Tower, and the ship-masts of the Tuscan port, it gave its waters to its life's grave—the sea.

The recollection blended sweetly now with my musings, over my garret grate, and offered a flowing image, to bear along upon its bosom the affections that were grouping in my Reverie.

It is a strange force of the mind and of the fancy, that can set the objects which are closest to the heart far down the lapse of time. Even now, as the fire fades slightly, and sinks slowly towards the bar, which is the dial of my hours, I seem to see that image of love which has played about the fire-glow of my grate—years hence. It still covers the same warm, trustful, religious heart. Trials have tried it; afflictions have weighed upon it; danger has scared it; and death is coming near to subdue it; but still it is the same.

The fingers are thinner; the face has lines of care, and sorrow, crossing each other in a web-work, that makes the golden tissue of humanity. But the heart is fond, and steady; it is the same dear heart, the same self-sacrificing heart, warming, like a fire, all around it. Affliction has tempered joy; and joy adorned affliction. Life and all its troubles have become distilled into an holy incense, rising ever from your fireside,—an offering to your household gods.

Your dreams of reputation, your swift determination, your impulsive pride, your deep uttered vows to win a name, have all sobered into affection—have all blended into that glow of feeling, which finds its centre, and hope, and joy in Home. From my soul I pity him whose soul does not leap at the mere utterance of that name.

A home!—it is the bright, blessed, adorable phantom which sits highest on the sunny horizon that girdeth Life! When shall it be reached? When shall it cease to be a glittering day-dream, and become fully and fairly yours?

It is not the house, though that may have its charms; nor the fields carefully tilled, and streaked with your own foot-paths;—nor the trees, though their shadow be to you like that of a great rock in a weary land;—nor yet is it the fireside, with its sweet blaze-play;—nor the pictures which tell of loved ones, nor the cherished books,—but more far than all these—it is the PRESENCE. The Lares[78] of your worship are there; the altar of your confidence there; the end of your worldly faith is there; and adorning it all, and sending your blood in passionate flow, is the ecstasy of the conviction, that *there* at least you are beloved; that there

---

77 River in northern Italy that the narrator goes on to follow until it empties into the sea.
78 Household gods.

you are understood; that there your errors will meet ever with gentlest forgiveness; that there your troubles will be smiled away; that there you may unburden your soul, fearless of harsh, unsympathizing ears; and that there you may be entirely and joyfully—yourself!

There may be those of coarse mould—and I have seen such even in the disguise of women—who will reckon these feelings puling sentiment. God pity them!—as they have need of pity.

——That image by the fireside, calm, loving, joyful, is there still: it goes not, however my spirit tosses, because my wish, and every will, keep it there, unerring.

The fire shows through the screen, yellow and warm, as a harvest sun. It is in its best age, and that age is ripeness.

A ripe heart!—now I know what Wordsworth meant, when he said,

> The good die first,
> And they whose hearts are dry as summer dust,
> Burn to the socket!

The town clock is striking midnight. The cold of the night-wind is urging its way in at the door and window-crevice; the fire has sunk almost to the third bar of the grate. Still my dream tires not, but wraps fondly round that image,—now in the far off, chilling mists of age, growing sainted. Love has blended into reverence; passion has subsided into joyous content.

——And what if age comes, said I, in a new flush of excitation,—what else proves the wine? What else gives inner strength, and knowledge, and a steady pilot-hand, to steer your boat out boldly upon that shoreless sea, where the river of life is running? Let the white ashes gather; let the silver hair lie, where lay the auburn; let the eye gleam farther back, and dimmer; it is but retreating toward the pure sky-depths, an usher to the land where you will follow after.

It is quite cold, and I take away the screen altogether; there is a little glow yet, but presently the coal slips down below the third bar, with a rumbling sound,—like that of coarse gravel falling into a new-dug grave.

——She is gone!

Well, the heart has burned fairly, evenly, generously, while there was mortality to kindle it; eternity will surely kindle it better.

——Tears indeed; but they are tears of thanksgiving, of resignation, and of hope!

And the eyes, full of those tears, which ministering angels bestow, climb with quick vision, upon the angelic ladder, and open upon the futurity where she has entered, and upon the country, which she enjoys.

It is midnight, and the sounds of life are dead.

You are in the death chamber of life; but you are also in the death chamber of care. The world seems sliding backward; and hope and you are sliding forward. The clouds, the agonies, the vain expectancies, the braggart noise, the fears, now vanish behind the curtain of the Past, and of the Night. They roll from your soul like a load.

In the dimness of what seems the ending Present, you reach out your prayerful hands toward that boundless Future, where God's eye lifts over the horizon, like sunrise on the ocean. Do you recognize it as an earnest of something better? Aye, if the heart has been pure, and steady,—burning like my fire—it has learned it without seeming to learn. Faith has grown upon it, as the blossom grows upon the bud, or the flower upon the slow-lifting stalk.

Cares cannot come into, the dream-land where I live. They sink with the dying street noise, and vanish with the embers of my fire. Even Ambition, with its hot and shifting flame, is all gone out. The heart in the dimness of the fading fire-glow is all itself. The memory of what good things have come over it in the troubled youth-life, bear it up; and hope and faith bear it on. There is no extravagant pulse-flow; there is no mad fever of the brain; but only the soul, forgetting—for once—all, save its destinies, and its capacities for good. And it mounts higher and higher on these wings of thought; and hope burns stronger and stronger out of the ashes of decaying life, until the sharp edge of the grave seems but a foot-scraper at the wicket of Elysium!

But what is paper; and what are words? Vain things! The soul leaves them behind; the pen staggers like a starveling cripple; and your heart is leaving it, a whole length of the life-course behind. The soul's mortal longings,—its poor baffled hopes, are dim now in the light of those infinite longings, which spread over it, soft and holy as day-dawn. Eternity has stretched a corner of its mantle toward you, and the breath of its waving fringe is like a gale of Araby.

A little rumbling, and a last plunge of the cinders within my grate, startled me, and dragged back my fancy from my flower chase, beyond the Phlegethon,[79] to the white ashes, that were now thick all over the darkened coals.

——And this—mused I—is only a bachelor-dream about a pure, and loving heart! And to-morrow comes cankerous life again:—— is it wished for? Or if not wished for, is the not wishing, wicked?

Will dreams satisfy, reach high as they can? Are we not after all poor grovelling mortals, tied to earth, and to each other; are there not sympathies, and hopes, and affections which can only find their issue, and blessing, in fellow absorption? Does not the heart, steady, and pure as it may be, and mounting on soul flights often as it dare, want a human sympathy, perfectly indulged, to make it healthful? Is there not a fount of love for this world, as there is a fount of love for the other? Is there not a certain store of tenderness, cooped in this heart, which must, and *will* be lavished, before the end comes? Does it not plead with the judgment, and make issue with prudence, year after year? Does it not dog your steps all through your social pilgrimage, setting up its claims in forms fresh, and odorous as new-blown heath bells, saying,—come away from the heartless, the factitious, the vain, and measure your heart not by its constraints, but by its fulness, and by its depth?—let it run, and be joyous!

Is there no demon that comes to your harsh night-dreams, like a taunting fiend, whispering—be satisfied; keep your heart from running over; bridle those affections; there is nothing worth loving?

Does not some sweet being hover over your spirit of reverie like a beckoning angel, crowned with halo, saying—hope on, hope ever; the heart and I are kindred; our mission will be fulfilled; nature shall accomplish its purpose; the soul shall have its Paradise!

——I threw myself upon my bed: and as my thoughts ran over the definite, sharp business of the morrow, my Reverie, and its glowing images, that made my heart bound, swept away, like those fleecy rain clouds of August, on which the sun paints rainbows—driven Southward, by a cool, rising wind from the North.

——I wonder,—thought I, as I dropped asleep,—if a married man with his sentiment made actual, is, after all, as happy as we poor fellows, in our dreams?

*   *   *

---

79 A river of fire in the ancient Greek underworld.

Editor's Note

Reveries of a Bachelor: **The End of the Story**

The bachelor continues to muse about the state of his single life in a third reverie. His fourth and final reverie is the longest. In it he travels to Europe and suffers the loss of one love to have it replaced by another. He marries this woman and has two children, thus bringing to an end a narrative arc that moves from bachelorhood to wedded bliss.

Chapter Ten

HARRIET BEECHER STOWE
(1811–1896)

Harriet Beecher Stowe was born into one of the most famous and influential Protestant clerical families of the nineteenth century. Her father, Lyman Beecher, and her younger brother, Henry Ward Beecher, were among the century's most popular preachers. Stowe's mother died when she was five years old and, although her father remarried, the strongest female influence on her life was her elder, proto-feminist sister, Catharine. In 1836, Harriet married Calvin Ellis Stowe, yet another influential Protestant clergyman, a professor at Lane Seminary in Cincinnati.

While the men in her family were all imbued with a high sense of calling when it came to nurturing religion and notions of civic virtue in the young nation, as a woman Stowe found her own options for political and religious influence to be limited. Such limitations did not stop her, however, when she became enraged by the Compromise of 1850, a political maneuver she referred to as a "pact with the devil." Particularly egregious in her mind was the way in which the Compromise continued to allow slavery to expand in the United States, and how it enacted the Fugitive Slave Act, a law that allowed slave owners great latitude in pursuing and reclaiming their runaway slaves in the Northern non-slave states.

Stowe turned to writing to give voice to her critique of American slavery. In 1851, she began to publish a serialized story titled *Uncle Tom's Cabin* in the abolitionist newspaper, the *National Era*. The story won a huge following, and when it was released in book form in 1852, it sold 10,000 copies within a week and 300,000 copies within a year. The book proved to be even more popular in England, where it sold 1.5 million copies in its first year of release.

Uncle Tom's Cabin is a long and complex work, intertwining several different story lines of slavery and oppression. It is also heavily inflected by Stowe's profound sense of grief over the death of her infant son, Charlie, in 1849. Many themes in the book revolve around children and the suffering caused by the loss—or potential loss—of a child. In the book's first arc, presented in the following excerpt, the reader is introduced to both Tom and Eliza, slaves on the Shelby plantation in Kentucky. In drastically different ways, Tom and Eliza face their fates of being sold—or having their loved ones sold—to new owners. In this powerfully charged moral work, Stowe presses her readers to confront the evils that emerge when a society allows its members to define some humans as nothing more than mere property.

UNCLE TOM'S CABIN;
OR, LIFE AMONG THE LOWLY

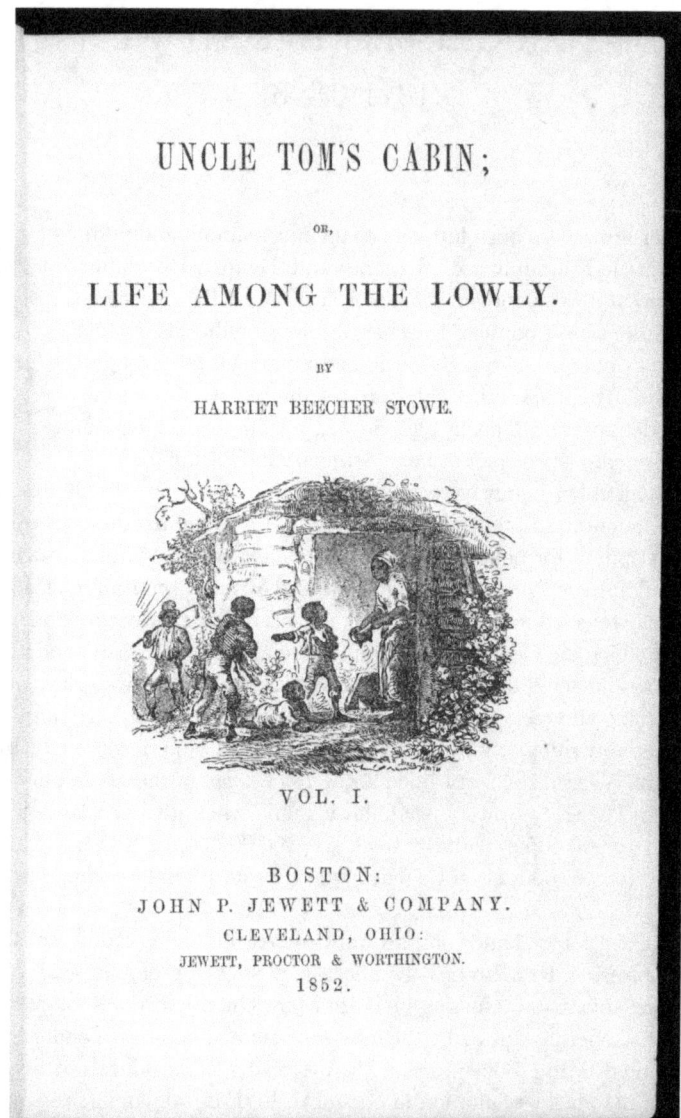

Title page from first book edition (Boston: John P. Jewett, 1852, Courtesy Lilly Library, Bloomington, IN).

Uncle Tom's Cabin originally appeared in serialized form in 1851–52 in the antislavery newspaper *The National Era*. The story was then turned into a two-volume set, published in 1852 by John P. Jewett and Company in Boston. This text is reprinted from the initial 1852 book edition.

Chapter 1

In Which the Reader Is Introduced to a Man of Humanity

Late in the afternoon of a chilly day in February, two gentlemen were sitting alone over their wine, in a well-furnished dining parlor, in the town of P—, in Kentucky. There were no servants present, and the gentlemen, with chairs closely approaching, seemed to be discussing some subject with great earnestness.

For convenience sake, we have said, hitherto, two *gentlemen*. One of the parties, however, when critically examined, did not seem, strictly speaking, to come under the species. He was a short, thick-set man, with coarse, commonplace features, and that swaggering air of pretension which marks a low man who is trying to elbow his way upward in the world. He was much over-dressed, in a gaudy vest of many colors, a blue neckerchief, bedropped gayly with yellow spots, and arranged with a flaunting tie, quite in keeping with the general air of the man. His hands, large and coarse, were plentifully bedecked with rings; and he wore a heavy gold watch-chain, with a bundle of seals of portentous size, and a great variety of colors, attached to it,—which, in the ardor of conversation, he was in the habit of flourishing and jingling with evident satisfaction. His conversation was in free and easy defiance of Murray's Grammar,[1] and was garnished at convenient intervals with various profane expressions, which not even the desire to be graphic in our account shall induce us to transcribe.

His companion, Mr. Shelby, had the appearance of a gentleman; and the arrangements of the house, and the general air of the housekeeping, indicated easy, and even opulent circumstances. As we before stated, the two were in the midst of an earnest conversation.

"That is the way I should arrange the matter," said Mr. Shelby.

"I can't make trade that way—I positively can't, Mr. Shelby," said the other, holding up a glass of wine between his eye and the light.

"Why, the fact is, Haley, Tom is an uncommon fellow; he is certainly worth that sum anywhere—steady, honest, capable, manages my whole farm like a clock."

"You mean honest, as niggers go," said Haley, helping himself to a glass of brandy.

"No; I mean, really, Tom is a good, steady, sensible, pious fellow. He got religion at a camp-meeting,[2] four years ago; and I believe he really *did* get it. I've trusted him, since then, with everything I have,—money, house, horses,—and let him come and go round the country; and I always found him true and square in everything."

"Some folks don't believe there is pious niggers, Shelby," said Haley, with a candid flourish of his hand, "but I *do*. I had a fellow, now, in this yer last lot I took to Orleans—'twas as good as a meetin', now, really, to hear that critter pray; and he was quite gentle and quiet like. He fetched me a good sum, too, for I bought him cheap of a man that was 'bliged to sell out; so I realized six hundred on him. Yes, I consider religion a valeyable thing in a nigger, when it's the genuine article, and no mistake."

"Well, Tom's got the real article, if ever a fellow had," rejoined the other. "Why, last fall, I let him go to Cincinnati[3] alone, to do business for me, and bring home five hundred

---

1 American grammarian Lindley Murray (1745–1826) published a widely used book entitled *English Grammar* (first edition, 1795).

2 A Christian revival meeting usually held in a tent or the open air in the early nineteenth century.

3 A city in southern Ohio across the river from Kentucky. Cincinnati was in a northern free state, but it did have economic and social ties to the South.

dollars. 'Tom,' says I to him, 'I trust you, because I think you're a Christian—I know you wouldn't cheat.' Tom comes back, sure enough; I knew he would. Some low fellows, they say, said to him—'Tom, why don't you make tracks for Canada?'[4] 'Ah, master trusted me, and I couldn't,'—they told me about it. I am sorry to part with Tom, I must say. You ought to let him cover the whole balance of the debt; and you would, Haley, if you had any conscience."

"Well, I've got just as much conscience as any man in business can afford to keep,—just a little, you know, to swear by, as 'twere," said the trader, jocularly; "and then, I'm ready to do anything in reason to 'blige friends; but this yer, you see, is a leetle too hard on a fellow—a leetle too hard." The trader sighed contemplatively, and poured out some more brandy.

"Well, then, Haley, how will you trade?" said Mr. Shelby, after an uneasy interval of silence.

"Well, haven't you a boy or gal that you could throw in with Tom?"

"Hum!—none that I could well spare; to tell the truth, it's only hard necessity makes me willing to sell at all. I don't like parting with any of my hands, that's a fact."

Here the door opened, and a small quadroon boy, between four and five years of age, entered the room. There was something in his appearance remarkably beautiful and engaging. His black hair, fine as floss silk, hung in glossy curls about his round, dimpled face, while a pair of large dark eyes, full of fire and softness, looked out from beneath the rich, long lashes, as he peered curiously into the apartment. A gay robe of scarlet and yellow plaid, carefully made and neatly fitted, set off to advantage the dark and rich style of his beauty; and a certain comic air of assurance, blended with bashfulness, showed that he had been not unused to being petted and noticed by his master.

"Hulloa, Jim Crow!"[5] said Mr. Shelby, whistling, and snapping a bunch of raisins towards him, "pick that up, now!"

The child scampered, with all his little strength, after the prize, while his master laughed.

"Come here, Jim Crow," said he. The child came up, and the master patted the curly head, and chucked him under the chin.

"Now, Jim, show this gentleman how you can dance and sing." The boy commenced one of those wild, grotesque songs common among the negroes, in a rich, clear voice, accompanying his singing with many comic evolutions of the hands, feet, and whole body, all in perfect time to the music.

"Bravo!" said Haley, throwing him a quarter of an orange.

"Now, Jim, walk like old Uncle Cudjoe, when he has the rheumatism," said his master.

Instantly the flexible limbs of the child assumed the appearance of deformity and distortion, as, with his back humped up, and his master's stick in his hand, he hobbled about the room, his childish face drawn into a doleful pucker, and spitting from right to left, in imitation of an old man.

Both gentlemen laughed uproariously.

---

4 Canada was not subject to the slave laws that might return fugitive slaves found in the North to their Southern owners.

5 Name frequently used for a black person, particularly an entertainer such as a clown or singer. The term originated from the folk song "Jim Crow."

"Now, Jim," said his master, "show us how old Elder Robbins leads the psalm." The boy drew his chubby face down to a formidable length, and commenced toning a psalm tune through his nose, with imperturbable gravity.

"Hurrah! bravo! what a young 'un!" said Haley; "that chap's a case, I'll promise. Tell you what," said he, suddenly clapping his hand on Mr. Shelby's shoulder, "fling in that chap, and I'll settle the business—I will. Come, now, if that ain't doing the thing up about the rightest!"

At this moment, the door was pushed gently open, and a young quadroon woman, apparently about twenty-five, entered the room.

There needed only a glance from the child to her, to identify her as its mother. There was the same rich, full, dark eye, with its long lashes; the same ripples of silky black hair. The brown of her complexion gave way on the cheek to a perceptible flush, which deepened as she saw the gaze of the strange man fixed upon her in bold and undisguised admiration. Her dress was of the neatest possible fit, and set off to advantage her finely moulded shape;—a delicately formed hand and a trim foot and ankle were items of appearance that did not escape the quick eye of the trader, well used to run up at a glance the points of a fine female article.

"Well, Eliza?" said her master, as she stopped and looked hesitatingly at him.

"I was looking for Harry, please, sir;" and the boy bounded toward her, showing his spoils, which he had gathered in the skirt of his robe.

"Well, take him away, then," said Mr. Shelby; and hastily she withdrew, carrying the child on her arm.

"By Jupiter," said the trader, turning to him in admiration, "there's an article, now! You might make your fortune on that ar gal in Orleans, any day. I've seen over a thousand, in my day, paid down for gals not a bit handsomer."

"I don't want to make my fortune on her," said Mr. Shelby, dryly; and, seeking to turn the conversation, he uncorked a bottle of fresh wine, and asked his companion's opinion of it.

"Capital, sir,—first chop!" said the trader; then turning, and slapping his hand familiarly on Shelby's shoulder, he added—

"Come, how will you trade about the gal?—what shall I say for her—what'll you take?"

"Mr. Haley, she is not to be sold," said Shelby. "My wife would not part with her for her weight in gold."

"Ay, ay! women always say such things, cause they ha'nt no sort of calculation. Just show 'em how many watches, feathers, and trinkets, one's weight in gold would buy, and that alters the case, I reckon."

"I tell you, Haley, this must not be spoken of; I say no, and I mean no," said Shelby decidedly.

"Well, you'll let me have the boy, though," said the trader; "you must own I've come down pretty handsomely for him."

"What on earth can you want with the child?" said Shelby.

"Why, I've got a friend that's going into this yer branch of the business—wants to buy up handsome boys to raise for the market. Fancy articles entirely—sell for waiters, and so on, to rich 'uns, that can pay for handsome 'uns. It sets off one of yer great places—a real handsome boy to open door, wait, and tend. They fetch a good sum; and this little devil is such a comical, musical concern, he's just the article."

"I would rather not sell him," said Mr. Shelby, thoughtfully; "the fact is, sir, I'm a humane man, and I hate to take the boy from his mother, sir."

"Oh, you do?—La! yes—something of that ar natur. I understand, perfectly. It is mighty onpleasant getting on with women, sometimes. I al'ays hates these yer screechin', screamin' times. They are *mighty* onpleasant; but, as I manages business, I generally avoids 'em, sir. Now, what if you get the girl off for a day, or a week, or so; then the thing's done quietly,— all over before she comes home. Your wife might get her some ear-rings, or a new gown, or some such truck, to make up with her."

"I'm afraid not."

"Lor bless ye, yes! These critters an't like white folks, you know; they get over things, only manage right. Now, they say," said Haley, assuming a candid and confidential air, "that this kind o' trade is hardening to the feelings; but I never found it so. Fact is, I never could do things up the way some fellers managed the business. I've seen 'em as would pull a woman's child out of her arms, and set him up to sell, and she screechin' like mad all the time;—very bad policy—damages the article—makes 'em quite unfit for service sometimes. I knew a real handsome gal once, in Orleans, as was entirely ruined by this sort o' handling. The fellow that was trading for her didn't want her baby; and she was one of your real high sort, when her blood was up. I tell you, she squeezed up her child in her arms, and talked, and went on real awful. It kinder makes my blood run cold to think on't; and when they carried off the child, and locked her up, she jest went ravin' mad, and died in a week. Clear waste, sir, of a thousand dollars, just for want of management,—there's where 'tis. It's always best to do the humane thing, sir; that's been my experience." And the trader leaned back in his chair, and folded his arms, with an air of virtuous decision, apparently considering himself a second Wilberforce.[6]

The subject appeared to interest the gentleman deeply; for while Mr. Shelby was thoughtfully peeling an orange, Haley broke out afresh, with becoming diffidence, but as if actually driven by the force of truth to say a few words more.

"It don't look well, now, for a feller to be praisin' himself; but I say it jest because it's the truth. I believe I'm reckoned to bring in about the finest droves of niggers that is brought in,—at least, I've been told so; if I have once, I reckon I have a hundred times,—all in good case,—fat and likely, and I lose as few as any man in the business. And I lays it all to my management, sir; and humanity, sir, I may say, is the great pillar of *my* management."

Mr. Shelby, not knowing what to say, said, "Indeed!"

"Now, I've been laughed at for my notions, sir, and I've been talked to. They an't pop'lar, and they an't common; but I stuck to 'em, sir; I've stuck to 'em, and realized well on 'em; yes, sir, they have paid their passage, I may say," and the trader laughed at his joke.

There was something so piquant and original in these elucidations of humanity, that Mr. Shelby could not help laughing in company. Perhaps you laugh too, dear reader; but you know humanity comes out in a variety of strange forms now-a-days, and there is no end to the odd things that humane people will say and do.

Mr. Shelby's laugh encouraged the trader to proceed.

"It's strange, now, but I never could beat this into people's heads. Now, there was Tom Loker, my old partner, down in Natchez; he was a clever fellow, Tom was, only the very

---

6 William Wilberforce (1759–1833), English politician and great crusader against slavery in England.

devil with niggers,—on principle 'twas, you see, for a better-hearted feller never broke bread; 'twas his system, sir. I used to talk to Tom. 'Why, Tom,' I used to say, 'when your gals takes on and cry, what's the use o' crackin' on 'em over the head, and knockin' on 'em round? It's ridiculous,' says I, 'and don't do no sort o' good. Why, I don't see no harm in their cryin',' says I; 'it's natur,' says I, 'and if natur can't blow off one way, it will another. Besides, Tom,' says I, 'it jest spiles your gals; they get sickly, and down in the mouth; and sometimes they gets ugly,—particular yellow gals do,—and it's the devil and all gettin' on 'em broke in. Now,' says I, 'why can't you kinder coax 'em up, and speak 'em fair? Depend on it, Tom, a little humanity, thrown in along, goes a heap further than all your jawin' and crackin'; and it pays better,' says I, 'depend on 't.' But Tom couldn't get the hang on 't; and he spiled so many for me, that I had to break off with him, though he was a good-hearted fellow, and as fair a business hand as is goin'."

"And do you find your ways of managing do the business better than Tom's?" said Mr. Shelby.

"Why, yes, sir, I may say so. You see, when I any ways can, I takes a leetle care about the unpleasant parts, like selling young uns and that,— get the gals out of the way—out of sight, out of mind, you know,—and when it's clean done, and can't be helped, they natu-rally gets used to it. 'Tan't, you know, as if it was white folks, that's brought up in the way of 'spectin' to keep their children and wives, and all that. Niggers, you know, that's fetched up properly, ha'n't no kind of 'spectations of no kind; so all these things comes easier."

"I'm afraid mine are not properly brought up, then," said Mr. Shelby.

"S'pose not; you Kentucky folks spile your niggers. You mean well by 'em, but 'tan't no real kindness, arter all. Now, a nigger, you see, what's got to be hacked and tumbled round the world, and sold to Tom, and Dick, and the Lord knows who, 'tan't no kindness to be givin' on him notions and expectations, and bringin' on him up too well, for the rough and tumble comes all the harder on him arter. Now, I venture to say, your niggers would be quite chop-fallen in a place where some of your plantation niggers would be singing and whooping like all possessed. Every man, you know, Mr. Shelby, naturally thinks well of his own ways; and I think I treat niggers just about as well as it's ever worth while to treat 'em."

"It's a happy thing to be satisfied," said Mr. Shelby, with a slight shrug, and some per-ceptible feelings of a disagreeable nature.

"Well," said Haley, after they had both silently picked their nuts for a season, "what do you say?"

"I'll think the matter over, and talk with my wife," said Mr. Shelby. "Meantime, Haley, if you want the matter carried on in the quiet way you speak of, you'd best not let your business in this neighborhood be known. It will get out among my boys, and it will not be a particularly quiet business getting away any of my fellows, if they know it, I'll promise you."

"Oh! certainly, by all means, mum! of course. But I'll tell you, I'm in a devil of a hurry, and shall want to know, as soon as possible, what I may depend on," said he, rising and putting on his overcoat.

"Well, call up this evening, between six and seven, and you shall have my answer," said Mr. Shelby, and the trader bowed himself out of the apartment.

"I'd like to have been able to kick the fellow down the steps," said he to himself, as he saw the door fairly closed, "with his impudent assurance; but he knows how much he has me at advantage. If anybody had ever said to me that I should sell Tom down south to one of those rascally traders, I should have said, 'Is thy servant a dog, that he should do this thing?' And now it must come, for aught I see. And Eliza's child, too! I know that I shall have some fuss with wife about that; and, for that matter, about Tom, too. So much for being in debt,—heigho! The fellow sees his advantage, and means to push it."

Perhaps the mildest form of the system of slavery is to be seen in the State of Kentucky. The general prevalence of agricultural pursuits of a quiet and gradual nature, not requiring those periodic seasons of hurry and pressure that are called for in the business of more southern districts, makes the task of the Negro a more healthful and reasonable one; while the master, content with a more gradual style of acquisition, has not those temptations to hardheartedness which always overcome frail human nature when the prospect of sudden and rapid gain is weighed in the balance, with no heavier counterpoise than the interests of the helpless and unprotected.

Whoever visits some estates there, and witnesses the good-humored indulgence of some masters and mistresses, and the affectionate loyalty of some slaves, might be tempted to dream the oft-fabled poetic legend of a patriarchal institution, and all that; but over and above the scene there broods a portentous shadow—the shadow of *law*. So long as the law considers all these human beings, with beating hearts and living affections, only as so many *things* belonging to a master,—so long as the failure, or misfortune, or imprudence, or death of the kindest owner, may cause them any day to exchange a life of kind protection and indulgence for one of hopeless misery and toil,—so long it is impossible to make anything beautiful or desirable in the best regulated administration of slavery.

Mr. Shelby was a fair average kind of man, good-natured and kindly, and disposed to easy indulgence of those around him, and there had never been a lack of anything which might contribute to the physical comfort of the Negroes on his estate. He had, however, speculated largely and quite loosely; had involved himself deeply, and his notes to a large amount had come into the hands of Haley; and this small piece of information is the key to the preceding conversation.

Now, it had so happened that, in approaching the door, Eliza had caught enough of the conversation to know that a trader was making offers to her master for somebody.

She would gladly have stopped at the door to listen, as she came out; but her mistress just then calling, she was obliged to hasten away.

Still she thought she heard the trader make an offer for her boy;— could she be mistaken? Her heart swelled and throbbed, and she involuntarily strained him so tight that the little fellow looked up into her face in astonishment.

"Eliza, girl, what ails you to-day?" said her mistress, when Eliza had upset the wash-pitcher, knocked down the work-stand, and finally was abstractedly offering her mistress a long night-gown in place of the silk dress she had ordered her to bring from the wardrobe.

Eliza started. "O, Missis!" she said, raising her eyes; then, bursting into tears, she sat down in a chair, and began sobbing.

"Why, Eliza child! what ails you?" said her mistress.

"O! Missis, Missis," said Eliza, "there's been a trader talking with master in the parlor. I heard him."

"Well, silly child, suppose there has."

"O, Missis, *do* you suppose Mas'r would sell my Harry?" And the poor creature threw herself into a chair, and sobbed convulsively.

"Sell him! No, you foolish girl! You know your master never deals with those southern traders, and never means to sell any of his servants, as long as they behave well. Why, you silly child, who do you think would want to buy your Harry? Do you think all the world are set on him as you are, you goosie? Come, cheer up, and hook my dress. There now, put my back hair up in that pretty braid you learnt the other day, and don't go listening at doors any more."

"Well, but Missis, *you* never would give your consent—to—to—"

"Nonsense, child! to be sure, I shouldn't. What do you talk so for? I would as soon have one of my own children sold. But really, Eliza, you are getting altogether too proud of that little fellow. A man can't put his nose into the door, but you think he must be coming to buy him."

Reassured by her mistress' confident tone, Eliza proceeded nimbly and adroitly with her toilet, laughing at her own fears, as she proceeded.

Mrs. Shelby was a woman of a high class, both intellectually and morally. To that natural magnanimity and generosity of mind which one often marks as characteristic of the women of Kentucky, she added high moral and religious sensibility and principle, carried out with great energy and ability into practical results. Her husband, who made no professions to any particular religious character, nevertheless reverenced and respected the consistency of hers, and stood, perhaps, a little in awe of her opinion. Certain it was that he gave her unlimited scope in all her benevolent efforts for the comfort, instruction, and improvement of her servants, though he never took any decided part in them himself. In fact, if not exactly a believer in the doctrine of the efficiency of the extra good works of saints, he really seemed somehow or other to fancy that his wife had piety and benevolence enough for two—to indulge a shadowy expectation of getting into heaven through her superabundance of qualities to which he made no particular pretension.

The heaviest load on his mind, after his conversation with the trader, lay in the foreseen necessity of breaking to his wife the arrangement contemplated,—meeting the importunities and opposition which he knew he should have reason to encounter.

Mrs. Shelby, being entirely ignorant of her husband's embarrassments, and knowing only the general kindliness of his temper, had been quite sincere in the entire incredulity with which she had met Eliza's suspicions. In fact, she dismissed the matter from her mind, without a second thought; and being occupied in preparations for an evening visit, it passed out of her thoughts entirely.

Chapter 2

The Mother

Eliza had been brought up by her mistress, from girlhood, as a petted and indulged favorite.

The traveller in the south must often have remarked that peculiar air of refinement, that softness of voice and manner, which seems in many cases to be a particular gift to the quadroon and mulatto women. These natural graces in the quadroon are often united with beauty of the most dazzling kind, and in almost every case with a personal appearance prepossessing and agreeable. Eliza, such as we have described her, is not a fancy sketch, but taken from remembrance, as we saw her, years ago, in Kentucky. Safe under the protecting care of her mistress, Eliza had reached maturity without those temptations which make beauty so fatal in inheritance to a slave. She had been married to a bright and talented young mulatto man, who was a slave on a neighboring estate, and bore the name of George Harris.

This young man had been hired out by his master to work in a bagging factory, where his adroitness and ingenuity caused him to be considered the first hand in the place. He had invented a machine for the cleaning of the hemp, which, considering the education and circumstances of the inventor, displayed quite as much mechanical genius as Whitney's[7] cotton-gin.[8]

He was possessed of a handsome person and pleasing manners, and was a general favorite in the factory. Nevertheless, as this young man was in the eye of the law not a man, but a thing, all these superior qualifications were subject to the control of a vulgar, narrow-minded, tyrannical master. This same gentleman, having heard of the fame of George's invention, took a ride over to the factory, to see what this intelligent chattel had been about. He was received with great enthusiasm by the employer, who congratulated him on possessing so valuable a slave.

He was waited upon over the factory, shown the machinery by George, who, in high spirits, talked so fluently, held himself so erect, looked so handsome and manly, that his master began to feel an uneasy consciousness of inferiority. What business had his slave to be marching round the country, inventing machines, and holding up his head among gentlemen? He'd soon put a stop to it. He'd take him back, and put him to hoeing and digging, and "see if he'd step about so smart." Accordingly, the manufacturer and all hands concerned were astounded when he suddenly demanded George's wages, and announced his intention of taking him home.

"But, Mr. Harris," remonstrated the manufacturer, "isn't this rather sudden?"

"What if it is?—isn't the man *mine?*"

"We would be willing, sir, to increase the rate of compensation."

"No object at all, sir. I don't need to hire any of my hands out, unless I've a mind to."

"But, sir, he seems peculiarly adapted to this business."

"Dare say he may be; never was much adapted to anything that I set him about, I'll be bound."

"But only think of his inventing this machine," interposed one of the workmen, rather unluckily.

"O yes!—a machine for saving work, is it? He'd invent that, I'll be bound; let a nigger alone for that, any time. They are all labor-saving machines themselves, every one of 'em. No, he shall tramp!"

George had stood like one transfixed, at hearing his doom thus suddenly pronounced by a power that he knew was irresistible. He folded his arms, tightly pressed in his lips, but a whole volcano of bitter feelings burned in his bosom, and sent streams of fire through his veins. He breathed short, and his large dark eyes flashed like live coals; and he might have broken out into some dangerous ebullition, had not the kindly manufacturer touched him on the arm, and said, in a low tone,

"Give way, George; go with him for the present. We'll try to help you, yet."

The tyrant observed the whisper, and conjectured its import, though he could not hear what was said; and he inwardly strengthened himself in his determination to keep the power he possessed over his victim.

---

7 In 1793 Eli Whitney (1765–1825) patented a machine that separated cotton from its seeds, revolutionizing the South's cotton industry. There were persistent rumors during his life and after his death that a slave had actually invented the machine. By law, slaves could not apply for invention patents.

8 [Author's Original Note] A machine of this description was really the invention of a young colored man in Kentucky.

George was taken home, and put to the meanest drudgery of the farm. He had been able to repress every disrespectful word; but the flashing eye, the gloomy and troubled brow, were part of a natural language that could not be repressed,—indubitable signs, which showed too plainly that the man could not become a thing.

It was during the happy period of his employment in the factory that George had seen and married his wife. During that period,—being much trusted and favored by his employer,—he had free liberty to come and go at discretion. The marriage was highly approved of by Mrs. Shelby, who, with a little womanly complacency in match-making, felt pleased to unite her handsome favorite with one of her own class who seemed in every way suited to her; and so they were married in her mistress' great parlor, and her mistress herself adorned the bride's beautiful hair with orange-blossoms, and threw over it the bridal veil, which certainly could scarce have rested on a fairer head; and there was no lack of white gloves, and cake and wine,—of admiring guests to praise the bride's beauty, and her mistress' indulgence and liberality. For a year or two Eliza saw her husband frequently, and there was nothing to interrupt their happiness, except the loss of two infant children, to whom she was passionately attached, and whom she mourned with a grief so intense as to call for gentle remonstrance from her mistress, who sought, with maternal anxiety, to direct her naturally passionate feelings within the bounds of reason and religion.

After the birth of little Harry, however, she had gradually become tranquillized and settled; and every bleeding tie and throbbing nerve, once more entwined with that little life, seemed to become sound and healthful, and Eliza was a happy woman up to the time that her husband was rudely torn from his kind employer, and brought under the iron sway of his legal owner.

The manufacturer, true to his word, visited Mr. Harris a week or two after George had been taken away, when as he hoped, the heat of the occasion had passed away, and tried every possible inducement to lead him to restore him to his former employment.

"You needn't trouble yourself to talk any longer," said he, doggedly; "I know my own business, sir."

"I did not presume to interfere with it, sir. I only thought that you might think it for your interest to let your man to us on the terms proposed."

"O, I understand the matter well enough. I saw your winking and whispering, the day I took him out of the factory; but you don't come it over me that way. It's a free country, sir; the man's mine, and I do what I please with him,—that's it!"

And so fell George's last hope;—nothing before him but a life of toil and drudgery, rendered more bitter by every little smarting vexation and indignity which tyrannical ingenuity could devise.

A very humane jurist once said, "The worst use you can put a man to is to hang him." No; there is another use that a man can be put to that is WORSE!

Chapter 3

The Husband and Father

Mrs. Shelby had gone on her visit, and Eliza stood in the verandah, rather dejectedly looking after the retreating carriage, when a hand was laid on her shoulder. She turned, and a bright smile lighted up her fine eyes.

"George, is it you? How you frightened me! Well; I am so glad you's come! Missis is gone to spend the afternoon; so come into my little room, and we'll have the time all to ourselves."

Saying this, she drew him into a neat little apartment opening on the verandah, where she generally sat at her sewing, within call of her mistress.

"How glad I am!—why don't you smile?—and look at Harry—how he grows." The boy stood shyly regarding his father through his curls, holding close to the skirts of his mother's dress. "Isn't he beautiful?" said Eliza, lifting his long curls and kissing him.

"I wish he'd never been born!" said George, bitterly. "I wish I'd never been born myself!"

Surprised and frightened, Eliza sat down, leaned her head on her husband's shoulder, and burst into tears.

"There now, Eliza, it's too bad for me to make you feel so, poor girl!" said he, fondly; "it's too bad. O, how I wish you never had seen me— you might have been happy!"

"George! George! how can you talk so? What dreadful thing has happened, or is going to happen? I'm sure we've been very happy, till lately."

"So we have, dear," said George. Then drawing his child on his knee, he gazed intently on his glorious dark eyes, and passed his hands through his long curls.

"Just like you, Eliza; and you are the handsomest woman I ever saw, and the best one I ever wish to see; but, oh, I wish I'd never seen you, nor you me!"

"O George, how can you!"

"Yes, Eliza, it's all misery, misery, misery! My life is bitter as wormwood;[9] the very life is burning out of me. I'm a poor, miserable, forlorn drudge; I shall only drag you down with me, that's all. What's the use of our trying to do anything, trying to know anything, trying to be anything? What's the use of living? I wish I was dead!"

"O, now, dear George, that is really wicked! I know how you feel about losing your place in the factory, and you have a hard master; but pray be patient, and perhaps something—"

"Patient!" said he, interrupting her; "haven't I been patient? Did I say a word when he came and took me away, for no earthly reason, from the place where everybody was kind to me? I'd paid him truly every cent of my earnings,—and they all say I worked well."

"Well, it is dreadful," said Eliza; "but, after all, he is your master, you know."

"My master! and who made him my master? That's what I think of— what right has he to me? I'm a man as much as he is. I'm a better man than he is. I know more about business than he does; I am a better manager than he is; I can read better than he can; I can write a better hand,— and I've learned it all myself, and no thanks to him,—I've learned it in spite of him; and now what right has he to make a dray-horse[10] of me?— to take me from things I can do, and do better than he can, and put me to work that any horse can do? He tries to do it; he says he'll bring me down and humble me, and he puts me to just the hardest, meanest and dirtiest work, on purpose!"

"O, George! George! you frighten me! Why, I never heard you talk so; I'm afraid you'll do something dreadful. I don't wonder at your feelings, at all; but oh, do be careful—do, do—for my sake—for Harry's!"

"I have been careful, and I have been patient, but it's growing worse and worse; flesh and blood can't bear it any longer;—every chance he can get to insult and torment me, he takes. I thought I could do my work well, and keep on quiet, and have some time to read and learn out of work hours; but the more he sees I can do, the more he loads on. He says that though I don't say anything, he sees I've got the devil in me, and he means to bring it out; and one of these days it will come out in a way that he won't like, or I'm mistaken!"

---

9 Proverbs 5:3–4.
10 Work horse.

"O dear! what shall we do?" said Eliza, mournfully.

"It was only yesterday," said George, "as I was busy loading stones into a cart, that young Mas'r Tom stood there, slashing his whip so near the horse that the creature was frightened. I asked him to stop, as pleasant as I could,—he just kept right on. I begged him again, and then he turned on me, and began striking me. I held his hand, and then he screamed and kicked and ran to his father, and told him that I was fighting him. He came in a rage, and said he'd teach me who was my master; and he tied me to a tree, and cut switches for young master, and told him that he might whip me till he was tired;—and he did it! If I don't make him remember it, some time!" and the brow of the young man grew dark, and his eyes burned with an expression that made his young wife tremble. "Who made this man my master? That's what I want to know!" he said.

"Well," said Eliza, mournfully, "I always thought that I must obey my master and mistress, or I couldn't be a Christian."

"There is some sense in it, in your case; they have brought you up like a child, fed you, clothed you, indulged you, and taught you, so that you have a good education; that is some reason why they should claim you. But I have been kicked and cuffed and sworn at, and at the best only let alone; and what do I owe? I've paid for all my keeping a hundred times over. I *won't* bear it. No, I *won't!*" he said, clenching his hand with a fierce frown.

Eliza trembled, and was silent. She had never seen her husband in this mood before; and her gentle system of ethics seemed to bend like a reed in the surges of such passions.

"You know poor little Carlo, that you gave me," added George; "the creature has been about all the comfort that I've had. He has slept with me nights, and followed me around days, and kind o' looked at me as if he understood how I felt. Well, the other day I was just feeding him with a few old scraps I picked up by the kitchen door, and Mas'r came along, and said I was feeding him up at his expense, and that he couldn't afford to have every nigger keeping his dog, and ordered me to tie a stone to his neck and throw him in the pond."

"O, George, you didn't do it!"

"Do it? not I!—but he did. Mas'r and Tom pelted the poor drowning creature with stones. Poor thing! he looked at me so mournful, as if he wondered why I didn't save him. I had to take a flogging because I wouldn't do it myself. I don't care. Mas'r will find out that I'm one that whipping won't tame. My day will come yet, if he don't look out."

"What are you going to do? O, George, don't do anything wicked; if you only trust in God, and try to do right, he'll deliver you."

"I an't a Christian like you, Eliza; my heart's full of bitterness; I can't trust in God. Why does he let things be so?"

"O, George, we must have faith. Mistress says that when all things go wrong to us, we must believe that God is doing the very best."

"That's easy to say for people that are sitting on their sofas and riding in their carriages; but let 'em be where I am, I guess it would come some harder. I wish I could be good; but my heart burns, and can't be reconciled, anyhow. You couldn't, in my place,—you can't now, if I tell you all I've got to say. You don't know the whole yet."

"What can be coming now?"

"Well, lately Mas'r has been saying that he was a fool to let me marry off the place; that he hates Mr. Shelby and all his tribe, because they are proud, and hold their heads up above him, and that I've got proud notions for you; and he says he won't let me come here any more, and that I shall take a wife and settle down on his place. At first he only scolded and grumbled these things; but yesterday he told me that I should take Mina for a wife, and settle down in a cabin with her, or he would sell me down river."

"Why—but you were married to *me*, by the minister, as much as if you'd been a white man!" said Eliza, simply.

"Don't you know a slave can't be married? There is no law in this country for that; I can't hold you for my wife, if he chooses to part us. That's why I wish I'd never seen you,— why I wish I'd never been born; it would have been better for us both,—it would have been better for this poor child if he had never been born. All this may happen to him yet!"

"O, but Master is so kind!"

"Yes, but who knows?—he may die—and then he may be sold to nobody knows who. What pleasure is it that he is handsome, and smart, and bright? I tell you, Eliza, that a sword will pierce through your soul for every good and pleasant thing your child is or has; it will make him worth too much for you to keep!"

The words smote heavily on Eliza's heart; the vision of the trader came before her eyes, and, as if some one had struck her a deadly blow, she turned pale and gasped for breath. She looked nervously out on the verandah, where the boy, tired of the grave conversation, had retired, and where he was riding triumphantly up and down on Mr. Shelby's walking-stick. She would have spoken to tell her husband her fears, but checked herself.

"No, no,—he has enough to bear, poor fellow!" she thought. "No, I won't tell him; besides, it ain't true; Missis never deceives us."

"So, Eliza, my girl," said the husband, mournfully, "bear up, now; and good-bye, for I'm going."

"Going, George! Going where?"

"To Canada," said he, straightening himself up; "and when I'm there, I'll buy you; that's all the hope that's left us. You have a kind master, that won't refuse to sell you. I'll buy you and the boy;—God helping me, I will!"

"O, dreadful! if you should be taken?"

"I won't be taken, Eliza; I'll *die* first! I'll be free, or I'll die!"

"You won't kill yourself!"

"No need of that. They will kill me, fast enough; they never will get me down the river alive!"

"Oh, George, for my sake, do be careful! Don't do anything wicked; don't lay hands on yourself, or anybody else! You are tempted too much—too much; but don't—go you must—but go carefully, prudently; pray God to help you."

"Well, then, Eliza, hear my plan. Mas'r took it into his head to send me right by here, with a note to Mr. Symmes, that lives a mile past. I believe he expected I should come here to tell you what I have. It would please him, if he thought it would aggravate 'Shelby's folks,' as he calls 'em. I'm going home quite resigned, you understand, as if all was over. I've got some preparations made,—and there are those that will help me; and, in the course of a week or so, I shall be among the missing, some day. Pray for me, Eliza, perhaps the good Lord will hear *you*."

"O, pray yourself, George, and go trusting in him; then you won't do anything wicked."

"Well, now, *good-by*," said George, holding Eliza's hands, and gazing into her eyes, without moving. They stood silent; then there were last words, and sobs, and bitter weeping,— such parting as those may make whose hope to meet again is as the spider's web,—and the husband and wife were parted.

Chapter 4

An Evening in Uncle Tom's Cabin

The cabin of Uncle Tom was a small log building, close adjoining to "the house," as the Negro *par excellence* designates his master's dwelling. In front it had a neat garden-patch, where, every summer, strawberries, raspberries, and a variety of fruits and vegetables, flourished under careful tending. The whole front of it was covered by a large scarlet bignonia and a native multiflora rose, which, entwisting and interlacing, left scarce a vestige of the rough logs to be seen. Here, also, in summer, various brilliant annuals, such as marigolds, petunias, four o'clocks, found an indulgent corner in which to unfold their splendors, and were the delight and pride of Aunt Chloe's[11] heart.

Let us enter the dwelling. The evening meal at the house is over, and Aunt Chloe, who presided over its preparation as head cook, has left to inferior officers in the kitchen the business of clearing away and washing dishes, and come out into her own snug territories, to "get her ole man's supper"; therefore, doubt not that it is her you see by the fire, presiding with anxious interest over certain frizzling items in a stew-pan, and anon with grave consideration lifting the cover of a bake-kettle, from whence steam forth indubitable intimations of "something good." A round, black, shining face is hers, so glossy as to suggest the idea that she might have been washed over with white of eggs, like one of her own tea rusks.[12] Her whole plump countenance beams with satisfaction and contentment from under her well-starched checked turban, bearing on it, however, if we must confess it, a little of that tinge of self-consciousness which becomes the first cook of the neighborhood, as Aunt Chloe was universally held and acknowledged to be.

A cook she certainly was, in the very bone and center of her soul. Not a chicken or turkey or duck in the barnyard but looked grave when they saw her approaching, and seemed evidently to be reflecting on their latter end; and certain it was that she was always meditating on trussing, stuffing and roasting, to a degree that was calculated to inspire terror in any reflecting fowl living. Her corn-cake, in all its varieties of hoe-cake, dodgers, muffins, and other species too numerous to mention, was a sublime mystery to all less practised compounders; and she would shake her fat sides with honest pride and merriment, as she would narrate the fruitless efforts that one and another of her compeers had made to attain to her elevation.

The arrival of company at the house, the arranging of dinners and suppers "in style," awoke all the energies of her soul; and no sight was more welcome to her than a pile of travelling trunks launched on the verandah, for then she foresaw fresh efforts and fresh triumphs.

Just at present, however, Aunt Chloe is looking into the bake-pan, in which congenial operation we shall leave her until we finish our picture of the cottage.

In one corner of it stood a bed, covered neatly with a snowy spread; and by the side of it was a piece of carpeting, of some considerable size. On this piece of carpeting Aunt Chloe took her stand, as being decidedly in the upper walks of life; and it and the bed by which it lay, and the whole corner, in fact, were treated with distinguished consideration, and made, so far as possible, sacred from the marauding inroads and desecrations of little folks. In fact,

---

11 "Aunt" and "Uncle" were frequently used familiar forms of address for older black women and men.

12 Breads that are baked twice to make them especially crisp.

that corner was the *drawing-room*[13] of the establishment. In the other corner was a bed of much humbler pretensions, and evidently designed for *use*. The wall over the fireplace was adorned with some very brilliant scriptural prints, and a portrait of General Washington, drawn and colored in a manner which would certainly have astonished that hero, if ever he had happened to meet with its like.

On a rough bench in the corner, a couple of woolly-headed boys, with glistening black eyes and fat shining cheeks, were busy in superintending the first walking operations of the baby, which, as is usually the case, consisted in getting up on its feet, balancing a moment, and then tumbling down,—each successive failure being violently cheered, as something decidedly clever.

A table, somewhat rheumatic in its limbs, was drawn out in front of the fire, and covered with a cloth, displaying cups and saucers of a decidedly brilliant pattern, with other symptoms of an approaching meal. At this table was seated Uncle Tom, Mr. Shelby's best hand, who, as he is to be the hero of our story, we must daguerreotype[14] for our readers. He was a large, broad-chested, powerfully-made man, of a fully glossy black, and a face whose truly African features were characterized by an expression of grave and steady good sense, united with much kindliness and benevolence. There was something about his whole air self-respecting and dignified, yet united with a confiding and humble simplicity.

He was very busily intent at this moment on a slate lying before him, on which he was carefully and slowly endeavoring to accomplish a copy of some letters, in which operation he was overlooked by young Mas'r George, a smart, bright boy of thirteen, who appeared fully to realize the dignity of his position as instructor.

"Not that way, Uncle Tom,—not that way," said he, briskly, as Uncle Tom laboriously brought up the tail of his g the wrong side out; "that makes a q, you see."

"La sakes, now, does it?" said Uncle Tom, looking with a respectful, admiring air, as his young teacher flourishingly scrawled *q*'s and *g*'s innumerable for his edification; and then, taking the pencil in his big, heavy fingers, he patiently recommenced.

"How easy white folks al'us does things!" said Aunt Chloe, pausing while she was greasing a griddle with a scrap of bacon on her fork, and regarding young Master George with pride. "The way he can write, now! and read, too! and then to come out here evenings and read his lessons to us,—it's mighty interestin'!"

"But, Aunt Chloe, I'm getting mighty hungry," said George. "Isn't that cake in the skillet almost done?"

"Mose done, Mas'r George," said Aunt Chloe, lifting the lid and peeping in,—"browning beautiful—a real lovely brown. Ah! let me alone for dat. Missis let Sally try to make some cake t'other day, jes to larn her, she said. 'O, go way, Missis,' says I; it really hurts my feelin's, now, to see good vittles spiled dat ar way! Cake ris all to one side—no shape at all; no more than my shoe;—go way!"

And with this final expression of contempt for Sally's greenness, Aunt Chloe whipped the cover off the bake-kettle, and disclosed to view a neatly-baked pound-cake, of which no city confectioner need to have been ashamed. This being evidently the central point of the entertainment, Aunt Chloe began now to bustle about earnestly in the supper department.

---

13 Formal reception room.
14 To describe in a lifelike manner, based on the early photographic technology invented by the French artist Louis Daguerre (1787–1851).

"Here you, Mose and Pete! get out de way, you niggers! Get away, Polly, honey,—mammy'll give her baby somefin, by and by. Now, Mas'r George, you jest take off dem books, and set down now with my old man, and I'll take up de sausages, and have de first griddle full of cakes on your plates in less dan no time."

"They wanted me to come to supper in the house," said George; "but I knew what was what too well for that, Aunt Chloe."

"So you did—so you did, honey," said Aunt Chloe, heaping the smoking battercakes on his plate; "you know'd your old aunty'd keep the best for you. O, let you alone for dat! Go way!" And, with that, aunty gave George a nudge with her finger, designed to be immensely facetious, and turned again to her griddle with great briskness.

"Now for the cake," said Mas'r George, when the activity of the griddle department had somewhat subsided; and, with that, the youngster flourished a large knife over the article in question.

"La bless you, Mas'r George!" said Aunt Chloe, with earnestness, catching his arm, "you wouldn't be for cuttin' it wid dat ar great heavy knife! Smash all down—spile all de pretty rise of it. Here, I've got a thin old knife, I keeps sharp a purpose. Dar now, see! comes apart light as a feather! Now eat away—you won't get anything to beat dat ar."

"Tom Lincon says," said George, speaking with his mouth full, "that their Jinny is a better cook than you."

"Dem Lincons an't much 'count, no way!" said Aunt Chloe, contemptuously; "I mean, set along side *our* folks. They's 'spectable folks enough in a kinder plain way; but, as to gettin' up anything in style, they don't begin to have a notion on't. Set Mas'r Lincon, now, alongside Mas'r Shelby! Good Lor! and Missis Lincon,—can she kinder sweep it into a room like my missis,—so kinder splendid, yer know! O, go way! don't tell me nothin' of dem Lincons!"—and Aunt Chloe tossed her head as one who hoped she did know something of the world.

"Well, though, I've heard you say," said George, "that Jinny was a pretty fair cook."

"So I did," said Aunt Chloe,—"I may say dat. Good, plain, common cookin', Jinny'll do;—make a good pone o' bread,—bile her taters *far*,— her corn cakes isn't extra, not extra now, Jinny's corn cakes isn't, but then they's far,—but, Lor, come to de higher branches, and what *can* she do? Why, she makes pies—sartin she does; but what kinder crust? Can she make your real flecky paste, as melts in your mouth, and lies all up like a puff? Now, I went over thar when Miss Mary was gwine to be married, and Jinny she jest showed me de weddin' pies. Jinny and I is good friends, ye know. I never said nothin'; but go long, Mas'r George! Why, I shouldn't sleep a wink for a week, if I had a batch of pies like dem ar. Why dey wan't no 'count't all."

"I suppose Jinny thought they were ever so nice," said George.

"Thought so!—didn't she? Thar she was, showing 'em, as innocent—ye see, it's jest here, Jinny *don't know*. Lor, the family an't nothing! She can't be spected to know! 'Ta'nt no fault o' hern. Ah, Mas'r George, you doesn't know half your privileges in yer family and bringin' up!" Here Aunt Chloe sighed, and rolled up her eyes with emotion.

"I'm sure, Aunt Chloe, I understand all my pie and pudding privileges," said George. "Ask Tom Lincon if I don't crow over him, every time I meet him."

Aunt Chloe sat back in her chair, and indulged in a hearty guffaw of laughter, at this witticism of young Mas'r's, laughing till the tears rolled down her black, shining cheeks, and varying the exercise with playfully slapping and poking Mas'r Georgey, and telling him to go way, and that he was a case—that he was fit to kill her, and that he sartin would kill her, one of these days; and, between each of these sanguinary predictions, going off into a laugh, each longer and stronger than the other, till George really began to think that he was a very dangerously witty fellow, and that it became him to be careful how he talked "as funny as he could."

"And so ye telled Tom, did ye? O, Lor! what young uns will be up ter! Ye crowed over Tom? O, Lor, Mas'r George, if ye wouldn't make a hornbug laugh!"

"Yes," said George, "I says to him, 'Tom, you ought to see some of Aunt Chloe's pies; they're the right sort,' says I."

"Pity, now, Tom couldn't," said Aunt Chloe, on whose benevolent heart the idea of Tom's benighted condition seemed to make a strong impression. "Ye oughter just ask him here to dinner, some o' these times, Mas'r George," she added; "it would look quite pretty of ye. Ye know, Mas'r George, ye oughtenter feel 'bove nobody, on 'count yer privileges, 'cause all our privileges is gi'n to us; we ought al'ays to 'member that," said Aunt Chloe, looking quite serious.

"Well, I mean to ask Tom here, some day next week," said George; "and you do your prettiest, Aunt Chloe, and we'll make him stare. Won't we make him eat so he won't get over it for a fortnight?"

"Yes, yes—sartin," said Aunt Chloe, delighted; "you'll see. Lor! to think of some of our dinners! Yer mind dat ar great chicken pie I made when we guv de dinner to Gineral Knox? I and Missis, we come pretty near quarrelling about dat ar crust. What does get into ladies sometimes, I don't know; but, sometimes, when a body has de heaviest kind o' 'sponsibility on 'em, as ye may say, and is all kinder 'seris' and taken up, dey takes dat ar time to be hangin' round and kinder interferin'! Now, Missis, she wanted me to do dis way, and she wanted me to do dat way; and, finally, I got kinder sarcy, and, says I, 'Now, Missis, do jist look at dem beautiful white hands o' yourn, with long fingers, and all a sparkling with rings, like my white lilies when de dew's on 'em; and look at my great black stumpin' hands. Now, don't ye think dat de Lord must have meant *me* to make de pie-crust, and you to stay in de parlor?' Dar! I was jist so sarcy, Mas'r George."

"And what did mother say?" said George.

"Say?—why, she kinder larfed in her eyes—dem great handsome eyes o' hern; and, says she, 'Well, Aunt Chloe, I think you are about in the right on't,' says she; and she went off in de parlor. She oughter cracked me over de head for bein' so sarcy; but dar's whar 't is—I can't do nothin' with ladies in de kitchen!"

"Well, you made out well with that dinner,—I remember everybody said so," said George.

"Didn't I? And wan't I behind de dinin'-room door dat bery day? and didn't I see de Gineral pass his plate three times for some more dat berry pie?—and, says he, 'You must have an uncommon cook, Mrs. Shelby.' Lor, I was fit to split myself."

"And de Gineral, he knows what cookin' is," said Aunt Chloe, drawing herself up with an air. "Bery nice man, de Gineral! He comes of one of de bery fustest families in Old Virginny! He knows what's what, as well as I do—de Gineral. Ye see, there's *pints* in all pies, Mas'r George; but tan't everybody knows what they is, or orter be. But the Gineral, he knows; I knew by his 'marks he made. Yes, he knows what de pints is!"

By this time, Master George had arrived at that pass to which even a boy can come (under uncommon circumstances), when he really could not eat another morsel and, therefore, he was at leisure to notice the pile of woolly heads and glistening eyes which were regarding their operations hungrily from the opposite corner.

"Here, you Mose, Pete," he said, breaking off liberal bits, and throwing it at them; "you want some, don't you? Come, Aunt Chloe, bake them some cakes."

And George and Tom moved to a comfortable seat in the chimney-corner while Aunt Chloe, after baking a goodly pile of cakes, took her baby on her lap, and began alternately filling its mouth and her own, and distributing to Mose and Pete, who seemed rather to prefer eating theirs as they rolled about on the floor under the table, tickling each other, and occasionally pulling the baby's toes.

"O! go long, will ye?" said the mother, giving now and then a kick, in a kind of general way, under the table, when the movement became too obstreperous. "Can't ye be decent when white folks comes to see ye? Stop dat ar, now, will ye? Better mind yerselves, or I'll take ye down a button-hole lower, when Mas'r George is gone!"

What meaning was crouched under this terrible threat, it is difficult to say; but certain it is that its awful indistinctness seemed to produce very little impression on the young sinners addressed.

"La, now!" said Uncle Tom, "they are so full of tickle all the while, they can't behave theirselves."

Here the boys emerged from under the table, and, with hands and faces well plastered with molasses, began a vigorous kissing of the baby.

"Get along wid ye!" said the mother, pushing away their woolly heads. "Ye'll all stick together, and never get clar, if ye do dat fashion. Go long to de spring and wash yerselves!" she said, seconding her exhortations by a slap, which resounded very formidably, but which seemed only to knock out so much more laugh from the young ones, as they tumbled precipitately over each other out of doors, where they fairly screamed with merriment.

"Did ye ever see such aggravating young uns?" said Aunt Chloe, rather complacently, as, producing an old towel, kept for such emergencies, she poured a little water out of the cracked tea-pot on it, and began rubbing off the molasses from the baby's face and hands; and, having polished her till she shone, she set her down in Tom's lap, while she busied herself in clearing away supper. The baby employed the intervals in pulling Tom's nose, scratching his face, and burying her fat hands in his woolly hair, which last operation seemed to afford her special content.

"Ain't she a peart young un?" said Tom, holding her from him to take a full-length view; then, getting up, he set her on his broad shoulder, and began capering and dancing with her, while Mas'r George snapped at her with his pocket-handkerchief, and Mose and Pete, now returned again, roared after her like bears, till Aunt Chloe declared that they "fairly took her head off" with their noise. As, according to her own statement, this surgical operation was a matter of daily occurrence in the cabin, the declaration no whit abated the merriment, till every one had roared and tumbled and danced themselves down to a state of composure.

"Well, now, I hopes you're done," said Aunt Chloe, who had been busy in pulling out a rude box of a trundle-bed; "and now, you Mose and you Pete, get into thar; for we's goin' to have the meetin'."

"O mother, we don't wanter. We wants to sit up to meetin',—meetin's is so curis. We likes 'em."

"La, Aunt Chloe, shove it under, and let 'em sit up," said Mas'r George, decisively, giving a push to the rude machine.

Aunt Chloe, having thus saved appearances, seemed highly delighted to push the thing under, saying, as she did so, "Well, mebbe 'twill do 'em some good."

The house now resolved itself into a committee of the whole, to consider the accommodations and arrangements for the meeting.

"What we's to do for cheers, now, I declare I don't know," said Aunt Chloe. As the meeting had been held at Uncle Tom's, weekly, for an indefinite length of time, without any more "cheers," there seemed some encouragement to hope that a way would be discovered at present.

"Old Uncle Peter sung both de legs out of dat oldest cheer, last week," suggested Mose.

"You go long! I'll boun' you pulled 'em out; some o' your shines," said Aunt Chloe.

"Well, it'll stand, if it only keeps jam up again de wall!" said Mose.

"Den Uncle Peter mus'n't sit in it, cause he al'ays hitches when he gets a singing. He hitched pretty nigh across de room, t' other night," said Pete.

"Good Lor! get him in it, then," said Mose, "and den he'd begin, 'Come saints and sinners, hear me tell,' and den down he'd go,"[15]—and Mose imitated precisely the nasal tones of the old man, tumbling on the floor, to illustrate the supposed catastrophe.

"Come now, be decent, can't ye?" said Aunt Chloe; "an't yer shamed?"

Mas'r George, however, joined the offender in the laugh, and declared decidedly that Mose was a "buster." So the maternal admonition seemed rather to fail of effect.

"Well, ole man," said Aunt Chloe, "you'll have to tote in them ar bar'ls."

"Mother's bar'ls is like dat ar widder's, Mas'r George was reading 'bout, in de good book,—dey never fails," said Mose, aside to Pete.

"I'm sure one on 'em caved in last week," said Pete, "and let 'em all down in de middle of de singin'; dat ar was failin', warn't it?"

During this aside between Mose and Pete, two empty casks had been rolled into the cabin, and being secured from rolling, by stones on each side, boards were laid across them, which arrangement, together with the turning down of certain tubs and pails, and the disposing of the rickety chairs, at last completed the preparation.

"Mas'r George is such a beautiful reader, now, I know he'll stay to read for us," said Aunt Chloe; "'pears like 'twill be so much more interestin'.'"

George very readily assented, for your boy is always ready for anything that makes him of importance.

The room was soon filled with a motley assemblage, from the old gray-headed patriarch of eighty, to the young girl and lad of fifteen. A little harmless gossip ensued on various themes, such as where old Aunt Sally got her new red handkerchief, and how "Missis was a going to give Lizy that spotted muslin gown, when she'd got her new berage made up;" and how Mas'r Shelby was thinking of buying a new sorrel colt, that was going to prove an addition to the glories of the place. A few of the worshippers belonged to families hard by, who had got permission to attend, and who brought in various choice scraps of information, about the sayings and doings at the house and on the place, which circulated as freely as the same sort of small change does in higher circles.

After a while the singing commenced, to the evident delight of all present. Not even all the disadvantage of nasal intonation could prevent the effect of the naturally fine voices, in airs at once wild and spirited. The words were sometimes the well-known and common hymns sung in the churches about, and sometimes of a wilder, more indefinite character, picked up at camp-meetings.

---

15 From the Methodist hymn "Come Saints and Sinners," also known as "Heavenly Union."

The chorus of one of them, which ran as follows, was sung with great energy and unction:

"Die on the field of battle,
Die on the field of battle.
Glory in my soul."[16]

Another special favorite had oft repeated the words—

"O, I'm going to glory,—won't you come along with me?
Don't you see the angels beck'ning, and a calling me away?
Don't you see the golden city and the everlasting day?"[17]

There were others, which made incessant mention of "Jordan's banks,"[18] and "Canaan's fields,"[19] and the "New Jerusalem;"[20] for the Negro mind, impassioned and imaginative, always attaches itself to hymns and expressions of a vivid and pictorial nature; and, as they sang, some laughed, and some cried, and some clapped hands, or shook hands rejoicingly with each other, as if they had fairly gained the other side of the river.

Various exhortations, or relations of experience, followed, and intermingled with the singing. One old gray-headed woman, long past work, but much revered as a sort of chronicle of the past, rose, and leaning on her staff, said—

"Well, chil'en! Well, I'm mighty glad to hear ye all and see ye all once more, 'cause I don't know when I'll be gone to glory; but I've done got ready, chil'en; 'pears like I'd got my little bundle all tied up, and my bonnet on, jest a waitin' for the stage to come along and take me home; sometimes, in the night, I think I hear the wheels a rattlin', and I'm lookin' out all the time; now, you jest be ready too, for I tell ye all, chil'en," she said, striking her staff hard on the floor, "dat ar *glory* is a mighty thing! It's a mighty thing, chil'en,—you don'no nothing about it,—it's *wonderful*." And the old creature sat down, with streaming tears, as wholly overcome, while the whole circle struck up—

"O Canaan, bright Canaan,
I'm bound for the land of Canaan."[21]

Mas'r George, by request, read the last chapters of Revelation,[22] often interrupted by such exclamations as "The *sakes* now!" "Only hear that!" "Jest think on't!" "Is all that a comin' sure enough?"

---

16 From the hymn "Die in the Field" by Samuel Wakefield (1799–1895).
17 Similar to the spiritual "Bound for the Promised Land."
18 Deuteronomy 11:31. The Jordan River marked the boundary of the Hebrews' Promised Land.
19 Exodus 6:4. Canaan is a reference to the land promised to the Israelites after their escape from slavery in Egypt.
20 Revelation 3:12 and 21:2. Reference to the heavenly city where Christians go after they are judged righteous.
21 From a famous Methodist hymn by John Wesley (1703–1791).
22 The last book in the New Testament; it tells of God's judgment for both the righteous and the unrighteous.

George, who was a bright boy, and well trained in religious things by his mother, finding himself an object of general admiration, threw in expositions of his own, from time to time, with a commendable seriousness and gravity, for which he was admired by the young and blessed by the old; and it was agreed, on all hands, that "a minister couldn't lay it off better than he did;" that " 'twas reely 'mazin'!"

Uncle Tom was a sort of patriarch in religious matters, in the neighborhood. Having, naturally, an organization in which the *morale*[23] was strongly predominant, together with a greater breadth and cultivation of mind than obtained among his companions, he was looked up to with great respect, as a sort of minister among them; and the simple, hearty, sincere style of his exhortations might have edified even better educated persons. But it was in prayer that he especially excelled. Nothing could exceed the touching simplicity, the child-like earnestness, of his prayer, enriched with the language of scripture, which seemed so entirely to have wrought itself into his being, as to have become a part of himself, and to drop from his lips unconsciously; in the language of a pious old Negro, he "prayed right up." And so much did his prayer always work on the devotional feelings of his audiences, that there seemed often a danger that it would be lost altogether in the abundance of the responses which broke out everywhere around him.

* * * *

While this scene was passing in the cabin of the man, one quite otherwise passed in the halls of the master.

The trader and Mr. Shelby were seated together in the dining room afore-named, at a table covered with papers and writing utensils.

Mr. Shelby was busy in counting some bundles of bills, which, as they were counted, he pushed over to the trader, who counted them likewise.

"All fair," said the trader; "and now for signing these yer."

Mr. Shelby hastily drew the bills of sale towards him, and signed them, like a man that hurries over some disagreeable business, and then pushed them over with the money. Haley produced, from a well-worn valise, a parchment, which, after looking over it a moment, he handed to Mr. Shelby, who took it with a gesture of suppressed eagerness.

"Wal, now, the thing's *done!*" said the trader, getting up.

"It's *done!*" said Mr. Shelby, in a musing tone; and, fetching a long breath, he repeated, "It's *done!*"

"Yer don't seem to feel much pleased with it, 'pears to me," said the trader.

"Haley," said Mr. Shelby, "I hope you'll remember that you promised, on your honor, you wouldn't sell Tom without knowing what sort of hands he's going into."

"Why, you've just done it, sir," said the trader.

"Circumstances, you well know, *obliged* me," said Shelby, haughtily.

"Wal, you know, they may 'blige *me*, too," said the trader. "Howsoever, I'll do the very best I can in gettin' Tom a good berth; as to my treatin' on him bad, you needn't be a grain afeard. If there's anything that I thank the Lord for, it is that I'm never noways cruel."

After the expositions which the trader had previously given of his humane principles, Mr. Shelby did not feel particularly reassured by these declarations; but, as they were the

---

23 French for moral faculties.

best comfort the case admitted of, he allowed the trader to depart in silence, and betook himself to a solitary cigar.

Chapter 5

Showing the Feelings of Living Property on Changing Owners

Mr. and Mrs. Shelby had retired to their apartment for the night. He was lounging in the large easy-chair, looking over some letters that had come in the afternoon mail, and she was standing before her mirror, brushing out the complicated braids and curls in which Eliza had arranged her hair; for, noticing her pale cheeks and haggard eyes, she had excused her attendance that night, and ordered her to bed. The employment, naturally enough, suggested her conversation with the girl in the morning; and, turning to her husband, she said, carelessly,

"By the by, Arthur, who was that low-bred fellow that you lugged in to our dinner table to-day?"

"Haley is his name," said Shelby, turning himself rather uneasily in his chair, and continuing with his eyes fixed on a letter.

"Haley! Who is he, and what may be his business here, pray?"

"Well, he's a man that I transacted some business with, last time I was at Natchez," said Mr. Shelby.

"And he presumed on it to make himself quite at home, and call and dine here, ay?"

"Why, I invited him; I had some accounts with him," said Shelby.

"Is he a Negro-trader?" said Mrs. Shelby, noticing a certain embarrassment in her husband's manner.

"Why, my dear, what put that into your head?" said Shelby, looking up.

"Nothing,—only Eliza came in here, after dinner, in a great worry, crying and taking on, and said you were talking with a trader, and that she heard him make an offer for her boy—the ridiculous little goose!"

"She did, hey?" said Mr. Shelby, returning to his paper, which he seemed for a few minutes quite intent upon, not perceiving that he was holding it bottom upwards.

"It will have to come out," said he, mentally; "as well now as ever."

"I told Eliza," said Mrs. Shelby, as she continued brushing her hair, "that she was a little fool for her pains, and that you never had anything to do with that sort of person. Of course, I knew you never meant to sell any of our people,—least of all, to such a fellow."

"Well, Emily," said her husband, "so I have always felt and said; but the fact is that my business lies so that I cannot get on without. I shall have to sell some of my hands."

"To that creature? Impossible! Mr. Shelby, you cannot be serious."

"I'm sorry to say that I am," said Mr. Shelby. "I've agreed to sell Tom."

"What! our Tom?—that good, faithful creature!—been your faithful servant from a boy! O, Mr. Shelby!—and you have promised him his freedom, too,—you and I have spoken to him a hundred times of it. Well, I can believe anything now,—I can believe *now* that you could sell little Harry, poor Eliza's only child!" said Mrs. Shelby, in a tone between grief and indignation.

"Well, since you must know all, it is so. I have agreed to sell Tom and Harry both; and I don't know why I am to be rated, as if I were a monster, for doing what every one does every day."

"But why, of all others, choose these?" said Mrs. Shelby. "Why sell them, of all on the place, if you must sell at all?"

"Because they will bring the highest sum of any,—that's why. I could choose another, if you say so. The fellow made me a high bid on Eliza, if that would suit you any better," said Mr. Shelby.

"The wretch!" said Mrs. Shelby, vehemently.

"Well, I didn't listen to it, a moment,—out of regard to your feelings, I wouldn't;—so give me some credit."

"My dear," said Mrs. Shelby, recollecting herself, "forgive me. I have been hasty. I was surprised, and entirely unprepared for this;—but surely you will allow me to intercede for these poor creatures. Tom is a noble-hearted, faithful fellow, if he is black. I do believe, Mr. Shelby, that if he were put to it, he would lay down his life for you."

"I know it,—I dare say;—but what's the use of all this?—I can't help myself."

"Why not make a pecuniary sacrifice? I'm willing to bear my part of the inconvenience. O, Mr. Shelby, I have tried—tried most faithfully, as a Christian woman should—to do my duty to these poor, simple, dependent creatures. I have cared for them, instructed them, watched over them, and known all their little cares and joys, for years; and how can I ever hold up my head again among them, if, for the sake of a little paltry gain, we sell such a faithful, excellent, confiding creature as poor Tom, and tear from him in a moment all we have taught him to love and value? I have taught them the duties of the family, of parent and child, and husband and wife; and how can I bear to have this open acknowledgment that we care for no tie, no duty, no relation, however sacred, compared with money? I have talked with Eliza about her boy—her duty to him as a Christian mother, to watch over him, pray for him, and bring him up in a Christian way; and now what can I say, if you tear him away, and sell him, soul and body, to a profane, unprincipled man, just to save a little money? I have told her that one soul is worth more than all the money in the world; and how will she believe me when she sees us turn round and sell her child?—sell him, perhaps, to certain ruin of body and soul!"

"I'm sorry you feel so about it, Emily,—indeed I am," said Mr. Shelby; "and I respect your feelings, too, though I don't pretend to share them to their full extent; but I tell you now, solemnly, it's of no use—I can't help myself. I didn't mean to tell you this, Emily; but, in plain words, there is no choice between selling these two and selling everything. Either they must go, or all must. Haley has come into possession of a mortgage, which, if I don't clear off with him directly, will take everything before it. I've raked, and scraped, and borrowed, and all but begged,—and the price of these two was needed to make up the balance, and I had to give them up. Haley fancied the child; he agreed to settle the matter that way, and no other. I was in his power, and had to do it. If you feel so to have them sold, would it be any better to have all sold?"

Mrs. Shelby stood like one stricken. Finally, turning to her toilet, she rested her face in her hands, and gave a sort of groan.

"This is God's curse on slavery!—a bitter, bitter, most accursed thing!—a curse to the master and a curse to the slave! I was a fool to think I could make anything good out of such a deadly evil. It is a sin to hold a slave under laws like ours,—I always felt it was,—I always thought so when I was a girl,—I thought so still more after I joined the church; but I thought I could gild it over,—I thought, by kindness, and care, and instruction, I could make the condition of mine better than freedom—fool that I was!"

"Why, wife, you are getting to be an abolitionist,[24] quite."

"Abolitionist! if they knew all I know about slavery, they *might* talk! We don't need them to tell us; you know I never thought that slavery was right—never fell willing to own slaves."

"Well, therein you differ from many wise and pious men," said Mr. Shelby. "You remember Mr. B's sermon, the other Sunday?"

"I don't want to hear such sermons; I never wish to hear Mr. B. in our church again. Ministers can't help the evil, perhaps,—can't cure it, any more than we can—but defend it!—it always went against my common sense. And I think you didn't think much of that sermon either."

"Well," said Shelby, "I must say these ministers sometimes carry matters further than we poor sinners would exactly dare to do. We men of the world must wink pretty hard at various things, and get used to a deal that isn't the exact thing. But we don't quite fancy, when women and ministers come out broad and square, and go beyond us in matters of either modesty or morals, that's a fact. But now, my dear, I trust you see the necessity of the thing, and you see that I have done the very best that circumstances would allow."

"O yes yes!" said Mrs. Shelby, hurriedly and abstractedly fingering her gold watch,—"I haven't any jewelry of any amount," she added, thoughtfully; "but would not this watch do something?—it was an expensive one, when it was bought. If I could only at least save Eliza's child, I would sacrifice anything I have."

"I'm sorry, very sorry, Emily," said Mr. Shelby. "I'm sorry this takes hold of you so; but it will do no good. The fact is, Emily, the thing's done; the bills of sale are already signed, and in Haley's hands; and you must be thankful it is no worse. That man has had it in his power to ruin us all,—and now he is fairly off. If you knew the man as I do, you'd think that we had had a narrow escape."

"Is he so hard, then?"

"Why, not a cruel man, exactly, but a man of leather—a man alive to nothing but trade and profit—cool, and unhesitating, and unrelenting, as death and the grave. He'd sell his own mother at a good per centage— not wishing the old woman any harm, either."

"And this wretch owns that good, faithful Tom, and Eliza's child!"

"Well, my dear, the fact is that this goes rather hard with me; it's a thing I hate to think of it. Haley wants to drive matters, and take possession to-morrow. I'm going to get out my horse bright and early, and be off. I can't see Tom, that's a fact; and you had better arrange a drive somewhere, and carry Eliza off. Let the thing be done when she is out of sight."

"No, no," said Mrs. Shelby; "I'll be in no sense accomplice or help in this cruel business. I'll go and see poor old Tom, God help him, in his distress! They shall see, at any rate, that their mistress can feel for and with them. As to Eliza, I dare not think about it. The Lord forgive us! What have we done, that this cruel necessity should come on us?"

There was one listener to this conversation whom Mr. and Mrs. Shelby little suspected.

Communicating with their apartment was a large closet, opening by a door into the outer passage. When Mrs. Shelby had dismissed Eliza for the night, her feverish and excited mind had suggested the idea of this closet; and she had hidden herself there, and, with her ear pressed close against the crack of the door, had lost not a word of the conversation.

---

24 A radical anti-slavery advocate seeking to abolish slavery throughout the entire United States.

When the voices died into silence, she rose and crept stealthily away. Pale, shivering, with rigid features and compressed lips, she looked an entirely altered being from the soft and timid creature she had been hitherto. She moved cautiously along the entry, paused one moment at her mistress' door, and raised her hands in mute appeal to Heaven, and then turned and glided into her own room. It was a quiet, neat apartment, on the same floor with her mistress. There was the pleasant sunny window, where she had often sat singing at her sewing; there a little case of books, and various little fancy articles, ranged by them, the gifts of Christmas holidays; there was her simple wardrobe in the closet and in the drawers:—here was, in short, her home; and, on the whole, a happy one it had been to her. But there, on the bed, lay her slumbering boy, his long curls falling negligently around his unconscious face, his rosy mouth half open, his little fat hands thrown out over the bed-clothes, and a smile spread like a sunbeam over his whole face.

"Poor boy! poor fellow!" said Eliza; "they have sold you! but your mother will save you yet!"

No tear dropped over that pillow; in such straits as these, the heart has no tears to give,—it drops only blood, bleeding itself away in silence. She took a piece of paper and a pencil, and wrote, hastily,

"O, Missis! dear Missis! don't think me ungrateful,—don't think hard of me, any way,—I heard all you and master said to-night. I am going to try to save my boy—you will not blame me! God bless and reward you for all your kindness!"

Hastily folding and directing this, she went to a drawer and made up a little package of clothing for her boy, which she tied with a handkerchief firmly round her waist; and, so fond is a mother's remembrance, that, even in the terrors of that hour, she did not forget to put in the little package one or two of his favorite toys, reserving a gayly painted parrot to amuse him, when she should be called on to awaken him. It was some trouble to arouse the little sleeper; but, after some effort, he sat up, and was playing with his bird, while his mother was putting on her bonnet and shawl.

"Where are you going, mother?" said he, as she drew near the bed, with his little coat and cap.

His mother drew near, and looked so earnestly into his eyes, that he at once divined that something unusual was the matter.

"Hush, Harry," she said; "mustn't speak loud, or they will hear us. A wicked man was coming to take little Harry away from his mother, and carry him 'way off in the dark; but mother won't let him—she's going to put on her little boy's cap and coat, and run off with him, so the ugly man can't catch him."

Saying these words, she had tied and buttoned on the child's simple outfit, and, taking him in her arms, she whispered to him to be very still; and, opening the door in her room which led into the outer verandah, she glided noiselessly out.

It was a sparkling, frosty, star-light night, and the mother wrapped the shawl close round her child, as perfectly quiet with vague terror, he clung round her neck.

Old Bruno, a great Newfoundland, who slept at the end of the porch, rose, with a low growl, as she came near. She gently spoke his name, and the animal, an old pet and play-mate of hers, instantly, wagging his tail, prepared to follow her, though apparently revolving much, in his simple dog's head, what such an indiscreet midnight promenade might mean. Some dim ideas of imprudence or impropriety in the measure seemed to embarrass him considerably; for he often stopped, as Eliza glided forward, and looked wistfully, first

Eliza comes to tell Uncle Tom that he is sold and she is running away to save her child (*Uncle Tom's Cabin*, Boston: John P. Jewett, 1852, Courtesy Lilly Library, Bloomington, Indiana).

at her and then at the house, and then, as if reassured by reflection, he pattered along after her again. A few minutes brought them to the window of Uncle Tom's cottage, and Eliza, stopping, tapped lightly on the window pane.

The prayer-meeting at Uncle Tom's had, in the order of hymn-singing, been protracted to a very late hour; and, as Uncle Tom had indulged himself in a few lengthy solos afterwards, the consequence was, that, although it was now between twelve and one o'clock, he and his worthy helpmeet were not yet asleep.

"Good Lord! what's that?" said Aunt Chloe, starting up and hastily drawing the curtain. "My sakes alive, if it an't Lizy! Get on your clothes, old man, quick!—there's old Bruno, too, a pawin' round; what on airth! I'm gwine to open the door."

And, suiting the action to the word, the door flew open, and the light of the tallow candle, which Tom had hastily lighted, fell on the haggard face and dark, wild eyes of the fugitive.

"Lord bless you!—I'm skeered to look at ye, Lizy! Are ye tuck sick, or what's come over ye?"

"I'm running away—Uncle Tom and Aunt Chloe—carrying off my child—Master sold him!"

"Sold him?" echoed both, lifting up their hands in dismay.

"Yes, sold him!" said Eliza, firmly; "I crept into the closet by Mistress' door to-night, and I heard Master tell Missis that he had sold my Harry, and you, Uncle Tom, both, to a trader; and that he was going off this morning on his horse, and that the man was to take possession today."

Tom had stood, during this speech, with his hands raised, and his eyes dilated, like a man in a dream. Slowly and gradually, as its meaning came over him, he collapsed, rather than seated himself, on his old chair, and sunk his head down upon his knees.

"The good Lord have pity on us!" said Aunt Chloe. "O! it don't seem as if it was true! What has he done, that Mas'r should sell *him?*"

"He hasn't done anything,—it isn't for that. Master don't want to sell; and Missis—she's always good. I heard her plead and beg for us; but he told her 'twas no use; that he was in this man's debt, and that this man had got the power over him; and that if he didn't pay him off clear, it would end in his having to sell the place and all the people, and move off. Yes, I heard him say there was no choice between selling these two and selling all, the man was driving him so hard. Master said he was sorry; but oh, Missis—you ought to have heard her talk! If she an't a Christian and an angel, there never was one. I'm a wicked girl to leave her so; but, then, I can't help it. She said, herself, one soul was worth more than the world; and this boy has a soul, and if I let him be carried off, who knows what'll become of it? It must be right: but, if it an't right, the Lord forgive me, for I can't help doing it!"

"Well, old man!" said Aunt Chloe, "why don't you go, too? Will you wait to be toted down river, where they kill niggers with hard work and starving? I'd a heap rather die than go there, any day! There's time for ye,—be off with Lizy,—you've got a pass to come and go any time. Come, bustle up, and I'll get your things together."

Tom slowly raised his head, and looked sorrowfully but quietly around, and said,

"No, no—I an't going. Let Eliza go—it's her right! I wouldn't be the one to say no— 'tan't in *natur* for her to stay; but you heard what she said! If I must be sold, or all the people on the place, and everything go to rack, why, let me be sold. I s'pose I can b'ar it as well as any on 'em," he added, while something like a sob and a sigh shook his broad, rough chest convulsively. "Mas'r always found me on the spot—he always will. I never have broke trust, nor used my pass no ways contrary to my word, and I never will. It's better for me alone to go, than to break up the place and sell all. Mas'r an't to blame, Chloe, and he'll take care of you and the poor—"

Here he turned to the rough trundle-bed full of little woolly heads, and broke fairly down. He leaned over the back of the chair, and covered his face with his large hands. Sobs, heavy, hoarse and loud, shook the chair, and great tears fell through his fingers on the floor; just such tears, sir, as you dropped into the coffin where lay your first-born son; such tears, woman, as you shed when you heard the cries of your dying babe. For, sir, he was a man,—and you are but another man. And, woman, though dressed in silk and jewels, you are but a woman, and, in life's great straits and mighty griefs, ye feel but one sorrow!

"And now," said Eliza, as she stood in the door, "I saw my husband only this afternoon, and I little knew then what was to come. They have pushed him to the very last standing-place, and he told me, to-day, that he was going to run away. Do try, if you can, to get word to him. Tell him how I went, and why I went; and tell him I'm going to try and find Canada. You must give my love to him, and tell him, if I never see him again,"—she turned away, and stood with her back to them for a moment, and then added, in a husky voice, "tell him to be as good as he can, and try and meet me in the kingdom of heaven."

"Call Bruno in there," she added. "Shut the door on him, poor beast! He mustn't go with me!"

A few last words and tears, a few simple adieus and blessings, and, clasping her wondering and affrighted child in her arms, she glided noiselessly away.

Chapter 6

Discovery

Mr. and Mrs. Shelby, after their protracted discussion of the night before, did not readily sink to repose, and, in consequence, slept somewhat later than usual, the ensuing morning.

"I wonder what keeps Eliza," said Mrs. Shelby, after giving her bell repeated pulls, to no purpose.

Mr. Shelby was standing before his dressing-glass, sharpening his razor; and just then the door opened, and a colored boy entered, with his shaving water.

"Andy," said his mistress, "step to Eliza's door, and tell her I have rung for her three times. Poor thing!" she added, to herself, with a sigh.

Andy soon returned, with eyes very wide in astonishment.

"Lor, Missis! Lizy's drawers is all open, and her things all lying every which way; and I believe she's just done clared out!"

The truth flashed upon Mr. Shelby and his wife at the same moment. He exclaimed,

"Then she suspected it, and she's off!"

"The Lord be thanked!" said Mrs. Shelby. "I trust she is."

"Wife, you talk like a fool! Really, it will be something pretty awkward for me, if she is. Haley saw that I hesitated about selling this child, and he'll think I connived at it, to get him out of the way. It touches my honor!" And Mr. Shelby left the room hastily.

There was great running and ejaculating, and opening and shutting of doors, and appearances of faces in all shades of color in different places, for about a quarter of an hour. One person only, who might have shed some light on the matter, was entirely silent, and that was the head cook, Aunt Chloe. Silently, and with a heavy cloud settled down over her once joyous face, she proceeded making out her breakfast biscuits, as if she heard and saw nothing of the excitement around her.

Very soon, about a dozen young imps were roosting, like so many crows, on the verandah railings, each one determined to be the first one to apprize the strange Mas'r of his ill luck.

"He'll be real mad, I'll be bound," said Andy.

"*Won't* he swar!" said little black Jake.

"Yes, for he *does* swar," said woolly-headed Mandy. "I hearn him yesterday, at dinner. I hearn all about it then, 'cause I got into the closet where Missis keeps the great jugs, and I hearn every word." And Mandy, who had never in her life thought of the meaning of a word she had heard, more than a black cat, now took airs of superior wisdom, and strutted about, forgetting to state that, though actually coiled up among the jugs at the time specified, she had been fast asleep all the time.

When, at last, Haley appeared, booted and spurred, he was saluted with the bad tidings on every hand. The young imps on the verandah were not disappointed in their hope of hearing him "swar," which he did with a fluency and fervency which delighted them all amazingly, as they ducked and dodged hither and thither, to be out of the reach of his riding-whip; and, all whooping off together, they tumbled, in a pile of immeasurable giggle, on the withered turf under the verandah, where they kicked up their heels and shouted to their full satisfaction.

"If I had the little devils!" muttered Haley, between his teeth.

"But you ha'nt got 'em though!" said Andy, with a triumphant flourish, and making a string of indescribable mouths at the unfortunate trader's back, when he was fairly beyond hearing.

"I say now, Shelby, this yer's a most extro'rnary business!" said Haley, as he abruptly entered the parlor. "It seems that gal's off, with her young un."

"Mr. Haley, Mrs. Shelby is present," said Mr. Shelby.

"I beg pardon, ma'am," said Haley, bowing slightly, with a still lowering brow; "but still I say, as I said before, this yer's a sing'lar report. Is it true, sir?"

"Sir," said Mr. Shelby, "if you wish to communicate with me, you must observe something of the decorum of a gentleman. Andy, take Mr. Haley's hat and riding-whip. Take a seat, sir. Yes, sir; I regret to say that the young woman, excited by overhearing, or having reported to her, something of this business, has taken her child in the night, and made off."

"I did expect fair dealing in this matter, I confess," said Haley.

"Well, sir," said Mr. Shelby, turning sharply round upon him, "what am I to understand by that remark? If any man calls my honor in question, I have but one answer for him."

The trader cowered at this, and in a somewhat lower tone said that "it was plaguy hard on a fellow, that had made a fair bargain, to be gulled that way."

"Mr. Haley," said Mr. Shelby, "if I did not think you had some cause for disappointment, I should not have borne from you the rude and unceremonious style of your entrance into my parlor this morning. I say thus much, however, since appearances call for it, that I shall allow of no insinuations cast upon me, as if I were at all partner to any unfairness in this matter. Moreover, I shall feel bound to give you every assistance, in the use of horses, servants, &c., in the recovery of your property. So, in short, Haley," said he, suddenly dropping from the tone of dignified coolness to his ordinary one of easy frankness, "the best way for you is to keep good-natured and eat some breakfast, and we will then see what it is to be done."

Mrs. Shelby now rose, and said her engagements would prevent her being at the breakfast-table that morning; and, deputing a very respectable mulatto woman to attend to the gentlemen's coffee at the sideboard, she left the room.

"Old lady don't like your humble servant, over and above," said Haley, with an uneasy effort to be very familiar.

"I am not accustomed to hear my wife spoken of with such freedom," said Mr. Shelby, dryly.

"Beg pardon; of course, only a joke, you know," said Haley, forcing a laugh.

"Some jokes are less agreeable than others," rejoined Shelby.

"Devilish free, now I've signed those papers, cuss him!" muttered Haley to himself; "quite grand, since yesterday!"

Never did fall of any prime minister at court occasion wider surges of sensation than the report of Tom's fate among his compeers on the place. It was the topic in every mouth, everywhere; and nothing was done in the house or in the field, but to discuss its probable results. Eliza's flight—an unprecedented event on the place—was also a great accessory in stimulating the general excitement.

Black Sam, as he was commonly called, from his being about three shades blacker than any other son of ebony on the place, was revolving the matter profoundly in all its phases and bearings, with a comprehensiveness of vision and a strict lookout to his own personal well-being, that would have done credit to any white patriot in Washington.

"It's an ill wind dat blows nowhar,—dat ar a fact," said Sam, sententiously, giving an additional hoist to his pantaloons, and adroitly substituting a long nail in place of a missing suspender-button, with which effort of mechanical genius he seemed highly delighted.

"Yes, it's an ill wind blows nowhar," he repeated. "Now, dar, Tom's down—wal, course der's room for some nigger to be up—and why not dis nigger?—dat's de idee. Tom, a ridin' round de country—boots blacked—pass in his pocket—all grand as Cuffee[25]—who but he? Now, why shouldn't Sam?—dat's what I want to know."

"Halloo, Sam—O Sam! Mas'r wants you to cotch Bill and Jerry," said Andy, cutting short Sam's soliloquy.

"High! what's afoot now, young un?"

"Why, you don't know, I s'pose, that Lizy's cut stick,[26] and clared out, with her young un?"

"You teach your granny!" said Sam, with infinite contempt; "knowed it a heap sight sooner than you did; this nigger an't so green, now!"

"Well, anyhow, Mas'r wants Bill and Jerry geared right up; and you and I's to go with Mas'r Haley, to look arter her."

"Good, now! dat's de time o' day!" said Sam. "It's Sam dat's called for in dese yer times. He's de nigger. See if I don't cotch her, now; Mas'r'll see what Sam can do!"

"Ah! but, Sam," said Andy, "you'd better think twice; for Missis don't want her cotched, and she'll be in yer wool."

"High!" said Sam, opening his eyes. "How you know dat?"

"Heard her say so, my own self, dis blessed mornin', when I bring in Mas'r's shaving-water. She sent me to see why Lizy didn't come to dress her; and when I telled her she was off, she jest ris up, and ses she, 'The Lord be praised;' and Mas'r, he seemed rael mad, and ses he, 'Wife, you talk like a fool.' But Lor! she'll bring him to! I knows well enough how that'll be,—it's allers best to stand Missis' side the fence, now I tell yer."

Black Sam, upon this, scratched his woolly pate, which, if it did not contain very profound wisdom, still contained a great deal of a particular species much in demand among politicians of all complexions and countries, and vulgarly denominated "knowing which side the bread is buttered;" so, stopping with grave consideration, he again gave a hitch to his pantaloons, which was his regularly organized method of assisting his mental perplexities.

"Der an't no sayin'—never—'bout no kind o' thing in *dis* yer world," he said, at last.

Sam spoke like a philosopher, emphasizing *this*—as if he had had a large experience in different sorts of worlds, and therefore had come to his conclusions advisedly.

"Now, sartin I'd a said that Missis would a scoured the varsal world after Lizy," added Sam, thoughtfully.

"So she would," said Andy; "but can't ye see through a ladder, ye black nigger? Missis don't want dis yer Mas'r Haley to get Lizy's boy; dat's de go!"

"High!" said Sam, with an indescribable intonation, known only to those who have heard it among the Negroes.

"And I'll tell yer more'n all," said Andy; "I specs you'd better be making tracks for dem hosses,—mighty sudden too,—for I hearn Missis 'quirin' arter yer,—so you've stood foolin' long enough."

Sam, upon this, began to bestir himself in real earnest, and after a while appeared, bearing down gloriously towards the house, with Bill and Jerry in a full canter, and adroitly throwing himself off before they had any idea of stopping, he brought them up alongside

---

25 A phrase denoting a Southern black man dressed in inappropriate, ridiculous splendor.
26 Slang for leaving quickly.

of the horse-post like a tornado. Haley's horse, which was a skittish young colt, winced, and bounced, and pulled hard at his halter.

"Ho, ho!" said Sam, "skerry, ar ye?" and his black visage lighted up with a curious, mischievous gleam. "I'll fix ye now!" said he.

There was a large beech-tree overshadowing the place, and the small, sharp, triangular beech-nuts lay scattered thickly on the ground. With one of these in his fingers, Sam approached the colt, stroked and patted, and seemed apparently busy in soothing his agitation. On pretence of adjusting the saddle, he adroitly slipped under it the sharp little nut, in such a manner that the least weight brought upon the saddle would annoy the nervous sensibilities of the animal, without leaving any perceptible graze or wound.

"Dar!" he said rolling his eyes with an approving grin; "me fix 'em!"

At this moment Mrs. Shelby appeared on the balcony, beckoning to him. Sam approached it with as good a determination to pay court as did ever suitor after a vacant place at St. James or Washington.[27]

"Why have you been loitering so, Sam? I sent Andy to tell you to hurry."

"Lord bless you, Missis!" said Sam, "horses won't be cotched all in a minit; they'd done clared out way down to the south pasture, and the Lord knows whar!"

"Sam, how often must I tell you not to say 'Lord bless you, and the Lord knows,' and such things? It's wicked."

"O Lord bless my soul; I done forgot, Missis! I won't say nothing of de sort no more."

"Why, Sam, you just *have* said it again."

"Did I? O, Lord! I mean—I didn't go fur to say it."

"You must be *careful*, Sam."

"Just let me get my breath, Missis, and I'll start fair. I'll be bery careful."

"Well, Sam, you are to go with Mr. Haley, to show him the road, and help him. Be careful of the horses, Sam; you know Jerry was a little lame last week; *don't ride them too fast.*"

Mrs. Shelby spoke the last words with a low voice, and strong emphasis.

"Let dis child alone for dat!" said Sam, rolling up his eyes with a volume of meaning. "Lord knows! High! Didn't say dat!" said he, suddenly catching his breath, with a ludicrous flourish of apprehension, which made his mistress laugh, 'spite of herself. "Yes, Missis, I'll look out for de hosses!"

"Now, Andy," said Sam, returning to his stand under the beech-trees, "you see I wouldn't be 'tall surprised if dat ar gen'lman's crittur should gib a fling, by and by, when he comes to be a gettin' up. You know, Andy, critturs will do such things;" and therewith Sam poked Andy in the side, in a highly suggestive manner.

"High!" said Andy, with an air of instant appreciation.

"Yes, you see, Andy, Missis wants to make time,—dat ar's clar to der most or'nary 'bserver. I jis make a little for her. Now, you see, get all dese yer hosses loose, caperin' permiscus round dis yer lot and down to de wood dar, and I spec Mas'r won't be off in a hurry."

Andy grinned.

"Yer see," said Sam, "yer see, Andy, if any such thing should happen as that Mas'r Haley's horse *should* begin to act contrary, and cut up, you and I jist lets go of our'n to help him, and *we'll help him*—oh yes!" And Sam and Andy laid their heads back on their

---

27 A person with high political ambitions, as St. James is the royal residence in England and Washington is the seat of the American government.

shoulders, and broke into a low, immoderate laugh, snapping their fingers and flourishing their heels with exquisite delight.

At this instant, Haley appeared on the verandah. Somewhat mollified by certain cups of very good coffee, he came out smiling and talking, in tolerably restored humor. Sam and Andy, clawing for certain fragmentary palm-leaves, which they were in the habit of considering as hats, flew to the horse-posts, to be ready to "help Mas'r."

Sam's palm-leaf had been ingeniously disentangled from all pretensions to braid, as respects its brim; and the slivers starting apart, and standing upright, gave it a blazing air of freedom and defiance, quite equal to that of any Fejee[28] chief; while the whole brim of Andy's being departed bodily, he rapped the crown on his head with a dexterous thump, and looked about well pleased, as if to say, "Who says I haven't got a hat?"

"Well, boys," said Haley, "look alive now; we must lose no time."

"Not a bit of him, Mas'r!" said Sam, putting Haley's rein in his hand, and holding his stirrup, while Andy was untying the other two horses.

The instant Haley touched the saddle, the mettlesome creature bounded from the earth with a sudden spring, that threw his master sprawling, some feet off, on the soft, dry turf. Sam, with frantic ejaculations, made a dive at the reins, but only succeeded in brushing the blazing palm-leaf afore-named into the horse's eyes, which by no means tended to allay the confusion of his nerves. So, with great vehemence, he overturned Sam, and, giving two or three contemptuous snorts, flourished his heels vigorously in the air, and was soon prancing away towards the lower end of the lawn, followed by Bill and Jerry, whom Andy had not failed to let loose, according to contract, speeding them off with various direful ejaculations. And now ensued a miscellaneous scene of confusion. Sam and Andy ran and shouted,—dogs barked here and there,—and Mike, Mose, Mandy, Fanny, and all the smaller specimens on the place, both male and female, raced, clapped hands, whooped, and shouted, with outrageous officiousness and untiring zeal.

Haley's horse, which was a white one, and very fleet and spirited, appeared to enter into the spirit of the scene with great gusto; and having for his coursing ground a lawn of nearly half a mile in extent, gently sloping down on every side into indefinite woodland, he appeared to take infinite delight in seeing how near he could allow his pursuers to approach him, and then, when within a hand's breadth, whisk off with a start and a snort, like a mischievous beast as he was, and career far down into some alley of the wood-lot. Nothing was further from Sam's mind than to have any one of the troop taken until such season as should seem to him most befitting,—and the exertions that he made were certainly most heroic. Like the sword of Cœur De Lion,[29] which always blazed in front and thickest of the battle, Sam's palm-leaf was to be seen everywhere when there was the least danger that a horse could be caught;— there he would bear down full tilt, shouting, "Now for it! cotch him! cotch him!" in a way that would set everything to indiscriminate rout in a moment.

Haley ran up and down, and cursed and swore and stamped miscellaneously. Mr. Shelby in vain tried to shout directions from the balcony, and Mrs. Shelby from her chamber window alternately laughed and wondered,—not without some inkling of what lay at the bottom of all this confusion.

---

28 South Pacific island of Fiji.
29 King Richard I of England (1157–1199), also known as Richard the Lionheart.

At last, about twelve o'clock, Sam appeared triumphant, mounted on Jerry, with Haley's horse by his side, reeking with sweat, but with flashing eyes and dilated nostrils, showing that the spirit of freedom had not yet entirely subsided.

"He's cotched!" he exclaimed, triumphantly. "If 't hadn't been for me, they might a bust theirselves, all on 'em; but I cotched him!"

"You!" growled Haley, in no amiable mood. "If it hadn't been for you, this never would have happened."

"Lord bless us, Mas'r," said Sam, in a tone of the deepest concern, "and me that has been racin' and chasin' till the sweat jest pours off me!"

"Well, well!" said Haley, "you've lost me near three hours, with your cursed nonsense. Now let's be off, and have no more fooling."

"Why, Mas'r," said Sam, in a deprecating tone, "I believe you mean to kill us all clar, horses and all. Here we are all just ready to drop down, and the critters all in a reek of sweat. Why, Mas'r won't think of startin' on now till arter dinner. Mas'r's hoss wants rubben down; see how he splashed hisself; and Jerry limps too; don't think Missis would be willin' to have us start dis yer way, no how. Lord bless you, Mas'r, we can ketch up, if we do stop. Lizy never was no great of a walker."

Mrs. Shelby, who, greatly to her amusement, had overheard this conversation from the verandah, now resolved to do her part. She came forward, and, courteously expressing her concern for Haley's accident, pressed him to stay to dinner, saying that the cook should bring it on the table immediately.

Thus, all things considered, Haley, with rather an equivocal grace, proceeded to the parlor, while Sam, rolling his eyes after him with unutterable meaning, proceeded gravely with the horses to the stable-yard.

"Did yer see him, Andy? *did* yer see him?" said Sam, when he had got fairly beyond the shelter of the barn, and fastened the horse to a post. "O, Lor, if it warn't as good as a meetin', now, to see him a dancin' and kickin' and swarin' at us. Didn't I hear him? Swar away, ole fellow (says I to myself); will yer have yer hoss now, or wait till you cotch him? (says I). Lor, Andy, I think I can see him now." And Sam and Andy leaned up against the barn, and laughed to their hearts' content.

"Yer oughter seen how mad he looked, when I brought the hoss up. Lord, he'd a killed me, if he durs' to; and there I was a standin' as inner-cent and as humble."

"Lor, I seed you," said Andy; "an't you an old hoss, Sam?"

"Rather specks I am," said Sam; "did you see Missis up stars at the winder? I seed her laughin'."

"I'm sure, I was racin' so, I didn't see nothing," said Andy.

"Well, yer see," said Sam, proceeding gravely to wash down Haley's pony, "I'se 'quired what yer may call a habit o' *bobservation*, Andy. It's a very 'portant habit, Andy; and I 'commend yer to be cultivatin' it, now yer young. Hist up that hind foot, Andy. Yer see, Andy, it's *bobservation* makes all de difference in niggers. Didn't I see which way the wind blew dis yer mornin'? Didn't I see what Missis wanted, though she never let on? Dat ar's bobservation, Andy. I 'spects it's what you may call a faculty. Faculties is different in different peoples, but cultivation of 'em goes a great way."

"I guess if I hadn't helped your bobservation dis mornin', yer wouldn't have seen your way so smart," said Andy.

"Andy," said Sam, "you's a promisin' child, der an't no manner o' doubt. I think lots of yer, Andy; and I don't feel no ways ashamed to take idees from you. We ought-enter overlook nobody, Andy, cause the smartest on us gets tripped up sometimes. And so, Andy, let's go up to the house now. I'll be boun' Missis'll give us an uncommon good bite, dis yer time."

Chapter 7

The Mother's Struggle

It is impossible to conceive of a human creature more wholly desolate and forlorn than Eliza, when she turned her footsteps from Uncle Tom's cabin.

Her husband's suffering and dangers, and the danger of her child, all blended in her mind, with a confused and stunning sense of the risk she was running, in leaving the only home she had ever known, and cutting loose from the protection of a friend whom she loved and revered. Then there was the parting from every familiar object,—the place where she had grown up, the trees under which she had played, the groves where she had walked many an evening in happier days, by the side of her young husband,—everything, as it lay in the clear, frosty starlight, seemed to speak reproachfully to her, and ask her whither could she go from a home like that?

But stronger than all was maternal love, wrought into a paroxysm of frenzy by the near approach of a fearful danger. Her boy was old enough to have walked by her side, and, in an indifferent case, she would only have led him by the hand; but now the bare thought of putting him out of her arms made her shudder, and she strained him to her bosom with a convulsive grasp, as she went rapidly forward.

The frosty ground creaked beneath her feet, and she trembled at the sound; every quaking leaf and fluttering shadow sent the blood backward to her heart, and quickened her footsteps. She wondered within herself at the strength that seemed to be come upon her; for she felt the weight of her boy as if it had been a feather, and every flutter of fear seemed to increase the supernatural power that bore her on, while from her pale lips burst forth, in frequent ejaculations, the prayer to a Friend above—"Lord, help! Lord, save me!"

If it were *your* Harry, mother, or your Willie, that were going to be torn from you by a brutal trader, to-morrow morning,—if you had seen the man, and heard that the papers were signed and delivered, and you had only from twelve o'clock till morning to make good your escape,— how fast could *you* walk? How many miles could you make in those few brief hours, with the darling at your bosom,—the little sleepy head on your shoulder,—the small, soft arms trustingly holding on to your neck?

For the child slept. At first, the novelty and alarm kept him waking; but his mother so hurriedly repressed every breath or sound, and so assured him that if he were only still she would certainly save him, that he clung quietly round her neck, only asking, as he found himself sinking to sleep,

"Mother, I don't need to keep awake, do I?"

"No, my darling; sleep, if you want to."

"But, mother, if I do get asleep, you won't let him get me?"

"No, so may God help me!" said his mother, with a paler cheek, and a brighter light in her large dark eyes.

"You're *sure*, an't you, mother?"

"Yes, *sure*!" said the mother, in a voice that startled herself; for it seemed to come from a spirit within, that was no part of her; and the boy dropped his little weary head on her shoulder, and was soon asleep. How the touch of those warm arms, the gentle breathings that came in her neck, seemed to add fire and spirit to her movements! It seemed to her as if strength poured into her in electric streams, from every gentle touch and movement of the sleeping, confiding child. Sublime is the dominion of the mind over the body, that, for a time, can make flesh and nerve impregnable, and string the sinews like steel, so that the weak become so mighty.

The boundaries of the farm, the grove, the wood-lot, passed by her dizzily, as she walked on; and still she went, leaving one familiar object after another, slacking not, pausing not, till reddening daylight found her many a long mile from all traces of any familiar objects upon the open highway.

She had often been, with her mistress, to visit some connections, in the little village of T——, not far from the Ohio river, and knew the road well. To go thither, to escape across the Ohio river, were the first hurried outlines of her plan of escape; beyond that, she could only hope in God.

When horses and vehicles began to move along the highway, with that alert perception peculiar to a state of excitement, and which seems to be a sort of inspiration, she became aware that her headlong pace and distracted air might bring on her remark and suspicion. She therefore put the boy on the ground, and, adjusting her dress and bonnet, she walked on at as rapid a pace as she thought consistent with the preservation of appearances. In her little bundle she had provided a store of cakes and apples, which she used as expedients for quickening the speed of the child, rolling the apple some yards before them, when the boy would run with all his might after it; and this ruse, often repeated, carried them over many a half-mile.

After a while, they came to a thick patch of woodland, through which murmured a clear brook. As the child complained of hunger and thirst, she climbed over the fence with him; and, sitting down behind a large rock which concealed them from the road, she gave him a breakfast out of her little package. The boy wondered and grieved that she could not eat; and when, putting his arms round her neck, he tried to wedge some of his cake into her mouth, it seemed to her that the rising in her throat would choke her.

"No, no, Harry darling! mother can't eat till you are safe! We must go on—on—till we come to the river!" And she hurried again into the road, and again constrained herself to walk regularly and composedly forward.

She was many miles past any neighborhood where she was personally known. If she should chance to meet any who knew her, she reflected that the well-known kindness of the family would be of itself a blind to suspicion, as making it an unlikely supposition that she could be a fugitive. As she was also so white as not to be known as of colored lineage, without a critical survey, and her child was white also, it was much easier for her to pass on unsuspected.

On this presumption, she stopped at noon at a neat farmhouse, to rest herself, and buy some dinner for her child and self; for, as the danger decreased with the distance, the supernatural tension of the nervous system lessened, and she found herself both weary and hungry.

The good woman, kindly and gossiping, seemed rather pleased than otherwise with having somebody come in to talk with; and accepted, without examination, Eliza's statement, that she "was going on a little piece, to spend a week with her friends,"—all which she hoped in her heart might prove strictly true.

An hour before sunset, she entered the village of T——, by the Ohio river, weary and foot-sore, but still strong in heart. Her first glance was at the river, which lay, like Jordan, between her and the Canaan of liberty on the other side.

It was now early spring, and the river was swollen and turbulent; great cakes of floating ice were swinging heavily to and fro in the turbid waters. Owing to the peculiar form of the shore on the Kentucky side, the land bending far out into the water, the ice had been lodged and detained in great quantities, and the narrow channel which swept round the bend was full of ice, piled one cake over another, thus forming a temporary barrier to the descending ice, which lodged, and formed a great, undulating raft, filling up the whole river, and extending almost to the Ohio shore.

Eliza stood, for a moment, contemplating this unfavorable aspect of things, which she saw at once must prevent the usual ferry-boat from running, and then turned into a small public house on the bank, to make a few inquiries.

The hostess, who was busy in various fizzing and stewing operations over the fire, preparatory to the evening meal, stopped, with a fork in her hand, as Eliza's sweet and plaintive voice arrested her.

"What is it?" she said.

"Isn't there any ferry or boat, that takes people over to B——, now?" she said.

"No, indeed!" said the woman; "the boats has stopped running."

Eliza's look of dismay and disappointment struck the woman, and she said inquiringly, "May be you're wanting to get over?—anybody sick? Ye seem mighty anxious?"

"I've got a child that's very dangerous," said Eliza. "I never heard of it till last night, and I've walked quite a piece today, in hopes to get to the ferry."

"Well, now, that's onlucky," said the woman, whose motherly sympathies were much aroused; "I'm re'lly consarned for ye. Solomon!" she called, from the window, towards a small back building. A man, in leather apron and very dirty hands, appeared at the door.

"I say, Sol," said the woman, "is that ar man going to tote them bar'ls over to-night?"

"He said he should try, if 'twas any way prudent," said the man.

"There's a man a piece down here, that's going over with some truck this evening, if he durs' to; he'll be in here to supper to-night, so you'd better set down and wait. That's a sweet little fellow," added the woman, offering him a cake.

But the child, wholly exhausted, cried with weariness. "Poor fellow! he isn't used to walking, and I've hurried him on so," said Eliza.

"Well, take him into this room," said the woman, opening into a small bedroom, where stood a comfortable bed. Eliza laid the weary boy upon it, and held his hands in hers till he was fast asleep. For her there was no rest. As a fire in her bones, the thought of the pursuer urged her on; and she gazed with longing eyes on the sullen, surging waters that lay between her and liberty.

Here we must take our leave of her for the present, to follow the course of her pursuers.

*   *   *   *

Though Mrs. Shelby had promised that the dinner should be hurried on table, yet it was soon seen, as the thing has often been seen before, that it required more than one to make a bargain. So, although the order was fairly given out in Haley's hearing, and carried to Aunt Chloe by at least half a dozen juvenile messengers, that dignitary only gave certain very gruff snorts, and tosses of her head, and went on with every operation in an unusually leisurely and circumstantial manner.

For some singular reason, an impression seemed to reign among the servants generally that Missis would not be particularly disobliged by delay; and it was wonderful what a number of counter accidents occurred constantly, to retard the course of things. One luckless wight contrived to upset the gravy; and then gravy had to be got up *de novo*,[30] with due care and formality, Aunt Chloe watching and stirring with dogged precision, answering shortly, to all suggestions of haste, that she "warn't a going to have raw gravy on the table, to help nobody's catchings." One tumbled down with the water, and had to go to the spring for more; and another precipitated the butter into the path of events; and there was from time to time giggling news brought into the kitchen that "Mas'r Haley was mighty oneasy, and that he couldn't sit in his cheer no ways, but was a walkin' and stalkin' to the winders and through the porch."

"Sarves him right!" said Aunt Chloe, indignantly. "He'll get wus nor oneasy, one of these days, if he don't mend his ways. His master'll be sending for him, and then see how he'll look!"

"He'll go to torment, and no mistake," said little Jake.

"He desarves it!" said Aunt Chloe, grimly; "he's broke a many, many, many hearts,—I tell ye all!" she said, stopping, with a fork uplifted in her hands; "it's like what Mas'r George reads in Ravelations,—souls a callin' under the altar! and a callin' on the Lord for vengeance on sich!— and by and by the Lord'll hear 'em—so he will!"[31]

Aunt Chloe, who was much revered in the kitchen, was listened to with open mouth; and, the dinner being now fairly sent in, the whole kitchen was at leisure to gossip with her, and to listen to her remarks.

"Sich'll be burnt up forever, and no mistake; won't ther?" said Andy.

"I'd be glad to see it, I'll be boun'," said little Jake.

"Chil'en!" said a voice, that made them all start. It was Uncle Tom, who had come in, and stood listening to the conversation at the door.

"Chil'en!" he said, "I'm afeard you don't know what ye're sayin'. Forever is a *dre'ful* word, chil'en; it's awful to think on't. You oughtenter wish that ar to any human crittur."

"We wouldn't to anybody but the soul-drivers," said Andy; "nobody can help wishing it to them, they's so awful wicked."

"Don't natur herself kinder cry out on em?" said Aunt Chloe. "Don't dey tear der suckin' baby right off his mother's breast, and sell him, and der little children as is crying and holding on by her clothes,—don't dey pull 'em off and sells em? Don't dey tear wife and husband apart?" said Aunt Chloe, beginning to cry, "when it's jest takin' the very life on 'em?—and all the while does they feel one bit,—don't dey drink and smoke, and take it on common easy? Lor, if the devil don't get them, what's he good for?" And Aunt Chloe covered her face with her checked apron, and began to sob in good earnest.

"Pray for them that 'spitefully use you,[32] the good book says," says Tom.

"Pray for 'em!" said Aunt Chloe; "Lor, it's too tough! I can't pray for 'em."

"It's natur, Chloe, and natur's strong," said Tom, "but the Lord's grace is stronger; besides, you oughter think what an awful state a poor crittur's soul's in that'll do them ar things.—you oughter thank God that you an't like him, Chloe. I'm sure I'd rather be sold, ten thousand times over, than to have all that ar poor crittur's got to answer for."

"So'd I, a heap," said Jake. "Lor, *shouldn't* we cotch it, Andy?"

Andy shrugged his shoulders, and gave an acquiescent whistle.

---

30 Latin for "anew."
31 Revelation 6:9–10. The passage refers to Jesus Christ on Judgment Day being asked when he will avenge the wrongs done against those who had placed their faith in Him.
32 Matthew 5:44–48.

"I'm glad Mas'r didn't go off this morning, as he looked to," said Tom; "that ar hurt me more than sellin', it did. Mebbe it might have been natural for him, but 'twould have come desp't hard on me, as has known him from a baby; but I've seen Mas'r, and I begin ter feel sort o' reconciled to the Lord's will now. Mas'r couldn't help hisself; he did right, but I'm feared things will be kinder goin' to rack, when I'm gone. Mas'r can't be spected to be a pryin' round everywhar, as I've done, a keepin' up all the ends. The boys all means well, but they's powerful car'less. That ar troubles me."

The bell here rang, and Tom was summoned to the parlor.

"Tom," said his master, kindly, "I want you to notice that I give this gentleman bonds to forfeit a thousand dollars if you are not on the spot when he wants you; he's going to-day to look after his other business, and you can have the day to yourself. Go anywhere you like, boy."

"Thank you, Mas'r," said Tom.

"And mind yerself," said the trader, "and don't come it over your master with any o' yer nigger tricks; for I'll take every cent out of him, if you an't thar. If he'd hear to me, he wouldn't trust any on ye—slippery as eels!"

"Mas'r," said Tom,—and he stood very straight,—"I was jist eight years old when ole Missis put you into my arms, and you wasn't a year old. 'Thar,' says she, 'Tom, that's to be *your* young Mas'r; take good care on him,' says she. And now I jist ask you, Mas'r, have I ever broke word to you, or gone contrary to you, 'specially since I was a Christian?'"

Mr. Shelby was fairly overcome, and the tears rose to his eyes.

"My good boy," said he, "the Lord knows you say but the truth; and if I was able to help it, all the world shouldn't buy you."

"And sure as I am a Christian woman," said Mrs. Shelby, "you shall be redeemed as soon as I can any way bring together means. Sir," she said to Haley, "take good account of who you sell him to, and let me know."

"Lor, yes, for that matter," said the trader, "I may bring him up in a year, not much the wuss for wear, and trade him back."

"I'll trade with you then, and make it for your advantage," said Mrs. Shelby.

"Of course," said the trader, "all's equal with me; lives trade 'em up as down, so I does a good business. All I want is a livin', you know, ma'am; that's all any on us wants, I s'pose."

Mr. and Mrs. Shelby both felt annoyed and degraded by the familiar impudence of the trader, and yet both saw the absolute necessity of putting a constraint on their feelings. The more hopelessly sordid and insensible he appeared, the greater became Mrs. Shelby's dread of his succeeding in recapturing Eliza and her child, and of course the greater her motive for detaining him by every female artifice. She therefore graciously smiled, assented, chatted familiarly, and did all she could to make time pass imperceptibly.

At two o'clock Sam and Andy brought the horses up to the posts, apparently greatly refreshed and invigorated by the scamper of the morning.

Sam was there new oiled from dinner, with an abundance of zealous and ready officiousness. As Haley approached, he was boasting, in flourishing style, to Andy of the evident and eminent success of the operation, now that he had "farly come to it."

"Your master, I s'pose, don't keep no dogs," said Haley, thoughtfully, as he prepared to mount.

"Heaps on 'em," said Sam, triumphantly; "thar's Bruno—he's a roarer! and, besides that, 'bout every nigger of us keeps a pup of some natur or uther."

"Poh!" said Haley,—and he said something else, too, with regard to the said dogs, at which Sam muttered,

"I don't see no use cussin' on 'em no way."

"But your master don't keep no dogs (I pretty much know he don't) for trackin' out niggers."

Sam knew exactly what he meant, but he kept on a look of earnest and desperate simplicity.

"Our dogs all smells round considable sharp. I spect they's the kind, though they han't never had no practice. They's far dogs, though, at most anything, if you'd get 'em started. Here, Bruno," he called, whistling to the lumbering Newfoundland, who came pitching tumultuously toward them.

"You go hang!" said Haley, getting up. "Come, tumble up now."

Sam tumbled up accordingly, dexterously contriving to tickle Andy as he did so, which occasioned Andy to split out into a laugh, greatly to Haley's indignation, who made a cut at him with his riding-whip.

"I's 'stonished at yer, Andy," said Sam, with awful gravity. "This yer's a seris bisness, Andy. Yer mustn't be a makin' game. This yer an't no way to help Mas'r."

"I shall take the straight road to the river," said Haley, decidedly, after they had come to the boundaries of the estate. "I know the way of all of 'em,—they make tracks for the underground."

"Sartin," said Sam, "dat's de idee. Mas'r Haley hits de thing right in de middle. Now, der's two roads to de river,—de dirt road and der pike,—which Mas'r mean to take?"

Andy looked up innocently at Sam, surprised at hearing this new geographical fact, but instantly confirmed what he said, by a vehement reiteration.

"Course," said Sam, "I'd rather be 'clined to 'magine that Lizy'd take de dirt road, bein' it's the least travelled."

Haley, notwithstanding that he was a very old bird, and naturally inclined to be suspicious of chaff, was rather brought up by this view of the case.

"If yer warn't both on yer such cussed liars!" he said, contemplatively, as he pondered a moment.

The pensive, reflective tone in which this was spoken appeared to amuse Andy prodigiously, and he drew a little behind, and shook so as apparently to run a great risk of falling off his horse, while Sam's face was immovably composed into the most doleful gravity.

"Course," said Sam, "Mas'r can do as he'd ruther; go de straight road, if Mas'r thinks best,—it's all one to us. Now, when I study 'pon it, I think de straight road de best, *deridedly*."

"She would naturally go a lonesome way," said Haley, thinking aloud, and not minding Sam's remark.

"Dar an't no sayin'," said Sam; "gals is pecular; they never does nothin' ye thinks they will; mose gen'lly the contrar. Gals is nat'lly made contrar; and so, if you thinks they've gone one road, it is sartin you'd better go t'other, and then you'll be sure to find 'em. Now, my private 'pinion is, Lizy took der dirt road; so I think we'd better take de straight one."

This profound generic view of the female sex did not seem to dispose Haley particularly to the straight road; and he announced decidedly that he should go the other, and asked Sam when they should come to it.

"A little piece ahead," said Sam, giving a wink to Andy with the eye which was on Andy's side of the head; and he added, gravely, "but I've studded on de matter, and I'm quite clar we ought not to go dat ar way. I nebber been over it no way. It's desp't lonesome, and we might lose our way,—what we'd come to, de Lord only knows."

"Nevertheless," said Haley, "I shall go that way."

"Now I think on't, I think I hearn 'em tell that dat ar road was all fenced up and down by der creek, and thar, an't it, Andy?"

Andy wasn't certain; he'd only "hearn tell" about that road, but never been over it. In short, he was strictly noncommittal.

Haley, accustomed to strike the balance of probabilities between lies of greater or lesser magnitude, thought that it lay in favor of the dirt road aforesaid. The mention of the thing he thought he perceived was involuntary on Sam's part at first, and his confused attempts to dissuade him he set down to a desperate lying on second thoughts, as being unwilling to implicate Eliza.

When, therefore, Sam indicated the road, Haley plunged briskly into it, followed by Sam and Andy.

Now, the road, in fact, was an old one, that had formerly been a thoroughfare to the river, but abandoned for many years after the laying of the new pike. It was open for about an hour's ride, and after that it was cut across by various farms and fences. Sam knew this fact perfectly well,—indeed, the road had been so long closed up, that Andy had never heard of it. He therefore rode along with an air of dutiful submission, only groaning and vociferating occasionally that 'twas "desp't rough, and bad for Jerry's foot."

"Now, I jest give yer warning," said Haley, "I know yer; yer won't get me to turn off this yer road, with all yer fussin'—so you shet up!"

"Mas'r will go his own way!" said Sam, with rueful submission, at the same time winking most portentously to Andy, whose delight was now very near to the explosive point.

Sam was in wonderful spirits,—professed to keep a very brisk lookout,—at one time exclaiming that he saw "a gal's bonnet" on the top of some distant eminence, or calling to Andy "if that thar wasn't 'Lizy' down in the hollow;" always making these exclamations in some rough or craggy part of the road, where the sudden quickening of speed was a special inconvenience to all parties concerned, and thus keeping Haley in a state of constant commotion.

After riding about an hour in this way, the whole party made a precipitate and tumultuous descent into a barnyard belonging to a large farming establishment. Not a soul was in sight, all the hands being employed in the fields; but, as the barn stood conspicuously and plainly square across the road, it was evident that their journey in that direction had reached a decided finale.

"Wan't dat ar what I told Mas'r?" said Sam, with an air of injured innocence. "How does strange gentleman spect to know more about a country dan de natives born and raised?"

"You rascal!" said Haley, "you knew all about this."

"Didn't I tell yer I *know'd*, and yer wouldn't believe me? I told Mas'r 'twas all shet up, and fenced up, and I didn't spect we could get through,—Andy heard me."

It was all too true to be disputed, and the unlucky man had to pocket his wrath with the best grace he was able, and all three faced to the right about, and took up their line of march for the highway.

In consequence of all the various delays, it was about three-quarters of an hour after Eliza had laid her child to sleep in the village tavern that the party came riding into the same place. Eliza was standing by the window, looking out in another direction, when Sam's quick eye caught a glimpse of her. Haley and Andy were two yards behind. At this crisis, Sam contrived to have his hat blown off, and uttered a loud and characteristic ejaculation, which startled her at once; she drew suddenly back; the whole train swept by the window, round to the front door.

A thousand lives seemed to be concentrated in that one moment to Eliza. Her room opened by a side door to the river. She caught her child, and sprang down the steps towards it. The trader caught a full glimpse of her, just as she was disappearing down the bank; and throwing himself from his horse, and calling loudly on Sam and Andy, he was after her like a hound after a deer. In that dizzy moment her feet to her scarce seemed to touch the ground, and a moment brought her to the water's edge. Right on behind they came and, nerved with strength such as God gives only to the desperate, with one wild cry and flying leap, she vaulted sheer over the turbid current by the shore, on to the raft of ice beyond. It was a desperate leap—impossible to anything but madness and despair; and Haley, Sam, and Andy, instinctively cried out, and lifted up their hands, as she did it.

The huge green fragment of ice on which she alighted pitched and creaked as her weight came on it, but she stayed there not a moment. With wild cries and desperate energy she leaped to another and still another cake;—stumbling—leaping—slipping—springing upwards again! Her shoes are gone—her stockings cut from her feet—while blood marked every step; but she saw nothing, felt nothing, till dimly, as in a dream, she saw the Ohio side, and a man helping her up the bank.

"Yer a brave gal, now, whoever ye ar!" said the man, with an oath.

Eliza recognized the voice and face of a man who owned a farm not far from her old home.

"O, Mr. Symmes!—save me—do save me—do hide me!" said Eliza.

"Why, what's this?" said the man. "Why, if 'tan't Shelby's gal!"

"My child!—this boy!—he'd sold him! There is his Mas'r," said she, pointing to the Kentucky shore. "O, Mr. Symmes, you've got a little boy!"

"So I have," said the man, as he roughly, but kindly, drew her up the steep bank. "Besides, you're a right brave gal. I like grit, wherever I see it."

When they had gained the top of the bank, the man paused.

"I'd be glad to do something for ye," said he; "but then there's nowhar I could take ye. The best I can do is to tell ye to go *thar*," said he, pointing to a large white house which stood by itself, off the main street of the village. "Go thar; they're kind folks. Thar's no kind o' danger but they'll help you,—they're up to all that sort o' thing."

"The Lord bless you!" said Eliza, earnestly.

"No 'casion, no 'casion in the world," said the man. "What I've done's of no 'count."

"And, oh, surely, sir, you won't tell any one!"

"Go to thunder, gal! What do you take a feller for? In course not," said the man. "Come, now, go along like a likely, sensible gal, as you are. You've arnt your liberty, and you shall have it, for all me."

The woman folded her child to her bosom, and walked firmly and swiftly away. The man stood and looked after her.

"Shelby, now, mebbe won't think this yer the most neighborly thing in the world; but what's a feller to do? If he catches one of my gals in the same fix, he's welcome to pay back. Somehow I never could see no kind o' critter a strivin' and pantin', and trying to clar themselves, with the dogs arter 'em, and go agin 'em. Besides, I don't see no kind of 'casion for me to be hunter and catcher for other folks, neither."

So spoke this poor, heathenish Kentuckian, who had not been instructed in his constitutional relations,[33] and consequently was betrayed into acting in a sort of Christianized

---

33 Slavery was accommodated by the Constitution. This phrase may also refer to the more general laws relating to slavery such as the ones found in the Compromise of 1850, including the Fugitive Slave Act that helped slave owners recover their escaped slaves in non-slave states.

manner, which, if he had been better situated and more enlightened, he would not have been left to do.

Haley had stood a perfectly amazed spectator of the scene, till Eliza had disappeared up the bank, when he turned a blank, inquiring look on Sam and Andy.

"That ar was a tolable fair stroke of business," said Sam.

"The gal's got seven devils in her, I believe!" said Haley. "How like a wildcat she jumped!"

"Wal, now," said Sam, scratching his head, "I hope Mas'r'll 'scuse us tryin' dat ar road. Don't think I feel spry enough for dat ar, no way!" and Sam gave a hoarse chuckle.

"You laugh!" said the trader, with a growl.

"Lord bless you, Mas'r, I couldn't help it, now," said Sam, giving way to the long pent-up delight of his soul. "She looked so curis, a leapin' and springin'—ice a crackin'—and only to hear her,—plump! ker chuck! ker splash! Spring! Lord! how she goes it!" and Sam and Andy laughed till the tears rolled down their cheeks.

"I'll make ye laugh t'other side yer mouths!" said the trader, laying about their heads with his riding-whip.

Both ducked, and ran shouting up the bank, and were on their horses before he was up.

"Good evening, Mas'r!" said Sam, with much gravity. "I bery much spect Missis be anxious 'bout Jerry. Mas'r Haley won't want us no longer. Missis wouldn't hear of our ridin' the critters over Lizy's bridge tonight;" and, with a facetious poke into Andy's ribs, he started off, followed by the latter, at full speed,—their shouts of laughter coming faintly on the wind.

Chapter 8

Eliza's Escape

Eliza made her desperate retreat across the river just in the dusk of twilight. The gray mist of evening, rising slowly from the river, enveloped her as she disappeared up the bank, and the swollen current and floundering masses of ice presented a hopeless barrier between her and her pursuer. Haley therefore slowly and discontentedly returned to the little tavern, to ponder further what was to be done. The woman opened to him the door of a little parlor, covered with a rag carpet, where stood a table with a very shining black oil-cloth, sundry lank high-backed wood chairs, with some plaster images in resplendent colors on the mantel-shelf, above a very dimly-smoking grate; a long hardwood settle extended its uneasy length by the chimney, and here Haley sat him down to meditate on the instability of human hopes and happiness in general.

"What did I want with the little cuss, now," he said to himself, "that I should have got myself treed like a coon, as I am, this yer way?" and Haley relieved himself by repeating over a not very select litany of imprecations on himself, which, though there was the best possible reason to consider them as true, we shall, as a matter of taste, omit.

He was startled by the loud and dissonant voice of a man who was apparently dismounting at the door. He hurried to the window.

"By the land! if this yer an't the nearest, now, to what I've heard folks call Providence," said Haley. "I do b'lieve that ar's Tom Loker."

Haley hastened out. Standing by the bar, in the corner of the room, was a brawny, muscular man, full six feet in height, and broad in proportion. He was dressed in a coat of buffalo-skin, made with the hair outward, which gave him a shaggy and fierce appearance, perfectly in keeping with the whole air of his physiognomy. In the head and face every organ and lineament expressive of brutal and unhesitating violence was in a state of the highest possible development. Indeed, could our readers fancy a bull-dog come unto man's estate, and walking about in a hat and coat, they would have no unapt idea of the general style and effect of his physique. He was accompanied by a travelling companion, in many respects an exact contrast to himself. He was short and slender, lithe and cat-like in his motions, and had a peering, mousing expression about his keen black eyes, with which every feature of his face seemed sharpened into sympathy; his thin, long nose ran out as if it was eager to bore into the nature of things in general; his sleek, thin, black hair was stuck eagerly forward, and all his emotions and evolutions expressed a dry, cautious acuteness. The great big man poured out a big tumbler half full of raw spirits, and gulped it down without a word. The little man stood tiptoe, and putting his head first to one side and then to the other, and snuffing considerably in the directions of the various bottles, ordered at last a mint julep, in a thin and quivering voice, and with an air of great circumspection. When poured out, he took it and looked at it with a sharp, complacent air, like a man who thinks he has done about the right thing, and hit the nail on the head, and proceeded to dispose of it in short and well-advised sips.

"Wal, now, who'd a thought this yer luck 'ad come to me? Why, Loker, how are ye?" said Haley, coming forward, and extending his hand to the big man.

"The devil!" was the civil reply. "What brought you here, Haley?"

The mousing man, who bore the name of Marks, instantly stopped his sipping, and, poking his head forward, looked shrewdly on the new acquaintance, as a cat sometimes looks at a moving dry leaf, or some other possible object of pursuit.

"I say, Tom, this yer's the luckiest thing in the world. I'm in a devil of a hobble, and you must help me out."

"Ugh? aw! like enough!" grunted his complacent acquaintance. "A body may be pretty sure of that, when *you're* glad to see 'em; something to be made off of 'em. What's the blow now?"

"You've got a friend here?" said Haley, looking doubtfully at Marks; "partner, perhaps?"

"Yes, I have. Here, Marks! here's that ar feller that I was in with in Natchez."

"Shall be pleased with his acquaintance," said Marks, thrusting out a long, thin hand, like a raven's claw. "Mr. Haley, I believe?"

"The same, sir," said Haley. "And now, gentlemen, seein' as we've met so happily, I think I'll stand up to a small matter of a treat in this here parlor. So, now, old coon," said he to the man at the bar, "get us hot water, and sugar, and cigars, and plenty of the *real stuff*, and we'll have a blow-out."

Behold, then, the candles lighted, the fire stimulated to the burning point in the grate, and our three worthies seated round a table, well spread with all the accessories to good fellowship enumerated before.

Haley began a pathetic recital of his peculiar troubles. Loker shut up his mouth, and listened to him with gruff and surly attention. Marks, who was anxiously and with much fidgeting compounding a tumbler of punch to his own peculiar taste, occasionally looked up from his employment, and, poking his sharp nose and chin almost into Haley's face, gave the most earnest heed to the whole narrative. The conclusion of it appeared to amuse him extremely, for he shook his shoulders and sides in silence, and perked up his thin lips with an air of great internal enjoyment.

"So then, ye'r fairly sewed up, an't ye?" he said; "he! he! he! It's neatly done, too."

"This yer young-un business makes lots of trouble in the trade," said Haley, dolefully.

"If we could get a breed of gals that didn't care, now, for their young uns," said Marks; "tell ye, I think 'twould be 'bout the greatest mod'rn improvement I knows on,"—and Marks patronized his joke by a quiet introductory sniggle.

"Jes so," said Haley; "I never couldn't see into it; young uns is heaps of trouble to 'em; one would think, now, they'd be glad to get clar on 'em; but they arn't. And the more trouble a young un is, and the more good for nothing, as a gen'l thing, the tighter they sticks to 'em."

"Wal, Mr. Haley," said Marks, "jest pass the hot water. Yes, sir; you say jest what I feel and all'us have. Now, I bought a gal once, when I was in the trade,—a tight, likely wench she was, too, and quite considerable smart,—and she had a young un that was mis'able sickly; it had a crooked back, or something or other; and I jest gin't away to a man that thought he'd take his chance raising on't, being it didn't cost nothin';— never thought, yer know, of the gal's takin' on about it,—but, Lord, yer oughter seen how she went on. Why, re'lly, she did seem to me to valley the child more 'cause 'twas sickly and cross, and plagued her; and she warn't making b'lieve, neither,—cried about it, she did, and lopped round, as if she'd lost every friend she had. It re'lly was droll to think on't. Lord, there an't no end to women's notions."

"Wal, jes so with me," said Haley. "Last summer, down on Red river, I got a gal traded off on me, with a likely lookin' child enough, and his eyes looked as bright as yourn; but, come to look, I found him stone blind. Fact—he was stone blind. Wal, ye see, I thought there warn't no harm in my jest passing him along, and not sayin' nothin"; and I'd got him nicely swapped off for a keg o' whiskey; but come to get him away from the gal, she was jest like a tiger. So 'twas before we started, and I hadn't got my gang chained up; so what should she do but ups on a cotton-bale, like a cat, ketches a knife from one of the deck hands, and, I tell ye, she made all fly for a minit, till she saw 'twan't no use; and she jest turns round, and pitches head first, young un and all, into the river,—went down plump, and never ris."

"Bah!" said Tom Loker, who had listened to these stories with ill-repressed disgust,—"shif'less, both on ye! my gals don't cut up no such shines, I tell ye!"

"Indeed! how do you help it?" said Marks, briskly.

"Help it? why I buys a gal, and if she's got a young un to be sold, I jest walks up and puts my fist to her face, and says, 'Look here, now, if you give me one word out of your head, I'll smash yer face in. I won't hear one word—not the beginning of a word.' I says to 'em, 'This yer young un's mine, and not yourn, and you've no kind o' business with it. I'm going to sell it, first chance; mind, you don't cut up none o' yer shines about it, or I'll make ye wish ye'd never been born.' I tell ye, they sees it an't no play, when I gets hold. I makes 'em as whist as fishes;[34] and if one on 'em begins and gives a yelp, why,—" and Mr. Loker brought down his fist with a thump that fully explained the hiatus.

"That ar's what ye may call *emphasis*," said Marks, poking Haley in the side, and going into another small giggle. "An't Tom peculiar? he! he! he! I say, Tom, I s'pect you make 'em *understand*, for all niggers' heads is woolly. They don't never have no doubt o' your meaning, Tom. If you an't the devil, Tom, you's his twin brother, I'll say that for ye!"

Tom received the compliment with becoming modesty, and began to look as affable as was consistent, as John Bunyan says, "with his doggish nature."[35]

---

34 Quiet.

35 A reference to the second part of John Bunyan's *Pilgrim's Progress* (1678), when Satan's attacks on the righteous are described as a part of his "doggish nature."

Haley, who had been imbibing very freely of the staple of the evening, began to feel a sensible elevation and enlargement of his moral faculties,—a phenomenon not unusual with gentlemen of a serious and reflective turn, under similar circumstances.

"Wal, now, Tom," he said, "ye re'lly is too bad, as I al'ays have told ye; ye know, Tom, you and I used to talk over these yer matters down in Natchez, and I used to prove to ye that we made full as much, and was as well off for this yer world, by treatin' on 'em well, besides keepin' a better chance for comin' in the kingdom at last, when wust comes to wust, and thar an't nothing else left to get, ye know."

"Boh!" said Tom, "*don't* I know?—don't make me too sick with any yer stuff,—my stomach is a little riled now;" and Tom drank half a glass of raw brandy.

"I say," said Haley, and leaning back in his chair and gesturing impressively; "I'll say this now, I al'ays meant to drive my trade so as to make money on't, *fust and foremost*, as much as any man; but, then, trade an't everything, and money an't everything, 'cause we's all got souls. I don't care, now, who hears me say it,—and I think a cussed sight on it,—so I may as well come out with it. I b'lieve in religion, and one of these days, when I've got matters tight and snug, I calculates to tend to my soul and them ar matters; and so what's the use of doin' any more wickedness than's re'lly necessary?—it don't seem to me it's 'tall prudent."

"Tend to yer soul!" repeated Tom, contemptuously; "take a bright look-out to find a soul in you,—save yourself any care on that score. If the devil sifts you through a hair sieve, he won't find one."

"Why, Tom, you're cross," said Haley; "why can't ye take it pleasant, now, when a feller's talking for your good?"

"Stop that ar jaw o' yourn, there," said Tom, gruffly. "I can stand most any talk o' yourn but your pious talk,—that kills me right up. After all, what's the odds between me and you? 'Tan't that you care one bit more, or have a bit more feelin',—it's clean, sheer, dog meanness, wanting to cheat the devil and save your own skin; don't I see through it? And your 'gettin' religion,' as you call it, arter all, is too p'isin mean for any crittur;—run up a bill with the devil all your life, and then sneak out when pay time comes! Boh!"

"Come, come, gentlemen, I say; this isn't business," said Marks. "There's different ways, you know, of looking at all subjects. Mr. Haley is a very nice man, no doubt, and has his own conscience; and, Tom, you have your ways, and very good ones, too, Tom; but quarrelling, you know, won't answer no kind of purpose. Let's go to business. Now, Mr. Haley, what is it?—you want us to undertake to catch this yer gal?"

"The gal's no matter of mine,—she's Shelby's; it's only the boy. I was a fool for buying the monkey!"

"You're generally a fool!" said Tom, gruffly.

"Come, now, Loker, none of your huffs," said Marks, licking his lips; "you see, Mr. Haley's a puttin' us in a way of a good job, I reckon; just hold still,—these yer arrangements is my forte. This yer gal, Mr. Haley, how is she? what is she?"

"Wal! white and handsome—well brought up. I'd a gin Shelby eight hundred or a thousand, and then made well on her."

"White and handsome—well brought up!" said Marks, his sharp eyes, nose and mouth, all alive with enterprise. "Look here, now, Loker, a beautiful opening. We'll do a business here on our own account;—we does the catchin'; the boy, of course, goes to Mr. Haley,—we takes the gal to Orleans to speculate on. An't it beautiful?"

Tom, whose great heavy mouth had stood ajar during this communication, now suddenly snapped it together, as a big dog closes on a piece of meat, and seemed to be digesting the idea at his leisure.

"Ye see," said Marks to Haley, stirring his punch as he did so, "ye see, we has justices convenient[36] at all p'ints along shore, that does up any-little jobs in our line quite reasonable. Tom, he does the knockin' down and that ar; and I come in all dressed up—shining boots—everything first chop, when the swearin's to be done. You oughter see, now," said Marks, in a glow of professional pride, "how I can tone it off. One day, I'm Mr. Twickem, from New Orleans; 'nother day, I'm just come from my plantation on Pearl river, where I works seven hundred niggers; then, again, I come out a distant relation of Henry Clay, or some old cock in Kentuck. Talents is different, you know. Now, Tom's a roarer when there's any thumping or fighting to be done; but at lying he an't good, Tom an't,—ye see it don't come natural to him; but, Lord, if thar's a feller in the country that can swear to anything and everything, and put in all the circumstances and flourishes with a longer face, and carry't through better'n I can, why, I'd like to see him, that's all! I b'lieve my heart, I could get along and snake through, even if justices were more particular than they is. Sometimes I rather wish they was more particular; 'twould be a heap more relishin' if they was,—more fun, yer know."

Tom Loker, who, as we have made it appear, was a man of slow thoughts and movements, here interrupted Marks by bringing his heavy fist down on the table, so as to make all ring again. "*It'll do!*" he said.

"Lord bless ye, Tom, ye needn't break all the glasses!" said Marks; "save your fist for time o' need."

"But, gentlemen, an't I to come in for a share of the profits?" said Haley.

"An't it enough we catch the boy for ye?" said Loker. "What do ye want?"

"Wal," said Haley, "if I gives you the job, its worth something,—say ten per cent, on the profits, expenses paid."

"Now," said Loker, with a tremendous oath, and striking the table with his heavy fist, "don't I know *you*, Dan Haley? Don't you think to come it over me! Suppose Marks and I have taken up the catchin' trade, jest to 'commodate gentlemen like you, and get nothin' for ourselves?— Not by a long chalk! we'll have the gal out and you keep quiet, or, ye see, we'll have both,—what's to hinder? Han't you show'd us the game? It's as free to us as you, I hope. If you or Shelby wants to chase us, look where the partridges was last year; if you find them or us, you're quite welcome."

"O, wal, certainly, jest let it go at that," said Haley, alarmed; "you catch the boy for the job;—you allers did trade *far* with me, Tom, and was up to yer word."

"Ye know that," said Tom; "I don't pretend none of your snivelling ways, but I won't lie in my 'counts with the devil himself. What I ses I'll do, I will do,—you know *that*, Dan Haley."

"Jes so, jes so,—I said so, Tom," said Haley; "and if you'd only promise to have the boy for me in a week, at any point you'll name, that's all I want."

"But it an't all I want, by a long jump," said Tom. "Ye don't think I did business with you, down in Natchez, for nothing, Haley; I've learned to hold an eel, when I catch him. You've got to fork over fifty dollars, flat down, or this child don't start a peg. I know yer."

"Why, when you have a job in hand that may bring a clean profit of somewhere about a thousand or sixteen hundred, why, Tom, you're on-reasonable," said Haley.

"Yes, and hasn't we business booked for five weeks to come,—all we can do? And suppose we leaves all, and goes to bushwhacking—round arter yer young un, and finally

---

36 Government officials willing to falsify documents or adjudicate testimony so that free African Americans might be kidnaped and sold into slavery.

doesn't catch the gal,—and gals allers is the devil to catch,—what's then? would you pay us a cent—would you? I think I see you a doin' it—ugh! No, no; flap down your fifty. If we get the job, and it pays, I'll hand it back; if we don't, it's for our trouble,— that's *far*, an't it, Marks?"

"Certainly, certainly," said Marks, with a conciliatory tone; "it's only a retaining fee, you see,—he! he! he!—we lawyers, you know. Wal, we must all keep good-natured,—keep easy, yer know. Tom'll have the boy for yer, anywhere ye'll name; won't ye, Tom?"

"If I find the young un, I'll bring him on to Cincinnati, and leave him at Granny Belcher's, on the landing," said Loker.

Marks had got from his pocket a greasy pocket-book, and taking a long paper from thence, he sat down, and fixing his keen black eyes on it, began mumbling over its contents: "Barnes—Shelby County[37]—boy Jim, three hundred dollars for him, dead or alive.

"Edwards—Dick and Lucy—man and wife, six hundred dollars; wench Polly and two children—six hundred for her or her head.

"I'm jest a runnin' over our business, to see if we can take up this yer handily. Loker," he said, after a pause, "we must set Adams and Springer on the track of these yer; they've been booked some time."

"They'll charge too much," said Tom.

"I'll manage that ar; they's young in the business, and must spect to work cheap," said Marks, as he continued to read. "Ther's three on 'em easy cases, 'cause all you've got to do is to shoot 'em, or swear they is shot; they couldn't, of course, charge much for that. Them other cases," he said, folding the paper, "will bear puttin' off a spell. So now let's come to the particulars. Now, Mr. Haley, you saw this yer gal when she landed?"

"To be sure,—plain as I see you."

"And a man helpin' her up the bank?" said Loker.

"To be sure, I did."

"Most likely," said Marks, "she's took in somewhere; but where, 's a question. Tom, what do you say?"

"We must cross the river to-night, no mistake," said Tom.

"But there's no boat about," said Marks. "The ice is running awfully, Tom; an't it dangerous?"

"Don'no nothing 'bout that,—only it's got to be done," said Tom, decidedly.

"Dear me," said Marks, fidgeting, "it'll be—I say," he said, walking to the window, "it's dark as a wolf's mouth, and, Tom—"

"The long and short is, you're scared, Marks; but I can't help that,— you've got to go. Suppose you want to lie by a day or two, till the gal's been carried on the underground line up to Sandusky or so, before you start."

"O, no; I an't a grain afraid," said Marks, "only—"

"Only what?" said Tom.

"Well, about the boat. Yer see there an't any boat."

"I heard the woman say there was one coming along this evening, and that a man was going to cross over in it. Neck or nothing, we must go with him," said Tom.

"I s'pose you've got good dogs," said Haley.

"First rate," said Marks. "But what's the use? you han't got nothin' o' hers to smell on."

---

37 A county east of Louisville in north-central Kentucky.

"Yes, I have," said Haley, triumphantly. "Here's her shawl she left on the bed in her hurry; she left her bonnet, too."

"That ar's lucky," said Loker; "fork over."

"Though the dogs might damage the gal, if they come on her unawares," said Haley.

"That ar's a consideration," said Marks. "Our dogs tore a feller half to pieces, once, down in Mobile, 'fore we could get 'em off."

"Well, ye see, for this sort that's to be sold for their looks, that ar won't answer, ye see," said Haley.

"I do see," said Marks. "Besides, if she's got took in, 'tan't no go, neither. Dogs is no 'count in these yer up states where these critters get carried; of course, ye can't get on their track. They only does down in plantations, where niggers, when they runs, has to do their own running, and don't get no help."

"Well," said Loker, who had just stepped out to the bar to make some inquiries, "they say the man's come with the boat; so, Marks—"

That worthy cast a rueful look at the comfortable quarters he was leaving, but slowly rose to obey. After exchanging a few words of further arrangement, Haley, with visible reluctance, handed over the fifty dollars to Tom, and the worthy trio separated for the night.

If any of our refined and Christian readers object to the society into which this scene introduces them, let us beg them to begin and conquer their prejudices in time. The catching business, we beg to remind them, is rising to the dignity of a lawful and patriotic profession. If all the broad land between the Mississippi and the Pacific becomes one great market for bodies and souls, and human property retains the locomotive tendencies of this nineteenth century, the trader and catcher may yet be among our aristocracy.

* * * *

While this scene was going on at the tavern, Sam and Andy, in a state of high felicitation, pursued their way home.

Sam was in the highest possible feather, and expressed his exultation by all sorts of supernatural howls and ejaculations, by divers odd motions and contortions of his whole system. Sometimes he would sit backward, with his face to the horse's tail and sides, and then, with a whoop and a somerset,[38] come right side up in his place again, and, drawing on a grave face, begin to lecture Andy in high-sounding tones for laughing and playing the fool. Anon, slapping his sides with his arms, he would burst forth in peals of laughter, that made the old woods ring as they passed. With all these evolutions, he contrived to keep the horses up to the top of their speed, until, between ten and eleven, their heels resounded on the gravel at the end of the balcony. Mrs. Shelby flew to the railings.

"Is that you, Sam? Where are they?"

"Mas'r Haley's a-restin' at the tavern; he's drefful fatigued, Missis."

"And Eliza, Sam?"

"Wal, she's clar 'cross Jordan. As a body may say, in the land o' Canaan."

"Why, Sam, what *do* you mean?" said Mrs. Shelby, breathless, and almost faint, as the possible meaning of these words came over her.

"Wal, Missis, de Lord he persarves his own. Lizy's done gone over the river into 'Hio, as 'markably as if de Lord took her over in a charrit of fire and two hosses," said Sam.

---

38 Somersault.

Sam's vein of piety was always uncommonly fervent in his mistress' presence; and he made great capital of scriptural figures and images.

"Come up here, Sam," said Mr. Shelby, who had followed on to the verandah, "and tell your mistress what she wants. Come, come, Emily," said he, passing his arm round her, "you are cold and all in a shiver; you allow yourself to feel too much."

"Feel too much! Am not I a woman,—a mother? Are we not both responsible to God for this poor girl? My God! lay not this sin to our charge."

"What sin, Emily? You see yourself that we have only done what we were obliged to."

"There's an awful feeling of guilt about it, though," said Mrs. Shelby. "I can't reason it away."

"Here, Andy, you nigger, be alive!" called Sam, under the verandah; "take these yer hosses to der barn; don't ye hear Mas'r a callin'?" and Sam soon appeared, palm-leaf in hand, at the parlor door.

"Now, Sam, tell us distinctly how the matter was," said Mr. Shelby. "Where is Eliza, if you know?"

"Wal, Mas'r, I saw her, with my own eyes, a crossin' on the floatin' ice. She crossed most 'markably; it wasn't no less nor a miracle; and I saw a man help her up the 'Hio side, and then she was lost in the dusk."

"Sam, I think this rather apocryphal,—this miracle. Crossing on floating ice isn't easily done," said Mr. Shelby.

"Easy! couldn't nobody a done it, widout de Lord. Why, now," said Sam, "'twas jist dis yer way. Mas'r Haley, and me, and Andy, we comes up to de little tavern by the river, and I rides a leetle ahead,—(I's so zealous to be a cotchin' Lizy, that I couldn't hold in, no way),—and when I comes by the tavern winder, sure enough there she was, right in plain sight, and dey diggin' on behind. Wal, I loses off my hat, and sings out nuff to raise the dead. Course Lizy she hars, and she dodges back, when Mas'r Haley he goes past the door; and then, I tell ye, she clared out de side door; she went down de river bank;—Mas'r Haley he seed her, and yelled out, and him, and me, and Andy, we took arter. Down she come to the river, and thar was the current running ten feet wide by the shore, and over t'other side ice a sawin' and a jiggling up and down, kinder as 'twere a great island. We come right behind her, and I thought my soul he'd got her sure enough,—when she gin sich a screech as I never hearn, and thar she was, clar over t'other side the current, on the ice, and then on she went, a screeching and a jumpin',—the ice went crack! c'wallop! cracking! chunk! and she a boundin' like a buck! Lord, the spring that ar gal's got in her an't common, I'm o' 'pinion."

Mrs. Shelby sat perfectly silent, pale with excitement, while Sam told his story.

"God be praised, she isn't dead!" she said; "but where is the poor child now?"

"De Lord will pervide," said Sam, rolling up his eyes piously. "As I've been a sayin', dis yer's a providence and no mistake, as Missis has allers been a instructin' on us. Thar's allers instruments ris up to do de Lord's will. Now, if 't hadn't been for me today, she'd a been took a dozen times. Warn't it I started off de hosses, dis yer mornin', and kept 'em chasin' till nigh dinner time? And didn't I car Mas'r Haley nigh five miles out of de road, dis evening, or else he'd come up with Lizy as easy as a dog arter a coon. These yer's all providences."

"They are a kind of providences that you'll have to be pretty sparing of Master Sam. I allow no such practices with gentlemen on my place," said Mr. Shelby, with as much stern-ness as he could command, under the circumstances.

Now, there is no more use in making believe to be angry with a Negro than with a child; both instinctively see the true state of the case, through all attempts to effect the contrary; and Sam was in no wise disheartened by this rebuke, though he assumed an air of doleful gravity, and stood with the corners of his mouth lowered in most penitential style.

"Mas'r's quite right,—quite; it was ugly on me,—there's no disputin' that ar; and of course Mas'r and Missis wouldn't encourage no such works. I'm sensible of dat ar; but a poor nigger like me's 'mazin' tempted to act ugly sometimes, when fellers will cut up such shines as dat ar Mas'r Haley; he an't no gen'lman no way; anybody's been raised as I've been can't help a seein' dat ar."

"Well, Sam," said Mrs. Shelby, "as you appear to have a proper sense of your errors, you may go now and tell Aunt Chloe she may get you some of that cold ham that was left of dinner to-day. You and Andy must be hungry."

"Missis is a heap too good for us," said Sam, making his bow with alacrity, and departing.

It will be perceived, as has been before intimated, that Master Sam had a native talent that might, undoubtedly, have raised him to eminence in political life,—a talent of making capital out of everything that turned up, to be invested for his own especial praise and glory; and having done up his piety and humility, as he trusted, to the satisfaction of the parlor, he clapped his palm-leaf on his head, with a sort of rakish, free-and-easy air, and proceeded to the dominions of Aunt Chloe, with the intention of flourishing largely in the kitchen.

"I'll speechify these yer niggers," said Sam to himself, "now I've got a chance. Lord, I'll reel it off to make 'em stare!"

It must be observed that one of Sam's especial delights had been to ride in attendance on his master to all kinds of political gatherings, where, roosted on some rail fence, or perched aloft in some tree, he would sit watching the orators, with the greatest apparent gusto, and then, descending among the various brethren of his own color, assembled on the same errand, he would edify and delight them with the most ludicrous burlesques and imitations, all delivered with the most imperturbable earnestness and solemnity; and though the auditors immediately about him were generally of his own color, it not unfrequently happened that they were fringed pretty deeply with those of a fairer complexion, who listened, laughing and winking, to Sam's great self-congratulation. In fact, Sam considered oratory as his vocation, and never let slip an opportunity of magnifying his office.

Now, between Sam and Aunt Chloe there had existed, from ancient times, a sort of chronic feud, or rather a decided coolness; but, as Sam was meditating something in the provision department, as the necessary and obvious foundation of his operations, he determined, on the present occasion, to be eminently conciliatory; for he well knew that although "Missis' orders" would undoubtedly be followed to the letter, yet he should gain a considerable deal by enlisting the spirit also. He therefore appeared before Aunt Chloe with a touchingly subdued, resigned expression, like one who has suffered immeasurable hardships in behalf of a persecuted fellow-creature,—enlarged upon the fact that Missis had directed him to come to Aunt Chloe for whatever might be wanting to make up the balance in his solids and fluids,—and thus unequivocally acknowledged her right and supremacy in the cooking department, and all thereto pertaining.

The thing took accordingly. No poor, simple, virtuous body was ever cajoled by the attentions of an electioneering politician with more ease than Aunt Chloe was won over by Master Sam's suavities; and if he had been the prodigal son himself, he could not have been overwhelmed with more maternal bountifulness; and he soon found himself seated, happy and glorious, over a large tin pan, containing a sort of *olla podrida*[39] of all that had appeared on the table for two or three days past. Savory morsels of ham, golden blocks of corn-cake, fragments of pie of every conceivable mathematical figure, chicken wings, gizzards, and drumsticks, all appeared in picturesque confusion; and Sam, as monarch of all he surveyed, sat with his palm-leaf cocked rejoicingly to one side, and patronizing Andy at his right hand.

The kitchen was full of all his compeers, who had hurried and crowded in, from the various cabins, to hear the termination of the day's exploits. Now was Sam's hour of glory. The story of the day was rehearsed, with all kinds of ornament and varnishing which might be necessary to heighten its effect; for Sam, like some of our fashionable dilettanti, never allowed a story to lose any of its gilding by passing through his hands. Roars of laughter attended the narration, and were taken up and prolonged by all the smaller fry, who were lying, in any quantity, about on the floor, or perched in every corner. In the height of the uproar and laughter, Sam, however, preserved an immovable gravity, only from time to time rolling his eyes up, and giving his auditors divers inexpressibly droll glances, without departing from the sententious elevation of his oratory.

"Yer see, fellow-countrymen," said Sam, elevating a turkey's leg, with energy, "yer see, now, what dis yer chile's up ter, for fendin' yer all,—yes, all on yer. For him as tries to get one o' our people, is as good as tryin' to get all; yer see the principle's de same,—dat ar's clar. And any one o' these yer drivers that comes smelling round arter any our people, why, he's got me in his way; I'm the feller he's got to set in with,—I'm the feller for yer all to come to, bredren,—I'll stand up for yer rights,— I'll fend 'em to the last breath!"

"Why, but Sam, yer telled me, only this mornin', that you'd help this yer Mas'r to cotch Lizy; seems to me yer talk don't hang together," said Andy.

"I tell you now, Andy," said Sam, with awful superiority, "don't yer be a talkin' 'bout what yer don't know nothin' on; boys like you, Andy, means well, but they can't be spected to collusitate the great principles of action."

Andy looked rebuked, particularly by the hard word collusitate, which most of the youngerly members of the company seemed to consider as a settler in the case, while Sam proceeded.

"Dat ar was *conscience*, Andy; when I thought of gwine arter Lizy, I railly spected Mas'r was sot dat way. When I found Missis was sot the contrar, dat ar was conscience *more yet*,— cause fellers allers get more by stickin' to Missis' side,—so yer see I's persistent either way, and sticks up to conscience, and holds on to principles. Yes, *principles*," said Sam, giving an enthusiastic toss to a chicken's neck,—"what's principles good for, if we isn't persistent, I wanter know? Thar, Andy, you may have dat ar bone,—'tan't picked quite clean."

Sam's audience hanging on his words with open mouths, he could not but proceed.

"Dis yer matter 'bout persistence, feller-niggers," said Sam, with the air of one entering into an abstruse subject, "dis yer 'sistency's a thing what an't seed into very clar, by most anybody. Now, yer see, when a feller stands up for a thing one day and night, de contrar de next, folks ses (and nat'rally enough dey ses), why he an't persistent,—hand me dat ar bit o' corn-cake, Andy. But let's look inter it. I hope the gen'lmen and der fair sex will scuse my usin' an or'nary sort o' 'parison. Here! I'm a tryin' to get top o' der hay. Wal, I puts up my larder dis yer side; 'tan't no go;—den, cause I don't try dere no more, but puts my larder

---

39 Spanish for a rich stew.

right de contrar side, an't I persistent? I'm persistent in wantin' to get up which ar side my larder is; don't you see, all on yer?"

"It's the only thing ye ever was persistent in, Lord knows!" muttered Aunt Chloe, who was getting rather restive; the merriment of the evening being to her somewhat after the scripture comparison,—like "vinegar upon nitre."[40]

"Yes, indeed!" said Sam, rising, full of supper and glory, for a closing effort. "Yes, my feller-citizens and ladies of de other sex in general, I has principles,—I'm proud to 'oon 'em,—they's perquisite to dese yer times, and ter all times. I has principles, and I sticks to 'em like forty,— jest anything that I thinks is principle, I goes in to't;—I wouldn't mind if dey burnt me 'live,—I'd walk right up to de stake. I would, and say, here I comes to shed my last blood fur my principles, fur my country, fur der gen'l interests of s'ciety."

"Well," said Aunt Chloe, "one o' yer principles will have to be to get to bed some time to-night, and not be a keepin' everybody up till mornin'; now, every one of you young uns that don't want to be cracked, had better be scase, mighty sudden."

"Niggers! all on yer," said Sam, waving his palm-leaf with benignity, "I give yer my blessin'; go to bed now, and be good boys."

And, with this pathetic benediction, the assembly dispersed.

Chapter 9

In Which It Appears That a Senator Is but a Man

The light of the cheerful fire shone on the rug and carpet of a cosy parlor, and glittered on the sides of the teacups and well-brightened tea-pot, as Senator Bird was drawing off his boots, preparatory to inserting his feet in a pair of new handsome slippers, which his wife had been working for him while away on his senatorial tour. Mrs. Bird, looking the very picture of delight, was superintending the arrangements of the table, ever and anon mingling admonitory remarks to a number of frolicsome juveniles, who were effervescing in all those modes of untold gambol and mischief that have astonished mothers ever since the flood.

"Tom, let the door-knob alone,—there's a man! Mary! Mary! don't pull the cat's tail,— poor pussy! Jim, you mustn't climb on that table,— no, no! You don't know my dear, what a surprise it is to us all, to see you here tonight!" said she, at last, when she found a space to say something to her husband.

"Yes, yes, I thought I'd just make a run down, spend the night, and have a little comfort at home. I'm tired to death, and my head aches!"

Mrs. Bird cast a glance at a camphor-bottle,[41] which stood in the half-open closet, and appeared to meditate an approach to it, but her husband interposed.

"No, no, Mary, no doctoring! a cup of your good hot tea, and some of our good home living, is what I want. It's a tiresome business, this legislating!"

And the senator smiled, as if he rather liked the idea of considering himself a sacrifice to his country.

"Well," said his wife, after the business of the tea-table was getting rather slack, "and what have they been doing in the Senate?"

---

40 Proverbs 25:20.
41 Camphor was used as a stimulant or as a medicine to treat stomach ailments.

Now, it was a very unusual thing for gentle little Mrs. Bird ever to trouble her head with what was going on in the house of the state, very wisely considering that she had enough to do to mind her own. Mr. Bird, therefore, opened his eyes in surprise, and said,

"Not very much of importance."

"Well; but is it true that they have been passing a law forbidding people to give meat and drink to those poor colored folks that come along? I heard they were talking of some such law, but I didn't think any Christian legislature would pass it!"

"Why, Mary, you are getting to be a politician, all at once."

"No, nonsense! I wouldn't give a fip for all your politics, generally, but I think this is something downright cruel and unchristian. I hope, my dear, no such law has been passed."

"There has been a law passed forbidding people to help off the slaves that come over from Kentucky, my dear; so much of that thing has been done by these reckless Abolitionists, that our brethren in Kentucky are very strongly excited, and it seems necessary, and no more than Christian and kind, that something should be done by our state to quiet the excitement."

"And what is the law? It don't forbid us to shelter these poor creatures a night, does it, and to give 'em something comfortable to eat, and a few old clothes, and send them quietly about their business?"

"Why, yes, my dear; that would be aiding and abetting, you know."

Mrs. Bird was a timid, blushing little woman, of about four feet in height, and with mild blue eyes, and a peach-blow complexion, and the gentlest, sweetest voice in the world;—as for courage, a moderate-sized cock-turkey had been known to put her to rout at the very first gobble, and a stout house-dog, of moderate capacity, would bring her into subjection merely by a show of his teeth. Her husband and children were her entire world, and in these she ruled more by entreaty and persuasion than by command or argument. There was only one thing that was capable of arousing her, and that provocation came in on the side of her unusually gentle and sympathetic nature;—anything in the shape of cruelty would throw her into a passion, which was the more alarming and inexplicable in proportion to the general softness of her nature. Generally the most indulgent and easy to be entreated of all mothers, still her boys had a very reverent remembrance of a most vehement chastisement she once bestowed on them, because she found them leagued with several graceless boys of the neighborhood, stoning a defenceless kitten.

"I'll tell you what," Master Bill used to say, "I was scared that time. Mother came at me so that I thought she was crazy, and I was whipped and tumbled off to bed, without any supper, before I could get over wondering what had come about; and, after that, I heard mother crying outside the door, which made me feel worse than all the rest. I'll tell you what," he'd say, "we boys never stoned another kitten!"

On the present occasion, Mrs. Bird rose quickly, with very red cheeks, which quite improved her general appearance, and walked up to her husband, with quite a resolute air, and said, in a determined tone,

"Now, John, I want to know if you think such a law as that is right and Christian?"

"You won't shoot me, now, Mary, if I say I do!"

"I never could have thought it of you, John; you didn't vote for it?"

"Even so, my fair politician."

"You ought to be ashamed, John! Poor, homeless, houseless creatures! It's a shameful, wicked, abominable law, and I'll break it, for one, the first time I get a chance; and I hope I *shall* have a chance, I do! Things have got to a pretty pass, if a woman can't give a warm supper and a bed to poor, starving creatures, just because they are slaves, and have been abused and oppressed all their lives, poor things!"

"But, Mary, just listen to me. Your feelings are all quite right, dear, and interesting, and I love you for them; but, then, dear, we mustn't suffer our feelings to run away with our judgment; you must consider it's not a matter of private feeling,—there are great public interests involved,—there is such a state of public agitation rising, that we must put aside our private feelings."

"Now, John, I don't know anything about politics, but I can read my Bible; and there I see that I must feed the hungry, clothe the naked, and comfort the desolate; and that Bible I mean to follow."

"But in cases where your doing so would involve a great public evil—"

"Obeying God never brings on public evils. I know it can't. It's always safest, all round, to *do as* He bids us."

"Now, listen to me, Mary, and I can state to you a very clear argument, to show—"

"O, nonsense, John! you can talk all night, but you wouldn't do it. I put it to you, John,—would *you* now turn away a poor, shivering, hungry creature from your door, because he was a runaway? *Would* you, now?"

Now, if the truth must be told, our senator had the misfortune to be a man who had a particularly humane and accessible nature, and turning away anybody that was in trouble never had been his forte; and what was worse for him in this particular pinch of the argument was, that his wife knew it, and, of course, was making an assault on rather an indefensible point. So he had recourse to the usual means of gaining time for such cases made and provided; he said "ahem," and coughed several times, took out his pocket-handkerchief, and began to wipe his glasses. Mrs. Bird, seeing the defenceless condition of the enemy's territory, had no more conscience than to push her advantage.

"I should like to see you doing that, John—I really should! Turning a woman out of doors in a snow-storm, for instance; or, may be you'd take her up and put her in jail, wouldn't you? You would make a great hand at that!"

"Of course, it would be a very painful duty," began Mr. Bird, in a moderate tone.

"Duty, John! don't use that word! You know it isn't a duty—it can't be a duty! If folks want to keep their slaves from running away, let 'em treat 'em well,—that's my doctrine. If I had slaves (as I hope I never shall have), I'd risk their wanting to run away from me, or you either, John. I tell you folks don't run away when they are happy; and when they do run, poor creatures! they suffer enough with cold and hunger and fear, without everybody's turning against them; and, law or no law, I never will, so help me God!"

"Mary! Mary! My dear, let me reason with you."

"I hate reasoning, John,—especially reasoning on such subjects. There's a way you political folks have of coming round and round a plain right thing; and you don't believe in it yourselves, when it comes to practice. I know you well enough, John. You don't believe it's right any more than I do; and you wouldn't do it any sooner than I."

At this critical juncture, old Cudjoe, the black man-of-all-work, put his head in at the door, and wished "Missis would come into the kitchen;" and our senator, tolerably relieved, looked after his little wife with a whimsical mixture of amusement and vexation, and, seating himself in the arm-chair, began to read the papers.

After a moment, his wife's voice was heard at the door, in a quick, earnest tone,—"John! John! I do wish you'd come here, a moment."

He laid down his paper, and went into the kitchen, and started, quite amazed at the sight that presented itself:—A young and slender woman, with garments torn and frozen, with one shoe gone, and the stocking torn away from the cut and bleeding foot, was laid back in a deadly swoon upon two chairs. There was the impress of the despised race on her face, yet none could help feeling its mournful and pathetic beauty, while its stony sharpness, its cold, fixed, deathly aspect, struck a solemn chill over him. He drew his breath short, and stood in silence. His wife, and their only colored domestic, old Aunt Dinah, were busily engaged in restorative measures; while old Cudjoe had got the boy on his knee, and was busy pulling off his shoes and stockings, and chafing his little cold feet.

"Sure, now, if she an't a sight to behold!" said old Dinah, compassionately; "'pears like 'twas the heat that made her faint. She was tol'able peart when she cum in, and asked if she couldn't warm herself here a spell; and I was just a askin' her where she cum from, and she fainted right down. Never done much hard work, guess, by the looks of her hands."

"Poor creature!" said Mrs. Bird, compassionately, as the woman slowly unclosed her large, dark eyes, and looked vacantly at her. Suddenly an expression of agony crossed her face, and she sprang up, saying, "O, my Harry! Have they got him?"

The boy, at this, jumped from Cudjoe's knee, and, running to her side, put up his arms. "O, he's here! he's here!" she exclaimed.

"O, ma'am!" said she, wildly, to Mrs. Bird, "do protect us! don't let them get him!"

"Nobody shall hurt you here, poor woman," said Mrs. Bird, encouragingly. "You are safe; don't be afraid."

"God bless you!" said the woman, covering her face and sobbing; while the little boy, seeing her crying, tried to get into her lap.

With many gentle and womanly offices, which none knew better how to render than Mrs. Bird, the poor woman was, in time, rendered more calm. A temporary bed was provided for her on the settle, near the fire; and, after a short time, she fell into a heavy slumber, with the child, who seemed no less weary, soundly sleeping on her arm; for the mother resisted, with nervous anxiety, the kindest attempts to take him from her; and, even in sleep, her arm encircled him with an unrelaxing clasp, as if she could not even then be beguiled of her vigilant hold.

Mr. and Mrs. Bird had gone back to the parlor, where, strange as it may appear, no reference was made, on either side, to the preceding conversation; but Mrs. Bird busied herself with her knitting-work, and Mr. Bird pretended to be reading the paper.

"I wonder who and what she is!" said Mr. Bird, at last, as he laid it down.

"When she wakes up and feels a little rested, we will see," said Mrs. Bird.

"I say, wife!" said Mr. Bird, after musing in silence over his newspaper.

"Well, dear!"

"She couldn't wear one of your gowns, could she, by any letting down, or such matter? She seems to be rather larger than you are."

A quite perceptible smile glimmered on Mrs. Bird's face, as she answered, "We'll see."

Another pause, and Mr. Bird again broke out,

"I say, wife!"

"Well! What now?"

"Why, there's that old bombazine[42] cloak, that you keep on purpose to put over me when I take my afternoon's nap; you might as well give her that,—she needs clothes."

---

42 A twilled fabric, often made of silk.

At this instant, Dinah looked in to say that the woman was awake, and wanted to see Missis.

Mr. and Mrs. Bird went into the kitchen, followed by the two eldest boys, the smaller fry having, by this time, been safely disposed of in bed.

The woman was now sitting up on the settle, by the fire. She was looking steadily into the blaze, with a calm, heartbroken expression, very different from her former agitated wildness.

"Did you want me?" said Mrs. Bird, in gentle tones. "I hope you feel better now, poor woman!"

A long-drawn, shivering sigh was the only answer; but she lifted her dark eyes, and fixed them on her with such a forlorn and imploring expression, that the tears came into the little woman's eyes.

"You needn't be afraid of anything; we are friends here, poor woman! Tell me where you came from, and what you want," said she.

"I came from Kentucky," said the woman.

"When?" said Mr. Bird, taking up the interrogatory.

"To-night."

"How did you come?"

"I crossed on the ice."

"Crossed on the ice!" said every one present.

"Yes," said the woman, slowly, "I did. God helping me, I crossed on the ice; for they were behind me—right behind—and there was no other way!"

"Law, Missis," said Cudjoe, "the ice is all in broken-up blocks, a swinging and a teetering up and down in the water!"

"I know it was—I know it!" said she, wildly; "but I did it! I wouldn't have thought I could,—I didn't think I should get over, but I didn't care! I could but die, if I didn't. The Lord helped me; nobody knows how much the Lord can help 'em, till they try," said the woman, with a flashing eye.

"Were you a slave?" said Mr. Bird.

"Yes, sir; I belonged to a man in Kentucky."

"Was he unkind to you?"

"No, sir; he was a good master."

"And was your mistress unkind to you?"

"No, sir—no! my mistress was always good to me."

"What could induce you to leave a good home, then, and run away, and go through such dangers?"

The woman looked up at Mrs. Bird, with a keen, scrutinizing glance, and it did not escape her that she was dressed in deep mourning.

"Ma'am," she said, suddenly, "have you ever lost a child?"

The question was unexpected, and it was a thrust on a new wound; for it was only a month since a darling child of the family had been laid in the grave.

Mr. Bird turned around and walked to the window, and Mrs. Bird burst into tears; but, recovering her voice, she said,

"Why do you ask that? I have lost a little one."

"Then you will feel for me. I have lost two, one after another,—left 'em buried there when I came away; and I had only this one left. I never slept a night without him; he was all I had. He was my comfort and pride, day and night; and, ma'am, they were going to take him away from me,—to sell him,—sell him down south, ma'am, to go all alone,— a baby that had never been away from his mother in his life! I couldn't stand it, ma'am. I knew I never should be good for anything, if they did; and when I knew the papers were signed, and he was sold, I took him and came off in the night; and they chased me,—the man that bought him, and some of Mas'r's folks,—and they were coming down right behind me, and I heard 'em. I jumped right on to the ice; and how I got across, I don't know,—but, first I knew, a man was helping me up the bank."

The woman did not sob nor weep. She had gone to a place where tears are dry; but every one around her was in some way characteristic of themselves, showing signs of hearty sympathy.

The two little boys, after a desperate rummaging in their pockets, in search of those pocket-handkerchiefs which mothers know are never to be found there, had thrown themselves disconsolately into the skirts of their mother's gown, where they were sobbing, and wiping their eyes and noses, to their hearts' content;—Mrs. Bird had her face fairly hidden in her pocket-handkerchief; and old Dinah, with tears streaming down her black, honest face, was ejaculating, "Lord have mercy on us!" with all the fervor of a camp-meeting;— while old Cudjoe, rubbing his eyes very hard with his cuffs, and making a most uncommon variety of wry faces, occasionally responded in the same key, with great fervor. Our senator was a statesman, and of course could not be expected to cry, like other mortals; and so he turned his back to the company, and looked out of the window, and seemed particularly busy in clearing his throat and wiping his spectacle-glasses, occasionally blowing his nose in a manner that was calculated to excite suspicion, had any one been in a state to observe critically.

"How came you to tell me you had a kind master?" he suddenly exclaimed, gulping down very resolutely some kind of rising in his throat, and turning suddenly round upon the woman.

"Because he was a kind master; I'll say that of him, any way;—and my mistress was kind; but they couldn't help themselves. They were owing money; and there was some way, I can't tell how, that a man had a hold on them, and they were obliged to give him his will. I listened, and heard him telling mistress that, and she begging and pleading for me,— and he told her he couldn't help himself, and that the papers were all drawn;—and then it was I took him and left my home, and came away. I knew 'twas no use of my trying to live, if they did it; for't 'pears like this child is all I have."

"Have you no husband?"

"Yes, but he belongs to another man. His master is real hard to him, and won't let him come to see me, hardly ever; and he's grown harder and harder upon us, and he threatens to sell him down south;—it's like I'll never see him again!"

The quiet tone in which the woman pronounced these words might have led a superficial observer to think that she was entirely apathetic; but there was a calm, settled depth of anguish in her large, dark eyes, that spoke of something far otherwise.

"And where do you mean to go, my poor woman?" said Mrs. Bird.

"To Canada, if I only knew where that was. Is it very far off, is Canada?" said she, looking up, with a simple, confiding air, to Mrs. Bird's face.

"Poor thing!" said Mrs. Bird, involuntarily.

"Is't a very great way off, think?" said the woman, earnestly.

"Much further than you think, poor child!" said Mrs. Bird; "but we will try to think what can be done for you. Here, Dinah, make her up a bed in your own room, close by the kitchen, and I'll think what to do for her in the morning. Meanwhile, never fear, poor woman; put your trust in God; he will protect you."

Mrs. Bird and her husband reëntered the parlor. She sat down in her little rocking-chair before the fire, swaying thoughtfully to and fro. Mr. Bird strode up and down the room, grumbling to himself. "Pish! pshaw! confounded awkward business!" At length, striding up to his wife, he said,

"I say, wife, she'll have to get away from here, this very night. That fellow will be down on the scent bright and early to-morrow morning; if 'twas only the woman, she could lie quiet till it was over, but that little chap can't be kept still by a troop of horse and foot, I'll warrant me; he'll bring it all out, popping his head out of some window or door. A pretty kettle of fish it would be for me, too, to be caught with them both here, just now! No; they'll have to be got off to-night."

"To-night! How is it possible?—where to?"

"Well, I know pretty well where to," said the senator, beginning to put on his boots, with a reflective air; and, stopping when his leg was half in, he embraced his knee with both hands, and seemed to go off in deep meditation.

"It's a confounded awkward, ugly business," said he, at last, beginning to tug at his boot-straps again, "and that's a fact!" After one boot was fairly on, the senator sat with the other in his hand, profoundly studying the figure of the carpet. "It will have to be done, though, for aught I see,—hang it all!" and he drew the other boot anxiously on, and looked out of the window.

Now, little Mrs. Bird was a discreet woman,—a woman who never in her life said, "I told you so!" and, on the present occasion, though pretty well aware of the shape her husband's meditations were taking, she very prudently forbore to meddle with them, only sat very quietly in her chair, and looked quite ready to hear her liege lord's intentions, when he should think proper to utter them.

"You see," he said, "there's my old client, Van Trompe, has come over from Kentucky, and set all his slaves free; and he has bought a place seven miles up the creek, here, back in the woods, where nobody goes, unless they go on purpose; and it's a place that isn't found in a hurry. There she'd be safe enough; but the plague of the thing is, nobody could drive a carriage there to-night, but me."

"Why not? Cudjoe is an excellent driver."

"Ay, ay, but here it is. The creek has to be crossed twice; and the second crossing is quite dangerous, unless one knows it as I do. I have crossed it a hundred times on horseback, and know exactly the turns to take. And so, you see, there's no help for it. Cudjoe must put in the horses, as quietly as may be, about twelve o'clock, and I'll take her over; and then, to give color to the matter, he must carry me on to the next tavern, to take the stage for Columbus, that comes by about three or four, and so it will look as if I had had the carriage only for that. I shall get into business bright and early in the morning. But I'm thinking I shall feel rather cheap there, after all that's been said and done; but, hang it, I can't help it!"

"Your heart is better than your head, in this case, John," said the wife, laying her little white hand on his. "Could I ever have loved you, had I not known you better than you know yourself?" And the little woman looked so handsome, with the tears sparkling in her eyes, that the senator thought he must be a decidedly clever fellow, to get such a pretty creature into such a passionate admiration of him; and so, what could he do but walk off soberly, to see about the carriage. At the door, however, he stopped a moment, and then coming back, he said, with some hesitation,

"Mary, I don't know how you'd feel about it, but there's that drawer full of things—of—of—poor little Henry's." So saying, he turned quickly on his heel, and shut the door after him.

His wife opened the little bed-room door adjoining her room, and taking the candle, set it down on the top of a bureau there; then from a small recess she took a key, and put it thoughtfully in the lock of a drawer, and made a sudden pause, while two boys, who, boy like, had followed close on her heels, stood looking, with silent, significant glances at their mother. And oh! mother that reads this, has there never been in your house a drawer, or a closet, the opening of which has been to you like the opening again of a little grave? Ah! happy mother that you are, if it has not been so.

Mrs. Bird slowly opened the drawer. There were little coats of many a form and pattern, piles of aprons, and rows of small stockings; and even a pair of little shoes, worn and rubbed at the toes, were peeping from the folds of a paper. There was a toy horse and wagon, a top, a ball,—memorials gathered with many a tear and many a heart-break! She sat down by the drawer, and, leaning her head on her hands over it, wept till the tears fell through her fingers into the drawer; then suddenly raising her head, she began, with nervous haste, selecting the plainest and most substantial articles, and gathering them into a bundle.

"Mamma," said one of the boys, gently touching her arm, "are you going to give away *those* things?"

"My dear boys," she said, softly and earnestly, "if our dear, loving little Henry looks down from heaven, he would be glad to have us do this. I could not find it in my heart to give them away to any common person—to anybody that was happy; but I give them to a mother more heartbroken and sorrowful than I am; and I hope God will send his blessings with them!"

There are in this world blessed souls, whose sorrows all spring up into joys for others; whose earthly hopes, laid in the grave with many tears, are the seed from which spring healing flowers and balm for the desolate and the distressed. Among such was the delicate woman who sits there by the lamp, dropping slow tears, while she prepares the memorials of her own lost one for the outcast wanderer.

After a while, Mrs. Bird opened a wardrobe, and, taking from thence a plain, serviceable dress or two, she sat down busily to her work-table, and with needle, scissors, and thimble, at hand, quietly commenced the "letting down" process which her husband had recommended, and continued busily at it till the old clock in the corner struck twelve, and she heard the low rattling of wheels at the door.

"Mary," said her husband, coming in, with his overcoat in his hand, "you must wake her up now; we must be off."

Mrs. Bird hastily deposited the various articles she had collected in a small plain trunk, and locking it, desired her husband to see it in the carriage, and then proceeded to call the woman. Soon, arrayed in a cloak, bonnet, and shawl, that had belonged to her benefactress, she appeared at the door with her child in her arms. Mr. Bird hurried her into the carriage, and Mrs. Bird pressed on after her to the carriage steps. Eliza leaned out of the carriage and put out her hand,—a hand as soft and beautiful as was given in return. She fixed her large, dark eyes, full of earnest meaning, on Mrs. Bird's face, and seemed going to speak. Her lips moved,—she tried once or twice, but there was no sound,—and pointing upward, with a look never to be forgotten, she fell back in the seat, and covered her face. The door was shut, and the carriage drove on.

What a situation, now, for a patriotic senator, that had been all the week before spurring up the legislature of his native state to pass more stringent resolutions against escaping fugitives, their harborers and abettors!

Our good senator in his native state had not been exceeded by any of his brethren at Washington, in the sort of eloquence which has won for them immortal renown! How sublimely he had sat with his hands in his pockets, and scouted all sentimental weakness of those who would put the welfare of a few miserable fugitives before great state interests!

He was as bold as a lion about it, and "mightily convinced" not only himself, but everybody that heard him;—but then his idea of a fugitive was only an idea of the letters that spell the word,—or, at the most, the image of a little newspaper picture of a man with a stick and bundle, with "Ran away from the subscriber" under it. The magic of the real presence of distress,—the imploring human eye, the frail, trembling human hand, the despairing appeal of helpless agony,—these he had never tried. He had never thought that a fugitive might be a hapless mother, a defenceless child,—like that one which was now wearing his lost boy's little well-known cap; and so, as our poor senator was not stone or steel,—as he was a man, and a downright noble-hearted one, too,—he was, as everybody must see, in a sad case for his patriotism. And you need not exult over him, good brother of the Southern States; for we have some inklings that many of you, under similar circumstances, would not do much better. We have reason to know, in Kentucky, as in Mississippi, are noble and generous hearts, to whom never was tale of suffering told in vain. Ah, good brother! is it fair for you to expect of us services which your own brave, honorable heart would not allow you to render, were you in our place?

Be that as it may, if our good senator was a political sinner, he was in a fair way to expiate it by his night's penance. There had been a long continuous period of rainy weather, and the soft, rich earth of Ohio, as every one knows, is admirably suited to the manufacture of mud,—and the road was an Ohio railroad of the good old times.

"And pray, what sort of a road may that be?" says some eastern traveller, who has been accustomed to connect no ideas with a railroad, but those of smoothness or speed.

Know, then, innocent eastern friend, that in benighted regions of the west, where the mud is of unfathomable and sublime depth, roads are made of round rough logs, arranged transversely side by side, and coated over in their pristine freshness with earth, turf, and whatsoever may come to hand, and then the rejoicing native calleth it a road, and straightway essayeth to ride thereupon. In process of time, the rains wash off all the turf and grass aforesaid, move the logs hither and thither, in picturesque positions, up, down and crosswise, with divers chasms and ruts of black mud intervening.

Over such a road as this our senator went stumbling along, making moral reflections as continuously as under the circumstances could be expected,—the carriage proceeding along much as follows,—bump! bump! bump! slush! down in the mud!—the senator, woman and child, reversing their positions so suddenly as to come, without any very accurate adjustment, against the windows of the down-hill side. Carriage sticks fast, while Cudjoe on the outside is heard making a great muster among the horses. After various ineffectual pullings and twitchings, just as the senator is losing all patience, the carriage suddenly rights itself with a bounce,—two front wheels go down into another abyss, and senator, woman, and child, all tumble promiscuously on to the front seat,— senator's hat is jammed over his eyes and nose quite unceremoniously, and he considers himself fairly extinguished;—child cries, and Cudjoe on the outside delivers animated addresses to the horses, who are kicking, and floundering, and straining, under repeated cracks of the whip. Carriage springs up, with another bounce,—down go the hind wheels,—senator, woman, and child, fly over on to the back seat, his elbows encountering her bonnet, and both her feet being jammed into his hat, which flies off in the concussion. After a few moments the "slough" is passed, and the horses stop, panting;—the senator finds his hat, the woman straightens her bonnet and hushes her child, and they brace themselves firmly for what is yet to come.

For a while only the continuous bump! bump! intermingled, just by way of variety, with divers side plunges and compound shakes; and they begin to flatter themselves that they are not so badly off, after all. At last, with a square plunge, which puts all on to their feet and then down into their seats with incredible quickness, the carriage stops,—and, after much outside commotion, Cudjoe appears at the door.

"Please, sir, it's powerful bad spot, this yer. I don't know how we's to get clar out. I'm a thinkin' we'll have to be a gettin' rails."

The senator despairingly steps out, picking gingerly for some firm foothold; down goes one foot an immeasurable depth,—he tries to pull it up, loses his balance, and tumbles over into the mud, and is fished out, in a very despairing condition, by Cudjoe.

But we forbear, out of sympathy to our readers' bones. Western travellers, who have beguiled the midnight hour in the interesting process of pulling down rail fences, to pry their carriages out of mud holes, will have a respectful and mournful sympathy with our unfortunate hero. We beg them to drop a silent tear, and pass on.

It was full late in the night when the carriage emerged, dripping and bespattered, out of the creek, and stood at the door of a large farmhouse.

It took no inconsiderable perseverance to arouse the inmates; but at last the respectable proprietor appeared, and undid the door. He was a great, tall, bristling Orson[43] of a fellow, full six feet and some inches in his stockings, and arrayed in a red flannel hunting-shirt. A very heavy mat of sandy hair, in a decidedly tousled condition, and a beard of some days' growth, gave the worthy man an appearance, to say the least, not particularly prepossessing. He stood for a few minutes holding the candle aloft, and blinking on our travellers with a dismal and mystified expression that was truly ludicrous. It cost some effort of our senator to induce him to comprehend the case fully; and while he is doing his best at that, we shall give him a little introduction to our readers.

Honest old John Van Trompe was once quite a considerable landholder and slave-owner in the State of Kentucky. Having "nothing of the bear about him but the skin," and being gifted by nature with a great, honest, just heart, quite equal to his gigantic frame, he had been for some years witnessing with repressed uneasiness the workings of a system equally bad for oppressor and oppressed. At last, one day, John's great heart had swelled altogether too big to wear his bonds any longer; so he just took his pocket-book out of his desk, and went over into Ohio, and bought a quarter of a township of good, rich land, made out free papers for all his people,—men, women, and children,—packed them up in wagons, and sent them off to settle down; and then honest John turned his face up the creek, and sat quietly down on a snug, retired farm, to enjoy his conscience and his reflections.

"Are you the man that will shelter a poor woman and child from slave-catchers?" said the senator, explicitly.

"I rather think I am," said honest John, with some considerable emphasis.

"I thought so," said the senator.

---

43 In the well-known medieval romance "Valentine and Orson," Orson is a wild and strong man who had been raised by a bear.

"If there's anybody comes," said the good man, stretching his tall, muscular form upward, "why here I'm ready for him: and I've got seven sons, each six foot high, and they'll be ready for 'em. Give our respects to 'em," said John; "tell 'em it's no matter how soon they call,—make no kinder difference to us," said John, running his fingers through the shock of hair that thatched his head, and bursting out into a great laugh.

Weary, jaded, and spiritless, Eliza dragged herself up to the door with her child lying in a heavy sleep on her arm. The rough man held the candle to her face, and uttering a kind of compassionate grunt, opened the door of a small bedroom adjoining to the large kitchen where they were standing, and motioned her to go in. He took down a candle, and lighting it, set it upon the table, and then addressed himself to Eliza.

"Now, I say, gal, you needn't be a bit afeard, let who will come here. I'm up to all that sort o' thing," said he, pointing to two or three goodly rifles over the mantel-piece; "and most people that know me know that 't wouldn't be healthy to try to get anybody out o' my house when I'm agin it. So now you jist go to sleep now, as quiet as if yer mother was a rockin' ye," said he, as he shut the door.

"Why, this is an uncommon handsome un," he said to the senator. "Ah, well; handsome uns has the greatest cause to run, sometimes, if they has any kind o' feelin', such as decent women should. I know all about that."

The senator, in a few words, briefly explained Eliza's history.

"O! ou! aw! now, I want to know?" said the good man, pitifully; "sho! now sho! That's natur now, poor crittur hunted down like a deer,— hunted down, jest for havin' natural feelin's, and doin' what no kind o' mother could help a doin'! I tell ye what, these yer things make me come the nighest to swearin', now, o' most anything," said honest John, as he wiped his eyes with the back of a great, freckled, yellow hand. "I tell yer what, stranger, it was years and years before I'd jine the church, 'cause the minister round in our parts used to preach that the Bible went in for these ere cuttings up,—and I couldn't be up to 'em with their Greek and Hebrew, and so I took up agin 'em, Bible and all. I never jined the church till I found a minister that was up to 'em all in Greek and all that, and he said right the contrary; and then I took right hold, and jined the church,—I did now, fact," said John, who had been all this time uncorking some very frisky bottled cider, which at this juncture he presented.

"Ye'd better just put up here, now, till daylight," said he, heartily, "and I'll call up the old woman, and have a bed got ready for you in no time."

"Thank you, my good friend," said the senator, "I must be along, to take the night stage for Columbus."

"Ah! well, then, if you must, I'll go a piece with you, and show you a cross road that will take you there better than the road you came on. That road's mighty bad."

John equipped himself, and, with a lantern in hand, was soon seen guiding the senator's carriage towards a road that ran down in a hollow, back of his dwelling. When they parted, the senator put into his hand a ten-dollar bill.

"It's for her," he said, briefly.

"Ay, ay," said John, with equal conciseness.

They shook hands, and parted.

* * *

Editor's Note

Uncle Tom's Cabin: **The End of the Story**

The remainder of the novel follows the twin stories of Eliza's escape north toward Canada and Uncle Tom's journey to the Deep South. Religious symbolism permeates the book as Canada comes to represent heaven with an immense reunion of Eliza's whole family (including her long-lost mother), while the Deep South comes to represent the tortures and deprivations of hell. Eliza and George Harris eventually go to Europe to be educated and then plan to settle with his family in Liberia. Near the end of the story, Tom is whipped to death by his wicked owner, Simon Legree. The brutal end of Tom's Christ-like life takes on the air of tragic martyrdom as he sacrifices himself rather than betray other slaves who have fled Legree's plantation in search of their freedom.

Chapter Eleven

TIMOTHY SHAY ARTHUR
(1809–1885)

Timothy Shay Arthur's literary reputation today rests almost solely on his 1854 temperance novel, *Ten Nights in a Bar-Room*. Like many of his successful contemporaries, Arthur's literary output showed far more range than this single work would imply. Beginning in the 1840s, he began writing what would eventually become a body of work that included 150 novels and collections of short stories. He also edited several influential periodicals, including *Arthur's Home Gazette* (later renamed *The Home Magazine*). Reportedly, more than a million copies of his works were circulating in the United States before the Civil War.

His *Ten Nights in a Bar-Room* was the most popular single piece of temperance literature to appear before the Civil War, no mean feat considering how much temperance material appeared in the first half of the nineteenth century. In 1826, the American Society for the Promotion of Temperance was founded, and by 1833 more than four thousand local temperance societies with more than half a million members dotted the American landscape. These societies helped generate and distribute hundreds of thousands of temperance tracts. More than 400,000 copies of *Ten Nights in a Bar-Room* joined these tracts to help reform what one antebellum writer called a "nation of drunkards."

Arthur's *Ten Nights in a Bar-Room* is noteworthy for the way it captures how drinking is far more than simply a private act. It is an activity that blends the personal and communal worlds of the individual. In a larger sense, Arthur was deeply concerned with individuals making choices whose consequences spread out like ever-widening concentric circles. Bad decisions could not only destroy an individual, but they could ultimately topple a nation. What was at stake in the temperance cause was but a mirror of what is at stake every time an individual makes a choice that adversely affects his family, his larger community, and his country.

TEN NIGHTS IN A BAR-ROOM,
AND WHAT I SAW THERE

Title Page, *Ten Nights in a Bar-Room* (Philadelphia: Porter and Coates, 1882—All illustrations in this selection are taken from this edition of the book).

The following text is taken from an 1856 edition of *Ten Nights in a Bar-Room* with only slight corrections to obvious errors in typesetting and proofreading. Timothy Shay Arthur, *Ten Nights in a Bar-Room and What I Saw There*. Philadelphia: Bradley, 1856.

Publisher's Preface

[From the 1854 Edition]

This new temperance volume, by Mr. Arthur, comes in just at the right time, when the subject of restrictive laws[1] is agitating the whole country, and good and true men everywhere are gathering up their strength for a prolonged and unflinching contest. It will prove a powerful auxiliary in the cause.

"Ten Nights in a Bar-Room" gives a series of sharply drawn sketches of scenes, some of them touching in the extreme, and some dark and terrible. Step by step the author traces the downward course of the tempting vender and his infatuated victims, until both are involved in hopeless ruin. The book is marred by no exaggerations, but exhibits the actualities of bar-room life, and the consequences flowing therefrom, with a severe simplicity, and adherence to truth, that gives to every picture a Daguerrean[2] vividness.

NIGHT THE FIRST

The "Sickle and Sheaf"

TEN years ago, business required me to pass a day in Cedarville. It was late in the afternoon when the stage set me down at the "Sickle and Sheaf," a new tavern, just opened by a new landlord, in a new house, built with the special end of providing "accommodations for man and beast." As I stepped from the dusty old vehicle in which I had been jolted along a rough road for some thirty miles, feeling tired and hungry, the good-natured face of Simon Slade, the landlord, beaming as it did with a hearty welcome, was really a pleasant sight to see, and the grasp of his hand was like that of a true friend.

I felt, as I entered the new and neatly furnished sitting-room adjoining the bar, that I had indeed found a comfortable resting-place after my wearisome journey.

"All as nice as a new pin," said I, approvingly, as I glanced around the room, up to the ceiling—white as the driven snow—and over the handsomely carpeted floor. "Haven't seen any thing so inviting as this. How long have you been open?"

"Only a few months," answered the gratified landlord. "But we are not yet in good going order. It takes time, you know, to bring every thing into the right shape. Have you dined yet?"

"No. Every thing looked so dirty at the stage-house, where we stopped to get dinner, that I couldn't venture upon the experiment of eating. How long before your supper will be ready?"

"In an hour," replied the landlord.

"That will do. Let me have a nice piece of tender steak, and the loss of dinner will soon be forgotten."

"You shall have that, cooked fit for an alderman," said the landlord. "I call my wife the best cook in Cedarville."

As he spoke, a neatly dressed girl, about sixteen years of age, with rather an attractive countenance, passed through the room.

---

1 The State of Maine passed an alcohol prohibition law in 1851, sparking animated discussions at both the state and the federal levels on whether other prohibition laws should be passed.
2 Daguerreotypes were the first successful form of photography, developed in France in the 1830s. The reference here is to the lifelike or photographic quality of the sketches.

"My daughter," said the landlord, as she vanished through the door. There was a sparkle of pride in the father's eyes, and a certain tenderness in the tones of his voice, as he said—"My daughter," that told me she was very dear to him.

"You are a happy man to have so fair a child," said I, speaking more in compliment than with a careful choice of words.

"I am a happy man," was the landlord's smiling answer; his fair, round face, unwrinkled by a line of care or trouble, beaming with self-satisfaction. "I have always been a happy man, and always expect to be. Simon Slade takes the world as it comes, and takes it easy. My son, sir"—he added, as a boy in his twelfth year, came in. "Speak to the gentleman."

The boy lifted to mine a pair of deep blue eyes, from which innocence beamed, as he offered me his hand, and said, respectfully—"How do you do, sir?" I could not but remark the girl-like beauty of his face, in which the hardier firmness of the boy's character was already visible.

"What is your name?" I asked.

"Frank, sir."

"Frank is his name," said the landlord—"we called him after his uncle. Frank and Flora—the names sound pleasant to our ears. But, you know, parents are apt to be a little partial and over fond."

"Better that extreme than its opposite," I remarked.

"Just what I always say. Frank, my son,"—the landlord spoke to the boy—"there's some one in the bar. You can wait on him as well as I can."

The lad glided from the room, in ready obedience.

"A handy boy that, sir; a very handy boy. Almost as good in the bar as a man. He mixes a toddy or a punch just as well as I can."

"But," I suggested, "are you not a little afraid of placing one so young in the way of temptation."

"Temptation!" The open brows of Simon Slade contracted a little. "No, sir!" he replied, emphatically. "The till is safer under his care than it would be in that of one man in ten. The boy comes, sir, of honest parents. Simon Slade never wronged anybody out of a farthing."

"Oh," said I, quickly, "you altogether misapprehend me. I had no reference to the till, but to the bottle."

The landlord's brows were instantly unbent, and a broad smile circled over his good-humored face.

"Is that all? Nothing to fear, I can assure you. Frank has no taste for liquor, and might pour it out for months without a drop finding its way to his lips. Nothing to apprehend there, sir—nothing."

I saw that further suggestions of danger would be useless, and so remained silent. The arrival of a traveler called away the landlord, and I was left alone for observation and reflection. The bar adjoined the neat sitting-room, and I could see, through the open door, the customer upon whom the lad was attending. He was a well-dressed young man—or rather boy, for he did not appear to be over nineteen years of age—with a fine, intelligent face, that was already slightly marred by sensual indulgence. He raised the glass to his lips, with a quick, almost eager motion, and drained it at a single draught.

"Just right," said he, tossing a sixpence to the young bar-tender. "You are first-rate at a brandy-toddy. Never drank a better in my life."

The lad's smiling face told that he was gratified by the compliment. To me the sight was painful, for I saw that this youthful tippler was on dangerous ground.

"Who is that young man in the bar?" I asked, a few minutes afterward, on being rejoined by the landlord.

Simon Slade stepped to the door and looked into the bar for a moment.

Two or three men were there by this time; but he was at no loss in answering my question.

"Oh, that's a son of Judge Hammond, who lives in the large brick house just as you enter the village. Willy Hammond, as everybody familiarly calls him, is about the finest young man in our neighborhood. There is nothing proud or put-on about him—nothing—even if his father is a judge, and rich into the bargain. Every one, gentle or simple, likes Willy Hammond. And then he is such good company. Always so cheerful, and always with a pleasant story on his tongue. And he's so high-spirited withal, and so honorable. Willy Hammond would lose his right hand rather than be guilty of a mean action."

"Landlord!" The voice came loud from the road in front of the house, and Simon Slade again left me to answer the demands of some new comer. I went into the bar-room, in order to take a closer observation of Willy Hammond, in whom an interest, not unmingled with concern, had already been awakened in my mind. I found him engaged in a pleasant conversation with a plain-looking farmer, whose homely, terse, common sense was quite as conspicuous as his fine play of words and lively fancy. The farmer was a substantial conservative, and young Hammond a warm admirer of new ideas and the quicker adaptation of means to ends. I soon saw that his mental powers were developed beyond his years, while his personal qualities were strongly attractive. I understood better, after being a silent listener and observer for ten minutes, why the landlord had spoken of him so warmly.

"Take a brandy-toddy, Mr. H—?" said Hammond, after the discussion closed, good humoredly. "Frank, our junior bar-keeper here, beats his father, in that line."

"I don't care if I do," returned the farmer; and the two passed up to the bar.

"Now, Frank, my boy, don't belie my praises," said the young man; "do your handsomest."

"Two brandy-toddies, did you say?" Frank made the inquiry with quite a professional air.

"Just what I did say; and let them be equal to Jove's nectar."[3]

Pleased at this familiarity, the boy went briskly to his work of mixing the tempting compound, while Hammond looked on with an approving smile.

"There," said the latter, as Frank passed the glasses across the counter, "if you don't call that first-rate, you're no judge." And he handed one of them to the farmer, who tasted the agreeable draught, and praised its flavor. As before, I noticed that Hammond drank eagerly, like one athirst—emptying his glass without once taking it from his lips.

Soon after the bar-room was empty; and then I walked around the premises, in company with the landlord, and listened to his praise of everything and his plans and purposes for the future. The house, yard, garden, and out-buildings were in the most perfect order; presenting, in the whole, a model of a village tavern.

"Whatever I do, sir," said the talkative Simon Slade, "I like to do well. I wasn't just raised to tavern-keeping, you must know; but I'm one who can turn his hand to almost any thing."

---

3 The chief drink of the ancient Roman gods.

"What was your business?" I inquired.

"I'm a miller, sir, by trade," he answered—"and a better miller, though I say it myself, is not to be found in Bolton county. I've followed milling these twenty years, and made some little money. But I got tired of hard work, and determined to lead an easier life. So I sold my mill, and built this house with the money. I always thought I'd like tavern-keeping. It's an easy life; and, if rightly seen after, one in which a man is sure to make money."

"You were still doing a fair business with your mill?"

"Oh, yes. Whatever I do, I do right. Last year, I put by a thousand dollars above all expenses, which is not bad, I can assure you, for a mere grist mill. If the present owner comes out even, he'll do well!"

"How is that?"

"Oh, he's no miller. Give him the best wheat that is grown, and he'll ruin it in grinding. He takes the life out of every grain. I don't believe he'll keep half the custom that I transferred with the mill."

"A thousand dollars, clear profit, in so useful a business, ought to have satisfied you," said I.

"There you and I differ," answered the landlord. "Every man desires to make as much money as possible, and with the least labor. I hope to make two or three thousand dollars a year, over and above all expenses, at tavern-keeping. My bar alone ought to yield me that sum. A man with a wife and children very naturally tries to do as well by them as possible."

"Very true; but," I ventured to suggest, "will this be doing as well by them as if you had kept on at the mill?"

"Two or three thousand dollars a year against one thousand! Where are your figures, man?"

"There may be something beyond the money to take into the account," said I.

"What?" inquired Slade, with a kind of half credulity.

"Consider the different influences of the two callings in life—that of a miller and a tavern-keeper."

"Well! say on."

"Will your children be as safe from temptation here as in their former home?"

"Just as safe," was the unhesitating answer. "Why not?"

I was about to speak of the alluring glass in the case of Frank, but remembering that I had already expressed a fear in that direction, felt that to do so again would be useless, and so kept silent.

"A tavern-keeper," said Slade, "is just as respectable as a miller—in fact, the very people who used to call me 'Simon' or 'Neighbor Dustycoat,' now say 'Landlord,' or Mr. Slade, and treat me in every way more as if I were an equal than ever they did before."

"The change," said I, "may be due to the fact of your giving evidence of possessing some means. Men are very apt to be courteous to those who have property. The building of the tavern has, without doubt, contributed to the new estimation in which you are held."

"That isn't all," replied the landlord. "It is because I am keeping a good tavern, and thus materially advancing the interests of Cedarville, that some of our best people look at me with different eyes."

"Advancing the interests of Cedarville! In what way?" I did not apprehend his meaning.

"A good tavern always draws people to a place, while a miserable old tumbledown of an affair, badly kept, such as we have had for years, as surely repels them. You can generally tell something about the condition of a town by looking at its taverns. If they are well kept, and doing a good business, you will hardly be wrong in the conclusion that the place is thriving. Why, already, since I built and opened the 'Sickle and Sheaf,' property has advanced over twenty per cent, along the whole street, and not less than five new houses have been commenced."

"Other causes, besides the simple opening of a new tavern, may have contributed to this result," said I.

"None of which I am aware. I was talking with Judge Hammond only yesterday—he owns a great deal of ground on the street—and he did not hesitate to say, that the building and opening of a good tavern here had increased the value of his property at least five thousand dollars. He said, moreover, that he thought the people of Cedarville ought to present me with a silver pitcher; and that, for one, he would contribute ten dollars for the purpose."

The ringing of the supper bell interrupted further conversation; and with the best of appetites, I took my way to the room, where a plentiful meal was spread. As I entered, I met the wife of Simon Slade, just passing out, after seeing that every thing was in order. I had not observed her before; and now could not help remarking that she had a flushed, excited countenance, as if she had been over a hot fire, and was both worried and fatigued. And there was, moreover, a peculiar expression of the mouth, never observed in one whose mind is entirely at ease—an expression that once seen is never forgotten. The face stamped itself, instantly, on my memory; and I can even now recall it with almost the original distinctness. How strongly it contrasted with that of her smiling, self-satisfied husband, who took his place at the head of his table with an air of conscious importance. I was too hungry to talk much, and so found greater enjoyment in eating than in conversation. The landlord had a more chatty guest by his side, and I left them to entertain each other, while I did ample justice to the excellent food with which the table was liberally provided.

After supper I went to the sitting-room, and remained there until the lamps were lighted. A newspaper occupied my time for perhaps half an hour; then the buzz of voices from the adjoining bar-room, which had been increasing for some time, attracted my attention, and I went in there to see and hear what was passing. The first person upon whom my eyes rested was young Hammond, who sat talking with a man older than himself by several years. At a glance, I saw that this man could only associate himself with Willy Hammond as a tempter. Unscrupulous selfishness was written all over his sinister countenance; and I wondered that it did not strike every one, as it did me, with instant repulsion. There could not be, I felt certain, any common ground of association, for two such persons, but the dead level of a village bar-room. I afterward learned, during the evening, that this man's name was Harvey Green, and that he was an occasional visitor at Cedarville, remaining a few days, or a few weeks at a time, as appeared to suit his fancy, and having no ostensible business or special acquaintance with anybody in the village.

"There is one thing about him," remarked Simon Slade, in answering some question that I put in reference to the man, "that I don't object to; he has plenty of money, and is not at all niggardly in spending it. He used to come here, so he told me, about once in five or six months; but his stay at the miserably kept tavern, the only one then in Cedarville, was so uncomfortable, that he had pretty well made up his mind never to visit us again. Now, however, he has engaged one of my best rooms, for which he pays me by the year, and I am to charge him full board for the time he occupies it. He says that there is something about Cedarville that always attracts him; and that his health is better while here than it is anywhere, except South during the winter season. He'll not leave less than two or three hundred dollars a year in our village—there is one item, for you, of advantage to a place in having a good tavern."

"What is his business?" I asked. "Is he engaged in any trading operations?"

The landlord shrugged his shoulders, and looked slightly mysterious, as he answered—

"I never inquire about the business of a guest. My calling is to entertain strangers. If they are pleased with my house, and pay my bills on presentation, I have no right to seek further. As a miller, I never asked a customer whether he raised, bought, or stole his wheat. It was my business to grind it, and I took care to do it well. Beyond that, it was all his own affair. And so it will be in my new calling. I shall mind my own business and keep my own place."

Besides young Hammond and this Harvey Green, there were in the bar-room, when I entered, four others besides the landlord. Among these was a Judge Lyman,—so he was addressed—a man between forty and fifty years of age, who had a few weeks before received the Democratic nomination for member of Congress. He was very talkative and very affable, and soon formed a kind of centre of attraction to the bar-room circle. Among other topics of conversation that came up was the new tavern, introduced by the landlord, in whose mind it was, very naturally, the uppermost thought.

"The only wonder to me is," said Judge Lyman, "that nobody had wit enough to see the advantage of a good tavern in Cedarville ten years ago, or enterprise enough to start one. I give our friend Slade the credit of being a shrewd, far-seeing man; and, mark my word for it, in ten years from to-day he will be the richest man in the county."

"Nonsense—Ho! ho! "Simon Slade laughed outright. "The richest man! You forget Judge Hammond."

"No, not even Judge Hammond, with all deference for our clever friend Willy,"—and Judge Lyman smiled pleasantly on the young man.

"If he gets richer, somebody will be poorer!" The individual who uttered these words had not spoken before, and I turned to look at him more closely. A glance showed him to be one of a class seen in all bar-rooms; a poor, broken-down inebriate, with the inward power of resistance gone—conscious of having no man's respect, and giving respect to none. There was a shrewd twinkle in his eyes, as lie fixed them on Slade, that gave added force to the peculiar tone in which his brief, but telling sentence was uttered. I noticed a slight contraction on the landlord's ample forehead, the first evidence I had yet seen of ruffled feelings. The remark, thrown in so untimely (or timely, some will say), and with a kind of prophetic malice, produced a temporary pause in the conversation. No one answered, or questioned the intruder, who, I could perceive, silently enjoyed the effect of his words. But soon the obstructed current ran on again.

"If our excellent friend, Mr. Slade," said Harvey Green, "is not the richest man in Cedarville at the end of ten years, he will at least enjoy the satisfaction of having made his town richer."

"A true word that," replied Judge Lyman—"as true a word as ever was spoken. What a dead-and-alive place this has been until within the last few months. All vigorous growth had stopped, and we were actually going to seed."

"And the graveyard too," muttered the individual who had before disturbed the self-satisfied harmony of the company, remarking upon the closing sentence of Harvey Green. "Come, landlord," he added, as he strode across to the bar, speaking in a changed, reckless sort of a way, "fix me up a good hot whisky-punch, and do it right; and there's another sixpence toward the fortune you are bound to make. It's the last one left—not a copper more in my pockets," and he turned them inside-out, with a half-solemn, half-ludicrous air. "I send it to keep company in your till with four others that have found their way into that snug place since morning, and which will be lonesome without their little friend."

I looked at Simon Slade; his eyes rested on mine for a moment or two, and then sunk beneath my earnest gaze. I saw that his countenance flushed, and that his motions were slightly confused. The incident, it was plain, did not awaken agreeable thoughts. Once I saw his hand move toward the sixpence that lay upon the counter; but, whether to push it back or draw it toward the till, I could not determine. The whisky-punch was in due time ready, and with it the man retired to a table across the room, and sat down to enjoy the tempting beverage. As he did so, the landlord quietly swept the poor unfortunate's last sixpence into his drawer. The influence of this strong potation[4] was to render the man a little more talkative. To the free conversation passing around him he lent an attentive ear, dropping in a word, now and then, that always told upon the company like a well-directed blow. At last, Slade lost all patience with him, and said, a little fretfully,—

"Look here, Joe Morgan, if you will be ill-natured, pray go somewhere else, and not interrupt good feeling among gentlemen."

"Got my last sixpence," retorted Joe, turning his pockets inside-out again. "No more use for me here tonight. That's the way of the world. How apt a scholar is our good friend Dustycoat, in this new school! Well, he was a good miller—no one ever disputed that—and it's plain to see that he is going to make a good landlord. I thought his heart was a little too soft; but the indurating process has begun, and, in less than ten years, if it isn't as hard as one of his old millstones, Joe Morgan is no prophet. Oh, you needn't knit your brows so, friend Simon, we're old friends; and friends are privileged to speak plain."

"I wish you'd go home. You're not yourself, tonight," said the landlord, a little coaxingly—for he saw that nothing was to be gained by quarreling with Morgan. "Maybe my heart *is* growing harder," he added, with affected good-humor; "and it is time, perhaps. One of my weaknesses, I have heard even you say, was being too woman-hearted."

"No danger of that now," retorted Joe Morgan. "I've known a good many land-lords in my time, but can't remember one that was troubled with the disease that once afflicted you."

Just at this moment the outer door was pushed open with a slow, hesitating motion; then a little pale face peered in, and a pair of soft blue eyes went searching about the room. Conversation was instantly hushed, and every face, excited with interest, turned toward the child, who had now stepped through the door. She was not over ten years of age; but it moved the heart to look upon the saddened expression of her young coun-tenance, and the forced bravery therein, that scarcely overcame the native timidity so touchingly visible.

"Father!" I have never heard this word spoken in a voice that sent such a thrill along every nerve. It was full of sorrowful love—full of a tender concern that had its origin too deep for the heart of a child. As she spoke, the little one sprang across the room, and laying her hands upon the arm of Joe Morgan, lifted her eyes, that were ready to gush over with tears, to his face.

"Come, father! won't you come home?" I hear that low, pleading voice even now, and my heart gives a quicker throb. Poor child! Darkly shadowed was the sky that bent gloomily over thy young life.

---

4 Drink.

"COME, FATHER! WON'T YOU COME HOME?"

"Come, Father! Won't you come home?"

Morgan arose, and suffered the child to lead him from the room. He seemed passive in her hands. I noticed that he thrust his fingers nervously into his pocket, and that a troubled look went over his face as they were withdrawn. His last sixpence was in the till of Simon Slade!

The first man who spoke was Harvey Green, and this not for a minute after the father and his child had vanished through the door.

"If I was in your place, landlord"—his voice was cold and unfeeling—"I'd pitch that fellow out of the bar-room the next time he stepped through the door. He's no business here, in the first place; and, in the second, he doesn't know how to behave himself. There's no telling how much a vagabond like him injures a respectable house."

"I wish he would stay away," said Simon, with a perplexed air.

"I'd *make* him stay away," answered Green.

"That may be easier said than done," remarked Judge Lyman. "Our friend keeps a public-house, and can't just say who shall or shall not come into it."

"But such a fellow has no business here. He's a good-for-nothing sot. If I kept a tavern, I'd refuse to sell him liquor."

"That you might do," said Judge Lyman—"and I presume your hint will not be lost on our friend Slade."

"He will have liquor, so long as he can get a cent to buy it with," remarked one of the company; "and I don't see why our landlord here, who has gone to so much expense to fit up a tavern, shouldn't have the sale of it as well as anybody else. Joe talks a little freely sometimes; but no one can say that he is quarrelsome. You've got to take him as he is, that's all."

"I'm one," retorted Harvey Green, with a slightly ruffled manner, "who is never disposed to take people as they are when they choose to render themselves disagreeable. If I was Mr. Slade, as I remarked in the beginning, I'd pitch that fellow into the road the next time he put his foot over my door-step."

"Not if I were present," remarked the other, coolly.

Green was on his feet in a moment; and I saw, from the flash of his eyes, that he was a man of evil passions. Moving a pace or two in the direction of the other, he said sharply—

"What is that, sir?"

The individual against whom his anger was so suddenly aroused was dressed plainly, and had the appearance of a working-man. He was stout and muscular.

"I presume you heard my words. They were spoken distinctly," he replied, not moving from where he sat, nor seeming to be in the least disturbed. But there was cool defiance in the tones of his voice and in the steady look of his eyes.

"You're an impertinent fellow, and I'm half tempted to chastise you."

Green had scarcely finished the sentence, ere he was lying at full length upon the floor! The other had sprung upon him like a tiger, and with one blow from his heavy fist, struck him down as if he had been a child. For a moment or two, Green lay stunned and bewildered—then, starting up with a savage cry, that sounded more bestial than human, he drew a long knife from a concealed sheath, and attempted to stab his assailant; but the murderous purpose was not accomplished, for the other man, who had superior strength and coolness, saw the design, and with a well-directed blow almost broke the arm of Green, causing the knife to leave his hand and glide far across the room.

"I'm half tempted to wring your neck off," exclaimed the man, whose name was Lyon, now much excited; and seizing Green by the throat, he strangled him until his face grew black. "Draw a knife on me, ha! You murdering villain!" And he gripped him tighter.

Judge Lyman and the landlord now interfered, and rescued Green from the hands of his fully aroused antagonist. For some time they stood growling at each other, like two parted dogs straggling to get free, in order to renew the conflict, but gradually cooled off. In a little while Judge Lyman drew Green aside, and the two men left the bar-room together. In the door, as they were retiring, the former slightly nodded to Willy Hammond, who soon followed them, going into the sitting-room; and from thence, as I could perceive, upstairs, to an apartment above.

"Not after much good," I heard Lyon mutter to himself. "If Judge Hammond don't look a little closer after that boy of his, he'll be sorry for it, that's all."

"Who is this Green?" I asked of Lyon, finding myself alone with him in the bar-room, soon after.

"A blackleg,[5] I take it," was his unhesitating answer.

"Does Judge Lyman suspect his real character?"

"I don't know any thing about that; but I wouldn't be afraid to bet ten dollars, that if you could look in upon them now, you would find cards in their hands."

"What a school, and what teachers for the youth who just went with them!" I could not help remarking.

"Willy Hammond?"

"Yes."

"You may well say that. What can his father be thinking about to leave him exposed to such influences!"

"He's one of the few who are in raptures about this tavern, because its erection has slightly increased the value of his property about here; but, if he is not the loser of fifty per cent, for every one gained, before ten years go by, I'm very much in error."

"How so?"

"It will prove, I fear, the open door to ruin for his son."

"That's bad," said I.

"Bad! It is awful to think of. There is not a finer young man in the country, nor one with better mind and heart, than Willy Hammond. So much the sadder will be his destruction. Ah, sir! this tavern-keeping is a curse to any place."

"But I thought, just now, that you spoke in favor of letting even the poor drunkard's money go into our landlord's till, in order to encourage his commendable enterprise in opening so good a tavern."

"We all speak with covert irony sometimes," answered the man, "as I did then. Poor Joe Morgan! He is an old and early friend of Simon Slade. They were boys together, and worked as millers under the same roof for many years. In fact, Joe's father owned the mill, and the two learned their trade with him. When old Morgan died, the mill came into Joe's hands. It was in rather a worn-out condition, and Joe went in debt for some pretty thorough repairs and additions of machinery. By and by, Simon Slade, who was hired by Joe to run the mill, received a couple of thousand dollars at the death of an aunt. This sum enabled him to buy a share in the mill, which Morgan was very glad to sell in order to get clear of his debt. Time passed on, and Joe left his milling interest almost entirely in the care of Slade, who, it must be said in his favor, did not neglect the business. But it somehow happened—I will not say unfairly—that at the end of ten years, Joe Morgan no longer owned a share in the mill. The whole property was in the hands of Slade. People did not much wonder at this; for while Slade was always to be found at the mill, industrious, active, and attentive to customers, Morgan was rarely seen on the premises. You would oftener find him in the woods, with a gun over his shoulder, or sitting by a trout brook, or lounging at the tavern. And yet everybody liked Joe, for he was companionable, quick-witted, and very kindhearted. He would say sharp things,

---

5 A swindler.

sometimes, when people manifested little meannesses; but there was so much honey in his gall, that bitterness rarely predominated.

"A year or two before his ownership in the mill ceased, Morgan married one of the sweetest girls in our town—Fanny Ellis, that was her name, and she could have had her pick of the young men. Everybody affected to wonder at her choice; and yet nobody really did wonder, for Joe was an attractive young man, take him as you would, and just the one to win the heart of a girl like Fanny. What if he had been seen, now and then, a little the worse for drink! What if he showed more fondness for pleasure than for business! Fanny did not look into the future with doubt or fear. She believed that her love was strong enough to win him from all evil allurements; and, as for this world's goods, they were matters in which her maiden fancies rarely busied themselves.

"Well. Dark days came for her, poor soul! And yet, in all the darkness of her earthly lot, she has never, it is said, been any thing but a loving, forbearing, self-denying wife to Morgan. And he—fallen as he is, and powerless in the grasp of the monster intemperance—has never, I am sure, hurt her with a cruel word. Had he added these, her heart would, long ere this, have broken. Poor Joe Morgan! Poor Fanny! Oh, what a curse is this drink!"

The man, warming with his theme, had spoken with an eloquence I had not expected from his lips. Slightly overmastered by his feelings, he paused for a moment or two, and then added:

"It was unfortunate for Joe, at least, that Slade sold his mill, and became a tavern-keeper; for Joe had a sure berth, and wages regularly paid. He didn't always stick to his work, but would go off on a spree every now and then; but Slade bore with all this, and worked harder himself to make up for his hand's shortcoming. And no matter what deficiency the little store-room at home might show, Fanny Morgan never found her meal barrel empty without knowing where to get it replenished.

"But, after Slade sold the mill, a sad change took place. The new owner was little disposed to pay wages to a hand who would not give him all his time during working hours; and in less than two weeks from the day he took possession, Morgan was discharged. Since then, he has been working about at one odd job and another, earning scarcely enough to buy the liquor it requires to feed the inordinate thirst that is consuming him. I am not disposed to blame Simon Slade for the wrong-doing of Morgan; but here is a simple fact in the case—if he had kept on at the useful calling of a miller, he would have saved this man's family from want, suffering, and a lower deep of misery than that into which they have already fallen. I merely state it, and you can draw your own conclusion. It is one of the many facts, on the other side of this tavern question, which it will do no harm to mention. I have noted a good many facts besides, and one is, that before Slade opened the "Sickle and Sheaf," he did all in his power to save his early friend from the curse of intemperance; now he has become his tempter. Heretofore, it was his hand that provided the means for his family to live in some small degree of comfort; now he takes the poor pittance the wretched man earns, and dropping it in his till, forgets the wife and children at home who are hungry for the bread this money should have purchased.

"Joe Morgan, fallen as he is, sir, is no fool. His mind sees quickly yet; and he rarely utters a sentiment that is not full of meaning. When he spoke of Slade's heart growing as hard in ten years as one of his old mill-stones, he was not uttering words at random, nor merely indulging in a harsh sentiment, little caring whether it were closely applicable or not. That the indurating process had begun, he, alas! was too sadly conscious."

The landlord had been absent from the room for some time. He left soon after Judge Lyman, Harvey Green, and Willy Hammond withdrew, and I did not see him again during the evening. His son Frank was left to attend at the bar; no very hard task, for not more than half a dozen called in to drink from the time Morgan left until the bar was closed.

While Mr. Lyon was giving me the brief history just recorded, I noticed a little incident that caused a troubled feeling to pervade my mind. After a man, for whom the landlord's son had prepared a fancy drink, had nearly emptied his glass, he sat it down upon the counter and went out. A tablespoonful or two remained in the glass, and I noticed Frank, after smelling at it two or three times, put the glass to his lips and sip the sweetened liquor. The flavor proved agreeable; for, after tasting it, he raised the glass again and drained every drop.

"Frank!" I heard a low voice, in a warning tone, pronounce the name, and glancing toward a door partly open, that led from the inside of the bar to the yard, I saw the face of Mrs. Slade. It had the same troubled expression I had noticed before, but now blended with more of anxiety.

The boy went out at the call of his mother; and when a new customer entered, I noticed that Flora, the daughter, came in to wait upon him. I noticed, too, that while she poured out the liquor, there was a heightened color on her face, in which I fancied that I saw a tinge of shame. It is certain that she was not in the least gracious to the person on whom she was waiting; and that there was little heart in her manner of performing the task.

Ten o'clock found me alone and musing in the bar-room over the occurrences of the evening. Of all the incidents, that of the entrance of Joe Morgan's child kept the most prominent place in my thoughts. The picture of that mournful little face was ever before me; and I seemed all the while to hear the word "Father," uttered so touchingly, and yet with such a world of childish tenderness. And the man, who would have opposed the most stubborn resistance to his fellow-men, had they sought to force him from the room, going passively, almost meekly out, led by that little child—I could not, for a time, turn my thoughts from the image thereof! And then thought bore me to the wretched home, back to which the gentle, loving child had taken her father, and my heart grew faint in me as imagination busied itself with all the misery there.

And Willy Hammond. The little that I had heard and seen of him greatly interested me in his favor. Ah! upon what dangerous ground was he treading. How many pitfalls awaited his feet—how near they were to the brink of a fearful precipice, down which to fall was certain destruction. How beautiful had been his life-promise! How fair the opening day of his existence! Alas! the clouds were gathering already, and the low rumble of the distant thunder presaged the coming of a fearful tempest. Was there none to warn him of the danger? Alas! all might now come too late, for so few who enter the path in which his steps were treading will hearken to friendly counsel, or heed the solemn warning. Where was he now? This question recurred over and over again. He had left the bar-room with Judge Lyman and Green early in the evening, and had not made his appearance since. Who and what was Green? And Judge Lyman, was he a man of principle? One with whom it was safe to trust a youth like Willy Hammond?

While I mused thus, the bar-room door opened, and a man past the prime of life, with a somewhat florid face, which gave a strong relief to the gray, almost white hair that, suffered to grow freely, was pushed back, and lay in heavy masses on his coat collar, entered with a hasty step. He was almost venerable in appearance; yet there was in his dark, quick eyes the brightness of unquenched loves, the fires of which were kindled at the altars of selfishness and sensuality. This I saw at a glance. There was a look of concern on his face, as he threw his eyes around the bar-room; and he seemed disappointed, I thought, at finding it empty.

"Is Simon Slade here?"

As I answered in the negative, Mrs. Slade entered through the door that opened from the yard, and stood behind the counter.

"Ah, Mrs. Slade! Good-evening, madam!" he said.

"Good-evening, Judge Hammond."

"Is your husband at home?"

"I believe he is," answered Mrs. Slade. "I think he's somewhere about the house."

"Ask him to step here, will you?"

Mrs. Slade went out. Nearly five minutes went by, during which time Judge Hammond paced the floor of the bar-room uneasily. Then the landlord made his appearance. The free, open, manly, self-satisfied expression of his countenance, which I had remarked on alighting from the stage in the afternoon, was gone. I noticed at once the change, for it was striking. He did not look steadily into the face of Judge Hammond, who asked him, in a low voice, if his son had been there during the evening.

"He was here," said Slade.

"When?"

"He came in some time after dark and stayed, maybe, an hour."

"And hasn't been here since?"

"It's nearly two hours since he left the bar-room," replied the landlord.

Judge Hammond seemed perplexed. There was a degree of evasion in Slade's manner that he could hardly help noticing. To me it was all apparent, for I had lively suspicions that made my observation acute.

Judge Hammond crossed his arms behind him, and took three or four strides about the floor.

"Was Judge Lyman here to-night?" he then asked.

"He was," answered Slade.

"Did he and Willy go out together?"

The question seemed an unexpected one for the landlord. Slade appeared slightly confused, and did not answer promptly.

"I—I rather think they did," he said, after a brief hesitation.

"Ah, well! Perhaps he is at Judge Lyman's. I will call over there."

And Judge Hammond left the bar-room.

"Would you like to retire, sir?" said the landlord, now turning to me, with a forced smile—I saw that it was forced.

"If you please," I answered.

He lit a candle and conducted me to my room, where, overwearied with the day's exertion, I soon fell asleep, and did not awake until the sun was shining brightly into my windows.

I remained at the village a portion of the day, but saw nothing of the parties in whom the incidents of the previous evening had awakened a lively interest. At four o'clock I left in the stage, and did not visit Cedarville again for a year.

Night the Second

The Changes of a Year

A CORDIAL grasp of the hand and a few words of hearty welcome greeted me as I alighted from the stage at the "Sickle and Sheaf," on my next visit to Cedarville. At the first glance, I saw no change in the countenance, manner, or general bearing of Simon Slade, the landlord. With him, the year seemed to have passed like a pleasant summer day. His face was round, and full, and rosy, and his eyes sparkled with that good-humor which flows from intense self-satisfaction. Every thing about him seemed to say—"All right with myself and the world."

I had scarcely expected this. From what I saw during my last brief sojourn at the "Sickle and Sheaf," the inference was natural, that elements had been called into activity, which must produce changes adverse to those pleasant states of mind that threw an almost perpetual sunshine over the landlord's countenance. How many hundreds of times had I thought of Joe Morgan and Willy Hammond—of Frank, and the temptations to which a bar-room exposed him. The heart of Slade must, indeed, be as hard as one of his old mill-stones, if he could remain an unmoved witness of the corruption and degradation of these.

"My fears have outrun the actual progress of things," said I to myself, with a sense of relief, as I mused alone in the still neatly arranged sitting-room, after the landlord, who sat and chatted for a few minutes, had left me. "There is, I am willing to believe, a basis of good in this man's character, which has led him to remove, as far as possible, the more palpable evils that ever attach themselves to a house of public entertainment. He had but entered on the business last year. There was much to be learned, pondered, and corrected. Experience, I doubt not, has led to many important changes in the manner of conducting the establishment, and especially in what pertains to the bar."

As I thought thus, my eyes glanced through the half-open door, and rested on the face of Simon Slade. He was standing behind his bar—evidently alone in the room—with his head bent in a musing attitude. At first I was in some doubt as to the identity of the singularly changed countenance. Two deep perpendicular seams lay sharply defined on his forehead—the arch of his eyebrows was gone, and from each corner of his compressed lips, lines were seen reaching halfway to the chin. Blending with a slightly troubled expression, was a strongly marked selfishness, evidently brooding over the consummation of its purpose. For some moments I sat gazing on his face, half doubting at times if it were really that of Simon Slade. Suddenly, a gleam flashed over it—an ejaculation was uttered, and one clenched hand brought down, with a sharp stroke, into the open palm of the other. The landlord's mind had reached a conclusion, and was resolved upon action. There were no warm rays in the gleam of light that irradiated his countenance—at least none for my heart, which felt under them an almost icy coldness.

"Just the man I was thinking about," I heard the landlord say, as some one entered the bar, while his whole manner underwent a sudden change.

"The old saying is true," was answered in a voice, the tones of which were familiar to my ears.

"Thinking of the old Harry?" said Slade.

"Yes."

"True, literally, in the present case," I heard the landlord remark, though in a much lower tone; "for, if you are not the devil himself, you can't be farther removed than a second cousin."

A low, gurgling laugh met this little sally. There was something in it so unlike a human laugh, that it caused my blood to trickle, for a moment, coldly along my veins.

I heard nothing more except the murmur of voices in the bar, for a hand shut the partly opened door that led from the sitting-room.

Whose was that voice? I recalled its tones, and tried to fix in my thought the person to whom it belonged, but was unable to do so. I was not very long in doubt, for on stepping out upon the porch in front of the tavern, the well-remembered face of Harvey Green presented itself. He stood in the bar-room door, and was talking earnestly to Slade, whose back was toward me. I saw that he recognized me, although I had not passed a word with him on the occasion of my former visit; and there was a lighting up of his countenance as if about to speak—but I withdrew my eyes from his face to avoid the unwelcome greeting. When I looked at him again, I saw that he was regarding me with a sinister glance, which was instantly withdrawn. In what broad, black characters was the word TEMPTER written on his face! How was it possible for any one to look thereon, and not read the warning inscription!

Soon after, he withdrew into the bar-room, and the landlord came and took a seat near me on the porch.

"How is the Sickle and Sheaf coming on?" I inquired.

"First-rate," was the answer—"First-rate."

"As well as you expected?"

"Better."

"Satisfied with your experiment?"

"Perfectly. Couldn't get me back to the rumbling old mill again, if you were to make me a present of it."

"What of the mill?" I asked. "How does the new owner come on?"

"About as I thought it would be."

"Not doing very well?"

"How could it be expected, when he didn't know enough of the milling business to grind a bushel of wheat right. He lost half of the custom I transferred to him in less than three months. Then he broke his main shaft, and it took over three weeks to get in a new one. Half of his remaining customers discovered by this time, that they could get far better meal from their grain at Harwood's mill near Lynwood, and so did not care to trouble him any more. The upshot of the whole matter is, he broke down next, and had to sell the mill at a heavy loss."

"Who has it now?"

"Judge Hammond is the purchaser."

"He is going to rent it, I suppose?"

"No; I believe he means to turn it into some kind of a factory—and, I rather think, will connect therewith a distillery. This is a fine grain-growing country, as you know. If he does set up a distillery, he'll make a fine thing of it. Grain has been too low in this section for some years; this all the farmers have felt, and they are very much pleased at the idea. It will help them wonderfully. I always thought my mill a great thing for the farmers; but what I did for them was a mere song compared to the advantage of an extensive distillery."

"Judge Hammond is one of your richest men?"

"Yes—the richest in the county. And what is more, he's a shrewd, far-seeing man, and knows how to multiply his riches."

"How is his son Willy coming on?"

"Oh! first-rate."

The landlord's eyes fell under the searching look I bent upon him.

"How old is he now?"

"Just twenty."

"A critical age," I remarked.

"So people say; but I didn't find it so," answered Slade, a little distantly.

"The impulses within and the temptations without, are the measure of its dangers. At his age, you were, no doubt, daily employed at hard work."

"I was, and no mistake."

"Thousands and hundreds of thousands are indebted to useful work, occupying many hours through each day, and leaving them with wearied bodies at night, for their safe passage from yielding youth to firm, resisting manhood. It might not be with you as it is now, had leisure and freedom to go in and out when you pleased been offered at the age of nineteen."

"I can't tell as to that," said the landlord, shrugging his shoulders. "But I don't see that Willy Hammond is in any especial danger. He is a young man with many admirable qualities —is social—liberal—generous almost to a fault—but has good common sense, and wit enough, I take it, to keep out of harm's way."

A man passing the house at the moment, gave Simon Slade an opportunity to break off a conversation that was not, I could see, altogether agreeable. As he left me, I arose and stepped into the bar-room. Frank, the landlord's son, was behind the bar. He had grown considerably in the year—and from a rather delicate, innocent-looking boy, to a stout, bold lad. His face was rounder, and had a gross, sensual expression, that showed itself particularly about the mouth. The man Green was standing beside the bar talking to him, and I noticed that Frank laughed heartily, at some low, half obscene remarks that he was making. In the midst of these, Flora, the sister of Frank, a really beautiful girl, came in to get something from the bar. Green spoke to her familiarly, and Flora answered him with a perceptibly heightening color.

I glanced toward Frank, half expecting to see an indignant flush on his young face. But no—he looked on with a smile! "Ah!" thought I, "have the boy's pure impulses so soon died out in this fatal atmosphere? Can he bear to see those evil eyes—he knows they are evil— rest upon the face of his sister? or to hear those lips, only a moment since polluted with vile words, address her with the familiarity of a friend?"

"Fine girl, that sister of yours, Frank! Fine girl!" said Green, after Flora had withdrawn— speaking of her with about as much respect in his voice as if he were praising a fleet racer or favorite hound.

The boy smiled, with a pleased air.

"I must try and find her a good husband, Frank. I wonder if she wouldn't have me?"

"You'd better ask her," said the boy, laughing.

"I would, if I thought there was any chance for me."

"Nothing like trying. Faint heart never won fair lady," returned Frank, more with the air of a man than a boy. How fast he was growing old!

"A banter, by George!" exclaimed Green, slapping his hands together. "You're a great boy, Frank! a great boy! I shall have to talk to your father about you. Coming on too fast. Have to be put back in your lessons—hey!"

And Green winked at the boy, and shook his finger at him. Frank laughed in a pleased way, as he replied:

"I guess I'll do."

"I guess you will," said Green, as, satisfied with his colloquy, he turned off and left the bar-room.

"Have something to drink, sir?" inquired Frank, addressing me in a bold, free way.

I shook my head.

"Here's a newspaper," he added.

I took the paper and sat down—not to read, but to observe. Two or three men soon came in, and spoke in a very familiar way to Frank, who was presently busy setting out the liquors they had called for. Their conversation, interlarded with much that was profane and vulgar, was of horses, horse-racing, gunning, and the like, to all of which the young bar-keeper lent an attentive ear, putting in a word now and then, and showing an intelligence in such matters quite beyond his age. In the midst thereof, Mr. Slade made his appearance. His presence caused a marked change in Frank, who retired from his place among the men, a step or two outside of the bar, and did not make a remark while his father remained. It was plain from this, that Mr. Slade was not only aware of Frank's dangerous precocity, but had already marked his forwardness by rebuke.

So far, all that I had seen and heard impressed me unfavorably, notwithstanding the declaration of Simon Slade, that every thing about the "Sickle and Sheaf" was coming on "first-rate," and that he was "perfectly satisfied" with his experiment. Why, even if the man had gained, in money, fifty thousand dollars by tavern-keeping in a year, he had lost a jewel in the innocence of his boy that was beyond all valuation. "Perfectly satisfied?" Impossible! He was not perfectly satisfied. How could he be? The look thrown upon Frank when he entered the bar-room, and saw him "hale fellow, well met," with three or four idle, profane, drinking customers, contradicted that assertion.

After supper, I took a seat in the bar-room, to see how life moved on in that place of rendezvous for the surface-population of Cedarville. Interest enough in the characters I had met there a year before remained for me to choose this way of spending the time, instead of visiting at the house of a gentleman who had kindly invited me to pass an evening with his family.

The bar-room custom, I soon found, had largely increased in a year. It now required, for a good part of the time, the active services of both the landlord and his son to meet the calls for liquor. What pained me most, was to see the large number of lads and young men who came in to lounge and drink; and there was scarcely one of them whose face did not show marks of sensuality, or whose language was not marred by obscenity, profanity, or vulgar slang. The subjects of conversation were varied enough, though politics was the most prominent. In regard to politics, I heard nothing in the least instructive; but only abuse of individuals and dogmatism on public measures. They were all exceedingly confident in assertion; but I listened in vain for exposition, or even for demonstrative facts. He who asseverated in the most positive manner, and swore the hardest, carried the day in the petty contests.

I noticed, early in the evening, and at a time when all the inmates of the room were in the best possible humor with themselves, the entrance of an elderly man, on whose face I instantly read a deep concern. It was one of those mild, yet strongly marked faces, that strike you at a glance. The forehead was broad, the eyes large and far back in their sockets, the lips full but firm. You saw evidences of a strong, but well-balanced character. As he came in, I noticed a look of intelligence pass from one to another; and then the eyes of two or three were fixed upon a young man who was seated not far from me, with his back to the entrance, playing at dominoes. He had a glass of ale by his side. The old man searched about the room for some moments, before his glance rested upon the individual I have mentioned. My eyes were full upon his face, as he advanced toward him, yet unseen. Upon it was not a sign of angry excitement, but a most touching sorrow.

"Edward!" he said, as he laid his hand gently on the young man's shoulder. The latter started at the voice, and crimsoned deeply. A few moments he sat irresolute.

"Edward, my son!" It would have been a cold, hard heart indeed that softened not under the melting tenderness of these tones. The call was irresistible, and obedience a necessity. The powers of evil had, yet, too feeble a grasp on the young man's heart to hold him in thrall. Rising with a half-reluctant manner, and with a shamefacedness that it was impossible to conceal, he retired as quietly as possible. The notice of only a few in the bar-room was attracted by the incident.

"I can tell you what," I heard the individual, with whom the young man had been play-ing at dominoes, remark—himself not twenty years of age—"if my old man were to make a fool of himself in this way—sneaking around after me in bar-rooms—he'd get only his trouble for his pains. I'd like to see him try it, though! There'd be a nice time of it, I guess. Wouldn't I creep off with him, as meek as a lamb! Ho! ho!"

"Who is that old gentleman who came in just now?" I inquired of the person who thus commented on the incident which had just occurred.

"Mr. Hargrove is his name."

"And that was his son?"

"Yes; and I'm only sorry he doesn't possess a little more spirit."

"How old is he?"

"About twenty."

"Not of legal age, then?"

"He's old enough to be his own master."

"The law says differently," I suggested.

In answer, the young man cursed the law, snapping his fingers in its imaginary face as he did so.

"At least you will admit," said I, "that Edward Hargrove, in the use of a liberty to go where he pleases, and do what he pleases, exhibits but small discretion."

"I will admit no such thing. What harm is there, I would like to know, in a social little game such as we were playing? There were no stakes—we were not gambling."

I pointed to the half-emptied glass of ale left by young Hargrove.

"Oh! oh!" half sneered, half laughed a man, twice the age of the one I had addressed, who sat near by, listening to our conversation. I looked at him for a moment, and then said—

"The great danger lies there, without doubt. If it were only a glass of ale and a game of dominoes—but it doesn't stop there, and well the young man's father knows it."

"Perhaps he does," was answered. "I remember him in his younger days; and a pretty high boy he was. He didn't stop at a glass of ale and a game at dominoes; not he! I've seen him as drunk as a lord many a time; and many a time at a horse-race, or cock-fight, betting with the bravest. I was only a boy, though a pretty old boy; but I can tell you, Hargrove was no saint."

"I wonder not, then, that he is anxious for his son," was my remark. "He knows well the lurking dangers in the path he seems inclined to enter."

"I don't see that they have done him much harm. He sowed his wild oats—then got married, and settled down into a good, substantial citizen. A little too religious and phari-saical, I always thought; but upright in his dealings. He had his pleasures in early life, as was befitting the season of youth—why not let his son taste of the same agreeable fruit? He's wrong, sir—wrong! And I've said as much to Ned. I only wish the boy had showed the right spunk this evening, and told the old man to go home about his business."

"So do I," chimed in the young disciple in this bad school. "It's what I'd say to my old man, in double-quick time, if he was to come hunting after me."

"He knows better than to do that," said the other, in a way that let me deeper into the young man's character.

"Indeed he does. He's tried his hand on me once or twice during the last year, but found it wouldn't do, no how; Tom Peters is out of his leading-strings."

"And can drink his glass with any one, and not be a grain the worse for it."

"Exactly, old boy!" said Peters, slapping his preceptor on the knee. "Exactly! I'm not one of your weak-headed ones. Oh no!"

"Look here, Joe Morgan!"—the half-angry voice of Simon Slade now rung through the bar-room,—"just take yourself off home!"

I had not observed the entrance of this person. He was standing at the bar, with an emptied glass in his hand. A year had made no improvement in his appearance. On the contrary, his clothes were more worn and tattered; his countenance more sadly marred. What he had said to irritate the landlord, I know not; but Slade's face was fiery with passion, and his eyes glared threateningly at the poor besotted one, who showed not the least inclination to obey.

"Off with you, I say! And never show your face here again. I won't have such low vagabonds as you are about my house. If you can't keep decent and stay decent, don't intrude yourself here."

"A rum-seller talk of decency!" retorted Morgan. "Pah! You were a decent man once, and a good miller into the bargain. But that time's past and gone. Decency died out when you exchanged the pick and facing-hammer for the glass and muddler. Decency! Pah! How you talk! As if it were any more decent to sell rum than to drink it."

There was so much of biting contempt in the tones, as well as the words of the half-intoxicated man, that Slade, who had himself been drinking rather more freely than usual, was angered beyond self-control. Catching up an empty glass from the counter, he hurled it with all his strength at the head of Joe Morgan. The missive just grazed one of his temples, and flew by on its dangerous course. The quick sharp cry of a child startled the air, followed by exclamations of alarm and horror from many voices.

"It's Joe Morgan's child!" "He's killed her!" "Good heavens!" Such were the exclamations that rang through the room. I was among the first to reach the spot where a little girl, just gliding in through the door, had been struck on the forehead by the glass, which had cut a deep gash, and stunned her into insensibility. The blood flowed instantly from the wound, and covered her face, which presented a shocking appearance. As I lifted her from the floor, upon which she had fallen, Morgan, into whose very soul the piercing cry of his child had penetrated, stood by my side, and grappled his arms around her insensible form, uttering as he did so heart-touching moans and lamentations.

"What's the matter? Oh, what's the matter?" It was a woman's voice, speaking in frightened tones.

"It's nothing! Just go out, will you, Ann?" I heard the landlord say.

But his wife—it was Mrs. Slade—having heard the shrieks of pain and terror uttered by Morgan's child, had come running into the bar-room—heeded not his words, but pressed forward into the little group that stood around the bleeding girl.

"IT'S JOE MORGAN'S CHILD! HE'S KILLED HER! GOOD HEAVENS!"

"It's Joe Morgan's child! He's killed her! Good Heavens!"

"Run for Doctor Green, Frank," she cried in an imperative voice, the moment her eyes rested on the little one's bloody face.

Frank came around from behind the bar, in obedience to the word; but his father gave a partial countermand, and he stood still. Upon observing which, his mother repeated the order, even more emphatically.

"Why don't you jump, you young rascal!" exclaimed Harvey Green. "The child may be dead before the doctor can get here."

Frank hesitated no longer, but disappeared instantly through the door.

"Poor, poor child!" almost sobbed Mrs. Slade, as she lifted the insensible form from my arms. "How did it happen? Who struck her?"

"Who? Curse him! Who but Simon Slade?" answered Joe Morgan, through his clenched teeth.

The look of anguish, mingled with bitter reproach, instantly thrown upon the landlord by his wife, can hardly be forgotten by any who saw it that night.

"Oh, Simon! Simon! And has it come to this already?" What a world of bitter memories, and sad forebodings of evil, did that little sentence express. "To this already"—Ah! In the downward way, how rapidly the steps do tread—how fast the progress!

"Bring me a basin of water, and a towel, quickly!" she now exclaimed.

The water was brought, and in a little while the face of the child lay pure and white as snow against her bosom. The wound from which the blood had flowed so freely was found on the upper part of the forehead, a little to the side, and extending several inches back, along the top of the head. As soon as the blood stains were wiped away, and the effusion partially stopped, Mrs. Slade carried the still insensible body into the next room, whither the distressed, and now completely sobered father, accompanied her. I went with them, but Slade remained behind.

The arrival of the doctor was soon followed by the restoration of life to the inanimate body. He happened to be at home, and came instantly. He had just taken the last stitch in the wound, which required to be drawn together, and was applying strips of adhesive plaster, when the hurried entrance of some one caused me to look up. What an apparition met my eyes! A woman stood in the door, with a face in which maternal anxiety and terror blended fearfully. Her countenance was like ashes—her eyes straining wildly—her lips apart, while the panting breath almost hissed through them.

"Joe! Joe! What is it? Where is Mary? Is she dead?" were her eager inquiries.

"No, Fanny," answered Joe Morgan, starting up from where he was actually kneeling by the side of the reviving little one, and going quickly to his wife. "She's better now. It's a bad hurt, but the doctor says it's nothing dangerous. Poor, dear child!"

The pale face of the mother grew paler—she gasped—caught for breath two or three times—a low shudder ran through her frame—and then she lay white and pulseless in the arms of her husband. As the doctor applied restoratives, I had opportunity to note more particularly the appearance of Mrs. Morgan. Her person was very slender, and her face so attenuated that it might almost be called shadowy. Her hair, which was a rich chestnut brown, with a slight golden lustre, had fallen from her comb, and now lay all over her neck and bosom in beautiful luxuriance. Back from her full temples it had been smoothed away by the hand of Morgan, that all the while moved over her brow and temples with a caressing motion that I saw was unconscious, and which revealed the tenderness of feeling with which, debased as he was, he regarded the wife of his youth, and the long suffering companion of his later and evil days. Her dress was plain and coarse, but clean and well fitting; and about her whole person was an air of neatness and taste. She could not now be called beautiful; yet in her marred features—marred by suffering and grief—were many lineaments of beauty; and much that told of a pure, true woman's heart beating in her bosom. Life came slowly back to the stilled heart, and it was nearly half an hour before the circle of motion was fully restored.

Then, the twain, with their child, tenderly borne in the arms of her father, went sadly homeward, leaving more than one heart heavier for their visit.

I saw more of the landlord's wife on this occasion than before. She had acted with a promptness and humanity that impressed me very favorably. It was plain, from her exclamations on learning that her husband's hand inflicted the blow that came so near destroying the child's life, that her faith for good in the tavern-keeping experiment had never been strong. I had already inferred as much. Her face, the few times I had seen her, wore a troubled look; and I could never forget its expression, nor her anxious, warning voice, when she discovered Frank sipping the dregs from a glass in the bar-room.

It is rarely, I believe, that wives consent freely to the opening of taverns by their husbands; and the determination on the part of the latter to do so, is not infrequently attended with a breach of confidence and good feeling, never afterward fully healed. Men look close to the money result; women to the moral consequences. I doubt if there be one dram-seller in ten, between whom and his wife there exists a good understanding—to say nothing of genuine affection. And, in the exceptional cases, it will generally be found that the wife is as mercenary, or careless of the public good, as her husband. I have known some women to set up grog-shops; but they were women of bad principles and worse hearts. I remember one case, where a woman, with a sober, church-going husband, opened a dram-shop. The husband opposed, remonstrated, begged, threatened—but all to no purpose. The wife, by working for the clothing stores, had earned and saved about three hundred dollars. The love of money, in the slow process of accumulation, had been awakened; and, in ministering to the depraved appetites of men who loved drink and neglected their families, she saw a quicker mode of acquiring the gold she coveted. And so the dram-shop was opened. And what was the result? The husband quit going to church. He had no heart for that; for, even on the Sabbath-day, the fiery stream was stayed not in his house. Next he began to tipple. Soon, alas! the subtle poison so pervaded his system that morbid desire came; and then he moved along quick-footed in the way to ruin. In less than three years, I think, from the time the grog-shop was opened by his wife, he was in a drunkard's grave. A year or two more, and the pit that was digged for others by the hands of the wife, she fell into herself. Ever breathing an atmosphere poisoned by the fumes of liquor, the love of tasting it was gradually formed, and she too, in the end, became a slave to the Demon of Drink. She died, at last, poor as a beggar in the street. Ah! this liquor-selling is the way to ruin; and they who open the gates, as well as those who enter the downward path, alike go to destruction. But this is digressing.

After Joe Morgan and his wife left the "Sickle and Sheaf," with that gentle child, who, as I afterward learned, had not, for a year or more, laid her little head to sleep until her father returned home—and who, if he stayed out beyond a certain hour, would go for him, and lead him back, a very angel of love and patience—I re-entered the bar-room, to see how life was passing there. Not one of all I had left in the room remained. The incident which had occurred was of so painful a nature, that no further unalloyed pleasure was to be had there during the evening, and so each had retired. In his little kingdom the landlord sat alone, his head resting on his hand, and his face shaded from the light. The whole aspect of the man was that of one in self-humiliation. As I entered he raised his head, and turned his face toward me. Its expression was painful.

"Rather an unfortunate affair," said he. "I'm angry with myself, and sorry for the poor child. But she'd no business here. As for Joe Morgan, it would take a saint to bear his tongue when once set a-going by liquor. I wish he'd stay away from the house. Nobody wants his company. Oh, dear!"

The ejaculation, or rather groan, that closed the sentence showed how little Slade was satisfied with himself, notwithstanding this feeble effort at self-justification.

"His thirst for liquor draws him hither," I remarked. "The attraction of your bar to his appetite is like that of the magnet to the needle. He cannot stay away."

"He *must* stay away!" exclaimed the landlord, with some vehemence of tone, striking his fist upon the table by which he sat. "He *must* stay away! There is scarcely an evening that he does not ruffle my temper, and mar good feelings in all the company. Just see what he provoked me to do this evening. I might have killed the child. It makes my blood run cold to think of it! Yes, sir—he must stay away. If no better can be done, I'll hire a man to stand at the door and keep him out."

"He never troubled you at the mill," said I. "No man was required at the mill door?"

"No!" And the landlord gave emphasis to the word by an oath, ejaculated with a heartiness that almost startled me. I had not heard him swear before. "No! the great trouble was to get him and keep him there, the good-for-nothing, idle fellow!"

"I'm afraid," I ventured to suggest, "that things don't go on quite so smoothly here as they did at the mill. Your customers are of a different class."

"I don't know about that; why not?" He did not just relish my remark.

"Between quiet, thrifty, substantial farmers, and drinking bar-room loungers, are many degrees of comparison."

"Excuse me, sir!" Simon Slade elevated his person. "The men who visit my bar-room, as a general thing, are quite as respectable, moral, and substantial as any who came to the mill—and I believe more so. The first people in the place, sir, are to be found here. Judge Lyman and Judge Hammond; Lawyer Wilks and Doctor Maynard; Mr. Grand and Mr. Lee; and dozens of others—all our first people. No, sir; you mustn't judge all by vagabonds like Joe Morgan."

There was a testy spirit manifested that I did not care to provoke. I could have met his assertion with facts and inferences of a character to startle any one occupying his position, who was in a calm, reflective state; but to argue with him then would have been worse than idle; and so I let him talk on until the excitement occasioned by my words died out for want of new fuel.

Night the Third

Joe Morgan's Child

"I DON'T see any thing of your very particular friend, Joe Morgan, this evening," said Harvey Green, leaning on the bar and speaking to Slade. It was the night succeeding that on which the painful and exciting scene with the child had occurred.

"No," was answered—and to the word was added a profane imprecation. "No; and if he'll just keep away from here, he may go to—on a hard-trotting horse and a porcupine saddle as fast as he pleases. He's tried my patience beyond endurance, and my mind is made up, that he gets no more drams at this bar. I've borne his vile tongue and seen my company annoyed by him just as long as I mean to stand it. Last night decided me. Suppose I'd killed that child?"

"You'd have had trouble then, and no mistake."

"Wouldn't I? Blast her little picture! What business has she creeping in here every night?"

"She must have a nice kind of a mother," remarked Green, with a cold sneer.

"I don't know what she is now," said Slade, a slight touch of feeling in his voice—"heartbroken, I suppose. I couldn't look at her last night; it made me sick. But there was a time when Fanny Morgan was the loveliest and best woman in Cedarville. I'll say that for her. Oh, dear! What a life her miserable husband has caused her to lead."

"Better that he were dead and out of the way."

"Better a thousand times," answered Slade. "If he'd only fall down some night and break his neck, it would be a blessing to his family."

"And to you in particular," laughed Green.

"You may be sure it wouldn't cost me a large sum for mourning," was the unfeeling response.

Let us leave the bar-room of the "Sickle and Sheaf," and its cold-hearted inmates, and look in upon the family of Joe Morgan, and see how it is in the home of the poor inebriate. We will pass by a quick transition.

"Joe!" The thin white hand of Mrs. Morgan clasps the arm of her husband, who has arisen up suddenly, and now stands by the partly opened door. "Don't go out to-night, Joe. Please, don't go out."

"Father!" A feeble voice calls from the corner of an old settee, where little Mary lies with her head bandaged.

"Well, I won't then!" is replied—not angrily, nor even fretfully—but in a kind voice.

"Come and sit by me, father." How tenderly, yet how full of concern is that low, sweet voice. "Come, won't you?"

"Yes, dear."

"Now bold my hand, father."

Joe takes the hand of little Mary, that instantly lightens upon his.

"You won't go away and leave me to-night, will you, father? Say you won't."

"How very hot your hand is, dear. Does your head ache?"

"A little; but it will soon feel better."

Up into the swollen and disfigured face of the fallen father, the large, earnest blue eyes of the child are raised. She does not see the marred lineaments; but, only the beloved countenance of her parent.

"Dear father!"

"What, love?"

"I wish you'd promise me something."

"What, dear?"

"Will you promise?"

"I can't say until I hear your request. If I can promise, I will."

"Oh! you can promise—you can, father!"

How the large blue eyes dance and sparkle!

"What is it, love?"

"That you'll never go into Simon Slade's bar any more."

The child raises herself, evidently with a painful effort; and leans nearer to her father.

Joe shakes his head, and poor Mary drops back upon her pillow with a sigh. Her lids fall, and the long lashes lie strongly relieved on her colorless cheeks.

"I won't go there to-night, dear. So let your heart be at rest."

Mary's lids unclose, and two round drops, released from their clasp, glide slowly over her face.

"Thank you, father—thank you. Mother will be so glad."

The eyes closed again; and the father moved uneasily. His heart is touched. There is a struggle within him. It is on his lips to say that he will never drink at the "Sickle and Sheaf" again; but resolution just lacks the force of utterance.

"Father!"

"Well, dear?"

"I don't think I'll be well enough to go out in two or three days. You know the doctor said that I would have to keep very still, for I had a great deal of fever."

"Yes, poor child."

"Now, won't you promise me one thing?"

"What is it, dear?"

"Not to go out in the evening until I get well."

Joe Morgan hesitated.

"Just promise me that, father. It won't be long; I shall be up again in a little while."

How well the father knows what is in the heart of his child. Her fears are all for him. Who is to go after her poor father, and lead him home when the darkness of inebriety is on his spirit, and external perception so dulled that not skill enough remains to shun the harm that lies in his path?

"Do promise just that, father, dear."

He cannot resist the pleading voice and look.

"I promise it, Mary; so shut your eyes now and go to sleep. I'm afraid this fever will increase."

"Oh! I'm so glad—so glad!"

Mary does not clasp her hands, nor show strong external signs of pleasure; but how full of a pure, unselfish joy is that low-murmured ejaculation, spoken in the depths of her spirit, as well as syllabled by her tongue!

Mrs. Morgan has been no unconcerned witness of all this; but knowing the child's influence over her father, she has not ventured a word. More was to be gained, she was sure, by silence on her part; and so she has kept silent. Now she comes nearer to them, and says, as she lets a hand rest on the shoulder of her husband—

"You feel better for that promise already; I know you do."

He looks up to her, and smiles faintly. He does feel better, but is hardly willing to acknowledge it.

Soon after Mary is sleeping. It does not escape the observation of Mrs. Morgan that her husband grows restless; for he gets up suddenly, every now and then, and walks quickly across the room, as if in search of something. Then sits down, listlessly—sighs—stretches himself, and says, "Oh, dear!" What shall she do for him? How is the want of his accustomed evening stimulus to be met? She thinks, and questions, and grieves inwardly. Poor Joe Morgan! His wife understands his case, and pities him from her heart. But, what can she do? Go out and get him something to drink? "Oh, no! no! no! never!" She answered the thought audibly almost, in the excitement of her feelings. An hour has passed—Joe's restlessness has increased instead of diminishing. What is to be done? Now Mrs. Morgan has left the room. She has resolved upon something, for the case must be met. Ah! here she comes, after an absence of five minutes, bearing in her hand a cup of strong coffee.

"It was kind and thoughtful in you, Fanny," says Morgan, as with a gratified look he takes the cup. But his hand trembles, and he spills a portion of the contents as he tries to raise it to his lips. How dreadfully his nerves are shattered! Unnatural stimulants have been applied so long, that all true vitality seems lost.

And now the hand of his wife is holding the cup to his lips, and he drinks eagerly.

"This is dreadful—dreadful! Where will it end? What is to be done?"

Fanny suppresses a sob, as she thus gives vent to her troubled feelings. Twice, already, has her husband been seized with the drunkard's madness; and, in the nervous prostration consequent upon even a brief withdrawal of his usual strong stimulants, she sees the fearful precursor of another attack of this dreadful and dangerous malady. In the hope of supplying the needed tone she has given him strong coffee; and this, for the time, produces the effect desired. The restlessness is allayed, and a quiet state of body and mind succeeds. It needs but a suggestion to induce him to retire for the night. After being a few minutes in bed, sleep steals over him, and his heavy breathing tells that he is in the world of dreams.

And now there comes a tap at the door.

"Come in," is answered.

The latch is lifted, the door swings open, and a woman enters.

"Mrs. Slade!" The name is uttered in a tone of surprise.

"Fanny, how are you this evening?" Kindly, yet half sadly, the words are said.

"Tolerable, I thank you."

The hands of the two women are clasped, and for a few moments they gaze into each other's face. What a world of tender commiseration is in that of Mrs. Slade!

"How is little Mary to-night?".

"Not so well, I'm afraid. She has a good deal of fever."

"Indeed! Oh, I'm sorry! Poor child! what a dreadful thing it was! Oh! Fanny! you don't know how it has troubled me. I've been intending to come around all day to see how she was, but couldn't get off until now."

"It came near killing her," said Mrs. Morgan.

"It's in God's mercy she escaped. The thought of it curdles the very blood in my veins. Poor child! is this her on the settee?"

"Yes."

Mrs. Slade takes a chair, and sitting by the sleeping child, gazes long upon her pale, sweet face. Now the lips of Mary part—words are murmured—what is she saying?

"No, no, mother; I can't go to bed yet. Father isn't home. And it's so dark. There's no one to lead him over the bridge. I'm not afraid. Don't—don't cry so, mother—I'm not afraid! Nothing will hurt me."

The child's face flushes. She moans, and throws her arms about uneasily. Hark again.

"I wish Mr. Slade wouldn't look so cross at me. He never did when I went to the mill. He doesn't take me on his knee now, and stroke my hair. Oh, dear! I wish father wouldn't go there any more. Don't! don't, Mr. Slade. Oh! oh!"—the ejaculation prolonged into a frightened cry, "My head! my head!"

A few choking sobs are followed by low moans; and then the child breathes easily again. But the flush does not leave her cheek; and when Mrs. Slade, from whose eyes the tears come forth drop by drop, and roll down her face, touches it lightly, she finds it hot with fever.

"Has the doctor seen her to-day, Fanny?"

"No, ma'am."

"He should see her at once. I will go for him;" and Mrs. Slade starts up and goes quickly from the room. In a little while she returns with Doctor Green, who sits down and looks at the child for some moments with a sober, thoughtful face. Then he lays his fingers on her pulse and times its beat by his watch—shakes his head, and looks graver still.

"How long has she had fever?" he asks.

"All day."

"You should have sent for me earlier."

"Oh, doctor! She is not dangerous, I hope?" Mrs. Morgan looks frightened.

"She's a sick child, madam."

"You've promised, father."—The dreamer is speaking again.—"I'm not well enough yet. Oh, don't go, father; don't! There! He's gone! Well, well! I'll try and walk there—I can sit down and rest by the way. Oh, dear! How tired I am! Father! Father!"

The child starts up and looks about her wildly.

"Oh, mother, is it you?" And she sinks back upon her pillow, looking now inquiringly from face to face.

"Father—where is father?" she asks.

"Asleep, dear."

"Oh! Is he? I'm glad."

"Her eyes close wearily."

"Do you feel any pain, Mary?" inquired the doctor.

"Yes, sir—in my head. It aches and beats so."

The cry of "Father" has reached the ears of Morgan, who is sleeping in the next room, and roused him into consciousness. He knows the doctor's voice. Why is he here at this late hour? "Do you feel any pain, Mary?" The question he hears distinctly, and the faintly uttered reply also. He is sober enough to have all his fears instantly excited. There is nothing in the world that he loves as he loves that child. And so he gets up and dresses himself as quickly as possible; the stimulus of anxiety giving tension to his relaxed nerves.

"Oh, father!" The quick ears of Mary detect his entrance first, and a pleasant smile welcomes him.

"Is she very sick, doctor?" he asks, in a voice full of anxiety.

"She's a sick child, sir; you should have sent for me earlier." The doctor speaks rather sternly, and with a purpose to rebuke.

The reply stirs Morgan, and he seems to cower half-timidly under the words, as if they were blows. Mary has already grasped her father's hand, and holds on to it tightly.

After examining the case a little more closely, the doctor prepares some medicine, and, promising to call early in the morning, goes away. Mrs. Slade follows soon after; but, in parting with Mrs. Morgan, leaves something in her hand, which, to the surprise of the latter, proves to be a ten-dollar bill. The tears start to her eyes; and she conceals the money in her bosom—murmuring a fervent "God bless her!"

A simple act of restitution is this on the part of Mrs. Slade, prompted as well by humanity as a sense of justice. With one hand her husband has taken the bread from the family of his old friend, and thus with the other he restores it.

And now Morgan and his wife are alone with their sick child. Higher the fever rises, and partial delirium seizes upon her over-excited brain. She talks for a time almost incessantly. All her trouble is about her father; and she is constantly referring to his promise not to go out in the evening until she gets well. How tenderly and touchingly she appeals to him; now looking up into his face in partial recognition; and now calling anxiously after him, as if he had left her and was going away.

"You'll not forget your promise, will you, father?" she says, speaking so calmly, that he thinks her mind has ceased to wander.

"No, dear; I will not forget it," he answers, smoothing her hair gently with his hand.

"You'll not go out in the evening again, until I get well?"

"No, dear."

"Father!"

"What, love?"

"Stoop down closer; I don't want mother to hear; it will make her feel so bad."

The father bends his ear close to the lips of Mary. How he starts and shudders! What has she said?—only these brief words—

"I shall not get well, father; I'm going to die."

The groans, impossible to repress, that issued through the lips of Joe Morgan, startled the ears of his wife, and she came quickly to the bed-side.

"What is it? What is the matter, Joe?" she inquired, with a look of anxiety.

"Hush, father. Don't tell her. I only said it to you." And Mary put a finger on her lips, and looked mysterious. "There, mother—you go away; you've got trouble enough, any how. Don't tell her, father."

But the words, which came to him like a prophecy, awoke such pangs of fear and remorse in the heart of Joe Morgan, that it was impossible for him to repress the signs of pain. For some moments he gazed at his wife—then stooping forward, suddenly, he buried his face in the bed-clothes, and sobbed bitterly.

A suggestion of the truth now flashed through the mind of Mrs. Morgan, sending a thrill of pain along every nerve. Ere she had time to recover herself, the low, sweet voice of Mary broke upon the hushed air of the room, and she sung—

Jesus can make a dying bed
    Feel soft as downy pillows are,
While on His breast I lean my head,
    And breathe my life out, sweetly, there.

It was impossible for Mrs. Morgan longer to repress her feelings. As the softly breathed strain died away, her sobs broke forth, and for a time she wept violently.

"There," said the child,—"I didn't mean to tell you. I only told father, because—because he promised not to go to the tavern any more until I got well; and I'm not going to get well. So, you see, mother, he'll never go again—never—never—never. Oh, dear! how my head pains. Mr. Slade threw it so hard. But it didn't strike father; and I'm so glad. How it would have hurt him—poor father! But he'll never go there any more; and that will be so good, won't it, mother?"

A light broke over her face; but seeing that her mother still wept, she said—

"Don't cry. Maybe I'll be better."

And then her eyes closed heavily, and she slept again.

"Joe," said Mrs. Morgan, after she had in a measure recovered herself—she spoke firmly—"Joe, did you hear what she said?"

Morgan only answered with a groan.

"Her mind wanders; and yet she may have spoken only the truth."

He groaned again.

"If she should die, Joe—"

"Don't; oh, don't talk so, Fanny. She's not going to die. It's only because she's a little light-headed."

"Why is she light-headed, Joe?"

"It's the fever—only the fever, Fanny."

"It was the blow, and the wound on her head, that caused the fever. How do we know the extent of injury on the brain? Doctor Green looked very serious. I'm afraid, husband, that the worst is before us. I've borne and suffered a great deal—only God knows how much—I pray that I may have strength to bear this trial also. Dear child!

She is better fitted for heaven than for earth, and it may be that God is about to take her to Himself. She's been a great comfort to me—and to you, Joe, more like a guardian angel than a child."

Mrs. Morgan had tried to speak very firmly; but as sentence followed sentence, her voice lost more and more of its even tone. With the closing words all self-control vanished; and she wept bitterly. What could her feeble erring husband do, but weep with her?

"Joe,"—Mrs. Morgan aroused herself as quickly as possible, for she had that to say which she feared she might not have the heart to utter—"Joe, if Mary dies, you cannot forget the cause of her death."

"Oh, Fanny! Fanny!"

"Nor the hand that struck the cruel blow."

"Forget it? Never! And if I forgive Simon Slade—"

"Nor the place where the blow was dealt," said Mrs. Morgan, interrupting him.

"Poor—poor child!" moaned the conscience-stricken man.

"Nor your promise, Joe—nor your promise given to our dying child."

"Father! Father! Dear father!" Mary's eyes suddenly unclosed, as she called her father eagerly.

"Here I am, love. What is it?" And Joe Morgan pressed up to the bed-side.

"Oh! it's you, father! I dreamed that you had gone out, and—and—but you won't, will you, dear father?"

"No, love—no."

"Never any more until I get well?"

"I must go out to work, you know, Mary."

"At night, father. That's what I mean. You won't, will you?"

"No, dear, no."

A soft smile trembled over the child's face; her eyelids drooped wearily, and she fell off into slumber again. She seemed not so restless as before—did not moan, nor throw herself about in her sleep.

"She's better, I think," said Morgan, as he bent over her, and listened to her softer breathing.

"It seems so," replied his wife. "And now, Joe, you must go to bed again. I will lie down here with Mary, and be ready to do any thing for her that she may want."

"I don't feel sleepy. I'm sure I couldn't close my eyes. So let me sit up with Mary. You are tired and worn out."

Mrs. Morgan looked earnestly into her husband's face. His eyes were unusually bright, and she noticed a slight nervous restlessness about his lips. She laid one of her hands on his, and perceived a slight tremor.

"You must go to bed," she spoke firmly. "I shall not let you sit up with Mary. So go at once." And she drew him almost by force into the next room.

"It's no use, Fanny. There's not a wink of sleep in my eyes. I shall lie awake anyhow. So do you get a little rest."

Even as he spoke there were nervous twitchings of his arms and shoulders; and as he entered the chamber, impelled by his wife, he stopped suddenly and said—

"What is that?"

"Where?" asked Mrs. Morgan.

"Oh, it's nothing—I see. Only one of my old boots. I thought it a great black cat."

Oh! what a shudder of despair seized upon the heart of the wretched wife. Too well she knew the fearful signs of that terrible mad-ness from which, twice before, he had suffered. She could have looked on calmly and seen him die—but, "Not this—not this! Oh, Father in heaven!" she murmured, with such a heart-sinking that it seemed as if life itself would go out.

"Get into bed, Joe; get into bed as quickly as possible."

Morgan was now passive in the hands of his wife, and obeyed her almost like a child. He had turned down the bed-clothes, and was about getting in, when he started back, with a look of disgust and alarm.

"There's nothing there, Joe. What's the matter with you?"

"I'm sure I don't know, Fanny," and his teeth rattled together, as he spoke. "I thought there was a great toad under the clothes."

"How foolish you are!"—yet tears were blinding her eyes as she said this. "It's only fancy. Get into bed and shut your eyes. I'll make you another cup of strong coffee. Perhaps that will do you good. You're only a little nervous. Mary's sickness has disturbed you."

Joe looked cautiously under the bedclothes, as he lifted them up still farther, and peered beneath.

"You know there's nothing in your bed; see!"

And Mrs. Morgan threw, with a single jerk, all the clothes upon the floor.

"There now! look for yourself. Now shut your eyes," she continued, as she spread the sheet and quilt over him, after his head was on the pillow. "Shut them tight and keep them so until I boil the water and make a cup of coffee. You know as well as I do that it's nothing but fancy."

Morgan closed his eyes firmly, and drew the clothes over his head.

"I'll be back in a very few minutes," said his wife, going hurriedly to the door. Ere leaving, however, she partly turned her head and glanced back. There sat her husband, upright and staring fearfully.

"Don't, Fanny! don't go away!" he cried, in a frightened voice.

"Joe! Joe! why will you be so foolish? It's nothing but imagination. Now do lie down and shut your eyes. Keep them shut. There now."

And she laid a hand over his eyes, and pressed it down tightly.

"I wish Doctor Green was here," said the wretched man. "He could give me some thing."

"Shall I go for him?"

"Go, Fanny! Run over right quickly."

"But you won't keep in bed."

"Yes, I will. There now." And he drew the clothes over his face. "There; I'll lie just so until you come back. Now run, Fanny, and don't stay a minute."

Scarcely stopping to think, Mrs. Morgan went hurriedly from the room, and drawing an old shawl over her head, started with swift feet for the residence of Doctor Green, which was not very far away. The kind doctor understood, at a word, the sad condition of her husband, and promised to attend him immediately. Back she flew at even a wilder speed, her heart throbbing with vague apprehension. Oh! what a fearful cry was that which smote her ears as she came within a few paces of home. She knew the voice, changed as it was by terror, and a shudder almost palsied her heart. At a single bound she cleared the intervening space, and in the next moment was in the room where she had left her husband. But he was not there! With suspended breath, and feet that scarcely obeyed her will, she passed into the chamber where little Mary lay. Not here!

"Joe! husband!" she called in a faint voice.

"Here he is, mother." And now she saw that Joe had crept into the bed behind the sick child, and that her arm was drawn tightly around his neck.

"You won't let them hurt me, will you, dear?" said the poor, frightened victim of a terrible mania.

"Nothing will hurt you, father," answered Mary, in a voice that showed her mind to be clear, and fully conscious of her parent's true condition.

She had seen him thus before Ah! what an experience for a child!

"You're an angel—my good angel, Mary," he murmured, in a voice yet trembling with fear. "Pray for me, my child. Oh, ask your Father in heaven to save me from these dreadful creatures. There now!" he cried, rising up suddenly, and looking toward the door. "Keep out! Go away! You can't come in here. This is Mary's room; and she's an angel. Ah, ha! I knew you wouldn't dare come in here—

A single saint can put to flight,
Ten thousand blustering sons of night."

He added in a half-wandering way, yet with an assured voice, as he laid himself back upon his pillow, and drew the clothes over his head.

"Poor father!" sighed the child, as she gathered both arms about his neck. "I will be your good angel. Nothing shall hurt you here."

"I knew I would be safe where you were," he whispered back—"I knew it, and so I came. Kiss me, love."

How pure and fervent was the kiss laid instantly upon his lips! There was a power in it to remand the evil influences that were surrounding and pressing in upon him like a flood. All was quiet now, and Mrs. Morgan neither by word nor movement disturbed the solemn stillness that reigned in the apartment. In a few minutes the deepened breathing of her husband gave a blessed intimation that he was sinking into sleep. Oh, sleep! sleep! How tearfully, in times past, had she prayed that he might sleep; and yet no sleep came for hours and days—even though powerful opiates were given—until exhausted nature yielded, and then sleep had a long, long struggle with death. Now the sphere of his loving, innocent child seemed to have overcome, at least for the time, the evil influences that were getting possession even of his external senses. Yes, yes, he was sleeping! Oh, what a fervent "Thank God!" went up from the heart of his stricken wife.

Soon the quick ears of Mrs. Morgan detected the doctor's approaching footsteps, and she met him at the door with a finger on her lips. A whispered word or two explained the better aspect of affairs, and the doctor said, encouragingly,

"That's good, if he will only sleep on."

"Do you think he will, doctor?" was asked anxiously.

"He may. But we cannot hope too strongly. It would be something very unusual."

Both passed noiselessly into the chamber. Morgan still slept, and by his deep breathing it was plain that he slept soundly. And Mary, too, was sleeping, her face now laid against her father's, and her arms still about his neck. The sight touched even the doctor's heart and moistened his eyes. For nearly half an hour he remained; and then, as Morgan continued to sleep, he left medicine to be given immediately, and went home, promising to call early in the morning.

It is now past midnight, and we leave the lonely, sad-hearted watcher with her sick ones.

I was sitting, with a newspaper in my hand—not reading, but musing—at the "Sickle and Sheaf," late in the evening marked by the incidents just detailed.

"Where's your mother?" I heard Simon Slade inquire. He had just entered an adjoining room.

"She's gone out somewhere," was answered by his daughter Flora.

"Where?"

"I don't know."

"How long has she been away?"

"More than an hour."

"And you don't know where she went to? "

"No, sir."

Nothing more was said, but I heard the landlord's heavy feet moving backward and forward across the room for some minutes.

"Why, Ann! where have you been?" The door of the next room had opened and shut.

"Where I wish you had been with me," was answered in a very firm voice.

"Where?"

"To Joe Morgan's."

"Humph!" Only this ejaculation met my ears. But something was said in a low voice, to which Mrs. Slade replied with some warmth,

"If you don't have his child's blood clinging for life to your garments, you may be thankful."

"What do you mean?" he asked quickly.

"All that my words indicate. Little Mary is very ill!"

"Well, what of it."

"Much. The doctor thinks her in great danger. The cut on her head has thrown her into a violent fever, and she is delirious. Oh, Simon! if you had heard what I heard to-night."

"What?" was asked in a growling tone.

"She is out of her mind, as I said, and talks a great deal. She talked about you."

"Of me! Well, what had she to say?"

"She said—so pitifully—'I wish Mr. Slade wouldn't look so cross at me. He never did when I went to the mill. He doesn't take me on his knee now, and stroke my hair. Oh, dear!' Poor child! She was always so good."

"Did she say that?" Slade seemed touched.

"Yes, and a great deal more. Once she screamed out, 'Oh, don't! don't, Mr. Slade! don't! My head! my head!' It made my very heart ache. I can never forget her pale, frightened face, nor her cry of fear. Simon—if she should die!"

There was a long silence.

"If we were only back to the mill." It was Mrs. Slade's voice.

"There, now! I don't want to hear that again," quickly spoke out the landlord. "I made a slave of myself long enough."

"You had at least a clear conscience," his wife answered.

"Do hush, will you?" Slade was now angry. "One would think, by the way you talk sometimes, that I had broken every command of the Decalogue."

"You will break hearts as well as commandments, if you keep on for a few years as you have begun—and ruin souls as well as fortunes."

Mrs. Slade spoke calmly, but with marked severity of tone. Her husband answered with an oath, and then left the room, banging the door after him. In the hush that followed I retired to my chamber, and lay for an hour awake, pondering on all I had just heard. What a revelation was in that brief passage of words between the landlord and his excited companion!

Night the Fourth

Death of Little Mary Morgan

"WHERE are you going, Ann?" It was the landlord's voice. Time—a little after dark.

"I'm going over to see Mrs. Morgan," answered his wife.

"What for?"

"I wish to go," was replied.

"Well, *I* don't wish you to go," said Slade, in a very decided way.

"I can't help that, Simon. Mary, I'm told, is dying, and Joe is in a dreadful way. I'm needed there—and so are you, as to that matter. There was a time when, if word came to you that Morgan or his family were in trouble—"

"Do hush, will you!" exclaimed the landlord, angrily. "I won't be preached to in this way any longer."

"Oh, well; then don't interfere with my movements, Simon; that's all I have to say. I'm needed over there, as I just said, and I'm going."

There were considerable odds against him, and Slade, perceiving this, turned off, muttering something that his wife did not hear, and she went on her way. A hurried walk brought her to the wretched home of the poor drunkard, whose wife met her at the door.

"How is Mary?" was the visitor's earnest inquiry.

Mrs. Morgan tried to answer the question; but, though her lips moved, no sounds issued therefrom.

Mrs. Slade pressed her hands tightly in both of hers; and then passed in with her to the room where the child lay. A glance sufficed to tell Mrs. Slade that death had already laid his icy fingers upon her brow.

"How are you, dear?" she asked, as she bent over and kissed her.

"Better, I thank you!" replied Mary, in a low whisper.

Then she fixed her eyes upon her mother's face with a look of inquiry.

"What is it, love?"

"Hasn't father waked up yet? "

"No, dear."

"Won't he wake up soon?"

"He's sleeping very soundly. I wouldn't like to disturb him."

"Oh, no; don't disturb him. I thought, maybe, he was awake."

And the child's lids drooped languidly, until the long lashes lay close against her cheeks.

There was silence for a little while, and then Mrs. Morgan said in a half-whisper to Mrs. Slade,

"Oh, we've had such a dreadful time with poor Joe. He got in that terrible way again last night. I had to go for Doctor Green and leave him all alone. When I came back, he was in bed with Mary; and she, dear child! had her arms around his neck, and was trying to comfort him; and would you believe it, he went off to sleep, and slept in that way for a long time. The doctor came, and when he saw how it was, left some medicine for him, and went away. I was in such hopes that he would sleep it all off. But about twelve o'clock he started up, and sprung out of bed with an awful scream. Poor Mary! she too had fallen asleep. The cry wakened her, and frightened her dreadfully. She's been getting worse ever since, Mrs. Slade.

"Just as he was rushing out of the room, I caught him by the arm, and it took all my strength to hold him.

" 'Father! father!' Mary called after him, as soon as she was awake enough to understand what was the matter—'Don't go out, father; there's nothing here.'

"THERE IT IS NOW! JUMP! OUT OF BED, QUICK! JUMP OUT, MARY! SEE! IT'S RIGHT OVER YOUR HEAD!"

"There it is now! Jump! Out of bed, quick! Jump out, Mary! See! It's right over your head!"

"He looked back toward the bed, in a frightful way.

"'See, father!' and the dear child turned down the quilt and sheet, in order to convince him that nothing was in the bed. 'I'm here,' she added. 'I'm not afraid. Come, father. If there's nothing here to hurt me, there's nothing to hurt you.'

"There was something so assuring in this, that Joe took a step or two toward the bed, looking sharply into it as he did so. From the bed his eyes wandered up to the ceiling, and the old look of terror came into his face.

"'There it is now! Jump out of bed, quick! Jump out, Mary!' he cried. 'See! it's right over your head.'

"Mary showed no sign of fear as she lifted her eyes to the ceiling, and gazed steadily for a few moments in that direction.

"'There's nothing there, father,' said she, in a confident voice.

"'It's gone now,' Joe spoke in a tone of relief. 'Your angel-look drove it away. Aha! There it is now, creeping along the floor!' he suddenly exclaimed, fearfully; starting away from where he stood.

"'Here, father! Here!' Mary called to him, and he sprung into the bed again; while she gathered her arms about him tightly, saying in a low, soothing voice,—'Nothing can harm you here, father.'

"Without a moment's delay, I gave him the morphine left by Doctor Green. He took it eagerly, and then crouched down in the bed, while Mary continued to assure him of perfect safety. So long as he was clearly conscious as to where he was, he remained perfectly still. But, as soon as partial slumber came, he would scream out, and spring from the bed in terror and then it would take us several minutes to quiet him again. Six times during the night did this occur; and as often, Mary coaxed him back. The morphine I continued to give as the doctor had directed. By morning, the opiates had done their work, and he was sleeping soundly. When the doctor came, we removed him to his own bed. He is still asleep; and I begin to feel uneasy, lest he should never awake again. I have heard of this happening."

"See if father isn't awake," said Mary, raising her head from the pillow. She had not heard what passed between her mother and Mrs. Slade, for the conversation was carried on in low voices.

Mrs. Morgan stepped to the door, and looked into the room where her husband lay.

"He is still asleep, dear," she remarked, coming back to the bed.

"Oh! I wish he was awake. I want to see him so much. Won't you call him, mother?"

"I have called him a good many times. But you know the doctor gave him opium. He can't wake up yet."

"He's been sleeping a very long time; don't you think so, mother?"

"Yes, dear, it does seem a long time. But it is best for him. He'll be better when he wakes."

Mary closed her eyes, wearily. How deathly white was her face—how sunken her eyes—how sharply contracted her features!

"I've given her up, Mrs. Slade," said Mrs. Morgan, in a low, rough, choking whisper, as she leaned nearer to her friend. "I've given her up! The worst is over; but, oh! it seemed as though my heart would break in the struggle. Dear child! In all the darkness of my way, she has helped and comforted me. Without her, it would have been the blackness of darkness."

"Father! father!" The voice of Mary broke out with a startling quickness.

Mrs. Morgan turned to the bed, and laying her hand on Mary's arm said—

"He's still sound asleep, dear."

"No, he isn't, mother. I heard him move. Won't you go in and see if he is awake?"

In order to satisfy the child, her mother left the room. To her surprise, she met the eyes of her husband as she entered the chamber where he lay. He looked at her calmly.

"What does Mary want with me?" he asked.

"She wishes to see you. She's called you so many, many times. Shall I bring her in here?"

"No. I'll get up and dress myself."

"I wouldn't do that. You've been sick."

"Oh, no. I don't feel sick."

"Father! father!" The clear, earnest voice of Mary was heard calling.

"I'm coming, dear," answered Morgan.

"Come quick, father, won't you?"

"Yes, love." And Morgan got up and dressed himself—but with unsteady hands, and every sign of nervous prostration. In a little while, with the assistance of his wife, he was ready, and supported by her, came tottering into the room where Mary was lying.

"Oh, father!"—What a light broke over her countenance.—"I've been waiting for you so long. I thought you were never going to wake up. Kiss me, father."

"What can I do for you, Mary?" asked Morgan, tenderly, as he laid his face down upon the pillow beside her.

"Nothing, father. I don't wish for anything. I only wanted to see you."

"I'm here, now, love."

"Dear father!" How earnestly, yet tenderly she spoke, laying her small hand upon his face. "You've always been good to me, father."

"Oh, no. I've never been good to anybody," sobbed the weak, broken-spirited man, as he raised himself from the pillow.

How deeply touched was Mrs. Slade, as she sat, the silent witness of this scene!

"You haven't been good to yourself, father—but you've always been good to us."

"Don't, Mary! don't say anything about that," interrupted Morgan. "Say that I've been very bad—very wicked. Oh, Mary, dear! I only wish that I was as good as you are; I'd like to die, then, and go right away from this evil world. I wish there was no liquor to drink—no taverns—no bar-rooms. Oh dear! Oh dear! I wish I was dead."

And the weak, trembling, half-palsied man laid his face again upon the pillow beside his child, and sobbed aloud.

What an oppressive silence reigned for a time through the room!

"Father." The stillness was broken by Mary. Her voice was clear and even. "Father, I want to tell you something."

"What is it, Mary?"

"There'll be nobody to go for you, father." The child's lips now quivered, and tears filled into her eyes.

"Don't talk about that, Mary. I'm not going out in the evening any more until you get well. Don't you remember I promised?"

"But, father"—She hesitated.

"What, dear?"

"I'm going away to leave you and mother."

"Oh, no—no—no, Mary! Don't say that."—The poor man's voice was broken.— "Don't say that! We can't let you go, dear."

"God has called me." The child's voice had a solemn tone, and her eyes turned reverently upward.

"I wish he would call me! Oh, I wish he would call me!" groaned Morgan, hiding his face in his hands. "What shall I do when you are gone? Oh, dear! Oh, dear!"

"Father! "Mary spoke calmly again. "You are not ready to go yet. God will let you live here longer, that you may get ready."

"How can I get ready without you to help me, Mary? My angel child!"

"Haven't I tried to help you, father, oh, so many times? "said Mary.

"Yes—yes—you've always tried."

"But it wasn't any use. You would go out—you would go to the tavern. It seemed almost as if you couldn't help it."

Morgan groaned in spirit.

"Maybe I can help you better, father, after I die. I love you so much, that I am sure God will let me come to you, and stay with you always, and be your angel. Don't you think he will, mother?"

But Mrs. Morgan's heart was too full. She did not even try to answer, but sat, with streaming eyes, gazing upon her child's face.

"Father, I dreamed something about you, while I slept to-day." Mary again turned to her father.

"What was it, dear?"

"I thought it was night, and that I was still sick. You promised not to go out again until I was well. But you did go out; and I thought you went over to Mr. Slade's tavern. When I knew this, I felt as strong as when I was well, and I got up and dressed myself, and started out after you. But I hadn't gone far, before I met Mr. Slade's great bull-dog, Nero, and he growled at me so dreadfully that I was frightened and ran back home. Then I started again, and went away round by Mr. Mason's. But there was Nero in the road, and this time he caught my dress in his mouth and tore a great piece out of the skirt. I ran back again, and he chased me all the way home. Just as I got to the door, I looked around, and there was Mr. Slade, setting Nero on me. As soon as I saw Mr. Slade, though he looked at me very wicked, I lost all my fear, and turning around, I walked past Nero, who showed his teeth, and growled as fiercely as ever, but didn't touch me. Then Mr. Slade tried to stop me. But I didn't mind him, and kept right on, until I came to the tavern, and there you stood in the door. And you were dressed so nice. You had on a new hat and a new coat; and your boots were new, and polished just like Judge Hammond's. I said—'O father! is this you?' And then you took me up in your arms and kissed me, and said— 'Yes, Mary, I am your real father. Not old Joe Morgan—but Mr. Morgan now.' It seemed all so strange, that I looked into the bar-room to see who was there. But it wasn't a bar-room any longer; but a store full of goods. The sign of the 'Sickle and Sheaf' was taken down; and over the door I now read your name, father. Oh! I was so glad, that I awoke—and then I cried all to myself, for it was only a dream."

The last words were said very mournfully, and with a drooping of Mary's lids, until the tear-gemmed lashes lay close upon her cheeks. Another period of deep silence followed—for the oppressed listeners gave no utterance to what was in their hearts. Feeling was too strong for speech. Nearly five minutes glided away, and then Mary whispered the name of her father, but without opening her eyes.

Morgan answered, and bent down his ear.

"You will only have mother left," she said—"only mother. And she cries so much when you are away,"

"I won't leave her, Mary, only when I go to work," said Morgan, whispering back to the child. "And I'll never go out at night any more."

"Yes; you promised me that."

"And I'll promise more."

"What, father?"

"Never to go into a tavern again."

"Never!"

"No, never. And I'll promise still more."

"Father?"

"Never to drink a drop of liquor as long as I live."

"Oh, father! dear, dear father!" And with a cry of joy Mary started up and flung herself upon his breast. Morgan drew his arms tightly around her, and sat for a long time, with his lips pressed to her cheek—while she lay against his bosom as still as death. As death? Yes; for, when the father unclasped his arms, the spirit of his child was with the angels of the resurrection!

It was my fourth evening in the bar-room of the "Sickle and Sheaf." The company was not large, nor in very gay spirits. All had heard of little Mary's illness; which followed so quickly on the blow from the tumbler, that none hesitated about connecting the one with the other. So regular had been the child's visits, and so gently exerted, yet powerful, her influence over her father, that most of the frequenters at the "Sickle and Sheaf" had felt for her a more than common interest; which the cruel treatment she received, and the subsequent illness, materially heightened.

"Joe Morgan hasn't turned up this evening," remarked some one.

"And isn't likely to for a while," was answered.

"Why not?" inquired the first speaker.

"They say, the man with the poker[6] is after him."

"Oh, dear! that's dreadful. It's the second or third chase, isn't it?"

"Yes."

"He'll be likely to catch him this time."

"I shouldn't wonder."

"Poor devil! It won't be much matter. His family will be a great deal better without him."

"It will be a blessing to them if he dies."

"Miserable, drunken wretch!" muttered Harvey Green, who was present. "He's only in the way of everybody. The sooner he's off, the better."

The landlord said nothing. He stood leaning across the bar, looking more sober than usual.

"That was rather an unlucky affair of yours, Simon. They say the child is going to die."

"Who says so?" Slade started, scowled, and threw a quick glance upon the speaker.

"Doctor Green."

"Nonsense! Doctor Green never said any such thing."

"Yes, he did, though."

"Who heard him?"

"I did."

"You did?"

"Yes."

"He wasn't in earnest?" A slight paleness overspread the countenance of the landlord.

"He was, though. They had an awful time there last night."

"Where?"

"At Joe Morgan's. Joe has the mania, and Mrs. Morgan was alone with him and her sick girl all night."

"He deserves to have it; that's all I've got to say." Slade tried to speak with a kind of rough indifference.

"That's pretty hard talk," said one of the company.

"I don't care if it is. It's the truth. What else could he expect?"

"A man like Joe is to be pitied," remarked the other.

"I pity his family," said Slade.

---

6 The devil with his pitchfork.

"Especially little Mary." The words were uttered tauntingly, and produced murmurs of satisfaction throughout the room.

Slade started back from where he stood, in an impatient manner, saying something that I did not hear.

"Look here, Simon, I heard some strong suggestions over at Lawyer Phillip's office to-day."

Slade turned his eyes upon the speaker.

"If that child should die, you'll probably have to stand a trial for manslaughter."

"No—girl-slaughter," said Harvey Green, with a cold, inhuman chuckle.

"But, I'm in earnest," said the other. "Mr. Phillips said that a case could be made out of it."

"It was only an accident, and all the lawyers in Christendom can't make anything more of it," remarked Green, taking the side of the landlord, and speaking with more gravity than before.

"Hardly an accident," was replied.

"He didn't throw at the girl."

"No matter. He threw a heavy tumbler at her father's head. The intention was to do an injury; and the law will not stop to make any nice discriminations in regard to the individual upon whom the injury was wrought. Moreover, who is prepared to say, that he didn't aim at the girl?"

"Any man who intimates such a thing is a cursed liar!" exclaimed the landlord, half maddened by the suggestion.

"I won't throw a tumbler at your head," coolly remarked the individual whose plain speaking had so irritated Simon Slade. "Throwing tumblers I never thought a very creditable kind of argument—though with some men, when cornered, it is a favorite mode of settling a question. Now, as for our friend the landlord, I am sorry to say, that his new business doesn't seem to have improved either his manners or his temper a great deal. As a miller, he was one of the best-tempered men in the world, and wouldn't have harmed a kitten. But, now, he can swear, and bluster, and throw glasses at people's heads, and all that sort of thing, with the best of brawling rowdies. I'm afraid he's taking lessons in a bad school—I am."

"I don't think you have any right to insult a man in his own house," answered Slade, in a voice dropped to a lower key than the one in which he had before spoken.

"I had no intention to insult you," said the other. "I was only speaking suppositiously, and in view of your position on a trial for manslaughter, when I suggested, that no one could prove, or say, that you didn't mean to strike little Mary, when you threw the tumbler."

"Well, I didn't mean to strike her: and I don't believe there is a man in this bar-room who thinks that I did—not one."

"I'm sure I do not," said the individual with whom he was in controversy. "Nor I"—

"Nor I"—went round the room.

"But, as I wished to set forth," was continued, "the case will not be so plain a one when it finds its way into court, and twelve men, to each of whom you may be a stranger, come to sit in judgment upon the act. The slightest twist in the evidence, the prepossessions of a witness, or the bad tact of the prosecution, may cause things to look so dark on your side as to leave you but little chance. For my part, if the child should die, I think your chances for a term in the state's prison are as eight to ten; and I should call that pretty close cutting."

I looked attentively at the man who said this, all the while he was speaking, but could not clearly make out whether he were altogether in earnest, or merely trying to worry the mind of Slade. That he was successful in accomplishing the latter, was very plain; for the landlord's countenance steadily lost color, and became overcast with alarm. With that evil delight which some men take in giving pain, others, seeing Slade's anxious looks, joined in the persecution, and soon made the landlord's case look black enough; and the landlord himself almost as frightened as a criminal just under arrest.

"It's bad business, and no mistake," said one.

"Yes, bad enough. I wouldn't be in his shoes for his coat," remarked another.

"For his coat? No, not for his whole wardrobe," said a third.

"Nor for the 'Sickle and Sheaf' thrown into the bargain," added a fourth.

"It will be a clear case of manslaughter, and no mistake. What is the penalty?"

"From two to ten years in the penitentiary," was readily answered.

"They'll give him five, I reckon."

"No—not more than two. It will be hard to prove malicious intention."

"I don't know that. I've heard him curse the girl and threaten her many a time. Haven't you?"

"Yes"—"Yes"—"I have, often," ran around the bar-room.

"You'd better hang me at once," said Slade, affecting to laugh.

At this moment, the door behind Slade opened, and I saw his wife's anxious face thrust in for a moment. She said something to her husband, who uttered a low ejaculation of surprise, and went out quickly.

"What's the matter now?" asked one of another.

"I shouldn't wonder if little Mary Morgan was dead," was suggested.

"I heard her say dead," remarked one who was standing near the bar.

"What's the matter, Frank?" inquired several voices, as the landlord's son came in through the door out of which his father had passed.

"Mary Morgan is dead," answered the boy.

"Poor child! Poor child!" sighed one, in genuine regret at the not unlooked for intelligence. "Her trouble is over."

And there was not one present, but Harvey Green, who did not utter some word of pity or sympathy. He shrugged his shoulders, and looked as much of contempt and indifference as he thought it prudent to express.

"See here, boys," spoke out one of the company, "can't we do something for poor Mrs. Morgan? Can't we make up a purse for her?"

"That's it," was quickly responded; "I'm good for three dollars; and there they are," drawing out the money and laying it upon the counter.

"And here are five to go with them," said I, quickly stepping forward, and placing a five dollar bill alongside of the first contribution.

"Here are five more," added a third individual And so it went on, until thirty dollars were paid down for the benefit of Mrs. Morgan.

"Into whose hands shall this be placed?" was next asked.

"Let me suggest Mrs. Slade," said I. "To my certain knowledge, she has been with Mrs. Morgan to-night. I know that she feels in her a true woman's interest."

"Just the person," was answered. "Frank, tell your mother we would like to see her. Ask her to step into the sitting-room."

In a few moments the boy came back, and said that his mother would see us in the next room, into which we all passed. Mrs. Slade stood near the table, on which burned a lamp.

I noticed that her eyes were red, and that there was on her countenance a troubled and sorrowful expression.

"We have just heard," said one of the company, "that little Mary Morgan is dead."

"Yes—it is too true," answered Mrs. Slade, mournfully. "I have just left there. Poor child! she has passed from an evil world."

"Evil it has indeed been to her," was remarked.

"You may well say that. And yet, amid all the evil, she has been an angel of mercy. Her last thought in dying was of her miserable father. For him, at any time, she would have laid down her life willingly."

"Her mother must be nearly broken-hearted. Mary is the last of her children."

"And yet the child's death may prove a blessing to her."

"How so?"

"Her father promised Mary, just at the last moment—solemnly promised her—that, henceforth, he would never taste liquor. That was all her trouble. That was the thorn in her dying pillow. But he plucked it out, and she went to sleep, lying against his heart. Oh, gentlemen! it was the most touching sight I ever saw."

All present seemed deeply moved.

"They are very poor and wretched" was said.

"Poor and miserable enough," answered Mrs. Slade.

"We have just been taking up a collection for Mrs. Morgan. Here is the money, Mrs. Slade—thirty dollars—we place it in your hands for her benefit. Do with it, for her, as you may see best."

"Oh, gentlemen!" What a quick gleam went over the face of Mrs. Slade. "I thank you, from my heart, in the name of that unhappy one, for this act of true benevolence. To you the sacrifice has been small; to her the benefit will be great indeed. A new life will, I trust, be commenced by her husband, and this timely aid will be something to rest upon, until he can get into better employment than he now has. Oh, gentlemen! let me urge on you, one and all, to make common cause in favor of Joe Morgan. His purposes are good now; he means to keep his promise to his dying child—means to reform his life. Let the good impulses that led to this act of relief further prompt you to watch over him, and, if you see him about going astray, to lead him kindly back into the right path. Never—oh! never encourage him to drink; but rather take the glass from his hand, if his own appetite lead him aside, and by all the persuasive influence you possess, induce him to go out from the place of temptation.

"Pardon my boldness in saying so much," added Mrs. Slade, recollecting herself, and coloring deeply as she did so. "My feelings have led me away."

And she took the money from the table where it had been placed, and retired toward the door.

"You have spoken well, madam," was answered. "And we thank you for reminding us of our duty."

"One word more—and forgive the earnest heart from which it comes "– said Mrs. Slade, in a voice that trembled on the words she uttered. "I cannot help speaking, gentlemen! Think if some of you be not entering the road wherein Joe Morgan has so long been walking. Save him, in heaven's name!—but see that ye do not yourselves become cast-always!"

As she said this, she glided through the door, and it closed after her.

"I don't know what her husband would say to that," was remarked after a few moments of surprised silence.

"I don't care what *he* would say; but I'll tell you what *I* will say," spoke out a man whom I had several times noticed as rather a free tippler. "The old lady has given us capital advice, and I mean to take it, for one. I'm going to try to save Joe Morgan, and—myself too. I've already entered the road she referred to; but I'm going to turn back. So good-night to you all; and if Simon Slade gets no more of my sixpences, he may thank his wife for it—God bless her?"

And the man drew his hat with a jerk over his forehead, and left immediately.

This seemed the signal for dispersion, and all retired—not by way of the bar-room, but out into the hall, and through the door leading upon the porch that ran along in front of the house. Soon after the bar was closed, and a dead silence reigned throughout the house. I saw no more of Slade that night. Early in the morning, I left Cedarville; the landlord looked a very sober when he bade me good-by through the stage-door, and wished me a pleasant journey.

Night the Fifth

Some of the Consequences of Tavern-Keeping

NEARLY five years glided away before business again called me to Cedarville. I knew little of what passed there in the interval, except that Simon Slade had actually been indicted for manslaughter, in causing the death of Morgan's child. He did not stand a trial, however, Judge Lyman having used his influence, successfully, in getting the indictment quashed. The judge, some people said, interested himself in Slade more than was just seemly— especially, as he had, on several occasions, in the discharge of his official duties, displayed what seemed an over-righteous indignation against individuals arraigned for petty offences. The impression made upon me by Judge Lyman had not been favorable. He seemed a cold, selfish, scheming man of the world. That he was an unscrupulous politician, was plain to me, in a single evening's observation of his sayings and doings among the common herd of a village bar-room.

As the stage rolled, with a gay flourish of our driver's bugle, into the village, I noted here and there familiar objects, and marked the varied evidences of change. Our way was past the elegant residence and grounds of Judge Hammond, the most beautiful and highly cultivated in Cedarville. At least, such it was regarded at the time of my previous visit. But, the moment my eyes rested upon the dwelling and its varied surroundings, I perceived an altered aspect. Was it the simple work of time? or, had familiarity with other and more elegantly arranged suburban homes, marred this in my eyes by involuntary contrast? Or had the hand of cultivation really been stayed, and the marring fingers of neglect suffered undisturbed to trace on every thing disfiguring characters?

Such questions were in my thoughts, when I saw a man in the large portico of the dwelling, the ample columns of which, capped in rich Corinthian, gave the edifice the aspect of a Grecian temple. He stood leaning against one of the columns—his hat off, and his long gray hair thrown back and resting lightly on his neck and shoulders. His head was bent down upon his breast, and he seemed in deep abstraction. Just as the coach swept by, he looked up, and in the changed features I recognized Judge Hammond. His complexion was still florid, but his face had grown thin, and his eyes were sunken. Trouble was written in every lineament. Trouble? How inadequately does the word express my meaning! Ah! at a single glance, what a volume of suffering was opened to the gazer's eye. Not lightly had the foot of time rested there, as if treading on odorous flowers, but heavily, and with iron-shod heel. This I saw at a glance; and then, only the image of the man was present to my inner vision, for the swiftly rolling stage-coach had borne me onward past the altered home of the wealthiest denizen of Cedarville. In a few minutes our driver reined up before the " 'Sickle and Sheaf," and as I stepped to the ground, a rotund, coarse, red-faced man, whom I failed to recognize as Simon Slade until he spoke, grasped my hand, and pronounced my name. I could not but contrast, in thought, his appearance with what it was when I first saw him, some six years previously; nor help saying to myself—

"So much for tavern-keeping!"

As marked a change was visible everywhere In and around the "Sickle and Sheaf." It, too, had grown larger by additions of wings and rooms; but it had also grown coarser in growing larger. When built, all the doors were painted white, and the shutters green, giving to the house a neat, even tasteful appearance. But the white and green had given place to a dark, dirty brown, that to my eyes was particularly unattractive. The bar-room had been extended, and now a polished brass rod, or railing, embellished the counter, and sundry ornamental attractions had been given to the shelving behind the bar—such as mirrors, gilding, etc. Pictures, too, were hung upon the walls, or more accurately speaking, coarse colored lithographs, the subjects of which, if not really obscene, were flashing, or vulgar. In the sitting-room, next to the bar, I noticed little change of objects, but much in their condition. The carpet, chairs, and tables were the same in fact, but far from being the same in appearance. The room had a close, greasy odor, and looked as if it had not been thoroughly swept and dusted for a week.

A smart young Irishman was in the bar, and handed me the book in which passenger's names were registered. After I had recorded mine, he directed my trunk to be carried to the room designated as the one I was to occupy. I followed the porter, who conducted me to the chamber which had been mine at previous visits. Here, too, were evidences of change; but not for the better. Then the room was as sweet and clean as it could be; the sheets and pillow-cases as white as snow, and the furniture shining with polish. Now all was dusty and dingy, the air foul, and the bed-linen scarcely whiter than tow.[7] No curtain made softer the light as it came through the window; nor would the shutters entirely keep out the glare, for several of the slats were broken. A feeling of disgust came over me, at the close smell and foul appearance of everything; so, after washing my hands and face, and brushing the dust from my clothes, I went down-stairs. The sitting-room was scarcely more attractive than my chamber; so I went out upon the porch and took a chair. Several loungers were here; hearty, strong-looking, but lazy fellows, who, if they had anything to do, liked idling better than working. One of them had leaned his chair back against the wall of the house, and was swinging his legs with a half circular motion, and humming "Old Folks at Home." Another set astride of his chair, with his face turned toward, and his chin resting upon, the back. He was in too lazy a condition of body and mind for motion or singing. A third had slidden down in his chair, until he sat on his back, while his feet were elevated above his head, and resting against one of the pillars that supported the porch; while a fourth lay stretched out on a bench, sleeping, his hat over his face to protect him from buzzing and biting flies.

Though all but the sleeping man eyed me inquisitively, as I took my place among them, not one changed his position. The rolling of eyeballs cost but little exertion; and with that effort they were contented.

---

7 Light brown.

"Hallo! who's that?" one of these loungers suddenly exclaimed, as a man went swiftly by in a light sulky; and he started up, and gazed down the road, seeking to penetrate the cloud of dust which the fleet rider had swept up with hoofs and wheels.

"I didn't see." The sleeping man aroused himself, rubbed his eyes, and gazed along the road.

"Who was it, Matthew?" The Irish bar-keeper now stood in the door.

"Willy Hammond," was answered by Matthew.

"Indeed! Is that his new three hundred dollar horse?"

"Yes."

"My! but he's a screamer!"

"Isn't he! Most as fast as his young master."

"Hardly," said one of the men, laughing. "I don't think anything in creation can beat Hammond. He goes it, with a perfect rush."

"Doesn't he! Well; you may say what you please of him, he's as good-hearted a fellow as ever walked; and generous to a fault."

"His old dad will agree with you in the last remark," said Matthew.

"No doubt of that, for he has to stand the bills," was answered.

"Yes, whether he will or no, for I rather think Willy has, somehow or other, got the upper hand of him."

"In what way?"

"It's Hammond and Son, over at the mill and distillery."

"I know; but what of that!"

"Willy was made the business man—ostensibly—in order, as the old man thought, to get him to feel the responsibility of the new position, and thus tame him down."

"Tame *him* down! Oh, dear! It will take more than business to do that. The curb was applied too late."

"As the old gentleman has already discovered, I'm thinking, to his sorrow."

"He never comes here any more; does he, Matthew?"

"Who?"

"Judge Hammond."

"Oh, dear, no. He and Slade had all sorts of a quarrel about a year ago, and he's never darkened our doors since."

"It was something about Willy and——." The speaker did not mention any name, but winked knowingly and tossed his head toward the entrance of the house, to indicate some member of Slade's family.

"I believe so."

"D'ye think Willy really likes her?"

Matthew shrugged his shoulders, but made no answer.

"She's a nice girl," was remarked in an under tone, "and good enough for Hammond's son any day; though, if she were my daughter, I'd rather see her in Jericho[8] than fond of his company."

"He'll have plenty of money to give her. She can live like a queen."

"For how long?"

"Hush!" came from the lips of Matthew. "There she is now."

---

8 Famous doomed city of the Old Testament (Joshua 5–6).

I looked up, and saw at a short distance from the house, and approaching, a young lady, in whose sweet, modest face, I at once recognized Flora Slade. Five years had developed her into a beautiful woman. In her alone, of all that appertained to Simon Slade, there was no deterioration. Her eyes were as mild and pure as when first I met her at gentle sixteen, and her father said "My daughter," with such a mingling of pride and affection in his tone. She passed near where I was sitting, and entered the house. A closer view showed me some marks of thought and suffering; but they only heightened the attractions of her face. I failed not to observe the air of respect with which all returned her slight nod and smile of recognition.

"She's a nice girl, and no mistake—the flower of this flock," was said, as soon as she passed into the house.

"Too good for Willy Hammond, in my opinion," said Matthew. "Clever and generous as people call him."

"Just my opinion," was responded. "She's as pure and good, almost, as an angel; and he?—I can tell you what—he's not the clear thing. He knows a little too much of the world—on its bad side, I mean."

The appearance of Slade put an end to this conversation. A second observation of his person and countenance did not remove the first unfavorable impression. His face had grown decidedly bad in expression, as well as gross and sensual. The odor of his breath, as he took a chair close to where I was sitting, was that of one who drank habitually and freely; and the red, swimming eyes evidenced, too surely, a rapid progress toward the sad condition of a confirmed inebriate. There was, too, a certain thickness of speech, that gave another corroborating sign of evil progress.

"Have you seen anything of Frank this afternoon?" He inquired of Matthew, after we had passed a few words.

"Nothing," was the bar-keeper's answer.

"I saw him with Tom Wilkins as I came over," said one of the men who was sitting in the porch.

"What was he doing with Tom Wilkins?" said Slade, in a fretted tone of voice. "He doesn't seem very choice of his company."

"They were gunning."

"Gunning!"

"Yes. They both had fowling-pieces. I wasn't near enough to ask where they were going."

This information disturbed Slade a good deal. After muttering to himself a little while, he started up and went into the house.

"And I could have told him a little more, had I been so inclined," said the individual who mentioned the fact that Frank was with Tom Wilkins.

"What more?" inquired Matthew.

"There was a buggy in the case; and a champagne basket. What the latter contained you can easily guess."

"Whose buggy?"

"I don't know anything about the buggy; but if 'Lightfoot' doesn't sink in value a hundred dollars or so before sundown, call me a false prophet."

"Oh, no," said Matthew, incredulously. "Frank wouldn't do an outrageous thing like that. Lightfoot won't be in a condition to drive for a month to come."

"I don't care. She's out now; and the way she was putting it down when I saw her, would have made a locomotive look cloudy."

"Where did he get her?" was inquired.

"She's been in the six-acre field, over by Mason's Bridge, for the last week or so," Matthew answered. "Well; all I have to say," he added, "is that Frank ought to be slung up and well horse-whipped. I never saw such a young rascal. He cares for no good, and fears no evil. He's the worst boy I ever saw."

"It would hardly do for you to call him a boy to his face," said one of the men, laughing.

"I don't have much to say to him in any way," replied Matthew, "for I know very well, that if we ever do get into a regular quarrel, there'll be a hard time of it. The same house will not hold us afterward—that's certain. So I steer clear of the young reprobate."

"I wonder his father don't put him to some business," was remarked. "The idle life he now leads will be his ruin."

"He was behind the bar for a year or two."

"Yes; and was smart at mixing a glass—but—"

"Was himself becoming too good a customer?"

"Precisely. He got drunk as a fool before reaching his fifteenth year."

"Good gracious!" I exclaimed, involuntarily.

"It's true, sir," said the last speaker, turning to me, "I never saw anything like it. And this wasn't all bar-room talk, which, as you may know, isn't the most refined and virtuous in the world. I wouldn't like my son to hear much of it. Frank was always an eager listener to everything that was said, and in a very short time became an adept in slang and profanity. I'm no saint myself; but it's often made my blood run cold to hear him swear."

"I pity his mother," said I; for my thought turned naturally to Mrs. Slade.

"You may well do that," was answered. "I doubt if Cedarville holds a sadder heart. It was a dark day for her, let me tell you, when Simon Slade sold his mill and built this tavern. She was opposed to it in the beginning."

"I have inferred as much."

"I know it," said the man. "My wife has been intimate with her for years. Indeed, they have always been like sisters. I remember very well her coming to our house, about the time the mill was sold, and crying about it as if her heart would break. She saw nothing but trouble and sorrow ahead. Tavern-keeping she had always regarded as a low business; and the change from a respectable miller to a lazy tavern-keeper, as she expressed it, was presented to her mind as something disgraceful. I remember, very well, trying to argue the point with her—assuming that it was quite as respectable to keep tavern as to do anything else; but I might as well have talked to the wind. She was always a pleasant, hopeful, cheerful woman before that time; but, really, I don't think I've seen a true smile on her face since."

"That was a great deal for a man to lose," said I.

"What?" he inquired, not clearly understanding me.

"The cheerful face of his wife."

"The face was but an index of her heart," said he.

"So much the worse."

"True enough for that. Yes, it was a great deal to lose."

"What has he gained that will make up for this?"

The man shrugged his shoulders.

"What has he gained?" I repeated. "Can you figure it up?"

"He's a richer man, for one thing."

"Happier?"

There was another shrug of the shoulders. "I wouldn't like to say that."

"How much richer?"

"Oh, a great deal. Somebody was saying, only yesterday, that he couldn't be worth less than thirty thousand dollars."

"Indeed? So much."

"Yes."

"How has he managed to accumulate so rapidly?"

"His bar has a large run of custom. And, you know, that pays wonderfully."

"He must have sold a great deal of liquor in six years."

"And he has. I don't think I'm wrong in saying, that in the six years which have gone by since the 'Sickle and Sheaf' was opened, more liquor has been drank than in the previous twenty years."

"Say forty," remarked a man who had been a listener to what we said.

"Let it be forty then," was the according answer.

"How comes this?" I inquired. "You had a tavern here before the 'Sickle and Sheaf' was opened."

"I know we had, and several places besides, where liquor was sold. But, everybody far and near knew Simon Slade the miller, and everybody liked him. He was a good miller, and a cheerful, social, chatty sort of a man, putting everybody in a good humor who came near him. So it became the talk everywhere, when he built this house, which he fitted up nicer than anything that had been seen in these parts. Judge Hammond, Judge Lyman, Lawyer Wilson, and all the big-bugs of the place at once patronized the new tavern; and, of course, everybody else did the same. So, you can easily see how he got such a run."

"It was thought, in the beginning," said I, "that the new tavern was going to do wonders for Cedarville."

"Yes," answered the man laughing, "and so it has."

"In what respect?"

"Oh, in many. It has made some men richer, and some poorer."

"Who has it made poorer?"

"Dozens of people. You may always take it for granted, when you see a tavern-keeper, who has a good run at his bar, getting rich, that a great many people are getting poor."

"How so?" I wished to hear in what way the man, who was himself, as was plain to see, a good customer at somebody's bar, reasoned on the subject.

"He does not add to the general wealth. He produces nothing. He takes money from his customers, but gives them no article of value in return—nothing that can be called property, personal or real. He is just so much richer and they just so much poorer for the exchange. Is it not so?"

I readily assented to the position as true, and then said—

"Who, in particular, is poorer?"

"Judge Hammond, for one."

"Indeed! I thought the advance in his property, in consequence of the building of this tavern, was so great, that he was reaping a rich pecuniary harvest."

"There was a slight advance in property along the street after the 'Sickle and Sheaf' was opened, and Judge Hammond was benefited thereby. Interested parties made a good deal of noise about it; but it didn't amount to much, I believe."

"What has caused the judge to grow poorer?"

"The opening of this tavern, as I just said."

"In what way did it affect him?"

"He was among Slade's warmest supporters, as soon as he felt the advance in the price of building lots, called him one of the most enterprising men in Cedarville—a real benefactor to the place—and all that stuff. To set a good example of patronage, he came over every day and took his glass of brandy, and encouraged everybody else that he could influence to do the same. Among those who followed his example was his son Willy. There was not, let me tell you, in all the country for twenty miles around, a finer young man than Willy, nor one of so much promise, when this man-trap"—he let his voice fall, and glanced around, as he thus designated Slade's tavern—"was opened; and now, there is not one dashing more recklessly along the road to ruin. When too late, his father saw that his son was corrupted, and that the company he kept was of a dangerous character. Two reasons led him to purchase Slade's old mill, and turn it into a factory and a distillery. Of course, he had to make a heavy outlay for additional buildings, machinery, and distilling apparatus. The reasons influencing him were the prospect of realizing a large amount of money, especially in distilling, and the hope of saving Willy, by getting him closely engaged and interested in business. To accomplish, more certainly, the latter end, he unwisely transferred to his son, as his own capital, twenty thousand dollars, and then formed with him a regular copartnership—giving Willy an active business control.

"But the experiment, sir," added the man, emphatically, "has proved a failure. I heard yesterday, that both mill and distillery were to be shut up, and offered for sale."

"They did not prove as money-making as was anticipated?"

"No, not under Willy Hammond's management. He had made too many bad acquaintances—men who clung to him because he had plenty of money at his command, and spent it as freely as water. One-half of his time he was away from the mill, and while there, didn't half attend to business. I've heard it said—and I don't much doubt its truth—that he's squandered his twenty thousand dollars, and a great deal more besides."

"How is that possible?"

"Well; people talk, and not always at random. There's been a man staying here, most of his time, for the last four or five years, named Green. He does not do any thing, and don't seem to have any friends in the neighborhood. Nobody knows where he came from, and he is not at all communicative on that head himself. Well, this man became acquainted with young Hammond after Willy got to visiting the bar here, and attached himself to him at once. They have, to all appearance, been fast friends ever since; riding about, or going off on gunning or fishing excursions almost every day, and secluding themselves somewhere nearly every evening. That man, Green, sir, it is whispered, is a gambler; and I believe it. Granted, and there is no longer a mystery as to what Willy does with his own and his father's money."

I readily assented to this view of the case.

"And so assuming that Green is a gambler," said I, "he has grown richer, in consequence of the opening of a new and more attractive tavern in Cedarville."

"Yes, and Cedarville is so much the poorer for all his gains; for I've never heard of his buying a foot of ground, or in any way encouraging productive industry. He's only a blood-sucker."

"It is worse than the mere abstraction of money," I remarked; "he corrupts his victims, at the same time that he robs them."

"True."

"Willy Hammond may not be his only victim," I suggested.

"Nor is he, in my opinion. I've been coming to this bar, nightly, for a good many years—a sorry confession for a man to make, I must own," he added, with a slight tinge of shame; "but so it is. Well, as I was saying, I've been coming to this bar, nightly, for a good many years, and I generally see all that is going on around me. Among the regular visitors are at least half a dozen young men, belonging to our best families—who have been raised with care, and well educated. That their presence here is unknown to their friends, I am quite certain—or, at least, unknown and unsuspected by some of them. They do not drink a great deal yet; but all try a glass or two. Toward nine o'clock, often at an earlier hour, you will see one and another of them go quietly out of the bar, through the sitting-room, preceded, or soon followed, by Green and Slade. At any hour of the night, up to one or two, and sometimes three o'clock, you can see light streaming through the rent in a curtain drawn before a particular window, which I know to be in the room of Harvey Green. These are facts, sir; and you can draw your own conclusion. I think it a very serious matter."

"Why does Slade go out with these young men?" I inquired. "Do you think he gambles also?"

"If he isn't a kind of a stool-pigeon for Harvey Green, then I'm mistaken again."

"Hardly. He cannot, already, have become so utterly unprincipled."

"It's a bad school, sir, this tavern-keeping," said the man.

"I readily grant you that."

"And it's nearly seven years since he commenced to take lessons. A great deal may be learned, sir, of good or evil, in seven years, especially if any interest be taken in the studies."

"True."

"And it's true in this case, you may depend upon it. Simon Slade is not the man he was, seven years ago. Anybody with half an eye can see that. He's grown selfish, grasping, unscrupulous, and passionate. There could hardly be a greater difference between men than exists between Simon Slade the tavern-keeper, and Simon Slade the miller."

"And intemperate, also?" I suggested.

"He's beginning to take a little too much," was answered.

"In that case, he'll scarcely be as well off five years hence as he is now."

"He's at the top of the wheel, some of us think."

"What has led to this opinion?"

"He's beginning to neglect his house, for one thing."

"A bad sign."

"And there is another sign. Heretofore, he has always been on hand, with the cash, when desirable property went off, under forced sale, at a bargain. In the last three or four months, several great sacrifices have been made, but Simon Slade showed no inclination to buy. Put this fact against another,—week before last, he sold a house and lot in the town for five hundred dollars less than he paid for them, a year ago—and for just that sum less than their true value."

"How came that?" I inquired.

"Ah! there's the question! He wanted money; though for what purpose he has not intimated to any one, as far as I can learn."

"What do you think of it?"

"Just this. He and Green have been hunting together in times past; but the professed gambler's instincts are too strong to let him spare even his friend in evil. They have commenced playing one against the other."

"Ah! you think so?"

"I do; and if I conjecture rightly, Simon Slade will be a poorer man, in a year from this time, than he is now."

Here our conversation was interrupted. Some one asked my talkative friend to go and take a drink, and he, nothing loath, left me without ceremony.

Very differently served was the supper I partook of on that evening, from the one set before me on the occasion of my first visit to the "Sickle and Sheaf." The table-cloth was not merely soiled, but offensively dirty; the plates, cups, and saucers, dingy and sticky; the knives and forks unpolished; and the food of a character to satisfy the appetite with a very few mouthfuls. Two greasy-looking Irish girls waited on the table, at which neither landlord nor landlady presided. I was really hungry when the supper-bell rang; but the craving of my stomach soon ceased in the atmosphere of the dining-room, and I was the first to leave the table.

Soon after the lamps were lighted, company began to assemble in the spacious bar-room, where were comfortable seats, with tables, newspapers, backgammon boards, dominoes, etc. The first act of nearly every one who came in was to call for a glass of liquor; and sometimes the same individual drank two or three times in the course of half an hour, on the invitation of new comers who were convivially inclined.

Most of those who came in were strangers to me. I was looking from face to face to see if any of the old company were present, when one countenance struck me as familiar. I was studying it, in order, if possible, to identify the person, when some one addressed him as "Judge."

Changed as the face was, I now recognized it as that of Judge Lyman. Five years had marred that face terribly. It seemed twice the former size; and all its bright expression was gone. The thickened and protruding eyelids half closed the leaden eyes, and the swollen lips and cheeks gave to his countenance a look of all-predominating sensuality. True manliness had bowed itself in debasing submission to the bestial. He talked loudly, and with a pompous dogmatism—mainly on political subjects—but talked only from memory; for any one could see, that thought came into but feeble activity. And yet, derationalized, so to speak, as he was, through drink, he had been chosen a representative in Congress, at the previous election, on the anti-temperance ticket, and by a very handsome majority. He was the rum candidate; and the rum interest, aided by the easily swayed "indifferents," swept aside the claims of law, order, temperance, and good morals; and the district from which he was chosen as a National Legislator sent him up to the National Councils, and said in the act—"Look upon him we have chosen as our representative, and see in him a type of our principles, our quality, and our condition as a community."

Judge Lyman, around whom a little circle soon gathered, was very severe on the temperance party, which, for two years, had opposed his election, and which, at the last struggle, showed itself to be a rapidly growing organization. During the canvass, a paper was published by this party, in which his personal habits, character, and moral principles were discussed in the freest manner, and certainly not in a way to elevate him in the estimation of men whose opinion was of any value.

It was not much to be wondered at, that he assumed to think temperance issues at the polls were false issues; and that when temperance men sought to tamper with elections, the liberties of the people were in danger; nor that he pronounced the whole body of temperance men as selfish schemers and canting hypocrites.

"The next thing we will have," he exclaimed, warming with his theme, and speaking so loud that his voice sounded throughout the room, and arrested every one's attention, "will be laws to fine any man who takes a chew of tobacco, or lights a cigar. Touch the liberties of the people in the smallest particular, and all guarantees are gone. The Stamp Act, against which our noble forefathers rebelled, was a light measure of oppression to that contemplated by these worse than fanatics."

"You are right there, judge; right for once in your life, if you (hic) were never right before!" exclaimed a battered looking specimen of humanity, who stood near the speaker, slapping Judge Lyman on the shoulder familiarly as he spoke. "There's no telling what they will do. There's (hic) my old uncle Josh Wilson, who's been keeper of the Poor-house these ten years. Well, they're going to turn him out, if ever they get the upper hand in Bolton county."

"If? That word involves a great deal, Harry!" said Lyman. "We mus'n't let them get the upper hand. Every man has a duty to perform to his country in this matter, and every one must do his duty. But what have they got against your Uncle Joshua? What has he been doing to offend this righteous party?"

"They've nothing against him, (hic) I believe. Only, they say, they're not going to have a Poor-house in the county at all."

"What! Going to turn the poor wretches out to starve?" said one.

"Oh no! (hic)," and the fellow grinned, half shrewdly and half maliciously, as he answered —"no, not that. But, when they carry the day, there'll be no need of Poor-houses. At least, that's their talk—and I guess maybe there's something in it, for I never knew a man to go to the Poor-house, who hadn't (hic) rum to blame for his poverty. But, you see, I'm interested in this matter. I go for keeping up the Poor-house (hic); for I guess I'm travelling that road, and I shouldn't like to get to the last milestone (hic) and find no snug quarters— no Uncle Josh. You're safe for one vote, anyhow, old chap, on next election day!" And the man's broad hand slapped the member's shoulder again. "Huzza for the rummies! That's (hic) the ticket! Harry Grimes never deserts his friends. True as steel!"

"You're a trump!" returned Judge Lyman, with low familiarity. "Never fear about the Poor-house and Uncle Josh. They're all safe."

"But look here, judge," resumed the man. "It isn't only the Poor-house, the jail is to go next."

"Indeed!"

"Yes, that's their talk; and I guess they ain't far out of the way neither. What takes men to jail? You can tell us something about that, judge, for you've jugged a good many in your time. Didn't pretty much all of 'em drink rum? (hic.)"

But the judge answered nothing.

"Silence (hic) gives consent," resumed Grimes. "And they say more; once give 'em the upper hand—and they're confident of beating us—and the Court-house will be to let. As for judges and lawyers, they'll starve, or go into some better business. So you see, (hic) judge, your liberties are in danger. But fight hard, old fellow; and if you must die, (hic) die game!"

How well Judge Lyman relished this mode of presenting the case, was not very apparent; he was too good a politician and office-seeker, to show any feeling on the subject, and thus endanger a vote. Harry Grimes' vote counted one, and a single vote, sometimes, gained or lost an election.

"One of their gags," he said, laughing. "But I'm too old a stager not to see the flimsiness of such pretensions. Poverty and crime have their origin in the corrupt heart, and their foundations are laid long and long before the first step is taken on the road to inebriety. It is easy to promise results; for only the few look at causes, and trace them to their effects."

"HUZZA FOR THE RUMMIES! THAT'S THE TICKET!"

"Huzza for the Rummies! That's the ticket!"

"Rum and ruin, (hic). Are they not cause and effect?" asked Grimes.

"Sometimes they are," was the half extorted answer.

"Oh, Green, is that you?" exclaimed the judge, as Harvey Green came in with a soft cat-like step. He was, evidently, glad of a chance to get rid of his familiar friend and elector.

I turned my eyes upon the man, and read his face closely. It was unchanged. The same cold, sinister eye; the same chiselled mouth, so firm now, and now yielding so elastically; the same smile "from the teeth outward"—the same lines that revealed his heart's deep, dark selfishness. If he had indulged in drink during the five intervening years, it had not corrupted his blood, nor added thereto a single degree of heat.

"Have you seen anything of Hammond this evening?" asked Judge Lyman.

"I saw him an hour or two ago," answered Green.

"How does he like his new horse?"

"He's delighted with him."

"What was the price?"

"Three hundred dollars."

"Indeed!"

The judge had already arisen, and he and Green were now walking side by side across the bar-room floor.

"I want to speak a word with you," I heard Lyman say.

And then the two went out together. I saw no more of them during the evening.

Not long afterward, Willy Hammond came in. Ah! there was a sad change here; a change that in no way belied the words of Matthew the bar-keeper. He went up to the bar, and I heard him ask for Judge Lyman. The answer was in so low a voice, that it did not reach my ear.

With a quick, nervous motion, Hammond threw his hand toward a row of decanters on the shelf behind the bar-keeper, who immediately set one of them containing brandy before him. From this he poured a tumbler half full, and drank it off at a single draught, unmixed with water.

He then asked some further question, which I could not hear, manifesting, as it appeared, considerable excitement of mind. In answering him, Matthew glanced his eyes upward, as if indicating some room in the house. The young man then retired, hurriedly, through the sitting-room.

"What's the matter with Willy Hammond to-night?" asked some one of the bar-keeper. "Who's he after in such a hurry?"

"He wants to see Judge Lyman," replied Matthew.

"Oh!"

"I guess they're after no good," was remarked.

"Not much, I'm afraid."

Two young men, well dressed, and with faces marked by intelligence, came in at the moment, drank at the bar, chatted a little while familiarly with the bar-keeper, and then quietly disappeared through the door leading into the sitting-room. I met the eyes of the man with whom I had talked during the afternoon, and his knowing wink brought to mind his suggestion, that in one of the upper rooms gambling went on nightly, and that some of the most promising young men of the town had been drawn, through the bar attraction, into this vortex of ruin. I felt a shudder creeping along my nerves.

The conversation that now went on among the company was of such an obscene and profane character that, in disgust, I went out. The night was clear, the air soft, and the moon shining down brightly. I walked for some time in the porch, musing on what I had seen and heard; while a constant stream of visitors came pouring into the bar-room. Only a few of these remained. The larger portion went in quickly, took their glass, and then left, as if to avoid observation as much as possible.

Soon after I commenced walking in the porch, I noticed an elderly lady go slowly by, who, in passing, slightly paused, and evidently tried to look through the bar-room door. The pause was but for an instant. In less than ten minutes she came back, again stopped—this time longer—and again moved of slowly, until she passed out of sight. I was yet thinking about her, when, on lifting my eyes from the ground, she was advancing along the road, but a few rods distant. I almost started at seeing her, for there no longer remained a doubt on my mind, that she was some trembling, heart-sick mother, in search of an erring son, whose feet were in dangerous paths. Seeing me, she kept on, though lingeringly. She went but a short distance before returning; and this time, she moved in closer to the house, and reached a position that enabled her eyes to range through a large portion of the bar-room. A nearer inspection appeared to satisfy her. She retired with quicker steps; and did not again return during the evening.

Ah! what a commentary upon the uses of an attractive tavern was here! My heart ached, as I thought of all that unknown mother had suffered; and, was doomed to suffer. I could not shut out the image of her drooping form as I lay upon my pillow that night; she even haunted me in my dreams.

Night the Sixth

More Consequences

THE landlord did not make his appearance on the next morning until nearly ten o'clock; and then he looked like a man who had been on a debauch. It was eleven before Harvey Green came down. Nothing about him indicated the smallest deviation from the most orderly habit. Clean shaved, with fresh linen, and a face every line of which was smoothed into calmness, he looked as if he had slept soundly on a quiet conscience, and now hailed the new day with a tranquil spirit.

The first act of Slade was to go behind the bar and take a stiff glass of brandy and water; the first act of Green, to order beefsteak and coffee for his breakfast. I noticed the meeting between the two men, on the appearance of Green. There was a slight reserve on the part of Green, and an uneasy embarrassment on the part of Slade. Not even the ghost of a smile was visible in either countenance. They spoke a few words together, and then separated as if from a sphere of mutual repulsion. I did not observe them again in company during the day.

"There's trouble over at the mill," was remarked by a gentleman with whom I had some business transactions in the afternoon. He spoke to a person who sat in his office.

"Ah! what's the matter?" said the other.

"All the hands were discharged at noon, and the mill shut down."

"How comes that?"

"They've been losing money from the start."

"Rather bad practice, I should say."

"It involves some bad practices, no doubt."

"On Willy's part?"

"Yes. He is reported to have squandered the means placed in his hands, after a shameless fashion."

"Is the loss heavy?"

"So it is said."

"How much?"

"Reaching to thirty or forty thousand dollars. But this is rumor, and, of course, an exaggeration."

"Of course. No such loss as that could have been made. But what was done with the money? How could Willy have spent it. He dashes about a great deal; buys fast horses, drinks rather freely, and all that; but thirty or forty thousand dollars couldn't escape in this way."

At the moment a swift trotting horse, bearing a light sulky and a man, went by.

"There goes young Hammond's three hundred dollar animal," said the last speaker.

It was Willy Hammond's yesterday. But there has been a change of ownership since then; I happen to know."

"Indeed."

"Yes. The man Green, who has been loafing about Cedarville for the last few years—after no good, I can well believe—came into possession to-day."

"Ah? Willy must be very fickle-minded. Does the possession of a coveted object so soon bring satiety?"

"There is something not clearly understood about the transaction. I saw Mr. Hammond during the forenoon, and he looked terribly distressed."

"The embarrassed condition of things at the mill readily accounts for this."

"True; but I think there are causes of trouble beyond the mere embarrassments."

"The dissolute, spendthrift habits of his son," was suggested. "These are sufficient to weigh down the father's spirits,—to bow him to the very dust."

"To speak out plainly," said the other, "I am afraid that the young man adds another vice to that of drinking and idleness."

"What?"

"Gaming."

"No!"

"There is little doubt of it in my mind. And it is further my opinion, that his fine horse, for which he paid three hundred dollars only a few days ago, has passed into the hands of this man Green, in payment of a debt contracted at the gaming table."

"You shock me. Surely, there can be no grounds for such a belief."

"I have, I am sorry to say, the gravest reasons for what I allege. That Green is a professional gambler, who was attracted here by the excellent company that assembled at the 'Sickle and Sheaf' in the beginning of the lazy miller's pauper-making experiment, I do not in the least question. Grant this, and take into account the fact that young Hammond has been much in his company, and you have sufficient cause for the most disastrous effects."

"If this be really so," observed the gentleman, over whose face a shadow of concern darkened, then Willy Hammond may not be his only victim."

"And is not, you may rest assured. If rumor be true, other of our promising young men are being drawn into the whirling circles that narrow toward a vortex of ruin."

In corroboration of this, I mentioned the conversation I had held with one of the frequenters of Slade's bar-room, on this very subject; and also what I had myself observed on the previous evening.

The man, who had until now been sitting quietly in a chair, started up, exclaiming as he did so—

"Merciful heaven! I never dreamed of this! Whose sons are safe?"

"No man's," was the answer of the gentleman in whose office we were sitting—"No man's—while there are such open doors to ruin as you may find at the 'Sickle and Sheaf.' Did not you vote the anti-temperance ticket at the last election?"

"I did," was the answer; "and from principle."

"On what were your principles based?" was inquired.

"On the broad foundations of civil liberty."

"The liberty to do good or evil, just as the individual may choose?"

"I would not like to say that. There are certain evils against which there can be no legislation that would not do harm. No civil power in this country has the right to say what a citizen shall eat or drink."

"But may not the people, in any community, pass laws, through their delegated lawmakers, restraining evil-minded persons from injuring the common good?"

"Oh, certainly—certainly."

"And are you prepared to affirm, that a drinking-shop, where young men are corrupted—ay, destroyed, body and soul—does not work an injury to the common good?"

"Ah! but there must be houses of public entertainment."

"No one denies this. But can that be a really Christian community which provides for the moral debasement of strangers, at the same time that it entertains them? Is it necessary that, in giving rest and entertainment to the traveler, we also lead him into temptation?"

"Yes—but—but—it is going too far to legislate on what we are to eat and drink. It is opening too wide a door for fanatical oppression. We must inculcate temperance as a right principle. We must teach our children the evils of intemperance, and send them out into the world as practical teachers of order, virtue, and sobriety. If we do this, the reform becomes radical, and in a few years there will be no bar-rooms, for none will crave the fiery poison."

"Of little value, my friend, will be, in far too many cases, your precepts, if temptation invites our sons at almost every step of their way through life. Thousands have fallen, and thousands are now tottering, soon to fall. Your sons are not safe; nor are mine. We cannot tell the day nor the hour when they may weakly yield to the solicitation of some companion, and enter the wide open door of ruin. And are we wise and good citizens to commission men to do the evil work of enticement? To encourage them to get gain in corrupting and destroying our children? To hesitate over some vague ideal of human liberty, when the sword is among us, slaying our best and dearest? Sir! while you hold back from the work of staying the flood that is desolating our fairest homes, the black waters are approaching your own doors."

There was a startling emphasis in the tones with which this last sentence was uttered; and I did not wonder at the look of anxious alarm that it called to the face of him whose fears it was meant to excite.

"What do you mean, sir?" was inquired.

"Simply, that your sons are in equal danger with others."

"And is that all?"

"They have been seen, of late, in the barroom of the 'Sickle and Sheaf.'"

"Who says so?"

"Twice within a week I have seen them going in there," was answered.

"Good heavens! No!"

"It is true, my friend. But who is safe? If we dig pits, and conceal them from view, what marvel if our own children fall therein?"

"My sons going to a tavern?" The man seemed utterly confounded. "How *can* I believe it? You must be in error, sir."

"No. What I tell you is the simple truth. And if they go there—"

The man paused not to hear the conclusion of the sentence, but went hastily from the office.

"We are beginning to reap as we have sown," remarked the gentleman, turning to me as his agitated friend left the office. "As I told them in the commencement it would be, so it is happening. The want of a good tavern in Cedarville was over and over again alleged as one of the chief causes of our want of thrift, and when Slade opened the 'Sickle and Sheaf,' the man was almost glorified. The gentleman who has just left us failed not in laudation of the enterprising landlord; the more particularly, as the building of the new tavern advanced the price of ground on the street, and made him a few hundred dollars richer. Really, for a time, one might have thought, from the way people went on, that Simon Slade was going to make every man's fortune in Cedarville. But all that has been gained by a small advance in property, is as a grain of sand to a mountain, compared with the fearful demoralization that has followed."

I readily assented to this, for I had myself seen enough to justify the conclusion.

As I sat in the bar-room of the "Sickle and Sheaf" that evening, I noticed, soon after the lamps were lighted, the gentleman referred to in the above conversation, whose sons were represented as visitors to the bar, come in quietly, and look anxiously about the room. He spoke to no one, and, after satisfying himself that those he sought were not there, went out.

"What sent him here, I wonder?" muttered Slade, speaking partly to himself, and partly aside to Matthew, the bar-keeper.

"After the boys, I suppose," was answered.

"I guess the boys are old enough to take care of themselves."

"They ought to be," returned Matthew.

"And are," said Slade. "Have they been here this evening?"

"No, not yet."

While they yet talked together, two young men whom I had seen on the night before, and noticed particularly as showing signs of intelligence and respectability beyond the ordinary visitors at a bar-room, came in.

"John," I heard Slade say, in a low, confidential voice, to one of them, "your old man was here just now."

"No!" The young man looked startled—almost confounded.

"It's a fact. So you'd better keep shady."

"What did he want?"

"I don't know."

"What did he say?"

"Nothing. He just came in, looked around, and then went out."

"His face was as dark as a thunder-cloud," remarked Matthew.

"Is No. 4 vacant?" inquired one of the young men.

"Yes."

"Send us up a bottle of wine and some cigars. And when Bill Harding and Harry Lee come in, tell them where they can find us."

"All right," said Matthew. "And now, take a friend's advice and make yourselves scarce."

The young men left the room hastily. Scarcely had they departed, ere I saw the same gentleman come in, whose anxious face had, a little while before, thrown its shadow over the apartment. He was the father in search of his sons. Again he glanced around, nervously; and this time appeared to be disappointed. As he entered, Slade went out.

"Have John and Wilson been here this evening?" he asked, coming up to the bar and addressing Matthew.

"They are not here," replied Matthew, evasively.

"But haven't they been here?"

"They *may* have been here; I only came in from my supper a little while ago."

"I thought I saw them entering, only a moment or two ago."

"They're not here, sir." Matthew shook his head and spoke firmly.

"Where is Mr. Slade?"

"In the house, somewhere."

"I wish you would ask him to step here."

Matthew went out, but in a little while came back with word that the landlord was not to be found.

"You are sure the boys are not here?" said the man, with a doubting, dissatisfied manner.

"See for yourself, Mr. Harrison!"

"Perhaps they are in the parlor?"

"Step in, sir," coolly returned Matthew. The man went through the door into the sitting-room, but came back immediately.

"Not there?" said Matthew. The man shook his head. "I don't think you will find them about here," added the bar-keeper.

Mr. Harrison—this was the name by which Matthew had addressed him—stood musing and irresolute for some minutes. He could not be mistaken about the entrance of his sons, and yet they were not there. His manner was much perplexed. At length he took a seat, in a far corner of the bar-room, somewhat beyond the line of observation, evidently with the purpose of waiting to see if those he sought would come in. He had not been there long, before two young men entered, whose appearance at once excited his interest. They went up to the bar and called for liquor. As Matthew set the decanter before them, he leaned over the counter, and said something in a whisper.

"Where?" was instantly ejaculated, in surprise, and both of the young men glanced uneasily about the room. They met the eyes of Mr. Harrison, fixed intently upon them. I do not think, from the way they swallowed their brandy and water, that it was enjoyed very much.

"What the deuce is he doing here?" I heard one of them say, in a low voice.

"After the boys, of course."

"Have they come yet?"

Matthew winked as he answered, "All safe."

"In No. 4?"

"Yes. And the wine and cigars all waiting for you."

"Good."

"You'd better not go through the parlor. Their old man's not at all satisfied. He half suspects they're in the house. Better go off down the street, and come back and enter through the passage."

The young men, acting on this hint, at once retired, the eyes of Harrison following them out.

For nearly an hour Mr. Harrison kept his position, a close observer of all that transpired. I am very much in error, if, before leaving that sink of iniquity, he was not fully satisfied as to the propriety of legislating on the liquor question. Nay, I incline to the opinion, that, if the power of suppression had rested in his hands, there would not have been, in the whole State, at the expiration of an hour, a single dram-selling establishment. The goring of his ox had opened his eyes to the true merits of the question. While he was yet in the bar-room, young Hammond made his appearance. His look was wild and excited. First he called for brandy, and drank with the eagerness of a man long athirst.

"Where is Green?" I heard him inquire, as he set his glass upon the counter.

"Haven't seen any thing of him since supper," was answered by Matthew.

"Is he in his room?"

"I think it probable."

"Has Judge Lyman been about here to-night?"

"Yes. He spouted here for half an hour against the temperance party, as usual, and then"—Matthew tossed his head toward the door leading to the sitting-room.

Hammond was moving toward this door, when, in glancing around the room, he encountered the fixed gaze of Mr. Harrison—a gaze that instantly checked his progress. Returning to the bar, and leaning over the counter, he said to Matthew:

"What has sent him here?"

Matthew winked knowingly.

"After the boys?" inquired Hammond.

"Yes."

"Where are they?"

"Up-stairs."

"Does he suspect this?"

"I can't tell. If he doesn't think them here now, he is looking for them to come in."

"Do they know he is after them?"

"O yes."

"All safe then?"

"As an iron chest. If you want to see them, just rap at No. 4."

Hammond stood for some minutes leaning on the bar, and then, not once again looking toward that part of the room where Mr. Harrison was seated, passed out through the door leading to the street. Soon afterward Mr. Harrison departed.

Disgusted, as on the night before, with the unceasing flow of vile, obscene, and profane language, I left my place of observation in the bar-room and sought the open air. The sky was unobscured by a single cloud, and the moon, almost at the full, shone abroad with more than common brightness. I had not been sitting long in the porch, when the same lady, whose movements had attracted my attention, came in sight, walking very slowly— the deliberate pace assumed, evidently, for the purpose of better observation. On coming opposite the tavern, she slightly paused, as on the evening before, and then kept on, passing down the street, until she was beyond observation.

"Poor mother!" I was still repeating to myself, when her form again met my eyes. Slowly she advanced, and now came in nearer to the house. The interest excited in my mind was so strong, that I could not repress the desire I felt to address her, and so stepped from the shadow of the porch. She seemed startled, and retreated backward several paces.

"Are you in search of any one?" I inquired, respectfully.

The woman now stood in a position that let the moon shine full upon her face, reveal-ing every feature. She was far past the meridian of life; and there were lines of suffering and sorrow on her fine countenance. I saw that her lips moved, but it was some time before I distinguished the words.

"Have you seen my son to-night? They say he comes here."

The manner in which this was said caused a cold thrill to run over me. I perceived that the woman's mind wandered. I answered—

"No, ma'am; I haven't seen any thing of him."

My tone of voice seemed to inspire her with confidence, for she came up close to me, and bent her face toward mine.

"It's a dreadful place," she whispered, huskily. "And they say he comes here. Poor boy! He isn't what he used to be."

"It is a very bad place," said I. "Come"—and I moved a step or two in the direction from which I had seen her approaching —"come, you'd better go away as quickly as possible."

"But if he's here," she answered, not moving from where she stood, "I might save him, you know."

"I am sure you won't find him, ma'am," I urged. "Perhaps he is home, now."

"Oh, no! no!" And she shook her head mournfully. "He never comes home until long after midnight. I wish I could see inside of the bar-room. I'm sure he must be there."

"If you will tell me his name, I will go in and search for him."

After a moment of hesitation, she answered:

"His name is Willy Hammond."

How the name, uttered so sadly, and yet with such moving tenderness by the mother's lips, caused me to start—almost to tremble.

"If he is in the house, ma'am," said I, firmly, "I will see him for you." And I left her and went into the bar. "In what room do you think I will find young Hammond?" I asked of the bar-keeper.

He looked at me curiously, but did not answer. The question had come upon him unanticipated.

"In Harvey Green's room?" I pursued.

"I don't know, I am sure. He isn't in the house to my knowledge. I saw him go out about half an hour since."

"Green's room is No.—?"

"Eleven," he answered.

"In the front part of the house?"

"Yes."

I asked no further question, but went to No. 11, and tapped on the door. But no one answered the summons. I listened, but could not distinguish the slightest sound within. Again I knocked; but louder. If my ears did not deceive me, the chink of coin was heard. Still there was neither voice nor movement.

I was disappointed. That the room had inmates, I felt sure. Remembering, now, what I had heard about light being seen in this room through a rent in the curtain, I went downstairs, and out into the street. A short distance beyond the house, I saw, dimly, the woman's form. She had only just passed in her movement to and fro. Glancing up at the window, which I now knew to be the one in Green's room, light through the torn curtain was plainly visible. Back into the house I went, and up to No. 11. This time I knocked imperatively; and this time made myself heard.

"What's wanted?" came from within. I knew the voice to be that of Harvey Green.

I only knocked louder. A hurried movement and the low murmur of voices was heard for some moments; then the door was unlocked and held partly open by Green, whose body so filled the narrow aperture that I could not look into the room. Seeing me, a dark scowl fell upon his countenance.

"What d'ye want?" he inquired, sharply.

"Is Mr. Hammond here? If so, he is wanted down-stairs."

"No, he's not," was the quick answer. "What sent you here for him, hey?"

"The fact that I expected to find him in your room," was my firm answer.

Green was about shutting the door in my face, when some one placed a hand on his shoulder, and said something to him that I could not hear.

"Who wants to see him?" he inquired of me.

Satisfied, now, that Hammond was in the room, I said, slightly elevating my voice:

"His mother."

The words were an "open sesame" to the room. The door was suddenly jerked open, and with a blanching face, the young man confronted me.

"Who says my mother is down-stairs?" he demanded.

"I come from her in search of you," I said. "You will find her in the road, walking up and down in front of the tavern."

Almost with a bound he swept by me, and descended the stairway at two or three long strides. As the door swung open, I saw, besides Green and Hammond, the landlord and Judge Lyman. It needed not the loose cards on the table near which the latter were sitting to tell me of their business in that room.

As quickly as seemed decorous, I followed Hammond. On the porch I met him, coming in from the road.

"You have deceived me, sir," said he, sternly—almost menacingly.

"No, sir!" I replied. "What I told you was but too true. Look! There she is now."

The young man sprung around, and stood before the woman, a few paces distant.

"Mother! oh, mother! what *has* brought you here?" he exclaimed, in an under tone, as he caught her arm, and moved away. He spoke—not roughly, nor angrily—but with respect—half reproachfulness—and an unmistakable tenderness.

"Oh, Willy! Willy!" I heard her answer. "Somebody said you came here at night, and I couldn't rest. Oh, dear! They'll murder you! I know they will. Don't, oh!——"

My ears took in the sense no further, though her pleading voice still reached my ears. A few moments, and they were out of sight.

Nearly two hours afterward, as I was ascending to my chamber, a man brushed quickly by me. I glanced after him, and recognized the person of young Hammond. He was going to the room of Harvey Green!

Night the Seventh

Sowing the Wind

THE state of affairs in Cedarville, it was plain, from the partial glimpses I had received, was rather desperate. Desperate, I mean, as regarded the various parties brought before my observation. An eating cancer was on the community, and so far as the eye could mark its destructive progress, the ravages were fearful. That its roots were striking deep, and penetrating, concealed from view, in many unsuspected directions, there could be no doubt. What appeared on the surface was but a milder form of the disease, compared with its hidden, more vital, and more dangerous advances.

I could not but feel a strong interest in some of these parties. The case of young Hammond had, from the first, awakened concern; and now a new element was added in the unlooked-for appearance of his mother on the stage, in a state that seemed one of partial derangement. The gentleman at whose office I met Mr. Harrison on the day before—the reader will remember Mr. H. as having come to the "Sickle and Sheaf" in search of his sons—was thoroughly conversant with the affairs of the village, and I called upon him early in the day in order to make some inquiries about Mrs. Hammond. My first question, as to whether he knew the lady, was answered by the remark—

"Oh, yes. She is one of my earliest friends."

The allusion to her did not seem to awaken agreeable states of mind. A slight shade obscured his face, and I noticed that he sighed involuntarily.

"Is Willy her only child?"

"Her only living child. She had four; another son, and two daughters; but she lost all but Willy when they were quite young. And," he added, after a pause— "it would have been better for her, and for Willy too, if be had gone to a better land with them."

"His course of life must be to her a terrible affliction," said I.

"It is destroying her reason," he replied, with emphasis. "He was her idol. No mother ever loved a son with more self-devotion than Mrs. Hammond loved her beautiful, fine-spirited, intelligent, affectionate boy. To say that she was proud of him, is but a tame expression. Intense love—almost idolatry—was the strong passion of her heart. How tender, how watchful was her love! Except when at school, he was scarcely ever separated from her. In order to keep him by her side, she gave up her thoughts to the suggestion and maturing of plans for keeping his mind active and interested in her society—and her success was perfect. Up to the age of sixteen or seventeen, I do not think he had a desire for other companionship than that of his mother. But this, you know, could not last. The boy's maturing thought must go beyond the home and social circle. The great world, that he was soon to enter, was before him; and through loopholes that opened here and there he obtained partial glimpses of what was beyond. To step forth into this world, where he was soon to be a busy actor and worker, and to step forth alone, next came in the natural order of progress. How his mother trembled with anxiety, as she saw him leave her side! Of the dangers that would surround his path, she knew too well; and these were magnified by her fears—at least so I often said to her. Alas! how far the sad reality has outrun her most fearful anticipations.

"When Willy was eighteen—he was then reading law—I think I never saw a young man of fairer promise. As I have often heard it remarked of him, he did not appear to have a single fault. But he had a dangerous gift—rare conversational powers, united with great urbanity of manner. Every one who made his acquaintance became charmed with his society; and he soon found himself surrounded by a circle of young men, some of whom were not the best companions he might have chosen. Still, his own pure instincts and honorable principles were his safeguard; and I never have believed that any social allurements would have drawn him away from the right path, if this accursed tavern had not been opened by Slade."

"There was a tavern here before the 'Sickle and Sheaf' was opened?" said I.

"Oh, yes. But it was badly kept, and the bar-room visitors were of the lowest class. No respectable young man in Cedarville would have been seen there. It offered no temptations to one moving in Willy's circle. But the opening of the 'Sickle and Sheaf' formed a new era. Judge Hammond—himself not the purest man in the world, I'm afraid—gave his countenance to the establishment, and talked of Simon Slade as an enterprising man who ought to be encouraged. Judge Lyman and other men of position in Cedarville followed his bad example; and the bar-room of the 'Sickle and Sheaf' was at once voted respectable. At all times of the day and evening you could see the flower of our young men going in and out, sitting in front of the bar-room, or talking hand and glove with the landlord, who, from a worthy miller, regarded as well enough in his place, was suddenly elevated into a man of importance, whom the best in the village were delighted to honor."

In the beginning, Willy went with the tide, and, in an incredibly short period, was acquiring a fondness for drink that startled and alarmed his friends. In going in through Slade's open door, he entered the downward way, and has been moving onward with fleet footsteps ever since. The fiery poison inflamed his mind, at the same time that it dimmed his noble perceptions. Fondness for mere pleasure followed, and this led him into various sensual indulgences, and exciting modes of passing the time. Every one liked him—he was so free, so companionable, and so generous—and almost every one encouraged, rather than repressed, his dangerous proclivities. Even his father, for a time, treated the matter lightly, as only the first flush of young life. 'I commenced sowing my wild oats at quite as early an age,' I have heard him say. 'He'll cool off, and do well enough. Never fear.' But his mother was in a state of painful alarm from the beginning. Her truer instincts, made doubly acute by her yearning love, perceived the imminent danger, and in all possible ways did she seek to lure him from the path in which he was moving at so rapid a pace. Willy was always very much attached to his mother, and her influence over him was strong; but in this case he regarded her fears as chimerical. The way in which he walked was, to him, so pleasant, and the companions of his journey so delightful, that he could not believe in the prophesied evil; and when his mother talked to him in her warning voice, and with a sad countenance, he smiled at her concern, and made light of her fears.

"And so it went on, month after month, and year after year, until the young man's sad declensions were the town talk. In order to throw his mind into a new channel—to awaken, if possible, a new and better interest in life—his father ventured upon the doubtful experiment we spoke of yesterday: that of placing capital in his hands, and making him an equal partner in the business of distilling and cotton-spinning. The disastrous—I might say disgraceful—result you know. The young man squandered his own capital, and heavily embarrassed his father.

"The effect of all this upon Mrs. Hammond has been painful in the extreme. We can only dimly imagine the terrible suffering through which she has passed. Her present aberration was first visible after a long period of sleeplessness, occasioned by distress of mind. During the whole of two weeks, I am told, she did not close her eyes; the most of that time walking the floor of her chamber, and weeping. Powerful anodynes, frequently repeated, at length brought relief. But, when she awoke from a prolonged period of unconsciousness, the brightness of her reason was gone. Since then, she has never been clearly conscious of what was passing around her, and well for her, I have sometimes thought it was, for even obscurity of intellect is a blessing in her case. Ah, me! I always get the heart-ache, when I think of her."

"Did not this event startle the young man from his fatal dream, if I may so call his mad infatuation?" I asked.

"No. He loved his mother, and was deeply afflicted by the calamity; but it seemed as if he could not stop. Some terrible necessity appeared to be impelling him onward. If he formed good resolutions—and I doubt not that he did—they were blown away like threads of gossamer, the moment he came within the sphere of old associations. His way to the mill was by the 'Sickle and Sheaf;' and it was not easy for him to pass there without being drawn into the bar, either by his own desire for drink, or through the invitation of some pleasant companion, who was lounging in front of the tavern."

"There may have been something even more impelling than his love of drink," said I. "What?"

I related, briefly, the occurrences of the preceding night.

"I feared—nay, I was certain—that he was in the toils of this man! And yet your confirmation of the fact startles and confounds me," said he, moving about his office in a disturbed manner. "If my mind has questioned and doubted in regard to young Hammond, it questions and doubts no longer. The word 'mystery' is not now written over the door of his habitation. Great Father! and is it thus that our young men are led into temptation? Thus that their ruin is premeditated, secured? Thus that the fowler is permitted to spread his net in the open day, and the destroyer licensed to work ruin in darkness? It is awful to contemplate!"

The man was strongly excited.

"Thus it is," he continued; "and we who see the whole extent, origin, and downward rushing force of a widely sweeping desolation, lift our voices of warning almost in vain. Men who have every thing at stake—sons to be corrupted, and daughters to become the wives of young men exposed to corrupting influences—stand aloof, questioning and doubting as to the expediency of protecting the innocent from the wolfish designs of bad men; who, to compass their own selfish ends, would destroy them body and soul. We are called fanatics, ultraists, designing, and all that, because we ask our law-makers to stay the fiery ruin. Oh, no! we must not touch the traffic. All the dearest and best interests of society may suffer; but the rum-seller must be protected. He must be allowed to get gain, if the jails and poor-houses are filled, and the graveyards made fat with the bodies of young men stricken down in the flower of their years, and of wives and mothers who have died of broken hearts. Reform, we are told, must commence at home. We must rear temperate children, and then we shall have temperate men. That when there are none to desire liquor, the rum-seller's traffic will cease. And all the while society's true benefactors are engaged in doing this, the weak, the unsuspecting, and the erring must be left an easy prey, even if the work requires for its accomplishment a hundred years. Sir! a human soul destroyed through the rum-seller's infernal agency, is a sacrifice priceless in value. No considerations of worldly gain can, for an instant, be placed in comparison therewith. And yet souls are destroyed by thousands every year; and they will fall by tens of thousands ere society awakens from its fatal indifference, and lays its strong hand of power on the corrupt men who are scattering disease, ruin, and death, broadcast over the land!

"I always get warm on this subject," he added, repressing his enthusiasm. "And who that observes and reflects can help growing excited? The evil is appalling; and the indifference of the community one of the strangest facts of the day."

While he was yet speaking, the elder Mr. Hammond came in. He looked wretched. The redness and humidity of his eyes showed want of sleep, and the relaxed muscles of his face exhaustion from weariness and suffering. He drew the person with whom I had been talking aside, and continued in earnest conversation with him for many minutes—often gesticulating violently. I could see his face, though I heard nothing of what he said. The play of his features was painful to look upon, for every changing muscle showed a new phase of mental suffering.

"Try and see him, will you not?" he said, as he turned, at length, to leave the office.

"I will go there immediately," was answered.

"Bring him home, if possible."

"My very best efforts shall be made."

Judge Hammond bowed, and went out hurriedly.

"Do you know the number of the room occupied by the man Green?" asked the gentleman, as soon as his visitor had retired.

"Yes. It is No. 11."

"Willy has not been home since last night. His father, at this late day, suspects Green to be a gambler! The truth flashed upon him only yesterday; and this, added to his other sources of trouble, is driving him, so he says, almost mad. As a friend, he wishes me to go to the 'Sickle and Sheaf,' and try and find Willy. Have you seen any thing of him this morning?"

I answered in the negative.

"Nor of Green?"

"No."

"Was Slade about when you left the tavern?"

"I saw nothing of him."

"What Judge Hammond fears may be all too true—that, in the present condition of Willy's affairs, which have reached the point of disaster, his tempter means to secure the largest possible share of property yet in his power to pledge or transfer,—to squeeze from his victim the last drop of blood that remains, and then fling him, ruthlessly, from his hands."

"The young man must have been rendered almost desperate, or he would never have returned, as he did, last night. Did you mention this to his father?"

"No. It would have distressed him the more, without effecting any good. He is wretched enough. But time passes, and none is to be lost now. Will you go with me?"

I walked to the tavern with him; and we went into the bar together. Two or three men were at the counter, drinking.

"Is Mr. Green about this morning?" was asked by the person who had come in search of young Hammond.

"Haven't seen any thing of him."

"Is he in his room?"

"I don't know."

"Will you ascertain for me?"

"Certainly. Frank,"—and he spoke to the landlord's son, who was lounging on a settee,—"I wish you would see if Mr. Green is in his room."

"Go and see yourself. I'm not your waiter," was growled back, in an ill-natured voice.

"In a moment I'll ascertain for you," said Matthew, politely.

After waiting on some new customers, who were just entering, Matthew went up-stairs to obtain the desired information. As he left the bar-room, Frank got up and went behind the counter, where he mixed himself a glass of liquor, and drank it off, evidently with real enjoyment.

"Rather a dangerous business for one so young as you are," remarked the gentleman with whom I had come, as Frank stepped out of the bar, and passed near where we were standing. The only answer to this was an ill-natured frown, and an expression of face which said, almost as plainly as words, "It's none of your business."

"Not there," said Matthew, now coming in.

"Are you certain?"

"Yes, sir."

But there was a certain involuntary hesitation in the bar-keeper's manner, which led to a suspicion that his answer was not in accordance with the truth. We walked out together, conferring on the subject, and both concluded that his word was not to be relied upon.

"What is to be done?" was asked.

"Go to Green's room," I replied, "and knock at the door. If he is there, he may answer, not suspecting your errand."

"Show me the room."

I went up with him, and pointed out No. 11. He knocked lightly, but there came no sound from within. He repeated the knock; all was silent. Again and again he knocked, but there came back only a hollow reverberation.

"There's no one there," said he, returning to where I stood, and we walked down-stairs together. On the landing, as we reached the lower passage, we met Mrs. Slade. I had not, during this visit at Cedarville, stood face to face with her before. Oh! what a wreck she presented, with her pale, shrunken countenance, hollow, lustreless eyes, and bent, feeble body. I almost shuddered as I looked at her. What a haunting and sternly rebuking spectre she must have moved, daily, before the eyes of her husband.

"Have you noticed Mr. Green about this morning?" I asked.

"He hasn't come down from his room yet," she replied.

"Are you certain?" said my companion. "I knocked several times at the door just now, but received no answer."

"What do you want with him?" asked Mrs. Slade, fixing her eyes upon us.

"We are in search of Willy Hammond; and it has been suggested that he is with Green."

"Knock twice lightly, and then three times more firmly," said Mrs. Slade; and as she spoke, she glided past us with noiseless tread.

"Shall we go up together?"

I did not object; for, although I had no delegated right of intrusion, my feelings were so much excited in the case, that I went forward, scarcely reflecting on the propriety of so doing.

The signal knock found instant answer. The door was softly opened, and the unshaven face of Simon Slade presented itself.

"Mr. Jacobs!" he said, with surprise in his tones. "Do you wish to see me?"

"No, sir; I wish to see Mr. Green," and with a quick, firm pressure against the door, he pushed it wide open. The same party was there that I had seen on the night before,— Green, young Hammond, Judge Lyman, and Slade. On the table at which the three former were sitting, were cards, slips of paper, an inkstand and pens, and a pile of bank-notes. On a side-table, or, rather, butler's tray, were bottles, decanters, and glasses.

"Judge Lyman! Is it possible?" exclaimed Mr. Jacobs, the name of my companion: "I did not expect to find you here."

Green instantly swept his hands over the table to secure the money and bills it contained; but, ere he had accomplished his purpose, young Hammond grappled three or four narrow strips of paper, and hastily tore them into shreds.

"You're a cheating scoundrel!" cried Green, fiercely, thrusting his hand into his bosom as if to draw from thence a weapon; but the words were scarcely uttered, ere Hammond sprung upon him with the fierceness of a tiger, bearing him down upon the floor. Both hands were already about the gambler's neck, and, ere the bewildered spectators could interfere, and drag him off, Green was purple in the face, and nearly strangled.

"Call me a cheating scoundrel!" said Hammond, foaming at the mouth, as he spoke,— "Me! whom you have followed like a thirsty bloodhound. Me! whom you have robbed, and cheated, and debased from the beginning! Oh! for a pistol to rid the earth of the blackest-hearted villain that walks its surface. Let me go, gentlemen! I have nothing left in

"WILLY HAMMOND MURDERED BY THE GAMBLER, HARVEY GREEN."

"Willy Hammond murdered by the gambler, Harvey Green."

the world to care for,—there is no consequence I fear. Let me do society one good service before I die!"

And, with one vigorous effort, he swept himself clear of the hands that were pinioning him, and sprung again upon the gambler with the fierce energy of a savage beast. By this time, Green had got his knife free from its sheath, and, as Hammond was closing upon him in his blind rage, plunged it into his side. Quick almost as lightning, the knife was withdrawn, and two more stabs inflicted ere we could seize and disarm the murderer. As we did so, Willy Hammond fell over with a deep groan, the blood flowing from his side.

In the terror and excitement that followed, Green rushed from the room. The doctor, who was instantly summoned, after carefully examining the wound, and the condition of the unhappy young man, gave it as his opinion that he was fatally injured.

Oh! the anguish of the father, who had quickly heard of the dreadful occurrence, when this announcement was made. I never saw such fearful agony in any human countenance. The calmest of all the anxious group was Willy himself. On his father's face his eyes were fixed as if by a kind of fascination.

"Are you in much pain, my poor boy!" sobbed the old man, stooping over him, until his long white hair mingled with the damp locks of the sufferer.

"Not much, father," was the whispered reply. "Don't speak of this to mother, yet. I'm afraid it will kill her."

What could the father answer? Nothing! And he was silent.

"Does she know of it?" A shadow went over his face.

Mr. Hammond shook his head.

Yet, even as he spoke, a wild cry of distress was heard below. Some indiscreet person had borne to the ears of the mother the fearful news about her son, and she had come wildly flying toward the tavern, and was just entering.

"It is my poor mother," said Willy, a flush coming into his pale face. "Who could have told her of this?"

Mr. Hammond started for the door, but ere he had reached it, the distracted mother entered.

"Oh! Willy, my boy! my boy!" she exclaimed, in tones of anguish that made the heart shudder. And she crouched down on the floor, the moment she reached the bed whereon he lay, and pressed her lips—oh, so tenderly and lovingly!—to his.

"Dear mother! Sweet mother! Best of mothers!" He even smiled as he said this; and, into the face that now bent over him, looked up with glances of unutterable fondness.

"Oh, Willy! Willy! Willy! my son, my son!" And again her lips were laid closely to his.

Mr. Hammond now interfered, and endeavored to remove his wife, fearing for the consequence upon his son.

"Don't, father!" said Willy; "let her remain. I am not excited nor disturbed. I am glad that she is here, now. It will be best for us both."

"You must not excite him, dear," said Mr. Hammond—"he is very weak."

"I'll not excite him," answered the mother. "I'll not speak a word. There, love"—and she laid her fingers softly upon the lips of her son —"don't speak a single word."

For only a few moments did she sit with the quiet formality of a nurse, who feels how much depends on the repose of her patient. Then she began, weeping, moaning, and wringing her hands.

"Mother!" The feeble voice of Willy stilled, instantly, the tempest of feeling. "Mother, kiss me!"

She bent down and kissed him.

"Are you there, mother?" His eyes moved about, with a straining motion.

"Yes, love, here I am."

"I don't see you, mother. It's getting so dark. Oh, mother! mother!" he shouted suddenly, starting up and throwing himself forward upon her bosom—"save me! save me!"

How quickly did the mother clasp her arms around him—how eagerly did she strain him to her bosom! The doctor, fearing the worst consequences, now came forward, and endeavored to release the arms of Mrs. Hammond, but she resisted every attempt to do so.

"I will save you, my son," she murmured in the ear of the young man. "Your mother will protect you. Oh! if you had never left her side, nothing on earth could have done you harm."

"He is dead!" I heard the doctor whisper; and, a thrill of horror went through me. The words reached the ears of Mr. Hammond, and his groan was one of almost mortal agony.

"Who says he is dead?" came sharply from the lips of the mother, as she pressed the form of her child back upon the bed from which he had sprung to her arms, and looked wildly upon his face. One long scream of horror told of her convictions, and she fell, lifeless, across the body of her dead son!

All in the room believed that Mrs. Hammond had only fainted. But the doctor's perplexed, troubled countenance, as he ordered her carried into another apartment, and the ghastliness of her face when it was upturned to the light, suggested to every one what proved to be true. Even to her obscured perceptions, the consciousness that her son was dead came with a terrible vividness—so terrible, that it extinguished her life.

Like fire among dry stubble ran the news of this fearful event through Cedarville. The whole town was wild with excitement. The prominent fact, that Willy Hammond had been murdered by Green, whose real profession was known by many, and now declared to all, was on every tongue; but a hundred different and exaggerated stories as to the cause and the particulars of the event were in circulation. By the time preparations to remove the dead bodies of mother and son from the "Sickle and Sheaf," to the residence of Mr. Hammond, were completed, hundreds of people, men, women, and children, were assembled around the tavern; and many voices were clamorous for Green; while some called out for Judge Lyman, whose name, it thus appeared, had become associated in the minds of the people with the murderous affair. The appearance, in the midst of this excitement, of the two dead bodies, borne forth on settees, did not tend to allay the feverish state of indignation that prevailed. From more than one voice, I heard the words, "Lynch the scoundrel!"

A part of the crowd followed the sad procession, while the greater portion, consisting of men, remained about the tavern. All bodies, no matter for what purpose assembled, quickly find leading spirits who, feeling the great moving impulse, give it voice and direction. It was so in this case. Intense indignation against Green was firing every bosom; and when a man elevated himself a few feet above the agitated mass of humanity, and cried out—

"The murderer must not escape!"

A wild responding shout, terrible in its fierceness, made the air quiver.

"Let ten men be chosen to search the house and premises," said the leading spirit.

"Ay! ay! Choose them! Name them!" was quickly answered.

Ten men were called by name, who instantly stepped in front of the crowd.

"Search everywhere; from garret to cellar; from hayloft to dog-kennel. Everywhere! everywhere!" cried the man.

And instantly the ten men entered the house. For nearly a quarter of an hour, the crowd waited with increasing signs of impatience. These delegates at length appeared, with the announcement that Green was nowhere about the premises. It was received with a groan.

"Let no man in Cedarville do a stroke of work until the murderer is found," now shouted the individual who still occupied his elevated position.

"Agreed! agreed! No work in Cedarville until the murderer is found," rang out fiercely.

"Let all who have horses, saddle and bridle them as quickly as possible, and assemble, mounted, at the Court House."

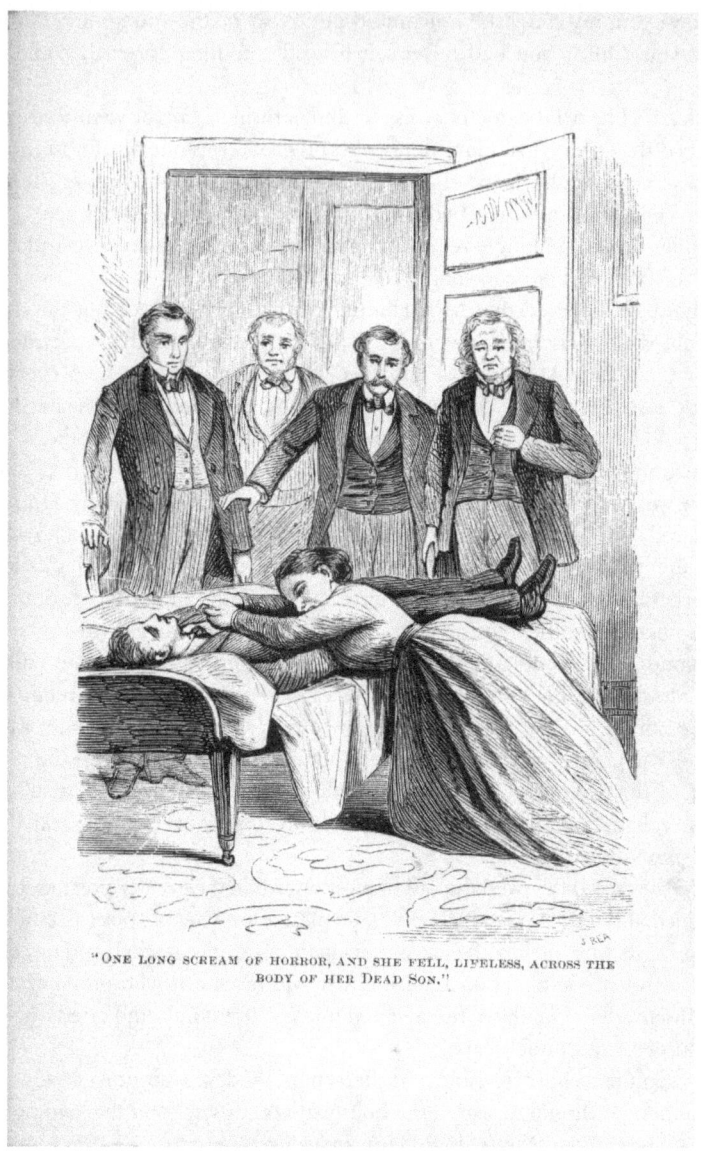

"ONE LONG SCREAM OF HORROR, AND SHE FELL, LIFELESS, ACROSS THE
BODY OF HER DEAD SON."

"One long scream of horror, and she fell, lifeless, across the body of her dead son."

About fifty men left the crowd hastily.

"Let the crowd part in the centre, up and down the road, starting from a line in front of me."

This order was obeyed.

"Separate again, taking the centre of the road for a line."

Four distinct bodies of men stood now in front of the tavern.

"Now search for the murderer in every nook and corner, for a distance of three miles from this spot; each party keeping to its own section; the road being one dividing line, and a line through the centre of this tavern the other. The horsemen will pursue the wretch to a greater distance."

More than a hundred acquiescing voices responded to this, as the man sprung down from his elevation and mingled with the crowd, which began instantly to move away on its appointed mission.

As the hours went by, one, and another, and another, of the searching party returned to the village, wearied with their efforts, or confident that the murderer had made good his escape. The horsemen, too, began to come in, during the afternoon, and by sundown, the last of them, worn out and disappointed, made their appearance.

For hours after the exciting events of the forenoon, there were but few visitors at the "Sickle and Sheaf." Slade, who did not show himself among the crowd, came down soon after its dispersion. He had shaved and put on clean linen; but still bore many evidences of a night spent without sleep. His eyes were red and heavy and the eyelids swollen; while his skin was relaxed and colorless. As he descended the stairs, I was walking in the passage. He looked shy at me, and merely nodded. Guilt was written plainly on his countenance; and with it was blended anxiety and alarm. That he might be involved in trouble, he had reason to fear; for, he was one of the party engaged in gambling in Green's room, as both Mr. Jacobs and I had witnessed.

"This is dreadful business," said he, as we met, face to face, half an hour afterward. He did not look me steadily in the eyes.

"It is horrible!" I answered. "To corrupt and ruin a young man, and then murder him! There are few deeds in the catalogue of crime blacker than this."

"It was done in the heat of passion," said the landlord, with something of apology in his manner. "Green never meant to kill him."

"In peaceful intercourse with his fellow men, why did he carry a deadly weapon? There was murder in his heart, sir."

"That is speaking very strongly."

"Not stronger than facts will warrant," I replied. "That Green is a murderer in heart, it needed not this awful consummation to show. With a cool, deliberate purpose, he has sought, from the beginning, to destroy young Hammond."

"It is hardly fair," answered Slade, "in the present feverish excitement against Green, to assume such a questionable position. It may do him a great wrong."

"Did Willy Hammond speak only idle words, when he accused Green of having followed him like a thirsty bloodhound?—of having robbed, and cheated, and debased him from the beginning?"

"He was terribly excited at the moment."

"Yet," said I, "no ear that heard his words could for an instant doubt that they were truthful utterances, wrung from a maddened heart."

My earnest, positive manner had its effect upon Slade. He knew that what I asserted, the whole history of Green's intercourse with young Hammond would prove; and he had, moreover, the guilty consciousness of being a party to the young man's ruin. His eyes cowered beneath the steady gaze I fixed upon him. I thought of him as one implicated in the murder, and my thought must have been visible in my face.

"One murder will not justify another," said he.

"There is no justification for murder on any plea," was my response.

"And yet, if these infuriated men find Green, they will murder him."

"I hope not. Indignation at a horrible crime has fearfully excited the people. But I think their sense of justice is strong enough to prevent the consequences you apprehend."

I would not like to be in Green's shoes," said the landlord, with an uneasy movement.

I looked him closely in the face. It was the punishment of the man's crime that seemed so fearful in his eyes; not the crime itself. Alas! how the corrupting traffic had debased him.

My words were so little relished by Slade, that he found some ready excuse to leave me. I saw but little more of him during the day.

As evening began to fall, the gambler's unsuccessful pursuers, one after another, found their way to the tavern, and by the time night had fairly closed in, the bar-room was crowded with excited and angry men, chafing over their disappointment, and loud in their threats of vengeance. That Green had made good his escape, was now the general belief; and the stronger this conviction became, the more steadily did the current of passion begin to set in a new direction. It had become known to every one, that, besides Green and young Hammond, Judge Lyman and Slade were in the room engaged in playing cards. The merest suggestion as to the complicity of these two men with Green in ruining Hammond, and thus driving him mad, was enough to excite strong feeling against them; and now that the mob had been cheated of its victim, its pent up indignation sought eagerly some new channel.

"Where's Slade?" some one asked, in a loud voice, from the centre of the crowded bar-room. "Why does he keep himself out of sight?"

"Yes; where's the landlord?" half a dozen voices responded.

"Did he go on the hunt?" some one inquired.

"No!" "No!" "No!" ran round the room. "Not he."

"And yet, the murder was committed in his own house, and before his own eyes!"

"Yes, before his own eyes!" repeated one and another, indignantly.

"Where's Slade? Where's the landlord? Has anybody seen him to-night? Matthew, where's Simon Slade?"

From lip to lip passed these interrogations; while the crowd of men became agitated, and swayed to and fro.

"I don't think he's home," answered the bar-keeper, in a hesitating manner, and with visible alarm.

"How long since he was here?"

"I haven't seen him for a couple of hours."

"That's a lie!" was sharply said.

"Who says it's a lie?" Matthew affected to be strongly indignant.

"I do!" And a rough, fierce-looking man confronted him.

"What right have you to say so?" asked Matthew, cooling off considerably.

"Because you lie!" said the man, boldly. "You've seen him within a less time than half an hour, and well you know it. Now, if you wish to keep yourself out of this trouble, answer truly. We are in no mood to deal with liars or equivocators. Where is Simon Slade?"

"I do not know," replied Matthew, firmly.

"Is he in the house?"

"He may be, or he may not be. I am just as ignorant of his exact whereabouts as you are."

"Will you look for him?"

Matthew stepped to the door, opening from behind the bar, and called the name of Frank.

"What's wanted?" growled the boy.

"Is your father in the house?"

"I don't know, nor don't care," was responded in the same ungracious manner.

"Some one bring him into the bar-room, and we'll see if we can't make him care a little."

The suggestion was no sooner made, than two men glided behind the bar, and passed into the room from which the voice of Frank had issued. A moment after they reappeared, each grasping an arm of the boy, and bearing him like a weak child between them. He looked thoroughly frightened at this unlooked-for invasion of his liberty.

"See here, young man." One of the leading spirits of the crowd addressed him, as soon as he was brought in front of the counter. "If you wish to keep out of trouble, answer our questions at once, and to the point. We are in no mood for trifling. Where's your father?"

"Somewhere about the house, I believe," Frank replied, in an humbled tone. He was no little scared at the summary manner with which he had been treated.

"How long since you saw him?"

"Not long ago."

"Ten minutes?"

"No: nearly half an hour."

"Where was he then?"

"He was going up-stairs."

"Very well, we want him. See him, and tell him so."

Frank went into the house, but came back into the bar-room after an absence of nearly five minutes, and said that he could not find his father anywhere.

"Where is he then?" was angrily demanded.

"Indeed, gentlemen, I don't know." Frank's anxious look and frightened manner showed that he spoke truly.

"There's something wrong about this—something wrong—wrong," said one of the men. "Why should he be absent now? Why has he taken no steps to secure the man who committed a murder in his own house, and before his own eyes?

"I shouldn't wonder if he aided him to escape," said another, making this serious charge with a restlessness and want of evidence that illustrated the reckless and unjust spirit by which a mob is ever governed.

"No doubt of it in the least!" was the quick and positive response. And at once this erroneous conviction seized upon every one. Not a single fact was presented. The simple, bold assertion, that no doubt existed in the mind of one man as to Slade's having aided Green to escape, was sufficient for the unreflecting mob.

"Where is he? Where is he? Let us find him. He knows where Green is, and he shall reveal the secret."

This was enough. The passions of the crowd were at fever heat again. Two or three men were chosen to search the house and premises, while others dispersed to take a wider range. One of the men who volunteered to go over the house was a person named Lyon, with whom I had formed some acquaintance, and several times conversed with on the state of affairs in Cedarville. He still remained too good a customer at the bar. I left the bar at the same time that he did, and went up to my room. We walked side by side, and parted at my door, I going in, and he continuing on to make his searches. I felt, of course, anxious and much excited, as well in consequence of the events of the day, as the present aspect of things. My head was aching violently, and in the hope of getting relief, I laid myself down. I had already lighted a candle, and turned the key in my door to prevent intrusion. Only for a short time did I lie, listening to the hum of voices that came with a hoarse murmur from below, to the sound of feet moving along the passages, and to the continual opening and shutting of doors, when something like suppressed breathing reached my ears. I started up instantly, and listened; but my quickened pulses were now audible to my own sense, and obscured what was external.

"It is only imagination," I said to myself. Still, I sat upright, listening.

Satisfied, at length, that all was mere fancy, I laid myself back on the pillow, and tried to turn my thoughts away from the suggested idea that some one was in the room. Scarcely had I succeeded in this, when my heart gave a new impulse, as a sound like a movement fell upon my ears.

"Mere fancy!" I said to myself, as some one went past the door at the moment. "My mind is over-excited."

Still I raised my head, supporting it with my hand, and listened, directing my attention inside, and not outside of the room. I was about letting my head fall back upon the pillow, when a slight cough, so distinct as not to be mistaken, caused me to spring to the floor, and look under the bed. The mystery was explained. A pair of eyes glittered in the candlelight. The fugitive, Green, was under my bed. For some moments I stood looking at him, so astonished that I had neither utterance nor decision; while he glared at me with a fierce defiance. I saw that he was clutching a revolver.

"Understand!" he said, in a grating whisper, "that I am not to be taken alive."

I let the blanket, which had concealed him from view, fall from my hand, and then tried to collect my thoughts.

"Escape is impossible," said I, again lifting the temporary curtain by which he was hid. "The whole town is armed, and on the search; and should you fall into the hands of the mob, in its present state of exasperation, your life would not be safe an instant. Remain, then, quiet, where you are, until I can see the sheriff, to whom you had better resign yourself, for there's little chance for you except under his protection."

After a brief parley, he consented that things should take this course, and I went out, locking the room door after me, and started in search of the sheriff. On the information I gave, the sheriff acted promptly. With five officers, fully armed for defense, in case an effort were made to get the prisoner out of their hands, he repaired immediately to the "Sickle and Sheaf." I had given the key of my room into his possession.

The appearance of the sheriff, with his *posse*, was sufficient to start the suggestion that Green was somewhere concealed in the house; and a suggestion was only needed to cause the fact to be assumed, and unhesitatingly declared. Intelligence went through the reassembling crowd like an electric current, and ere the sheriff could manacle and lead forth his prisoner, the stairway down which he had to come was packed with bodies, and echoing with oaths and maledictions.

"Gentlemen, clear the way!" cried the sheriff, as he appeared with the white and trembling culprit at the head of the stairs. "The murderer is now in the hands of the law, and will meet the sure consequences of his crime."

A shout of execration rent the air; but not a single individual stirred.

"Give way, there! Give way!" And the sheriff took a step or two forward, but the prisoner held back.

"Oh, the murdering villain! The cursed blackleg! Where's Willy Hammond?" was heard distinctly above the confused mingling of voices.

"Gentlemen! the law must have its course; and no good citizen will oppose the law. It is made for your protection—for mine—and for that of the prisoner."

"Lynch law is good enough for him," shouted a savage voice. "Hand him over to us, sheriff, and we'll save you the trouble of hanging him, and the county the cost of a gallows. We'll do the business right."

Five men, each armed with a revolver, now ranged themselves around the sheriff, and the latter said firmly,

"It is my duty to see this man safely conveyed to prison; and I'm going to do my duty. If there is any more blood shed here, the blame will rest with you." And the body of officers pressed forward, the mob slowly retreating before them.

Green, overwhelmed with terror, held back. I was standing where I could see his face. It was ghastly with mortal fear. Grasping his pinioned arms, the sheriff forced him onward. After contending with the crowd for nearly ten minutes, the officers gained the passage below; but the mob was denser here, and blocking up the door, resolutely maintained their position.

Again and again the sheriff appealed to the good sense and justice of the people.

"The prisoner will have to stand a trial and the law will execute sure vengeance."

"No, it won't!" was sternly responded.

"Who'll be judge in the case?" was asked.

"Why, Judge Lyman!" was contemptuously answered.

"A blackleg himself!" was shouted by two or three voices.

"Blackleg judge, and blackleg lawyers! Oh, yes! The law will execute sure vengeance! Who was in the room gambling with Green and Hammond?"

"Judge Lyman!" "Judge Lyman!" was answered back.

"It won't do, sheriff! There's no law in the country to reach the case but Lynch law; and that the scoundrel must have. Give him to us!"

"Never! On, men, with the prisoner!" cried the sheriff resolutely, and the *posse* made a rush toward the door, bearing back the resisting and now infuriated crowd. Shouts, cries, oaths, and savage imprecations blended in wild discord; in the midst of which my blood was chilled by the sharp crack of a pistol. Another and another shot followed; and then, as a cry of pain thrilled the air, the fierce storm hushed its fury in an instant.

"Who's shot? Is he killed?"

There was a breathless eagerness for the answer.

"It's the gambler!" was replied. "Somebody has shot Green."

A low muttered invective against the victim was heard here and there; but the announcement was not received with a shout of exultation, though there was scarcely a heart that did not feel pleasure at the sacrifice of Harvey Green's life.

It was true as had been declared. Whether the shot were aimed deliberately, or guided by an unseen hand to the heart of the gambler, was never known; nor did the most careful examination, instituted afterward by the county, elicit any information that even directed suspicion toward the individual who became the agent of his death.

At the coroner's inquest, held over the dead body of Harvey Green, Simon Slade was present. Where he had concealed himself while the mob were in search of him, was not known. He looked haggard; and his eyes were anxious and restless. Two murders in his house, occurring in a single day, were quite enough to darken his spirits; and the more so, as his relations with both the victims were not of a character to awaken any thing but self-accusation.

As for the mob, in the death of Green its eager thirst for vengeance was satisfied. Nothing more was said against Slade, as a participator in the ruin and death of young Hammond.

The popular feeling was one of pity rather than indignation toward the landlord; for it was seen that he was deeply troubled.

One thing I noticed, and it was that the drinking at the bar was not suspended for a moment. A large proportion of those who made up the crowd of Green's angry pursuers, were excited by drink as well as indignation, and I am very sure that, but for the maddening effects of liquor, the fatal shot would never have been fired. After the fearful catastrophe, and when every mind was sobered, or ought to have been sobered, the crowd returned to the bar-room, where the drinking was renewed. So rapid were the calls for liquor, that both Matthew and Frank, the landlord's son, were kept busy mixing the various compounds demanded by the thirsty customers.

From the constant stream of human beings that flowed toward the "Sickle and Sheaf," after the news of Green's discovery and death went forth, it seemed as if every man and boy within a distance of two or three miles had received intelligence of the event. Few, very, of those who came, but went first into the bar-room; and nearly all who entered the bar-room called for liquor. In an hour after the death of Green, the fact that his dead body was laid out in the room immediately adjoining, seemed utterly to pass from the consciousness of every one in the bar. The calls for liquor were incessant; and, as the excitement of drink increased, voices grew louder, and oaths more plentiful, while the sounds of laughter ceased not for an instant.

"They're giving him a regular Irish wake," I heard remarked, with a brutal laugh. I turned to the speaker, and, to my great surprise, saw that it was Judge Lyman, more under the influence of drink than I remembered to have seen him. He was about the last man I expected to find here. If he knew of the strong indignation expressed toward him a little while before, by some of the very men now excited with liquor, his own free drinking had extinguished fear.

"Yes, curse him!" was the answer. "If they have a particularly hot corner 'away down below,' I hope he's made its acquaintance before this."

"Most likely he's smelled brimstone," chuckled the judge.

"Smelled it! If old Clubfoot[9] hasn't treated him with a brimstone-bath long before this, he hasn't done his duty. If I thought as much, I'd vote for sending his majesty a remonstrance forthwith."

"Ha! ha!" laughed the judge. "You're warm on the subject."

"Ain't I? The blackleg scoundrel! Hell's too good for him."

"H-u-s-h! Don't let your indignation run into profanity," said Judge Lyman, trying to assume a serious air; but the muscles of his face but feebly obeyed his will's feeble effort.

"Profanity! Poh! I don't call that profanity. It's only speaking out in meeting, as they say,—it's only calling black, black—and white, white. You believe in a hell, don't you, judge?"

"I suppose there is one; though I don't know very certain."

"You'd better be certain!" said the other, meaningly.

"Why so?"

"Oh! because if there is one, and you don't cut your cards a little differently, you'll be apt to find it at the end of your journey."

"What do you mean by that?" asked the judge, retreating somewhat into himself, and trying to look dignified.

---

9 The devil.

"Just what I say," was unhesitatingly answered.

"Do you mean to insinuate any thing?" asked the judge, whose brows were beginning to knit themselves.

"Nobody thinks you a saint," replied the man, roughly.

"I never professed to be."

"And it is said,"—the man fixed his gaze almost insultingly upon Judge Lyman's face— "that you'll get about as hot a corner in the lower regions as is to be found there, whenever you make the journey in that direction."

"You are insolent!" exclaimed the judge, his face becoming inflamed.

"Take care what you say, sir!" The man spoke threateningly.

"You'd better take care what *you* say."

"So I will," replied the other. "But—"

"What's to pay here?" inquired a third party, coming up at the moment, and interrupting the speaker.

"The devil will be to pay," said Judge Lyman, "if somebody don't look out sharp."

"Do you mean that for me, ha?" The man, between whom and himself this slight contention had so quickly sprung up, began stripping back his coat sleeves, like one about to commence boxing.

"I mean it for anybody who presumes to offer me an insult."

The raised voices of the two men now drew toward them the attention of every one in the bar-room.

"The devil! There's Judge Lyman!" I heard some one exclaim, in a tone of surprise.

"Wasn't he in the room with Green when Willy Hammond was murdered?" asked another.

"Yes, he was; and what's more, it is said he had been playing against him all night, he and Green sharing the plunder."

This last remark came distinctly to the ears of Lyman, who started to his feet instantly, exclaiming fiercely—

"Whoever says that is a cursed liar!"

The words were scarcely out of his mouth, before a blow staggered him against the wall, near which he was standing. Another blow felled him, and then his assailant sprang over his prostrate body, kicking him, and stamping upon his face and breast in the most brutal, shocking manner.

"Kill him! He's worse than Green!" somebody cried out, in a voice so full of cruelty and murder that it made my blood curdle. "Remember Willy Hammond!"

The terrible scene that followed, in which were heard a confused mingling of blows, cries, yells, and horrible oaths, continued for several minutes, and ceased only when the words—"Don't, don't strike him any more! He's dead!" were repeated several times. Then the wild strife subsided. As the crowd parted from around the body of Judge Lyman, and gave way, I caught a single glance at his face. It was covered with blood, and every feature seemed to have been literally trampled down, until all was a level surface! Sickened at the sight, I passed hastily from the room into the open air, and caught my breath several times, before respiration again went on freely. As I stood in front of the tavern, the body of Judge Lyman was borne out by three or four men, and carried off in the direction of his dwelling.

"Is he dead?" I inquired of those who had him in charge.

"No," was the answer. "He's not dead, but terribly beaten," and they passed on.

Again the loud voices of men in angry strife arose in the bar-room. I did not return there to learn the cause, or to witness the fiend-like conduct of men, all whose worst passions were stimulated by drink into the wildest fervor. As I was entering my room, the thought flashed through my mind that, as Green was found there, it needed only the bare suggestion that I had aided in his concealment, to direct toward me the insane fury of the drunken mob.

"It is not safe to remain here." I said this to myself, with the emphasis of a strong internal conviction.

Against this, my mind opposed a few feeble arguments; but the more I thought of the matter, the more clearly did I become satisfied, that to attempt to pass the night in that room was to me a risk it was not prudent to assume.

So I went in search of Mrs. Slade, to ask her to have another room prepared for me. But she was not in the house; and I learned, upon inquiry, that since the murder of young Hammond, she had been suffering from repeated hysterical and fainting fits, and was now, with her daughter, at the house of a relative, whither she had been carried early in the afternoon.

It was on my lip to request the chambermaid to give me another room; but this I felt to be scarcely prudent, for if the popular indignation should happen to turn toward me, the servant would be the one questioned, most likely, as to where I had removed my quarters.

It isn't safe to stay in the house," said I, speaking to myself. "Two, perhaps three, murders have been committed already. The tiger's thirst for blood has been stimulated, and who can tell how quickly he may spring again, or in what direction?"

Even while I said this, there came up from the bar-room louder and madder shouts. Then blows were heard, mingled with cries and oaths. A shuddering sense of danger oppressed me, and I went hastily down-stairs, and out into the street. As I gained the passage, I looked into the sitting-room, where the body of Green was laid out. Just then, the bar-room door was burst open by a fighting party, who had been thrown, in their fierce contention, against it. I paused only for a moment or two; and even in that brief period of time, saw blows exchanged over the dead body of the gambler!

"This is no place for me," I said, almost aloud, and hurried from the house, and took my way to the residence of a gentleman who had shown me many kindnesses during my visits at Cedarville. There was needed scarcely a word of representation on my part, to secure the cordial tender of a bed.

What a change! It seemed almost like a passage from Pandemonium[10] to a heavenly region, as I seated myself alone in the quiet chamber a cheerful hospitality had assigned me, and mused on the exciting and terrible incidents of the day. They that sow the wind shall reap the whirlwind.[11] How marked had been the realization of this prophecy, couched in such strong but beautiful imagery!

On the next day I was to leave Cedarville. Early in the morning I repaired to the "Sickle and Sheaf." The storm was over, and all was calm and silent as desolation. Hours before, the tempest had subsided; but the evidences left behind of its ravaging fury were fearful to look upon. Doors, chairs, windows, and tables were broken, and even the strong brass rod

---

10 Pandemonium was the name of Satan's palace in John Milton's (1608–1674) *Paradise Lost* (1667).

11 Hosea 8:7.

that ornamented the bar had been partially wrenched from its fastenings by strong hands, under an impulse of murder, that only lacked a weapon to execute its fiendish purpose. Stains of blood, in drops, marks, and even dried-up pools, were to be seen all over the bar-room and passage floors, and in many places on the porch.

In the sitting-room still lay the body of Green. Here, too, were many signs to indicate a fierce struggle. The looking-glass was smashed to a hundred pieces, and the shivered fragments lay yet untouched upon the floor. A chair, which it was plain had been used as a weapon of assault, had two of its legs broken short off, and was thrown into a corner. And even the bearers, on which the dead man lay, were pushed from their true position, showing that even in its mortal sleep, the body of Green had felt the jarring strife of elements he had himself helped to awaken into mad activity. From his face, the sheet had been drawn aside; but no hand ventured to replace it; and there it lay, in its ghastly paleness, exposed to the light, and covered with restless flies, attracted by the first faint odors of putridity. With gaze averted, I approached the body, and drew the covering decently over it.

No person was in the bar. I went out into the stable-yard, where I met the hostler with his head bound up. There was a dark blue circle around one of his eyes, and an ugly-looking red scar on his cheek.

"Where is Mr. Slade? "I inquired.

"In bed, and likely to keep it for a week," was answered.

"How comes that?"

"Naturally enough. There was fighting all around last night, and he had to come in for a share. The fool! If he'd just held his tongue, he might have come out of it with a whole skin. But, when the rum is in, the wit is out, with him. It's cost me a black eye and a broken head; for how could I stand by and see him murdered outright?"

"Is he very badly injured?"

"I rather think he is. One eye is clean gone."

"Oh, shocking!"

"It's shocking enough, and no mistake."

"Lost an eye!"

"Too true, sir. The doctor saw him this morning, and says the eye was fairly gouged out, and broken up. In fact, when we carried him up-stairs for dead, last night, his eye was lying upon his cheek. I pushed it back with my own hand!"

"Oh, horrible!" The relation made me sick. "Is he otherwise much injured?"

"The doctor thinks there are some bad hurts inside. Why, they kicked and trampled upon him, as if he had been a wild beast! I never saw such a pack of blood-thirsty devils in my life."

"So much for rum," said I.

"Yes, sir; so much for rum," was the emphatic response. "It was the rum, and nothing else. Why, some of the very men who acted the most like tigers and devils, are as harmless persons as you will find in Cedarville when sober. Yes, sir; it was the rum, and nothing else. Rum gave me this broken head and black eye."

"So you had been drinking also?"

"Oh, yes. There's no use in denying that."

"Liquor does you harm."

"Nobody knows that better than I do."

"Why do you drink, then?"

"Oh, just because it comes in the way. Liquor is under my eyes and nose all the time, and it's as natural as breathing to take a little now and then. And when I don't think of it myself, somebody will think of it for me, and say—'Come, Sam, let's take something.' So you see, for a body such as I am, there isn't much help for it."

"But ain't you afraid to go on in this way? Don't you know where it will all end?"

"Just as well as anybody. It will make an end of me—or of all that is good in me. Rum and ruin, you know, sir. They go together like twin brothers."

"Why don't you get out of the way of temptation?" said I.

"It's easy enough to ask that question, sir; but how am I to get out of the way of temptation? Where shall I go, and not find a bar in my road, and somebody to say—'Come, Sam, let's take a drink?' It can't be done, sir, no how. I'm a hostler, and don't know how to be any thing else."

"Can't you work on a farm?"

"Yes; I can do something in that way. But, when there are taverns and bar-rooms, as many as three or four in every mile all over the country, how are you to keep clear of them? Figure me out that."

"I think you'd better vote on the Maine Law[12] side at next election," said I.

"Faith, and I did it last time!" replied the man, with a brightening face— and if I'm spared, I'll go the same ticket next year."

"What do you think of the Law?" I asked.

"Think of it! Bless your heart! if I was a praying man, which I'm sorry to say I ain't—my mother was a pious woman, sir"—his voice fell and slightly trembled—"if I was a praying man, sir, I'd pray, night and morning, and twenty times every day of my life, for God to put it into the hearts of the people to give us that Law. I'd have some hope then. But I haven't much as it is. There's no use in trying to let liquor alone."

"Do many drinking men think as you do?"

"I can count up a dozen or two myself. It isn't the drinking men who are so much opposed to the Maine Law as your politicians. They throw dust in the people's eyes about it, and make a great many, who know nothing at all of the evils of drinking in themselves, believe some bugbear story about trampling on the rights of I don't know who, nor they either. As for rum-sellers' rights, I never could see any right they had to get rich by ruining poor devils such as I am. I think, though, that we have some right to be protected against them."

The ringing of a bell here announced the arrival of some traveler, and the hostler left me.

I learned, during the morning, that Matthew, the bar-keeper, and also the son of Mr. Slade, were both considerably hurt during the affrays in the bar-room, and were confined, temporarily, to their beds. Mrs. Slade still continued in a distressing and dangerous state. Judge Lyman, though shockingly injured, was not thought to be in a critical condition.

A busy day the sheriff had of it, making arrests of various parties engaged in the last night's affairs. Even Slade, unable as he was to lift his head from his pillow, was required to give heavy bail for his appearance at court. Happily, I escaped the inconvenience of being held to appear as a witness, and early in the afternoon had the satisfaction of finding myself rapidly borne away in the stage-coach. It was two years before I entered the pleasant village of Cedarville again.

---

12 In 1851, Neal Dow (1804–1897) helped pass an alcohol prohibition law in the State of Maine.

Night the Eighth

Reaping the Whirlwind

I WAS in Washington City during the succeeding month. It was the short, or closing session of a regular Congressional term. The implication of Judge Lyman in the affair of Green and young Hammond had brought him into such bad odor in Cedarville, and the whole district from which he had been chosen, that his party deemed it wise to set him aside, and take up a candidate less likely to meet with so strong, and, it might be, successful an opposition. By so doing, they were able to secure the election, once more, against the growing temperance party, which succeeded, however, in getting a Maine Law man into the State Legislature. It was, therefore, Judge Lyman's last winter at the Federal Capital.

While seated in the reading-room at Fuller's Hotel, about noon, on the day after my arrival in Washington, I noticed an individual, whose face looked familiar, come in and glance about, as if in search of some one. While yet questioning in my mind who he could be, I heard a man remark to a person with whom he had been conversing—

"There's that vagabond member away from his place in the House, again."

"Who?" inquired the other.

"Why, Judge Lyman," was answered.

"Oh!" said the other, indifferently; "it isn't of much consequence. Precious little wisdom does he add to that intelligent body."

"His vote is worth something, at least, when important questions are at stake."

"What does he charge for it?" was coolly inquired.

There was a shrug of the shoulders, and an arching of the eyebrows, but no answer.

"I'm in earnest, though, in the question," said the last speaker.

"Not in saying that Lyman will sell his vote to the highest bidders?"

"That will depend altogether upon whom the bidders may be. They must be men who have something to lose as well as gain—men not at all likely to bruit[13] the matter, and in serving whose personal interests no abandonment of party is required. Judge Lyman is always on good terms with the lobby members, and may be found in company with some of them daily. Doubtless, his absence from the House, now, is for the purpose of a special meeting with gentlemen who are ready to pay well for votes in favor of some bill making appropriations of public money for private or corporate benefit."

"You certainly cannot mean all you say to be taken in its broadest sense," was replied to this.

"Yes; in its very broadest. Into just this deep of moral and political degradation has this man fallen, disgracing his constituents, and dishonoring his country."

"His presence at Washington doesn't speak very highly in favor of the community he represents."

"No; still, as things are now, we cannot judge of the moral worth of a community by the men sent from it to Congress. Representatives show merely the strength of parties. The candidate chosen in party primary meetings is not selected because he is the best man they have, and the one fittest to legislate wisely in national affairs; but he who happens to have the strongest personal friends among those who nominate, or who is most likely to poll

---

13 A report.

the highest vote. This is why we find, in Congress, such a large preponderance of tenth-rate men."

"A man such as you represent Judge Lyman to be, would sell his country, like another Arnold."[14]

"Yes; if the bid were high enough."

"Does he gamble?"

"Gambling, I might say, is a part of his profession. Very few nights pass, I am told, without finding him at the gaming-table."

I heard no more. At all this, I was not in the least surprised; for my knowledge of the man's antecedents had prepared me for allegations quite as bad as these.

During the week I spent at the Federal Capital, I had several opportunities of seeing Judge Lyman, in the House and out of it,—in the House only when the yeas and nays were called on some important measure, or a vote taken on a bill granting special privileges. In the latter case, his vote, as I noticed, was generally cast on the affirmative side. Several times I saw him staggering on the Avenue, and once brought into the House for the purpose of voting, in so drunken a state, that he had to be supported to his seat. And even worse than this—when his name was called, he was asleep, and had to be shaken several times before he was sufficiently aroused to give his vote!

Happily, for the good of his country, it was his last winter in Washington. At the next session, a better man took his place.

Two years from the period of my last visit to Cedarville, I found myself approaching that quiet village again. As the church-spire came in view, and house after house became visible, here and there, standing out in pleasant relief against the green background of woods and fields, all the exciting events which rendered my last visit so memorable, came up fresh in my mind. I was yet thinking of Willy Hammond's dreadful death, and of his broken-hearted mother, whose life went out with his, when the stage rolled by their old homestead. Oh, what a change was here! Neglect, decay, and dilapidation were visible, let the eye fall where it would. The fences were down, here and there; the hedges, once so green and nicely trimmed, had grown rankly in some places, but were stunted and dying in others; all the beautiful walks were weedy and grass-grown, and the box-borders dead; the garden, rainbow-hued in its wealth of choice and beautiful flowers when I first saw it, was lying waste,—a rooting-ground for hogs. A glance at the house showed a broken chimney, the bricks unremoved from the spot where they struck the ground; a moss-grown roof, with a large limb from a lightning-rent tree lying almost balanced over the eaves, and threatening to fall at the touch of the first wind-storm that swept over. Half of the vines that clambered about the portico were dead, and the rest, untrained, twined themselves in wild disorder, or fell groveling to the earth. One of the pillars of the portico was broken, as were, also, two of the steps that went up to it. The windows of the house were closed, but the door stood open, and, as the stage went past, my eyes rested, for a moment, upon an old man seated in the hall. He was not near enough to the door for me to get a view of his face; but the white flowing hair left me in no doubt as to his identity. It was Judge Hammond.

The "Sickle and Sheaf" was yet the stage-house of Cedarville, and there, a few minutes afterward, I found myself. The hand of change had been here also. The first object that attracted my attention was the sign-post, which, at my earlier arrival, some eight or

---

14 Benedict Arnold (1741–1801) was a brilliant American general who shifted his allegiance to the British in the middle of the American Revolution.

nine years before, stood up in its new white garment of paint, as straight as a plummet-line, bearing proudly aloft the golden sheaf and gleaming sickle. Now, the post, dingy and shattered, and worn from the frequent contact of wheels, and gnawing of restless horses, leaned from its trim perpendicular at an angle of many degrees, as if ashamed of the faded, weather-worn, lying symbol it bore aloft in the sunshine. Around the post was a filthy mud-pool, in which a hog lay grunting out its sense of enjoyment. Two or three old empty whisky barrels lumbered up the dirty porch, on which a coarse, bloated, vulgar-looking man sat leaning against the wall—his chair tipped back on its hind legs—squinting at me from one eye, as I left the stage and came forward toward the house.

"Ah! is this you?" said he, as I came near to him, speaking thickly, and getting up with a heavy motion. I now recognized the altered person of Simon Slade. On looking at him closer, I saw that the eye which I had thought only shut was in fact destroyed. How vividly, now, uprose in imagination the scenes I had witnessed during my last night in his bar-room; the night when a brutal mob, whom he had inebriated with liquor, came near murdering him.

"Glad to see you once more, my boy! Glad to see you! I—I—I'm not just—you see. How are you? How are you?"

And he shook my hand with a drunken show of cordiality.

I felt shocked and disgusted. Wretched man! down the crumbling sides of the pit he had digged for other feet, he was himself sliding, while not enough strength remained even to struggle with his fate.

I tried for a few minutes to talk with him; but his mind was altogether beclouded, and his questions and answers incoherent; so I left him, and entered the bar-room.

"Can I get accommodations here for a couple of days?" I inquired of a stupid, sleepy-looking man, who was sitting in a chair behind the bar.

"I reckon so," he answered, but did not rise.

I turned, and walked a few paces toward the door, and then walked back again.

"I'd like to get a room," said I.

The man got up slowly, and going to a desk, fumbled about in it for a while. At length he brought out an old, dilapidated blank-book, and throwing it open on the counter, asked me, with an indifferent manner, to write down my name.

"I'll take a pen, if you please."

"Oh, yes!" And he hunted about again in the desk, from which, after a while, he brought forth the blackened stump of a quill, and pushed it toward me across the counter.

"Ink," said I—fixing my eyes upon him with a look of displeasure.

"I don't believe there is any," he muttered. "Frank," and he called the landlord's son, going to the door behind the bar as he did so.

"What d'ye want?" a rough, ill-natured voice answered.

"Where's the ink?"

"Don't know any thing about it."

"You had it last. What did you do with it?"

"Nothing!" was growled back.

"Well, I wish you'd find it."

"Find it yourself, and——" I cannot repeat the profane language he used.

"Never mind," said I. "A pencil will do just as well." And I drew one from my pocket. The attempt to write with this, on the begrimed and greasy page of the register, was only partially successful. It would have puzzled almost any one to make out the name. From the date of the last entry, it appeared that mine was the first arrival, for over a week, of any person desiring a room.

As I finished writing my name, Frank came stalking in, with a cigar in his mouth, and a cloud of smoke around his head. He had grown into a stout man—though his face presented little that was manly, in the true sense of the word. It was disgustingly sensual. On seeing me, a slight flush tinged his cheeks.

"How do you do?" he said, offering me his hand. "Peter,"—he turned to the lazy-looking bar-keeper—"tell Jane to have No. 11 put in order for a gentleman immediately, and tell her to be sure and change the bed-linen."

"Things look rather dull here," I remarked, as the bar-keeper went out to do as he had been directed.

"Rather; it's a dull place, anyhow."

"How is your mother?" I inquired.

A slight, troubled look came into his face, as he answered:

"No better."

"She's sick, then?"

"Yes; she's been sick a good while; and I'm afraid will never be much better." His manner was not altogether cold and indifferent, but there was a want of feeling in his voice.

"Is she at home?"

"No, sir."

As he showed no inclination to say more on the subject, I asked no further questions, and he soon found occasion to leave me.

The bar-room had undergone no material change, so far as its furniture and arrangements were concerned; but a very great change was apparent in the condition of these. The brass rod around the bar, which, at my last visit, was brightly polished, was now a greenish-black, and there came from it an unpleasant odor of verdigris.[15] The walls were fairly coated with dust, smoke, and fly-specks, and the windows let in the light but feebly through the dirt-obscured glass. The floor was filthy. Behind the bar, on the shelves designed for a display of liquors, was a confused mingling of empty or half-filled decanters, cigar-boxes, lemons and lemon-peel, old newspapers, glasses, a broken pitcher, a hat, a soiled vest, and a pair of blacking-brushes, with other incongruous things, not now remembered. The air of the room was loaded with offensive vapors.

Disgusted with every thing about the bar, I went into the sitting-room. Here, there was some order in the arrangement of the dingy furniture; but you might have written your name in dust on the looking-glass and table. The smell of the torpid atmosphere was even worse than that of the bar-room. So I did not linger here, but passed through the hall, and out upon the porch, to get a draught of pure air.

Slade still sat leaning against the wall.

"Fine day this," said he, speaking in a mumbling kind of voice.

"Very fine," I answered.

"Yes, very fine."

"Not doing so well as you were a few years ago," said I.

"No—you see—these—these 'ere blamed temperance people are ruining every thing."

"Ah! Is that so?"

---

15 A greenish poisonous pigment that collects on corroding copper.

"Yes. Cedarville isn't what it was when you first came to the 'Sickle and Sheaf.' I——I—— you see. Curse the temperance people! They've ruined every thing, you see. Everything! Ruined—"

And he muttered, and mouthed his words in such a way, that I could understand but little he said; and, in that little, there was scarcely any coherency. So I left him, with a feeling of pity in my heart for the wreck he had become, and went into the town to call upon one or two gentlemen with whom I had business.

In the course of the afternoon, I learned that Mrs. Slade was in an insane asylum, about five miles from Cedarville. The terrible events of the day on which young Hammond was murdered completed the work of mental ruin, begun at the time her husband abandoned the quiet, honorable calling of a miller, and became a tavern-keeper. Reason could hold its position no longer. When word came to her that Willy and his mother were both dead, she uttered a wild shriek, and fell down in a fainting fit. From that period the balance of her mind was destroyed. Long before this, her friends saw that reason wavered. Frank had been her idol. A pure, bright, affectionate boy he was, when she removed with him from their pleasant cottage-home, where all the surrounding influences were good, into a tavern, where an angel could scarcely remain without corruption. From the moment this change was decided on by her husband, a shadow fell upon her heart. She saw, before her husband, her children, and herself, a yawning pit, and felt that, in a very few years, all of them must plunge down into its fearful darkness.

Alas! how quickly began the realization of her worst fears in the corruption of her worshiped boy! And how vain proved all effort and remonstrance, looking to his safety, whether made with himself or his father! From the day the tavern was opened, and Frank drew into his lungs full draughts of the changed atmosphere by which he was now surrounded, the work of moral deterioration commenced. The very smell of the liquor exhilarated him unnaturally; while the subjects of conversation, so new to him, that found discussion in the bar-room, soon came to occupy a prominent place in his imagination, to the exclusion of those humane, child-like, tender, and heavenly thoughts and impressions it had been the mother's care to impart and awaken.

Ah! with what an eager zest does the heart drink in of evil. And how almost hopeless is the case of a boy, surrounded, as Frank was, by the corrupting, debasing associations of a barroom! Had his father meditated his ruin, he could not have more surely laid his plans for the fearful consummation; and he reaped as he had sown. With a selfish desire to get gain, he embarked in the trade of corruption, ruin, and death, weakly believing that he and his could pass through the fire harmless. How sadly a few years demonstrated his error, we have seen.

Flora, I learned, was with her mother, devoting her life to her. The dreadful death of Willy Hammond, for whom she had conceived a strong attachment, came near depriving her of reason also. Since the day on which that awful tragedy occurred, she had never even looked upon her old home. She went away with her unconscious mother, and ever since had remained with her—devoting her life to her comfort. Long before this, all her own and mother's influence over her brother had come to an end. It mattered not how she sought to stay his feet, so swiftly moving along the downward way, whether by gentle entreaty, earnest remonstrance, or tears; in either case, wounds for her own heart were the sure consequences, while his steps never lingered a moment. A swift destiny seemed hurrying him on to ruin. The change in her father—once so tender, so cheerful in his tone, so proud of and loving toward his daughter—was another source of deep grief to her pure young spirit. Over him, as well as over her brother, all her power was lost; and he even avoided her, as though her presence were an offense to him. And so, when she went out from her unhappy home, she took with her no desire to return. Even when imagination bore her back to the "Sickle and Sheaf," she felt an intense, heart-sickening repulsion toward the place where she had first felt the poisoned arrows of life; and in the depths of her spirit she prayed that her eyes might never look upon it again. In her almost cloister-like seclusion, she sought to gather the mantle of oblivion about her heart.

Had not her mother's condition made Flora's duty a plain one, the true, unselfish instincts of her heart would have doubtless led her back to the polluted home she had left, there, in a kind of living death, to minister as best she could to the comfort of a debased father and brother. But she was spared that trial—that fruitless sacrifice.

Evening found me once more in the bar-room of the "Sickle and Sheaf." The sleepy, indifferent bar-keeper, was now more in his element—looked brighter, and had quicker motions. Slade, who had partially recovered from the stupefying effects of the heavy draughts of ale with which he washed down his dinner, was also in a better condition, though not inclined to talk. He was sitting at a table, alone, with his eyes wandering about the room. Whether his thoughts were agreeable or disagreeable, it was not easy to determine. Frank was there, the centre of a noisy group of coarse fellows, whose vulgar sayings and profane expletives continually rung through the room. The noisiest, coarsest, and most profane was Frank Slade; yet did not the incessant volume of bad language that flowed from his tongue appear in the least to disturb his father.

Outraged, at length, by this disgusting exhibition, that had not even the excuse of an exciting cause, I was leaving the bar-room, when I heard some one remark to a young man who had just come in—

"What! you here again, Ned? Ain't you afraid your old man will be after you, as usual?"

"No," answered the person addressed, chuckling inwardly, "he's gone to a prayer-meeting."

"You'll at least have the benefit of his prayers," was lightly remarked.

I turned to observe the young man more closely. His face I remembered, though I could not identify him at first. But, when I heard him addressed soon after as Ned Hargrove, I had a vivid recollection of a little incident that occurred some years before, and which then made a strong impression. The reader has hardly forgotten the visit of Mr. Hargrove to the bar-room of the "Sickle and Sheaf," and the conversation among some of its inmates, which his withdrawal, in company with his son, then occasioned. The father's watchfulness over his boy, and his efforts to save him from the allurements and temptations of a barroom, had proved, as now appeared, unavailing. The son was several years older; but it was sadly evident, from the expression of his face, that he had been growing older in evil faster than in years.

The few words that I have mentioned as passing between this young man and another inmate of the bar-room, caused me to turn back from the door, through which I was about passing, and take a chair near to where Hargrove had seated himself. As I did so, the eyes of Simon Slade rested on the last-named individual.

"Ned Hargrove!" he said, speaking roughly —"if you want a drink, you'd better get it, and make yourself scarce."

"Don't trouble yourself," retorted the young man, "you'll get your money for the drink in good time."

This irritated the landlord, who swore at Hargrove violently, and said something about not wanting boys about his place who couldn't stir from home without having "daddy or mammy running after them."

"Never fear!" cried out the person who had first addressed Hargrove—"his old man's gone to a prayer-meeting. We shan't have the light of his pious countenance here to-night."

I fixed my eyes upon the young man to see what effect this coarse and irreverent allusion to his father would have. A slight tinge of shame was in his face; but I saw that he had not sufficient moral courage to resent the shameful desecration of a parent's name. How should he, when he was himself the first to desecrate that name?

"If he were forty fathoms deep in the infernal regions," answered Slade, "he'd find out that Ned was here, and get half an hour's leave of absence to come after him. The fact is, I'm tired of seeing his solemn, sanctimonious face here every night. If the boy hasn't spirit enough to tell him to mind his own business, as I have done more than fifty times, why, let the boy stay away himself."

"Why don't you send him off with a flea in his ear, Ned?" said one of the company, a young man scarcely his own age. "My old man tried that game with me, but he soon found that I could hold the winning cards."

"Just what I'm going to do the very next time he comes after me."

"Oh, yes! So you've said twenty times," remarked Frank Slade, in a sneering, insolent manner.

Edward Hargrove had not the spirit to resent this; he only answered,

"Just let him show himself here to-night, and you will see."

"No, we won't see," sneered Frank.

"Wouldn't it be fun!" was exclaimed. "I hope to be on hand, should it ever come off."

"He's as 'fraid as death of the old chap," laughed a sottish-looking man, whose age ought to have inspired him with some respect for the relation between father and son, and doubtless would, had not a long course of drinking and familiarity with debasing associates blunted his moral sense.

"Now for it!" I heard uttered, in a quick, delighted voice. "Now for fun! Spunk up to him, Ned! Never say die!"

I turned toward the door, and there stood the father of Edward Hargrove. How well I remembered the broad, fine forehead, the steady, yet mild eyes, the firm lips, the elevated, superior bearing of the man I had once before seen in that place, and on a like errand. His form was slightly bent now; his hair was whiter; his eyes farther back in his head; his face thinner and marked with deeper lines; and there was in the whole expression of his face a touching sadness. Yet, superior to the marks of time and suffering, an unflinching resolution was visible in his countenance, that gave to it a dignity, and extorted involuntary respect. He stood still, after advancing a few paces, and then, his searching eyes having discovered his son, he said mildly, yet firmly, and with such a strength of parental love in his voice that resistance was scarcely possible:

"Edward! Edward! Come, my son."

"Don't go." The words were spoken in an under-tone, and he who uttered them turned his face away from Mr. Hargrove, so that the old man could not see the motion of his lips. A little while before, he had spoken bravely against the father of Edward; now, he could not stand up in his presence.

I looked at Edward. He did not move from where he was sitting, and yet I saw that to resist his father cost him no light struggle.

"Edward." There was nothing imperative—nothing stern—nothing commanding in the father's voice; but its great, its almost irresistible power, lay in its expression of the father's belief that his son would instantly leave the place. And it was this power that prevailed. Edward arose, and, with eyes cast upon the floor, was moving away from his companions, when Frank Slade exclaimed:

"Poor, weak fool!"

It was a lightning flash of indignation, rather than a mere glance from the human eye, that Mr. Hargrove threw instantly upon Frank; while his fine form sprung up erect. He did not speak, but merely transfixed him with a look. Frank curled his lip impotently, as he tried to return the old man's withering glances.

"Now look here!" said Simon Slade, in some wrath, "there's been just about enough of this. I'm getting tired of it. Why don't you keep Ned at home? Nobody wants him here."

"Refuse to sell him liquor," returned Mr. Hargrove.

"It's my trade to sell liquor," answered Slade, boldly.

"I wish you had a more honorable calling," said Hargrove, almost mournfully.

"If you insult my father, I'll strike you down!" exclaimed Frank Slade, starting up and assuming a threatening aspect.

"I respect filial devotion, meet it where I will," calmly replied Mr. Hargrove,—"I only wish it had a better foundation in this case. I only wish the father had merited—"

I will not stain my page with the fearful oath that Frank Slade yelled, rather than uttered, as, with clenched fist, he sprung toward Mr. Hargrove. But ere he had reached the unruffled old man—who stood looking at him as one would look into the eyes of a wild beast, confident that he could not stand the gaze—a firm hand grasped his arm, and a rough voice said—

"Avast, there, young man! Touch a hair of that white head, and I'll wring your neck off"

"Lyon!" As Frank uttered the man's name, he raised his fist to strike him. A moment the clenched hand remained poised in the air; then it fell slowly to his side, and he contented himself with an oath and a vile epithet.

"You can swear to your heart's content. It will do nobody any harm but yourself," coolly replied Mr. Lyon, whom I now recognized as the person with whom I had held several conversations during previous visits.

"Thank you, Mr. Lyon," said Mr. Hargrove, "for this manly interference. It is no more than I should have expected from you."

"I never suffer a young man to strike an old man," said Lyon, firmly. "Apart from that, Mr. Hargrove, there are other reasons why your person must be free from violence where I am."

"This is a bad place for you, Lyon," said Mr. Hargrove; "and I've said so to you a good many times." He spoke in rather an under tone. "Why *will* you come here?"

"It's a bad place, I know," replied Lyon, speaking out boldly, "and we all know it. But habit, Mr. Hargrove—habit. That's the cursed thing! If the bar-rooms were all shut up, there would be another story to tell. Get us the Maine law, and there will be some chance for us."

"Why don't you vote the temperance ticket?" asked Mr. Hargrove.

"Why did I? you'd better ask," said Lyon.

"I thought you voted against us."

"Not I. Ain't quite so blind to my own interests as that. And, if the truth were known, I should not at all wonder if every man in this room, except Slade and his son, voted on your side of the house."

"It's a little strange, then," said Mr. Hargrove, "that with the drinking men on our side, we failed to secure the election."

"You must blame that on your moderate men, who see no danger and go blind with their party," answered Lyon. "We have looked the evil in the face, and know its direful quality."

"Come! I would like to talk with you, Mr. Lyon."

Mr. Hargrove, his son, and Mr. Lyon went out together. As they left the room, Frank Slade said—

"What a cursed liar and hypocrite he is!"

"Who?" was asked.

"Why, Lyon," answered Frank, boldly.

"You'd better say that to his face."

"It wouldn't be good for him," remarked one of the company.

At this Frank started to his feet, stalked about the room, and put on all the disgusting airs of a drunken braggart. Even his father saw the ridiculous figure he cut, and growled out—

"There, Frank, that'll do. Don't make a miserable fool of yourself!"

At which Frank retorted, with so much of insolence that his father flew into a towering passion, and ordered him to leave the bar-room.

"You can go out yourself if you don't like the company. I'm very well satisfied," answered Frank.

"Leave this room, you impudent young scoundrel!"

"Can't go, my amiable friend," said Frank, with a cool self-possession that maddened his father, who got up hastily, and moved across the bar-room to the place where he was standing.

"Go out, I tell you!" Slade spoke resolutely.

"Would be happy to oblige you," Frank said, in a taunting voice; "but, 'pon my word, it isn't at all convenient."

Half intoxicated as he was, and already nearly blind with passion, Slade lifted his hand to strike his son. And the blow would have fallen had not some one caught his arm, and held him back from the meditated violence. Even the debased visitors of this bar-room could not stand by and see nature outraged in a bloody strife between father and son; for it was plain from the face and quickly assumed attitude of Frank, that if his father had laid his hand upon him, he would have struck him in return.

I could not remain to hear the awful imprecations that father and son, in their impotent rage, called down from heaven upon each other's heads. It was the most shocking exhibition of depraved human nature that I had ever seen. And so I left the bar-room, glad to escape from its stifling atmosphere and revolting scenes.

Night the Ninth

A Fearful Consummation

NEITHER Slade nor his son was present at the breakfast-table on the next morning. As for myself, I did not eat with much appetite. Whether this defect arose from the state of my mind, or the state of the food set before me, I did not stop to inquire; but left the stifling, offensive atmosphere of the dining-room in a very few moments after entering that usually attractive place for a hungry man.

A few early drinkers were already in the bar-room—men with shattered nerves and cadaverous faces, who could not begin the day's work without the stimulus of brandy or whisky. They came in, with gliding footsteps, asked for what they wanted in low voices, drank in silence, and departed. It was a melancholy sight to look upon.

About nine o'clock the landlord made his appearance. He, too, came gliding into the bar-room, and his first act was to seize upon a brandy decanter, pour out nearly half a pint of the fiery liquid, and drink it off. How badly his hand shook—so badly that he spilled the brandy both in pouring it out and in lifting the glass to his lips! What a shattered wreck he was! He looked really worse now than he did on the day before, when drink gave an artificial vitality to his system, a tension to his muscles, and light to his countenance. The miller of ten years ago, and the tavern-keeper of to-day! Who could have identified them as one?

Slade was turning from the bar, when a man came in. I noticed an instant change in the landlord's countenance. He looked startled; almost frightened. The man drew a small package from his pocket, and after selecting a paper therefrom, presented it to Slade, who received it with a nervous reluctance, opened, and let his eye fall upon the writing within. I was observing him closely at the time, and saw his countenance flush deeply. In a moment or two it became pale again—paler even than before.

"Very well—all right. I'll attend to it," said the landlord, trying to recover himself, yet swallowing with every sentence.

The man, who was no other than a sheriff's deputy, and who gave him a sober, professional look, then went out with a firm step, and an air of importance. As he passed through the outer door, Slade retired from the bar-room.

"Trouble coming," I heard the bar-keeper remark, speaking partly to himself, and partly with the view, as was evident from his manner, of leading me to question him. But this I did not feel that it was right to do.

"Got the sheriff on him at last," added the bar-keeper.

"What's the matter, Bill?" inquired a man who now came in with a bustling, important air, and leaned familiarly over the bar. "Who was Jenkins after?"

"The old man," replied the bar-keeper, in a voice that showed pleasure rather than regret.

"No!"

"It's a fact." Bill, the bar-keeper, actually smiled.

"What's to pay?" said the man.

"Don't know, and don't care much."

"Did he serve a summons or an execution?"[16]

"Can't tell."

"Judge Lyman's suit went against him."

"Did it?"

"Yes; and I heard Judge Lyman swear, that if he got him on the hip, he'd sell him out, bag and basket. And he's the man to keep his word."

"I never could just make out," said the barkeeper, "how he ever came to owe Judge Lyman so much. I've never known of any business transactions between them."

"It's been dog eat dog, I rather guess," said the man.

"What do you mean by that?" inquired the bar-keeper.

"You've heard of dogs hunting in pairs?"

"Oh, yes."

---

16 Enforcing a legal judgment.

"Well, since Harvey Green got his deserts, the business of fleecing our silly young fellows, who happened to have more money than wit or discretion, has been in the hands of Judge Lyman and Slade. They hunted together, Slade holding the game, while the Judge acted as blood-sucker. But that business was interrupted about a year ago; and game got so scarce that, as I suggested, dog began to eat dog. And here comes the end of the matter, if I'm not mistaken. So mix us a stiff toddy. I want one more good drink at the 'Sickle and Sheaf,' before the colors are struck."

And the man chuckled at his witty effort.

During the day, I learned that affairs stood pretty much as this man had conjectured. Lyman's suits had been on sundry notes payable on demand; but nobody knew of any property transactions between him and Slade. On the part of Slade, no defense had been made—the suit going by default. The visit of the sheriff's officer was for the purpose of serving an execution.

As I walked through Cedarville on that day, the whole aspect of the place seemed changed. I questioned with myself, often, whether this were really so, or only the effect of imagination. The change was from cheerfulness and thrift, to gloom and neglect. There was, to me, a brooding silence in the air; a pause in the life-movement; a folding of the hands, so to speak, because hope had failed from the heart. The residence of Mr. Harrison, who, some two years before, had suddenly awakened to a lively sense of the evil of rum-selling, because his own sons were discovered to be in danger, had been one of the most tasteful in Cedarville. I had often stopped to admire the beautiful shrubbery and flowers with which it was surrounded; the walks so clear—the borders so fresh and even—the arbors so cool and inviting. There was not a spot upon which the eye could rest, that did not show the hand of taste. When I now came opposite to this house, I was no longer in doubt as to the actuality of a change. There were no marked evidences of neglect; but the high cultivation and nice regard for the small details were lacking. The walks were cleanly swept; but the box-borders were not so carefully trimmed. The vines and bushes that in former times were cut and tied so evenly, could hardly have felt the keen touch of the pruning-knife for months.

As I paused to note the change, a lady, somewhat beyond the middle age, came from the house. I was struck by the deep gloom that overshadowed her countenance. Ah! said I to myself, as I passed on, how many dear hopes, that once lived in that heart, must have been scattered to the winds. As I conjectured, this was Mrs. Harrison, and I was not unprepared to hear, as I did a few hours afterward, that her two sons had fallen into drinking habits; and, not only this, had been enticed to the gaming table. Unhappy mother! What a lifetime of wretchedness was compressed for thee into a few short years!

I walked on, noting, here and there, changes even more marked than appeared about the residence of Mr. Harrison. Judge Lyman's beautiful place showed utter neglect; and so did one or two others that, on my first visit to Cedarville, charmed me with their order, neatness, and cultivation. In every instance, I learned, on inquiring, that the owners of these, or some members of their families, were, or had been, visitors at the "Sickle and Sheaf;" and that the ruin, in progress or completed, began after the establishment of that point of attraction in the village.

Something of a morbid curiosity, excited by what I saw, led me on to take a closer view of the residence of Judge Hammond than I had obtained on the day before. The first thing that I noticed, on approaching the old, decaying mansion, were handbills, posted on the gate, the front-door, and on one of the windows. A nearer inspection revealed their import. The property had been seized; and was now offered at sheriff's sale!

Ten years before, Judge Hammond was known as the richest man in Cedarville: and now, the homestead he had once so loved to beautify—where all that was dearest to him in life once gathered—worn, disfigured, and in ruins, was about being wrested from him. I paused at the gate, and leaning over it, looked in with saddened feelings upon the dreary waste within. No sign of life was visible. The door was shut—the windows closed—not the faintest wreath of smoke was seen above the blackened chimney-tops. How vividly did imagination restore the life, and beauty, and happiness, that made their home there only a few years before,—the mother and her noble boy, one looking with trembling hope, the other with joyous confidence, into the future,—the father, proud of his household treasures, but not their wise and jealous guardian.

Ah! that his hands should have unbarred the door, and thrown it wide, for the wolf to enter that precious fold! I saw them all in their sunny life before me; yet, even as I looked upon them, their sky began to darken. I heard the distant mutterings of the storm, and soon the desolating tempest swept down fearfully upon them. I shuddered as it passed away, to look upon the wrecks left scattered around. What a change!

"And all this," said I, "that one man, tired of being useful, and eager to get gain, might gather in accursed gold!"

Pushing open the gate, I entered the yard, and walked around the dwelling, my footsteps echoing in the hushed solitude of the deserted place. Hark! was that a human voice?

I paused to listen.

The sound came, once more, distinctly to my ears. I looked around, above, everywhere, but perceived no living sign. For nearly a minute I stood still, listening. Yes: there it was again—a low, moaning voice, as of one in pain or grief. I stepped onward a few paces; and now saw one of the doors standing ajar. As I pushed this door wide open, the moan was repeated. Following the direction from which the sound came, I entered one of the large drawing-rooms. The atmosphere was stifling, and all as dark as if it were midnight. Groping my way to a window, I drew back the bolt and threw open a shutter. Broadly the light fell across the dusty, uncarpeted floor, and on the dingy furniture of the room. As it did so, the moaning voice which had drawn me thither swelled on the air again; and now I saw, lying upon an old sofa, the form of a man. It needed no second glance to tell me that this was Judge Hammond. I put my hand upon him, and uttered his name: but he answered not. I spoke more firmly, and slightly shook him; but only a piteous moan was returned.

"Judge Hammond!" I now called aloud, and somewhat imperatively.

But it availed nothing. The poor old man aroused not from the stupor in which mind and body were enshrouded.

"He is dying!" thought I; and instantly left the house in search of some friends to take charge of him in his last, sad extremity. The first person to whom I made known the fact shrugged his shoulders, and said it was no affair of his, and that I must find somebody whose business it was to attend to him. My next application was met in the same spirit; and no better success attended my reference of the matter to a third party. No one to whom I spoke seemed to have any sympathy for the broken-down old man. Shocked by this indifference, I went to one of the county officers, who, on learning the condition of Judge Hammond, took immediate steps to have him removed to the Alms-house, some miles distant.

"But why to the Alms-house?" I inquired, on learning his purpose. "He has property."

"Every thing has been seized for debt," was the reply.

"Will there be nothing left after his creditors are satisfied?"

"Very few, if any, will be satisfied," he answered. "There will not be enough to pay half the judgments against him."

"And is there no friend to take him in,—no one, of all who moved by his side in the days of prosperity, to give a few hours' shelter, and soothe the last moments of his unhappy life?"

"Why did you make application here?" was the officer's significant question.

I was silent.

"Your earnest appeals for the poor old man met with no words of sympathy? "

"None."

"He has, indeed, fallen low. In the days of his prosperity, he had many friends, so called. Adversity has shaken them all like dead leaves from sapless branches."

"But why? This is not always so."

"Judge Hammond was a selfish, worldly man. People never liked him much. His favoring, so strongly, the tavern of Slade, and his distillery operations, turned from him some of his best friends. The corruption and terrible fate of his son—and the insanity and death of his wife—all were charged upon him in people's minds; and every one seemed to turn from him instinctively after the fearful tragedy was completed. He never held up his head afterward. Neighbors shunned him as they would a criminal. And here has come the end at last. He will be taken to the Poor-house, to die there—a pauper!"

"And all," said I, partly speaking to myself, "because a man, too lazy to work at an honest calling, must needs go to rum-selling."

"The truth, the whole truth, and nothing but the truth," remarked the officer with emphasis, as he turned from me to see that his directions touching the removal of Mr. Hammond to the Poor-house were promptly executed.

In my wanderings about Cedarville during that day, I noticed a small but very neat cottage, a little way from the centre of the village. There was not around it a great profusion of flowers and shrubbery; but the few vines, flowers, and bushes that grew green and flourishing about the door, and along the clean walks, added to the air of taste and comfort that so peculiarly marked the dwelling.

"Who lives in that pleasant little spot?" I asked of a man whom I had frequently seen in Slade's bar-room. He happened to be passing the house at the same time that I was.

"Joe Morgan," was answered.

"Indeed!" I spoke in some surprise. "And what of Morgan? How is he doing?"

"Very well."

"Doesn't he drink?"

"No. Since the death of his child, he has never taken a drop. That event sobered him, and he has remained sober ever since."

"What is he doing?"

"Working at his old trade."

"That of a miller?"

"Yes. After Judge Hammond broke down, the distillery apparatus and cotton spinning machinery were all sold and removed from Cedarville. The purchaser of what remained, having something of the fear of God, as well as regard for man, in his heart, set himself to the restoration of the old order of things, and in due time the revolving mill-wheel was at its old and better work of grinding corn and wheat for bread. The only two men in Cedarville competent to take charge of the mill were Simon Slade and Joe Morgan. The first could not be had, and the second came in as a matter of course."

"And he remains sober and industrious?"

"As any man in the village," was the answer.

I saw but little of Slade or his son during the day. But both were in the bar-room at night, and both in a condition sorrowful to look upon. Their presence, together, in the bar-room, half intoxicated as they were, seemed to revive the unhappy temper of the previous evening, as freshly as if the sun had not risen and set upon their anger.

During the early part of the evening, considerable company was present, though not of a very select class. A large proportion were young men. To most of them the fact that Slade had fallen into the sheriff's hands was known; and I gathered from some aside conversation which reached my ears, that Frank's idle, spendthrift habits had hastened the present crisis in his father's affairs. He, too, was in debt to Judge Lyman—on what account, it was not hard to infer.

It was after nine o'clock, and there were not half a dozen persons in the room, when I noticed Frank Slade go behind the bar for the third or fourth time. He was just lifting a decanter of brandy, when his father, who was considerably under the influence of drink, started forward, and laid his hand upon that of his son. Instantly a fierce light gleamed from the eyes of the young man.

"Let go of my hand!" he exclaimed.

"No, I won't. Put up that brandy bottle—you're drunk now."

"Don't meddle with me, old man!" angrily retorted Frank. "I'm not in the mood to bear any thing more from *you*."

"You're drunk as a fool now," returned Slade, who had seized the decanter. "Let go the bottle."

For only an instant did the young man hesitate. Then he drove his half-clenched hand against the breast of his father, who went staggering away several paces from the counter. Recovering himself, and now almost furious, the landlord rushed forward upon his son, his hand raised to strike him.

"Keep off!" cried Frank. "Keep off! If you touch me, I'll strike you down!" At the same time raising the half-filled bottle threateningly.

But his father was in too maddened a state to fear any consequences, and so pressed forward upon his son, striking him in the face the moment he came near enough to do so.

Instantly, the young man, infuriated by drink and evil passions, threw the bottle at his father's head. The dangerous missile fell, crashing upon one of his temples, shivering it into a hundred pieces. A heavy, jarring fall too surely marked the fearful consequences of the blow. When we gathered around the fallen man, and made an effort to lift him from the floor, a thrill of horror went through every heart. A mortal paleness was already on his marred face, and the death-gurgle in his throat! In three minutes from the time the blow was struck, his spirit had gone upward to give an account of the deeds done in the body.

"Frank Slade! you have murdered your father!"

Sternly were these terrible words uttered. It was some time before the young man seemed to comprehend their meaning. But the moment he realized the awful truth, he uttered an exclamation of horror. Almost at the same instant, a pistol-shot came sharply on the ear. But the meditated self-destruction was not accomplished. The aim was not surely taken; and the ball struck harmlessly against the ceiling.

Half an hour afterward, and Frank Slade was a lonely prisoner in the county jail!

Does the reader need a word of comment on this fearful consummation? No: and we will offer none.

"FRANK SLADE! YOU HAVE MURDERED YOUR FATHER!"

"Frank Slade! You have murdered your father!"

Night the Tenth

The Closing Scene at the "Sickle and Sheaf"

ON the day that succeeded the evening of this fearful tragedy, placards were to be seen all over the village, announcing a mass meeting at the "Sickle and Sheaf" that night.

By early twilight, the people commenced assembling. The bar, which had been closed all day, was now thrown open, and lighted; and in this room, where so much of evil had been originated, encouraged, and consummated, a crowd of earnest-looking men were soon gathered. Among them I saw the fine person of Mr. Hargrove. Joe Morgan—or rather, Mr. Morgan—was also of the number. The latter I would scarcely have recognized, had not some one near me called him by name. He was well dressed, stood erect, and though there were many deep lines on his thoughtful countenance, all traces of his former habits were gone. While I was observing him, he arose, and addressing a few words to the assemblage, nominated Mr. Hargrove as chairman of the meeting. To this a unanimous assent was given.

On talking the chair, Mr. Hargrove made a brief address, something to this effect.

"Ten years ago," said he, his voice evincing a slight unsteadiness as he began, but growing firmer as he proceeded, "there was not a happier spot in Bolton county than Cedarville. Now, the marks of ruin are everywhere. Ten years ago, there was a kind-hearted, industrious miller in Cedarville, liked by every one, and as harmless as a little child. Now, his bloated, disfigured body lies in that room. His death was violent, and by the hand of his own son!"

Mr. Hargrove's words fell slowly, distinctly, and marked by the most forcible emphasis. There was scarcely one present who did not feel a low shudder run along his nerves, as the last words were spoken in a husky whisper.

"Ten years ago," he proceeded, "the miller had a happy wife, and two innocent, gladhearted children. Now, his wife, bereft of reason, is in a mad-house, and his son the occupant of a felon's cell, charged with the awful crime of parricide!"

Briefly he paused, while his audience stood gazing upon him with half-suspended respiration.

"Ten years ago," he went on, "Judge Hammond was accounted the richest man in Cedarville. Yesterday he was carried, a friendless pauper, to the Alms-house; and to-day he is the unmourned occupant of a pauper's grave! Ten years ago, his wife was the proud, hopeful, loving mother of a most promising son. I need not describe what Willy Hammond was. All here knew him well. Ah! What shattered the fine intellect of that noble-minded woman? Why did her heart break? Where is she? Where is Willy Hammond?"

A low, half-repressed groan answered the speaker.

"Ten years ago, you, sir," pointing to a sad-looking old man, and calling him by name, "had two sons—generous, promising, manly-hearted boys. What are they now? You need not answer the question. Too well is their history and your sorrow known. Ten years ago, I had a son,—amiable, kind, loving, but weak. Heaven knows how I sought to guard and protect him! But he fell also. The arrows of destruction darkened the very air of our once secure and happy village. And who was safe? Not mine, nor yours!

"Shall I go on? Shall I call up and pass in review before you, one after another, all the wretched victims who have fallen in Cedarville during the last ten years? Time does not permit. It would take hours for the enumeration! No; I will not throw additional darkness into the picture. Heaven knows it is black enough already! But what is the root of this great evil? Where lies the fearful secret? Who understands the disease? A direful pestilence is in the air—it walketh in darkness, and wasteth at noonday. It is slaying the first-born in our houses, and the cry of anguish is swelling on every gale. Is there no remedy?"

"Yes! yes! There is a remedy!" was the spontaneous answer from many voices.

"Be it our task, then, to find and apply it this night," answered the chairman, as he took his seat.

"And there is but one remedy," said Morgan, as Mr. Hargrove sat down. "The accursed traffic must cease among us. You must cut off the fountain, if you would dry up the stream. If you would save the young, the weak, and the innocent—on you God has laid the solemn duty of their protection—you must cover them from the tempter. Evil is strong, wily, fierce, and active in the pursuit of its ends. The young, the weak, and the innocent can no more resist its assaults, than the lamb can resist the wolf. They are helpless, if you abandon them to the powers of evil. Men and brethren! as one who has himself been well-nigh lost—as one who, daily, feels and trembles at the dangers that beset his path—I do conjure you to stay the fiery stream that is bearing every thing good and beautiful among you to destruction. Fathers! for the sake of your young children, be up now and doing. Think of Willy Hammond, Frank Slade, and a dozen more whose names I could repeat, and hesitate no longer! Let us resolve, this night, that from henceforth the traffic shall cease in Cedarville. Is there not a large majority of citizens in favor of such a measure? And whose rights or interests can be affected by such a restriction? Who, in fact, has any right to sow disease and death in our community? The liberty, under sufferance, to do so, wrongs the individual who uses it, as well as those who become his victims. Do you want proof of this? Look at Simon Slade, the happy, kind-hearted miller; and at Simon Slade, the tavern-keeper. Was he benefited by the liberty to work harm to his neighbor? No! no! In heaven's name, then, let the traffic cease! To this end, I offer these resolutions:—

"Be it resolved by the inhabitants of Cedarville, That from this day henceforth, no more intoxicating drink shall be sold within the limits of the corporation.

"Resolved, further, That all the liquors in the 'Sickle and Sheaf' be forthwith destroyed, and that a fund be raised to pay the creditors of Simon Slade therefor, should they demand compensation.

"Resolved, That in closing up all other places where liquor is sold, regard shall be had to the right of property which the law secures to every man.

"Resolved, That with the consent of the legal authorities, all the liquor for sale in Cedarville be destroyed; provided the owners thereof be paid its full value out of a fund specially raised for that purpose."

But for the calm yet resolute opposition of one or two men, these resolutions would have passed by acclamation. A little sober argument showed the excited company that no good end is ever secured by the adoption of wrong means.

There were, in Cedarville, regularly constituted authorities, which alone had the power to determine public measures; or to say what business might or might not be pursued by individuals. And through these authorities they must act in an orderly way.

There was some little chafing at this view of the case. But good sense and reason prevailed. Somewhat modified, the resolutions passed, and the more ultra-inclined contented themselves with carrying out the second resolution, to destroy forthwith all the liquor to be found on the premises; which was immediately done. After which the people dispersed to their homes, each with a lighter heart, and better hopes for the future of their village.

On the next day, as I entered the stage that was to bear me from Cedarville, I saw a man strike his sharp axe into the worn, faded, and leaning post that had, for so many years, borne aloft the "Sickle and Sheaf;" and, just as the driver gave word to his horses, the false emblem which had invited so many to enter the way of destruction, fell crashing to the earth.

THE END

Chapter Twelve

ANN SOPHIA WINTERBOTHAM STEPHENS
(1810–1886)

Born into a well-to-do Connecticut wool merchant family, Ann Stephens received a good education, both formally in dame schools and less formally through her family's highly educated social circles. Early in her career she wrote poetry and later joined the editorial staffs of a number of important American periodicals, including the *Ladies Companion*, *Graham's Magazine* (where she worked alongside fellow editor Edgar Allan Poe), and *Frank Leslie's Ladies Gazette of Fashion*. She even published her own magazine for a time, *Mrs. Stephen's Illustrated New Monthly* (1856–58). Her writing gained her such fame that when she visited Europe, she was entertained by both Charles Dickens and William Makepeace Thackeray, as well as the famous explorer and naturalist Alexander von Humboldt.

Along with being an immensely prolific author and editor, Stephens had a voracious appetite for learning. After traveling on the Ohio frontier and studying various Native American languages, she wrote *Malaeska* for the *Ladies Companion* as a three-part serial in 1839. Later, at the height of her literary fame, the newly established publishing firm of Irwin P. Beadle chose Stephens's *Malaeska* as the inaugural volume in its revolutionary new dime novel library—a series of books that promised exciting reading material for the masses. For the Beadle edition, Stephens complicated the story's plot and enriched its descriptive passages, as well as added epigraphs to its chapters and modernized its punctuation. It is estimated that as a dime novel, and in its other printed forms, *Malaeska* sold some half million copies in the nineteenth century.

Malaeska is the account of a strong and resourceful Native American woman, who marries a white man only to see him killed by her father. The resulting events tell the tortuous story of Malaeska coming to terms with the doomed nature of cross-racial encounters and relationships on the American frontier. It is a tragic tale that underlines—through a personal, domestic story of love and loss—the plight of Native Americans in the midst of the unremitting westward expansion of white civilization in the early nineteenth century.

MALAESKA; THE INDIAN WIFE
OF THE WHITE HUNTER

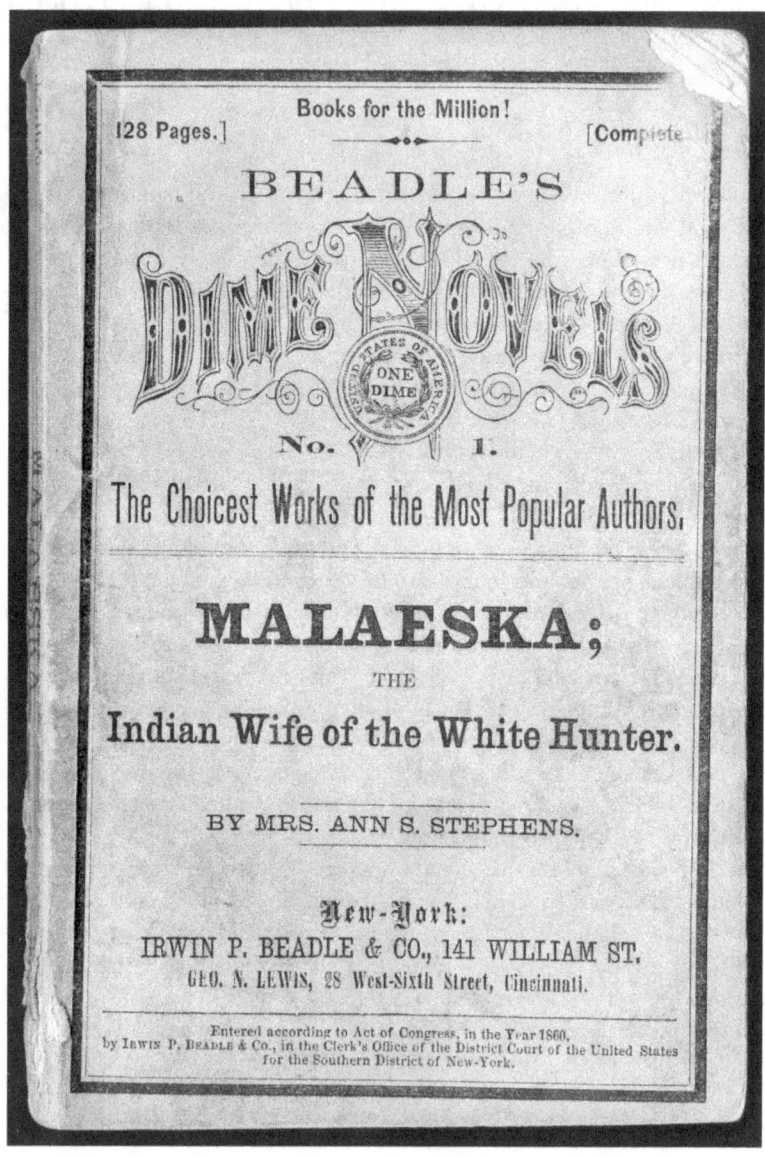

Dime Novel Cover of *Malaeska* (New York: Irwin P. Beadle, 1860, Courtesy Lilly Library, Bloomington, IN).

This text is reprinted from the Beadle's Dime Novels edition of *Malaeska; The Indian Wife of the White Hunter*, published in New York by Irwin P. Beadle in 1860.

Publishers' Notice from the First Edition

WE take pleasure in introducing the reader to the following romance by Mrs. Ann
S. Stephens. It is one of the most interesting and fascinating works of this eminent author.
It is chosen as the initial volume of the Dime Novel series, from the chaste character of its
delineations, from the interest which attaches to its fine pictures of border life and Indian
adventure, and from the real romance of its incidents. It is American in all its features,
pure in its tone, elevating in its sentiments; and may be referred to as a work representative of the series that is to follow—every volume of which will be of the highest order of
merit, from the pens of authors whose intellectual and moral excellencies have already
given the writers an enviable name, in this country and in Europe. By the publication of
the series contemplated, it is hoped to reach all classes, old and young, male and female, in
a manner at once to captivate and to enliven—to answer to the popular demand for works
of romance, but also to instill a pure and elevating sentiment in the hearts and minds of
the people.

BEADLE & Co.
New York,
June, 1860.

Chapter I

The brake hung low on the rifted rock
　With sweet and holy dread;
The wild-flowers trembled to the shock
　Of the red man's stealthy tread;
And all around fell a fitful gleam
　Through the light and quivering spray,
While the noise of a restless mountain-stream
　Rush'd out on the stilly day.

THE traveler who has stopped at Catskill, on his way up the Hudson, will remember that
a creek of no insignificant breadth washes one side of the village, and that a heavy stone
dwelling stands a little up from the water on a point of verdant meadow-land, which forms
a lip of the stream, where it empties into the more majestic river. This farm-house is the
only object that breaks the green and luxuriant beauty of the point, on that side, and its
quiet and entire loneliness contrasts pleasantly with the bustling and crowded little village
on the opposite body of land. There is much to attract attention to that dwelling. Besides
occupying one of the most lovely sites on the river, it is remarkable for an appearance of
old-fashioned comfort at variance with the pillared houses and rustic cottages which meet
the eye everywhere on the banks of the Hudson. There are no flowers to fling fragrance
about it, and but little of embellishment is manifest in its grounds; but it is surrounded by an
abundance of thrifty fruit-trees; an extensive orchard sheds its rich foliage to the sunshine
on the bank, and the sward is thick and heavy which slopes greenly from the front door
down to the river's brink.

　The interior of the house retains an air of substantial comfort which answers well to
the promise conveyed without. The heavy furniture has grown old with its occupants; rich
it has been in its time, and now it possesses the rare quality of fitness, and of being in

harmony with surrounding things. Every thing about that house is in perfect keeping with the character and appearance of its owner. The occupant himself, is a fine stately farmer of the old class—shrewd, penetrating, and intelligent —one of those men who contrive to keep the heart green when the frost of age is chilling the blood and whitening upon the brow. He has already numbered more than the threescore years and ten allotted to man. His habits and the fashion of his attire are those of fifty years ago. He still clings to huge wood-fires, apples, and cider in the winter-season, and allows a bevy of fine cows to pasture on the rich grass in front of his dwelling in the summer. All the hospitable feeling of former years remains warm at his heart. He is indeed a fine specimen of the staunch old republi- can farmer of the last century, occupying the house which his father erected, and enjoying a fresh old age beneath the roof tree which shadowed his infancy.

During a sojourn in this vicinity last season, it was one of our greatest pleasures to spend an evening with the old gentleman, listening to legends of the Indians, reminis- cences of the Revolution, and pithy remarks on the present age, with which he loved to entertain us, while we occasionally interrupted him by comparing knitting-work with the kind old lady, his wife, or by the praises of a sweet little grandchild, who would cling about his knees and play with the silver buckles on his shoes as he talked. That tall, stately old man, and the sweet child made a beautiful picture of "age at play with infancy," when the fire-light flickered over them, to the ancient family pictures, painted in Holland, hang- ing on the wall behind us, in the old-fashioned oval frames, which, with the heavy Dutch Bible, which lay on the stand, secured with hasps and brass hinges, ponderous as the fas- tenings of a prison-door, were family relics precious to the old gentleman from antiquity and association. Yes, the picture was pleasant to look upon; but there was pleasure in listening to his legends and stories. If the one here related is not exactly as he told it, he will not fail to recognize the beautiful young Indian girl, whom he described to us, in the character of Malaeska.

At the time of our story, the beautiful expanse of country which stretches from the foot of the Catskill mountains[1] to the Hudson was one dense wilderness. The noble stream glided on in the solemn stillness of nature, shadowed with trees that had battled with storms for centuries, its surface as yet unbroken, save by the light prow of the Indian's canoe. The lofty rampart of mountains frowned against the sky as they do now, but ren- dered more gloomy by the thick growth of timber which clothed them at the base; they loomed up from the dense sea of foliage like the outposts of a darker world. Of all the cultivated acres which at the present day sustain thousands with their products, one little clearing alone smiled up from the heart of the wilderness. A few hundred acres had been cleared by a hardy band of settlers, and a cluster of log-houses was erected in the heart of the little valley which now contains Catskill village. Although in the neighborhood of a savage Indian tribe, the little band of pioneers remained unmolested in their hum- ble occupations, gradually clearing the land around their settlement, and sustaining their families on the game which was found in abundance in the mountains. They held little intercourse with the Indians, but hitherto no act of hostility on either side had aroused discontent between the settler and the savages.

It was early in May, about a year after the first settlement of the whites, when some six or eight of the stoutest men started for the woods in search of game. A bear had been seen

---

1 A region in southeastern New York State, with high mountains to the west, that is linked by the Hudson River to Albany and New York City.

on the brink of the clearing at break of day, and while the greater number struck off in search of more humble game, three of the most resolute followed his trail, which led to the mountains.

The foremost of the three hunters was an Englishman of about forty, habited in a threadbare suit of blue broadcloth, with drab gaiters buttoned up to his knees, and a hat sadly shorn of its original nap. His hunting apparatus bespoke the peculiar care which all of his country so abundantly bestow on their implements of sport. The other two were much younger, and dressed in home-made cloth, over which were loose frocks manufactured from the refuse flax or swingled tow. Both were handsome, but different in the cast of their features. The character of the first might be read in his gay air and springy step, as he followed close to the Englishman, dashing away the brushwood with the muzzle of his gun, and detecting with a quick eye the broken twigs or disturbed leaves which betrayed the course of the hunted bear. There was also something characteristic in the wearing of his dress, in the fox-skin cap thrown carelessly on one side of his superb head, exposing a mass of short brown curls around the left ear and temple, and in the bosom of his coarse frock, thrown open so as to give free motion to a neck Apollo might have coveted. He was a hunter, who had occasionally visited the settlement of late, but spent whole weeks in the woods, professedly in collecting furs by his own efforts, or by purchase from the tribe of Indians encamped at the foot of the mountains.

The last was more sedate in his looks, and less buoyant in his air. There was an intellectual expression in his high, thoughtful brow, embrowned though it was by exposure. A depth of thought in his serious eye, and a graceful dignity in his carriage, bespoke him as one of those who hide deep feeling under an appearance of coldness and apathy. He had been a schoolmaster in the Bay State,[2] from whence he had been drawn by the bright eyes and merry laugh of one Martha Fellows, a maiden of seventeen, whose father had moved to the settlement at Catskill the preceding summer, and to whom, report said, he was to be married whenever a minister, authorized to perform the ceremony, should find his way to the settlement.

The three hunters bent their way in a southwestern direction from the settlement, till the forest suddenly opened into a beautiful and secluded piece of meadow-land, known to this day by its Dutch title of "the Straka," which means, our aged friend informed us, a strip of land. The Straka lay before them of an oblong form, some eight or ten acres in expanse, with all its luxuriance of trees, grass, and flowers, bathed in the dew and sunshine of a warm summer's morning. It presented a lovely contrast to the dense wilderness from which the hunters emerged, and they halted for a moment beneath the boughs of a tall hickory to enjoy its delicious freshness. The surface of the inclosure was not exactly level, but down the whole length it curved gently up from the middle, on either side, to the magnificent trees that hedged it in with a beautiful and leafy rampart. The margin was irregular; here and there a clump of trees shot down into the inclosure, and the clearing occasionally ran up into the forest in tiny glades and little grassy nooks, in which the sunlight slumbered like smiles on the face of a dreaming infant. On every side the trunks of huge trees shot up along the margin beneath their magnificent canopy of leaves, like the ivied columns of a ruin, or fell back in the misty perspective of the forest, scarcely discernible in its gloom of shadow. The heavy piles of foliage, which fell amid the boughs like a

2 Massachusetts.

wealth of drapery flung in masses to the summer wind, was thrifty and ripe with the warm breath of August. No spirit of decay had as yet shed a gorgeous breath over its deep, rich green, but all was wet with dew, and kindled up by the sunlight to a thousand varying tints of the same color. A bright spring gushed from a swell of ground in the upper part of the inclosure, and the whole surface of the beautiful spot was covered with a vigorous growth of tall meadow-grass, which rose thicker and brighter and of a more delicate green down the middle, where the spring curved onward in a graceful rivulet, musical as the laugh of a child. As if called to life by the chime of a little brook, a host of white wild-flowers unfolded their starry blossoms along the margin, and clumps of swamp-lilies shed an azure hue along the grass.

Until that day, our hunters had ever found "the Straka" silent and untenanted, save by singing-birds, and wild deer which came down from the mountains to feed on its rich verdure; but now a dozen wreaths of smoke curled up from the trees at the north-ern extremity, and a camp of newly-erected wigwams might be seen through a vista in the wood. One or two were built even on the edge of the clearing; the grass was much trampled around them, and three or four half-naked Indian children lay rolling upon it, laughing, shouting, and flinging up their limbs in the pleasant morning air. One young Indian woman was also frolicking among them, tossing an infant in her arms, caroling and playing with it. Her laugh was musical as a bird song, and as she darted to and fro, now into the forest and then out into the sunshine, her long hair glowed like the wing of a raven, and her motion was graceful as an untamed gazelle. They could see that the child, too, was very beautiful, even from the distance at which they stood, and occasionally, as the wind swept toward them, his shout came ringing upon it like the gush of waters leap-ing from their fount.

"This is a little *too* bad," muttered the Englishman, fingering his gun-lock. "Can they find no spot to burrow in but 'the Straka?' St. George! but I have a mind to shoot the squaw and wring the neck of every red imp among them."

"Do it!" exclaimed Danforth, turning furiously upon him; "touch but a hair of her head, and by the Lord that made me, I will bespatter that tree with your brains!"

The Englishman dropped the stock of his musket hard to the ground, and a spot of fiery red flashed into his cheek at this savage burst of anger so uncalled for and so insolent. He gazed a moment on the frowning face of the young hunter, and then lifting his gun, turned carelessly away.

"Tut, man, have done with this," he said; "I did but jest. Come, we have lost the trail, and shall miss the game, too, if we tarry longer; come."

The Englishman shouldered his musket, as he spoke, and turned into the woods. Jones followed, but Danforth lingered behind.

"I must see what this means," he muttered, glancing after his companions, and then at the group of young Indians; "what can have brought them so near the settlement?"

He gave another quick glance toward the hunters, and then hurried across "the Straka" toward the wigwams. Jones and the Englishman had reached the little lake or pond, which lies about a mile south of "the Straka," when they were again joined by Danforth. His brow was unclouded, and he seemed anxious to do away the effect of his late violence by more than ordinary cheerfulness. Harmony was restored, and they again struck into the trail of the bear, and pursued toward the mountains.

Noon found our hunters deep in the ravines which cut into the ridge of the Catskill on which the Mountain House now stands. Occupied by the wild scenery which surrounded him, Jones became separated from his companions, and long before he was aware of it, they had proceeded far beyond the reach of his voice. When he became sensible of his situation, he found himself in a deep ravine sunk into the very heart of the mountains. A small stream crept along the rocky bottom, untouched by a single sun's ray, though it was now high noon. Every thing about him was wild and fearfully sublime, but the shadows were refreshing and cool, and the stream, rippling along its rocky bed, sent up a pleasant murmur as he passed. Gradually a soft, flowing sound, like the rush of a current of air through a labyrinth of leaves and blossoms, came gently to his ear. As he proceeded, it became more musical and liquid, swelled upon the ear gradually and with a richer burden of sound, till he knew that it was the rush and leap of waters at no great distance. The ravine had sunk deeper and deeper, and fragments of rock lay thickly in the bed of the stream. Arthur Jones paused, and looked about him bewildered, and yet with a lofty, poetical feeling at his heart, aroused by a sense of the glorious handiwork of the Almighty encompassing him. He stood within the heart of the mountain, and it seemed to heave and tremble beneath his feet with some unknown influence as he gazed. Precipices, and rocks piled on rocks were heaped to the sky on either side. Large forest-trees stood rooted in the wide clefts, and waved their heavy boughs abroad like torn banners streaming upon the air. A strip of the blue heavens arched gently over the whole, and that was beautiful. It smiled softly, and like a promise of love over that sunless ravine. Another step, and the waterfall was before him. It was sublime, but beautiful—oh, very beautiful—that little body of water, curling and foaming downward like a wreath of snow sifted from the clouds, breaking in a shower of spray over the shelf of rocks which stayed its progress, then leaping a second foaming mass, down, down, like a deluge of flowing light, another hundred feet to the shadowy depths of the ravine. A shower of sunlight played amid the foliage far overhead, and upon the top of the curving precipice where the waters made their first leap. As the hunter became more calm, he remarked how harmoniously the beautiful and sublime were blended in the scene. The precipices were rugged and frowning, but soft, rich mosses and patches of delicate white wild-flowers clung about them. So profusely were those gentle flowers lavished upon the rocks, that it seemed as if the very spray drops were breaking into blossoms as they fell. The hunter's heart swelled with pleasure as he drank in the extreme beauty of the scene. He rested his gun against a fragment of rock, and sat down with his eyes fixed on the waterfall. As he gazed, it seemed as if the precipices were moving upward—upward to the very sky. He was pondering on this strange optical illusion, which has puzzled many a dizzy brain since, when the click of a gunlock struck sharply on his ear. He sprang to his feet. A bullet whistled by his head, cutting through the dark locks which curled in heavy masses above his temples, and as a sense of giddiness cleared from his brain, he saw a half-naked savage crouching upon the ledge of rocks which ran along the foot of the fall. The spray fell upon his bronzed shoulders and sprinkled the stock of his musket as he lifted it to discharge the other barrel. With the quickness of thought, Jones drew his musket to his eye and fired. The savage sent forth a fierce, wild yell of agony, and springing up with the bound of a wild animal, fell headlong from the shelf. Trembling with excitement, yet firm and courageous, the hunter reloaded his gun, and stood ready to sell his life as clearly as possible, for he believed that the ravine was full of concealed savages, who would fall upon him like a pack of wolves. But every thing remained quiet, and when he found that he was alone, a terrible consciousness of bloodshed came upon him. His knees trembled, his cheek burned, and, with an impulse of fierce excitement, he leaped over the intervening rocks and stood by the slain savage. He was lying with his face to the earth, quite dead; Jones drew forth his knife, and lifting the long, black hair, cut it away from the crown. With the trophy in his hand, he sprang across the ravine. The fearless spirit of a madness seemed upon him, for he rushed up the steep ascent, and plunged into the forest, apparently careless what direction he took. The sound of a musket stopped his aimless career. He listened, and bent his steps more calmly toward the eminence on which the Mountain House now stands. Here he found the Englishman with the carcass of a huge bear stretched at his feet, gazing on the glorious expanse of country, spread out like a map, hundreds of fathoms beneath him. His face was flushed, and the perspiration rolled freely from his forehead. Danforth stood beside him, also bearing traces of recent conflict.

"So you have come to claim a share of the meat," said the old hunter, as Jones approached. "It is brave to leave your skulking-place in the bushes, when the danger is over. Bless me, lad! what have you there?" he exclaimed, starting up and pointing to the scalp.

Jones related his encounter with the savage. The Englishman shook his head forebodingly.

"We shall have hot work for this job before the week is over," he said. "It was a foolish shot; but keep a good heart, my lad, for, hang me, if I should not have done the same thing if the red devil had sent a bullet so near my head. Come, we will go and bury the fellow the best way we can."

Jones led the way to the fall, but they found only a few scattered locks of black hair, and a pool of blood half washed from the rock by the spray. The body of the savage and his rifle had disappeared—how, it was in vain to conjecture.

One of the largest log-houses in the settlement had been appropriated as a kind of tavern, or place of meeting for the settlers when they returned from their hunting excursions. Here a store of spirits was kept, under the care of John Fellows and pretty Martha Fellows, his daughter, the maiden before mentioned. As the sun went down, the men who had gone to the woods in the morning, began to collect with their game. Two stags, raccoons and meaner game in abundance, were lying before the door, when the three hunters came in with the slain bear. They were greeted with a boisterous shout, and the hunters crowded eagerly forward to examine the prize; but when Jones cast the Indian's scalp on the pile, they looked in each other's faces with ominous silence, while the young hunter stood pale and collected before them. It was the first time that Indian life had been taken by any of their number, and they felt that in the shedding of red blood, the barriers of their protection were broken down.

"It is a bad business," said one of the elder settlers, waving his head and breaking the general silence. "There'll be no clear hunting in the woods after this; but how did it all come about, Jones? Let us know how you came by that scalp—did the varmint fire at you, or how was it?"

The hunters gathered around Jones, who was about to account for his possession of the scalp, when the door of the house was opened, and he happened to look into the little room thus exposed. It was scantily furnished with a few benches and stools; a bed was in one corner, and Martha Fellows, his promised wife, stood by a rough deal table, on which were two or three drinking-cups, a couple of half-empty bottles, with a pitcher of water, backed by a broken mug, filled to the fractured top with maple molasses. Nothing of the kind could have been more beautiful than pretty Martha as she bent forward, listening with rapt attention to the animated whisper of William Danforth, who stood by her, divested of his coarse frock, his cap lying on the table before him, and his athletic figure displayed to the best advantage by the roundabout buttoned closely over his bosom. A red silk handkerchief, tied like a scarf round his waist, gave a picturesque gracefulness to his costume, altogether in harmony with his fine proportions, and with the bold cast of his head, which certainly was a model of muscular beauty.

A flash of anger shot athwart Arthur Jones' forehead, and a strange jealous feeling came to his heart. He began a confused account of his adventure, but the Englishman interrupted him, and took it upon himself to gratify the clamorous curiosity of the hunters, leaving Jones at liberty to scrutinize each look and motion of his lady-love. He watched with a jealous feeling the blush as it deepened and glowed on her embrowned cheek; he saw the sparkling pleasure of her hazel eyes, and the pretty dimples gathering about her red lips, like spots of sunlight flickering through the leaves of a red rose, and his heart sickened with distrust. But when the handsome hunter laid his hand on hers and bent his head, till the short curls on his temples almost mingled with her glossy ringlets, the lover could bear the sight no more. Breaking from the little band of hunters, he stalked majestically into the house, and approaching the object of his uneasiness, exclaimed, "Martha Fellows," in a voice which caused the pretty culprit to snatch her hand from under the hunter's, and to overturn two empty tin cups in her fright.

"Sir," said Martha, recovering herself, and casting a mischievous glance at Danforth, which was reciprocated with interest.

Mr. Arthur Jones felt that he was making himself ridiculous, and suppressing his wrath, he finished his magnificent commencement: "Will you give me a drink of water?" At which Martha pointed with her little embrowned hand to the pitcher, saying:

"There it is;" then, turning her back to her lover, she cast another arch glance at Danforth, and taking his cap from the table, began to blow upon the yellow fur, and put it to her cheek, as if it had been a pet kitten she was caressing, and all for the laudable purpose of tormenting the man who loved her, and whom she loved better than any thing in existence. Jones turned on her a bitter contemptuous look, and raising the pitcher to his lips, left the room. In a few minutes the other hunters entered, and Jason Fellows, father to Martha, announced it as decided by the hunters, who had been holding a kind of council without, that Arthur Jones and William Danforth, as the two youngest members of the community, should be dispatched to the nearest settlement to request aid to protect them from the Indians, whose immediate attack they had good reason to fear.

Martha, on hearing the names of the emissaries mentioned, dropped the cup she had been filling.

"Oh, not him—not them, I mean—they will be overtaken and tomahawked by the way!" she exclaimed, turning to her father with a look of affright.

"Let Mr. Danforth remain," said Jones, advancing to the table; "I will undertake the mission alone."

Tears came into Martha's eyes, and she turned them reproachfully to her lover; but, full of his heroic resolution to be tomahawked and comfortably scalped on his own responsibility, he turned majestically, without deigning to meet the tearful glance which was well calculated to mitigate his jealous wrath.

Danforth, on being applied to, requested permission to defer his answer till the morning, and the hunters left the house to divide the game, which had been forgotten in the general excitement.

Danforth, who had lingered to the last, took up his cap, and whispering good-night to Martha, left the house. The poor girl scarcely heeded his departure. Her eyes filled with tears, and seating herself on a settee which ran along one end of the room, she folded her arms on a board which served as a back, and burying her face upon them, wept violently.

As she remained in this position, she heard a familiar step on the floor. Her heart beat quick, fluttered a moment, and then settled to its regular pulsations again, for her lover had seated himself beside her. Martha wiped the tears from her eyes and remained quiet, for she knew that he had returned, and with that knowledge, the spirit of coquetry had revived; and when Jones, softened by her apparent sorrow—for he had seen her parting with Danforth—put his hand softly under her forehead and raised her face, the creature was laughing—laughing at his folly, as he thought.

"Martha, you are doing wrong—wrong to yourself and to me," said the disappointed lover, rising indignantly and taking his hat, with which he advanced to the door.

"Don't go," said Martha, turning her head till one cheek only rested on her arm, and casting a glance, half-repentant, half-comic, on her retreating lover; "don't go off so; if you do, you'll be very sorry for it."

Jones hesitated—she became very serious—the tears sprang to her eyes, and she looked exceedingly penitent. He returned to her side. Had he appealed to her feelings then—had he spoken of the pain she had given him in her encouragement of another, she would have acknowledged the fault with all proper humility; but he did no such thing—he was a common-sense man, and he resolved to end his first love-quarrel in a common-sense manner, as if common-sense ever had any thing to do with lovers' quarrels. "I will reason with her," he thought. "He will say I have made him very wretched, and I will tell him I am very sorry," *she* thought.

"Martha," he said, very deliberately, "why do I find you on terms of such familiarity with this Manhattan[3] fellow?"

Martha was disappointed. He spoke quite too calmly, and there was a sarcastic emphasis in the word "fellow," that roused her pride. The lips, which had just begun to quiver with repentance, worked themselves into a pouting fullness, till they resembled the rose-bud just as it bursts into leaves. Her rounded shoulder was turned pettishly toward her lover, with the air of a spoiled child, and she replied that "he was always finding fault."

Jones took her hand, and was proceeding in his sensible manner to convince her that she was wrong, and acted wildly, foolishly, and with a careless disregard to her own happiness.

As might be expected, the beautiful rustic snatched her hand away, turned her shoulder more decidedly on her lover, and bursting into tears, declared that she would thank him if he would stop scolding, and that she did not care if she never set eyes on him again.

He would have remonstrated; "Do listen to common-sense," he said, extending his hand to take hers.

"I hate common-sense!" she exclaimed, dashing away his hand; "I won't hear any more of your lecturing,—leave the house, and never speak to me again as long as you live."

Mr. Arthur Jones took up his hat, placed it deliberately on his head, and walked out of the house. With a heavy heart Martha watched his slender form as it disappeared in the darkness, and then stole away to her bed in the garret.

"He will call in the morning before he starts; he won't have the heart to go away without saying one word,—I am sure he won't," she repeated to herself over and over again, as she lay sobbing and weeping penitent tears on her pillow that night.

---

3 The Dutch gave the island of Manhattan its first permanent European settlement in 1624.

When William left the log tavern, he struck into the woods, and took his course toward the Pond. There was a moon, but the sky was clouded, and the little light which struggled to the earth, was too faint to penetrate the thick foliage of the wilderness. Danforth must have been familiar with the track, for he found his way without difficulty through the wilderness, and never stopped till he came out on the northern brink of the Pond. He looked anxiously over the face of the little lake. The fitful moon had broken from a cloud, and was touching the tiny waves with beauty, while the broken, rocky shore encompassed it with shadow, like a frame-work of ebony. No speck was on its bosom; no sound was abroad, but the evening breeze as it rippled on the waters, and made a sweet whispering melody in the tree-tops.

Suddenly a light, as from a pine torch, was seen on a point of land jutting out from the opposite shore. Another and another flashed out, each bearing to a particular direction, and then a myriad of flames rose high and bright, illuminating the whole point, and shooting its fiery reflection, like a meteor, almost across the bosom of the waters.

"Yes, they are preparing for work," muttered Danforth, as he saw a crowd of painted warriors arrange themselves around the camp-fire, each with his firelock in his hand. There was a general movement. Dark faces flittered in quick succession between him and the blaze, as the warriors performed the heavy march, or war-dance, which usually preceded the going out of a hostile party.

Danforth left the shore, and striking out in an oblique direction, arrived, after half an hour of quick walking, at the Indian encampment. He threaded his way through the cluster of bark wigwams, till he came to one standing on the verge of the inclosure. It was of logs, and erected with a regard to comfort which the others wanted. The young hunter drew aside the mat which hung over the entrance, and looked in. A young Indian girl was sitting on a pile of furs at the opposite extremity. She wore no paint—her cheek was round and smooth, and large gazelle-like eyes gave a soft brilliancy to her countenance, beautiful beyond expression. Her dress was a robe of dark chintz, open at the throat, and confined at the waist by a narrow belt of wampum, which, with the bead bracelets on her naked arms, and the embroidered moccasins laced over her feet, was the only Indian ornament about her. Even her hair, which all of her tribe wore laden with ornaments, and hanging down the back, was braided and wreathed in raven bands over her smooth forehead. An infant, almost naked, was lying in her lap, throwing its unfettered limbs about, and lifting his little hands to his mother's mouth, as she rocked back and forth on her seat of skins, chanting, in a sweet, mellow voice, the burden of an Indian lullaby. As the form of the hunter darkened the entrance, the Indian girl started up with a look of affectionate joy, and laying her child on the pile of skins, advanced to meet him.

"Why did the white man leave his woman so many nights?" she said, in her broken English, hanging fondly about him; "the boy and his mother have listened long for the sound of his moccasins."

Danforth passed his arm around the waist of his Indian wife, and drawing her to him, bent his cheek to hers, as if that slight caress was sufficient answer to her gentle greeting, and so it was; her untutored heart, rich in its natural affections, had no aim, no object, but what centered in the love she bore her white husband. The feelings which in civilized life are scattered over a thousand objects, were, in her bosom, centered in one single being; he supplied the place of all the high aspirations—of all the passions and sentiments which are fostered into strength by society, and as her husband bowed his head to hers, the blood darkened her cheek, and her large, liquid eyes were flooded with delight.

"And what has Malaeska been doing since the boy's father went to the wood?" inquired Danforth, as she drew him to the couch where the child was lying half buried in the rich fur.

"Malaeska has been alone in the wigwam, watching the shadow of the big pine. When her heart grew sick, she looked in the boy's eyes and was glad," replied the Indian mother, laying the infant in his father's arms.

Danforth kissed the child, whose eyes certainly bore a striking resemblance to his own; and parting the straight, black hair from a forehead which scarcely bore a tinge of its mother's blood, muttered, "It's a pity the little fellow is not quite white."

The Indian mother took the child, and with a look of proud anguish, laid her finger on its cheek, which was rosy with English blood.

"Malaeska's father is a great chief—the boy will be a chief in her father's tribe; but Malaeska never thinks of that when she sees the white man's blood come into the boy's face." She turned mournfully to her seat again.

"He will make a brave chief," said Danforth, anxious to soften the effects of his inadvertent speech; "but tell me, Malaeska, why have the warriors kindled the council fire? I saw it blaze by the pond as I came by."

Malaeska could only inform that the body of a dead Indian had been brought to the encampment about dusk, and that it was supposed he had been shot by some of the whites from the settlement. She said that the chief had immediately called a council to deliberate on the best means of revenging their brother's death.

Danforth had feared this movement in the savages, and it was to mitigate their wrath that he sought the encampment at so late an hour. He had married the daughter of their chief, and, consequently, was a man of considerable importance in the tribe. But he felt that his utmost exertion might fail to draw them from their meditated vengeance, now that one of their number had been slain by the whites. Feeling the necessity of his immediate presence at the council, he left the wigwam and proceeded at a brisk walk to the brink of the Pond. He came out of the thick forest which fringed it a little above the point on which the Indians were collected. Their dance was over, and from the few guttural tones which reached him, Danforth knew that they were planning the death of some particular individuals, which was probably to precede their attack on the settlement. The council fire still streamed high in the air, reddening the waters and lighting up the trees and foreground with a beautiful effect, while the rocky point seemed of emerald pebbles, so brilliant was the reflection cast over it, and so distinctly did it display the painted forms of the savages as they sat in a circle round the blaze, each with his weapon lying idly by his side. The light lay full on the glittering wampum and feathery crest of one who was addressing them with more energy than is common to the Indian warrior.

Danforth was too far off to collect a distinct hearing of the discourse, but with a feeling of perfect security, he left the deep shadow in which he stood, and approached the council fire. As the light fell upon him, the Indians leaped to their feet, and a savage yell rent the air, as if a company of fiends had been disturbed in their orgies. Again and again was the fierce cry reiterated, till the woods resounded with the wild echo rudely summoned from the caves. As the young hunter stood lost in astonishment at the strange commotion, he was seized by the savages, and dragged before their chief, while the group around furiously demanded vengeance, quick and terrible, for the death of their slain brother. The truth flashed across the hunter's mind. It was his death they had been planning. It was he they supposed to be the slayer of the Indian. He remonstrated and declared himself guiltless of the red man's death. It was in vain. He had been seen on the mountain by one of the tribe, not five minutes before the dead body of the Indian was found. Almost in despair the hunter turned to the chief.

"Am I not your son—the father of a young chief—one of your own tribe?" he said, with appealing energy.

The saturnine face of the chief never changed, as he answered in his own language: "The red man has taken a rattlesnake to warm in his wigwam—the warriors shall crush his head!" and with a fierce grin, he pointed to the pile of resinous wood which the savages were heaping on the council fire.

Danforth looked round on the group preparing for his destruction. Every dusky face was lighted up with a demoniac thirst for blood, the hot flames quivering into the air, their gorgeous tints amalgamating and shooting upward like a spire of living rainbows, while a thousand fiery tongues, hissing and darting onward like vipers eager for their prey, licked the fresh pine-knots heaped for his death-pyre. It was a fearful sight, and the heart of the brave hunter quailed within him as he looked. With another wild whoop, the Indians seized their victim, and were about to strip him for the sacrifice. In their blind fury they tore him from the grasp of those who held him, and were too intent on divesting him of his clothes to remark that his limbs were free. But he was not so forgetful. Collecting his strength for a last effort, he struck the nearest savage a blow in the chest, which sent him reeling among his followers, then taking advantage of the confusion, he tore off his cap, and springing forward with the bound of an uncaged tiger, plunged into the lake. A shout rent the air, and a score of dark heads broke the water in pursuit.

Fortunately, a cloud was over the moon, and the fugitive remained under the water till he reached the shadow thrown by the thickly-wooded bank, when, rising for a moment, he supported himself and hurled his cap out toward the center of the pond. The ruse succeeded, for the moon came out just at the instant, and with renewed shouts the savages turned in pursuit of the empty cap. Before they learned their mistake, Danforth had made considerable headway under the friendly bank, and took to the woods just as the shoal of Indians' heads entered the shadow in eager chase.

The fugitive stood for a moment on the brink of the forest, irresolute, for he knew not which course to take.

"I have it; they will never think of looking for me there," he exclaimed, dashing through the undergrowth and taking the direction toward "the Straka." The whoop of the pursuers smote his ear as they made the land. On, on he bounded with the swiftness of a hunted stag, through swamp and brushwood, and over rocks. He darted till he came in sight of his own wigwam. The sound of pursuit had died away, and he began to hope that the savages had taken the track which led to the settlement.

Breathless with exertion he entered the hut. The boy was asleep, but his mother was listening for the return of her husband.

"Malaeska," he said, catching her to his panting heart; "Malaeska, we must part; your tribe seek my life; the warriors are on my track now—now! Do you hear their shouts?" he added.

A wild whoop came from the woods below, and forcing back the arms she flung about him, he seized a war-club and stood ready for the attack.

Malaeska sprang to the door, and looked out with the air of a frightened doe. Darting back to the pile of furs, she laid the sleeping child on the bare earth, and motioning her husband to lie down, heaped the skins over his prostrate form; then taking the child in her arms, she stretched herself on the pile, and drawing a bear-skin over her, pretended to be asleep.

She had scarcely composed herself, when three savages entered the wigwam. One bore a blazing pine-knot, with which he proceeded to search for the fugitive. While the others were busy among the scanty furniture, he approached the trembling wife, and after feeling about among the furs without effect, lifted the bear-skins which covered her; but her sweet face in apparent slumber, and the beautiful infant lying across her bosom, were all that rewarded his search. As if her beauty had power to tame the savage, he carefully replaced the covering over her person, and speaking to his companions, left the hut without attempting to disturb her further.

Malaeska remained in her feigned slumber till she heard the Indians take to the woods again. Then she arose and lifted the skins from off her husband, who was nearly suffocated under them. When he had regained his feet, she placed the war-club in his hand, and taking up the babe, led the way to the entrance of the hut. Danforth saw by the act, that she intended to desert her tribe and accompany him in his flight. He had never thought of introducing her as his wife among the whites, and now that circumstances made it necessary for him to part with her forever, or to take her among his people for shelter, a pang, such as he had never felt, came to his heart. His affections struggled powerfully with his pride. The picture of his disgrace—of the scorn with which his parents and sisters would receive the Indian wife and half-Indian child, presented itself before him, and he had not the moral courage to risk the degradation which her companionship would bring upon him. These conflicting thoughts flashed through his mind in an instant, and when his wife stopped at the door, and, looking anxiously in his face, beckoned him to follow, he said, sharply, for his conscience was ill at ease:

"Malaeska, I go alone; you and the boy must remain with your people."

His words had a withering effect on the poor Indian. Her form drooped, and she raised her eyes with a look so mingled with humiliation and reproach, that the hunter's heart thrilled painfully in his bosom. Slowly, and as if her soul and strength were paralyzed, she crept to her husband's feet, and sinking to her knees, held up the babe.

"Malaeska's breast will die, and the boy will have no one to feed him," she said.

That beautiful child—that young mother kneeling in her humiliation—those large dark eyes, dim with the intensity of her solicitude, and that voice so full of tender entreaty—the husband's heart could not withstand them. His bosom heaved, tears gathered in his eyes, and raising the Indian and her child of his bosom, he kissed them both again and again.

"Malaeska," he said, folding her close to his heart, "Malaeska, I must go now; but when seven suns have passed, I will come again; or, if the tribe still seek my life, take the child and come to the settlement. I shall be there."

The Indian woman bowed her head in humble submission.

"The white man is good. Malaeska will come," she said.

One more embrace, and the poor Indian wife was alone with her child.

Poor Martha Fellows arose early, and waited with nervous impatience for the appearance of her lover; but the morning passed, the hour of noon drew near, and he came not. The heart of the maiden grew heavy, and when her father came in to dine, her eyes were red with weeping, and a cloud of mingled sorrow and petulance darkened her handsome face. She longed to question her father about Jones, but he had twice replenished his brown earthen bowl with pudding and milk, before she could gather courage to speak.

"Have you seen Arthur Jones this morning?" she at length questioned, in a low, timid voice.

The answer she received, was quite sufficient punishment for all her coquettish folly of the previous night. Jones had left the settlement—left it in anger with her, without a word of explanation—without even saying farewell. It really was hard. The little coquette had the heart-ache terribly, till he frightened it away by telling her of the adventure which Danforth had met with among the Indians, and of his departure with Arthur Jones in search of aid from the nearest settlement. The old man gloomily added, that the savages would doubt-less burn the houses over their heads, and massacre every living being within them, long before the two brave fellows would return with men. Such, indeed, were the terrible fears of almost every one in the little neighborhood. Their apprehensions, however, were prema-ture. Part of the Indian tribe had gone out on a hunting-party among the hills, and were ignorant of the fatal shot with which Jones had aroused the animosity of their brethren; while those who remained, were dispersed in a fruitless pursuit after Danforth.

On the afternoon of the fifth day after the departure of their emissaries, the whites began to see unequivocal symptoms of an attack; and now their fears did not deceive them. The hunting-party had returned to their encampment, and the detached parties were gath-ering around "the Straka." About dark, an Indian appeared in the skirts of the clearing, as if to spy out the position of the whites. Soon after, a shot was fired at the Englishman, before mentioned, as he returned from his work, which passed through the crown of his hat. That hostilities were commencing, was now beyond a doubt, and the males of the settlement met in solemn conclave, to devise measures for the defence of their wives and children. Their slender preparations were soon made; all were gathered around one of the largest houses in gloomy apprehension; the women and children within, and the men standing in front, sternly resolving to die in the defence of their loved ones. Suddenly there came up a sound from the wood, the trampling of many feet, and the crackling of brush-wood, as if some large body of men were forcing a way through the tangled forest. The women bowed their pallid faces, and gathering their children in their arms, waited appalled for the attack. The men stood ready, each grasping his weapon, their faces pallid, and their eyes kindled with stern courage, as they heard the stifled groans of the loved objects cower-ing behind them for protection. The sound became nearer and more distinct; dark forms were seen dimly moving among the trees, and then a file of men came out into the clear-ing. They were whites, led on by William Danforth and Arthur Jones. The settlers uttered a boisterous shout, threw down their arms, and ran in a body to meet the new-comers. The women sprang to their feet, some weeping, others laughing in hysterical joy, and all embracing their children with frantic energy.

Never were there more welcome guests than the score of weary men who refreshed themselves in the various houses of the settlement that night. Sentinels were placed, and each settler returned to his dwelling, accompanied by three or four guests; every heart beat high, save one—Martha Fellows; she, poor girl, was sad among the general rejoicing; her lover had not spoken to her, though she lingered near his side in the crowd, and had once almost touched him. Instead of going directly to her father's house, as had been his custom, he accepted the Englishman's invitation, and departed to sleep in his dwelling.

Now this same Englishman had a niece residing with him, who was considered by some to be more beautiful than Martha herself. The humble maiden thought of Jones, and of the bright blue eyes of the English girl, till her heart burned with the very same jealous feelings she had so ridiculed in her lover.

"I will see him! I will see them both!" she exclaimed, starting up from the settle where she had remained, full of jealous anxiety, since the dispersing of the crowd; and unheeded by her father, who was relating his hunting exploits to the five strangers quartered on him, she dashed away her tears, threw a shawl over her head, and taking a cup, as an excuse for borrowing something, left the house.

The Englishman's dwelling stood on the outward verge of the clearing, just within the shadow of the forest. Martha had almost reached the entrance, when a dark form rushed from its covert in the brushwood, and rudely seizing her, darted back into the wilderness. The terrified girl uttered a fearful shriek; for the fierce eyes gazing down upon her, were those of a savage. She could not repeat the cry, for the wretch crushed her form to his naked chest with a grasp of iron, and winding his hand in her hair, was about to dash her to the ground. That moment a bullet whistled by her cheek. The Indian tightened his hold with spasmodic violence, staggered back, and fell to the ground, still girding her in his death-grasp; a moment he writhed in mortal agony—warm blood gushed over his victim—the heart under her struggled fiercely in its last throes; then the lifeless arms relaxed, and she lay fainting on a corpse.

Chapter II

He lay upon the trampled ground,
     She knelt beside him there,
While a crimson stream gush'd slowly
     'Neath the parting of his hair.
His head was on her bosom thrown—
     She sobb'd his Christian name—
He smiled, for still he knew her,
     And strove to do the same.

—FRANK LEE BENEDICT.[4]

"Oh, Arthur! dear Arthur, I am glad it was you that saved me," whispered Martha, about an hour after her rescue, as she lay on the settle in her father's house, with Arthur Jones bending anxiously over her.

Jones dropped the hand he had been holding, and turned away with troubled features.

Martha looked at him, and her eyes were brimming with tears. "Jones," she said humbly and very affectionately, "Jones, I did wrong the other night, and I am sorry for it; will you forgive me?"

"I will—but never again—never, as I live," he replied, with a stern determination in his manner, accompanied by a look that humbled her to the heart. In after years, when Martha was Arthur Jones' wife, and when the stirrings of vanity would have led her to trifle with his feelings, she remembered that look, and dared not brave it a second time.

At sunrise, the next morning, an armed force went into the forest, composed of all who could be spared from the settlement, amounting to about thirty fighting-men. The Indians, encamped about "the Straka," more than doubled that number, yet the handful of brave whites resolved to offer them a decisive combat.

---

4 An American poet and novelist (1834–1910) who also co-edited *Peterson's Ladies National Magazine* with Ann Stephens.

The little band was approaching the northeastern extremity of the Pond, when they halted for a moment to rest. The spot on which they stood was level, and thinly timbered. Some were sitting on the grass, and others leaning on their guns, consulting on their future movements, when a fiendish yell arose like the howl of a thousand wild beasts, and, as if the very earth had yawned to emit them, a band of warriors sprang up in appalling numbers, on the front and rear, and approaching them, three abreast, fired into the group with terrible slaughter.

The whites returned their fire, and the sounds of murderous strife were indeed horrible. Sternly arose the white man's shout amid the blazing of guns and the whizzing of tomahawks, as they flashed though the air on their message of blood. Above all burst out the war-whoop of the savages, sometimes rising hoarse, and like the growling of a thousand bears; then, as the barking of as many wolves, and again, sharpening to the shrill, unearthly cry of a tribe of wild-cats. Oh, it was fearful, that scene of slaughter. Heart to heart, and muzzle to muzzle, the white and red man battled in horrid strife. The trees above them drooped under a cloud of smoke, and their trunks were scarred with gashes, cut by the tomahawks which had missed their more deadly aim. The ground was burdened with the dead, and yet the strife raged fiercer and fiercer, till the going down of the sun.

In the midst of the fight was William Danforth. Many a dusky form bit the dust, and many a savage howl followed the discharge of his trusty gun. But at length it became foul with continued use, and he went to the brink of the Pond to wash it. He was stooping to the water, when the dark form of an Indian chief cast its shadow a few feet from him. He, too, had come down to clean his gun. The moment he had accomplished his purpose, he turned to the white man, who had been to him as a son, and drawing his muscular form up to its utmost height, uttered a defiance in the Indian tongue. Instantly the weapons of both were loaded and discharged. The tall form of the chief wavered unsteadily for a moment, and fell forward, half its length, into the Pond. He strove to rise. His hands dashed wildly on the crimson water, the blows grew fainter, and the chief was dead.

The setting sun fell brilliantly over the glittering raiment of the prostrate chief—his long, black hair streamed out upon the water, and the tiny waves rippled playfully among the gorgeous feathers which had been his savage crown. A little back on the green bank, lay Danforth, wounded unto death. He strove to creep to the battle-field, but the blood gushed afresh from his wounds, and he fell back upon the earth faint and in despair.

The savages retreated; the sounds of strife became more distant, and the poor youth was left alone with the body of the slain warrior. He made one more desperate effort, and secured the gun which had belonged to the chief; though faint with loss of blood, he loaded that as well as his own, and placing them beside him, resolved to defend the remnant of life, yet quivering at his heart, to the last moment. The sun went slowly down; the darkness fell like a veil over the lake, and there he lay, wounded and alone, in the solitude of the wilderness. Solemn and regretful were the thoughts of the forsaken man as that night of agony went by. Now his heart lingered with strange and terrible dread around the shadowy portals of eternity which were opening before him; again it turned with a strong feeling of self-condemnation to his Indian wife and the infant pledge of the great love, which had made him almost forsake kindred and people for their sakes.

The moon arose, and the dense shadow of a hemlock, beneath which he had fallen, lay within a few feet of him like the wing of a great bird, swayed slowly forward with an imperceptible and yet certain progress. The eyes of the dying man were fixed on the margin of the shadow with a keen, intense gaze. There was something terrible in its stealthy creeping and silent advance, and he strove to elude it as if it had been a living thing; but with every motion the blood gushed afresh from his heart, and he fell back upon the sod, his white teeth clenched with pain, and his hands clutched deep into the damp moss. Still his keen eyes glittered in the moonlight with the fevered workings of pain and imagination. The shadow on which they turned was to him no shadow, but now a nest of serpents, creeping with their insidious coils toward him; and again, a pall—a black funereal pall, dragged forward by invisible spirits, and about to shut him out from the light forever. Slowly and surely it crept across his damp forehead and over his glowing eyes. His teeth unclenched, his hands relaxed, and a gentle smile broke over his pale lips, when he felt with what a cool and spirit-like touch it visited him. Just then a human shadow mingled with that of the tree, and the wail of a child broke on the still night air. The dying hunter struggled and strove to cry out,—"Malaeska—Ma—Ma—Mala—"

The poor Indian girl heard the voice, and with a cry, half of frenzied joy and half of fear, sprang to his side. She flung her child on the grass and lifted her dying husband to her heart, and kissed his damp forehead in a wild, eager agony of sorrow.

"Malaeska," said the young man, striving to wind his arms about her, "my poor girl, what will become of you? O God! who will take care of my boy?"

The Indian girl pushed back the damp hair from his forehead, and looked wildly down into his face. A shiver ran through her frame when she saw the cold, gray shadows of death gathering there; then her black eyes kindled, her beautiful lip curved to an expression more lofty than a smile, her small hand pointed to the West, and the wild religion of her race gushed up from her heart, a stream of living poetry.

"The hunting-ground of the Indian is yonder, among the purple clouds of the evening. The stars are very thick there, and the red light is heaped together like mountains in the heart of a forest. The sugar-maple gives its waters all the year round, and the breath of the deer is sweet, for it feeds on the golden spire-bush and the ripe berries. A lake of bright waters is there. The Indian's canoe flies over it like a bird high up in the morning. The West has rolled back its clouds, and a great chief has passed through. He will hold back the clouds that his white son may go up to the face of the Great Spirit. Malaeska and her boy will follow. The blood of the red man is high in her heart, and the way is open. The lake is deep, and the arrow sharp; death will come when Malaeska calls him. Love will make her voice sweet in the land of the Great Spirit; the white man will hear it, and call her to his bosom again!"

A faint, sad smile flitted over the dying hunter's face, and his voice was choked with a pain which was not death. "My poor girl," he said, feebly drawing her kindling face to his lips, "there is no great hunting-ground as you dream. The whites have another faith, and—O God! I have taken away her trust, and have none to give in return!"

The Indian's face drooped forward, the light of her wild, poetic faith had departed with the hunter's last words, and a feeling of cold desolation settled on her heart. He was dying on her bosom, and she knew not where he was going, nor that their parting might not be eternal.

The dying man's lips moved as if in prayer. "Forgive me, O Father of mercies! forgive me that I have left this poor girl in her heathen ignorance," he murmured, faintly, and his lips continued to move though there was no perceptible sound. After a few moments of exhaustion, he fixed his eyes on the Indian girl's face with a look of solemn and touching earnestness.

"Malaeska," he said, "talk not of putting yourself and the boy to death. That would be a sin, and God would punish it. To meet me in another world, Malaeska, you must learn to love the white man's God, and wait patiently till he shall send you to me. Go not back to your tribe when I am dead. Down at the mouth of the great river are many whites; among them are my father and mother. Find your way to them, tell them how their son died, and beseech them to cherish you and the boy for his sake. Tell them how much he loved you, my poor girl. Tell them—I can not talk more. There is a girl at the settlement, one Martha Fellows; go to her. She knows of you, and has papers—a letter to my father. I did not expect this, but had prepared for it. Go to her—you will do this—promise, while I can understand."

Malaeska had not wept till now, but her voice was choked, and tears fell like rain over the dying man's face as she made the promise.

He tried to thank her, but the effort died away in a faint smile and a tremulous motion of the white lips—"Kiss me, Malaeska."

The request was faint as a breath of air, but Malaeska heard it. She flung herself on his bosom with a passionate burst of grief, and her lips clung to his as if they would have drawn him back from the very grave. She felt the cold lips moving beneath the despairing pressure of hers, and lifted her head.

"The boy, Malaeska; let me look on my son."

The child had crept to his mother's side, and crouching on his hands and knees, sat with his large black eyes filled with a strange awe, gazing on the white face of his father. Malaeska drew him closer, and with instinctive feelings he wound his arms round the neck, and nestled his face close to the ashy cheek of the dying man. There was a faint motion of the hands as if the father would have embraced his child, and then all was still. After a time, the child felt the cheek beneath his waxing hard and cold. He lifted his head and pored with breathless wonder over the face of his father's corpse. He looked up at his mother. She, too, was bending intently over the face of the dead, and her eyes were full of a wild, melancholy light. The child was bewildered. He passed his tiny hand once more over the cold face, and then crept away, buried his head in the folds of his mother's dress, and began to cry.

Morning dawned upon the little lake, quietly and still, as if nothing but the dews of heaven and the flowers of earth had ever tasted its freshness; yet all under the trees, the tender grass and the white blossoms, were crushed to the ground, stained and trampled in human blood. The delicious light broke, like a smile from heaven, over the still bosom of the waters, and flickered cheeringly through the dewy branches of the hemlock which shadowed the prostrate hunter. Bright dew-drops lay thickly on his dress, and gleamed, like a shower of seed pearls, in his rich, brown hair. The green moss on either side was soaked with a crimson stain, and the pale, leaden hue of dissolution had settled on his features. He was not alone; for on the same mossy couch lay the body of the slaughtered chief; the limbs were composed, as if on a bier—the hair wiped smooth, and the crescent of feathers, broken and wet, were arranged with care around his bronzed temples. A little way off, on a hillock, purple with flowers, lay a beautiful child, beckoning to the birds as they fluttered by—plucking up the flowers, and uttering his tiny shout of gladness, as if death and sorrow were not all around him. There, by the side of the dead hunter, sat Malaeska, the widow, her hands dropping nervously by her side, her long hair sweeping the moss, and her face bowed on her bosom, stupefied with the overwhelming poignancy of her grief. Thus she remained, motionless and lost in sorrow, till the day was at its noon. Her child, hungry and tired with play, had cried itself to sleep among the flowers; but the mother knew it not—her heart and all her faculties seemed closed as with a portal of ice.

That night when the moon was up, the Indian widow dug a grave, with her own hands, on the green margin of the lake. She laid her husband and her father side by side, and piled sods upon them. Then she lifted the wretched and hungry babe from the earth, and, with a heavy heart, bent her way to "the Straka."

Chapter III

The sunset fell to the deep, deep stream,
    Ruddy as gold could be,
While russet brown and a crimson gleam
    Slept in each forest-tree;
But the heart of the Indian wife was sad
    As she urged her light canoe,
While her boy's young laugh rose high and glad
    When the wild birds o'er them flew.

MARTHA FELLOWS and her lover were alone in her father's cabin on the night after the Indian engagement. They were both paler than usual, and too anxious about the safety of their little village for any thing like happiness, or tranquil conversation. The old man had been stationed as sentinel on the verge of the clearing; and as the two sat together in silence, with hands interlocked, and gazing wistfully in each other's face, a rifle-shot cut sharply from the old man's station. They both started to their feet, and Martha clung shrieking to her lover. Jones forced her back to the settle—and, snatching his rifle, sprang to the door. There was a sound of approaching footsteps, and with it was mingled the voice of old Fellows, and the sweeter and more imperfect tones of a female, with the sobbing breath of a child. As Jones stood wondering at the strange sound, a remarkable group darkened the light which streamed from the cabin door. It was Fellows partly supporting and partly dragging forward a pale and terrified Indian girl. The light glittered upon her picturesque raiment, and revealed the dark, bright eyes of a child which was fastened to her back, and which clung to her neck silent with terror and exhaustion.

"Come along, you young porcupine! You skulking copper-colored little squaw, you! We shan't kill you, nor the little pappoose, neither; so you needn't shake so. Come along! There's Martha Fellows, if you can find enough of your darnationed queer English to tell her what you want."

As he spoke, the rough, but kind-hearted old man entered the hut, pushing the wretched Malaeska and her child before him.

"Martha! why what in the name of nature makes you look so white about the mouth? You needn't be afraid of this little varmint, no how. She's as harmless as a gartersnake. Come, see if you can find out what she wants of you. She can talk the drollest you ever heard. But I've scared away her senses, and she only stares at me like a shot deer."

When the Indian heard the name of the astonished girl, into whose presence she had been dragged, she withdrew from the old man's grasp and stole timidly toward the settle.

"The white man left papers with the maiden—Malaeska only wants the papers," she pleaded, placing her small palms beseechingly together.

Martha turned still more pale, and started to her feet. "It is true then," she said, almost wildly. "Poor Danforth is dead, and these forlorn creatures, his widow and child, have come to me at last. Oh! Jones, he was telling me of this the night you got so angry. I could not tell you why we were talking so much together; but I knew all the time that he had an Indian wife—it seemed as if he had a forewarning of his death, and must tell some one. The last time I saw him, he gave me a letter, sealed with black, and bade me seek his wife, and persuade her to carry it to his father, if he was killed in the fight. It is that letter she has come after; but how will she find her way to Manhattan?"

"Malaeska knows which way the waters run: she can find a path down the big river. Give her the papers that she may go!" pleaded the sad voice of the Indian.

"Tell us first," said Jones, addressing her kindly, "have the Indians left our neighborhood? Is there no danger of an attack?"

"The white man need not fear. When the great chief died, the smoke of his wigwam went out; and his people have gone beyond the mountains. Malaeska is alone."

There was wretchedness and touching pathos in the poor girl's speech, that affected the little group even to tears.

"No you ain't, by gracious!" exclaimed Fellows, dashing his hand across his eyes. "You shall stay and live with me, and help Matt, you shall—and that's the end on't. I'll make a farmer of the little pappoose. I'll bet a beaver-skin that he'll larn to gee and haw the oxen and hold plow afore half the Dutch boys that are springing up here as thick as clover-tops in a third year's clearing."

Malaeska did not perfectly understand the kind settler's proposition; but the tone and manner were kindly, and she knew that he wished to help her.

"When the boy's father was dying, he told Malaeska to go to his people, and they would tell her how to find the white man's God. Give her the papers, and she will go. Her heart will be full when she thinks of the kind words and the soft looks which the white chiefs and the bright-haired maiden have given her."

"She goes to fulfill a promise to the dead—we ought not to prevent her," said Jones.

Malaeska turned her eyes eagerly and gratefully upon him as he spoke, and Martha went to her bed and drew the letter, which had been intrusted to her care, from beneath the pillow. The Indian took it between her trembling hands, and pressing it with a gesture almost of idolatry to her lips, thrust it into her bosom.

"The white maiden is good! Farewell!" she turned toward the door as she spoke.

"Stay! It will take many days to reach Manhattan—take something to eat, or you will starve on the way," said Martha, compassionately.

"Malaeska has her bow and arrow, and she can use them; but she thanks the white maiden. A piece of bread for the boy—he has cried to his mother many times for food; but her bosom was full of tears, and she had none to give him."

Martha ran to the cupboard and brought forth a large fragment of bread and a cup of milk. When the child saw the food, he uttered a soft, hungry murmur, and his little fingers began to work eagerly on his mother's neck. Martha held the cup to his lips, and smiled through her tears to see how hungrily he swallowed, and with what a satisfied and pleased look his large, black eyes were turned up to hers as he drank. When the cup was withdrawn, the boy breathed a deep sigh of satisfaction, and let his head fall sleepily on his mother's shoulder; her large eyes seemed full of moonlight, and a gleam of pleasure shot athwart her sad features; she unbound a bracelet of wampum from her arm and placed it in Martha's hand. The next instant she was lost in the darkness without. The kind settler rushed out, and hallooed for her to come back; but her step was like that of a fawn, and while he was wandering fruitlessly around the settlement, she reached the margin of the creek; and, unmooring a canoe, which lay concealed in the sedge, placed herself in it, and shot round the point to the broad bosom of the Hudson.

Night and morning, for many successive days, that frail canoe glided down the current, amid the wild and beautiful scenery of the Highlands, and along the park-like shades of a more level country. There was something in the sublime and lofty handiwork of God which fell soothingly on the sad heart of the Indian. Her thoughts were continually dwelling on the words of her dead husband, ever picturing to themselves the land of spirits where he had promised that she should join him. The perpetual change of scenery, the sunshine playing with the foliage, and the dark, heavy masses of shadow, flung from the forests and the rocks on either hand, were continually exciting her untamed imagination to comparison with the heaven of her wild fancy. It seemed, at times, as if she had but to close her eyes and open them again to be in the presence of her lost one. There was something heavenly in the solemn, perpetual flow of the river, and in the music of the leaves as they rippled to the wind, that went to the poor widow's heart like the soft voice of a friend. After a day or two, the gloom which hung about her young brow, partially departed. Her cheek again dimpled to the happy laugh of her child, and when he nestled down to sleep in the furs at the bottom of the canoe, her soft, plaintive lullaby would steal over the waters like the song of a wild bird seeking in vain for its mate.

Malaeska never went on shore, except to gather wild fruit, and occasionally to kill a bird, which her true arrow seldom failed to bring down. She would strike a fire and prepare her game in some shady nook by the river side, while the canoe swung at its mooring, and her child played on the fresh grass, shouting at the cloud of summer insects that flashed by, and clapping his tiny hands at the humming-birds that came to rifle honey from the flowers that surrounded him.

The voyage was one of strange happiness to the widowed Indian. Never did Christian believe in the pages of Divine Writ with more of trust, than she placed in the dying promise of her husband, that she should meet him again in another world. His spirit seemed forever about her, and to her wild, free imagination, the passage down the magnificent stream seemed a material and glorious path to the white man's heaven. Filled with strange, sweet thoughts, she looked abroad on the mountains looming up from the banks of the river—on the forest-trees so various in their tints, and so richly clothed, till she was inspired almost to forgetfulness of her affliction. She was young and healthy, and every thing about her was so lovely, so grand and changing, that her heart expanded to the sunshine like a flower which has been bowed down, but not crushed beneath the force of a storm. Part of each day she spent in a wild, dreamy state of imagination. Her mind was lulled to sweet musings by the gentle sounds that hovered in the air from morning till evening, and through the long night, when all was hushed save the deep flow of the river. Birds came out with their cheerful voices at dawn, and at midday she floated in the cool shadow of the hills, or shot into some cove for a few hours' rest. When the sunset shed its gorgeous dyes over the river—and the mountain ramparts, on either side, were crimson as with the track of contending armies— when the boy was asleep, and the silent stars came out to kindle up her night path, then a clear, bold melody gushed from the mother's lips like a song from the heart of a nightingale. Her eye kindled, her cheek grew warm, the dip of her paddle kept a liquid accompaniment to her rich, wild voice, as the canoe floated downward on waves that seemed rippling over a world of crushed blossoms, and were misty with the approach of evening.

Malaeska had been out many days, when the shady gables and the tall chimneys of Manhattan broke upon her view, surrounded by the sheen of its broad bay, and by the forest which covered the uninhabited part of the island. The poor Indian gazed upon it with an unstable but troublesome fear. She urged her canoe into a little cove on the Hoboken shore,[5] and her heart grew heavy as the grave, as she pondered on the means of fulfilling her charge. She took the letter from her bosom; the tears started to her eyes, and she kissed it with a regretful sorrow, as if a friend were about to be rendered up from her affections forever. She took the child to her heart, and held him there till its throbbings grew audible, and the strength of her misgivings could not be restrained. After a time she became more calm. She lifted the child from her bosom, laved his hands and face in the stream, and brushed his black hair with her palm till it glowed like the neck of a raven. Then she girded his little crimson robe with a string of wampum, and after arranging her own attire, shot the canoe out of the cove and urged it slowly across the mouth of the river. Her eyes were full of tears all the way, and when the child murmured, and strove to comfort her with his infant caress, she sobbed aloud, and rowed steadily forward.

It was a strange sight to the phlegmatic inhabitants of Manhattan, when Malaeska passed through their streets in full costume, and with the proud, free tread of her race. Her hair hung in long braids down her back, each braid fastened at the end with a tuft of scarlet feathers. A coronet of the same bright plumage circled her small head, and her robe was gorgeous with beads, and fringed with porcupine quills. A bow of exquisite workmanship was in her hand, and a scarf of scarlet cloth bound the boy to her back. Nothing could be more strikingly beautiful than the child. His spirited head was continually turning from one strange object to another, and his bright, black eyes were brim-full of childish wonder. One little arm was flung around his young mother's neck, and its fellow rested on the feathered arrow-shafts which crowded the quiver slung against her left shoulder. The timid, anxious look of the mother, was in strong contrast with the eager gaze of the boy. She had caught much of the delicacy and refinement of civilized life from her husband, and her manner became startled and fawnlike beneath the rude gaze of the passers-by. The modest blood burned in her cheek, and the sweet, broken English trembled on her lips, when several persons, to whom she showed the letter passed by without answering her. She did not know that they were of another nation than her husband, and spoke another language than that which love had taught her. At length she accosted an aged man who could comprehend her imperfect language. He read the name on the letter, and saw that it was addressed to his master, John Danforth, the richest fur-trader in Manhattan. The old serving-man led the way to a large, irregular building, in the vicinity of what is now Hanover Square. Malaeska followed with a lighter tread, and a heart relieved of its fear. She felt that she had found a friend in the kind old man who was conducting her to the home of her husband's father.

The servant entered this dwelling and led the way to a low parlor, paneled with oak and lighted with small panes of thick, greenish glass. A series of Dutch tiles—some of them most exquisite in finish and design, surrounded the fire-place, and a coat-of-arms, elaborately carved in oak, stood out in strong relief from the paneling above. A carpet, at that time an uncommon luxury, covered a greater portion of the floor, and the furniture was rich in its material, and ponderous with heavy carved work. A tall, and rather hard-featured man sat in an arm-chair by one of the narrow windows, reading a file of papers

5 Hoboken is a settlement in what is now New Jersey on the west shore of the Hudson River across from Manhattan Island.

which had just arrived in the last merchant-ship from London. A little distance from him, a slight and very thin lady of about fifty was occupied with household sewing; her work-box stood on a small table before her, and a book of common-prayer lay beside it. The servant had intended to announce his strange guests, but, fearful of losing sight of him, Malaeska followed close upon his footsteps, and before he was aware of it, stood within the room, holding her child by the hand.

"A woman, sir,—an Indian woman, with a letter," said the embarrassed servant, motioning his charge to draw back. But Malaeska had stepped close to the merchant, and was looking earnestly in his face when he raised his eyes from the papers. There was something cold in his severe gaze as he fixed it on her through his spectacles. The Indian felt chilled and repulsed; her heart was full, and she turned with a look of touching appeal to the lady. That face was one to which a child would have fled for comfort; it was tranquil and full of kindness. Malaeska's face brightened as she went up to her, and placed the letter in her hands without speaking a word; but the palpitation of her heart was visible through her heavy garments, and her hands shook as she relinquished the precious paper.

"The seal is black," said the lady, turning very pale as she gave the letter to her husband, "but it is *his* writing," she added, with a forced smile. "He could not have sent word himself, were he —ill." She hesitated at the last word, for, spite of herself, the thoughts of death lay heavily at her heart.

The merchant composed himself in his chair, settled his spectacles, and after another severe glance at the bearer, opened the letter. His wife kept her eyes fixed anxiously on his face as he read. She saw that his face grew pale, that his high, narrow forehead contracted, and that the stern mouth became still more rigid in its expression. She knew that some evil had befallen her son—her only son, and she grasped a chair for support; her lips were bloodless, and her eyes became keen with agonizing suspense. When her husband had read the letter through, she went close to him, but looked another way as she spoke.

"Tell me! has any harm befallen my son?" Her voice was low and gentle, but husky with suspense.

Her husband did not answer, but his hand fell heavily upon his knee, and the letter rattled in his unsteady grasp; his eyes were fixed on his trembling wife with a look that chilled her to the heart. She attempted to withdraw the letter from his hand, but he clenched it the firmer.

"Let it alone—he is dead—murdered by the savages—why should you know more?"

The poor woman staggered back, and the fire of anxiety went out from her eyes.

"Can there be any thing worse than death— the death of the first-born of our youth—cut off in his proud manhood?" she murmured, in a low, broken voice.

"Yes, woman!" said the husband, almost fiercely; "there is a thing worse than death—disgrace!"

"Disgrace coupled with my son? You are his father, John. Do not slander him now that he is dead—before his mother, too." There was a faint, red spot then upon that mild woman's face, and her mouth curved proudly as she spoke. All that was stern in her nature had been aroused by the implied charge against the departed.

"Read, woman, read! Look on that accursed wretch and her child! They have enticed him into their savage haunts, and murdered him. Now they come to claim protection and reward for the foul deed."

Malaeska drew her child closer to her as she listened to this vehement language, and shrank slowly back to a corner of the room, where she crouched, like a frightened hare, looking wildly about, as if seeking some means to evade the vengeance which seemed to threaten her.

After the first storm of feeling, the old man buried his face in his hands and remained motionless, while the sobs of his wife, as she read her son's letter, alone broke the stillness of the room.

Malaeska felt those tears as an encouragement, and her own deep feelings taught her how to reach those of another. She drew timidly to the mourner and sank at her feet.

"Will the white woman look upon Malaeska?" she said, in a voice full of humility and touching earnestness. "She loved the young white chief, and when the shadows fell upon his soul, he said that his mother's heart would grow soft to the poor Indian woman who had slept in his bosom while she was very young. He said that her love would open to his boy like a flower to the sunshine. Will the white woman look upon the boy? He is like his father."

"He is, poor child, he is!" murmured the bereaved mother, looking on the boy through her tears—"like him, as he was when we were both young, and he the blessing of our hearts. Oh, John, do you remember his smile?—how his cheek would dimple when we kissed it! Look upon this poor, fatherless creature; they are all here again; the sunny eye and the broad forehead. Look upon him, John, for my sake—for the sake of our dead son, who prayed us with his last breath to love *his* son. Look upon him!"

The kind woman led the child to her husband as she spoke, and resting her arm on his shoulder, pressed her lips upon his swollen temples. The pride of his nature was touched. His bosom heaved, and tears gushed through his rigid fingers. He felt a little form draw close to his knee, and a tiny, soft hand strive with its feeble might to uncover his face. The voice of nature was strong within him. His hands dropped, and he pored with a troubled face over the uplifted features of the child.

Tears were in those young, bright eyes as they returned his grandfather's gaze, but when a softer expression came into the old man's face, a smile broke through them, and the little fellow lifted both his arms and clasped them over the bowed neck of his grandfather. There was a momentary struggle, and then the merchant folded the boy to his heart with a burst of strong feeling such as his iron nature had seldom known.

"He *is* like his father. Let the woman go back to her tribe; we will keep the boy."

Malaeska sprang forward, clasped her hands, and turned with an air of wild, heart-thrilling appeal to the lady.

"You will not send Malaeska from her child. No—no, white woman. Your boy has slept against your heart, and you have felt his voice in your ear, like the song of a young mocking-bird. You would not send the poor Indian back to the woods without her child. She has come to you from the forest, that she may learn the path to the white man's heaven, and see her husband again, and you will not show it her. Give the Indian woman her boy; her heart is growing very strong; she will not go back to the woods alone!"

As she spoke these words, with an air more energetic even than her speech, she snatched the child from his grandfather's arms, and stood like a lioness guarding her young, her lips writhing and her black eyes flashing fire, for the savage blood kindled in her veins at the thought of being separated from her son.

"Be quiet, girl, be quiet. If you go, the child shall go with you," said the gentle Mrs. Danforth. "Do not give way to this fiery spirit; no one will wrong you."

Malaeska dropped her air of defiance, and placing the child humbly at his grandfather's feet, drew back, and stood with her eyes cast down, and her hands clasped deprecatingly together, a posture of supplication in strong contrast with her late wild demeanor.

"Let them stay. Do not separate the mother and the child!" entreated the kind lady, anxious to soothe away the effect of her husband's violence. "The thoughts of a separation drives her wild, poor thing. *He* loved her;—why should we send her back to her savage haunts? Read this letter once more, my husband. You can not refuse the dying request of our first-born."

With gentle and persuasive words like these, the kind lady prevailed. Malaeska was allowed to remain in the house of her husband's father, but it was only as the nurse of her own son. She was not permitted to acknowledge herself as his mother; and it was given out that young Danforth had married in one of the new settlements—that the young couple had fallen victims to the savages, and that their infant son had been rescued by an Indian girl, who brought him to his grandfather. The story easily gained credit, and it was no matter of wonder that the old fur merchant soon became fondly attached to the little orphan, or that the preserver of his grandchild was made an object of grateful attention in his household.

Chapter IV

> Her heart is in the wild wood;
>   Her heart is not here.
> Her heart is in the wild wood;
>   It was hunting the deer.

It would have been an unnatural thing, had that picturesque young mother abandoned the woods, and prisoned herself in a quaint old Dutch house, under the best circumstances. The wild bird, which has fluttered freely from its nest through a thousand forests, might as well be expected to love its cage, as this poor wild girl her new home, with its dreary stillness and its leaden regularity. But love was all-powerful in that wild heart. It had brought Malaeska from her forest home, separated her from her tribe in its hour of bitter defeat, and sent her a forlorn wanderer among strangers that regarded her almost with loathing.

The elder Danforth was a just man, but hard as granite in his prejudices. An only son had been murdered by the savages to whom this poor young creature belonged. His blood—all of his being that might descend to posterity—had been mingled with the accursed race who had sacrificed him. Gladly would he have rent the two races asunder, in the very person of his grandchild, could the pure half of his being been thus preserved.

But he was a proud, childless old man, and there was something in the boy's eyes, in the brave lift of his head, and in his caressing manner, which filled the void in his heart, half with love and half with pain. He could no more separate the two passions in his own soul, than he could drain the savage blood from the little boy's veins.

But the house-mother, the gentle wife, could see nothing but her son's smile in that young face, nothing but his look in the large eyes, which, black in color, still possessed something of the azure light that had distinguished those of the father.

The boy was more cheerful and bird-like than his mother, for all her youth had gone out on the banks of the pond where her husband died. Always submissive, always gentle, she was nevertheless a melancholy woman. A bird which had followed its young out into strange lands, and caged it there, could not have hovered around it more hopelessly.

Nothing but her husband's dying wish would have kept Malaeska in Manhattan. She thought of her own people incessantly—of her broken, harassed tribe, desolated by the death of her father, and whose young chief she had carried off and given to strangers.

But shame dyed Malaeska's cheek as she thought of these things. What right had she, an Indian of the pure blood, to bring the grandchild of her father under the roof of his enemies? Why had she not taken the child in her arms and joined her people as they sang the death-chant for her father, "who," she murmured to herself again and again, "was a great chief," and retreated with them deep into the wilderness, to which they were driven, giving them a chief in her son?

But no! passion had been too strong in Malaeska's heart. The woman conquered the patriot; and the refinement which affection had given her, enslaved the wild nature without returning a compensation of love for the sacrifice. She pined for her people—all the more that they were in peril and sorrow. She longed for the shaded forest-paths, and the pretty lodge, with its couches of fur and its floor of blossoming turf. To her the very winds seemed chained among the city houses; and when she heard them sighing through the gables, it seemed to her that they were moaning for freedom, as she was in the solitude of her lonely life.

They had taken the child from her. A white nurse was found, who stepped in between the young heir and his mother, thrusting her ruthlessly aside. In this the old man was obstinate. The wild blood of the boy must be quenched; he must know nothing of the race from which his disgrace sprang. If the Indian woman remained under his roof, it must be as a menial, and on condition that all natural affection lay crushed within her—unexpressed, unguessed at by the household.

But Mrs. Danforth had compassion on the poor mother. She remembered the time when her own child had made all the pulses of her being thrill with love, which now took the form of a thousand tender regrets. She could not watch the lone Indian stealing off to her solitary room under the gable roof—a mother, yet childless—without throbs of womanly sorrow. She was far too good a wife to brave her husband's authority, but, with the cowardliness of a kind heart, she frequently managed to evade it. Sometimes in the night she would creep out of her prim chamber, and steal the boy from the side of his nurse, whom she bore on her own motherly bosom to the solitary bed of Malaeska.

As if Malaeska had a premonition of the kindliness, she was sure to be wide awake, thinking of her child, and ready to gush forth in murmurs of thankfulness for the joy of clasping her own son a moment to that lonely heart.

Then the grandmother would steal to her husband's side again, charging it upon her memory to awake before daylight, and carry the boy back to the stranger's bed, making her gentle charity a secret as if it had been a sin.

It was pitiful to see Malaeska haunting the footsteps of her boy all the day long. If he was taken into the garden, she was sure to be hovering around the old pear-trees, where she could sometimes unseen lure him from his play, and lavish kisses on his mouth as he laughed recklessly, and strove to abandon her for some bright flower or butterfly that crossed his path. This snatch of affection, this stealthy way of appeasing a hungry nature, was enough to drive a well-tutored woman mad; as for Malaeska, it was a marvel that she could tame her erratic nature into the abject position allotted her in that family. She had neither the occupation of a servant, nor the interests of an equal.

Forbidden to associate with the people in the kitchen, yet never welcomed in the formal parlor when its master was at home, she hovered around the halls and corners of the house, or hid herself away in the gable chambers, embroidering beautiful trifles on scraps of silk and fragments of bright cloth, with which she strove to bribe the woman who controlled her child, into forbearance and kindness.

But alas, poor woman! submission to the wishes of the dead was a terrible duty; her poor heart was breaking all the time; she had no hope, no life; the very glance of her eye was an appeal for mercy; her step, as it fell on the turf, was leaden with despondency—she had nothing on earth to live for.

This state of things arose when the child was a little boy; but as he grew older the bitterness of Malaeska's lot became more intense. The nurse who had supplanted her went away; for he was becoming a fine lad, and far removed from the need of woman's care. But this brought her no nearer to his affections. The Indian blood was strong in his young veins; he loved such play as brought activity and danger with it, and broke from the Indian woman's caresses with a sort of scorn, and she knew that the old grandfather's prejudice was taking root in his heart, and dared not utter a protest. She was forbidden to lavish tenderness on her son, or to call forth his in return, lest it might create suspicion of the relationship.

In his early boyhood, she could steal to his chamber at night, and give free indulgence to the wild tenderness of her nature; but after a time even the privilege of watching him in his sleep was denied to her. Once, when she broke the tired boy's rest by her caresses, he became petulant, and chided her for her obtrusiveness. The repulse went to her heart like iron. She had no power to plead; for her life, she dared not tell him the secret of that aching love which she felt—too cruelly felt—oppressed his boyhood; for that would be to expose the disgrace of blood which embittered the old man's pride.

She was his mother; yet her very existence in that house was held as a reproach. Every look that she dared to cast on her child, was watched jealously as a fault. Poor Malaeska! hers was a sad, sad life.

She had borne every thing for years, dreaming, poor thing, that the eternal cry that went up from her heart would be answered, as the boy grew older; but when he began to shrink proudly from her caresses, and question the love that was killing her, the despair which smoldered at her heart broke forth, and the forest blood spoke out with a power that not even a sacred memory of the dead could oppose. A wild idea seized upon her. She would no longer remain in the white man's house, like a bird beating its wings against the wires of a cage. The forests were wide and green as ever. Her people might yet be found. She would seek them in the wilderness. The boy should go with her, and become the chief of his tribe, as her father had been. That old man should not forever trample down her heart. There was a free life which she would find or die.

The boy's childish petulance had created this wild wish in his mother's heart. The least sign of repulsion drove her frantic. She began to thirst eagerly for her old free existence in the woods; but for the blood of her husband, which ran in the old man's veins, she would have given way to the savage hate of her people, against the house-hold in which she had been so unhappy. As it was, she only panted to be away with her child, who must love her when no white man stood by to rebuke him. With her aroused energies the native reticence of her tribe came to her aid. The stealthy art of warfare against an enemy awoke. They should not know how wretched she was. Her plans must be securely made. Every step toward freedom should be carefully considered. These thoughts occupied Malaeska for days and weeks. She became active in her little chamber. The bow and sheaf of arrows that had given her the appearance of a young Diana when she came to Manhattan in her canoe, was taken down from the wall, newly strung, and the stone arrow-heads patiently sharpened. Her dress, with its gorgeous embroidery of fringe and wampum, was examined with care. She must return to her people as she had left them. The daughter of a chief—the mother of a chief—not a fragment of the white man's bounty should go with her to the forest.

Cautiously, and with something of native craft, Malaeska made her preparations. Down upon the shores of the Hudson, lived an old carpenter who made boats for a living. Malaeska had often seen him at his work, and her rude knowledge of his craft gave peculiar interest to the curiosity with which she regarded him. The Indian girl had long been an object of his especial interest, and the carpenter was flattered by her admiration of his work.

One day she came to his house with a look of eager watchfulness. Her step was hurried, her eye wild as a hawk's when its prey is near. The old man was finishing a fanciful little craft, of which he was proud beyond any thing. It was so light, so strong, so beautifully decorated with bands of red and white around the edge—no wonder the young woman's eyes brightened when she saw it.

"What would he take for the boat?" That was a droll question from her. Why he had built it to please his own fancy. A pair of oars would make it skim the water like a bird. He had built it with an eye to old Mr. Danforth, who had been down to look at his boats for that dark-eyed grandson, whom he seemed to worship. None of his boats were fanciful or light enough for the lad. So he had built this at a venture.

Malaeska's eyes kindled brighter and brighter. Yes, yes; she, too, was thinking of the young gentleman; she would bring him to look at the boat. Mrs. Danforth often trusted the boy out with her; if he would only tell the price, perhaps they might be able to bring the money, and give the boat a trial on the Hudson.

The old man laughed, glanced proudly at his handiwork, and named a price. It was not too much; Malaeska had double that amount in the embroidered pouch that hung in her little room at home—for the old gentleman had been liberal to her in every thing but kindness. She went home elated and eager; all was in readiness. The next day—oh, how her heart glowed as she thought of the next day!

Chapter V

Her boat is on the river,
    With the boy by her side;
With her bow and her quiver
    She stands in her pride.

THE next afternoon old Mr. Danforth was absent from home. A municipal meeting, or something of that kind, was to be attended, and he was always prompt in the performance of public duties. The good housewife had not been well for some days. Malaeska, always a gentle nurse, attended her with unusual assiduity. There was something evidently at work in the Indian woman's heart. Her lips were pale, her eyes full of pathetic trouble. After a time, when weariness made the old lady sleepy, Malaeska stole to the bedside, and kneeling down, kissed the withered hand that fell over the bed, with strange humility. This action was so light that the good lady did not heed it, but afterward it came to her like a dream, and as such she remembered this leave-taking of the poor mother.

William—for the lad was named after his father—was in a moody state that afternoon. He had no playfellows, for the indisposition of his grandmother had shut all strangers from the house, so he went into the garden, and began to draw the outlines of a rude fortification from the white pebbles that paved the principal walk. He was interrupted in the work by a pair of orioles, that came dashing through the leaves of an old apple-tree in a far end of the garden, in full chase and pursuit, making the very air vibrate with their rapid motion.

After chasing each other up and down, to and fro in the clear sunshine, they were attracted by something in the distance, and darted off like a couple of golden arrows, sending back wild gushes of music in the start.

The boy had been watching them with his great eyes full of envious delight. Their riotous freedom charmed him; he felt chained and caged even in that spacious garden, full of golden fruit and bright flowers as it was. The native fire kindled in his frame.

"Oh, if I were only a bird, that could fly home when I pleased, and away to the woods again—the bright, beautiful woods that I can see across the river, but never must play in. How the birds love it though!"

The boy stopped speaking, for, like any other child kept to himself, he was talking over his thoughts aloud. But a shadow fell across the white pebbles on which he sat, and this it was which disturbed him.

It was the Indian woman, Malaeska, with a forced smile on her face and looking wildly strange. She seemed larger and more stately than when he had seen her last. In her hand she held a light bow tufted with yellow and crimson feathers. When she saw his eyes brighten at the sight of the bow, Malaeska took an arrow from the sheaf which she carried under her cloak, and fitted it to the string.

"See, this is what we learn in the woods."

The two birds were wheeling to and fro across the garden and out into the open space; their plumage flashed in the sunshine and gushes of musical triumph floated back as one shot ahead of the other. Malaeska lifted her bow with something of her old forest gracefulness—a faint twang of the bowstring—a sharp whiz of the arrow, one of the birds fluttered downward, with a sad little cry, and fell upon the ground, trembling like a broken poplar flower.

The boy started up—his eye brightened and his thin nostrils dilated, the savage instincts of his nature broke out in all his features.

"And you learned how to do this in the woods, Malaeska?" he said, eagerly.

"Yes; will you learn too?"

"Oh, yes—give hold here—quick—quick!"

"Not here; we learn these things in the woods; come with me, and I will show you all about it." Malaeska grew pale as she spoke, and trembled in all her limbs. What if the boy refused to go with her?

"What! over the river to the woods that look so bright and so brown when the nuts fall? Will you take me there, Malaeska?"

"Yes, over the river where it shines like silver."

"You will? oh my!—but how?"

"Hush! not so loud. In a beautiful little boat."

"With white sails, Malaeska?"

"No—with paddles."

"Ah, me!—but I can't make them go in the water; once grandfather let me try, but I had to give it up."

"But I can make them go."

"You! why, that isn't a woman's work."

"No, but everybody learns it in the woods."

"Can I?"

"Yes!"

"Then come along before grandfather comes to say we shan't; come along, I say; I want to shoot and run and live in the woods—come along, Malaeska. Quick, or somebody will shut the gate."

Malaeska looked warily around—on the windows of the house, through the thickets, and along the gravel walks. No one was in sight. She and her boy were all alone. She breathed heavily and lingered, thinking of the poor lady within.

"Come!" cried the boy, eagerly; "I want to go—come along to the woods."

"Yes, yes," whispered Malaeska, "to the woods—it is our home. There I shall be a mother once more."

With the steps of a young deer, starting for its covert, she left the garden. The boy kept bravely on with her, bounding forward with a laugh when her step was too rapid for him to keep up with it. Thus, in breathless haste, they passed through the town into the open country and along the rough banks of the river.

A little inlet, worn by the constant action of the water, ran up into the shore, which is now broken with wharves and bristling with masts. A clump of old forest-hemlocks bent over the waters, casting cool, green shadows upon it till the sun was far in the west.

In these shadows, rocking sleepily on the ripples, lay the pretty boat which Malaeska had purchased. A painted basket, such as the peaceful Indians sometimes sent to market, stood in the stern stored with bread; a tiger-skin, edged with crimson cloth, according to the Indian woman's fancy, lay along the bottom of the boat, and cushions of scarlet cloth, edged with an embroidery of beads, lay on the seat.

William Danforth broke into a shout when he saw the boat and its appointments. "Are we going in this? May I learn to row, now—now?" With a leap he sprang into the little craft, and seizing the oars, called for her to come on, for he was in a hurry to begin.

Malaeska loosened the cable, and holding the end in her hand, sprang to the side of her child.

"Not yet, my chief, not yet; give the oars to me a little while; when we can no longer see the steeples, you shall pull them," she said.

The boy gave up his place with an impatient toss of his head, which sent the black curls flying over his temples. But the boat shot out into the river with a velocity that took away his breath, and he sat down in the bow, laughing as the silver spray rained over him. With her face to the north, and her eyes flashing with the eager joy of escape, Malaeska dashed up the river; every plunge of the oars was a step toward freedom—every gleam of the sun struck her as a smile from the Great Spirit to whom her husband and father had gone.

When the sun went down, and the twilight came on, the little boat was far up the river. It had glided under the shadows of Weehawken,[6] and was skirting the western shore toward the Highlands, at that time crowned by an unbroken forest, and savage in the grandeur of wild nature.

Now Malaeska listened to the entreaties of her boy, and gave the oars into his small hands. No matter though the boat receded under his brave but imperfect efforts; once out of sight of the town, Malaeska had less fear, and smiled securely at the energy with which

---

6 Weehawken is a settlement in what is now New Jersey on the west shore of the Hudson River across from Manhattan Island. It was made famous in 1804 as the place where Aaron Burr killed Alexander Hamilton in duel.

the little fellow beat the waters. He was indignant if she attempted to help him, and the next moment was sure to send a storm of rain over her in some more desperate effort to prove how capable he was of taking the labor from her hands.

Thus the night came on, soft and calm, wrapping the mother and child in a world of silvery moonbeams. The shadows which lay along the hills bounded their watery path with gloom. This made the boy sad, and he began to feel mournfully weary; but scenes like this were familiar with Malaeska, and her old nature rose high and free in this solitude which included all that she had in the living world—her freedom and the son of her white husband.

"Malaeska," said the boy, creeping to her side, and laying his head on her lap, "Malaeska, I am tired—I want to go home."

"Home! but you have not seen the woods. Courage, my chief, and we will go on shore."

"But it is black—so black, and something is crying there—something that is sick or wants to get home like me."

"No, no,—it is only a whippowil singing to the night."

"A whippowil? Is that a little boy, Malaeska? Let us bring him into the boat."

"No, my child, it is only a bird."

"Poor bird!" sighed the boy; "how it wants to get home."

"No, it loves the woods. The bird would die if you took it from the shade of the trees," said Malaeska, striving to pacify the boy, who crept upward into her lap and laid his cheek against hers. She felt that he trembled, and that tears lay cold on his cheeks. "Don't, my William, but look up and see how many stars hang over us—the river is full of them."

"Oh, but grandfather will be missing me," pleaded the boy.

Malaeska felt herself chilled; she had taken the boy but not his memory; that went back to the opulent home he had left. With her at his side, and the beautiful universe around, he thought of the old man who had made her worse than a serf in his household—who had stolen away the human soul that God had given into her charge. The Indian woman grew sad to the very depths of her soul when the boy spoke of his grandfather.

"Come," she said, with mournful pathos, "now we will find an open place in the woods. You shall have a bed like the pretty flowers. I will build a fire, and you shall see it grow red among the branches."

The boy smiled in the moonlight.

"A fire out of doors! Yes, yes, let's go into the woods. Will the birds talk to us there?"

"The birds talk to us always when we get into the deep of the woods."

Malaeska urged her boat into a little inlet that ran up between two great rocks upon the shore, where it was sheltered and safe; then she took the tiger-skin and the cushions in her arms, and, cautioning the boy to hold on to her dress, began to mount a little elevation where the trees were thin and the grass abundant, as she could tell from the odor of wild-flowers that came with the wind. A rock lay embedded in this rich forest-grass, and over it a huge white poplar spread its branches like a tent.

Upon this rock Malaeska enthroned the boy, talking to him all the time, as she struck sparks from a flint which she took from her basket, and began to kindle a fire from the dry sticks which lay around in abundance. When William saw the flames rise up high and clear, illuminating the beautiful space around, and shooting gleams of gold through the poplar's branches he grew brave again, and coming down from his eminence, began to gather brushwood that the fire might keep bright. Then Malaeska took a bottle of water and some bread, with fragments of dried beef, from her basket, and the boy came smiling from his work. He was no longer depressed by the dark, and the sight of food made him hungry.

How proudly the Indian mother broke the food and surrendered it to his eager appetite. The bright beauty of her face was something wonderful to look upon as she watched him by the firelight. For the first time, since he was a little infant, he really seemed to belong to her.

When he was satisfied with food, and she saw that his eyelids began to droop, Malaeska went to some rocks at a little distance, and tearing up the moss in great green fleeces, brought it to the place she had chosen under the poplar-tree, and heaped a soft couch for the child. Over this she spread the tiger-skin with its red border, and laid the crimson pillows whose fringes glittered in the firelight like gems around the couch of a prince.

To this picturesque bed Malaeska took the boy, and seating herself by his side, began to sing as she had done years ago under the roof of her wigwam. The lad was very weary, and fell asleep while her plaintive voice filled the air and was answered mournfully back by a night-bird deep in the blackness of the forest.

When certain that the lad was asleep, Malaeska lay down on the hard rock by his side, softly stealing one arm over him and sighing out her troubled joy as she pressed his lips with her timid kisses.

Thus the poor Indian sunk to a broken rest, as she had done all her life, piling up soft couches for those she loved, and taking the cold stone for herself. It was her woman's destiny, not the more certain because of her savage origin. Civilization does not always reverse this mournful picture of womanly self-abnegation.

When the morning came, the boy was aroused by a full chorus of singing-birds that fairly made the air vibrate with their melody. In and out through the branches rang their wild minstrelsy, till the sunshine came laughing through the greenness, giving warmth and pleasant light to the music. William sat up, rubbing his eyes, and wondering at the strange noises. Then he remembered where he was, and called aloud for Malaeska. She came from behind a clump of trees, carrying a partridge in her hand, pierced through the heart with her arrow. She flung the bird on the rock at William's feet, and kneeling down before him, kissed his feet, his hands, and the folds of his tunic, smoothing his hair and his garments with pathetic fondness.

"When shall we go home, Malaeska?" cried the lad, a little anxiously. "Grandfather will want us."

"This is the home for a young chief," replied the mother, looking around upon the pleasant sky and the forest-turf, enameled with wild-flowers. "What white man has a tent like this?"

The boy looked up and saw a world of golden tulip-blossoms starring the branches above him.

"It lets in the cold and the rain," he said, shaking the dew from his glossy hair. "I don't like the woods, Malaeska."

"But you will—oh yes, you will," answered the mother, with anxious cheerfulness; "see, I have shot a bird for your breakfast."

"A bird? and I am so hungry."

"And see here, what I have brought from the shore."

She took a little leaf-basket from a recess in the rocks, and held it up full of black raspberries with the dew glittering upon them.

The boy clapped his hands, laughing merrily.

"Give me the raspberries—I will eat them all. Grandfather isn't here to stop me, so I will eat and eat till the basket is empty. After all, Malaeska, it is pleasant being in the woods—come, pour the berries on the moss, just here, and get another basketful while I eat these; but don't go far—I am afraid when you are out of sight. No, no, let me build the fire—see how I can make the sparks fly."

Down he came from the rock, forgetting his berries, and eager to distinguish himself among the brushwood, while Malaeska withdrew a little distance and prepared her game for roasting.

The boy was quick and full of intelligence; he had a fire blazing at once, and shouted back a challenge to the birds as its flames rose in the air, sending up wreaths of delicate blue smoke into the poplar branches, and curtaining the rocks with mist.

Directly the Indian woman came forward with her game, nicely dressed and pierced with a wooden skewer; to this she attached a piece of twine, which, being tied to a branch overhead, swung its burden gently to and fro before the fire.

While this rustic breakfast was in preparation, the boy went off in search of flowers or berries—any thing that he could find. He came back with a quantity of green wild cherries in his tunic, and a bird's nest, with three speckled eggs in it, which he had found under a tuft of fern leaves. A striped squirrel, that ran down a chestnut-limb, looked at him with such queer earnestness, that he shouted lustily to Malaeska, saying that he loved the beautiful woods and all the pretty things in it.

When he came back, Malaeska had thrown off her cloak, and crowned herself with a coronal of scarlet and green feathers, which rendered her savage dress complete, and made her an object of wondering admiration to the boy, as she moved in and out through the trees, with her face all aglow with proud love.

While the partridge was swaying to and fro before the fire, Malaeska gathered a handful of chestnut-leaves and wove them together in a sort of mat; upon this cool nest she laid the bird, and carved it with a pretty poniard which William's father had given her in his first wooing; then she made a leaf-cup, and, going to a little spring which she had discovered, filled it with crystal water. So, upon the flowering turf, with wild birds serenading them, and the winds floating softly by, the mother and boy took their first regular meal in the forest. William was delighted; every thing was fresh and beautiful to him. He could scarcely contain his eagerness to be in action long enough to eat the delicate repast which Malaeska diversified with smiles and caresses. He wanted to shoot the birds that sang so sweetly in the branches, all unconscious that the act would inflict pain on the poor little songsters; he could not satisfy himself with gazing on the gorgeous raiment of his mother—it was something wonderful in his eyes.

At last the rustic meal was ended, and with his lips reddened by the juicy fruit, he started up, pleading for the bow and arrow.

Proud as a queen and fond as a woman, Malaeska taught him how to place the arrow on the bowstring, and when to lift it gradually toward his face. He took to it naturally, the young rogue, and absolutely danced for joy when his first arrow leaped from his bow and went rifling through the poplar-leaves. How Malaeska loved this practice! how she triumphed in each graceful lift of his arm! how her heart leaped to the rich tumult of his shouts! He wanted to go off alone and try his skill among the squirrels, but Malaeska was afraid, and followed him step by step, happy and watchful. Every moment increased his skill; he would have exhausted the sheaf of arrows, but that Malaeska patiently searched for them after each shot, and thus secured constant amusement till he grew tired even of that rare sport.

Toward noon, Malaeska left him at rest on the tiger-skin, and went herself in search of game for the noonday meal; never had she breathed so freely, never had the woods seemed so like her home. A sense of profound peace stole over her. These groves were her world, and on the rock near by lay her other life—all that she had on earth to love. She was in no haste to find her tribe. What care had she for any thing while the boy was with her, and the forest so pleasant? What did she care for but his happiness?

It required but few efforts of her woodcraft to obtain game enough for another pleasant meal; so, with a light step, she returned to her fairy-like encampment. Tired with his play, the boy had fallen asleep on the rock. She saw the graceful repose of his limbs, and the sunshine shimmering softly through his black hair. Her step grew lighter; she was afraid of rustling a leaf, lest the noise might disturb him. Thus, softly and almost holding her breath, she drew nearer and nearer to the rock. All at once a faint gasping breath bespoke some terrible emotion—she stood motionless, rooted to the earth. A low rattle checked her first, and then she saw the shimmer of a serpent, coiled upon the very rock where her boy was lying. Her approach had aroused the reptile, and she could see him preparing to lance out. His first fling would be at the sleeping boy. The mother was frozen into marble; she dared not move—she could only stare at the snake with a wild glitter of the eye.

The stillness seemed to appease the creature. The noise of his rattle grew fainter, and his eyes sank like waning fire-sparks into the writhing folds that settled on the moss. But the child was disturbed by a sunbeam that slanted through the leaves overhead, and turned upon the tiger-skin. Instantly the rattle sounded sharp and clear, and out from the writhing folds shot the venomous head with its vicious eyes fixed on the boy. Malaeska had, even in her frozen state, some thought of saving her boy. With her cold hands she had fitted the arrow and lifted the bow, but as the serpent grew passive, the weapon dropped again; for he lay on the other side of the child, and to kill him she was obliged to shoot over that sleeping form. But the reptile crested himself again, and now with a quiver of horrible dread at her heart, but nerves strained like steel, she drew the bowstring, and, aiming at the head, which glittered like a jewel, just beyond her child, let the arrow fly. She went blind on the instant—the darkness of death fell upon her brain; the coldness of death lay upon her heart; she listened for some cry—nothing but a sharp rustling of leaves and then profound stillness met her strained senses.

The time in which Malaeska was struck with darkness seemed an eternity to her, but it lasted only an instant, in fact; then her eyes opened wide in the agonized search, and terrible thrills shot through her frame. A laugh rang up through the trees, and then she saw her boy sitting up on the tiger-skin, his cheeks all rosy with sleep and dimpled with surprise, gazing down upon the headless rattlesnake that had uncoiled convulsively in its death-spasms, and lay quivering across his feet.

"Ha! ha!" he shouted, clapping his hands, "this is a famous fellow—prettier than the birds, prettier than the squirrels. Malaeska! Malaeska! see what this checkered thing is with no head, and rings on its tail."

Malaeska was so weak she could hardly stand, but, trembling in every limb, she staggered toward the rock, and seizing upon the still quivering snake, hurled it with a shuddering cry into the undergrowth.

Then she fell upon her knees, and clasped the boy close, close to her bosom till he struggled and cried out that she was hurting him. But she could not let him go; it seemed as if the serpent would coil around him the moment her arms were loosened; she clung to his garments—she kissed his hands, his hair, and his flushed forehead with passionate energy.

He could not understand all this. Why did Malaeska breathe so hard, and shake so much? He wished she had not flung away the pretty creature which had crept to his bed while he slept, and looked so beautiful. But when she told how dangerous the reptile was, he began to be afraid, and questioned her with vague terror about the way she had killed him.

Some yards from the rock, Malaeska found her arrow on which the serpent's head was impaled, and she carried it with trembling exultation to the boy, who shrank away with new-born dread, and began to know what fear was.

Chapter VI

Mid forests and meadow lands, though we may roam,
Be it ever so humble, there's no place like home;
      Home, home, sweet, sweet, home,
      There's no place like home;
      There's no place like home.

THIS event troubled Malaeska, and gathering up her little property, she unmoored the boat, and made progress up the river. The child was delighted with the change, and soon lost all unpleasant remembrance of the rattlesnake. But Malaeska was very careful in the selection of her encampment that afternoon, and kindled a bright fire before she spread the tiger-skin for William's bed, which she trusted would keep all venomous things away. They ate their supper under a huge white pine, that absorbed the firelight in its dusky branches, and made every thing gloomy around. As the darkness closed over them William grew silent, and by the heaviness of his features Malaeska saw that he was oppressed by thoughts of home. She had resolved not to tell him of the relationship which was constantly in her thoughts, till they should stand at the council-fires of the tribe, when the Indians should know him as their chief, and he recognize a mother in poor Malaeska.

Troubled by his sad look, the Indian woman sought for something in her stores that should cheer him. She found some seed-cakes, golden and sweet, which only brought tears into the child's eyes, for they reminded him of home and all its comforts.

"Malaeska," he said, "when shall we go back to grandfather and grandmother? I know they want to see us."

"No, no; we must not think about that," said Malaeska, anxiously.

"But I can't help it—how can I?" persisted the boy, mournfully.

"Don't—don't say you love them—I mean your grandfather—more than you love Malaeska. She would die for you."

"Yes; but I don't want you to die, only to go back home," he pleaded.

"We are going home—to our beautiful home in the woods, which I told you of."

"Dear me, I'm so tired of the woods."

"Tired of the woods?"

"Yes, I *am* tired. They are nice to play in, but it isn't home, no way. How far is it, Malaeska, to where grandfather lives?"

"I don't know—I don't want to know. We shall never—never go there again," said the Indian, passionately. "You are mine, all mine."

The boy struggled in her embrace restively.

"But I won't stay in the woods. I want to be in a real house, and sleep in a soft bed, and—and— there, now, it is going to rain; I hear it thunder. Oh, how I want to go home!"

There was in truth a storm mustering over them; the wind rose and moaned hoarsely through the pines. Malaeska was greatly distressed, and gathered the tired boy lovingly to her bosom for shelter.

"Have patience, William; nothing shall hurt you. Tomorrow we will row the boat all day. You shall pull the oars yourself."

"Shall I, though?" said the boy, brightening a little; "but will it be on the way home?"

"We shall go across the mountains where the Indians live. The brave warriors who will make William their king."

"But I don't want to be a king, Malaeska!"

"A chief—a great chief—who shall go to the war-path and fight battles."

"Ah, I should like that, with your pretty bow and arrow, Malaeska; wouldn't I shoot the wicked red-skins?"

"Ah, my boy, don't say that."

"Oh," said the child, shivering, "the wind is cold; how it sobs in the pine boughs. Don't you wish we were at home now?"

"Don't be afraid of the cold," said Malaeska, in a troubled voice; "see, I will wrap this cloak about you, and no rain can come through the fur blanket. We are brave, you and I—what do we care for a little thunder and rain—it makes me feel brave."

"But you don't care for home; you love the woods and the rain. The thunder and lightning makes your eyes bright, but I don't like it; so take me home, please, and then you may go to the woods; I won't tell."

"Oh, don't—don't. It breaks my heart," cried the poor mother. "Listen, William: the Indians—my people—the brave Indians want you for a chief. In a few years you shall lead them to war."

"But I hate the Indians."

"No, no."

"They are fierce and cruel."

"Not to you—not to you!"

"I won't live with the Indians!"

"They are a brave people—you shall be their chief."

"They killed my father."

"But I am of those people. I saved you and brought you among the white people."

"Yes, I know; grandmother told me that."

"And I belonged to the woods."

"Among the Indians?"

"Yes. Your father loved these Indians, William."

"Did he—but they killed him."

"But it was in battle."

"In fair battle; did you say that?"

"Yes, child. Your father was friendly with them, but they thought he had turned enemy. A great chief met him in the midst of the fight, and they killed each other. They fell and died together."

"Did you know this great chief, Malaeska?"

"He was my father," answered the Indian woman, hoarsely; "my own father."

"Your father and mine; how strange that they should hate each other," said the boy, thoughtfully.

"Not always," answered Malaeska, struggling against the tears that choked her words; "at one time they loved each other."

"Loved each other! that is strange; and did my father love you, Malaeska?"

White as death the poor woman turned; a hand was clenched under her deer-skin robe, and pressed hard against her heart; but she had promised to reveal nothing, and bravely kept her word.

The boy forgot his reckless question the moment it was asked, and did not heed her pale silence, for the storm was gathering darkly over them. Malaeska wrapped him in her cloak, and sheltered him with her person. The rain began to patter heavily overhead; but the pine-tree was thick with foliage, and no drops, as yet, could penetrate to the earth.

"See, my boy, we are safe from the rain; nothing can reach us here," she said, cheering his despondency. "I will heap piles of dry wood on the fire, and shelter you all night long."

She paused a moment, for flashes of blue lightning began to play fiercely through the thick foliage overhead, revealing depths of darkness that was enough to terrify a brave man. No wonder the boy shrank and trembled as it flashed and quivered over him.

Malaeska saw how frightened he was, and piled dry wood recklessly on the fire, hoping that its steady blaze would reassure him.

They were encamped on a spur of the Highlands that shot in a precipice over the stream, and the light of Malaeska's fire gleamed far and wide, casting a golden track far down the Hudson.

Four men, who were urging a boat bravely against the storm, saw the light, and shouted eagerly to each other.

"Here she is; nothing but an Indian would keep up a fire like that. Pull steadily, and we have them."

They did pull steadily, and defying the storm, the boat made harbor under the cliff where Malaeska's fire still burned. Four men stole away from the boat, and crept stealthily up the hill, guided by the lightning and the gleaming fire above. The rain, beating among the branches, drowned their footsteps; and they spoke only in hoarse whispers, which were lost on the wind.

William had dropped asleep with tears on his thick eyelashes, which the strong firelight revealed to Malaeska, who regarded him with mournful affection. The cold wind chilled her through and through, but she did not feel it. So long as the boy slept comfortably she had no want.

I have said that the storm muffled all other sounds; and the four men who had left their boat at the foot of the cliff stood close by Malaeska before she had the least idea of their approach. Then a blacker shadow than fell from the pine, darkened the space around her, and looking suddenly up, she saw the stern face of old Mr. Danforth between her and the firelight.

Malaeska did not speak or cry aloud, but snatching the sleeping boy close to her heart, lifted her pale face to his, half-defiant, half-terrified.

"Take my grandson from the woman and bring him down to the boat," said the old man, addressing those that came with him.

"No, no, he is mine!" cried Malaeska, fiercely. "Nothing but the Great Spirit shall take him from me again!"

The sharp anguish in her voice awoke the boy. He struggled in her arms, and looking around, saw the old man.

"Grandfather, oh! grandfather, take me home. I do want to go home," he cried, stretching out his arms.

"Oh!" I have not the power of words to express the bitter anguish of that single exclamation, when it broke from the mother's pale lips. It was the cry of a heart that snapped its strongest fiber there and then. The boy wished to leave her. She had no strength after that, but allowed them to force him from her arms without a struggle. The rattlesnake had not paralyzed her so completely.

So they took the boy ruthlessly from her embrace, and carried him away. She followed after without a word of protest, and saw them lift him into the boat and push off, leaving her to the pitiless night. It was a cruel thing—bitterly cruel—but the poor woman was stupefied with the blow, and watched the boat with heavy eyes. All at once she heard the boy calling after her:

"Malaeska, come too. Malaeska—Malaeska!"

She heard the cry, and her icy heart swelled passionately. With the leap of a panther she sprang to her own boat, and dashed after her tormenters, pulling fiercely through the storm. But with all her desperate energy, she was not able to overtake those four powerful men. They were out of sight directly, and she drifted after them alone—all alone.

Malaeska never went back to Mr. Danforth's house again, but she built a lodge on the Weehawken shore, and supported herself by selling painted baskets and such embroideries as the Indians excel in. It was a lonely life, but sometimes she met her son in the streets of Manhattan, or sailing on the river, and this poor happiness kept her alive.

After a few months, the lad came to her lodge. His grandmother consented to the visit, for she still had compassion on the lone Indian, and would not let the youth go beyond sea without bidding her farewell. In all the bitter anguish of that parting Malaeska kept her faith, and smothering the great want of her soul, saw her son depart without putting forth the holy claim of her motherhood. One day Malaeska stood upon the shore and saw a white-sailed ship veer from her moorings and pass away with cruel swiftness toward the ocean, the broad, boundless ocean, that seemed to her like eternity.

Chapter VII

Alone in the forest, alone,
    When the night is dark and late—
Alone on the waters, alone,
    She drifts to her woman's fate.

AGAIN Malaeska took to her boat and, all alone, began her mournful journey to the forest. After the fight at Catskill, her brethren had retreated into the interior. The great tribe, which gave its name to the richest intervale in New York State, was always munificent in its hospitality to less fortunate brethren, to whom its hunting-grounds were ever open. Malaeska knew that her people were mustered somewhere near the amber-colored falls of Genesee,[7] and she began her mournful voyage with vague longings to see them again, now that she had nothing but memories to live upon.

With a blanket in the bow of her boat, a few loaves of bread, and some meal in a coarse linen bag, she started up the river. The boat was battered and beginning to look old—half

---

7 In west-central New York State, roughly three hundred miles from Manhattan Island.

the gorgeous paint was worn from its sides, and the interior had been often washed by the tempests that beat over the little cove near her lodge where she had kept it moored. She made no attempt to remedy its desolate look. The tigerskin was left behind in her lodge. No crimson cushions rendered the single seat tempting to sit upon. These fanciful comforts were intended for the boy—motherly love alone provided them; but now she had no care for things of this kind. A poor lone Indian woman, trampled on by the whites, deserted by her own child, was going back to her kinsfolk for shelter. Why should she attempt to appear less desolate than she was?

Thus, dreary and abandoned, Malaeska sat in her boat, heavily urging it up the stream. She had few wants, but pulled at the oars all day long, keeping time to the slow movement with her voice, from which a low funereal chant swelled continually.

Sometimes she went ashore, and building a fire in the loneliness, cooked the fish she had speared or the bird her arrow had brought down; but these meals always reminded her of the few happy days spent, after the sylvan fashion, with her boy, and she would sit moaning over the untested food till the very birds that hovered near would pause in their singing to look askance at her. So she relaxed in her monotonous toil but seldom, and generally slept in her little craft, with the current rippling around her, wrapped only in a coarse, gray blanket.

No one cared about her movements, and no one attempted to bring her back, or she might have been traced at intervals by some rock close to the shore, blackened with embers, where she had baked her corn-bread, or by the feathers of a bird which she had dressed, without caring to eat it.

Day after day—day after day, Malaeska kept on her watery path till she came to the mouth of the Mohawk.[8] There she rested a little, with a weary, heavy-hearted dread of pursuing her journey further. What if her people should reject her as a renegade? She had deserted them in their hour of deep trouble—fled from the grave of her father, their chief, and had carried his grandson away to his bitterest enemy, the white man.

Would the people of her tribe forgive this treason, and take her back? She scarcely cared; life had become so dreary, the whole world so dark, that the poor soul rather courted pain, and would have smiled to know that death was near. Some vague ideas of religion, that the gentle grandmother of her son had taken pains to instill into that wild nature, kept her from self-destruction; but she counted the probabilities that the tribe might put her to death, with vague hope.

Weary days, and more weary nights, she spent upon the Mohawk, creeping along the shadows and seeking the gloomiest spots for her repose: under the wild grape-vines that bent down the young elms with their purple fruit—under the golden willows and dusky pines she sought rest, never caring for danger; for, what had she to care how death or pain presented itself, so long as she had no fear of either?

At last she drew up her boat under a shelving precipice, and making it safe, took to the wilderness with nothing but a little corn meal, her blanket, and bow. With the same heavy listlessness that had marked her entire progress, she threaded the forest-paths, knowing by the hacked trees that her tribe had passed that way. But her path was rough, and the encampment far off, and she had many a heavy mile to walk before it could be reached.

---

8   The Mohawk River joins the Hudson north of Albany; these waters flow southward through the Hudson River Valley, with the Catskill Mountains to the west. This river was a critical trading route in the region for both whites and Native Americans.

Her moccasins were worn to tatters, and her dress, once so gorgeous, all rent and weather stained when she came in sight of the little prairie, hedged in by lordly forest-trees, in which her broken tribe had built their lodges.

Malaeska threw away her scant burden of food, and took a prouder bearing when she came in sight of those familiar lodges. In all her sorrow, she could not forget that she was the daughter of a great chief and a princess among the people whom she sought.

Thus, with an imperial tread, and eyes bright as the stars, she entered the encampment and sought the lodge which, by familiar signs, she knew to be that of the chief who had superseded her son.

It was near sunset, and many of the Indian women had gathered in front of this lodge, waiting for their lords to come forth; for there was a council within the lodge, and like the rest of their sex, the dusky sisterhood liked to be in the way of intelligence. Malaeska had changed greatly during the years that she had been absent among the whites. If the lightness and grace of youth were gone, a more imposing dignity came in their place. Habits of refinement had kept her complexion clear and her hair bright. She had left them a slender, spirited young creature; she returned a serious woman, modest, but queenly withal.

The women regarded her first with surprise and then with kindling anger, for, after pausing to look at them without finding a familiar face, she walked on toward the lodge, and lifting the mat, stood within the opening in full view both of the warriors assembled there and the wrathful glances of the females on the outside.

When the Indians saw the entrance to their council darkened by a woman, dead silence fell upon them, followed by a fierce murmur that would have made a person who feared death tremble. Malaeska stood undismayed, surveying the savage group with a calm, regretful look; for, among the old men, she saw some that had been upon the war-path with her father. Turning to one of these warriors, she said:

"It is Malaeska, daughter of the Black Eagle."

A murmur of angry surprise ran through the lodge, and the women crowded together, menacing her with their glances.

"When my husband, the young white chief, died," continued Malaeska, "he told me to go down the great water and carry my son to his own people. The Indian wife obeys her chief."

A warrior, whom Malaeska knew as the friend of her father, arose with austere gravity, and spoke:

"It is many years since Malaeska took the young chief to his white fathers. The hemlock that was green has died at the top since then. Why does Malaeska come back to her people alone? Is the boy dead?"

Malaeska turned pale in the twilight, and her voice faltered.

"The boy is not dead—yet Malaeska is alone!" she answered plaintively.

"Has the woman made a white chief of the boy? Has he become the enemy of our people?" said another of the Indians, looking steadily at Malaeska.

Malaeska knew the voice and the look; it was that of a brave who, in his youth, had besought her to share his wigwam. A gleam of proud reproach came over her features, but she bent her head without answering.

Then the old chief spoke again. "Why does Malaeska come back to her tribe like a bird with its wings broken? Has the white chief driven her from his wigwam?"

Malaeska's voice broke out; the gentle pride of her character rose as the truth of her position presented itself.

"Malaeska obeyed the young chief, her husband, but her heart turned back to her own people. She tried to bring the boy into the forest again, but they followed her up the great river and took him away; Malaeska stands here alone."

Again the Indian spoke. "The daughter of the Black Eagle forsook her tribe when the death-song of her father was loud in the woods. She comes back when the corn is ripe, but there is no wigwam open to her. When a women of the tribe goes off to the enemy, she returns only to die. Have I said well?"

A guttural murmur of assent ran through the lodge. The women heard it from their place in the open air, and gathering fiercely around the door, cried out, "Give her to us! She has stolen our chief—she has disgraced her tribe. It is long since we have danced at the fire-festival."

The rabble of angry women came on with their taunts and menaces, attempting to seize Malaeska, who stood pale and still before them; but the chief, whom she had once rejected, stood up, and with a motion of his hands repulsed them.

"Let the women go back to their wigwams. The daughter of a great chief dies only by the hands of a chief. To the warrior of her tribe, whom she has wronged, her life belongs."

Malaeska lifted her sorrowful eyes to his face—how changed it was since the day he had asked her to share his lodge.

"And it is you that want my life?" she said.

"By the laws of the tribe it is mine," he answered. "Turn your face to the east—it is growing dark; the forest is deep; no one shall hear Malaeska's cries when the hatchet cleaves her forehead. Come!"

Malaeska turned in pale terror, and followed him. No one interfered with the chief, whom she had refused for a white man. Her life belonged to him. He had a right to choose the time and place of her execution. But the women expressed their disappointment in fiendish sneers, as she glided like a ghost through their ranks and disappeared in the blackness of the forest.

Not a word was spoken between her and the chief. Stern and silent he struck into a trail which she knew led to the river, for she had traveled over it the day before. Thus, in darkness and profound silence, she walked on all night till her limbs were so weary that she longed to call out and pray the chief to kill her then and there; but he kept on a little in advance, only turning now and then to be sure that she followed.

Once she ventured to ask him why he put off her death so long; but he pointed along the trail, and walked along without deigning a reply. During the day he took a handful of parched corn from his pouch and told her to eat; but for himself, through that long night and day, he never tasted a morsel.

Toward sunset they came out on the banks of the Mohawk, near the very spot where she had left her boat. The Indian paused here and looked steadily at his victim.

The blood grew cold in Malaeska's veins—death was terrible when it came so near. She cast one look of pathetic pleading on his face, then, folding her hands, stood before him waiting for the moment.

"Malaeska!"

His voice was softened, his lips quivered as the name once so sweet to his heart passed through them.

"Malaeska, the river is broad and deep. The keel of your boat leaves no track. Go! the Great Spirit will light you with his stars. Here is corn and dried venison. Go in peace!"

She looked at him with her wild tender eyes; her lips began to tremble, her heart swelled with gentle sweetness, which was the grace of her civilization. She took the red hand of the savage and kissed it reverently.

"Farewell," she said; "Malaeska has no words; her heart is full."

The savage began to tremble; a glow of the old passion came over him.

"Malaeska, my wigwam is empty; will you go back? It is my right to save or kill."

"*He* is yonder, in the great hunting-ground, waiting for Malaeska to come. Could she go blushing from another chief's wigwam?"

For one instant those savage features were convulsed; then they settled down into the cold gravity of his former expression, and he pointed to the boat.

She went down to the edge of the water, while he took the blanket from his shoulders and placed it in the boat. Then he pushed the little craft from its mooring, and motioned her to jump in; he forbore to touch her hand, or even look on her face, but saw her take up the oars and leave the shore without a word; but when she was out of sight, his head fell forward on his bosom, and he gradually sank to an attitude of profound grief.

While he sat upon a fragment of rock, with a rich sunset crimsoning the water at his feet, a canoe came down the river, urged by a white man, the only one who ever visited his tribe. This man was a missionary among the Indians, who held him in reverence as a great medicine chief, whose power of good was something to marvel at.

The chief beckoned to the missionary, who seemed in haste, but he drew near the shore. In a few brief but eloquent words the warrior spoke of Malaeska, of the terrible fate from which she had just been rescued, and of the forlorn life to which she must henceforth be consigned. There was something grand in this compassion that touched a thousand generous impulses in the missionary's heart. He was on his course down the river—for his duties lay with the Indians of many tribes—so he promised to overtake the lonely woman, to comfort and protect her from harm till she reached some settlement.

The good man kept his word. An hour after his canoe was attached to Malaeska's little craft by its slender cable, and he was conversing kindly with her of those things that interested his pure nature most.

Malaeska listened with meek and grateful attention. No flower ever opened to the sunshine more sweetly than her soul received the holy revelations of that good man. He had no time or place for teaching, but seized any opportunity that arose where a duty could be performed. His mission lay always where human souls required knowledge. So he never left the lonely woman till long after they had passed the mouth of the Mohawk, and were floating on the Hudson. When they came in sight of the Catskill range, Malaeska was seized with an irresistible longing to see the graves of her husband and father. What other place in the wide, wide world had she to look for? Where could she go, driven forth as she was by her own people, and by the father of her husband?

Surely among the inhabitants of the village she could sell such trifles as her inventive talent could create, and if any of the old lodges stood near "the Straka," that would be shelter enough.

With these thoughts in her mind, Malaeska took leave of the missionary with many a whispered blessing, and took her way to "the Straka." There she found an old lodge, through whose crevices the winds had whistled for years; but she went diligently to work, gathering moss and turf with which this old home, connected with so many sweet and bitter associations, was rendered habitable again. Then she took possession, and proceeded to invent many objects of comfort and even taste, with which to beautify the spot she had consecrated with memories of her passionate youth, and its early, only love.

The woods were full of game, and wild fruits were abundant; so that it was a long, long time before Malaeska's residence in the neighborhood was known. She shrank from approaching a people who had treated her so cruelly, and so kept in utter loneliness so long as solitude was possible.

In all her life Malaeska retained but one vague hope, and that was for the return of her son from that far-off country to which the cruel whites had sent him. She had questioned the missionary earnestly about these lands, and had now a settled idea of their extent and distance across the ocean. The great waters no longer seemed like eternity to her, or absence so much like death. Some time she might see her child again; till then she would wait and pray to the white man's God.

Chapter VIII

Huzza, for the forests and hills!
    Huzza, for the berries so blue!
Our baskets we'll cheerily fill,
    While the thickets are sparkling with dew.

YEARS before the scene of our story returns to Catskill, Arthur Jones and the pretty Martha Fellows had married and settled down in life. The kind-hearted old man died soon after the union, and left the pair inheritors of his little shop and of a respectable landed property. Arthur made an indulgent, good husband, and Martha soon became too much confined by the cares of a rising family, for any practice of the teasing coquetry which had characterized her girlhood. She seconded her husband in all his money-making projects; was an economical and thrifty housekeeper; never allowed her children to go barefooted, except in the very warmest weather; and, to use her own words, made a point of holding her head as high as any woman in the settlement.

If an uninterrupted course of prosperity could entitle a person to this privilege, Mrs. Jones certainly made no false claim to it. Every year added something to her husband's possessions. Several hundred acres of cleared land were purchased beside that which he inherited from his father-in-law; the humble shop gradually increased to a respectable variety-store, and a handsome frame-house occupied the site of the old log-cabin.

Besides all this, Mr. Jones was a justice of the peace and a dignitary in the village; and his wife, though a great deal stouter than when a girl, and the mother of six children, had lost none of her healthy good looks, and at the age of thirty-eight continued to be a very handsome woman indeed.

Thus was the family situated at the period when our story returns to them. One warm afternoon, in the depth of summer, Mrs. Jones was sitting in the porch of her dwelling occupied in mending a garment of home-made linen, which, from its size, evidently belonged to some one of her younger children. A cheese-press, with a rich heavy mass of curd compressed between the screws, occupied one side of the porch; and against it stood a small double flax-wheel, unbanded, and with a day's work yet unreeled from the spools. A hatchel and a pair of hand-cards,[9] with a bunch of spools tied together by a tow string,

---

9 Combing tools to aid with turning flax into yarn.

lay in a corner, and high above, on rude wooden pegs, hung several enormous bunches of tow and linen yarn, the products of many weeks' hard labor.

Her children had gone into the woods after whortleberries, and the mother now and then laid down her work and stepped out to the greensward beyond the porch to watch their coming, not anxiously, but as one who feels restless and lost without her usual companions. After standing on the grass for awhile, shading her eyes with her hand and looking toward the woods, she at last returned to the porch, laid down her work, and entering the kitchen, filled the tea-kettle and began to make preparations for supper. She had drawn a long pine table to the middle of the floor, and was proceeding to spread it, when her eldest daughter came through the porch, with a basket of whortleberries on her arm. Her pretty face was flushed with walking, and a profusion of fair tresses flowed in some disorder from her pink sun-bonnet, which was falling partly back from her head.

"Oh, mother, I have something so strange to tell you," she said, setting down the basket with its load of ripe, blue fruit, and fanning herself with a bunch of chestnut-leaves gathered from the woods. "You know the old wigwam by 'the Straka?' Well, when we went by it, the brush, which used to choke up the door, was all cleared off; the crevices were filled with green moss and leaves, and a cloud of smoke was curling beautifully up from the roof among the trees. We could not tell what to make of it, and were afraid to look in at first; but finally I peeped through an opening in the logs, and as true as you are here, mother, there sat an Indian woman reading—reading, mother! did you know that Indians could read? The inside of the wigwam was hung with straw matting, and there was a chest in it, and some tools, and a little shelf of books, and another with some earthen dishes and a china cup and saucer, sprigged with gold, standing upon it. I did not see any bed, but there was a pile of fresh, sweet fern in one corner, with a pair of clean sheets spread on it, which I suppose she sleeps on, and there certainly was a feather pillow lying at the top.

"Well, the Indian woman looked kind and harmless; so I made an excuse to go in, and ask for a cup to drink out of.

"As I went round to the other side of the wigwam, I saw that the smoke came up from a fire on the outside; a kettle was hanging in the flame, and several other pots and kettles stood on a little bench by the trunk of an oak-tree, close by. I must have made some noise, for the Indian woman was looking toward the door when I opened it, as if she were a little afraid, but when she saw who it was, I never saw any one smile so pleasantly; she gave me the china cup, and went with me out to the spring where the boys were playing.

"As I was drinking, my sleeve fell back, and she saw the little wampum bracelet which you gave me, you know, mother. She started and took hold of my arm, and stared in my face, as if she would have looked me through; at last she sat down on the grass by the spring, and asked me to sit down by her and tell her my name. When I told her, she seemed ready to cry with joy; tears came into her eyes, and she kissed my hand two or three times, as if I had been the best friend she ever had on earth.

"I told her that a poor Indian girl had given the bracelet to you, before you were married to my father. She asked a great many questions about it, and you.

"When I began to describe the Indian fight, and the chief's grave down by the lake, she sat perfectly still till I had done; then I looked in her face: great tears were rolling one by one down her cheeks, her hands were locked in her lap, and her eyes were fixed upon my face with a strange stare, as if she did not know what she was gazing so hard at. She looked in my face, in this way, more than a minute after I had done speaking.

"The boys stopped their play, for they had begun to dam up the spring, and stood with their hands full of turf, huddled together, and staring at the poor woman as if they had never seen a person cry before. She did not seem to mind them, but went into the wigwam again without speaking a word."

"And was that the last you saw of her?" inquired Mrs. Jones, who had become interested in her daughter's narration.

"Oh, no; she came out again just as we were going away from the spring. Her voice was more sweet and mournful than it had been, and her eyes looked heavy and troubled. She thanked me for the story I had told her, and gave me this pair of beautiful moccasins."

Mrs. Jones took the moccasins from her daughter's hand. They were of neatly dressed deer-skin, covered with beads and delicate needlework in silk.

"It is strange!" muttered Mrs. Jones; "one might almost think it possible. But nonsense; did not the old merchant send us word that the poor creature and her child were lost in the Highlands—that they died of hunger? Well, Sarah," she added, turning to her daughter, "is this all? What did the woman say when she gave you the moccasins? I don't wonder that you are pleased with them."

"She only told me to come again, and——"

Here Sarah was interrupted by a troop of noisy boys, who came in a body through the porch, flourishing their straw hats and swinging their whortleberry[10] baskets heavy with fruit, back and forth at each step.

"Hurra! hurra! Sarah's fallen in love with an old squaw. How do you do, Miss Jones? Oh, mother, I wish you coulda-seen her hugging and kissing the copper-skin—it was beautiful!"

Here the boisterous rogues set up a laugh that rang through the house, like the breaking up of a military muster.

"Mother, do make them be still; they have done nothing but tease and make fun of me all the way home," said the annoyed girl, half crying.

"How did the old squaw's lips taste, hey?" persisted the eldest boy, pulling his sister's sleeve, and looking with eyes full of saucy mischief up into her face. "Sweet as maple-sugar, wasn't it? Come, tell."

"Arthur—Arthur! you had better be quiet, if you know when you're well off!" exclaimed the mother, with a slight motion of the hand, which had a great deal of significant meaning to the mischievous group.

"Oh, don't—please, don't!" exclaimed the spoiled urchin, clapping his hands to his ears and running off to a corner, where he stood laughing in his mother's face. "I say, Sarah, was it sweet?"

"Arthur, don't let me speak to you again, I say," cried Mrs. Jones, making a step forward and doing her utmost to get up a frown, while her hand gave additional demonstration of its hostile intent.

"Well, then, make her tell me; you ought to cuff *her* ears for not answering a civil question—hadn't she, boys?"

There was something altogether too ludicrous in this impudent appeal, and in the look of demure mischief put on by the culprit. Mrs. Jones bit her lips and turned away, leaving the boy, as usual, victor of the field. "He isn't worth minding, Sarah," she said, evidently ashamed of her want of resolution; "come into the 'out-room,' I've something to tell you."

---

10 Any of a range of berries including blueberries and huckleberries.

When the mother and daughter were alone, Mrs. Jones sat down and drew the young girl into her lap.

"Well, Sarah," she said, smoothing down the rich hair that lay against her bosom, "your father and I have been talking about you to-day. You are almost sixteen, and can spin your day's work with any girl in the settlement. Your father says that after you have learned to weave and make cheese, he will send you down to Manhattan to school."

"Oh, mother, did he say so? in real, real earnest?" cried the delighted girl, flinging her arms round her mother's neck and kissing her yet handsome mouth with joy at the information it had just conveyed. "When will he let me go? I can learn to weave and make cheese in a week."

"If you learn all that he thinks best for you to know in two years, it will be as much as we expect. Eighteen is quite young enough. If you are very smart at home, you shall go when you are eighteen."

"Two years is a long, long time," said the girl, in a tone of disappointment; "but then father is kind to let me go at all. I will run down to the store and thank him. But, mother," she added, turning back from the door, "was there really any harm in talking with the Indian woman? There was nothing about her that did not seem like the whites but her skin, and that was not so *very* dark."

"Harm? No child; how silly you are to let the boys tease you so."

"I will go and see her again, then—may I?"

"Certainly—but see; your father is coming to supper; run out and cut the bread. You must be very smart, now; remember the school."

During the time which intervened between Sarah Jones' sixteenth and eighteenth year, she was almost a daily visitor at the wigwam. The little footpath which led from the village to "the Straka," though scarcely definable to others, became as familiar to her as the grounds about her father's house. If a day or two passed in which illness or some other cause prevented her usual visit, she was sure to receive some token of remembrance from the lone Indian woman. Now, it reached her in the form of a basket of ripe fruit, or a bunch of wild flowers, tied together with the taste of an artist; again, it was a cluster of grapes, with the purple bloom lying fresh upon them, or a young mocking-bird, with notes as sweet as the voice of a fountain, would reach her by the hands of some village boy.

These affectionate gifts could always be traced to the inhabitant of the wigwam, even though she did not, as was sometimes the case, present them in person.

There was something strange in the appearance of this Indian woman, which at first excited the wonder, and at length secured the respect of the settlers. Her language was pure and elegant, sometimes even poetical beyond their comprehension, and her sentiments were correct in principle, and full of simplicity. When she appeared in the village with moccasins or pretty painted baskets for sale, her manner was apprehensive and timid as that of a child. She never sat down, and seldom entered any dwelling, preferring to sell her merchandise in the open air, and using as few words as possible in the transaction. She was never seen to be angry, and a sweet patient smile always hovered about her lips when she spoke. In her face there was more than the remains of beauty; the poetry of intellect and of warm, deep feeling, shed a loveliness over it seldom witnessed on the brow of a savage. In truth, Malaeska was a strange and incomprehensible being to the settlers. But she was so quiet, so timid and gentle, that they all loved her, bought her little wares, and supplied her wants as if she had been one of themselves.

There was something beautiful in the companionship which sprang up between the strange woman and Sarah Jones. The young girl was benefited by it in a manner which was little to be expected from an intercourse so singular and, seemingly, so unnatural. The mother was a kind-hearted worldly woman, strongly attached to her family, but utterly devoid of those fine susceptibilities which make at once the happiness and the misery of so many human beings. But all the elements of an intellectual, delicate, and high-souled woman slumbered in the bosom of her child. They beamed in the depths of her large blue eyes, broke over her pure white forehead, like perfume from the leaves of a lily, and made her small mouth eloquent with smiles and the beauty of unpolished thoughts.

At sixteen the character of the young girl had scarcely begun to develop itself; but when the time arrived when she was to be sent away to school, there remained little except mere accomplishments for her to learn. Her mind had become vigorous by a constant intercourse with the beautiful things of nature. All the latent properties of a warm, youthful heart, and of a superior intellect, had been gently called into action by the strange being who had gained such an ascendency over her feelings.

The Indian woman, who in herself combined all that was strong, picturesque, and imaginative in savage life, with the delicacy, sweetness, and refinement which follows in the train of civilization, had trod with her the wild beautiful scenery of the neighborhood. They had breathed the pure air of the mountain together, and watched the crimson and amber clouds of sunset melt into evening, when pure sweet thoughts came to their hearts naturally, as light shines from the bosom of the star.

It is strange that the pure and simple religion which lifts the soul up to God, should have been first taught to the beautiful young white from the lips of a savage, when inspired by the dying glory of a sunset sky. Yet so it was; she had sat under preaching all her life, had imbibed creeds and shackled her spirit down with the opinions and traditions of other minds, nor dreamed that the love of God may sometimes kindle in the human heart, like fire flashing up from an altar-stone; and again, may expand gradually to the influence of the Divine Spirit, unfolding so gently that the soul itself scarcely knows at what time it burst into flower—that every effect we make, for the culture of the heart and the expanding of the intellect, is a step toward the attainment of religion, if nothing more.

When the pure, simple faith of the Indian was revealed—when she saw how beautifully high energies and lofty feelings were mingled with the Christian meekness and enduring faith of her character, she began to love goodness for its own exceeding beauty, and to cultivate those qualities that struck her as so worthy in her wild-wood friend. Thus Sarah attained a refinement of the soul which no school could have given her, and no superficial gloss could ever conceal or dim. This refinement of principle and feeling lifted the young girl far out of her former commonplace associations; and the gentle influence of her character was felt not only in her father's household, but through all the neighborhood.

Chapter IX

She long'd for her mother's loving kiss,
    And her father's tender words,
And her little sister's joyous mirth,
    Like the song of summer birds.

Her heart went back to the olden home
　　That her memory knew so well,
Till the veriest trifle of the past
　　Swept o'er her like a spell.

SARAH JONES went to Manhattan at the appointed time, with a small trunk of clothing and a large basket of provisions; for a sloop in those days was a long time in coming down the Hudson, even with a fair wind, and its approach to a settlement made more commotion than the largest Atlantic steamer could produce at the present day. So the good mother provided her pretty pilgrim with a lading of wonder-cakes, with biscuits, dried beef, and cheese, enough to keep a company of soldiers in full ration for days.

Besides all this plenteousness in the commissary department, the good lady brought out wonderful specimens of her own handiwork in the form of knit muffles, fine yarn stockings, and colored wristlets, that she had been years in knitting for Sarah's outfit when she should be called upon to undertake this perilous adventure into the great world.

Beyond all this, Sarah had keepsakes from the children, with a store of pretty bracelets and fancy baskets from Malaeska, who parted with her in tenderness and sorrow; for once more like a wild grape-vine, putting out its tendrils everywhere for support, she was cast to the earth again.

After all, Sarah did not find the excitement of her journey so very interesting, and but for the presence of her father on the sloop, she would have been fairly homesick before the white sails of the sloop had rounded the Point. As it was, she grew thoughtful and almost sad as the somber magnificence of the scenery unrolled itself. A settlement here and there broke the forest with smiles of civilization, which she passed with a proud consciousness of seeing the world; but, altogether, she thought more of the rosy mother and riotous children at home than of new scenes or new people.

At last Manhattan, with its girdle of silver waters, its gables and its overhanging trees, met her eager look. Here was her destiny—here she was to be taught and polished into a marvel of gentility. The town was very beautiful, but after the first novelty gave way, she grew more lonely than ever; every thing was so strange—the winding streets, the gay stores, and the quaint houses, with their peaks and dormer windows, all seeming to her far too grand for comfort.

To one of these houses Arthur Jones conducted his daughter, followed by a porter who carried her trunk on one shoulder, while Jones took charge of the provision-basket, in person.

There was nothing in all this very wonderful, but people turned to look at the group with more than usual interest, as it passed, for Sarah had all her mother's fresh beauty, with nameless graces of refinement, which made her a very lovely young creature to look upon.

When so many buildings have been raised in a city, so many trees uprooted, and ponds filled up, it is impossible to give the localities that formerly existed; for all the rural landmarks are swept away. But, in the olden times, houses had breathing space for flowers around them in Manhattan, and a man of note gave his name to the house he resided in. The aristocratic portion of the town was around the Bowling Green[11] and back into the neighboring streets.

---

11 A place in the southernmost part of Manhattan, near the first Dutch fort established on the island.

Somewhere in one of these streets, I can not tell the exact spot, for a little lake in the neighborhood disappeared soon after our story, and all the pretty points of the scene were destroyed with it—but somewhere, in one of the most respectable streets, stood a house with the number of gables and windows requisite to perfect gentility, and a large brass plate spread its glittering surface below the great brass knocker. This plate set forth, in bright, gold letters, the fact that Madame Monot, relict of Monsieur Monot who had so distinguished himself as leading teacher in one of the first female seminaries in Paris, could be found within, at the head of a select school for young ladies.

Sarah was overpowered by the breadth and brightness of this door-plate, and startled by the heavy reverberations of the knocker. There was something too solemn and grand about the entrance for perfect tranquillity.

Mr. Jones looked back at her, as he dropped the knocker, with a sort of tender self-complacency, for he expected that she would be rather taken aback by the splendor to which he was bringing her; but Sarah only trembled and grew timid; she would have given the world to turn and run away any distance so that in the end she reached home.

The door opened, at least the upper half, and they were admitted into a hall paved with little Dutch tiles, spotlessly clean, through which they were led into a parlor barren and prim in all its appointments, but which was evidently the grand reception-room of the establishment. Nothing could have been more desolate than the room, save that it was redeemed by two narrow windows which overlooked the angle of the green inclosure in which the house stood. This angle was separated by a low wall from what seemed a broad and spacious garden, well filled with fruit-trees and flowering shrubbery.

The spring was just putting forth its first buds, and Sarah forgot the chilliness within as she saw the branches of a young apple-tree, flushed with the first tender green, drooping over the wall. It reminded her pleasantly of the orchard at home.

The door opened, and, with a nervous start, Sarah arose with her father to receive the little Frenchwoman who came in with a fluttering courtesy, eager to do the honors of her establishment.

Madame Monot took Sarah out of her father's hands with a graceful dash that left no room for appeal. "She knew it all—exactly what the young lady required—what would best please her very respectable parents—there was no need of explanations—the young lady was fresh as a rose—very charming—in a few months they should see—that was all—Monsieur Jones need have no care about his child—Madame would undertake to finish her education very soon—music, of course—an instrument had just come from Europe on purpose for the school—then French, nothing easier—Madame could promise that the young lady should speak French beautifully in one—two—three—four months, without doubt—Monsieur Jones might retire very satisfied—his daughter should come back different—perfect, in fact."

"With all this volubility, poor Jones was half talked, half courtesied out of the house, without having uttered a single last word of farewell, or held his daughter one moment against the honest heart that yearned to carry her off again, despite his great ambition to see her a lady.

Poor Sarah gazed after him till her eyes were blinded with unshed tears; then she arose with a heavy heart and followed Madame to the room which was henceforth to be her refuge from the most dreary routine of duties that ever a poor girl was condemned to. It was a comfort that the windows overlooked that beautiful garden. That night, at a long, narrow table, set out with what the unsuspecting girl at first considered the preliminaries of a meal, Sarah met the score of young ladies who were to be her schoolmates. Fortunately she had no appetite and did not mind the scant fare. Fifteen or twenty girls, some furtively, others boldly, turning their eyes upon her, was enough to frighten away the appetite of a less timid person.

Poor Sarah! of all the homesick school-girls that ever lived, she was the most lonely. Madame's patronizing kindness only sufficed to bring the tears into her eyes which she was struggling so bravely to keep back.

But Sarah was courageous as well as sensitive. She came to Manhattan to study; no matter if her heart ached, the brain must work; her father had made great sacrifices to give her six months at this expensive school; his money and kindness must not be thrown away.

Thus the brave girl reasoned, and, smothering the haunting wish for home, she took up her tasks with energy.

Meantime Jones returned home with a heavy heart and a new assortment of spring goods, that threw every female heart in Catskill into a flutter of excitement. Every hen's nest in the neighborhood was robbed before the eggs were cold, and its contents transported to the store. As for butter, there was a universal complaint of its scarcity on the home table, while Jones began to think seriously of falling a cent on the pound, it came in so abundantly.

Chapter X

'Twas a dear, old-fashion'd garden,
    Half sunshine and half shade,
Where all day long the birds and breeze
    A pleasant music made;
And hosts of bright and glowing flowers
    Their perfume shed around,
Till it was like a fairy haunt
    That knew no human sound.
                —FRANK LEE BENEDICT.

IT was a bright spring morning, the sky full of great fleecy clouds that chased each other over the clear blue, and a light wind stirring the trees until their opening buds sent forth a delicious fragrance, that was like a perfumed breath from the approaching summer.

Sarah Jones stood by the window of her little room, looking wistfully out into the neighboring garden, oppressed by a feeling of loneliness and home-sickness, which made her long to throw aside her books, relinquish her half-acquired accomplishments, and fly back to her quiet country home.

It seemed to her that one romp with her brothers through the old orchard, pelting each other with the falling buds, would be worth all the French and music she could learn in a score of years. The beat of her mother's lathe in the old-fashioned loom, would have been pleasanter music to her ear, than that of the pianoforte, which she had once thought so grand an affair; but since then she had spent so many weary hours over it, shed so many tears upon the cold white keys, which made her fingers ache worse than ever the spinning-wheel had done, that, like any other schoolgirl, she was almost inclined to regard the vaunted piano as an instrument of torture, invented expressly for her annoyance.

She was tired of thinking and acting by rule, and though Madame Monot was kind enough in her way, the discipline to which Sarah was forced to submit, was very irksome to the untrained country girl. She was tired of having regular hours for study—tired of walking out for a stated time in procession with the other girls—nobody daring to move with any thing like naturalness or freedom—and very often she felt almost inclined to write home and ask them to send for her.

It was in a restive, unhappy mood, like the one we have been describing, that she stood that morning at the window, when she ought to have been hard at work over the pile of books which lay neglected upon her little table.

That pretty garden which she looked down upon, was a sore temptation to her; and had Madame Monot known how it distracted Sarah's attention, there is every reason to believe that she would have been removed in all haste to the opposite side of the house, where, if she chose to idle at her casement, there would be nothing more entertaining than a hard brick wall to look at. Just then, the garden was more attractive than at any other season of the year. The spring sunshine had made the shorn turf like a green carpet, the trim flower-beds were already full of early blossoms, the row of apple-trees was one great mass of flowers, and the tall pear-tree in the corner was just beginning to lose its delicate white leaves, sprinkling them daintily over the grass, where they fluttered about like a host of tiny butterflies.

The old-fashioned stoop that opened from the side of the house into the garden, was covered with a wild grape-vine, that clambered up to the pointed Dutch gables, hung down over the narrow windows, and twined and tangled itself about as freely and luxuriantly as it could have done in its native forest.

Sarah watched the gardener as he went soberly about his various duties, and she envied him the privilege of wandering at will among the graveled walks, pausing under the trees and bending over the flower-beds.

Perhaps in these days, when nothing but scentless japonicas and rare foreign plants are considered endurable, that garden would be an ordinary affair enough, at which no well-trained boarding-school miss would condescend to look for an instant; but to Sarah Jones it was a perfect little paradise.

The lilac bushes nodded in the wind, shaking their purple and white plumes, like groups of soldiers on duty; great masses of snow-balls stood up in the center of the beds; peonies, violets, lilies of the valley, tulips, syringas, and a host of other dear old-fashioned flowers, lined the walks; and, altogether, the garden was lovely enough to justify the poor girl's admiration. There she stood, quite forgetful of her duties; the clock in the hall struck its warning note—she did not even hear it; some one might at any moment enter and surprise her in the midst of her idleness and disobedience—she never once thought of it, so busily was she watching every thing in the garden.

The man finished his morning's work and went away, but Sarah did not move. A pair of robins had flown into the tall pear-tree, and were holding an animated conversation, interspersed with bursts and gushes of song. They flew from one tree to another, once hovering near the grape-vine, but returned to the pear-tree at last, sang, chirped, and danced about in frantic glee, and at last made it evident that they intended to build a nest in that very tree. Sarah could have clapped her hands with delight! It was just under her window—she could watch them constantly, study or no study. She worked herself into such a state of excitement at the thought, that Madame Monot would have been shocked out of her proprieties at seeing one of her pupils guilty of such folly.

The clock again struck—that time in such a sharp, reproving way, that it reached even Sarah's ear. She started, looked nervously round, and saw the heap of books upon the table. "Oh, dear me," she sighed; "those tiresome lessons! I had forgotten all about them. Well, I will go to studying in a moment," she added, as if addressing her conscience or her fears. "Oh, that robin—how he does sing."

She forgot her books again, and just at that moment there was a new object of interest added to those which the garden already possessed.

The side door of the house opened, and an old gentleman stepped out upon the broad stoop, stood there for a few moments, evidently enjoying the morning air, then passed slowly down the steps into the garden, supporting himself by his stout cane, and walking with considerable care and difficulty, like any feeble old man.

Sarah had often seen him before, and she knew very well who he was. He was the owner of the house that the simple girl so coveted, and his name was Danforth.

She had learned every thing about him, as a school-girl is sure to do concerning any person or thing that strikes her fancy. He was very wealthy indeed, and had no family except his wife, the tidiest, darling old lady, who often walked in the garden herself, and always touched the flowers, as she passed, as if they had been pet children.

The venerable old pair had a grandson, but he was away in Europe, so they lived in their pleasant mansion quite alone, with the exception of a few domestics, who looked nearly as aged and respectable as their master and mistress.

Sarah had speculated a great deal about her neighbors. She did so long to know them, to be free to run around in their garden, and sit in the pleasant rooms that overlooked it, glimpses of which she had often obtained through the open windows, when the housemaid was putting things to rights.

Sarah thought that she might possibly be a little afraid of the old gentleman, he looked so stern; but his wife she longed to kiss and make friends with at once; she looked so gentle and kind, that even a bird could not have been afraid of her.

Sarah watched Mr. Danforth walk slowly down the principal garden-path, and seat himself in a little arbor overrun by a trumpet honeysuckle, which was not yet in blossom, although there were faint traces of red among the green leaves, which gave promise of an ample store of blossoms before many weeks.

He sat there some time, apparently enjoying the sunshine that stole in through the leaves. At length Sarah saw him rise, move toward the entrance, pause an instant, totter, then fall heavily upon the ground.

She did not wait even to think or cry out—every energy of her free, strong nature was aroused. She flew out of her room down the stairs, fortunately encountering neither teachers nor pupils, and hurried out of the street-door.

The garden was separated from Madame Monot's narrow yard by a low stone wall, along the top of which ran a picket fence. Sarah saw a step-ladder that had been used by a servant in washing windows; she seized it, dragged it to the wall, and sprang lightly from thence into the garden.

It seemed to her that she would never reach the spot where the poor gentleman was lying, although, in truth, scarcely three minutes had elapsed between the time that she saw him fall and reached the place where he lay.

Sarah stooped over him, raised his head, and knew at once what was the matter—he had been seized with apoplexy. She had seen her grandfather die with it, and recognized the symptoms at once. It was useless to think of carrying him; so she loosened his neckcloth, lifted his head upon the arbor seat, and darted toward the house, calling with all her might the name by which she had many times heard the gardener address the black cook.

"Eunice! Eunice!"

At her frantic summons, out from the kitchen rushed the old woman, followed by several of her satellites, all screaming at once to know what was the matter, and wild with astonishment at the sight of a stranger in the garden.

"Quick! quick!" cried Sarah. "Your master has been taken with a fit; come and carry him into the house. One of you run for a doctor."

"Oh, de laws! oh, dear! oh, dear!" resounded on every side; but Sarah directed them with so much energy that the women, aided by an old negro who had been roused by the disturbance, conveyed their master into the house, and laid him upon a bed in one of the lower rooms.

"Where is your mistress?" questioned Sarah.

"Oh, she's gwine out," sobbed the cook; "oh, my poor ole masser, my poor ole masser!"

"Have you sent for the doctor?"

"Yes, young miss, yes; he'll be here in a minit, bress yer pooty face."

Sarah busied herself over the insensible man, applying every remedy that she could remember of having seen her mother use when her grandfather was ill, and really did the very things that ought to have been done.

It was not long before the doctor arrived, bled his patient freely, praised Sarah's presence of mind, and very soon the old gentleman returned to consciousness.

Sarah heard one of the servants exclaim: "Oh, dar's missus! praise de Lord!"

A sudden feeling of shyness seized the girl, and she stole out of the room and went into the garden, determined to escape unseen. But before she reached the arbor she heard one of the servants calling after her.

"Young miss! young miss! Please to wait; ole missus wants to speak to you."

Sarah turned and walked toward the house, ready to burst into tears with timidity and excitement. But the lady whom she had so longed to know, came down the steps and moved toward her, holding out her hand. She was very pale, and shaking from head to foot; but she spoke with a certain calmness, which it was evident she would retain under the most trying circumstances.

"I can not thank you," she said; "if it had not been for you, I should never have seen my husband alive again."

Sarah began to sob, the old lady held out her arms, and the frightened girl actually fell into them. There they stood for a few moments, weeping in each other's embrace, and by those very tears establishing a closer intimacy than years of common intercourse would have done.

"How did you happen to see him fall?" asked the old lady.

"I was looking out of my window," replied Sarah, pointing to her open casement, "and when I saw it I ran over at once."

"You are a pupil of Madame Monot's, then?"

"Yes—and, oh my, I must go back! They will scold me dreadfully for being away so long."

"Do not be afraid," said Mrs. Danforth, keeping fast hold of her hand when she tried to break away. "I will make your excuses to Madame; come into the house. I can not let you go yet."

She led Sarah into the house, and seated her in an easy chair in the old-fashioned sitting-room.

"Wait here a few minutes, if you please, my dear. I must go to my husband."

She went away and left Sarah quite confused with the strangeness of the whole affair. Here she was, actually seated in the very apartment she had so desired to enter—the old lady she had so longed to know addressing her as if she had been a favorite child.

She peeped out of the window toward her late prison; every thing looked quiet there, as usual. She wondered what dreadful penance she would be made to undergo, and decided that even bread and water for two days would not be so great a hardship, when she had the incident of the morning to reflect upon.

She looked about the room, with its quaint furniture, every thing so tidy and elegant, looking as if a speck of dust had never by any accident settled in the apartment, and thinking it the prettiest place she had seen in her life.

Then she began thinking about the poor sick man, and worked herself into a fever of anxiety to hear tidings concerning him. Just then a servant entered with a tray of refreshments, and set it on the table near her, saying:

"Please, miss, my missus says you must be hungry, 'cause it's your dinner-time."

"And how is your master?" Sarah asked.

"Bery comferble now; missee'll be here in a minit. Now please to eat sumfin."

Sarah was by no means loth to comply with the invitation, for the old cook had piled the tray with all sorts of delicacies, that presented a pleasing contrast to the plain fare she had been accustomed to of late.

By the time she had finished her repast Mrs. Danforth returned, looking more composed and relieved.

"The doctor gives me a great deal of encouragement," she said; "my husband is able to speak; by to-morrow he will thank you better than I can."

"Oh, no," stammered Sarah; "I don't want any thanks, please. I didn't think—I"

She fairly broke down, but Mrs. Danforth patted her hand and said, kindly:

"I understand. But at least you must let me love you very much."

Sarah felt her heart flutter and her cheeks glow. The blush and smile on that young face were a more fitting answer than words could have given.

"I have sent an explanation of your absence to Madame Monot," continued Mrs. Danforth, "and she has given you permission to spend the day with me; so you need have no fear of being blamed."

The thought of a whole day's freedom was exceedingly pleasant to Sarah, particularly when it was to be spent in that old house, which had always appeared as interesting to her as a story. It required but a short time for Mrs. Danforth and her to become well acquainted, and the old lady was charmed with her loveliness, and natural, graceful manners.

She insisted upon accompanying Mrs. Danforth into the sick room, and made herself so useful there, that the dear lady mentally wondered how she had ever got on without her.

When Sarah returned to her home that night, she felt that sense of relief which any one who has led a monotonous life for months must have experienced, when some sudden event has changed its whole current, and given a new coloring to things that before appeared tame and insignificant.

During the following days Sarah was a frequent visitor at Mr. Danforth's house, and after that, circumstances occurred which drew her into still more intimate companionship with her new friend.

One of Madame Monot's house-servants was taken ill with typhus fever, and most of the young ladies left the school for a few weeks. Mrs. Danforth insisted upon Sarah's making her home at their house during the interval, an invitation which she accepted with the utmost delight.

Mr. Danforth still lingered—could speak and move—but the favorable symptoms which at first presented themselves had entirely disappeared, and there was little hope given that he could do more than linger for a month or two longer. During that painful season Mrs. Danforth found in Sarah a sympathizing and consoling friend. The sick man himself became greatly attached to her, and could not bear that she should even leave his chamber.

The young girl was very happy in feeling herself thus prized and loved, and the quick weeks spent in that old house were perhaps among the happiest of her life, in spite of the saddening associations which surrounded her.

One morning while she was sitting with the old gentleman, who had grown so gentle and dependent that those who had known him in former years would scarcely have recognized him, Mrs. Danforth entered the room, bearing several letters in her hand.

"European letters, my dear," she said to her husband, and while she put on her glasses and seated herself to read them, Sarah stole out into the garden.

She had not been there long, enjoying the fresh loveliness of the day, before she heard Mrs. Danforth call her.

"Sarah, my dear; Sarah."

The girl went back to the door where the old lady stood.

"Share a little good news with me in the midst of all our trouble," she said; "my dear, my boy—my grandson—is coming home."

Sarah's first thought was one of regret—every thing would be so changed by the arrival of a stranger; but that was only a passing pang of selfishness; her next reflection was one of unalloyed delight, for the sake of that aged couple.

"I am very glad, dear madam; his coming will do his grandfather so much good."

"Yes, indeed; more than all the doctors in the world."

"When do you expect him?"

"Any day, now; he was to sail a few days after the ship that brought these letters, and as this vessel has been detained by an accident, he can not be far away."

"I am to go back to school to-day," said Sarah, regretfully.

"But you will be with us almost as much," replied Mrs. Danforth. "I have your mother's permission, and will go myself to speak with Madame. You will run over every day to your lessons, but you will live here; we can not lose our pet so soon."

"You are very kind—oh, so kind," Sarah said, quite radiant at the thought of not being confined any longer in the dark old school-building.

"It is you who are good to us. But come, we will go over now; I must tell Madame Monot at once."

The explanations were duly made, and Sarah returned to her old routine of lessons; but her study-room was now the garden, or any place in Mr. Danforth's house that she fancied.

The old gentleman was better again; able to be wheeled out of doors into the sunshine; and there was nothing he liked so much as sitting in the garden, his wife knitting by his side, Sarah studying at his feet, and the robins singing in the pear-trees overhead, as if feeling it a sacred duty to pay their rent by morning advances of melody.

Chapter XI

A welcome to the homestead—
    The gables and the trees
And welcome to the true hearts,
    As the sunshine and the breeze.

ONE bright morning, several weeks after Mr. Danforth's attack, the three were seated in their favorite nook in the garden.

It was a holiday with Sarah; there were no lessons to study; no exercises to practice; no duty more irksome than that of reading the newspaper aloud to the old gentleman, who particularly fancied her fresh, happy voice.

Mrs. Danforth was occupied with her knitting, and Sarah sat at their feet upon a low stool, looking so much like a favorite young relative that it was no wonder if the old pair forgot that she was unconnected with them, save by the bonds of affection, and regarded her as being, in reality, as much a part of their family as they considered her in their hearts.

While they sat there, some sudden noise attracted Mrs. Danforth's attention; she rose and went into the house so quietly that the others scarcely noticed her departure.

It was not long before she came out again, walking very hastily for her, and with such a tremulous flutter in her manner, that Sarah regarded her in surprise.

"William!" she said to her husband, "William!"

He roused himself from the partial doze into which he had fallen, and looked up.

"Did you speak to me?" he asked.

"I have good news for you. Don't be agitated—it is all pleasant."

He struggled up from his seat, steadying his trembling hands upon his staff.

"My boy has come!" he exclaimed, louder and more clearly than he had spoken for weeks; "William, my boy!"

At the summons, a young man came out of the house and ran toward them. The old gentleman flung his arms about his neck and strained him close to his heart.

"My boy!" was all he could say; "my William!"

When they had all grown somewhat calmer, Mrs. Danforth called Sarah, who was standing at a little distance.

"I want you to know and thank this young lady, William," she said; "your grandfather and I owe her a great deal."

She gave him a brief account of the old gentleman's fall, and Sarah's presence of mind; but the girl's crimson cheeks warned her to pause.

"No words can repay such kindness," said the young man, as he relinquished her hand, over which he had bowed with the ceremonious respect of the time.

"It is I who owe a great deal to your grandparents," Sarah replied, a little tremulously, but trying to shake off the timidity which she felt beneath his dark eyes. "I was a regular prisoner, like any other school-girl, and they had the goodness to open the door and let me out."

"Then fidgety old Madame Monot had you in charge?" young Danforth said, laughing; "I can easily understand that it must be a relief to get occasionally where you are not obliged to wait and think by rule."

"There—there!" said the old lady; "William is encouraging insubordination already; you will be a bad counselor for Sarah."

Both she and her husband betrayed the utmost satisfaction at the frank and cordial conversation which went on between the young pair; and in an hour Sarah was as much at ease as if she had been gathering wild-flowers in her native woods.

Danforth gave them long and amusing accounts of his adventures, talked naturally and well of the countries he had visited, the notable places he had seen, and never had man three more attentive auditors.

That was a delightful day to Sarah; and as William Danforth had not lost, in his foreign wanderings, the freshness and enthusiasm pleasant in youth, it was full of enjoyment to him likewise.

There was something so innocent in Sarah's loveliness—something so unstudied in her graceful manner, that the very contrast she presented to the artificial women of the world with whom he had been of late familiar, gave her an additional charm in the eye of the young man.

Many times, while they talked, Mrs. Danforth glanced anxiously toward her husband; but his smile reassured her, and there stole over her pale face a light from within which told of some pleasant vision that had brightened the winter season of her heart, and illuminated it with a reflected light almost as beautiful as that which had flooded it in its spring-time, when her dreams were of her own future, and the aged, decrepit man by her side a stalwart youth, noble and brave as the boy in whom their past seemed once more to live.

"If Madame Monot happens to see me she will be shocked," Sarah said, laughingly. "She told me that she hoped I would improve my holiday by reading some French sermons that she gave me."

"And have you looked at them?" Danforth asked.

"I am afraid they are mislaid," she replied, mischievously.

"Not greatly to your annoyance, I fancy? I think if I had been obliged to learn French from old-fashioned sermons, it would have taken me a long time to acquire the language."

"I don't think much of French sermons," remarked Mrs. Danforth, with a doubtful shake of the head.

"Nor of the people," added her husband; "you never did like them, Therese."

She nodded assent, and young Danforth addressed Sarah in Madame Monot's much-vaunted language. She answered him hesitatingly, and they held a little chat, he laughing good-naturedly at her mistakes and assisting her to correct them, a proceeding which the old couple enjoyed as much as the young pair, so that a vast amount of quiet amusement grew out of the affair.

They spent the whole morning in the garden, and when Sarah went up to her room for a time to be alone with the new world of thought which had opened upon her, she felt as if she had known William Danforth half her life. She did not attempt to analyze her feelings; but they were very pleasant and filled her soul with a delicious restlessness like gushes of agony struggling from the heart of a song-bird. Perhaps Danforth made no more attempt than she to understand the emotions which had been aroused within him; but they were both very happy, careless as the young are sure to be, and so they went on toward the beautiful dream that brightens every life, and which spread before them in the nearing future.

And so the months rolled on, and that pleasant old Dutch house grew more and more like a paradise each day. Another and another quarter was added to Sarah's school-term. She saw the fruit swell from its blossoms into form till its golden and mellow ripeness filled the garden with fragrance. Then she saw the leaves drop from the trees and take a thousand gorgeous dyes from the frost. Still the old garden was a paradise. She saw those leaves grow crisp and sere, rustling to her step with mournful sighs, and giving themselves with shudders to the cold wind. Still the garden was paradise. She saw the snow fall, white and cold, over lawn and gravel-walk, bending down the evergreens and tender shrubs, while long, bright icicles hung along the gables or broke into fragments on the ground beneath. Still the garden was paradise; for love has no season, and desolation is unknown where he exists, even though his sacred presence is unsuspected. Long before the promised period arrived, there was no falsehood in Madame Monot's assertion that her pupil should be perfect; for a lovelier or more graceful young creature than Sarah Jones could not well exist. How it would have been had she been entirely dependent on the school-teachers for her lessons, I can not pretend to say; but the pleasant studies which were so delicately aided in that old summer-house, while the old people sat by just out of ear-shot—as nice old people should on such occasions—were effective enough to build up half a dozen schools, if the progress of one pupil would suffice.

At such times old Mrs. Danforth would look up blandly from her work and remark in an innocent way to her husband, "That it was really beautiful to see how completely Sarah took to her lessons and how kindly William stayed at home to help her. Really," she thought, "traveling abroad did improve a person's disposition wonderfully. It gives a young man so much steadiness of character. There was William, now, who was so fond of excitement, and never could be persuaded to stay at home before, he could barely be driven across the threshold now."

The old man listened to these remarks with a keen look of the eye; he was asking himself the reason of this change in his grandson, and the answer brought a grim smile to his lips. The fair girl, who was now almost one of his household, had become so endeared to him that he could not bear the idea of even parting with her again, and the thought that the line of his name and property might yet persuade her to make the relationship closer still, had grown almost into a passion with the old man.

This state of things lasted only a few months. Before the leaves fell, a change came upon Mr. Danforth. He was for some time more listless and oppressed than usual, and seemed to be looking into the distance for some thought that had disturbed him. One day, without preliminaries, he began to talk with his wife about William's father, and, for the first time in years, mentioned his unhappy marriage.

"I have sometimes thought," said the lady, bending over her work to conceal the emotion that stirred her face, "I have sometimes thought that we should have told our grandson of all this years ago."

The old man's hand began to tremble on the top of his cane. His eyes grew troubled and he was a long time in answering.

"It is too late now—we must let the secret die with us. It would crush him forever. I was a proud man in those days," he said, at last; "proud and stubborn. God has smitten me, therefore, I sometimes think. The thought of that poor woman, whose child I took away, troubles me at nights. Tell me, Therese, if you know any thing about her. The day of my sickness I went to the lodge in Weehawken where she was last seen, hoping to find her, praying for time to make atonement; but the lodge was in ruins—no one could be found who even remembered her. It had cost me a great effort to go, and when the disappointment came, I fell beneath it. Tell me, Therese, if you have heard any thing of Malaeska?"

The good lady was silent; but she grew pale, and the work trembled in her hands.

"You will not speak?" said the old man, sharply.

"Yes," said the wife, gently laying down her work, and lifting her compassionate eyes to the keen face bending toward her, "I did hear, from some Indians that came to the fur-stations up the river, that an—that Malaeska went back to her tribe."

"There is something more," questioned the old man—"something you keep back."

The poor wife attempted to shake her head, but she could not, even by a motion, force herself to an untruth. So, dropping both hands in her lap, she shrunk away from his glance, and the tears began to roll down her cheeks.

"Speak!" said the old man, hoarsely.

She answered, in a voice low and hoarse as his own, "Malaeska went to her tribe; but they have cruel laws, and looking upon her as a traitor in giving her son to us, sent her into the woods with one who was chosen to kill her."

The old man did not speak, but his eyes opened wildly and he fell forward upon his face.

William and Sarah were coquetting, with her lessons, under the old pear-tree, between the French phrases; he had been whispering something sweeter than words ever sounded to her before in any language, and her cheeks were one flush of roses as his breath floated over them.

"Tell me—look at me—any thing to say that you have known this all along," he said, bending his flashing eyes on her face with a glance that made her tremble.

She attempted to look up, but failed in the effort. Like a rose that feels the sunshine too warmly, she drooped under the glow of her own blushes.

"Do speak," he pleaded.

"Yes," she answered, lifting her face with modest firmness to his, "Yes, I do love you."

As the words left her lips, a cry made them both start.

"It is grandmother's voice; he is ill again," said the young man.

They moved away, shocked by a sudden recoil of feelings. A moment brought them in sight of the old man, who lay prostrate on the earth. His wife was bending over him, striving to loosen his dress with her withered little hands.

"Oh, come," she pleaded, with a look of helpless distress; "help me untie this, or he will never breathe again."

It was all useless; the old man never did breathe again. A single blow had smitten him down. They bore him into the house, but the leaden weight of his body, the limp fall of his limbs, all revealed the mournful truth too plainly. It was death—sudden and terrible death.

If there is an object on earth calculated to call forth the best sympathies of humanity, it is an "old widow"—a woman who has spent the spring, noon, and autumn of life, till it verges into winter, with one man, the first love of her youth, the last love of her age—the spring-time when love is a passionate sentiment, the winter-time when it is august.

In old age men or women seldom resist trouble—it comes, and they bow to it. So it was with this widow: she uttered no complaints, gave way to no wild outbreak of sorrow—"she was lonesome—very lonesome without him," that was all her moan; but the raven threads that lay in the snow of her hair, were lost in the general whiteness before the funeral was over, and after that she began to bend a little, using his staff to lean on. It was mournful to see how fondly her little wrinkled hands would cling around the head, and the way she had of resting her delicate chin upon it, exactly as he had done.

But even his staff, the stout prop of his waning manhood, was not strong enough to keep that gentle old woman from the grave. She carried it to the last, but one day it stood unused by the bed, which was white and cold as the snow-drift through which they dug many feet before they could lay her by her husband's side.

Chapter XII

Put blossoms on the mantle-piece,
　Throw sand upon the floor,
A guest is coming to the house,
　That never came before.

SARAH JONES had been absent several months, when a rumor got abroad in the village, that the school-girl had made a proud conquest in Manhattan. It was said that Squire Jones had received letters from a wealthy merchant of that place, and that he was going down the river to conduct his daughter home, when a wedding would soon follow, and Sarah Jones be made a lady.

This report gained much of its probability from the demeanor of Mrs. Jones. Her port became more lofty when she appeared in the street, and she was continually throwing out insinuations and half-uttered hints, as if her heart were panting to unburden itself of some proud secret, which she was not yet at liberty to reveal.

When Jones actually started for Manhattan, and it was whispered about that his wife had taken a dress-pattern of rich chintz from the store, for herself, and had bought each of the boys a new wool hat, conjecture became almost certainty; and it was asserted boldly, that Sarah Jones was coming home to be married to a man as rich as all outdoors, and that her mother was beginning to hold her head above common folks on the strength of it.

About three weeks after this report was known, Mrs. Jones, whose motions were watched with true village scrutiny, gave demonstrations of a thorough house-cleaning. An old woman, who went out to days' work, was called in to help, and there were symptoms of slaughter observable in the barn-yard one night after the turkeys and chickens had gone to roost; all of which kept the public mind in a state of pleasant excitement.

Early the next morning, after the barn-yard massacre, Mrs. Jones was certainly a very busy woman. All the morning was occupied in sprinkling white sand on the nicely-scoured floor of the out-room, or parlor, which she swept very expertly into a series of angular figures called herringbones, with a new splint broom. After this, she filled the fire-place with branches of hemlock and white pine, wreathed a garland of asparagus, crimson with berries, around the little looking-glass, and, dropping on one knee, was filling a large pitcher on the hearth from an armful of wild-flowers, which the boys had brought her from the woods, when the youngest son came hurrying up from the Point, to inform her that a sloop had just hove in sight and was making full sail up the river.

"Oh, dear, I shan't be half ready!" exclaimed the alarmed housekeeper, snatching up a handful of meadow-lilies, mottled so heavily with dark-crimson spots, that the golden bells seemed drooping beneath a weight of rubies and small garnet stones, and crowding them down into the pitcher amid the rosy spray of wild honeysuckle-blossoms, and branches of flowering dogwood.

"Here, Ned, give me the broom, quick! and don't shuffle over the sand so. There, now," she continued, gathering up the fragments of leaves and flowers from the hearth, and glancing hastily around the room, "I wonder if any thing else is wanting?"

Every thing seemed in order, even to her critical eye. The tea-table stood in one corner, its round top turned down and its polished surface reflecting the herring-bones drawn in the sand, with the distinctness of a mirror. The chairs were in their exact places, and the new crimson moreen[12] cushions and valance decorated the settee, in all the brilliancy of their first gloss. Yes, nothing more was to be done, still the good woman passed her apron over the speckless table and flirted it across a chair or two, before she went out, quite determined that no stray speck of dust should disgrace her child on coming home.

Mrs. Jones closed the door, and hurried up to the square bedroom, to be certain that all was right there also. A patch-work quilt, pieced in what old ladies call "a rising sun,"

---

12 A heavy wool fabric.

radiated in tints of red, green, and yellow, from the center of the bed down to the snow-white valances. A portion of the spotless homespun sheet was carefully turned over the upper edge of the quilt, and the whole was surmounted by a pair of pillows, white as a pile of newly-drifted snow-flakes. A pot of roses, on the window-sill, shed a delicate reflection over the muslin curtains looped up on either side of the sash; and the fresh wind, as it swept through, scattered their fragrant breath deliciously through the little room.

Mrs. Jones gave a satisfied look and then hurried to the chamber prepared for her daughter, and began to array her comely person in the chintz dress, which had created such a sensation in the village. She had just encased her arms in the sleeves, when the door partly opened, and the old woman, who had been hired for a few days as "help," put her head through the opening. "I say, Miss Jones, I can't find nothin' to make the stuffin' out on."

"My goodness! isn't that turkey in the oven yet? I do believe, if I could be cut into a hundred pieces, it wouldn't be enough for this house. What do you come to me for?—don't you know enough to make a little stuffing, without my help?"

"Only give me enough to do it with, and if I don't, why, there don't nobody, that's all; but I've been a looking all over for some sausengers, and can't find none, nowhere."

"Sausages? Why, Mrs. Bates, you don't think that I would allow that fine turkey to be stuffed with sausages?"

"I don't know nothin' about it, but I tell you just what it is, Miss Jones, if you are a-growing so mighty partic'lar about your victuals, just cause your darter's a-coming home with a rich beau, you'd better cook 'em yourself; nobody craves the job," retorted the old woman, in her shrillest voice, shutting the door with a jar that shook the whole apartment.

"Now the cross old thing will go off just to spite me," muttered Mrs. Jones, trying to smother her vexation, and, opening the door, she called to the angry "help:"

"Why, Mrs. Bates, do come back, you did not stay to hear me out. Save the chickens' livers and chop them up with bread and butter; season it nicely, and, I dare say, you will be as well pleased with it as can be."

"Well, and if I du, what shall I season with—sage or summer-savory? I'm sure I'm willing to du my best," answered the partially mollified old woman.

"A little of both, Mrs. Bates—oh, dear! won't you come back and see if you can make my gown meet? There—do I look fit to be seen?"

"Now, what do you ask that for, Miss Jones? you know you look as neat as a new pin. This is a mighty purty calerco, ain't it, though?"

The squire's lady had not forgotten all the feelings of her younger days, and the old woman's compliment had its effect.

"I will send down to the store for some tea and molasses for you to take home to-night, Mrs. Bates, and—"

"Mother! mother!" shouted young Ned, bolting into the room, "the sloop has tacked, and is making for the creek. I see three people on the deck, and I'm almost sure father was one of them—they will be here in no time."

"Gracious me!" muttered the old woman, hurrying away to the kitchen.

Mrs. Jones smoothed down the folds of her new dress with both hands, as she ran down to the "out-room." She took her station in a stiff, high-backed chair by the window, with a look of consequential gentility, as if she had done nothing but sit still and receive company all her life.

After a few minutes' anxious watching, she saw her husband and daughter coming up from the creek, accompanied by a slight, dark, and remarkably graceful young man, elaborately, but not gayly dressed, for the fashion of the time, and betraying even in his air and walk peculiar traits of high-breeding and refinement. His head was slightly bent, and he seemed to be addressing the young lady who leaned on his arm.

The mother's heart beat high with mingled pride and affection, as she gazed on her beautiful daughter thus proudly escorted home. There was triumph in the thought, that almost every person in the village might witness the air of gallantry and homage with which she was regarded by the handsomest and richest merchant of Manhattan. She saw that her child looked eagerly toward the house as they approached, and that her step was rapid, as if impatient of the quiet progress of her companions. Pride was lost in the sweet thrill of maternal affection which shot through the mother's heart. She forgot all her plans, in the dear wish to hold her first-born once more to her bosom; and ran to the door, her face beaming with joy, her arms outstretched, and her lips trembling with the warmth of their own welcome.

The next moment her child was clinging about her, lavishing kisses on her handsome mouth, and checking her caresses to gaze up through the mist of tears and smiles which deluged her own sweet face, to the glad eyes that looked down so fondly upon her.

"Oh, mother! dear, dear mother, how glad I am to get home! Where are the boys? where is little Ned?" inquired the happy girl, rising from her mother's arms, and looking eagerly round for other objects of affectionate regard.

"Sarah, don't you intend to let me speak to your mother?" inquired the father, in a voice which told how truly his heart was in the scene.

Sarah withdrew from her mother's arms, blushing and smiling through her tears; the husband and wife shook hands half a dozen times over; Mrs. Jones asked him how he had been, what kind of a voyage he had made, how he liked Manhattan, and a dozen other questions, all in a breath; and then the stranger was introduced. Mrs. Jones forgot the dignified courtesy which she had intended to perpetrate on the entrance of her guest, and shook him heartily by the hand, as if she had been acquainted with him from his cradle.

When the happy group entered the parlor, they found Arthur, who had been raised to the dignity of storekeeper in the father's absence, ready to greet his parent and sister; and the younger children huddled together at the door which led to the kitchen, brimful of eager joy at the father's return, and yet too much afraid of the stranger to enter the room.

Altogether, it was as cordial, warm-hearted a reception as a man could reasonably wish on his return home; and, fortunately for Mrs. Jones, the warmth of her own natural feeling saved her the ridicule of trying to get up a genteel scene, for the edification of her future son-in-law.

About half an hour after the arrival of her friends, Mrs. Jones was passing from the kitchen, where she had seen the turkey placed in the oven, with his portly bosom rising above the rim of a dripping-pan, his legs tied together, and his wings tucked snugly over his back, when she met her husband in the passage.

"Well," said the wife, in a cautious voice, "has every thing turned out well—is he so awful rich as your letter said?"

"There is no doubt about that; he is as rich as a Jew, and as proud as a lord. I can tell you what, Sarah's made the best match in America, let the other be what it will," replied the squire, imitating the low tone of his questioner.

"What an eye he's got, hasn't he? I never saw any thing so black and piercing in my life. He's very handsome, too, only a little darkish—I don't wonder the girl took a fancy to him. I say, has any thing been said about the wedding?"

"It must be next week, at any rate, for he wants to go back to Manhattan in a few days; he and Sarah will manage it without our help, I dare say." Here Mr. and Mrs. Jones looked at each other and smiled.

"I say, squire, I want to ask you one question," interrupted Mrs. Bates, coming through the kitchen door and sidling up to the couple, "is that watch which the gentleman carries rale genuine gold, or on'y pinchbeck? I'd give any thing on 'arth to find out."

"I believe it's gold, Mrs. Bates."

"Now, du tell! What, rale Guinea gold? Now, if that don't beat all natur. I ruther guess Miss Sarah's feathered her nest this time, any how. Now, squire, du tell a body, when is the wedding to be? I won't tell a single 'arthly critter, if you'll on'y jest give me a hint."

"You must ask Sarah," replied Mr. Jones, following his wife into the parlor; "I never meddle with young folks' affairs."

"Now, did you ever?" muttered the old woman, when she found herself alone in the passage. "Never mind; if I don't find out afore I go home to-night, I lose my guess, that's all. I should just like to know what they're a talking about this minute."

Here the old woman crouched down and put her ear to the crevice under the parlor door; in a few moments she scrambled up and hurried off into the kitchen again, just in time to save herself from being pushed over by the opening door.

Sarah Jones returned home the same warmhearted, intelligent girl as ever. She was a little more delicate in person, more quiet and graceful in her movements; and love had given depth of expression to her large blue eyes, a richer tone to her sweet voice, and had mellowed down the buoyant spirit of the girl to the softness and grace of womanhood. Thoroughly and trustfully had she given her young affections, and her person seemed imbued with gentleness from the fount of love, that gushed up so purely in her heart. She knew that she was loved in return—not as she loved, fervently, and in silence, but with the fire of a passionate nature; with the keen, intense feeling which mingles pain even with happiness, and makes sorrow sharp as the tooth of a serpent.

Proud, fastidious, and passionate was the object of her regard; his prejudices had been strengthened and his faults matured, in the lap of luxury and indulgence. He was high-spirited and generous to a fault, a true friend and a bitter enemy—one of those men who have lofty virtues and strong counterbalancing faults. But with all his heart and soul he loved the gentle girl to whom he was betrothed. In that he had been thoroughly unselfish and more than generous; but not the less proud. The prejudices of birth and station had been instilled into his nature, till they had become a part of it; yet he had unhesitatingly offered hand and fortune to the daughter of a plain country farmer.

In truth, his predominating pride might be seen in this, mingled with the powerful love which urged him to the proposal. He preferred bestowing wealth and station on the object of his choice, rather than receiving any worldly advantage from her. It gratified him that his love would be looked up to by its object, as the source from which all benefits must be derived. It was a feeling of refined selfishness; he would have been startled had any one told him so; and yet, a generous pride was at the bottom of all. He gloried in exalting his chosen one; while his affianced wife, and her family, were convinced that nothing could be more noble than his conduct, in thus selecting a humble and comparatively portionless girl to share his brilliant fortune.

On the afternoon of the second day after her return home, Sarah entered the parlor with her bonnet on and a shawl flung over her arm, prepared for a walk. Her lover was lying on the crimson cushions of the settee, with his fine eyes half-closed, and a book nearly falling from his listless hand.

"Come," said Sarah, taking the volume playfully from his hand, "I have come to persuade you to a long walk. Mother has introduced all her friends, now you must go and see mine—the dearest and best."

"Spare me," said the young man, half-rising, and brushing the raven hair from his forehead with a graceful motion of the hand; "I will go with *you* anywhere, but *do* excuse me these horrid introductions—I am overwhelmed with the hospitality of your neighborhood." He smiled, and attempted to regain the book as he spoke.

"Oh, but this is quite another kind of person; you never saw any thing at all like her—there is something picturesque and romantic about her. You like romance?"

"What is she, Dutch or English? I can't speak Dutch, and your own sweet English is enough for me. Come, take off that bonnet and let me read to you."

"No, no; *I* must visit the wigwam, if *you* will not."

"The wigwam, Miss Jones?" exclaimed the youth, starting up, his face changing its expression, and his large black eyes flashing on her with the glance of an eagle. "Am I to understand that your friend is an Indian?"

"Certainly, she *is* an Indian, but not a common one, I assure you."

"She *is* an Indian. Enough, I will *not* go; and I can only express my surprise at a request so extraordinary. I have no ambition to cultivate the copper-colored race, or to find my future wife seeking her friends in the woods."

The finely cut lip of the speaker curved with a smile of haughty contempt, and his manner was disturbed and irritable, beyond any thing the young girl had ever witnessed in him before. She turned pale at this violent burst of feeling, and it was more than a minute before she addressed him again.

"This violence seems unreasonable—why should my wish to visit a harmless, solitary fellow-being create so much opposition," she said, at last.

"Forgive me, if I have spoken harshly, dear Sarah," he answered, striving to subdue his irritation, but spite of his effort it blazed out again the next instant. "It is useless to strive against the feeling; I hate the whole race! If there is a thing I abhor on earth, it is a savage—a fierce, bloodthirsty wild beast in human form!"

There was something in the stern expression of his face which pained and startled the young girl who gazed on it; a brilliancy of the eye, and an expansion of the thin nostrils, which bespoke terrible passions when once excited to the full.

"This is a strange prejudice," she murmured, unconsciously, while her eyes sank from their gaze on his face.

"It is no prejudice, but a part of my nature," he retorted, sternly, pacing up and down the room. "An antipathy rooted in the cradle, which grew stronger and deeper with my manhood. I loved my grandfather, and from him I imbibed this early hate. His soul loathed the very name of Indian. When he met one of the prowling creatures in the highway, I have seen his lips writhe, his chest heave, and his face grow white, as if a wild beast had started up in his path. There was one in our family, an affectionate, timid creature, as the sun ever shone upon. I can remember loving her very dearly when I was a mere child, but my grandfather recoiled at the very sound of her name, and seemed to regard her presence as a curse, which for some reason he was compelled to endure. I could never imagine why he kept her. She was very kind to me, and I tried to find her out after my return from Europe, but you remember that my grandparents died suddenly during my absence, and no one could give me any information about her. Save that one being, there is not a savage, male or female, whom I should not rejoice to see exterminated from the face of the earth. Do not, I pray you, look so terribly shocked, my sweet girl; I acknowledge the feeling to be a prejudice too violent for adequate foundation; but it was grounded in my nature by one whom I respected and loved as my own life, and it will cling to my heart as long as there is a pulse left in it."

"I have no predilection for savages as a race," said Sarah, after a few moments' silence, gratified to find some shadow of reason for her lover's violence; "but you make one exception, may I not also be allowed a favorite especially as she is a white in education, feeling, every thing but color? You would not have me neglect one of the kindest, best friends I ever had on earth, because the tint of her skin is a shade darker than my own?"

Her voice was sweet and persuasive, a smile trembled on her lips, and she laid a hand gently on his arm as she spoke. He must have been a savage indeed, had he resisted her winning ways.

"I would have you forgive my violence and follow your own sweet impulses," he said, putting back the curls from her uplifted forehead, and drawing her to his bosom; "say you have forgiven me, dear, and then go where you will."

It was with gentle words like these, that he had won the love of that fair being; they fell upon her heart, after his late harshness, like dew to a thirsty violet. She raised her glistening eyes to his with a language more eloquent than words, and disengaging herself from his arms, glided softly out of the room.

These words could hardly be called a lovers' quarrel, and yet they parted with all the sweet feelings of reconciliation, warm at the heart of each.

Chapter XIII

By that forest-grave she mournful stood,
 While her soul went forth in prayer;
Her life was one long solitude,
 Which she offer'd, meekly, there.

SARAH pursued the foot-path, which she had so often trod through the forest, with a fawn-like lightness of step, and a heart that beat quicker at the sight of each familiar bush or forest-tree, which had formerly been the waymark of her route.

"Poor woman, she must have been very lonely," she murmured, more than once, when the golden blossoms of a spice-bush, or the tendrils of a vine trailing over the path, told how seldom it had been traveled of late, and her heart imperceptibly became saddened by the thoughts of her friend; spite of this, she stopped occasionally to witness the gambols of a gray squirrel among the tall branches, that swayed and rustled in the sun-shine overhead, and smiled at her usual timidity, when, thus employed, a slender grass-snake crept across her foot and coiled itself up in the path like a chain of living emeralds; his small eyes glittering like sparks of fire, his tiny jaw open, and a sharp little tongue playing within like a red-hot needle cleft at the point. She forced herself to look upon the harmless reptile, without a fear which she knew to be childish, and turning aside, pursued her way to "the Straka."

To her disappointment, she found the wigwam empty, but a path was beaten along the edge of the woods, leading toward the Pond, which she had never observed before. She turned into it with a sort of indefinite expectation of meeting her friend; and after winding through the depths of the forest for nearly a mile, the notes of a wild, plaintive song rose and fell—a sad, sweet melody—on the still air.

A few steps onward brought the young girl to a small open space surrounded by young saplings and flowering shrubs; tall grass swept from a little mound which swelled up from the center, to the margin of the inclosure, and a magnificent hemlock shadowed the whole space with its drooping boughs.

A sensation of awe fell upon the heart of the young girl, for, as she gazed, the mound took the form of a grave. A large rose-tree, heavy with blossoms, drooped over the head, and the sheen of rippling waters broke through a clump of sweet-brier, which hedged it in from the lake.

Sarah remembered that the Indian chief's grave was on the very brink of the water, and that she had given a young rose-tree to Malaeska years ago, which must have shot up into the solitary bush standing before her, lavishing fragrance from its pure white flowers over the place of the dead.

This would have been enough to convince her that she stood by the warrior's grave, had the place been solitary, but at the foot of the hemlock, with her arms folded on her bosom and her calm face uplifted toward heaven, sat Malaeska. Her lips were slightly parted, and the song which Sarah had listened to afar off broke from them—a sad pleasant strain, that blended in harmony with the rippling waters and the gentle sway of the hemlock branches overhead.

Sarah remained motionless till the last note of the song died away on the lake, then she stepped forward into the inclosure. The Indian woman saw her and arose, while a beautiful expression of joy beamed over her face.

"The bird does not feel more joyful at the return of spring, when snows have covered the earth all winter, than does the poor Indian's heart at the sight of her child again," she said, taking the maiden's hand and kissing it with a graceful movement of mingled respect and affection. "Sit down, that I may hear the sound of your voice once more."

They sat down together at the foot of the hemlock.

"You have been lonely, my poor friend, and ill, I fear; how thin you have become during my absence," said Sarah, gazing on the changed features of her companion.

"I shall be happy again now," replied the Indian, with a faint sweet smile, "you will come to see me every day."

"Yes, while I remain at home, but—but—I'm going back again soon."

"You need not tell me more in words, I can read it in the tone of your voice, in the light of that modest eye, though the silken lash does droop over it like leaves around a wet violet—in the color coming and going on those cheeks; another is coming to take you from home," said the Indian, with a playful smile. "Did you think the lone woman could not read the signs of love—that she has never loved herself?"

"You?"

"Do not look so wild, but tell me of yourself. Are you to be married so *very* soon?"

"In four days."

"Then where will your home be?"

"In Manhattan."

There were a few moments of silence. Sarah sat gazing on the turf, with the warm blood mantling to her cheek, ashamed and yet eager to converse more fully on the subject which flooded her young heart with supreme content. The Indian continued motionless, lost in a train of sad thoughts conjured up by the last word uttered; at length she laid her hand on that of her companion, and spoke; her voice was sad, and tears stood in her eyes.

"In a few days you go from me again—oh, it is very wearisome to be always alone; the heart pines for something to love. I have been petting a little wren, that has built his nest under the eaves of my wigwam, since you went away; it was company for me, and will be again. Do not look so pitiful, but tell me who is he that calls the red blood to your cheek? What are his qualities? Does he love you as one like you should be loved? Is he good, brave?"

"He says that he loves me," replied the young girl, blushing more deeply, and a beautiful smile broke into her eyes as she raised them for a moment to the Indian's face.

"And you?"

"I have neither experience nor standard to judge love by. If to think of one from morning to night, be love—to feel his presence color each thought even when he is far away—to know that he is haunting your beautiful day-dreams, wandering with you through the lovely places which fancy is continually presenting to one in solitude, filling up each space and thought of your life, and yet in no way diminishing the affection which the heart bears to others, but increasing it rather—if to be made happy with the slightest trait of noble feeling, proud in his virtues, and yet quick-sighted and doubly sensitive to all his faults, clinging to him in spite of those faults—if this be love, then I do love with the whole strength of my being. They tell me it is but a dream, which will pass away, but I do not believe it; for in my bosom the first sweet flutter of awakened affection, has already settled down to a deep feeling of contentment. My heart is full of tranquillity, and, like that white rose which lies motionless in the sunshine burdened with the wealth of its own sweetness, it unfolds itself day by day to a more pure and subdued state of enjoyment. This feeling may not be the love which men talk so freely of, but it can not change—never—not even in death, unless William Danforth should prove utterly unworthy!"

"William Danforth! Did I hear aright? Is William Danforth the name of your affianced husband?" inquired the Indian, in a voice of overwhelming surprise, starting up with sudden impetuosity and then slowly sinking back to her seat again. "Tell me," she added, faintly, and yet in a tone that thrilled to the heart, "has this boy—this young gentleman, I mean—come of late from across the big waters?"

"He came from Europe a year since, on the death of his grandparents," was the reply.

"A year, a whole year!" murmured the Indian, clasping her hands over her eyes with sudden energy. Her head sunk forward upon her knees, and her whole frame shivered with a rush of strong feeling, which was perfectly unaccountable to the almost terrified girl who gazed upon her. "Father of Heaven, I thank thee! my eyes shall behold him once more. O God, make me grateful!" These words, uttered so fervently, were muffled by the locked hands of the Indian woman, and Sarah could only distinguish that she was strongly excited by the mention of her lover's name.

"Have you ever known Mr. Danforth?" she inquired, when the agitation of the strange woman had a little subsided. The Indian did not answer, but raising her head, and brushing the tears from her eyes, she looked in the maiden's face with an expression of pathetic tenderness that touched her to the heart.

"And *you* are to be *his* wife? You, my bird of birds."

She fell upon the young girl's neck as she spoke, and wept like an infant; then, as if conscious of betraying too deep emotion, she lifted her head, and tried to compose herself;

while Sarah sat gazing on her, agitated, bewildered, and utterly at a loss to account for this sudden outbreak of feeling, in one habitually so subdued and calm in her demeanor. After sitting musingly and in silence several moments, the Indian again lifted her eyes; they were full of sorrowful meaning, yet there was an eager look about them which showed a degree of excitement yet unsubdued.

"Dead—are they both dead? his grandparents, I mean?" she said, earnestly.

"Yes, they are both dead; he told me so."

"And he—the young man—where is he now?"

"I left him at my father's house, not three hours since."

"Come, let us go."

The two arose, passed through the inclosure, and threaded the path toward the wigwam slowly and in silence. The maiden was lost in conjecture, and her companion seemed pondering in some hidden thought of deep moment. Now her face was sad and regretful in its look, again it lighted up a thrilling expression of eager and yearning tenderness.

The afternoon shadows were gathering over the forest, and being anxious to reach home before dark, Sarah refused to enter the wigwam when they reached it. The Indian went in for a moment, and returned with a slip of birch bark, on which a few words were lightly traced in pencil.

"Give this to the young man," she said, placing the bark in Sarah's hand; "and now good-night— good-night."

Sarah took the bark and turned with a hurried step to the forest track. She felt agitated, and as if something painful were about to happen. With a curiosity aroused by the Indian's strange manner, she examined the writing on the slip of bark in her hand; it was only a request that William Danforth would meet the writer at a place appointed, on the bank of the Catskill Creek, that evening. The scroll was signed, "Malaeska."

Malaeska! It was singular, but Sarah Jones had never learned the Indian's name before.

Chapter XIV

Wild was her look, wild was her air,
Back from her shoulders stream'd the hair—
The locks, that wont her brow to shade,
Started erectly from her head;
Her figure seem'd to rise more high—
From her pale lips a frantic cry
Rang sharply through the moon's pale light—
And life to her was endless night.

THE point of land, which we have described in the early part of this story, as hedging in the outlet of Catskill Creek, gently ascends from the juncture of the two streams and rolls upward into a broad and beautiful hill, which again sweeps off toward the mountains and down the margin of the Hudson in a vast plain, at the present day cut up into highly cultivated farms, and diversified by little eminences, groves, and one large tract of swamp-land. Along the southern margin of the creek the hill forms a lofty and picturesque bank, in some places dropping to the water in a sheer descent of forty or fifty feet, and others, sloping down in a more gradual but still abrupt fall, broken into little ravines, and thickly covered with a fine growth of young timber.

A foot-path winds up from the stone dwelling, which we have already described, along the upper verge of this bank to the level of the plain, terminating in a singular projection of earth which shoots out from the face of the bank some feet over the stream, taking the form of a huge serpent's head. This projection commands a fine view of the village, and is known to the inhabitants by the title of "Hoppy Nose," from a tradition attached to it. The foot-path, which terminates at this point, receives a melancholy interest from the constant presence of a singular being who has trod it regularly for years. Hour after hour, and day after day, through sunshine and storm, he is to be seen winding among the trees, or moving with a slow monotonous walk along this track, where it verges into the rich sward. Speechless he has been for years, not from inability, but from a settled unbroken habit of silence. He is perfectly gentle and inoffensive, and from his quiet bearing a slight observer might mistake him for a meditative philosopher, rather than a man slightly and harmlessly insane as a peculiar expression in his clear, blue eyes and his resolute silence must surely proclaim him to be.

But we are describing subsequent things, rather than the scenery as it existed at the time of our story. Then, the hillside and all the broad plain was a forest of heavy timbered land, but the bank of the creek was much in its present condition. The undergrowth throve a little more luxuriantly, and the "Hoppy Nose" shot out from it covered with a thick coating of grass, but shrubless, with the exception of two or three saplings and a few clumps of wild-flowers.

As the moon arose on the night after Sarah Jones' interview with the Indian woman, that singular being stood upon the "Hoppy Nose," waiting the appearance of young Danforth. More than once she went out to the extreme verge of the projection, looked eagerly up and down the stream, then back into the shadow again, with folded arms, continued her watch as before.

At length a slight sound came from the opposite side; she sprang forward, and supporting herself by a sapling, bent over the stream, with one foot just touching the verge of the projection, her lips slightly parted, and her left hand holding back the hair from her temples, eager to ascertain the nature of the sound. The sapling bent and almost snapped beneath her hold, but she remained motionless, her eyes shining in the moonlight with a strange, uncertain luster, and fixed keenly on the place whence the sound proceeded.

A canoe cut out into the river, and made toward the spot where she was standing.

"It is he!" broke from her parted lips, as the moonlight fell on the clear forehead and graceful form of a young man, who stood upright in the little shallop, and drawing a deep breath, she settled back, folded her arms, and waited his approach.

The sapling had scarcely swayed back to its position, when the youth curved his canoe round to a hollow in the bank, and climbing along the ascent, he drew himself up the steep side of the "Hoppy Nose" by the brushwood, and sprang to the Indian woman's side.

"Malaeska," he said, extending his hand with a manner and voice of friendly recognition; "my good, kind nurse, believe me, I am rejoiced to have found you again."

Malaeska did not take his hand, but after an intense and eager gaze into his face, flung herself on his bosom, sobbing aloud, murmuring soft, broken words of endearment, and trembling all over with a rush of unconquerable tenderness.

The youth started back, and a frown gathered on his haughty forehead. His prejudices were offended, and he strove to put her from his bosom; even gratitude for all her goodness could not conquer the disgust with which he recoiled from the embrace of a savage.

"Malaeska," he said, almost sternly, attempting to unclasp her arms from his neck, "You forget—I am no longer a boy—be composed, and say what I can do for you?"

But she only clung to him the more passionately, and answered with an appeal that thrilled to his very heart.

"Put not your mother away—she has waited long—my son! my son!"

The youth did not comprehend the whole meaning of her words. They were more energetic and full of pathos than he had ever witnessed before; but she had been his nurse, and he had been long absent from her, and the strength of her attachment made him, for a moment, forgetful of her race. He was affected almost to tears.

"Malaeska," he said kindly, "I did not know till now how much you loved me. Yet it is not strange—I can remember when you were almost a mother to me."

"*Almost!*" she exclaimed, throwing back her head till the moonlight revealed her face. "Almost! William Danforth, as surely as there is a God to witness my words, you are my own son!"

The youth started, as if a dagger had been thrust to his heart. He forced the agitated woman from his bosom, and, bending forward, gazed sternly into her eyes.

"Woman, are you mad? Dare you assert this to *me?*"

He grasped her arm almost fiercely, and seemed as if tempted to offer some violence, for the insult her words had conveyed; but she lifted her eyes to his with a look of tenderness, in painful contrast with his almost insane gaze.

"Mad, my son?" she said, in a voice that thrilled with a sweet and broken earnestness on the still air. "It was a blessed madness—the madness of two warm young hearts that forgot every thing in the sweet impulse with which they clung together; it was madness which led your father to take the wild Indian girl to his bosom, when in the bloom of early girlhood. Mad! oh, I could go mad with very tenderness, when I think of the time when your little form was first placed in my arms; when my heart ached with love to feel your little hand upon my bosom, and your low murmur fill my ear. Oh, it was a sweet madness. I would die to know it again."

The youth had gradually relaxed his hold on her arm, and stood looking upon her as one in a dream, his arms dropping helpless as if they had been suddenly paralyzed; but when she again drew toward him, he was aroused to frenzy.

"Great God!" he almost shrieked, dashing his hand against his forehead. "No, no! it can not—I, an Indian? a half-blood? the grandson of my father's murderer? Woman, speak the truth; word for word, give me the accursed history of my disgrace. If I am your son, give me proof—proof, I say!"

When the poor woman saw the furious passion she had raised, she sunk back in silent terror, and it was several minutes before she could answer his wild appeal. When she did speak, it was gaspingly and in terror. She told him all—of his birth; his father's death; of her voyage to Manhattan; and of the cruel promise that had been wrung from her, to conceal the relationship between herself and her child. She spoke of her solitary life in the wigwam, of the yearning power which urged her mother's heart to claim the love of her only child, when that child appeared in her neighborhood. She asked not to be acknowledged as his parent, but only to live with him, even as a bond servant, if he willed it, so as to look upon his face and to claim his love in private, when none should be near to witness it.

He stood perfectly still, with his pale face bent to hers, listening to her quick gasping speech, till she had done. Then she could see that his face was convulsed in the moonlight, and that he trembled and grasped a sapling which stood near for support. His voice was that of one utterly overwhelmed and broken-hearted.

"Malaeska," he said, "unsay all this, if you would not see me die at your feet. I am young, and a world of happiness was before me. I was about to be married to one so gentle—so pure—I, an Indian—was about to give my stained hand to a lovely being of untainted blood. I, who was so proud of lifting her to my lofty station. Oh, Malaeska!" he exclaimed, vehemently grasping her hand with a clutch of iron, "say that this was a story— a sad, pitiful story got up to punish my pride; say but this, and I will give you all I have on earth—every farthing. I will love you better than a thousand sons. Oh, if you have mercy, contradict the wretched falsehood!" His frame shook with agitation, and he gazed upon her as one pleading for his life.

When the wretched mother saw the hopeless misery which she had heaped upon her proud and sensitive child, she would have laid down her life could she have unsaid the tale which had wrought such agony, without bringing a stain of falsehood on her soul.

But words are fearful weapons, never to be checked when once put in motion. Like barbed arrows they enter the heart, and can not be withdrawn again, even by the hand that has shot them. Poisoned they are at times, with a venom that clings to the memory forever. Words are, indeed, fearful things! The poor Indian mother could not recall hers, but she tried to soothe the proud feelings which had been so terribly wounded.

"Why should my son scorn the race of his mother? The blood which she gave him from her heart was that of a brave and kingly line, warriors and chieftains, all——"

The youth interrupted her with a low, bitter laugh. The deep prejudices which had been instilled into his nature—pride, despair, every feeling which urges to madness and evil—were a fire in his heart.

"So I have a patent of nobility to gild my sable birthright, an ancestral line of dusky chiefs to boast of. I should have known this, when I offered my hand to that lovely girl. She little knew the dignity which awaited her union. Father of heaven, my heart will break—I am going mad!"

He looked wildly around as he spoke, and his eyes settled on the dark waters, flowing so tranquilly a few feet beneath him. Instantly he became calm, as one who had found an unexpected resource in his affliction. His face was perfectly colorless and gleamed like marble as he turned to his mother, who stood in a posture of deep humility and supplication a few paces off, for she dared not approach him again either with words of comfort or tenderness. All the sweet hopes which had of late been so warm in her heart, were utterly crushed. She was a heart-broken, wretched woman, without a hope on this side the grave. The young man drew close to her, and taking both her hands, looked sorrowfully into her face. His voice was tranquil and deep-toned, but a slight husky sound gave an unnatural solemnity to his words.

"Malaeska," he said, raising her hands toward heaven, "swear to me by the God whom we both worship, that you have told me nothing but the truth; I would have no doubt."

There was something sublime in his position, and in the solemn calmness which had settled upon him. The poor woman had been weeping, but the tears were checked in her eyes, and her pale lips ceased their quivering motion and became firm, as she looked up to the white face bending over her.

"As I hope to meet you, my son, before that God, I have spoken nothing but the truth."

"Malaeska!"

"Will you not call me mother?" said the meek woman, with touching pathos. "I know that I am an Indian, but your father loved me."

"Mother? Yes, God forbid that I should refuse to call you mother; I am afraid that I have often been harsh to you, but I did not know your claim on my love. Even now, I have been unkind."

"No, no, my son."

"I remember you were always meek and forgiving—you forgive me now, my poor mother?"

Malaeska could not speak, but she sank to her son's feet, and covered his hand with tears and kisses.

"There is one who will feel this more deeply than either of us. You will comfort her, Mala—mother, will you not?"

Malaeska rose slowly up, and looked into her son's face. She was terrified by his child-like gentleness; her breath came painfully. She knew not why it was, but a shudder ran through her frame, and her heart grew heavy, as if some terrible catastrophe were about to happen. The young man stepped a pace nearer the bank, and stood, motionless, gazing down into the water. Malaeska drew close to him, and laid her hand on his arm.

"My son, why do you stand thus? Why gaze so fearfully upon the water?"

He did not answer, but drew her to his bosom, and pressed his lips down upon her forehead. Tears sprang afresh to the mother's eyes, and her heart thrilled with an exquisite sensation, which was almost pain. It was the first time he had kissed her since his childhood. She trembled with mingled awe and tenderness as he released her from his embrace, and put her gently from the brink of the projection. The action had placed her back toward him. She turned—saw him clasp his hands high over his head, and spring into the air. There was a plunge; the deep rushing sound of waters flowing back to their place, and then a shriek, sharp and full of terrible agony, rung over the stream like the death-cry of a human being.

The cry broke from the wretched mother, as she tore off her outer garments and plunged after the self-murderer. Twice the moonlight fell upon her pallid face and her long hair, as it streamed out on the water. The third time another marble face rose to the surface, and with almost superhuman strength the mother bore up the lifeless body of her son with one arm, and with the other struggled to the shore. She carried him up the steep bank where, at another time, no woman could have clambered even without incumbrance, and laid him on the grass. She tore open his vest, and laid her hand upon the heart. It was cold and pulseless. She chafed his palms, rubbed his marble forehead, and stretching herself on his body, tried to breathe life into his marble lips from her own cold heart. It was in vain. When convinced of this, she ceased all exertion; her face fell forward to the earth, and, with a low sobbing breath, she lay motionless by the dead.

The villagers heard that fearful shriek, and rushed down to the stream. Boats were launched, and when their crews reached the "Hoppy Nose," it was to find two human beings lying upon it.

The next morning found a sorrowful household in Arthur Jones' dwelling. Mrs. Jones was in tears, and the children moved noiselessly around the house, and spoke in timid whispers, as if the dead could be aroused. In the "out-room" lay the body of William Danforth, shrouded in his winding-sheet. With her heavy eyes fixed on the marble features of her son, sat the wretched Indian mother. Until the evening before, her dark hair had retained the volume and gloss of youth, but now it fell back from her hollow temples profusely as ever, but perfectly gray. The frost of grief had changed it in a single night. Her features were sunken, and she sat by the dead, motionless and resigned. There was nothing of stubborn grief about her. She answered when spoken to, and was patient in her suffering; but all could see that it was but the tranquillity of a broken heart, mild in its utter desolation. When the villagers gathered for the funeral, Malaeska, in a few gentle words, told them of her relationship to the dead, and besought them to bury him by the side of his father.

The coffin was carried out, and a solemn train followed it through the forest. Women and children all went forth to the burial.

When the dead body of her affianced husband was brought home, Sarah Jones had been carried senseless to her chamber. The day wore on, the funeral procession passed forth, and she knew nothing of it. She was falling continually from one fainting fit to another, murmuring sorrowfully in her intervals of consciousness, and dropping gently away with the sad words on her lips, like a child mourning itself to sleep. Late in the night, after her lover's interment, she awoke to a consciousness of misfortune. She turned feebly upon her pillow, and prayed earnestly and with a faith which turned trustingly to God for strength. As the light dawned, a yearning wish awoke in her heart to visit the grave of her betrothed. She arose, dressed herself, and bent her way with feeble step toward the forest. Strength returned to her as she went forward. The dew lay heavily among the wild-flowers in her path, and a squirrel, which had made her walk cheerful two days before, was playing among the branches overhead. She remembered the happy feeling with which she had witnessed his gambols then, and covered her face as if a friend had attempted to comfort her.

The wigwam was desolate, and the path which led to the grave lay with the dew yet unbroken on its turf. The early sunshine was playing among the wet, heavy branches of the hemlock, when she reached the inclosure. A sweet fragrance was shed over the trampled grass from the white rose-tree which bent low beneath the weight of its pure blossoms. A shower of damp petals lay upon the chieftain's grave, and the green leaves quivered in the air as it sighed through them with a pleasant and cheering motion. But Sarah saw nothing but a newly-made grave, and stretched upon its fresh sods the form of a human being. A feeling of awe came over the maiden's heart. She moved reverently onward, feeling that she was in the sanctuary of the dead. The form was Malaeska's. One arm fell over the grave, and her long hair, in all its mournful change of color, had been swept back from her forehead, and lay tangled amid the rank grass. The sod on which her head rested was sprinkled over with tiny white blossoms. A handful lay crushed beneath her cheek, and sent up a faint odor over the marble face. Sarah bent down and touched the forehead. It was cold and hard, but a tranquil sweetness was there which told that the spirit had passed away without a struggle. Malaeska lay dead among the graves of her household, the heart-broken victim of an unnatural marriage.

* * * *

Years passed on—the stern, relentless years that have at last swept away every visible trace which links the present with the past. The old house in Manhattan, where Sarah Jones had known so much happiness, which had been brightened for a little season by the sunshine of two young hearts, then darkened by the gloom of death, had long stood silent and untenanted.

After the death of William Danforth, there had been no relative in America to claim the estate left by his grandfather. In those days it took much time for tidings to cross the sea, and after they had reached England, there was such struggle and contention between those who claimed the property, that it was long before any actual settlement of it was made.

At last the old house was to be torn down, and its garden destroyed, to give place to a block of stores, the usual fate of every relic of old time in our restless city.

The day came upon which the solitary dwelling was to be demolished. The roof was torn off, the stout walls rudely pulled down, the timbers creaking as if suffering actual agony from their destruction; the grape-vine was buried beneath the fragments, the rose-bushes uprooted and thrown out upon the pavement to die, and in a few hours the only trace left of the once pleasant spot, was a shapeless mass of broken bricks and mortar, above which the swallows flew in wild circles, deploring the loss of their old nesting-places.

While that devastation was in progress, a lady stood upon the opposite side of the street, watching every blow with painful interest. She was many years past the bloom of youth, but the features had a loveliness almost saint-like from the holy resignation which illumi-nated them.

So when the work of ruin was complete, Sarah Jones stole quietly away, stilling the wave of anguish that surged over her heart from the past, and going back to her useful life, with-out a murmur against the Providence that had made it so lonely.

Chapter Thirteen

HORATIO ALGER JR.
(1832–1899)

Horatio Alger Jr. has become synonymous with the American rags-to-riches mythology, but his many stories might be more aptly described as morality tales tracing personal journeys from rags-to-respectability. Born in Massachusetts, the son of a Unitarian minister, Alger studied at Harvard University and then Harvard Divinity School. He became a  Unitarian minister in 1864 only to be soon accused of molesting boys in his congregation—charges that he never denied. He was forced to resign after less than two years in his post, whereupon he moved to New York to devote himself full-time to his literary aspirations.

After writing a number of books and short stories, Alger published *Ragged Dick* in 1868. Eventually Alger published nearly one hundred novels along with countless short stories and poems. *Ragged Dick*, however, would stand as his most famous and popular work. Many of his later tales are little more than thinly disguised retellings of the *Ragged Dick* storyline with slight variations and appropriately adjusted titles such as *Luck and Pluck* and *Bound to Rise*. Taken as a whole, these stories and the success formula they espoused helped canonize Alger as the literary patron saint of the American ideal that even the lowliest boy might make something of himself in the great United States.

Ragged Dick is the story of a young New York City shoeshine boy who has been given precious few material and familial advantages in life, but he has a wealth of natural talent and personal fortitude. The story explores many of Alger's favorite themes: the development of character through adversity; the ability to better oneself by embracing American cultural bulwarks, such as religion, education, and finance; and an unstoppable drive toward self-improvement. Several aspects of Alger's formula for personal success can be traced back to earlier American literary figures, such as Benjamin Franklin, but his ability to translate this formula into dozens of highly popular books for boys left an indelible mark on the cultural belief that America was indeed a land of endless opportunities for those who had enough ambition and determination to grab them.

RAGGED DICK;
OR,
STREET LIFE IN NEW YORK WITH THE BOOT-BLACKS

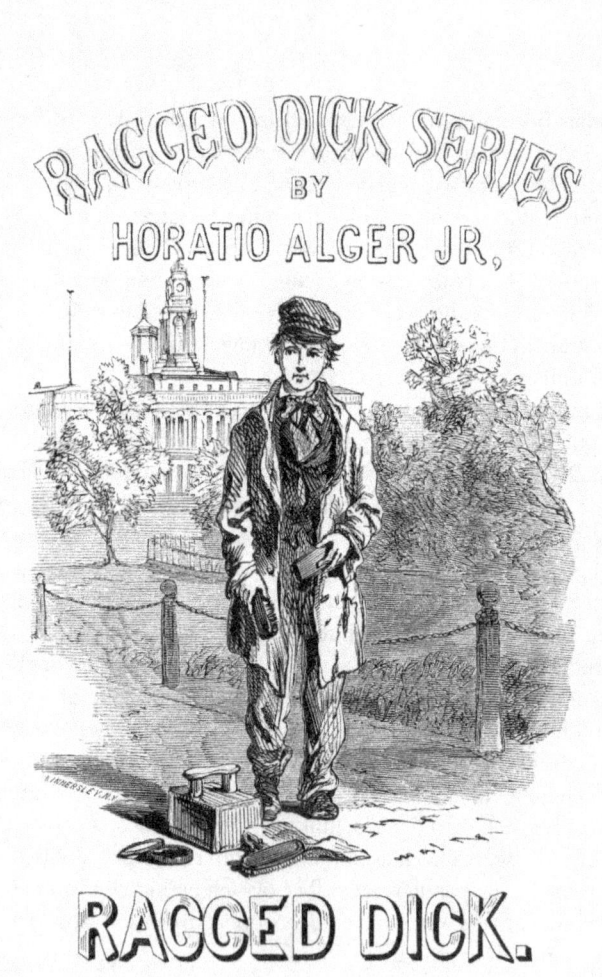

Title page from early book edition (*Ragged Dick*; Boston: Loring, 1868)

This text is reprinted from: *Ragged Dick; or, Street Life in New York with the Boot-Blacks.* Boston: Loring, 1868.

Preface

"RAGGED DICK" was contributed as a serial story to the pages of the *Schoolmate*, a well-known juvenile magazine, during the year 1867. While in course of publication, it was received with so many evidences of favor that it has been rewritten and considerably enlarged, and is now presented to the public as the first volume of a series intended to illustrate the life and experiences of the friendless and vagrant children who are now numbered by thousands in New York and other cities.

Several characters in the story are sketched from life. The necessary information has been gathered mainly from personal observation and conversations with the boys themselves. The author is indebted also to the excellent Superintendent of the Newsboys' Lodging House, in Fulton Street, for some facts of which he has been able to make use. Some anachronisms may be noted. Wherever they occur, they have been admitted, as aiding in the development of the story, and will probably be considered as of little importance in an unpretending volume, which does not aspire to strict historical accuracy.

The author hopes that, while the volumes in this series may prove interesting as stories, they may also have the effect of enlisting the sympathies of his readers in behalf of the unfortunate children whose life is described, and of leading them to co-operate with the praiseworthy efforts now being made by the Children's Aid Society and other organizations to ameliorate their condition.

New York, April, 1868

Chapter I

Ragged Dick Is Introduced to the Reader

"WAKE up there, youngster," said a rough voice.

Ragged Dick opened his eyes slowly, and stared stupidly in the face of the speaker, but did not offer to get up.

"Wake up, you young vagabond!" said the man a little impatiently; "I suppose you'd lay there all day, if I hadn't called you."

"What time is it?" asked Dick.

"Seven o'clock."

"Seven o'clock! I oughter've been up an hour ago. I know what 'twas made me so precious sleepy. I went to the Old Bowery last night, and didn't turn in till past twelve."

"You went to the Old Bowery?[1] Where'd you get your money?" asked the man, who was a porter in the employ of a firm doing business on Spruce Street.

"Made it by shines, in course. My guardian don't allow me no money for theatres, so I have to earn it."

"Some boys get it easier than that," said the porter significantly.

"You don't catch me stealin', if that's what you mean," said Dick.

"Don't you ever steal, then?"

---

1 A section of southern Manhattan Island full of theaters, cheap concert halls, pawn shops, brothels, beer gardens and inexpensive boarding houses.

"No, and I wouldn't. Lots of boys does it, but I wouldn't."

"Well, I'm glad to hear you say that. I believe there's some good in you, Dick, after all."

"Oh, I'm a rough customer!" said Dick. "But I wouldn't steal. It's mean."

"I'm glad you think so, Dick," and the rough voice sounded gentler than at first. "Have you got any money to buy your breakfast?"

"No, but I'll soon get some."

While this conversation has been going on, Dick had got up. His bedchamber had been a wooden box half full of straw, on which the young boot-black had reposed his weary limbs, and slept as soundly as if it had been a bed of down. He dumped down into the straw without taking the trouble of undressing. Getting up too was an equally short process. He jumped out of the box, shook himself, picked out one or two straws that had found their way into rents in his clothes, and, drawing a well-worn cap over his uncombed locks, he was all ready for the business of the day.

Dick's appearance as he stood beside the box was rather peculiar. His pants were torn in several places, and had apparently belonged in the first instance to a boy two sizes larger than himself. He wore a vest, all the buttons of which were gone except two, out of which peeped a shirt which looked as if it had been worn a month. To complete his costume he wore a coat too long for him, dating back, if one might judge from its general appearance, to a remote antiquity.

Washing the face and hands is usually considered proper in commencing the day, but Dick was above such refinement. He had no particular dislike to dirt, and did not think it necessary to remove several dark streaks on his face and hands. But in spite of his dirt and rags there was something about Dick that was attractive. It was easy to see that if he had been clean and well dressed he would have been decidedly good-looking. Some of his companions were sly, and their faces inspired distrust; but Dick had a frank, straight-forward manner that made him a favorite.

Dick's business hours had commenced. He had no office to open. His little blacking-box was ready for use, and he looked sharply in the faces of all who passed, addressing each with, "Shine yer boots, sir?"

"How much?" asked a gentleman on his way to his office.

"Ten cents," said Dick, dropping his box, and sinking upon his knees on the sidewalk, flourishing his brush with the air of one skilled in his profession.

"Ten cents! Isn't that a little steep?"

"Well, you know 'taint all clear profit," said Dick, who had already set to work. "There's the *blacking* costs something, and I have to get a new brush pretty often."

"And you have a large rent too," said the gentleman quizzically, with a glance at a large hole in Dick's coat.

"Yes, sir," said Dick, always ready to joke; "I have to pay such a big rent for my manshun up on Fifth Avenoo, that I can't afford to take less than ten cents a shine. I'll give you a bully shine, sir."

"Be quick about it, for I am in a hurry. So your house is on Fifth Avenue, is it?"

"It isn't anywhere else," said Dick, and Dick spoke the truth there.

"What tailor do you patronize?" asked the gentleman, surveying Dick's attire.

"Would you like to go to the same one?" asked Dick, shrewdly.

"Well, no; it strikes me that he didn't give you a very good fit."

"This coat once belonged to General Washington,"[2] said Dick, comically. "He wore it all through the Revolution, and it got torn some, 'cause he fit so hard. When he died he told his widder to give it to some smart young feller that hadn't got none of his own; so she gave it to me. But if you'd like it, sir, to remember General Washington by, I'll let you have it reasonable."

"Thank you, but I wouldn't want to deprive you of it. And did your pants come from General Washington too?"

"No, they was a gift from Lewis Napoleon.[3] Lewis had outgrown 'em and sent 'em to me,—he's bigger than me, and that's why they don't fit."

"It seems you have distinguished friends. Now, my lad, I suppose you would like your money."

"I shouldn't have any objection," said Dick.

"I believe," said the gentleman, examining his pocket-book, "I haven't got anything short of twenty-five cents. Have you got any change?"

"Not a cent," said Dick. "All my money's invested in the Erie Railroad."[4]

"That's unfortunate."

"Shall I get the money changed, sir?"

"I can't wait; I've got to meet an appointment immediately. I'll hand you twenty-five cents, and you can leave the change at my office any time during the day."

"All right, sir. Where is it?"

"No. 125 Fulton Street. Shall you remember?"

"Yes, sir. What name?"

"Greyson—office on second floor."

"All right, sir; I'll bring it."

"I wonder whether the little scamp will prove honest," said Mr. Greyson to himself, as he walked away. "If he does, I'll give him my custom regularly. If he don't, as is most likely, I shan't mind the loss of fifteen cents."

Mr. Greyson didn't understand Dick. Our ragged hero wasn't a model boy in all respects. I am afraid he swore sometimes, and now and then he played tricks upon unsophisticated boys from the country, or gave a wrong direction to honest old gentlemen unused to the city. A clergyman in search of the Cooper Institute[5] he once directed to the Tombs Prison,[6] and, following him unobserved, was highly delighted when the unsuspicious stranger walked up the front steps of the great stone building on Centre Street, and tried to obtain admission.

"I guess he wouldn't want to stay long if he did get in," thought Ragged Dick, hitching up his pants. "Leastways I shouldn't. They're so precious glad to see you that they won't let you go, but board you gratooitous, and never send in no bills."

---

2 George Washington (1732–1799), commanding general of the American forces during the Revolution, and the first president of the United States.

3 Louis-Napoleon Bonaparte (1808–1873) was a nephew of Napoleon Bonaparte and the first president of France elected by a popular vote.

4 Railroad connecting New York City to Lake Erie. Stock was sold in order to build and run this railroad.

5 The Cooper Union was one of the oldest schools of higher education in New York City.

6 Nickname of the Manhattan Detention Complex, a prison designed to look like a magnificent ancient Egyptian building.

Another of Dick's faults was his extravagance. Being always wide-awake and ready for business, he earned enough to have supported him comfortably and respectably. There were not a few young clerks who employed Dick from time to time in his professional capacity, who scarcely earned as much as he, greatly as their style and dress exceeded his. But Dick was careless of his earnings. Where they went he could hardly have told himself. However much he managed to earn during the day, all was generally spent before morning. He was fond of going to the Old Bowery Theatre, and to Tony Pastor's,[7] and if he had any money left afterwards, he would invite some of his friends in somewhere to have an oyster stew; so it seldom happened that he commenced the day with a penny.

Then I am sorry to add that Dick had formed the habit of smoking. This cost him considerable, for Dick was rather fastidious about his cigars, and wouldn't smoke the cheapest. Besides, having a liberal nature, he was generally ready to treat his companions. But of course the expense was the smallest objection. No boy of fourteen can smoke without being affected injuriously. Men are frequently injured by smoking, and boys always. But large numbers of the newsboys and boot-blacks form the habit. Exposed to the cold and wet they find that it warms them up, and the self-indulgence grows upon them. It is not uncommon to see a little boy, too young to be out of his mother's sight, smoking with all the apparent satisfaction of a veteran smoker.

There was another way in which Dick sometimes lost money. There was a noted gambling-house on Baxter Street, which in the evening was sometimes crowded with these juvenile gamesters, who staked their hard earnings, generally losing of course, and refreshing themselves from time to time with a vile mixture of liquor at two cents a glass. Sometimes Dick strayed in here, and played with the rest.

I have mentioned Dick's faults and defects, because I want it understood, to begin with, that I don't consider him a model boy. But there were some good points about him nevertheless. He was above doing anything mean or dishonorable. He would not steal, or cheat, or impose upon younger boys, but was frank and straight-forward, manly and self-reliant. His nature was a noble one, and had saved him from all mean faults. I hope my young readers will like him as I do, without being blind to his faults. Perhaps, although he was only a boot-black, they may find something in him to imitate.

And now, having fairly introduced Ragged Dick to my young readers, I must refer them to the next chapter for his further adventures.

Chapter II

Johnny Nolan

AFTER Dick had finished polishing Mr. Greyson's boots he was fortunate enough to secure three other customers, two of them reporters in the Tribune establishment, which occupies the corner of Spruce Street and Printing House Square.

When Dick had got through with his last customer the City Hall clock indicated eight o'clock. He had been up an hour, and hard at work, and naturally began to think of breakfast. He went up to the head of Spruce Street, and turned into Nassau. Two blocks further,

---

7 Tony Pastor, a successful theater owner in New York City, is sometimes called the father of vaudeville because he so favored presenting a wide variety of entertainment.

and he reached Ann Street. On this street was a small, cheap restaurant, where for five cents Dick could get a cup of coffee, and for ten cents more, a plate of beef-steak with a plate of bread thrown in. These Dick ordered, and sat down at a table.

It was a small apartment with a few plain tables unprovided with cloths, for the class of customers who patronized it were not very particular. Our hero's breakfast was soon before him. Neither the coffee nor the steak were as good as can be bought at Delmonico's; but then it is very doubtful whether, in the present state of his wardrobe, Dick would have been received at that aristocratic restaurant, even if his means had admitted of paying the high prices there charged.

Dick had scarcely been served when he espied a boy about his own size standing at the door, looking wistfully into the restaurant. This was Johnny Nolan, a boy of fourteen, who was engaged in the same profession as Ragged Dick. His wardrobe was in very much the same condition as Dick's.

"Had your breakfast, Johnny?" inquired Dick, cutting off a piece of steak.

"No."

"Come in, then. Here's room for you."

"I aint got no money," said Johnny, looking a little enviously at his more fortunate friend.

"Haven't you had any shines?"

"Yes, I had one, but I shan't get any pay till to-morrow."

"Are you hungry?"

"Try me, and see."

"Come in. I'll stand treat this morning."

Johnny Nolan was nowise slow to accept this invitation, and was soon seated beside Dick.

"What'll you have, Johnny?"

"Same as you."

"Cup o' coffee and beefsteak," ordered Dick.

These were promptly brought, and Johnny attacked them vigorously.

Now, in the boot-blacking business, as well as in higher avocations, the same rule prevails, that energy and industry are rewarded, and indolence suffers. Dick was energetic and on the alert for business, but Johnny the reverse. The consequence was that Dick earned probably three times as much as the other.

"How do you like it?" asked Dick, surveying Johnny's attacks upon the steak with evident complacency. "It's hunky."

I don't believe "hunky" is to be found in either Webster's or Worcester's big dictionary;[8] but boys will readily understand what it means.

"Do you come here often?" asked Johnny.

"Most every day. You'd better come too."

"I can't afford it."

"Well, you'd ought to, then," said Dick. "What do you do with your money, I'd like to know?"

"I don't get near as much as you, Dick."

"Well, you might if you tried. I keep my eyes open—that's the way I get jobs. You're lazy, that's what's the matter."

---

8 Noah Webster (1758–1843) and Joseph Worcester (1784–1865) were the authors of the first two great dictionaries published by Americans. Both dictionaries became famous for their attention to uniquely American vocabulary usage and spelling issues.

Johnny did not see fit to reply to this charge. Probably he felt the justice of it, and preferred to proceed with the breakfast, which he enjoyed the more as it cost him nothing.

Breakfast over, Dick walked up to the desk, and settled the bill. Then, followed by Johnny, he went out into the street.

"Where are you going, Johnny?"

"Up to Mr. Taylor's, on Spruce Street, to see if he don't want a shine."

"Do you work for him reg'lar?"

"Yes. Him and his partner wants a shine most every day. Where are you goin'?"

"Down front of the Astor House.[9] I guess I'll find some customers there."

At this moment Johnny started, and, dodging into an entry way, hid behind the door, considerably to Dick's surprise.

"What's the matter now?" asked our hero.

"Has he gone?" asked Johnny, his voice betraying anxiety.

"Who gone, I'd like to know?"

"That man in the brown coat."

"What of him. You aint scared of him, are you?"

"Yes, he got me a place once."

"Where?"

"Ever so far off."

"What if he did?"

"I ran away."

"Didn't you like?"

"No, I had to get up too early. It was on a farm, and I had to get up at five to take care of the cows. I like New York best."

"Didn't they give you enough to eat?"

"Oh, yes, plenty."

"And you had a good bed?"

"Yes."

"Then you'd better have stayed. You don't get either of them here. Where'd you sleep last night?"

"Up an alley in an old wagon."

"You had a better bed than that in the country, didn't you?"

"Yes, it was as soft as—as cotton."

Johnny had once slept on a bale of cotton, the recollection supplying him with a comparison.

"Why didn't you stay?"

"I felt lonely," said Johnny.

Johnny could not exactly explain his feelings, but it is often the case that the young vagabond of the streets, though his food is uncertain, and his bed may be any old wagon or barrel that he is lucky enough to find unoccupied when night sets in, gets so attached to his precarious but independent mode of life, that he feels discontented in any other. He is accustomed to the noise and bustle and ever-varied life of the streets, and in the quiet scenes of the country misses the excitement in the midst of which he has always dwelt.

---

9 The first grand luxury hotel in New York City.

Johnny had but one tie to bind him to the city. He had a father living, but he might as well have been without one. Mr. Nolan was a confirmed drunkard, and spent the greater part of his wages for liquor. His potations made him ugly, and inflamed a temper never very sweet, working him up sometimes to such a pitch of rage that Johnny's life was in danger. Some months before, he had thrown a flat-iron at his son's head with such terrific force that unless Johnny had dodged he would not have lived long enough to obtain a place in our story. He fled the house, and from that time had not dared to re-enter it. Somebody had given him a brush and box of blacking, and he had set up in business on his own account. But he had not energy enough to succeed, as has already been stated, and I am afraid the poor boy had met with many hardships, and suffered more than once from cold and hunger. Dick had befriended him more than once, and often given him a breakfast or dinner, as the case might be.

"How'd you get away?" asked Dick, with some curiosity. "Did you walk?"

"No, I rode on the cars."

"Where'd you get your money? I hope you didn't steal it."

"I didn't have none."

"What did you do, then?"

"I got up about three o'clock, and walked to Albany."

"Where's that?" asked Dick, whose ideas on the subject of geography were rather vague.

"Up the river."

"How far?"

"About a thousand miles," said Johnny, whose conceptions of distance were equally vague.

"Go ahead. What did you do then?"

"I hid on top of a freight car, and came all the way without their seeing me.[10] That man in the brown coat was the man that got me the place, and I'm afraid he'd want to send me back."

"Well," said Dick, reflectively, "I dunno as I'd like to live in the country. I couldn't go to Tony Pastor's, or the Old Bowery. There wouldn't be no place to spend my evenings. But I say, it's tough in winter, Johnny, 'specially when your overcoat's at the tailor's, an' likely to stay there."

"That's so, Dick. But I must be goin', or Mr. Taylor'll get somebody else to shine his boots."

Johnny walked back to Nassau Street, while Dick kept on his way to Broadway.

"That boy," soliloquized Dick, as Johnny took his departure, "aint got no ambition. I'll bet he won't get five shines to-day. I'm glad I aint like him. I couldn't go to the theatre, nor buy no cigars, nor get half as much as I wanted to eat.—Shine yer boots, sir?"

Dick always had an eye to business, and this remark was addressed to a young man, dressed in a stylish manner, who was swinging a jaunty cane.

"I've had my boots blacked once already this morning, but this confounded mud has spoiled the shine."

"I'll make 'em all right, sir, in a minute."

"Go ahead, then."

---

10 [Author's Original Note] A fact.

The boots were soon polished in Dick's best style, which proved very satisfactory, our hero being a proficient in the art.

"I haven't got any change," said the young man, fumbling in his pocket, "but here's a bill you may run somewhere and get changed. I'll pay you five cents extra for your trouble."

He handed Dick a two-dollar bill, which our hero took into a store close by.

"Will you please change that, sir?" said Dick, walking up to the counter.

The salesman to whom he proffered it took the bill, and, slightly glancing at it, exclaimed angrily, "Be off, you young vagabond, or I'll have you arrested."

"What's the row?"

"You've offered me a counterfeit bill."

"I didn't know it," said Dick.

"Don't tell me. Be off, or I'll have you arrested."

Chapter III

Dick Makes a Proposition

THOUGH Dick was somewhat startled at discovering that the bill he had offered was counterfeit, he stood his ground bravely.

"Clear out of this shop, you young vagabond," repeated the clerk.

"Then give me back my bill."

"That you may pass it again? No, sir, I shall do no such thing."

"It doesn't belong to me," said Dick. "A gentleman that owes me for a shine gave it to me to change."

"A likely story," said the clerk; but he seemed a little uneasy.

"I'll go and call him," said Dick.

He went out, and found his late customer standing on the Astor House steps.

"Well, youngster, have you brought back my change? You were a precious long time about it. I began to think you had cleared out with the money."

"That aint my style," said Dick, proudly.

"Then where's the change?"

"I haven't got it."

"Where's the bill then?"

"I haven't got that either."

"You young rascal!"

"Hold on a minute, mister," said Dick, "and I'll tell you all about it. The man what took the bill said it wasn't good, and kept it."

"The bill was perfectly good. So he kept it, did he? I'll go with you to the store, and see whether he won't give it back to me."

Dick led the way, and the gentleman followed him into the store. At the reappearance of Dick in such company, the clerk flushed a little, and looked nervous. He fancied that he could browbeat a ragged boot-black, but with a gentleman he saw that it would be a different matter. He did not seem to notice the new-comers, but began to replace some goods on the shelves.

"Now," said the young man, "point out the clerk that has my money."

"That's him," said Dick, pointing out the clerk.

The gentleman walked up to the counter.

"I will trouble you," he said a little haughtily, "for a bill which that boy offered you, and which you still hold in your possession."

"It was a bad bill," said the clerk, his cheek flushing, and his manner nervous.

"It was no such thing. I require you to produce it, and let the matter be decided."

The clerk fumbled in his vest-pocket, and drew out a bad-looking bill.

"This is a bad bill, but it is not the one I gave the boy."

"It is the one he gave me."

The young man looked doubtful.

"Boy," he said to Dick, "is this the bill you gave to be changed?"

"No, it isn't."

"You lie, you young rascal!" exclaimed the clerk, who began to find himself in a tight place, and could not see the way out.

This scene naturally attracted the attention of all in the store, and the proprietor walked up from the lower end, where he had been busy

"What's all this, Mr. Hatch?" he demanded.

"That boy," said the clerk, "came in and asked change for a bad bill. I kept the bill, and told him to clear out. Now he wants it again to pass on somebody else."

"Show the bill."

The merchant looked at it. "Yes, that's a bad bill," he said. "There is no doubt about that."

"But it is not the one the boy offered," said Dick's patron. "It is one of the same denomination, but on a different bank."

"Do you remember what bank it was on?"

"It was on the Merchant's Bank of Boston."

"Are you sure of it?"

"I am."

"Perhaps the boy kept it and offered the other."

"You may search me if you want to," said Dick, indignantly.

"He doesn't look as if he was likely to have any extra bills. I suspect that your clerk pocketed the good bill, and has substituted the counterfeit note. It is a nice little scheme of his for making money."

"I haven't seen any bill on the Merchant's Bank," said the clerk, doggedly.

"You had better feel in your pockets."

"This matter must be investigated," said the merchant, firmly. "If you have the bill, produce it."

"I haven't got it," said the clerk; but he looked guilty notwithstanding.

"I demand that he be searched," said Dick's patron.

"I tell you I haven't got it."

"Shall I send for a police officer, Mr. Hatch, or will you allow yourself to be searched quietly?" said the merchant.

Alarmed at the threat implied in these words, the clerk put his hand into his vest-pocket, and drew out a two-dollar bill on the Merchants' Bank.

"Is this your note?" asked the shopkeeper, showing it to the young man.

"It is."

"I must have made a mistake," faltered the clerk.

"I shall not give you a chance to make such another mistake in my employ," said the merchant sternly. "You may go up to the desk and ask for what wages are due you. I shall have no further occasion for your services."

"Now, youngster," said Dick's patron, as they went out of the store, after he had finally got the bill changed. "I must pay you something extra for your trouble. Here's fifty cents."

"Thank you, sir," said Dick. "You're very kind. Don't you want some more bills changed?"

"Not to-day," said he with a smile. "It's too expensive."

"I'm in luck," thought our hero complacently. "I guess I'll go to Barnum's[11] to-night, and see the bearded lady, the eight-foot giant, the two-foot dwarf, and the other curiosities, too numerous to mention."

Dick shouldered his box and walked up as far as the Astor House. He took his station on the sidewalk, and began to look about him.

Just behind him were two persons,—one, a gentleman of fifty; the other, a boy of thirteen or fourteen. They were speaking together, and Dick had no difficulty in hearing what was said.

"I am sorry, Frank, that I can't go about, and show you some of the sights of New York, but I shall be full of business to-day. It is your first visit to the city too."

"Yes, sir."

"There's a good deal worth seeing here. But I'm afraid you'll have to wait till next time. You can go out and walk by yourself, but don't venture too far, or you may get lost."

Frank looked disappointed.

"I wish Tom Miles knew I was here," he said. "He would go around with me."

"Where does he live?"

"Somewhere up town, I believe."

"Then, unfortunately, he is not available. If you would rather go with me than stay here, you can, but as I shall be most of the time in merchants' counting-rooms, I am afraid it would not be very interesting."

"I think," said Frank, after a little hesitation, "that I will go off by myself. I won't go very far, and if I lose my way, I will inquire for the Astor House."

"Yes, anybody will direct you here."

"Very well, Frank, I am sorry I can't do better for you."

"Oh, never mind, uncle, I shall be amused in walking around, and looking at the shop-windows. There will be a great deal to see."

Now Dick had listened to all this conversation. Being an enterprising young man, he thought he saw a chance for a speculation, and determined to avail himself of it.

Accordingly he stepped up to the two just as Frank's uncle was about leaving, and said, "I know all about the city, sir; I'll show him around, if you want me too."

The gentleman looked a little curiously at the ragged figure before him.

"So you are a city boy, are you?"

"Yes, sir," said Dick, "I've lived here ever since I was a baby."

"And you know all about the public buildings, I suppose?"

"Yes, sir."

---

11 Barnum's American Museum was on Broadway and housed a great variety of curiosities along with a lecture hall and a theater.

"And the Central Park?"[12]

"Yes, sir. I know my way all round."

The gentleman looked thoughtful.

"I don't know what to say, Frank," he remarked after a while. "It is rather a novel proposal. He isn't exactly the sort of guide I would have picked out for you. Still he looks honest. He has an open face, and I think can be depended upon."

"I wish he wasn't so ragged and dirty," said Frank, who felt a little shy about being seen with such a companion.

"I'm afraid you haven't washed your face this morning," said Mr. Whitney, for that was the gentleman's name.

"They didn't have no wash-bowls at the hotel where I stopped," said Dick.

"What hotel did you stop at?"

"The Box Hotel."

"The Box Hotel?"

"Yes, sir, I slept in a box on Spruce Street."

Frank surveyed Dick curiously.

"How did you like it?" he asked.

"I slept bully."

"Suppose it had rained."

"Then I'd have wet my best clothes," said Dick.

"Are these all the clothes you have?"

"Yes, sir."

Mr. Whitney spoke a few words to Frank, who seemed pleased with the suggestion.

"Follow me, my lad," he said.

Dick in some surprise obeyed orders, following Mr. Whitney and Frank into the hotel, past the office, to the foot of the staircase. Here a servant of the hotel stopped Dick, but Mr. Whitney explained that he had something for him to do, and he was allowed to proceed.

They entered a long entry, and finally paused before a door. This being opened a pleasant chamber was disclosed.

"Come in, my lad," said Mr. Whitney

Dick and Frank entered.

Chapter IV

Dick's New Suit

"Now," said Mr. Whitney to Dick, "my nephew here is on his way to a boarding-school. He had a suit of clothes in his trunk about half worn. He is willing to give them to you. I think they will look better than those you have on."

Dick was so astonished that he hardly knew what to say. Presents were something that he knew very little about, never having received any to his knowledge. That so large a gift should be made to him by a stranger seemed very wonderful.

The clothes were brought out, and turned out to be a neat gray suit.

---

12 Central Park opened in 1857 and covered a nearly 800-acre rectangular area in central Manhattan, beginning near 59th Street and stretching toward the north.

"Before you put them on, my lad, you must wash yourself. Clean clothes and a dirty skin don't go very well together. Frank, you may attend to him. I am obliged to go at once. Have you got as much money as you require?"

"Yes, uncle."

"One more word, my lad," said Mr. Whitney, addressing Dick; "I may be rash in trusting a boy of whom I know nothing, but I like your looks, and I think you will prove a proper guide for my nephew."

"Yes, I will, sir," said Dick, earnestly. "Honor bright!"

"Very well. A pleasant time to you."

The process of cleansing commenced. To tell the truth Dick needed it, and the sensation of cleanliness he found both new and pleasant. Frank added to his gift a shirt, stockings, and an old pair of shoes. "I am sorry I haven't any cap," said he.

"I've got one," said Dick.

"It isn't so new as it might be," said Frank, surveying an old felt hat, which had once been black, but was now dingy, with a large hole in the top and a portion of the rim torn off.

"No," said Dick; "my grandfather used to wear it when he was a boy, and I've kep' it ever since out of respect for his memory. But I'll get a new one now. I can buy one cheap on Chatham Street."

"Is that near here?"

"Only five minutes' walk."

"Then we can get one on the way."

When Dick was dressed in his new attire, with his face and hands clean, and his hair brushed, it was difficult to imagine that he was the same boy.

He now looked quite handsome, and might readily have been taken for a young gentleman, except that his hands were red and grimy.

"Look at yourself," said Frank, leading him before the mirror.

"By gracious!" said Dick, starting back in astonishment, "that isn't me, is it?"

"Don't you know yourself?" asked Frank, smiling.

"It reminds me of Cinderella," said Dick, "when she was changed into a fairy princess. I see it one night at Barnum's. What'll Johnny Nolan say when he sees me? He won't dare to speak to such a young swell as I be now. Ain't it rich?" and Dick burst into a loud laugh. His fancy was tickled by the anticipation of his friend's surprise. Then the thought of the valuable gifts he had received occurred to him, and he looked gratefully at Frank.

"You're a brick," he said.

"A what?"

"A brick! You're a jolly good fellow to give me such a present."

"You're quite welcome, Dick," said Frank, kindly. "I'm better off than you are, and I can spare the clothes just as well as not. You must have a new hat though. But that we can get when we go out. The old clothes you can make into a bundle."

"Wait a minute till I get my handkercher," and Dick pulled from the pocket of the pants a dirty rag, which might have been white once, though it did not look like it, and had apparently once formed a part of a sheet or shirt.

"You mustn't carry that," said Frank.

"But I've got a cold," said Dick.

"Oh, I don't mean you to go without a handkerchief. I'll give you one."

Frank opened his trunk and pulled out two, which he gave to Dick.

"I wonder if I aint dreamin'," said Dick, once more surveying himself doubtfully in the glass. "I'm afraid I'm dreamin', and shall wake up in a barrel, as I did night afore last."

"Shall I pinch you so you can wake here?" asked Frank, playfully.

"Yes," said Dick, seriously, "I wish you would."

He pulled up the sleeve of his jacket, and Frank pinched him pretty hard, so that Dick winced.

"Yes, I guess I'm awake," said Dick; "you've got a pair of nippers, you have."

"But what shall I do with my brush and blacking?" he asked.

"You can leave them here till we come back," said Frank. "They will be safe."

"Hold on a minute," said Dick, surveying Frank's boots with a professional eye, "you aint got a good shine on them boots. I'll make 'em shine so you can see your face in 'em."

And he was as good as his word.

"Thank you," said Frank; "now you had better brush your own shoes."

This had not occurred to Dick, for in general the professional boot-black considers his blacking too valuable to expend on his own shoes or boots, if he is fortunate enough to possess a pair.

The two boys now went downstairs together. They met the same servant who had spoken to Dick a few minutes before, but there was no recognition.

"He don't know me," said Dick. "He thinks I'm a young swell like you."

"What's a swell?"

"Oh, a feller that wears nobby clothes like you."

"And you, too, Dick."

"Yes," said Dick, "who'd ever have thought as I should have turned into a swell?"

They had now got out on Broadway, and were slowly walking along the west side by the Park, when who should Dick see in front of him, but Johnny Nolan?

Instantly Dick was seized with a fancy for witnessing Johnny's amazement at his change in appearance. He stole up behind him, and struck him on the back.

"Hallo, Johnny, how many shines have you had?"

Johnny turned round expecting to see Dick, whose voice he recognized, but his astonished eyes rested on a nicely dressed boy (the hat alone excepted) who looked indeed like Dick, but so transformed in dress that it was difficult to be sure of his identity.

"What luck, Johnny?" repeated Dick.

Johnny surveyed him from head to foot in great bewilderment.

"Who be you?" he said.

"Well, that's a good one," laughed Dick; "so you don't know Dick?"

"Where'd you get all them clothes?" asked Johnny. "Have you been stealin'?"

"Say that again, and I'll lick you. No, I've lent my clothes to a young feller as was goin' to a party, and didn't have none fit to wear, and so I put on my second-best for a change."

Without deigning any further explanation, Dick went off, followed by the astonished gaze of Johnny Nolan, who could not quite make up his mind whether the neat-looking boy he had been talking with was really Ragged Dick or not.

In order to reach Chatham Street it was necessary to cross Broadway. This was easier proposed than done. There is always such a throng of omnibuses, drays, carriages, and vehicles of all kinds in the neighborhood of the Astor House, that the crossing is formidable to one who is not used to it. Dick made nothing of it, dodging in and out among the horses and wagons with perfect self-possession. Reaching the opposite sidewalk, he looked back, and found that Frank had retreated in dismay, and that the width of the street was between them.

"Come across!" called out Dick.

"I don't see any chance," said Frank, looking anxiously at the prospect before him. "I'm afraid of being run over."

"If you are, you can sue 'em for damages," said Dick.

Finally Frank got safely over after several narrow escapes, as he considered them.

"Is it always so crowded?" he asked.

"A good deal worse sometimes," said Dick. "I knowed a young man once who waited six hours for a chance to cross, and at last got run over by an omnibus, leaving a widder and a large family of orphan children. His widder, a beautiful young woman, was obliged to start a peanut and apple stand. There she is now."

"Where?"

Dick pointed to a hideous old woman, of large proportions, wearing a bonnet of immense size, who presided over an apple-stand close by.

Frank laughed.

"If that is the case," he said, "I think I will patronize her."

"Leave it to me," said Dick, winking.

He advanced gravely to the apple-stand, and said, 'Old lady, have you paid your taxes?"

The astonished woman opened her eyes.

"I'm a gov'ment officer," said Dick, "sent by the mayor to collect your taxes. I'll take it in apples just to oblige. That big red one will about pay what you're owin' to the gov'ment."

"I don't know nothing about no taxes," said the old woman, in bewilderment.

"Then," said Dick, "I'll let you off this time. Give us two of your best apples, and my friend here, the President of the Common Council, will pay you."

Frank smiling, paid three cents apiece for the apples, and they sauntered on, Dick remarking, "If these apples aint good, old lady, we'll return 'em, and get our money back." This would have been rather difficult in his case, as the apple was already half consumed.

Chatham Street, where they wished to go, being on the East side, the two boys crossed the Park. This is an enclosure of about ten acres, which years ago was covered with a green sward, but is now a great thoroughfare for pedestrians and contains several important public buildings. Dick pointed out the City Hall, the Hall of Records, and the Rotunda. The former is a white building of large size, and surmounted by a cupola.

"That's where the mayor's office is," said Dick. "Him and me are very good friends. I once blacked his boots by partic'lar appointment. That's the way I pay my city taxes."

Chapter V

Chatham Street and Broadway

THEY were soon in Chatham Street, walking between rows of ready-made clothing shops, many of which had half their stock in trade exposed on the sidewalk. The proprietors of these establishments stood at the doors, watching attentively the passersby, extending urgent invitations to any who even glanced at the goods, to enter.

"Walk in, young gentlemen," said a stout man, at the entrance of one shop.

"No, I thank you," replied Dick, "as the fly said to the spider."

"We're selling off at less than cost."

"Of course you be. That's where you makes your money," said Dick. "There aint nobody of any enterprise that pretends to make any profit on his goods."

The Chatham Street trader looked after our hero as if he didn't quite comprehend him; but Dick, without waiting for a reply, passed on with his companion.

In some of the shops auctions seemed to be going on.

"I am only offered two dollars, gentlemen, for this elegant pair of doeskin pants, made of the very best of cloth. It's a frightful sacrifice. Who'll give an eighth? Thank you, sir. Only seventeen shillings! Why the cloth cost more by the yard!"

This speaker was standing on a little platform haranguing to three men, holding in his hand meanwhile a pair of pants very loose in the legs, and presenting a cheap Bowery look.

Frank and Dick paused before the shop door, and finally saw them knocked down to rather a verdant-looking individual at three dollars.

"Clothes seem to be pretty cheap here," said Frank.

"Yes, but Baxter Street is the cheapest place."

"Is it?"

"Yes. Johnny Nolan got a whole rig-out there last week, for a dollar,—coat, cap, vest, pants, and shoes. They was very good measure, too, like my best clothes that I took off to oblige you."

"I shall know where to come for clothes next time," said Frank, laughing. "I had no idea the city was so much cheaper than the country. I suppose the Baxter Street tailors are fashionable?"

"In course they are. Me and Horace Greeley[13] always go there for clothes. When Horace gets a new suit, I always have one made just like it; but I can't go the white hat. It aint becomin' to my style of beauty."

A little farther on a man was standing out on the sidewalk, distributing small printed handbills. One was handed to Frank, which he read as follows,—

"Grand Closing-Out Sale!—A variety of Beautiful and Costly Articles for Sale, at a Dollar apiece. Unparalleled Inducements! Walk in, Gentlemen!"

"Whereabouts is this sale?" asked Frank.

"In here, young gentlemen," said a black-whiskered individual, who appeared suddenly on the scene. "Walk in."

"Shall we go in, Dick?"

"It's a swindlin' shop," said Dick, in a low voice. "I've been there. That man's a reg'lar cheat. He's seen me before, but he don't know me coz of my clothes."

"Step in and see the articles," said the man, persuasively. "You needn't buy, you know."

"Are all the articles worth more'n a dollar?" asked Dick.

"Yes," said the other, "and some worth a great deal more."

"Such as what?"

"Well, there's a silver pitcher worth twenty dollars."

"And you sell it for a dollar. That's very kind of you," said Dick, innocently.

"Walk in, and you'll understand it."

"No, I guess not," said Dick. "My servants is so dishonest that I wouldn't like to trust 'em with a silver pitcher. Come along, Frank. I hope you'll succeed in your charitable enterprise of supplyin' the public with silver pitchers at nineteen dollars less than they are worth."

"How does he manage, Dick?" asked Frank, as they went on.

---

13 Horace Greeley (1811–1872) was a politician and the editor of the *New York Tribune*, one of the largest and most important newspapers of its day in Manhattan.

"All his articles are numbered, and he makes you pay a dollar, and then shakes some dice, and whatever the figgers come to, is the number of the article you draw. Most of 'em aint worth sixpence."

A hat and cap store being close at hand, Dick and Frank went in. For seventy-five cents, which Frank insisted on paying, Dick succeeded in getting quite a neat-looking cap, which corresponded much better with his appearance than the one he had on. The last, not being considered worth keeping, Dick dropped on the sidewalk, from which, on looking back, he saw it picked up by a brother boot-black who appeared to consider it better than his own.

They retraced their steps and went up Chambers Street to Broadway. At the corner of Broadway and Chambers Street is a large white marble warehouse, which attracted Frank's attention.

"What building is that?" he asked, with interest.

"That belongs to my friend. A. T. Stewart," said Dick. "It's the biggest store on Broadway.[14] If I ever retire from boot-blackin', and go into mercantile pursuits, I may buy him out, or build another store that'll take the shine off this one."

"Were you ever in the store?" asked Frank.

"No," said Dick; "but I'm intimate with one of Stewart's partners. He is a cash boy, and does nothing but take money all day."

"A very agreeable employment," said Frank, laughing.

"Yes," said Dick, "I'd like to be in it."

The boys crossed to the West side of Broadway, and walked slowly up the street. To Frank it was a very interesting spectacle. Accustomed to the quiet of the country, there was something fascinating in the crowds of people thronging the sidewalks, and the great variety of vehicles constantly passing and repassing in the street. Then again the shop-windows with their multifarious contents interested and amused him, and he was constantly checking Dick to look in at some well-stocked window.

"I don't see how so many shopkeepers can find people enough to buy of them," he said. "We haven't got but two stores in our village, and Broadway seems to be full of them."

"Yes," said Dick; "and it's pretty much the same in the avenoos, 'specially the Third, Sixth, and Eighth avenoos. The Bowery, too, is a great place for shoppin'. There everybody sells cheaper'n anybody else, and nobody pretends to make no profit on their goods."

"Where's Barnum's Museum?" asked Frank.

"Oh, that's down nearly opposite the Astor House," said Dick. "Didn't you see a great building with lots of flags?"

"Yes."

"Well, that's Barnum's.[15] That's where the Happy Family live, and the lions, and bears, and curiosities generally. It's a tip-top place. Haven't you ever been there? It's most as good as the Old Bowery, only the plays isn't quite so excitin'."

"I'll go if I get time," said Frank. "There is a boy at home who came to New York a month ago, and went to Barnum's, and has been talking about it ever since, so I suppose it must be worth seeing."

---

14 [Author's Original Note] Mr. Stewart's Tenth Street store was not open at the time Dick spoke.
15 [Author's Original Note] Since destroyed by fire, and rebuilt farther up Broadway, and again burned down in February.

"They've got a great play at the Old Bowery now," pursued Dick. "'Tis called the 'Demon of the Danube.' The Demon falls in love with a young woman, and drags her by the hair up to the top of a steep rock where his castle stands."

"That's a queer way of showing his love," said Frank, laughing.

"She didn't want to go with him, you know, but was in love with another chap. When he heard about his girl bein' carried off, he felt awful, and swore an oath not to rest till he had got her free. Well, at last he got into the castle by some under-ground passage, and he and the Demon had a fight. Oh, it was bully seein' 'em roll round on the stage, cuttin' and slashin' at each other."

"And which got the best of it?"

"At first the Demon seemed to be ahead, but at last the young Baron got him down, and struck a dagger into his heart, sayin', 'Die, false and perjured villain! The dogs shall feast upon thy carcass!' and then the Demon give an awful howl and died. Then the Baron seized his body, and threw it over the precipice."

"It seems to me the actor who plays the Demon ought to get extra pay, if he has to be treated that way."

"That's so," said Dick; "but I guess he's used to it. It seems to agree with his constitution."

"What building is that?" asked Frank, pointing to a structure several rods back from the street, with a large yard in front. It was an unusual sight for Broadway, all the other buildings in that neighborhood being even with the street.

"That is the New York Hospital," said Dick. "They're a rich institution, and take care of sick people on very reasonable terms."

"Did you ever go in there?"

"Yes," said Dick; "there was a friend of mine, Johnny Mullen, he was a newsboy, got run over by a omnibus as he was crossin' Broadway down near Park Place. He was carried to the Hospital, and me and some of his friends paid his board while he was there. It was only three dollars a week, which was very cheap, considerin' all the care they took of him. I got leave to come and see him while he was here. Everything looked so nice and comfortable, that I thought a little of coaxin' a omnibus driver to run over me, so I might go there too."

"Did your friend have to have his leg cut off?" asked Frank, interested.

"No," said Dick; "though there was a young student there that was very anxious to have it cut off; but it wasn't done, and Johnny is around the streets as well as ever."

While this conversation was going on they reached No. 365, at the corner of Franklin Street.[16]

"That's Taylor's Saloon," said Dick. "When I come into a fortun' I shall take my meals there reg'lar."

"I have heard of it very often," said Frank. "It is said to be very elegant. Suppose we go in and take an ice-cream. It will give us a chance to see it to better advantage."

"Thank you," said Dick; "I think that's the most agreeable way of seein' the place myself."

The boys entered, and found themselves in a spacious and elegant saloon, resplendent with gilding, and adorned on all sides by costly mirrors. They sat down to a small table with a marble top, and Frank gave the order.

"It reminds me of Aladdin's palace," said Frank, looking about him.

---

16 [Author's Original Note] Now the office of the Merchants' Union Express Company.

"Does it?" said Dick; "he must have had plenty of money."

"He had an old lamp, which he had only to rub, when the Slave of the Lamp would appear, and do whatever he wanted."

"That must have been a valooable lamp. I'd be willin' to give all my Erie shares for it."

There was a tall, gaunt individual at the next table, who apparently heard this last remark of Dick's. Turning towards our hero, he said, "May I inquire, young man, whether you are largely interested in this Erie Railroad?"

"I haven't got no property except what's invested in Erie," said Dick, with a comical side-glance at Frank.

"Indeed! I suppose the investment was made by your guardian."

"No," said Dick; "I manage my property myself."

"And I presume your dividends have not been large?"

"Why, no," said Dick; "you're about right there. They haven't."

"As I supposed. It's poor stock. Now, my young friend, I can recommend a much better investment, which will yield you a large annual income. I am agent of the Excelsior Copper Mining Company, which possesses one of the most productive mines in the world. It's sure to yield fifty per cent. on the investment. Now, all you have to do is to sell out your Erie shares, and invest in our stock, and I'll insure you a fortune in three years. How many shares did you say you had?"

"I didn't say, that I remember," said Dick. "Your offer is very kind and obligin', and as soon as I get time I'll see about it."

"I hope you will," said the stranger. "Permit me to give you my card. 'Samuel Snap, No.— Wall Street.' I shall be most happy to receive a call from you, and exhibit the maps of our mine. I should be glad to have you mention the matter also to your friends. I am confident you could do no greater service than to induce them to embark in our enterprise."

"Very good," said Dick.

Here the stranger left the table, and walked up to the desk to settle his bill.

"You see what it is to be a man of fortun', Frank," said Dick, "and wear good clothes. I wonder what that chap'll say when he sees me blackin' boots to-morrow in the street?"

"Perhaps you earn your money more honorably than he does, after all," said Frank. "Some of these mining companies are nothing but swindles, got up to cheat people out of their money."

"He's welcome to all he gets out of me," said Dick.

Chapter VI

Up Broadway to Madison Square

As the boys pursued their way up Broadway, Dick pointed out the prominent hotels and places of amusement. Frank was particularly struck with the imposing fronts of the St. Nicholas and Metropolitan Hotels, the former of white marble, the latter of a subdued brown hue, but not less elegant in its internal appointments. He was not surprised to be informed that each of these splendid structures cost with the furnishing not far from a million dollars.

At Eighth Street Dick turned to the right, and pointed out the Clinton Hall Building now occupied by the Mercantile Library, comprising at that time over fifty thousand volumes.[17]

A little farther on they came to a large building standing by itself just at the opening of Third and Fourth Avenues, and with one side on each.

"What is that building?" asked Frank.

"That's the Cooper Institute," said Dick; "built by Mr. Cooper, a particular friend of mine. Me and Peter Cooper used to go to school together."

"What is there inside?" asked Frank.

"There's a hall for public meetins' and lectures in the basement, and a readin' room and a picture gallery up above," said Dick.

Directly opposite Cooper Institute, Frank saw a very large building of brick, covering about an acre of ground.

"Is that a hotel?" he asked.

"No," said Dick; "that's the Bible House.[18] It's the place where they make Bibles. I was in there once,— saw a big pile of 'em."

"Did you ever read the Bible?" asked Frank, who had some idea of the neglected state of Dick's education.

"No," said Dick; "I've heard it's a good book, but I never read one. I aint much on readin'. It makes my head ache."

"I suppose you can't read very fast."

"I can read the little words pretty well, but the big ones is what stick me."

"If I lived in the city, you might come every evening to me, and I would teach you."

"Would you take so much trouble about me?" asked Dick, earnestly.

"Certainly; I should like to see you getting on. There isn't much chance of that if you don't know how to read and write."

"You're a good feller," said Dick, gratefully. "I wish you did live in New York. I'd like to know somethin'. Whereabouts do you live?"

"About fifty miles off, in a town on the left bank of the Hudson. I wish you'd come up and see me sometime. I would like to have you come and stop two or three days."

"Honor bright?"

"I don't understand."

"Do you mean it?" asked Dick, incredulously.

"Of course I do. Why shouldn't I?"

"What would your folks say if they knowed you asked a boot-black to visit you?"

"You are none the worse for being a boot-black, Dick."

"I aint used to genteel society," said Dick. "I shouldn't know how to behave."

"Then I could show you. You won't be a boot-black all your life, you know."

"No," said Dick; "I'm goin' to knock off when I get to be ninety."

"Before that, I hope," said Frank, smiling.

"I really wish I could get somethin' else to do," said Dick, soberly. "I'd like to be a office boy, and learn business, and grow up 'spectable."

---

17 [Author's Original Note] Now not far from one hundred thousand.

18 The home of the American Bible Society (founded in 1816), a Christian printing establishment that published hundreds of thousands of copies of the Scriptures each year.

"Why don't you try, and see if you can't get a place, Dick?"

"Who'd take Ragged Dick?"

"But you aint ragged now, Dick."

"No," said Dick; "I look a little better than I did in my Washington coat and Louis Napoleon pants. But if I got in a office, they wouldn't give me more'n three dollars a week, and I couldn't live 'spectable on that."

"No, I suppose not," said Frank, thoughtfully. "But you would get more at the end of the first year."

"Yes," said Dick; "but by that time I'd be nothin' but skin and bones."

Frank laughed. "That reminds me," he said, "of the story of an Irishman, who, out of economy, thought he would teach his horse to feed on shavings. So he provided the horse with a pair of green spectacles which made the shavings look eatable. But unfortunately, just as the horse got learned, he up and died."

"The hoss must have been a fine specimen of architectur' by the time he got through," remarked Dick.

"Whereabouts are we now?" asked Frank, as they emerged from Fourth Avenue into Union Square.

"That is Union Park," said Dick, pointing to a beautiful enclosure, in the centre of which was a pond, with a fountain playing.

"Is that the statue of General Washington?" asked Frank, pointing to a bronze equestrian statue on a granite pedestal.

"Yes," said Dick; "he's growed some since he was President. If he'd been as tall as that when he fit in the Revolution, he'd have walloped the Britishers some, I reckon."

Frank looked up at the statue, which is fourteen and a half feet high, and acknowledged the justice of Dick's remark.

"How about the coat, Dick?" he asked. "Would it fit you?"

"Well, it might be rather loose," said Dick, "I aint much more'n ten feet high with my boots off."

"No, I should think not," said Frank, smiling. "You're a queer boy, Dick."

"Well, I've been brought up queer. Some boys is born with a silver spoon in their mouth. Victoria's boys is born with a gold spoon, set with di'monds; but gold and silver was scarce when I was born, and mine was pewter."

"Perhaps the gold and silver will come by and by, Dick. Did you ever hear of Dick Whittington?"

"Never did. Was he a Ragged Dick?"

"I shouldn't wonder if he was. At any rate he was very poor when he was a boy, but he didn't stay so. Before he died, he became Lord Mayor of London."

"Did he?" asked Dick, looking interested. "How did he do it?"

"Why, you see, a rich merchant took pity on him, and gave him a home in his own house, where he used to stay with the servants, being employed in little errands. One day the merchant noticed Dick picking up pins and needles that had been dropped, and asked him why he did it. Dick told him he was going to sell them when he got enough. The merchant was pleased with his saving disposition, and when soon after, he was going to send a vessel to foreign parts, he told Dick he might send anything he pleased in it, and it should be sold to his advantage. Now Dick had nothing in the world but a kitten which had been given him a short time before."

"How much taxes did he have to pay on it?" asked Dick.

"Not very high, probably. But having only the kitten, he concluded to send it along. After sailing a good many months, during which the kitten grew up to be a strong cat, the ship touched at an island never before known, which happened to be infested with rats and mice to such an extent that they worried everybody's life out, and even ransacked the king's palace. To make a long story short, the captain, seeing how matters stood, brought Dick's cat ashore, and she soon made the rats and mice scatter. The king was highly delighted when he saw what havoc she made among the rats and mice, and resolved to have her at any price. So he offered a great quantity of gold for her, which, of course, the captain was glad to accept. It was faithfully carried back to Dick, and laid the foundation of his fortune. He prospered as he grew up, and in time became a very rich merchant, respected by all, and before he died was elected Lord Mayor of London."

"That's a pretty good story," said Dick; "but I don't believe all the cats in New York will ever make me mayor."

"No, probably not, but you may rise in some other way. A good many distinguished men have once been poor boys. There's hope for you, Dick, if you'll try."

"Nobody ever talked to me so before," said Dick. "They just called me Ragged Dick, and told me I'd grow up to be a vagabone (boys who are better educated need not be surprised at Dick's blunders) and come to the gallows."

"Telling you so won't make it turn out so, Dick. If you'll try to be somebody, and grow up into a respectable member of society, you will. You may not become rich—it isn't everybody that becomes rich, you know—but you can obtain a good position, and be respected."

"I'll try," said Dick, earnestly. "I needn't have been Ragged Dick so long if I hadn't spent my money in goin' to the theatre, and treatin' boys to oyster-stews, and bettin' money on cards, and such like."

"Have you lost money that way?"

"Lots of it. One time I saved up five dollars to buy me a new rig-out, cos my best suit was all in rags, when Limpy Jim wanted me to play a game with him."

"Limpy Jim?" said Frank, interrogatively.

"Yes, he's lame; that's what makes us call him Limpy Jim."

"I suppose you lost?"

"Yes, I lost every penny, and had to sleep out, cos I hadn't a cent to pay for lodgin'. 'Twas a awful cold night, and I got most froze."

"Wouldn't Jim let you have any of the money he had won to pay for a lodging?"

"No; I axed him for five cents, but he wouldn't let me have it."

"Can you get lodging for five cents?" asked Frank, in surprise.

"Yes," said Dick, "but not at the Fifth Avenue Hotel. That's it right out there."

Chapter VII

The Pocket-Book

THEY had reached the junction of Broadway and of Fifth Avenue. Before them was a beautiful park of ten acres. On the left-hand side was a large marble building, presenting a fine appearance with its extensive white front. This was the building at which Dick pointed.

"Is that the Fifth Avenue Hotel?" asked Frank. "I've heard of it often. My Uncle William always stops there when he comes to New York."

"I once slept on the outside of it," said Dick. "They was very reasonable in their charges, and told me I might come again."

"Perhaps sometime you'll be able to sleep inside," said Frank.

"I guess that'll be when Queen Victoria goes to the Five Points to live."

"It looks like a palace," said Frank. "The queen needn't be ashamed to live in such a beautiful building as that."

Though Frank did not know it, one of the queen's palaces is far from being as fine a looking building as the Fifth Avenue Hotel. St. James' Palace is a very ugly-looking brick structure, and appears much more like a factory than like the home of royalty. There are few hotels in the world as fine-looking as this democratic institution.

At that moment a gentleman passed them on the sidewalk, who looked back at Dick, as if his face seemed familiar.

"I know that man," said Dick, after he had passed. "He's one of my customers."

"What is his name?"

"I don't know."

"He looked back as if he thought he knew you."

"He would have knowed me at once if it hadn't been for my new clothes," said Dick. "I don't look much like Ragged Dick now."

"I suppose your face looked familiar."

"All but the dirt," said Dick, laughing. "I don't always have the chance of washing my face and hands in the Astor House."

"You told me," said Frank, "that there was a place where you could get lodging for five cents. Where's that?"

"It's the News-boys' Lodgin' House, on Fulton Street,"[19] said Dick, "up over the 'Sun' office. It's a good place. I don't know what us boys would do without it. They give you supper for six cents, and a bed for five cents more."

"I suppose some boys don't even have the five cents to pay,—do they?"

"They'll trust the boys," said Dick. "But I don't like to get trusted. I'd be ashamed to get trusted for five cents, or ten either. One night I was comin' down Chatham Street, with fifty cents in my pocket. I was goin' to get a good oyster-stew, and then go to the lodgin' house; but somehow it slipped through a hole in my trowses-pocket, and I hadn't a cent left. If it had been summer I shouldn't have cared, but it's rather tough stayin' out winter nights."

Frank, who had always possessed a good home of his own, found it hard to realize that the boy who was walking at his side had actually walked the streets in the cold without a home, or money to procure the common comfort of a bed.

"What did you do?" he asked, his voice full of sympathy.

"I went to the 'Times' office. I knowed one of the pressmen, and he let me set down in a comer, where I was warm, and I soon got fast asleep."

"Why don't you get a room somewhere, and so always have a home to go to?"

"I dunno," said Dick. "I never thought of it. P 'rhaps I may hire a furnished house on Madison Square."

---

19 The first home for newsboys founded in New York City in 1854. It had beds for 85 boys, who were charged a small sum for nightly room and board. It also had printing offices, as well as educational lecture rooms that could accommodate up to 100 boys at a time.

"That's where Flora McFlimsey[20] lived."

"I don't know her," said Dick, who had never read the popular poem of which she is the heroine.

While this conversation was going on, they had turned into Twenty-fifth Street, and had by this time reached Third Avenue.

Just before entering it, their attention was drawn to the rather singular conduct of an individual in front of them. Stopping suddenly, he appeared to pick up something from the sidewalk, and then looked about him in rather a confused way.

"I know his game," whispered Dick. "Come along and you'll see what it is."

He hurried Frank forward until they overtook the man, who had come to a stand-still.

"Have you found anything?" asked Dick.

"Yes," said the man, "I've found this."

He exhibited a wallet which seemed stuffed with bills, to judge from its plethoric appearance.

"Whew!" exclaimed Dick; "you're in luck."

"I suppose somebody has lost it," said the man, "and will offer a handsome reward."

"Which you'll get."

"Unfortunately I am obliged to take the next train to Boston. That's where I live. I haven't time to hunt up the owner."

"Then I suppose you'll take the pocket-book with you," said Dick, with assumed simplicity.

"I should like to leave it with some honest fellow who would see it returned to the owner," said the man, glancing at the boys.

"I'm honest," said Dick.

"I've no doubt of it," said the other. "Well, young man, I'll make you an offer. You take the pocket-book—"

"All right. Hand it over, then."

"Wait a minute. There must be a large sum inside. I shouldn't wonder if there might be a thousand dollars. The owner will probably give you a hundred dollars reward."

"Why don't you stay and get it?" asked Frank.

"I would, only there is sickness in my family, and I must get home as soon as possible. Just give me twenty dollars, and I'll hand you the pocket-book, and let you make whatever you can out of it. Come, that's a good offer. What do you say?"

Dick was well dressed, so that the other did not regard it as at all improbable that he might possess that sum. He was prepared, however, to let him have it for less, if necessary.

"Twenty dollars is a good deal of money," said Dick, appearing to hesitate.

"You'll get it back, and a good deal more," said the stranger, persuasively.

"I don't know but I shall. What would you do, Frank?"

"I don't know but I would," said Frank, "if you've got the money." He was not a little surprised to think that Dick had so much by him.

"I don't know but I will," said Dick, after some irresolution. "I guess I won't lose much."

"You can't lose anything," said the stranger briskly. "Only be quick, for I must be on my way to the cars. I am afraid I shall miss them now."

---

20 Flora McFlimsey was the heroine of the poem "Nothing to Wear" by William Allen Butler (1825–1902).

Dick pulled out a bill from his pocket, and handed it to the stranger, receiving the pocket-book in return. At that moment a policeman turned the corner, and the stranger, hurriedly thrusting the bill into his pocket, without looking at it, made off with rapid steps.

"What is there in the pocket-book, Dick?" asked Frank in some excitement. "I hope there's enough to pay you for the money you gave him."

Dick laughed.

"I'll risk that," said he.

"But you gave him twenty dollars. That's a good deal of money."

"If I had given him as much as that, I should deserve to be cheated out of it."

"But you did,—didn't you?"

"He thought so."

"What was it, then?"

"It was nothing but a dry-goods circular got up to imitate a bank-bill."

Frank looked sober.

"You ought not to have cheated him, Dick," he said, reproachfully.

"Didn't he want to cheat me?"

"I don't know."

"What do you s'pose there is in that pocket-book?" asked Dick, holding it up.

Frank surveyed its ample proportions, and answered sincerely enough, "Money, and a good deal of it."

"There aint stamps enough in it to buy a oyster-stew," said Dick. "If you don't believe it, just look while I open it."

So saying he opened the pocket-book, and showed Frank that it was stuffed out with pieces of blank paper, carefully folded up in the shape of bills. Frank, who was unused to city life, and had never heard anything of the "drop-game" looked amazed at this unexpected development.

"I knowed how it was all the time," said Dick. "I guess I got the best of him there. This wallet's worth somethin'. I shall use it to keep my stiffkit's of Erie stock in, and all my other papers what aint of no use to anybody but the owner."

"That's the kind of papers it's got in it now," said Frank, smiling.

"That's so!" said Dick.

"By hokey!" he exclaimed suddenly, "if there aint the old chap comin' back ag'in. He looks as if he'd heard bad news from his sick family."

By this time the pocket-book dropper had come up.

Approaching the boys, he said in an undertone to Dick, "Give me back that pocket-book, you young rascal!"

"Beg your pardon, mister," said Dick, "but was you addressin' me?"

"Yes, I was."

"'Cause you called me by the wrong name. I've knowed some rascals, but I aint the honor to belong to the family."

He looked significantly at the other as he spoke, which didn't improve the man's temper. Accustomed to swindle others, he did not fancy being practised upon in return.

"Give me back that pocket-book," he repeated in a threatening voice.

"Couldn't do it," said Dick, coolly. "I'm go'n' to restore it to the owner. The contents is so valooable that most likely the loss has made him sick, and he'll be likely to come down liberal to the honest finder."

"You gave me a bogus bill," said the man.

"It's what I use myself," said Dick.

"You've swindled me."

"I thought it was the other way."

"None of your nonsense," said the man angrily. "If you don't give up that pocket-book, I'll call a policeman."

"I wish you would," said Dick. "They'll know most likely whether it's Stewart or Astor that's lost the pocket-book, and I can get 'em to return it."

The "dropper," whose object it was to recover the pocket-book, in order to try the same game on a more satisfactory customer, was irritated by Dick's refusal, and above all by the coolness he displayed. He resolved to make one more attempt.

"Do you want to pass the night in the Tombs?" he asked.

"Thank you for your very obligin' proposal," said Dick; "but it aint convenient to-day. Any other time, when you'd like to have me come and stop with you, I'm agreeable; but my two youngest children is down with the measles, and I expect I'll have to set up all night to take care of 'em. Is the Tombs, in gineral, a pleasant place of residence?"

Dick asked this question with an air of so much earnestness that Frank could scarcely forbear laughing, though it is hardly necessary to say that the dropper was by no means so inclined.

"You'll know sometime," he said, scowling.

"I'll make you a fair offer," said Dick. "If I get more'n fifty dollars as a reward for my honesty, I'll divide with you. But I say, aint it most time to go back to your sick family in Boston?"

Finding that nothing was to be made out of Dick, the man strode away with a muttered curse.

"You were too smart for him, Dick," said Frank.

"Yes," said Dick, "I aint knocked round the city streets all my life for nothin'."

Chapter VIII

Dick's Early History

"Have you always lived in New York, Dick?" asked Frank, after a pause.

"Ever since I can remember."

"I wish you'd tell me a little about yourself. Have you got any father or mother?"

"I aint got no mother. She died when I wasn't but three years old. My father went to sea; but he went off before mother died, and nothin' was ever heard of him. I expect he got wrecked, or died at sea."

"And what became of you when your mother died?"

"The folks she boarded with took care of me, but they was poor, and they couldn't do much. When I was seven the woman died, and her husband went out West, and then I had to scratch for myself."

"At seven years old!" exclaimed Frank, in amazement.

"Yes," said Dick, "I was a little feller to take care of myself, but," he continued with pardonable pride, "I did it."

"What could you do?"

"Sometimes one thing, and sometimes another," said Dick. "I changed my business accordin' as I had to. Sometimes I was a newsboy, and diffused intelligence among the masses, as I heard somebody say once in a big speech he made in the Park. Them was the times when Horace Greeley and James Gordon Bennett made money."

"Through your enterprise?" suggested Frank.

"Yes," said Dick; "but I give it up after a while."

"What for?"

"Well, they didn't always put news enough in their papers, and people wouldn't buy 'em as fast as I wanted 'em to. So one mornin' I was stuck on a lot of *Heralds*, and I thought I'd make a sensation. So I called out 'GREAT NEWS! QUEEN VICTORIA ASSASSINATED!' All my *Heralds* went off like hot cakes, and I went off, too, but one of the gentlemen what got sold remembered me, and said he'd have me took up, and that's what made me change my business."

"That wasn't right, Dick," said Frank.

"I know it," said Dick; "but lots of boys does it."

"That don't make it any better."

"No," said Dick, "I was sort of ashamed at the time, 'specially about one poor old gentleman,—a Englishman he was. He couldn't help cryin' to think the queen was dead, and his hands shook when he handed me the money for the paper."

"What did you do next?"

"I went into the match business," said Dick; "but it was small sales and small profits. Most of the people I called on had just laid in a stock, and didn't want to buy. So one cold night, when I hadn't money enough to pay for a lodgin', I burned the last of my matches to keep me from freezin'. But it cost too much to get warm that way, and I couldn't keep it up."

"You've seen hard times, Dick," said Frank, compassionately.

"Yes," said Dick, "I've knowed what it was to be hungry and cold, with nothin' to eat or to warm me; but there's one thing I never could do," he added proudly.

"What's that?"

"I never stole," said Dick. "It's mean and I wouldn't do it."

"Were you ever tempted to?"

"Lots of times. Once I had been goin' round all day, and hadn't sold any matches, except three cents' worth early in the mornin'. With that I bought an apple, thinkin' I should get some more bimeby.[21] When evenin' come I was awful hungry. I went into a baker's just to look at the bread. It made me feel kind o' good just to look at the bread and cakes, and I thought maybe they would give me some. I asked 'em wouldn't they give me a loaf, and take their pay in matches. But they said they'd got enough matches to last three months; so there wasn't any chance for a trade. While I was standin' at the stove warmin' me, the baker went into a back room, and I felt so hungry I thought I would take just one loaf, and go off with it. There was such a big pile I don't think he'd have known it."

"But you didn't do it?"

"No, I didn't, and I was glad of it, for when the man came in ag'in, he said he wanted some one to carry some cake to a lady in St. Mark's Place. His boy was sick, and he hadn't no one to send; so he told me he'd give me ten cents if I would go. My business wasn't very pressin' just then, so I went, and when I come back, I took my pay in bread and cakes. Didn't they taste good, though?"

---

21 By and by, eventually.

"So you didn't stay long in the match business, Dick?"

"No, I couldn't sell enough to make it pay. Then there was some folks that wanted me to sell cheaper to them; so I couldn't make any profit. There was one old lady—she was rich, too, for she lived in a big brick house—beat me down so, that I didn't make no profit at all; but she wouldn't buy without, and I hadn't sold none that day; so I let her have them. I don't see why rich folks should be so hard upon a poor boy that wants to make a livin'."

"There's a good deal of meanness in the world, I'm afraid, Dick."

"If everybody was like you and your uncle," said Dick, "there would be some chance for poor people. If I was rich I'd try to help 'em along."

"Perhaps you will be rich sometime, Dick."

Dick shook his head.

"I'm afraid all my wallets will be like this," said Dick, indicating the one he had received from the dropper, "and will be full of papers what aint of no use to anybody except the owner."

"That depends very much on yourself, Dick," said Frank. "Stewart wasn't always rich, you know."

"Wasn't he?"

"When he first came to New York as a young man he was a teacher, and teachers are not generally very rich. At last he went into business, starting in a small way, and worked his way up by degrees. But there was one thing he determined in the beginning; that he would be strictly honorable in all his dealings, and never overreach any one for the sake of making money. If there was a chance for him, Dick, there is a chance for you."

"He knowed enough to be a teacher, and I'm awful ignorant," said Dick.

"But you needn't stay so."

"How can I help it?"

"Can't you learn at school?"

"I can't go to school 'cause I've got my livin' to earn. It wouldn't do me much good if I learned to read and write, and just as I'd got learned I starved to death."

"But are there no night-schools?"

"Yes."

"Why don't you go? I suppose you don't work in the evenings."

"I never cared much about it," said Dick, "and that's the truth. But since I've got to talkin' with you, I think more about it. I guess I'll begin to go."

"I wish you would, Dick. You'll make a smart man if you only get a little education."

"Do you think so?" asked Dick, doubtfully.

"I know so. A boy who has earned his own living ever since he was seven years old must have something in him. I feel very much interested in you, Dick. You've had a hard time of it so far in life, but I think better times are in store. I want you to do well, and I feel sure you can if you only try."

"You're a good fellow," said Dick, gratefully. "I'm afraid I'm a pretty rough customer, but I aint as bad as some. I mean to turn over a new leaf, and try to grow up 'spectable."

"There've been a great many boys begin as low down as you, Dick, that have grown up respectable and honored. But they had to work pretty hard for it."

"I'm willin' to work hard," said Dick. "And you must not only work hard, but work in the right way."

"What's the right way?"

"You began in the right way when you determined never to steal, or do anything mean or dishonorable, however strongly tempted to do so. That will make people have confidence in you when they come to know you. But, in order to succeed well, you must manage to get as good an education as you can. Until you do, you cannot get a position in an office or counting-room, even to run errands."

"That's so," said Dick, soberly. "I never thought how awful ignorant I was till now."

"That can be remedied with perseverance," said Frank. "A year will do a great deal for you."

"I'll go to work and see what I can do," said Dick, energetically.

Chapter IX

A Scene in a Third Avenue Car

THE boys had turned into Third Avenue, a long street, which, commencing just below the Cooper Institute, runs out to Harlem. A man came out of a side street, uttering at intervals a monotonous cry which sounded like "glass puddin'."

"Glass pudding!" repeated Frank, looking in surprised wonder at Dick. "What does he mean?"

"Perhaps you'd like some," said Dick.

"I never heard of it before."

"Suppose you ask him what he charges for his puddin'."

Frank looked more narrowly at the man, and soon concluded that he was a glazier.

"Oh, I understand," he said. "He means 'glass put in.'"

Frank's mistake was not a singular one. The monotonous cry of these men certainly sounds more like "glass puddin," than the words they intend to utter.

"Now," said Dick, "where shall we go?"

"I should like to see Central Park," said Frank. "Is it far off?"

"It is about a mile and a half from here," said Dick. "This is Twenty-ninth Street, and the Park begins at Fifty-ninth Street."

It may be explained, for the benefit of readers who have never visited New York, that about a mile from the City Hall the cross-streets begin to be numbered in regular order. There is a continuous line of houses as far as One Hundred and Thirtieth Street, where may be found the terminus of the Harlem line of horse-cars. When the entire island is laid out and settled, probably the numbers will reach two hundred or more. Central Park, which lies between Fifty-ninth Street on the south, and One Hundred and Tenth Street on the north, is true to its name, occupying about the centre of the island. The distance between two parallel streets is called a block, and twenty blocks make a mile. It will therefore be seen that Dick was exactly right, when he said they were a mile and a half from Central Park.

"That is too far to walk," said Frank.

" 'Twon't cost but six cents to ride," said Dick.

"You mean in the horse-cars?"

"Yes."

"All right then. We'll jump aboard the next car."

The Third Avenue and Harlem line of horse-cars is better patronized than any other in New York, though not much can be said for the cars, which are usually dirty and overcrowded. Still, when it is considered that only seven cents are charged for the entire distance to Harlem, about seven miles from the City Hall, the fare can hardly be complained of. But of course most of the profit is made from the way-passengers who only ride a short distance.

A car was at that moment approaching, but it seemed pretty crowded.

"Shall we take that, or wait for another?" asked Frank.

"The next'll most likely be as bad," said Dick.

The boys accordingly signalled to the conductor to stop, and got on the front platform. They were obliged to stand up till the car reached Fortieth Street, when so many of the passengers had got off that they obtained seats.

Frank sat down beside a middle-aged woman, or lady, as she probably called herself, whose sharp visage and thin lips did not seem to promise a very pleasant disposition. When the two gentlemen who sat beside her arose, she spread her skirts in the endeavor to fill two seats. Disregarding this, the boys sat down.

"There aint room for two," she said looking sourly at Frank.

"There were two here before."

"Well, there ought not to have been. Some people like to crowd in where they're not wanted."

"And some like to take up a double allowance of room," thought Frank; but he did not say so. He saw that the woman had a bad temper, and thought it wisest to say nothing.

Frank had never ridden up the city as far as this, and it was with much interest that he looked out of the car windows at the stores on either side. Third Avenue is a broad street, but in the character of its houses and stores it is quite inferior to Broadway, though better than some of the avenues further east. Fifth Avenue, as most of my readers already know, is the finest street in the city, being lined with splendid private residences, occupied by the wealthier classes. Many of the cross streets also boast houses which may be considered palaces, so elegant are they externally and internally. Frank caught glimpses of some of these as he was carried towards the Park.

After the first conversation, already mentioned, with the lady at his side, he supposed he should have nothing further to do with her. But in this he was mistaken. While he was busy looking out of the car window, she plunged her hand into her pocket in search of her purse, which she was unable to find. Instantly she jumped to the conclusion that it had been stolen, and her suspicions fastened upon Frank, with whom she was already provoked for "crowding her," as she termed it.

"Conductor!" she exclaimed in a sharp voice.

"What's wanted, ma'am?" returned that functionary.

"I want you to come here right off."

"What's the matter?"

"My purse has been stolen. There was four dollars and eighty cents in it. I know, because I counted it when I paid my fare."

"Who stole it?"

"That boy," she said pointing to Frank, who listened to the charge in the most intense astonishment. "He crowded in here on purpose to rob me, and I want you to search him right off."

"That's a lie!" exclaimed Dick, indignantly.

"Oh, you're in league with him, I dare say," said the woman spitefully. "You're as bad as he is, I'll be bound."

"You're a nice female, you be!" said Dick, ironically.

"Don't you dare to call me a female, sir," said the lady, furiously.

"Why, you aint a man in disguise, be you?" said Dick.

"You are very much mistaken, madam," said Frank, quietly. "The conductor may search me, if you desire it."

A charge of theft, made in a crowded car, of course made quite a sensation. Cautious passengers instinctively put their hands on their pockets, to make sure that they, too, had not been robbed. As for Frank, his face flushed, and he felt very indignant that he should even be suspected of so mean a crime. He had been carefully brought up, and been taught to regard stealing as low and wicked.

Dick, on the contrary, thought it a capital joke that such a charge should have been made against his companion. Though he had brought himself up, and known plenty of boys and men, too, who would steal, he had never done so himself. He thought it mean. But he could not be expected to regard it as Frank did. He had been too familiar with it in others to look upon it with horror.

Meanwhile the passengers rather sided with the boys. Appearances go a great ways, and Frank did not look like a thief.

"I think you must be mistaken, madam," said a gentleman sitting opposite. "The lad does not look as if he would steal."

"You can't tell by looks," said the lady, sourly. "They're deceitful; villains are generally well dressed."

"Be they?" said Dick. "You'd ought to see me with my Washington coat on. You'd think I was the biggest villain ever you saw."

"I've no doubt you are," said the lady, scowling in the direction of our hero.

"Thank you, ma'am," said Dick. "'Tisn't often I get such fine compliments."

"None of your impudence," said the lady, wrathfully. "I believe you're the worst of the two."

Meanwhile the car had been stopped.

"How long are we going to stop here?" demanded a passenger, impatiently. "I'm in a hurry, if none of the rest of you are."

"I want my pocket-book," said the lady, defiantly.

"Well, ma'am, I haven't got it, and I don't see as it's doing you any good detaining us all here."

"Conductor, will you call a policeman to search that young scamp?" continued the aggrieved lady.

"You don't expect I'm going to lose my money, and do nothing about it."

"I'll turn my pockets inside out if you want me to," said Frank, proudly. "There's no need of a policeman. The conductor, or any one else, may search me."

"Well, youngster," said the conductor, "if the lady agrees, I'll search you."

The lady signified her assent.

Frank accordingly turned his pockets inside out; but nothing was revealed except his own porte-monnaie and a penknife.

"Well, ma'am, are you satisfied?" asked the conductor.

"No, I aint," said she, decidedly.

"You don't think he's got it still?"

"No, but he's passed it over to his confederate, that boy there that's so full of impudence."

"That's me," said Dick, comically.

"He confesses it," said the lady; "I want him searched."

"All right," said Dick, "I'm ready for the operation, only as I've got valooable property about me be careful not to drop any of my Erie Bonds."

The conductor's hand forthwith dove into Dick's pocket, and drew out a rusty jack-knife, a battered cent, about fifty cents in change, and the capacious pocket-book which he had received from the swindler who was anxious to get back to his sick family in Boston.

"Is that yours, ma'am?" asked the conductor, holding up the wallet which excited some amazement, by its size, among the other passengers.

"It seems to me you carry a large pocket-book for a young man of your age," said the conductor.

"That's what I carry my cash and valooable papers in," said Dick.

"I suppose that isn't yours, ma'am," said the conductor, turning to the lady.

"No," said she, scornfully. "I wouldn't carry round such a great wallet at that. Most likely he's stolen it from somebody else."

"What a prime detective you'd be!" said Dick. "p'rhaps you know who I took it from."

"I don't know but my money's in it," said the lady, sharply. "Conductor, will you open that wallet, and see what there is in it?"

"Don't disturb the valooable papers," said Dick, in a tone of pretended anxiety.

The contents of the wallet excited some amusement among the passengers.

"There don't seem to be much money here," said the conductor, taking out a roll of tissue paper cut out in the shape of bills, and rolled up.

"No," said Dick. "Didn't I tell you them were papers of no valoo to anybody but the owner? If the lady'd like to borrow, I won't charge no interest."

"Where is my money, then?" said the lady, in some discomfiture. "I shouldn't wonder if one of the young scamps had thrown it out of the window."

"You'd better search your pocket once more," said the gentleman opposite. "I don't believe either of the boys is in fault. They don't look to me as if they would steal."

"Thank you, sir," said Frank.

The lady followed out the suggestion, and, plunging her hand once more into her pocket, drew out a small porte-monnaie. She hardly knew whether to be glad or sorry at this discovery. It placed her in rather an awkward position after the fuss she had made, and the detention to which she had subjected the passengers, now, as it proved, for nothing.

"Is that the pocket-book you thought stolen?" asked the conductor.

"Yes," said she, rather confusedly.

"Then you've been keeping me waiting all this time for nothing," he said, sharply. "I wish you'd take care to be sure next time before you make such a disturbance for nothing. I've lost five minutes, and shall not be on time."

"I can't help it," was the cross reply; "I didn't know it was in my pocket."

"It seems to me you owe an apology to the boys you accused of a theft which they have not committed," said the gentleman opposite.

"I shan't apologize to anybody," said the lady, whose temper was not of the best; "least of all to such whipper-snappers as they are."

"Thank you, ma'am," said Dick, comically, "your handsome apology is accepted. It aint of no consequence, only I didn't like to expose the contents of my valooable pocket-book, for fear it might excite the envy of some of my poor neighbors."

"You're a character," said the gentleman who had already spoken, with a smile.

"A bad character!" muttered the lady.

But it was quite evident that the sympathies of those present were against the lady, and on the side of the boys who had been falsely accused, while Dick's drollery had created considerable amusement.

The cars had now reached Fifty-ninth Street, the southern boundary of the Park, and here our hero and his companion got off.

"You'd better look out for pickpockets, my lad," said the conductor, pleasantly. "That big wallet of yours might prove a great temptation."

"That's so," said Dick. "That's the misfortin' of being rich. Astor and me don't sleep much for fear of burglars breakin' in and robbin' us of our valooable treasures. Sometimes I think I'll give all my money to an Orphan Asylum, and take it out in board. I guess I'd make money by the operation."

While Dick was speaking, the car rolled away, and the boys turned up Fifty-ninth Street, for two long blocks yet separated them from the Park.

Chapter X

Introduces a Victim of Misplaced Confidence

"WHAT a queer chap you are, Dick!" said Frank laughing. "You always seem to be in good spirits."

"No, I aint always. Sometimes I have the blues."

"When?"

"Well, once last winter it was awful cold, and there was big holes in my shoes, and my gloves and all my warm clothes was at the tailor's. I felt as if life was sort of tough, and I'd like it if some rich man would adopt me, and give me plenty to eat and drink and wear, without my havin' to look so sharp after it. Then agin' when I've seen boys with good homes, and fathers, and mothers, I've thought I'd like to have somebody to care for me."

Dick's tone changed as he said this, from his usual levity, and there was a touch of sadness in it. Frank, blessed with a good home and indulgent parents, could not help pitying the friendless boy who had found life such up-hill work.

"Don't say you have no one to care for you, Dick," he said, lightly laying his hand on Dick's shoulder. "I will care for you."

"Will you?"

"If you will let me."

"I wish you would," said Dick, earnestly. "I'd like to feel that I have one friend who cares for me."

Central Park was now before them, but it was far from presenting the appearance which it now exhibits. It had not been long since work had been commenced upon it, and it was still very rough and unfinished. A rough tract of land, two miles and a half from north to south, and a half a mile broad, very rocky in parts, was the material from which the Park Commissioners have made the present beautiful enclosure. There were no houses of good appearance near it, buildings being limited mainly to rude temporary huts used by the workmen who were employed in improving it. The time will undoubtedly come when the Park will be surrounded by elegant residences, and compare favorably in this respect with the most attractive parts of any city in the world. But at the time when Frank and Dick visited it, not much could be said in favor either of the Park or its neighborhood.

"If this is Central Park," said Frank, who naturally felt disappointed, "I don't think much of it. My father's got a large pasture that is much nicer."

"It'll look better some time," said Dick. "There aint much to see now but rocks. We will take a walk over it if you want to."

"No," said Frank, "I've seen as much of it as I want to. Besides, I feel tired."

"Then we'll go back. We can take the Sixth Avenue cars. They will bring us out at Vesey Street, just beside the Astor House."

"All right," said Frank. "That will be the best course. I hope," he added, laughing, "our agreeable lady friend won't be there. I don't care about being accused of *stealing* again."

"She was a tough one," said Dick. "Wouldn't she make a nice wife for a man that likes to live in hot water, and didn't mind bein' scalded two or three times a day?"

"Yes, I think she'd just suit him. Is that the right car, Dick?"

"Yes, jump in, and I'll follow."

The Sixth Avenue is lined with stores, many of them of very good appearance, and would make a very respectable principal street for a good-sized city. But it is only one of several long business streets which run up the island, and illustrate the extent and importance of the city to which they belong.

No incidents worth mentioning took place during their ride down town. In about three-quarters of an hour the boys got out of the car beside the Astor House.

"Are you goin' in now, Frank?" asked Dick.

"That depends upon whether you have anything else to show me."

"Wouldn't you like to go to Wall Street?"

"That's the street where there are so many bankers and brokers,—isn't it?"

"Yes, I s'pose you aint afraid of bulls and bears, —are you?"

"Bulls and bears?" repeated Frank, puzzled.

"Yes."

"What are they?"

"The bulls is what tries to make the stocks go up, and the bears is what try to growl 'em down."

"Oh, I see. Yes, I'd like to go."

Accordingly they walked down on the west side of Broadway as far as Trinity Church,[22] and then, crossing, entered a street not very wide or very long, but of very great importance. The reader would be astonished if he could know the amount of money involved in the transactions which take place in a single day in this street. It would be found that although Broadway is much greater in length, and lined with stores, it stands second to Wall Street in this respect.

"What is that large marble building?" asked Frank, pointing to a massive structure on the corner of Wall and Nassau Streets. It was in the form of a parallelogram, two hundred feet long by ninety wide, and about eighty feet in height, the ascent to the entrance being by eighteen granite steps.

"That's the Custom House,"[23] said Dick.

---

22 A large Episcopal church in lower Manhattan on Broadway. Newly renovated in 1846, the church's grand spire was the highest point in the city until the 1890s.

23 Located on Wall Street, the Custom House was a great building designed in the Greek Revival style, fronted by giant columns. It served as the central inspection and taxation point for the large shipping and merchant businesses that made use of New York City's extensive harbor.

"It looks like pictures I've seen of the Parthenon at Athens," said Frank, meditatively.
"Where's Athens?" asked Dick. "It aint in York State,—is it?"

"Not the Athens I mean, at any rate. It is in Greece, and was a famous city two thousand years ago."

"That's longer than I can remember," said Dick. "I can't remember distinctly more'n about a thousand years."

"What a chap you are, Dick! Do you know if we can go in?"

The boys ascertained, after a little inquiry, that they would be allowed to do so. They accordingly entered the Custom House and made their way up to the roof, from which they had a fine view of the harbor, the wharves crowded with shipping, and the neighboring shores of Long Island and New Jersey. Towards the north they looked down for many miles upon continuous lines of streets, and thousands of roofs, with here and there a church-spire rising above its neighbors. Dick had never before been up there, and he, as well as Frank, was interested in the grand view spread before them.

At length they descended, and were going down the granite steps on the outside of the building, when they were addressed by a young man, whose appearance is worth describing.

He was tall, and rather loosely put together, with small eyes and rather a prominent nose. His clothing had evidently not been furnished by a city tailor. He wore a blue coat with brass buttons, and pantaloons of rather scanty dimensions, which were several inches too short to cover his lower limbs. He held in his hand a piece of paper, and his countenance wore a look of mingled bewilderment and anxiety.

"Be they a-payin' out money inside there?" he asked, indicating the interior by a motion of his hand.

"I guess so," said Dick. "Are you a goin' in for some?"

"Wal, yes. I've got an order here for sixty dollars,—made a kind of speculation this morning."

"How was it?" asked Frank.

"Wal, you see I brought down some money to put in the bank, fifty dollars it was, and I hadn't justly made up my mind what bank to put it into, when a chap came up in a terrible hurry, and said it was very unfortunate, but the bank wasn't open, and he must have some money right off. He was obliged to go out of the city by the next train. I asked him how much he wanted. He said fifty dollars. I told him I'd got that, and he offered me a check on the bank for sixty, and I let him have it. I thought that was a pretty easy way to earn ten dollars, so I counted out the money and he went off. He told me I'd hear a bell ring when they began to pay out money. But I've waited most two hours, and I hain't heard it yet. I'd ought to be goin', for I told dad I'd be home to-night. Do you think I can get the money now?"

"Will you show me the check?" asked Frank, who had listened attentively to the countryman's story, and suspected that he had been made the victim of a swindler. It was made out upon the "Washington Bank," in the sum of sixty dollars, and was signed "Ephraim Smith."

"Washington Bank!" repeated Frank. "Dick, is there such a bank in the city?"

"Not as I knows on," said Dick. "Leastways I don't own any shares in it."

"Ain't this the Washington Bank?" asked the countryman, pointing to the building on the steps of which the three were now standing.

"No, it's the Custom House."

"And won't they give me any money for this?" asked the young man, the perspiration standing on his brow.

"I am afraid the man who gave it to you was a swindler," said Frank, gently.

"And won't I ever see my fifty dollars again?" asked the youth in agony.

"I am afraid not."

"What'll dad say?" ejaculated the miserable youth. "It makes me feel sick to think of it. I wish I had the feller here. I'd shake him out of his boots."

"What did he look like? I'll call a policeman and you shall describe him. Perhaps in that way you can get track of your money."

Dick called a policeman, who listened to the description, and recognized the operator as an experienced swindler. He assured the countryman that there was very little chance of his ever seeing his money again. The boys left the miserable youth loudly bewailing his bad luck, and proceeded on their way down the street.

"He's a baby," said Dick, contemptuously. "He'd ought to know how to take care of himself and his money. A feller has to look sharp in this city, or he'll lose his eye-teeth before he knows it."

"I suppose you never got swindled out of fifty dollars, Dick?"

"No, I don't carry no such small bills. I wish I did," he added.

"So do I, Dick. What's that building there at the end of the street?"

"That's the Wall-Street Ferry to Brooklyn."

"How long does it take to go across?"

"Not more'n five minutes."

"Suppose we just ride over and back."

"All right!" said Dick. "It's rather expensive; but if you don't mind, I don't."

"Why, how much does it cost?"

"Two cents apiece."

"I guess I can stand that. Let us go."

They passed the gate, paying the fare to a man who stood at the entrance, and were soon on the ferry-boat, bound for Brooklyn.

They had scarcely entered the boat, when Dick, grasping Frank by the arm, pointed to a man just outside of the gentlemen's cabin.

"Do you see that man, Frank?" he inquired.

"Yes, what of him?"

"He's the man that cheated the country chap out of his fifty dollars."

Chapter XI

Dick as a Detective

Dick's ready identification of the rogue who had cheated the countryman, surprised Frank.

"What makes you think it is he?" he asked.

"Because I've seen him before, and I know he's up to them kind of tricks. When I heard how he looked, I was sure I knowed him."

"Our recognizing him won't be of much use," said Frank. "It won't give back the countryman his money."

"I don't know," said Dick, thoughtfully. "Maybe I can get it."

"How?" asked Frank, incredulously.

"Wait a minute, and you'll see."

Dick left his companion, and went up to the man whom he suspected.

"Ephraim Smith," said Dick, in a low voice.

The man turned suddenly, and looked at Dick uneasily.

"What did you say?" he asked.

"I believe your name is Ephraim Smith," continued Dick.

"You're mistaken," said the man, and was about to move off.

"Stop a minute," said Dick. "Don't you keep your money in the Washington Bank?"

"I don't know any such bank. I'm in a hurry, young man, and I can't stop to answer any foolish questions."

The boat had by this time reached the Brooklyn pier, and Mr. Ephraim Smith seemed in a hurry to land.

"Look here," said Dick, significantly; "you'd better not go on shore unless you want to jump into the arms of a policeman."

"What do you mean?" asked the man, startled.

"That little affair of yours is known to the police," said Dick; "about how you got fifty dollars out of a greenhorn on a false check, and it mayn't be safe for you to go ashore."

"I don't know what you're talking about," said the swindler with affected boldness, though Dick could see that he was ill at ease.

"Yes you do," said Dick. "There isn't but one thing to do. Just give me back that money, and I'll see that you're not touched. If you don't, I'll give you up to the first p'liceman we meet."

Dick looked so determined, and spoke so confidently, that the other, overcome by his fears, no longer hesitated, but passed a roll of bills to Dick and hastily left the boat.

All this Frank witnessed with great amazement, not understanding what influence Dick could have obtained over the swindler sufficient to compel restitution.

"How did you do it?" he asked eagerly.

"I told him I'd exert my influence with the president to have him tried by *habeas corpus,*" said Dick.

"And of course that frightened him. But tell me, without joking, how you managed."

Dick gave a truthful account of what occurred, and then said, "Now we'll go back and carry the money."

"Suppose we don't find the poor countryman?"

"Then the p'lice will take care of it."

They remained on board the boat, and in five minutes were again in New York. Going up Wall Street, they met the countryman a little distance from the Custom House. His face was marked with the traces of deep anguish; but in his case even grief could not subdue the cravings of appetite. He had purchased some cakes of one of the old women who spread out for the benefit of passers-by an array of apples and seed-cakes, and was munching them with melancholy satisfaction.

"Hilloa!" said Dick. "Have you found your money?"

"No," ejaculated the young man, with a convulsive gasp. "I shan't ever see it again. The mean skunk's cheated me out of it. Consarn his picter! It took me most six months to save it up. I was workin' for Deacon Pinkham in our place. Oh, I wish I'd never come to New York! The deacon, he told me he'd keep it for me; but I wanted to put it in the bank, and now it's all gone, boo hoo!"

And the miserable youth, having despatched his cakes, was so overcome by the thought of his loss that he burst into tears.

"I say," said Dick, "dry up, and see what I've got here."

The youth no sooner saw the roll of bills, and comprehended that it was indeed his lost treasure, than from the depths of anguish he was exalted to the most ecstatic joy. He seized Dick's hand, and shook it with so much energy that our hero began to feel rather alarmed for its safety.

"'Pears to me you take my arm for a pump-handle," said he. "Couldn't you show your gratitood some other way? It's just possible I may want to use my arm ag'in some time." .

The young man desisted, but invited Dick most cordially to come up and stop a week with him at his country home, assuring him that he wouldn't charge him anything for board.

"All right!" said Dick. "If you don't mind I'll bring my wife along, too. She's delicate, and the country air might do her good."

Jonathan stared at him in amazement, uncertain whether to credit the fact of his marriage. Dick walked on with Frank, leaving him in an apparent state of stupefaction, and it is possible that he has not yet settled the affair to his satisfaction.

"Now," said Frank, "I think I'll go back to the Astor House. Uncle has probably got through his business and returned."

"All right," said Dick.

The two boys walked up to Broadway, just where the tall steeple of Trinity faces the street of bankers and brokers, and walked leisurely to the hotel. When they arrived at the Astor House, Dick said, "Good-by, Frank."

"Not yet," said Frank; "I want you to come in with me."

Dick followed his young patron up the steps. Frank went to the reading-room, where, as he had thought probable, he found his uncle already arrived, and reading a copy of "The Evening Post," which he had just purchased outside.

"Well, boys," he said, looking up, "have you had a pleasant jaunt?"

"Yes, sir," said Frank. "Dick's a capital guide."

"So this is Dick," said Mr. Whitney, surveying him with a smile. "Upon my word, I should hardly have known him. I must congratulate him on his improved appearance."

"Frank's been very kind to me," said Dick, who, rough street-boy as he was, had a heart easily touched by kindness, of which he had never experienced much. "He's a tip-top fellow."

"I believe he is a good boy," said Mr. Whitney. "I hope, my lad, you will prosper and rise in the world. You know in this free country poverty in early life is no bar to a man's advancement. I haven't risen very high myself," he added, with a smile, "but have met with moderate success in life; yet there was a time when I was as poor as you."

"Were you, sir?" asked Dick, eagerly.

"Yes, my boy, I have known the time when I have been obliged to go without my dinner because I didn't have enough money to pay for it."

"How did you get up in the world?" asked Dick, anxiously.

"I entered a printing-office as an apprentice, and worked for some years. Then my eyes gave out and I was obliged to give that up. Not knowing what else to do, I went into the country, and worked on a farm. After a while I was lucky enough to invent a machine, which has brought me in a great deal of money. But there was one thing I got while I was in the printing-office which I value more than money."

"What was that, sir?"

"A taste for reading and study. During my leisure hours I improved myself by study, and acquired a large part of the knowledge which I now possess. Indeed, it was one of my books that first put me on the track of the invention, which I afterwards made. So you see, my lad, that my studious habits paid me in money, as well as in another way."

"I'm awful ignorant," said Dick, soberly.

"But you are young, and, I judge, a smart boy. If you try to learn, you can, and if you ever expect to do anything in the world, you must know something of books."

"I will," said Dick, resolutely. "I aint always goin' to black boots for a livin'."

"All labor is respectable, my lad, and you have no cause to be ashamed of any honest business; yet when you can get something to do that promises better for your future prospects, I advise you to do so. Till then earn your living in the way you are accustomed to, avoid extravagance, and save up a little money if you can."

"Thank you for your advice," said our hero. "There aint many that takes an interest in Ragged Dick."

"So that's your name," said Mr. Whitney. "If I judge you rightly, it won't be long before you change it. Save your money, my lad, buy books, and determine to be somebody, and you may yet fill an honorable position."

"I'll try," said Dick. "Good-night, sir."

"Wait a minute, Dick," said Frank. "Your blacking-box and old clothes are upstairs. You may want them."

"In course," said Dick. "I couldn't get along without my best clothes, and my stock in trade."

"You may go up to the room with him, Frank," said Mr. Whitney. "The clerk will give you the key. I want to see you, Dick, before you go."

"Yes, sir," said Dick.

"Where are you going to sleep to-night, Dick?" asked Frank, as they went upstairs together.

"P'r'aps at the Fifth Avenue Hotel—on the outside," said Dick.

"Haven't you any place to sleep, then?"

"I slept in a box, last night."

"In a box?"

"Yes, on Spruce Street."

"Poor fellow!" said Frank, compassionately.

"Oh, 'twas a bully bed—full of straw! I slept like a top."

"Don't you earn enough to pay for a room, Dick?"

"Yes," said Dick; "only I spend my money foolish, goin' to the Old Bowery, and Tony Pastor's, and sometimes gamblin' in Baxter Street."

"You won't gamble any more,—will you, Dick?" said Frank, laying his hand persuasively on his companion's shoulder.

"No, I won't," said Dick.

"You'll promise?"

"Yes, and I'll keep it. You're a good feller. I wish you was goin' to be in New York."

"I am going to a boarding-school in Connecticut. The name of the town is Barnton. Will you write to me, Dick?"

"My writing would look like hens' tracks," said our hero.

"Never mind. I want you to write. When you write you can tell me how to direct, and I will send you a letter."

"I wish you would," said Dick. "I wish I was more like you."

"I hope you will make a much better boy, Dick. Now we'll go in to my uncle. He wishes to see you before you go."

They went into the reading-room. Dick had wrapped up his blacking-brush in a newspaper with which Frank had supplied him, feeling that a guest of the Astor House should hardly be seen coming out of the hotel displaying such a professional sign.

"Uncle, Dick's ready to go," said Frank.

"Good-by, my lad," said Mr. Whitney. "I hope to hear good accounts of you sometime. Don't forget what I have told you. Remember that your future position depends mainly upon yourself, and that it will be high or low as you choose to make it."

He held out his hand, in which was a five-dollar bill. Dick shrunk back.

"I don't like to take it," he said. "I haven't earned it."

"Perhaps not," said Mr. Whitney; "but I give it to you because I remember my own friendless youth. I hope it may be of service to you. Sometime when you are a prosperous man, you can repay it in the form of aid to some poor boy, who is struggling upward as you are now."

"I will, sir," said Dick, manfully.

He no longer refused the money, but took it gratefully, and, bidding Frank and his uncle good-by, went out into the street. A feeling of loneliness came over him as he left the presence of Frank, for whom he had formed a strong attachment in the few hours he had known him.

Chapter XII

Dick Hires a Room on Mott Street

GOING out into the fresh air Dick felt the pangs of hunger. He accordingly went to a restaurant and got a substantial supper. Perhaps it was the new clothes he wore, which made him feel a little more aristocratic. At all events, instead of patronizing the cheap restaurant where he usually procured his meals, he went into the refectory attached to Lovejoy's Hotel, where the prices were higher and the company more select. In his ordinary dress, Dick would have been excluded, but now he had the appearance of a very respectable, gentlemanly boy, whose presence would not discredit any establishment. His orders were therefore received with attention by the waiter and in due time a good supper was placed before him.

"I wish I could come here every day," thought Dick. "It seems kind o' nice and 'spectable, side of the other place. There's a gent at that other table that I've shined boots for more'n once. He don't know me in my new clothes. Guess he don't know his boot-black patronizes the same establishment."

His supper over, Dick went up to the desk, and, presenting his check, tendered in payment his five-dollar bill, as if it were one of a large number which he possessed. Receiving back his change he went out into the street.

Two questions now arose: How should he spend the evening, and where should he pass the night? Yesterday, with such a sum of money in his possession, he would have answered both questions readily. For the evening, he would have passed it at the Old Bowery, and gone to sleep in any out-of-the-way place that offered. But he had turned over a new leaf, or resolved to do so. He meant to save his money for some useful purpose,—to aid his advancement in the world. So he could not afford the theatre. Besides, with his new clothes, he was unwilling to pass the night out of doors.

"I should spile 'em," he thought, "and that wouldn't pay."

So he determined to hunt up a room which he could occupy regularly, and consider as his own, where he could sleep nights, instead of depending on boxes and old wagons for a chance shelter. This would be the first step towards respectability, and Dick determined to take it.

He accordingly passed through the City Hall Park, and walked leisurely up Centre Street.

He decided that it would hardly be advisable for him to seek lodgings in Fifth Avenue, although his present cash capital consisted of nearly five dollars in money, besides the valuable papers contained in his wallet. Besides, he had reason to doubt whether any in his line of business lived on that aristocratic street. He took his way to Mott Street, which is considerably less pretentious, and halted in front of a shabby brick lodging-house kept by a Mrs. Mooney, with whose son Tom, Dick was acquainted.

Dick rang the bell, which sent back a shrill metallic response.

The door was opened by a slatternly servant, who looked at him inquiringly, and not without curiosity. It must be remembered that Dick was well dressed, and that nothing in his appearance bespoke his occupation. Being naturally a good-looking boy, he might readily be mistaken for a gentleman's son.

"Well, Queen Victoria," said Dick, "is your missus at home?"

"My name's Bridget," said the girl.

"Oh, indeed!" said Dick. "You looked so much like the queen's picter what she gave me last Christmas in exchange for mine, that I couldn't help calling you by her name."

"Oh, go along wid ye!" said Bridget. "It's makin' fun ye are."

"If you don't believe me," said Dick, gravely, "all you've got to do is to ask my partic'lar friend, the Duke of Newcastle."

"Bridget!" called a shrill voice from the basement.

"The missus is calling me," said Bridget, hurriedly. "I'll tell her ye want her."

"All right!" said Dick.

The servant descended into the lower regions, and in a short time a stout, red-faced woman appeared on the scene.

"Well, sir, what's your wish?" she asked.

"Have you got a room to let?" asked Dick.

"Is it for yourself you ask?" questioned the woman, in some surprise.

Dick answered in the affirmative.

"I haven't got any very good rooms vacant. There's a small room in the third story."

"I'd like to see it," said Dick.

"I don't know as it would be good enough for you," said the woman, with a glance at Dick's clothes.

"I aint very partic'lar about accommodations," said our hero. "I guess I'll look at it."

Dick followed the landlady up two narrow staircases, uncarpeted and dirty, to the third landing, where he was ushered into a room about ten feet square. It could not be considered a very desirable apartment. It had once been covered with an oilcloth carpet, but this was now very ragged, and looked worse than none. There was a single bed in the corner, covered with an indiscriminate heap of bed-clothing, rumpled and not over-clean. There was a bureau, with the veneering scratched and in some parts stripped off, and a small glass, eight inches by ten, cracked across the middle; also two chairs in rather a disjointed condition. Judging from Dick's appearance, Mrs. Mooney thought he would turn from it in disdain.

But it must be remembered that Dick's past experience had not been of a character to make him fastidious. In comparison with a box, or an empty wagon, even this little room seemed comfortable. He decided to hire it if the rent proved reasonable.

"Well, what's the tax?" asked Dick.

"I ought to have a dollar a week," said Mrs. Mooney, hesitatingly.

"Say seventy-five cents, and I'll take it," said Dick.

"Every week in advance?"

"Yes."

"Well, as times is hard, and I can't afford to keep it empty, you may have it. When will you come?"

"To-night," said Dick.

"It aint lookin' very neat. I don't know as I can fix it up to-night."

"Well, I'll sleep here to-night, and you can fix it up to-morrow."

"I hope you'll excuse the looks. I'm a lone woman, and my help is so shiftless, I have to look after everything myself; so I can't keep things as straight as I want to."

"All right!" said Dick.

"Can you pay me the first week in advance?" asked the landlady, cautiously.

Dick responded by drawing seventy-five cents from his pocket, and placing it in her hand.

"What's your business, sir, if I may inquire?" said Mrs. Mooney.

"Oh, I'm professional!" said Dick.

"Indeed!" said the landlady, who did not feel much enlightened by this answer.

"How's Tom?" asked Dick.

"Do you know my Tom?" said Mrs. Mooney in surprise. "He's gone to sea,—to Californy. He went last week."

"Did he?" said Dick. "Yes, I knew him."

Mrs. Mooney looked upon her new lodger with increased favor, on finding that he was acquainted with her son, who, by the way, was one of the worst young scamps in Mott Street, which is saying considerable.

"I'll bring over my baggage from the Astor House this evening," said Dick in a tone of importance.

"From the Astor House!" repeated Mrs. Mooney, in fresh amazement.

"Yes, I've been stoppin' there a short time with some friends," said Dick.

Mrs. Mooney might be excused for a little amazement at finding that a guest from the Astor House was about to become one of her lodgers—such transfers not being common.

"Did you say you was purfessional?" she asked.

"Yes, ma'am," said Dick, politely.

"You aint a—a—" Mrs. Mooney paused, uncertain what conjecture to hazard.

"Oh, no, nothing of the sort," said Dick, promptly. "How could you think so, Mrs. Mooney?"

"No offense, sir," said the landlady, more perplexed than ever.

"Certainly not," said our hero. "But you must excuse me now, Mrs. Mooney, as I have business of great importance to attend to."

"You'll come round this evening?"

Dick answered in the affirmative, and turned away.

"I wonder what he is!" thought the landlady, following him with her eyes as he crossed the street. "He's got good clothes on, but he don't seem very particular about his room. Well; I've got all my rooms full now. That's one comfort."

Dick felt more comfortable now that he had taken the decisive step of hiring a lodging, and paying a week's rent in advance. For seven nights he was sure of a shelter and a bed to sleep in. The thought was a pleasant one to our young vagrant, who hitherto had seldom known when he rose in the morning where he should find a resting-place at night.

"I must bring my traps round," said Dick to himself. "I guess I'll go to bed early to-night. It'll feel kinder good to sleep in a reg'lar bed. Boxes is rather hard to the back, and aint comfortable in case of rain. I wonder what Johnny Nolan would say if he knew I'd got a room of my own."

Chapter XIII

Micky Maguire

ABOUT nine o'clock Dick sought his new lodgings. In his hands he carried his professional wardrobe, namely, the clothes which he had worn at the commencement of the day, and the implements of his business. These he stowed away in the bureau drawers, and by the light of a flickering candle took off his clothes and went to bed. Dick had a good digestion and a reasonably good conscience; consequently he was a good sleeper. Perhaps, too, the soft feather bed conduced to slumber. At any rate his eyes were soon closed, and he did not awake until half-past six the next morning.

He lifted himself on his elbow, and stared around him in transient bewilderment.

"Blest if I hadn't forgot where I was," he said to himself. "So this is my room, is it? Well, it seems kind of 'spectable to have a room and a bed to sleep in. I'd orter be able to afford seventy-five cents a week. I've throwed away more money than that in one evenin'. There aint no reason why I shouldn't live 'spectable. I wish I knowed as much as Frank. He's a tip-top feller. Nobody ever cared enough for me before to give me good advice. It was kicks, and cuffs, and swearin' at me all the time. I'd like to show him I can do something."

While Dick was indulging in these reflections, he had risen from bed, and, finding an accession to the furniture of his room, in the shape of an ancient wash-stand bearing a cracked bowl and broken pitcher, indulged himself in the rather unusual ceremony of a good wash. On the whole, Dick preferred to be clean, but it was not always easy to gratify his desire. Lodging in the street as he had been accustomed to do, he had had no opportunity to perform his toilet in the customary manner. Even now he found himself unable to arrange his dishevelled locks, having neither comb nor brush. He determined to purchase a comb, at least, as soon as possible, and a brush too, if he could get one cheap. Meanwhile he combed his hair with his fingers as well as he could, though the result was not quite so satisfactory as it might have been.

A question now came up for consideration. For the first time in his life Dick possessed two suits of clothes. Should he put on the clothes Frank had given him, or resume his old rags?

Now, twenty-four hours before, at the time Dick was introduced to the reader's notice, no one could have been less fastidious as to his clothing than he. Indeed, he had rather a contempt for good clothes, or at least he thought so. But now, as he surveyed the ragged and dirty coat and the patched pants, Dick felt ashamed of them. He was unwilling to appear in the streets with them. Yet, if he went to work in his new suit, he was in danger of spoiling it, and he might not have it in his power to purchase a new one. Economy dictated a return to the old garments. Dick tried them on, and surveyed himself in the cracked glass; but the reflection did not please him.

"They don't look 'spectable," he decided; and forthwith taking them off again, he put on the new suit of the day before.

"I must try to earn a little more," he thought, "to pay for my room, and to buy some new clo'es when these is wore out."

He opened the door of his chamber, and went downstairs and into the street, carrying his blacking-box with him.

It was Dick's custom to commence his business before breakfast; generally it must be owned, because he began the day penniless, and must earn his meal before he ate it. To-day it was different. He had four dollars left in his pocket-book; but this he had previously determined not to touch. In fact he had formed the ambitious design of starting an account at a savings' bank, in order to have something to fall back upon in case of sickness or any other emergency, or at any rate as a reserve fund to expend in clothing or other necessary articles when he required them. Hitherto he had been content to live on from day to day without a penny ahead; but the new vision of respectability which now floated before Dick's mind, owing to his recent acquaintance with Frank, was beginning to exercise a powerful effect upon him.

In Dick's profession as in others there are lucky days, when everything seems to flow prosperously. As if to encourage him in his new-born resolution, our hero obtained no less than six jobs in the course of an hour and a half. This gave him sixty cents, quite abundant to purchase his breakfast, and a comb besides. His exertions made him hungry, and, entering a small eating-house he ordered a cup of coffee and a beefsteak. To this he added a couple of rolls. This was quite a luxurious breakfast for Dick, and more expensive than he was accustomed to indulge himself with. To gratify the curiosity of my young readers, I will put down the items with their cost, —

Coffee,	5 cts.
Beefsteak,	15
A couple of rolls,	5
	—— 25 cts.

It will thus be seen that our hero had expended nearly one-half of his morning's earnings. Some days he had been compelled to breakfast on five cents, and then he was forced to content himself with a couple of apples, or cakes. But a good breakfast is a good preparation for a busy day, and Dick sallied forth from the restaurant lively and alert, ready to do a good stroke of business.

Dick's change of costume was liable to lead to one result of which he had not thought. His brother boot-blacks might think he had grown aristocratic, and was putting on airs,—that, in fact, he was getting above his business, and desirous to outshine his associates. Dick had not dreamed of this, because in fact, in spite of his new-born ambition, he entertained no such feelings. There was nothing of what boys call "big-feeling" about him. He was a thorough democrat, using the word not politically, but in its proper sense, and was disposed to fraternize with all whom he styled "good fellows," without regard to their position. It may seem a little unnecessary to some of my readers to make this explanation; but they must remember that pride and "big-feeling" are confined to no age or class, but may be found in boys as well as men, and in boot-blacks as well as those of a higher rank.

The morning being a busy time with the bootblacks, Dick's changed appearance had not as yet attracted much attention. But when business slackened a little, our hero was destined to be reminded of it.

Among the down-town boot-blacks was one hailing from the Five Points,—a stout, red-haired, freckled-faced boy of fourteen, bearing the name of Micky Maguire. This boy, by his boldness and recklessness, as well as by his personal strength, which was considerable, had acquired an ascendency among his fellow professionals, and had a gang of subservient followers, whom he led on to acts of ruffianism, not unfrequently terminating in a month or two at Blackwell's Island.[24] Micky himself had served two terms there; but the confinement appeared to have had very little effect in amending his conduct, except, perhaps, in making him a little more cautious about an encounter with the "copps," as the members of the city police are, for some unknown reason, styled among the Five-Point[25] boys.

Now Micky was proud of his strength, and of the position of leader which it had secured him. Moreover he was democratic in his tastes, and had a jealous hatred of those who wore good clothes and kept their faces clean. He called it putting on airs, and resented the implied superiority. If he had been fifteen years older, and had a trifle more education, he would have interested himself in politics, and been prominent at ward meetings, and a terror to respectable voters on election day. As it was, he contented himself with being the leader of a gang of young ruffians, over whom he wielded a despotic power.

Now it is only justice to Dick to say that, so far as wearing good clothes was concerned, he had never hitherto offended the eyes of Micky Maguire. Indeed, they generally looked as if they patronized the same clothing establishment. On this particular morning it chanced that Micky had not been very fortunate in a business way, and, as a natural consequence, his temper, never very amiable, was somewhat ruffled by the fact. He had had a very frugal breakfast,—not because he felt abstemious, but owing to the low state of his finances. He was walking along with one of his particular friends, a boy nicknamed Limpy Jim, so called from a slight peculiarity in his walk, when all at once he espied our friend Dick in his new suit.

"My eyes!" he exclaimed, in astonishment; "Jim, just look at Ragged Dick. He's come into a fortun', and turned gentleman. See his new clothes."

"So he has," said Jim. "Where'd he get 'em, I wonder?"

"Hooked 'em, p'r'aps. Let's go and stir him up a little. We don't want no gentlemen on our beat. So he's puttin' on airs,—is he? I'll give him a lesson."

So saying the two boys walked up to our hero, who had not observed them, his back being turned, and Micky Maguire gave him a smart slap on the shoulder.

Dick turned round quickly.

---

24 A narrow island in New York City's East River, Blackwell's Island contained a number of buildings including a prison, as well as an insane asylum and a hospital.

25 The Five Points area of lower Manhattan was notorious for its high crime rates and vicious criminal activity.

Chapter XIV

A Battle and a Victory

"WHAT'S that for?" demanded Dick, turning round to see who had struck him.

"You're gettin' mighty fine!" said Micky Maguire, surveying Dick's new clothes with a scornful air.

There was something in his words and tone, which Dick, who was disposed to stand up for his dignity, did not at all relish.

"Well, what's the odds if I am?" he retorted. "Does it hurt you any?"

"See him put on airs, Jim," said Micky, turning to his companion. "Where'd you get them clo'es?"

"Never mind where I got 'em. Maybe the Prince of Wales gave 'em to me."

"Hear him, now, Jim," said Micky. "Most likely he stole 'em."

"Stealin' aint in *my* line."

It might have been unconscious the emphasis which Dick placed on the word "my." At any rate Micky chose to take offence.

"Do you mean to say *I* steal?" he demanded, doubling up his fist, and advancing towards Dick in a threatening manner.

"I don't say anything about it," answered Dick, by no means alarmed at this hostile demonstration. "I know you've been to the island twice. P'r'aps 'twas to make a visit along of the Mayor and Aldermen. Maybe you was a innocent victim of oppression. I aint a goin' to say."

Mickey's freckled face grew red with wrath, for Dick had only stated the truth.

"Do you mean to insult me?" he demanded shaking the fist already doubled up in Dick's face. "Maybe you want a lickin'?"

"I aint partic'larly anxious to get one," said Dick, coolly. "They don't agree with my constitution which is nat'rally delicate. I'd rather have a good dinner than a lickin' any time."

"You're afraid," sneered Micky. "Isn't he, Jim?"

"In course he is."

"P'r'aps I am," said Dick, composedly, "but it don't trouble me much."

"Do you want to fight?" demanded Micky, encouraged by Dick's quietness, fancying he was afraid to encounter him.

"No, I don't," said Dick. "I aint fond of fightin'. It's a very poor amusement, and very bad for the complexion, 'specially for the eyes and nose, which is apt to run red, white, and blue."

Micky misunderstood Dick, and judged from the tenor of his speech that he would be an easy victim. As he knew, Dick very seldom was concerned in any street fight,—not from cowardice, as he imagined, but because he had too much good sense to do so. Being quarrelsome, like all bullies, and supposing that he was more than a match for our hero, being about two inches taller, he could no longer resist an inclination to assault him, and tried to plant a blow in Dick's face which would have hurt him considerably if he had not drawn back just in time.

Now, though Dick was far from quarrelsome, he was ready to defend himself on all occasions, and it was too much to expect that he would stand quiet and allow himself to be beaten.

He dropped his blacking-box on the instant, and returned Micky's blow with such good effect that the young bully staggered back, and would have fallen, if he had not been propped up by his confederate, Limpy Jim.

"Go in, Micky!" shouted the latter, who was rather a coward on his own account, but liked to see others fight. "Polish him off, that's a good feller."

Micky was now boiling over with rage and fury, and required no urging. He was fully determined to make a terrible example of poor Dick. He threw himself upon him, and strove to bear him to the ground; but Dick, avoiding a close hug, in which he might possibly have got the worst of it, by an adroit movement, tripped up his antagonist, and stretched him on the sidewalk.

"Hit him, Jim!" exclaimed Micky, furiously.

Limpy Jim did not seem inclined to obey orders. There was a quiet strength and coolness about Dick, which alarmed him. He preferred that Micky should incur all the risks of battle, and accordingly set himself to raising his fallen comrade.

"Come, Micky," said Dick, quietly, "you'd better give it up. I wouldn't have touched you if you hadn't hit me first. I don't want to fight. It's low business."

"You're afraid of hurtin' your clo'es," said Micky, with a sneer.

"Maybe I am," said Dick. "I hope I haven't hurt yours."

Micky's answer to this was another attack, as violent and impetuous as the first. But his fury was in the way. He struck wildly, not measuring his blows, and Dick had no difficulty in turning aside, so that his antagonist's blow fell upon the empty air, and his momentum was such that he nearly fell forward headlong. Dick might readily have taken advantage of his unsteadiness, and knocked him down; but he was not vindictive, and chose to act on the defensive, except when he could not avoid it.

Recovering himself, Micky saw that Dick was a more formidable antagonist than he had supposed, and was meditating another assault, better planned, which by its impetuosity might bear our hero to the ground. But there was an unlooked-for interference.

"Look out for the 'copp,'" said Jim, in a low voice.

Micky turned round and saw a tall policeman heading towards him, and thought it might be prudent to suspend hostilities. He accordingly picked up his blacking-box, and hitching up his pants, walked off, attended by Limpy Jim.

"What's that chap been doing?" asked the policeman of Dick.

"He was amoosin' himself by pitchin' into me," replied Dick.

"What for?"

"He didn't like it 'cause I patronized a different tailor from him."

"Well, it seems to me you *are* dressed pretty smart for a boot-black," said the policeman.

"I wish I wasn't a boot-black," said Dick.

"Never mind, my lad. It's an honest business," said the policeman, who was a sensible man and a worthy citizen. "It's an honest business. Stick to it till you get something better."

"I mean to," said Dick. "It aint easy to get out of it, as the prisoner remarked, when he was asked how he liked his residence."

"I hope you don't speak from experience."

"No," said Dick; "I don't mean to get into prison if I can help it."

"Do you see that gentleman over there?" asked the officer, pointing to a well-dressed man who was walking on the other side of the street.

"Yes."

"Well, he was once a newsboy."

"And what is he now?"

"He keeps a bookstore, and is quite prosperous."

Dick looked at the gentleman with interest, wondering if he should look as respectable when he was a grown man.

It will be seen that Dick was getting ambitious. Hitherto he had thought very little of the future, but was content to get along as he could, dining as well as his means would allow, and spending the evenings in the pit of the Old Bowery, eating peanuts between the acts if he was prosperous, and if unlucky supping on dry bread or an apple, and sleeping in an old box or a wagon. Now, for the first time, he began to reflect that he could not black boots all his life. In seven years he would be a man, and, since his meeting with Frank, he felt he would like to be a respectable man. He could see and appreciate the difference between Frank and such a boy as Micky Maguire, and it was not strange that he preferred the society of the former.

In the course of the next morning, in pursuance of his new resolutions for the future, he called at a savings bank, and held out four dollars in bills besides another dollar in change. There was a high railing, and a number of clerks busily writing at desks behind it. Dick, never having been in a bank before, did not know where to go. He went, by mistake, to the desk where money was paid out.

"Where's your book?" asked the clerk.

"I haven't got any."

"Have you any money deposited here?"

"No, sir, I want to leave some here."

"Then go to the next desk."

Dick followed directions, and presented himself before an elderly man with gray hair, who looked at him over the rims of his spectacles.

"I want you to keep that for me," said Dick, awkwardly emptying his money out on the desk.

"How much is there?"

"Five dollars."

"Have you got an account here?"

"No, sir."

"Of course you can write?"

The "of course" was said on account of Dick's neat dress.

"Have I got to do any writing?" asked our hero, a little embarrassed.

"We want you to sign your name in this book," and the old gentleman shoved round a large folio volume containing the names of depositors.

Dick surveyed the book with some awe.

"I aint much on writin'," he said.

"Very well, write as well as you can."

The pen was put into Dick's hand, and, after dipping it in the inkstand, he succeeded after a hard effort, accompanied by many contortions of the face, in inscribing upon the book of the bank the name

DICK HUNTER.

"Dick!—that means Richard, I suppose," said the bank officer, who had some difficulty in making out the signature.

"No; Ragged Dick is what folks call me."

"You don't look very ragged."

"No, I've left my rags to home. They might get wore out if I used 'em too common."

"Well, my lad, I'll make out a book in the name of Dick Hunter, since you seem to prefer Dick to Richard. I hope you will save up your money and deposit more with us."

Our hero took his bank-book, and gazed on the entry "Five Dollars" with a new sense of importance. He had been accustomed to joke about Erie shares, but now, for the first time, he felt himself a capitalist; on a small scale, to be sure, but still it was no small thing for Dick to have five dollars which he could call his own. He firmly determined that he would lay by every cent he could spare from his earnings towards the fund he hoped to accumulate.

But Dick was too sensible not to know that there was something more than money needed to win a respectable position in the world. He felt that he was very ignorant. Of reading and writing he only knew the rudiments, and that, with a slight acquaintance with arithmetic, was all he did know of books. Dick knew he must study hard, and he dreaded it. He looked upon learning as attended with greater difficulties than it really possesses. But Dick had good pluck. He meant to learn, nevertheless, and resolved to buy a book with his first spare earnings.

When Dick went home at night he locked up his bank-book in one of the drawers of the bureau. It was wonderful how much more independent he felt whenever he reflected upon the contents of that drawer, and with what an important air of joint ownership he regarded the bank building in which his small savings were deposited.

Chapter XV

Dick Secures a Tutor

THE next morning Dick was unusually successful, having plenty to do, and receiving for one job twenty-five cents,—the gentleman refusing to take change. Then flashed upon Dick's mind the thought that he had not yet returned the change due to the gentleman whose boots he had blacked on the morning of his introduction to the reader.

"What'll he think of me?" said Dick to himself. "I hope he won't think I'm mean enough to keep the money."

Now Dick was scrupulously honest, and though the temptation to be otherwise had often been strong, he had always resisted it. He was not willing on any account to keep money which did not belong to him, and he immediately started for 125 Fulton Street (the address which had been given him) where he found Mr. Greyson's name on the door of an office on the first floor.

The door being open, Dick walked in.

"Is Mr. Greyson in?" he asked of a clerk who sat on a high stool before a desk.

"Not just now. He'll be in soon. Will you wait?"

"Yes," said Dick.

"Very well; take a seat then."

Dick sat down and took up the morning "Tribune," but presently came to a word of four syllables, which he pronounced to himself a "sticker," and laid it down. But he had not long to wait, for five minutes later Mr. Greyson entered.

"Did you wish to speak to me, my lad?" said he to Dick, whom in his new clothes he did not recognize.

"Yes, sir," said Dick. "I owe you some money."

"Indeed!" said Mr. Greyson, pleasantly; "that's an agreeable surprise. I didn't know but you had come for some. So you are a debtor of mine, and not a creditor?"

"I b'lieve that's right," said Dick, drawing fifteen cents from his pocket, and placing in Mr. Greyson's hand.

"Fifteen cents!" repeated he, in some surprise. "How do you happen to be indebted to me in that amount?"

"You gave me a quarter for a-shinin' your boots, yesterday mornin', and couldn't wait for the change. I meant to have brought it before, but I forgot all about it till this mornin'.

"It had quite slipped my mind also. But you don't look like the boy I employed. If I remember rightly he wasn't as well dressed as you."

"No," said Dick. "I was dressed for a party, then, but the clo'es was too well ventilated to be comfortable in cold weather."

"You're an honest boy," said Mr. Greyson. "Who taught you to be honest?"

"Nobody," said Dick. "But it's mean to cheat and steal. I've always knowed that."

"Then you've got ahead of some of our business men. Do you read the Bible?"

"No," said Dick. "I've heard it's a good book, but I don't know much about it."

"You ought to go to some Sunday School. Would you be willing?"

"Yes," said Dick, promptly. "I want to grow up 'spectable. But I don't know where to go."

"Then I'll tell you. The church I attend is at the corner of Fifth Avenue and Twenty-first Street."

"I've seen it," said Dick.

"I have a class in the Sunday School there. If you'll come next Sunday, I'll take you into my class, and do what I can to help you."

"Thank you," said Dick, "but p'r'aps you'll get tired of teaching me. I'm awful ignorant."

"No, my lad," said Mr. Greyson, kindly. "You evidently have some good principles to start with, as you have shown by your scorn of dishonesty. I shall hope good things of you in the future."

"Well, Dick," said our hero, apostrophizing himself, as he left the office; "you're gettin' up in the world. You've got money invested, and are goin' to attend church, by partic'lar invitation, on Fifth Avenue. I shouldn't wonder much if you should find cards, when you get home, from the Mayor, requestin' the honor of your company to dinner, along with other distinguished guests."

Dick felt in very good spirits. He seemed to be emerging from the world in which he had hitherto lived, into a new atmosphere of respectability, and the change seemed very pleasant to him.

At six o'clock Dick went into a restaurant on Chatham Street, and got a comfortable supper. He had been so successful during the day that, after paying for this, he still had ninety cents left. While he was despatching his supper, another boy came in, smaller and slighter than Dick, and sat down beside him. Dick recognized him as a boy who three months before had entered the ranks of the boot-blacks, but who, from a natural timidity, had not been able to earn much. He was ill-fitted for the coarse companionship of the street boys, and shrank from the rude jokes of his present associates. Dick had never troubled him; for our hero had a certain chivalrous feeling which would not allow him to bully or disturb a younger and weaker boy than himself.

"How are you, Fosdick?" said Dick, as the other seated himself.

"Pretty well," said Fosdick. "I suppose you're all right."

"Oh, yes, I'm right side up with care. I've been havin' a bully supper. What are you goin' to have?"

"Some bread and butter."

"Why don't you get a cup o' coffee?"

"Why," said Fosdick, reluctantly, "I haven't got money enough to-night."

"Never mind," said Dick; "I'm in luck to-day. I'll stand treat."

"That's kind in you," said Fosdick, gratefully.

"Oh, never mind that," said Dick.

Accordingly he ordered a cup of coffee, and a plate of beef-steak, and was gratified to see that his young companion partook of both with evident relish. When the repast was over, the boys went out into the street together, Dick pausing at the desk to settle for both suppers.

"Where are you going to sleep to-night, Fosdick?" asked Dick, as they stood on the sidewalk.

"I don't know," said Fosdick, a little sadly. "In some door-way, I expect. But I'm afraid the police will find me out, and make me move on."

"I'll tell you what," said Dick, "you must go home with me. I guess my bed will hold two."

"Have you got a room?" asked the other, in surprise.

"Yes," said Dick, rather proudly, and with a little excusable exultation. "I've got a room over in Mott Street; there I can receive my friends. That'll be better than sleepin' in a door-way,—won't it?"

"Yes, indeed it will," said Fosdick. "How lucky I was to come across you! It comes hard to me living as I do. When my father was alive I had every comfort."

"That's more'n I ever had," said Dick. "But I'm goin' to try to live comfortable now. Is your father dead?"

"Yes," said Fosdick, sadly. "He was a printer; but he was drowned one dark night from a Fulton ferry-boat, and, as I had no relations in the city, and no money, I was obliged to go to work as quick as I could. But I don't get on very well."

"Didn't you have no brothers nor sisters?" asked Dick.

"No," said Fosdick; "father and I used to live alone. He was always so much company to me that I feel very lonesome without him. There's a man out West somewhere that owes him two thousand dollars. He used to live in the city, and father lent him all his money to help him go into business; but he failed, or pretended to, and went off. If father hadn't lost that money he would have left me well off; but no money would have made up his loss to me."

"What's the man's name that went off with your father's money?"

"His name is Hiram Bates."

'P'r'aps you'll get the money again, sometime."

"There isn't much chance of it," said Fosdick. "I'd sell out my chances of that for five dollars."

"Maybe I'll buy you out some time," said Dick. "Now, come round and see what sort of a room I've got. I used to go to the theatre evenings, when I had money; but now I'd rather go to bed early, and have a good sleep."

"I don't care much about theatres," said Fosdick. "Father didn't use to let me go very often. He said it wasn't good for boys."

"I like to go to the Old Bowery sometimes. They have tip-top plays there. Can you read and write well?" he asked, as a sudden thought came to him.

"Yes," said Fosdick. "Father always kept me at school when he was alive, and I stood pretty well in my classes. I was expecting to enter at the Free Academy[26] next year."

"Then I'll tell you what," said Dick; "I'll make a bargain with you. I can't read much more'n a pig; and my writin' looks like hens' tracks. I don't want to grow up knowin' no more'n a four-year-old boy. If you'll teach me readin' and writin' evenin's, you shall sleep in my room every night. That'll be better'n door-steps or old boxes, where I've slept many a time."

"Are you in earnest?" said Fosdick, his face lighting up hopefully.

"In course I am," said Dick. "It's fashionable for young gentlemen to have private tootors to introduce 'em into the flower-beds of literatoor and science, and why should't I foller the fashion? You shall be my perfessor; only you must promise not to be very hard if my writin' looks like a rail-fence or a bender."

"I'll try not to be too severe," said Fosdick, laughing. "I shall be thankful for such a chance to get a place to sleep. Have you got anything to read out of?"

"No," said Dick. "My extensive and well-selected library was lost overboard in a storm, when I was sailin' from the Sandwich Islands to the desert of Sahara. But I'll buy a paper. That'll do me a long time."

Accordingly Dick stopped at a paper-stand, and bought a copy of a weekly paper, filled with the usual variety of reading matter,—stories, sketches, poems, etc.

They soon arrived at Dick's lodging-house. Our hero, procuring a lamp from the land-lady, led the way into his apartment, which he entered with the proud air of a proprietor.

"Well, how do you like it, Fosdick?" he asked, complacently.

The time was when Fosdick would have thought it untidy and not particularly attractive. But he had served a severe apprenticeship in the streets, and it was pleasant to feel himself under shelter, and he was not disposed to be critical.

"It looks very comfortable, Dick," he said.

"The bed aint very large," said Dick; "but I guess we can get along."

"Oh, yes," said Fosdick, cheerfully. "I don't take up much room."

"Then that's all right. There's two chairs, you see, one for you and one for me. In case the mayor comes in to spend the evenin' socially, he can sit on the bed."

The boys seated themselves, and five minutes later, under the guidance of his young tutor, Dick had commenced his studies.

Chapter XVI

The First Lesson

FORTUNATELY for Dick, his young tutor was well qualified to instruct him. Henry Fosdick, though only twelve years old, knew as much as many boys of fourteen. He had always been studious and ambitious to excel. His father, being a printer, employed in an office where books were printed, often brought home new books in sheets, which Henry was always glad to read. Mr. Fosdick had been, besides, a subscriber to the Mechanics' Apprentices' Library, which contains many thousands of well-selected and instructive books. Thus Henry had acquired an amount of general information, unusual in a boy of his age. Perhaps he had

---

26 [Author's Original Note] Now the [C]ollege of the [C]ity of New York.

devoted too much time to study, for he was not naturally robust. All this, however, fitted him admirably for the office to which Dick had appointed him,—that of his private instructor.

The two boys drew up their chairs to the rickety table, and spread out the paper before them.

"The exercises generally commence with ringing the bell," said Dick; "but as I aint got none, we'll have to do without."

"And the teacher is generally provided with a rod," said Fosdick. "Isn't there a poker handy, that I can use in case my scholar doesn't behave well?"

"'Taint lawful to use fire-arms," said Dick.

"Now, Dick," said Fosdick, "before we begin, I must find out how much you already know. Can you read any?"

"Not enough to hurt me," said Dick. "All I know about readin' you could put in a nut-shell, and there'd be room left for a small family."

"I suppose you know your letters?"

"Yes," said Dick, "I know 'em all, but not intimately. I guess I can call 'em all by name."

"Where did you learn them? Did you ever go to school?"

"Yes; I went two days."

"Why did you stop?"

"It didn't agree with my constitution."

"You don't look very delicate," said Fosdick.

"No," said Dick, "I aint troubled much that way; but I found lickins didn't agree with me."

"Did you get punished?"

"Awful," said Dick.

"What for?"

"For indulgin' in a little harmless amoosement," said Dick. "You see the boy that was sittin' next to me fell asleep, which I considered improper in school-time; so I thought I'd help the teacher a little by wakin' him up. So I took a pin and stuck into him; but I guess it went a little too far, for he screeched awful. The teacher found out what it was that made him holler, and whipped me with a ruler till I was black and blue. I thought 'twas about time to take a vacation; so that's the last time I went to school."

"You didn't learn to read in that time, of course?"

"No," said Dick; "but I was a newsboy a l'ttle while; so I learned a little, just so's to find out what the news was. Sometimes I didn't read straight and called the wrong news. One mornin' I asked another boy what the paper said, and he told me the King of Africa was dead. I thought it was all right till folks began to laugh."

"Well, Dick, if you'll only study well, you won't be liable to make such mistakes."

"I hope so," said Dick. "My friend Horace Greeley told me the other day that he'd get me to take his place now and then when he was off makin' speeches if my edication hadn't been neglected."

"I must find a good piece for you to begin on," said Fosdick, looking over the paper.

"Find an easy one," said Dick, "with words of one story."

Fosdick at length found a piece which he thought would answer. He discovered on trial that Dick had not exaggerated his deficiencies. Words of two syllables he seldom pronounced right, and was much surprised when he was told how "through" was sounded.

"Seems to me it's throwin' away letters to use all them," he said.

"How would you spell it?" asked his young teacher.

"T-h-r-u," said Dick.

"Well," said Fosdick, "there's a good many other words that are spelt with more letters than they need to have. But it's the fashion, and we must follow it."

But if Dick was ignorant, he was quick, and had an excellent capacity. Moreover he had perseverance, and was not easily discouraged. He had made up his mind he must know more, and was not disposed to complain of the difficulty of his task. Fosdick had occasion to laugh more than once at his ludicrous mistakes; but Dick laughed too, and on the whole both were quite interested in the lesson.

At the end of an hour and a half the boys stopped for the evening.

"You're learning fast, Dick," said Fosdick. "At this rate you will soon learn to read well."

"Will I?" asked Dick with an expression of satisfaction. "I'm glad of that. I don't want to be ignorant. I didn't use to care, but I do now. I want to grow up 'spectable."

"So do I, Dick. We will both help each other, and I am sure we can accomplish something. But I am beginning to feel sleepy."

"So am I," said Dick. "Them hard words make my head ache. I wonder who made 'em all?"

"That's more than I can tell. I suppose you've seen a dictionary."

"That's another of 'em. No, I can't say I have, though I may have seen him in the street without knowin' him."

"A dictionary is a book containing all the words in the language."

"How many are there?"

"I don't rightly know; but I think there are about fifty thousand."

"It's a pretty large family," said Dick. "Have I got to learn 'em all?"

"That will not be necessary. There are a large number which you would never find occasion to use."

"I'm glad of that," said Dick; "for I don't expect to live to be more'n a hundred, and by that time I wouldn't be more'n half through."

By this time the flickering lamp gave a decided hint to the boys that unless they made haste they would have to undress in the dark. They accordingly drew off their clothes, and Dick jumped into bed. But Fosdick, before doing so, knelt down by the side of the bed, and said a short prayer.

"What's that for?" asked Dick, curiously.

"I was saying my prayers," said Fosdick, as he rose from his knees. "Don't you ever do it?"

"No," said Dick. "Nobody ever taught me."

"Then I'll teach you. Shall I?"

"I don't know," said Dick, dubiously. "What's the good?"

Fosdick explained as well as he could, and perhaps his simple explanation was better adapted to Dick's comprehension than one from an older person would have been. Dick felt more free to ask questions, and the example of his new friend, for whom he was beginning to feel a warm attachment, had considerable effect upon him. When, therefore, Fosdick asked again if he should teach him a prayer, Dick consented, and his young bedfellow did so. Dick was not naturally irreligious. If he had lived without a knowledge of God and of religious things, it was scarcely to be wondered at in a lad who, from an early age, had been thrown upon his own exertions for the means of living, with no one to care for him or give him good advice. But he was so far good that he could appreciate goodness in others, and this it was that had drawn him to Frank in the first place, and now to Henry Fosdick. He did not, therefore, attempt to ridicule his companion, as some boys better brought up might have done, but was willing to follow his example in what something told him was right. Our young hero had taken an important step towards securing that genuine respectability which he was ambitious to attain.

Weary with the day's work, and Dick perhaps still more fatigued by the unusual mental effort he had made, the boys soon sank into a deep and peaceful slumber, from which they did not awaken till six o'clock the next morning. Before going out Dick sought Mrs. Mooney, and spoke to her on the subject of taking Fosdick as a room-mate. He found that she had no objection, provided he would allow her twenty-five cents a week extra, in consideration of the extra trouble which his companion might be expected to make. To this Dick assented, and the arrangement was definitely concluded.

This over, the two boys went out and took stations near each other. Dick had more of a business turn than Henry, and less shrinking from publicity, so that his earnings were greater. But he had undertaken to pay the entire expenses of the room, and needed to earn more. Sometimes, when two customers presented themselves at the same time, he was able to direct one to his friend. So at the end of the week both boys found themselves with surplus earnings. Dick had the satisfaction of adding two dollars and a half to his deposits in the Savings Bank, and Fosdick commenced an account by depositing seventy-five cents.

On Sunday morning Dick bethought himself of his promise to Mr. Greyson to come to the church on Fifth Avenue. To tell the truth, Dick recalled it with some regret. He had never been inside a church since he could remember, and he was not much attracted by the invitation he had received. But Henry, finding him wavering, urged him to go, and offered to go with him. Dick gladly accepted the offer, feeling that he required some one to lend him countenance under such unusual circumstances.

Dick dressed himself with scrupulous care, giving his shoes a "shine" so brilliant that it did him great credit in a professional point of view, and endeavored to clean his hands thoroughly; but, in spite of all he could do, they were not so white as if his business had been of a different character.

Having fully completed his preparations, he descended into the street, and, with Henry by his side, crossed over to Broadway.

The boys pursued their way up Broadway, which on Sunday presents a striking contrast in its quietness to the noise and confusion of ordinary weekdays, as far as Union Square then turned down Fourteenth Street, which brought them to Fifth Avenue.

"Suppose we dine at Delmonico's,"[27] said Fosdick, looking towards that famous restaurant.

"I'd have to sell some of my Erie shares," said Dick.

A short walk now brought them to the church of which mention has already been made. They stood outside, a little abashed, watching the fashionably attired people who were entering, and were feeling a little undecided as to whether they had better enter also, when Dick felt a light touch upon his shoulder.

Turning round, he met the smiling glance of Mr. Greyson.

"So, my young friend, you have kept your promise," he said. "And whom have you brought with you?"

---

27 One of New York City's most famous and expensive restaurants. It opened in 1827 and moved several times as it grew ever more famous. Eventually most famous for its steaks, it has the reputation of being the first restaurant to make use of a wine list.

"A friend of mine," said Dick. "His name is Henry Fosdick."

"I am glad you have brought him. Now follow me, and I will give you seats."

Chapter XVII

Dick's First Appearance in Society

It was the hour for morning service. The boys followed Mr. Greyson into the handsome church, and were assigned seats in his own pew.

There were two persons already seated in it,—a good-looking lady of middle age, and a pretty little girl of nine. They were Mrs. Greyson and her only daughter Ida. They looked pleasantly at the boys as they entered, smiling a welcome to them.

The morning service commenced. It must be acknowledged that Dick felt rather awkward. It was an unusual place for him, and it need not be wondered at that he felt like a cat in a strange garret. He would not have known when to rise if he had not taken notice of what the rest of the audience did, and followed their example. He was sitting next to Ida and as it was the first time he had ever been near so well-dressed a young lady, he naturally felt bashful. When the hymns were announced, Ida found the place, and offered a hymn-book to our hero. Dick took it awkwardly, but his studies had not yet been pursued far enough for him to read the words readily. However, he resolved to keep up appearances, and kept his eyes fixed steadily on the hymn-book.

At length the service was over. The people began to file slowly out of church, and among them, of course, Mr. Greyson's family and the two boys. It seemed very strange to Dick to find himself in such different companionship from what he had been accustomed, and he could not help thinking, "Wonder what Johnny Nolan 'ould say if he could see me now!"

But Johnny's business engagements did not often summon him to Fifth Avenue, and Dick was not likely to be seen by any of his friends in the lower part of the city.

"We have our Sunday school in the afternoon," said Mr. Greyson. "I suppose you live at some distance from here?"

"In Mott Street, sir," answered Dick.

"That is too far to go and return. Suppose you and your friend come and dine with us, and then we can come here together in the afternoon."

Dick was as much astonished at this invitation as if he had really been invited by the Mayor to dine with him and the Board of Aldermen. Mr. Greyson was evidently a rich man, and yet he had actually invited two boot-blacks to dine with him.

"I guess we'd better go home, sir," said Dick, hesitating.

"I don't think you can have any very pressing engagements to interfere with your accepting my invitation," said Mr. Greyson, good-humoredly, for he understood the reasons of Dick's hesitation. "So I take it for granted that you both accept."

Before Dick fairly knew what he intended to do, he was walking down Fifth Avenue with his new friends.

Now, our young hero was not naturally bashful; but he certainly felt so now, especially as Miss Ida Greyson chose to walk by his side, leaving Henry Fosdick to walk with her father and mother.

"What is your name?" asked Ida, pleasantly.

Our hero was about to answer "Ragged Dick," when it occurred to him that in the present company he had better forget his old nickname.

"Dick Hunter," he answered.

"Dick!" repeated Ida. "That means Richard doesn't it?"

"Everybody calls me Dick."

"I have a cousin Dick," said the young lady, sociably. "His name is Dick Wilson. I suppose you don't know him?"

"No," said Dick.

"I like the name of Dick," said the young lady, with charming frankness.

Without being able to tell why, Dick felt rather glad she did. He plucked up courage to ask her name.

"My name is Ida," answered the young lady. "Do you like it?"

"Yes," said Dick. "It's a bully name."

Dick turned red as soon as he had said it, for he felt that he had not used the right expression.

The little girl broke into a silvery laugh.

"What a funny boy you are!" she said.

"I didn't mean, it," said Dick, stammering. "I meant it's a tip-top name."

Here Ida laughed again, and Dick wished himself back in Mott Street.

"How old are you?" inquired Ida, continuing her examination.

"I'm fourteen,—goin' on fifteen," said Dick.

"You're a big boy of your age," said Ida. "My cousin Dick is a year older than you, but he isn't as large."

Dick looked pleased. Boys generally like to be told that they are large of their age.

"How old be you?" asked Dick, beginning to feel more at his ease.

"I'm nine years old," said Ida. "I go to Miss Jarvis's school. I've just begun to learn French. Do you know French?"

"Not enough to hurt me," said Dick.

Ida laughed again, and told him that he was a droll boy.

"Do you like it?" asked Dick.

"I like it pretty well, except the verbs. I can't remember them well. Do you go to school?"

"I'm studying with a private tutor," said Dick.

"Are you? So is my cousin Dick. He's going to college this year. Are you going to college?"

"Not this year."

"Because, if you did, you know you'd be in the same class with my cousin. It would be funny to have two Dicks in one class."

They turned down Twenty-fourth Street, passing the Fifth Avenue Hotel on the left, and stopped before an elegant house with a brown stone front. The bell was rung, and the door being opened, the boys, somewhat abashed, followed Mr. Greyson into a handsome hall. They were told where to hang their hats, and a moment afterwards were ushered into a comfortable dining-room, where a table was spread for dinner.

Dick took his seat on the edge of a sofa, and was tempted to rub his eyes to make sure that he was really awake. He could hardly believe that he was a guest in so fine a mansion.

Ida helped to put the boys at their ease.

"Do you like pictures?" she asked.

"Very much," answered Henry.

The little girl brought a book of handsome engravings, and, seating herself beside Dick, to whom she seemed to have taken a decided fancy, commenced showing them to him.

"There are the Pyramids of Egypt," she said, pointing to one engraving. "What are they for?" asked Dick, puzzled. "I don't see any winders." "No," said Ida, "I don't believe anybody lives there. Do they, papa?" "No, my dear. They are used for the burial of the dead. The largest of them is said to be the loftiest building in the world with one exception. The spire of the Cathedral of Strasburg is twenty-four feet higher, if I remember rightly." "Is Egypt near here?" asked Dick. "Oh, no, it's ever so many miles off; about four or five hundred. Didn't you know?" "No," said Dick. "I never heard." "You don't appear to be very accurate in your information, Ida," said her mother. "Four or five thousand miles would be considerably nearer the truth."

After a little more conversation they sat down to dinner. Dick seated himself in an embarrassed way. He was very much afraid of doing or saying something which would be considered an impropriety, and had the uncomfortable feeling that everybody was looking at him, and watching his behavior.

"Where do you live, Dick?" asked Ida, familiarly.

"In Mott Street."

"Where is that?"

"More than a mile off."

"Is it a nice street?"

"Not very," said Dick. "Only poor folks live there."

"Are you poor?"

"Little girls should be seen and not heard," said her mother, gently.

"If you are," said Ida, "I'll give you the five-dollar gold-piece aunt gave me for a birthday present."

"Dick cannot be called poor, my child," said Mrs. Greyson, "since he earns his living by his own exertions."

"Do you earn your living?" asked Ida, who was a very inquisitive young lady, and not easily silenced. "What do you do?"

Dick blushed violently. At such a table, and in presence of the servant who was standing at that moment behind his chair, he did not like to say that he was a shoe-black, although he well knew that there was nothing dishonorable in the occupation.

Mr. Greyson perceived his feelings, and to spare them said, "You are too inquisitive, Ida. Some time Dick may tell you, but you know we don't talk of business on Sundays."

Dick in his embarrassment had swallowed a large spoonful of hot soup, which made him turn red in the face. For the second time, in spite of the prospect of the best dinner he had ever eaten, he wished himself back in Mott Street. Henry Fosdick was more easy and unembarrassed than Dick, not having led such a vagabond and neglected life. But it was to Dick that Ida chiefly directed her conversation, having apparently taken a fancy to his frank and handsome face. I believe I have already said that Dick was a very good-looking boy, especially now since he kept his face clean. He had a frank, honest expression, which generally won its way to the favor of those with whom he came in contact.

Dick got along pretty well at the table by dint of noticing how the rest acted, but there was one thing he could not manage, eating with his fork, which, by the way, he thought a very singular arrangement.

At length they arose from the table, somewhat to Dick's relief. Again Ida devoted herself to the boys, and exhibited a profusely illustrated Bible for their entertainment. Dick was interested in looking at the pictures, though he knew very little of their subjects. Henry Fosdick was much better informed; as might have been expected.

When the boys were about to leave the house with Mr. Greyson for the Sunday school, Ida placed her hand on Dick's, and said persuasively, "You'll come again, Dick, won't you?"

"Thank you," said Dick, "I'd like to," and he could not help thinking Ida the nicest girl he had ever seen.

"Yes," said Mrs. Greyson, hospitably, "we shall be glad to see you both here again."

"Thank you very much," said Henry Fosdick, gratefully. "We shall like very much to come."

I will not dwell upon the hour spent in Sunday school, nor upon the remarks of Mr. Greyson to his class. He found Dick's ignorance of religious subjects so great that he was obliged to begin at the beginning with him. Dick was interested in hearing the children sing, and readily promised to come again the next Sunday.

When the service was over Dick and Henry walked homewards. Dick could not help letting his thoughts rest on the sweet little girl who had given him so cordial a welcome, and hoping that he might meet her again.

"Mr. Greyson is a nice man,—isn't he, Dick?" asked Henry, as they were turning into Mott Street, and were already in sight of their lodging-house.

"Ain't he, though?" said Dick. "He treated us just as if we were young gentlemen."

"Ida seemed to take a great fancy to you."

"She's a tip-top girl," said Dick, "but she asked so many questions that I didn't know what to say."

He had scarcely finished speaking, when a stone whizzed by his head, and, turning quickly, he saw Micky Maguire running round the corner of the street which they had just passed.

Chapter XVIII

Micky Maguire's Second Defeat

DICK was no coward. Nor was he in the habit of submitting passively to an insult. When, therefore, he recognized Micky Maguire as his assailant, he instantly turned and gave chase. Micky anticipated pursuit, and ran at his utmost speed. It is doubtful if Dick would have overtaken him, but Micky had the ill luck to trip just as he had entered a narrow alley, and, falling with some violence, received a sharp blow from the hard stones, which made him scream with pain.

"Ow!" he whined. "Don't you hit a feller when he's down."

"What made you fire that stone at me?" demanded our hero, looking down at the fallen bully.

"Just for fun," said Micky.

"It would have been a very agreeable s'prise if it had hit me," said Dick. "S'posin' I fire a rock at you jest for fun."

"Don't!" exclaimed Micky, in alarm.

"It seems you don't like agreeable s'prises," said Dick, "any more'n the man did what got hooked by a cow one mornin, before breakfast. It didn't improve his appetite much."

"I've most broke my arm," said Micky, ruefully, rubbing the affected limb.

"If it's broke you can't fire no more stones, which is a very cheerin' reflection," said Dick. "Ef you haven't money enough to buy a wooden one I'll lend you a quarter. There's one good thing about wooden ones, they aint liable to get cold in winter, which is another cheerin' reflection."

"I don't want none of yer cheerin' reflections," said Micky, sullenly. "Yer company aint wanted here."

"Thank you for your polite invitation to leave," said Dick, bowing ceremoniously. "I'm willin' to go, but ef you throw any more stones at me, Micky Maguire, I'll hurt you worse than the stones did."

The only answer made to this warning was a scowl from his fallen opponent. It was quite evident that Dick had the best of it, and he thought it prudent to say nothing.

"As I've got a friend waitin' outside, I shall have to tear myself away," said Dick. "You'd better not throw any more stones, Micky Maguire, for it don't seem to agree with your constitution."

Micky muttered something which Dick did not stay to hear. He backed out of the alley, keeping watchful eye on his fallen foe, and rejoined Henry Fosdick, who was waiting his return.

"Who was it, Dick?" he asked.

"A partic'lar friend of mine, Micky Maguire," said Dick. "He playfully fired a rock at my head as a mark of his 'fection. He loves me like a brother, Micky does."

"Rather a dangerous kind of a friend, I should think," said Fosdick. "He might have killed you."

"I've warned him not to be so 'fectionate another time," said Dick.

"I know him," said Henry Fosdick. "He's at the head of a gang of boys living at the Five-Points. He threatened to whip me once because a gentleman employed me to black his boots instead of him."

"He's been at the Island two or three times for stealing," said Dick. "I guess he won't touch me again. He'd rather get hold of small boys. If he ever does anything to you, Fosdick, just let me know, and I'll give him a thrashing."

Dick was right. Micky Maguire was a bully, and like most bullies did not fancy tackling boys whose strength was equal or superior to his own. Although he hated Dick more than ever, because he thought our hero was putting on airs, he had too lively a remembrance of his strength and courage to venture upon another open attack. He contented himself, therefore, whenever he met Dick, with scowling at him. Dick took this very philosophically, remarking that, "if it was soothin' to Micky's feelings, he might go ahead, as it didn't hurt him much."

It will not be necessary to chronicle the events of the next few weeks. A new life had commenced for Dick. He no longer haunted the gallery of the Old Bowery; and even Tony Pastor's hospitable doors had lost their old attractions. He spent two hours every evening in study. His progress was astonishingly rapid. He was gifted with a natural quickness; and he was stimulated by the desire to acquire a fair education as a means of "growin' up 'spectable," as he termed it. Much was due also to the patience and perseverance of Henry Fosdick, who made a capital teacher.

"You're improving wonderfully, Dick," said his friend, one evening, when Dick had read an entire paragraph without a mistake.

"Am I?" said Dick, with satisfaction.

"Yes. If you'll buy a writing-book to-morrow, we can begin writing to-morrow evening."

"What else do you know, Henry?" asked Dick.

"Arithmetic, and geography, and grammar."

"What a lot you know!" said Dick, admiringly.

"I don't *know* any of them," said Fosdick. "I've only studied them. I wish I knew a great deal more."

"I'll be satisfied when I know as much as you," said Dick.

"It seems a great deal to you now, Dick, but in a few months you'll think differently. The more you know, the more you'll want to know."

"Then there aint any end to learnin'?" said Dick.

"No."

"Well," said Dick, "I guess I'll be as much as sixty before I know everything."

"Yes; as old as that, probably," said Fosdick, laughing.

"Anyway, you know too much to be blackin' boots. Leave that to ignorant chaps like me."

"You won't be ignorant long, Dick."

"You'd ought to get into some office or countin'-room."

"I wish I could," said Fosdick, earnestly. "I don't succeed very well at blacking boots. You make a great deal more than I do."

"That's cause I aint troubled with bashfulness," said Dick. "Bashfulness aint as natural to me as it is to you. I'm always on hand, as the cat said to the milk. You'd better give up shines, Fosdick, and give your 'tention to mercantile pursuits."

"I've thought of trying to get a place," said Fosdick; "but no one would take me with these clothes;" and he directed his glance to his well-worn suit, which he kept as neat as he could, but which, in spite of all his care, began to show decided marks of use. There was also here and there a stain of blacking upon it, which, though an advertisement of his profession, scarcely added to its good appearance.

"I almost wanted to stay at home from Sunday school last Sunday," he continued, "because I thought everybody would notice how dirty and worn my clothes had got to be."

"If my clothes wasn't two sizes too big for you," said Dick, generously, "I'd change. You'd look as if you'd got into your great-uncle's suit by mistake."

"You're very kind, Dick, to think of changing," said Fosdick, "for your suit is much better than mine; but I don't think that mine would suit you very well. The pants would show a little more of your ankles than is the fashion, and you couldn't eat a very hearty dinner without bursting the buttons off the vest."

"That wouldn't be very convenient," said Dick. "I aint fond of lacin' to show my elegant figger. But I say," he added with a sudden thought, "how much money have we got in the savings' bank?"

Fosdick took a key from his pocket, and went to the drawer in which the bank-books were kept, and, opening it, brought them out for inspection.

It was found that Dick had the sum of eighteen dollars and ninety cents placed to his credit, while Fosdick had six dollars and forty-five cents. To explain the large difference, it must be remembered that Dick had deposited five dollars before Henry deposited anything, being the amount he had received as a gift from Mr. Whitney.

"How much does that make, the lot of it?" asked Dick. "I aint much on figgers yet, you know."

"It makes twenty-five dollars and thirty-five cents, Dick," said his companion, who did not understand the thought which suggested the question.

"Take it, and buy some clothes, Henry," said Dick, shortly.

"What, your money too?"

"In course."

"No, Dick, you are too generous. I couldn't think of it. Almost three-quarters of the money is yours. You must spend it on yourself."

"I don't need it," said Dick.

"You may not need it now, but you will some time."

"I shall have some more then."

"That may be; but it wouldn't be fair for me to use your money, Dick. I thank you all the same for your kindness."

"Well, I'll lend it to you, then," persisted Dick, "and you can pay me when you get to be a rich merchant."

"But it isn't likely I ever shall be one."

"How d'you know? I went to a fortun' teller once, and she told me I was born under a lucky star with a hard name, and I should have a rich man for my particular friend, who would make my fortun'. I guess you are going to be the rich man."

Fosdick laughed, and steadily refused for some time to avail himself of Dick's generous proposal; but at length, perceiving that our hero seemed much disappointed, and would be really glad if his offer were accepted, he agreed to use as much as might be needful.

This at once brought back Dick's good-humor, and he entered with great enthusiasm into his friend's plans.

The next day they withdrew the money from the bank, and, when business got a little slack, in the afternoon, set out in search of a clothing store. Dick knew enough of the city to be able to find a place where a good bargain could be obtained. He was determined that Fosdick should have a good serviceable suit, even if it took all the money they had. The result of their search was that for twenty three dollars Fosdick obtained a very neat outfit, including a couple of shirts, a hat, and a pair of shoes, besides a dark mixed suit, which appeared stout and of good quality.

"Shall I send the bundle home?" asked the salesman, impressed by the off-hand manner in which Dick drew out the money in payment for the clothes.

"Thank you," said Dick, "you're very kind, but I'll take it home myself, and you can allow me something for my trouble."

"All right," said the clerk, laughing; "I'll allow it on your next purchase."

Proceeding to their apartment in Mott Street, Fosdick at once tried on his new suit, and it was found to be an excellent fit. Dick surveyed his new friend with much satisfaction.

"You look like a young gentleman of fortun'," he said, "and do credit to your governor."

"I suppose that means you, Dick," said Fosdick, laughing.

"In course it does."

"You should say *of* course," said Fosdick, who, in virtue of his position as Dick's tutor, ventured to correct his language from time to time.

"How dare you correct your gov'nor?" said Dick, with comic indignation. "'I'll cut you off with a shillin', you young dog,' as the Markis says to his nephew in the play at the Old Bowery."

Chapter XIX

Fosdick Changes His Business

Fosdick did not venture to wear his new clothes while engaged in his business. This he felt would have been wasteful extravagance. About ten o'clock in the morning, when business slackened, he went home, and dressing himself went to a hotel where he could see copies of the *Morning Herald* and *Sun,* and, noting down the places where a boy was wanted, went on a round of applications. But he found it no easy thing to obtain a place. Swarms of boys seemed to be out of employment, and it was not unusual to find from fifty to a hundred applicants for a single place.

There was another difficulty. It was generally desired that the boy wanted should reside with his parents. When Fosdick, on being questioned, revealed the fact of his having no parents, and being a boy of the street, this was generally sufficient of itself to insure a refusal. Merchants were afraid to trust one who had led such a vagabond life. Dick, who was always ready for an emergency, suggested borrowing a white wig, and passing himself off for Fosdick's father or grandfather. But Henry thought this might be rather a difficult character for our hero to sustain. After fifty applications and as many failures, Fosdick began to get discouraged. There seemed to be no way out of his present business, for which he felt unfitted.

"I don't know but I shall have to black boots all my life," he said, one day, despondently, to Dick.

"Keep a stiff upper lip," said Dick. "By the time you get to be a gray-headed veteran, you may get a chance to run errands for some big firm on the Bowery, which is a very cheerin' reflection."

So Dick by his drollery and perpetual good spirits kept up Fosdick's courage.

"As for me," said Dick, "I expect by that time to lay up a colossal fortun' out of shines, but live in princely style on the Avenoo."

But one morning, Fosdick, straying into French's Hotel, discovered the following advertisement in the columns of "The Herald,"—

"Wanted—A smart, capable boy to run of errands, and make himself generally useful in a hat and cap store. Salary three dollars a week at first. Inquire at No.— Broadway, after ten o'clock, A.M."

He determined to make application, and, as the City Hall clock just then struck the hour indicated, lost no time in proceeding to the store, which was only a few blocks distant from the Astor House. It was easy to find the store, as from a dozen to twenty boys were already assembled in front of it. They surveyed each other askance, feeling that they were rivals, and mentally calculating each other's chances.

"There isn't much chance for me," said Fosdick to Dick, who had accompanied him. "Look at all these boys. Most of them have good homes, I suppose, and good recommendations, while I have nobody to refer to."

"Go ahead," said Dick. "Your chance is as good as anybody's."

While this was passing between Dick and his companion, one of the boys, a rather supercilious-looking young gentleman, genteelly dressed, and evidently having a very high opinion of his dress and himself turned suddenly to Dick, and remarked,—

"I've seen you before."

"Oh, have you?" said Dick, whirling round; "then p'r'aps you'd like to see me behind."

At this unexpected answer all the boys burst into a laugh with the exception of the questioner, who, evidently considered that Dick had been disrespectful.

"I've seen you somewhere," he said, in a surly tone, correcting himself.

"Most likely you have," said Dick. "That's where I generally keep myself."

There was another laugh at the expense of Roswell Crawford, for that was the name of the young aristocrat. But he had his revenge ready. No boy relishes being an object of ridicule, and it was with a feeling of satisfaction that he retorted,—

"I know you for all your impudence. You're nothing but a boot-black."

This information took the boys who were standing around by surprise, for Dick was well-dressed, and had none of the implements of his profession with him.

"S'pose I be," said Dick. "Have you got any objection?"

"Not at all," said Roswell, curling his lip; "only you'd better stick to blacking boots, and not try to get into a store."

"Thank you for your kind advice," said Dick. "Is it gratooitous, or do you expect to be paid for it?"

"You're an impudent fellow."

"That's a very cheerin' reflection," said Dick, good-naturedly.

"Do you expect to get this place when there's gentlemen's sons applying for it? A boot-black in a store! That would be a good joke."

Boys as well as men are selfish, and, looking upon Dick as a possible rival, the boys who listened seemed disposed to take the same view of the situation.

"That's what I say," said one of them, taking sides with Roswell.

"Don't trouble yourselves," said Dick. "I aint agoin' to cut you out. I can't afford to give up a independent and loocrative profession for a salary of three dollars a week."

"Hear him talk!" said Roswell Crawford, with an unpleasant sneer. "If you are not trying to get the place, what are you here for?"

"I came with a friend of mine," said Dick, indicating Fosdick, "who's goin' in for the situation."

"Is he a boot-black, too?" demanded Roswell, superciliously.

"He!" retorted Dick, loftily. "Didn't you know his father was a member of Congress, and intimately acquainted with all the biggest men in the State?"

The boys surveyed Fosdick as if they did not quite know whether to credit this statement, which, for the credit of Dick's veracity, it will be observed he did not assert, but only propounded in the form of a question. There was no time for comment, however, as just then the proprietor of the store came to the door, and, casting his eyes over the waiting group, singled out Roswell Crawford, and asked him to enter.

"Well, my lad, how old are you?"

"Fourteen years old," said Roswell, consequentially.

"Are your parents living?"

"Only my mother. My father is dead. He was a gentleman," he added complacently.

"Oh, was he?' said the shop-keeper. "Do you live in the city?"

"Yes, sir. In Clinton Place."

"Have you ever been in a situation before?"

"Yes, sir," said Roswell, a little reluctantly.

"Where was it?"

"In an office on Dey Street."

"How long were you there?"

"A week."

"It seems to me that was a short time. Why did you not stay longer?"

"Because," said Rosewell, loftily, "the man wanted me to get to the office at eight o'clock, and make the fire. I'm a gentleman's son, and am not used to such dirty work."

"Indeed!" said the shop-keeper. "Well young gentleman, you may step aside a few minutes. I will speak with some of the other boys before making my selection."

Several other boys were called in and questioned. Roswell stood by and listened with an air of complacency. He could not help thinking his chances the best. "The man can see I'm a gentleman, and will do credit to his store," he thought.

At length it came to Fosdick's turn. He entered with no very sanguine anticipations of success. Unlike Roswell, he set a very low estimate upon his qualifications when compared with those of other applicants. But his modest bearing, and quiet, gentlemanly manner, entirely free from pretension, prepossessed the shop-keeper, who was a sensible man, in his favor.

"Do you reside in the city?" he asked.

"Yes, sir," said Henry.

"What is your age?"

"Twelve."

"Have you ever been in any situation?"

"No, sir."

"I should like to see a specimen of your hand writing. Here, take the pen and write your name."

Henry Fosdick had a very handsome handwriting for a boy of his age, while Roswell, who had submitted to the same test, could do little more than scrawl.

"Do you reside with your parents?"

"No, sir, they are dead."

"Where do you live, then?"

"In Mott Street."

Roswell curled his lip when this name was pronounced, for Mott Street, as my New York readers know, is in the immediate neighborhood of the Five-Points, and very far from a fashionable locality.

"Have you any testimonials to present?" asked Mr. Henderson, for that was his name.

Fosdick hesitated. This was the question which he had foreseen would give him trouble.

But at this moment it happened most opportunely that Mr. Greyson entered the shop with the intention of buying a hat.

"Yes," said Fosdick, promptly; "I will refer to this gentleman."

"How do you do, Fosdick?" asked Mr. Greyson, noticing him for the first time. "How do you happen to be here?"

"I am applying for a place, sir," said Fosdick. "May I refer the gentleman to you?"

"Certainly, I shall be glad to speak a good word for you. Mr. Henderson, this is a member of my Sunday-school class, for whose good qualities and good abilities I can speak confidently."

"That will be sufficient," said the shop-keeper, who knew Mr. Greyson's high character and position. "He could have no better recommendation. You may come to the store to-morrow morning at half-past seven o'clock. The pay will be three dollars a week for the first six months. If I am satisfied with you, I shall then raise it to five dollars."

The other boys looked disappointed, but none more so than Roswell Crawford. He would have cared less if any one else had obtained the situation; but for a boy who lived in Mott Street to be preferred to him, a gentleman's son, he considered indeed humiliating. In a spirit of petty spite, he was tempted to say, "He's a boot-black. Ask him if he isn't."

"He's an honest and intelligent lad," said Mr. Greyson. "As for you, young man, I only hope you have one-half his good qualities."

Roswell Crawford left the store in disgust, and the other unsuccessful applicants with him.

"What luck, Fosdick?" asked Dick, eagerly, as his friend came out of the store.

"I've got the place," said Fosdick, in accents of satisfaction; "but it was only because Mr. Greyson spoke up for me."

"He's a trump," said Dick, enthusiastically.

The gentleman, so denominated, came out before the boys went away, and spoke with them kindly.

Both Dick and Henry were highly pleased at the success of the application. The pay would indeed be small, but, expended economically, Fosdick thought he could get along on it, receiving his room rent, as before, in return for his services as Dick's private tutor. Dick determined, as soon as his education would permit, to follow his companion's example.

"I don't know as you'll be willin' to room with a boot-black," he said, to Henry, "now you're goin' into business."

"I couldn't room with a better friend, Dick," said Fosdick, affectionately, throwing his arm round our hero. "When we part, it'll be because you wish it."

So Fosdick entered upon a new career.

Chapter XX

Nine Months Later

THE next morning Fosdick rose early, put on his new suit, and, after getting breakfast, set out for the Broadway store in which he had obtained a position. He left his little blacking-box in the room.

"It'll do to brush my own shoes," he said. "Who knows but I may have to come back to it again?"

"No danger," said Dick; "I'll take care of the feet, and you'll have to look after the heads, now you're in a hat-store."

"I wish you had a place too," said Fosdick.

"I don't know enough yet," said Dick. "Wait till I've gradooated."

"And can put A. B. after your name."

"What's that?"

"It stands for Bachelor of Arts. It's a degree that students get when they graduate from college."

"Oh," said Dick, "I didn't know but it meant A Boot-black. I can put that after my name now. Wouldn't Dick Hunter, A. B., sound tip-top?"

"I must be going," said Fosdick. "It won't do for me to be late the very first morning."

"That's the difference between you and me," said Dick. "I'm my own boss, and there aint no one to find fault with me if I'm late. But I might as well be goin' too. There's a gent as comes down to his store pretty early that generally wants a shine."

The two boys parted at the Park. Fosdick crossed it, and proceeded to the hat-store, while Dick, hitching up his pants, began to look about him for a customer. It was seldom that Dick had to wait long. He was always on the alert, and if there was any business to do he was always sure to get his share of it. He had now a stronger inducement than ever to attend strictly to business; his little stock of money in the savings bank having been nearly exhausted by his liberality to his room-mate. He determined to be as economical as possible, and moreover to study as hard as he could, that he might be able to follow Fosdick's example, and obtain a place in a store or counting-room. As there were no striking incidents occurring in our hero's history within the next nine months, I propose to pass over that period, and recount the progress he made in that time.

Fosdick was still at the hat-store, having succeeded in giving perfect satisfaction to Mr. Henderson. His wages had just been raised to five dollars a week. He and Dick still kept house together at Mrs. Mooney's lodging-house, and lived very frugally, so that both were able to save up money. Dick had been unusually successful in business. He had several regular patrons, who had been drawn to him by his ready wit, and quick humor, and from two of them he had received presents of clothing, which had saved him any expense on that score. His income had averaged quite seven dollars a week in addition to this. Of this amount he was now obliged to pay one dollar weekly for the room which he and Fosdick occupied, but he was still able to save one half the remainder. At the end of nine months therefore, or thirty-nine weeks, it will be seen that he had accumulated no less a sum than one hundred and seventeen dollars. Dick may be excused for feeling like a capitalist when he looked at the long row of deposits in his little bank-book. There were other boys in the same business who had earned as much money, but they had had little care for the future, and spent as they went along, so that few could boast a bank-account, however small.

"You'll be a rich man some time, Dick," said Henry Fosdick, one evening.

"And live on Fifth Avenoo," said Dick.

"Perhaps so. Stranger things have happened."

"Well," said Dick, "if such a misfortin' should come upon me I should bear it like a man. When you see a Fifth Avenoo manshun for sale for a hundred and seventeen dollars, just let me know and I'll buy it as an investment."

"Two hundred and fifty years ago you might have bought one for that price, probably. Real estate wasn't very high among the Indians."

"Just my luck," said Dick; "I was born too late. I'd orter have been an Indian, and lived in splendor on my present capital."

"I'm afraid you'd have found your present business rather unprofitable at that time."

But Dick had gained something more valuable than money. He had studied regularly every evening, and his improvement had been marvellous. He could now read well, write a fair hand, and had studied arithmetic as far as Interest. Besides this he had obtained some knowledge of grammar and geography. If some of my boy readers, who have been study-ing for years, and got no farther than this, should think it incredible that Dick, in less than a year, and studying evenings only, should have accomplished it, they must remember that our hero was very much in earnest in his desire to improve. He knew that, in order to grow up respectable, he must be well advanced, and he was willing to work. But then the reader must not forget that Dick was naturally a smart boy. His street education had sharpened his faculties, and taught him to rely upon himself. He knew that it would take him a long time to reach the goal which he had set before him, and he had patience to keep on trying. He knew that he had only himself to depend upon, and he determined to make the most of himself,—a resolution which is the secret of success in nine cases out of ten.

"Dick," said Fosdick, one evening, after they had completed their studies, "I think you'll have to get another teacher soon."

"Why?" asked Dick, in some surprise. "Have you been offered a more loocrative position?"

"No," said Fosdick, "but I find I have taught you all I know myself. You are now as good a scholar as I am."

"Is that true?" said Dick, eagerly, a flush of gratification coloring his brown cheek.

"Yes," said Fosdick. "You've made wonderful progress. I propose, now that evening schools have begun, that we join one, and study together through the winter."

"All right," said Dick. "I'd be willin' to go now; but when I first began to study I was ashamed to have anybody know that I was so ignorant. Do you really mean, Fosdick, that I know as much as you?"

"Yes, Dick, it's true."

"Then I've got you to thank for it," said Dick, earnestly. "You've made me what I am."

"And haven't you paid me, Dick?"

"By payin' the room rent," said Dick, impulsively. "What's that? It isn't half enough. I wish you'd take half my money; you deserve it."

"Thank you, Dick, but you're too generous. You've more than paid me. Who was it took my part when all the other boys imposed upon me? And who gave me money to buy clothes, and so got me my situation?"

"Oh, that's nothing!" said Dick.

"It's a great deal, Dick. I shall never forget it. But now it seems to me you might try to get a situation yourself."

"Do I know enough?"

"You know as much as I do."

"Then I'll try," said Dick, decidedly.

"I wish there was a place in our store," said Fosdick. "It would be pleasant for us to be together."

"Never mind," said Dick; "there'll be plenty of other chances. P'r'aps A. T. Stewart might like a partner. I wouldn't ask more'n a quarter of the profits."

"Which would be a very liberal proposal on your part," said Fosdick, smiling. "But perhaps Mr. Stewart might object to a partner living on Mott Street."

"I'd just as lieves move to Fifth Avenoo," said Dick. "I aint got no prejudices in favor of Mott Street."

"Nor I," said Fosdick, "and in fact I have been thinking it might be a good plan for us to move as soon as we could afford. Mrs. Mooney doesn't keep the room quite so neat as she might."

"No," said Dick." She aint got no prejudices against dirt. Look at that towel."

Dick held up the article indicated, which had now seen service nearly a week, and hard service at that, —Dick's avocation causing him to be rather hard on towels.

"Yes," said Fosdick, "I've got about tired of it. I guess we can find some better place without having to pay much more. When we move, you must let me pay my share of the rent."

"We'll see about that," said Dick. "Do you propose to move to Fifth Avenoo?"

"Not just at present, but to some more agreeable neighborhood than this. We'll wait till you get a situation, and then we can decide."

A few days later, as Dick was looking about for customers in the neighborhood of the Park, his attention was drawn to a fellow boot-black, a boy about a year younger than himself, who appeared to have been crying.

"What's the matter, Tom?" asked Dick. "Haven't you had luck to-day?"

"Pretty good," said the boy; "but we're havin' hard times at home. Mother fell last week and broke her arm, and to-morrow we've got to pay the rent, and if we don't the landlord says he'll turn us out."

"Haven't you got anything except what you earn?" asked Dick.

"No," said Tom, "not now. Mother used to earn three or four dollars a week; but she can't do nothin' now, and my little sister and brother are too young."

Dick had quick sympathies. He had been so poor himself, and obliged to submit to so many privations that he knew from personal experience how hard it was. Tom Wilkins he knew as an excellent boy who never squandered his money, but faithfully carried it home to his mother. In the days of his own extravagance and shiftlessness he had once or twice asked Tom to accompany him to the Old Bowery or Tony Pastor's, but Tom had always steadily refused.

"I am sorry for you, Tom," he said. "How much do you owe for rent?"

"Two weeks now," said Tom.

"How much is it a week?"

"Two dollars a week—that makes four."

"Have you got anything towards it?"

"No; I've had to spend all my money for food for mother and the rest of us. I've had pretty hard work to do that. I don't know what we'll do. I haven't any place to go to, and I'm afraid mother'll get cold in her arm."

"Can't you borrow the money somewhere?" asked Dick.

Tom shook his head despondingly.

"All the people I know are as poor as I am," said he. "They'd help me if they could, but it's hard work for them to get along themselves."

"I'll tell you what, Tom," said Dick, impulsively, "I'll stand your friend."

"Have you got any money?" asked Tom, doubtfully.

"Got any money!" repeated Dick. "Don't you know that I run a bank on my own account? How much is it you need?"

"Four dollars," said Tom. "If we don't pay that before to-morrow night, out we go. You haven't got as much as that, have you?"

"Here are three dollars," said Dick, drawing out his pocket-book. "I'll let you have the rest to-morrow, and maybe a little more."

"You're a right down good fellow, Dick," said Tom; "but won't you want it yourself?"

"Oh, I've got some more," said Dick.

"Maybe I'll never be able to pay you."

"'Spose you don't," said Dick; "I guess I won't fail."

"I won't forget it, Dick. I hope I'll be able to do somethin' for you sometime."

"All right," said Dick. "I'd ought to help you. I haven't got no mother to look out for. I wish I had."

There was a tinge of sadness in his tone, as he pronounced the last four words; but Dick's temperament was sanguine, and he never gave way to unavailing sadness. Accordingly he began to whistle as he turned away, only adding, "I'll see you to-morrow, Tom."

The three dollars which Dick had handed to Tom Wilkins were his savings for the present week. It was now Thursday afternoon. His rent, which amounted to a dollar, he expected to save out of the earnings of Friday and Saturday. In order to give Tom the additional assistance he had promised, Dick would be obliged to have recourse to his bank-savings. He would not have ventured to trench upon it for any other reason but this. But he felt that it would be selfish to allow Tom and his mother to suffer when he had it in his power to relieve them. But Dick was destined to be surprised, and that in a disagreeable manner, when he reached home.

Chapter XXI

Dick Loses His Bank-Book

It was hinted at the close of the last chapter that Dick was destined to be disagreeably surprised on reaching home.

Having agreed to give further assistance to Tom Wilkins, he was naturally led to go to the drawer where he and Fosdick kept their bank-books. To his surprise and uneasiness *the drawer proved to be empty.*

"Come here a minute, Fosdick," he said.

"What's the matter, Dick?"

"I can't find my bank-book, nor yours either. What's 'come of them?"

"I took mine with me this morning, thinking I might want to put in a little more money. I've got it in my pocket, now."

"But where's mine?" asked Dick, perplexed.

"I don't know. I saw it in the drawer when I took mine this morning."

"Are you sure?"

"Yes, positive, for I looked into it to see how much you had got."

"Did you lock it again?" asked Dick.

"Yes; didn't you have to unlock it just now?"

"So I did," said Dick. "But it's gone now. Somebody opened it with a key that fitted the lock, and then locked it ag'in."

"That must have been the way."

"It's rather hard on a feller," said Dick, who, for the first time since we became acquainted with him, began to feel down-hearted.

"Don't give it up, Dick. You haven't lost the money, only the bank-book."

"Ain't that the same thing?"

"No. You can go to the bank to-morrow morning, as soon as it opens, and tell them you have lost the book, and ask them not to pay the money to any one except yourself."

"So I can," said Dick, brightening up. "That is, if the thief hasn't been to the bank to-day."

"If he has, they might detect him by his hand writing."

"I'd like to get ahold of the one that stole it," said Dick, indignantly. "I'd give him a good lickin'."

"It must have been somebody in the house. Suppose we go and see Mrs. Mooney. She may know whether anybody came into our room to-day."

The two boys went downstairs, and knocked at the door of a little back sitting-room where Mrs. Mooney generally spent her evenings. It was a shabby little room, with a threadbare carpet on the floor, the walls covered with a certain large-figured paper, patches of which had been stripped off here and there, exposing the plaster, the remainder being defaced by dirt and grease. But Mrs. Mooney had one of those comfortable temperaments which are tolerant of dirt, and didn't mind it in the least. She was seated beside a small pine work-table, industriously engaged in mending stockings.

"Good-evening, Mrs. Mooney," said Fosdick, politely.

"Good-evening," said the landlady. "Sit down, if you can find chairs. I'm hard at work as you see, but a poor lone widder can't afford to be idle."

"We can't stop long, Mrs. Mooney, but my friend here has had something taken from his room to-day, and we thought we'd come and see you about it."

"What is it?" asked the landlady. "You don't think I'd take anything? If I am poor, it's an honest name I've always had, as all my lodgers can testify."

"Certainly not, Mrs. Mooney; but there are others in the house that may not be honest. My friend has lost his bank-book. It was safe in the drawer this morning, but to-night it is not to be found."

"How much money was there in it?" asked Mrs. Mooney.

"Over a hundred dollars," said Fosdick.

"It was my whole fortun'," said Dick. "I was goin' to buy a house next year."

Mrs. Mooney was evidently surprised to learn the extent of Dick's wealth, and was disposed to regard him with increased respect.

"Was the drawer locked?" she asked.

"Yes."

"Then it couldn't have been Bridget. I don't think she has any keys."

"She wouldn't know what a bank-book was," said Fosdick. "You didn't see any of the lodgers go into our room to-day, did you?"

"I shouldn't wonder if it was Jim Travis," said Mrs. Mooney, suddenly.

This James Travis was a bar-tender in a low groggery in Mulberry Street, and had been for a few weeks an inmate of Mrs. Mooney's lodging-house. He was a coarse-looking fellow who, from his appearance, evidently patronized liberally the liquor he dealt out to others. He occupied a room opposite Dick's, and was often heard by the two boys reeling upstairs in a state of intoxication, uttering shocking oaths.

This Travis had made several friendly overtures to Dick and his room-mate, and had invited them to call round at the bar-room where he tended, and take something. But this invitation had never been accepted, partly because the boys were better engaged in the evening, and partly because neither of them had taken a fancy to Mr. Travis; which certainly was not strange, for nature had not gifted him with many charms, either of personal appearance or manners. The rejection of his friendly proffers had caused him to take a dislike to Dick and Henry, whom he considered stiff and unsocial.

"What makes you think it was Travis?" asked Fosdick. "He isn't at home in the daytime."

"But he was to-day. He said he had got a bad cold, and had to come home for a clean handkerchief."

"Did you see him?" asked Dick.

"Yes," said Mrs. Mooney. "Bridget was hanging out clothes, and I went to the door to let him in."

"I wonder if he had a key that would fit our drawer," said Fosdick.

"Yes," said Mrs. Mooney. "The bureaus in the two rooms are just alike. I got 'em at auction, and most likely the locks is the same."

"It must have been he," said Dick, looking towards Fosdick.

"Yes," said Fosdick, "it looks like it."

"What's to be done? That's what I'd like to know," said Dick. "Of course he'll say he hasn't got it; and he won't be such a fool as to leave it in his room."

"If he hasn't been to the bank, it's all right," said Fosdick. "You can go there the first thing to-morrow morning, and stop their paying any money on it."

"But I can't get any money on it myself," said Dick. "I told Tom Wilkins I'd let him have some more money to-morrow, or his sick mother'll have to turn out of their lodgin's."

"How much money were you going to give him?"

"I gave him three dollars to-day, and was goin' to give him two dollars to-morrow."

"I've got the money, Dick. I didn't go to the bank this morning."

"All right. I'll take it, and pay you back next week."

"No, Dick; if you've given three dollars, you must let me give two."

"No, Fosdick, I'd rather give the whole. You know I've got more money than you. No, I haven't, either," said Dick, the memory of his loss flashing upon him. "I thought I was rich this morning, but now I'm in destitoot circumstances."

"Cheer up, Dick; you'll get your money back."

"I hope so," said our hero, rather ruefully.

The fact was, that our friend Dick was beginning to feel what is so often experienced by men who do business of a more important character and on a larger scale than he, the bitterness of a reverse of circumstances. With one hundred dollars and over carefully laid away in the savings bank, he had felt quite independent. Wealth is comparative, and Dick probably felt as rich as many men who are worth a hundred thousand dollars. He was beginning to feel the advantages of his steady self-denial, and to experience the pleasures of property. Not that Dick was likely to be unduly attached to money. Let it be said to his credit that it had never given him so much satisfaction as when it enabled him to help Tom Wilkins in his trouble.

Besides this, there was another thought that troubled him. When he obtained a place he could not expect to receive as much as he was now making from blacking boots,—probably not more than three dollars a week,—while his expenses without clothing would amount to four dollars. To make up the deficiency he had confidently relied upon his savings, which would be sufficient to carry him along for a year, if necessary. If he should not recover his money, he would be compelled to continue a boot-black for at least six months longer; and this was rather a discouraging reflection. On the whole it is not to be wondered at that Dick felt unusually sober this evening, and that neither of the boys felt much like studying.

The two boys consulted as to whether it would be best to speak to Travis about it. It was not altogether easy to decide. Fosdick was opposed to it.

"It will only put him on his guard," said he, "and I don't see it will do any good. Of course he will deny it. We'd better keep quiet, and watch him, and, by giving notice at the bank, we can make sure that he doesn't get any money on it. If he does present himself at the bank, they will know at once that he is a thief, and he can be arrested."

This view seemed reasonable, and Dick resolved to adopt it. On the whole, he began to think prospects were brighter than he had at first supposed, and his spirits rose a little.

"How'd he know I had any bank-book? That's what I can't make out," he said.

"Don't you remember?" said Fosdick, after a moment's thought, "we were speaking of our savings, two or three evenings since?"

"Yes," said Dick.

"Our door was a little open at the time, and I heard somebody come upstairs, and stop a minute in front of it. It must have been Jim Travis. In that way he probably found out about your money, and took the opportunity to-day to get hold of it."

This might or might not be the correct explanation. At all events it seemed probable.

The boys were just on the point of going to bed, later in the evening, when a knock was heard at the door, and, to their no little surprise, their neighbor, Jim Travis, proved to be the caller. He was a sallow-complexioned young man, with dark hair and bloodshot eyes.

He darted a quick glance from one to the other as he entered, which did not escape the boys' notice.

"How are ye, to-night?" he said, sinking into one of the two chairs with which the room was scantily furnished.

"Jolly," said Dick. "How are you?"

"Tired as a dog," was the reply. "Hard work and poor pay; that's the way with me. I wanted to go to the theatre, to-night, but I was hard up, and couldn't raise the cash."

Here he darted another quick glance at the boys; but neither betrayed anything.

"You don't go out much, do you?" he said.

"Not much," said Fosdick. "We spend our evenings in study."

"That's precious slow," said Travis, rather contemptuously. "What's the use of studying so much? You don't expect to be a lawyer, do you, or anything of that sort?"

"Maybe," said Dick. "I haven't made up my mind yet. If my feller-citizens should want me to go to Congress some time, I shouldn't want to disapp'int 'em; and then readin' and writin' might come handy."

"Well," said Travis, rather abruptly, "I'm tired, and I guess I'll turn in."

"Good-night," said Fosdick.

The boys looked at each other as their visitor left the room.

"He came in to see if we'd missed the bank-book," said Dick.

"And to turn off suspicion from himself, by letting us know he had no money," added Fosdick.

"That's so," said Dick. "I'd like to have searched them pockets of his."

Chapter XXII

Tracking the Thief

FOSDICK was right in supposing that Jim Travis had stolen his bank-book. He was also right in supposing that that worthy young man had come to the knowledge of Dick's savings by what he had accidentally overheard. Now, Travis, like a very large number of young men of his class, was able to dispose of a larger amount of money than he was able to earn. Moreover, he had no great fancy for work at all, and would have been glad to find some other way of obtaining money enough to pay his expenses. He had recently received a letter from an old companion, who had strayed out to California, and going at once to the mines had been lucky enough to get possession of a very remunerative claim. He wrote to Travis that he had already realized two thousand dollars from it, and expected to make his fortune within six months.

Two thousand dollars! This seemed to Travis a very large sum, and quite dazzled his imagination. He was at once inflamed with the desire to go out to California and try his luck. In his present situation he only received thirty dollars a month, which was probably all that his services were worth, but went a very little way towards gratifying his expensive tastes. Accordingly he determined to take the next steamer to the land of gold, if he could possibly manage to get money enough to pay the passage.

The price of a steerage passage at that time was seventy-five dollars,—not a large sum, certainly,—but it might as well have been seventy-five hundred for any chance James Travis had of raising the amount at present. His available funds consisted of precisely two dollars and a quarter; of which sum, one dollar and a half was due to his washerwoman. This, however, would not have troubled Travis much, and he would conveniently have forgotten all about it; but, even leaving this debt unpaid, the sum at his command would not help him materially towards paying his passage money.

Travis applied for help to two or three of his companions; but they were all of that kind who never keep an account with savings banks, but carry all their spare cash about with them. One of these friends offered to lend him thirty-seven cents, and another a dollar; but neither of these offers seemed to encourage him much. He was about giving up his project in despair, when he learned, accidentally, as we have already said, the extent of Dick's savings.

One hundred and seventeen dollars! Why, that would not only pay his passage, but carry him up to the mines, after he had arrived in San Francisco. He could not help thinking it over, and the result of this thinking was that he determined to borrow it of Dick without leave. Knowing that neither of the boys were in their rooms in the daytime, he came back in the course of the morning, and, being admitted by Mrs. Mooney herself, said, by way of accounting for his presence, that he had a cold, and had come back for a handkerchief. The landlady suspected nothing, and, returning at once to her work in the kitchen, left the coast clear.

Travis at once entered Dick's room, and, as there seemed to be no other place for depositing money, tried the bureau-drawers. They were all readily opened, except one, which proved to be locked. This he naturally concluded must contain the money, and going back to his own chamber for the key of the bureau, tried it on his return, and found to his satisfaction that it would fit. When he discovered the bank-book, his joy was mingled with disappointment. He had expected to find bank-bills instead. This would have saved all further trouble, and would have been immediately available. Obtaining money at the savings bank would involve fresh risk. Travis hesitated whether to take it or not; but finally decided that it would be worth the trouble and hazard.

He accordingly slipped the book into his pocket, locked the drawer again, and, forgetting all about the handkerchief for which he had come home, went downstairs, and into the street.

There would have been time to go to the savings bank that day, but Travis had already been absent from his place of business some time, and did not venture to take the additional time required. Besides, not being very much used to savings banks, never having had occasion to use them, he thought it would be more prudent to look over the rules and regulations, and see if he could not get some information as to the way he ought to proceed. So the day passed, and Dick's money was left in safety at the bank.

In the evening, it occurred to Travis that it might be well to find out whether Dick had discovered his loss. This reflection it was that induced the visit which is recorded at the close of the last chapter. The result was that he was misled by the boys' silence on the subject, and concluded that nothing had yet been discovered.

"Good!" thought Travis, with satisfaction. "If they don't find out for twenty-four hours, it'll be too late, then, and I shall be all right."

There being a possibility of the loss being discovered before the boys went out in the morning, Travis determined to see them at that time, and judge whether such was the case. He waited, therefore, until he heard the boys come out, and then opened his own door.

"Morning, gents," said he, sociably. "Going to business?"

"Yes," said Dick. "I'm afraid my clerks'll be lazy if I aint on hand."

"Good joke!" said Travis. "If you pay good wages, I'd like to speak for a place."

"I pay all I get myself," said Dick. "How's business with you?"

"So so. Why don't you call round, some time?"

"All my evenin's is devoted to literatoor and science," said Dick. "Thank you all the same."

"Where do you hang out?" inquired Travis, in choice language, addressing Fosdick.

"At Henderson's hat and cap store, on Broadway."

"I'll look in upon you some time when I want a title," said Travis. "I suppose you sell cheaper to your friends."

"I'll be as reasonable as I can," said Fosdick, not very cordially; for he did not much fancy having it supposed by his employer that such a disreputable-looking person as Travis was a friend of his.

However, Travis had no idea of showing himself at the Broadway store, and only said this by way of making conversation, and encouraging the boys to be social.

"You haven't any of you gents seen a pearl-handled knife, have you?" he asked.

"No," said Fosdick; "have you lost one?"

"Yes," said Travis, with unblushing falsehood. "I left it on my bureau a day or two since. I've missed one or two other little matters. Bridget don't look to me any too honest. Likely she's got 'em."

"What are you goin' to do about it?" said Dick.

"I'll keep mum unless I lose something more, and then I'll kick up a row, and haul her over the coals. Have you missed anything?"

"No," said Fosdick, answering for himself, as he could do without violating the truth.

There was a gleam of satisfaction in the eyes of Travis, as he heard this.

"They haven't found it out yet," he thought. "I'll bag the money to-day, and then they may whistle for it."

Having no further object to serve in accompanying the boys, he bade them good-morning, and turned down another street.

"He's mighty friendly all of a sudden," said Dick.

"Yes," said Fosdick; "it's very evident what it all means. He wants to find out whether you have discovered your loss or not."

"But he didn't find out."

"No; we've put him on the wrong track. He means to get his money to-day, no doubt."

"My money," suggested Dick.

"I accept the correction," said Fosdick.

"Of course, Dick, you'll be on hand as soon as the bank opens."

"In course I shall. Jim Travis'll find he's walked into the wrong shop."

"The bank opens at ten o'clock, you know."

"I'll be there on time."

The two boys separated.

"Good luck, Dick," said Fosdick, as he parted from him. "It'll all come out right, I think."

"I hope 'twill," said Dick.

He had recovered from his temporary depression, and made up his mind that the money would be recovered. He had no idea of allowing himself to be outwitted by Jim Travis, and enjoyed already, in anticipation, the pleasure of defeating his rascality.

It wanted two hours and a half yet to ten o'clock, and this time to Dick was too precious to be wasted. It was the time of his greatest harvest. He accordingly repaired to his usual place of business, succeeded in obtaining six customers, which yielded him sixty cents. He then went to a restaurant, and got some breakfast. It was now half-past nine, and Dick, feeling that it wouldn't do to be late, left his box in charge of Johnny Nolan, and made his way to the bank.

The officers had not yet arrived, and Dick lingered on the outside, waiting till they should come. He was not without a little uneasiness, fearing that Travis might be as prompt as himself, and finding him there, might suspect something, and so escape the snare. But, though looking cautiously up and down the street, he could discover no traces of the supposed thief. In due time ten o'clock struck, and immediately afterwards the doors of the bank were thrown open, and our hero entered.

As Dick had been in the habit of making a weekly visit for the last nine months, the cashier had come to know him by sight.

"You're early, this morning, my lad," he said pleasantly. "Have you got some more money to deposit? You'll be getting rich, soon."

"I don't know about that," said Dick. "My bank-book's been stole."

"Stolen!" echoed the cashier. "That's unfortunate. Not so bad as it might be, though. The thief can't collect the money."

"That's what I came to see about," said Dick. "I was afraid he might have got it already."

"He hasn't been here yet. Even if he had, I remember you, and should have detected him. When was it taken?"

"Yesterday," said Dick. "I missed it in the evenin' when I got home."

"Have you any suspicion as to the person who took it?" asked the cashier.

Dick thereupon told all he knew as to the general character and suspicious conduct of Jim Travis, and the cashier agreed with him that he was probably the thief. Dick also gave his reason for thinking that he would visit the bank that morning, to withdraw the funds.

"Very good," said the cashier. "We'll be ready for him. What is the number of your book?"

"No. 5,678," said Dick.

"Now give me a little description of this Travis whom you suspect."

Dick accordingly furnished a brief outline sketch of Travis, not particularly complimentary to the latter.

"That will answer. I think I shall know him," said the cashier. "You may depend upon it that he shall receive no money on your account."

"Thank you," said Dick.

Considerably relieved in mind, our hero turned towards the door, thinking that there would be nothing gained by his remaining longer, while he would of course lose time.

He had just reached the doors, which were of glass, when through them he perceived James Travis himself just crossing the street, and apparently coming towards the bank. It would not do, of course, for him to be seen.

"Here he is," he exclaimed, hurrying back. "Can't you hide me somewhere? I don't want to be seen."

The cashier understood at once how the land lay. He quickly opened a little door, and admitted Dick behind the counter.

"Stoop down," he said, "so as not to be seen."

Dick had hardly done so when Jim Travis opened the outer door, and, looking about him in a little uncertainty, walked up to the cashier's desk.

Chapter XXIII

Travis Is Arrested

JIM TRAVIS advanced into the bank with a doubtful step, knowing well that he was on a dishonest errand, and heartily wishing that he were well out of it. After a little hesitation, he approached the paying-teller, and, exhibiting the bank-book, said, "I want to get my money out."

The bank-officer took the book, and, after looking at it a moment, said, "How much do you want?"

"The whole of it," said Travis.

"You can draw out any part of it, but to draw out the whole requires a week's notice."

"Then I'll take a hundred dollars."

"Are you the person to whom the book belongs?"

"Yes, sir," said Travis, without hesitation.

"Your name is—"

"Hunter."

The bank-clerk went to a large folio volume, containing the names of depositors, and began to turn over the leaves. While he was doing this, he managed to send out a young man connected with the bank for a policeman. Travis did not perceive this, or did not suspect that it had anything to do with himself. Not being used to savings banks, he supposed the delay only what was usual. After a search, which was only intended to gain time that a policeman might be summoned, the cashier came back, and, sliding out a piece of paper to Travis, said, "It will be necessary for you to write an order for the money."

Travis took a pen, which he found on the ledge outside, and wrote the order, signing his name "Dick Hunter," having observed that name on the outside of the book.

"Your name is Dick Hunter, then?" said the cashier, taking the paper, and looking at the thief over his spectacles.

"Yes," said Travis, promptly.

"But," continued the cashier, "I find Hunter's age is put down on the bank-book as fourteen. Surely you must be more than that."

Travis would gladly have declared that he was only fourteen; but, being in reality twenty-three, and possessing a luxuriant pair of whiskers, this was not to be thought of. He began to feel uneasy.

"Dick Hunter's my younger brother," he said. "I'm getting out the money for him."

"I thought you said your own name was Dick Hunter," said the cashier.

"I said my name was Hunter," said Travis, ingeniously. "I didn't understand you."

"But you've signed the name of Dick Hunter to this order. How is that?" questioned the troublesome cashier.

Travis saw that he was getting himself into a tight place; but his self-possession did not desert him.

"I thought I must give my brother's name," he answered.

"What is your own name?"

"Henry Hunter."

"Can you bring any one to testify that the statement you are making is correct?"

"Yes, a dozen if you like," said Travis, boldly. "Give me the book, and I'll come back this afternoon. I didn't think there'd be such a fuss about getting out a little money."

"Wait a moment. Why don't your brother come himself?"

"Because he's sick. He's down with the measles," said Travis.

Here the cashier signed to Dick to rise and show himself. Our hero accordingly did so.

"You will be glad to find that he has recovered," said the cashier, pointing to Dick.

With an exclamation of anger and dismay, Travis, who saw the game was up, started for the door, feeling that safety made such a course prudent. But he was too late. He found himself confronted by a burly policeman, who seized him by the arm, saying, "Not so fast, my man. I want you."

"Let me go," exclaimed Travis, struggling to free himself.

"I'm sorry I can't oblige you," said the officer. "You'd better not make a fuss, or I may have to hurt you a little."

Travis sullenly resigned himself to his fate, darting a look of rage at Dick, whom he considered the author of his present misfortune.

"This is your book," said the cashier, handing back his rightful property to our hero. "Do you wish to draw out any money?"

"Two dollars," said Dick.

"Very well. Write an order for that amount."

Before doing so, Dick, who now that he saw Travis in the power of the law began to pity him, went up to the officer, and said,—

"Won't you let him go? I've got my bank-book back, and I don't want anything done to him."

"Sorry I can't oblige you," said the officer; "but I'm not allowed to do it. He'll have to stand his trial."

"I'm sorry for you, Travis," said Dick. "I didn't want you arrested. I only wanted my bank-book back."

"Curse you!" said Travis, scowling vindictively. "Wait till I get free. See if I don't fix you."

"You needn't pity him too much," said the officer. "I know him now. He's been on the Island before."

"It's a lie," said Travis, violently.

"Don't be too noisy, my friend," said the officer. "If you've got no more business here, we'll be going."

He withdrew with the prisoner in charge, and Dick, having drawn his two dollars, left the bank. Notwithstanding the violent words the prisoner had used towards himself, and his attempted robbery, he could not help feeling sorry that he had been instrumental in causing his arrest.

"I'll keep my book a little safer hereafter," thought Dick. "Now I must go and see Tom Wilkins."

Before dismissing the subject of Travis and his theft, it may be remarked that he was duly tried, and, his guilt being clear, was sent to Blackwell's Island for nine months. At the end of that time, on his release, he got a chance to work his passage on a ship to San Francisco, where he probably arrived in due time. At any rate, nothing more has been heard of him, and probably his threat of vengeance against Dick will never be carried into effect.

Returning to the City Hall Park, Dick soon fell in with Tom Wilkins.

"How are you, Tom?" he said. "How's your mother?"

"She's better, Dick, thank you. She felt worried about bein' turned out into the street; but I gave her that money from you, and now she feels a good deal easier."

"I've got some more for you, Tom," said Dick, producing a two-dollar bill from his pocket.

"I ought not to take it from you, Dick."

"Oh, it's all right, Tom. Don't be afraid."

"But you may need it yourself."

"There's plenty more where that came from."

"Any way, one dollar will be enough. With that we can pay the rent."

"You'll want the other to buy something to eat."

"You're very kind, Dick."

"I'd ought to be. I've only got myself to take care of."

"Well, I'll take it for my mother's sake. When you want anything done just call on Tom Wilkins."

"All right. Next week, if your mother doesn't get better, I'll give you some more."

Tom thanked our hero very gratefully, and Dick walked away, feeling the self-approval which always accompanies a generous and disinterested action. He was generous by nature, and, before the period at which he is introduced to the reader's notice, he frequently treated his friends to cigars and oyster-stews. Sometimes he invited them to accompany him to the theatre at his expense. But he never derived from these acts of liberality the same degree of satisfaction as from this timely gift to Tom Wilkins. He felt that his money was well bestowed, and would save an entire family from privation and discomfort. Five dollars would, to be sure, make something of a difference in the amount of his savings. It was more than he was able to save up in a week. But Dick felt fully repaid for what he had done, and he felt prepared to give as much more, if Tom's mother should continue to be sick, and should appear to him to need it.

Besides all this, Dick felt a justifiable pride in his financial ability to afford so handsome a gift. A year before, however much he might have desired to give, it would have been quite out of his power to give five dollars. His cash balance never reached that amount. It was seldom, indeed, that it equalled one dollar. In more ways than one Dick was beginning to reap the advantage of his self-denial and judicious economy.

It will be remembered that when Mr. Whitney at parting with Dick presented him with five dollars, he told him that he might repay it to some other boy who was struggling upward. Dick thought of this, and it occurred to him that after all he was only paying up an old debt.

When Fosdick came home in the evening, Dick announced his success in recovering his lost money, and described the manner in which it had been brought about.

"You're in luck, Dick," said Fosdick. "I guess we'd better not trust the bureau-drawer again."

"I mean to carry my book round with me," said Dick.

"So shall I, as long as we stay at Mrs. Mooney's. I wish we were in a better place."

"I must go down and tell her she needn't expect Travis back. Poor chap, I pity him!"

Travis was never more seen in Mrs. Mooney's establishment. He was owing that lady for a fortnight's rent of his room, which prevented her feeling much compassion for him. The room was soon after let to a more creditable tenant, who proved a less troublesome neighbor than his predecessor.

Chapter XXIV

Dick Receives a Letter

IT was about a week after Dick's recovery of his bank-book, that Fosdick brought home with him in the evening a copy of the "Daily Sun."

"Would you like to see your name in print, Dick?" he asked.

"Yes," said Dick, who was busy at the wash-stand, endeavoring to efface the marks which his day's work had left upon his hands. "They haven't put me up for mayor, have they? 'Cause if they have, I shan't accept. It would interfere too much with my private business."

"No," said Fosdick, "they haven't put you up for office yet, though that may happen sometime. But if you want to see your name in print, here it is."

Dick was rather incredulous, but, having dried his hands on the towel, took the paper, and following the directions of Fosdick's finger, observed in the list of advertised letters the name of "RAGGED DICK."

"By gracious, so it is," said he. "Do you s'pose it means me?"

"I don't know of any other Ragged Dick,—do you?"

"No," said Dick, reflectively; "it must be me. But I don't know of anybody that would be likely to write to me."

"Perhaps it is Frank Whitney," suggested Fosdick, after a little reflection. "Didn't he promise to write to you?"

"Yes," said Dick, "and he wanted me to write to him."

"Where is he now?"

"He was going to a boarding-school in Connecticut, he said. The name of the town was Barnton."

"Very likely the letter is from him."

"I hope it is. Frank was a tip-top boy, and he was the first that made me ashamed of bein' so ignorant and dirty."

"You had better go to the post-office to-morrow morning, and ask for the letter."

"P'r'aps they won't give it to me."

"Suppose you wear the old clothes you used to a year ago, when Frank first saw you? They won't have any doubt of your being Ragged Dick then."

"I guess I will. I'll be sort of ashamed to be seen in 'em though," said Dick, who had considerable more pride in a neat personal appearance than when we were first introduced to him.

"It will be only for one day, or one morning," said Fosdick.

"I'd do more'n that for the sake of gettin' a letter from Frank. I'd like to see him."

The next morning, in accordance with the suggestion of Fosdick, Dick arrayed himself in the long disused Washington coat and Napoleon pants, which he had carefully preserved, for what reason he could hardly explain.

When fairly equipped, Dick surveyed himself in the mirror,—if the little seven-by-nine-inch looking-glass, with which the room was furnished, deserved the name. The result of the survey was not on the whole a pleasing one. To tell the truth, Dick was quite ashamed of his appearance, and, on opening the chamber-door, looked around to see that the coast was clear, not being willing to have any of his fellow-boarders see him in his present attire.

He managed to slip out into the street unobserved, and, after attending to two or three regular customers who came down-town early in the morning, he made his way down Nassau Street to the post-office. He passed along until he came to a compartment on which he read ADVERTISED LETTERS, and, stepping up to the little window, said,—

"There's a letter for me. I saw it advertised in the 'Sun' yesterday."

"What name?" demanded the clerk.

"Ragged Dick," answered our hero.

"That's a queer name," said the clerk, surveying him a little curiously. "Are you Ragged Dick?"

"If you don't believe me, look at my clo'es," said Dick.

"That's pretty good proof, certainly," said the clerk, laughing. "If that isn't your name, it deserves to be."

"I believe in dressin' up to your name," said Dick.

"Do you know any one in Barnton, Connecticut?" asked the clerk, who had by this time found the letter.

"Yes," said Dick. "I know a chap that's at boardin'-school there."

"It appears to be in a boy's hand. I think it must be yours."

The letter was handed to Dick through the window. He received it eagerly, and drawing back so as not to be in the way of the throng who were constantly applying for letters, or slipping them into the boxes provided for them, hastily opened it, and began to read. As the reader may be interested in the contents of the letter as well as Dick, we transcribe it below.

It was dated Barnton, Conn., and commenced thus,—

"Dear Dick,—You must excuse my addressing this letter to 'Ragged Dick'; but the fact is, I don't know what your last name is, nor where you live. I am afraid there is not much chance of your getting this letter; but I hope you will. I have thought of you very often, and wondered how you were getting along, and I should have written to you before if I had known where to direct.

"Let me tell you a little about myself. Barnton is a very pretty country town, only about six miles from Hartford. The boarding-school which I attend is under the charge of Ezekiel Munroe, A.M. He is a man of about fifty, a graduate of Yale College, and has always been a teacher. It is a large two-story house, with an addition containing a good many small bed-chambers for the boys. There are about twenty of us, and there is one assistant teacher who teaches the English branches. Mr. Munroe, or Old Zeke, as we call him behind his back, teaches Latin and Greek. I am studying both these languages, because father wants me to go to college.

"But you won't be interested in hearing about our studies. I will tell you how we amuse ourselves. There are about fifty acres of land belonging to Mr. Munroe; so that we have plenty of room for play. About a quarter of a mile from the house there is a good-sized pond. There is a large, round-bottomed boat, which is stout and strong. Every Wednesday and Saturday afternoon, when the weather is good, we go out rowing on the pond. Mr. Barton, the assistant teacher, goes with us, to look after us. In the summer we are allowed to go in bathing. In the winter there is splendid skating on the pond.

"Besides this, we play ball a good deal, and we have various other plays. So we have a pretty good time, although we study pretty hard too. I am getting on very well in my studies. Father has not decided yet where he will send me to college.

"I wish you were here, Dick. I should enjoy your company, and besides I should like to feel that you were getting an education. I think you are naturally a pretty smart boy; but I suppose, as you have to earn your own living, you don't get much chance to learn. I only wish I had a few hundred dollars of my own. I would have you come up here, and attend school with us. If I ever have a chance to help you in any way, you may be sure that I will.

"I shall have to wind up my letter now, as I have to hand in a composition to-morrow, on the life and character of Washington. I might say that I have a friend who wears a coat that once belonged to the general. But I suppose that coat must be worn out by this time. I don't much like writing compositions. I would a good deal rather write letters.

"I have written a longer letter than I meant to. I hope you will get it, though I am afraid not. If you do, you must be sure to answer it, as soon as possible. You needn't mind if your writing does look like 'hens-tracks,' as you told me once.

"Good-by, Dick. You must always think of me, as your very true friend,

"Frank Whitney."

Dick read this letter with much satisfaction. It is always pleasant to be remembered, and Dick had so few friends that it was more to him than to boys who are better provided. Again, he felt a new sense of importance in having a letter addressed to him. It was the first letter he had ever received. If it had been sent to him a year before, he would not have been able to read it. But now, thanks to Fosdick's instructions, he could not only read writing, but he could write a very good hand himself.

There was one passage in the letter which pleased Dick. It was where Frank said that if he had the money he would pay for his education himself.

"He's a tip-top feller," said Dick. "I wish I could see him ag'in."

There were two reasons why Dick would like to have seen Frank. One was, the natural pleasure he would have in meeting a friend; but he felt also that he would like to have Frank witness the improvement he had made in his studies and mode of life.

"He'd find me a little more 'spectable than when he first saw me," thought Dick.

Dick had by this time got up to Printing House Square. Standing on Spruce Street, near the "Tribune" office, was his old enemy, Micky Maguire.

It has already been said that Micky felt a natural enmity towards those in his own condition in life who wore better clothes than himself. For the last nine months, Dick's neat appearance had excited the ire of the young Philistine. To appear in neat attire and with a clean face Micky felt was a piece of presumption, and an assumption of superiority on the part of our hero, and he termed it "tryin' to be a swell."

Now his astonished eyes rested on Dick in his ancient attire, which was very similar to his own. It was a moment of triumph to him. He felt that "pride had had a fall," and he could not forbear reminding Dick of it.

"Them's nice clo'es you've got on," said he, sarcastically, as Dick came up.

"Yes," said Dick, promptly. "I've been employin' your tailor. If my face was only dirty we'd be taken for twin brothers."

"So you've give up tryin' to be a swell?"

"Only for this partic'lar occasion," said Dick. "I wanted to make a fashionable call, so I put on my regimentals."

"I don't b'lieve you've got any better clo'es," said Micky.

"All right," said Dick, "I won't charge you nothin' for what you believe."

Here a customer presented himself for Micky, and Dick went back to his room to change his clothes, before resuming business.

Chapter XXV

Dick Writes His First Letter

WHEN Fosdick reached home in the evening, Dick displayed his letter with some pride.

"It's a nice letter," said Fosdick, after reading it. "I should like to know Frank."

"I'll bet you would," said Dick. "He's a trump."

"When are you going to answer it?"

"I don't know," said Dick dubiously. "I never writ a letter."

"There's no reason why you shouldn't. There's always a first time, you know."

"I don't know what to say," said Dick.

"Get some paper and sit down to it, and you'll find enough to say. You can do that this evening instead of studying."

"If you'll look it over afterwards, and shine it up a little."

"Yes, if it needs it; but I rather think Frank would like it best just as you wrote it."

Dick decided to adopt Fosdick's suggestion. He had very serious doubts as to his ability to write a letter. Like a good many other boys, he looked upon it as a very serious job, not reflecting that, after all, letter-writing is nothing but talking upon paper. Still, in spite of his misgivings, he felt that the letter ought to be answered, and he wished Frank to hear from him. After various preparations, he at last got settled down to his task, and, before the evening was over, a letter was written. As the first letter which Dick had ever produced, and because it was characteristic of him, my readers may like to read it.

Here it is,—

"Dear Frank,—I got your letter this mornin', and was very glad to hear you hadn't forgotten Ragged Dick. I aint so ragged as I was. Openwork coats and trousers has gone out of fashion. I put on the Washington coat and Napoleon pants to go to the post-office, for fear they wouldn't think I was the boy that was meant. On my way back I received the congratulations of my intimate friend, Micky Maguire, on my improved appearance.

"I've give up sleepin' in boxes, and old wagons, findin' it didn't agree with my constitution. I've hired a room in Mott Street, and have got a private tooter, who rooms with me and looks after my studies in the evenin'. Mott Street aint very fashionable; but my manshun on Fifth Avenoo isn't finished yet, and I'm afraid it won't be till I'm a gray-haired veteran. I've got a hundred dollars towards it, which I've saved from my earnin's. I haven't forgot what you and your uncle said to me, and I'm trying to grow up 'spectable. I haven't been to Tony Pastor's, or the Old Bowery, for ever so long. I'd rather save up my money to support me in my old age. When my hair gets gray, I'm goin' to knock off blackin' boots, and go into some light, genteel employment, such as keepin' an apple-stand, or disseminatin' pea-nuts among the people.

"I've got so as to read pretty well, so my tooter says. I've been studyin' geography and grammar also. I've made such astonishin' progress that I can tell a noun from a conjunction as far away as I can see 'em. Tell Mr. Munroe that if he wants an accomplished teacher in his school, he can send for me, and I'll come on by the very next train. Or, if he wants to sell out for a hundred dollars, I'll buy the whole concern, and agree to teach the scholars all I know myself in less than six months. Is teachin' as good business, generally speakin', as blackin' boots? My private tooter combines both, and is makin' a fortun' with great rapidity. He'll be as rich as Astor some time, *if he only lives long enough.*

"I should think you'd have a bully time at your school. I should like to go out in the boat, or play ball with you. When are you comin' to the city? I wish you'd write and let me know when you do, and I'll call and see you. I'll leave my business in the hands of my numerous clerks, and go round with you. There's lots of things you didn't see when you was here before. They're getting on fast at the Central Park. It looks better than it did a year ago.

"I aint much used to writin' letters. As this is the first one I ever wrote, I hope you'll excuse the mistakes. I hope you'll write to me again soon. I can't write so good a letter as you; but I'll do my best, as the man said when he was asked if he could swim over to Brooklyn backwards. Good-by, Frank. Thank you for all your kindness. Direct your next letter to No. — Mott Street.

"Your true friend,

"Dick Hunter."

When Dick had written the last word, he leaned back in his chair, and surveyed the letter with much satisfaction.

"I didn't think I could have wrote such a long letter, Fosdick," said he.

"Written would be more grammatical, Dick," suggested his friend.

"I guess there's plenty of mistakes in it," said Dick. "Just look at it, and see."

Fosdick took the letter, and read it over carefully.

"Yes, there are some mistakes," he said; "but it sounds so much like you that I think it would be better to let it go just as it is. It will be more likely to remind Frank of what you were when he first saw you."

"Is it good enough to send?" asked Dick, anxiously.

"Yes, it seems to me to be quite a good letter. It is written just as you talk. Nobody but you could have written such a letter, Dick. I think Frank will be amused at your proposal to come up there as teacher."

"P'r'aps it would be a good idea for us to open a seleck school here in Mott Street," said Dick, humorously. "We could call it 'Professor Fosdick and Hunter's Mott Street Seminary.' Boot-blackin' taught by Professor Hunter."

The evening was so far advanced that Dick decided to postpone copying his letter till the next evening. By this time he had come to have a very fair handwriting, so that when the letter was complete it really looked quite creditable, and no one would have suspected that it was Dick's first attempt in this line. Our hero surveyed it with no little complacency. In fact, he felt rather proud of it, since it reminded him of the great progress he had made. He carried it down to the post-office, and deposited it with his own hands in the proper box. Just on the steps of the building, as he was coming out, he met Johnny Nolan, who had been sent on an errand to Wall Street by some gentleman, and was just returning.

"What are you doin' down here, Dick?" asked Johnny.

"I've been mailin' a letter."

"Who sent you?"

"Nobody."

"I mean, who writ the letter?"

"I wrote it myself."

"Can you write letters?" asked Johnny, in amazement.

"Why shouldn't I?"

"I didn't know you could write. I can't."

"Then you ought to learn."

"I went to school once; but it was too hard work, so I give it up."

"You're lazy, Johnny,—that's what's the matter. How'd you ever expect to know anything, if you don't try?"

"I can't learn."

"You can, if you want to."

Johnny Nolan was evidently of a different opinion. He was a good-natured boy, large of his age, with nothing particularly bad about him, but utterly lacking in that energy, ambition, and natural sharpness, for which Dick was distinguished. He was not adapted to succeed in the life which circumstances had forced upon him; for in the street-life of the metropolis a boy needs to be on the alert, and have all his wits about him, or he will find himself wholly distanced by his more enterprising competitors for popular favor. To succeed in his profession, humble as it is, a boot-black must depend upon the same qualities which gain success in higher walks in life. It was easy to see that Johnny, unless very much favored by circumstances, would never rise much above his present level. For Dick, we cannot help hoping much better things.

Chapter XXVI

An Exciting Adventure

DICK now began to look about for a position in a store or counting-room. Until he should obtain one he determined to devote half the day to blacking boots, not being willing to break in upon his small capital. He found that he could earn enough in half a day to pay all his necessary expenses, including the entire rent of the room. Fosdick desired to pay his half; but Dick steadily refused, insisting upon paying so much as compensation for his friend's services as instructor.

It should be added that Dick's peculiar way of speaking and use of slang terms had been somewhat modified by his education and his intimacy with Henry Fosdick. Still he continued to indulge in them to some extent, especially when he felt like joking, and it was natural to Dick to joke, as my readers have probably found out by this time. Still his manners were considerably improved, so that he was more likely to obtain a situation than when first introduced to our notice.

Just now, however, business was very dull, and merchants, instead of hiring new assistants, were disposed to part with those already in their employ. After making several ineffectual applications, Dick began to think he should be obliged to stick to his profession until the next season. But about this time something occurred which considerably improved his chances of preferment.

This is the way it happened.

As Dick, with a balance of more than a hundred dollars in the savings bank, might fairly consider himself a young man of property, he thought himself justified in occasionally taking a half holiday from business, and going on an excursion. On Wednesday afternoon Henry Fosdick was sent by his employer on an errand to that part of Brooklyn near Greenwood Cemetery. Dick hastily dressed himself in his best, and determined to accompany him.

The two boys walked down to the South Ferry, and, paying their two cents each, entered the ferry boat. They remained at the stern, and stood by the railing, watching the great city, with its crowded wharves, receding from view. Beside them was a gentleman with two children—a girl of eight and a little boy of six. The children were talking gayly to their father. While he was pointing out some object of interest to the little girl, the boy managed to creep, unobserved, beneath the chain that extends across the boat, for the protection of passengers, and, stepping incautiously to the edge of the boat, fell over into the foaming water.

At the child's scream, the father looked up, and, with a cry of horror, sprang to the edge of the boat. He would have plunged in, but, being unable to swim, would only have endangered his own life, without being able to save his child.

"My child!" he exclaimed in anguish,—"who will save my child? A thousand—ten thousand dollars to any one who will save him!"

There chanced to be but few passengers on board at the time, and nearly all these were either in the cabins or standing forward. Among the few who saw the child fall was our hero.

Now Dick was an expert swimmer. It was an accomplishment which he had possessed for years, and he no sooner saw the boy fall than he resolved to rescue him. His determination was formed before he heard the liberal offer made by the boy's father. Indeed, I must do Dick the justice to say that, in the excitement of the moment, he did not hear it at all, nor would it have stimulated the alacrity with which he sprang to the rescue of the little boy.

Little Johnny had already risen once, and gone under for the second time, when our hero plunged in. He was obliged to strike out for the boy, and this took time. He reached him none too soon. Just as he was sinking for the third and last time, he caught him by the jacket. Dick was stout and strong, but Johnny clung to him so tightly, that it was with great difficulty he was able to sustain himself.

"Put your arms round my neck," said Dick.

The little boy mechanically obeyed, and clung with a grasp strengthened by his terror. In this position Dick could bear his weight better. But the ferryboat was receding fast. It was quite impossible to reach it. The father, his face pale with terror and anguish, and his hands clasped in suspense, saw the brave boy's struggles, and prayed with agonizing fervor that he might be successful. But it is probable, for they were now midway of the river, that both Dick and the little boy whom he had bravely undertaken to rescue would have been drowned, had not a row-boat been fortunately near. The two men who were in it witnessed the accident, and hastened to the rescue of our hero.

"Keep up a little longer," they shouted, bending to their oars, "and we will save you."

Dick heard the shout, and it put fresh strength into him. He battled manfully with the treacherous sea, his eyes fixed longingly upon the approaching boat.

"Hold on tight, little boy," he said. "There's a boat coming."

The little boy did not see the boat. His eyes were closed to shut out the fearful water, but he clung the closer to his young preserver. Six long, steady strokes, and the boat dashed along side. Strong hands seized Dick and his youthful burden, and drew them into the boat, both dripping with water.

"God be thanked!" exclaimed the father, as from the steamer he saw the child's rescue. "That brave boy shall be rewarded, if I sacrifice my whole fortune to compass it."

"You've had a pretty narrow escape, young chap," said one of the boatman to Dick. "It was a pretty tough job you undertook."

"Yes," said Dick. "That's what I thought when I was in the water. If it hadn't been for you, I don't know what would have 'come of us."

"Anyhow you're a plucky boy, or you wouldn't have dared to jump into the water after this little chap. It was a risky thing to do."

"I'm used to the water," said Dick, modestly. "I didn't stop to think of the danger, but I wasn't going to let that little fellow drown without tryin' to save him."

The boat at once headed for the ferry wharf on the Brooklyn side. The captain of the ferry-boat, seeing the rescue, did not think it necessary to stop his boat, but kept on his way. The whole occurrence took place in less time than I have occupied in telling it.

The father was waiting on the wharf to receive his little boy, with what feelings of gratitude and joy can be easily understood. With a burst of happy tears he clasped him to his arms. Dick was about to withdraw modestly, but the gentleman perceived the movement, and, putting down the child, came forward, and, clasping his hand, said with emotion, "My brave boy, I owe you a debt I can never repay. But for your timely service I should now be plunged into an anguish which I cannot think of without a shudder."

Our hero was ready enough to speak on most occasions, but always felt awkward when he was praised.

"It wasn't any trouble," he said, modestly. "I can swim like a top."

"But not many boys would have risked their lives for a stranger," said the gentleman. "But," he added with a sudden thought, as his glance rested on Dick's dripping garments, "both you and my little boy will take cold in wet clothes. Fortunately I have a friend living close at hand, at whose house you will have an opportunity of taking off your clothes, and having them dried."

Dick protested that he never took cold; but Fosdick, who had now joined them, and who, it is needless to say, had been greatly alarmed at Dick's danger, joined in urging compliance with the gentleman's proposal, and in the end our hero had to yield. His new friend secured a hack, the driver of which agreed for extra recompense to receive the dripping boys into his carriage, and they were whirled rapidly to a pleasant house in a side street, where matters were quickly explained, and both boys were put to bed.

"I aint used to goin' to bed quite so early," thought Dick. "This is the queerest excursion I ever took."

Like most active boys Dick did not enjoy the prospect of spending half a day in bed; but his confinement did not last as long as he anticipated.

In about an hour the door of his chamber was opened, and a servant appeared, bringing a new and handsome suit of clothes throughout.

"You are to put on these," said the servant to Dick; "but you needn't get up till you feel like it."

"Whose clothes are they?" asked Dick.

"They are yours."

"Mine! Where did they come from?"

"Mr. Rockwell sent out and bought them for you. They are the same size as your wet ones."

"Is he here now?"

"No. He bought another suit for the little boy, and has gone back to New York. Here's a note he asked me to give you."

Dick opened the paper, and read as follows,—

"Please accept this outfit of clothes as the first instalment of a debt which I can never repay. I have asked to have your wet suit dried, when you can reclaim it. Will you oblige me by calling to-morrow at my counting room, No.—, Pearl Street.

"Your friend,

"James Rockwell."

Chapter XXVII

Conclusion

WHEN Dick was dressed in his new suit, he surveyed his figure with pardonable complacency. It was the best he had ever worn, and fitted him as well as if it had been made expressly for him.

"He's done the handsome thing," said Dick to himself; "but there wasn't no 'casion for his givin' me these clothes. My lucky stars are shinin' pretty bright now. Jumpin' into the water pays better than shinin' boots; but I don't think I'd like to try it more'n once a week."

About eleven o'clock the next morning Dick repaired to Mr. Rockwell's counting-room on Pearl Street. He found himself in front of a large and handsome warehouse. The counting-room was on the lower floor. Our hero entered, and found Mr. Rockwell sitting at a desk. No sooner did that gentleman see him than he arose, and, advancing, shook Dick by the hand in the most friendly manner.

"My young friend," he said, "you have done me so great service that I wish to be of some service to you in return. Tell me about yourself, and what plans or wishes you have formed for the future."

Dick frankly related his past history, and told Mr. Rockwell of his desire to get into a store or counting room, and of the failure of all his applications thus far. The merchant listened attentively to Dick's statement, and, when he had finished, placed a sheet of paper before him, and, handing him a pen, said, "Will you write your name on this piece of paper?"

Dick wrote in a free, bold hand, the name Richard Hunter. He had very much improved in his penmanship, as has already been mentioned, and now had no cause to be ashamed of it.

Mr. Rockwell surveyed it approvingly.

"How would you like to enter my counting-room as clerk, Richard?" he asked.

Dick was about to say "Bully," when he recollected himself, and answered, "Very much."

"I suppose you know something of arithmetic, do you not?"

"Yes, sir."

"Then you may consider yourself engaged at a salary of ten dollars a week. You may come next Monday morning."

"Ten dollars!" repeated Dick, thinking he must have misunderstood.

"Yes; will that be sufficient?"

"It's more than I can earn," said Dick, honestly.

"Perhaps it is at first," said Mr. Rockwell, smiling; "but I am willing to pay you that. I will besides advance you as fast as your progress will justify it."

Dick was so elated than he hardly restrained himself from some demonstration which would have astonished the merchant; but he exercised self-control, and only said, "I'll try to serve you so faithfully, sir, that you won't repent having taken me into your service."

"And I think you will succeed," said Mr. Rockwell, encouragingly. "I will not detain you any longer, for I have some important business to attend to. I shall expect to see you on Monday morning."

Dick left the counting-room, hardly knowing whether he stood on his head or his heels, so overjoyed was he at the sudden change in his fortunes. Ten dollars a week was to him a fortune, and three times as much as he had expected to obtain at first. Indeed he would have been glad, only the day before, to get a place at three dollars a week. He reflected that with the stock of clothes which he had now on hand, he could save up at least half of it, and even then live better than he had been accustomed to do; so that his little fund in the savings bank, instead of being diminished, would be steadily increasing. Then he was to be advanced if he deserved it. It was indeed a bright prospect for a boy who, only a year before, could neither read nor write, and depended for a night's lodging upon the chance hospitality of an alley-way or old wagon. Dick's great ambition to "grow up 'spectable" seemed likely to be accomplished after all.

"I wish Fosdick was as well off as I am," he thought generously. But he determined to help his less fortunate friend, and assist him up the ladder as he advanced himself.

When Dick entered his room on Mott Street, he discovered that some one else had been there before him, and two articles of wearing apparel had disappeared.

"By gracious!" he exclaimed; "somebody's stole my Washington coat and Napoleon pants. Maybe it's an agent of Barnum's, who expects to make a fortun' by exhibitin' the valooable wardrobe of a gentleman of fashion."

Dick did not shed many tears over his loss, as, in his present circumstances, he never expected to have any further use for the well-worn garments. It may be stated that he afterwards saw them adorning the figure of Micky Maguire; but whether that estimable young man stole them himself, he never ascertained. As to the loss, Dick was rather pleased that it had occurred. It seemed to cut him off from the old vagabond life which he hoped never to resume. Henceforward he meant to press onward, and rise as high as possible.

Although it was yet only noon, Dick did not go out again with his brush. He felt that it was time to retire from business. He would leave his share of the public patronage to other boys less fortunate than himself. That evening Dick and Fosdick had a long conversation.

Fosdick rejoiced heartily in his friend's success, and on his side had the pleasant news to communicate that his pay had been advanced to six dollars a week.

"I think we can afford to leave Mott Street now," he continued. "This house isn't as neat as it might be, and I should like to live in a nicer quarter of the city."

"All right," said Dick. "We'll hunt up a new room to-morrow. I shall have plenty of time, having retired from business. I'll try to get my reg'lar customers to take Johnny Nolan in my place. That boy hasn't any enterprise. He needs somebody to look out for him."

"You might give him your box and brush, too, Dick."

"No," said Dick; "I'll give him some new ones, but mine I want to keep, to remind me of the hard times I've had, when I was an ignorant boot-black, and never expected to be anything better."

"When, in short, you were 'Ragged Dick.' You must drop that name, and think of yourself now as—"

"Richard Hunter, Esq.," said our hero, smiling.

"A young gentleman on the way to fame and fortune," added Fosdick.

Here ends the story of Ragged Dick. As Fosdick said, he is Ragged Dick no longer. He has taken a step upward, and is determined to mount still higher. There are fresh adventures in store for him, and for others who have been introduced in these pages. Those who have felt interested in his early life will find his history continued in a new volume, forming the second of the series, to be called,—

FAME AND FORTUNE;

Or,

THE PROGRESS OF RICHARD HUNTER.

Chapter Fourteen

LOUISA MAY ALCOTT
(1832–1888)

Louisa May Alcott was the second of four daughters born to Bronson
Alcott, the famous Transcendentalist thinker and social reformer. Her
father's intellectual prominence introduced Louisa May to some of
the leading American literary lights of her age, including Nathaniel
Hawthorne, Margaret Fuller, Henry David Thoreau and Ralph Waldo
Emerson.

Alcott's father may have had a certain ethereal intellectual brilliance,
but he had no great gift for managing the more mundane matters of life,
and his family lived in a perpetually impoverished state. Alcott worked a number of jobs to
help financially support her family, including as a domestic companion, a teacher, a seamstress and even a nurse in a Civil War army hospital in Washington, DC. She also began
writing novels and short stories to supplement her family's income, but it was only with the
great success of *Little Women, or Meg, Beth, Jo and Amy* in 1868 (it sold over 80,000 copies in its
first two years) that the financial fortunes of her family finally stabilized. The royalties from
this work, and her future books, allowed the Alcott family to escape the shadow of constant
debt that had hung over it since Alcott's youth.

A semi-autobiographical work based on her own experience of growing up with three
sisters, a beloved mother, and a largely absent father figure, *Little Women* is a contemporary
retelling of John Bunyan's *Pilgrim's Progress* for a new generation of postbellum American
youngsters. It is a highly didactic work that lays great stress on Alcott's belief in the importance of personal virtue, intellectual vibrancy and moral fortitude. The firebrand of the
novel, Jo, is based on Alcott's own independent spirit, and it is Jo's strong devotion to family
amid her personal failings that trumpets Alcott's primary message that it is a heart focused
on doing good that matters most in a world that too often only offers poor moral examples,
temptations against virtue, and trying material circumstances.

LITTLE WOMEN,
OR, MEG, JO, BETH, AND AMY

They all drew to the fire, mother in the big chair, with Beth at
her feet; Meg and Amy perched on either arm of the chair, and Jo
leaning on the back. — PAGE 12.

Frontispiece from first book edition (*Little Women, or, Meg, Jo, Beth, and Amy*, Boston: Robert Brothers, 1868, Courtesy Lilly Library, Bloomington, IN).

This text is reprinted from the following edition: *Little Women, or, Meg, Jo, Beth, and Amy*. Boston: Roberts Brothers, 1868.

Preface

"Go then, my little Book, and show to all
That entertain and bid thee welcome shall,
What thou dost keep close shut up in thy breast;
And wish what thou dost show them may be blest
To them for good, may make them choose to be
Pilgrims better, by far, than thee or me.
Tell them of Mercy; she is one
Who early hath her pilgrimage begun.
Yea, let young damsels learn of her to prize
The world which is to come, and so be wise;
For little tripping maids may follow God
Along the ways which saintly feet have trod."

ADAPTED FROM JOHN BUNYAN.[1]

1

Playing Pilgrims

"Christmas won't be Christmas without any presents," grumbled Jo, lying on the rug. "It's so dreadful to be poor!" sighed Meg, looking down at her old dress.

"I don't think it's fair for some girls to have plenty of pretty things, and other girls nothing at all," added little Amy, with an injured sniff.

"We've got father and mother and each other," said Beth contentedly from her corner.

The four young faces on which the firelight shone brightened at the cheerful words, but darkened again as Jo said sadly, "We haven't got father, and shall not have him for a long time." She didn't say "perhaps never," but each silently added it, thinking of father far away, where the fighting was.

Nobody spoke for a minute; then Meg said in an altered tone,—

"You know the reason mother proposed not having any presents this Christmas was because it is going to be a hard winter for every one; and she thinks we ought not to spend money for pleasure, when our men are suffering so in the army. We can't do much, but we can make our little sacrifices, and ought to do it gladly. But I am afraid I don't;" and Meg shook her head, as she thought regretfully of all the pretty things she wanted.

"But I don't think the little we should spend would do any good. We've each got a dollar, and the army wouldn't be much helped by our giving that. I agree not to expect anything from mother or you, but I do want to buy Undine and Sintram[2] for myself. I've wanted it *so* long," said Jo, who was a bookworm.

---

1 Adapted from Part II of John Bunyan's classic religious allegory *Pilgrim's Progress* (1684), which tells the story of an everyman character named Christian and his journey to the Celestial City (Heaven).

2 Two stories by the German novelist and poet Friedrich De La Motte-Fouqué (1777–1843), which were immensely popular with nineteenth-century American children.

"I planned to spend mine in new music," said Beth, with a little sigh, which no one heard but the hearth-brush and kettle-holder.

"I shall get a nice box of Faber's drawing pencils. I really need them," said Amy, decidedly.

"Mother didn't say anything about our money, and she won't wish us to give up everything. Let's each buy what we want, and have a little fun, I'm sure we work hard enough to earn it," cried Jo, examining the heels of her shoes in a gentlemanly manner.

"I know I do, — teaching those tiresome children nearly all day, when I'm longing to enjoy myself at home," began Meg, in the complaining tone again.

"You don't have half such a hard time as I do," said Jo. "How would you like to be shut up for hours with a nervous, fussy old lady, who keeps you trotting, is never satisfied, and worries you till you're ready to fly out of the window or box her ears?"

"It's naughty to fret, — but I do think washing dishes and keeping things tidy is the worst work in the world. It makes me cross; and my hands get so stiff, I can't practice well at all." And Beth looked at her rough hands with a sigh that any one could hear that time.

"I don't believe any of you suffer as I do," cried Amy; "for you don't have to go to school with impertinent girls, who plague you if you don't know your lessons, and laugh at your dresses, and label your father if he isn't rich, and insult you when your nose isn't nice."

"If you mean *libel*, I'd say so, and not talk about *labels*, as if Papa was a pickle-bottle," advised Jo, laughing.

"I know what I mean, and you needn't be 'statirical' about it. It's proper to use good words, and improve your *vocabilary*," returned Amy, with dignity.

"Don't peck at one another, children. Don't you wish we had the money Papa lost when we were little, Jo? Dear me, how happy and good we'd be, if we had no worries," said Meg, who could remember better times.

"You said the other day you thought we were a deal happier than the King children, for they were fighting and fretting all the time, in spite of their money."

"So I did, Beth. Well, I guess we are; for though we do have to work, we make fun for ourselves, and are a pretty jolly set, as Jo would say."

"Jo does use such slang words," observed Amy, with a reproving look at the long figure stretched on the rug. Jo immediately sat up, put her hands in her pockets, and began to whistle.

"Don't, Jo; it's so boyish."

"That's why I do it."

"I detest rude, unlady-like girls."

"I hate affected, niminy piminy chits!"

"Birds in their little nests agree," sang Beth, the peace-maker, with such a funny face that both sharp voices softened to a laugh, and the "pecking" ended for that time.

"Really, girls, you are both to be blamed," said Meg, beginning to lecture in her elder sisterly fashion. "You are old enough to leave off boyish tricks, and to behave better, Josephine. It didn't matter so much when you were a little girl; but now you are so tall, and turn up your hair, you should remember that you are a young lady."

"I ain't! and if turning up my hair makes me one, I'll wear it in two tails till I'm twenty," cried Jo, pulling off her net, and shaking down a chestnut mane. "I hate to think I've got to grow up and be Miss March, and wear long gowns, and look as prim as a China-aster.[3] It's bad enough to be a girl, any-way, when I like boy's games and work, and manners. I can't get over my disappointment in not being a boy, and it's worse than ever now, for I'm dying to go and fight with papa, and I can only stay at home and knit like a poky old woman;" and Jo shook the blue army-sock till the needles rattled like castanets, and her ball bounded across the room.

"Poor Jo; it's too bad! But it can't be helped, so you must try to be contented with making your name boyish, and playing brother to us girls," said Beth, stroking the rough head at her knee with a hand that all the dishwashing and dusting in the world could not make ungentle in its touch.

"As for you, Amy," continued Meg, "you are altogether too particular and prim. Your airs are funny now, but you'll grow up an affected little goose if you don't take care. I like your nice manners, and refined ways of speaking, when you don't try to be elegant; but your absurd words are as bad as Jo's slang."

"If Jo is a tom-boy, and Amy a goose, what am I, please?" asked Beth, ready to share the lecture.

"You're a dear, and nothing else," answered Meg, warmly; and no one contradicted her, for the "Mouse" was the pet of the family.

As young readers like to know "how people look," we will take this moment to give them a little sketch of the four sisters, who sat knitting away in the twilight, while the December snow fell quietly without, and the fire crackled cheerfully within. It was a comfortable old room, though the carpet was faded and the furniture very plain, for a good picture or two hung on the walls, books filled the recesses, chrysanthemums and Christmas roses bloomed in the windows, and a pleasant atmosphere of home-peace pervaded it.

Margaret, the eldest of the four, was sixteen, and very pretty, being plump and fair, with large eyes, plenty of soft brown hair, a sweet mouth, and white hands, of which she was rather vain. Fifteen-year old Jo was very tall, thin, and brown, and reminded one of a colt; for she never seemed to know what to do with her long limbs, which were very much in her way. She had a decided mouth, a comical nose, and sharp gray eyes, which appeared to see everything, and were by turns fierce, funny, or thoughtful. Her long, thick hair was her one beauty; but it was usually bundled into a net, to be out of her way. Round shoulders had Jo, big hands and feet, a fly-away look to her clothes, and the uncomfortable appearance of a girl who was rapidly shooting up into a woman, and didn't like it. Elizabeth, — or Beth, as everyone called her, — was a rosy, smooth-haired, bright-eyed girl of thirteen, with a shy manner, a timid voice, and a peaceful expression, which was seldom disturbed. Her father called her "Little Tranquillity," and the name suited her excellently; for she seemed to live in a happy world of her own, only venturing out to meet the few whom she trusted and loved. Amy, though the youngest, was a most important person, in her own opinion at least. A regular snow maiden, with blue eyes, and yellow hair curling on her shoulders; pale and slender, and always carrying herself like a young lady mindful of her manners. What the characters of the four sisters were, we will leave to be found out.

The clock struck six; and, having swept up the hearth, Beth put a pair of slippers down to warm. Somehow the sight of the old shoes had a good effect upon the girls, for mother

3 A beautiful annual plant that flowers in a wide range of colors.

was coming, and everyone brightened to welcome her. Meg stopped lecturing, and lit the lamp, Amy got out of the easy-chair without being asked, and Jo forgot how tired she was as she sat up to hold the slippers nearer to the blaze.

"They are quite worn out; Marmee must have a new pair."

"I thought I'd get her some with my dollar," said Beth.

"No, I shall!" cried Amy.

"I'm the oldest," began Meg, but Jo cut in with a decided —

"I'm the man of the family now papa is away, and *I* shall provide the slippers, for he told me to take special care of mother while he was gone."

"I'll tell you what we'll do," said Beth; "let's each get her something for Christmas, and not get anything for ourselves."

"That's like you, dear! What will we get?" exclaimed Jo.

Every one thought soberly for a minute; then Meg announced, as if the idea was suggested by the sight of her own pretty hands, "I shall give her a nice pair of gloves."

"Army shoes, best to be had," cried Jo.

"Some handkerchiefs, all hemmed," said Beth.

"I'll get a little bottle of Cologne; she likes it, and it won't cost much, so I'll have some left to buy something for me," added Amy.

"How will we give the things?" asked Meg.

"Put 'em on the table, and bring her in and see her open the bundles. Don't you remember how we used to do on our birthdays?" answered Jo.

"I used to be *so* frightened when it was my turn to sit in the big chair with the crown on, and see you all come marching round to give the presents, with a kiss. I liked the things and the kisses, but it was dreadful to have you sit looking at me while I opened the bundles," said Beth, who was toasting her face and the bread for tea, at the same time.

"Let Marmee think we are getting things for ourselves, and then surprise her. We must go shopping to-morrow afternoon, Meg; there is lots to do about the play for Christmas night," said Jo, marching up and down with her hands behind her back, and her nose in the air.

"I don't mean to act any more after this time; I'm getting too old for such things," observed Meg, who was as much a child as ever about "dressing up" frolics.

"You won't stop, I know, as long as you can trail round in a white gown with your hair down, and wear gold-paper jewelry. You are the best actress we've got, and there'll be an end of everything if you quit the boards,"[4] said Jo. "We ought to rehearse to-night; come here, Amy, and do the fainting scene, for you are as stiff as a poker in that."

"I can't help it; I never saw anyone faint, and I don't choose to make myself all black and blue, tumbling flat as you do. If I can go down easily, I'll drop; if I can't, I shall fall into a chair and be graceful; I don't care if Hugo does come at me with a pistol," returned Amy, who was not gifted with dramatic power, but was chosen because she was small enough to be borne out shrieking by the hero of the piece.

"Do it this way; clasp your hands so, and stagger across the room, crying frantically, 'Roderigo! save me! save me!'" and away went Jo, with a melodramatic scream which was truly thrilling.

Amy followed, but she poked her hands out stiffly before her, and jerked herself along as if she went by machinery; and her "Ow!" was more suggestive of pins being run into

---

4 The stage.

her than of fear and anguish. Jo gave a despairing groan, and Meg laughed outright, while Beth let her bread burn as she watched the fun, with interest.

"It's no use! do the best you can when the time comes, and if the audience shout, don't blame me. Come on, Meg."

Then things went smoothly, for Don Pedro defied the world in a speech of two pages without a single break; Hagar, the witch, chanted an awful incantation over her kettleful of simmering toads, with weird effect; Roderigo rent his chains asunder manfully, and Hugo died in agonies of remorse and arsenic, with a wild "Ha! ha!"

"It's the best we've had yet," said Meg, as the dead villain sat up and rubbed his elbows.

"I don't see how you can write and act such splendid things, Jo. You're a regular Shakespeare!" exclaimed Beth, who firmly believed that her sisters were gifted with wonderful genius in all things.

"Not quite," replied Jo, modestly. "I do think 'The Witch's Curse, an Operatic Tragedy'[5] is rather a nice thing, but I'd like to try Macbeth, if we only had a trapdoor for Banquo. I always wanted to do the killing part. 'Is that a dagger that I see before me?'"[6] muttered Jo, rolling her eyes and clutching at the air, as she had seen a famous tragedian do.

"No, it's the toasting fork, with mother's shoe on it instead of the bread. Beth's stage struck!" cried Meg, and the rehearsal ended in a general burst of laughter.

"Glad to find you so merry, my girls," said a cheery voice at the door, and actors and audience turned to welcome a stout, motherly lady with a "can-I-help-you" look about her which was truly delightful. She wasn't a particularly handsome person, but mothers are always lovely to their children, and the girls thought the gray cloak and unfashionable bonnet covered the most splendid woman in the world.

"Well, dearies, how have you got on to-day? There was so much to do, getting the boxes ready to go to-morrow, that I didn't come home to dinner. Has anyone called, Beth? How is your cold, Meg? Jo, you look tired to death. Come and kiss me, baby."

While making these maternal inquiries Mrs. March got her wet things off, her hot slippers on, and sitting down in the easy-chair, drew Amy to her lap, preparing to enjoy the happiest hour of her busy day. The girls flew about, trying to make things comfortable, each in her own way. Meg arranged the tea-table; Jo brought wood and set chairs, dropping, overturning, and clattering everything she touched; Beth trotted to and fro between parlor and kitchen, quiet and busy; while Amy gave directions to everyone, as she sat with her hands folded.

As they gathered about the table, Mrs. March said, with a particularly happy face, "I've got a treat for you after supper."

A quick, bright smile went round like a streak of sunshine. Beth clapped her hands, regardless of the hot biscuit she held, and Jo tossed up her napkin, crying, "A letter! a letter! Three cheers for father!"

"Yes, a nice long letter. He is well, and thinks he shall get through the cold season better than we feared. He sends all sorts of loving wishes for Christmas, and an especial message to you girls," said Mrs. March, patting her pocket as if she had got a treasure there.

---

5 When Alcott was 16 and living in Boston, she wrote a number of plays for her family, including: *Norna; or, The Witches' Curse*.

6 Shakespeare, *Macbeth* 2.1.

"Hurry up, and get done! Don't stop to quirk your little finger, and prink over your plate, Amy," cried Jo, choking in her tea, and dropping her bread, butter side down, on the carpet, in her haste to get at the treat.

Beth ate no more, but crept away to sit in her shadowy corner and brood over the delight to come, till the others were ready.

"I think it was so splendid in father to go as a chaplain when he was too old to be draughted, and not strong enough for a soldier," said Meg, warmly.

"Don't I wish I could go as a drummer, a *vivan*[7] — what's its name? or a nurse, so I could be near him and help him," exclaimed Jo, with a groan.

"It must be very disagreeable to sleep in a tent, and eat all sorts of bad-tasting things, and drink out of a tin mug," sighed Amy.

"When will he come home, Marmee?" asked Beth, with a little quiver in her voice.

"Not for many months, dear, unless he is sick. He will stay and do his work faithfully as long as he can, and we won't ask for him back a minute sooner than he can be spared. Now come and hear the letter."

They all drew to the fire, mother in the big chair with Beth at her feet, Meg and Amy perched on either arm of the chair, and Jo leaning on the back, where no one would see any sign of emotion if the letter should happen to be touching.

Very few letters were written in those hard times that were not touching, especially those which fathers sent home. In this one little was said of the hardships endured, the dangers faced, or the homesickness conquered; it was a cheerful, hopeful letter, full of lively descriptions of camp life, marches, and military news; and only at the end did the writer's heart overflow with fatherly love and longing for the little girls at home.

"Give them all my dear love and a kiss. Tell them I think of them by day, pray for them by night, and find my best comfort in their affection at all times. A year seems very long to wait before I see them, but remind them that while we wait we may all work, so that these hard days need not be wasted. I know they will remember all I said to them, that they will be loving children to you, will do their duty faithfully, fight their bosom enemies bravely, and conquer themselves so beautifully, that when I come back to them I may be fonder and prouder than ever of my little women."

Everybody sniffed when they came to that part; Jo wasn't ashamed of the great tear that dropped off the end of her nose, and Amy never minded the rumpling of her curls as she hid her face on her mother's shoulder and sobbed out, "I *am* a selfish girl! but I'll truly try to be better, so he mayn't be disappointed in me by and by."

"We all will!" cried Meg. "I think too much of my looks, and hate to work, but won't any more, if I can help it."

"I'll try and be what he loves to call me, 'a little woman,' and not be rough and wild; but do my duty here instead of wanting to be somewhere else," said Jo, thinking that keeping her temper at home was a much harder task than facing a rebel or two down South.

Beth said nothing, but wiped away her tears with the blue army-sock, and began to knit with all her might, losing no time in doing the duty that lay nearest her, while she resolved in her quiet little soul to be all that father hoped to find her when the year brought round the happy coming home.

Mrs. March broke the silence that followed Jo's words, by saying in her cheery voice, "Do you remember how you used to play Pilgrim's Progress when you were little things?

---

7 A *vivandière* is French for a woman who accompanies an army to sell it provisions.

Nothing delighted you more than to have me tie my piece-bags[8] on your backs for burdens, give you hats and sticks and rolls of paper, and let you travel through the house from the cellar, which was the City of Destruction, up, up, to the house-top, where you had all the lovely things you could collect to make a Celestial City."

"What fun it was, especially going by the lions, fighting Apollyon, and passing through the Valley where the hobgoblins were!" said Jo.

"I liked the place where the bundles fell off and tumbled downstairs," said Meg.

"My favorite part was when we came out on the flat roof where our flowers and arbors, and pretty things were, and all stood and sung for joy up there in the sunshine," said Beth, smiling, as if that pleasant moment had come back to her.

"I don't remember much about it, except that I was afraid of the cellar and the dark entry, and always liked the cake and milk we had up at the top. If I wasn't too old for such things, I'd rather like to play it over again," said Amy, who began to talk of renouncing childish things at the mature age of twelve.

"We never are too old for this, my dear, because it is a play we are playing all the time in one way or another. Our burdens are here, our road is before us, and the longing for goodness and happiness is the guide that leads us through many troubles and mistakes to the peace which is a true Celestial City. Now, my little pilgrims, suppose you begin again, not in play, but in earnest, and see how far on you can get before father comes home."

"Really, mother? where are our bundles?" asked Amy, who was a very literal young lady.

"Each of you told what your burden was just now, except Beth; I rather think she hasn't got any," said her mother.

"Yes, I have; mine is dishes and dusters, and envying girls with nice pianos, and being afraid of people."

Beth's bundle was such a funny one that everybody wanted to laugh; but nobody did, for it would have hurt her feelings very much.

"Let us do it," said Meg thoughtfully. "It is only another name for trying to be good, and the story may help us; for though we do want to be good, it's hard work and we forget, and don't do our best."

"We were in the Slough of Despond[9] to-night, and mother came and pulled us out as Help did in the book. We ought to have our roll of directions, like Christian. What shall we do about that?" asked Jo, delighted with the fancy which lent a little romance to the very dull task of doing her duty.

"Look under your pillows Christmas morning, and you will find your guide-book," replied Mrs. March.

They talked over the new plan while old Hannah cleared the table; then out came the four little work-baskets, and the needles flew as the girls made sheets for Aunt March. It was uninteresting sewing, but to-night no one grumbled. They adopted Jo's plan of dividing the long seams into four parts, and calling the quarters Europe, Asia, Africa and America, and in that way got on capitally, especially when they talked about the different countries as they stitched their way through them.

At nine they stopped work, and sang, as usual, before they went to bed. No one but Beth could get much music out of the old piano; but she had a way of softly touching the

---

8 Bags full of cloth remnants.

9 In John Bunyan's *Pilgrim's Progress*, the Slough of Despond is a deep bog where the main character, Christian, struggles to pass through as he sinks under the weight of his sins.

yellow keys, and making a pleasant accompaniment to the simple songs they sung. Meg had a voiced like a flute, and she and her mother led the little choir. Amy chirped like a cricket, and Jo wandered through the airs at her own sweet will, always coming out at the wrong place with a crook or a quaver that spoiled the most pensive tune. They had always done this from the time they could lisp

"Crinkle, crinkle, 'ittle 'tar,"

and it had become a household custom, for the mother was a born singer. The first sound in the morning was her voice, as she went about the house singing like a lark; and the last sound at night was the same cheery sound, for the girls never grew too old for that familiar lullaby.

2

A Merry Christmas

Jo was the first to wake in the gray dawn of Christmas morning. No stockings hung at the fireplace, and for a moment she felt as much disappointed as she did long ago, when her little sock fell down because it was so crammed with goodies. Then she remembered her mother's promise, and slipping her hand under her pillow, drew out a little crimson-covered book.[10] She knew it very well, for it was that beautiful old story of the best life ever lived, and Jo felt that it was a true guide-book for any pilgrim going the long journey. She woke Meg with a "Merry Christmas," and bade her see what was under her pillow. A green-covered book appeared, with the same picture inside, and a few words written by their mother, which made their one present very precious in their eyes. Presently Beth and Amy woke, to rummage and find their little books also, — one dove-colored, the other blue; and all sat looking at and talking about them, while the East grew rosy with the coming day.

In spite of her small vanities, Margaret had a sweet and pious nature, which unconsciously influenced her sisters, especially Jo, who loved her very tenderly, and obeyed her because her advice was so gently given.

"Girls," said Meg seriously, looking from the tumbled head beside her to the two little night-capped ones in the room beyond, "mother wants us to read and love and mind these books, and we must begin at once. We used to be faithful about it; but since father went away, and all this war trouble unsettled us, we have neglected many things. You can do as you please; but *I* shall keep my book on the table here, and read a little every morning as soon as I wake, for I know it will do me good, and help me through the day."

Then she opened her new book and began to read. Jo put her arm round her, and, leaning cheek to cheek, read also, with the quiet expression so seldom seen on her restless face.

"How good Meg is! Come, Amy, let's do as they do. I'll help you with the hard words, and they'll explain things if we don't understand," whispered Beth, very much impressed by the pretty books and her sisters' example.

---

10 Either a copy of the Bible or *The Pilgrim's Progress.*

"I'm glad mine is blue," said Amy; and then the rooms were very still while the pages were softly turned, and the winter sunshine crept in to touch the bright heads and serious faces with a Christmas greeting.

"Where is mother?" asked Meg, as she and Jo ran down to thank her for their gifts, half an hour later.

"Goodness only knows. Some poor creeter come a-beggin', and your ma went straight off to see what was needed. There never *was* such a woman for givin' away vittles and drink, clothes and firin'," replied Hannah, who had lived with the family since Meg was born, and was considered by them all more as a friend than a servant.

"She will be back soon, I guess; so do your cakes, and have everything ready," said Meg, looking over the presents which were collected in a basket and kept under the sofa, ready to be produced at the proper time. "Why, where is Amy's bottle of Cologne?" she added, as the little flask did not appear.

"She took it out a minute ago, and went off with it to put a ribbon on it, or some such notion," replied Jo, dancing about the room to take the first stiffness off the new army-slippers.

How nice my handkerchiefs look, don't they? Hannah washed and ironed them for me, and I marked them all myself," said Beth, looking proudly at the somewhat uneven letters which had cost her such labor.

"Bless the child, she's gone and put 'Mother' on them instead of 'M. March;' how funny!" cried Jo, taking up one.

"Isn't it right? I thought it was better to do it so, because Meg's initials are 'M. M.,' and I don't want any one to use these but Marmee," said Beth, looking troubled.

"It's all right, dear, and a very pretty idea; quite sensible, too, for no one can ever mistake now. It will please her very much, I know," said Meg, with a frown for Jo and a smile for Beth.

"There's mother; hide the basket, quick!" cried Jo, as a door slammed and steps sounded in the hall.

Amy came in hastily, and looked rather abashed when she saw her sisters all waiting for her.

"Where have you been, and what are you hiding behind you?" asked Meg, surprised to see, by her hood and cloak, that lazy Amy had been out so early.

"Don't laugh at me, Jo! I didn't mean any one should know till the time came. I only meant to change the little bottle for a big one, and I gave *all* my money to get it, and I'm truly trying not to be selfish any more."

As she spoke, Amy showed the handsome flask which replaced the cheap one; and looked so earnest and humble in her little effort to forget herself, that Meg hugged her on the spot, and Jo pronounced her "a trump,"[11] while Beth ran to the window, and picked her finest rose to ornament the stately bottle.

"You see I felt ashamed of my present, after reading and talking about being good this morning, so I ran round the corner and changed it the minute I was up; and I'm *so* glad, for mine is the handsomest now."

Another bang of the street-door sent the basket under the sofa, and the girls to the table eager for breakfast.

---

11 Slang referring to a great person.

"Merry Christmas, Marmee! Lots of them! Thank you for our books; we read some, and mean to every day," they cried, in chorus.

"Merry Christmas, little daughters! I'm glad you began at once, and hope you will keep on. But I want to say one word before we sit down. Not far away from here lies a poor woman with a little newborn baby. Six children are huddled into one bed to keep from freezing, for they have no fire. There is nothing to eat over there; and the oldest boy came to tell me they were suffering hunger and cold. My girls, will you give them your breakfast as a Christmas present?"

They were all unusually hungry, having waited nearly an hour, and for a minute no one spoke; only a minute, for Jo exclaimed impetuously,—

"I'm so glad you came before we began!"

"May I go and help carry the things to the poor little children?" asked Beth, eagerly.

"*I* shall take the cream and the muffins," added Amy, heroically giving up the articles she most liked.

Meg was already covering the buckwheats, and piling the bread into one big plate.

"I thought you'd do it," said Mrs. March, smiling as if satisfied. 'You shall all go and help me, and when we come back we will have bread and milk for breakfast, and make it up at dinner-time."

They were soon ready, and the procession set out. Fortunately it was early, and they went through back streets, so few people saw them, and no one laughed at the funny party.

A poor, bare, miserable room it was, with broken windows, no fire, ragged bed-clothes, a sick mother, wailing baby, and a group of pale, hungry children cuddled under one old quilt, trying to keep warm. How the big eyes stared, and the blue lips smiled, as the girls went in!

"Ach, mein Gott![12] it is good angels come to us!" said the poor woman, crying for joy.

"Funny angels in hoods and mittens," said Jo, and set them laughing.

In a few minutes it really did seem as if kind spirits had been at work there. Hannah, who had carried wood, made a fire, and stopped up the broken panes with old hats, and her own cloak. Mrs. March gave the mother tea and gruel, and comforted her with promises of help, while she dressed the little baby as tenderly as if it had been her own. The girls meantime, spread the table, set the children round the fire, and fed them like so many hungry birds; laughing, talking, and trying to understand the funny broken English.

"Das ist gute!" "Der angel-kinder!"[13] cried the poor things, as they ate, and warmed their purple hands at the comfortable blaze.

The girls had never been called angel children before, and thought it very agreeable, especially Jo, who had been considered a "Sancho"[14] ever since she was born. That was a very happy breakfast, though they didn't get any of it; and when they went away, leaving comfort behind, I think there were not in all the city four merrier people than the hungry little girls who gave away their breakfasts, and contented themselves with bread and milk on Christmas morning.

"That's loving our neighbor better than ourselves, and I like it," said Meg, as they set out their presents, while their mother was upstairs collecting clothes for the poor Hummels.

---

12 German for "Oh, my God!"

13 German for "That is good! The angel-children."

14 A comical sidekick character found in the novel *Don Quixote* (1605) by Miguel de Cervantes.

Not a very splendid show, but there was a great deal of love done up in the few little bundles; and the tall vase of red roses, white chrysanthemums, and trailing vines, which stood in the middle, gave quite an elegant air to the table.

"She's coming! strike up, Beth, open the door, Amy. Three cheers for Marmee!" cried Jo, prancing about, while Meg went to conduct mother to the seat of honor.

Beth played her gayest march, Amy threw open the door, and Meg enacted escort with great dignity. Mrs. March was both surprised and touched; and smiled with her eyes full as she examined her presents and read the little notes which accompanied them. The slippers went on at once, a new handkerchief was slipped into her pocket, well scented with Amy's Cologne, the rose was fastened in her bosom, and the nice gloves were pronounced a "perfect fit."

There was a good deal of laughing, and kissing, and explaining, in the simple, loving fashion which makes these home-festivals so pleasant at the time, so sweet to remember long afterward, and then all fell to work.

The morning charities and ceremonies took so much time, that the rest of the day was devoted to preparations for the evening festivities. Being still too young to go often to the theater, and not rich enough to afford any great outlay for private performances, the girls put their wits to work, and, necessity being the mother of invention, made whatever they needed. Very clever were some of their productions; pasteboard guitars, antique lamps made of old-fashioned butter-boats, covered with silver paper, gorgeous robes of old cotton, glittering with tin spangles from a pickle factory, and armor covered with the same useful diamond-shaped bits, left in sheets when the lids of tin preserve pots were cut out. The furniture was used to being turned topsy-turvy, and the big chamber was the scene of many innocent revels.

No gentlemen were admitted; so Jo played male parts to her heart's content, and took immense satisfaction in a pair of russet-leather boots given her by a friend, who knew a lady who knew an actor. These boots, an old foil, and a slashed doublet once used by an artist for some picture, were Jo's chief treasures, and appeared on all occasions. The smallness of the company made it necessary for the two principal actors to take several parts apiece; and they certainly deserved some credit for the hard work they did in learning three or four different parts, whisking in and out of various costumes, and managing the stage besides. It was excellent drill for their memories, a harmless amusement, and employed many hours which otherwise would have been idle, lonely, or spent in less profitable society.

On Christmas night, a dozen girls piled onto the bed, which was the dress circle, and sat before the blue and yellow chintz curtains, in a most flattering state of expectancy. There was a good deal of rustling and whispering behind the curtain, a trifle of lamp-smoke, and an occasional giggle from Amy, who was apt to get hysterical in the excitement of the moment. Presently a bell sounded, the curtains flew apart, and the Operatic Tragedy began.

"A gloomy wood," according to the one play-bill, was represented by a few shrubs in pots, a green baize[15] on the floor, and a cave in the distance. This cave was made with a clothes-horse[16] for a roof, bureaus for walls; and in it was a small furnace in full blast, with a black pot on it. and an old witch bending over it. The stage was dark, and the glow of the furnace had a fine effect, especially as real steam issued from the kettle when the witch

---

15 A thick, felt-like fabric.
16 A wooden frame used to hang clothes upon.

took off the cover. A moment was allowed for the first thrill to subside; then Hugo, the villain, stalked in with a clanking sword at his side, a slouched hat, black beard, mysterious cloak, and the boots. After pacing to and fro in much agitation, he struck his forehead, and burst out in a wild strain, singing of his hatred to Roderigo, his love for Zara, and his pleasing resolution to kill the one and win the other. The gruff tones of Hugo's voice, with an occasional shout when his feelings overcame him, were very impressive, and the audience applauded the moment he paused for breath. Bowing with the air of one accustomed to public praise, he stole to the cavern and ordered Hagar to come forth with a commanding, "What ho, minion! I need thee!"

Out came Meg, with gray horse-hair hanging about her face, a red and black robe, a staff, and cabalistic signs upon her cloak. Hugo demanded a potion to make Zara adore him, and one to destroy Roderigo. Hagar, in a fine dramatic melody, promised both, and proceeded to call up the spirit who would bring the love philter:—[17]

> *"Hither, hither, from thy home,*
> *Airy sprite, I bid thee come!*
> *Born of roses, fed on dew,*
> *Charms and potions canst thou brew?*
> *Bring me here, with elfin speed,*
> *The fragrant philter which I need;*
> *Make it sweet, and swift and strong,*
> *Spirit, answer now my song!"*

A soft strain of music sounded, and then at the back of the cave appeared a little figure in cloudy white, with glittering wings, golden hair, and a garland of roses on its head. Waving a wand, it sung: —

> *"Hither I come,*
> *From my airy home,*
> *Afar in the silver moon;*
> *Take the magic spell,*
> *Oh, use it well!*
> *Or its power will vanish soon!"*

and dropping a small gilded bottle at the witch's feet, the spirit vanished. Another chant from Hagar produced another apparition, — not a lovely one, for, with a bang, an ugly, black imp appeared, and having croaked a reply, tossed a dark bottle at Hugo, and disappeared with a mocking laugh. Having warbled his thanks, and put the potions in his boots, Hugo departed; and Hagar informed the audience that, as he had killed a few of her friends in times past, she has cursed him, and intends to thwart his plans, and be revenged on him. Then the curtain fell, and the audience reposed and ate candy while discussing the merits of the play.

A good deal of hammering went on before the curtain rose again; but when it became evident what a masterpiece of stage carpentering had been got up, no one murmured at the delay. It was truly superb! A tower rose to the ceiling; half-way up appeared a window

---

17 Magic potion.

with a lamp burning at it, and behind the white curtain appeared Zara in a lovely blue and silver dress, waiting for Roderigo. He came, in gorgeous array, with plumed cap, red cloak, chestnut love-locks,[18] a guitar, and the boots, of course. Kneeling at the foot of the tower, he sung a serenade in melting tones. Zara replied, and after a musical dialogue, consented to fly. Then came the grand effect of the play. Roderigo produced a rope-ladder with five steps to it, threw up one end, and invited Zara to descend. Timidly she crept from her lattice, put her hand on Roderigo's shoulder, and was about to leap gracefully down, when, "Alas! alas for Zara!" she forgot her train, — it caught in the window; the tower tottered, leaned forward, fell with a crash, and buried the unhappy lovers in the ruins!

A universal shriek arose as the russet boots waved wildly from the wreck and a golden head emerged, exclaiming, "I told you so! I told you so!" With wonderful presence of mind Don Pedro, the cruel sire, rushed in, dragged out his daughter with a hasty aside,—

"Don't laugh, act as if it was all right!" and, ordering Roderigo up, banished him from the kingdom with wrath and scorn. Though decidedly shaken by the fall of the tower upon him, Roderigo defied the old gentleman, and refused to stir. This dauntless example fired Zara; she also defied her sire, and he ordered them both to the deepest dungeons of the castle. A stout little retainer came in with chains and led them away, looking very much frightened and evidently forgetting the speech he ought to have made.

Act third was the castle hall, and here Hagar appeared, having come to free the lovers and finish Hugo. She hears him coming, and hides; sees him put the potions into two cups of wine, and bid the timid little servant "Bear them to the captives in their cells, and tell them I shall come anon." The servant takes Hugo aside to tell him something, and Hagar changes the cups for two others which are harmless. Ferdinando, the "minion," carries them away, and Hagar puts back the cup which holds the poison meant for Roderigo. Hugo, getting thirsty after a long warble, drinks it, loses his wits, and after a good deal of clutching and stamping, falls flat and dies; while Hagar informs him what she has done in a song of exquisite power and melody.

This was a truly thrilling scene; though some persons might have thought that the sudden tumbling down of a quantity of long hair rather marred the effect of the villain's death. He was called before the curtain, and with great propriety appeared leading Hagar, whose singing was considered more wonderful than all the rest of the performance put together.

Act fourth displayed the despairing Roderigo on the point of stabbing himself, because he has been told that Zara has deserted him. Just as the dagger is at his heart, a lovely song is sung under his window, informing him that Zara is true, but in danger, and he can save her if he will. A key is thrown in, which unlocks the door, and in a spasm of rapture he tears off his chains, and rushes away to find and rescue his lady-love.

Act fifth opened with a stormy scene between Zara and Don Pedro. He wishes her to go into a convent, but she won't hear of it; and, after a touching appeal, is about to faint when Roderigo dashes in and demands her hand. Don Pedro refuses, because he is not rich. They shout and gesticulate tremendously, but cannot agree, and Roderigo is about to bear away the exhausted Zara, when the timid servant enters with a letter and a bag from Hagar, who has mysteriously disappeared. The latter informs the party that she bequeaths untold wealth to the young pair, and an awful doom to Don Pedro, if he doesn't make them happy. The bag is opened, and several quarts of tin money shower down upon the stage, till it is quite glorified with the glitter. This entirely softens the "stern sire;" he consents without a

---

18 Long locks of hair.

murmur, all join in a joyful chorus, and the curtain falls upon the lovers kneeling to receive Don Pedro's blessing, in attitudes of the most romantic grace.

Tumultuous applause followed, but received an unexpected check; for the cot-bed on which the "dress circle" was built, suddenly shut up, and extinguished the enthusiastic audience. Roderigo and Don Pedro flew to the rescue, and all were taken out unhurt, though many were speechless with laughter. The excitement had hardly subsided when Hannah appeared, with "Mrs. March's compliments, and would the ladies walk down to supper."

This was a surprise, even to the actors; and when they saw the table they looked at one another in rapturous amazement. It was like "Marmee" to get up a little treat for them, but anything so fine as this was unheard of since the departed days of plenty. There was ice cream, actually two dishes of it,— pink and white,— and cake, and fruit, and distracting French bonbons, and in the middle of the table four great bouquets of hothouse flowers!

It quite took their breath away; and they stared first at the table and then at their mother, who looked as if she enjoyed it immensely.

"Is it fairies?" asked Amy.

"It's Santa Claus," said Beth.

"Mother did it;" and Meg smiled her sweetest, in spite of her gray beard and white eyebrows.

"Aunt March had a good fit, and sent the supper," cried Jo, with a sudden inspiration.

"All wrong; old Mr. Laurence sent it," replied Mrs. March.

"The Laurence boy's grandfather! What in the world put such a thing into his head? We don't know him," exclaimed Meg.

"Hannah told one of his servants about your breakfast party; he is an odd old gentleman, but that pleased him. He knew my father, years ago, and he sent me a polite note this afternoon, saying he hoped I would allow him to express his friendly feeling toward my children by sending them a few trifles in honor of the day. I could not refuse, and so you have a little feast at night to make up for the bread and milk breakfast."

"That boy put it into his head, I know he did! He's a capital fellow, and I wish we could get acquainted. He looks as if he'd like to know us; but he's bashful, and Meg is so prim she won't let me speak to him when we pass," said Jo, as the plates went round, and the ice began to melt out of sight, with ohs! and ahs! of satisfaction.

"You mean the people who live in the big house next door, don't you?" asked one of the girls. "My mother knows old Mr. Laurence, but says he's very proud, and don't like to mix with his neighbors. He keeps his grandson shut up when he isn't riding or walking with his tutor, and makes him study dreadful hard. We invited him to our party, but he didn't come. Mother says he's very nice, though he never speaks to us girls."

"Our cat ran away once, and he brought her back, and we talked over the fence, and were getting on capitally, all about cricket, and so on, when he saw Meg coming, and walked off. I mean to know him some day, for he needs fun, I'm sure he does," said Jo, decidedly.

"I like his manners, and he looks like a little gentleman, so I've no objection to your knowing him if a proper opportunity comes. He brought the flowers himself, and I should have asked him in, if I had been sure what was going on upstairs. He looked so wistful as he went away, hearing the frolic, and evidently having none of his own."

"It's a mercy you didn't, mother!" laughed Jo, looking at her boots. "But we'll have another play some time, that he *can* see. Perhaps he'll help act; wouldn't that be jolly?"

"I never had a bouquet before; how pretty it is," and Meg examined her flowers with great interest.

"They *are* lovely, but Beth's roses are sweeter to me," said Mrs. March, sniffing at the half dead posy in her belt.

Beth nestled up to her, and whispered softly, "I wish I could send my bunch to father. I'm afraid he isn't having such a merry Christmas as we are."

3

The Laurence Boy

Jo! Jo! Where are you?" cried Meg, at the foot of the garret stairs.

"Here," answered a husky voice from above; and running up, Meg found her sister eating apples and crying over the "Heir of Redclyffe,"[19] wrapped up in a comforter on an old three-legged sofa by the sunny window. This was Jo's favorite refuge; and here she loved to retire with half a dozen russets and a nice book, to enjoy the quiet and the society of a pet rat who lived near by, and didn't mind her a particle. As Meg appeared, Scrabble whisked into his hole. Jo shook the tears off her cheeks, and waited to hear the news.

"Such fun! Only see! a regular note of invitation from Mrs. Gardiner for to-morrow night!" cried Meg, waving the precious paper, and then proceeding to read it, with girlish delight.

" 'Mrs. Gardiner would be happy to see Miss March and Miss Josephine at a little dance on New-Year's-Eve.' Marmee is willing we should go; now what *shall* we wear?"

"What's the use of asking that, when you know we shall wear our poplins, because we haven't got anything else?" answered Jo, with her mouth full.

"If I only had a silk!" sighed Meg; "mother says I may when I'm eighteen, perhaps; but two years is an everlasting time to wait."

"I'm sure our pops look like silk, and they are nice enough for us. Yours is as good as new, but I forgot the burn and the tear in mine; whatever shall I do? the burn shows horridly, and I can't take any out."

"You must sit still all you can, and keep your back out of sight; the front is all right. I shall have a new ribbon for my hair, and Marmee will lend me her little pearl pin, and my new slippers are lovely, and my gloves will do, though they aren't as nice as I'd like."

"Mine are spoiled with lemonade, and I can't get any new ones, so I shall have to go without," said Jo, who never troubled herself much about dress.

"You *must* have gloves, or I won't go," cried Meg, decidedly. "Gloves are more important than anything else; you can't dance without them, and if you don't I should be *so* mortified."

"Then I'll stay still; I don't care much for company dancing; it's no fun to go sailing round, I like to fly about and cut capers."

"You can't ask mother for new ones, they are so expensive, and you are so careless. She said, when you spoiled the others, that she shouldn't get you any more this winter. Can't you fix them any way?" asked Meg, anxiously.

"I can hold them crumpled up in my hand, so no one will know how stained they are; that's all I can do. No! I'll tell you how we can manage — each wear one good one and carry a bad one; don't you see?"

---

19 1853 novel by Charlotte M. Yonge involving a complicated plot to disinherit the title character.

Your hands are bigger than mine, and you will stretch my glove dreadfully," began Meg, whose gloves were a tender point with her.

"Then I'll go without. I don't care what people say," cried Jo, taking up her book.

"You may have it, you may! only don't stain it, and do behave nicely; don't put your hands behind you, or stare, or say 'Christopher Columbus!' will you?"

"Don't worry about me; I'll be as prim as a dish, and not get into any scrapes, if I can help it. Now go and answer your note, and let me finish this splendid story."

So Meg went away to "accept with thanks," look over her dress, and sing blithely as she did up her one real lace frill; while Jo finished her story, her four apples, and had a game of romps with Scrabble.

On New-Year's-Eve the parlor was deserted, for the two younger girls played dressing maids, and the two elder were absorbed in the all-important business of "getting ready for the party." Simple as the toilets were, there was a great deal of running up and down, laughing and talking, and at one time a strong smell of burnt hair pervaded the house. Meg wanted a few curls about her face, and Jo undertook to pinch the papered locks with a pair of hot tongs.

"Ought they to smoke like that?" asked Beth, from her perch on the bed.

"It's the dampness drying," replied Jo.

"What a queer smell! it's like burnt feathers," observed Amy, smoothing her own pretty curls with a superior air.

"There, now I'll take off the papers and you'll see a cloud of little ringlets," said Jo, putting down the tongs.

She did take off the papers, but no cloud of ringlets appeared, for the hair came with the papers, and the horrified hair-dresser laid a row of little scorched bundles on the bureau before her victim.

"Oh, oh, oh! what *have* you done? I'm spoilt! I can't go! my hair, oh, my hair!" wailed Meg, looking with despair at the uneven frizzle on her forehead.

"Just my luck! you shouldn't have asked me to do it. I always spoil everything. I'm no end sorry, but the tongs were too hot, and so I've made a mess," groaned poor Jo, regarding the black pancakes with tears of regret.

"It isn't spoilt; just frizzle it, and tie your ribbon so the ends come on your forehead a bit, and it will look like the last fashion. I've seen lots of girls do it so," said Amy consolingly.

"Serves me right for trying to be fine. I wish I'd let my hair alone," cried Meg, petulantly.

"So do I, it was so smooth and pretty. But it will soon grow out again," said Beth, coming to kiss and comfort the shorn sheep.

After various lesser mishaps, Meg was finished at last, and by the united exertions of the family Jo's hair was got up, and her dress on. They looked very well in their simple suits, Meg in silvery drab,[20] with a blue velvet snood, lace frills, and the pearl pin; Jo in maroon, with a stiff, gentlemanly linen collar, and a white chrysanthemum or two for her only ornament. Each put on one nice light glove, and carried one soiled one, and all pronounced the effect "quite easy and fine." Meg's high-heeled slippers were dreadfully tight, and hurt her, though she would not own it, and Jo's nineteen hair-pins all seemed stuck straight into her head, which was not exactly comfortable; but, dear me, let us be elegant or die.

---

20 Brown or gray cloth, dull in sheen.

"Have a good time, dearies," said Mrs. March, as the sisters went daintily down the walk. "Don't eat much supper, and come away at eleven, when I send Hannah for you." As the gate clashed behind them, a voice cried from a window, —

"Girls, girls! *have* you both got nice pocket-hand-kerchiefs?"

"Yes, yes, spandy nice,[21] and Meg has Cologne on hers," cried Jo, adding, with a laugh, as they went on, "I do believe Marmee would ask that if we were all running away from an earthquake."

"It is one of her aristocratic tastes, and quite proper, for a real lady is always known by neat boots, gloves, and handkerchief," replied Meg, who had a good many little "aristocratic tastes" of her own.

"Now don't forget to keep the bad breadth[22] out of sight, Jo. Is my sash right; and does my hair look *very* bad?" said Meg, as she turned from the glass in Mrs. Gardiner's dressing-room after a prolonged prink.[23]

"I know I shall forget. If you see me doing anything wrong, just remind me by a wink, will you?" returned Jo, giving her collar a twitch and her head a hasty brush.

"No, winking isn't lady-like; I'll lift my eyebrows if anything is wrong, and nod if you are all right. Now hold your shoulders straight, and take short steps, and don't shake hands if you are introduced to anyone, it isn't the thing."

"How *do* you learn all the proper quirks? I never can. Isn't that music gay?"

Down they went, feeling a trifle timid, for they seldom went to parties, and, informal as this little gathering was, it was an event to them. Mrs. Gardiner, a stately old lady, greeted them kindly, and handed them over to the eldest of her six daughters. Meg knew Sallie, and was at her ease very soon; but Jo, who didn't care much for girls or girlish gossip, stood about with her back carefully against the wall, and felt as much out of place as a colt in a flower-garden. Half a dozen jovial lads were talking about skates in another part of the room, and she longed to go and join them, for skating was one of the joys of her life. She telegraphed her wish to Meg, but the eyebrows went up so alarmingly that she dared not stir. No one came to talk to her, and one by one the group near her dwindled away, till she was left alone. She could not roam about and amuse herself, for the burnt breadth would show, so she stared at people rather forlornly till the dancing began. Meg was asked at once, and the tight slippers tripped about so briskly that none would have guessed the pain their wearer suffered smilingly. Jo saw a big redheaded youth approaching her corner, and fearing he meant to engage her, she slipped into a curtained recess, intending to peep and enjoy herself in peace. Unfortunately, another bashful person had chosen the same refuge; for, as the curtain fell behind her, she found herself face to face with the "Laurence boy."

"Dear me, I didn't know anyone was here!" stammered Jo, preparing to back out as speedily as she had bounced in.

But the boy laughed, and said, pleasantly, though he looked a little startled,—

"Don't mind me, stay if you like."

"Shan't I disturb you?"

"Not a bit; I only came here because I don't know many people, and felt rather strange at first, you know."

"So did I. Don't go away, please, unless you'd rather."

---

21 Expression for something thought to be very good.
22 Portion of burned fabric.
23 Variation of "primp," to carefully groom.

The boy sat down again and looked at his boots, till Jo said, trying to be polite and easy,—

"I think I've had the pleasure of seeing you before; you live near us, don't you?"

"Next door;" and he looked up and laughed outright, for Jo's prim manner was rather funny when he remembered how they had chatted about cricket when he brought the cat home.

That put Jo at her ease; and she laughed too, as she said, in her heartiest way,—

"We did have such a good time over your nice Christmas present."

"Grandpa sent it."

"But you put it into his head, didn't you, now?"

"How is your cat, Miss March?" asked the boy, trying to look sober, while his black eyes shone with fun.

"Nicely, thank you, Mr. Laurence; but I ain't Miss March, I'm only Jo," returned the young lady.

"I'm not Mr. Laurence, I'm only Laurie."

"Laurie Laurence; what an odd name."

"My first name is Theodore, but I don't like it, for the fellows called me Dora, so I made them say Laurie instead."

"I hate my name, too — so sentimental! I wish every one would say Jo, instead of Josephine. How did you make the boys stop calling you Dora?"

"I thrashed 'em."

"I can't thrash Aunt March, so I suppose I shall have to bear it;" and Jo resigned herself with a sigh.

"Don't you like to dance, Miss Jo?" asked Laurie, looking as if he thought the name suited her.

"I like it well enough if there is plenty of room, and every one is lively. In a place like this I'm sure to upset something, tread on people's toes, or do something dreadful, so I keep out of mischief, and let Meg do the pretty. Don't you dance?"

"Sometimes; you see I've been abroad a good many years, and haven't been about enough yet to know how you do things here."

"Abroad!" cried Jo, "oh, tell me about it! I love dearly to hear people describe their travels."

Laurie didn't seem to know where to begin; but Jo's eager questions soon set him going, and he told her how he had been at school in Vevey,[24] where the boys never wore hats, and had a fleet of boats on the lake, and for holiday fun went on walking trips about Switzerland with their teachers.

"Don't I wish I'd been there!" cried Jo. "Did you go to Paris?"

"We spent last winter there."

"Can you talk French?"

"We were not allowed to speak anything else at Vevay."

"Do say some. I can read it, but can't pronounce."

"Quel nom à cette jeune demoiselle en les pantoufles jolis?" said Laurie, good-naturedly.

"How nicely you do it! Let me see — you said, 'Who is the young lady in the pretty slippers,' didn't you?"

"Oui, mademoiselle."

---

24 Popular tourist resort in Switzerland on Lake Geneva.

"It's my sister Margaret, and you knew it was! Do you think she is pretty?"

"Yes; she makes me think of the German girls, she looks so fresh and quiet, and dances like a lady."

Jo quite glowed with pleasure at this boyish praise of her sister, and stored it up to repeat to Meg. Both peeped, and criticized, and chatted, till they felt like old acquaintances. Laurie's bashfulness soon wore off, for Jo's gentlemanly demeanor amused and set him at his ease, and Jo was her merry self again, because her dress was forgotten, and nobody lifted their eyebrows at her. She liked the "Laurence boy" better than ever, and took several good looks at him, so that she might describe him to the girls; for they had no brothers, very few male cousins, and boys were almost unknown creatures to them.

"Curly black hair, brown skin, big black eyes, long nose, nice teeth, little hands and feet, tall than I am; very polite for a boy, and altogether jolly. Wonder how old he is?"

It was on the tip of Jo's tongue to ask; but she checked herself in time, and, with unusual tact, tried to find out in a roundabout way.

"I suppose you are going to college soon? I see you pegging away at your books — no, I mean studying hard;" and Jo blushed at the dreadful "pegging" which had escaped her.

Laurie smiled, but didn't seem shocked, and answered, with a shrug,—

"Not for two or three years yet; I won't go before seventeen, any-way."

"Aren't you but fifteen?" asked Jo, looking at the tall lad, whom she had imagined seventeen already.

"Sixteen, next month."

"How I wish I was going to college; you don't look as if you liked it."

"I hate it! nothing but grinding or sky-larking;[25] and I don't like the way fellows do either, in this country."

"What do you like?"

"To live in Italy, and to enjoy myself in my own way."

Jo wanted very much to ask what his own way was; but his black brows looked rather threatening as he knit them, so she changed the subject by saying, as her foot kept time, "That's a splendid polka; why don't you go and try it?"

"If you will come too," he answered, with a queer little French bow.

"I can't; for I told Meg I wouldn't, because —" there Jo stopped, and looked undecided whether to tell or to laugh.

"Because what?" asked Laurie, curiously.

"You won't tell?"

"Never!"

"Well, I have a bad trick of standing before the fire, and so I burn my frocks, and I scorched this one; and, though it's nicely mended, it shows, and Meg told me to keep still, so no one would see it. You may laugh if you want to; it is funny, I know."

But Laurie didn't laugh; he only looked down a minute, and the expression of his face puzzled Jo, when he said very gently,—

"Never mind that; I'll tell you how we can manage: there's a long hall out there, and we can dance grandly, and no one will see us. Please come."

Jo thanked him, and gladly went, wishing she had two neat gloves, when she saw the nice pearl-colored ones her partner put on. The hall was empty, and they had a

---

25 To study hard or, to frolic.

grand polka, for Laurie danced well, and taught her the German step, which delighted Jo, being full of swing and spring. When the music stopped they sat down on the stairs to get their breath, and Laurie was in the midst of an account of a student's festival at Heidelberg,[26] when Meg appeared in search of her sister. She beckoned, and Jo reluctantly followed her into a side-room, where she found her on a sofa holding her foot, and looking pale.

"I've sprained my ankle. That stupid high heel turned, and gave me a horrid wrench. It aches so, I can hardly stand, and I don't know how I'm ever going to get home," she said, rocking to and fro in pain.

"I knew you'd hurt your feet with those silly shoes. I'm sorry; but I don't see what you can do, except get a carriage, or stay here all night," answered Jo, softly rubbing the poor ankle, as she spoke.

"I can't have a carriage without its costing ever so much; I dare say I can't get one at all, for most people come in their own, and it's a long way to the stable, and no one to send."

"I'll go."

"No, indeed; it's past ten, and dark as Egypt. I can't stop here, for the house is full; Sallie has some girls staying with her. I'll rest till Hannah comes, and then do the best I can."

"I'll ask Laurie; he will go," said Jo, looking relieved as the idea occurred to her.

"Mercy, no! don't ask or tell anyone. Get me my rubbers,[27] and put these slippers with our things. I can't dance any more; but as soon as supper is over, watch for Hannah and tell me the minute she comes."

"They are going out to supper now. I'll stay with you; I'd rather."

"No, dear, run along, and bring me some coffee. I'm so tired, I can't stir."

So Meg reclined, with rubbers well hidden, and Jo went blundering away to the dining-room, which she found after going into a china-closet, and opening the door of a room where old Mr. Gardiner was taking a little private refreshment. Making a dart at the table, she secured the coffee, which she immediately spilt, thereby making the front of her dress as bad as the back.

"Oh, dear! what a blunderbuss I am!" exclaimed Jo, finishing Meg's glove by scrubbing her gown with it.

"Can I help you?" said a friendly voice; and there was Laurie, with a full cup in one hand and a plate of ice in the other.

"I was trying to get something for Meg, who is very tired, and someone shook me, and here I am in a nice state," answered Jo, glancing dismally, from the stained skirt to the coffee-colored glove.

"Too bad! I was looking for someone to give this to; may I take it to your sister?"

"Oh, thank you; I'll show you where she is. I don't offer to take it myself, for I should only get into another scrape if I did."

Jo led the way; and, as if used to waiting on ladies, Laurie drew up a little table, brought a second installment of coffee and ice for Jo, and was so obliging that even particular Meg pronounced him a "nice boy." They had a merry time over the bonbons and mottos, and were in the midst of a quiet game of "buzz" with two or three other young people who had

---

26 City in southwestern Germany and home to one of the oldest and most distinguished universities in Europe.
27 Rubber, waterproof overshoes.

strayed in, when Hannah appeared. Meg forgot her foot, and rose so quickly that she was forced to catch hold of Jo, with an exclamation of pain.

"Hush! Don't say anything," she whispered; adding aloud, "It's nothing; I turned my foot a little,— that's all," and limped up stairs to put her things on.

Hannah scolded, Meg cried, and Jo was at her wits' end, till she decided to take things into her own hands. Slipping out, she ran down, and finding a servant, asked if he could get her a carriage. It happened to be a hired waiter, who knew nothing about the neighborhood; and Jo was looking round for help, when Laurie, who had heard what she said, came up and offered his grandfather's carriage, which had just come for him, he said.

"It's so early,— you can't mean to go yet?" began Jo, looking relieved, but hesitating to accept the offer.

"I always go early,— I do, truly. Please let me take you home; it's all on my way, you know, and it rains, they say."

That settled it; and telling him of Meg's mishap, Jo gratefully accepted, and rushed up to bring down the rest of the party. Hannah hated rain as much as a cat does; so she made no trouble, and they rolled away in the luxurious closed carriage, feeling very festive and elegant. Laurie went on the box, so Meg could keep her foot up, and the girls talked over their party in freedom.

"I had a capital time; did you?" asked Jo, rumpling up her hair, and making herself comfortable.

"Yes, till I hurt myself. Sallie's friend, Annie Moffat, took a fancy to me, and asked me to come and spend a week with her when Sallie does. She is going in the spring, when the opera comes, and it will be perfectly splendid if mother only lets me go," answered Meg, cheering up at the thought.

"I saw you dancing with the red-headed man I ran away from; was he nice?"

"Oh, very! His hair is auburn, not red; and he was very polite, and I had a delicious redowa[28] with him!"

"He looked like a grasshopper in a fit, when he did the new step. Laurie and I couldn't help laughing; did you hear us?"

"No, but it was very rude. What *were* you about all that time, hidden away there?"

Jo told her adventures, and by the time she had finished they were at home. With many thanks, they said "Good Night," and crept in, hoping to disturb no one; but the instant their door creaked, two little night-caps bobbed up, and two sleepy but eager voices cried out,—

"Tell about the party! tell about the party!"

With what Meg called "a great want of manners," Jo had saved some bonbons for the little girls, and they soon subsided, after hearing the most thrilling events of the evening.

"I declare, it really seems like being a fine young lady, to come home from my party in my carriage, and sit in my dressing-gown with a maid to wait on me," said Meg, as Jo bound up her foot with arnica,[29] and brushed her hair.

"I don't believe fine young ladies enjoy themselves a bit more than we do, in spite of our burned hair, old gowns, one glove apiece, and tight slippers, that sprain our ankles when we are silly enough to wear them." And I think Jo was quite right.

---

28 A quick-stepping Eastern European folk dance.
29 Herb used to ease the pain of sprains and bruises.

4

Burdens

Oh dear, how hard it does seem to take up our packs and go on," sighed Meg, the morning after the party; for now the holidays were over, the week of merry-making did not fit her for going on easily with the task she never liked.

"I wish it was Christmas or New-Year all the time; wouldn't it be fun?" answered Jo, yawning dismally.

"We shouldn't enjoy ourselves half so much as we do now. But it does seem so nice to have little suppers and bouquets, and go to parties, and drive home in a carriage, and read and rest, and not grub. It's like other people, you know, and I always envy girls who do such things; I'm so fond of luxury," said Meg, trying to decide which of two shabby gowns was the least shabby.

"Well, we can't have it, so don't let us grumble, but shoulder our bundles and trudge along as cheerfully as Marmee does. I'm sure Aunt March is a regular Old Man of the Sea[30] to me, but I suppose when I've learned to carry her without complaining, she will tumble off, or get so light that I shan't mind her."

This idea tickled Jo's fancy, and put her in good spirits; but Meg didn't brighten, for her burden, consisting of four spoilt children, seemed heavier than ever. She hadn't heart enough even to make herself pretty, as usual, by putting on a blue neck-ribbon and dressing her hair in the most becoming way.

"Where's the use of looking nice, when no one sees me but those cross midgets, and no one cares whether I'm pretty or not," she muttered, shutting her drawer with a jerk. "I shall have to toil and moil[31] all my days, with only little bits of fun now and then, and get old and ugly and sour, because I'm poor, and can't enjoy my life as other girls do. It's a shame!"

So Meg went down, wearing an injured look, and wasn't at all agreeable at breakfast-time. Every one seemed rather out of sorts, and inclined to croak. Beth had a headache, and lay on the sofa trying to comfort herself with the cat and three kittens; Amy was fretting because her lessons were not learned, and she couldn't find her rubbers; Jo *would* whistle, and make a great racket getting ready; Mrs. March was very busy trying to finish a letter, which must go at once; and Hannah had the grumps, for being up late didn't suit her.

"There never *was* such a cross family!" cried Jo, losing her temper when she had upset an inkstand, broken both boot-lacings, and sat down upon her hat.

"You're the crossest person in it!" returned Amy, washing out the sum, that was all wrong, with the tears that had fallen on her slate.

"Beth, if you don't keep these horrid cats down cellar I'll have them drowned," exclaimed Meg, angrily, as she tried to get rid of the kitten, who had swarmed up her back, and stuck like a burr just out of reach.

Jo laughed, Meg scolded, Beth implored, and Amy wailed, because she couldn't remember how much nine times twelve was.

"Girls! girls! do be quiet one minute. I *must* get this off by the early mail, and you drive me distracted with your worry," cried Mrs. March, crossing out the third spoilt sentence in her letter.

---

30 A character in *The Thousand and One Nights* collection of Arabian folk tales who sits atop the shoulders of a sailor (by the name of Sinbad) and refuses to get down.

31 Work.

There was a momentary lull, broken by Hannah, who bounced in, laid two hot turn-overs on the table, and bounced out again. These turn-overs were an institution; and the girls called them "muffs," for they had no others, and found the hot pies very comforting to their hands on cold mornings. Hannah never forgot to make them, no matter how busy or grumpy she might be, for the walk was long and bleak; the poor things got no other lunch and were seldom home before three.

"Cuddle your cats and get over your headache, Bethy. Good-by, Marmee; we are a set of rascals this morning, but we'll come home regular angels. Now then, Meg," and Jo tramped away, feeling that the pilgrims were not setting out as they ought to do.

They always looked back before turning the corner, for their mother was always at the window, to nod, and smile, and wave her hand to them. Somehow it seemed as if they couldn't have got through the day without that, for whatever their mood might be, the last glimpse of that motherly face was sure to affect them like sunshine.

"If Marmee shook her fist instead of kissing her hand to us, it would serve us right, for more ungrateful minxes than we are were never seen," cried Jo, taking a remorseful satis-faction in the slushy road and bitter wind.

"Don't use such dreadful expressions," said Meg, from the depths of the veil in which she had shrouded herself like a nun sick of the world.

"I like good, strong words, that mean something," replied Jo, catching her hat as it took a leap off her head, preparatory to flying away altogether.

"Call yourself any names you like; but *I* am neither a rascal nor a minx, and I don't choose to be called so."

"You're a blighted being, and decidedly cross to-day, because you can't sit in the lap of luxury all the time. Poor dear! just wait till I make my fortune, and you shall revel in carriages, and ice-cream, and high-heeled slippers, and posies, and redheaded boys to dance with."

"How ridiculous you are, Jo!" but Meg laughed at the nonsense, and felt better in spite of herself.

"Lucky for you I am; for if I put on crushed airs, and tried to be dismal, as you do, we should be in a nice state. Thank goodness, I can always find something funny to keep me up. Don't croak any more, but come home jolly, there's a dear."

Jo gave her sister an encouraging pat on the shoulder as they parted for the day, each going a different way, each hugging her little warm turn-over, and each trying to be cheerful in spite of wintry weather, hard work, and the unsatisfied desires of pleasure-loving youth.

When Mr. March lost his property in trying to help an unfortunate friend, the two oldest girls begged to be allowed to do something toward their own support, at least. Believing that they could not begin too early to cultivate energy, industry, and independence, their parents consented, and both fell to work with the hearty good-will which, in spite of all obstacles, is sure to succeed at last. Margaret found a place as nursery governess, and felt rich with her small salary. As she said, she *was* "fond of luxury," and her chief trouble was poverty. She found it harder to bear than the others, because she could remember a time when home was beautiful, life full of ease and pleasure, and want of any kind unknown. She tried not to be envious or discontented, but it was very natural that the young girl should long for pretty things, gay friends, accomplishments, and a happy life. At the Kings she daily saw all she wanted, for the children's older sisters were just out,[32] and Meg caught frequent glimpses

---

32 The girls had been officially presented to society.

of dainty ball-dresses and bouquets, heard lively gossip about theaters, concerts, sleighing parties and merry-makings of all kinds, and saw money lavished on trifles which would have been so precious to her. Poor Meg seldom complained, but a sense of injustice made her feel bitter toward every one sometimes, for she had not yet learned to know how rich she was in the blessings which alone can make life happy.

Jo happened to suit Aunt March, who was lame and needed an active person to wait upon her. The childless old lady had offered to adopt one of the girls when the troubles came, and was much offended because her offer was declined. Other friends told the Marches that they had lost all chance of being remembered in the rich old lady's will; but the unworldly Marches only said, —

"We can't give up our girls for a dozen fortunes. Rich or poor, we will keep together and be happy in one another."

The old lady wouldn't speak to them for a time, but, happening to meet Jo at a friend's, something in her comical face and blunt manners struck the old lady's fancy, and she proposed to take her for a companion. This did not suit Jo at all; but she accepted the place, since nothing better appeared and, to every one's surprise, got on remarkably well with her irascible relative. There was an occasional tempest, and once Jo had marched home, declaring she couldn't bear it any longer; but Aunt March always cleared up quickly, and sent for her back again with such urgency that she could not refuse, for in her heart she rather liked the peppery old lady.

I suspect that the real attraction was a large library of fine books, which was left to dust and spiders since Uncle March died. Jo remembered the kind old gentleman who used to let her build railroads and bridges with his big dictionaries, tell her stories about the queer pictures in his Latin books, and buy her cards of gingerbread whenever he met her in the street. The dim, dusty room, with the busts staring down from the tall book-cases, the cozy chairs, the globes, and, best of all, the wilderness of books, in which she could wander where she liked, made the library a region of bliss to her. The moment Aunt March took her nap, or was busy with company, Jo hurried to this quiet place, and, curling herself up in the big chair, devoured poetry, romance, history, travels, and pictures, like a regular book-worm. But, like all happiness, it did not last long; for as sure as she had just reached the heart of the story, the sweetest verse of the song, or the most perilous adventure of her traveller, a shrill voice called, "Josy-phine! Josy-phine!" and she had to leave her paradise to wind yarn, wash the poodle, or read Belsham's Essays,[33] by the hour together.

Jo's ambition was to do something very splendid; what it was she had no idea, but left it for time to tell her; and, meanwhile, found her greatest affliction in the fact that she couldn't read, run, and ride as much as she liked. A quick temper, sharp tongue, and restless spirit were always getting her into scrapes, and her life was a series of ups and downs, which were both comic and pathetic. But the training she received at Aunt March's was just what she needed; and the thought that she was doing something to support herself made her happy, in spite of the perpetual "Josy-phine!"

Beth was too bashful to go to school; it had been tried, but she suffered so much that it was given up, and she did her lessons at home, with her father. Even when he went away, and her mother was called to devote her skill and energy to Soldiers' Aid Societies, Beth

---

33 William Belsham (1752–1827) was a British political theorist and historian who, among his many writings, published two famous volumes entitled *Essays, Philosophical, Historical, and Literary* (1789, 1791).

went faithfully on by herself, and did the best she could. She was a housewifely little creature, and helped Hannah keep home neat and comfortable for the workers, never thinking of any reward but to be loved. Long, quiet days she spent, not lonely nor idle, for her little world was peopled with imaginary friends, and she was by nature a busy bee. There were six dolls to be taken up and dressed every morning, for Beth was a child still, and loved her pets as well as ever; not one whole or handsome one among them; all were outcasts till Beth took them in; for, when her sisters outgrew these idols, they passed to her, because Amy would have nothing old or ugly. Beth cherished them all the more tenderly for that very reason, and set up a hospital for infirm dolls. No pins were ever stuck into their cotton vitals; no harsh words or blows were ever given them; no neglect ever saddened the heart of the most repulsive, but all were fed and clothed, nursed and caressed, with an affection which never failed. One forlorn fragment of *dollanity* had belonged to Jo; and, having led a tempestuous life, was left a wreck in the rag-bag, from which dreary poor-house it was rescued by Beth, and taken to her refuge. Having no top to its head, she tied on a neat little cap, and as both arms and legs were gone, she hid these deficiencies by folding it in a blanket, and devoting her best bed to this chronic invalid. If anyone had known the care lavished on that dolly, I think it would have touched their hearts, even while they laughed. She brought it bits of bouquets; she read to it, took it out to breathe the air, hidden under her coat; she sung it lullabys, and never went to bed without kissing its dirty face, and whispering tenderly, "I hope you'll have a good night, my poor dear."

Beth had her troubles as well as the others; and not being an angel, but a very human little girl, she often "wept a little weep," as Jo said, because she couldn't take music lessons and have a fine piano. She loved music so dearly, tried so hard to learn, and practiced away so patiently at the jingling old instrument, that it did seem as if someone (not to hint Aunt March) ought to help her. Nobody did, however, and nobody saw Beth wipe the tears off the yellow keys, that wouldn't keep in tune when she was all alone. She sung like a little lark about her work, never was too tired to play for Marmee and the girls, and day after day said hopefully to herself, "I know I'll get my music some time, if I'm good."

There are many Beths in the world, shy and quiet, sitting in corners till needed, and living for others so cheerfully, that no one sees the sacrifices till the little cricket on the hearth stops chirping, and the sweet, sunshiny presence vanishes, leaving silence and shadow behind.

If anybody had asked Amy what the greatest trial of her life was, she would have answered at once, "My nose." When she was a baby, Jo had accidentally dropped her into the coal-hod,[34] and Amy insisted that the fall had ruined her nose forever. It was not big, nor red, like poor "Petrea's;" it was only rather flat, and all the pinching in the world could not give it an aristocratic point. No one minded it but herself, and it was doing its best to grow, but Amy felt deeply the want of a Grecian nose, and drew whole sheets of handsome ones to console herself.

"Little Raphael,"[35] as her sisters called her, had a decided talent for drawing, and was never so happy as when copying flowers, designing fairies, or illustrating stories with queer specimens of art. Her teachers complained that instead of doing her sums, she covered

---

34 A metal pail for carrying coal.
35 Raphael Sanzio (1483–1520) was a famous Italian Renaissance painter and architect, considered along with Michelangelo and Leonardo da Vinci to be one of the great masters of the period.

her slate with animals; the blank pages of her atlas were used to copy maps on, and caricatures of the most ludicrous description came fluttering out of all her books at unlucky
moments. She got through her lessons as well as she could, and managed to escape rep-
rimands by being a model of deportment. She was a great favorite with her mates, being
good-tempered, and possessing the happy art of pleasing without effort. Her little airs and
graces were much admired, so were her accomplishments; for beside her drawing, she
could play twelve tunes, crochet, and read French without mispronouncing more than two-
thirds of the words. She had a plaintive way of saying, "When Papa was rich we did so-
and-so," which was very touching; and her long words were considered "perfectly elegant"
by the girls.

Amy was in a fair way to be spoilt, for every one petted her, and her small vanities and
selfishnesses were growing nicely. One thing, however, rather quenched the vanities; she
had to wear her cousin's clothes. Now Florence's mamma hadn't a particle of taste, and
Amy suffered deeply at having to wear a red instead of a blue bonnet, unbecoming gowns,
and fussy aprons that did not fit. Everything was good, well made, and little worn; but
Amy's artistic eyes were much afflicted, especially this winter, when her school dress was a
dull purple, with yellow dots, and no trimming.

"My only comfort," she said to Meg, with tears in her eyes, "is, that mother doesn't take
tucks in my dresses whenever I'm naughty, as Maria Parks' mother does. My dear, it's really
dreadful; for sometimes she is so bad, her frock is up to her knees, and she can't come to
school. When I think of this *deggerredation*, I feel that I can bear even my flat nose and purple
gown, with yellow sky-rockets on it."

Meg was Amy's confidante and monitor, and, by some strange attraction of oppo-
sites, Jo was gentle Beth's. To Jo alone did the shy child tell her thoughts; and over her
big, harum-scarum sister, Beth unconsciously exercised more influence than anyone in
the family. The two older girls were a great deal to each other, but both took one of the
younger into their keeping, and watched over them in their own way; "playing mother"
they called it, and put their sisters in the places of discarded dolls, with the maternal
instinct of little women.

"Has anybody got anything to tell? It's been such a dismal day I'm really dying for some
amusement," said Meg, as they sat sewing together that evening.

"I had a queer time with aunt to-day, and, as I got the best of it, I'll tell you about it,"
began Jo, who dearly loved to tell stories. "I was reading that everlasting Belsham, and
droning away as I always do, for aunt soon drops off, and then I take out some nice book,
and read like fury, till she wakes up. I actually made myself sleepy; and before she began to
nod, I gave such a gape that she asked me what I meant by opening my mouth wide enough
to take the whole book in at once.

" 'I wish I could, and be done with it,' said I, trying not to be saucy.

"Then she gave me a long lecture on my sins, and told me to sit and think them over
while she just 'lost' herself for a moment. She never finds herself very soon; so the minute
her cap began to bob, like a top-heavy dahlia, I whipped the 'Vicar of Wakefield'[36] out of
my pocket, and read away, with one eye on him, and one on aunt. I'd just got to where they
all tumbled into the water, when I forgot, and laughed out loud. Aunt woke up; and, being

---

36 Immensely popular novel by the Irish writer Oliver Goldsmith, which tells the story of a
reverend, his wife and their six children after they lose their fortune.

more good-natured after her nap, told me to read a bit, and show what frivolous work I preferred to the worthy and instructive Belsham. I did my very best, and she liked it, though she only said, —

"'I don't understand what it's all about; go back and begin it, child.'

"Back I went, and made the Primroses as interesting as ever I could. Once I was wicked enough to stop in a thrilling place, and say meekly, 'I'm afraid it tires you, ma'am; shan't I stop now?'

"She caught up her knitting which had dropped out of her hands, gave me a sharp look through her specs, and said, in her short way,—

"'Finish the chapter, and don't be impertinent, miss.'"

"Did she own she liked it?" asked Meg.

"Oh, bless you, no! but she let old Belsham rest; and, when I ran back after my gloves this afternoon, there she was, so hard at the Vicar, that she didn't hear me laugh as I danced a jig in the hall, because of the good time coming. What a pleasant life she might have, if she only chose. I don't envy her much, in spite of her money, for after all rich people have about as many worries as poor ones, I guess," added Jo.

"That reminds me," said Meg, "that I've got something to tell. It isn't funny, like Jo's story, but I thought about it a good deal as I came home. At the Kings' to-day I found everybody in a flurry, and one of the children said that her oldest brother had done something dreadful, and papa had sent him away. I heard Mrs. King crying, and Mr. King talking very loud, and Grace and Ellen turned away their faces when they passed me, so I shouldn't see how red their eyes were. I didn't ask any questions, of course; but I felt so sorry for them, and was rather glad I hadn't any wild brothers to do wicked things, and disgrace the family."

"I think being disgraced in school is a great deal try*inger* than anything bad boys can do," said Amy, shaking her head, as if her experience of life had been a deep one. "Susie Perkins came to school to-day with a lovely red carnelian ring; I wanted it dreadfully, and wished I was her with all my might. Well, she drew a picture of Mr. Davis, with a monstrous nose and a hump, and the words, 'Young ladies, my eye is upon you!' coming out of his mouth in a balloon thing. We were laughing over it, when all of a sudden his eye *was* on us, and he ordered Susie to bring up her slate. She was *parry*lized with fright, but she went, and oh, what *do* you think he did? He took her by the ear, the ear! just fancy how horrid! and led her to the recitation platform, and made her stand there half an hour, holding that slate so everyone could see."

"Didn't the girls shout at the picture?" asked Jo, who relished the scrape.

"Laugh! not a one; they sat as still as mice, and Susie cried quarts, I know she did. I didn't envy her then, for I felt that millions of carnelian rings would'nt have made me happy after that. I never, never should have got over such a agonizing mortification;" and Amy went on with her work, in the proud consciousness of virtue, and the successful utterance of two long words in a breath.

"I saw something that I liked this morning, and I meant to tell it at dinner, but I forgot," said Beth, putting Jo's topsy-turvy basket in order as she talked. "When I went to get some oysters for Hannah, Mr. Laurence was in the fish shop, but he didn't see me, for I kept behind a barrel, and he was busy with Mr. Cutter, the fish-man. A poor woman came in with a pail and a mop, and asked Mr. Cutter if he would let her do some scrubbing for a bit of fish, because she hadn't any dinner for her children, and had been disappointed of a day's work. Mr. Cutter was in a hurry, and said 'No,' rather crossly; so she was going away, looking hungry and sorry, when Mr. Laurence hooked up a big fish with the crooked end of his cane, and held it out to her. She was so glad and surprised she took it right in her arms, and thanked him over and over. He told her to 'go along and cook it,' and she hurried off, so happy! wasn't it nice of him? Oh, she did look so funny, hugging the big, slippery fish, and hoping Mr. Laurence's bed in heaven would be 'aisy.'"

When they had laughed at Beth's story, they asked their mother for one; and, after a moment's thought, she said soberly,—

"As I sat cutting out blue flannel jackets to-day, at the rooms, I felt very anxious about father, and thought how lonely and helpless we should be if anything happened to him. It was not a wise thing to do, but I kept on worrying, till an old man came in with an order for some things. He sat down near me, and I began to talk to him, for he looked poor, and tired, and anxious.

"'Have you sons in the army?' I asked, for the note he brought was not to me.

"'Yes, ma'am; I had four, but two were killed; one is a prisoner, and I'm going to the other, who is very sick in a Washington hospital,' he answered quietly.

"'You have done a great deal for your country, sir,' I said, feeling respect now, instead of pity.

"'Not a mite more than I ought, ma'am. I'd go myself, if I was any use; as I ain't, I give my boys, and give 'em free.'

"He spoke so cheerfully, looked so sincere, and seemed so glad to give his all, that I was ashamed of myself. I'd given one man and thought it too much, while he gave four, without grudging them; I had all my girls to comfort me at home, and his last son was waiting, miles away, to say 'good-by' to him, perhaps. I felt so rich, so happy, thinking of my blessings, that I made him a nice bundle, gave him some money, and thanked him heartily for the lesson he had taught me."

"Tell another story, mother; one with a moral to it, like this. I like to think about them afterwards, if they are real, and not too preachy," said Jo, after a minute's silence.

Mrs. March smiled, and began at once; for she had told stories to this little audience for many years, and knew how to please them.

"Once upon a time there were four girls, who had enough to eat, and drink, and wear; a good many comforts and pleasures, kind friends and parents, who loved them dearly, and yet they were not contented." (Here the listeners stole sly looks at one another, and began to sew diligently.) "These girls were anxious to be good, and made many excellent resolutions, but somehow they did not keep them very well, and were constantly saying, 'If we only had this,' or 'If we could only do that,' quite forgetting how much they already had, and how many pleasant things they actually could do; so they asked an old woman what spell they could use to make them happy, and she said, 'When you feel discontented, think over your blessings, and be grateful'" (Here Jo looked up quickly, as if about to speak, but changed her mind, seeing that the story was not done yet.)

"Being sensible girls, they decided to try her advice, and soon were surprised to see how well off they were. One discovered that money couldn't keep shame and sorrow out of rich people's houses; another that, though she was poor, she was a great deal happier, with her youth, health, and good spirits, than a certain fretful, feeble old lady, who couldn't enjoy her comforts; a third, that, disagreeable as it was to help get dinner, it was harder still to have to go begging for it; and the fourth, that even carnelian rings were not so valuable as good behavior. So they agreed to stop complaining, to enjoy the blessings already possessed, and try to deserve them, lest they should be taken away entirely, instead of increased; and I believe they were never disappointed, or sorry that they took the old woman's advice."

"Now, Marmee, that is very cunning of you to turn our own stories against us, and give us a sermon instead of a 'spin'" cried Meg.

"I like that kind of sermon; it's the sort father used to tell us," said Beth, thoughtfully, putting the needles straight on Jo's cushion.

"I don't complain near as much as the others do, and I shall be more careful than ever now, for I've had warning from Susie's downfall," said Amy, morally.

"We needed that lesson, and we won't forget it. If we do, you just say to us as old Chloe did in Uncle Tom,— 'Tink ob yer marcies, chillen! tink ob yer marcies!'"[37] added Jo, who could not for the life of her help getting a morsel of fun out of the little sermon, though she took it to heart as much as any of them.

5

Being Neighborly

What in the world are you going to do now, Jo?" asked Meg, one snowy afternoon, as her sister came clumping through the hall, in rubber boots, old sack[38] and hood, with a broom in one hand and a shovel in the other.

"Going out for exercise," answered Jo, with a mischievous twinkle in her eyes.

"I should think two long walks this morning would have been enough. It's cold and dull out, and I advise you to stay, warm and dry, by the fire, as I do," said Meg, with a shiver.

"Never take advice; can't keep still all day, and not being a pussy-cat, I don't like to doze by the fire. I like adventures, and I'm going to find some."

Meg went back to toast her feet, and read "Ivanhoe,"[39] and Jo began to dig paths with great energy. The snow was light; and with her broom she soon swept a path all round the garden, for Beth to walk in when the sun came out; and the invalid dolls needed air. Now, the garden separated the Marches house from that of Mr. Laurence; both stood in a suburb of the city, which was still country-like, with groves and lawns, large gardens, and quiet streets. A low hedge parted the two estates. On one side was an old brown house, looking rather bare and shabby, robbed of the vines that in summer covered its walls, and the flowers which then surrounded it. On the other side was a stately stone mansion, plainly betokening every sort of comfort and luxury, from the big coach-house and well-kept grounds to the conservatory, and the glimpses of lovely things one caught between the rich curtains. Yet it seemed a lonely, lifeless sort of house; for no children frolicked on the lawn, no motherly face ever smiled at the windows, and few people went in and out, except the old gentleman and his grandson.

To Jo's lively fancy this fine house seemed a kind of enchanted palace, full of splendors and delights, which no one enjoyed. She had long wanted to behold these hidden

---

37 The slave wife of Uncle Tom in Harriet Beecher Stowe's anti-slavery novel *Uncle Tom's Cabin* (1852), who reminds those around her to "think on your mercies."
38 Expression for a loose-fitting woman's coat, also spelled "sacque."
39 A novel of medieval romance and adventure by the Scottish author Sir Walter Scott, published in 1819 and widely read in the United States. It centers on the story of a disinherited knight who must fight to reclaim his birthright.

glories, and to know the "Laurence boy," who looked as if he would like to be known, if he only knew how to begin. Since the party she had been more eager than ever, and had planned many ways of making friends with him; but he had not been lately seen, and Jo began to think he had gone away, when she one day spied a brown face at an upper window, looking wistfully down into their garden, where Beth and Amy were snowballing one another.

"That boy is suffering for society and fun," she said to herself. "His grandpa don't know what's good for him, and keeps him shut up all alone. He needs a party of jolly boys to play with, or somebody young and lively. I've a great mind to go over and tell the old gentleman so."

The idea amused Jo, who liked to do daring things, and was always scandalizing Meg by her queer performances. The plan of "going over" was not forgotten; and when the snowy afternoon came, Jo resolved to try what could be done. She saw Mr. Laurence drive off, and then sallied out to dig her way down to the hedge, where she paused, and took a survey. All quiet; curtains down at the lower windows; servants out of sight, and nothing human visible but a curly black head leaning on a thin hand at the upper window.

"There he is," thought Jo; "poor boy! all alone, and sick, this dismal day! It's a shame! I'll toss up a snow-ball and make him look out, and then say a kind word to him."

Up went a handful of soft snow, and the head turned at once, showing a face which lost its listless look in a minute, as the big eyes brightened, and the mouth began to smile. Jo nodded, and laughed, and flourished her broom as she called out, —

"How do you do? Are you sick?"

Laurie opened the window and croaked out as hoarsely as a raven, —

"Better, thank you. I've had a horrid cold, and been shut up a week."

"I'm sorry. What do you amuse yourself with?"

"Nothing; it's as dull as tombs up here."

"Don't you read?"

"Not much; they won't let me."

"Can't somebody read to you?"

"Grandpa does, sometimes; but my books don't interest him, and I hate to ask Brooke all the time."

"Have some one come and see you, then."

"There isn't any one I'd like to see. Boys make such a row, and my head is weak."

"Isn't there some nice girl who'd read and amuse you? Girls are quiet, and like to play nurse."

"Don't know any."

"You know me," began Jo, then laughed, and stopped.

"So I do! Will you come, please?" cried Laurie.

"I'm not quiet and nice; but I'll come, if mother will let me. I'll go ask her. Shut that window, like a good boy, and wait till I come."

With that, Jo shouldered her broom and marched into the house, wondering what they would all say to her. Laurie was in a flutter of excitement at the idea of having company, and flew about to get ready; for, as Mrs. March said, he was "a little gentleman," and did honor to the coming guest by brushing his curly pate, putting on a fresh collar, and trying to tidy up the room, which, in spite of half a dozen servants, was anything but neat. Presently, there came a loud ring, then a decided voice, asking for "Mr. Laurie," and a surprised-looking servant came running up to announce a young lady.

"All right, show her up, it's Miss Jo," said Laurie, going to the door of his little parlor to meet Jo, who appeared, looking rosy and kind, and quite at her ease, with a covered dish in one hand, and Beth's three kittens in the other.

"Here I am, bag and baggage," she said briskly. "Mother sent her love, and was glad if I could do anything for you. Meg wanted me to bring some of her blanc-mange;[40] she makes it very nice, and Beth thought her cats would be comforting. I knew you'd laugh at them, but I couldn't refuse, she was so anxious to do something."

It so happened that Beth's funny loan was just the thing; for, in laughing over the kits, Laurie forgot his bashfulness, and grew sociable at once.

"That looks too pretty to eat," he said, smiling with pleasure, as Jo uncovered the dish, and showed the blanc-mange, surrounded by a garland of green leaves, and the scarlet flowers of Amy's pet geranium.

"It isn't anything, only they all felt kindly, and wanted to show it. Tell the girl to put it away for your tea; it's so simple, you can eat it; and, being soft, it will slip down without hurting your sore throat. What a cozy room this is."

"It might be, if it was kept nice; but the maids are lazy, and I don't know how to make them mind. It worries me, though."

"I'll right it up in two minutes; for it only needs to have the hearth brushed, so, — and the things stood straight on the mantel-piece, so, — and the books put here, and the bottles there, and your sofa turned from the light, and the pillows plumped up a bit. Now, then, you're fixed."

And so he was; for, as she laughed and talked, Jo had whisked things into place, and given quite a different air to the room. Laurie watched her in respectful silence; and, when she beckoned him to his sofa, he sat down with a sigh of satisfaction, saying, gratefully, —

"How kind you are! Yes, that's what it wanted. Now please take the big chair, and let me do something to amuse my company."

"No; I came to amuse you. Shall I read aloud?" and Jo looked affectionately toward some inviting books near by.

"Thank you; I've read all those, and if you don't mind, I'd rather talk," answered Laurie.

"Not a bit; I'll talk all day if you'll only set me going. Beth says I never know when to stop."

"Is Beth the rosy one, who stays at home a good deal, and sometimes goes out with a little basket?" asked Laurie, with interest.

"Yes, that's Beth; she's my girl, and a regular good one she is, too."

"The pretty one is Meg, and the curly-haired one is Amy, I believe?"

"How did you find that out?"

Laurie colored up, but answered frankly, "Why, you see, I often hear you calling to one another, and when I'm alone up here, I can't help looking over at your house, you always seem to be having such good times. I beg your pardon for being so rude, but sometimes you forget to put down the curtain at the window where the flowers are; and, when the lamps are lighted, it's like looking at a picture to see the fire, and you all round the table with your mother; her face is right opposite, and it looks so sweet behind the flowers, I can't help watching it. I haven't got any mother, you know;" and Laurie poked the fire to hide a little twitching of the lips that he could not control.

---

40 A sweet, white pudding.

The solitary, hungry look in his eyes went straight to Jo's warm heart. She had been so simply taught that there was no nonsense in her head, and at fifteen she was as innocent and frank as any child. Laurie was sick and lonely; and feeling how rich she was in home-love and happiness, she gladly tried to share it with him. Her brown face was very friendly, and her sharp voice unusually gentle, as she said, —

"We'll never draw that curtain any more, and I give you leave to look as much as you like. I just wish, though, instead of peeping, you'd come over and see us. Mother is so splendid, she'd do you heaps of good, and Beth would sing to you if *I* begged her to, and Amy would dance; Meg and I would make you laugh over our funny stage properties, and we'd have jolly times. Wouldn't your grandpa let you?"

"I think he would, if your mother asked him. He's very kind, though he don't look it; and he lets me do what I like, pretty much, only he's afraid I might be a bother to strangers," began Laurie, brightening more and more.

"We are not strangers, we are neighbors, and you needn't think you'd be a bother. We *want* to know you, and I've been trying to do it this ever so long. We haven't been here a great while, you know, but we have got acquainted with all our neighbors but you."

"You see grandpa lives among his books, and don't mind much what happens outside. Mr. Brooke, my tutor, doesn't stay here, you know, and I have no one to go about with me, so I just stop at home and get on as I can."

"That's bad; you ought to make a dive, and go visiting everywhere you are asked; then you'll have lots of friends, and pleasant places to go to. Never mind being bashful; it won't last long if you keep going."

Laurie turned red again, but wasn't offended at being accused of bashfulness; for there was so much good-will in Jo, it was impossible not to take her blunt speeches as kindly as they were meant.

"Do you like your school?" asked the boy, changing the subject, after a little pause, during which he stared at the fire, and Jo looked about her well pleased.

"Don't go to school; I'm a business man — girl, I mean. I go to wait on my aunt, and a dear, cross old soul she is, too," answered Jo.

Laurie opened his mouth to ask another question; but remembering just in time that it wasn't manners to make too many inquiries into people's affairs, he shut it again, and looked uncomfortable. Jo liked his good breeding, and didn't mind having a laugh at Aunt March, so she gave him a lively description of the fidgety old lady, her fat poodle, the parrot that talked Spanish, and the library where she revelled. Laurie enjoyed that immensely; and when she told about the prim old gentleman who came once to woo Aunt March, and, in the middle of a fine speech, how Poll had tweaked his wig off to his great dismay, the boy lay back and laughed till the tears ran down his cheeks, and a maid popped her head in to see what was the matter.

"Oh! that does me lots of good; tell on, please," he said, taking his face out of the sofa-cushion, red and shining with merriment.

Much elated with her success, Jo did "tell on," all about their plays and plans, their hopes and fears for father, and the most interesting events of the little world in which the sisters lived. Then they got to talking about books; and to Jo's delight she found that Laurie loved them as well as she did, and had read even more than herself.

"If you like them so much, come down and see ours. Grandpa is out, so you needn't be afraid," said Laurie, getting up.

"I'm not afraid of anything," returned Jo, with a toss of the head.

"I don't believe you are!" exclaimed the boy, looking at her with much admiration, though he privately thought she would have good reason to be a trifle afraid of the old gentleman, if she met him in some of his moods.

The atmosphere of the whole house being summer-like, Laurie led the way from room to room, letting Jo stop to examine whatever struck her fancy; and so at last they came to the library, where she clapped her hands, and pranced, as she always did when especially delighted. It was lined with books, and there were pictures and statues, and distracting little cabinets full of coins and curiosities, and Sleepy-Hollow chairs,[41] and queer tables, and bronzes; and, best of all, a great, open fireplace, with quaint tiles all round it.

"What richness!" sighed Jo, sinking into the depths of a velvet chair, and gazing about her with an air of intense satisfaction. "Theodore Laurence, you ought to be the happiest boy in the world," she added impressively.

"A fellow can't live on books," said Laurie, shaking his head, as he perched on a table opposite.

Before he could say more, a bell rung, and Jo flew up, exclaiming with alarm, "Mercy me! It's your grandpa!"

"Well, what if it is? You are not afraid of anything, you know," returned the boy, looking wicked.

"I think I am a little bit afraid of him, but I don't know why I should be. Marmee said I might come, and I don't think you're any the worse for it," said Jo, composing herself, though she kept her eyes on the door.

"I'm a great deal better for it, and ever so much obliged. I'm only afraid you are very tired talking to me; it was *so* pleasant, I couldn't bear to stop," said Laurie, gratefully.

"The doctor to see you, sir," and the maid beckoned as she spoke.

"Would you mind if I left you for a minute? I suppose I must see him," said Laurie.

"Don't mind me. I'm as happy as a cricket here," answered Jo.

Laurie went away, and his guest amused herself in her own way. She was standing before a fine portrait of the old gentleman, when the door opened again, and, without turning, she said decidedly, "I'm sure now that I shouldn't be afraid of him, for he's got kind eyes, though his mouth is grim, and he looks as if he had a tremendous will of his own. He isn't as handsome as *my* grandfather, but I like him."

"Thank you, ma'am," said a gruff voice behind her; and there, to her great dismay, stood old Mr. Laurence.

Poor Jo blushed till she couldn't blush any redder, and her heart began to beat uncomfortably fast as she thought what she had said. For a minute a wild desire to run away possessed her; but that was cowardly, and the girls would laugh at her; so she resolved to stay, and get out of the scrape as she could. A second look showed her that the living eyes, under the bushy gray eyebrows, were kinder even than the painted ones; and there was a sly twinkle in them, which lessened her fear a good deal. The gruff voice was gruffer than ever, as the old gentleman said abruptly, after the dreadful pause, "So, you're not afraid of me, hey?"

"Not much, sir."

"And you don't think me as handsome as your grandfather?"

---

41 Deep, slope-backed chairs with rich upholstery.

"Not quite, sir."

"And I've got a tremendous will, have I?"

"I only said I thought so."

"But you like me, in spite of it?"

"Yes, I do, sir."

That answer pleased the old gentleman; he gave a short laugh, shook hands with her, and, putting his finger under her chin, turned up her face, examined it gravely, and let it go, saying, with a nod, "You've got your grandfather's spirit, if you haven't his face. He *was* fine man, my dear; but, what is better, he was a brave and an honest one, and I was proud to be his friend."

"Thank you, sir." And Jo was quite comfortable after that, for it suited her exactly.

"What have you been doing to this boy of mine, hey?" was the next question, sharply put.

"Only trying to be neighborly, sir;" and Jo told how her visit came about.

"You think he needs cheering up a bit, do you?"

"Yes, sir; he seems a little lonely, and young folks would do him good, perhaps. We are only girls, but we should be glad to help if we could, for we don't forget the splendid Christmas present you sent us," said Jo, eagerly.

"Tut, tut, tut; that was the boy's affair. How is the poor woman?"

"Doing nicely, sir;" and off went Jo, talking very fast, as she told all about the Hummels, in whom her mother had interested richer friends than they were.

"Just her father's way of doing good. I shall come and see your mother some fine day. Tell her so. There's the tea-bell; we have it early, on the boy's account. Come down, and go on being neighborly."

"If you'd like to have me, sir."

"Shouldn't ask you, if I didn't;" and Mr. Laurence offered her his arm with old-fashioned courtesy.

"What *would* Meg say to this?" thought Jo, as she was marched away, while her eyes danced with fun as she imagined herself telling the story at home.

"Hey! why, what the dickens has come to the fellow?" said the old gentleman, as Laurie came running downstairs and brought up with a start of surprise at the astonishing sight of Jo arm in arm with his redoubtable grandfather.

"I didn't know you'd come, sir," he began, as Jo gave him a triumphant little glance.

"That's evident, by the way you racket down stairs. Come to your tea, sir, and behave like a gentleman;" and having pulled the boy's hair by way of a caress, Mr. Laurence walked on, while Laurie went through a series of comic evolutions behind their backs, which nearly produced an explosion of laughter from Jo.

The old gentleman did not say much as he drank his four cups of tea, but he watched the young people, who soon chatted away like old friends, and the change in his grandson did not escape him. There was color, light and life in the boy's face now, vivacity in his manner, and genuine merriment in his laugh.

"She's right; the lad *is* lonely. I'll see what these little girls can do for him," thought Mr. Laurence, as he looked and listened. He liked Jo, for her odd, blunt ways suited him; and she seemed to understand the boy almost as well as if she had been one herself.

If the Laurences had been what Jo called "prim and poky," she would not have got on at all, for such people always made her shy and awkward; but finding them free and easy, she was so herself, and made a good impression. When they rose she proposed to go, but Laurie said he had something more to show her, and took her away to the conservatory, which had been lighted for her benefit. It seemed quite fairy-like to Jo, as she went up and down the walks, enjoying the blooming walls on either side,— the soft light, the damp, sweet air, and the wonderful vines and trees that hung about her,— while her new friend cut the finest flowers till his hands were full; then he tied them up, saying, with the happy look Jo liked to see, "Please give these to your mother, and tell her I like the medicine she sent me very much."

They found Mr. Laurence standing before the fire in the great drawing-room, but Jo's attention was entirely absorbed by a grand piano which stood open.

"Do you play?" she asked, turning to Laurie with a respectful expression.

"Sometimes," he answered, modestly.

"Please do now; I want to hear it, so I can tell Beth."

"Won't you first?"

"Don't know how; too stupid to learn, but I love music dearly."

So Laurie played, and Jo listened, with her nose luxuriously buried in heliotrope and tea roses. Her respect and regard for the "Laurence boy" increased very much, for he played remarkably well, and didn't put on any airs. She wished Beth could hear him, but she did not say so; only praised him till he was quite abashed, and his grandfather came to the rescue. "That will do, that will do, young lady; too many sugar-plums are not good for him. His music isn't bad, but I hope he will do as well in more important things. Going? Well, I'm much obliged to you, and I hope you'll come again. My respects to your mother; good-night, Doctor Jo."

He shook hands kindly, but looked as if something did not please him. When they got into the hall, Jo asked Laurie if she had said anything amiss; he shook his head.

"No, it was me; he don't like to hear me play."

"Why not?"

"I'll tell you some day. John is going home with you, as I can't."

"No need of that; I ain't a young lady, and it's only a step. Take care of yourself, won't you?"

"Yes, but you will come again, I hope?"

"If you promise to come and see us after you are well."

"I will."

"Good-night, Laurie."

"Good-night, Jo, good-night."

When all the afternoon's adventures had been told, the family felt inclined to go visiting in a body, for each found something very attractive in the big house on the other side of the hedge. Mrs. March wanted to talk of her father with the old man who had not forgotten him; Meg longed to walk in the conservatory; Beth sighed for the grand piano, and Amy was eager to see the fine pictures and statues.

"Mother, why didn't Mr. Laurence like to have Laurie play?" asked Jo, who was of an inquiring disposition.

"I am not sure, but I think it was because his son, Laurie's father, married an Italian lady, a musician, which displeased the old man, who is very proud. The lady was good and lovely and accomplished, but he did not like her, and never saw his son after he married. They both died when Laurie was a little child, and then his grandfather took him home. I fancy the boy, who was born in Italy, is not very strong, and the old man is afraid of losing him, which makes him so careful. Laurie comes naturally by his love of music, for he is like his mother, and I dare say his grandfather fears that he may want to be a musician; at any rate, his skill reminds him of the woman he did not like, and so he 'glowered,' as Jo said."

"Dear me, how romantic!" exclaimed Meg.

"How silly," said Jo; "let him be a musician, if he wants to, and not plague his life out sending him to college, when he hates to go."

"That's why he has such handsome black eyes and pretty manners, I suppose; Italians are always nice," said Meg, who was a little sentimental.

"What do you know about his eyes and his manners? you never spoke to him, hardly;" cried Jo, who was *not* sentimental.

"I saw him at the party, and what you tell shows that he knows how to behave. That was a nice little speech about the medicine mother sent him."

"He meant the blanc-mange, I suppose."

"How stupid you are, child; he meant you, of course."

"Did he?" and Jo opened her eyes as if it had never occurred to her before.

"I never saw such a girl! You don't know a compliment when you get it," said Meg, with the air of a young lady who knew all about the matter.

"I think they are great nonsense, and I'll thank you not to be silly, and spoil my fun. Laurie's a nice boy, and I like him, and I won't have any sentimental stuff about compliments and such rubbish. We'll all be good to him, because he hasn't got any mother, and he *may* come over and see us, mayn't he, Marmee?"

"Yes, Jo, your little friend is very welcome, and I hope Meg will remember that children should be children as long as they can."

"I don't call myself a child, and I'm not in my teens yet," observed Amy. "What do you say, Beth?"

"I was thinking about our 'Pilgrim's Progress,'" answered Beth, who had not heard a word. "How we got out of the Slough and through the Wicket Gate[42] by resolving to be good, and up the steep hill, by trying; and that maybe the house over there, full of splendid things, is going to be our Palace Beautiful."

"We have got to get by the lions[43] first," said Jo, as if she rather liked the prospect.

6

Beth Finds the Palace Beautiful

The big house did prove a Palace Beautiful, though it took some time for all to get in, and Beth found it very hard to pass the lions. Old Mr. Laurence was the biggest one; but, after he had called, said something funny or kind to each one of the girls, and talked over old times with their mother, nobody felt much afraid of him, except timid Beth. The other lion was the fact that they were poor and Laurie rich; for this made them shy of accepting favors which they could not return. But after a while they found that he considered them the benefactors, and could not do enough to show how grateful he was for Mrs. March's motherly welcome, their cheerful society, and the comfort he took in that humble home

---

42 In Bunyan's *The Pilgrim's Progress*, the Wicked Gate leads into the Celestial City. It bears the inscription: "Knock and it shall be opened unto you."

43 Lions guard the Palace Beautiful, a place where Bunyan has Christian stop to rest on his way to the Celestial City.

of theirs; so they soon forgot their pride, and interchanged kindnesses without stopping to think which was the greater.

All sorts of pleasant things happened about that time, for the new friendship flourished like grass in spring. Every one liked Laurie, and he privately informed his tutor that "the Marches were regularly splendid girls." With the delightful enthusiasm of youth, they took the solitary boy into their midst, and made much of him, and he found something very charming in the innocent companionship of these simple-hearted girls. Never having known mother or sisters, he was quick to feel the influences they brought about him; and their busy, lively ways made him ashamed of the indolent life he led. He was tired of books, and found people so interesting now, that Mr. Brooke was obliged to make very unsatisfactory reports; for Laurie was always playing truant and running over to the Marches.

"Never mind, let him take a holiday, and make it up afterward," said the old gentleman. "The good lady next door says he is studying too hard, and needs young society, amusement, and exercise. I suspect she is right, and that I've been coddling the fellow as if I'd been his grandmother. Let him do what he likes, as long as he is happy; he can't get into mischief in that little nunnery over there, and Mrs. March is doing more for him than we can."

What good times they had, to be sure! Such plays and tableaux;[44] such sleigh-rides and skating frolics; such pleasant evenings in the old parlor, and now and then such gay little parties at the great house. Meg could walk in the conservatory whenever she liked, and revel in bouquets; Jo browsed over the new library voraciously, and convulsed the old gentleman with her criticisms; Amy copied pictures and enjoyed beauty to her heart's content, and Laurie played lord of the manor in the most delightful style.

But Beth, though yearning for the grand piano, could not pluck up courage to go to the "mansion of bliss," as Meg called it. She went once with Jo, but the old gentleman, not being aware of her infirmity, stared at her so hard from under his heavy eyebrows, and said "hey!" so loud, that he frightened her so much her "feet chattered on the floor," she told her mother; and she ran away, declaring she would never go there any more, not even for the dear piano. No persuasions or enticements could overcome her fear, till the fact coming to Mr. Laurence's ear in some mysterious way, he set about mending matters. During one of the brief calls he made, he artfully led the conversation to music, and talked away about great singers whom he had seen, fine organs he had heard, and told such charming anecdotes, that Beth found it impossible to stay in her distant corner, but crept nearer and nearer, as if fascinated. At the back of his chair she stopped, and stood listening, with her great eyes wide open, and her cheeks red with the excitement of this unusual performance. Taking no more notice of her than if she had been a fly, Mr. Laurence talked on about Laurie's lessons and teachers; and presently, as if the idea had just occurred to him, he said to Mrs. March, —

"The boy neglects his music now, and I'm glad of it, for he was getting too fond of it. But the piano suffers for want of use; wouldn't some of your girls like to run over, and practice on it now and, then just to keep it in tune, you know, ma'am?"

Beth took a step forward, and pressed her hands tightly together, to keep from clapping them, for this was an irresistible temptation; and the thought of practicing on that splendid instrument quite took her breath away. Before Mrs. March could reply, Mr. Laurence went on with an odd little nod and smile, —

"They needn't see or speak to anyone, but run in at any time, for I'm shut up in my study at the other end of the house, Laurie is out a great deal, and the servants are never near the

---

44 A picturesque, motionless grouping of people posed to represent a striking scene.

drawing-room after nine o'clock." Here he rose, as if going, and Beth made up her mind to speak, for that last arrangement left nothing to be desired. "Please tell the young ladies what I say, and if they don't care to come, why, never mind;" here a little hand slipped into his, and Beth looked up at him with a face full of gratitude, as she said, in her earnest yet timid way, —

"Oh, sir! they do care, very, very much!"

"Are you the musical girl?" he asked, without any startling "hey!" as he looked down at her very kindly.

"I'm Beth; I love it dearly, and I'll come if you are quite sure nobody will hear me — and be disturbed," she added, fearing to be rude, and trembling at her own boldness as she spoke.

"Not a soul, my dear; the house is empty half the day, so come and drum away as much as you like, and I shall be obliged to you."

"How kind you are, sir."

Beth blushed like a rose under the friendly look he wore, but she was not frightened now, and gave the big hand a grateful squeeze, because she had no words to thank him for the precious gift he had given her. The old gentleman softly stroked the hair off her forehead, and, stooping down, he kissed her, saying, in a tone few people ever heard, —

"I had a little girl once with eyes like these; God bless you, my dear; good-day, madam," and away he went, in a great hurry.

Beth had a rapture with her mother, and then rushed up to impart the glorious news to her family of invalids, as the girls were not at home. How blithely she sang that evening, and how they all laughed at her, because she woke Amy in the night by playing the piano on her face in her sleep. Next day, having seen both the old and young gentleman out of the house, Beth, after two or three retreats, fairly got in at the side-door, and made her way as noiselessly as any mouse to the drawing-room, where her idol stood. Quite by accident, of course, some pretty, easy music lay on the piano; and, with trembling fingers, and frequent stops to listen and look about, Beth at last touched the great instrument, and straightway forgot her fear, herself, and everything else but the unspeakable delight which the music gave her, for it was like the voice of a beloved friend.

She stayed till Hannah came to take her home to dinner; but she had no appetite, and could only sit and smile upon every one in a general state of beatitude.

After that, the little brown hood slipped through the hedge nearly every day, and the great drawing-room was haunted by a tuneful spirit that came and went unseen. She never knew that Mr. Laurence often opened his study door to hear the old-fashioned airs he liked; she never saw Laurie mount guard in the hall, to warn the servants away; she never suspected that the exercise-books and new songs which she found in the rack were put there for her especial benefit; and when he talked to her about music at home, she only thought how kind he was to tell things that helped her so much. So she enjoyed herself heartily, and found, what isn't always the case, that her granted wish was all she had hoped. Perhaps it was because she was so grateful for this blessing that a greater was given her; at any rate, she deserved both.

"Mother, I'm going to work Mr. Laurence a pair of slippers. He is so kind to me I must thank him, and I don't know any other way. Can I do it?" asked Beth, a few weeks after that eventful call of his.

"Yes, dear; it will please him very much, and be a nice way of thanking him. The girls will help you about them, and I will pay for the making up," replied Mrs. March, who took peculiar pleasure in granting Beth's requests, because she so seldom asked anything for herself.

After many serious discussions with Meg and Jo, the pattern was chosen, the materials bought, and the slippers begun. A cluster of grave yet cheerful pansies, on a deeper purple ground was pronounced very appropriate and pretty, and Beth worked away early and late, with occasional lifts over hard parts. She was a nimble little needle-woman, and they were finished before any one got tired of them. Then she wrote a very short, simple note, and, with Laurie's help, got them smuggled on to the study-table one morning before the old gentleman was up.

When this excitement was over, Beth waited to see what would happen. All that day passed, and a part of the next, before any acknowledgment arrived, and she was beginning to fear she had offended her crotchety friend. On the afternoon of the second day she went out to do an errand, and give poor Joanna, the invalid doll, her daily exercise. As she came up the street on her return, she saw three, — yes, four heads popping in and out of the parlor windows; and the moment they saw her, several hands were waved, and several joyful voices screamed, —

"Here's a letter from the old gentleman; come quick, and read it!"

"Oh Beth! he's sent you —" began Amy, gesticulating with unseemly energy; but she got no further, for Jo quenched her by slamming down the window.

Beth hurried on in a flutter of suspense; at the door her sisters seized and bore her to the parlor in a triumphal procession, all pointing, and all saying at once, "Look there! look there!" Beth did look, and turned pale with delight and surprise; for there stood a little cabinet piano, with a letter lying on the glossy lid, directed like a sign-board to, "Miss Elizabeth March."

"For me?" gasped Beth, holding onto Jo, and feeling as if she should tumble down, it was such an overwhelming thing altogether.

"Yes; all for you, my precious! Isn't it splendid of him? Don't you think he's the dearest old man in the world? Here's the key in the letter; we didn't open it, but we are dying to know what he says," cried Jo, hugging her sister, and offering the note.

"You read it; I can't, I feel so queer. Oh, it is too lovely!" and Beth hid her face in Jo's apron, quite upset by her present.

Jo opened the paper, and began to laugh, for the first words she saw were:—

"Miss MARCH:

"*Dear Madam* —"

"How nice it sounds! I wish some one would write to me so!" said Amy, who thought the old-fashioned address very elegant.

"'I have had many pairs of slippers in my life, but I never had any that suited me so well as yours,'" continued Jo. "'Heart's-ease is my favorite flower, and these will always remind me of the gentle giver. I like to pay my debts, so I know you will allow "the old gentleman" to send you something which once belonged to the little granddaughter he lost. With hearty thanks, and best wishes, I remain,

"'Your grateful friend and humble servant,
"'JAMES LAURENCE.'"

"There, Beth, that's an honor to be proud of, I'm sure! Laurie told me how fond Mr. Laurence used to be of the child who died, and how he kept all her little things carefully. Just think; he's given you her piano! That comes of having big blue eyes and loving music," said Jo, trying to soothe Beth, who trembled, and looked more excited than she had ever been before.

"See the cunning brackets to hold candles, and the nice green silk, puckered up with a gold rose in the middle, and the pretty rack and stool, all complete," added Meg, opening the instrument and displaying its beauties.

' "Your humble servant, James Laurence;' only think of his writing that to you. I'll tell the girls; they'll think it's killing," said Amy, much impressed by the note.

"Try it, honey; let's hear the sound of the baby pianny," said Hannah, who always took a share in the family joys and sorrows.

So Beth tried it, and everyone pronounced it the most remarkable piano ever heard. It had evidently been newly tuned and put in apple-pie order; but, perfect as it was, I think the real charm of it lay in the happiest of all happy faces which leaned over it, as Beth lovingly touched the beautiful black and white keys, and pressed the bright pedals.

"You'll have to go and thank him," said Jo, by way of a joke; for the idea of the child's really going, never entered her head.

"Yes, I mean to; I guess I'll go now, before I get frightened thinking about it;" and, to the utter amazement of the assembled family, Beth walked deliberately down the garden, through the hedge, and in at the Laurences door.

"Well, I wish I may die, if it ain't the queerest thing I ever see! The pianny has turned her head; she'd never have gone, in her right mind," cried Hannah, staring after her, while the girls were rendered quite speechless by the miracle.

They would have been still more amazed, if they had seen what Beth did afterward. If you will believe me, she went and knocked at the study door, before she gave herself time to think; and when a gruff voice called out, "Come in!" she did go in, right up to Mr. Laurence, who looked quite taken aback, and held out her hand, saying, with only a small quaver in her voice, "I came to thank you, sir, for—" but she didn't finish, for he looked so friendly that she forgot her speech; and, only remembering that he had lost the little girl he loved, she put both arms round his neck, and kissed him.

If the roof of the house had suddenly flown off, the old gentleman wouldn't have been more astonished; but he liked it — oh, dear, yes! he liked it amazingly; and was so touched and pleased by that confiding little kiss, that all his crustiness vanished; and he just set her on his knee, and laid his wrinkled cheek against her rosy one, feeling as if he had got his own little granddaughter back again. Beth ceased to fear him from that moment, and sat there talking to him as cosily as if she had known him all her life; for love casts out fear, and gratitude can conquer pride. When she went home, he walked with her to her own gate, shook hands cordially, and touched his hat as he marched back again, looking very stately and erect, like a handsome, soldierly old gentleman, as he was.

When the girls saw that performance, Jo began to dance a jig, by way of expressing her satisfaction; Amy nearly fell out of the window in her surprise, and Meg exclaimed, with uplifted hands, "Well, I do believe the world is coming to an end!"

7

Amy's Valley of Humiliation[45]

That boy is a perfect Cyclops, isn't he?" said Amy, one day, as Laurie clattered by on horseback, with a flourish of his whip as he passed.

"How dare you say so, when he's got both his eyes? and very handsome ones they are, too;" cried Jo, who resented any slighting remarks about her friend.

---

45 In Bunyan's *The Pilgrim's Progress*, Christian descends into the Valley of Humiliation accompanied by Discretion, Piety, Charity and Prudence. They give him food at the bottom of the valley and help him on his way.

"I didn't say anything about his eyes, and I don't see why you need fire up when I admire his riding."

"Oh, my goodness! that little goose means a centaur, and she called him a Cyclops," exclaimed Jo, with a burst of laughter.

"You needn't be so rude, it's only a 'lapse of lingy;'[46] as Mr. Davis says," retorted Amy, finishing Jo with her Latin. "I just wish I had a little of the money Laurie spends on that horse," she added, as if to herself, yet hoping her sisters would hear.

"Why?" asked Meg, kindly, for Jo had gone off in another laugh at Amy's second blunder.

"I need it so much; I'm dreadfully in debt, and it won't be my turn to have the rag money for a month."

"In debt, Amy? what do you mean?" And Meg looked sober.

"Why, I owe at least a dozen pickled limes, and I can't pay them, you know, till I have money, for Marmee forbade my having anything charged at the shop."

"Tell me all about it. Are limes the fashion now? It used to be pricking bits of rubber to make balls;" and Meg tried to keep her countenance, Amy looked so grave and important.

"Why, you see, the girls are always buying them, and unless you want to be thought mean, you must do it, too. It's nothing but limes now, for every one is sucking them in their desks in school-time, and trading them off for pencils, bead-rings, paper dolls, or something else, at recess. If one girl likes another, she gives her a lime; if she's mad with her, she eats one before her face, and doesn't offer even a suck. They treat by turns; and I've had ever so many, but haven't returned them, and I ought, for they are debts of honor, you know."

"How much will pay them off, and restore your credit?" asked Meg, taking out her purse.

"A quarter would more than do it, and leave a few cents over for a treat for you. Don't you like limes?"

"Not much; you may have my share. Here's the money, — make it last as long as you can, for it isn't very plenty, you know."

"Oh, thank you! it must be so nice to have pocket-money! I'll have a grand feast, for I haven't tasted a lime this week. I felt delicate about taking any, as I couldn't return them, and I'm actually suffering for one."

Next day Amy was rather late at school; but could not resist the temptation of displaying, with pardonable pride, a moist brown paper parcel, before she consigned it to the inmost recesses of her desk. During the next few minutes the rumor that Amy March had got twenty-four delicious limes (she ate one on the way) and was going to treat, circulated through her "set," and the attentions of her friends became quite overwhelming. Katy Brown invited her to her next party on the spot; Mary Kingsley insisted on lending her her watch till recess, and Jenny Snow, a satirical young lady who had basely twitted Amy upon her limeless state, promptly buried the hatchet, and offered to furnish answers to certain appalling sums. But Amy had not forgotten Miss Snow's cutting remarks about "some persons whose noses were not too flat to smell other people's limes, and stuck-up people, who were not too proud to ask for them;" and she instantly crushed "that Snow girl's" hopes by the withering telegram, "You needn't be so polite all of a sudden, for you won't get any."

---

46 *Lapsus linguae* is Latin for "slip of the tongue."

A distinguished personage happened to visit the school that morning, and Amy's beauti-fully drawn maps received praise, which honor to her foe rankled in the soul of Miss Snow, and caused Miss March to assume the airs of a studious young peacock. But, alas, alas! pride goes before a fall, and the revengeful Snow turned the tables with disastrous success. No sooner had the guest paid the usual stale compliments, and bowed himself out, than Jenny, under pretense of asking an important question, informed Mr. Davis, the teacher, that Amy March had pickled limes in her desk.

Now Mr. Davis had declared limes a contraband article, and solemnly vowed to pub-licly ferule[47] the first person who was found breaking the law. This much-enduring man had succeeded in banishing chewing gum after a long and stormy war, had made a bonfire of the confiscated novels and newspapers, had suppressed a private post-office, had forbidden distortions of the face, nicknames, and caricatures, and done all that one man could do to keep half a hundred rebellious girls in order. Boys are trying enough to human patience, goodness knows! but girls are infinitely more so, especially to nervous gentlemen with tyr-annical tempers and no more talent for teaching than "Dr. Blimber."[48] Mr. Davis knew any quantity of Greek, Latin, Algebra, and ologies of all sorts, so he was called a fine teacher; and manners, morals, feelings, and examples were not considered of any particular import-ance. It was a most unfortunate moment for denouncing Amy, and Jenny knew it. Mr. Davis had evidently taken his coffee too strong that morning; there was an east wind, which always affected his neuralgia, and his pupils had not done him the credit which he felt he deserved; therefore, to use the expressive, if not elegant, language of a school-girl, "he was as nervous as a witch and as cross as a bear." The word "limes" was like fire to powder; his yellow face flushed, and he rapped on his desk with an energy which made Jenny skip to her seat with unusual rapidity.

'Young ladies, attention, if you please!"

At the stern order the buzz ceased, and fifty pairs of blue, black, gray, and brown eyes were obediently fixed upon his awful countenance.

"Miss March, come to the desk."

Amy rose to comply, with outward composure, but a secret fear oppressed her, for the limes weighed upon her conscience.

"Bring with you the limes you have in your desk," was the unexpected command which arrested her before she got out of her seat.

"Don't take all," whispered her neighbor, a young lady of great presence of mind.

Amy hastily shook out half a dozen, and laid the rest down before Mr. Davis, feeling that any man possessing a human heart would relent when that delicious perfume met his nose. Unfortunately, Mr. Davis particularly detested the odor of the fashionable pickle, and disgust added to his wrath.

"Is that all?"

"Not quite," stammered Amy.

"Bring the rest, immediately."

With a despairing glance at her set she obeyed.

"You are sure there are no more?"

"I never lie, sir."

"So I see. Now take these disgusting things, two by two, and throw them out of the window."

---

47 A punishment that involves hitting the open hand with a flat piece of wood, often a ruler.
48 Harsh schoolmaster from Charles Dicken's novel *Dombey and Son* (1848).

There was a simultaneous sigh, which created quite a little gust as the last hope fled, and the treat was ravished from their longing lips. Scarlet with shame and anger, Amy went to and fro twelve mortal times; and as each doomed couple, looking, oh, so plump and juicy! fell from her reluctant hands, a shout from the street completed the anguish of the girls, for it told them that their feast was being exulted over by the little Irish children, who were their sworn foes. This — this was too much; all flashed indignant or appealing glances at the inexorable Davis, and one passionate lime-lover burst into tears.

As Amy returned from her last trip, Mr. Davis gave a portentous "hem," and said, in his most impressive manner, —

"Young ladies, you remember what I said to you a week ago. I am sorry this has happened; but I never allow my rules to be infringed, and I *never* break my word. Miss March, hold out your hand."

Amy started, and put both hands behind her, turning on him an imploring look, which pleaded for her better than the words she could not utter. She was rather a favorite with "old Davis," as, of course, he was called, and it's my private belief that he *would* have broken his word if the indignation of one irrepressible young lady had not found vent in a hiss. That hiss, faint as it was, irritated the irascible gentleman, and sealed the culprit's fate.

"Your hand, Miss March!" was the only answer her mute appeal received; and, too proud to cry or beseech, Amy set her teeth, threw back her head defiantly, and bore without flinching several tingling blows on her little palm. They were neither many nor heavy, but that made no difference to her. For the first time in her life she had been struck; and the disgrace, in her eyes, was as deep as if he had knocked her down.

"You will now stand on the platform till recess," said Mr. Davis, resolved to do the thing thoroughly, since he had begun.

That was dreadful; it would have been bad enough to go to her seat, and see the pitying faces of her friends, or the satisfied ones of her few enemies; but to face the whole school, with that shame fresh upon her, seemed impossible, and for a second she felt as if she could only drop down where she stood, and break her heart with crying. A bitter sense of wrong, and the thought of Jenny Snow, helped her to bear it; and, taking the ignominious place, she fixed her eyes on the stove-funnel above what now seemed a sea of faces, and stood there so motionless and white, that the girls found it very hard to study, with that pathetic little figure before them.

During the fifteen minutes that followed, the proud and sensitive little girl suffered a shame and pain which she never forgot. To others it might seem a ludicrous or trivial affair, but to her it was a hard experience; for during the twelve years of her life she had been governed by love alone, and a blow of that sort had never touched her before. The smart of her hand, and the ache of her heart, were forgotten in the sting of the thought, —

"I shall have to tell at home, and they will be so disappointed in me!"

The fifteen minutes seemed an hour; but they came to an end at last, and the word "recess!" had never seemed so welcome to her before.

"You can go, Miss March," said Mr. Davis, looking, as he felt, uncomfortable.

He did not soon forget the reproachful look Amy gave him, as she went, without a word to any one, straight into the anteroom, snatched her things, and left the place "forever," as she passionately declared to herself. She was in a sad state when she got home; and when the older girls arrived, some time later, an indignation meeting was held at once. Mrs. March did not say much, but looked disturbed, and comforted her afflicted little daughter in her tenderest manner. Meg bathed the insulted hand with glycerine and tears; Beth felt that even her beloved kittens would fail as a balm for griefs like this, and Jo wrathfully proposed that Mr. Davis be arrested without delay, while Hannah shook her fist at the "villain," and pounded potatoes for dinner as if she had him under her pestle.

No notice was taken of Amy's flight, except by her mates; but the sharp-eyed demoiselles discovered that Mr. Davis was quite benignant in the afternoon, also unusually nervous. Just before school closed, Jo appeared, wearing a grim expression, as she stalked up to the desk, and delivered a letter from her mother; then collected Amy's property, and departed, carefully scraping the mud from her boots on the door-mat, as if she shook the dust of the place off her feet.[49]

"Yes, you can have a vacation from school, but I want you to study a little every day, with Beth," said Mrs. March, that evening. "I don't approve of corporal punishment, especially for girls. I dislike Mr. Davis' manner of teaching, and don't think the girls you associate with are doing you any good, so I shall ask your father's advice before I send you anywhere else."

"That's good! I wish all the girls would leave, and spoil his old school. It's perfectly maddening to think of those lovely limes," sighed Amy, with the air of a martyr.

"I am not sorry you lost them, for you broke the rules, and deserved some punishment for disobedience," was the severe reply, which rather disappointed the young lady, who expected nothing but sympathy.

"Do you mean you are glad I was disgraced before the whole school?" cried Amy.

"I should not have chosen that way of mending a fault," replied her mother; "but I'm not sure that it won't do you more good than a milder method. You are getting to be altogether too conceited and together, my dear, and it is quite time you set about correcting it. You have a good many little gifts and virtues, but there is no need of parading them, for conceit spoils the finest genius. There is not much danger that real talent or goodness will be overlooked long; even if it is, the consciousness of possessing and using it well should satisfy one, and the great charm of all power is modesty."

"So it is!" cried Laurie, who was playing chess in a corner with Jo. "I knew a girl, once, who had a really remarkable talent for music, and she didn't know it; never guessed what sweet little things she composed when she was alone, and wouldn't have believed it if any one had told her."

"I wish I'd known that nice girl, maybe she would have helped me, I'm so stupid," said Beth, who stood beside him, listening eagerly.

"You do know her, and she helps you better than any one else could," answered Laurie, looking at her with such mischievous meaning in his merry black eyes, that Beth suddenly turned very red, and hid her face in the sofa-cushion, quite overcome by such an unexpected discovery.

Jo let Laurie win the game, to pay for that praise of her Beth, who could not be prevailed upon to play for them after her compliment. So Laurie did his best, and sang delightfully, being in a particularly lively humor, for to the Marches he seldom showed the moody side of his character. When he was gone, Amy, who had been pensive all the evening, said, suddenly, as if busy over some new idea, —

"Is Laurie an accomplished boy?"

---

49 Luke 9:5. Jesus instructed his disciples to shake the dust off their feet when they left towns that would not receive them.

"Yes; he has had an excellent education, and has much talent; he will make a fine man, if not spoilt by petting," replied her mother.

"And he isn't conceited, is he?" asked Amy.

"Not in the least; that is why he is so charming, and we all like him so much."

"I see; it's nice to have accomplishments, and be elegant; but not to show off, or get perked up,"[50] said Amy, thoughtfully.

"These things are always seen and felt in a person's manner and conversation, if modestly used; but it is not necessary to display them," said Mrs. March.

"Any more than it's proper to wear all your bonnets, and gowns, and ribbons, at once, that folks may know you've got 'em," added Jo; and the lecture ended in a laugh.

8

Jo Meets Apollyon[51]

Girls, where are you going?" asked Amy, coming into their room one Saturday afternoon, and finding them getting ready to go out, with an air of secresy which excited her curiosity.

"Never mind; little girls shouldn't ask questions," returned Jo, sharply.

Now if there *is* anything mortifying to our feelings, when we are young, it is to be told that; and to be bidden to "run away, dear," is still more trying to us. Amy bridled up at this insult, and determined to find out the secret, if she teased for an hour. Turning to Meg, who never refused her anything very long, she said, coaxingly, "Do tell me! I should think you might let me go, too; for Beth is fussing over her dolls, and I haven't got anything to do, and am *so* lonely."

"I can't, dear, because you aren't invited," began Meg; but Jo broke in impatiently, "Now, Meg, be quiet or you will spoil it all. You can't go, Amy; so don't be a baby, and whine about it."

"You are going somewhere with Laurie, I know you are; you were whispering and laughing together, on the sofa, last night, and you stopped when I came in. Aren't you going with him?"

"Yes, we are; now do be still, and stop bothering."

Amy held her tongue, but used her eyes, and saw Meg slip a fan into her pocket.

"I know! I know! you're going to the theater to see the 'Seven Castles'!" she cried, adding, resolutely, "and I *shall* go, for mother said I might see it; and I've got my rag-money,[52] and it was mean not to tell me in time."

"Just listen to me a minute, and be a good child," said Meg soothingly. "Mother doesn't wish you to go this week, because your eyes are not well enough yet to bear the light of this fairy piece. Next week you can go with Beth and Hannah, and have a nice time."

---

50 Puffed up with pride.

51 In Bunyan's *Pilgrim's Progress*, Christian meets Apollyon, the embodiment of dangerous wrath, in the Valley of Humiliation. Apollyon wounds Christian by showering him with dangerous darts of fire.

52 Money earned by collecting rags and selling them to be used for purposes such as making paper.

"I don't like that half as well as going with you and Laurie. Please let me; I've been sick with this cold so long, and shut up, I'm dying for some fun. Do, Meg! I'll be ever so good," pleaded Amy, looking as pathetic as she could.

"Suppose we take her. I don't believe mother would mind, if we bundle her up well," began Meg.

"If *she* goes *I* shan't; and if I don't, Laurie won't like it; and it will be very rude, after he invited only us, to go and drag in Amy. I should think she'd hate to poke herself where she isn't wanted," said Jo, crossly, for she disliked the trouble of overseeing a fidgety child, when she wanted to enjoy herself.

Her tone and manner angered Amy, who began to put her boots on, saying, in her most aggravating way, "I *shall* go; Meg says I may; and if I pay for myself, Laurie hasn't anything to do with it."

"You can't sit with us, for our seats are reserved, and you mustn't sit alone; so Laurie will give you his place, and that will spoil our pleasure; or he'll get another seat for you, and that isn't proper, when you weren't asked. You shan't stir a step, so you may just stay where you are," scolded Jo, crosser than ever, having just pricked her finger in her hurry.

Sitting on the floor, with one boot on, Amy began to cry, and Meg to reason with her, when Laurie called from below, and the two girls hurried down, leaving their sister wailing; for now and then she forgot her grown-up ways, and acted like a spoilt child. Just as the party was setting out, Amy called over the banisters, in a threatening tone, 'You'll be sorry for this, Jo March! see if you ain't."

"Fiddlesticks!" returned Jo, slamming the door.

They had a charming time, for "The Seven Castles of the Diamond Lake"[53] was as brilliant and wonderful as heart could wish. But, in spite of the comical red imps, sparkling elves, and gorgeous princes and princesses, Jo's pleasure had a drop of bitterness in it; the fairy queen's yellow curls reminded her of Amy; and between the acts she amused herself with wondering what her sister would do to make her "sorry for it." She and Amy had had many lively skirmishes in the course of their lives, for both had quick tempers, and were apt to be violent when fairly roused. Amy teased Jo, and Jo irritated Amy, and semi-occasional explosions occurred, of which both were much ashamed afterward. Although the oldest, Jo had the least self-control, and had hard times trying to curb the fiery spirit which was continually getting her into trouble; her anger never lasted long, and, having humbly confessed her fault, she sincerely repented, and tried to do better. Her sisters used to say, that they rather liked to get Jo into a fury, because she was such an angel afterward. Poor Jo tried desperately to be good, but her bosom enemy was always ready to flame up and defeat her; and it took years of patient effort to subdue it.

When they got home, they found Amy reading in the parlor. She assumed an injured air as they came in; never lifted her eyes from her book, or asked a single question. Perhaps curiosity might have conquered resentment, if Beth had not been there to inquire, and receive a glowing description of the play. On going up to put away her best hat, Jo's first look was toward the bureau; for, in their last quarrel, Amy had soothed her feelings by turning Jo's top drawer upside down, on the floor. Everything was in its place, however; and after a hasty glance into her various closets, bags, and boxes, Jo decided that Amy had forgiven and forgotten her wrongs.

---

53 An invented title.

There Jo was mistaken; for next day she made a discovery which produced a tempest. Meg, Beth, and Amy were sitting together, late in the afternoon, when Jo burst into the room, looking excited, and demanding, breathlessly, "Has anyone taken my book?"

Meg and Beth said "No," at once, and looked surprised; Amy poked the fire, and said nothing. Jo saw her color rise, and was down upon her in a minute.

"Amy, you've got it!"

"No, I haven't."

"You know where it is, then!"

"No, I don't."

"That's a fib!" cried Jo, taking her by the shoulders, and looking fierce enough to frighten a much braver child than Amy.

"It isn't. I haven't got it, don't know where it is now, and don't care."

"You know something about it, and you'd better tell at once, or I'll make you," and Jo gave her a slight shake.

"Scold as much as you like, you'll never get your silly old story again," cried Amy, getting excited in her turn.

"Why not?"

"I burned it up."

"What! my little book I was so fond of, and worked over, and meant to finish before father got home? Have you really burnt it?" said Jo, turning very pale, while her eyes kindled and her hands clutched Amy nervously.

"Yes, I did! I told you I'd make you pay for being so cross yesterday, and I have, so—"

Amy got no farther, for Jo's hot temper mastered her, and she shook Amy till her teeth chartered in her head; crying, in a passion of grief and anger, —

"You wicked, wicked girl! I never can write it again, and I'll never forgive you as long as I live."

Meg flew to rescue Amy, and Beth to pacify Jo, but Jo was quite beside herself; and, with a parting box on her sister's ear, she rushed out of the room up to the old sofa in the garret, and finished her fight alone.

The storm cleared up below, for Mrs. March came home, and, having heard the story, soon brought Amy to a sense of the wrong she had done her sister. Jo's book was the pride of her heart, and was regarded by her family as a literary sprout of great promise. It was only half a dozen little fairy tales, but Jo had worked over them patiently, putting her whole heart into her work, hoping to make something good enough to print. She had just copied them with great care, and had destroyed the old manuscript, so that Amy's bonfire had consumed the loving work of several years. It seemed a small loss to others, but to Jo it was a dreadful calamity, and she felt that it never could be made up to her. Beth mourned as for a departed kitten, and Meg refused to defend her pet; Mrs. March looked grave and grieved, and Amy felt that no one would love her till she had asked pardon for the act which she now regretted more than any of them.

When the tea-bell rang, Jo appeared, looking so grim and unapproachable, that it took all Amy's courage to say, meekly, —

"Please, forgive me, Jo; I'm very, very sorry."

"I never shall forgive you" was Jo's stern answer; and, from that moment, she ignored Amy entirely.

No one spoke of the great trouble, — not even Mrs. March, — for all had learned by experience that when Jo was in that mood words were wasted; and the wisest course was to wait till some little accident, or her own generous nature, softened Jo's resentment, and healed the breach. It was not a happy evening; for, though they sewed as usual, while their mother read aloud from Bremer, Scott, or Edgeworth,[54] something was wanting, and the sweet home-peace was disturbed. They felt this most when singing-time came; for Beth could only play, Jo stood dumb as a stone, and Amy broke down, so Meg and mother sung alone. But, in spite of their efforts to be as cheery as larks, the flute-like voices did not seem to chord as well as usual, and all felt out of tune.

As Jo received her good-night kiss, Mrs. March whispered, gently, —

"My dear, don't let the sun go down upon your anger; forgive each other, help each other, and begin again to-morrow."

Jo wanted to lay her head down on that motherly bosom, and cry her grief and anger all away; but tears were an unmanly weakness, and she felt so deeply injured that she really *couldn't* quite forgive yet. So she winked hard, shook her head, and said, gruffly, because Amy was listening, —

"It was an abominable thing, and she don't deserve to be forgiven."

With that she marched off to bed, and there was no merry or confidential gossip that night.

Amy was much offended that her overtures of peace had been repulsed, and began to wish she had not humbled herself, to feel more injured than ever, and to plume herself on her superior virtue in a way which was particularly exasperating. Jo still looked like a thunder-cloud, and nothing went well all day. It was bitter cold in the morning; she dropped her precious turn-over in the gutter, Aunt March had an attack of fidgets, Meg was pensive, Beth *would* look grieved and wistful when she got home, and Amy kept making remarks about people who were always talking about being good, and yet wouldn't try, when other people set them a virtuous example.

"Everybody is so hateful, I'll ask Laurie to go skating. He is always kind and jolly, and will put me to rights, I know," said Jo to herself, and off she went.

Amy heard the clash of skates, and looked out with an impatient exclamation, —

"There! she promised I should go next time, for this is the last ice we shall have. But it's no use to ask such a cross patch to take me."

"Don't say that; you *were* very naughty, and it *is* hard to forgive the loss of her precious little book; but I think she might do it now, and I guess she will, if you try her at the right minute," said Meg. "Go after them; don't say anything till Jo has got good-natured with Laurie, then take a quiet minute, and just kiss her, or do some kind thing, and I'm sure she'll be friends again, with all her heart."

"I'll try," said Amy, for the advice suited her; and, after a flurry to get ready, she ran after the friends, who were just disappearing over the hill.

It was not far to the river, but both were ready before Amy reached them. Jo saw her coming, and turned her back; Laurie did not see, for he was carefully skating along the shore, sounding the ice, for a warm spell had preceded the cold snap.

"I'll go on to the first bend, and see if it's all right, before we begin to race," Amy heard him say, as he shot away, looking like a young Russian, in his fur-trimmed coat and cap.

Jo heard Amy panting after her run, stamping her feet, and blowing her fingers, as she tried to put her skates on; but Jo never turned, and went slowly zigzagging down the river,

---

54 Fredrick Bremer (1801–1865), Sir Walter Scott (1771–1832) and Maria Edgeworth (1767–1849) all wrote novels and moral tales that were widely read in this period.

taking a bitter, unhappy sort of satisfaction in her sister's troubles. She had cherished her anger till it grew strong, and took possession of her, as evil thoughts and feelings always do, unless cast out at once. As Laurie turned the bend, he shouted back, —

"Keep near the shore; it isn't safe in the middle."

Jo heard, but Amy was just struggling to her feet, and did not catch a word. Jo glanced over her shoulder, and the little demon she was harboring said in her ear, —

"No matter whether she heard or not, let her take care of herself."

Laurie had vanished round the bend; Jo was just at the turn, and Amy, far behind, striking out toward the smoother ice in the middle of the river. For a minute Jo stood still, with a strange feeling at her heart; then she resolved to go on, but something held and turned her round, just in time to see Amy throw up her hands and go down, with the sudden crash of rotten ice, the splash of water, and a cry that made Jo's heart stand still with fear. She tried to call Laurie, but her voice was gone; she tried to rush forward, but her feet seemed to have no strength in them; and, for a second, she could only stand motionless, staring, with a terror-stricken face, at the little blue hood above the black water. Something rushed swiftly by her, and Laurie's voice cried out, —

"Bring a rail; quick, quick!"

How she did it, she never knew; but for the next few minutes she worked as if possessed, blindly obeying Laurie, who was quite self-possessed, and, lying flat, held Amy up by his arm and hockey,[55] till Jo dragged a rail from the fence, and together they got the child out, more frightened than hurt.

"Now then, we must walk her home as fast as we can; pile our things on her, while I get off these confounded skates," cried Laurie, wrapping his coat round Amy, and tugging away at the straps, which never seemed so intricate before.

Shivering, dripping, and crying, they got Amy home; and, after an exciting time of it, she fell asleep, rolled in blankets, before a hot fire. During the bustle Jo had scarcely spoken; but flown about, looking pale and wild, with her things half off, her dress torn, and her hands cut and bruised by ice and rails. and refractory buckles. When Amy was comfortably asleep, the house quiet, and Mrs. March sitting by the bed, she called Jo to her, and began to bind up the hurt hands.

"Are you sure she is safe?" whispered Jo, looking remorsefully at the golden head, which might have been swept away from her sight forever, under the treacherous ice.

"Quite safe, dear; she is not hurt, and won't even take cold, I think, you were so sensible in covering and getting her home quickly," replied her mother, cheerfully.

"Laurie did it all; I only let her go. Mother, if she *should* die, it would be my fault;" and Jo dropped clown beside the bed in a passion of penitent tears, telling all that had happened, bitterly condemning her hardness of heart, and sobbing out her gratitude for being spared the heavy punishment which might have come upon her.

"It's my dreadful temper! I try to cure it; I think I have, and then it breaks out worse than ever. Oh, mother! what shall I do! What shall I do?" cried poor Jo, in despair.

"Watch and pray, dear; never get tired of trying; and never think it is impossible to conquer your fault," said Mrs. March, drawing the blowzy head to her shoulder, and kissing the wet cheek so tenderly, that Jo cried harder than ever.

"You don't know; you can't guess how bad it is! It seems as if I could do anything when I'm in a passion; I get so savage, I could hurt any one and enjoy it. I'm afraid I *shall* do

---

55 Hockey stick.

something dreadful some day, and spoil my life, and make everybody hate me. Oh, mother! help me, do help me!"

"I will, my child; I will. Don't cry so bitterly, but remember this day, and resolve, with all your soul, that you will never know another like it. Jo, dear, we all have our temptations, some far greater than yours, and it often takes us all our lives to conquer them. You think your temper is the worst in the world; but mine used to be just like it."

"Yours, mother? Why, you are never angry!" and, for the moment, Jo forgot remorse in surprise.

"I've been trying to cure it for forty years, and have only succeeded in controlling it. I am angry nearly every day of my life, Jo; but I have learned not to show it; and I still hope to learn not to feel it, though it may take me another forty years to do so."

The patience and the humility of the face she loved so well, was a better lesson to Jo than the wisest lecture, the sharpest reproof. She felt comforted at once by the sympathy and confidence given her; the knowledge that her mother had a fault like hers, and tried to mend it, made her own easier to bear, and strengthened her resolution to cure it; though forty years seemed rather a long time to watch and pray, to a girl of fifteen.

"Mother, are you angry when you fold your lips tight together, and go out of the room sometimes, when Aunt March scolds, or people worry you?" asked Jo, feeling nearer and dearer to her mother than ever before.

"Yes, I've learned to check the hasty words that rise to my lips; and when I feel that they mean to break out against my will, I just go away a minute, and give myself a little shake, for being so weak and wicked," answered Mrs. March, with a sigh and a smile, as she smoothed and fastened up Jo's disheveled hair.

"How did you learn to keep still? That is what troubles me — for the sharp words fly out before I know what I'm about; and the more I say the worse I get, till it's a pleasure to hurt people's feelings, and say dreadful things. Tell me how you do it, Marmee dear."

"My good mother used to help me —"

"As you do us —" interrupted Jo, with a grateful kiss.

"But I lost her when I was a little older than you are, and for years had to struggle on alone, for I was too proud to confess my weakness to any one else. I had a hard time, Jo, and shed a good many bitter tears over my failures; for, in spite of my efforts, I never seemed to get on. Then your father came, and I was so happy that I found it easy to be good. But by and by, when I had four little daughters round me, and we were poor, then the old trouble began again; for I am not patient by nature, and it tried me very much to see my children wanting anything."

"Poor mother! What helped you then?"

"Your father, Jo. He never loses patience, — never doubts or complains, — but always hopes, and works and waits so cheerfully, that one is ashamed to do otherwise before him. He helped and comforted me, and showed me that I must try to practice all the virtues I would have my little girls possess, for I was their example. It was easier to try for your sakes than for my own; a startled or surprised look from one of you, when I spoke, sharply rebuked me more than any words could have done; and the love, respect, and confidence of my children was the sweetest reward I could receive for my efforts to be the woman I would have them copy."

"Oh, mother! if I'm ever half as good as you, I shall be satisfied," cried Jo, much touched.

"I hope you will be a great deal better, dear; but you must keep watch over your 'bosom enemy,' as father calls it, or it may sadden, if not spoil your life. You have had a warning; remember it, and try with heart and soul to master this quick temper, before it brings you greater sorrow and regret than you have known today."

"I will try, mother, I truly will. But you must help me, remind me, and keep me from flying out. I used to see father sometimes put his finger on his lips, and look at you with a very kind, but sober face; and you always folded your lips tight, or went away; was he reminding you then?" asked Jo, softly.

"Yes; I asked him to help me so, and he never forgot it, but saved me from many a sharp word by that little gesture and kind look."

Jo saw that her mother's eyes filled, and her lips trembled, as she spoke; and, fearing that she had said too much, she whispered anxiously, "Was it wrong to watch you, and to speak of it? I didn't mean to be rude, but it's so comfortable to say all I think to you, and feel so safe and happy here."

"My Jo, you may say anything to your mother, for it is my greatest happiness and pride to feel that my girls confide in me, and know how much I love them."

"I thought I'd grieved you."

"No, dear; but speaking of father reminded me how much I miss him, how much I owe him, and how faithfully I should watch and work to keep his little daughters safe and good for him."

"Yet you told him to go, mother, and didn't cry when he went, and never complain now, or seem as if you needed any help," said Jo, wondering.

"I gave my best to the country I love, and kept my tears till he was gone. Why should I complain, when we both have merely done our duty, and will surely be the happier for it in the end? If I don't seem to need help, it is because I have a better friend, even than father, to comfort and sustain me. My child, the troubles and temptations of your life are beginning, and may be many; but you can overcome and outlive them all, if you learn to feel the strength and tenderness of your Heavenly father as you do that of your earthly one. The more you love and trust Him, the nearer you will feel to Him, and the less you will depend on human power and wisdom. His love and care never tire or change, can never be taken from you, but may become the source of lifelong peace, happiness, and strength. Believe this heartily, and go to God with all your little cares, and hopes, and sins, and sorrows, as freely and confidingly as you come to your mother."

Jo's only answer was to hold her mother close, and, in the silence which followed, the sincerest prayer she had ever prayed left her heart, without words; for in that sad, yet happy hour, she had learned not only the bitterness of remorse and despair, but the sweetness of self-denial and self-control; and, led by her mother's hand, she had drawn nearer to the Friend who welcomes every child with a love stronger than that of any father, tenderer than that of any mother.

Amy stirred, and sighed in her sleep; and, as if eager to begin at once to mend her fault, Jo looked up with an expression on her face which it had never worn before.

"I let the sun go down on my anger; I wouldn't forgive her, and today, if it hadn't been for Laurie, it might have been too late! How could I be so wicked?" said Jo, half aloud, as she leaned over her sister, softly stroking the wet hair scattered on the pillow.

As if she heard, Amy opened her eyes, and held out her arms, with a smile that went straight to Jo's heart. Neither said a word, but they hugged one another close, in spite of the blankets, and everything was forgiven and forgotten in one hearty kiss.

9

Meg Goes to Vanity Fair[56]

I do think it was the most fortunate thing in the world, that those children should have the measles just now," said Meg, one April day, as she stood packing the "go abroady" trunk in her room, surrounded by her sisters.

"And so nice of Annie Moffat, not to forget her promise. A whole fortnight of fun will be regularly splendid," replied Jo, looking like a windmill, as she folded skirts with her long arms.

"And such lovely weather; I'm so glad of that," added Beth, tidily sorting neck and hair ribbons in her best box, lent for the great occasion.

"I wish I was going to have a fine time, and wear all these nice things," said Amy with her mouth full of pins, as she artistically replenished her sister's cushion.

"I wish you were all going; but, as you can't, I shall keep my adventures to tell you when I come back. I'm sure it's the least I can do, when you have been so kind, lending me things and helping me get ready," said Meg, glancing round the room at the very simple outfit, which seemed nearly perfect in their eyes.

"What did mother give you out of the treasure box?" asked Amy, who had not been present at the opening of a certain cedar chest, in which Mrs. March kept a few relics of past splendor, as gifts for her girls when the proper time came.

"A pair of silk stockings, that pretty carved fan, and a lovely blue sash. I wanted the violet silk; but there isn't time to make it over, so I must be contented with my old tarleton."[57]

"It will look nicely over my new muslin skirt, and the sash will set it off beautifully. I wish I hadn't smashed my coral bracelet, for you might have had it," said Jo, who loved to give and lend, but whose possessions were usually too dilapidated to be of much use.

"There is a lovely old-fashioned pearl set in the treasure box; but mother said real flowers were the prettiest ornament for a young girl, and Laurie promised to send me all I want," replied Meg. "Now, let me see; there's my new gray walking suit, —just curl up the feather in my hat, Beth, — then my poplin, for Sunday, and the small party, — it looks heavy for spring, don't it? the violet silk would be so nice; oh, dear!"

"Never mind; you've got the tarleton for the big party, and you always look like an angel in white," said Amy, brooding over the little store of finery in which her soul delighted.

"It isn't low-necked, and it don't sweep enough, but it will have to do. My blue house-dress looks so well, turned and freshly trimmed, that I feel as if I'd got a new one. My silk sacque[58] isn't a bit the fashion, and my bonnet doesn't look like Sallie's; I didn't like to say anything, but I was dreadfully disappointed in my umbrella. I told mother black, with a white handle, but she forgot, and bought a green one, with a yellowish handle. It's strong and neat, so I ought not to complain, but I know I shall feel ashamed of it beside Annie's silk one, with a gold top," sighed Meg, surveying the little umbrella with great disfavor.

"Change it," advised Jo.

"I won't be so silly, or hurt Marmee's feelings, when she took so much pains to get my things. It's a nonsensical notion of mine, and I'm not going to give up to it. My silk stockings

---

56 In Bunyan's *Pilgrim's Progress*, Christian travels to Vanity Fair, where he is tempted with all sorts of items (which come to nothing but vanity) by various vendors.

57 A thin, plain-weave, cotton fabric.

58 Silk coat.

and two pairs of spandy gloves are my comfort. You are a dear, to lend me yours, Jo; I feel so rich, and sort of elegant, with two new pairs, and the old ones cleaned up for common;" and Meg took a refreshing peep at her glove-box.

"Annie Moffat has blue and pink bows on her night-caps; would you put some on mine?" she asked, as Beth brought up a pile of snowy muslins, fresh from Hannah's hands.

"No, I wouldn't; for the smart caps won't match the plain gowns, without any trimming on them. Poor folks shouldn't rig,"[59] said Jo, decidedly.

"I wonder if I shall *ever* be happy enough to have real lace on my clothes, and bows on my caps?" said Meg, impatiently.

"You said the other day that you'd be perfectly happy if you could only go to Annie Moffat's," observed Beth in her quiet way.

"So I did! Well, I *am* happy, and I *won't* fret; but it does seem as if the more one gets the more one wants, don't it? There, now, the trays are ready, and everything in but my ball-dress, which I shall leave for mother," said Meg, cheering up, as she glanced from the half-filled trunk to the many-times pressed and mended white tarleton, which she called her "ball dress," with an important air.

The next day was fine, and Meg departed, in style, for a fortnight of novelty and pleasure. Mrs. March had consented to the visit rather reluctantly, fearing that Margaret would come back more discontented than she went. But she had begged so hard, and Sallie had promised to take good care of her, and a little pleasure seemed so delightful after a winter of hard work that the mother yielded, and the daughter went to take her first taste of fashionable life.

The Moffats *were* very fashionable, and simple Meg was rather daunted, at first, by the splendor of the house, and the elegance of its occupants. But they were kindly people, in spite of the frivolous life they led, and soon put their guest at her ease. Perhaps Meg felt, without understanding why, that they were not particularly cultivated or intelligent people, and that all their gilding could not quite conceal the ordinary material of which they were made. It certainly was agreeable to fare sumptuously, drive in a fine carriage, wear her best frock every day, and do nothing but enjoy herself. It suited her exactly; and soon she began to imitate the manners and conversation of those about her; to put on little airs and graces, use French phrases, crimp her hair, take in her dresses, and talk about the fashions, as well as she could. The more she saw of Annie Moffat's pretty things, the more she envied her, and sighed to be rich. Home now looked bare and dismal as she thought of it, work grew harder than ever, and she felt that she was a very destitute and much injured girl, in spite of the new gloves and silk stockings.

She had not much time for repining, however, for the three young girls were busily employed in "having a good time." They shopped, walked, rode, and called all day; went to theaters and operas, or frolicked at home in the evening; for Annie had many friends, and knew how to entertain them. Her older sisters were very fine young ladies, and one was engaged, which was extremely interesting and romantic, Meg thought. Mr. Moffat was a fat, jolly old gentleman, who knew her father; and Mrs. Moffat, a fat, jolly old lady, who took as great a fancy to Meg as her daughter had done. Everyone petted her; and "Daisy," as they called her, was in a fair way to have her head turned.

When the evening for the "small party" came, she found that the poplin wouldn't do at all, for the other girls were putting on thin dresses, and making themselves very fine indeed;

---

59 Dress above their proper social station.

so out came the tarleton, looking older, limper, and shabbier than ever, beside Sallie's crisp new one. Meg saw the girls glance at it, and then at one another, and her cheeks began to burn; for, with all her gentleness, she was very proud. No one said a word about it, but Sallie offered to dress her hair, and Annie to tie her sash, and Belle, the engaged sister, praised her white arms; but, in their kindness Meg saw only pity for her poverty, and her heart felt very heavy as she stood by herself, while the others laughed chattered, prinked, and flew about like gauzy butterflies. The hard, bitter feeling was getting pretty bad, when the maid brought in a box of flowers. Before she could speak, Annie had the cover off, and all were exclaiming at the lovely roses, heath, and fern within.

"It's for Belle, of course; George always sends her some, but these are altogether ravishing," cried Annie, with a great sniff.

"They are for Miss March," the man said. "And here's a note," put in the maid, holding it to Meg.

"What fun! Who are they from? Didn't know you had a lover," cried the girls, fluttering about Meg in a high state of curiosity and surprise.

"The note is from mother, and the flowers from Laurie," said Meg simply, yet much gratified that he had not forgotten her.

"Oh, indeed!" said Annie, with a funny look, as Meg slipped the note into her pocket, as a sort of talisman against envy, vanity, and false pride; for the few loving words had done her good, and the flowers cheered her up by their beauty.

Feeling almost happy again, she laid by a few ferns and roses for herself, and quickly made up the rest in dainty bouquets for the breasts, hair, or skirts of her friends, offering them so prettily, that Clara, the elder sister, told her she was "the sweetest little thing she ever saw;" and they looked quite charmed with her small attention. Somehow the kind act finished her despondency; and, when all the rest went to show themselves to Mrs. Moffat, she saw a happy, bright-eyed face in the mirror, as she laid her ferns against her rippling hair, and fastened the roses in the dress that didn't strike her as so *very* shabby now.

She enjoyed herself very much that evening, for she danced to her heart's content; every one was very kind, and she had three compliments. Annie made her sing, and some one said she had a remarkably fine voice; Major Lincoln asked who "the fresh little girl, with the beautiful eyes, was;" and Mr. Moffat insisted on dancing with her, because she "didn't dawdle, but had some spring in her," as he gracefully expressed it. So, altogether she had a very nice time, till she overheard a bit of a conversation, which disturbed her extremely. She was sitting just inside the conservatory, waiting for her partner to bring her an ice, when she heard a voice ask, on the other side of the flowery wall, —

"How old is he?"

"Sixteen or seventeen, I should say," replied another voice.

"It would be a grand thing for one of those girls, wouldn't it? Sallie says they are very intimate now, and the old man quite dotes on them."

"Mrs. M. has made her plans, I dare say, and will play her cards well, early as it is. The girl evidently doesn't think of it yet," said Mrs. Moffat.

"She told that fib about her mamma, as if she did know, and colored up when the flowers came, quite prettily. Poor thing! she'd be so nice if she was only got up in style. Do you think she'd be offended if we offered to lend her a dress for Thursday?" asked another voice.

"She's proud, but I don't believe she'd mind, for that dowdy tarleton is all she has got. She may tear it to-night, and that will be a good excuse for offering a decent one."

"We'll see; I shall ask that Laurence, as a compliment to her, and we'll have fun about it afterward."

Here Meg's partner appeared, to find her looking much flushed and rather agitated. She was proud, and her pride was useful just then, for it helped her hide her mortification, anger, and disgust, at what she had just heard; for, innocent and unsuspicious as she was, she could not help understanding the gossip of her friends. She tried to forget it, but could not, and kept repeating to herself, "Mrs. M. has her plans," "that fib about her mamma," and "dowdy tarleton," till she was ready to cry, and rush home to tell her troubles, and ask for advice. As that was impossible, she did her best to seem gay; and, being rather excited, she succeeded so well, that no one dreamed what an effort she was making. She was very glad when it was all over, and she was quiet in her bed, where she could think and wonder and fume till her head ached, and her hot cheeks were cooled by a few natural tears. Those foolish, yet well-meant words, had opened a new world to Meg, and much disturbed the peace of the old one, in which, till now, she had lived as happily as a child. Her innocent friendship with Laurie was spoilt by the silly speeches she had overheard; her faith in her mother was a little shaken by the worldly plans attributed to her by Mrs. Moffat, who judged others by herself; and the sensible resolution to be contented with the simple wardrobe which suited a poor man's daughter, was weakened by the unnecessary pity of girls, who thought a shabby dress one of the greatest calamities under heaven.

Poor Meg had a restless night, and got up heavy-eyed, unhappy, half resentful toward her friends, and half ashamed of herself for not speaking out frankly, and setting everything right. Everybody dawdled that morning, and it was noon before the girls found energy enough even to take up their worsted work. Something in the manner of her friends struck Meg at once; they treated her with more respect, she thought; took quite a tender interest in what she said, and looked at her with eyes that plainly betrayed curiosity. All this surprised and flattered her, though she did not understand it till Miss Belle looked up from her writing, and said, with a sentimental air, —

"Daisy, dear, I've sent an invitation to your friend, Mr. Laurence, for Thursday. We should like to know him, and it's only a proper compliment to you."

Meg colored, but a mischievous fancy to tease the girls made her reply demurely, —

"You are very kind, but I'm afraid he won't come."

"Why not, chérie?"[60] asked Miss Belle.

"He's too old."

"My child, what do you mean? What is his age, I beg to know!" cried Miss Clara.

"Nearly seventy, I believe," answered Meg, counting stitches, to hide the merriment in her eyes.

"You sly creature! of course, we meant the young man," exclaimed Miss Belle, laughing.

"There isn't any; Laurie is only a little boy," and Meg laughed also at the queer look which the sisters exchanged, as she thus described her supposed lover.

"About your age," Nan said.

"Nearer my sister Jo's; *I* am seventeen in August," returned Meg, tossing her head.

"It's very nice of him to send you flowers, isn't it?" said Annie, looking wise about nothing.

---

60 French for "Dear" or "Sweetheart."

"Yes, he often does, to all of us; for their house is full, and we are so fond of them. My mother and old Mr. Laurence are friends, you know, so it is quite natural that we children should play together;" and Meg hoped they would say no more.

"It's evident Daisy isn't out yet," said Miss Clara to Belle with a nod.

"Quite a pastoral state of innocence all round," returned Miss Belle, with a shrug.

"I'm going out to get some little matters for my girls; can I do anything for you, young ladies?" asked Mrs. Moffat, lumbering in, like an elephant, in silk and lace.

"No, thank you, ma'am," replied Sallie; "I've got my new pink silk for Thursday, and don't want a thing."

"Nor I—" began Meg, but stopped, because it occurred to her that she *did* want several things, and could not have them.

"What shall you wear?" asked Sallie.

"My old white one again, if I can mend it fit to be seen; it got sadly torn last night," said Meg, trying to speak quite easily, but feeling very uncomfortable.

"Why don't you send home for another?" said Sallie, who was not an observing young lady.

"I haven't got any other." It cost Meg an effort to say that, but Sallie did not see it, and exclaimed, in amiable surprise, —

"Only that? how funny—." She did not finish her speech, for Belle shook her head at her, and broke in, saying, kindly, —

"Not at all; where is the use of having a lot of dresses when she isn't out? There's no need of sending home, Daisy, even if you had a dozen, for I've got a sweet blue silk laid away, which I've outgrown, and you shall wear it, to please me; won't you, dear?"

"You are very kind, but I don't mind my old dress, if you don't; it does well enough for a little girl like me," said Meg.

"Now do let me please myself by dressing you up in style. I admire to do it, and you'd be a regular little beauty, with a touch here and there. I shan't let anyone see you till you are done, and then we'll burst upon them like Cinderella and her godmother, going to the ball," said Belle, in her persuasive tone.

Meg couldn't refuse the offer so kindly made, for a desire to see if she would be "a little beauty" after touching up caused her to accept, and forget all her former uncomfortable feelings towards the Moffats.

On the Thursday evening, Belle shut herself up with her maid; and, between them, they turned Meg into a fine lady. They crimped and curled her hair, they polished her neck and arms with some fragrant powder, touched her lips with coralline salve, to make them redder, and Hortense would have added "a *soupçon*[61] of rouge," if Meg had not rebelled. They laced her into a sky-blue dress, which was so tight she could hardly breathe, and so low in the neck that modest Meg blushed at herself in the mirror. A set of silver filigree was added, bracelets, necklace, brooch, and even ear-rings, for Hortense tied them on, with a bit of pink silk, which did not show. A cluster of tea rose-buds at the bosom, and a *ruche*,[62] reconciled Meg to the display of her pretty white shoulders, and a pair of high-heeled blue silk boots satisfied the last wish of her heart. A laced handkerchief, a plumy fan, and a bouquet in a silver holder, finished her off; and Miss Belle surveyed her with the satisfaction of a little girl with a newly dressed doll.

---

61 French for "a touch."
62 A ruffle.

"Mademoiselle is charmante, tres jolie,[63] is she not?" cried Hortense, clasping her hands in an affected rapture.

"Come and show yourself," said Miss Belle, leading the way to the room where the others were waiting.

As Meg went rustling after, with her long skirts trailing, her ear-rings tinkling, her curls waving, and her heart beating, she felt as if her "fun" had really begun at last, for the mirror had plainly told her that she *was* "a little beauty." Her friends repeated the pleasing phrase enthusiastically; and, for several minutes, she stood, like the jackdaw in the fable,[64] enjoying her borrowed plumes, while the rest chattered like a party of magpies.

"While I dress, do you drill her, Nan, in the management of her skirt, and those French heels, or she will trip herself up. Put your silver butterfly in the middle of that white barbe, and catch up that long curl on the left side of her head, Clara, and don't any of you disturb the charming work of my hands," said Belle, as she hurried away, looking well pleased with her success.

"I'm afraid to go down, I feel so queer and stiff, and half-dressed," said Meg to Sallie, as the bell rang, and Mrs. Moffat sent to ask the young ladies to appear at once.

"You don't look a bit like yourself, but you are very nice. I'm nowhere beside you, for Belle has heaps of taste, and you're quite French, I assure you. Let your flowers hang; don't be so careful of them, and be sure you don't trip," returned Sallie, trying not to care that Meg was prettier than herself.

Keeping that warning carefully in mind, Margaret got safely down stairs, and sailed into the drawing-rooms, where the Moffats and a few early guests were assembled. She very soon discovered that there is a charm about fine clothes which attracts a certain class of people, and secures their respect. Several young ladies, who had taken no notice of her before, were very affectionate all of a sudden; several young gentlemen, who had only stared at her at the other party, now not only stared, but asked to be introduced, and said all manner of foolish, but agreeable things to her; and several old ladies, who sat on sofas, and criticised the rest of the party, inquired who she was, with an air of interest. She heard Mrs. Moffat reply to one of them, —

"Daisy March — father a colonel in the army — one of our first families, but reverses of fortune, you know; intimate friends of the Laurences; sweet creature, I assure you; my Ned is quite wild about her."

"Dear me!" said the old lady, putting up her glass for another observation of Meg, who tried to look as if she had not heard, and been rather shocked at Mrs. Moffat's fibs.

The "queer feeling" did not pass away, but she imagined herself acting the new part of fine lady, and so got on pretty well, though the tight dress gave her a side-ache, the train kept getting under her feet, and she was in constant fear lest her ear-rings should fly off, and get lost or broken. She was flirting her fan, and laughing at the feeble jokes of a young gentleman who tried to be witty, when she suddenly stopped laughing and looked confused; for, just opposite, she saw Laurie. He was staring at her with undisguised surprise, and disapproval also, she thought; for, though he bowed and smiled, yet something in his honest eyes made her blush, and wish she had her old dress on. To complete her confusion, she saw

---

63 French for "charming, very pretty."
64 A jackdaw is a black bird of the crow family. In Aesop's fable, a plain jackdaw struts around dressed up in peacock feathers only to end up being rejected both by jackdaws and peacocks.

Belle nudge Annie, and both glance from her to Laurie, who, she was happy to see, looked unusually boyish and shy.

"Silly creatures, to put such thoughts into my head! I won't care for it, or let it change me a bit," thought Meg, and rustled across the room to shake hands with her friend.

"I'm glad you came, for I was afraid you wouldn't," she said, with her most grown-up air.

"Jo wanted me to come, and tell her how you looked, so I did;" answered Laurie, without turning his eyes upon her, though he half smiled at her maternal tone.

"What shall you tell her?" asked Meg, full of curiosity to know his opinion of her, yet feeling ill at ease with him, for the first time.

"I shall say I didn't know you; for you look so grown-up. and unlike yourself, I'm quite afraid of you," he said, fumbling at his glove button.

"How absurd of you! The girls dressed me up for fun, and I rather like it. Wouldn't Jo stare if she saw me?" said Meg, bent on making him say whether he thought her improved or not.

"Yes, I think she would," returned Laurie gravely.

"Don't you like me so?" asked Meg.

"No, I don't," was the blunt reply.

"Why not?" in an anxious tone.

He glanced at her frizzled[65] head, bare shoulders, and fantastically trimmed dress, with an expression that abashed her more than his answer, which had not a particle of his usual politeness about it.

"I don't like fuss and feathers."

That was altogether too much from a lad younger than herself; and Meg walked away, saying, petulantly,—

"You are the rudest boy I ever saw."

Feeling very much ruffled, she went and stood at a quiet window, to cool her cheeks, for the tight dress gave her an uncomfortably brilliant color. As she stood there, Major Lincoln passed by; and, a minute after, she heard him saying to his mother, —

"They are making a fool of that little girl; I wanted you to see her, but they have spoilt her entirely; she's nothing but a doll, to-night."

"Oh, dear!" sighed Meg; "I wish I'd been sensible, and worn my own things; then I should not have disgusted other people, or felt so uncomfortable and ashamed myself."

She leaned her forehead on the cool pane, and stood half hidden by the curtains, never minding that her favorite waltz had begun, till some one touched her; and, turning, she saw Laurie looking penitent, as he said, with his very best bow, and his hand out, —

"Please forgive my rudeness, and come and dance with me."

"I'm afraid it will be too disagreeable to you," said Meg, trying to look offended, and failing entirely.

"Not a bit of it; I'm dying to do it. Come, I'll be good; I don't like your gown, but I do think you are — just splendid;" and he waved his hands, as if words failed to express his admiration.

Meg smiled, and relented, and whispered, as they stood waiting to catch the time,

"Take care my skirt doesn't trip you up; it's the plague of my life and I was a goose to wear it."

---

65 Curled.

"Pin it round your neck, and then it will be useful," said Laurie, looking down at the little blue boots, which he evidently approved of.

Away they went, fleetly and gracefully; for, having practiced at home, they were well matched, and the blithe young couple were a pleasant sight to see, as they twirled merrily round and round, feeling more friendly than ever after their small tiff.

"Laurie, I want you to do me a favor; will you?" said Meg, as he stood fanning her, when her breath gave out, which it did, very soon, though she would not own why.

"Won't I!" said Laurie, with alacrity.

"Please don't tell them at home about my dress to-night. They won't understand the joke, and it will worry mother."

"Then why did you do it?" said Laurie's eyes, so plainly, that Meg hastily added, —

"I shall tell them, myself, all about it, and 'fess' to mother how silly I've been. But I'd rather do it myself; so you'll not tell, will you?"

"I give you my word I won't; only what shall I say when they ask me?"

"Just say I looked nice, and was having a good time."

"I'll say the first, with all my heart; but how about the other? You don't look as if you were having a good time; are you?" and Laurie looked at her with an expression which made her answer, in a whisper, —

"No; not just now. Don't think I'm horrid; I only wanted a little fun, but this sort don't pay, I find, and I'm getting tired of it."

"Here comes Ned Moffat; what does he want?" said Laurie, knitting his black brows, as if he did not regard his young host in the light of a pleasant addition to the party.

"He put his name down for three dances, and I suppose he's coming for them; what a bore!" said Meg, assuming a languid air. which amused Laurie immensely.

He did not speak to her again till supper-time, when he saw her drinking champagne with Ned, and his friend Fisher, who were behaving "like a pair of fools," as Laurie said to himself, for he felt a brotherly sort of right to watch over the Marches, and fight their battles whenever a defender was needed.

"You'll have a splitting headache to-morrow, if you drink much of that. I wouldn't, Meg; your mother don't like it, you know," he whispered, leaning over her chair, as Ned turned to refill her glass, and Fisher stooped to pick up her fan.

"I'm not Meg, to-night; I'm 'a doll,' who does all sorts of crazy things. To-morrow I shall put away my 'fuss and feathers.' and be desperately good again," she answered, with an affected little laugh.

"Wish to-morrow was here, then," muttered Laurie, walking off, ill-pleased at the change he saw in her.

Meg danced and flirted, chattered and giggled, as the other girls did; after supper she undertook the German,[66] and blundered through it, nearly upsetting her partner with her long skirt, and romping in a way that scandalized Laurie, who looked on and meditated a lecture. But he got no chance to deliver it, for Meg kept away from him till he came to say good-night.

"Remember!" she said, trying to smile, for the splitting headache had already begun.

"Silence à la mort,"[67] replied Laurie, with a melodramatic flourish, as he went away.

---

66 Complex dance for couples.
67 French for "silence to the death."

This little bit of by-play excited Annie's curiosity; but Meg was too tired for gossip, and went to bed, feeling as if she had been to a masquerade, and hadn't enjoyed herself as much as she expected. She was sick all the next day, and on Saturday went home, quite used up with her fortnight's fun, and feeling that she had sat in the lap of luxury long enough.

"It does seem pleasant to be quiet, and not have company manners on all the time. Home *is* a nice place, though it isn't splendid," said Meg, looking about her with a restful expression, as she sat with her mother and Jo on the Sunday evening.

"I'm glad to hear you say so, dear, for I was afraid home would seem dull and poor to you, after your fine quarters," replied her mother, who had given her many anxious looks that day; for motherly eyes are quick to see any change in children's faces.

Meg had told her adventures gaily, and said over and over what a charming time she had had; but something still seemed to weigh upon her spirits, and, when the younger girls were gone to bed, she sat thoughtfully staring at the fire, saying little, and looking worried. As the clock struck nine, and Jo proposed bed, Meg suddenly left her chair, and, taking Beth's stool, leaned her elbows on her mother's knee, saying, bravely,—

"Marmee, I want to 'fess.'"

"I thought so; what is it, dear?"

"Shall I go away?" asked Jo, discreetly.

"Of course not; don't I always tell you everything? I was ashamed to speak of it before the children, but I want you to know all the dreadful things I did at the Moffats."

"We are prepared," said Mrs. March, smiling, but looking a little anxious.

"I told you they rigged me up, but I didn't tell you that they powdered, and squeezed, and frizzled, and made me look like a fashion-plate. Laurie thought I wasn't proper; I know he did, though he didn't say so, and one man called me 'a doll.' I knew it was silly, but they flattered me and said I was a beauty, and quantities of nonsense, so I let them make a fool of me."

"Is that all?" asked Jo, as Mrs. March looked silently at the downcast face of her pretty daughter, and could not find it in her heart to blame her little follies.

"No; I drank champagne, and romped, and tried to flirt, and was, altogether, abominable," said Meg self-reproachfully.

"There is something more, I think;" and Mrs. March smoothed the soft cheek, which suddenly grew rosy, as Meg answered, slowly, —

"Yes; it's very silly, but I want to tell it, because I hate to have people say and think such things about us and Laurie."

Then she told the various bits of gossip she had heard at the Moffats; and as she spoke, Jo saw her mother fold her lips tightly, as if ill pleased that such ideas should be put into Meg's innocent mind.

"Well, if that isn't the greatest rubbish I ever heard," cried Jo, indignantly. "Why didn't you pop out and tell them so, on the spot?"

"I couldn't, it was so embarrassing for me. I couldn't help hearing, at first, and then I was so angry and ashamed, I didn't remember that I ought to go away."

"Just wait till *I* see Annie Moffat, and I'll show you how to settle such ridiculous stuff. The idea of having 'plans,' and being kind to Laurie, because he's rich, and may marry us by and by! Won't he shout, when I tell him what those silly things say about us poor children?" and Jo laughed, as if, on second thoughts, the thing struck her as a good joke.

"If you tell Laurie, I'll never forgive you! She mustn't, must she, mother?" said Meg, looking distressed.

"No; never repeat that foolish gossip, and forget it as soon as you can," said Mrs. March, gravely. "I was very unwise to let you go among people of whom I know so little; kind, I dare say, but worldly, ill-bred, and full of these vulgar ideas about young people. I am more sorry than I can express for the mischief this visit may have done you, Meg."

"Don't be sorry, I won't let it hurt me; I'll forget all the bad, and remember only the good; for I did enjoy a great deal, and thank you very much for letting me go. I'll not be sentimental or dissatisfied, mother; I know I'm a silly little girl, and I'll stay with you till I'm fit to take care of myself. But it *is* nice to be praised and admired, and I can't help saying I like it," said Meg, looking half ashamed of the confession.

"That is perfectly natural, and quite harmless, if the liking does not become a passion, and lead one to do foolish or unmaidenly things. Learn to know and value the praise which is worth having, and to excite the admiration of excellent people, by being modest as well as pretty, Meg."

Margaret sat thinking a moment, while Jo stood with her hands behind her, looking both interested and a little perplexed; for it was a new thing to see Meg blushing and talking about admiration, lovers, and things of that sort; and Jo felt as if during that fortnight her sister had grown up amazingly, and was drifting away from her into a world where she could not follow.

"Mother, do you have 'plans,' as Mrs. Moffat said?" asked Meg, bashfully.

"Yes, my dear, I have a great many; all mothers do, but mine differ somewhat from Mrs. Moffat's, I suspect. I will tell you some of them, for the time has come when a word may set this romantic little head and heart of yours right, on a very serious subject. You are young, Meg; but not too young to understand me, and mothers' lips are the fittest to speak of such things to girls like you. Jo, your turn will come in time, perhaps, so listen to my 'plans,' and help me carry them out, if they are good."

Jo went and sat on one arm of the chair, looking as if she thought they were about to join in some very solemn affair. Holding a hand of each, and watching the two young faces wistfully, Mrs. March said, in her serious yet cheery way, —

"I want my daughters to be beautiful, accomplished, and good; to be admired, loved, and respected, to have a happy youth, to be well and wisely married, and to lead useful, pleasant lives, with as little care and sorrow to try them as God sees fit to send. To be loved and chosen by a good man is the best and sweetest thing which can happen to a woman; and I sincerely hope my girls may know this beautiful experience. It is natural to think of it, Meg; right to hope and wait for it, and wise to prepare for it; so that, when the happy time comes, you may feel ready for the duties, and worthy of the joy. My dear girls, I *am* ambitious for you, but not to have you make a dash in the world, — marry rich men merely because they are rich, or have splendid houses, which are not homes, because love is wanting. Money is a needful and precious thing, — and, when well used, a noble thing, — but I never want you to think it is the first or only prize to strive for. I'd rather see you poor men's wives, if you were happy, beloved, contented, than queens on thrones, without self-respect and peace."

"Poor girls don't stand any chance, Belle says, unless they put themselves forward," sighed Meg.

"Then we'll be old maids," said Jo, stoutly.

"Right, Jo; better be happy old maids than unhappy wives, or unmaidenly girls, running about to find husbands," said Mrs. March, decidedly. "Don't be troubled, Meg; poverty seldom daunts a sincere lover. Some of the best and most honored women I know were poor girls, but so love-worthy that they were not allowed to be old maids. Leave these things to time; make this home happy, so that you may be fit for homes of your own, if they are offered you, and contented here if they are not. One thing remember, my girls, mother is always ready to be your confidant, father to be your friend; and both of us trust and hope that our daughters, whether married or single, will be the pride and comfort of our lives."

"We will, Marmee, we will!" cried both, with all their hearts, as she bade them good night.

* * *

Editor's Note

Little Women: **The End of the Story**

Little Women, or Meg, Beth, Jo and Amy was so popular that Louisa May Alcott soon embarked on writing a sequel to the story, which she named *Good Wives* (1869). Both these volumes are now commonly bound in the same book under the title *Little Women*. In the second volume, three of the girls grow up to get married. Meg marries Laurie's tutor, John Brooke, while Alcott refused to give in to her readers who cried out for Jo to marry Laurie. Instead, Jo refuses Laurie's advances, breaking his heart (for a time), but also—Jo believes—clearing the way for Beth, who is deeply in love with Laurie. Beth, however, is not given the chance to marry Laurie. Too good and pure for an earthly existence of any duration, Beth dies in the sequel, opening the way for Laurie to eventually marry Amy. Jo is the last to marry, and her marriage choice is interesting. She chooses to wed an older "bear" of a German man appropriately named Bhaer. Thus, all the surviving March girls end up being "good wives."

Chapter Fifteen

ELIZABETH STUART PHELPS
(1844–1911)

The horrific, destructive magnitude of the Civil War (1861–65) still presents a staggering picture today. Over 623,000 soldiers died in the conflict, and there is no accurate estimation of the civilian dead. Other American wars pale in comparison. The combined American casualties of the Revolution, the War of 1812, the Mexican War, the Spanish-American War, both World Wars and the Korean War roughly equal the number of men killed during the Civil War. Approximately one out of every 11 American males of service age died in this war, leaving it difficult—if not impossible—to find an American family untouched by its deadly grip.

Into this profound and pervasive culture of grief came Elizabeth Stuart Phelps's first novel, *The Gates Ajar* (1868), a story partly inspired by the deaths of her mother, stepmother and fiancé, a man who had died in the Battle of Antietam (1862). Almost overnight *The Gates Ajar* became an international bestseller, catapulting Phelps to fame when she was just 24 years old. The book helped launch a literary career that would include some 56 other novels, along with countless stories, pamphlets, essays and poems. Phelps would write two sequels to the 1868 novel (*The Gates Between* in 1887 and *Within the Gates* in 1901), but none of her work ever again approached the astounding popularity of her first novel. It went through more than fifty printings in the nineteenth century.

In *The Gates Ajar*, Phelps offers her readers an extended biblically grounded argument—in novel form—describing the nature of heaven. It posits heaven as a natural continuation of earthly life, a view portrayed not through a typical wise and theologically informed male character, but through a woman whose deep spiritual sensitivity is capable of comprehending the true depth of God's love. Phelps targets her work most directly at the spiritual hearts, not the theological heads, of her readers, and she uses her novel to underline her belief that women have an absolutely pivotal role to play in spreading the message of God's comforting love to a nation—particularly to that nation's women—still reeling from the most terrible war it had ever experienced.

THE GATES AJAR

"Splendor! Immensity! Eternity! Grand words! Great things!
A little definite happiness would be more to the purpose."

MADAME DE GASPARIN.[1]

To my father,[2] whose life, like a perfume from beyond the Gates, penetrates every life which approaches it, the readers of this little book will owe whatever pleasant thing they may find within its pages.

E. S. P.

ANDOVER, October 22, 1868.

Frontispiece, Aunt Winifred, Mary and Faith (*The Gates Ajar*, Illustrated Edition, Boston: Fields, Osgood & Co., 1870).

The book was first released in November 1868. The text used here is reprinted from the second printing of the book: *The Gates Ajar*. Boston: Fields, Osgood and Company, 1869. Phelps took over two years to write the novel and later recounted that it was divinely inspired, saying that "The Angel said unto me 'Write' and I wrote."

1 Comtesse de Gasparin (1813–1894), writer of travel and religious works. This quotation comes from "The Paradise We Fear," in *The Near and the Heavenly Horizons* (1862).

2 Austin Phelps (1820–1890) was a minister and a famous Christian educator and writer. He served as the president of Andover Seminary in Massachusetts for ten years.

I

ONE WEEK; only one week to-day, this twenty-first of February.

I had been sitting here in the dark and thinking about it, till it seems so horribly long and so horribly short; it has been such a week to live through, and it is such a small part of the weeks that must be lived through, that I could think no longer, but lighted my lamp and opened my desk to find something to do.

I was tossing my paper about,— only my own: the packages in the yellow envelopes I have not been quite brave enough to open yet,—when I came across this poor little book in which I used to keep memoranda of the weather, and my lovers, when I was a school-girl. I turned the leaves, smiling to see how many blank pages were left, and took up my pen, and now I am not smiling any more.

If it had not come exactly as it did, it seems to me as if I could bear it better. They tell me that it should not have been such a shock. "Your brother had been in the army so long that you should have been prepared for anything. Everybody knows by what a hair a soldier's life is always hanging," and a great deal more that I am afraid I have not listened to. I suppose it is all true; but that never makes it any easier.

The house feels like a prison. I walk up and down and wonder that I ever called it home. Something is the matter with the sunsets; they come and go, and I do not notice them. Something ails the voices of the children, snowballing down the street; all the music has gone out of them, and they hurt me like knives. The harmless, happy children!—and Roy loved the little children.

Why, it seems to me as if the world were spinning around in the light and wind and laughter, and God just stretched down His hand one morning and put it out.

It was such a dear, pleasant world to be put out!

It was never dearer or more pleasant than it was on that morning. I had not been as happy for weeks. I came up from the Post-Office singing to myself. His letter was so bright and full of mischief! I had not had one like it all the winter. I have laid it away by itself, filled with his jokes and pet names, "Mamie" or "Queen Mamie" every other line, and signed

"Until next time, your happy
"ROY."

I wonder if all brothers and sisters keep up the baby-names as we did. I wonder if I shall ever become used to living without them.

I read the letter over a great many times, and stopped to tell Mrs. Bland the news in it, and wondered what had kept it so long on the way, and wondered if it could be true that he would have a furlough in May. It seemed too good to be true. If I had been fourteen instead of twenty-four, I should have jumped up and down and clapped my hands there in the street. The sky was so bright that I could scarcely turn up my eyes to look at it. The sunshine was shivered into little lances all over the glaring white crust. There was a snowbird chirping and pecking on the maple-tree as I came in.

I went up and opened my window; sat down by it and drew a long breath, and began to count the days till May. I must have sat there as much as half an hour. I was so happy counting the days that I did not hear the front gate, and when I looked down a man stood there,— a great rough man,—who shouted up that he was in a hurry, and wanted seventy-five cents for a telegram that he had brought over from East Homer. I believe I went down and paid him, sent him away, came up here and locked the door before I read it.

Phoebe found me here at dinner-time.

If I could have gone to him, could have busied myself with packing and journeying, could have been forced to think and plan, could have had the shadow of a hope of one more look, one word, I suppose I should have taken it differently. Those two words— "Shot dead"—shut me up and walled me in, as I think people must feel shut up and walled in, in Hell. I write the words most solemnly, for I know that there has been Hell in my heart.

It is all over now. He came back, and they brought him up the steps, and I listened to their feet,—so many feet; he used to come bounding in. They let me see him for a minute, and there was a funeral, and Mrs. Bland came over, and she and Phoebe attended to everything, I suppose. I did not notice nor think till we had left him out there in the cold and had come back. The windows of his room were opened, and the bitter wind swept in. The house was still and damp. Nobody was there to welcome me. Nobody would ever be * * * *

Poor old Phoebe! I had forgotten her. She was waiting at the kitchen window in her black bonnet; she took off my things and made me a cup of tea, and kept at work near me for a little while, wiping her eyes. She came in just now, when I had left my unfinished sentence to dry, sitting here with my face in my hands.

"Laws now, Miss Mary, my dear! This won't never do,—a rebellin' agin Providence, and singein' your hair on the lamp chimney this way! The dining-room fire's goin' beautiful, and the salmon is toasted to a brown. Put away them papers and come right along!"

II

February 23.

Who originated that most exquisite of inquisitions, the condolence system?

A solid blow has in itself the elements of its rebound; it arouses the antagonism of the life on which it falls; its relief is the relief of a combat.

But a hundred little needles pricking at us,—what is to be done with them? The hands hang down, the knees are feeble. We cannot so much as gasp, because they *are* little needles.

I know that there are those who like these calls; but why, in the name of all sweet pity, must we endure them without respect of persons, as we would endure a wedding reception or make a party-call?

Perhaps I write excitedly and hardly. I feel excited and hard.

I am sure I do not mean to be ungrateful for real sorrowful sympathy, however imperfectly it may be shown, or that near friends (if one has them), cannot give, in such a time as this, actual strength, even if they fail of comfort, by look and tone and love. But it is not near friends who are apt to wound, nor real sympathy which sharpens the worst of the needles. It is the fact that all your chance acquaintances feel called upon to bring their curious eyes and jarring words right into the silence of your first astonishment; taking you in a round of morning calls with kid gloves and parasol, and the liberty to turn your heart about and cut into it at pleasure. You may quiver at every touch, but there is no escape, because it is "the thing."

For instance: Meta Tripp came in this afternoon,—I have refused myself to everybody but Mrs. Bland, before, but Meta caught me in the parlor, and there was no escape.

She had come, it was plain enough, because she must, and she had come early, because, she too having lost a brother in the war, she was expected to be very sorry for me. Very likely she was, and very likely she did the best she knew how, but she was—not as uncomfortable as I, but as uncomfortable as she could be, and was evidently glad when it was over. She observed, as she went out, that I shouldn't feel so sad by and by. She felt very sad at first when Jack died, but everybody got over that after a time. The girls were going to sew for the Fair next week at Mr. Quirk's, and she hoped I would exert myself and come.

Ah, well: —

> "First learn to love one living man,
> Then mayst thou think upon the dead."[3]

It is not that the child is to be blamed for not knowing enough to stay away; but her coming here has made me wonder whether I am different from other women; why Roy was so much more to me than many brothers are to many sisters. I think it must be that there never *was* another like Roy. Then we have lived together so long, we two alone, since father died, that he had grown to me, heart of my heart, and life of my life. It did not seem as if he *could* be taken, and I be left.

Besides, I suppose most young women of my age have their dreams, and a future probable or possible, which makes the very incompleteness of life sweet, because of the symmetry which is waiting somewhere. But that was settled so long ago for me that it makes it very different. Roy was all there was.

February 26.

Death and Heaven could not seem very different to a Pagan from what they seem to me.

I say this deliberately. It has been deliberately forced upon me. That of which I had a faint consciousness in the first shock takes shape now. I do not see how one with such thoughts in her heart as I have had can possibly be "regenerate," or stand any chance of ever becoming "one of the redeemed." And here I am, what I have been for six years, a member of an Evangelical church, in good and regular standing!

The bare, blank sense of physical repulsion from death, which was all the idea I had of anything when they first brought him home, has not gone yet. It is horrible. It was cruel. Roy, all I had in the wide world,—Roy, with the flash in his eyes, with his smile that lighted the house all up; with his pretty, soft hair that I used to kiss and curl about my fingers, his bounding step, his strong arms that folded me in and cared for me,—Roy snatched away in an instant by a dreadful God, and laid out there in the wet and snow,—in the hideous wet and snow,—never to kiss him, never to see him any more! * * * *

He was a good boy. Roy was a good boy. He must have gone to Heaven. But I know nothing about Heaven. It is very far off. In my best and happiest days, I never liked to think of it. If I were to go there, it could do me no good, for I should not see Roy. Or if by chance I should see him standing up among the grand, white angels, he would not be the old dear Roy. I should grow so tired of singing! Should long and fret for one little talk,—for I never said good by, and —

---

3 From "A Poet's Epitaph" by William Wordsworth (1770–1850).

I will stop this.

A scrap from the German of Bürger,[4] which I came across to-day, shall be copied here.

"Be calm, my child, forget thy woe,
And think of God and Heaven;
Christ thy Redeemer hath to thee
Himself for comfort given.

"O mother, mother, what is Heaven?
O mother, what is Hell?
To be with Wilhelm,—that's my Heaven;
Without him,—that's my Hell."

February 27.

Miss Meta Tripp, in the ignorance of her little silly heart, has done me a great mischief.

Phoebe prepared me for it, by observing, when she came up yesterday to dust my room, that "folks was all sayin' that Mary Cabot"—(Homer is not an aristocratic town, and Phoebe doffs and dons my title at her own sweet will)—"that Mary Cabot was dreadful low sence Royal died, and hadn't ought to stay shut up by herself, day in and day out. It was behaving con-trary to the will of Providence, and very bad for her health, too." Moreover, Mrs. Bland, who called this morning with her three babies,—she never is able to stir out of the house without those children, poor thing!—lingered awkwardly on the door-steps as she went away, and hoped that Mary my dear wouldn't take it unkindly, but she did wish that I would exert myself more to see my friends and receive comfort in my affliction. She didn't want to interfere, or bother me, or—but—people would talk, and —

My good little minister's wife broke down all in a blush, at this point in her "porochial duties" (I more than suspect that her husband had a hand in the matter), so I took pity on her embarrassment, and said smiling that I would think about it.

I see just how the leaven has spread. Miss Meta, a little overwhelmed and a good deal mystified by her call here, pronounces "poor Mary Cabot *so* sad; she wouldn't talk about Royal; and you couldn't persuade her to come to the Fair; and she was so *sober!*—why, it was dreadful!"

Therefore, Homer has made up its mind that I shall become resigned in an arithmetical manner, and comforted according to the Rule of Three.

I wish I could go away! I wish I could go away and creep into the ground and die! If nobody need ever speak any more words to me! If anybody only knew *what* to say!

Little Mrs. Bland has ever been very kind, and I thank her with all my heart. But she does not know. She does not understand. Her happy heart is bound up in her little live children. She never laid anybody away under the snow without a chance to say good by.

As for the minister, he came, of course, as it was proper that he should, before the funeral, and once after. He is a very good man, but I am afraid of him, and I am glad that he has not come again.

---

4 Gottfried August Bürger (1747–1794) was a German poet who was a prolific writer of immensely popular poetry, especially ballads.

Night.

I can only repeat and re-echo what I wrote this noon. If anybody knew *what* to say!

Just after supper I heard the door-bell, and, looking out of the window, I caught a glimpse of Deacon Quirk's old drab felt hat, on the upper step. My heart sank, but there was no help for me. I waited for Phoebe to bring up his name, desperately listening to her heavy steps, and letting her knock three times before I answered. I confess to having taken my hair down twice, washed my hands to a most unnecessary extent, and been a long time brushing my dress; also to forgetting my handkerchief, and having to go back for it after I was down stairs. Deacon Quirk looked tired of waiting. I hope he was.

O, what an ill-natured thing to say! What is coming over me? What would Roy think? What could he?

"Good evening, Mary," said the Deacon, severely, when I went in. Probably he did not mean to speak severely, but the truth is, I think he was a little vexed that I had kept him waiting. I said good evening, and apologized for my delay, and sat down as far from him as I conveniently could. There was an awful silence.

"I came in this evening," said the Deacon, breaking it with a cough, "I came—hem!—to confer with you—"

I looked up. "I thought somebody had ought to come," continued the Deacon, "to confer with you as a Christian brother on your spiritooal condition."

I opened my eyes.

"To confer with you on your spiritooal condition," repeated my visitor. "I understand that you have had some unfortoonate exercises of mind under your affliction, and I observed that you absented yourself from the Communion Table last Sunday."

"I did."

"Intentionally?"

"Intentionally."

He seemed to expect me to say something more; and, seeing that there was no help for it, I answered.

"I did not feel fit to go. I should not have dared to go. God does not seem to me just now what He used to. He has dealt very bitterly with me. But, however wicked I may be, I will not mock Him. I think, Deacon Quirk, that I did right to stay away."

"Well," said the Deacon, twirling his hat with a puzzled look, "perhaps you did. But I don't see the excuse for any such feelings as would make it necessary. I think it my duty to tell you, Mary, that I am sorry to see you in such a rebellious state of mind."

I made no reply.

"Afflictions come from God," he observed, looking at me as impressively as if he supposed that I had never heard the statement before. "Afflictions come from God, and, however afflictin' or however crushin' they may be, it is our duty to submit to them. Glory in triboolation, St. Paul says, glory in triboolation."

I continued silent.

"I sympathize with you in this sad dispensation," he proceeded. "Of course you was very fond of Royal; it's natural you should be, quite natural—" He stopped, perplexed, I suppose, by something in my face. "Yes, it's very natural; poor human nature sets a great deal by earthly props and affections. But it's your duty, as a Christian and a church-member, to be resigned."

I tapped the floor with my foot. I began to think that I could not bear much more.

"To be resigned, my dear young friend. To say 'Abba, Father,' and pray that the will of the Lord be done."[5]

"Deacon Quirk!" said I, "I am *not* resigned. I pray the dear Lord with all my heart to make me so, but I will not say that I am, until I am,—if ever that time comes. As for those words about the Lord's will, I would no more take them on my lips than I would blasphemy, unless I could speak them honestly,—and that I cannot do. We had better talk of something else now, had we not?"

Deacon Quirk looked at me. It struck me that he would look very much so at a Mormon or a Hottentot, and I wondered whether he were going to excommunicate me on the spot.

As soon as he began to speak, however, I saw that he was only bewildered,—honestly bewildered, and honestly shocked: I do not doubt that I had said bewildering and shocking things.

"My friend," he said solemnly, "I shall pray for you and leave you in the hands of God. Your brother, whom He has removed from this earthly life for His own wise—"

"We will not talk any more about Roy, if you please," I interrupted; "*he* is happy and safe."

"Hem!—I hope so," he replied, moving uneasily in his chair; "I believe he never made a profession of religion, but there is no limit to the mercy of God. It is very unsafe for the young to think that they can rely on a death-bed repentance, but our God is a covenant-keeping God, and Royal's mother was a pious woman. If you cannot say with certainty that he is numbered among the redeemed, you are justified, perhaps, in hoping so."

I turned sharply on him, but words died on my lips. How could I tell the man of that short, dear letter that came to me in December,—that Roy's was no death-bed repentance, but the quiet, natural growth of a life that had always been the life of the pure in heart; of his manly beliefs and unselfish motives; of that dawning sense of friendship with Christ of which he used to speak so modestly, dreading lest he should not be honest with himself? "Perhaps I ought not to call myself a Christian," he wrote,—I learned the words by heart,—"and I shall make no profession to be such, till I am sure of it, but my life has not seemed to me for a long time to be my own. 'Bought with a price'[6] just expresses it. I can point to no time at which I was conscious by any revolution of feeling of 'experiencing a change of heart,' but it seems to me that a man's heart might be changed for all that. I do not know that it is necessary for us to be able to watch every footprint of God. The *way* is all that concerns us,—to see that we follow it and Him. This I am sure of; and knocking about in this army life only convinces me of what I felt in a certain way before,—that it is the only way, and He the only guide *to* follow."

But how could I say anything of this to Deacon Quirk?—this my sealed and sacred treasure, of all that Roy left me the dearest. At any rate I did not. It seemed both obstinate and cruel in him to come there and say what he had been saying. He might have known that I would not say that Roy had gone to Heaven, if—why, if there had been the breath of a doubt. It is a possibility of which I cannot rationally conceive, but I suppose that his name would never have passed my lips.

---

5 Mark 14:36.
6 1 Corinthians 6:20.

So I turned away from Deacon Quirk, and shut my mouth, and waited for him to finish. Whether the idea began to struggle into his mind that he *might* not have been making a very comforting remark, I cannot say; but he started very soon to go.

"Supposing you are right, and Royal was saved at the eleventh hour," he said at parting, with one of his stolid efforts to be consolatory, that are worse than his rebukes, "if he is singing the song of Moses and the Lamb (he pointed with his big, dingy thumb at the ceiling), *he* doesn't rebel against the doings of Providence. All *his* affections are subdued to God,— merged, as you might say,—merged in worshipping before the great White Throne.[7] He doesn't think this miser'ble earthly sphere of any importance, compared with that eternal and exceeding weight of glory. In the appropriate words of the poet, —

'O, not to one created thing
 Shall our embrace be given,
But all our joy shall be in God,
 For only God is Heaven.'

Those are very spiritooal and scripteral lines, and it's very proper to reflect how true they are."

I saw him go out, and came up here and locked myself in, and have been walking round and round the room. I must have walked a good while, for I feel as weak as a baby.

Can the man in any state of existence be made to comprehend that he has been holding me on the rack this whole evening?

Yet he came under a strict sense of duty, and in the kindness of all the heart he has! I know, or I ought to know, that he is a good man,—far better in the sight of God to-night, I do not doubt, than I am.

But it hurts,—it cuts,—that thing which he said as he went out; because I suppose it must be true; because it seems to me greater than I can bear to have it true.

Roy, away in that dreadful Heaven, can have no thought of me, cannot remember how I loved him, how he left me all alone. The singing and the worshipping must take up all his time. God wants it all. He is a "Jealous God."[8] I am nothing any more to Roy.

March 2.

And once I was much,—very much to him!

His Mamie, his poor Queen Mamie,—dearer, he used to say, than all the world to him,—I don't see how he can like it so well up there as to forget her. Though Roy was a very good boy. But this poor, wicked little Mamie,—why, I fall to pitying her as if she were some one else, and wish that some one would cry over her a little. I can't cry.

Roy used to say a thing,—I have not the words, but it was like this,—that one must be either very young or very ungenerous, if one could find time to pity one's self.

I have lain for two nights, with my eyes open all night long. I thought that perhaps I might see him. I have been praying for a touch, a sign, only for something to break the silence into which he has gone. But there is no answer, none. The light burns blue, and I see at last that it is morning, and go down stairs alone, and so the day begins.

---

7 Revelation 20:11. The throne upon which Jesus Christ sits to judge the righteous and the unrighteous.
8 Exodus 20:5.

Something of Mrs. Browning's has been keeping a dull mechanical time in my brain all day.

> "God keeps a niche
> In Heaven to hold our idols: ... albeit
> He brake them to our faces, and denied
> That our close kisses should impair their white."[9]

But why must He take them? And why should He keep them there? Shall we ever see them framed in their glorious gloom? Will He let us touch them *then?* Or must we stand like a poor worshipper at a Cathedral, looking up at his pictured saint afar off upon the other side?

Has everything stopped just here? Our talks together in the twilight, our planning and hoping and dreaming together; our walks and rides and laughing; our reading and singing and loving,—these then are all gone out forever?

God forgive the words! but Heaven will never be Heaven to me without them.

March 4.

Perhaps I had better not write any more here after this.

On looking over the leaves, I see that the little green book has become an outlet for the shallower part of pain.

Meta Tripp and Deacon Quirk, gossip and sympathy that have buzzed into my trouble and annoyed me like wasps (we are apt to make more fuss over a wasp-sting than a sabre-cut), just that proportion of suffering which alone can ever be put into words,—the surface.

I begin to understand what I never understood till now,—what people mean by the luxury of grief. No, I am sure that I never understood it, because my pride suffered as much as any part of me in that other time. I would no more have spent two consecutive hours drifting at the mercy of my thoughts, than I would have put my hand into the furnace fire. The right to mourn makes everything different. Then, as to mother, I was very young when she died, and father, though I loved him, was never to me what Roy has been.

This luxury of grief, like all luxuries, is pleasurable. Though, as I was saying, it is only the shallow part of one's heart—I imagine that the deepest hearts have their shallows— which can be filled by it, still it brings a shallow relief.

Let it be confessed to this honest book, that, driven to it by desperation, I found in it a wretched sort of content.

Being a little stronger now physically, I shall try to be a little braver; it will do no harm to try. So I seem to see that it was the content of poison,—salt-water poured between ship-wrecked lips.

At any rate, I mean to put the book away and lock it up. Roy used to say that he did not believe in journals. I begin to see why.

---

9 From the poem "Futurity" by Elizabeth Barrett Browning (1806–1861).

III

March 7.

I HAVE taken out my book, and am going to write again. But there is an excellent reason. I have something else than myself to write about.

This morning Phoebe persuaded me to walk down to the office, "To keep up my spirits and get some salt pork."

She brought my things and put them on me while I was hesitating; tied my victorine and buttoned my gloves; warmed my boots, and fussed about me as if I had been a baby. It did me good to be taken care of, and I thanked her softly; a little more softly than I am apt to speak to Phoebe.

"Bless your soul, my dear!" she said, winking briskly, "I don't want no thanks. It's thanks enough jest to see one of your old looks comin' over you for a spell, sence —"

She knocked over a chair with her broom, and left her sentence unfinished. Phoebe has always had a queer, clinging, superior sort of love for us both. She dandled us on her knees, and made all our rag-dolls, and carried us through measles and mumps and the rest. Then mother's early death threw all the care upon her. I believe that in her secret heart she considers me more her child than her mistress. It cost a great many battles to become established as "Miss Mary."

"I should like to know," she would say, throwing back her great, square shoulders and towering up in front of me,—"I should like to know if you s'pose I'm a goin' to 'Miss' anybody that I've trotted to Bamberry Cross as many times as I have you, Mary Cabot! Catch me!"

I remember how she would insist on calling me "her baby" after I was in long dresses, and that it mortified me cruelly once when Meta Tripp was here to tea with some Boston cousins. Poor, good Phoebe! Her rough love seems worth more to me, now that it is all I have left me in the world. It occurs to me that I may not have taken notice enough of her lately. She has done her honest best to comfort me, and she loved Roy, too.

But about the letter. I wrapped my face up closely in the *crêpe*, so that, if I met Deacon Quirk, he should not recognize me, and, thinking that the air was pleasant as I walked, came home with the pork for Phoebe and a letter for myself. I did not open it; in fact, I forgot all about it, till I had been at home for half an hour. I cannot bear to open a letter since that morning when the lances of light fell on the snow. They have written to me from everywhere,—uncles and cousins and old school-friends; well-meaning people; saying each the same thing in the same way,—no, not that exactly, and very likely I should feel hurt and lonely if they did not write; but sometimes I wish it did not all have to be read.

So I did not notice much about my letter this morning, till presently it occurred to me that what must be done had better be done quickly; so I drew up my chair to the desk, prepared to read and answer on the spot. Something about the writing and the signature rather pleased me: it was dated from Kansas, and was signed with the name of my mother's youngest sister, Winifred Forceythe. I will lay the letter in between these two leaves, for it seems to suit the pleasant, spring-like day; besides, I took out the green book again on account of it.

LAWRENCE, KANSAS, February 21.

MY DEAR CHILD,—I have been thinking how happy you will be by and by because Roy is happy.

And yet I know—I understand —

You have been in all my thoughts, and they have been such pitiful, tender thoughts, that I cannot help letting you know that somebody is sorry for you. For the rest, the heart knoweth its own, and I am, after all, too much of a stranger to my sister's child to intermeddle.

So my letter dies upon my pen. You cannot bear words yet. How should I dare to fret you with them? I can only reach you by my silence, and leave you with the Heart that bled and broke for you and Roy.

Your Aunt,

WINIFRED FORCEYTHE.

POSTSCRIPT, February 23.

I open my letter to add, that I am thinking of coming to New England with Faith,—you know Faith and I have nobody but each other now. Indeed, I may be on my way by the time this reaches you. It is just possible that I may not come back to the West. I shall be for a time at your uncle Calvin's, and then my husband's friends think that they must have me. I should like to see you for a day or two, but if you do not care to see me, say so. If you let me come because you think you must, I shall find it out from your face in an hour. I should like to be something to you, or do something for you; but if I cannot, I would rather not come.

I like that letter.

I have written to her to come, and in such a way that I think she will understand me to mean what I say. I have not seen her since I was a child. I know that she was very much younger than my mother; that she spent her young ladyhood teaching at the South;—grandfather had enough with which to support her, but I have heard it said that she preferred to take care of herself;—that she finally married a poor minister, whose sermons people liked, but whose coat was shockingly shabby; that she left the comforts and elegances and friends of New England to go to the West and bury herself in an unheard-of little place with him (I think she must have loved him); that he afterwards settled in Lawrence; that there, after they had been married some childless years, this little Faith was born; and that there Uncle Forceythe died about three years ago; that is about all I know of her. I suppose her share of Grandfather Burleigh's little property supports her respectably. I understand that she has been living a sort of missionary life among her husband's people since his death, and that they think they shall never see her like again. It is they who keep her from coming home again, Uncle Calvin's wife told me once; they and one other thing,—her husband's grave.

I hope she will come to see me. I notice one strange thing about her letter. She does not use the ugly words "death" and "dying." I don't know exactly what she put in their places, but something that had a pleasant sound.

"To be happy because Roy is happy." I wonder if she really thinks it is possible.

I wonder what makes the words chase me about.

IV

May 5.

I AM afraid that my brave resolutions are all breaking down.

The stillness of the May days is creeping into everything; the days in which the furlough was to come; in which the bitter Peace has come instead, and in which he would have been at home, never to go away from me any more.

The lazy winds are choking me. Their faint sweetness makes me sick. The moist, rich loam is ploughed in the garden; the grass, more golden than green, springs in the warm hollow by the front gate; the great maple, just reaching up to tap at the window, blazes and bows under its weight of scarlet blossoms. I cannot bear their perfume; it comes up in great breaths, when the window is opened. I wish that little cricket, just waked from his winter's nap, would not sit there on the sill and chirp at me. I hate the bluebirds flashing in and out of the carmine cloud that the maple makes, and singing, singing, everywhere.

It is easy to understand how Bianca heard "The nightingales sing through her head," how she could call them "Owl-like birds," who sang "for spite," who sang "for hate," who sang "for doom."[10]

Most of all I hate the maple. I wish winter were back again to fold it away in white, with its bare, black fingers only to come tapping at the window. "Roy's maple" we used to call it. How much fun he had out of that old tree!

As far back as I can remember, we never considered spring to be officially introduced till we had had a fight with the red blossoms. Roy used to pelt me well; but with that pretty chivalry of his, which was rare in such a little fellow, which developed afterwards into that rarer treatment of women, of which every one speaks who speaks of him, he would stop the play the instant it threatened roughness. I used to be glad, though, that I had strength and courage enough to make it some fun to him.

The maple is full of pictures of Roy. Roy, not yet over the dignity of his first boots, aiming for the cross-barred branch, coming to the ground with a terrible wrench on his ankle, straight up again before anybody could stop him, and sitting there on the ugly swaying bough as white as a sheet, to wave his cap,—"There, I meant to do it, and I have!" Roy, chopping off the twigs for kindling-wood in his mud oven, and sending his hatchet right through the parlor window. Roy cutting leaves for me, and then pulling all my wreaths down over my nose every time I put them on! Roy making me jump half-way across the room with a sudden thump on my window, and, looking out, I would see him with his hat off and hair blown from his forehead, framed in by the scented blossoms, or the quivering green, or the flame of blood-red leaves. But there is no end to them if I begin.

I had planned, if he came this week, to strip the richest branches, and fill his room.

May 6.

The May-day stillness, the lazy winds, the sweetness in the air, are all gone. A miserable northeasterly storm has set in. The garden loam is a mass of mud; the golden grass is drenched; the poor little cricket is drowned in a mud-puddle; the bluebirds are huddled among the leaves, with their heads under their drabbled wings, and the maple blossoms, dull and shrunken, drip against the glass.

It begins to be evident that it will never do for me to live alone. Yet who is there in the wide world that I could bear to bring here—into Roy's place?

A little old-fashioned book, bound in green and gold, attracted my attention this morning while I was dusting the library. It proved to be my mother's copy of "Elia,"[11]—one

---

10 References to the poem "Bianca among the Nightingales" by Elizabeth Barrett Browning (1806–1861).

11 *Essays of Elia* was a collection of personal and conversational essays by Charles Lamb (1775–1834).

that father had given her, I saw by the fly-leaf, in their early engagement days. It is some time since I read Charles Lamb; indeed, since the middle of February I have read nothing of any sort. Phoebe dries the Journal for me every night, and sometimes I glance at the Telegraphic Summary, and sometimes I don't.

"You used to be fond enough of books," Mrs. Bland says, looking puzzled,—"regular blue-stocking, Mr. Bland called you (no personal objection to you, of course, my dear, but he *doesn't* like literary women, which is a great comfort to me). Why don't you read and divert yourself now?"

But my brain, like the rest of me, seems to be crushed. I could not follow three pages of history with attention. Shakespeare, Wordsworth, Whittier, Mrs. Browning, are filled with Roy's marks,—and so down the shelf. Besides, poetry strikes as nothing else does, deep into the roots of things. One finds everywhere some strain at the fibres of one's heart. A mind must be healthily reconciled to actual life, before a poet—at least most poets—can help it. We must learn to bear and to work, before we can spare strength to dream.

To hymns and hymn-like poems, exception should be made. Some of them are like soft hands stealing into ours in the dark, and holding us fast without a spoken word. I do not know how many times Whittier's "Psalm,"[12] and that old cry of Cowper's, "God moves in a mysterious way,"[13] have quieted me,—just the sound of the words; when I was too wild to take in their meaning, and too wicked to believe them if I had.

As to novels, (by the way, Meta Tripp sent me over four yesterday afternoon, among which notice "Aurora Floyd" and "Uncle Silas,") the author of "Rutledge" expresses my feeling about them precisely.[14] I do not remember her exact words, but they are not unlike these. "She had far outlived the passion of ordinary novels; and the few which struck the depths of her experience gave her more pain than pleasure."

However, I took up poor "Elia" this morning, and stumbled upon "Dream Children,"[15] to which, for pathos and symmetry, I have read few things superior in the language. Years ago, I almost knew it by heart, but it has slipped out of memory with many other things of late. Any book, if it be one of those which Lamb calls "books which *are* books," put before us at different periods of life, will unfold to us new meanings,—wheels within wheels, delicate springs of purpose to which, at the last reading, we were stone-blind; gems which perhaps the author ignorantly cut and polished.

A sentence in this "Dream Children," which at eighteen I passed by with a compassionate sort of wonder, only thinking that it gave me "the blues" to read it, and that I was glad Roy was alive, I have seized upon and learned all over again now. I write it down to the dull music of the rain.

"And how, when he died, though he had not been dead an hour, it seemed as if he had died a great while ago, such a distance there is betwixt life and death; and how I bore his

---

12 John Greenleaf Whittier (1807–1892) was a popular Quaker poet and abolitionist. His poem "My Psalm" deals with the themes of death and God's providence.

13 William Cowper (1731–1800) was a British hymn writer and poet. "God moves in a mysterious way" is the opening line to the last hymn he ever wrote.

14 *Uncle Silas* (1864) was a mystery novel by J. Sheridan Le Fanu; *Rutledge* (1860) was a novel published anonymously by Miriam Coles Harris; *Aurora Floyd* (1863), also a novel, was written by Mary Elizabeth Braddon.

15 "Dream-Children; A Reverie" is a short essay by Charles Lamb that deals with the haunting presence of those dear to us who have died.

death, as I thought, pretty well at first, but afterwards it haunted and haunted me; and though I did not cry or take it to heart as some do, and as I think he would have done if I had died, yet I missed him all day long, and knew not till then how much I had loved him. I missed his kindness and I missed his crossness, and wished him to be alive again to be quarrelling with him (for we quarrelled sometimes), rather than not have him again."

How still the house is! I can hear the coach rumbling away at the half-mile corner, coming up from the evening train. A little arrow of light has just cut the gray gloom of the West.

Ten o'clock

The coach to which I sat listening rumbled up to the gate and stopped. Puzzled for the moment, and feeling as inhospitable as I knew how, I went down to the door. The driver was already on the steps, with a bundle in his arms that proved to be a rather minute child; and a lady, veiled, was just stepping from the carriage into the rain. Of course I came to my senses at that, and, calling to Phoebe that Mrs. Forceythe had come, sent her out an umbrella.

She surprised me by running lightly up the steps. I had imagined a somewhat advanced age and a sedate amount of infirmities, to be necessary concomitants of aunthood. She came in all sparkling with rain-drops, and, gently pushing aside the hand with which I was trying to pay her driver, said, laughing: —

"Here we are, bag and baggage, you see, 'big trunk, little trunk,' &c., &c. You did not expect me? Ah, my letter missed then. It is too bad to take you by storm in this way. Come, Faith! No, don't trouble about the trunks just now. Shall I go right in here?"

Her voice had a sparkle in it, like the drops on her veil, but it was low and very sweet. I took her in by the dining-room fire, and was turning to take off the little girl's things, when a soft hand stayed me, and I saw that she had drawn off the wet veil. A face somewhat pale looked down at me,—she is taller than I,—with large, compassionate eyes.

"I am too wet to kiss you, but I must have a look," she said, smiling. "That will do. You are like your mother, very like."

I don't know what possessed me, whether it was the sudden, sweet feeling of kinship with something alive, or whether it was her face or her voice, or all together, but I said: —

"I don't think you are too wet to be kissed," and threw my arms about her neck,—I am not of the kissing kind, either, and I had on my new bombazine, and she *was* very wet.

I thought she looked pleased.

Phoebe was sent to open the register in the blue room, and as soon as it was warm I went up with them, leading Faith by the hand. I am unused to children, and she kept stepping on my dress, and spinning around and tipping over, in the most astonishing manner. It strikingly reminded me of a top at the last gasp. Her mother observed that she was tired and sleepy. Phoebe was waiting around awkwardly up stairs, with fresh towels on her arm. Aunt Winifred turned and held out her hand.

"Well, Phoebe, I am glad to see you. This is Phoebe, I am sure? You have altered with everything else since I was here before. You keep bright and well, I hope, and take good care of Miss Mary?"

It was a simple enough thing, to be sure, her taking the trouble to notice the old servant with whom she had scarcely ever exchanged a half-dozen words; but I liked it. I liked the way, too, in which it was done. It reminded me of Roy's fine, well-bred manner towards his inferiors,—always cordial, yet always appropriate; I have heard that our mother had much the same.

I tried to make things look as pleasant as I could down stairs, while they were making ready for tea. The grate was raked up a little, a bright supper-cloth laid on the table, and the curtains drawn. Phoebe mixed a hasty cake of some sort, and brought out the heavier pieces of silver,—tea-pot, &c., which I do not use when I am alone, because it is so much trouble to take care of them, and because I like the little Wedgwood set that Roy had for his chocolate.

"How pleasant!" said Aunt Winifred, as she sat down with Faith in a high chair beside her. Phoebe had a great hunt up garret for that chair; it has been stowed away there since it and I parted company. "How pleasant everything is here! I believe in bright dining-rooms. There is an indescribable dinginess to most that I have seen, which tends to any-thing but thankfulness. Homesick, Faith? No; that's right. I don't think we shall be homesick at Cousin Mary's."

If she had not said that, the probabilities are that they would have been, for I have fallen quite out of the way of active housekeeping, and have almost forgotten how to entertain a friend. But I do not want her good opinion wasted, and mean they shall have a good time if I can make it for them.

It was a little hard at first to see her opposite me at the table; it was Roy's place.

While she was sitting there in the light, with the dust and weariness of travel brushed away a little, I was able to make up my mind what this aunt of mine looks like.

She is young, then, to begin with, and I find it necessary to reiterate the fact, in order to get it into my stupid brain. The cape and spectacles, the little old woman's shawl and inva-lid's walk, for which I had prepared myself, persist in hovering before my bewildered eyes, ready to drop down on her at a moment's notice. Just thirty-five she is by her own showing; older than I, to be sure; but as we passed in front of the mirror together, once to-night, I could not see half that difference between us. The peace of her face and the pain of mine contrast sharply, and give me an old, worn look, beside her. After all, though, to one who had seen much of life, hers would be the true maturity perhaps,—the maturity of repose. A look in her eyes once or twice gave me the impression that she thinks me rather young, though she is far too wise and delicate to show it. I don't like to be treated like a girl. I mean to find out what she does think.

My eyes have been on her face the whole evening, and I believe it is the sweetest face—woman's face—that I have ever seen. Yet she is far from being a beautiful woman. It is difficult to say what makes the impression; scarcely any feature is accurate, yet the *tout ensemble*[16] seems to have no fault. Her hair, which must have been bright bronze once, has grown gray—quite gray—before its time. I really do not know of what color her eyes are; blue, perhaps, most frequently, but they change with every word that she speaks; when quiet, they have a curious, far-away look, and a steady, lambent light shines through them. Her mouth is well cut and delicate, yet you do not so much notice that as its expression. It looks as if it held a happy secret, with which, however near one may come to her, one can never intermeddle. Yet there are lines about it and on her forehead, which are proof plain enough that she has not always floated on summer seas. She yet wears her widow's black, but relieves it pleasantly by white at the throat and wrists. Take her altogether, I like to look at her.

---

16 French for "general effect."

Faith is a round, rolling, rollicking little piece of mischief, with three years and a half of experience in this very happy world. She has black eyes and a pretty chin, funny little pink hands all covered with dimples, and a dimple in one cheek besides. She has tipped over two tumblers of water, scratched herself all over playing with the cat, and set her apron on fire already since she has been here. I stand in some awe of her; but, after I have become initiated, I think we shall be very good friends.

"Of all names in the catalogue," I said to her mother, when she came down into the parlor after putting her to bed, "Faith seems to be about the *most* inappropriate for this solid-bodied, twinkling little bairn of yours, with her pretty red cheeks, and such an appetite for supper!"

"Yes," she said, laughing, "there is nothing *spirituelle* about Faith. But she means just that to me. I could not call her anything else. Her father gave her the name." Her face changed, but did not sadden; a quietness crept into it and into her voice, but that was all.

"I will tell you about it sometime,—perhaps," she added, rising and standing by the fire. "Faith looks like him." Her eyes assumed their distant look, "like the eyes of those who see the dead," and gazed away,—so far away, into the fire, that I felt that she would not be listening to anything that I might say, and therefore said nothing.

We spent the evening chatting cosily. After the fire had died down in the grate (I had Phoebe light a pine-knot there, because I noticed that Aunt Winifred fancied the blaze in the dining-room), we drew up our chairs into the corner by the register, and roasted away to our hearts' content. A very bad habit, to sit over the register, and Aunt Winifred says she shall undertake to break me of it. We talked about everything under the sun,—uncles, aunts, cousins, Kansas and Connecticut, the surrenders and the assassination, books, pictures, music, and Faith,—O, and Phoebe and the cat. Aunt Winifred talks well, and does not gossip nor exhaust her resources; one feels always that she has material in reserve on any subject that is worth talking about.

For one thing I thank her with all my heart: she never spoke of Roy.

Upon reflection, I find that I have really passed a pleasant evening.

She knocked at my door just now, after I had written the last sentence, and had put away the book for the night. Thinking that it was Phoebe, I called, "Come in," and did not turn. She had come to the bureau where I stood unbraiding my hair, and touched my arm, before I saw who it was. She had on a crimson dressing-gown of warm flannel, and her hair hung down on her shoulders. Although so gray, her hair is massive yet, and coils finely when she is dressed.

"I beg your pardon," she said, "but I thought you would not be in bed, and I came in to say,—let me sit somewhere else at the breakfast-table, if you like. I saw that I had taken 'the vacant place.' Good night, my dear."

It was such a little thing! I wonder how many people would have noticed it or taken the trouble to speak of it. The quick perception, the unusual delicacy,—these, too, are like Roy.

I almost wish that she had stayed a little longer. I almost think that I could bear to have her speak to me about him.

Faith, in the next room, seems to have wakened from a frightened dream, and I can hear their voices through the wall. Her mother is soothing and singing to her in the broken words of some old lullaby with which Phoebe used to sing Roy and me to sleep, years and years ago. The unfamiliar, home-like sound is pleasant in the silent house. Phoebe, on her way to bed, is stopping on the garret-stairs to listen to it. Even the cat comes mewing up to the door, and purring as I have not heard the creature purr since the old Sunday-night singing, hushed so long ago.

V

May 7.

I WAS awakened and nearly smothered this morning by a pillow thrown directly at my head.

Somewhat unaccustomed, in the respectable, old maid's life that I lead, to such a pleasant little method of salutation, I jerked myself upright, and stared. There stood Faith in her night-dress, laughing as if she would suffocate, and her mother in search of her was just knocking at the open door.

"She insisted on going to wake Cousin Mary, and wouldn't be washed till I let her; but I stipulated that she should kiss you softly on both your eyes."

"I did," said Faith, stoutly; "I kissed her eyes, both two of 'em, and her nose, and her mouth and her neck; then I pulled her hair, and then I spinched her; but I thought she'd have to be banged a little. *Wasn't* it a bang, though!"

It really did me good to begin the day with a hearty laugh. The days usually look so long and blank at the beginning, that I can hardly make up my mind to step out into them. Faith's pillow was the famous pebble in the pond, to which authors of original imagination invariably resort; I felt its little circles widening out all through the day. I wonder if Aunt Winifred thought of that. She thinks of many things.

For instance, afraid apparently that I should think I was afflicted with one of those professional visitors who hold that a chance relationship justifies them in imposing on one from the beginning to the end of the chapter, she managed to make me understand, this morning, that she was expecting to go back to Uncle Forceythe's brother on Saturday. I was surprised at myself to find that this proposition struck me with dismay. I insisted with all my heart on keeping her for a week at the least, and sent forth a fiat that her trunks should be unpacked.

We have had a quiet, homelike day. Faith found her way to the orchard, and installed herself there for the day, overhauling the muddy grass with her bare hands to find dandelions. She came in at dinner-time as brown as a little nut, with her hat hanging down her neck, her apron torn, and just about as dirty as I should suppose it possible for a clean child to succeed in making herself. Her mother, however, seemed to be quite used to it, and the expedition with which she made her presentable I regard as a stroke of genius.

While Faith was disposed of, and the house still, auntie and I took our knitting and spent a regular old woman's morning at the south window in the dining-room. In the afternoon Mrs. Bland came over, babies and all, and sent up her card to Mrs. Forceythe.

Supper-time came, and still there had not been a word of Roy. I began to wonder at, while I respected, this unusual silence.

While her mother was putting Faith to bed, I went into my room alone, for a few moments' quiet. An early dark had fallen, for it had clouded up just before sunset. The dull, gray sky and narrow horizon shut down and crowded in everything. A soldier from the village, who has just come home, was walking down the street with his wife and sister. The crickets were chirping in the meadows. The faint breath of the maple came up.

I sat down by the window, and hid my face in both my hands. I must have sat there some time, for I had quite forgotten that I had company to entertain, when the door softly opened and shut, and some one came and sat down on the couch beside me. I did not speak, for I could not, and, the first I knew, a gentle arm crept about me, and she had gathered me into her lap and laid my head on her shoulder, as she might have gathered Faith.

"There," she said, in her low, lulling voice, "now tell Auntie all about it."

I don't know what it was, whether the voice, or touch, or words, but it came so suddenly,—and nobody had held me for so long,—that everything seemed to break up and unlock in a minute, and I threw up my hands and cried. I don't know how long I cried.

She passed her hand softly to and fro across my hair, brushing it away from my temples, while they throbbed and burned; but she did not speak. By and by I sobbed out: —

"Auntie, Auntie, Auntie!" as Faith sobs out in the dark. It seemed to me that I must have help or die.

"Yes, dear. I understand. I know how hard it is. And you have been bearing it alone so long! I am going to help you, and you must tell me all you can."

The strong, decided words, "I am going to help you," gave me the first faint hope I have had, that I *could* be helped, and I could tell her—it was not sacrilege—the pent-up story of these weeks. All the time her hand went softly to and fro across my hair.

Presently, when I was weak and faint with the new comfort of my tears, "Aunt Winifred," I said, "I don't know what it means to be resigned; I don't know what it *means!*"

Still her hand passed softly to and fro across my hair.

"To have everything stop all at once! without giving me any time to learn to bear it. Why, you do not know,—it is just as if a great black gate had swung to and barred out the future, and barred out him, and left me all alone in any world that I can ever live in, forever and forever."

"My child," she said, with emphasis solemn and low upon the words,—"my child, I *do* know. I think you forget—my husband."

I had forgotten. How could I? We are most selfishly blinded by our own griefs. No other form than ours ever seems to walk with us in the furnace. Her few words made me feel, as I could not have felt if she had said more, that this woman who was going to help me had suffered too; had suffered perhaps more than I,—that, if I sat as a little child at her feet, she could teach me through the kinship of her pain.

"O my dear," she said, and held me close, "I have trodden every step of it before you,— every single step."

"But you never were so wicked about it! You never felt—why, I have been *afraid* I should hate God! You never were so wicked as that."

Low under her breath she answered "Yes,"—this sweet, saintly woman who had come to me in the dark as an angel might.

Then, turning suddenly, her voice trembled and broke: —

"Mary, Mary, do you think He *could* have lived those thirty-three years,[17] and be cruel to you now? Think that over and over; only that. It may be the only thought you dare to have,—it was all I dared to have once,—but cling to it; *cling with both hands*, Mary, and keep it."

I only put both hands about her neck and clung there; but I hope—it seems, as if I clung a little to the thought besides; it was as new and sweet to me as if I had never heard of it in all my life; and it has not left me yet.

---

17 Reference to Jesus Christ's life (33 years) on earth.

"And then, my dear," she said, when she had let me cry a little longer, "when you have once found out that Roy's God loves you more than Roy does, the rest comes more easily. It will not be as long to wait as it seems now. It isn't as if you never were going to see him again."

I looked up bewildered.

"What's the matter, dear?"

"Why, do you think I shall see him,—really see him?"

"Mary Cabot," she said abruptly, turning to look at me, "who has been talking to you about this thing?"

"Deacon Quirk," I answered faintly,—"Deacon Quirk and Dr. Bland."

She put her other arm around me with a quick movement, as if she would shield me from Deacon Quirk and Dr. Bland.

"Do I think you will see him again? You might as well ask me if I thought God made you and made Roy, and gave you to each other. See him! Why, of course you will see him as you saw him here."

"As I saw him here! Why, here I looked into his eyes, I saw him smile, I touched him. Why, Aunt Winifred, Roy is an angel!"

She patted my hand with a little, soft, comforting laugh.

"But he is not any the less Roy for that,—not any the less your own real Roy, who will love you and wait for you and be very glad to see you, as he used to love and wait and be glad when you came home from a journey on a cold winter night."

"And he met me at the door, and led me in where it was light and warm!" I sobbed.

"So he will meet you at the door in this other home, and lead you into the light and the warmth. And cannot that make the cold and dark a little shorter? Think a minute!"

"But there is God,—I thought we went to Heaven to worship Him, and—"

"Shall you worship more heartily or less, for having Roy again? Did Mary love the Master more or less, after Lazarus came back?[18] Why, my child, where did you get your ideas of God? Don't you suppose He *knows* how you love Roy?"

I drank in the blessed words without doubt or argument. I was too thirsty to doubt or argue. Some other time I may ask her how she knows this beautiful thing, but not now. All I can do now is to take it into my heart and hold it there.

Roy my own again,—not only to look at standing up among the singers,—but close to me; somehow or other to be as near as—to be nearer than—he was here, *really* mine again! I shall never let this go.

After we had talked awhile, and when it came time to say good night, I told her a little about my conversation with Deacon Quirk, and what I said to him about the Lord's will. I did not know but that she would blame me.

"Some time," she said, turning her great, compassionate eyes on me,—I could feel them in the dark,—and smiling, "you will find out all at once, in a happy moment, that you can say those words with all your heart, and with all your soul, and with all your strength; it will come, even in this world, if you will only let it. But, until it does, you do right, quite right, not to scorch your altar with a false burnt-offering. God is not a God to be mocked. He would rather have only the old cry: 'I believe; help mine unbelief,'[19] and wait till you can say the rest.

---

18 John 11:1–44. Jesus raises Lazarus (the brother of Mary of Bethany) from the dead.
19 Mark 9:24.

"It has often grated on my ears," she added, "to hear people speak those words unworthily. They seem to me the most solemn words that the Bible contains, or that Christian experience can utter. As far as my observation goes, the good people—for they are good people—who use them when they ought to know better are of two sorts. They are people in actual agony, bewildered, racked with rebellious doubts, unaccustomed to own even to themselves the secret seethings of sin; really persuaded that because it is a Christian duty to have no will but the Lord's, they are under obligations to affirm that they have no will but the Lord's. Or else they are people who know no more about this pain of bereavement than a child. An affliction has passed over them, put them into mourning, made them feel uncomfortable till the funeral was over, or even caused them a shallow sort of grief, of which each week evaporates a little, till it is gone. These mourners air their trouble the longest, prate loudest about resignation, and have the most to say to you or me about our 'rebellious state of mind.' Poor things! One can hardly be vexed at them for pity. Think of being made so!"

"There is still another class of the cheerfully resigned," I suggested, "who are even more ready than these to tell you of your desperate wickedness—"

"People who have never had even the semblance of a trouble in all their lives," she interrupted. "Yes. I was going to speak of them. Of all miserable comforters, they are the most arrogant."

"As to real instant submission," she said presently, "there *is* some of it in the world. There are sweet, rare lives capable of great loves and great pains, which yet are kept so attuned to the life of Christ, that the cry in the Garden[20] comes scarcely less honestly from their lips, than from his. Such, like the St. John, are but one among the Twelve. Such, it will do you and me good, dear, at least to remember."

"Such," I thought when I was left alone, "you new dear friend of mine, who have come with such a blessed coming into my lonely days,—such you must be now, whatever you were once."

If I should tell her that, how she would open her soft eyes!

VI

May 9.

As I WAS looking over the green book last night, Aunt Winifred came up behind me and softly laid a bunch of violets down between the leaves.

By an odd contrast, the contented, passionless things fell against those two verses that were copied from the German, and completely covered them from sight. I lifted the flowers, and held up the page for her to see.

As she read, her face altered strangely; her eyes dilated, her lip quivered, a flush shot over her cheeks and dyed her forehead up to the waves of her hair. I turned away quickly, feeling that I had committed a rudeness in watching her, and detecting in her, however involuntarily, some far, inner sympathy, or shadow of a long-past sympathy, with the desperate words.

"Mary," she said, laying down the book, "I believe Satan wrote that."

---

20 Matt. 26:42. A reference to Jesus acknowledging God's providence by saying "Thy will be done."

She laughed a little then, nervously, and paled back into her quiet, peaceful self.

"I mean that he inspired it. They are wicked words. You must not read them over. You will outgrow them sometime with a beautiful growth of trust and love. Let them alone till that time comes. See, I will blot them out of sight for you with colors as blue as heaven,—the *real* heaven, where God *will* be loved the most."

She shook apart the thick, sweet nosegay, and, taking a half-dozen of the little blossoms, pinned them, dripping with fragrant dew, upon the lines. There I shall let them stay, and, since she wishes it, I shall not lift them to see the reckless words till I can do it safely.

This afternoon Aunt Winifred has been telling me about herself. Somewhat more, or of a different kind, I should imagine, from what she has told most people. She seems to love me a little, not in a proper kind of way, because I happen to be her niece, but for my own sake. It surprises me to find how pleased I am that she should.

That Kansas life must have been very hard to her, in contrast as it was with the smooth elegance of her girlhood; she was very young, too, when she undertook it. I said something of the sort to her.

"They have been the hardest and the easiest, the saddest and the happiest, years of all my life," she answered.

I pondered the words in my heart, while I listened to her story. She gave me vivid pictures of the long, bright bridal journey, overshadowed with a very mundane weariness of jolting coaches and railway accidents before its close; of the little neglected hamlet which waited for them, twenty miles from a post-office and thirty from a school-house; of the parsonage, a log-hut among log-huts, distinguished and adorned by a little lath and plastering, glass windows, and a doorstep;—they drew in sight of it at the close of a tired day, with a red sunset lying low on the flats.

Uncle Forceythe wanted mission-work, and mission-work he found here with—I should say with a vengeance, if the expression were exactly suited to an elegantly constructed and reflective journal.

"My heart sank for a moment, I confess," she said, "but it never would do, you know, to let him suspect that, so I smiled away as well as I knew how, shook hands with one or two women in red calico who had been "slickin up inside," they said; went in by the fire,—it was really a pleasant fire,—and, as soon as they had left us alone, I climbed into John's lap, and, with both arms around his neck, told him that I knew we should be very happy. And I said—"

"Said what?"

She blushed a little, like a girl.

"I believe I said I should be happy in Patagonia,—with him. I made him laugh at last, and say that my face and words were like a beautiful prophecy. And, Mary, if they were, it was beautifully fulfilled. In the roughest times,—times of ragged clothes and empty flour-barrels, of weakness and sickness and quack doctors, of cold and discouragement, of prairie fires and guerillas,—from trouble to trouble, from year's end to year's end, we were happy together, we two. As long as we could have each other, and as long as we could be about our Master's business, we felt as if we did not dare to ask for anything more, lest it should seem that we were ungrateful for such wealth of mercy."

It would take too long to write out here the half that she told me, though I wish I could, for it interested me more than any story that I have ever read.

After years of Christ-like toiling to help those rough old farmers and wicked bushwhackers to Heaven, the call to Lawrence came, and it seemed to Uncle Forceythe that he had better go. It was a pleasant, influential parish, and there, though not less hard at work, they found fewer rubs and more comforts; there Faith came, and there were their pleasant days, till the war.—I held my breath to hear her tell about Quantrell's raid.[21] There, too, Uncle wasted through that death-in-life, consumption;[22] there he "fell on sleep," she said, and there she buried him.

She gave me no further description of his death than those words, and she spoke them with her far-away, tearless eyes looking off through the window, and after she had spoken she was still for a time.

The heart knoweth its own bitterness; that grew distinct to me, as I sat, shut out by her silence. Yet there was nothing bitter about her face.

"Faith was six months old when we went," she said presently. "We had never named her: Baby was name enough at first for such a wee thing; then she was the only one, and had come so late, that it seemed to mean more to us than to most to have a baby all to ourselves, and we liked the sound of the word. When it became quite certain that John must go, we used to talk it over, and he said that he would like to name her, but what, he did not tell me.

"At last, one night, after he had lain for a while thinking with closed eyes, he bade me bring the child to him. The sun was setting, I remember, and the moon was rising. He had had a hard day; the life was all scorched out of the air. I moved the bed up by the window, that he might have the breath of the rising wind. Baby was wide awake, cooing softly to herself in the cradle, her bits of damp curls clinging to her head, and her pink feet in her hands. I took her up and brought her just as she was, and knelt down by the bed. The street was still. We could hear the frogs chanting a mile away. He lifted her little hands upon his own, and said—no matter about the words—but he told me that as he left the child, so he left the name, in my sacred charge,—that he had chosen it for me,—that, when he was out of sight, it might help me to have it often on my lips.

"So there in the sunset and the moonrise, we two alone together, he baptized her, and we gave our little girl to God."

When she had said this, she rose and went over to the window, and stood with her face from me. By and by, "It was the fourteenth," she said, as if musing to herself,—"the fourteenth of June."

I remember now that Uncle Forceythe died on the fourteenth of June. It may have been that the words of that baptismal blessing were the last that they heard, either child or mother.

                                                                        May 10.

It has been a pleasant day; the air shines like transparent gold; the wind sweeps like somebody's strong arms over the flowers, and gathers up a crowd of perfumes that wander up and down about one. The church bells have rung out like silver all day. Those bells— especially the Second Advent at the farther end of the village—are positively ghastly when it rains.

Aunt Winifred was dressed bright and early for church. I, in morning dress and slippers, sighed and demurred.

---

21 On August 21, 1863, the Southern guerilla fighter, William Quantrill, led his men on a meticulously planned and extremely brutal raid on Lawrence, Kansas. The raid later became known as the Lawrence Massacre. Quantrill's raiders looted the town's banks and stores and killed nearly 200 men and boys.

22 Lung disease, most often tuberculosis.

"Auntie, *do* you expect to hear anything new?"

"Judging from your diagnosis of Dr. Bland,—no."

"To be edified, refreshed, strengthened, or instructed?"

"Perhaps not."

"Bored, then?"

"Not exactly."

"What do you expect?"

"There are the prayers and singing. Generally one can, if one tries, wring a little devotion from the worst of them. As to a minister, if he is good and commonplace, young and earnest and ignorant, and I, whom he cannot help one step on the way to Heaven, consequently stay at home, Deacon Quirk, whom he might carry a mile or two, by and by stays at home also. If there is to be a 'building fitly joined together,'[23] each stone must do its part of the upholding. I feel better to go half a day always. I never compel Faith to go, but I never have a chance, for she teases not to be left at home."

"I think it's splendid to go to church most the time," put in Faith, who was squatted on the carpet, counting sugared caraway seeds,—"all but the sermon. That isn't splendid. I don't like the great big prayers 'n' things. I like caramary seeds,[24] though; mother always gives 'em to me in meeting 'cause I'm a good girl. Don't you wish *you* were a good girl, Cousin Mary, so's you could have some? Besides, I've got on my best hat and my button-boots. Besides, there used to be a real funny little boy up in meeting at home, and he gave me a little tin dorg once over the top the pew. Only mother made me give it back. O, you ought to seen the man that preached down at Uncle Calvin's! I tell you he was a bully old minister,—*he banged the Bible like everything!*"

"There's a devotional spirit for you!" I said to her mother.

"Well," she answered, laughing, "it is better than that she should be left to play dolls and eat preserves, and be punished for disobedience. Sunday would invariably become a guilty sort of holiday at that rate. Now, caraways or 'bully old ministers' notwithstanding, she carries to bed with her a dim notion that this has been holy time and pleasant time. Besides, the associations of a church-going childhood, if I can manage them genially, will be a help to her when she is older. Come, Faith! go and pull off Cousin Mary's slippers, and bring down her boots, and then she'll have to go to church. No, I *didn't* say that you might tickle her feet!"

Feeling the least bit sorry that I had set the example of a stay-at-home Christian before the child, I went directly up stairs to make ready, and we started after all in good season.

Dr. Bland was in the pulpit. I observed that he looked—as indeed did the congregation bodily—with some curiosity into our slip, where it has been a rare occurrence of late to find me, and where the light, falling through the little stained glass oriel, touched Aunt Winifred's thoughtful smile. I wonder whether Dr. Bland thought it was wicked for people to smile in church. No, of course he has too much sense. I wonder what it is about Dr. Bland that always suggests such questions.

It has been very warm all day,—that aggravating, unseasonable heat, which is apt to come in spasms in the early part of May, and which, in thick spring alpaca and heavy sack, one finds intolerable. The thermometer stood at 75° on the church-porch; every window

---

23 Ephesians 2:21.
24 Caraway seeds.

was shut, and everybody's fan was fluttering. Now, with this sight before him, what should our observant minister do, but give out as his first hymn: "Thine earthly Sabbaths." "Thine earthly Sabbaths" would be a beautiful hymn, if it were not for those lines about the weather: —

"No midnight shade, *no clouded sun,*
But sacred, high, eternal noon"!

There was a great hot sunbeam striking directly on my black bonnet. My fan was broken. I gasped for air. The choir went over and over and *over* the words, spinning them into one of those indescribable tunes, in which everybody seems to be trying to get through first. I don't know what they called them,—they always remind me of a game of "Tag."

I looked at Aunt Winifred. She took it more coolly than I, but an amused little smile played over her face. She told me after church that she had repeatedly heard that hymn given out at noon of an intense July day. Her husband, she said, used to save it for the winter, or for cloudy afternoons. "Using means of grace," he called that.

However, Dr. Bland did better the second time, Aunt Winifred joined in the singing, and I enjoyed it, so I will not blame the poor man. I suppose he was so far lifted above this earth, that he would not have known whether he was preaching in Greenland's icy mountains, or on India's coral strand.

When he announced his text, "For our conversation is in Heaven,"[25] Aunt Winifred and I exchanged glances of content. We had been talking about heaven on the way to church; at least, till Faith, not finding herself entertained, interrupted us by some severe speculations as to whether Maltese kitties were mulattoes, and "why the bell-ringer didn't jump off the steeple some night, and see if he couldn't fly right up, the way Elijah did."[26]

I listened to Dr. Bland as I have not listened for a long time. The subject was of all subjects nearest my heart. He is a scholarly man, in his way. He ought to know, I thought, more about it than Aunt Winifred. Perhaps he could help me.

His sermon, as nearly as I can recall it, was substantially this.

"The future life presented a vast theme to our speculation. Theories 'too numerous to mention' had been held concerning it. Pagans had believed in a coming state of rewards and punishments. What natural theology had dimly foreshadowed, Revelation had brought in, like a full-orbed day, with healing on its wings." I am not positive about the metaphors.

"As it was fitting that we should at times turn our thoughts upon the threatenings of Scripture, it was eminently suitable also that we should consider its promises.

"He proposed in this discourse to consider the promise of Heaven, the reward offered by Christ to his good and faithful servants.

"In the first place: What is heaven?"

I am not quite clear in my mind what it was, though I tried my best to find out. As nearly as I can recollect, however, —

"Heaven is an eternal state.

"Heaven is a state of holiness.

---

25 Philippians 3:20.
26 II Kings 2:1. God took Elijah up to heaven in a whirlwind.

"Heaven is a state of happiness."

Having heard these observations before, I will not enlarge as he did upon them, but leave that for the "vivid imagination" of the green book.

"In the second place: What will be the employments of heaven?

"We shall study the character of God.

"An infinite mind must of necessity be eternally an object of study to a finite mind. The finite mind must of necessity find in such study supreme delight. All lesser joys and interests will pale. He felt at moments, in reflecting on this theme, that that good brother who, on being asked if he expected to see the dead wife of his youth in heaven, replied, 'I expect to be so overwhelmed by the glory of the presence of God, that it may be thousands of years before I shall think of my wife,'—he felt that perhaps this brother was near the truth."

Poor Mrs. Bland looked exceedingly uncomfortable.

"We shall also glorify God."

He enlarged upon this division, but I have forgotten exactly how. There was something about adoration, and the harpers harping with their harps, and the sea of glass, and crying, Worthy the Lamb! and a great deal more that bewildered and disheartened me so that I could scarcely listen to it. I do not doubt that we shall glorify God primarily and happily, but can we not do it in some other way than by harping and praying?

"We shall moreover love each other with a universal and unselfish love."

"That we shall recognize our friends in heaven, he was inclined to think, after mature deliberation, was probable. But there would be no special selfish affections there. In this world we have enmities and favoritisms. In the world of bliss our hearts would glow with holy love alike to all other holy hearts."

I wonder if he really thought *that* would make "a world of bliss." Aunt Winifred slipped her hand into mine under her cloak. Ah, Dr. Bland, if you had known how that little soft touch was preaching against you!

"In the words of an eminent divine, who has long since entered into the joys of which he spoke: 'Thus, whenever the mind roves through the immense region of heaven, it will find, among all its innumerable millions, not an enemy, not a stranger, not an indifferent heart, not a reserved bosom. Disguise here, and even concealment, will be unknown. The soul will have no interests to conceal, *no thoughts to disguise*. A window will be opened in every breast, and show to every eye the rich and beautiful furniture within!'

"Thirdly: How shall we fit for heaven?"

He mentioned several ways, among which,—

"We should subdue our earthly affections to God.

"We must not love the creature as the Creator. My son, give *me* thy heart. When he removes our friends from the scenes of time (with a glance in my direction), we should resign ourselves to his will, remembering that the Lord gave and the Lord hath taken away in mercy; that He is all in all; that He will never leave us nor forsake us; that *He* can never change or die."

As if that made any difference with the fact, that his best treasures change or die!

"In conclusion, —

"We infer from our text that our hearts should not be set upon earthly happiness. (Enlarged.)

"That the subject of heaven should be often in our thoughts and on our lips." (Enlarged.)

Of course I have not done justice to the filling up of the sermon; to the illustrations, metaphors, proof-texts, learning, and eloquence,—for, though Dr. Bland cannot seem to think outside of the old grooves, a little eloquence really flashes through the tameness of his style sometimes, and when he was talking about the harpers, etc., some of his words were well chosen. "To be drowned in light," I have somewhere read, "may be beautiful; it is still to be drowned." But I have given the skeleton of the discourse, and I have given the sum of the impressions that it left on me, an attentive hearer. It is fortunate that I did not hear it while I was alone; it would have made me desperate. Going hungry, hopeless, blinded, I came back empty, uncomforted, groping. I wanted something actual, something pleasant, about this place into which Roy has gone. He gave me glittering generalities, cold commonplace, vagueness, unreality, a God and a future at which I sat and shivered.

Dr. Bland is a good man. He had, I know, written that sermon with prayer. I only wish that he could be made to *see* how it glides over and sails splendidly away from wants like mine.

But thanks be to God who has provided a voice to answer me out of the deeps.

Auntie and I walked home without any remarks (we overheard Deacon Quirk observe to a neighbor: "That's what I call a good gospel sermon, now!"), sent Faith away to Phoebe, sat down in the parlor, and looked at each other.

"Well?" said I.

"I know it," said she.

Upon which we both began to laugh.

"But did he say the dreadful truth?"

"Not as I find it in my Bible."

"That it is probable, only *probable* that we shall recognize—"

"My child, do not be troubled about that. It is not probable, it is sure. If I could find no proof for it, I should none the less believe it, as long as I believe in God. He gave you Roy, and the capacity to love him. He has taught you to sanctify that love through love to Him. Would it be *like* Him to create such beautiful and unselfish loves,—most like the love of heaven of any type we know,—just for our threescore years and ten of earth? Would it be like Him to suffer two souls to grow together here, so that the separation of a day is pain, and then wrench them apart for all eternity? It would be what Madame de Gasparin calls, 'fearful irony on the part of God.'"[27]

"But there are lost loves. There are lost souls."

"How often would I have gathered you, and ye would not! That is not his work. He would have saved both soul and love. They had their own way. We were speaking of His redeemed. The object of having this world at all, you know, is to fit us for another. Of what use will it have been, if on passing out of it we must throw by forever its gifts, its lessons, its memories? God links things together better than that. Be sure, as you are sure of Him, that we shall be *ourselves* in heaven. Would you be yourself not to recognize Roy?—consequently, not to love Roy, for to love and to be separated is misery, and heaven is joy."

"I understand. But you said you had other proof."

"So I have; plenty of it. If 'many shall come from the East and from the West, and shall sit down in the kingdom of God with Abraham, Isaac, and Jacob,' will they not be likely

---

27 Comtesse de Gasparin (1813–1894), writer of travels and religious works. This quotation comes from "The Paradise We Fear," in *The Near and the Heavenly Horizons* (1862), a work that expresses thoughts on heaven very like those in *The Gates Ajar*, such as "Paradise […] is my native country, not a foreign land; it is the house of my father, not the temple of an abstract divinity. I do not see an indistinguishable throng of phantoms; I meet brothers and dear friends."

to know that they are with Abraham, Isaac, and Jacob? or will they think it is Shadrach, Meshach, and Abednego?[28]

"What is meant by such expressions as 'risen *together*,' 'sitting *together* at the right hand of God,' 'sitting *together* in heavenly places'? If they mean anything, they mean recognitions, friendships, enjoyments.

"Did not Peter and the others know Moses when they saw him?—know Elias when they saw him? Yet these men were dead hundreds of years before the favored fishermen were born.

"How was it with those 'saints which slept and arose' when Christ hung dead there in the dark? Were they not seen of many?"

"But that was a miracle."

"They were risen dead, such as you and I shall be some day. The miracle consisted in their rising then and there. Moreover, did not the beggar recognize Abraham? and—Well, one might go through the Bible finding it full of this promise in hints or assertions, in parables or visions. We are 'heirs of God,' 'joint heirs with Christ'; having suffered with Him, we shall be 'glorified *together*.'[29] Christ himself has said many sure things: 'I will come and receive you, that where I am, there ye may be.' 'I will that they be with me where I am.' Using, too, the very type of Godhead to signify the eternal nearness and eternal love of just such as you and Roy, as John and me, he prays: 'Holy Father, keep them whom Thou hast given me, that *they may be one as we are.*'[30]

"There is one place, though, where I find what I like better than all the rest; you remember that old cry wrung from the lips of the stricken king,—'I shall go to him; but he will not return to me.'"

"I never thought before how simple and direct it is, and that, too, in those old blinded days."

"The more I study the Bible," she said, "and I study not entirely in ignorance of the commentators and the mysteries, the more perplexed I am to imagine where the current ideas of our future come from. They certainly are not in this book of gracious promises. That heaven which we heard about to-day was Dr. Bland's, not God's. 'It's aye a wonderfu' thing to me,' as poor Lauderdale said, 'the way some preachers take it upon themselves to explain matters to the Almighty!'"[31]

"But the harps and choirs, the throne, the white robes, are all in Revelation. Deacon Quirk would put his great brown finger on the verses, and hold you there triumphantly."

"Can't people tell picture from substance, a metaphor from its meaning? That book of Revelation is precisely what it professes to be,—a vision, a symbol. A symbol of something, to be sure, and rich with pleasant hopes, but still a symbol. Now, I really believe that a large proportion of Christian church-members, who have studied their Bible, attended Sabbath schools, listened to sermons all their lives, if you could fairly come at

---

28 All the men mentioned here are important Old Testament characters. Abraham, Isaac and Jacob lived centuries before Shadrach, Meshach and Abednego.

29 Romans 8:17.

30 There are multiple references in this paragraph to Jesus's prayer for his disciples in John 17.

31 Lauderdale is a character in Margaret Oliphant's (1828–1897) supernaturalist novel, *Son of the Soil* (1865). He is quoted frequently in *The Gates Ajar*.

their most definite idea of the place where they expect to spend eternity, would own it to be the golden city, with pearl gates, and jewels in the wall. It never occurs to them, that, if one picture is literal, another must be. If we are to walk golden streets, how can we stand on a sea of glass? How can we 'sit on thrones'? How can untold millions of us 'lie in Abraham's bosom'?

"But why have given us empty symbols? Why not a little fact?"

"They are not *empty* symbols. And why God did not give us actual descriptions of actual heavenly life, I don't trouble myself to wonder. He certainly had his reasons, and that is enough for me. I find from these symbols, and from his voice in my own heart, many beautiful things,—I will tell you some more of them at another time,—and, for the rest, I am content to wait. He loves me, and he loves mine. As long as we love Him, He will never separate Himself from us, or us from each other. That, at least, is *sure*."

"If that is sure, the rest is of less importance;—yes. But Dr. Bland said an awful thing!"

"The quotation from a dead divine?"

"Yes. That there will be no separate interests, no thoughts to conceal."

"Poor good man! He has found out by this time that he should not have laid down nonsense like that, without qualification or demur, before a Bible-reading hearer. It was simply *his* opinion, not David's, or Paul's, or John's, or Isaiah's. He had a perfect right to put it in the form of a conjecture. Nobody would forbid his conjecturing that the inhabitants of heaven are all deaf and dumb, or wear green glasses, or shave their heads, if he chose, provided he stated that it was conjecture, not revelation."

"But where does the Bible say that we shall have power to conceal our thoughts?—and I would rather be annihilated than to spend eternity with heart laid bare,—the inner temple thrown open to be trampled on by every passing stranger!"

"The Bible specifies very little about the minor arrangements of eternity in any way. But I doubt if, under any circumstances, it would have occurred to inspired men to inform us that our thoughts shall continue to be our own. The fact is patent on the face of things. The dead minister's supposition would destroy individuality at one fell swoop. We should be like a man walking down a room lined with mirrors, who sees himself reflected in all sizes, colors, shades, at all angles and in all proportions, according to the capacity of the mirror, till he seems no longer to belong to himself, but to be cut up into ellipses and octagons and prisms. How soon would he grow frantic in such companionship, and beg for a corner where he might hide and hush himself in the dark?

"That we shall in a higher life be able to do what we cannot in this,—judge fairly of each other's *moral* worth,—is undoubtedly true. Whatever the Judgment Day may mean, that is the substance of it. But this promiscuous theory of refraction;—never!

"Besides, wherever the Bible touches the subject, it premises our individuality as a matter of course. What would be the use of talking, if everybody knew the thoughts of everybody else?"

"You don't suppose that people talk in heaven?"

"I don't suppose anything else. Are we to spend ages of joy, a company of mutes together? Why not talk?"

"I supposed we should sing,—but—"

"Why not talk as well as sing? Does not song involve the faculty of speech?—unless you would like to make canaries of us."

"Ye-es. Why, yes."

"There are the visitors at the beautiful Mount of Transfiguration again. Did not they *talk* with each other and with Christ?[32] Did not John *talk* with the angel who 'shewed him those things'?"

"And you mean to say—"

"I mean to say that if there is such a thing as common sense, you will talk with Roy as you talked with him here,—only not as you talked with him here, because there will be no troubles nor sins, no anxieties nor cares, to talk about; no ugly shades of cross words or little quarrels to be made up; no fearful looking-for of separation."

I laid my head upon her shoulder, and could hardly speak for the comfort that she gave me.

"Yes, I believe we shall talk and laugh and joke and play—"

"Laugh and joke in heaven!"

"Why not?"

"But it seems so—so—why, so wicked and irreverent and all that, you know."

Just then Faith, who, mounted out on the kitchen table, was preaching at Phoebe in comical mimicry of Dr. Bland's choicest intonations, laughed out like the splash of a little wave.

The sound came in at the open door, and we stopped to listen till it had rippled away.

"There!" said her mother, "put that child, this very minute, with all her little sins forgiven, into one of our dear Lord's many mansions, and do you suppose that she would be any the less holy or less reverent for a laugh like that? Is he going to check all the sparkle and blossom of life when he takes us to himself? I don't believe any such thing.

"There were both sense and Christianity in what somebody wrote on the death of a humorous poet: —

'Does nobody laugh there, where he has gone, —
This man of the smile and the jest?'

— provided there was any hope that the poor fellow *had* gone to heaven; if not, it was bad philosophy and worse religion.

"Did not David dance before the Lord with all his might? A Bible which is full of happy battle-cries: 'Rejoice in the Lord! make a joyful noise unto him![33] Give thanks unto the Lord, for his mercy endureth!'—a Bible which exhausts its splendid wealth of rhetoric to make us understand that the coming life is a life of *joy*, no more threatens to make nuns than mutes of us. I expect that you will hear some of Roy's very old jokes, see the sparkle in his eye, listen to his laughing voice, lighten up the happy days as gleefully as you may choose; and that—"

Faith appeared upon the scene just then, with the interesting information that she had bitten her tongue; so we talked no more.

How pleasant—how pleasant this is! I never supposed before that God would let any one laugh in heaven.

I wonder if Roy has seen the President. Aunt Winifred says she does not doubt it. She thinks that all the soldiers must have crowded up to meet him, and "O," she says, "what a sight to see!"

---

32 Matthew 17:1–13.
33 Psalm 97:12; Psalm 66:1; Psalm 81:1; 1 Chronicles 16:34.

VII

May 12.

AUNT WINIFRED has said something about going, but I cannot yet bear to hear of such a thing. She is to stay a while longer.

16th.

We have been over to-night to the grave.

She proposed to go by herself, thinking, I saw, with the delicacy with which she always thinks, that I would rather not be there with another. Nor should I, nor could I, with any other than this woman. It is strange. I wished to go there with her. I had a vague, unreasoning feeling that she would take away some of the bitterness of it, as she has taken the bitterness of much else.

It is looking very pleasant there now. The turf has grown fine and smooth. The low arbor-vitæ hedge and knots of Norway spruce, that father planted long ago for mother, drop cool, green shadows that stir with the wind. My English ivy has crept about and about the cross. Roy used to say that he should fancy a cross to mark the spot where he might lie; I think he would like this pure, unveined marble. May-flowers cover the grave now, and steal out among the clover-leaves with a flush like sunrise. By and by there will be roses, and in August, August's own white lilies.

We went silently over, and sat silently down on the grass, the field-path stretching away to the little church behind us, and beyond, in front, the slope, the flats, the river, the hills cut in purple distance melting far into the east. The air was thick with perfume. Golden bees hung giddily over the blush in the grass. In the low branches that swept the grave a little bird had built her nest.

Aunt Winifred did not speak to me for a time, nor watch my face. Presently she laid her hand upon my lap, and I put mine into it.

"It is very pleasant here," she said then, in her very pleasant voice.

"I meant that it should be," I answered, trying not to let her see my lips quiver. "At least it must not look neglected. I don't suppose it makes any difference to *him.*"

"I do not feel sure of that."

"What do you mean?"

"I do not feel sure that anything he has left makes no 'difference' to him."

"But I don't understand. He is in heaven. He would be too happy to care for anything that is going on in this woful world."

"Perhaps that is so," she said, smiling a sweet contradiction to her words, "but I don't believe it."

"What do you believe?"

"Many things that I have to say to you, but you cannot bear them now."

"I have sometimes wondered, for I cannot help it," I said, "whether he is shut off from all knowledge of me for all these years till I can go to him. It will be a great while. It seems hard. Roy would want to know something, if it were only a little, about me."

"I believe that he wants to know, and that he knows, Mary; though, since the belief must rest on analogy and conjecture, you need not accept it as demonstrated mathematics," she answered, with another smile.

"Roy never forgot me here!" I said, not meaning to sob.

"That is just it. He was not constituted so that he, remaining himself, Roy, could forget you. If he goes out into this other life forgetting, he becomes another than himself. That is a far more unnatural way of creeping out of the difficulty than to assume that he loves and remembers. Why not assume that? In fact, why assume anything else? Neither reason, nor the Bible, nor common sense, forbids it. Instead of starting with it as an hypothesis to be proved if we can, I lay it down as one of those probabilities for which Butler[34] would say, 'the presumption amounts nearly to certainty'; and if any one can disprove it, I will hear what he has to say. There!" she broke off, laughing softly, "that is a sufficient dose of meta-physics for such a simple thing. It seems to me to lie just here: Roy loved you. Our Father, for some tender, hidden reason, took him out of your sight for a while. Though changed much, he can have forgotten nothing. Being *only out of sight*, you remember, not lost, nor asleep, nor annihilated, he goes on loving. To love must mean to think of, to care for, to hope for, to pray for, not less out of a body than in it."

"But that must mean—why, that must mean—"

"That he is near you. I do not doubt it."

The sunshine quivered in among the ivy-leaves, and I turned to watch it, thinking.

"I do not doubt," she went on, speaking low,—"I cannot doubt that our absent dead are very present with us. He said, 'I am with you alway,' knowing the need we have of him, even to the end of the world. He must understand the need we have of them. I cannot doubt it."

I watched her as she sat with her absent eyes turned eastward, and her peculiar look—I have never seen it on another face—as of one who holds a happy secret; and while I watched I wondered.

"There is a reason for it," she said, rousing as if from a pleasant dream,—"a good sens-ible reason, too, it strikes me, independent of Scriptural or other proof."

"What is that?"

"That God keeps us briskly at work in this world."

I did not understand.

"Altogether too briskly, considering that it is a preparative world, to intend to put us from it into an idle one. What more natural than that we shall spend our best energies as we spent them here,—in comforting, teaching, helping, saving people whose very souls we love better than our own? In fact, it would be very *un*natural if we did not."

"But I thought that God took care of us, and angels, like Gabriel and the rest, if I ever thought anything about it, which I am inclined to doubt."

"'God works by the use of means,' as the preachers say. Why not use Roy as well as Gabriel? What archangel could understand and reach the peculiarities of your nature as he could? or, even if understanding, could so love and bear with you? What is to be done? Will they send Roy to the planet Jupiter to take care of somebody's else sister?"

I laughed in spite of myself; nor did the laugh seem to jar upon the sacred stillness of the place. Her words were drawing away the bitterness, as the sun was blotting the dull, dead greens of the ivy into its glow of golden color.

"But the Bible, Aunt Winifred."

"The Bible does *not* say a great deal on this point," she said, "but it does not contradict me. In fact, it helps me; and, moreover, it would uphold me in black and white if it weren't for one little obstacle."

"And that?"

---

34 The English bishop and theologian Joseph Butler (1692–1752), whose sermons and collected works argued (often by analogy) for God's intimate involvement in His Creation.

"That frowning 'original Greek,' which Gail Hamilton denounces with her righteous indignation.[35] No sooner do I find a pretty verse that is exactly what I want, than up hops a commentator, and says, this isn't according to text, and means something entirely different; and Barnes says this, and Stuart believes that, and Olshausen has demonstrated the other, and very ignorant it is in you, too, not to know it![36] Here the other day I ferreted out a sentence in Revelation that seemed to prove beyond question that angels and redeemed men were the same; where the angel says to John, you know, 'Am I not of thy brethren the prophets?'[37] I thought that I had discovered a delightful thing which all the Fathers of the church had overlooked, and went in great glee to your Uncle Calvin, to be told that something was the matter,—a noun left out, or some other unanswerable and unreasonable horror, I don't know what; and that it didn't mean that he was of thy brethren the prophets at all!

"You see, if it could be proved that the Christian dead become angels, we could have all that we need, direct from God, about—to use the beautiful old phrase—the communion of saints. From Genesis to Revelation the Bible is filled with angels who are at work on earth. They hold sweet converse with Abraham in his tent. They are intrusted to save the soul of Lot. An angel hears the wail of Hagar. The beautiful feet of an angel bring the good tidings to maiden Mary. An angel's noiseless step guides Peter through the barred and bolted gate. Angels rolled the stone from the buried Christ, and angels sat there in the solemn morning,—O Mary! if we could have seen them!

"Then there is that one question, direct, comprehensive,—we should not need anything else,—'Are they not all ministering spirits, sent forth to minister to the heirs of salvation?'

"But you see it never seems to have entered those commentators' heads that all these beautiful things refer to any but a superior race of beings, like those from whose ranks Lucifer fell."

"How stupid in them!"

"I take comfort in thinking so; but, to be serious, even admitting that these passages refer to a superior race, must there not be some similarity in the laws which govern existence in the heavenly world? Since these gracious deeds are performed by what we are accustomed to call 'spiritual beings,' why may they not as well be done by people from this world as from anywhere else? Besides, there is another point, and a reasonable one, to be made. The word angel in the original[38] means, strictly, a messenger. It applies to any servant of God, animate or inanimate. An east wind is as much an angel as Michael. Again, the generic terms, 'spirits,' 'gods,' 'sons of God,' are used interchangeably for saints and for angels. So, you see, I fancy that I find a way for you and Roy and me and all of us, straight into the shining ministry. Mary, Mary, wouldn't you like to go this very afternoon?"

She lay back in the grass, with her face upturned to the sky, and drew a long breath, wearily. I do not think she meant me to hear it. I did not answer her, for it came over me

---

35 Gail Hamilton was a pseudonym for Mary Abigail Dodge, a friend of Phelps and the editor of the periodical *Our Young Folks* (1865–1867).

36 Albert Barnes (1798–1870), Moses Stuart (1780–1852) and Hermann Olshausen (1796–1839) were all professors of theology and writers of famous biblical commentaries. Stuart was also Phelps's grandfather.

37 Revelation 22:9.

38 [Author's Original Note] ἄγγελος

with such a hopeless thrill, how good it would be to be taken to Roy, there by his beautiful grave, with the ivy and the May-flowers and the sunlight and the clover-leaves round about; and that it could not be, and how long it was to wait,—it came over me so that I could not speak.

"There!" she said, suddenly rousing, "what a thoughtless, wicked thing it was to say! And I meant to give you only the good cheer of a cheery friend. No, I do not care to go this afternoon, nor any afternoon, till my Father is ready for me. Wherever he has most for me to do, there I wish,—yes, I think I *wish* to stay. He knows best."

After a pause, I asked again, "Why did He not tell us more about this thing,—about their presence with us? You see if I could *know* it!"

"The mystery of the Bible lies not so much in what it says, as in what it does not say," she replied. "But I suppose that we have been told all that we can comprehend in this world. Knowledge on one point might involve knowledge on another, like the links of a chain, till it stretched far beyond our capacity. At any rate, it is not for me to break the silence. That is God's affair. I can only accept the fact. Nevertheless, as Dr. Chalmers says: 'It were well for us all could we carefully draw the line between the secret things which belong to God and the things which are revealed and belong to us and to our children.'[39] Some one else,—Whately, I think,—I remember to have noticed as speaking about these very subjects to this effect,—that precisely because we know so little of them, it is the more important that we 'should endeavor so to dwell on them as to make the most of what little knowledge we have.'"[40]

"Aunt Winifred, you are such a comfort!"

"It needs our best faith," she said, "to bear this reticence of God. I cannot help thinking sometimes of a thing Lauderdale said,—I am always quoting him,—from 'Son of the Soil,' you remember: 'It's an awfu' marvel, beyond my reach, when a word of communication would make a' the difference, why it's no permitted, if it were but to keep a heart from breaking now and then.' Think of poor Eugénie de Guèrin, trying to continue her little journal 'To Maurice in Heaven,' till the awful, answerless stillness shut up the book and laid aside the pen.[41]

"But then," she continued, "there is this to remember,— I may have borrowed the idea, or it may be my own,—that if we could speak to them, or they to us, there would be no death, for there would be no separation. The last, the surest, in some cases the only test of loyalty to God, would thus be taken away. Roman Catholic nature is human nature, when it comes upon its knees before a saint. Many lives—all such lives as yours and mine—would become—"

"Would become what?"

"One long defiance to the First Commandment."[42]

I cannot become used to such words from such quiet lips. Yet they give me a curious sense of the trustworthiness of her peace. "Founded upon a rock," it seems to be. She has done what it takes a lifetime for some of us to do; what some of us go into eternity, leaving undone; what I am afraid I shall never do,—sounded her own nature. She knows the worst

39 Thomas Chalmers (1780–1847) was a Scottish clergyman and mathematician. This line is from his sermon on 1 John 16 entitled "On the Nature of Sin Unto Death."
40 Richard Whately of Dublin (1787–1863) was an Anglican archbishop, logician and apologist. Phelps refers here to his work *Christian Evidences* (1837).
41 Eugénie de Guèrin (1805–1848) was a religious mystic whose *Journals* mourned the loss of her brother and often theorized the form the afterlife might take.
42 Exodus 20:2: "Thou shalt have no other gods before me."

of herself, and faces it as fairly, I believe, as anybody can do in this world. As for the best of herself, she trusts that to Christ, and he knows it, and we. I hope she, in her sweet humbleness, will know it some day.

"I suppose, nevertheless," she said, "that Roy knows what you are doing and feeling as well as, perhaps better than, he knew it three months ago. So he can help you without harming you."

I asked her, turning suddenly, how that could be, and yet heaven be heaven,—how he could see me suffer what I had suffered, could see me sometimes when I supposed none but God had seen me,—and sing on and be happy.

"You are not the first, Mary, and you will not be the last, to ask that question. I cannot answer it, and I never heard of any who could. I feel sure only of this,—that he would suffer far less to see you than to know nothing about you; and that God's power of inventing happiness is not to be blocked by an obstacle like this. Perhaps Roy sees the end from the beginning, and can bear the sight of pain for the peace that he watches coming to meet you. I do not know,—that does not perplex me now; it only makes me anxious for one thing."

"What is that?"

"That you and I shall not do anything to make them sorry."

"To make them sorry?"

"Roy would care. Roy would be disappointed to see you make life a hopeless thing for his sake, or to see you doubt his Saviour."

"Do you think *that?*"

"Some sort of mourning over sin enters that happy life. God himself 'was grieved' forty years long over his wandering people. Among the angels there has been 'silence,' whatever that mysterious pause may mean, just as there is joy over one sinner that repenteth; another of my proof-texts that, to show that they are allowed to keep us in sight."

"Then you think, you really think, that Roy remembers and loves and takes care of me; that he has been listening, perhaps, and is—why, you don't think he may be *here?*"

"Yes, I do. Here, close beside you all this time, trying to speak to you through the blessed sunshine and the flowers, trying to help you and sure to love you,—right here, dear. I do not believe God means to send him away from you, either."

My heart was too full to answer her. Seeing how it was, she slipped away, and, strolling out of sight with her face to the eastern hills, left me alone.

And yet I did not seem alone. The low branches swept with a little soft sigh across the grave; the May-flowers wrapped me in with fragrance thick as incense; the tiny sparrow turned her soft eyes at me over the edge of the nest, and chirped contentedly; the "blessed sunshine" talked with me as it touched the edges of the ivy-leaves to fire.

I cannot write it even here, how these things stole into my heart and hushed me. If I had seen him standing by the stainless cross, it would not have frightened or surprised me. There—not dead or gone, but *there*—it helps me and makes me strong!

"Mamie! little Mamie!"

O Roy, I will try to bear it all, if you will only stay!

VIII

May 20.

THE NEARER the time has come for Aunt Winifred to go, the more it has seemed impossible to part with her. I have run away from the thought like a craven, till she made me face it this morning, by saying decidedly that she should go on the first of the week.

I dropped my sewing; the work-basket tipped over, and all my spools rolled away under the chairs. I had a little time to think while I was picking them up.

"There is the rest of my visit at Norwich to be made, you know," she said, "and while I am there I shall form some definite plans for the summer; I have hardly decided what, yet. I had better leave here by the seven o'clock train, if such an early start will not incommode you."

I wound up the last spool, and turned away to the window. There was a confused, dreary sky of scurrying clouds, and a cold wind was bruising the apple-buds. I hate a cold wind in May. It made me choke a little, thinking how I should sit and listen to it after she was gone,—of the old, blank, comfortless days that must come and go,—of what she had brought, and what she would take away. I was a bit faint, I think, for a minute. I had not really thought the prospect through, before.

"Mary," she said, "what's the matter. Come here."

I went over, and she drew me into her lap, and I put my arms about her neck.

"I can *not* bear it," said I, "and that is the matter."

She smiled, but her smile faded when she looked at me.

And then I told her, sobbing, how it was; that I could not go into my future alone,—I could not do it! that she did not know how weak I was,—and reckless,—and wicked; that she did not know what she had been to me. I begged her not to leave me. I begged her to stay and help me bear my life.

"My dear! you are as bad as Faith when I put her to bed alone."

"But," I said, "when Faith cries, you go to her, you know."

"Are you quite in earnest, Mary?" she asked, after a pause. "You don't know very much about me, after all, and there is the child. It is always an experiment, bringing two families into lifelong relations under one roof. If I could think it best, you might repent your bargain."

"*I* am not 'a family,'" I said, feebly trying to laugh. "Aunt Winifred, if you and Faith only *will* make this your home, I can never thank you, never. I shall be entertaining my good angels, and that is the whole of it."

"I have had some thought of not going back," she said at last, in a low, constrained voice, as if she were touching something that gave her great pain, "for Faith's sake. I should like to educate her in New England, if—I had intended if we stayed to rent or buy a little home of our own somewhere, but I had been putting off a decision. We are most weak and most selfish sometimes when we think ourselves strongest and noblest, Mary. I love my husband's people. I think they love me. I was almost happy with them. It seemed as if I were carrying on his work for him. That was so pleasant!"

She put me down out of her arms and walked across the room.

"I will think the matter over," she said, by and by, in her natural tones, "and let you know to-night."

She went away up stairs then, and I did not see her again until to-night. I sent Faith up with her dinner and tea, judging that she would rather see the child than me. I observed, when the dishes came down, that she had touched nothing but a cup of coffee.

I began to understand, as I sat alone in the parlor through the afternoon, how much I had asked of her. In my selfish distress at losing her, I had not thought of that. Faces that her husband loved, meadows and hills and sunsets that he has watched, the home where his last step sounded and his last word was spoken, the grave where she has laid him,—this last more than all,—call after her, and cling to her with yearning closeness. To leave them, is to leave the last faint shadow of her beautiful past. It hurts, but she is too brave to cry out.

Tea was over, and Faith in bed, but still she did not come down. I was sitting by the window, watching a little crescent moon climb over the hills, and wondering whether I had better go up, when she came in and stood behind me, and said, attempting to laugh: —

"Very impolite in me to run off so, wasn't it? Cowardly, too, I think. Well, Mary?"

"Well, Auntie?"

"Have you not repented your proposition yet?"

"You would excel as an inquisitor, Mrs. Forceythe!"

"Then it shall be as you say; as long as you want us you shall have us,—Faith and me."

I turned to thank her, but could not when I saw her face. It was very pale; there was something inexpressibly sad about her mouth, and her eyelids drooped heavily, like one weary from a great struggle.

Feeling for the moment guilty and ashamed before her, as if I had done her wrong, "It is going to be very hard for you," I said.

"Never mind about that," she answered, quickly. "We will not talk about that. I knew, though I did not *wish* to know, that it was best for Faith. Your hands about my neck have settled it. Where the work is, there the laborer must be. It is quite plain now. I have been talking it over with them all the afternoon; it seems to be what they want."

"With *them*"? I started at the words; who had been in her lonely chamber? Ah, it is simply real to her. Who, indeed, but her Saviour and her husband?

She did not seem inclined to talk, and stole away from me presently, and out of doors; she was wrapped in her blanket shawl, and had thrown a shimmering white hood over her gray hair. I wondered where she could be going, and sat still at the window watching her. She opened and shut the gate softly; and, turning her face towards the churchyard, walked up the street and out of my sight.

She feels nearer to him in the resting-place of the dead. Her heart cries after the grave by which she will never sit and weep again; on which she will never plant the roses any more.

As I sat watching and thinking this, the faint light struck her slight figure and little shimmering hood again, and she walked down the street and in with steady step.

When she came up and stood beside me, smiling, with the light knitted thing thrown back on her shoulders, her face seemed to rise from it as from a snowy cloud; and for her look,—I wish Raphael could have had it for one of his rapt Madonnas.[43]

"Now, Mary," she said, with the sparkle back again in her voice, "I am ready to be entertaining, and promise not to play the hermit again very soon. Shall I sit here on the sofa with you? Yes, my dear, I am happy, quite happy."

So then we took this new promise of home that has come to make my life, if not joyful, something less than desolate, and analyzed it in its practical bearings. What a pity that all pretty dreams have to be analyzed! I had some notion about throwing our little incomes into a joint family fund, but she put a veto to that; I suppose because mine is the larger. She prefers to take board for herself and Faith; but, if I know myself, she shall never be suffered to have the feeling of a boarder, and I will make her so much at home in my house that she shall not remember that it is not her own.

---

43 Raphael was a sixteenth-century Italian artist who created several renowned paintings that portrayed the Madonna with a beautiful, serene face.

Her visit to Norwich she has decided to put off until the autumn, so that I shall have her to myself undisturbed all summer.

I have been looking at Roy's picture a long time, and wondering how he would like the new plan. I said something of the sort to her.

"Why put any 'would' in that sentence?" she said, smiling. "It belongs in the present tense."

"Then I am sure he likes it," I answered,—"he likes it," and I said the words over till I was ready to cry for rest in their sweet sound.

22d.

It is Roy's birthday. But I have not spoken of it. We used to make a great deal of these little festivals,—but it is of no use to write about that.

I am afraid I have been bearing it very badly all day. She noticed my face, but said nothing till to-night. Mrs. Bland was down stairs, and I had come away alone up here in the dark. I heard her asking for me, but would not go down. By and by Aunt Winifred knocked, and I let her in.

"Mrs. Bland cannot understand why you don't see her, Mary," she said, gently. "You know you have not thanked her for those English violets that she sent the other day. I only thought I would remind you; she might feel a little pained."

"I can't to-night,—not to-night, Aunt Winifred. You must excuse me to her somehow. I don't want to go down."

"Is it that you don't 'want to,' or *is* it that you can't?" she said, in that gentle, motherly way of hers, at which I can never take offence. "Mary, I wonder if Roy would not a little rather that you would go down?"

It might have been Roy himself who spoke.

I went down.

IX

June 1.

AUNT WINIFRED went to the office this morning, and met Dr. Bland, who walked home with her. He always likes to talk with her.

A woman who knows something about fate, free-will, and foreknowledge absolute, who is not ignorant of politics, and talks intelligently of Agassiz's latest fossil,[44] who can understand a German quotation, and has heard of Strauss and Neander,[45] who can dash her sprightliness ably against his old dry bones of metaphysics and theology, yet never speak an accent above that essentially womanly voice of hers, is, I imagine, a phenomenon in his social experience.

I was sitting at the window when they came up and stopped at the gate. Dr. Bland lifted his hat to me in his grave way, talking the while; somewhat eagerly, too, I could see. Aunt Winifred answered him with a peculiar smile and a few low words that I could not hear.

"But, my dear madam," he said, "the glory of God, you see, the glory of God is the primary consideration."

---

44 Louis Agassiz (1807–1873) was a European-trained geologist and botanist who taught at Harvard for much of his career.

45 David Friedrich Strauss (1808–1874) and John August Wilhelm Neander (1789–1850) were both famous liberal Protestant German theologians. Strauss's internationally renowned *Life of Jesus* (1835) stressed the humanity of Christ.

"But the glory of God *involves* these lesser glories, as a sidereal system, though a splendid whole, exists by the multiplied differing of one star from another star. Ah, Dr. Bland, you make a grand abstraction out of it, but it makes me cold,"—she shivered, half playfully, half involuntarily,—"it makes me cold. I am very much alive and human; and Christ was human God."

She came in smiling a little sadly, and stood by me, watching the minister walk over the hill.

"How much does that man love his wife and children?" she asked abruptly.

"A good deal. Why?"

"I am afraid that he will lose one of them, then, before many more years of his life are past."

"What! he hasn't been telling you that they are consumptive or anything of the sort?"

"O dear me, no," with a merry laugh, which died quickly away: "I was only thinking,—there is trouble in store for him; some intense pain,—if he is capable of intense pain,—which shall shake his cold, smooth theorizing to the foundation. He speaks a foreign tongue when he talks of bereavement, of death, of the future life. No argument could convince him of that, though, which is the worst of it."

"He must think you shockingly heterodox."

"I don't doubt it. We had a little talk this morning, and he regarded me with an expression of mingled consternation and perplexity that was curious. He is a very good man. He is not a stupid man. I only wish that he would stop preaching and teaching things that he knows nothing about.

"He is only drifting with the tide, though," she added, "in his views of this matter. In our recoil from the materialism of the Romish Church,[46] we have, it seems to me, nearly stranded ourselves on the opposite shore. Just as, in a rebound from the spirit which would put our Saviour on a level with Buddha or Mahomet, we have been in danger of forgetting 'to begin as the Bible begins,' with his humanity. It is the grandeur of inspiration, that it knows how to *balance* truth."

It had been in my mind for several days to ask Aunt Winifred something, and, feeling in the mood, I made her take off her things and devote herself to me. My question concerned what we call the "intermediate state."

"I have been expecting that," she said; "what about it?"

"What *is* it?"

"Life and activity."

"We do not go to sleep, of course."

"I believe that notion is about exploded, though clear thinkers like Whately have appeared to advocate it. Where it originated, I do not know, unless from the frequent comparisons in the Scriptures of death with sleep, which refer solely, I am convinced, to the condition of body, and which are voted down by an overwhelming majority of decided statements relative to the consciousness, happiness, and tangibility of the life into which we immediately pass."

"It is intermediate, in some sense, I suppose."

"It waits between two other conditions,—yes; I think the drift of what we are taught about it leads to that conclusion. I expect to become at once sinless, but to have a broader Christian character many years hence; to be happy at once, but to be happier by and by; to

---

46 Roman Catholic Church.

find in myself wonderful new tastes and capacities, which are to be immeasurably ennobled and enlarged after the Resurrection, whatever that may mean."

"What does it mean?"

"I know no more than you, but you shall hear what I think, presently. I was going to say that this seems to be plain enough in the Bible. The angels took Lazarus at once to Abraham.[47] Dives[48] seems to have found no interval between death and consciousness of suffering."

"They always tell you that that is only a parable."

"But it must mean *something*. No story in the Bible has been pulled to pieces and twisted about as that has been. We are in danger of pulling and twisting all sense out of it. Then Judas, having hanged his wretched self, went to his own place. Besides, there was Christ's promise to the thief."

I told her that I had heard Dr. Bland say that we could not place much dependence on that passage, because "Paradise" did not necessarily mean heaven.

"But it meant living, thinking, enjoying; for 'To-day thou shalt *be with me.*'[49] Paul's beautiful perplexed revery, however, would be enough if it stood alone; for he did not know whether he would rather stay in this world, or depart and be with Christ, which is far better. *With Christ*, you see; and His three mysterious days, which typify our intermediate state, were over then, and he had ascended to his Father. Would it be 'far better'[50] either to leave this actual tangible life throbbing with hopes and passions, to leave its busy, Christ-like working, its quiet joys, its very sorrows which are near and human, for a nap of several ages, or even for a vague, lazy, half-alive, disembodied existence?"

"Disembodied? I supposed, of course, that it was disembodied."

"I do not think so. And that brings us to the Resurrection. All the *tendency* of Revelation is to show that an embodied state is superior to a disembodied one. Yet certainly we who love God are promised that death will lead us into a condition which shall have the advantage of this: for the good apostle to die 'was gain.' I don't believe, for instance, that Adam and Eve have been wandering about in a misty condition all these thousands of years. I suspect that we have some sort of body immediately after passing out of this, but that there is to come a mysterious change, equivalent, perhaps, to a re-embodiment, when our capacities for action will be greatly improved, and that in some manner this new form will be connected with this 'garment by the soul laid by.'"

"Deacon Quirk expects to rise in his own entire, original body, after it has lain in the First Church cemetery a proper number of years, under a black slate headstone, adorned by a willow, and such a 'cherubim' as that poor boy shot,—by the way, if I've laughed at that story once, I have fifty times."

"Perhaps Deacon Quirk would admire a work of art that I found stowed away on the top of your Uncle Calvin's bookcases. It was an old woodcut—nobody knows how old—of an interesting skeleton rising from his grave, and, in a sprightly and modest manner, drawing on his skin, while Gabriel, with apoplectic cheeks, feet uppermost in the air, was blowing a good-sized tin trumpet in his ear!

"No; some of the popular notions of resurrection are simple physiological impossibilities, from causes 'too tedious to specify.' Imagine, for instance, the resurrection of two

---

47 Luke 16:22.
48 Religious divines or scholars.
49 Luke 23:43.
50 Philippians 1:21–23.

Hottentots, one of whom has happened to make a dinner of the other some fine day. A little complication there! Or picture the touching scene, when that devoted husband, King Mausolas,[51] whose widow had him burned and ate the ashes, should feel moved to institute a search for his body! It is no wonder that the infidel argument has the best of it, when we attempt to enforce a natural impossibility. It is worth while to remember that Paul expressly stated that we shall *not* rise in our entire earthly bodies. The simile which he used is the seed sown, dying in, and mingling with, the ground. How many of its original particles are found in the full-grown corn?"

"Yet you believe that *something* belonging to this body is preserved for the completion of another?"

"Certainly. I accept God's statement about it, which is as plain as words can make a statement. I do not know, and I do not care to know, how it is to be effected. God will not be at a loss for a way, any more than he is at a loss for a way to make his fields blossom every spring. For aught we know, some invisible compound of an annihilated body may hover, by a divine decree, around the site of death till it is wanted,—sufficient to preserve identity as strictly as a body can ever be said to preserve it; and stranger things have happened. You remember the old Mohammedan belief in the one little bone which is imperishable. Prof. Bush's idea of our triune existence is suggestive, for a notion.[52] He believed, you know, that it takes a material body, a spiritual body, and a soul, to make a man. The spiritual body is enclosed within the material, the soul within the spiritual. Death is simply the slipping off of the outer body, as a husk slips off from its kernel. The deathless frame stands ready then for the soul's untrammelled occupation. But it is a waste of time to speculate over such useless fancies, while so many remain that will vitally affect our happiness."

It is singular; but I never gave a serious thought—and I have done some thinking about other matters—to my heavenly body, till that moment, while I sat listening to her. In fact, till Roy went, the Future was a miserable, mysterious blank, to be drawn on and on in eternal and joyless monotony, and to which, at times, annihilation seemed preferable. I remember, when I was a child, asking father once, if I were so good that I *had* to go to heaven, whether, after a hundred years, God would not let me "die out." More or less of the disposition of that same desperate little sinner I suspect has always clung to me. So I asked Aunt Winifred, in some perplexity, what she supposed our bodies would be like.

"It must be nearly all 'suppose,'" she said, "for we are nowhere definitely told. But this is certain. They will be as real as these."

"But these you can see, you can touch."

"What would be the use of having a body that you can't see and touch? A body is a *body*, not a spirit. Why should you not, having seen Roy's old smile and heard his own voice, clasp his hand again, and feel his kiss on your happy lips?

"It is really amusing," she continued, "to sum up the notions that good people—excellent people—even thinking people—have of the heavenly body. Vague visions of floating about in the clouds, of balancing—with a white robe on, perhaps—in stiff rows about a throne,

---

51 King Mausolas was the ruler of Caria (377–353 BCE). After his death, his wife built a shrine to him that was so magnificent that it was considered one of the seven wonders of the ancient world.

52 George Bush (1796–1859) was professor of Hebrew at New York University and later in life became a devoted spiritualist who believed the soul could exist without a body on earth. The allusion is to Bush's *Anastasis: or, the Doctrine of the Resurrection of the Body, Rationally and Scripturally Considered* (1844).

like the angels in the old pictures, converging to an apex, or ranged in semi-circles like so many marbles. Murillo has one charming exception. I always take a secret delight in that little cherub of his, kicking the clouds in the right-hand upper corner of the Immaculate Conception; he seems to be having a good time of it, in genuine baby-fashion. The truth is, that the ordinary idea, if sifted accurately, reduces our eternal personality to—*gas.*

"Isaac Taylor holds, that, as far as the abstract idea of spirit is concerned, it may just as reasonably be granite as ether.[53]

"Mrs. Charles says a pretty thing about this.[54] She thinks these 'super-spiritualized angels' very 'unsatisfactory' beings, and that 'the heart returns with loving obstinacy to the young men in long white garments' who sat waiting in the sepulchre.

"Here again I cling to my conjecture about the word 'angel'; for then we should learn emphatically something about our future selves.

" 'As the angels in heaven,' or 'equal unto the angels,' we are told in another place,—that may mean simply what it says. At least, if we are to resemble them in the particular respect of which the words were spoken,—and that one of the most important which could well be selected,—it is not unreasonable to infer that we shall resemble them in others. 'In the Resurrection,' by the way, means, in that connection and in many others, simply future state of existence, without any reference to the time at which the great bodily change is to come.

" 'But this is a digression,' as the novelists say. I was going to say, that it bewilders me to conjecture where students of the Bible have discovered the usual foggy nonsense about the corporeity of heaven.

"If there is anything laid down in plain statement, devoid of metaphor or parable, simple and unequivocal, it is the definite contradiction of all that. Paul, in his preface to that sublime apostrophe to death, repeats and reiterates it, lest we should make a mistake in his meaning.

" 'There are celestial *bodies.*' 'It is raised a spiritual *body.*' 'There is a spiritual *body.*' 'It *is* raised in incorruption.' 'It *is* raised in glory.' 'It *is* raised in power.'[55] Moses, too, when he came to the transfigured mount in glory, had as real a *body* as when he went into the lonely mount to die."

"But they will be different from these?"

"The glory of the terrestrial is one, the glory of the celestial another. Take away sin and sickness and misery, and that of itself would make difference enough."

"You do not suppose that we shall look as we look now?"

"I certainly do. At least, I think it more than possible that the 'human form divine,' or something like it, is to be retained. Not only from the fact that risen Elijah bore it; and Moses, who, if he had not passed through his resurrection, does not seem to have looked different from the other,—I have to use those two poor prophets on all occasions, but, as we are told of them neither by parable nor picture, they are important,—and that angels never appeared in any other, but because, in sinless Eden, God chose it for Adam

---

53 Isaac Taylor (1787–1865) was an English philosopher and historical writer whose *Physical Theory of Another Life* (1836) is frequently referenced in *The Gates Ajar.*

54 Elizabeth Rundle Charles (1828–1896) was an English writer who wrote a famous fictional account of Martin Luther's life, *Chronicles of the Schönberg-Cotta Family* (1863). These quotes are found in another of her writings, "Heaven" (1884).

55 1 Corinthians 15:40–43.

and Eve. What came in unmarred beauty direct from His hand cannot be unworthy of His other Paradise 'beyond the stars.' It would chime in pleasantly, too, with the idea of Redemption, that our very bodies, free from all the distortion of guilt, shall return to something akin to the pure ideal in which He moulded them. Then there is another reason, and stronger."

"What is that?"

"The human form has been borne and dignified forever by Christ. And, further than that, he ascended to His Father in it, and lives there in it as human God to-day."

I had never thought of that, and said so.

"Yes, with the very feet which trod the dusty road to Emmaus; the very wounded hands which Thomas touched, believing; the very lips which ate of the broiled fish and honeycomb; the very voice which murmured 'Mary!' in the garden, and which told her that He ascended unto His Father and her Father, to His God and her God, He 'was parted from them,' and was 'received up into heaven.' His death and resurrection stand forever the great prototype of ours. Otherwise, what is the meaning of such statements as these: 'When He shall appear, we shall be like Him';[56] 'The first man (Adam) is of the earth; the second man is the Lord. As we have borne the image of the earthy, we shall also bear the image of the heavenly'?[57] And what of this, when we are told that our 'vile bodies,' being changed, shall be fashioned 'like unto His glorious body'?"[58]

I asked her if she inferred from that, that we should have just such bodies as the freedom from pain and sin would make of these.

"Flesh and blood cannot inherit the kingdom," she said. "There is no escaping that, even if I had the smallest desire to escape it, which I have not. Whatever is essentially earthly and temporary in the arrangements of this world will be out of place and unnecessary there. Earthly and temporary, flesh and blood certainly are."

"Christ said 'A spirit hath not flesh and bones, as ye see me have.'[59]

"A spirit hath not; and who ever said that it did? His body had something that appeared like them, certainly. That passage, by the way, has led some ingenious writer on the Chemistry of Heaven to infer that our bodies there will be like these, minus blood! I don't propose to spend my time over such investigations. Summing up the meaning of the story of those last days before the Ascension, and granting the shade of mystery which hangs over them, I gather this,—that the spiritual body is real, is tangible, is visible, is human, but that 'we shall be changed.'[60] Some indefinable but thorough change had come over Him. He could withdraw Himself from the recognition of Mary, and from the disciples, whose 'eyes were holden,'[61] as it pleased Him. He came and went through barred and bolted doors. He appeared suddenly in a certain place, without sound of footstep or flutter of garment to announce His approach. He vanished, and was not, like a cloud. New and wonderful powers had been given to Him, of which, probably, His little bewildered group of friends saw but a few illustrations.

"And He was yet man?"

---

56 1 John 3:2.
57 1 Thessalonians 15:49.
58 Philippians 3:2.
59 Luke 24:39.
60 1 Corinthians 15:52.
61 Luke 24:16.

"He was Jesus of Nazareth until the sorrowful drama of human life that He had taken upon Himself was thoroughly finished, from manger to sepulchre, and from sepulchre to the right hand of His Father."

"I like to wonder," she said, presently, "what we are going to look like and be like. *Ourselves*, in the first place. 'It is I Myself,' Christ said. Then to be perfectly well, never a sense of pain or weakness,—imagine how much solid comfort, if one had no other, in being forever rid of all the ills that flesh is heir to! Beautiful, too, I suppose we shall be, every one. Have you never had that come over you, with a thrill of compassionate thankfulness, when you have seen a poor girl shrinking, as only girls can shrink, under the life-long affliction of a marred face or form? The loss or presence of beauty is not as slight a deprivation or blessing as the moralists would make it out. Your grandmother, who was the most beautiful woman I ever saw, the belle of the county all her young days, and the model for artists' fancy sketching even in her old ones, as modest as a violet and as honest as the sunshine, used to have the prettiest little way when we girls were in our teens, and she thought that we must be lectured a bit on youthful vanity, of adding, in her quiet voice, smoothing down her black silk apron as she spoke, 'But still it is a thing to be thankful for, my dear, to have a *comely countenance*.'

"But to return to the track and our future bodies. We shall find them vastly convenient, undoubtedly, with powers of which there is no dreaming. Perhaps they will be so one with the soul that to will will be to do, hindrance out of the question. I, for instance, sitting here by you, and thinking that I should like to be in Kansas, would be there. There is an interesting bit of a hint in Daniel about Gabriel, who, 'being caused to fly swiftly, touched him about the time of the evening oblation.'"[62]

"But do you not make a very material kind of heaven out of such suppositions?"

"It depends upon what you mean by 'material.' The term does not, to my thinking, imply degradation, except so far as it is associated with sin. Dr. Chalmers[63] has the right of it, when he talks about '*spiritual materialism*.' He says in his sermon on the New Heavens and Earth,—which, by the way, you should read, and from which I wish a few more of our preachers would learn something,—that we 'forget that on the birth of materialism, when it stood out in the freshness of those glories which the great Architect of Nature had impressed upon it, that then the "morning stars sang together, and all the sons of God shouted for joy."' I do not believe in a *gross* heaven, but I believe in a *reasonable* one."

4th.

We have been devoting ourselves to feminine vanities all day out in the orchard. Aunt Winifred has been making her summer bonnet, and I some linen collars. I saw, though she said nothing, that she thought the *crêpe* a little gloomy, and I am going to wear these in the mornings to please her.

She has an accumulation of work on hand, and in the afternoon I offered to tuck a little dress for Faith,—the prettiest pink *barège* affair pale as a blush rose, and about as delicate. Faith, who had been making mud-pies in the swamp, and was spattered with black peat from curls to stockings, looked on approvingly, and wanted it to wear on a flag-root expedition to-morrow. It seemed to do me good to do something for somebody after all this lonely and—I suspect—selfish idleness.

6th.

---

62 Daniel 9:21.
63 Thomas Chalmers (1780–1847) was a Scottish clergyman and mathematician.

I read a little of Dr. Chalmers to-day, and went laughing to Aunt Winifred with the first sentence.

"There is a limit to the revelations of the Bible about futurity, and it were a mental or spiritual trespass to go beyond it."

"Ah! but," she said, "look a little farther down."

And I read, "But while we attempt not to be 'wise above that which is written,' we should attempt, and that most studiously, to be wise *up to* that which is written."

8th.

It occurred to me to-day, that it was a noticeable fact, that, among all the visits of angels to this world of which we are told, no one seems to have discovered in any the presence of a dead friend. If redeemed men are subject to the same laws as they, why did such a thing never happen? I asked Aunt Winifred, and she said that the question reminded her of St. Augustine's lonely cry thirty years after the death of Monica: "Ah, the dead do not come back; for, had it been possible, there has not been a night when I should not have seen my mother!" There seemed to be two reasons, she said, why there should be no exceptions to the law of silence imposed between us and those who have left us; one of which was, that we should be over-powered with familiar curiosity about them, which nobody seems to have dared to express in the presence of angels, and the secrets of their life God has decreed that it is unlawful to utter.

"But Lazarus, and Jairus's little daughter, and the dead raised at the Crucifixion,—what of them?" I asked.

"I cannot help conjecturing that they were suffered to forget their glimpse of spiritual life," she said. "Since their resurrection was a miracle, there might be a miracle throughout. At least, their lips must have been sealed, for not a word of their testimony has been saved. When Lazarus dined with Simon, after he had come back to life,—and of that feast we have a minute account in, I believe, every Gospel,—nobody seems to have asked, or he to have answered, any questions about it.

"The other reason is a sorrowfully sufficient one. It is that *every* lost darling has not gone to heaven. Of all the mercies that our Father has given, this blessed uncertainty, this long unbroken silence, may be the dearest. Bitterly hard for you and me, but what are thousands like you and me weighed against one who stands beside a hopeless grave? Think a minute what mourners there have been, and *whom* they have mourned! Ponder one such solitary instance as that of Vittoria Colonna[64] wondering, through her widowed years, if she could ever be 'good enough' to join wicked Pescara in another world! This poor earth holds— God only knows how many, God make them very few!—Vittorias. Ah, Mary, what right have *we* to complain?"

9th.

To-night Aunt Winifred had callers,—Mrs. Quirk and (O Homer aristocracy!) the butcher's wife,—and it fell to my lot to put Faith to bed.

The little maiden seriously demurred. Cousin Mary was very good,—O yes, she was good enough,—but her mamma was a great deal gooder; and why couldn't little peoples sit up till nine o'clock as well as big peoples, she should like to know!

Finally, she came to the gracious conclusion that perhaps I'd *do*, made me carry her all the way up stairs, and dropped, like a little lump of lead, half asleep, on my shoulder, before two buttons were unfastened.

---

64 Vittoria Colonna (1492–1547) was an Italian noblewoman and poet. She became a young widow who yearned to be reunited with her dead husband.

Feeling under some sort of theological obligation to hear her say her prayers, I pulled her curls a little till she awoke, and went through with "Now I lay me down to sleep, I pway ve Lord," triumphantly. I supposed that was the end, but it seems that she has been also taught the Lord's Prayer, which she gave me promptly to understand.

"O, see here! That isn't all. I can say Our Father, and you've got to help me a lot!"

This very soon became a self-evident proposition; but by our united efforts we managed, after tribulations manifold, to arrive successfully at "For ever 'n' ever 'n' ever 'n' *A*-men."

"Dear me," she said, jumping up with a yawn. "I think that's a *dreadful long-tailed prayer,*—don't you, Cousin Mary?"

"Now I must kiss mamma good night," she announced, when she was tucked up at last.

"But mamma kissed you good night before you came up."

"O, so she did. Yes, I 'member. Well, it's papa I've got to kiss. I knew there was somebody."

I looked at her in perplexity.

"Why, there!" she said, "in the upper drawer,—my pretty little papa in a purple frame. Don't you know?"

I went to the bureau-drawer, and found in a case of velvet a small ivory painting of her father. This I brought, wondering, and the child took it reverently and kissed the pictured lips.

"Faith," I said, as I laid it softly back, "do you always do this?"

"Do what? Kiss papa good night? O yes, I've done that ever since I was a little girl, you know. I guess I've always kissed him pretty much. When I'm a naughty girl he feels *real* sorry. He's gone to heaven. I like him. O yes, and then, when I'm through kissing, mamma kisses him too."

X

June 11.

I was in her room this afternoon while she was dressing. I like to watch her brush her beautiful gray hair; it quite alters her face to have it down; it seems to shrine her in like a cloud, and the outlines of her cheeks round out, and she grows young.

"I used to be proud of my hair when I was a girl," she said with a slight blush, as she saw me looking at her; "it was all I had to be vain of, and I made the most of it. Ah well! I was dark-haired three years ago.

"O you regular old woman!" she added, smiling at herself in the mirror, as she twisted the silver coils flashing through her fingers. "Well, when I am in heaven, I shall have my pretty brown hair again."

It seemed odd enough to hear that; then the next minute it did not seem odd at all, but the most natural thing in the world.

June 14.

She said nothing to me about the anniversary and, though it has been in my thoughts all the time, I said nothing to her. I thought that she would shut herself up for the day, and was rather surprised that she was about as usual busily at work, chatting with me, and playing with Faith. Just after tea, she went away alone for a time, and came back a little quiet, but that was all. I was for some reason impressed with the feeling that she kept the day in memory, not so much as the day of her mourning, as of his release.

Longing to do something for her, yet not knowing what to do, I went into the garden while she was away, and, finding some carnations, that shone like stars in the dying light, I gathered them all, and took them to her room, and, filling my tiny porphyry[65] vase, left them on the bracket, under the photograph of Uncle Forceythe that hangs by the window.

When she found them, she called me, and kissed me.

"Thank you, dear," she said, "and thank God too, Mary, for me. That he should have been happy,—happy and out of pain, for three long beautiful years! O, think of that!"

When I was in her room with the flowers, I passed the table on which her little Bible lay open. A mark of rich ribbon—a black ribbon—fell across the pages; it bore in silver text these words: —

"Thou shalt have no other gods before me"[66]

20th.

"I thank thee, my God, the river of Lethe[67] may indeed flow through the Elysian Fields,—it does not water the Christian's Paradise."

Aunt Winifred was saying that over to herself in a dreamy undertone this morning, and I happened to hear her.

"Just a quotation, dear," she said, smiling, in answer to my look of inquiry, "I couldn't originate so pretty a thing. *Isn't* it pretty?"

"Very; but I am not sure that I understand it."

"You thought that forgetfulness would be necessary to happiness?"

"Why,—yes; as far as I had ever thought about it; that is, after our last ties with this world are broken. It does not seem to me that I could be happy to remember all that I have suffered and all that I have sinned here."

"But the last of all the sins will be as if it had never been. Christ takes care of that. No shadow of a sense of guilt can dog you, or affect your relations to Him or your other friends. The last pain borne, the last tear, the last sigh, the last lonely hour, the last unsatisfied dream, forever gone by; why should not the dead past bury its dead?"

"Then why remember it?"

"'Save but to swell the sense of being blest.' Besides, forgetfulness of the disagreeable things of this life implies forgetfulness of the pleasant ones. They are all tangled together."

"To be sure. I don't know that I should like that."

"Of course you wouldn't. Imagine yourself in a state of being where you and Roy had lost your past; all that you had borne and enjoyed, and hoped and feared, together; the pretty little memories of your babyhood, and first 'half-days' at school, when he used to trudge along beside you,—little fellow! how many times I have watched him!—holding you tight by the apron-sleeve or hat-string, or bits of fat fingers, lest you should run away or fall. Then the old Academy pranks, out of which you used to help each other; his little chivalry and elder-brotherly advice; the mischief in his eyes; some of the 'Sunday-night talks'; the first novel that you read and dreamed over together; the college stories; the chats over the

---

65 Dark in color with small pieces that glitter like gold.
66 Exodus 20:3.
67 In Greek mythology, the river of Lethe flowed through the land of the afterlife. Those who drank from it forgot their previous lives.

corn-popper by firelight; the earliest, earnest looking-on into life together, its temptations conquered, its lessons learned, its disappointments faced together,—always you two,—would you like to, are you *likely* to, forget all this?

"Roy might as well be not Roy, but a strange angel, if you should. Heaven will be not less heaven, but more, for this pleasant remembering. So many other and greater and happier memories will fill up the time then, that after years these things may—probably will—seem smaller than it seems to us now they can ever be; but they will, I think, be always dear; just as we look back to our baby-selves with a pitying sort of fondness, and, though the little creatures are of small enough use to us now, yet we like to keep good friends with them for old times' sake.

"I have no doubt that you and I shall sit down some summer afternoon in heaven and talk over what we have been saying to-day, and laugh perhaps at all the poor little dreams we have been dreaming of what has not entered into the heart of man. You see it is certain to be so much *better* than anything that I can think of; which is the comfort of it. And Roy —"

"Yes; some more about Roy, please."

"Supposing he were to come right into the room now,—and I slipped out,—and you had him all to yourself again—Now, dear, don't cry, but wait a minute!" Her caressing hand fell on my hair. "I did not mean to hurt you, but to say that your first talk with him, after you stand face to face, may be like that.

"Remembering this life is going to help us amazingly, I fancy, to appreciate the next," she added, by way of period. "Christ seems to have thought so, when he called to the minds of those happy people what, in that unconscious ministering of lowly faith which may never reap its sheaf in the field where the seed was sown, they had not had the comfort of finding out before,—'I was sick and in prison, and ye visited me.'[68] And to come again to Abraham in the parable, did he not say, 'Son, *remember* that thou in thy lifetime hadst good things and Lazarus evil'?"[69]

"I wonder what it is going to look like," I said, as soon as I could put poor Dives out of my mind.

"Heaven? Eye hath not seen, but I have my fancies. I think I want some mountains, and very many trees."

"Mountains and trees!"

"Yes; mountains as we see them at sunset and sunrise, or when the maples are on fire and there are clouds enough to make great purple shadows chase each other into lakes of light, over the tops and down the sides,—the *ideal* of mountains which we catch in rare glimpses, as we catch the ideal of everything. Trees as they look when the wind cooes through them on a June afternoon; elms or lindens or pines as cool as frost, and yellow sunshine trickling through on moss. Trees in a forest so thick that it shuts out the world, and you walk like one in a sanctuary. Trees pierced by stars, and trees in a bath of summer moons to which the thrill of 'Love's young dream'[70] shall cling forever—But there is no end to one's fancies. Some water, too, I would like."

"There shall be no more sea."

---

68 Matthew 25:36.
69 Luke 16:25.
70 The title of a poem by the Irish poet and musician Thomas Moore (1779–1852).

"Perhaps not; though, as the sea is the great type of separation and of destruction, that may be only figurative. But I'm not particular about the sea, if I can have rivers and little brooks, and fountains of just the right sort; the fountains of this world don't please me generally. I want a little brook to sit and sing to Faith by. O, I forgot! she will be a large girl probably, won't she?"

"Never too large to like to hear your mother sing, will you, Faith?"

"O no," said Faith, who bobbed in and out again like a canary just then,—"not unless I'm *dreadful* big, with long dresses and a waterfall, you know. I s'pose, maybe, I'd have to have little girls myself to sing to, then. I hope they'll behave better'n Mary Ann does. She's lost her other arm, and all her sawdust is just running out. Besides, Kitty thought she was a mouse, and ran down cellar with her, and she's all shooken up, somehow. She don't look very pretty."

"Flowers, too," her mother went on, after the interruption. "*Not* all amaranth and asphodel, but of variety and color and beauty unimagined; glorified lilies of the valley, heavenly tea-rose buds, and spiritual harebells among them. O, how your poor mother used to say,—you know flowers were her poetry,—coming in weak and worn from her garden in the early part of her sickness, hands and lap and basket full: 'Winifred, if I only supposed I *could* have some flowers in heaven I shouldn't be half so afraid to go!' I had not thought as much about these things then as I have now, or I should have known better how to answer her. I should like, if I had my choice, to have day-lilies and carnations fresh under my windows all the time."

"Under your windows?"

"Yes. I hope to have a home of my own."

"Not a house?"

"Something not unlike it. In the Father's house are many mansions.[71] Sometimes I fancy that those words have a literal meaning which the simple men who heard them may have understood better than we, and that Christ is truly 'preparing' my home for me. He must be there, too, you see,—I mean John."

I believe that gave me some thoughts that I ought not to have, and so I made no reply.

"If we have trees and mountains and flowers and books," she went on, smiling, "I don't see why not have houses as well. Indeed, they seem to me as supposable as anything can be which is guess-work at the best; for what a homeless, desolate sort of sensation it gives one to think of people wandering over the 'sweet fields beyond the flood' without a local habitation and a name. What could be done with the millions who, from the time of Adam, have been gathering there, unless they lived under the conditions of organized society? Organized society involves homes, not unlike the homes of this world.

"What other arrangement could be as pleasant, or could be pleasant at all? Robertson's definition of a church exactly fits. 'More united in each other, because more united in God.'[72] A happy home is the happiest thing in the world. I do not see why it should not be in any world. I do not believe that all the little tendernesses of family ties are thrown by and lost with this life. In fact, Mary, I cannot think that anything which has in it the elements of permanency is to be lost, but sin. Eternity cannot be—it cannot be the great blank ocean

---

71 John 14:2.
72 Frederick William Robertson (1816–1853) was a British preacher, popular among Oxford undergraduates, who emphasized the humanity of Christ. Robertson became famous for his preaching to the poor and laboring classes.

which most of us have somehow or other been brought up to feel that it is, which shall swallow up, in a pitiless, glorified way, all the little brooks of our delight. So I expect to have my beautiful home, and my husband, and Faith, as I had them here; with many differences and great ones, but *mine* just the same. Unless Faith goes into a home of her own,—the little creature! I suppose she can't always be a baby.

"Do you remember what a pretty little wistful way Charles Lamb has of wondering about all this?

"'Shall I enjoy friendships there, wanting the smiling indications which point me to them here,—"the sweet assurance of a look"? Sun, and sky, and breeze, and solitary walks, and summer holidays, and the greenness of fields, and the delicious juices of meats and fish, and society, ... and candle-light and fireside conversations, and innocent vanities, and jests, and *irony itself,*—do these things go out with life?'"

"Now, Aunt Winifred!" I said, sitting up straight, "what am I to do with these beautiful heresies? If Deacon Quirk *should* hear!"

"I do not see where the heresy lies. As I hold fast by the Bible, I cannot be in much danger."

"But you don't glean your conjectures from the Bible."

"I conjecture nothing that the Bible contradicts. I do not believe as truth indisputable anything that the Bible does not give me. But I reason from analogy about this, as we all do about other matters. Why should we not have pretty things in heaven? If this 'bright and beautiful economy' of skies and rivers, of grass and sunshine, of hills and valleys, is not too good for such a place as this world, will there be any less variety of the bright and beautiful in the next? There is no reason for supposing that the voice of God will speak to us in thunder-claps, or that it will not take to itself the thousand gentle, suggestive tongues of a nature built on the ruins of this, an unmarred system of beneficence.

"There is a pretty argument in the fact that just such sunrises, such opening of buds, such fragrant dropping of fruit, such bells in the brooks, such dreams at twilight, and such hush of stars, were fit for Adam and Eve, made holy man and woman. How do we know that the abstract idea of a heaven needs imply anything very much unlike Eden? There is some reason as well as poetry in the conception of a 'Paradise Regained.' A 'new earth wherein dwelleth righteousness.'"[73]

"But how far is it safe to trust to this kind of argument?"

"Bishop Butler will answer you better than I. Let me see,—Isaac Taylor says something about that."

She went to the bookcase for his "Physical Theory of Another Life," and, finding her place, showed me this passage: —

"If this often repeated argument from analogy is to be termed, as to the conclusions it involves, a conjecture merely, we ought then to abandon altogether every kind of abstract reasoning; nor will it be easy afterwards to make good any principle of natural theology. In truth, the very basis of reasoning is shaken by a scepticism so sweeping as this."

And in another place: —

"None need fear the consequences of such endeavors who have well learned the prime principle of sound philosophy, namely, not to allow the most plausible and pleasing

---

73 2 Peter 3:13.

conjectures to unsettle our convictions of truth … resting upon positive evidence. If there be any who frown upon all such attempts, … they would do well to consider, that although individually, and from the constitution of their minds, they may find it very easy to abstain from every path of excursive meditation, it is not so with others who almost irresistibly are borne forward to the vast field of universal contemplation,—a field from which the human mind is not to be barred, and which is better taken possession of by those who reverently bow to the authority of Christianity, than left open to impiety."

"Very good," I said, laying down the book. "But about those trees and houses, and the rest of your 'pretty things'? Are they to be like these?"

"I don't suppose that the houses will be made of oak and pine and nailed together, for instance. But I hope for heavenly types of nature and of art. *Something that will be to us then what these are now.* That is the amount of it. They may be as 'spiritual' as you please; they will answer all the purpose to us. As we are not spiritual beings yet, however, I am under the necessity of calling them by their earthly names. You remember Plato's old theory, that the ideal of everything exists eternally in the mind of God. If that is so,—and I do not see how it can be otherwise,—then whatever of God is expressed to us in this world by flower, or blade of grass, or human face, why should not that be expressed forever in heaven by something corresponding to flower, or grass, or human face? I do not mean that the heavenly creation will be less real than these, but more so. Their 'spirituality' is of such a sort that our gardens and forests and homes are but shadows of them.

"You don't know how I amuse myself at night thinking this all over before I go to sleep; wondering what one thing will be like, and another thing; planning what I should like; thinking that John has seen it all, and wondering if he is laughing at me because I know so little about it! I tell you, Mary, there's a 'deal o' comfort in 't,' as Phoebe says about her cup of tea."

July 5.

Aunt Winifred has been hunting up a Sunday-school class for herself and one for me; which is a venture that I never was persuaded into undertaking before. She herself is fast becoming acquainted with the poorer people of the town.

I find that she is a thoroughly busy Christian, with a certain "week-day holiness" that is strong and refreshing, like a west wind. Church-going, and conversations on heaven, by no means exhaust her vitality.

She told me a pretty thing about her class; it happened the first Sabbath that she took it. Her scholars are young girls of from fourteen to eighteen years of age, children of church-members, most of them. She seemed to have taken their hearts by storm. *She* says, "They treated me very prettily, and made me love them at once."

Clo Bentley is in the class; Clo is a pretty, soft-eyed little creature, with a shrinking mouth, and an absorbing passion for music, which she has always been too poor to gratify. I suspect that her teacher will make a pet of her. She says that in the course of her lesson, or, in her words, —

"While we were all talking together, somebody pulled my sleeve, and there was Clo in the corner, with her great brown eyes fixed on me. 'See here!' she said in a whisper, 'I can't be good! I would be good if I could *only* just have a piano!' 'Well, Clo,' I said, 'if you will be a good girl, and go to heaven, I think you will have a piano there, and play just as much as you care to.'

"You ought to have seen the look the child gave me! Delight and fear and incredulous bewilderment tumbled over each other, as if I had proposed taking her into a forbidden fairy-land.

" 'Why, Mrs. Forceythe! Why, they won't let anybody have a piano up there! not in *heaven?*'

"I laid down the question-book, and asked what kind of place she supposed that heaven was going to be.

" 'O,' she said, with a dreary sigh, 'I never think about it when I can help it. I suppose we *shall all just stand there!*'

" 'And you?' I asked of the next, a bright girl with snapping eyes.

" 'Do you want me to talk good, or tell the truth?' she answered me. Having been given to understand that she was not expected to 'talk good' in my class, she said, with an approving, decided nod: 'Well, then! I don't think it's going to be *anything nice* anyway. No, I don't! I told my last teacher so, and she looked just as shocked, and said I never should go there as long as I felt so. That made me mad, and I told her I didn't see but I should be as well off in one place as another, except for the fire.'

"A silent girl in the corner began at this point to look interested. 'I always supposed,' said she, 'that you just floated round in heaven—you know—all together—something like ju-jube paste!'

"Whereupon I shut the question-book entirely, and took the talking to myself for a while.

" 'But I *never* thought it was anything like that,' interrupted little Clo, presently, her cheeks flushed with excitement. 'Why, I should like to go, if it is like that! I never supposed people talked, unless it was about converting people, and saying your prayers, and all that.'

"Now, weren't those ideas[74] alluring and comforting for young girls in the blossom of warm human life? They were trying with all their little hearts to 'be good,' too, some of them, and had all of them been to church and Sunday school all their lives. Never, never, if Jesus Christ had been Teacher and Preacher to them, would He have pictured their blessed endless years with Him in such bleak colors. They are not the hues of his Bible."

XI

July 16.

WE TOOK a trip to-day to East Homer for butter. Neither angels nor principalities could convince Phœbe that any butter but "Stephen David's" might, could, would, or should be used in this family. So to Mr. Stephen David's, a journey of four miles, I meekly betake myself at stated periods in the domestic year, burdened with directions about firkins[75] and half-firkins, pounds and half-pounds, salt and no salt, churning and "working over"; some of which I remember and some of which I forget, and to all of which Phœbe considers me sublimely incapable of attending.

The afternoon was perfect, and we took things leisurely, letting the reins swing from the hook,—an arrangement to which Mr. Tripp's old gray was entirely agreeable,—and,

---

74 [Author's Original Note] Facts.
75 A British unit of measurement equal to a quarter of a barrel.

leaning back against the buggy-cushions, wound along among the strong, sweet pine-smells, lazily talking, or lazily silent, as the spirit moved, and as only two people who thoroughly understand and like each other can talk or be silent.

We rode home by Deacon Quirk's, and, as we jogged by, there broke upon our view a blooming vision of the Deacon himself, at work in his potato-field with his son and heir, who, by the way, has the reputation of being the most awkward fellow in the township.

The amiable church-officer, having caught sight of us, left his work, and coming up to the fence "in rustic modesty unscared," guiltless of coat or vest, his calico shirt-sleeves rolled up to his huge brown elbows, and his dusty straw hat flapping in the wind, rapped on the rails with his hoe-handle as a sign for us to stop.

"Are we in a hurry?" I asked, under my breath.

"O no," said Aunt Winifred. "He has somewhat to say unto me, I see by his eyes. I have been expecting it. Let us hear him out. Good afternoon, Deacon Quirk."

"Good afternoon, ma'am. Pleasant day?"

She assented to the statement, novel as it was.

"A very pleasant day," repeated the Deacon, looking for the first time in his life, to my knowledge, a little undecided as to what he should say next. "Remarkable fine day for riding. In a hurry?"

"Well, not especially. Did you want anything of me?"

"You're a church-member, aren't you, ma'am?" asked the Deacon, abruptly.

"I am."

"Orthodox?"

"O yes," with a smile. "You had a reason for asking?"

"Yes, ma'am; I had, as you might say, a reason for asking."

The Deacon laid his hoe on the top of the fence, and his arms across it, and pushed his hat on the back of his head in a becoming and argumentative manner.

"I hope you don't consider that I'm taking liberties if I have a little religious conversation with you, Mrs. Forceythe."

"It is no offence to me if you are," replied Mrs. Forceythe, with a twinkle in her eye; but both twinkle and words glanced off from the Deacon.

"My wife was telling me last night," he began, with an ominous cough, "that her niece, Clotildy Bentley,—Moses Bentley's daughter, you know, and one of your sentimental girls that reads poetry, and is easy enough led away by vain delusions and false doctrine—was under your charge at Sunday school. Now Clotildy is intimate with my wife,—who is her aunt on her mother's side, and always tries to do her duty by her,—and she told Mrs. Quirk what you'd been a saying to those young minds on the Sabbath."

He stopped, and observed her impressively, as if he expected to see the guilty blushes of arraigned heresy covering her amused, attentive face.

"I hope you will pardon me, ma'am, for repeating it, but Clotildy said that you told her she should have a pianna in heaven. A *pianna*, ma'am!"

"I certainly did," she said, quietly.

"You did? Well, now, I didn't believe it, nor I wouldn't believe it, till I'd asked you! I thought it warn't more than fair that I should ask you, before repeating it, you know. It's none of my business, Mrs. Forceythe, any more than that I take a general interest in the spiritooal welfare of the youth of our Sabbath school; but I am very much surprised! I am *very* much surprised!"

"I am surprised that you should be, Deacon Quirk. Do you believe that God would take a poor little disappointed girl like Clo, who has been all her life here forbidden the enjoyment of a perfectly innocent taste, and keep her in His happy heaven eternal years, without finding means to gratify it? I don't."

"I tell Clotildy I don't see what she wants of a pianna-forte," observed "Clotildy's" uncle, sententiously. "She can go to singin' school, and she's been in the choir ever since I have, which is six years come Christmas. Besides, I don't think it's our place to speckylate on the mysteries of the heavenly spere. My wife told her that she mustn't believe any such things as that, which were very irreverent, and contrary to the Scriptures, and Clo went home crying. She said, 'It was so pretty to think about.' It is very easy to impress these delusions of fancy on the young."

"Pray, Deacon Quirk," said Aunt Winifred, leaning earnestly forward in the carriage, "will you tell me what there is 'irreverent' or 'unscriptural' in the idea that there will be instrumental music in heaven?"

"Well," replied the Deacon after some consideration, "come to think of it, there will be harps, I suppose. Harpers harping with their harps on the sea of glass. But I don't believe there will be any piannas. It's a dreadfully material way to talk about that glorious world, to my thinking."

"If you could show me wherein a harp is less 'material' than a piano, perhaps I should agree with you."

Deacon Quirk looked rather nonplussed for a minute.

"What *do* you suppose people will do in heaven?" she asked again.

"Glorify God," said the Deacon, promptly recovering himself,—"glorify God, and sing Worthy the Lamb! We shall be clothed in white robes with palms in our hands, and bow before the Great White Throne. We shall be engaged in such employments as befit sinless creatures in a spiritooal state of existence."

"Now, Deacon Quirk," replied Aunt Winifred, looking him over from head to foot,— old straw hat, calico shirt, blue overalls, and cowhide boots, coarse, work-worn hands, and "narrow forehead braided tight,"—"just imagine yourself, will you? taken out of this life this minute, as you stand here in your potato-field (the Deacon changed his position with evident uneasiness), and put into another life,—not anybody else, but yourself, just as you left this spot,—and do you honestly think that you should be happy to go and put on a white dress and stand still in a choir with a green branch in one hand and a singing-book in the other, and sing and pray and never do anything but sing and pray, this year, next year, and every year forever?"

"We-ell," he replied, surprised into a momentary flash of carnal candor, "I can't say that I shouldn't wonder for a minute, maybe, *how Abinadab would ever get those potatoes hoed without me.—*Abinadab! go back to your work!"

The graceful Abinadab had sauntered up during the conversation, and was listening, hoe in hand and mouth open. He slunk away when his father spoke, but came up again presently on tiptoe when Aunt Winifred was talking. There was an interested, intelligent look about his square and pitifully embarrassed face, which attracted my notice.

"But then," proceeded the Deacon, re-enforced by the sudden recollection of his duties as a father and a church-member, "that couldn't be a permanent state of feeling, you know. I expect to be transformed by the renewing of my mind to appreciate the glories of the New Jerusalem, descending out of heaven from God.[76] That's what I expect, marm. Now

---

76 Revelation 21:2.

I heerd that you told Mrs. Bland, or that Mary told her, or that she heerd it someway, that you said you supposed there were trees and flowers and houses and such in heaven. I told my wife I thought your deceased husband was a Congregational minister, and I didn't believe you ever said it; but that's the rumor."

Without deeming it necessary to refer to her "deceased husband," Aunt Winifred replied that "rumor" was quite right.

"Well!" said the Deacon, with severe significance, "*I* believe in a spiritooal heaven."

I looked him over again,—hat, hoe, shirt, and all; scanned his obstinate old face with its stupid, good eyes and animal mouth. Then I glanced at Aunt Winifred as she leaned forward in the afternoon light; the white, finely cut woman, with her serene smile and rapt, saintly eyes,—every inch of her, body and soul, refined not only by birth and training, but by the long nearness of her heart to Christ.

"Of the earth, earthy. Of the heavens, heavenly." The two faces sharpened themselves into two types. Which, indeed, was the better able to comprehend a "spiritooal heaven"?

"It is distinctly stated in the Bible, by which I suppose we shall both agree," said Aunt Winifred, gently, "that there shall be a *new earth*,[77] as well as new heavens. It is noticeable, also, that the descriptions of heaven, although a series of metaphors, are yet singularly earthlike and tangible ones. Are flowers and skies and trees less 'spiritual' than white dresses and little palm-branches? In fact, where are you going to get your little branches without trees? What could well be more suggestive of material modes of living, and material industry, than a city marked into streets and alleys, paved solidly with gold, walled in and barred with gates whose jewels are named and counted, and whose very length and breadth are measured with a celestial surveyor's chain?"

"But I think we'd ought to stick to what the Bible says," answered the Deacon, stolidly. "If it says golden cities and doesn't say flowers, it means cities and doesn't mean flowers. I dare say you're a good woman, Mrs. Forceythe, if you do hold such oncommon doctrine, and I don't doubt you mean well enough, but I don't think that we ought to trouble ourselves about these mysteries of a future state, *I*'m willing to trust them to God!"

The evasion of a fair argument by this self-sufficient spasm of piety was more than I could calmly stand, and I indulged in a subdued explosion.—Auntie says it sounded like Fourth of July crackers touched off under a wet barrel.

"Deacon Quirk! do you mean to imply that Mrs. Forceythe does not trust it to God? The truth is, that the existence of such a world as heaven is a fact from which you shrink. You know you do! She has twenty thoughts about it where you have one; yet you set up a claim to superior spirituality!"

"Mary, Mary, you are a little excited, I fear. God is a spirit, and they that worship him must worship him in spirit and in truth!"[78]

The relevancy of this last, I confess myself incapable of perceiving, but the good man seemed to be convinced that he had made a point, and we rode off leaving him under that blissful delusion.

"If he *weren't* a good man!" I sighed. "But he is, and I must respect him for it."

"Of course you must; nor is he to blame that he is narrow and rough. I should scarcely have argued as seriously as I did with him, but that, as I fancy him to be a representative

---

77 Revelation 21:1.
78 John 4:23.

of a class, I want to try an experiment. Isn't he amusing, though? He is precisely one of
Mr. Stopford Brooke's men 'who can understand nothing which is original.' "[79]

"Are there, or are there not, more of such men in our church than in others?"

"Not more proportionately to numbers. But I would not have them thinned out. The better we do Christ's work, the more of uneducated, neglected, or debased mind will be drawn
to try and serve Him with us. He sought out the lame, the halt, the blind, the stupid, the
crotchety, the rough, as well as the equable, the intelligent, the refined. Untrained Christians
in any sect will always have their eccentricities and their littlenesses, at which the silken judgment of high places, where the Carpenter's Son would be a strange guest, will sneer. That
never troubles me. It only raises the question in my mind whether cultivated Christians generally are sufficiently *cultivators*, scattering their golden gifts on wayside ground."

"Now take Deacon Quirk," I suggested, when we had ridden along a little way under
the low, green arches of the elms, "and put him into heaven as you proposed, just as he is,
and what *is* he going to do with himself? He can dig potatoes and sell them without cheating, and give generously of their proceeds to foreign missions; but take away his potatoes,
and what would become of him? I don't know a human being more incapacitated to live in
such a heaven as he believes in."

"Very true, and a good, common-sense argument against such a heaven. I don't profess
to surmise what will be found for him to do, beyond this,—that it will be some very palpable
work that he can understand. How do we know that he would not be appointed guardian
of his poor son here, to whom I suspect he has not been all that father might be in this life,
and that he would not have his body as well as his soul to look after, his farm as well as his
prayers? to him might be committed the charge of the dews and the rains and the hundred
unseen influences that are at work on this very potato-field."

"But when his son has gone in his turn, and we have all gone, and there are no more
potato-fields? An Eternity remains."

"You don't know that there wouldn't be any potato-fields; there may be some kind of
agricultural employments even then. To whomsoever a talent is given, it will be given him
wherewith to use it. Besides, by that time the good Deacon will be immensely changed.
I suppose that the simple transition of death, which rids him of sin and of grossness, will
not only wonderfully refine him, but will have its effect upon his intellect."

"If a talent is given, use will be found for it? Tell me some more about that."

"I fancy many things about it; but of course can feel sure of only the foundation principle. This life is a great school-house. The wise Teacher trains in us such gifts as, if we
graduate honorably, will be of most service in the perfect manhood and womanhood that
come after. He sees, as we do not, that a power is sometimes best trained by repression. 'We
do not always lose an advantage when we dispense with it,' Goethe says. But the suffocated
lives, like little Clo's there, make my heart ache sometimes. I take comfort in thinking how
they will bud and blossom up in the air, by and by. There are a great many of them. We
tread them underfoot in our careless stepping now and then, and do not see that they have
not the elasticity to rise from our touch. 'Heaven may be a place for those who failed on
earth,' the Country Parson says."[80]

---

79 Stopford Brooke (1832–1916) was an Irish clergyman who held to a conservative view of
    interpreting Scripture.
80 The Scottish clergyman, Andrew Kennedy Hutchinson Boyd (1825–1899), used the pen name
    "The Country Parson," and his works cast an observant eye on human nature and religion. His

"Then there will be air enough for all?"

"For all; for those who have had a little bloom in this world, as well. I suppose the artist will paint his pictures, the poet sing his happy songs; the orator and author will not find their talents hidden in the eternal darkness of a grave; the sculptor will use his beautiful gift in the moulding of some heavenly Carrara; 'as well the singer as the player on instruments shall be there.'[81] Christ said a thing that has grown on me with new meanings lately:—'He that *loseth his life for my sake shall find it.*'[82] *It*, you see,—not another man's life, not a strange compound of powers and pleasures, but his own familiar aspirations. So we shall best 'glorify God,' not less there than here, by doing it in the peculiar way that He himself marked out for us. But—ah, Mary, you see it is only the life 'lost' for His sake that shall be so beautifully found. A great man never goes to heaven because he is great. He must go, as the meanest of his fellow-sinners go, with face towards Calvary, and every golden treasure used for love of Him who showed him how."

"What would the old Pagans—and modern ones, too, for that matter—say to that? Wasn't it Tacitus[83] who announced it as his belief, that immortality was granted as a special gift to a few superior minds? For the people who persisted in making up the rest of the world, poor things! as it could be of little consequence what became of them, they might die as the brute dieth."

"It seems an unbearable thing to me sometimes," she went on, "the wreck of a gifted soul. A man who can be, if he chooses, as much better and happier than the rest of us as the ocean reflects more sky than a mill-pond, must also be, if he chooses, more wicked and more miserable. It takes longer to reach sea-shells than river-pebbles. I am compelled to think, also, that intellectual rank must in heaven bear some proportion to goodness. There are last and there are first that shall have changed places. As the tree falleth, there shall it lie, and with that amount of holiness of which a man leaves this life the possessor, he must start in another. I have seen great thinkers, 'foremost men'· in science, in theology, in the arts, who, I solemnly believe, will turn aside in heaven,—and will turn humbly and heartily,—to let certain day-laborers and paupers whom I have known go up before them as kings and priests unto God."

"I believe that. But I was going to ask,—for poor creatures like your respected niece, who hasn't a talent, nor even a single absorbing taste, for one thing above another thing,— what shall she do?"

"Whatever she liketh best; something very useful, my dear, don't be afraid, and very pleasant. Something, too, for which this life has fitted you; though you may not understand how that can be, better than did poor Heine on his 'matrazzen-gruft,' reading all the books that treated of his disease.[84] 'But what good this reading is to do me I don't know,' he said, 'except that it will qualify me to give lectures in heaven on the ignorance of doctors on earth about diseases of the spinal marrow.' "

---

writings, *Autumn Holidays of a Country Parson* (1865) and *Recreations of a Country Parson* (1859, 1861, 1878), were widely read in America.

81 Psalm 87:7.

82 Matthew16:25.

83 Tacitus (56–117) was a Roman senator and one of the empire's most famous historians.

84 Christian Johann Heinrich Heine (1797–1856) was a German poet and essayist. In the last years of his life he developed a medical condition he called "mattress-grave" or "matrazzengruft." It left him largely paralyzed and confined to bed.

"I don't know how many times I have thought of—I believe it was the poet Gray,[85] who said that his idea of heaven was to lie on the sofa and read novels. That touches the lazy part of us, though."

"Yes, they will be the active, outgoing, generous elements of our nature that will be brought into use then, rather than the self-centred and dreamy ones. Though I suppose that we shall read in heaven,—being influenced to be better and nobler by good and noble teachers of the pen, not less there than here."

"O think of it? To have books, and music,—and pictures?"

"All that Art, 'the handmaid of the Lord,'[86] can do for us, I have no doubt will be done. Eternity will never become monotonous. Variety without end, charms unnumbered within charms, will be devised by Infinite ingenuity to minister to our delight. Perhaps,—this is just my fancying,—perhaps there will be whole planets turned into galleries of art, over which we may wander at will; or into orchestral halls where the highest possibilities of music will be realized to singer and to hearer. Do you know, I have sometimes had a flitting notion that music would be the language of heaven? It certainly differs in some indescribable manner from the other arts. We have most of us felt it in our different ways. It always seems to me like the cry of a great, sad life dragged to use in this world against its will. Pictures and statues and poems fit themselves to their work more contentedly. Symphony and song struggle in fetters. That sense of conflict is not good for me. It is quite as likely to harm as to help. Then perhaps the mysteries of sidereal systems will be spread out like a child's map before us. Perhaps we shall take journeys to Jupiter and to Saturn and to the glittering haze of nebulæ, and to the site of ruined worlds whose 'extinct light is yet travelling through space.' Occupation for explorers there, you see!"

"You make me say with little Clo, 'O, why, I want to go!' every time I hear you talk. But there is one thing,—you spoke of families living together."

"Yes."

"And you spoke of—your husband. But the Bible—"

"Says there shall be no marrying nor giving in marriage.[87] I know that. Nor will there be such marrying or giving in marriage as there is in a world like this. Christ expressly goes on to state, that we shall be *as* the angels in heaven. How do we know what heavenly unions of heart with heart exist among the angels? It leaves me margin enough to live and be happy with John forever, and it holds many possibilities for the settlement of all perplexing questions brought about by the relations of this world. It is of no use to talk much about them. But it is on that very verse that I found my unshaken belief that they will be smoothed out in some natural and happy way, with which each one shall be content."

"But O, there is a great gulf fixed; and on one side one, and on the other another, and they loved each other."

Her face paled,—it always pales, I notice, at the mention of this mystery,—but her eyes never lost by a shade their steadfast trust.

"Mary, don't question me about *that*. That belongs to the unutterable things. God will take care of it. I *think* I could leave it to Him even if he brought it for me myself to face. I feel sure that He will make it all come out right. Perhaps He will be so dear to us, that we could not love any one who hated him. In some way the void *must* be filled, for he shall

---

85 Thomas Gray (1716–1771) was an English poet and a professor at Cambridge University.

86 Luke 1:38.

87 Mark 12:25.

wipe away tears. But it seems to me that the only thought in which there can be any *rest*, and in that there *can*, is this: that Christ, who loves us even as His Father loves Him, can be happy in spite of the existence of a hell. If it is possible to him, surely he can make it possible to us."

"Two things that He has taught us," she said after a silence, "give me beautiful assurance that none of these dreams with which I help myself can be beyond His intention to fulfil, One is, that eye hath not seen it, nor ear heard it, nor the heart conceived it,[88]—this lavishness of reward which He is keeping for us. Another is, that 'I shall be *satisfied* when I awake.'"[89]

"With his likeness."

"With his likeness. And about that I have other things to say."

But Old Gray stopped at the gate and Phœbe was watching for her butter, and it was no time to say them then.

XII

July 22.

AUNT WINIFRED has connected herself with our church. I think it was rather hard for her, breaking the last tie that bound her to her husband's people; but she had a feeling, that, if her work is to be done and her days ended here, she had better take up all such little threads of influence to make herself one with us.

25th.

To-day what should Deacon Quirk do but make a solemn call on Mrs. Forceythe, for the purpose of asking—and this with a hint that he wished he had asked before she became a member of the Homer First Congregational Church—whether there were truth in the rumors, now rife about town, that she was a Swedenborgian![90]

Aunt Winifred broke out laughing, and laughed merrily. The Deacon frowned.

"I used to fancy that I believed in Swedenborg," she said, as soon as she could sober down a little.

The Deacon pricked up his ears, with visions of excommunications and councils reflected on every feature.

"Until I read his books," she finished.

"Oh!" said the Deacon. He waited for more, but she seemed to consider the conversation at an end.

"So then you—if I understand—are *not* a Swedenborgian, ma'am?"

"If I were, I certainly should have had no inducement to join myself to your church," she replied, with gentle dignity. "I believe, with all my heart, in the same Bible and the same creed that you believe in, Deacon Quirk."

"And you *live* your creed, which all such genial Christians do not find it necessary to do," I thought, as the Deacon in some perplexity took his departure, and she returned with a smile to her sewing.

---

88 1 Corinthians 2:9.
89 Psalm 139:18.
90 Emmanuel Swedenborg (1688–1772) was a Swedish scientist and theologian. His voluminous writings were built upon his belief that he could visit heaven and hell and speak with angels.

I suppose the call came about in this way. We had the sewing-circle here last week, and just before the lamps were lighted, and when people had dropped their work to group and talk in the corners, Meta Tripp came up with one or two other girls to Aunt Winifred, and begged "to hear some of those queer things people said she believed about heaven." Auntie is never obtrusive with her views on this or any other matter, but, being thus urged, she answered a few questions that they put to her, to the extreme scandal of one or two old ladies, and the secret delight of the rest.

"Well," said little Mrs. Bland, squeezing and kissing her youngest, who was at that moment vigorously employed in sticking very long darning-needles into his mother's water-fall, "I hope there'll be a great many babies there. I should be perfectly happy if I always could have babies to play with!"

The look that Aunt Winifred shot over at me was worth seeing.

She merely replied, however, that she supposed all our "highest aspirations,"—with an indescribable accent to which Mrs. Bland was safely deaf,—if good ones, would be realized; and added, laughing, that Swedenborg said that the babies in heaven—who outnumber the grown people—will be given into the charge of those women especially fond of them.

"Swedenborg is suggestive, even if you can't accept what seem to the uninitiated to be his natural impossibilities," she said, after we had discussed Deacon Quirk awhile. "He says a pretty thing, too, occasionally. Did I ever read you about the houses?"

She had not, and I wished to hear, so she found the book on Heaven and Hell, and read: —

"As often as I have spoken with the angels mouth to mouth, so often I have been with them in their habitations: their habitations are altogether like the habitations on earth which are called houses, but more beautiful; in them are parlors, rooms, and chambers in great numbers; there are also courts, and round about are gardens, shrubberies, and fields. Palaces of heaven have been seen, which were so magnificent that they could not be described; above, they glittered as if they were of pure gold, and below, as if they were of precious stones; one palace was more splendid than another; within, it was the same the rooms were ornamented with such decorations as neither words nor sciences are sufficient to describe. On the side which looked to the south there were paradises, where all things in like manner glittered, and in some places the leaves were as of silver, and the fruits as of gold; and the flowers on their beds presented by colors as it were rainbows; at the boundaries again were palaces, in which the view terminated."

Aunt Winifred says that our hymns, taken all together, contain the worst and the best pictures of heaven that we have in any branch of literature.

"It seems to me incredible," she says, "that the Christian Church should have allowed that beautiful 'Jerusalem' in its hymnology so long, with the ghastly couplet, —

'Where congregations ne'er break up,
　　And Sabbaths have no end.'

The dullest preachers are sure to give it out, and that when there are the greatest number of restless children wondering when it will be time to go home. It is only within ten years that modern hymn-books have altered it, returning in part to the original.

"I do not think we have chosen the best parts of that hymn for our 'service of song.' You never read the whole of it? You don't know how pretty it is! It is a relief from the customary palms and choirs. One's whole heart is glad of the outlet of its sweet refrain, —

'Would God that I were there!'

before one has half read it. You are quite ready to believe that

'There is no hunger, heat, nor cold,
But *pleasure every way*.'

Listen to this: —

'Thy houses are of ivory,
Thy windows crystal clear,
Thy tiles are made of beaten gold;
O God, that I were there!

'We that are here in banishment
Continually do moan.
* * * * *

'Our sweet is mixed with bitter gall,
Our pleasure is but pain,
Our joys scarce last the looking on,
Our sorrows still remain.

'But there they live in such delight,
Such pleasure and such play,
As that to them a thousand years
Doth seem as yesterday.'

And this: —

'Thy gardens and thy gallant walks
Continually are green;
There grow such sweet and pleasant flowers
As nowhere else are seen.

'There cinnamon, there sugar grows,
There nard and balm abound,
What tongue can tell, or heart conceive
The joys that there are found?

'Quite through the streets, with silver sound,
The flood of life doth flow,
Upon whose banks, on every side,
The wood of life doth grow.'

I tell you we may learn something from that grand old Catholic singer.[91] He is far nearer to the Bible than the innovators on his MSS. Do you not notice how like his images are to the inspired ones, and yet how pleasant and natural is the effect of the entire poem?

---

91 "That grand old Catholic singer" probably refers to St. Augustine (354–430). The hymn "Jerusalem" is traditionally attributed to him.

"There is nobody like Bonar, though, to sing about heaven.[92] There is one of his, 'We shall meet and rest,'—do you know it?"

I shook my head, and knelt down beside her and watched her face,—it was quite unconscious of me, the musing face,—while she repeated dreamily: —

"Where the faded flower shall freshen, —
    Freshen nevermore to fade;
Where the shaded sky shall brighten, —
    Brighten nevermore to shade;
Where the sun-blaze never scorches;
    Where the star-beams cease to chill;
Where no tempest stirs the echoes
    Of the wood or wave or hill; ...
Where no shadow shall bewilder;
    Where life's vain parade is o'er;
Where the sleep of sin is broken,
    And the dreamer dreams no more
Where the bond is never severed, —
    Partings, claspings, sob and moan,
Midnight waking, twilight weeping,
    Heavy noontide,—all are done;
Where the child has found its mother;
    Where the mother finds the child;
Where dear families are gathered,
    That were scattered on the wild; ...
Where the hidden wound is healed;
    Where the blighted life reblooms;
Where the smitten heart the freshness
    Of its buoyant youth resumes; ...
Where we find the joy of loving,
    As we never loved before, —
Loving on, unchilled, unhindered,
    Loving once, forevermore." ...

                                                                                        30th.

Aunt Winifred was weeding her day-lilies this morning, when the gate creaked timidly, and then swung noisily, and in walked Abinadab Quirk, with a bouquet of China pinks in the button-hole of his green-gray linen coat. He had taken evident pains to smarten himself up a little, for his hair was combed into two horizontal *dabs* over his ears, and the green-gray coat and blue-checked shirt-sleeves were quite clean; but he certainly is the most uncouth specimen of six feet five that it has ever been my privilege to behold. I feel sorry for him, though. I heard Meta Tripp laughing at him in Sunday school the other day,—"Quadrangular Quirk," she called him, a little too loud, and the poor fellow heard her. He half turned, blushing fiercely; then slunk down in his corner with as pitiable a look as is often seen upon a man's face.

---

92 Horatius Bonar (1818–1889) was a Scottish clergyman, poet and hymn writer.

He came up to Auntie awkwardly,—a part of the scene I saw from the window, and the rest she told me,—head hanging, and the tiny bouquet held out.

"Clo sent these to you," he stammered out,—"my cousin Clo. I was coming 'long, and she thought, you know,—she'd get me, you see, to—to—that is, to—bring them. She sent her—that is—let me see. She sent her respect—ful—respectful—no, her love; that was it. She sent her love 'long with 'em."

Mrs. Forceythe dropped her weeds, and held out her white, shapely hands, wet with the heavy dew, to take the flowers.

"O, thank you! Clo knows my fancy for pinks. How kind in you to bring them! Won't you sit down a few moments? I was just going to rest a little. Do you like flowers?"

Abinadab eyed the white hands, as his huge fingers just touched them, with a sort of awe; and, sighing, sat down on the very edge of the garden bench beside her. After a singular variety of efforts to take the most uncomfortable position of which he was capable, he succeeded to his satisfaction, and, growing then somewhat more at his ease, answered her question.

"Flowers are sech *gassy* things. They just blow out and that's the end of 'em. I like machine-shops best."

"Ah! well, that is a very useful liking. Do you ever invent machinery yourself?"

"Sometimes," said Abinadab, with a bashful smile. "There's a little improvement of mine for carpet-sweepers up before the patent-office now. Don't know whether they'll run it through. Some of the chaps I saw in Boston told me they thought they would do't in time; it takes an awful sight of time. I'm alwers fussing over something of the kind; alwers did, sence I was a baby; had my little wind-mills and carts and things; used to sell 'em to the other young uns. Father don't like it. He wants me to stick to the farm. I don't like farming. I feel like a fish out of water.—Mrs. Forceythe, marm!"

He turned on her with an abrupt change of tone, so funny that she could with difficulty retain her gravity.

"I heard you saying a sight of queer things the other day about heaven. Clo, she's been telling me a sight more. Now, *I* never believed in heaven!"

"Why?"

"Because I don't believe," said the poor fellow, with sullen decision, "that a benevolent God ever would ha' made sech a derned awkward chap as I am!"

Aunt Winifred replied by stepping into the house, and bringing out a fine photograph of one of the best of the St. Georges,—a rapt, yet very manly face, in which the saint and the hero are wonderfully blended.

"I suppose," she said, putting it into his hands, "that if you should go to heaven! you would be as much fairer than that picture as that picture is fairer than you are now."

"No! Why, would I, though? Jim-miny! Why, it would be worth going for, wouldn't it?"

The words were no less reverently spoken than the vague rhapsodies of his father; for the sullenness left his face, and his eyes—which are pleasant, and not unmanly, when one fairly sees them—sparkled softly, like a child's.

"Make it all up there, maybe?" musing,—"the girls laughing at you all your life, and all? That would be the bigger heft of the two then, wouldn't it? for they say there ain't any end to things up there. Why, so it might be fair in Him after all; more'n fair, perhaps. See here, Mrs. Forceythe, I'm not a church-member, you know, and father, he's dreadful troubled about me; prays over me like a span of ministers, the old gentleman does, every Sunday night. Now, I don't want to go to the other place any more than the next man, and I've had my times, too, of thinking I'd keep steady and say my prayers reg'lar,—it makes a chap feel on a sight better terms with himself,—but I don't see how *I'm* going to wear white frocks and stand up in a choir,—never could sing no more'n a frog with a cold in his head,—it tires me more now, honest, to think of it, than it does to do a week's mowing. Look at me! Do you s'pose I'm fit for it? Father, he's always talking about the thrones, and the wings, and the praises, and the palms, and having new names in your foreheads (shouldn't object to that, though, by any means), till he drives me into the tool-house, or off on a spree. I tell him if God hain't got a place where chaps like me can do something He's fitted 'em to do in this world, there's no use thinking about it anyhow."

So Auntie took the honest fellow into her most earnest thought for half an hour, and argued, and suggested, and reproved, and helped him, as only she could do; and at the end of it seemed to have worked into his mind some distinct and not unwelcome ideas of what a Christ-like life must mean to him, and of the coming heaven which is so much more real to her than any life outside of it.

"And then," she told him, "I imagine that your fancy for machinery will be employed in some way. Perhaps you will do a great deal more successful inventing there than you ever will here."

"You don't say so!" said radiant Abinadab.

"God will give you something to do, certainly, and something that you will like."

"I might turn it to some religious purpose, you know!" said Abinadab, looking bright. "Perhaps I could help 'em build a church, or hist some of their pearl gates, or something like!"

Upon that he said that it was time to be at home and see to the oxen, and shambled awkwardly away.

Clo told us this afternoon that he begged the errand and the flowers from her. She says: "'Bin thinks there never was anybody like you, Mrs. Forceythe, and 'Bin isn't the only one, either." At which Mrs. Forceythe smiles absently, thinking—I wonder of what.

Monday night.

I saw as funny and as pretty a bit of drama this afternoon as I have seen for a long time.

Faith had been rolling out in the hot hay ever since three o'clock, with one of the little Blands, and when the shadows grew long they came in with flushed cheeks and tumbled hair, to rest and cool upon the door-steps. I was sitting in the parlor, sewing energetically on some sun-bonnets for some of Aunt Winifred's people down town,—I found the heat to be more bearable if I kept busy,—and could see, unseen, all the little *tableaux* into which the two children grouped themselves; a new one every instant; in the shadow now,—now in a quiver of golden glow; the wind tossing their hair about, and their chatter chiming down the hall like bells.

"O what a funny little sunset there's going to be behind the maple-tree," said the blond-haired Bland, in a pause.

"Funny enough," observed Faith, with her superior smile, "but it's going to be a great deal funnier up in heaven, I tell you, Molly Bland."

"Funny in heaven? Why, Faith!" Molly drew herself up with a religious air, and looked the image of her father.

"Yes, to be sure. I'm going to have some little pink blocks made out of it when I go; pink and yellow and green and purple and—O, so many blocks! I'm going to have a little red cloud to sail round in, like that one up over the house, too, I shouldn't wonder."

Molly opened her eyes.

"O, I don't believe it!"

"*You* don't know much!" said Miss Faith, superbly. "I shouldn't s'pose you would believe it. P'r'aps I'll have some strawberries too, and some ginger-snaps,—I'm not going to have any old bread and butter up there,—O, and some little gold apples, and a lot of playthings; nicer playthings—why, nicer than they have in the shops in Boston, Molly Bland! God's keeping 'em up there a purpose."

"Dear me!" said incredulous Molly, "I should just like to know who told you that much. My mother never told it at me. Did your mother tell it at you?"

"O, she told me some of it, and the rest I thinked out myself."

"Let's go and play One Old Cat," said Molly, with an uncomfortable jump; "I wish I hadn't got to go to heaven!"

"Why, Molly Bland! why, I think heaven's splendid! I've got my papa up there, you know. 'Here's my little girl!' That's what he's going to say. Mamma, she'll be there, too, and we're all going to live in the prettiest house. I have dreadful hurries to go this afternoon sometimes when Phœbe's cross and won't give me sugar. They don't let you in, though, 'nless you're a good girl."

"Who gets it all up?" asked puzzled Molly.

"Jesus Christ will give me all these beautiful fings," said Faith, evidently repeating her mother's words,—the only catechism that she has been taught.

"And what will he do when he sees you?" asked her mother, coming down the stairs and stepping up behind her.

"Take me up in His arms and kiss me."

"And what will Faith say?"

"*Fank—you!*" said the child, softly.

In another minute she was absorbed, body and soul, in the mysteries of One Old Cat.

"But I don't think she will feel much like being naughty for half an hour to come," her mother said; "hear how pleasantly her words drop! Such a talk quiets her, like a hand laid on her head. Mary, sometimes I think it is His very hand, as much as when He touched those other little children. I wish Faith to feel at home with Him and His home. Little thing! I really do not think that she is conscious of any fear of dying; I do not think it means anything to her but Christ, and her father, and pink blocks, and a nice time, and never disobeying me or being cross. Many a time she wakes me up in the morning talking away to herself, and when I turn and look at her, she says: 'O mamma, won't we go to heaven to-day, you fink? *When* will we go, mamma?'"

"If there had been any pink blocks and ginger-snaps for me when I was at her age, I should not have prayed every night to 'die out.' I think the horrors of death that children live through, unguessed and unrelieved, are awful. Faith may thank you all her life that she has escaped them."

"I should feel answerable to God for the child's soul, if I had not prevented that. I always wanted to know what sort of mother that poor little thing had, who asked, if she were *very* good up in heaven, whether they wouldn't let her go down to hell Saturday afternoons, and play a little while!"

"I know. But think of it,—blocks and ginger-snaps!"

"I treat Faith just as the Bible treats us, by dealing in *pictures* of truth that she can under-stand. I can make Clo and Abinadab Quirk comprehend that their pianos and machinery may not be made of literal rosewood and steel, but will be some synonyme of the thing, which will answer just such wants of their changed natures as rosewood and steel must answer now. There will be machinery and pianos in the same sense in which there will be pearl gates and harps. Whatever enjoyment any or all of them represent now, something will represent then.

"But Faith, if I told her that her heavenly ginger-snaps would not be made of molasses and flour, would have a cry, for fear that she was not going to have any ginger-snaps at all; so, until she is older, I give her unqualified ginger-snaps. The principal joy of a child's life consists in eating. Faith begins, as soon as the light wanes, to dream of that gum-drop which she is to have at bedtime. I don't suppose she can outgrow that at once by passing out of her little round body. She must begin where she left off,—nothing but a baby, though it will be as holy and happy a baby as Christ can make it. When she says: 'Mamma, I shall be hungery and want my dinner, up there,' I never hesitate to tell her that she shall have her dinner. She would never, in her secret heart, though she might not have the honesty to say so, expect to be otherwise than miserable in a dinnerless eternity."

"You are not afraid of misleading the child's fancy?"

"Not so long as I can keep the two ideas—that Christ is her best friend, and that heaven is not meant for naughty girls—pre-eminent in her mind. And I sincerely believe that He would give her the very pink blocks which she anticipates, no less than He would give back a poet his lost dreams, or you your brother. He has been a child; perhaps, incidentally to the unsolved mysteries of atonement, for this very reason,—that He may know how to 'prepare their places' for them, whose angels do always behold His Father. Ah, you may be sure that, if of such is the happy Kingdom, He will not scorn to stoop and fit it to their little needs.

"There was that poor little fellow whose guinea-pig died,—do you remember?"

"Only half; what was it?"

" 'O mamma,' he sobbed out, behind his handkerchief, 'don't great big elephants have souls?'

" 'No, my son.'

" 'Nor camels, mamma?'

" 'No.'

" 'Nor bears, nor alligators, nor chickens?'

" 'O no, dear.'

" 'O mamma, mamma! Don't little CLEAN—*white*—*guinea-pigs* have souls?'

"I never should have had the heart to say no to that; especially as we have no positive proof to the contrary.

"Then that scrap of a boy who lost his little red balloon the morning he bought it, and, broken-hearted, wanted to know whether it had gone to heaven. Don't I suppose if he had been taken there himself that very minute, that he would have found a little balloon in waiting for him? How can I help it?"

"It has a pretty sound. If people would not think it so material and shocking—"

"Let people read Martin Luther's letter to his little boy. There is the testimony of a pillar in good and regular standing! I don't think you need be afraid of my balloon, after that."

I remembered that there was a letter of his on heaven, but, not recalling it distinctly, I hunted for it to-night, and read it over. I shall copy it, the better to retain it in mind.[93]

---

93 Phelps found this letter in Mrs. Charles's *Chronicles of the Schönberg-Cotta Family*, but she adjusts its language and meaning to foreground the concrete nature of heaven.

"Grace and peace in Christ, my dear little son. I see with pleasure that thou learnest well, and prayed diligently. Do so, my son, and continue. When I come home I will bring thee a pretty fairing.

"I know a pretty, merry garden wherein are many children. They have little golden coats, and they gather beautiful apples under the trees, and pears, cherries, plums, and wheat-plums;—they sing, and jump, and are merry. They have beautiful little horses, too, with gold bits and silver saddles. And I asked the man to whom the garden belongs, whose children they were. And he said: 'They are the children that love to pray and to learn, and are good.' Then said I: 'Dear man, I have a son, too; his name is Johnny Luther. May he not also come into this garden and eat these beautiful apples and pears, and ride these fine horses?' Then the man said: 'If he loves to pray and to learn, and is good, he shall come into this garden, and Lippus and Jost too; and when they all come together, they shall have fifes and trumpets, lutes and all sorts of music, and they shall dance, and shoot with little cross-bows.'

"And he showed me a fine meadow there in the garden, made for dancing. There hung nothing but golden fifes, trumpets, and fine silver cross-bows. But it was early, and the children had not yet eaten; therefore I could not wait the dance, and I said to the man: 'Ah, dear sir! I will immediately go and write all this to my little son Johnny, and tell him to pray diligently, and to learn well, and to be good, so that he also may come to this garden. But he has an Aunt Lehne, he must bring her with him.' Then the man said: 'It shall be so; go, and write him so.'

"Therefore, my dear little son Johnny, learn and pray away! and tell Lippus and Jost, too that they must learn and pray. And then you shall come to the garden together. Herewith I commend thee to Almighty God. And greet Aunt Lehne, and give her a kiss for my sake.

"Thy dear Father,
"Martinus Luther.[94]
"Anno 1530."

XIII

August 3.

The summer is sliding quietly away,—my desolate summer which I dreaded; with the dreams gone from its wild flowers, the crown from its sunsets, the thrill from its winds and its singing.

But I have found out a thing. One can live without dreams and crowns and thrills.

I have not lost them. They lie under the ivied cross with Roy for a little while. They will come back to me with him. "Nothing is lost," she teaches me. And until they come back, I see—for she shows me—fields groaning under their white harvest, with laborers very few. Ruth followed the sturdy reapers, gleaning a little. I, perhaps, can do as much. The ways in which I must work seem so small and insignificant, so pitifully trivial sometimes, that I do not even like to write them down here. In fact, they are so small that, six months ago, I did not see them at all. Only to be pleasant to old Phœbe, and charitable to Meta Tripp, and

---

94 Latin for "Martin Luther" (1483–1546), who was a German theologian and professor. He was
   a pivotal figure in the Protestant Reformation.

faithful to my *not* very interesting little scholars, and a bit watchful of worn-out Mrs. Bland, and—But dear me, I won't! They *are* so little!

But one's self becomes of less importance, which seems to be the point.

It seems very strange to me sometimes, looking back to those desperate winter days, what a change has come over my thoughts of Roy. Not that he is any less—O, never any less to me. But it is almost as if she had raised him from the grave. Why seek ye the living among the dead?[95] Her soft, compassionate eyes shine with the question every hour. And every hour he is helping me,—ah, Roy, we understand one another now.

How he must love Aunt Winifred! How pleasant the days will be when we can talk her over, and thank her together!

"To be happy because Roy is happy." I remember how those first words of hers struck me. It does not seem to me impossible, now.

Aunt Winifred and I laugh at each other for talking so much about heaven. I see that the green book is filled with my questions and her answers. The fact is, not that we do not talk as much about mundane affairs as other people, but that this one thing interests us more.

If, instead, it had been flounces, or babies, or German philosophy, the green book would have filled itself just as unconsciously with flounces, or babies, or German philosophy. This interest in heaven is of course no sign of especial piety in me, nor could people with young, warm, uncrushed hopes throbbing through their days be expected to feel the same. It is only the old principle of, where the treasure is—the heart.

"How spiritual-minded Mary has grown!" Mrs. Bland observes, regarding me respectfully. I try in vain to laugh her out of the conviction. If Roy had not gone before, I should think no more, probably, about the coming life, than does the minister's wife herself.

But now—I cannot help it—that is the reality, this the dream; that the substance, this the shadow.

The other day Aunt Winifred and I had a talk which has been of more value to me than all the rest.

Faith was in bed; it was a cold, rainy evening; we were secure from callers; we lighted a few kindlers in the parlor grate; she rolled up the easy-chair, and I took my cricket at her feet.

"Paul at the feet of Gamaliel![96] This is what I call comfort. Now, Auntie, let us go to heaven awhile."

"Very well. What do you want there now?"

I paused a moment, sobered by a thought that has been growing steadily upon me of late.

"Something more, Aunt Winifred. All these other things are beautiful and dear; but I believe I want—God.

"You have not said much about Him. The Bible says a great deal about Him. You have given me the filling-up of heaven in all its pleasant promise, but—I don't know—there seems to be an outline wanting."

She drew my hand up into hers, smiling.

"I have not done my painting by artistic methods, I know; but it was not exactly accidental.

---

95 Luke 24:5.
96 St. Paul, when he was young, trained under the famous Jewish rabbi, Gamaliel.

"Tell me, honestly,—is God more to you or less, a more distinct Being or a more vague one, than He was six months ago? Is He, or is He not, dearer to you now than then?" I thought about it a minute, and then turned my face up to her.

"Mary, what a light in your eyes! How is it?"

It came over me slowly, but it came with such a passion of gratitude and unworthiness, that I scarcely knew how to tell her—that He never has been to me, in all my life, what he is now at the end of these six months. He was once an abstract Grandeur which I struggled more in fear than love to please. He has become a living Presence, dear and real.

"No dead fact stranded on the shore
    Of the oblivious years;
But warm, sweet, tender, even yet
    A present help." … .

He was an inexorable Mystery who took Roy from me to lose him in the glare of a more inexorable heaven. He is a Father who knew better than we that we should be parted for a while; but He only means it to be a little while. He is keeping him for me to find in the flush of some summer morning, on which I shall open my eyes no less naturally than I open them on June sunrises now. I always have that fancy of going in the morning.

She understood what I could not tell her, and said, "I thought it would be so."

"You, His interpreter, have done it," I answered her. "His heaven shows what He is,— don't you see?—like a friend's letter. I could no more go back to my old groping relations to Him, than I could make of you the dim and somewhat apocryphal Western Auntie that you were before I saw you."

"Which was precisely why I have dealt with this subject as I have," she said. "You had all your life been directed to an indefinite heaven, where the glory of God was to crowd out all individuality and all human joy from His most individual and human creatures, till the 'Glory of God' had become nothing but a name and a dread to you. So I let those three words slide by, and tried to bring you to them, as Christ brought the Twelve to believe in him, 'for the works' sake.'[97]

"Yes, my child; clinging human loves, stifled longings, cries for rest, forgotten hopes, shall have their answer. Whatever the bewilderment of beauties folded away for us in heavenly nature and art, they shall strive with each other to make us glad. These things have their pleasant place. But, through eternity, there will be always something beyond and dearer than the dearest of them. God himself will be first,—naturally and of necessity, without strain or struggle, *first*."

When I sat here last winter with my dead in my house, those words would have roused in me an agony of wild questionings. I should have beaten about them and beaten against them, and cried in my honest heart that they were false. I *knew* that I loved Roy more than I loved such a Being as God seemed to me then to be. Now, they strike me as simply and pleasantly true. The more I love Roy, the more I love Him. He loves us both.

"You see it could not be otherwise," she went on, speaking low. "Where would you be, or I, or they who seem to us so much dearer and better than ourselves, if it were not for Jesus Christ? What can heaven be to us, but a song of the love that is the same to us yesterday,

---

97 John 14:11.

to-day, and forever,—that, in the mystery of an intensity which we shall perhaps never understand, could choose death and be glad in the choosing, and, what is more than that, could live *life* for us for three-and-thirty years?

"I cannot strain my faith—or rather my common sense—to the rhapsodies with which many people fill heaven. But it seems to me like this: A friend goes away from us, and it may be seas or worlds that lie between us, and we love him. He leaves behind him his little keepsakes; a lock of hair to curl about our fingers; a picture that has caught the trick of his eyes or smile; a book, a flower, a letter. What we do with the curling hair, what we say to the picture, what we dream over the flower and the letter, nobody knows but ourselves. People have risked life for such mementos. Yet who loves the senseless gift more than the giver,—the curl more than the young forehead on which it fell,—the letter more than the hand which traced it?

"So it seems to me that we shall learn to see in God the centre of all possibilities of joy. The greatest of these lesser delights is but the greater measure of His friendship. They will not mean less of pleasure, but more of Him. They will not 'pale,' as Dr. Bland would say. Human dearness will wax, not wane, in heaven; but human friends will be loved for love of Him."

"I see; that helps me; like a torch in a dark room. But there will be shadows in the corners. Do you suppose that we shall ever *fully* feel it in the body?"

"In the body, probably not. We see through a glass so darkly that the temptation to idolatry is always our greatest. Golden images did not die with Paganism. At times I fancy that, somewhere between this world and another, a revelation will come upon us like a flash, of what *sin* really is,—such a revelation, lighting up the lurid background of our past in such colors, that the consciousness of what Christ has done for us will be for a time as much as heart can bear. After that, the mystery will be, not how to love Him most, but that we ever *could* have loved any creature or thing as much."

"We serve God quite as much by active work as by special prayer, here," I said after some thought; "how will it be there?"

"We must be busily at work certainly; but I think there must naturally be more communion with Him then. Now, this phrase 'communion with God' has been worn, and not always well worn.

"Prayer means to us, in this life, more often penitent confession than happy interchange of thought with Him. It is associated, too, with aching limbs and sleepy eyes, and nights when the lamp goes out. Obstacles, moral and physical, stand in the way of our knowing exactly what it may mean in the ideal of it.

"My best conception of it lies in the *friendship* of the man Christ Jesus. I suppose he will bear with him, eternally, the humanity which he took up with him from the Judean hills. I imagine that we shall see him in visible form like ourselves, among us, yet not of us; that he, himself, is "Gott mit ihnen";[98] that we shall talk with him as a man talketh with his friend. Perhaps, bowed and hushed at his dear feet, we shall hear from his own lips the story of Nazareth, of Bethany, of Golgotha, of the chilly mountains where he used to pray all night long for us; of the desert places where he hungered; of his cry for help—think, Mary—*His!*—when there was not one in all the world to hear it, and there was silence in heaven, while angels strengthened him and man forsook him. Perhaps his voice —the very voice which has sounded whispering through our troubled life—"Could ye not watch one

---

98 German for "God with you."

hour?"[99]—shall unfold its perplexed meanings; shall make its rough places plain; shall show us step by step the merciful way by which he led us to that hour; shall point out to us, joy by joy, the surprises that he has been planning for us, just as the old father in the story planned to surprise his wayward boy come home.

"And such a 'communion,'—which is not too much, nor yet enough, to dare to expect of a God who was the 'friend' of Abraham, who 'walked' with Enoch, who did not call fishermen his servants,—*such* will be that 'presence of God,' that 'adoration,' on which we have looked from afar off with despairing eyes that wept, they were so dazzled, and turned themselves away as from the thing they greatly feared."

I think we neither of us cared to talk for a while after this. Something made me forget even that I was going to see Roy in heaven. "Three-and-thirty years. Three-and-thirty years." The words rang themselves over.

"It is on the humanity of Christ," she said after some musing, "that all my other reasons for hoping for such a heaven as I hope for, rest for foundation. He knows exactly what we are, for he has been one of us; exactly what we hope and fear and crave, for he has hoped and feared and craved, not the less humanly, but only more intensely.

"'*If* it were not so,'—do you take in the thoughtful tenderness of that? A mother, stilling her frightened child in the dark, might speak just so,—*if it were not so, I would have told you*'[100] That brooding love makes room for all that we can want. He has sounded every deep of a troubled and tempted life. Who so sure as he to understand how to prepare a place where troubled and tempted lives may grow serene? Further than this; since he stands as our great Type, no less in death and after than before it, he answers for us many of these lesser questions on the event of which so much of our happiness depends.

"Shall we lose our personality in a vague ocean of ether,—you one puff of gas, I another? —

"He, with his own wounded body, rose and ate and walked and talked.

"Is all memory of this life to be swept away? —

"He, arisen, has forgotten nothing. He waits to meet his disciples at the old, familiar places; as naturally as if he had never been parted from them, he falls in with the current of their thoughts.

"Has any one troubled us with fears that in the glorified crowds of heaven we may miss a face dearer than all the world to us? —

"He made himself known to his friends,—Mary, and the two at Emmaus, and the bewildered group praying and perplexed in their bolted room.

"Do we weary ourselves with speculations whether human loves can outlive the shock of death? —

"Mary knew how He loved her, when, turning, she heard him call her by her name. They knew, whose hearts 'burned within them while he talked with them by the way, and when he tarried with them, the day being far spent.'"

"And for the rest?"

"For the rest, about which He was silent, we can trust him, and if, trusting, we please ourselves with fancies, he would be the last to think it blame to us. There is one promise which grows upon me the more I study it, 'He that spared not his own Son, how shall he not also *with him freely give us all things.*'[101] Sometimes I wonder if that does not infold a beautiful

99 Matthew 26:40.
100 John 14:2.
101 Romans 8:32.

double entendre, a hint of much that you and I have conjectured,— as one throws down a hint of a surprise to a child.

"Then there is that pledge to those who seek first His kingdom: '*All these things shall be added unto you.*'[102] 'These things,' were food and clothing, were varieties of material delight, and the words were spoken to men who lived hungry, beggared, and died the death of outcasts. If this passage could be taken literally, it would be very significant in its bearing on the future life; for Christ must keep his promise to the letter, in one world or another. It may be wrenching the verse, not as a verse, but from the grain of the argument, to insist on the literal interpretation,—though I am not sure."

XIV

August 15.

I ASKED the other day, wondering whether all ministers were like Dr. Bland, what Uncle Forceythe used to believe about heaven.

"Very much what I do," she said. "These questions were brought home to him, early in life, by the death of a very dear sister; he had thought much about them. I think one of the things that so much attached his people to him was the way he had of weaving their future life in with this, till it grew naturally and pleasantly into their frequent thought. O yes, your uncle supplied me with half of my proof-texts."

Aunt Winifred has not looked quite well of late, I fancy; though it may be only fancy. She has not spoken of it, except one day when I told her that she looked pale. It was the heat, she said.

20th.

Little Clo came over to-night. I believe she thinks Aunt Winifred the best friend she has in the world. Auntie has become much attached to all her scholars, and has a rare power of winning her way into their confidence. They come to her with all their little interests,—everything, from saving their souls to trimming a bonnet. Clo, however, is the favorite, as I predicted.

She looked a bit blue to-night, as girls will look; in fact, her face always has a tinge of sadness about it. Aunt Winifred, understanding at a glance that the child was not in a mood to talk before a third, led her away into the garden, and they were gone a long time. When it grew dark, I saw them coming up the path, Clo's hand locked in her teacher's, and her face, which was wet, upturned like a child's. They strolled to the gate, lingered a little to talk, and then Clo said good night without coming in.

Auntie sat for a while after she had gone, thinking her over, I could see.

"Poor thing!" she said at last, half to herself, half to me,—"poor little foolish thing! This is where the dreadful individuality of a human soul irks me. There comes a point, beyond which you *can't* help people."

"What has happened to Clo?"

"Nothing, lately. It has been happening for two years. Two miserable years are an eternity, at Clo's age. It is the old story,—a summer boarder; a little flirting; a little dreaming; a little pain; then autumn, and the nuts dropping on the leaves, and he was gone,—and knew not what he did,—and the child waked up. There was the future; to bake and sweep, to go to sewing-circles, and sing in the choir, and bear the moonlight nights,—and she loved him.

---

102 Matthew 6:33.

She has lived through two years of it, and she loves him now. Reason will not reach such a passion in a girl like Clo. I did not tell her that she would put it away with other girlish things, and laugh at it herself some happy day, as women have laughed at their young fancies before her; partly because that would be a certain way of repelling her confidence,—she does not believe it, and my believing could not make her; partly because I am not quite sure about it myself. Clo has a good deal of the woman about her; her introspective life is intense. She may cherish this sweet misery as she does her musical tastes, till it has struck deep root. There is nothing in the excellent Mrs. Bentley's household, nor in Homer anywhere, to draw the girl out from herself in time to prevent the dream from becoming a reality."

"Poor little thing! What did you say to her?"

"You ought to have heard what she said to me! I wish I were at liberty to tell you the whole story. What troubles her most is that it is not going to help the matter any to die. 'O Mrs. Forceythe,' she says, in a tone that is enough to give the heart-ache, even to such an old woman as Mrs. Forceythe, 'O Mrs. Forceythe, what is going to become of me up there? He never loved me, you see, and he never, never will, and he will have some beautiful, good wife of his own, and I won't have *any*body! For I can't love anybody else,—I've tried; I tried just as hard as I could to love my cousin 'Bin; he's real good, and—I'm—afraid 'Bin likes me, though I guess he likes his carpet-sweepers better. O, sometimes I think, and think, till it seems as if I could not bear it! I don't see how God can *make* me happy. I wish I could be buried up and go to sleep, and never have any heaven!' "

"And you told her—?"

"That she should have him there. That is, if not himself, something,—somebody who would so much more than fill his place, that she would never have a lonely or unloved minute. Her eyes brightened, and shaded, and pondered, doubting. She 'didn't see how it could ever be.' I told her not to try and see how, but to leave it to Christ. He knew all about this little trouble of hers, and he would make it right.

" 'Will he?' she questioned, sighing; 'but there are so many of us! There's 'Bin, and a plenty more, and I don't see how it's going to be smoothed out. Everything is in a jumble, Mrs. Forceythe, don't you see? for some people *can't* like and keep liking so many times.' Something came into my mind about the rough places that shall be made plain, and the crooked things straight. I tried to explain to her, and at last I kissed away her tears, and sent her home, if not exactly comforted, a little less miserable, I think, than when she came. Ah, well,—I wonder myself sometimes about these 'crooked things'; but, though I wonder, I never doubt."

She finished her sentence somewhat hurriedly, and half started from her chair, raising both hands with a quick, involuntary motion that attracted my notice. The lights came in just then, and, unless I am much mistaken, her face showed paler than usual; but when I asked her if she felt faint, she said, 'O no, I believe I am a little tired, and will go to bed."

September 1.

I am glad that the summer is over. This heat has certainly worn on Aunt Winifred, with that kind of wear which slides people into confirmed invalidism. I suppose she would bear it in her saintly way, as she bears everything, but it would be a bitter cup for her. I know she was always pale, but this is a paleness which —

Night.

A dreadful thing has happened!

I was in the middle of my sentence, when I heard a commotion in the street, and a child's voice shouting incoherently something about the doctor, and *"mother's killed! O, mother's killed! mother's burnt to death!"* I was at the window in time to see a blond-haired girl running wildly past the house, and to see that it was Molly Bland.

At the same moment I saw Aunt Winifred snatching her hat from its nail in the entry. She beckoned to me to follow, and we were half-way over to the parsonage before I had a distinct thought of what I was about.

We came upon a horrible scene. Dr. Bland was trying to do everything alone; there was not a woman in the house to help him, for they have never been able to keep a servant, and none of the neighbors had had time to be there before us. The poor husband was growing faint, I think. Aunt Winifred saw by a look that he could not bear much more, sent him after Molly for the doctor, and took everything meantime into her own charge.

I shall not write down a word of it. It was a sight that, once seen, will never leave me as long as I live. My nerves are thoroughly shaken by it, and it must be put out of thought as far as possible.

It seems that the little boy—the baby—crept into the kitchen by himself, and began to throw the contents of the match-box on the stove, "to make a bonfire," the poor little fellow said. In five minutes his apron was ablaze. His mother was on the spot at his first cry, and smothered the little apron, and saved the child, but her dress was muslin, and everybody was too far off to hear her at first,—and by the time her husband came in from the garden it was too late.

She is living yet. Her husband, pacing the room back and forth, and crouching on his knees by the hour, is praying God to let her die before the morning.

Morning.

There is no chance of life, the doctor says. But he has been able to find something that has lessened her sufferings. She lies partially unconscious.

Wednesday night.

Aunt Winifred and I were over to the parsonage to-night, when she roused a little from her stupor and recognized us. She spoke to her husband, and kissed me good by, and asked for the children. They were playing softly in the next room; we sent for them, and they came in,—the four unconscious, motherless little things,—with the sunlight in their hair.

The bitterness of death came into her marred face at sight of them, and she raised her hands to Auntie—to the only other mother there —with a sudden helpless cry: "I could bear it, I could bear it, if it weren't for *them*. Without any mother all their lives,—such little things,—and to go away where I can't do a single *thing* for them!"

Aunt Winifred stooped down and spoke low, but decidedly.

"You *will* do for them. God knows all about it. He will not send you away from them. You shall be just as much their mother, every day of their lives, as you have been here. Perhaps there is something to do for them which you never could have done here. He sees. He loves them. He loves you."

If I could paint, I might paint the look that struck through and through that woman's dying face; but words cannot touch it. If I were Aunt Winifred, I should bless God on my knees to-night for having shown me how to give such ease to a soul in death.

Thursday morning.

God is merciful. Mrs. Bland died at five o'clock.

10th.

How such a voice from the heavens shocks one out of the repose of calm sorrows and of calm joys. This has come and gone so suddenly that I cannot adjust it to any quiet and trustful thinking yet.

The whole parish mourns excitedly; for, though they worked their minister's wife hard, they loved her well. I cannot talk it over with the rest. It jars. Horror should never be dissected. Besides, my heart is too full of those four little children with the sunlight in their hair and the unconsciousness in their eyes.

15th.

Mrs. Quirk came over to-day in great perplexity. She had just come from the minister's. "I don't know what we're a goin' to do with him!" she exclaimed in a gush of impatient, uncomprehending sympathy; "you can't let a man take on that way much longer. He'll worry himself sick, and then we shall either lose him or have to pay his bills to Europe! Why, he jest stops in the house, and walks his study up and down, day and night; or else he jest sets and sets and don't notice nobody but the children. Now I've jest ben over makin' him some chicken-pie,— he used to set a sight by my chicken-pie,—and he made believe to eat it, 'cause I'd ben at the trouble, I suppose, but how much do you suppose he swallowed? Jest three mouthfuls! Thinks says I, I won't spend my time over chicken-pie for the afflicted agin, and on ironing-day, too! When I knocked at the study door, he said 'Come in,' and stopped his walkin' and turned as quick.

"'O,' says he, 'good morning. I thought it was Mrs. Forceythe.'

"I told him no, I wasn't Mrs. Forceythe, but I'd come to comfort him in his sorrer all the same. But that's the only thing I have agin our minister. He won't *be* comforted. Mary Ann Jacobs, who's been there kind of looking after the children and things for him, you know, sence the funeral—she says he's asked three or four times for you, Mrs. Forceythe. There's ben plenty of his people in to see him, but you haven't ben nigh him, Mary Ann says."

"I stayed away because I thought the presence of friends at this time would be an intrusion," Auntie said; "but if he would like to see me, that alters the case. I will go, certainly."

"I don't know," suggested Mrs. Quirk, looking over the top of her spectacles,—"I s'pose it's proper enough, but you bein' a widow, you know, and his wife—"

Aunt Winifred's eyes shot fire. She stood up and turned upon Mrs. Quirk with a look the like of which I presume that worthy lady had never seen before, and is not likely to see soon again (it gave the beautiful scorn of a Zenobia[103] to her fair, slight face), moved her lips slightly, but said nothing, put on her bonnet, and went straight to Dr. Bland's.

The minister, they told her, was in his study. She knocked lightly at the door, and was bidden in a lifeless voice to enter.

Shades and blinds were drawn, and the glare of the sun quite shut out. Dr. Bland sat by his study-table, with his face upon his hands. A Bible lay open before him. It had been lately used; the leaves were wet.

He raised his head dejectedly, but smiled when he saw who it was. He had been thinking about her, he said, and was glad that she had come.

I do not know all that passed between them, but I gather, from such hints as Auntie in her unconsciousness throws out, that she had things to say which touched some comfortless places in the man's heart. No Greek and Hebrew "original," no polished dogma, no link in his stereotyped logic, not one of his eloquent sermons on the future state, came to his relief.

These were meant for happy days. They rang cold as steel upon the warm needs of an afflicted man. Brought face to face, and sharply, with the blank heaven of his belief, he

---

103 Zenobia (240–275) was a famous Syrian queen who led a revolt against the Roman Empire.

stood up from before his dead, and groped about it, and cried out against it in the bitterness of his soul.

"I had no chance to prepare myself to bow to the will of God," he said, his reserved ministerial manner in curious contrast with the caged way in which he was pacing the room,—"I had no chance. I am taken by surprise, as by a thief in the night. I had a great deal to say to her, and there was no time. She could tell me what to do with my poor little children. I wanted to tell her other things. I wanted to tell her—Perhaps we all of us have our regrets when the Lord removes our friends; we may have done or left undone many things; we might have made them happier. My mind does not rest with assurance in its conceptions of the heavenly state. If I never can tell her—"

He stopped abruptly, and paced into the darkest shadows of the shadowed room, his face turned away.

"You said once some pleasant things about heaven?" he said at last, half appealingly, stopping in front of her, hesitating; like a man and like a minister, hardly ready to come with all the learning of his schools and commentators and sit at the feet of a woman.

She talked with him for a time in her unobtrusive way, deferring, when she honestly could, to his clerical judgment, and careful not to wound him by any word; but frankly and clearly, as she always talks.

When she rose to go he thanked her quietly.

"This is a somewhat novel train of thought to me," he said; "I hope it may not prove an unscriptural one. I have been reading the Book of Revelation to-day with these questions especially in mind. We are never too old to learn. Some passages may be capable of other interpretations than I have formerly given them. No matter what I *wish*, you see, I must be guided by the Word of my God."

Auntie says that she never respected the man so much as she did when, hearing those words, she looked up into his haggard face, convulsed with its human pain and longing.

"I hope you do not think that *I* am not guided by the Word of God," she answered. "I mean to be."

"I know you mean to be," he said cordially. "I do not say that you are not. I may come to see that you are, and that you are right. It will be a peaceful day for me if I can ever quite agree with your methods of reasoning. But I must think these things over. I thank you once more for coming. Your sympathy is grateful to me."

Just as she closed the door he called her back.

"See," he said, with a saddened smile. "At least I shall never preach *this* again. It seems to me that life is always undoing for us something that we have just laboriously done."

He held up before her a mass of old blue manuscript, and threw it, as he spoke, upon the embers left in his grate. It smoked and blazed up and burned out.

It was that sermon on heaven of which there is an abstract in this journal.

20th.

Aunt Winifred hired Mr. Tripp's gray this afternoon, and drove to East Homer on some unexplained errand. She did not invite me to go with her, and Faith, though she teased impressively, was left at home. Her mother was gone till late,—so late that I had begun to be anxious about her, and heard through the dark the first sound of the buggy wheels, with great relief. She looked very tired when I met her at the gate. She had not been able, she said, to accomplish her errand at East Homer, and from there had gone to Worcester by railroad, leaving Old Gray at the East Homer Eagle till her return. She told me nothing more, and I asked no questions.

XV

Sunday.

FAITH has behaved like a witch all day. She knocked down three crickets and six hymn-books in church this morning, and this afternoon horrified the assembled and devout congregation by turning round in the middle of the long prayer, and, in a loud and distinct voice, asking Mrs. Quirk, for "'nother those pepp'mints such as you gave me one Sunday a good many years ago, you 'member." After church, her mother tried a few Bible questions to keep her still.

"Faith, who was Christ's father?"

"Jerusalem!" said Faith, promptly.

"Where did his parents take Jesus when they fled from Herod?"

"O, to Europe. Of course I knew that! Everybody goes to Europe."

To-night, when her mother had put her to bed, she came down laughing.

"Faith does seem to have a hard time with the Lord's Prayer. To-night, being very sleepy and in a hurry to finish, she proceeded with great solemnity:—'Our Father who art in heaven, hallowed be thy name; six days shalt thou labor and do all thy work, and—Oh!'

"I was just thinking how amused her father must be."

Auntie says many such things. I cannot explain how pleasantly they strike me, nor how they help me.

29th.

Dr. Bland gave us a good sermon yesterday. There is an indescribable change in all his sermons. There is a change, too, in the man, and that something more than the haggardness of grief. I not only respect him and am sorry for him, but I feel more ready to be taught by him than ever before. A certain indefinable *humanness* softens his eyes and tones, and seems to be creeping into everything that he says. Yet, on the other hand, his people say that they have never heard him speak such pleasant, helpful things concerning his and their relations to God. I met him the other night, coming away from his wife's grave, and was struck by the expression of his face. I wondered if he were not slowly finding the "peaceful day," of which he told Aunt Winifred.

She, by the way, has taken another of her mysterious trips to Worcester.

30th.

We were wondering to-day where it will be,—I mean heaven.

"It is impossible to do more than wonder," Auntie said, "though we are explicitly told that there will be new heavens *and* a new earth,[104] which seems, if anything can be taken literally in the Bible, to point to this world as the future home of at least some of us."

"Not for all of us, of course?"

"I don't feel sure. I know that somebody spent his valuable time in estimating that all the people who have lived and died upon the earth would cover it, alive or buried, twice over; but I know that somebody else claims with equal solemnity to have discovered that they could all be buried in the State of Pennsylvania! But it would be of little consequence if we could not all find room here, since there must be other provision for us."

"Why?"

"Certainly there is 'a place' in which we are promised that we shall be 'with Christ,' this world being yet the great theatre of human life and battle-ground of Satan; no place,

---

104 Isaiah 65:17.

certainly, in which to confine a happy soul without prospect of release. The Spiritualistic notion of 'circles' of dead friends revolving over us is to me intolerable. I want my husband with me when I need him, but I hope he has a place to be happy in, which is out of this woful world.

"The old astronomical idea, stars around a sun, and systems around a centre, and that centre the Throne of God, is not an unreasonable one. Isaac Taylor, among his various conjectures, inclines, I fancy, to suppose that the sun of each system is the heaven of that system. Though the glory of God may be more directly and impressively exhibited in one place than in another, we may live in different planets, and some of us, after its destruction and renovation, on this same dear old, happy and miserable, loved and maltreated earth. I hope I shall be one of them. I should like to come back and build me a beautiful home in Kansas,—I mean in what was Kansas,—among the happy people and the familiar, transfigured spots where John and I worked for God so long together. That—with my dear Lord to see and speak with every day—would be 'Heaven our Home.'"

"There will be no *days*, then?"

"There will be succession of time. There may not be alternations of twenty-four hours dark or light, but 'I use with thee an earthly language,' as the wife said in that beautiful little 'Awakening,' of Therrmin's. Do you remember it? Do read it over, if you haven't read it lately.

"As to our coming back here, there is an echo to Peter's assertion, in the idea of a world under a curse, destroyed and regenerated,—the atonement of Christ reaching, with something more than poetic force, the very sands of the earth which he trod with bleeding feet to make himself its Saviour. That makes me feel—don't you see?—what a taint there is in sin. If dumb dust is to have such awful cleansing, what must be needed for you and me?

"How many pleasant talks we have had about these things, Mary! Well, it cannot be long, at the longest, before we know, even as we are known."

I looked at her smiling white face,—it is always very white now,—and something struck slowly through me, like a chill.

October 16, midnight.

There is no such thing as sleep at present. Writing is better than thinking.

Aunt Winifred went again to Worcester to-day. She said that she had to buy trimming for Faith's sack.

She went alone, as usual, and Faith and I kept each other company through the afternoon,—she on the floor with Mary Ann, I in the easy-chair with Macaulay. As the light began to fall level on the floor, I threw the book aside,—being at the end of a volume,—and, Mary Ann having exhausted her attractions, I surrendered unconditionally to the little maiden.

She took me up garret, and down cellar, on top of the wood-pile, and into the apple-trees; I fathomed the mysteries of Old Man's Castle and Still Palm; I was her grandmother, I was her baby, I was a rabbit, I was a chestnut horse, I was a watch-dog, I was a mild-tempered giant, I was a bear "warranted not to eat little girls," I was a roaring hippopotamus and a canary-bird, I was Jeff Davis[105] and I was Moses in the bulrushes, and of what I was, the time faileth me to tell.

It comes over me with a curious, mingled sense of the ludicrous and the horrible, that I should have spent the afternoon like a baby and almost as happily, laughing out with the

---

105 Jefferson Davis (1808–1889) was the president of the Confederate States of America during the Civil War.

child, past and future forgotten, the tremendous risks of "I spy" absorbing all my present; while what was happening was happening, and what was to come was coming. Not an echo in the air, not a prophecy in the sunshine, not a note of warning in the song of the robins that watched me from the apple-boughs!

As the long, golden afternoon slid away, we came out by the front gate to watch for the child's mother. I was tired, and, lying back on the grass, gave Faith some pink and purple larkspurs, that she might amuse herself in making a chain of them. The picture that she made sitting there on the short, dying grass—the light which broke all about her and over her at the first, creeping slowly down and away to the west, her little fingers linking the rich, bright flowers tube into tube, the dimple on her cheek and the love in her eyes—has photographed itself into my thinking.

How her voice rang out, when the wheels sounded at last, and the carriage, somewhat slowly driven, stopped!

"Mamma, mamma! see what I've got for you, mamma!"

Auntie tried to step from the carriage, and called me: "Mary, can you help me a little? I am—tired."

I went to her, and she leaned heavily on my arm, and we came up the path.

"Such a pretty little chain, all for you, mamma," began Faith, and stopped, struck by her mother's look.

"It has been a long ride, and I am in pain. I believe I will lie right down on the parlor sofa. Mary, would you be kind enough to give Faith her supper and put her to bed?"

Faith's lip grieved.

"Cousin Mary isn't *you*, mamma. I want to be kissed. You haven't kissed me."

Her mother hesitated for a moment; then kissed her once, twice; put both arms about her neck; and turned her face to the wall without a word.

"Mamma is tired, dear," I said; "come away."

She was lying quite still when I had done what was to be done for the child, and had come back. The room was nearly dark. I sat down on my cricket by her sofa.

"Shall Phœbe light the lamp?"

"Not just yet."

"Can't you drink a cup of tea if I bring it? "

"Not just yet."

"Did you find the sack-trimming?" I ventured, after a pause.

I believe so,—yes."

She drew a little package from her pocket, held it a moment, then let it roll to the floor forgotten. When I picked it up, the soft, tissue-paper wrapper was wet and hot with tears.

"Mary?"

"Yes."

"I never thought of the little trimming till the last minute. I had another errand."

I waited.

"I thought at first I would not tell you just yet. But I suppose the time has come; it will be no more easy to put it off. I have been to Worcester all these times to see a doctor."

I bent my head in the dark, and listened for the rest.

"He has his reputation; they said he could help me if anybody could. He thought at first he could. But to-day—Mary, see here."

She walked feebly towards the window, where a faint, gray light struggled in, and opened the bosom of her dress … .

There was silence between us for a long while after that; she went back to the sofa, and I took her hand and bowed my face over it, and so we sat.

The leaves rustled out of doors. Faith, up stairs, was singing herself to sleep with a droning sound.

"He talked of risking an operation," she said, at length, "but decided to-day that it was quite useless. I suppose I must give up and be sick now; I am feeling the reaction from having kept up so long. He thinks I shall not suffer a very great deal. He thinks he can relieve me, and that it may be soon over."

"There is no chance?"

"No chance."

I took both of her hands, and cried out, I believe, as I did that first night when she spoke to me of Roy, "Auntie, Auntie, Auntie!" and tried to think what I was doing, but only cried out the more.

"Why, Mary!" she said,—"why, Mary!" and again, as before, she passed her soft hand to and fro across my hair, till by and by I began to think, as I had thought before, that I could bear anything which God who loved us all—who *surely* loved us all— should send.

So then, after I had grown still, she began to tell me about it in her quiet voice, and the leaves rustled, and Faith had sung herself to sleep, and I listened wondering. For there was no pain in the quiet voice,—no pain, nor tone of fear. Indeed, it seemed to me that I detected, through its subdued sadness, a secret, suppressed buoyancy of satisfaction, with which something struggled.

"And you?" I asked, turning quickly upon her.

"I should thank God with all my heart, Mary, if it were not for Faith and you. But it *is* for Faith and you. That's all."

When I had locked the front door, and was creeping up here to my room, my foot crushed something, and a faint, wounded perfume came up. It was the little pink and purple chain.

XIV

October 17.

"THE Lord God a'mighty help us! but His ways are past finding out. What with one thing and another thing, that child without a mother, and you with the crape not yet rusty for Mr. Roy'l, it doos seem to me as if His manner of treating folks beats all! But I tell you this, Miss Mary, my dear; you jest say your prayers reg'lar and *stick to Him*, and He'll pull you through, sure!"

This was what Phœbe said when I told her.

November 8.

To-night, for the first time, Auntie fairly gave up trying to put Faith to bed. She had insisted on it until now, crawling up by the banisters like a wounded thing. This time she tottered and sank upon the second step. She cried out, feebly: "I am afraid I must give it up to

Cousin Mary. Faith!"—the child clung with both hands to her—"Faith, Faith! Mother's little girl?"

It was the last dear care of motherhood yielded; the last link snapped. It seemed to be the very bitterness of parting.

I turned away, that they might bear it together, they two alone.

19th.

Yet I think that took away the sting.

The days are slipping away now very quietly, and—to her I am sure, and to me for her sake—very happily.

She suffers less than I had feared, and she lies upon the bed and smiles, and Faith comes in and plays about, and the cheery morning sunshine falls on everything, and when her strong hours come, we have long talks together, hand clasped in hand.

Such pleasant talks! We are quite brave to speak of anything, since we know that what is to be is best just so, and since we fear no parting. I tell her that Faith and I will soon learn to shut our eyes and think we see her, and try to make it *almost* the same, for she will never be very far away, will she? And then she shakes her head smiling, for it pleases her, and she kisses me softly. Then we dream of how it will all be, and how we shall love and try to please each other quite as much as now.

"It will be like going around a corner, don't you see?" she says. "You will know that I am there all the while, though hidden, and that if you call me I shall hear." Then we talk of Faith, and of how I shall comfort her; that I shall teach her this, and guard her from that, and how I shall talk with her about heaven and her mother. Sometimes Faith comes up and wants to know what we are saying, and lays poor Mary Ann, sawdust and all, upon the pillow, and wants "her toof-ache kissed away." So Auntie kisses away the dolly's "toof-ache"; and kisses the dolly's little mother, sometimes with a quiver on her lips, but more often with a smile in her eyes, and Faith runs back to play, and her laugh ripples out, and her mother listens—listens —

Sometimes, too, we talk of some of the people for whom she cares; of her husband's friends; of her scholars, or Dr. Bland, or Clo, or poor 'Bin Quirk, or of somebody down town whom she was planning to help this winter. Little Clo comes in as often as she is strong enough to see her, and sends over untold jellies and blanc-manges, which Faith and I have to eat. "But don't let the child know that," Auntie says.

But more often we talk of the life which she is so soon to begin; of her husband and Roy; of what she will try to say to Christ; how much dearer He has grown to her since she has lain here in pain at His bidding, and how He helps her, at morning and at eventide and in the night-watches.

We talk of the trees and the mountains and the lilies in the garden, on which the glory of the light that is not the light of the sun may shine; of the "little brooks" by which she longs to sit and sing to Faith; of the treasures of art which she may fancy to have about her; of the home in which her husband may be making ready for her coming, and wonder what he has there, and if he knows how near the time is now.

But I notice lately that she more often and more quickly wearies of these things; that she comes back, and comes back again to some loving thought—as loving as a child's—of Jesus Christ. He seems to be—as she once said she tried that He should be to Faith—her "*best* friend."

Sometimes, too, we wonder what it means to pass out of the body, and what one will be first conscious of.

"I used to have a very human, and by no means slight, dread of the physical pain of death," she said to-day; "but, for some reason or other, that is slowly leaving me. I imagine that the suffering of any fatal sickness is worse than the immediate process of dissolution. Then there is so much beyond it to occupy one's thoughts. One thing I have thought much about; it is that, whatever may be our first experience after leaving the body, it is not likely to be a *revolutionary* one. It is more in analogy with God's dealings that a quiet process, a gentle accustoming, should open our eyes on the light that would blind if it came in a flash. Perhaps we shall not see Him,—perhaps we could not bear it to see Him at once. It may be that the faces of familiar human friends will be the first to greet us; it may be that the touch of the human hand dearer than any but His own shall lead us, as we are able, behind the veil, till we are a little used to the glory and the wonder, and lead us so to Him.

"Be that as it may, and be heaven where it may, I am not afraid. With all my guessing and my studying and my dreaming over these things, I am only a child in the dark. 'Nevertheless, I am not afraid of the dark.' God bless Mr. Robertson for saying that! I'm going to bless him when I see him. How pleasant it will be to see him, and some other friends whose faces I never saw in this world. David, for instance, or Paul, or Cowper, or President Lincoln, or Mrs. Browning. The only trouble is that *I* am nobody to them! However, I fancy that they will let me shake hands with them.

"No, I am quite willing to trust all these things to God.

'And what if much be still unknown?
　　Thy Lord shall teach thee that,
When thou shalt stand before His throne,
　　Or sit as Mary sat.'

I may find them very different from what I have supposed. I know that I shall find them infinitely *more* satisfying than I have supposed. As Schiller[106] said of his philosophy, 'Perhaps I may be ashamed of my raw design, at sight of the true original. This may happen; I expect it; but then, if reality bears no resemblance to my dreams, it will be a more majestic, a more delightful surprise.'

"I believe nothing that God denies. I cannot overrate the beauty of his promise. So it surely can have done no harm for me to take the comfort of my fancying till I am there; and what a comfort it has been to me, God only knows. I could scarcely have borne some things without it."

"You are never afraid that anything proving a little different from what you expect might—"

"Might disappoint me? No; I have settled that in my heart with God. I do not *think* I shall be disappointed. The truth is, he has obviously not *opened* the gates which bar heaven from our sight, but he has as obviously not *shut* them; they stand ajar, with the Bible and reason in the way, to keep them from closing; surely we should look in as far as we can, and surely, if we look with reverence, our eyes will be holden, that we may not cheat ourselves

---

106 Johann Christoph Friedrich von Schiller (1759–1805) was a famous German philosopher, playwright and poet. The quote is from Schiller's essay, "God," in his collection *The Philosophical Letters*, which was available to American readers through a Boston publisher as early as 1845.

with mirages. And, as the little Swedish girl said, the first time she saw the stars: 'O father, if the *wrong side* of heaven is so beautiful, what must the *right side* be?'"

January.

I write little now, for I am living too much. The days are stealing away and lessening one by one, and still Faith plays about the room, though very softly now, and still the cheery sunshine shimmers in, and still we talk with clasping hands, less often and more pleasantly. Morning and noon and evening come and go; the snow drifts down and the rain falls softly; clouds form and break and hurry past the windows; shadows melt and lights are shattered, and little rainbows are prisoned by the icicles that hang from the eaves.

I sit and watch them, and watch the sick-lamp flicker in the night, and watch the blue morning crawl over the hills; and the old words are stealing down my thought: *That is the substance, this the shadow; that the reality, this the dream.*

I watch her face upon the pillow; the happy secret on its lips; the smile within its eyes. It is nearly a year now since God sent the face to me. What it has done for me He knows; what the next year and all the years are to be without it. He knows, too.

It is slipping away,—slipping. And I—must—lose it.

Perhaps I should not have said what I said to-night; but being weak from watching, and seeing how glad she was to go, seeing how all the peace was for her, all the pain for us, I cried, "O Auntie, Auntie, why can't we go too? Why *can't* Faith and I go with you?"

But she answered me only, "Mary, He knows."

We will be brave again to-morrow. A little more sunshine in the room! A little more of Faith and the dolly!

The Sabbath.

She asked for the child at bedtime to-night, and I laid her down in her night-dress on her mother's arm. She kissed her, and said her prayers, and talked a bit about Mary Ann, and to-morrow, and her snow man. I sat over by the window in the dusk, and watched a little creamy cloud that was folding in the moon. Presently their voices grew low, and at last Faith's stopped altogether. Then I heard in fragments this: —

"Sleepy, dear? But you won't have many more talks with mamma. Keep awake just a minute, Faith, and hear—can you hear? Mamma will never, *never* forget her little girl; she won't go away very far; she will always love you. Will you remember as long as you live? She will always see you, though you can't see her, perhaps. Hush, my darling, *don't* cry! Isn't God naughty? No, God is good; God is always good. He won't take mamma a great way off. One more kiss? There! now you may go to sleep. One more! Come, Cousin Mary."

June 6.

It is a long time since I have written here. I did not want to open the book till I was sure that I could open it quietly, and could speak as she would like to have me speak, of what remains to be written.

But a very few words will tell it all.

It happened so naturally and so happily, she was so glad when the time came, and she made me so glad for her sake, that I cannot grieve. I say it from my honest heart, I cannot grieve. In the place out of which she has gone, she has left me peace. I think of something that Miss Procter said about the opening of that golden gate,[107]

---

107 The quotation is from "The Golden Gate," a poem by Adelaide Procter (1825–1864), published in her poetry collection *Legends and Lyrics* (1858).

"round which the kneeling spirits wait.
The halo seems to linger round those kneeling closest to the door:
The joy that lightened from that place shines still upon the watcher's face."
I think more often of some things that she herself said in the very last of those pleasant talks, when, turning a leaf in her little Bible, she pointed out to me the words: —
"It is expedient for you that I go away; for, if I go not away, the Comforter will not come."[108]
It was one spring-like night,—the twenty-ninth of March.
She had been in less pain, and had chatted and laughed more with us than for many a day. She begged that Faith might stay till dark, and might bring her Noah's ark and play down upon the foot of the bed where she could see her. I sat in the rocking-chair with my face to the window. We did not light the lamps.
The night came on slowly. Showery clouds flitted by, but there was a blaze of golden color behind them. It broke through and scattered them; it burned them and melted them; it shot great pink and purple jets up to the zenith; it fell and lay in amber mist upon the hills. A soft wind swept by, and darted now and then into the glow, and shifted it about, color away from color, and back again.
"See, Faith!" she said softly; "put down the little camel a minute, and look!" and added after, but neither to the child nor to me, it seemed: "At eventide there shall be light." Phœbe knocked presently, and I went out to see what was wanted, and planned a little for Auntie's breakfast, and came back.
Faith, with her little ark, was still playing quietly upon the bed. I sat down again in my rocking-chair with my face to the window. Now and then the child's voice broke the silence, asking Where should she put the elephant, and was there room there for the yellow bird? and now and then her mother answered her, and so presently the skies had faded, and so the night came on.
I was thinking that it was Faith's bedtime, and that I had better light the lamp, when a few distinct, hurried words from the bed attracted my attention.
"Faith, I think you had better kiss mamma now, and get down."
There was a change in the voice. I was there in a moment, and lifted the child from the pillow, where she had crept. But she said, "Wait a minute, Mary; wait a minute,"—for Faith clung to her, with one hand upon her cheek, softly patting it.
I went over and stood by the window.
It was her mother herself who gently put the little fingers away at last.
"Mother's own little girl! Good night, my darling, my darling."
So I took the child away to Phœbe, and came back, and shut the door.
"I thought you might have some message for Roy," she said.
"Now?"
"Now, I think."
We had often talked of this, and she had promised to remember it, whatever it might be. So I told her—But I will not write what I told her.
I saw that she was playing weakly with her wedding-ring, which hung very loosely below its little worn guard.
"Take the little guard," she said, "and keep it for Faith; but bury the other with me: he put it on: nobody else must take it—"

---

108 John 16:7.

The sentence dropped, unfinished.

I crept up on the bed beside her, for she seemed to wish it. I asked if I should light the lamp, but she shook her head. The room seemed light, she said, quite light. She wondered then if Faith were asleep, and if she would waken early in the morning.

After that I kissed her, and then we said nothing more, only presently she asked me to hold her hand.

It was quite dark when she turned her face at last towards the window. "John!" she said,—"why, John!"

*   *   *   *   *   *   *

They came in, with heads uncovered and voices hushed, to see her, in the days while she was lying down stairs among the flowers.

Once when I thought that she was alone, I went in,—it was at twilight,—and turned, startled by a figure that was crouched sobbing on the floor.

"O, I want to go too, I *want* to go too!" it cried.

"She's ben there all day long," said Phœbe, wiping her eyes, "and she won't go home for a mouthful of victuals, poor creetur! but she jest sets there and cries and cries, an' there's no stoppin' of her!"

It was little Clo.

At another time, I was there with fresh flowers, when the door opened, creaking a little, and 'Bin Quirk came in on tiptoe, trying in vain to still the noise of his new boots. His eyes were red and wet, and he held out to me timidly a single white carnation.

"Could you put it somewhere, where it wouldn't do any harm? I walked way over to Worcester and back to get it. If you could jest hide it under the others out of sight, seems to me it would do me a sight of good to feel it was there, you know."

I motioned to him to lay it himself between her fingers.

"O, I darsn't. I'm not fit, *I'*m not. She'd rether have you."

But I told him that I knew she would be as pleased that he should give it to her himself as she was when he gave her the China pinks on that distant summer day. So the great awkward fellow bent down, as simply as a child, as tenderly as a woman, and left the flower in its place.

"*She* liked 'em," he faltered; "maybe, if what she used to say is all so, she'll like 'em now. She liked 'em better than she did machines. I've just got my carpet-sweeper through; I was thinking how pleased she'd be; I wanted to tell her. If I should go to the good place,—if ever I do go, it will be just her doin's,—I'll tell her then, maybe, I—"

He forgot that anybody was there, and, sobbing, hid his face in his great hands.

So we are waiting for the morning when the gates shall open,—Faith and I. I from my stiller watches, am not saddened by the music of her life. I feel sure that her mother wishes it to be a cheery life. I feel sure that she is showing me, who will have no motherhood by which to show myself, how to help her little girl.

And Roy,—ah, well, and Roy,—he knows. Our hour is not yet come. If the Master will that we should be about His Father's business,[109] what is that to us?

---

109 Luke 2:49.

Chapter Sixteen

BRET HARTE
(1836–1902)

Bret Harte began his literary career early, publishing some short verse when he was 11 years old. In 1853, Harte left Brooklyn, New York, for the mining country of California. Once there, he became a newspaper writer, gaining a modest reputation as a satirist who, in a series of "condensed novels," wrote parodies of such popular and famous authors as James Fenimore Cooper, Charles Dickens, Victor Hugo and Timothy Shay Arthur. In 1868, he published "The Luck of Roaring Camp," a short story that for the first time moved his reputation beyond its local confines and set him on the road to a national recognition.

Harte's early writings gained immense popularity because they offered Americans a glimpse of Western life. Beginning with the California gold rush of 1849, hundreds of thousands of Americans began a westward movement that would colonize both the Midwest and Far West regions of the country. Harte's Western writings, with their folksy morals, realism, quirky humor and pathos found an admiring audience all across the country.

Harte's writings on the American Far West are studies on what it means to be civilized and on civilization itself. His own engagement with social causes—such as protesting a massacre of Indians (which cost him a newspaper job in Northern California), and his work with various abolitionist groups—made him keenly aware of issues of race, class and regionalism in America. His work serves as a vivid reminder that Americans lived in a country made up of humorous contrasts and violent contradictions, constantly probing not only what it meant to be an American, but a member of the human race.

THE LUCK OF ROARING CAMP

As the Procession Filed in, Comments Were Audible . . .

"As the Procession filed in, comments were audible. […]" (*The Luck of Roaring Camp and Selected Stories and Poems*, New York: The Macmillan Company, 1929).

These selections follow the text as published in the Houghton, Mifflin 1896 multivolume set: *The Writings of Bret Harte*. Boston: Houghton, Mifflin and Co., 1896, vols. 1 and 12.

There was commotion in Roaring Camp. It could not have been a fight, for in 1850 that was not novel enough to have called together the entire settlement. The ditches and claims were not only deserted, but "Tuttle's grocery" had contributed its gamblers, who, it will be remembered, calmly continued their game the day that French Pete and Kanaka Joe shot each other to death over the bar in the front room. The whole camp was collected before a rude cabin on the outer edge of the clearing. Conversation was carried on in a low tone, but the name of a woman was frequently repeated. It was a name familiar enough in the camp,—"Cherokee Sal."

Perhaps the less said of her the better. She was a coarse and, it is to be feared, a very sinful woman. But at that time she was the only woman in Roaring Camp, and was just then lying in sore extremity, when she most needed the ministration of her own sex. Dissolute, abandoned, and irreclaimable, she was yet suffering a martyrdom hard enough to bear even when veiled by sympathizing womanhood, but now terrible in her loneliness. The primal curse had come to her in that original isolation which must have made the punishment of the first transgression so dreadful. It was, perhaps, part of the expiation of her sin that, at a moment when she most lacked her sex's intuitive tenderness and care, she met only the half-contemptuous faces of her masculine associates. Yet a few of the spectators were, I think, touched by her sufferings. Sandy Tipton thought it was "rough on Sal," and, in the contemplation of her condition, for a moment rose superior to the fact that he had an ace and two bowers[1] in his sleeve.

It will be seen also that the situation was novel. Deaths were by no means uncommon in Roaring Camp, but a birth was a new thing. People had been dismissed the camp effectively, finally, and with no possibility of return; but this was the first time that anybody had been introduced *ab initio*.[2] Hence the excitement.

"You go in there, Stumpy," said a prominent citizen known as "Kentuck," addressing one of the loungers. "Go in there, and see what you kin do. You've had experience in them things."

Perhaps there was a fitness in the selection. Stumpy, in other climes, had been the putative head of two families; in fact, it was owing to some legal informality in these proceedings that Roaring Camp—a city of refuge—was indebted to his company. The crowd approved the choice, and Stumpy was wise enough to bow to the majority. The door closed on the extempore surgeon and midwife, and Roaring Camp sat down outside, smoked its pipe, and awaited the issue.

The assemblage numbered about a hundred men. One or two of these were actual fugitives from justice, some were criminal, and all were reckless. Physically they exhibited no indication of their past lives and character. The greatest scamp had a Raphael face,[3] with a profusion of blonde hair; Oakhurst, a gambler, had the melancholy air and intellectual abstraction of a Hamlet; the coolest and most courageous man was scarcely over five feet in height, with a soft voice and an embarrassed, timid manner. The term "roughs" applied to them was a distinction rather than a definition. Perhaps in the minor details of fingers, toes, ears, etc., the camp may have been deficient, but these slight omissions did not detract from their aggregate force. The strongest man had but three fingers on his right hand; the best shot had but one eye.

---

1 Trump, or winning, cards.
2 From the beginning.
3 A face of an angel.

Such was the physical aspect of the men that were dispersed around the cabin. The camp lay in a triangular valley between two hills and a river. The only outlet was a steep trail over the summit of a hill that faced the cabin, now illuminated by the rising moon. The suffering woman might have seen it from the rude bunk whereon she lay,—seen it winding like a silver thread until it was lost in the stars above.

A fire of withered pine boughs added sociability to the gathering. By degrees the natural levity of Roaring Camp returned. Bets were freely offered and taken regarding the result. Three to five that "Sal would get through with it;" even that the child would survive; side bets as to the sex and complexion of the coming stranger. In the midst of an excited discussion an exclamation came from those nearest the door, and the camp stopped to listen. Above the swaying and moaning of the pines, the swift rush of the river, and the crackling of the fire rose a sharp, querulous cry,—a cry unlike anything heard before in the camp. The pines stopped moaning, the river ceased to rush, and the fire to crackle. It seemed as if Nature had stopped to listen too.

The camp rose to its feet as one man! It was proposed to explode a barrel of gunpowder; but in consideration of the situation of the mother, better counsels prevailed, and only a few revolvers were discharged; for whether owing to the rude surgery of the camp, or some other reason, Cherokee Sal was sinking fast. Within an hour she had climbed, as it were, that rugged road that led to the stars, and so passed out of Roaring Camp, its sin and shame, forever. I do not think that the announcement disturbed them much, except in speculation as to the fate of the child. "Can he live now?" was asked of Stumpy. The answer was doubtful. The only other being of Cherokee Sal's sex and maternal condition in the settlement was an ass. There was some conjecture as to fitness, but the experiment was tried. It was less problematical than the ancient treatment of Romulus and Remus,[4] and apparently as successful.

When these details were completed, which exhausted another hour, the door was opened, and the anxious crowd of men, who had already formed themselves into a queue, entered in single file. Beside the low bunk or shelf, on which the figure of the mother was starkly outlined below the blankets, stood a pine table. On this a candle-box was placed, and within it, swathed in staring red flannel, lay the last arrival at Roaring Camp. Beside the candle-box was placed a hat. Its use was soon indicated. "Gentlemen," said Stumpy, with a singular mixture of authority and *ex officio* complacency,—"gentlemen will please pass in at the front door, round the table, and out at the back door. Them as wishes to contribute anything toward the orphan will find a hat handy." The first man entered with his hat on; he uncovered, however, as he looked about him, and so unconsciously set an example to the next. In such communities good and bad actions are catching. As the procession filed in comments were audible,—criticisms addressed perhaps rather to Stumpy in the character of showman: "Is that him?" "Mighty small specimen;" "Hasn't more'n got the color;" "Ain't bigger nor a derringer."[5] The contributions were as characteristic: A silver tobacco box; a doubloon; a navy revolver, silver mounted; a gold specimen; a very beautifully embroidered lady's handkerchief (from Oakhurst the gambler); a diamond breastpin; a diamond ring (suggested by the pin, with the remark from the giver that he "saw that pin and went two diamonds better"); a slung-shot; a Bible (contributor not detected); a golden

---

4 Romulus and Remus were the legendary founders of Rome who, as infants, were nursed by a wolf.

5 A small pistol, named for its inventor Henry Deringer (1796–1868)

spur; a silver teaspoon (the initials, I regret to say were not the giver's); a pair of surgeon's shears; a lancet; a Bank of England note for £5; and about $200 in loose gold and silver coin. During these proceedings Stumpy maintained a silence as impassive as the dead on his left, a gravity as inscrutable as that of the newly born on his right. Only one incident occurred to break the monotony of the curious procession. As Kentuck bent over the candle-box half curiously, the child turned, and, in a spasm of pain, caught at his groping finger, and held it fast for a moment. Kentuck looked foolish and embarrassed. Something like a blush tried to assert itself in his weather-beaten cheek. "The d—d little cuss!" he said, as he extricated his finger, with perhaps more tenderness and care than he might have been deemed capable of showing. He held that finger a little apart from its fellows as he went out, and examined it curiously. The examination provoked the same original remark in regard to the child. In fact, he seemed to enjoy repeating it. "He rastled with my finger," he remarked to Tipton, holding up the member, "the d—d little cuss!"

It was four o'clock before the camp sought repose. A light burnt in the cabin where the watchers sat, for Stumpy did not go to bed that night. Nor did Kentuck. He drank quite freely, and related with great gusto his experience, invariably ending with his characteristic condemnation of the newcomer. It seemed to relieve him of any unjust implication of sentiment, and Kentuck had the weaknesses of the nobler sex. When everybody else had gone to bed, he walked down to the river and whistled reflectingly. Then walked up the gulch past the cabin, still whistling with demonstrative unconcern. At a large redwood-tree he paused and retraced his steps, and again passed the cabin. Halfway down to the river's bank he again paused, and then returned and knocked at the door. It was opened by Stumpy. "How goes it?" said Kentuck, looking past Stumpy toward the candle-box. "All serene!" replied Stumpy. "Anything up?" "Nothing." There was a pause—an embarrassing one— Stumpy still holding the door. Then Kentuck had recourse to his finger, which he held up to Stumpy. "Rastled with it, —the d—d little cuss," he said, and retired.

The next day Cherokee Sal had such rude sepulture[6] as Roaring Camp afforded. After her body had been committed to the hillside, there was a formal meeting of the camp to discuss what should be done with her infant. A resolution to adopt it was unanimous and enthusiastic. But an animated discussion in regard to the manner and feasibility of providing for its wants at once sprang up. It was remarkable that the argument partook of none of those fierce personalities with which discussions were usually conducted at Roaring Camp. Tipton proposed that they should send the child to Red Dog,—a distance of forty miles,— where female attention could be procured. But the unlucky suggestion met with fierce and unanimous opposition. It was evident that no plan which entailed parting from their new acquisition would for a moment be entertained. "Besides," said Tom Ryder, "them fellows at Red Dog would swap it, and ring in somebody else on us." A disbelief in the honesty of other camps prevailed at Roaring Camp, as in other places.

The introduction of a female nurse in the camp also met with objection. It was argued that no decent woman could be prevailed to accept Roaring Camp as her home, and the speaker urged that "they didn't want any more of the other kind." This unkind allusion to the defunct mother, harsh as it may seem, was the first spasm of propriety,— the first symptom of the camp's regeneration. Stumpy advanced nothing. Perhaps he felt a certain delicacy in interfering with the selection of a possible successor in office. But when questioned, he averred stoutly that he and "Jinny"—the mammal before alluded to—could manage

---

6 Burial.

to rear the child. There was something original, independent, and heroic about the plan that pleased the camp. Stumpy was retained. Certain articles were sent for to Sacramento. "Mind," said the treasurer, as he pressed a bag of gold-dust into the expressman's hand, "the best that can be got,—lace, you know, and filigree-work and frills, —d—n the cost!"

Strange to say, the child thrived. Perhaps the invigorating climate of the mountain camp was compensation for material deficiencies. Nature took the foundling to her broader breast. In that rare atmosphere of the Sierra foothills,—that air pungent with balsamic odor, that ethereal cordial at once bracing and exhilarating,—he may have found food and nourishment, or a subtle chemistry that transmuted ass's milk to lime and phosphorus. Stumpy inclined to the belief that it was the latter and good nursing. "Me and that ass," he would say, "has been father and mother to him! Don't you," he would add, apostrophizing the helpless bundle before him, "never go back on us."

By the time he was a month old the necessity of giving him a name became apparent. He had generally been known as "The Kid," "Stumpy's Boy," "The Coyote" (an allusion to his vocal powers), and even by Kentuck's endearing diminutive of "The d—d little cuss." But these were felt to be vague and unsatisfactory, and were at last dismissed under another influence. Gamblers and adventurers are generally superstitious, and Oakhurst one day declared that the baby had brought "the luck" to Roaring Camp. It was certain that of late they had been successful. "Luck" was the name agreed upon, with the prefix of Tommy for greater convenience. No allusion was made to the mother, and the father was unknown. "It's better," said the philosophical Oakhurst, "to take a fresh deal all round. Call him Luck, and start him fair." A day was accordingly set apart for the christening. What was meant by this ceremony the reader may imagine who has already gathered some idea of the reckless irreverence of Roaring Camp. The master of ceremonies was one "Boston," a noted wag, and the occasion seemed to promise the greatest facetiousness. This ingenious satirist had spent two days in preparing a burlesque of the Church service, with pointed local allusions. The choir was properly trained, and Sandy Tipton was to stand godfather. But after the procession had marched to the grove with music and banners, and the child had been deposited before a mock altar, Stumpy stepped before the expectant crowd. "It ain't my style to spoil fun, boys," said the little man, stoutly eying the faces around him, "but it strikes me that this thing ain't exactly on the squar. It's playing it pretty low down on this yer baby to ring in fun on him that he ain't goin' to understand. And ef there's goin' to be any godfathers round, I'd like to see who's got any better rights than me." A silence followed Stumpy's speech. To the credit of all humorists be it said that the first man to acknowledge its justice was the satirist thus stopped of his fun. "But," said Stumpy, quickly following up his advantage, "we're here for a christening, and we'll have it. I proclaim you Thomas Luck, according to the laws of the United States and the State of California, so help me God." It was the first time that the name of the Deity had been otherwise uttered than profanely in the camp. The form of christening was perhaps even more ludicrous than the satirist had conceived; but strangely enough, nobody saw it and nobody laughed. "Tommy" was christened as seriously as he would have been under a Christian roof, and cried and was comforted in as orthodox fashion.

And so the work of regeneration began in Roaring Camp. Almost imperceptibly a change came over the settlement. The cabin assigned to "Tommy Luck"—or "The Luck," as he was more frequently called—first showed signs of improvement. It was kept scrupulously clean and whitewashed. Then it was boarded, clothed, and papered. The rosewood cradle, packed eighty miles by mule, had, in Stumpy's way of putting it, "sorter killed the rest of the furniture." So the rehabilitation of the cabin became a necessity. The men who were in the habit of lounging in at Stumpy's to see "how 'The Luck' got on" seemed to appreciate the change, and in self-defense the rival establishment of "Tuttle's grocery" bestirred itself and imported a carpet and mirrors. The reflections of the latter on the appearance of Roaring Camp tended to produce stricter habits of personal cleanliness. Again Stumpy imposed a kind of quarantine upon those who aspired to the honor and privilege of holding The Luck. It was a cruel mortification to Kentuck—who, in the carelessness of a large nature and the habits of frontier life, had begun to regard all garments as a second cuticle, which, like a snake's, only sloughed off through decay—to be debarred this privilege from certain prudential reasons. Yet such was the subtle influence of innovation that he thereafter appeared regularly every afternoon in a clean shirt and face still shining from his ablutions. Nor were moral and social sanitary laws neglected. "Tommy," who was supposed to spend his whole existence in a persistent attempt to repose, must not be disturbed by noise. The shouting and yelling, which had gained the camp its infelicitous title, were not permitted within hearing distance of Stumpy's. The men conversed in whispers or smoked with Indian gravity. Profanity was tacitly given up in these sacred precincts, and throughout the camp a popular form of expletive, known as "D—n the luck!" and "Curse the luck!" was abandoned, as having a new personal bearing. Vocal music was not interdicted, being supposed to have a soothing, tranquilizing quality; and one song, sung by "Man-o'-War Jack," an English sailor from her Majesty's Australian colonies, was quite popular as a lullaby. It was a lugubrious recital of the exploits of "the Arethusa, Seventy-four,"[7] in a muffled minor, ending with a prolonged dying fall at the burden of each verse, "On b-oo-o-ard of the Arethusa." It was a fine sight to see Jack holding The Luck, rocking from side to side as if with the motion of a ship, and crooning forth this naval ditty. Either through the peculiar rocking of Jack or the length of his song,—it contained ninety stanzas, and was continued with conscientious deliberation to the bitter end,—the lullaby generally had the desired effect. At such times the men would lie at full length under the trees in the soft summer twilight, smoking their pipes and drinking in the melodious utterances. An indistinct idea that this was pastoral happiness pervaded the camp. "This 'ere kind o' think," said the Cockney Simmons, meditatively reclining on his elbow, "is 'evingly." It reminded him of Greenwich.

On the long summer days The Luck was usually carried to the gulch from whence the golden store of Roaring Camp was taken. There, on a blanket spread over pine boughs, he would lie while the men were working in the ditches below. Latterly there was a rude attempt to decorate this bower with flowers and sweet-smelling shrubs, and generally some one would bring him a cluster of wild honeysuckles, azaleas, or the painted blossoms of Las Mariposas. The men had suddenly awakened to the fact that there were beauty and significance in these trifles, which they had so long trodden carelessly beneath their feet. A flake of glittering mica, a fragment of variegated quartz, a bright pebble from the bed of the creek, became beautiful to eyes thus cleared and strengthened, and were invariably put aside for The Luck. It was wonderful how many treasures the woods and hillsides yielded that "would do for Tommy." Surrounded by playthings such as never child out of fairyland had before, it is to be hoped that Tommy was content. He appeared to be serenely happy, albeit there was an infantine gravity about him, a contemplative light in his round gray eyes, that sometimes worried Stumpy. He was always tractable and quiet, and it is recorded

---

7 A large British warship with 74 guns.

that once, having crept beyond his "corral,"—a hedge of tessellated pine boughs, which surrounded his bed,—he dropped over the bank on his head in the soft earth, and remained with his mottled legs in the air in that position for at least five minutes with unflinching gravity. He was extricated without a murmur. I hesitate to record the many other instances of his sagacity, which rest, unfortunately, upon the statements of prejudiced friends. Some of them were not without a tinge of superstition. "I crep' up the bank just now," said Kentuck one day, in a breathless state of excitement, "and dern my skin if he wasn't a-talking to a jaybird as was a-sittin' on his lap. There they was, just as free and sociable as anything you please, a-jawin' at each other just like two cherrybums." Howbeit, whether creeping over the pine boughs or lying lazily on his back blinking at the leaves above him, to him the birds sang, the squirrels chattered, and the flowers bloomed. Nature was his nurse and playfellow. For him she would let slip between the leaves golden shafts of sunlight that fell just within his grasp; she would send wandering breezes to visit him with the balm of bay and resinous gum: to him the tall redwoods nodded familiarly and sleepily, the bumblebees buzzed, and the rooks cawed a slumbrous accompaniment.

Such was the golden summer of Roaring Camp. They were "flush times," and the luck was with them. The claims had yielded enormously. The camp was jealous of its privileges and looked suspiciously on strangers. No encouragement was given to immigration, and, to make their seclusion more perfect, the land on either side of the mountain wall that surrounded the camp they duly preëmpted. This, and a reputation for singular proficiency with the revolver, kept the reserve of Roaring Camp inviolate. The expressman—their only connecting link with the surrounding world—sometimes told wonderful stories of the camp. He would say, "They've a street up there in 'Roaring' that would lay over any street in Red Dog. They've got vines and flowers round their houses, and they wash themselves twice a day. But they're mighty rough on strangers, and they worship an Ingin baby."

With the prosperity of the camp came a desire for further improvement. It was proposed to build a hotel in the following spring, and to invite one or two decent families to reside there for the sake of The Luck, who might perhaps profit by female companionship. The sacrifice that this concession to the sex cost these men, who were fiercely skeptical in regard to its general virtue and usefulness, can only be accounted for by their affection for Tommy. A few still held out. But the resolve could not be carried into effect for three months, and the minority meekly yielded in the hope that something might turn up to prevent it. And it did.

The winter of 1851 will long be remembered in the foothills. The snow lay deep on the Sierras, and every mountain creek became a river, and every river a lake. Each gorge and gulch was transformed into a tumultuous watercourse that descended the hillsides, tearing down giant trees and scattering its drift and debris along the plain. Red Dog had been twice under water, and Roaring Camp had been forewarned. "Water put the gold into them gulches," said Stumpy. "It's been here once and will be here again!" And that night the North Fork suddenly leaped over its banks and swept up the triangular valley of Roaring Camp.

In the confusion of rushing water, crashing trees, and crackling timber, and the darkness which seemed to flow with the water and blot out the fair valley, but little could be done to collect the scattered camp. When the morning broke, the cabin of Stumpy, nearest the river-bank, was gone. Higher up the gulch they found the body of its unlucky owner; but the pride, the hope, the joy, The Luck, of Roaring Camp had disappeared. They were returning with sad hearts when a shout from the bank recalled them.

It was a relief-boat from down the river. They had picked up, they said, a man and an infant, nearly exhausted, about two miles below. Did anybody know them, and did they belong here?

It needed but a glance to show them Kentuck lying there, cruelly crushed and bruised, but still holding The Luck of Roaring Camp in his arms. As they bent over the strangely assorted pair, they saw that the child was cold and pulseless. "He is dead," said one. Kentuck opened his eyes. "Dead?" he repeated feebly. "Yes, my man, and you are dying too." A smile lit the eyes of the expiring Kentuck. "Dying!" he repeated; "he's a-taking me with him. Tell the boys I've got The Luck with me now;" and the strong man, clinging to the frail babe as a drowning man is said to cling to a straw, drifted away into the shadowy river that flows forever to the unknown sea.

*   *   *

JOHN JENKINS
Or,
The Smoker Reformed
BY T. S. A–TH–R[8]

Chapter I

"One cigar a day!" said Judge Boompointer.

"One cigar a day!" repeated John Jenkins, as with trepidation he dropped his half-consumed cigar under his work-bench.

"One cigar a day is three cents a day," remarked Judge Boompointer gravely; "and do you know, sir, what one cigar a day, or three cents a day, amounts to in the course of four years?"

John Jenkins, in his boyhood, had attended the village school, and possessed considerable arithmetical ability. Taking up a shingle which lay upon his work-bench, and producing a piece of chalk, with a feeling of conscious pride he made an exhaustive calculation.

"Exactly forty-three dollars and eighty cents," he replied, wiping the perspiration from his heated brow, while his face flushed with honest enthusiasm.

"Well, sir, if you saved three cents a day, instead of wasting it, you would now be the possessor of a new suit of clothes, an illustrated Family Bible, a pew in the church, a complete set of Patent Office Reports, a hymn-book, and a paid subscription to 'Arthur's Home Magazine,'[9] which could be purchased for exactly forty-three dollars and eighty cents; and," added the Judge, with increasing sternness, "if you calculate leap-year, which you seem to have strangely omitted, you have three cents more, sir—*three cents more!* What would that buy you, sir?"

"A cigar," suggested John Jenkins; but, coloring again deeply, he hid his face.

"No, sir," said the Judge, with a sweet smile of benevolence stealing over his stern features; "properly invested, it would buy you that which passeth all price. Dropped into the

---

8 Timothy Shay Arthur (1809–1885) was one of the most prolific writers of the antebellum period, producing more than 150 novels and collections of short stories. He also edited several influential periodicals. Among his many works, he wrote countless reform tales. The best known of these was his immensely popular temperance story, "Ten Nights in a Bar-Room" (1854), reprinted in this volume pp. 445–547.

9 *Arthur's Home Magazine* was a popular Philadelphia-based magazine edited by Timothy Shay Arthur.

missionary-box, who can tell what heathen, now idly and joyously wantoning in nakedness and sin, might be brought to a sense of his miserable condition, and made, through that three cents, to feel the torments of the wicked?"

With these words the Judge retired, leaving John Jenkins buried in profound thought. "Three cents a day," he muttered. "In forty years I might be worth four hundred and thirty-eight dollars and ten cents,—and then I might marry Mary. Ah, Mary!" The young carpenter sighed, and drawing a twenty-five cent daguerreotype[10] from his vest-pocket, gazed long and fervidly upon the features of a young girl in book muslin and a coral necklace. Then, with a resolute expression, he carefully locked the door of his work-shop, and departed.

Alas! his good resolutions were too late. We trifle with the tide of fortune, which too often nips us in the bud and casts the dark shadow of misfortune over the bright lexicon of youth! That night the half-consumed fragment of John Jenkins's cigar set fire to his work-shop and burned it up, together with all his tools and materials. There was no insurance.

Chapter II

The Downward Path

"Then you still persist in marrying John Jenkins?" queried Judge Boompointer, as he playfully, with paternal familiarity, lifted the golden curls of the village belle, Mary Jones.

"I do," replied the fair young girl, in a low voice that resembled rock candy in its saccharine firmness,—"I do. He has promised to reform. Since he lost all his property by fire"—

"The result of his pernicious habit, though he illogically persists in charging it to me," interrupted the Judge.

"Since then," continued the young girl, "he has endeavored to break himself of the habit. He tells me that he has substituted the stalks of the Indian rattan,[11] the outer part of a leguminous plant called the smoking-bean, and the fragmentary and unconsumed remainder of cigars, which occur at rare and uncertain intervals along the road, which, as he informs me, though deficient in quality and strength, are comparatively inexpensive." And blushing at her own eloquence, the young girl hid her curls on the Judge's arm.

"Poor thing!" muttered Judge Boompointer. "Dare I tell her all? Yet I must."

"I shall cling to him," continued the young girl, rising with her theme, "as the young vine clings to some hoary ruin. Nay, nay, chide me not, Judge Boompointer. I will marry John Jenkins!"

The Judge was evidently affected. Seating himself at the table, he wrote a few lines hurriedly upon a piece of paper, which he folded and placed in the fingers of the destined bride of John Jenkins.

"Mary Jones," said the Judge, with impressive earnestness, "take this trifle as a wedding gift from one who respects your fidelity and truthfulness. At the altar let it be a reminder of me." And covering his face hastily with a handkerchief, the stern and iron-willed man

---

10 A daguerreotype was a picture produced by an early photographic process developed in France in the 1830s.

11 Palm plant with long, tough stems.

left the room. As the door closed, Mary unfolded the paper. It was an order on the corner grocery for three yards of flannel, a paper of needles, four pounds of soap, one pound of starch, and two boxes of matches!

"Noble and thoughtful man!" was all Mary Jones could exclaim, as she hid her face in her hands and burst into a flood of tears.

* * *

The bells of Cloverdale are ringing merrily. It is a wedding. "How beautiful they look!" is the exclamation that passes from lip to lip, as Mary Jones, leaning timidly on the arm of John Jenkins, enters the church. But the bride is agitated, and the bridegroom betrays a feverish nervousness. As they stand in the vestibule, John Jenkins fumbles earnestly in his vest-pocket. Can it be the ring he is anxious about? No. He draws a small brown substance from his pocket, and biting off a piece, hastily replaces the fragment and gazes furtively around. Surely no one saw him? Alas! the eyes of two of that wedding party saw the fatal act. Judge Boompointer shook his head sternly. Mary Jones sighed and breathed a silent prayer. Her husband chewed!

Chapter III and Last

"What! more bread?" said John Jenkins gruffly. "You're always asking for money for bread. D—nation! Do you want to ruin me by your extravagance?" and as he uttered these words he drew from his pocket a bottle of whiskey, a pipe, and a paper of tobacco. Emptying the first at a draught, he threw the empty bottle at the head of his eldest boy, a youth of twelve summers. The missile struck the child full in the temple, and stretched him a lifeless corpse. Mrs. Jenkins, whom the reader will hardly recognize as the once gay and beautiful Mary Jones, raised the dead body of her son in her arms, and carefully placing the unfortunate youth beside the pump in the back yard, returned with saddened step to the house. At another time, and in brighter days, she might have wept at the occurrence. She was past tears now.

"Father, your conduct is reprehensible!" said little Harrison Jenkins, the youngest boy. "Where do you expect to go when you die?"

"Ah!" said John Jenkins fiercely; "this comes of giving children a liberal education; this is the result of Sabbath-schools. Down, viper!"

A tumbler thrown from the same parental fist laid out the youthful Harrison cold. The four other children had, in the mean time, gathered around the table with anxious expectancy. With a chuckle, the now changed and brutal John Jenkins produced four pipes, and filling them with tobacco, handed one to each of his offspring and bade them smoke. "It's better than bread!" laughed the wretch hoarsely.

Mary Jenkins, though of a patient nature, felt it her duty now to speak. "I have borne much, John Jenkins," she said. "But I prefer that the children should not smoke. It is an unclean habit, and soils their clothes. I ask this as a special favor!"

John Jenkins hesitated,—the pangs of remorse began to seize him.

"Promise me this, John!" urged Mary upon her knees.

"I promise!" reluctantly answered John.

"And you will put the money in a savings-bank?"

"I will," repeated her husband; "and I'll give up smoking, too."

"'Tis well, John Jenkins!" said Judge Boompointer, appearing suddenly from behind the door, where he had been concealed during this interview. "Nobly said! my man. Cheer up! I will see that the children are decently buried." The husband and wife fell into each other's arms. And Judge Boompointer, gazing upon the affecting spectacle, burst into tears.

From that day John Jenkins was an altered man.

Chapter Seventeen

LEW WALLACE
(1827–1905)

A native of Indiana, Lew Wallace had a life marked by forays into military service and the practice of law and politics. When the Civil War broke out, Wallace became involved in the recruitment of men from Indiana for Lincoln's Union army. He was soon promoted to the rank of general, proving capable in the field and popular among his men. Wallace's military service was inconsistent, but by the end of the war he had sufficiently distinguished himself to be named to the military tribunal that tried Lincoln's assassins.

After the war, Wallace resumed pursuing a career in politics (appointed governor of the Territory of New Mexico) but also increasingly turned his energies to writing. He was most interested in the genre of historical romance and published a novel on Cortez's conquest of Mexico, titled *The Fair God* (1873). His greatest literary success came in 1880 with the publication of *Ben-Hur: A Tale of the Christ*. This novel turned out to be an astounding hit. By 1890, it had been translated into several languages and had sold over 400,000 copies. Harper and Brothers proudly proclaimed, by the end of the nineteenth century, that *Ben-Hur* had outsold even Harriet Beecher Stowe's phenomenally popular *Uncle Tom's Cabin*. The book's famous chariot race became a staple across the country in Sunday-school lessons and messages from the pulpit, and the novel was adapted by William Young into a play that was so popular that it is estimated to have been performed over six thousand times for nearly 20 million people on three continents.

Although the novel is subtitled *A Tale of the Christ*, Jesus hardly appears in the story. It is primarily about the trials and tribulations of Judah Ben-Hur, a young Jewish nobleman, who is betrayed by childhood friend, Messala, and spends the rest of the novel exacting revenge and restoring his family to its proper place in Jewish society. It is a story full of bloodthirsty intrigue set against the backdrop of the life of Jesus Christ. This combination established the book as an interesting bridge between religious and secular reading material, offering adventure, full of revenge and romance, and set in biblical times.

BEN-HUR

A TALE OF THE CHRIST

Wallace's *Ben-Hur* was so popular that it has been used to market over one hundred products, ranging from the flour, seen above, to luxury cars, coffee, nutmeg, poultry seasoning, meat freezers, perfume, doorknobs and soap.

This text is reprinted from the following edition: *Ben-Hur: A Tale of the Christ*. New York: Harper and Brothers, 1880.

"Learn of the philosophers always to look for natural causes in all extraordinary events; and when such natural causes are wanting, recur to God."

COUNT DE GABALIS

"But this repetition of the old story is just the fairest charm of domestic discourse. If we can often repeat to ourselves sweet thoughts without *ennui*, why shall not another be suffered to awaken them within us still oftener."— *Hesp.*: JEAN PAUL F. RICHTER.

> "See how from far upon the eastern road
> The star-led wisards haste with odours sweet.
> But peaceful was the night
> Wherein the Prince of Light
>   His reign of peace upon the earth began;
> The winds with wonder whist
> Smoothly the waters kist,
>   Whispering new joys to the mild ocean—
> Who now hath quite forgot to rave,
> While birds of calm sit brooding on the charmed wave."
> *Christ's Nativity: The Hymn.*—*Milton.*

Book Second[1]

"There is a fire
And motion of the soul which will not dwell
In its own narrow being, but aspire
Beyond the fitting medium of desire;
And, but once kindled, quenchless evermore,
Preys upon high adventure, nor can tire
Of aught but rest."
Childe Harold.[2]

Chapter I

IT is necessary now to carry the reader forward twenty-one years, to the beginning of the administration of Valerius Gratus,[3] the fourth imperial governor of Judea—a period which

---

1 The novel *Ben-Hur* is divided into eight books. Four of the eight, in whole or in part, are represented in this anthology. The first book (not included here) sets the Middle Eastern scene and tells of the birth of Jesus in Bethlehem and the visit of the Three Wise Men from the East bearing gifts for him. One of these wise men is the Egyptian Balthasar, who plays an important role later in the novel.

2 Narrative poem by Lord Byron (published between 1812 and 1818) that describes the pilgrimage of a world-weary man looking for meaning. "Childe" is the medieval term for one who is a candidate for knighthood.

3 Began his governorship in the year 15 and served until 26, when he was replaced by Pontius Pilate.

will be remembered as rent by political agitations in Jerusalem, if, indeed, it be not the precise time of the opening of the final quarrel between the Jew and the Roman.

In the interval Judea had been subjected to changes affecting her in many ways, but in nothing so much as her political status. Herod the Great died within one year after the birth of the Child[4]—died so miserably that the Christian world had reason to believe him overtaken by the Divine wrath. Like all great rulers who spend their lives in perfecting the power they create, he dreamed of transmitting his throne and crown—of being the founder of a dynasty. With that intent, he left a will dividing his territories between his three sons, Antipas, Philip, and Archelaus, of whom the last was appointed to succeed to the title. The testament was necessarily referred to Augustus,[5] the emperor, who ratified all its provisions with one exception: he withheld from Archelaus the title of king until he proved his capacity and loyalty; in lieu thereof, he created him ethnarch[6], and as such permitted him to govern nine years, when, for misconduct and inability to stay the turbulent elements that grew and strengthened around him, he was sent into Gaul as an exile.

Cæsar was not content with deposing Archelaus; he struck the people of Jerusalem in a manner that touched their pride, and keenly wounded the sensibilities of the haughty habitués of the Temple. He reduced Judea to a Roman province, and annexed it to the prefecture of Syria. So, instead of a king ruling royally from the palace left by Herod on Mount Zion, the city fell into the hands of an officer of the second grade, an appointee called procurator, who communicated with the court in Rome through the Legate of Syria, residing in Antioch. To make the hurt more painful, the procurator was not permitted to establish himself in Jerusalem; Cæsarea was his seat of government. Most humiliating, however, most exasperating, most studied, Samaria,[7] of all the world the most despised—Samaria was joined to Judea as a part of the same province! What ineffable misery the bigoted Separatists or Pharisees endured at finding themselves elbowed and laughed at in the procurator's presence in Cæsarea by the devotees of Gerizim![8]

In this rain of sorrows, one consolation, and one only, remained to the fallen people: the high-priest occupied the Herodian palace in the market-place, and kept the semblance of a court there. What his authority really was is a matter of easy estimate. Judgment of life and death was retained by the procurator. Justice was administered in the name and according to the decretals of Rome. Yet more significant, the royal house was jointly occupied by the imperial exciseman, and all his corps of assistants, registrars, collectors, publicans, informers, and spies. Still, to the dreamers of liberty to come, there was a certain satisfaction in the fact that the chief ruler in the palace was a Jew. His mere presence there day after day kept them reminded of the covenants and promises of the prophets, and the ages when Jehovah governed the tribes through the sons of Aaron; it was to them a certain sign that he had not abandoned them: so their hopes lived, and served their patience, and helped them wait grimly the son of Judah who was to rule Israel.

Judea had been a Roman province eighty years and more—ample time for the Cæsars to study the idiosyncrasies of the people—time enough, at least, to learn that the Jew, with

---

4 Jesus Christ.
5 Augustus Caesar was the first emperor of the Roman Empire and ruled from 27 BCE to 14 CE.
6 Governor.
7 A land bordering Judea, inhabited by a people descended from Jewish stock but holding different religious beliefs considered heretical by their Jewish neighbors.
8 A holy mountain revered by the Samaritans, but not by the neighboring Jewish population.

all his pride, could be quietly governed if his religion were respected. Proceeding upon that policy, the predecessors of Gratus had carefully abstained from interfering with any of the sacred observances of their subjects. But he chose a different course: almost his first official act was to expel Hannas from the high-priesthood, and give the place to Ishmael, son of Fabus.

Whether the act was directed by Augustus, or proceeded from Gratus himself, its impolicy became speedily apparent. The reader shall be spared a chapter on Jewish politics; a few words upon the subject, however, are essential to such as may follow the succeeding narration critically. At this time, leaving origin out of view, there were in Judea the party of the nobles and the Separatist or popular party. Upon Herod's death, the two united against Archelaus; from temple to palace, from Jerusalem to Rome, they fought him; sometimes with intrigue, sometimes with the actual weapons of war. More than once the holy cloisters on Moriah resounded with the cries of fighting-men. Finally, they drove him into exile. Meantime throughout this struggle the allies had their diverse objects in view. The nobles hated Joazar, the high-priest; the Separatists, on the other hand, were his zealous adherents. When Herod's settlement went down with Archelaus, Joazar shared the fall. Hannas, the son of Seth, was selected by the nobles to fill the great office; thereupon the allies divided. The induction of the Sethian brought them face to face in fierce hostility.

In the course of the struggle with the unfortunate ethnarch, the nobles had found it expedient to attach themselves to Rome. Discerning that when the existing settlement was broken up some form of government must needs follow, they suggested the conversion of Judea into a province. The fact furnished the Separatists an additional cause for attack; and, when Samaria was made part of the province, the nobles sank into a minority, with nothing to support them but the imperial court and the prestige of their rank and wealth; yet for fifteen years—down, indeed, to the coming of Valerius Gratus—they managed to maintain themselves in both palace and Temple.

Hannas, the idol of his party, had used his power faithfully in the interest of his imperial patron. A Roman garrison held the Tower of Antonia;[9] a Roman guard kept the gates of the palace; a Roman judge dispensed justice civil and criminal; a Roman system of taxation, mercilessly executed, crushed both city and country; daily, hourly, and in a thousand ways, the people were bruised and galled, and taught the difference between a life of independence and a life of subjection; yet Hannas kept them in comparative quiet. Rome had no truer friend; and he made his loss instantly felt. Delivering his vestments to Ishmael, the new appointee, he walked from the courts of the Temple into the councils of the Separatists, and became the head of a new combination, Bethusian and Sethian.

Gratus, the procurator, left thus without a party, saw the fires which, in the fifteen years, had sunk into sodden smoke begin to glow with returning life. A month after Ishmael took the office, the Roman found it necessary to visit him in Jerusalem. When from the walls, hooting and hissing him, the Jews beheld his guard enter the north gate of the city and march to the Tower of Antonia, they understood the real purpose of the visit—a full cohort of legionaries was added to the former garrison, and the keys of their yoke could now be tightened with impunity. If the procurator deemed it important to make an example, alas for the first offender!

---

9 A castle connected to the Temple in Jerusalem.

Chapter II

WITH the foregoing explanation in mind, the reader is invited to look into one of the gardens of the palace on Mount Zion.[10] The time was noonday in the middle of July, when the heat of summer was at its highest.

The garden was bounded on every side by buildings, which in places arose two stories, with verandas shading the doors and windows of the lower story, while retreating galleries, guarded by strong balustrades, adorned and protected the upper. Here and there, moreover, the structures fell into what appeared low colonnades, permitting the passage of such winds as chanced to blow, and allowing other parts of the house to be seen, the better to realize its magnitude and beauty. The arrangement of the ground was equally pleasant to the eye. There were walks, and patches of grass and shrubbery, and a few large trees, rare specimens of the palm, grouped with the carob, apricot, and walnut. In all directions the grade sloped gently from the centre, where there was a reservoir, or deep marble basin, broken at intervals by little gates which, when raised, emptied the water into sluices bordering the walks—a cunning device for the rescue of the place from the aridity too prevalent elsewhere in the region.

Not far from the fountain, there was a small pool of clear water nourishing a clump of cane and oleander, such as grow on the Jordan and down by the Dead Sea. Between the clump and the pool, unmindful of the sun shining full upon them in the breathless air, two boys, one about nineteen, the other seventeen, sat engaged in earnest conversation.

They were both handsome, and, at first glance, would have been pronounced brothers. Both had hair and eyes black; their faces were deeply browned; and, sitting, they seemed of a size proper for the difference in their ages.

The elder was bareheaded. A loose tunic, dropping to the knees, was his attire complete, except sandals and a light-blue mantle spread under him on the seat. The costume left his arms and legs exposed, and they were brown as the face; nevertheless, a certain grace of manner, refinement of features, and culture of voice decided his rank. The tunic, of softest woollen, gray-tinted, at the neck, sleeves, and edge of the skirt bordered with red, and bound to the waist by a tasselled silken cord, certified him the Roman he was. And if in speech he now and then gazed haughtily at his companion and addressed him as an inferior, he might almost be excused, for he was of a family noble even in Rome—a circumstance which in that age justified any assumption. In the terrible wars between the first Cæsar and his great enemies, a Messala had been the friend of Brutus.[11] After Philippi,[12] without sacrifice of his honor, he and the conqueror became reconciled. Yet later, when Octavius disputed for the empire, Messala supported him. Octavius, as the Emperor Augustus, remembered the service, and showered the family with honors. Among other things, Judea being reduced to a province, he sent the son of his old client or retainer to Jerusalem, charged with the receipt and management of the taxes levied in that region; and in that service the son had since remained, sharing the palace with the high-priest. The youth just described was his son, whose habit it was to carry about with him all too faithfully a remembrance of the relation between his grandfather and the great Romans of his day.

---

10 A hill just outside the older parts of the city of Jerusalem.
11 Marcus Junius Brutus (85 BCE–42 BCE) was one of the assassins of Julius Caesar in 44 BCE.
12 Pivotal battle (42 BCE) in which Augustus and his allies defeated the assassins of Julius Caesar.

The associate of the Messala was slighter in form, and his garments were of fine white linen and of the prevalent style in Jerusalem; a cloth covered his head, held by a yellow cord, and arranged so as to fall away from the forehead down low over the back of the neck. An observer skilled in the distinctions of race, and studying his features more than his costume, would have soon discovered him to be of Jewish descent. The forehead of the Roman was high and narrow, his nose sharp and aquiline, while his lips were thin and straight, and his eyes cold and close under the brows. The front of the Israelite, on the other hand, was low and broad; his nose long, with expanded nostrils; his upper lip, slightly shading the lower one, short and curving to the dimpled corners, like a Cupid's bow; points which, in connection with the round chin, full eyes, and oval checks reddened with a wine-like glow, gave his face the softness, strength, and beauty peculiar to his race. The comeliness of the Roman was severe and chaste, that of the Jew rich and voluptuous.

"Did you not say the new procurator is to arrive tomorrow?"

The question proceeded from the younger of the friends, and was couched in Greek, at the time, singularly enough, the language everywhere prevalent in the politer circles of Judea; having passed from the palace into the camp and college; thence, nobody knew exactly when or how, into the Temple itself, and, for that matter, into precincts of the Temple far beyond the gates and cloisters—precincts of a sanctity intolerable for a Gentile.

"Yes, to-morrow," Messala answered.

"Who told you?"

"I heard Ishmael, the new governor in the palace—you call him high-priest—tell my father so last night. The news had been more credible, I grant you, coming from an Egyptian, who is of a race that has forgotten what truth is, or even from an Idumæan, whose people never knew what truth was; but, to make quite certain, I saw a centurion from the Tower this morning, and he told me preparations were going on for the reception; that the armorers were furbishing the helmets and shields, and regilding the eagles and globes; and that apartments long unused were being cleansed and aired as if for an addition to the garrison—the body-guard, probably, of the great man."

A perfect idea of the manner in which the answer was given cannot be conveyed, as its fine points continually escape the power behind the pen. The reader's fancy must come to his aid; and for that he must be reminded that reverence as a quality of the Roman mind was fast breaking down, or, rather, it was becoming unfashionable. The old religion had nearly ceased to be a faith; at most it was a mere habit of thought and expression, cherished principally by the priests who found service in the Temple profitable, and the poets who, in the turn of their verses, could not dispense with the familiar deities: there are singers of this age who are similarly given. As philosophy was taking the place of religion, satire was fast substituting reverence; insomuch that in Latin opinion it was to every speech, even to the little diatribes of conversation, salt to viands, and aroma to wine. The young Messala, educated in Rome, but lately returned, had caught the habit and manner; the scarce perceptible movement of the outer corner of the lower eyelid, the decided curl of the corresponding nostril, and a languid utterance affected as the best vehicle to convey the idea of general indifference, but more particularly because of the opportunities it afforded for certain rhetorical pauses thought to be of prime importance to enable the listener to take the happy conceit or receive the virus of the stinging epigram. Such a stop occurred in the answer just given, at the end of the allusion to the Egyptian and Idumæan. The color in the Jewish lad's cheeks deepened, for he remained silent, looking absently into the depths of the pool.

"Our farewell took place in this garden. 'The peace of the Lord go with you!'—your last words. 'The gods keep you!' I said. Do you remember? How many years have passed since then?"

"Five," answered the Jew, gazing into the water.

"Well, you have reason to be thankful to—whom shall I say? The gods? No matter. You have grown handsome; the Greeks would call you beautiful—happy achievement of the years! If Jupiter would stay content with one Ganymede,[13] what a cup-bearer you would make for the emperor! Tell me, my Judah, how the coming of the procurator is of such interest to you."

Judah bent his large eyes upon the questioner; the gaze was grave and thoughtful, and caught the Roman's, and held it while he replied, "Yes, five years. I remember the parting; you went to Rome; I saw you start, and cried, for I loved you. The years are gone, and you have come back to me accomplished and princely—I do not jest; and yet—yet—I wish you were the Messala you went away."

The fine nostril of the satirist stirred, and he put on a longer drawl as he said, "No, no; not a Ganymede—an oracle, my Judah. A few lessons from my teacher of rhetoric hard by the Forum—I will give you a letter to him when you become wise enough to accept a suggestion which I am reminded to make you—a little practice of the art of mystery, and Delphi[14] will receive you as Apollo himself. At the sound of your solemn voice, the Pythia will come down to you with her crown. Seriously, O my friend, in what am I not the Messala I went away? I once heard the greatest logician in the world. His subject was Disputation. One saying I remember —'Understand your antagonist before you answer him.' Let me understand you."

The lad reddened under the cynical look to which he was subjected; yet he replied, firmly, "You have availed yourself, I see, of your opportunities; from your teachers you have brought away much knowledge and many graces. You talk with the case of a master; yet your speech carries a sting. My Messala, when he went away, had no poison in his nature; not for the world would he have hurt the feelings of a friend."

The Roman smiled as if complimented, and raised his patrician head a toss higher.

"O my solemn Judah, we are not at Dodona or Pytho.[15] Drop the oracular, and be plain. Wherein have I hurt you?"

The other drew a long breath, and said, pulling at the cord about his waist, "In the five years, I, too, have learned somewhat. Hillel may not be the equal of the logician you heard, and Simeon and Shammai[16] are, no doubt, inferior to your master hard by the Forum. Their learning goes not out into forbidden paths; those who sit at their feet arise enriched simply with knowledge of God, the law, and Israel; and the effect is love and reverence for everything that pertains to them. Attendance at the Great College, and study of what I heard there, have taught me that Judea is not as she used to be. I know the space that lies between an independent kingdom and the petty province Judea is. I were meaner, viler,

---

13 An ancient Trojan hero said to be the most handsome of all mortal men.
14 An ancient site for the worship of Apollo. It was serviced by a priestess always named "Pythia," who was thought to be able to see the future.
15 Sites of ancient Greek religious oracles.
16 Hillel, Simeon and Shammai were renowned ancient Hebrew leaders and scholars.

than a Samaritan not to resent the degradation of my country. Ishmael is not lawfully high-priest, and he cannot be while the noble Hannas lives; yet he is a Levite; one of the devoted who for thousands of years have acceptably served the Lord God of our faith and worship. His—"

Messala broke in upon him with a biting laugh.

"Oh, I understand you now. Ishmael, you say, is a usurper, yet to believe an Idumæan sooner than Ishmael is to sting like an adder. By the drunken son of Semele,[17] what it is to be a Jew! All men and things, even heaven and earth, change; but a Jew never. To him there is no backward, no forward; he is what his ancestor was in the beginning. In this sand I draw you a circle—there! Now tell me what more a Jew's life is? Round and round, Abraham here, Isaac and Jacob yonder, God in the middle. And the circle—by the master of all thunders! the circle is too large. I draw it again—" He stopped, put his thumb upon the ground, and swept the fingers about it. "See, the thumb spot is the Temple, the finger-lines Judea. Outside the little space is there nothing of value? The arts! Herod was a builder; therefore he is accursed. Painting, sculpture! to look upon them is sin. Poetry you make fast to your altars. Except in the synagogue, who of you attempts eloquence? In war all you conquer in the six days you lose on the seventh. Such your life and limit; who shall say no if I laugh at you? Satisfied with the worship of such a people, what is your God to our Roman Jove, who lends us his eagles that we may compass the universe with our arms? Hillel, Simeon, Shammai, Abtalion—what are they to the masters who teach that everything is worth knowing that can be known?"

The Jew arose, his face much flushed.

"No, no; keep your place, my Judah, keep your place," Messala cried, extending his hand.

"You mock me."

"Listen a little further. Directly"—the Roman smiled derisively—" directly Jupiter and his whole family, Greek and Latin, will come to me, as is their habit, and make an end of serious speech. I am mindful of your goodness in walking from the old house of your fathers to welcome me back and renew the love of our childhood—if we can. 'Go.' said my teacher, in his last lecture—'Go, and, to make your lives great, remember Mars reigns and Eros has found his eyes.' He meant love is nothing, war everything. It is so in Rome. Marriage is the first step to divorce. Virtue is a tradesman's jewel. Cleopatra, dying, bequeathed her arts, and is avenged; she has a successor in every Roman's house. The world is going the same way; so, as to our future, down Eros, up Mars! I am to be a soldier; and you, O my Judah, I pity yon; what can you be?"

The Jew moved nearer the pool; Messala's drawl deepened.

"Yes, I pity you, my fine Judah. From the college to the synagogue; then to the Temple; then—oh, a crowning glory!—the seat in the Sanhedrim.[18] A life without opportunities; the gods help you! But I—"

Judah looked at him in time to see the flush of pride that kindled in his haughty face as he went on.

---

17 Referring to Semele and Zeus's son Dionysus, the Greek God of wine, fertility and revelry.
18 More commonly called the "Sanhedrin," this body comprised the highest, and therefore the most powerful, religious court in Jerusalem.

"But I—ah, the world is not all conquered. The sea has islands unseen. In the north there are nations yet unvisited. The glory of completing Alexander's march to the Far East remains to some one. See what possibilities lie before a Roman."

Next instant he resumed his drawl.

"A campaign into Africa; another after the Scythian; then—a legion! Most careers end there; but not mine. I—by Jupiter! what a conception!—I will give up my legion for a prefecture. Think of life in Rome with money—money, wine, women, games—poets at the banquet, intrigues in the court, dice all the year round. Such a rounding of life may be—a fat prefecture, and it is mine. O my Judah, here is Syria! Judea is rich; Antioch a capital for the gods. I will succeed Cyrenius, and you—shall share my fortune."

The sophists and rhetoricians who thronged the public resorts of Rome, almost monopolizing the business of teaching her patrician youth, might have approved these sayings of Messala, for they were all in the popular vein; to the young Jew, however, they were new, and unlike the solemn style of discourse and conversation to which he was accustomed. He belonged, moreover, to a race whose laws, modes, and habits of thought forbade satire and humor; very naturally, therefore, he listened to his friend with varying feelings; one moment indignant, then uncertain how to take him. The superior airs assumed had been offensive to him in the beginning; soon they became irritating, and at last an acute smart. Anger lies close by this point in all of us; and that the satirist evoked in another way. To the Jew of the Herodian period patriotism was a savage passion scarcely hidden under his common humor, and so related to his history, religion, and God that it responded instantly to derision of them. Wherefore it is not speaking too strongly to say that Messala's progress down to the last pause was exquisite torture to his hearer; at that point the latter said, with a forced smile,

"There are a few, I have heard, who can afford to make a jest of their future; you convince me, O my Messala, that I am not one of them."

The Roman studied him; then replied, "Why not the truth in a jest as well as a parable? The great Fulvia[19] went fishing the other day; she caught more than all the company besides. They said it was because the barb of her hook was covered with gold."

"Then you were not merely jesting?"

"My Judah, I see I did not offer you enough," the Roman answered, quickly, his eyes sparkling. "When I am prefect, with Judea to enrich me, I—will make you high-priest."

The Jew turned off angrily.

"Do not leave me," said Messala.

The other stopped irresolute.

"Gods, Judah, how hot the sun shines!" cried the patrician, observing his perplexity. "Let us seek a shade."

Judah answered, coldly,

"We had better part. I wish I had not come. I sought a friend and find a—"

"Roman," said Messala, quickly.

The hands of the Jew clenched, but controlling himself again, he started off. Messala arose, and, taking the mantle from the bench, flung it over his shoulder, and followed after; when he gained his side, he put his hand upon his shoulder and walked with him.

---

19 The wife of Mark Antony, one of Augustus's early allies in the fight against those who killed Julius Caesar. The reference here is how she used gold to buy friends in the power struggle after Caesar's death.

"This is the way—my hand thus—we used to walk when we were children. Let us keep it as far as the gate."

Apparently Messala was trying to be serious and kind, though he could not rid his countenance of the habitual satirical expression. Judah permitted the familiarity.

"You are a boy; I am a man; let me talk like one."

The complacency of the Roman was superb. Mentor lecturing the young Telemachus[20] could not have been more at ease.

"Do you believe in the Parcæ?[21] Ah, I forgot, you are a Sadducee: the Essenes[22] are your sensible people; they believe in the sisters. So do I. How everlastingly the three are in the way of our doing what we please! I sit down scheming. I run paths here and there. *Perpol!* Just when I am reaching to take the world in hand, I hear behind me the grinding of scissors. I look, and there she is, the accursed Atropos![23] But, my Judah, why did you get mad when I spoke of succeeding old Cyrenius? You thought I meant to enrich myself plundering your Judea. Suppose so; it is what some Roman will do. Why not I?"

Judah shortened his step.

"There have been strangers in mastery of Judea before the Roman," he said, with lifted hand. "Where are they, Messala? She has outlived them all. What has been will be again."

Messala put on his drawl.

"The Parcæ have believers outside the Essenes. Welcome, Judah, welcome to the faith!"

"No, Messala, count me not with them. My faith rests on the rock which was the foundation of the faith of my fathers back further than Abraham; on the covenants of the Lord God of Israel."

"Too much passion, my Judah. How my master would have been shocked had I been guilty of so much heat in his presence! There were other things I had to tell you, but I fear to now."

When they had gone a few yards, the Roman spoke again.

"I think you can hear me now, especially as what I have to say concerns yourself. I would serve you, O handsome as Ganymede; I would serve you with real good-will. I love you—all I can. I told you I meant to be a soldier. Why not you also? Why not you step out of the narrow circle which, as I have shown, is all of noble life your laws and customs allow?"

Judah made no reply.

"Who are the wise men of our day?" Messala continued. "Not they who exhaust their years quarrelling about dead things; about Baals, Joves, and Jehovahs;[24] about philosophies and religions. Give me one great name, O Judah; I care not where you go to find it—to Rome, Egypt, the East, or here in Jerusalem—Pluto[25] take me if it belong not to a man who wrought his fame out of the material furnished him by the present; holding nothing sacred that did not contribute to the end, scorning nothing that did! How was it with Herod! How

---

20 The son of Odysseus who helped his father avenge wrongs done to him while he was away at the Trojan War.
21 Roman divine beings associated with destiny, often called the Fates.
22 A religious sect that also had a firm sense of each person having a destiny to fulfill.
23 The oldest of the three sisters of Fate in Greek mythology.
24 Gods of pagan, Roman and Jewish religions.
25 Greek god of death and the underworld.

with the Maccabees? How with the first and second Cæsars? Imitate them. Begin now. At hand see—Rome, as ready to help you as she was the Idumæan Antipater."

The Jewish lad trembled with rage; and, as the garden gate was close by, he quickened his steps, eager to escape.

"O Rome, Rome!" he muttered.

"Be wise," continued Messala. "Give up the follies of Moses and the traditions; see the situation as it is. Dare look the Parcæ in the face, and they will tell you, Rome is the world. Ask them of Judea, and they will answer, She is what Rome wills."

They were now at the gate. Judah stopped, and took the hand gently from his shoulder, and confronted Messala, tears trembling in his eyes.

"I understand you, because you are a Roman; you cannot understand me—I am an Israelite. You have given me suffering to-day by convincing me that we can never be the friends we have been—never! Here we part. The peace of the God of my fathers abide with you!"

Messala offered him his hand; the Jew walked on through the gateway. When he was gone, the Roman was silent awhile; then he, too, passed through, saying to himself, with a toss of the head,

"Be it so. Eros is dead, Mars reigns!"

Chapter III

From the entrance to the Holy City, equivalent to what is now called St. Stephen's Gate,[26] a street extended westwardly, on a line parallel with the northern front of the Tower of Antonia, though a square from that famous castle. Keeping the course as far as the Tyropœon Valley, which it followed a little way south, it turned and again ran west until a short distance beyond what tradition tells us was the Judgment Gate, from whence it broke abruptly south. The traveller or the student familiar with the sacred locality will recognize the thoroughfare described as part of the Via Dolorosa[27]—with Christians of more inter-est, though of a melancholy kind, than any street in the world. As the purpose in view does not at present require dealing with the whole street, it will be sufficient to point out a house standing in the angle last mentioned as marking the change of direction south, and which, as an important centre of interest, needs somewhat particular description.

The building fronted north and west, probably four hundred feet each way, and, like most pretentious Eastern structures, was two stories in height, and perfectly quadrangular. The street on the west side was about twelve feet wide, that on the north not more than ten; so that one walking close to the walls, and looking up at them, would have been struck by the rude, unfinished, uninviting, but strong and imposing, appearance they presented; for they were of stone laid in large blocks, undressed—on the outer side, in fact, just as they were taken from the quarry. A critic of this age would have pronounced the house fortelesque in style, except for the windows, with which it was unusually garnished, and the ornate finish of the doorways or gates. The western windows were four in number, the northern only two, all set on the line of the second story in such manner as to overhang the

---

26 One of seven gates into the city of Jerusalem, located on the city's eastern wall.
27 A street that runs through Jerusalem, reported to have been walked by Jesus before his crucifixion.

thoroughfares below. The gates were the only breaks of wall externally visible in the first story; and, besides being so thickly riven with iron bolts as to suggest resistance to battering-rams, they were protected by cornices of marble, handsomely executed, and of such bold projection as to assure visitors well informed of the people that the rich man who resided there was a Sadducee in politics and creed.

Not long after the young Jew parted from the Roman at the palace up on the Market-place, he stopped before the western gate of the house described, and knocked. The wicket (a door hung in one of the valves of the gate) was opened to admit him. He stepped in hastily, and failed to acknowledge the low salaam of the porter.

To get an idea of the interior arrangement of the structure, as well as to see what more befell the youth, we will follow him.

The passage into which he was admitted appeared not unlike a narrow tunnel with panelled walls and pitted ceiling. There were benches of stone on both sides, stained and polished by long use. Twelve or fifteen steps carried him into a court-yard, oblong north and south, and in every quarter, except the east, bounded by what seemed the fronts of two-story houses; of which the lower floor was divided into lewens, while the upper was terraced and defended by strong balustrading. The servants coming and going along the terraces; the noise of millstones grinding; the garments fluttering from ropes stretched from point to point; the chickens and pigeons in full enjoyment of the place; the goats, cows, donkeys, and horses stabled in the lewens; a massive trough of water, apparently for the common use, declared this court appurtenant to the domestic management of the owner. Eastwardly there was a division wall broken by another passage-way in all respects like the first one.

Clearing the second passage, the young man entered a second court, spacious, square, and set with shrubbery and vines, kept fresh and beautiful by water from a basin erected near a porch on the north side. The lewens here were high, airy, and shaded by curtains striped alternate white and red. The arches of the lewens rested on clustered columns. A flight of steps on the south ascended to the terraces of the upper story, over which great awnings were stretched as a defence against the sun. Another stairway reached from the terraces to the roof, the edge of which, all around the square, was defined by a sculptured cornice, and a parapet of burned-clay tiling, sexangular and bright red. In this quarter, moreover, there was everywhere observable a scrupulous neatness, which, allowing no dust in the angles, not even a yellow leaf upon a shrub, contributed quite as much as anything else to the delightful general effect; insomuch that a visitor, breathing the sweet air, knew, in advance of introduction, the refinement of the family he was about calling upon.

A few steps within the second court, the lad turned to the right, and, choosing a walk through the shrubbery, part of which was in flower, passed to the stairway, and ascended to the terrace—a broad pavement of white and brown flags closely laid, and much worn. Making way under the awning to a doorway on the north side, he entered an apartment which the dropping of the screen behind him returned to darkness. Nevertheless, he proceeded, moving over a tiled floor to a divan, upon which he flung himself, face downwards, and lay at rest, his forehead upon his crossed arms.

About nightfall a woman came to the door and called; he answered, and she went in.

"Supper is over, and it is night. Is not my son hungry?" she asked.

"No," he replied.

"Are you sick?"

"I am sleepy."

"Your mother has asked for you."

"Where is she?"

"In the summer-house on the roof."

He stirred himself, and sat up.

"Very well. Bring me something to eat."

"What do you want?"

"What you please, Amrah. I am not sick, but indifferent. Life does not seem as pleasant as it did this morning. A new ailment, O my Amrah; and you who know me so well, who never failed me, may think of the things now that answer for food and medicine. Bring me what you choose."

Amrah's questions, and the voice in which she put them—low, sympathetic, and solicitous—were significant of an endeared relation between the two. She laid her hand upon his forehead; then, as satisfied, went out, saying, "I will see."

After a while she returned, bearing on a wooden platter a bowl of milk, some thin cakes of white bread broken, a delicate paste of brayed wheat, a bird broiled, and honey and salt. On one end of the platter there was a silver goblet full of wine, on the other a brazen hand-lamp lighted.

The room was then revealed: its walls smoothly plastered; the ceiling broken by great oaken rafters, brown with rain stains and time; the floor of small diamond-shaped white and blue tiles, very firm and enduring; a few stools with legs carved in imitation of the legs of lions; a divan raised a little above the floor, trimmed with blue cloth, and partially covered by an immense striped woollen blanket or shawl—in brief, a Hebrew bedroom.

The same light also gave the woman to view. Drawing a stool to the divan, she placed the platter upon it, then knelt close by ready to serve him. Her face was that of a woman of fifty, dark-skinned, dark-eyed, and at the moment softened by a look of tenderness almost maternal. A white turban covered her head, leaving the lobes of the ear exposed, and in them the sign that settled her condition—an orifice bored by a thick awl. She was a slave, of Egyptian origin, to whom not even the sacred fiftieth year could have brought freedom; nor would she have accepted it, for the boy she was attending was her life. She had nursed him through babyhood, tended him as a child, and could not break the service. To her love he could never be a man.

He spoke but once during the meal.

"You remember, O my Amrah," he said, "the Messala who used to visit me here days at a time."

"I remember him."

"He went to Rome some years ago, and is now back. I called upon him to-day."

A shudder of disgust seized the lad.

"I knew something had happened," she said, deeply interested. "I never liked the Messala. Tell me all."

But he fell into musing, and to her repeated inquiries only said, "He is much changed, and I shall have nothing more to do with him."

When Amrah took the platter away, he also went out, and up from the terrace to the roof.

The reader is presumed to know somewhat of the uses of the house-top in the East. In the matter of customs, climate is a lawgiver everywhere. The Syrian summer day drives the seeker of comfort into the darkened lewen; night, however, calls him forth early, and the shadows deepening over the mountain-sides seem veils dimly covering Circean singers;

but they are far off, while the roof is close by, and raised above the level of the shimmering plain enough for the visitation of cool airs, and sufficiently above the trees to allure the stars down closer, down at least into brighter shining. So the roof became a resort—became playground, sleeping-chamber, boudoir, rendezvous for the family, place of music, dance, conversation, reverie, and prayer.

The motive that prompts the decoration, at whatever cost, of interiors in colder climes suggested to the Oriental the embellishment of his house-top. The parapet ordered by Moses became a potter's triumph; above that, later, arose towers, plain and fantastic; still later, kings and princes crowned their roofs with summer-houses of marble and gold. When the Babylonian hung gardens in the air, extravagance could push the idea no further.

The lad whom we are following walked slowly across the house-top to a tower built over the northwest corner of the palace. Had he been a stranger, he might have bestowed a glance upon the structure as he drew nigh it, and seen all the dimness permitted—a darkened mass, low, latticed, pillared, and domed. He entered, passing under a half-raised curtain. The interior was all darkness, except that on four sides there were arched openings like doorways, through which the sky, lighted with stars, was visible. In one of the openings, reclining against a cushion from a divan, he saw the figure of a woman, indistinct even in white floating drapery. At the sound of his steps upon the floor, the fan in her hand stopped, glistening where the starlight struck the jewels with which it was sprinkled, and she sat up, and called his name.

"Judah, my son!"

"It is I, mother," he answered, quickening his approach.

Going to her, he knelt, and she put her arms around him, and with kisses pressed him to her bosom.

Chapter IV

THE mother resumed her easy position against the cushion, while the son took place on the divan, his head in her lap. Both of them, looking out of the opening, could see a stretch of lower house-tops in the vicinity, a bank of blue blackness over in the west which they knew to be mountains, and the sky, its shadowy depths brilliant with stars. The city was still. Only the winds stirred.

"Amrah tells me something has happened to you," she said, caressing his cheek. "When my Judah was a child, I allowed small things to trouble him, but he is now a man. He must not forget"—her voice became very soft—"that one day he is to be my hero."

She spoke in the language almost lost in the land, but which a few—and they were always as rich in blood as in possessions—cherished in its purity, that they might be more certainly distinguished from Gentile peoples—the language in which the loved Rebekah and Rachel sang to Benjamin.

The words appeared to set him thinking anew; after a while, however, he caught the hand with which she fanned him, and said, "Today, O my mother, I have been made to think of many things that never had place in my mind before. Tell me, first, what am I to be?"

"Have I not told you? You are to be my hero."

He could not see her face, yet he knew she was in play. He became more serious.

"You are very good, very kind, O my mother. No one will ever love me as you do."

He kissed the hand over and over again.

"I think I understand why you would have me put off the question," he continued. "Thus far my life has belonged to you. How gentle, how sweet your control has been! I wish it could last forever. But that may not be. It is the Lord's will that I shall one day become owner of myself—a day of separation, and therefore a dreadful day to you. Let us be brave and serious. I will be your hero, but you must put me in the way. You know the law—every son of Israel must have some occupation. I am not exempt, and ask now, shall I tend the herds? or till the soil? or drive the saw? or be a clerk or a lawyer? What shall I be? Dear, good mother, help me to an answer."

"Gamaliel[28] has been lecturing to-day," she said, thoughtfully.

"If so, I did not hear him."

"Then you have been walking with Simeon, who, they tell me, inherits the genius of his family."

"No, I have not seen him. I have been up on the Market-place, not to the Temple. I visited the young Messala."

A certain change in his voice attracted the mother's attention. A presentiment quickened the beating of her heart; the fan became motionless again.

"The Messala!" she said. "What could he say to so trouble you?"

"He is very much changed."

"You mean he has come back a Roman."

"Yes."

"Roman!" she continued, half to herself. "To all the world the word means master. How long has he been away?"

"Five years."

She raised her head, and looked off into the night.

"The airs of the Via Sacra[29] are well enough in the streets of the Egyptian and in Babylon; but in Jerusalem—our Jerusalem—the covenant abides."

And, full of the thought, she settled back into her easy place. He was first to speak.

"What Messala said, my mother, was sharp enough in itself; but, taken with the manner, some of the sayings were intolerable."

"I think I understand you. Rome, her poets, orators, senators, courtiers, are mad with affectation of what they call satire."

"I suppose all great peoples are proud," he went on, scarcely noticing the interruption; "but the pride of that people is unlike all others; in these latter days it is so grown the gods barely escape it."

"The gods escape!" said the mother, quickly. "More than one Roman has accepted worship as his divine right."

"Well, Messala always had his share of the disagreeable quality. When he was a child, I have seen him mock strangers whom even Herod condescended to receive with honors; yet he always spared Judea. For the first time, in conversation with me to-day, he trifled with our customs and God. As you would have had me do, I parted with him finally. And now, O

---

28   A great first-century Jewish teacher who counted among his students a young Jewish man who would later convert to Christianity and become known as Saint Paul.

29   A main street in ancient Rome that ran through the Roman Forum, where great philosophers often taught their students.

my dear mother, I would know with more certainty if there be just ground for the Roman's contempt. In what am I his inferior? Is ours a lower order of people? Why should I, even in Cæsar's presence, feel the shrinking of a slave? Tell me especially why, if I have the soul, and so choose, I may not hunt the honors of the world in all its fields? Why may not I take sword and indulge the passion of war? As a poet, why may not I sing of all themes? I can be a worker in metals, a keeper of flocks, a merchant, why not an artist like the Greek? Tell me, O my mother—and this is the sum of my trouble —why may not a son of Israel do all a Roman may?"

The reader will refer these questions back to the conversation in the Market-place; the mother, listening with all her faculties awake, from something which would have been lost upon one less interested in him—from the connections of the subject, the pointing of the questions, possibly his accent and tone—was not less swift in making the same reference. She sat up, and in a voice quick and sharp as his own, replied, "I see, I see! From association Messala, in boyhood, was almost a Jew; had he remained here, he might have become a proselyte, so much do we all borrow from the influences that ripen our lives; but the years in Rome have been too much for him. I do not wonder at the change; yet"—her voice fell—"he might have dealt tenderly at least with you. It is a hard, cruel nature which in youth can forget its first loves."

Her hand dropped lightly upon his forehead, and the fingers caught in his hair and lingered there lovingly, while her eyes sought the highest stars in view. Her pride responded to his, not merely in echo, but in the unison of perfect sympathy. She would answer him; at the same time, not for the world would she have had the answer unsatisfactory: an admission of inferiority might weaken his spirit for life. She faltered with misgivings of her own powers.

"What you propose, O my Judah, is not a subject for treatment by a woman. Let me put its consideration off till to-morrow, and I will have the wise Simeon—"

"Do not send me to the Rector," he said, abruptly.

"I will have him come to us."

"No, I seek more than information; while he might give me that better than you, O my mother, you can do better by giving me what he cannot—the resolution which is the soul of a man's soul."

She swept the heavens with a rapid glance, trying to compass all the meaning of his questions.

"While craving justice for ourselves, it is never wise to be unjust to others. To deny valor in the enemy we have conquered is to underrate our victory; and if the enemy be strong enough to hold us at bay, much more to conquer us"—she hesitated—"self-respect bids us seek some other explanation of our misfortunes than accusing him of qualities inferior to our own."

Thus, speaking to herself rather than to him, she began:

"Take heart, O my son. The Messala is nobly descended; his family has been illustrious through many generations. In the days of Republican Rome—how far back I cannot tell—they were famous, some as soldiers, some as civilians. I can recall but one consul of the name; their rank was senatorial, and their patronage always sought because they were always rich. Yet if to-day your friend boasted of his ancestry, you might have shamed him by recounting yours. If he referred to the ages through which the line is traceable, or to deeds, rank, or wealth—such allusions, except when great occasion demands them, are tokens of small minds—if he mentioned them in proof of his superiority, then without dread, and standing on each particular, you might have challenged him to a comparison of records."

Taking a moment's thought, the mother proceeded:

"One of the ideas of fast hold now is that time has much to do with the nobility of races and families. A Roman boasting his superiority on that account over a son of Israel will always fail when put to the proof. The founding of Rome was his beginning; the very best of them cannot trace their descent beyond that period; few of them pretend to do so; and of such as do, I say not one could make good his claim expect by resort to tradition. Messala certainly could not. Let us look now to ourselves. Could we better?"

A little more light would have enabled him to see the pride that diffused itself over her face.

"Let us imagine the Roman putting us to the challenge. I would answer him, neither doubting nor boastful."

Her voice faltered; a tender thought changed the form of the argument.

"Your father, O my Judah, is at rest with his fathers; yet I remember, as though it were this evening, the day he and I, with many rejoicing friends, went up into the Temple to present you to the Lord. We sacrificed the doves, and to the priest I gave your name, which he wrote in my presence—'Judah, son of Ithamar, of the House of Hur.' The name was then carried away, and written in a book of the division of records devoted to the saintly family.

"I cannot tell you when the custom of registration in this mode began. We know it prevailed before the flight from Egypt. I have heard Hillel[30] say Abraham caused the record to be first opened with his own name, and the names of his sons, moved by the promises of the Lord which separated him and them from all other races, and made them the highest and noblest, the very chosen of the earth. The covenant with Jacob was of like effect. 'In thy seed shall all the nations of the earth be blessed'—so said the angel to Abraham in the place Jehovah-jireh.[31] 'And the land whereon thou liest, to thee will I give it, and to thy seed'[32]— so the Lord himself said to Jacob asleep at Bethel on the way to Haran. Afterwards the wise men looked forward to a just division of the land of promise; and, that it might be known in the day of partition who were entitled to portions, the Book of Generations[33] was begun. But not for that alone. The promise of a blessing to all the earth through the patriarch reached far into the future. One name was mentioned in connection with the blessing—the benefactor might be the humblest of the chosen family, for the Lord our God knows no distinctions of rank or riches. So, to make the performance clear to men of the generation who were to witness it, and that they might give the glory to whom it belonged, the record was required to be kept with absolute certainty. Has it been so kept?"

The fan played to and fro, until, becoming impatient, he repeated the question, "Is the record absolutely true?"

"Hillel said it was, and of all who have lived no one was so well-informed upon the subject. Our people have at times been heedless of some parts of the law, but never of

---

30 Several great Jewish teachers came from the same line, fathered by the renowned Hillel the Elder (110 BCE—10 CE).

31 One of the traditional Hebrew names for God, meaning, "God will provide."

32 Gen. 28:13.

33 A book, now lost, reportedly being a genealogical record of the principal ancestors of the Israelites.

this part. The good rector himself has followed the Books of Generations through three periods—from the promises to the opening of the Temple; thence to the Captivity; thence, again, to the present. Once only were the records disturbed, and that was at the end of the second period; but when the nation returned from the long exile, as a first duty to God, Zerubbabel[34] restored the Books, enabling us once more to carry the lines of Jewish descent back unbroken fully two thousand years. And now—"

She paused as if to allow the hearer to measure the time comprehended in the statement.

"And now," she continued, "what becomes of the Roman boast of blood enriched by ages? By that test, the sons of Israel watching the herds on old Rephaim yonder are nobler than the noblest of the Marcii."

"And I, mother—by the Books, who am I?"

"What I have said thus far, my son, had reference to your question. I will answer you. If Messala were here, he might say, as others have said, that the exact trace of your lineage stopped when the Assyrian took Jerusalem, and razed the Temple, with all its precious stores; but you might plead the pious action of Zerubbabel, and retort that all verity in Roman genealogy ended when the barbarians from the West took Rome, and camped six months upon her desolated site. Did the government keep family histories? If so, what became of them in those dreadful days? No, no; there is verity in our Books of Generations; and, following them back to the Captivity, back to the foundation of the first Temple, back to the march from Egypt, we have absolute assurance that you are lineally sprung from Hur,[35] the associate of Joshua. In the matter of descent sanctified by time, is not the honor perfect? Do you care to pursue further? If so, take the *Torah*, and search the Book of Numbers,[36] and of the seventy-two generations after Adam, you can find the very progenitor of your house."

There was silence for a time in the chamber on the roof.

"I thank you, O my mother," Judah next said, clasping both her hands in his; "I thank you with all my heart. I was right in not having the good rector called in; he could not have satisfied me more than you have. Yet to make a family truly noble, is time alone sufficient?"

"Ah, you forget, you forget; our claim rests not merely upon time; the Lord's preference is our especial glory."

"You are speaking of the race, and I, mother, of the family—our family. In the years since Father Abraham, what have they achieved? What have they done? What great things to lift them above the level of their fellows?"

She hesitated, thinking she might all this time have mistaken his object. The information he sought might have been for more than satisfaction of wounded vanity. Youth is but the painted shell within which, continually growing, lives that wondrous thing the spirit of a man, biding its moment of apparition, earlier in some than in others. She trembled under a perception that this might be the supreme moment come to him; that as children at birth reach out their untried hands grasping for shadows, and crying the while, so his spirit might, in temporary blindness, be struggling to take hold of its impalpable future. They to

---

34 Governor of Judah who, along with Joshua, helped restore the Temple in Jerusalem around 520 BCE.

35 Exod. 17:10.

36 Num. 31:8.

whom a boy comes asking, Who am I, and what am I to be? have need of ever so much care. Each word in answer may prove to the after-life what each finger-touch of the artist is to the clay he is modelling.

"I have a feeling, O my Judah," she said, patting his cheek with the hand he had been caressing—"I have the feeling that all I have said has been in strife with an antagonist more real than imaginary. If Messala is the enemy, do not leave me to fight him in the dark. Tell me all he said."

Chapter V

THE young Israelite proceeded then, and rehearsed his conversation with Messala, dwelling with particularity upon the latter's speeches in contempt of the Jews, their customs, and much pent round of life.

Afraid to speak the while, the mother listened, discerning the matter plainly. Judah had gone to the palace on the Market-place, allured by love of a playmate whom he thought to find exactly as he had been at the parting years before; a man met him, and, in place of laughter and references to the sports of the past, the man had been full of the future, and talked of glory to be won, and of riches and power. Unconscious of the effect, the visitor had come away hurt in pride, yet touched with a natural ambition; but she, the jealous mother, saw it, and, not knowing the turn the aspiration might take, became at once Jewish in her fear. What if it lured him away from the patriarchal faith? In her view, that consequence was more dreadful than any or all others. She could discover but one way to avert it, and she set about the task, her native power reinforced by love to such degree that her speech took a masculine strength and at times a poet's fervor.

"There never has been a people," she began, "who did not think themselves at least equal to any other; never a great nation, my son, that did not believe itself the very superior. When the Roman looks down upon Israel and laughs, he merely repeats the folly of the Egyptian, the Assyrian, and the Macedonian; and as the laugh is against God, the result will be the same."

Her voice became firmer.

"There is no law by which to determine the superiority of nations; hence the vanity of the claim, and the idleness of disputes about it. A people risen, run their race, and die either of themselves or at the hands of another, who, succeeding to their power, take possession of their place, and upon their monuments write new names; such is history. If I were called upon to symbolize God and man in the simplest form, I would draw a straight line and a circle; and of the line I would say, 'This is God, for he alone moves forever straightforward,' and of the circle, 'This is man—such is his progress.' I do not mean that there is no difference between the careers of nations; no two are alike. The difference, however, is not, as some say, in the extent of the circle they describe or the space of earth they cover, but in the sphere of their movement, the highest being nearest God.

"To stop here, my son, would be to leave the subject where we began. Let us go on. There are signs by which to measure the height of the circle each nation runs while in its course. By them let us compare the Hebrew and the Roman.

"The simplest of all the signs is the daily life of the people. Of this I will only say, Israel has at times forgotten God, while the Roman never knew him; consequently comparison is not possible.

"Your friend—or your former friend—charged, if I understood you rightly, that we have had no poets, artists, or warriors; by which he meant, I suppose, to deny that we have had great men, the next most certain of the signs. A just consideration of this charge requires a definition at the commencement. A great man, O my boy, is one whose life proves him to have been recognized, if not called, by God. A Persian was used to punish our recreant fathers, and he carried them into captivity; another Persian was selected to restore their children to the Holy Land; greater than either of them, however, was the Macedonian through whom the desolation of Judea and the Temple was avenged.[37] The special distinction of the men was that they were chosen by the Lord, each for a divine purpose; and that they were Gentiles docs not lessen their glory. Do not lose sight of this definition while I proceed.

"There is an idea that war is the most noble occupation of men, and that the most exalted greatness is the growth of battle-fields. Because the world has adopted the idea, be not you deceived. That we must worship something is a law which will continue as long as there is anything we cannot understand. The prayer of the barbarian is a wail of fear addressed to Strength, the only divine quality he can clearly conceive; hence his faith in heroes. What is Jove but a Roman hero? The Greeks have their great glory because they were the first to set Mind above Strength. In Athens the orator and philosopher were more revered than the warrior. The charioteer and the swiftest runner are still idols of the arena; yet the immortelles are reserved for the sweetest singer. The birthplace of one poet was contested by seven cities. But was the Hellene the first to deny the old barbaric faith? No. My son, that glory is ours; against brutalism our fathers erected God; in our worship, the wail of fear gave place to the Hosanna and the Psalm. So the Hebrew and the Greek would have carried all humanity forward and upward. But, alas! the government of the world presumes war as an eternal condition; wherefore, over Mind and above God, the Roman has enthroned his Cæsar, the absorbent of all attainable power, the prohibition of any other greatness.

"The sway of the Greek was a flowering time for genius. In return for the liberty it then enjoyed, what a company of thinkers the Mind led forth? There was a glory for every excellence, and a perfection so absolute that in everything but war even the Roman has stooped to imitation. A Greek is now the model of the orators in the Forum; listen, and in every Roman song you will hear the rhythm of the Greek; if a Roman opens his mouth speaking wisely of moralities, or abstractions, or of the mysteries of nature, he is either a plagiarist or the disciple of some school which had a Greek for its founder. In nothing but war, I say again, has Rome a claim to originality. Her games and spectacles are Greek inventions, dashed with blood to gratify the ferocity of her rabble; her religion, if such it may be called, is made up of contributions from the faiths of all other peoples; her most venerated gods are from Olympus—even her Mars, and, for that matter, the Jove she much magnifies. So it happens, O my son, that of the whole world our Israel alone can dispute the superiority of the Greek, and with him contest the palm of original genius.

---

37 The Chaldean King Nebuchadnezzar captured Jerusalem in 597 BCE. The Persian King Cyrus then restored the Jews to their homeland some sixty years later. Approximately two centuries later, Alexander the Great (356–323 BCE) of Macedon, led the Greek conquest of Persia.

"To the excellences of other peoples the egotism of a Roman is a blindfold, impenetrable as his breastplate. Oh, the ruthless robbers! Under their trampling the earth trembles like a floor beaten with flails. Along with the rest we are fallen—alas that I should say it to you, my son! They have our highest places, and the holiest, and the end no man can tell; but this I know—they may reduce Judea as an almond broken with hammers, and devour Jerusalem, which is the oil and sweetness thereof; yet the glory of the men of Israel will remain a light in the heavens overhead out of reach: for their history is the history of God, who wrote with their hands, spake with their tongues, and was himself in all the good they did, even the least; who dwelt with them, a Lawgiver on Sinai, a Guide in the wilderness, in war a Captain, in government a King; who once and again pushed back the curtains of the pavilion which is his resting-place, intolerably bright, and, as a man speaking to men, showed them the right, and the way to happiness, and how they should live, and made them promises binding the strength of his Almightiness with covenants sworn to everlastingly. O my son, could it be that they with whom Jehovah thus dwelt, an awful familiar, derived nothing from him?—that in their lives and deeds the common human qualities should not in some degree have been mixed and colored with the divine? that their genius should not have in it, even after the lapse of ages, some little of heaven?"

For a time the rustling of the fan was all the sound heard in the chamber.

"In the sense which limits art to sculpture and painting, it is true," she next said, "Israel has had no artists."

The admission was made regretfully, for it must be remembered she was a Sadducee,[38] whose faith, unlike that of the Pharisees,[39] permitted a love of the beautiful in every form, and without reference to its origin.

"Still he who would do justice," she proceeded, "will not forget that the cunning of our hands was bound by the prohibition, 'Thou shalt not make unto thee any graven image, or any likeness of anything;'[40] which the Sopherim[41] wickedly extended beyond its purpose and time. Nor should it be forgotten that long before Dædalus[42] appeared in Attica and with his wooden statues so transformed sculpture as to make possible the schools of Corinth and Ægina, and their ultimate triumphs the Pœcile and Capitolium— long before the age of Dædalus, I say, two Israelites, Bezaleel and Aholiab, the master-builders of the first tabernacle, said to have been skilled 'in all manner of workmanship,' wrought the cherubim of the mercy-seat above the ark. Of gold beaten, not chiselled, were they; and they were statues in form both human and divine. 'And they shall stretch forth their wings on high, … and their faces shall look one to another.' Who will say they were not beautiful? or that they were not the first statues?"

---

38 A Jewish sect that held only the first five books of the Old Testament to be sacred. They are often compared to the Pharisee sect as a less rigorously religious and more open-minded group.

39 A strict Jewish sect that believed all truth and beauty originated from God and the people who love Him. The meaning of the term "Pharisee" is "separated one," denoting the sect's commitment to being set apart from the less religious and the non-religious of their day.

40 Exod. 20:4.

41 A group of Jewish teachers who built up traditions based on the Jewish laws that not all believed to be necessary or in even in accordance with the laws themselves.

42 The Greek god of handiwork and art, and considered to be the guiding inspiration behind Greek sculpture.

"Oh, I see now why the Greek outstripped us," said Judah, intensely interested. "And the ark; accursed be the Babylonians who destroyed it!"

"Nay, Judah, be of faith. It was not destroyed, only lost, hidden away too safely in some cavern of the mountains. One day—Hillel and Shammai both say so—one day, in the Lord's good time, it will be found and brought forth, and Israel dance before it, singing as of old. And they who look upon the faces of the cherubim then, though they have seen the face of the ivory Minerva, will be ready to kiss the hand of the Jew from love of his genius, asleep through all the thousands of years."

The mother, in her eagerness, had risen into something like the rapidity and vehemence of a speech-maker; but now, to recover herself, or to pick up the thread of her thought, she rested awhile.

"You are so good, my mother," he said, in a grateful way. "And I will never be done saying so. Shammai could not have talked better, nor Hillel. I am a true son of Israel again."

"Flatterer!" she said. "You do not know that I am but repeating what I heard Hillel say in an argument he had one day in my presence with a sophist from Rome."

"Well, the hearty words are yours."

Directly all her earnestness returned.

"Where was I? Oh yes, I was claiming for our Hebrew fathers the first statues. The trick of the sculptor, Judah, is not all there is of art, any more than art is all there is of greatness. I always think of great men marching down the centuries in groups and goodly companies, separable according to nationalities; here the Indian, there the Egyptian, yonder the Assyrian; above them the music of trumpets and the beauty of banners; and on their right hand and left, as reverent spectators, the generations from the beginning, numberless. As they go, I think of the Greek, saying, 'Lo! the Hellene leads the way.' Then the Roman replies, 'Silence! what was your place is ours now; we have left you behind as dust trodden on.' And all the time, from the far front back over the line of march, as well as forward into the farthest future, streams a light of which the wranglers know nothing, except that it is forever leading them on—the Light of Revelation! Who are they that carry it? Ah, the old Judean blood! How it leaps at the thought! By the light we know them. Thrice blessed, O our fathers, servants of God, keepers of the covenants! Ye are the leaders of men, the living and the dead. The front is thine; and though every Roman were a Cæsar, ye shall not lose it!"

Judah was deeply stirred.

"Do not stop, I pray you," he cried. "You give me to hear the sound of timbrels. I wait for Miriam and the women who went after her dancing and singing."[43]

She caught his feeling, and, with ready wit, wove it into her speech.

"Very well, my son. If you can hear the timbrel of the prophetess, you can do what I was about to ask; you can use your fancy, and stand with me, as if by the wayside, while the chosen of Israel pass us at the head of the procession. Now they come—the patriarchs first; next the fathers of the tribes. I almost hear the bells of their camels and the lowing of their herds. Who is he that walks alone between the companies? An old man, yet his eye is not dim, nor his natural force abated. He knew the Lord face to face![44] Warrior, poet, orator, lawgiver, prophet, his greatness is as the sun at morning, its flood of splendor quenching

---

43 Exod. 15:20.
44 Moses. Exod. 33:11.

all other lights, even that of the first and noblest of the Cæsars. After him the judges. And then the kings—the son of Jesse,[45] a hero in war, and a singer of songs eternal as that of the sea; and his son, who, passing all other kings in riches and wisdom, and while making the Desert habitable, and in its waste places planting cities, forgot not Jerusalem which the Lord had chosen for his seat on earth. Bend lower, my son! These that come next are the first of their kind, and the last. Their faces are raised, as if they heard a voice in the sky and were listening. Their lives were full of sorrows. Their garments smell of tombs and caverns. Hearken to a woman among them—'Sing ye to the Lord, for he hath triumphed gloriously!'[46] Nay, put your forehead in the dust before them! They were tongues of God, his servants, who looked through heaven, and, seeing all the future, wrote what they saw, and left the writing to be proven by time. Kings turned pale as they approached them, and nations trembled at the sound of their voices. The elements waited upon them. In their hands they carried every bounty and every plague. See the Tishbite and his servant Elisha![47] See the sad son of Hilkiah, and him, the seer of visions, by the river of Chebar![48] And of the three children of Judah who refused the image of the Babylonian,[49] lo! that one who, in the feast to the thousand lords, so confounded the astrologers. And yonder—O my son, kiss the dust again!— yonder the gentle son of Amoz,[50] from whom the world has its promise of the Messiah to come!"

In this passage the fan had been kept in rapid play; it stopped now, and her voice sank low.

"You are tired," she said.

"No," he replied, "I was listening to a new song of Israel."

The mother was still intent upon her purpose, and passed the pleasant speech.

"In such light as I could, my Judah, I have set our great men before you—patriarchs, legislators, warriors, singers, prophets. Turn we to the best of Rome. Against Moses place Cæsar, and Tarquin against David; Sylla against either of the Maccabees; the best of the consuls against the judges; Augustus against Solomon, and you are done: comparison ends there. But think then of the prophets—greatest of the great."

She laughed scornfully.

"Pardon me. I was thinking of the soothsayer who warned Caius Julius against the ides of March, and fancied him looking for the omens of evil which his master despised in the entrails of a chicken. From that picture turn to Elijah sitting on the hill-top on the way to Samaria, amid the smoking bodies of the captains and their fifties, warning the son of Ahab of the wrath of our God.[51] Finally, O my Judah—if such speech be reverent—how shall we judge Jehovah and Jupiter unless it be by what their servants have done in their names? And as for what you shall do—"

---

45 David, first king of a united Israel. 1 Sam. 16.

46 Exod. 15:1.

47 Old Testament prophets Elijah and Elisha, 2 Kings 3:11.

48 Refers to the prophet Ezekiel, Ezek. 43:3.

49 Allusion to Meshach, Shadrach and Abednego, who stayed faithful to the Lord even when under Babylonian rule. Daniel was also friends with these three and had the ability to prophesy and interpret dreams. Daniel 1–3.

50 Isaiah the prophet, whose writings included several references to the coming Messiah of the Jewish nation. 2 Kings 19:2.

51 1 Kings 21:21.

She spoke the latter words slowly, and with a tremulous utterance.

"As for what you shall do, my boy—serve the Lord, the Lord God of Israel, not Rome. For a child of Abraham there is no glory except in the Lord's ways, and in them there is much glory."

"I may be a soldier then?" Judah asked.

"Why not? Did not Moses call God a man of war?"

There was then a long silence in the summer chamber.

"You have my permission," she said, finally; "if only you serve the Lord instead of Cæsar."

He was content with the condition, and by-and-by fell asleep. She arose then, and put the cushion under his head, and, throwing a shawl over him and kissing him tenderly, went away.

Chapter VI

THE good man, like the bad, must die; but, remembering the lesson of our faith, we say of him and the event, "No matter, lie will open his eyes in heaven." Nearest this in life is the waking from healthful sleep to a quick consciousness of happy sights and sounds.

When Judah awoke, the sun was up over the mountains; the pigeons were abroad in flocks, filling the air with the gleams of their white wings; and off southeast he beheld the Temple, an apparition of gold in the blue of the sky. These, however, were familiar objects, and they received but a glance; upon the edge of the divan, close by him, a girl scarcely fifteen sat singing to the accompaniment of a *nebel*,[52] which she rested upon her knee, and touched gracefully. To her he turned listening; and this was what she sang:

The Song

"Wake not, but hear me, love!
   Adrift, adrift on slumber's sea,
   Thy spirit call to list to me.
Wake not, but hear me, love!
   A gift from Sleep, the restful king,
   All happy, happy dreams I bring.
"Wake not, but hear me, love!
   Of all the world of dreams 'tis thine
   This once to choose the most divine.
So choose, and sleep, my love!
   But ne'er again in choice be free,
   Unless, unless—thou dream'st of me."

She put the instrument down, and, resting her hands in her lap, waited for him to speak. And as it has become necessary to tell somewhat of her, we will avail ourselves of the chance, and add such particulars of the family into whose privacy we are brought as the reader may wish to know.

---

52 A small harp.

The favors of Herod had left surviving him many persons of vast estate. Where this fortune was joined to undoubted lineal descent from some famous son of one of the tribes, especially Judah, the happy individual was accounted a Prince of Jerusalem—a distinction which sufficed to bring him the homage of his less favored countrymen, and the respect, if nothing more, of the Gentiles with whom business and social circumstance brought him into dealing. Of this class none had won in private or public life a higher regard than the father of the lad whom we have been following. With a remembrance of his nationality which never failed him, he had yet been true to the king, and served him faithfully at home and abroad. Some offices had taken him to Rome, where his conduct attracted the notice of Augustus, who strove without reserve to engage his friendship. In his house, accordingly, were many presents, such as had gratified the vanity of kings—purple togas, ivory chairs, golden *pateræ*⁵³—chiefly valuable on account of the imperial hand which had honorably conferred them. Such a man could not fail to be rich; yet his wealth was not altogether the largess of royal patrons. He had welcomed the law that bound him to some pursuit; and, instead of one, he entered into many. Of the herdsmen watching flocks on the plains and hill-sides, far as old Lebanon, numbers reported to him as their employer; in the cities by the sea, and in those inland, he founded houses of traffic; his ships brought him silver from Spain, whose mines were then the richest known; while his caravans came twice a year from the East, laden with silks and spices. In faith he was a Hebrew, observant of the law and every essential rite; his place in the synagogue and Temple knew him well; he was thoroughly learned in the Scriptures; he delighted in the society of the college-masters, and carried his reverence for Hillel almost to the point of worship. Yet he was in no sense a Separatist; his hospitality took in strangers from every land; the carping Pharisees even accused him of having more than once entertained Samaritans⁵⁴ at his table. Had he been a Gentile, and lived, the world might have heard of him as the rival of Herodes Atticus:⁵⁵ as it was, he perished at sea some ten years before this second period of our story, in the prime of life, and lamented everywhere in Judea. We are already acquainted with two members of his family —his widow and son; the only other was a daughter—she whom we have seen singing to her brother.

Tirzah was her name, and as the two looked at each other, their resemblance was plain. Her features had the regularity of his, and were of the same Jewish type; they had also the charm of childish innocency of expression. Home-life and its trustful love permitted the negligent attire in which she appeared. A chemise buttoned upon the right shoulder, and passing loosely over the breast and back and under the left arm, but half concealed her person above the waist, while it left the arms entirely nude. A girdle caught the folds of the garment, marking the commencement of the skirt. The coiffure was very simple and becoming—a silken cap, Tyrian-dyed; and over that a striped scarf of the same material, beautifully embroidered, and wound about in thin folds so as to show the shape of the head without enlarging it; the whole finished by a tassel dropping from the crown point of the cap. She had rings, ear and finger; anklets and bracelets, all of gold; and around her neck there was a collar of gold, curiously garnished with a network of delicate chains, to

---

53 An ornate ceramic or metal bowl.

54 Neighbors of Judea who were much despised by the Jewish population because of their intermixed Jewish roots and commitment to a non-Judaic monotheism.

55 Wallace shifts his timeline here. Herodes Atticus was a Roman senator and philosopher who lived after the time of this novel (101–77).

which were pendants of pearl. The edges of her eyelids were painted, and the tips of her fingers stained. Her hair fell in two long plaits down her back. A curled lock rested upon each cheek in front of the ear. Altogether it would have been impossible to deny her grace, refinement, and beauty.

"Very pretty, my Tirzah, very pretty!" he said, with animation.

"The song?" she asked.

"Yes—and the singer, too. It has the conceit of a Greek. Where did you get it?"

"You remember the Greek who sang in the theatre last month? They said he used to be a singer at the court for Herod and his sister Salome. He came out just after an exhibition of wrestlers, when the house was full of noise. At his first note everything became so quiet that I heard every word. I got the song from him."

"But he sang in Greek."

"And I in Hebrew."

"Ah, yes. I am proud of my little sister. Have you another as good?"

"Very many. But let them go now. Amrah sent me to tell you she will bring you your breakfast, and that you need not come down. She should be here by this time. She thinks you sick—that a dreadful accident happened you yesterday. What was it? Tell me, and I will help Amrah doctor you. She knows the cures of the Egyptians, who were always a stupid set; but I have a great many recipes of the Arabs who—"

"Are even more stupid than the Egyptians," he said, shaking his head.

"Do you think so? Very well, then," she replied, almost without pause, and putting her hands to her left ear. "We will have nothing to do with any of them. I have here what is much surer and better—the amulet which was given to some of our people—I cannot tell when, it was so far back—by a Persian magician. See, the inscription is almost worn out."

She offered him the ear-ring, which he took, looked at, and handed back, laughing.

"If I were dying, Tirzah, I could not use the charm. It is a relic of idolatry, forbidden every believing son and daughter of Abraham. Take it, but do not wear it any more."

"Forbidden! Not so," she said. "Our father's mother wore it I do not know how many Sabbaths in her life. It has cured I do not know how many people—more than three anyhow. It is approved—look, here is the mark of the rabbis."

"I have no faith in amulets."

She raised her eyes to his in astonishment.

"What would Amrah say?"

"Amrah's father and mother tended *sakiyeh*[56] for a garden on the Nile."

"But Gamaliel!"

"He says they are godless inventions of unbelievers and Shechemites."[57]

Tirzah looked at the ring doubtfully.

"What shall I do with it?"

"Wear it, my little sister. It becomes you—it helps make you beautiful, though I think you that without help."

Satisfied, she returned the amulet to her ear just as Amrah entered the summer chamber, bearing a platter, with wash-bowl, water, and napkins.

Not being a Pharisee, the ablution was short and simple with Judah. The servant then went out, leaving Tirzah to dress his hair. When a lock was disposed to her satisfaction, she

---

56 A water wheel used in irrigating gardens.
57 Samaritans who inhabited Schecem, a large city in Samaria.

would unloose the small metallic mirror which, as was the fashion among her fair country-women, she wore at her girdle, and give it to him, that he might see the triumph, and how handsome it made him. Meanwhile they kept up their conversation.

"What do you think, Tirzah?—I am going away."

She dropped her hands with amazement.

"Going away! When? Where? For what?"

He laughed.

"Three questions, all in a breath! What a body you are!" Next instant he became serious. "You know the law requires me to follow some occupation. Our good father set me an example. Even you would despise me if I spent in idleness the results of his industry and knowledge. I am going to Rome."

"Oh, I will go with you."

"You must stay with mother. If both of us leave her she will die."

The brightness faded from her face.

"Ah, yes, yes! But—must you go? Here in Jerusalem you can learn all that is needed to be a merchant—if that is what you are thinking of."

"But that is not what I am thinking of. The law does not require the son to be what the father was."

"What else can you be?"

"A soldier," he replied, with a certain pride of voice.

Tears came into her eyes.

"You will be killed."

"If God's will, be it so. But, Tirzah, the soldiers are not all killed."

She threw her arms around his neck, as if to hold him back.

"We are so happy! Stay at home, my brother."

"Home cannot always be what it is. You yourself will be going away before long."

"Never!"

He smiled at her earnestness.

"A prince of Judah, or some other of one of the tribes, will come soon and claim my Tirzah, and ride away with her, to be the light of another house. What will then become of me?"

She answered with sobs.

"War is a trade," he continued, more soberly. "To learn it thoroughly, one must go to school, and there is no school like a Roman camp."

"You would not fight for Rome?" she asked, holding her breath.

"And you—even you hate her. The whole world hates her. In that, O Tirzah, find the reason of the answer I give you— Yes, I will fight for her, if, in return, she will teach me how one day to fight against her."

"When will you go?"

Amrah's steps were then heard returning.

"Hist!" he said. "Do not let her know of what I am thinking."

The faithful slave came in with breakfast, and placed the waiter holding it upon a stool before them; then, with white napkins upon her arm, she remained to serve them. They dipped their fingers in a bowl of water, and were rinsing them, when a noise arrested their attention. They listened, and distinguished martial music in the street on the north side of the house.

"Soldiers from the Prætorium! I must see them," he cried, springing from the divan, and running out.

In a moment more he was leaning over the parapet of tiles which guarded the roof at the extreme northeast corner, so absorbed that he did not notice Tirzah by his side, resting one hand upon his shoulder.

Their position—the roof being the highest one in the locality—commanded the house-tops eastward as far as the huge irregular Tower of Antonia, which has been already mentioned as a citadel for the garrison and military headquarters for the governor. The street, not more than ten feet wide, was spanned here and there by bridges, open and covered, which, like the roofs along the way, were beginning to be occupied by men, women, and children, called out by the *music*. The word is used, though it is hardly fitting; what the people heard when they came forth was rather an uproar of trumpets and the shriller *lituï*[58] so delightful to the soldiers.

The array after a while came into view of the two upon the house of the Hurs. First, a vanguard of the light-armed—mostly slingers and bowmen—marching with wide intervals between their ranks and files; next a body of heavy-armed infantry, bearing large shields, and *hastœ longœ*, or spears identical with those used in the duels before Ilium; then the musicians; and then an officer riding alone, but followed closely by a guard of cavalry; after them again, a column of infantry also heavy-armed, which, moving in close order, crowded the street from wall to wall, and appeared to be without end.

The brawny limbs of the men; the cadenced motion from right to left of the shields; the sparkle of scales, buckles, and breastplates and helms, all perfectly burnished; the plumes nodding above the tall crests; the sway of ensigns and iron-shod spears; the bold, confident step, exactly timed and measured; the demeanor, so grave, yet so watchful; the machine-like unity of the whole moving mass—made an impression upon Judah, but as something felt rather than seen. Two objects fixed his attention—the eagle of the legion first—a gilded effigy perched on a tall shaft, with wings outspread until they met above its head. He knew that, when brought from its chamber in the Tower, it had been received with divine honors.

The officer riding alone in the midst of the column was the other attraction. His head was bare; otherwise he was in full armor. At his left hip he wore a short sword; in his hand, however, he carried a truncheon, which looked like a roll of white paper. He sat upon a purple cloth instead of a saddle, and that, and a bridle with a forestall of gold and reins of yellow silk broadly fringed at the lower edge, completed the housings of the horse.

While the man was yet in the distance, Judah observed that his presence was sufficient to throw the people looking at him into angry excitement. They would lean over the parapets or stand boldly out, and shake their fists at him; they followed him with loud cries, and spit at him as he passed under the bridges; the women even flung their sandals, sometimes with such good effect as to hit him. When he was nearer, the yells became distinguishable—"Robber, tyrant, dog of a Roman! Away with Ishmael! Give us back our Hannas!"

When quite near, Judah could see that, as was but natural, the man did not share the indifference so superbly shown by the soldiers; his face was dark and sullen, and the glances he occasionally cast at his persecutors were full of menace; the very timid shrank from them.

Now the lad had heard of the custom, borrowed from a habit of the first Cæsar, by which chief commanders, to indicate their rank, appeared in public with only a laurel vine

---

58 A curved trumpet, favored by the Roman legions, and that produced a shrill tone.

upon their heads. By that sign he knew this officer—Valerius Gratus, the New Procurator of Judea!

To say truth now, the Roman under the unprovoked storm had the young Jew's sympathy; so that when he reached the corner of the house, the latter leaned yet farther over the parapet to see him go by, and in the act rested a hand upon a tile which had been a long time cracked and allowed to go unnoticed. The pressure was strong enough to displace the outer piece, which started to fall. A thrill of horror shot through the youth. He reached out to catch the missile. In appearance the motion was exactly that of one pitching something from him. The effort failed—nay, it served to push the descending fragment farther out over the wall. He shouted with all his might. The soldiers of the guard looked up; so did the great man, and that moment the missile struck him, and he fell from his seat as dead.

The cohort halted; the guards leaped from their horses, and hastened to cover the chief with their shields. On the other hand, the people who witnessed the affair, never doubting that the blow had been purposely dealt, cheered the lad as he yet stooped in full view over the parapet, transfixed by what he beheld, and by anticipation of the consequences flashed all too plainly upon him.

A mischievous spirit flew with incredible speed from roof to roof along the line of march, seizing the people, and urging them all alike. They laid hands upon the parapets and tore up the tiling and the sunburnt mud of which the house-tops were for the most part made, and with blind fury began to fling them upon the legionaries halted below. A battle then ensued. Discipline, of course, prevailed. The struggle, the slaughter, the skill of one side, the desperation of the other, are alike unnecessary to our story. Let us look rather to the wretched author of it all.

He arose from the parapet, his face very pale.

"O Tirzah, Tirzah! What will become of us?"

She had not seen the occurrence below, but was listening to the shouting and watching the mad activity of the people in view on the houses. Something terrible was going on, she knew; but what it was, or the cause, or that she or any of those dear to her were in danger, she did not know.

"What has happened? What does it all mean?" she asked, in sudden alarm.

"I have killed the Roman governor. The tile fell upon him."

An unseen hand appeared to sprinkle her face with the dust of ashes—it grew white so instantly. She put her arm around him, and looked wistfully, but without a word, into his eyes. His fears had passed to her, and the sight of them gave him strength.

"I did not do it purposely, Tirzah—it was an accident," he said, more calmly.

"What will they do?" she asked.

He looked off over the tumult momentarily deepening in the street and on the roofs, and thought of the sullen countenance of Gratus. If he were not dead, where would his vengeance stop? And if he were dead, to what height of fury would not the violence of the people lash the legionaries? To evade an answer, he peered over the parapet again, just as the guard were assisting the Roman to remount his horse.

"He lives, he lives, Tirzah! Blessed be the Lord God of our fathers!"

With that outcry, and a brightened countenance, he drew back and replied to her question.

"Be not afraid, Tirzah. I will explain how it happened, and they will remember our father and his services, and not hurt us."

He was leading her to the summer-house, when the roof jarred under their feet, and a crash of strong timbers being burst away, followed by a cry of surprise and agony, arose apparently from the court-yard below. He stopped and listened. The cry was repeated; then came a rush of many feet, and voices lifted in rage blent with voices in prayer; and then the screams of women in mortal terror. The soldiers had beaten in the north gate, and were in possession of the house. The terrible sense of being hunted smote him. His first impulse was to fly; but where? Nothing but wings would serve him. Tirzah, her eyes wild with fear, caught his arm.

"O Judah, what does it mean?"

The servants were being butchered—and his mother! Was not one of the voices he heard hers? With all the will left him, he said, "Stay here, and wait for me, Tirzah. I will go down and see what is the matter, and come back to you."

His voice was not steady as he wished. She clung closer to him.

Clearer, shriller, no longer a fancy, his mother's cry arose. He hesitated no longer.

"Come, then, let us go."

The terrace or gallery at the foot of the steps was crowded with soldiers. Other soldiers with drawn swords ran in and out of the chambers. At one place a number of women on their knees clung to each other or prayed for mercy. Apart from them, one with torn garments, and long hair streaming over her face, struggled to tear loose from a man all whose strength was tasked to keep his hold. Her cries were shrillest of all; cutting through the clamor, they had risen distinguishably to the roof. To her Judah sprang—his steps were long and swift, almost a winged flight—"Mother, mother!" he shouted. She stretched her hands towards him; but when almost touching them he was seized and forced aside. Then he heard some one say, speaking loudly.

"That is he!"

Judah looked, and saw—Messala.

"What, the assassin—that?" said a tall man, in legionary armor of beautiful finish. "Why, he is but a boy."

"Gods!" replied Messala, not forgetting his drawl. "A new philosophy! What would Seneca say to the proposition that a man must be old before he can hate enough to kill? You have him; and that is his mother; yonder his sister. You have the whole family."

For love of them, Judah forgot his quarrel.

"Help them, O my Messala! Remember our childhood and help them. I—Judah—pray you."

Messala affected not to hear.

"I cannot be of further use to you," he said to the officer. "There is richer entertainment in the street. Down Eros, up Mars!"

With the last words he disappeared. Judah understood him, and, in the bitterness of his soul, prayed to Heaven.

"In the hour of thy vengeance, O Lord," he said, "be mine the hand to put it upon him!"

By great exertion, he drew nearer the officer.

"O sir, the woman you hear is my mother. Spare her, spare my sister yonder. God is just, he will give you mercy for mercy."

The man appeared to be moved.

"To the Tower with the women!" he shouted, "but do them no harm. I will demand them of you." Then to those holding Judah, he said, "Get cords, and bind his hands, and take him to the street. His punishment is reserved."

The mother was carried away. The little Tirzah, in her home attire, stupefied with fear, went passively with her keepers. Judah gave each of them a last look, and covered his face with his hands, as if to possess himself of the scene fadelessly. He may have shed tears, though no one saw them.

There took place in him then what may be justly called the wonder of life. The thoughtful reader of these pages has ere this discerned enough to know that the young Jew in disposition was gentle even to womanliness—a result that seldom fails the habit of loving and being loved. The circumstances through which he had come had made no call upon the harsher elements of his nature, if such he had. At times he had felt the stir and impulses of ambition, but they had been like the formless dreams of a child walking by the sea and gazing at the coming and going of stately ships. But now, if we can imagine an idol, sensible of the worship it was accustomed to, dashed suddenly from its altar, and lying amidst the wreck of its little world of love, an idea may be had of what had befallen the young Ben-Hur, and of its effect upon his being. Yet there was no sign, nothing to indicate that he had undergone a change, except that when he raised his head, and held his arms out to be bound, the bend of the Cupid's bow had vanished from his lips. In that instant he had put off childhood and become a man.

A trumpet sounded in the court-yard. With the cessation of the call, the gallery was cleared of the soldiery; many of whom, as they dared not appear in the ranks with visible plunder in their hands, flung what they had upon the floor, until it was strewn with articles of richest *virtù*. When Judah descended, the formation was complete, and the officer waiting to see his last order executed.

The mother, daughter, and entire household were led out of the north gate, the ruins of which choked the passageway. The cries of the domestics, some of whom had been born in the house, were most pitiable. When, finally, the horses and all the dumb tenantry of the place were driven past him, Judah began to comprehend the scope of the procurator's vengeance. The very structure was devoted. Far as the order was possible of execution, nothing living was to be left within its walls. If in Judea there were others desperate enough to think of assassinating a Roman governor, the story of what befell the princely family of Hur would be a warning to them, while the ruin of the habitation would keep the story alive.

The officer waited outside while a detail of men temporarily restored the gate.

In the street the fighting had almost ceased. Upon the houses here and there clouds of dust told where the struggle was yet prolonged. The cohort was, for the most part, standing at rest, its splendor, like its ranks, in nowise diminished. Borne past the point of care for himself, Judah had heart for nothing in view but the prisoners, among whom he looked in vain for his mother and Tirzah.

Suddenly, from the earth where she had been lying, a woman arose and started swiftly back to the gate. Some of the guards reached out to seize her, and a great shout followed their failure. She ran to Judah, and, dropping down, clasped his knees, the coarse black hair powdered with dust veiling her eyes.

"O Amrah, good Amrah," he said to her, "God help you; I cannot."

She could not speak.

He bent down, and whispered, "Live, Amrah, for Tirzah and my mother. They will come back, and—"

A soldier drew her away; whereupon she sprang up and rushed through the gateway and passage into the vacant court-yard.

"Let her go," the officer shouted. "We will seal the house, and she will starve."

The men resumed their work, and, when it was finished there, passed round to the west side. That gate was also secured, after which the palace of the Hurs was lost to use.

The cohort at length marched back to the Tower, where the procurator stayed to recover from his hurts and dispose of his prisoners. On the tenth day following, he visited the Market-place.

Chapter VII

Next day a detachment of legionaries went to the desolated palace, and, closing the gates permanently, plastered the corners with wax, and at the sides nailed a notice in Latin:

"THIS IS THE PROPERTY OF THE EMPEROR."

In the haughty Roman idea, the sententious announcement was thought sufficient for the purpose—and it was.

The day after that again, about noon, a decurion with his command of ten horsemen approached Nazareth from the south—that is, from the direction of Jerusalem. The place was then a straggling village, perched on a hill-side, and so insignificant that its one street was little more than a path well beaten by the coming and going of flocks and herds. The great plain of Esdraelon crept close to it on the south, and from the height on the west a view could be had of the shores of the Mediterranean, the region beyond the Jordan, and Hermon. The valley below, and the country on every side, were given to gardens, vineyards, orchards, and pasturage. Groves of palm-trees Orientalized the landscape. The houses, in irregular assemblage, were of the humbler class—square, one-story, flat-roofed, and covered with bright-green vines. The drought that had burned the hills of Judea to a crisp, brown and lifeless, stopped at the boundary-line of Galilee.

A trumpet, sounded when the cavalcade drew near the village, had a magical effect upon the inhabitants. The gates and front doors cast forth groups eager to be the first to catch the meaning of a visitation so unusual.

Nazareth, it must be remembered, was not only aside from any great highway, but within the sway of Judas of Gamala;[59] wherefore it should not be hard to imagine the feelings with which the legionaries were received. But when they were up and traversing the street, the duty that occupied them became apparent, and then fear and hatred were lost in curiosity, under the impulse of which the people, knowing there must be a halt at the well in the northeastern part of the town, quit their gates and doors, and closed in after the procession.

A prisoner whom the horsemen were guarding was the object of curiosity. He was afoot, bareheaded, half naked, his hands bound behind him. A thong fixed to his wrists was looped over the neck of a horse. The dust went with the party when in movement, wrapping him in yellow fog, sometimes in a dense cloud. He dropped forward, footsore and faint. The villagers could see he was young.

At the well the decurion halted, and, with most of the men, dismounted. The prisoner sank down in the dust of the road, stupefied, and asking nothing: apparently he was in the

---

59 Judas was a Jewish rebel in Galilee who fought against the Roman occupation of Judea.

last stage of exhaustion. Seeing, when they came near, that he was but a boy, the villagers would have helped him had they dared.

In the midst of their perplexity, and while the pitchers were passing among the soldiers, a man was descried coming down the road from Sepphoris. At sight of him a woman cried out, "Look! Yonder comes the carpenter. Now we will hear something."

The person spoken of was quite venerable in appearance. Thin white locks fell below the edge of his full turban, and a mass of still whiter beard flowed down the front of his coarse gray gown. He came slowly, for, in addition to his age, he carried some tools—an axe, a saw, and a drawing-knife, all very rude and heavy—and had evidently travelled some distance without rest.

He stopped close by to survey the assemblage.

"O Rabbi, good Rabbi Joseph!" cried a woman, running to him. "Here is a prisoner; come ask the soldiers about him, that we may know who he is, and what he has done, and what they are going to do with him."

The rabbi's face remained stolid; he glanced at the prisoner, however, and presently went to the officer.

"The peace of the Lord be with you!" he said, with unbending gravity.

"And that of the gods with you," the decurion replied.

"Are you from Jerusalem?"

"Yes."

"Your prisoner is young."

"In years, yes."

"May I ask what he has done?"

"He is an assassin."

The people repeated the word in astonishment, but Rabbi Joseph pursued his inquest.

"Is he a son of Israel?"

"He is a Jew," said the Roman, dryly.

The wavering pity of the bystanders came back.

"I know nothing of your tribes, but can speak of his family," the speaker continued. "You may have heard of a prince of Jerusalem named Hur—Ben-Hur, they called him. He lived in Herod's day."

"I have seen him," Joseph said.

"Well, this is his son."

Exclamations became general, and the decurion hastened to stop them.

"In the streets of Jerusalem, day before yesterday, he nearly killed the noble Gratus by flinging a tile upon his head from the roof of a palace—his father's, I believe."

There was a pause in the conversation during which the Nazarenes gazed at the young Ben-Hur as at a wild beast.

"Did he kill him?" asked the rabbi.

"No."

"He is under sentence."

"Yes—the galleys for life."

"The Lord help him!" said Joseph, for once moved out of his stolidity.

Thereupon a youth who came up with Joseph, but had stood behind him unobserved, laid down an axe he had been carrying, and, going to the great stone standing by the well, took from it a pitcher of water. The action was so quiet that before the guard could interfere, had they been disposed to do so, he was stooping over the prisoner, and offering him drink.

The hand laid kindly upon his shoulder awoke the unfortunate Judah, and, looking up, he saw a face he never forgot—the face of a boy about his own age, shaded by locks of yellowish bright chestnut hair; a face lighted by dark-blue eyes, at the time so soft, so appealing, so full of love and holy purpose, that they had all the power of command and will. The spirit of the Jew, hardened though it was by days and nights of suffering, and so embittered by wrong that its dreams of revenge took in all the world, melted under the stranger's look, and became as a child's. He put his lips to the pitcher, and drank long and deep. Not a word was said to him, nor did he say a word.

When the draught was finished, the hand that had been resting upon the sufferer's shoulder was placed upon his head, and stayed there in the dusty locks time enough to say a blessing; the stranger then returned the pitcher to its place on the stone, and, taking his axe again, went back to Rabbi Joseph. All eyes went with him, the decurion's as well as those of the villagers.

This was the end of the scene at the well. When the men had drunk, and the horses, the march was resumed. But the temper of the decurion was not as it had been; he himself raised the prisoner from the dust, and helped him on a horse behind a soldier. The Nazarenes went to their houses—among them Rabbi Joseph and his apprentice.

And so, for the first time, Judah and the son of Mary met and parted.

Book Third

    "Cleopatra… Our size of sorrow,
Proportion'd to our cause, must be as great
As that which makes it.—
      Enter, below, DIOMEDES.
                    How now? is he dead?
Diomedes. His death's upon him, but not dead."
        Antony and Cleopatra (act iv., sc. xiii.).

Chapter I

THE city of Misenum gave name to the promontory which it crowned, a few miles southwest of Naples. An account of ruins is all that remains of it now; yet in the year of our Lord 24— to which it is desirable to advance the reader—the place was one of the most important on the western coast of Italy.[60]

In the year mentioned, a traveller coming to the promontory to regale himself with the view there offered, would have mounted a wall, and, with the city at his back, looked over the bay of Neapolis, as charming then as now; and then, as now, he would have seen the matchless shore, the smoking cone, the sky and waves so softly, deeply blue, Ischia here and Capri yonder; from one to the other and back again, through the purpled air, his gaze would have sported; at last—for the eyes do weary of the beautiful as the palate with sweets—at last it would have dropped upon a spectacle which the modern tourist cannot see—half the reserve navy of Rome astir or at anchor below him. Thus regarded, Misenum was a very proper place for three masters to meet, and at leisure parcel the world among them.

---

60 [Author's Original Note] The Roman government, it will be remembered, had two harbors in which great fleets were constantly kept—Ravenna and Misenum.

In the old time, moreover, there was a gateway in the wall at a certain point fronting the sea—an empty gateway forming the outlet of a street which, after the exit, stretched itself, in the form of a broad mole, out many stadia into the waves.

The watchman on the wall above the gateway was disturbed, one cool September morning, by a party coming down the street in noisy conversation. He gave one look, then settled into his drowse again.

There were twenty or thirty persons in the party, of whom the greater number were slaves with torches which flamed little and smoked much, leaving on the air the perfume of the Indian nard. The masters walked in advance arm-in-arm. One of them, apparently fifty years old, slightly bald, and wearing over his scant locks a crown of laurel, seemed, from the attentions paid him, the central object of some affectionate ceremony. They all sported ample togas of white wool broadly bordered with purple. A glance had sufficed the watchman. He knew, without question, they were of high rank, and escorting a friend to ship after a night of festivity. Further explanation will be found in the conversation they carried on.

"No, my Quintus," said one, speaking to him with the crown, "it is ill of Fortune to take thee from us so soon. Only yesterday thou didst return from the seas beyond the Pillars. Why, thou hast not even got back thy land legs."

"By Castor! if a man may swear a woman's oath," said another, somewhat worse of wine, "let us not lament. Our Quintus is but going to find what he lost last night. Dice on a rolling ship is not dice on shore—eh, Quintus?"

"Abuse not Fortune!" exclaimed a third. "She is not blind or fickle. At Antium, where our Arrius questions her, she answers him with nods, and at sea she abides with him holding the rudder. She takes him from us, but does she not always give him back with a new victory?"

"The Greeks are taking him away," another broke in. "Let us abuse them, not the gods. In learning to trade they forgot how to fight."

With these words, the party passed the gateway, and came upon the mole, with the bay before them beautiful in the morning light. To the veteran sailor the plash of the waves was like a greeting. He drew a long breath, as if the perfume of the water were sweeter than that of the nard, and held his hand aloft.

"My gifts were at Præneste, not Antium—and see! Wind from the west. Thanks, O Fortune, my mother!" he said, earnestly.

The friends all repeated the exclamation, and the slaves waved their torches.

"She comes—yonder!" he continued, pointing to a galley outside the mole. "What need has a sailor for other mistress? Is your Lucrece more graceful, my Caius?"

He gazed at the coming ship, and justified his pride. A white sail was bent to the low mast, and the oars dipped, arose, poised a moment, then dipped again, with wing-like action, and in perfect time.

"Yes, spare the gods," he said, soberly, his eyes fixed upon the vessel. "They send us opportunities. Ours the fault if we fail. And as for the Greeks, you forget, O my Lentulus, the pirates I am going to punish are Greeks. One victory over them is of more account than a hundred over the Africans."

"Then thy way is to the Ægean?"

The sailor's eyes were full of his ship.

"What grace, what freedom! A bird hath not less care for the fretting of the waves. See!" he said, but almost immediately added, "Thy pardon, my Lentulus. I am going to the Ægean; and as my departure is so near, I will tell the occasion—only keep it under the rose. I would not that you abuse the duumvir when next you meet him. He is my friend. The trade between Greece and Alexandria, as ye may have heard, is hardly inferior to that between Alexandria and Rome. The people in that part of the world forgot to celebrate the Cerealia, and Triptolemus[61] paid them with a harvest not worth the gathering. At all events, the trade is so grown that it will not brook interruption a day. Ye may also have heard of the Chersonesan pirates, nested up in the Euxine; none bolder, by the Bacchæ! Yesterday word came to Rome that, with a fleet, they had rowed down the Bosphorus, sunk the galleys off Byzantium and Chalcedon, swept the Propontis, and, still unsated, burst through into the Ægean. The corn-merchants who have ships in the East Mediterranean are frightened. They had audience with the Emperor himself, and from Ravenna there go to-day a hundred galleys, and from Misenum"—he paused as if to pique the curiosity of his friends, and ended with an emphatic—"one."

"Happy Quintus! We congratulate thee!"

"The preferment forerunneth promotion. We salute thee duumvir;[62] nothing less."

"Quintus Arrius, the duumvir, hath a better sound than Quintus Arrius, the tribune." In such manner they showered him with congratulations.

"I am glad with the rest," said the bibulous friend, "very glad; but I must be practical, O my duumvir; and not until I know if promotion will help thee to knowledge of the tesseræ will I have an opinion as to whether the gods mean thee ill or good in this—this business."

"Thanks, many thanks!" Arrius replied, speaking to them collectively. "Had ye but lanterns, I would say ye were augurs. *Perpol!* I will go further, and show what master diviners ye are! See—and read."

From the folds of his toga he drew a roll of paper, and passed it to them, saying, "Received while at table last night from—Sejanus."

The name was already a great one in the Roman world; great, and not so infamous as it afterwards became.

"Sejanus!" they exclaimed, with one voice, closing in to read what the minister had written.

"Sejanus to C. Cæcilius Rufus, Duumvir.

"ROME, *XIX. Kal. Sept.*

"Cæsar hath good report of Quintus Arrius, the tribune. In particular he hath heard of his valor, manifested in the western seas; insomuch that it is his will that the said Quintus be transferred instantly to the East.

"It is our Cæsar's will, further, that you cause a hundred triremes, of the first class, and full appointment, to be despatched without delay against the pirates who have appeared in the Ægean, and that Quintus be sent to command the fleet so despatched.

"Details are thine, my Cæcilius.

---

61 The Cerealia was a major Roman festival celebrating the harvest, while Triptolemus was the mythical figure who taught humans the agricultural arts.

62 A Roman magistrate who usually worked with another magistrate or army officer of equal rank on a specific task.

"The necessity is urgent, as thou wilt be advised by the reports enclosed for thy perusal and the information of the said Quintus.

"SEJANUS."

Arrius gave little heed to the reading. As the ship drew more plainly out of the perspective, she became more and more an attraction to him. The look with which he watched her was that of an enthusiast. At length he tossed the loosened folds of his toga in the air; in reply to the signal, over the *aplustre*, or fan-like fixture at the stern of the vessel, a scarlet flag was displayed; while several sailors appeared upon the bulwarks, and swung themselves hand over hand up the ropes to the *antenna*, or yard, and furled the sail. The bow was put round, and the time of the oars increased one half; so that at racing speed she bore down directly towards him and his friends. He observed the manœuvring with a perceptible brightening of the eyes. Her instant answer to the rudder, and the steadiness with which she kept her course, were especially noticeable as virtues to be relied upon in action.

"By the Nymphæ!" said one of the friends, giving back the roll, "we may not longer say our friend will be great; he is already great. Our love will now have famous things to feed upon. What more hast thou for us?"

"Nothing more," Arrius replied. "What ye have of the affair is by this time old news in Rome, especially between the palace and the Forum. The duumvir is discreet; what I am to do, where go to find my fleet, he will tell on the ship, where a sealed package is waiting me. If, however, ye have offerings for any of the altars to-day, pray the gods for a friend plying oar and sail somewhere in the direction of Sicily. But she is here, and will come to," he said, reverting to the vessel. "I have interest in her masters; they will sail and fight with me. It is not an easy thing to lay ship side on a shore like this; so let us judge their training and skill."

"What, is she new to thee?"

"I never saw her before; and, as yet, I know not if she will bring me one acquaintance."

"Is that well?"

"It matters but little. We of the sea come to know each other quickly; our loves, like our hates, are born of sudden dangers."

The vessel was of the class called *naves liburnicæ* —long, narrow, low in the water, and modelled for speed and quick maneuver. The bow was beautiful. A jet of water spun from its foot as she came on, sprinkling all the prow, which rose in graceful curvature twice a man's stature above the plane of the deck. Upon the bending of the sides were figures of Tritons blowing shells. Below the bow, fixed to the keel, and projecting forward under the water-line, was the *rostrum*, or beak, a device of solid wood, reinforced and armed with iron, in action used as a ram. A stout moulding extended from the bow the full length of the ship's sides, defining the bulwarks, which were tastefully crenelated; below the moulding, in three rows, each covered with a cap or shield of bull-hide, were the holes in which the oars were worked—sixty on the right, sixty on the left. In further ornamentation, *caducei* leaned against the lofty prow. Two immense ropes passing across the bow marked the number of anchors stowed on the foredeck.

The simplicity of the upper works declared the oars the chief dependence of the crew. A mast, set a little forward of midship, was held by fore and back stays and shrouds fixed to rings on the inner side of the bulwarks. The tackle was that required for the management of one great square sail and the yard to which it was hung. Above the bulwarks the deck was visible.

Save the sailors who had reefed the sail, and yet lingered on the yard, but one man was to be seen by the party on the mole, and he stood by the prow helmeted and with a shield.

The hundred and twenty oaken blades, kept white and shining by pumice and the constant wash of the waves, rose and fell as if operated by the same hand, and drove the galley forward with a speed rivalling that of a modern steamer.

So rapidly, and apparently so rashly, did she come that the landsmen of the tribune's party were alarmed. Suddenly the man by the prow raised his hand with a peculiar gesture; whereupon all the oars flew up, poised a moment in the air, then fell straight down. The water boiled and bubbled about them; the galley shook in every timber, and stopped as if scared. Another gesture of the hand, and again the oars arose, feathered, and fell; but this time those on the right, dropping towards the stern, pushed forward; while those on the left, dropping towards the bow, pulled backward. Three times the oars thus pushed and pulled against each other. Round to the right the ship swung as upon a pivot; then, caught by the wind, she settled gently broadside to the mole.

The movement brought the stern to view, with all its garniture—Tritons like those at the bow; name in large raised letters; the rudder at the side; the elevated platform upon which the helmsman sat, a stately figure in full armor, his hand upon the rudder-rope; and the *aplustre*, high, gilt, carved, and bent over the helmsman like a great runcinate leaf.

In the midst of the rounding-to, a trumpet was blown brief and shrill, and from the hatchways out poured the marines, all in superb equipment, brazen helms, burnished shields, and javelins. While the fighting-men thus went to quarters as for action, the sailors proper climbed the shrouds and perched themselves along the yard. The officers and musicians took their posts. There was no shouting or needless noise. When the oars touched the mole, a bridge was sent out from the helmsman's deck. Then the tribune turned to his party and said, with a gravity he had not before shown:

"Duty now, O my friends."

He took the chaplet from his head and gave it to the dice-player.

"Take thou the myrtle, O favorite of the tesseræ!" he said. "If I return, I will seek my sesterce[63] again; if I am not victor, I will not return. Hang the crown in thy atrium."

To the company he opened his arms, and they came one by one and received his parting embrace.

"The gods go with thee, O Quintus!" they said.

"Farewell," he replied.

To the slaves waving their torches he waved his hand; then he turned to the waiting ship, beautiful with ordered ranks and crested helms, and shields and javelins. As he stepped upon the bridge, the trumpets sounded, and over the aplustre rose the *vexillum purpureum*, or pennant of a commander of a fleet.

Chapter II

THE tribune, standing upon the helmsman's deck with the order of the duumvir open in his hand, spoke to the chief of the rowers.[64]

"What force hast thou?"

"Of oarsmen, two hundred and fifty-two; ten supernumeraries."

"Making reliefs of—"

---

63 Ancient Roman coins.
64 [Author's Original Note] Called *hortator*.

"Eighty-four."

"And thy habit?"

"It has been to take off and put on every two hours."

The tribune mused a moment.

"The division is hard, and I will reform it, but not now. The oars may not rest day or night."

Then to the sailing-master he said,

"The wind is fair. Let the sail help the oars."

When the two thus addressed were gone, he turned to the chief pilot.[65]

"What service hast thou had?"

"Two-and-thirty years."

"In what seas chiefly?"

"Between our Rome and the East."

"Thou art the man I would have chosen."

The tribune looked at his orders again.

"Past the Camponellan cape, the course will be to Messina. Beyond that, follow the bend of the Calabrian shore till Melito is on thy left, then— Knowest thou the stars that govern in the Ionian Sea?"

"I know them well."

"Then from Melito course eastward for Cythera. The gods willing, I will not anchor until in the Bay of Antemona. The duty is urgent. I rely upon thee."

A prudent man was Arrius—prudent, and of the class which, while enriching the altars at Præneste and Antium, was of opinion, nevertheless, that the favor of the blind goddess depended more upon the votary's care and judgment than upon his gifts and vows. All night as master of the feast he had sat at table drinking and playing; yet the odor of the sea returned him to the mood of the sailor, and he would not rest until he knew his ship. Knowledge leaves no room for chances. Having begun with the chief of the rowers, the sailing-master, and the pilot, in company with the other officers—the commander of the marines, the keeper of the stores, the master of the machines, the overseer of the kitchen or fires—he passed through the several quarters. Nothing escaped his inspection. When he was through, of the community crowded within the narrow walls he alone knew perfectly all there was of material preparation for the voyage and its possible incidents; and, finding the preparation complete, there was left him but one thing further—thorough knowledge of the *personnel* of his command. As this was the most delicate and difficult part of his task, requiring much time, he set about it his own way.

At noon that day the galley was skimming the sea off Pæstum. The wind was yet from the west, filling the sail to the master's content. The watches had been established. On the foredeck the altar had been set and sprinkled with salt and barley, and before it the tribune had offered solemn prayers to Jove and to Neptune and all the Oceanidæ, and, with vows, poured the wine and burned the incense. And now, the better to study his men, he was seated in the great cabin, a very martial figure.

The cabin, it should be stated, was the central compartment of the galley, in extent quite sixty-five by thirty feet, and lighted by three broad hatchways. A row of stanchions ran from end to end, supporting the roof, and near the centre the mast was visible, all bristling with axes and spears and javelins. To each hatchway there were double stairs descending

---

65 [Author's Original Note] Called *rector*.

right and left, with a pivotal arrangement at the top to allow the lower ends to be hitched to the ceiling; and, as these were now raised, the compartment had the appearance of a skylighted hall.

The reader will understand readily that this was the heart of the ship, the home of all aboard— eating-room, sleeping-chamber, field of exercise, lounging-place off duty—uses made possible by the laws which reduced life there to minute details and a routine relentless as death.

At the after-end of the cabin there was a platform, reached by several steps. Upon it the chief of the rowers sat; in front of him a sounding-table, upon which, with a gavel, he beat time for the oarsmen; at his right a clepsydra, or water-clock, to measure the reliefs and watches. Above him, on a higher platform, well guarded by gilded railing, the tribune had his quarters, overlooking everything, and furnished with a couch, a table, and a *cathedra*, or chair, cushioned, and with arms and high back—articles which the imperial dispensation permitted of the utmost elegance.

Thus at ease, lounging in the great chair, swaying with the motion of the vessel, the military cloak half draping his tunic, sword in belt, Arrius kept watchful eye over his command, and was as closely watched by them. He saw critically everything in view, but dwelt longest upon the rowers. The reader would doubtless have done the same: only he would have looked with much sympathy, while, as is the habit with masters, the tribune's mind ran forward of what he saw, inquiring for results.

The spectacle was simple enough of itself. Along the sides of the cabin, fixed to the ship's timbers, were what at first appeared to be three rows of benches; a closer view, however, showed them a succession of rising banks, in each of which the second bench was behind and above the first one, and the third above and behind the second. To accommodate the sixty rowers on a side, the space devoted to them permitted nineteen banks separated by intervals of one yard, with a twentieth bank divided so that what would have been its upper seat or bench was directly above the lower seat of the first bank. The arrangement gave each rower when at work ample room, if he timed his movements with those of his associates, the principle being that of soldiers marching with cadenced step in close order. The arrangement also allowed a multiplication of banks, limited only by the length of the galley.

As to the rowers, those upon the first and second benches sat, while those upon the third, having longer oars to work, were suffered to stand. The oars were loaded with lead in the handles, and near the point of balance hung to pliable thongs, making possible the delicate touch called feathering, but, at the same time, increasing the need of skill, since an eccentric wave might at any moment catch a heedless fellow and hurl him from his seat. Each oar-hole was a vent through which the laborer opposite it had his plenty of sweet air. Light streamed down upon him from the grating which formed the floor of the passage between the deck and the bulwark over his head. In some respects, therefore, the condition of the men might have been much worse. Still, it must not be imagined that there was any pleasantness in their lives. Communication between them was not allowed. Day after day they filled their places without speech; in hours of labor they could not see each other's faces; their short respites were given to sleep and the snatching of food. They never laughed; no one ever heard one of them sing. What is the use of tongues when a sigh or a groan will tell all men feel while, perforce, they think in silence? Existence with the poor wretches was like a stream under ground sweeping slowly, laboriously on to its outlet, wherever that might chance to be.

O Son of Mary! The sword has now a heart—and thine the glory! So now; but, in the days of which we are writing, for captivity there was drudgery on walls, and in the streets and mines, and the galleys both of war and commerce were insatiable. When Druilius won the first sea-fight for his country, Romans plied the oars, and the glory was to the rower not less than the marine. These benches which now we are trying to see as they were testified to the change come with conquest, and illustrated both the policy and the prowess of Rome. Nearly all the nations had sons there, mostly prisoners of war, chosen for their brawn and endurance. In one place a Briton; before him a Libyan; behind him a Crimean. Elsewhere a Scythian, a Gaul, and a Thebasite. Roman convicts cast down to consort with Goths and Longobardi, Jews, Ethiopians, and barbarians from the shores of Mæotis. Here an Athenian, there a red-haired savage from Hibernia, yonder blue-eyed giants of the Cimbri.

In the labor of the rowers there was not enough art to give occupation to their minds, rude and simple as they were. The reach forward, the pull, the feathering the blade, the dip, were all there was of it; motions most perfect when most automatic. Even the care forced upon them by the sea outside grew in time to be a thing instinctive rather than of thought. So, as the result of long service, the poor wretches became imbruted—patient, spiritless, obedient—creatures of vast muscle and exhausted intellects, who lived upon recollections generally few but dear, and at last lowered into the semi-conscious alchemic state wherein misery turns to habit, and the soul takes on incredible endurance.

From right to left, hour after hour, the tribune, swaying in his easy-chair, turned with thought of everything rather than the wretchedness of the slaves upon the benches. Their motions, precise, and exactly the same on both sides of the vessel, after a while became monotonous; and then he amused himself singling out individuals. With his stylus he made note of objections, thinking, if all went well, he would find among the pirates of whom he was in search better men for the places.

There was no need of keeping the proper names of the slaves brought to the galleys as to their graves; so, for convenience, they were usually identified by the numerals painted upon the benches to which they were assigned. As the sharp eyes of the great man moved from seat to seat on either hand, they came at last to number sixty, which, as has been said, belonged properly to the last bank on the left-hand side, but, wanting room aft, had been fixed above the first bench of the first bank. There they rested.

The bench of number sixty was slightly above the level of the platform, and but a few feet away. The light glinting through the grating over his head gave the rower fairly to the tribune's view—erect, and, like all his fellows, naked, except a cincture about the loins. There were, however, some points in his favor. He was very young, not more than twenty. Furthermore, Arrius was not merely given to dice; he was a connoisseur of men physically, and when ashore indulged a habit of visiting the gymnasia to see and admire the most famous athlete. From some professor, doubtless, he had caught the idea that strength was as much of the quality as the quantity of the muscle, while superiority in performance required a certain mind as well as strength. Having adopted the doctrine, like most men with a hobby, he was always looking for illustrations to support it.

The reader may well believe that while the tribune, in the search for the perfect, was often called upon to stop and study, he was seldom perfectly satisfied—in fact, very seldom held as long as on this occasion.

In the beginning of each movement of the oar, the rower's body and face were brought into profile view from the platform; the movement ended with the body reversed, and in a pushing posture. The grace and ease of the action at first suggested a doubt of the honesty of the effort put forth; but it was speedily dismissed; the firmness with which the oar was held while in the reach forward, its bending under the push, were proofs of the force applied; not that only, they as certainly proved the rower's art, and put the critic in the great arm-chair in search of the combination of strength and cleverness which was the central idea of his theory.

In course of the study, Arrius observed the subject's youth; wholly unconscious of tenderness on that account, he also observed that he seemed of good height, and that his limbs, upper and nether, were singularly perfect. The arms, perhaps, were too long, but the objection was well hidden under a mass of muscle which, in some movements, swelled and knotted like kinking cords. Every rib in the round body was discernible; yet the leanness was the healthful reduction so strained after in the palæstræ. And altogether there was in the rower's action a certain harmony which, besides addressing itself to the tribune's theory, stimulated both his curiosity and general interest.

Very soon he found himself waiting to catch a view of the man's face in full. The head was shapely, and balanced upon a neck broad at the base, but of exceeding pliancy and grace. The features in profile were of Oriental outline, and of that delicacy of expression which has always been thought a sign of blood and sensitive spirit. With these observations, the tribune's interest in the subject deepened.

"By the gods," he said to himself, "the fellow impresses me! He promises well. I will know more of him."

Directly the tribune caught the view he wished—the rower turned and looked at him.

"A Jew! and a boy!"

Under the gaze then fixed steadily upon him, the large eyes of the slave grew larger—the blood surged to his very brows—the blade lingered in his hands. But instantly, with an angry crash, down fell the gavel of the hortator. The rower started, withdrew his face from the inquisitor, and, as if personally chidden, dropped the oar half feathered. When he glanced again at the tribune, he was vastly more astonished—he was met with a kindly smile.

Meantime the galley entered the Straits of Messina, and, skimming past the city of that name, was after a while turned eastward, leaving the cloud over Ætna in the sky astern.

Often as Arrius returned to his platform in the cabin he returned to study the rower, and he kept saying to himself, "The fellow hath a spirit. A Jew is not a barbarian. I will know more of him."

Chapter III

The fourth day out, and the *Astræa*—so the galley was named—speeding through the Ionian Sea. The sky was clear, and the wind blew as if bearing the good-will of all the gods.

As it was possible to overtake the fleet before reaching the bay east of the island of Cythera, designated for assemblage, Arrius, somewhat impatient, spent much time on deck. He took note diligently of matters pertaining to his ship, and, as a rule, was well pleased. In the cabin, swinging in the great chair, his thought continually reverted to the rower on number sixty.

"Knowest thou the man just come from yon bench?" he at length asked of the hortator. A relief was going on at the moment.

"From number sixty?" returned the chief.

"Yes."

The chief looked sharply at the rower then going forward.

"As thou knowest," he replied, "the ship is but a month from the maker's hand, and the men are as new to me as the ship."

"He is a Jew," Arrius remarked, thoughtfully.

"The noble Quintus is shrewd."

"He is very young," Arrius continued.

"But our best rower," said the other. "I have seen his oar bend almost to breaking."

"Of what disposition is he?"

"He is obedient; further I know not. Once he made request of me."

"For what?"

"He wished me to change him alternately from the right to the left,"

"Did he give a reason?"

"He had observed that the men who are confined to one side become misshapen. He also said that some day of storm or battle there might be sudden need to change him, and he might then be unserviceable."

"*Perpol!* The idea is new. What else hast thou observed of him?"

"He is cleanly above his companions."

"In that he is Roman," said Arrius, approvingly. "Have you nothing of his history?"

"Not a word."

The tribune reflected awhile, and turned to go to his own seat.

"If I should be on deck when his time is up," he paused to say, "send him to me. Let him come alone."

About two hours later Arrius stood under the aplustre of the galley; in the mood of one who, seeing himself carried swiftly towards an event of mighty import, has nothing to do but wait—the mood in which philosophy vests an even-minded man with the utmost calm, and is ever so serviceable. The pilot sat with a hand upon the rope by which the rudder paddles, one on each side of the vessel, were managed. In the shade of the sail some sailors lay asleep, and up on the yard there was a lookout. Lifting his eyes from the solarium set under the aplustre for reference in keeping the course, Arrius beheld the rower approaching.

"The chief called thee the noble Arrius, and said it was thy will that I should seek thee here. I have come."

Arrius surveyed the figure, tall, sinewy, glistening in the sun, and tinted by the rich red blood within—surveyed it admiringly, and with a thought of the arena; yet the manner was not without effect upon him: there was in the voice a suggestion of life at least partly spent under refining influences; the eyes were clear and open, and more curious than defiant. To the shrewd, demanding, masterful glance bent upon it, the face gave back nothing to mar its youthful comeliness—nothing of accusation or sullenness or menace, only the signs which a great sorrow long borne imprints, as time mellows the surface of pictures. In tacit acknowledgment of the effect, the Roman spoke as an older man to a younger, not as a master to a slave.

"The hortator tells me thou art his best rower."

"The hortator is very kind," the rower answered.

"Hast thou seen much service?"

"About three years."

"At the oars?"

"I cannot recall a day of rest from them."

"The labor is hard; few men bear it a year without breaking, and thou—thou art but a boy."

"The noble Arrius forgets that the spirit hath much to do with endurance. By its help the weak sometimes thrive, when the strong perish."

"From thy speech, thou art a Jew."

"My ancestors further back than the first Roman were Hebrews."

"The stubborn pride of thy race is not lost in thee," said Arrius, observing a flush upon the rower's face.

"Pride is never so loud as when in chains."

"What cause hast thou for pride?"

"That I am a Jew."

Arrius smiled.

"I have not been to Jerusalem," he said; "but I have heard of its princes. I knew one of them. He was a merchant, and sailed the seas. He was fit to have been a king. Of what degree art thou?"

"I must answer thee from the bench of a galley. I am of the degree of slaves. My father was a prince of Jerusalem, and, as a merchant, he sailed the seas. He was known and honored in the guest-chamber of the great Augustus."

"His name?"

"Ithamar, of the house of Hur."

The tribune raised his hand in astonishment.

"A son of Hur—thou?"

After a silence, he asked,

"What brought thee here?"

Judah lowered his head, and his breast labored hard. When his feelings were sufficiently mastered, he looked the tribune in the face, and answered,

"I was accused of attempting to assassinate Valerius Gratus, the procurator."

"Thou!" cried Arrius, yet more amazed, and retreating a step. "Thou that assassin! All Rome rang with the story. It came to my ship in the river by Lodinum."

The two regarded each other silently.

"I thought the family of Hur blotted from the earth," said Arrius, speaking first.

A flood of tender recollections carried the young man's pride away; tears shone upon his cheeks.

"Mother—mother! And my little Tirzah! Where are they? O tribune, noble tribune, if thou knowest anything of them"—he clasped his hands in appeal—"tell me all thou knowest. Tell me if they are living—if living, where are they? and in what condition? Oh, I pray thee, tell me!"

He drew nearer Arrius, so near that his hands touched the cloak where it dropped from the latter's folded arms.

"The horrible day is three years gone," he continued—"three years, O tribune, and every hour a whole lifetime of misery—a lifetime in a bottomless pit with death, and no relief but in labor—and in all that time not a word from any one, not a whisper. Oh, if, in being forgotten, we could only forget! If only I could hide from that scene—my sister torn from me, my mother's last look! I have felt the plague's breath, and the shock of ships in battle; I have heard the tempest lashing the sea, and laughed, though others prayed: death would have been a riddance. Bend the oar—yes, in the strain of mighty effort trying to escape the haunting of what that day occurred. Think what little will help me. Tell me they are dead, if no more, for happy they cannot be while I am lost. I have heard them call me in the night; I have seen them on the water walking. Oh, never anything so true as my mother's love! And Tirzah—her breath was as the breath of white lilies. She was the youngest branch of the palm—so fresh, so tender, so graceful, so beautiful! She made my day all morning. She came and went in music. And mine was the hand that laid them low! I—"

"Dost thou admit thy guilt?" asked Arrius, sternly.

The change that came upon Ben-Hur was wonderful to see, it was so instant and extreme. The voice sharpened; the hands arose tight-clenched; every fibre thrilled; his eyes flamed.

"Thou hast heard of the God of my fathers," he said; "of the infinite Jehovah. By his truth and almightiness, and by the love with which he hath followed Israel from the beginning, I swear I am innocent!"

The tribune was much moved.

"O noble Roman!" continued Ben-Hur, "give me a little faith, and, into my darkness, deeper darkening every day, send a light!"

Arrius turned away, and walked the deck.

"Didst thou not have a trial?" be asked, stopping suddenly.

"No!"

The Roman raised his head, surprised.

"No trial—no witnesses! Who passed judgment upon thee?"

Romans, it should be remembered, were at no time such lovers of the law and its forms as in the ages of their decay.

"They bound me with cords, and dragged me to a vault in the Tower. I saw no one. No one spoke to me. Next day soldiers took me to the seaside. I have been a galley-slave ever since."

"What couldst thou have proven?"

"I was a boy, too young to be a conspirator. Gratus was a stranger to me. If I had meant to kill him, that was not the time or the place. He was riding in the midst of a legion, and it was broad day. I could not have escaped. I was of a class most friendly to Rome. My father had been distinguished for his services to the emperor. We had a great estate to lose. Ruin was certain to myself, my mother, my sister. I had no cause for malice, while every consideration—property, family, life, conscience, the Law—to a son of Israel as the breath of his nostrils—would have stayed my hand, though the foul intent had been ever so strong. I was not mad. Death was preferable to shame; and, believe me, I pray, it is so yet,"

"Who was with thee when the blow was struck?"

"I was on the house-top—my father's house. Tirzah was with me—at my side—the soul of gentleness. Together we leaned over the parapet to see the legion pass. A tile gave way under my hand, and fell upon Gratus. I thought I had killed him. Ah, what horror I felt!"

"Where was thy mother?"

"In her chamber below."

"What became of her?"

Ben-Hur clenched his hands, and drew a breath like gasp.

"I do not know. I saw them drag her away—that is all I know. Out of the house they drove every living thing, even the dumb cattle, and they sealed the gates. The purpose was that she should not return. I, too, ask for her. Oh for one word! She, at least, was innocent. I can forgive—but I pray thy pardon, noble tribune! A slave like me should not talk of forgiveness or of revenge. I am bound to an oar for life."

Arrius listened intently. He brought all his experience with slaves to his aid. If the feeling shown in this instance were assumed, the acting was perfect; on the other hand, if it were real, the Jew's innocence might not be doubted; and if he were innocent, with what blind fury the power had been exercised! A whole family blotted out to atone an accident! The thought shocked him.

There is no wiser providence than that our occupations, however rude or bloody, cannot wear us out morally; that such qualities as justice and mercy, if they really possess us, continue to live on under them, like flowers under the snow. The tribune could be inexorable, else he had not been fit for the usages of his calling; he could also be just; and to excite his sense of wrong was to put him in the way to right the wrong. The crews of the ships in which he served came after a time to speak of him as the good tribune. Shrewd readers will not want a better definition of his character.

In this instance there were many circumstances certainly in the young man's favor, and some to be supposed. Possibly Arrius knew Valerius Gratus without loving him. Possibly he had known the elder Hur. In the course of his appeal, Judah had asked him of that; and, as will be noticed, he had made no reply.

For once the tribune was at loss, and hesitated. His power was ample. He was monarch of the ship. His prepossessions all moved him to mercy. His faith was won. Yet, he said to himself, there was no haste—or, rather, there was haste to Cythera; the best rower could not then be spared; he would wait; he would learn more; he would at least be sure this was the prince Ben-Hur, and that he was of a right disposition. Ordinarily, slaves were liars.

"It is enough," he said aloud. "Go back to thy place."

Ben-Hur bowed; looked once more into the master's face, but saw nothing for hope. He turned away slowly, looked back, and said,

"If thou dost think of me again, O tribune, let it not be lost in thy mind that I prayed thee only for word of my people—mother, sister."

He moved on.

Arrius followed him with admiring eyes.

"*Perpol!*" he thought. "With teaching, what a man for the arena! What a runner! Ye gods! what an arm for the sword or the cestus!—Stay!" he said aloud.

Ben-Hur stopped, and the tribune went to him.

"If thou wert free, what wouldst thou do?"

"The noble Arrius mocks me!" Judah said, with trembling lips.

"No; by the gods, no!"

"Then I will answer gladly. I would give myself to duty the first of life. I would know no other. I would know no rest until my mother and Tirzah were restored to home. I would give every day and hour to their happiness. I would wait upon them; never a slave more faithful. They have lost much, but, by the God of my fathers, I would find them more!"

The answer was unexpected by the Roman. For a moment he lost his purpose.

"I spoke to thy ambition," he said, recovering. "If thy mother and sister were dead, or not to be found, what wouldst thou do?"

A distinct pallor overspread Ben-Hur's face, and he looked over the sea. There was a struggle with some strong feeling; when it was conquered, he turned to the tribune.

"What pursuit would I follow?" he asked.

"Yes."

"Tribune, I will tell thee truly. Only the night before the dreadful day of which I have spoken, I obtained permission to be a soldier. I am of the same mind yet; and, as in all the earth there is but one school of war, thither I would go."

"The palæstra![66]" exclaimed Arrius.

"No; a Roman camp."

"But thou must first acquaint thyself with the use of arms."

Now a master may never safely advise a slave. Arrius saw his indiscretion, and, in a breath, chilled his voice and manner.

"Go now," he said, "and do not build upon what has passed between us. Perhaps I do but play with thee. Or"—he looked away musingly—"or, if thou dost think of it with any hope, choose between the renown of a gladiator and the service of a soldier. The former may come of the favor of the emperor; there is no reward for thee in the latter. Thou art not a Roman. Go!"

A short while after Ben-Hur was upon his bench again.

A man's task is always light if his heart is light. Handling the oar did not seem so toilsome to Judah. A hope had come to him, like a singing bird. He could hardly see the visitor or hear its song; that it was there, though, he knew; his feelings told him so. The caution of the tribune—"Perhaps I do but play with thee"—was dismissed often as it recurred to his mind. That he had been called by the great man and asked his story was the bread upon which he fed his hungry spirit. Surely something good would come of it. The light about his bench was clear and bright with promises, and he prayed.

"O God! I am a true son of the Israel thou hast so loved! Help me, I pray thee!"

Chapter IV

In the Bay of Antemona, east of Cythera the island, the hundred galleys assembled. There the tribune gave one day to inspection. He sailed then to Naxos, the largest of the Cyclades, midway the coasts of Greece and Asia, like a great stone planted in the centre of a highway, from which he could challenge everything that passed; at the same time, he would be in position to go after the pirates instantly, whether they were in the Ægean or out on the Mediterranean.

As the fleet, in order, rowed in towards the mountain shores of the island, a galley was descried coming from the north. Arrius went to meet it. She proved to be a transport just from Byzantium, and from her commander he learned the particulars of which he stood in most need.

The pirates were from all the farther shores of the Euxine. Even Tanais, at the mouth of the river which was supposed to feed Palus Mæotis, was represented among them. Their preparations had been with the greatest secrecy. The first known of them was their appearance off the entrance to the Thracian Bosphorus, followed by the destruction of the fleet in station there. Thence to the outlet of the Hellespont everything afloat had fallen their prey.

---

66 Gymnasium or wrestling school.

There were quite sixty galleys in the squadron, all well manned and supplied. A few were biremes, the rest stout triremes. A Greek was in command, and the pilots, said to be familiar with all the Eastern seas, were Greek. The plunder had been incalculable. The panic, consequently, was not on the sea alone; cities, with closed gates, sent their people nightly to the walls. Traffic had almost ceased.

Where were the pirates now?

To this question, of most interest to Arrius, he received answer.

After sacking Hephæstia, on the island of Lemnos, the enemy had coursed across to the Thessalian group, and, by last account, disappeared in the gulfs between Eubœa and Hellas.

Such were the tidings.

Then the people of the island, drawn to the hill-tops by the rare spectacle of a hundred ships careering in united squadron, beheld the advance division suddenly turn to the north, and the others follow, wheeling upon the same point like cavalry in a column. News of the piratical descent had reached them, and now, watching the white sails until they faded from sight up between Rhene and Syros, the thoughtful among them took comfort, and were grateful. What Rome seized with strong hand she always defended: in return for their taxes, she gave them safety.

The tribune was more than pleased with the enemy's movements; he was doubly thankful to Fortune. She had brought swift and sure intelligence, and had lured his foes into the waters where, of all others, destruction was most assured. He knew the havoc one galley could play in a broad sea like the Mediterranean, and the difficulty of finding and overhauling her; he knew, also, how those very circumstances would enhance the service and glory if, at one blow, he could put a finish to the whole piratical array.

If the reader will take a map of Greece and the Ægean, he will notice the island of Eubœa lying along the classic coast like a rampart against Asia, leaving a channel between it and the continent quite a hundred and twenty miles in length, and scarcely an average of eight in width. The inlet on the north had admitted the fleet of Xerxes, and now it received the bold raiders from the Euxine. The towns along the Pelasgic and Meliac gulfs were rich and their plunder seductive. All things considered, therefore, Arrius judged that the robbers might be found somewhere below Thermopylæ. Welcoming the chance, he resolved to enclose them north and south, to do which not an hour could be lost; even the fruits and wines and women of Naxos must be left behind. So he sailed away without stop or tack until, a little before nightfall, Mount Ocha was seen upreared against the sky, and the pilot reported the Eubœan coast.

At a signal the fleet rested upon its oars. When the movement was resumed, Arrius led a division of fifty of the galleys, intending to take them up the channel, while another division, equally strong, turned their prows to the outer or seaward side of the island, with orders to make all haste to the upper inlet, and descend sweeping the waters.

To be sure, neither division was equal in number to the pirates; but each had advantages in compensation, among them, by no means least, a discipline impossible to a lawless horde, however brave. Besides, it was a shrewd count on the tribune's side, if, peradventure, one should be defeated, the other would find the enemy shattered by his victory, and in condition to be easily overwhelmed.

Meantime Ben-Hur kept his bench, relieved every six hours. The rest in the Bay of Antemona had freshened him, so that the oar was not troublesome, and the chief on the platform found no fault.

People, generally, are not aware of the ease of mind there is in knowing where they are, and where they are going. The sensation of being lost is a keen distress; still worse is the feeling one has in driving blindly into unknown places. Custom had dulled the feeling with Ben-Hur, but only measurably. Pulling away hour after hour, sometimes days and nights together, sensible all the time that the galley was gliding swiftly along some of the many tracks of the broad sea, the longing to know where he was, and whither going, was always present with him; but now it seemed quickened by the hope which had come to new life in his breast since the interview with the tribune. The narrower the abiding-place happens to be, the more intense is the longing; and so he found. He seemed to hear every sound of the ship in labor, and listened to each one as if it were a voice come to tell him something; he looked to the grating overhead, and through it into the light of which so small a portion was his, expecting, he knew not what; and many times he caught himself on the point of yielding to the impulse to speak to the chief on the platform, than which no circumstance of battle would have astonished that dignitary more.

In his long service, by watching the shifting of the meagre sunbeams upon the cabin floor when the ship was under way, he had come to know, generally, the quarter into which she was sailing. This, of course, was only of clear days like those good-fortune was sending the tribune. The experience had not failed him in the period succeeding the departure from Cythera. Thinking they were tending towards the old Judean country, he was sensitive to every variation from the course. With a pang, he had observed the sudden change northward which, as has been noticed, took place near Naxos: the cause, however, he could not even conjecture; for it must be remembered that, in common with his fellow-slaves, he knew nothing of the situation, and had no interest in the voyage. His place was at the oar, and he was held there inexorably, whether at anchor or under sail. Once only in three years had he been permitted an outlook from the deck. The occasion we have seen. He had no idea that, following the vessel he was helping drive, there was a great squadron close at hand and in beautiful order; no more did he know the object of which it was in pursuit.

When the sun, going down, withdrew his last ray from the cabin, the galley still held northward. Night fell, yet Ben-Hur could discern no change. About that time the smell of incense floated down the gangways from the deck.

"The tribune is at the altar," he thought. "Can it be we are going into battle?"

He became observant.

Now he had been in many battles without having seen one. From his bench he had heard them above and about him, until he was familiar with all their notes, almost as a singer with a song. So, too, he had become acquainted with many of the preliminaries of an engagement, of which, with a Roman as well as a Greek, the most invariable was the sacrifice to the gods. The rites were the same as those performed at the beginning of a voyage, and to him, when noticed, they were always an admonition.

A battle, it should be observed, possessed for him and his fellow-slaves of the oar an interest unlike that of the sailor and marine; it came, not of the danger encountered, but of the fact that defeat, if survived, might bring an alteration of condition—possibly freedom—at least a change of masters, which might be for the better.

In good time the lanterns were lighted and hung by the stairs, and the tribune came down from the deck. At his word the marines put on their armor. At his word again, the machines were looked to, and spears, javelins, and arrows, in great sheaves, brought and laid upon the floor, together with jars of inflammable oil, and baskets of cotton balls wound loose like the wicking of candles. And when, finally, Ben-Hur saw the tribune mount his platform and don his armor, and get his helmet and shield out, the meaning of the preparations might not be any longer doubted, and he made ready for the last ignominy of his service.

To every bench, as a fixture, there was a chain with heavy anklets. These the hortator proceeded to lock upon the oarsmen, going from number to number, leaving no choice but to obey, and, in event of disaster, no possibility of escape.

In the cabin, then, a silence fell, broken, at first, only by the sough of the oars turning in the leathern cases. Every man upon the benches felt the shame, Ben-Hur more keenly than his companions. He would have put it away at any price. Soon the clanking of the fetters notified him of the progress the chief was making in his round. He would come to him in turn; but would not the tribune interpose for him?

The thought may be set down to vanity or selfishness, as the reader pleases; it certainly, at that moment, took possession of Ben-Hur. He believed the Roman would interpose; anyhow, the circumstance would test the man's feelings. If, intent upon the battle, he would but think of him, it would be proof of his opinion formed—proof that he had been tacitly promoted above his associates in misery—such proof as would justify hope.

Ben-Hur waited anxiously. The interval seemed like an age. At every turn of the oar he looked towards the tribune, who, his simple preparations made, lay down upon the couch and composed himself to rest; whereupon number sixty chid himself, and laughed grimly, and resolved not to look that way again.

The hortator approached. Now he was at number one—the rattle of the iron links sounded horribly. At last number sixty! Calm from despair, Ben-Hur held his oar at poise, and gave his foot to the officer. Then the tribune stirred—sat up—beckoned to the chief.

A strong revulsion seized the Jew. From the hortator, the great man glanced at him; and when he dropped his oar all the section of the ship on his side seemed aglow. He heard nothing of what was said; enough that the chain hung idly from its staple in the bench, and that the chief, going to his seat, began to beat the sounding-board. The notes of the gavel were never so like music. With his breast against the leaded handle, he pushed with all his might—pushed until the shaft bent as if about to break.

The chief went to the tribune, and, smiling, pointed to number sixty.

"What strength!" he said.

"And what spirit!" the tribune answered. "*Perpol!* He is better without the irons. Put them on him no more."

So saying, he stretched himself upon the couch again.

The ship sailed on hour after hour under the oars in water scarcely rippled by the wind. And the people not on duty slept, Arrius in his place, the marines on the floor.

Once—twice—Ben-Hur was relieved; but he could not sleep. Three years of night, and through the darkness a sunbeam at last! At sea adrift and lost, and now land! Dead so long, and lo! the thrill and stir of resurrection. Sleep was not for such an hour. Hope deals with the future; now and the past are but servants that wait on her with impulse and suggestive circumstance. Starting from the favor of the tribune, she carried him forward indefinitely. The wonder is, not that things so purely imaginative as the results she points us to can make us so happy, but that we can receive them as so real. They must be as gorgeous poppies under the influence of which, under the crimson and purple and gold, reason lies down the while, and is not. Sorrows assuaged; home and the fortunes of his house restored; mother and sister in his arms once more—such were the central ideas which made him happier that moment than he had ever been. That he was rushing, as on wings, into horrible battle had, for the time, nothing to do with his thoughts. The things thus in hope were unmixed with doubts—they *were*. Hence his joy so full, so perfect, there was no room in his heart for revenge. Messala, Gratus, Rome, and all the bitter, passionate memories connected with them, were as dead plagues—miasms of the earth above which he floated, far and safe, listening to singing stars.

The deeper darkness before the dawn was upon the waters, and all things going well with the *Astræa*, when a man, descending from the deck, walked swiftly to the platform where the tribune slept, and awoke him. Arrius arose, put on his helmet, sword, and shield, and went to the commander of the marines.

"The pirates are close by. Up and ready!" he said, and passed to the stairs, calm, confident, insomuch that one might have thought, "Happy fellow! Apicius has set a feast for him."

Chapter V

Every soul aboard, even the ship, awoke. Officers went to their quarters. The marines took arms, and were led out, looking in all respects like legionaries. Sheaves of arrows and arm-fuls of javelins were carried on deck. By the central stairs the oil-tanks and fire-balls were set ready for use. Additional lanterns were lighted. Buckets were filled with water. The rowers in relief assembled under guard in front of the chief. As Providence would have it, Ben-Hur was one of the latter. Overhead he heard the muffled noise of the final preparations—of the sailors furling sail, spreading the nettings, unslinging the machines, and hanging the armor of bull-hide over the side. Presently quiet settled about the galley again; quite full of vague dread and expectation, which, interpreted, means *ready*.

At a signal passed down from the deck, and communicated to the hortator by a petty officer stationed on the stairs, all at once the oars stopped.

What did it mean?

Of the hundred and twenty slaves chained to the benches, not one but asked himself the question. They were without incentive. Patriotism, love of honor, sense of duty, brought them no inspiration. They felt the thrill common to men rushed helpless and blind into danger. It may be supposed the dullest of them, poising his oar, thought of all that might happen, yet could promise himself nothing; for victory would but rivet his chains the firmer, while the chances of the ship were his; sinking or on fire, he was doomed to her fate.

Of the situation without they might not ask. And who were the enemy? And what if they were friends, brethren, countrymen? The reader, carrying the suggestion forward, will see the necessity which governed the Roman when, in such emergencies, he locked the hapless wretches to their seats.

There was little time, however, for such thought with them. A sound like the rowing of galleys astern attracted Ben-Hur, and the *Astræa* rocked as if in the midst of countering waves. The idea of a fleet at hand broke upon him—a fleet in maneuver—forming probably for attack. His blood started with the fancy.

Another signal order came down from deck. The oars dipped, and the galley started imperceptibly. No sound from without, none from within, yet each man in the cabin instinctively poised himself for a shock; the very ship seemed to catch the sense, and hold its breath, and go crouched tiger-like.

In such a situation time is inappreciable; so that Ben-Hur could form no judgment of distance gone. At last there was a sound of trumpets on deck, full, clear, long blown. The chief beat the sounding-board until it rang; the rowers reached forward full length, and, deepening the dip of their oars, pulled suddenly with all their united force. The galley, quivering in every timber, answered with a leap. Other trumpets joined in the clamor—all from the rear, none forward—from the latter quarter only a rising sound of voices in tumult heard briefly. There was a mighty blow; the rowers in front of the chief's platform reeled, some of them fell; the ship bounded back, recovered, and rushed on more irresistibly than before. Shrill and high arose the shrieks of men in terror; over the blare of trumpets, and the grind and crash of the collision, they arose; then under his feet, under the keel, pounding, rumbling, breaking to pieces, drowning, Ben-Hur felt something overridden. The men about him looked at each other afraid. A shout of triumph from the deck—the beak of the Roman had won! But who were they whom the sea had drunk? Of what tongue, from what land were they?

No pause, no stay! Forward rushed the *Astræa;* and, as it went, some sailors ran down, and plunging the cotton balls into the oil-tanks, tossed them dripping to comrades at the head of the stairs: fire was to be added to other horrors of the combat.

Directly the galley heeled over so far that the oarsmen on the uppermost side with difficulty kept their benches. Again the hearty Roman cheer, and with it despairing shrieks. An opposing vessel, caught by the grappling-hooks of the great crane swinging from the prow, was being lifted into the air that it might be dropped and sunk.

The shouting increased on the right hand and on the left; before, behind, swelled an indescribable clamor. Occasionally there was a crash, followed by sudden peals of fright, telling of other ships ridden down, and their crews drowned in the vortexes.

Nor was the fight all on one side. Now and then a Roman in armor was borne down the hatchway, and laid bleeding, sometimes dying, on the floor.

Sometimes, also, puffs of smoke, blended with steam, and foul with the scent of roasting human flesh, poured into the cabin, turning the dimming light into yellow murk. Gasping for breath the while, Ben-Hur knew they were passing through the cloud of a ship on fire, and burning up with the rowers chained to the benches.

The *Astræa* all this time was in motion. Suddenly she stopped. The oars forward were dashed from the hands of the rowers, and the rowers from their benches. On deck, then, a furious trampling, and on the sides a grinding of ships afoul of each other. For the first time the beating of the gavel was lost in the uproar. Men sank on the floor in fear or looked about seeking a hiding-place. In the midst of the panic a body plunged or was pitched headlong down the hatchway, falling near Ben-Hur. He beheld the half-naked carcass, a mass of hair blackening the face, and under it a shield of bull-hide and wicker-work—a barbarian from the white-skinned nations of the North whom death had robbed of plunder and revenge. How came he there? An iron hand had snatched him from the opposing deck—no, the *Astræa* had been boarded! The Romans were fighting on their own deck? A chill smote the young Jew: Arrius was hard pressed—he might be defending his own life. If he should be slain! God of Abraham forefend! The hopes and dreams so lately come, were they only hopes and dreams? Mother and sister—house—home—Holy Land—was he not to see them, after all? The tumult thundered above him; he looked around; in the cabin all was confusion—the rowers on the benches paralyzed; men running blindly hither and thither; only the chief on his scat imperturbable, vainly beating the sounding-board, and waiting the order of the tribune—in the red murk illustrating the matchless discipline which had won the world.

The example had a good effect upon Ben-Hur. He controlled himself enough to think. Honor and duty bound the Roman to the platform; but what had he to do with such motives then? The bench was a thing to run from; while, if he were to die a slave, who would be the better of the sacrifice? With him living was duty, if not honor. His life belonged to his people. They arose before him never more real: he saw them, their arms outstretched; he heard them imploring him. And he would go to them. He started—stopped. Alas! a Roman judgment held him in doom. While it endured, escape would be profitless. In the wide, wide earth there was no place in which he would be safe from the imperial demand; upon the land none, nor upon the sea. Whereas he required freedom according to the forms of law, so only could he abide in Judea and execute the filial purpose to which he would devote himself: in other land he would not live. Dear God! How he had waited and watched and prayed for such a release! And how it had been delayed! But at last he had seen it in the promise of the tribune. What else the great man's meaning? And if the benefactor so belated should now be slain! The dead come not back to redeem the pledges of the living. It should not be—Arrius should not die. At least, better perish with him than survive a galley-slave.

Once more Ben-Hur looked around. Upon the roof of the cabin the battle yet beat; against the sides the hostile vessels yet crushed and grinded. On the benches, the slaves struggled to tear loose from their chains, and, finding their efforts vain, howled like madmen; the guards had gone upstairs; discipline was out, panic in. No, the chief kept his chair, unchanged, calm as ever—except the gavel, weaponless. Vainly with his clangor he filled the lulls in the din. Ben Hur gave him a last look, then broke away—not in flight, but to seek the tribune.

A very short space lay between him and the stairs of the hatchway aft. He took it with a leap, and was half-way up the steps—up far enough to catch a glimpse of the sky blood-red with fire, of the ships alongside, of the sea covered with ships and wrecks, of the fight closed in about the pilot's quarter, the assailants many, the defenders few—when suddenly his foothold was knocked away, and he pitched backward. The floor, when he reached it, seemed to be lifting itself and breaking to pieces; then, in a twinkling, the whole after-part of the hull broke asunder, and, as if it had all the time been lying in wait, the sea, hissing and foaming, leaped in, and all became darkness and surging water to Ben-Hur.

It cannot be said that the young Jew helped himself in this stress. Besides his usual strength, he had the indefinite extra force which nature keeps in reserve for just such perils to life; yet the darkness, and the whirl and roar of water, stupefied him. Even the holding his breath was involuntary.

The influx of the flood tossed him like a log forward into the cabin, where he would have drowned but for the refluence of the sinking motion. As it was, fathoms under the surface the hollow mass vomited him forth, and he arose along with the loosed debris. In the act of rising, he clutched something, and held to it. The time he was under seemed an age longer than it really was; at last he gained the top; with a great gasp he filled his lungs afresh, and, tossing the water from his hair and eyes, climbed higher upon the plank he held, and looked about him.

Death had pursued him closely under the waves; he found it waiting for him when he was risen—waiting multiform.

Smoke lay upon the sea like a semitransparent fog, through which here and there shone cores of intense brilliance. A quick intelligence told him that they were ships on fire. The battle was yet on; nor could he say who was victor. Within the radius of his vision now and then ships passed, shooting shadows athwart lights. Out of the dun clouds farther on he

BEN-HUR AND ARRIUS. THE RESCUE.—*Act II. Scene 2*

Ben-Hur and Arrius, the rescue. Act 2, scene 2 (*Ben-Hur*, The Player's edition, New York: Harper and Brothers, 1903, Courtesy Lilly Library, Bloomington, Indiana).

caught the crash of other ships colliding. The danger, however, was closer at hand. When the *Astræa* went down, her deck, it will be recollected, held her own crew, and the crews of the two galleys which had attacked her at the same time, all of whom were ingulfed. Many of them came to the surface together, and on the same plank or support of whatever kind continued the combat, begun possibly in the vortex fathoms down. Writhing and twisting in deadly embrace, sometimes striking with sword or javelin, they kept the sea around them in agitation, at one place inky-black, at another aflame with fiery reflections. With their struggles he had nothing to do; they were all his enemies: not one of them but would kill him for the plank upon which lie floated. He made haste to get away.

About that time he heard oars in quickest movement, and beheld a galley coming down upon him. The tall prow seemed doubly tall, and the red light playing upon its gilt and carving gave it an appearance of snaky life. Under its foot the water churned to flying foam.

He struck out, pushing the plank, which was very broad and unmanageable. Seconds were precious—half a second might save or lose him. In the crisis of the effort, up from the sea, within arm's reach, a helmet shot like a gleam of gold. Next came two hands with fingers extended—large hands were they, and strong—their hold once fixed, might not be loosed. Ben-Hur swerved from them appalled. Up rose the helmet and the head it encased—then two arms, which began to beat the water wildly—the head turned back, and gave the face to the light. The mouth gaping wide; the eyes open, but sightless, and the bloodless pallor of a drowning man—never anything more ghastly! Yet he gave a cry of joy at the sight, and as the face was going under again, he caught the sufferer by the chain which passed from the helmet beneath the chin, and drew him to the plank.

The man was Arrius, the tribune.

For a while the water foamed and eddied violently about Ben-Hur, taxing all his strength to hold to the support and at the same time keep the Roman's head above the surface. The galley had passed, leaving the two barely outside the stroke of its oars. Right through the floating men, over heads helmeted as well as heads bare, she drove, in her wake nothing but the sea sparkling with fire. A muffled crash, succeeded by a great outcry, made the rescuer look again from his charge. A certain savage pleasure touched his heart—the *Astræa* was avenged.

After that the battle moved on. Resistance turned to flight. But who were the victors? Ben-Hur was sensible how much his freedom and the life of the tribune depended upon that event. He pushed the plank under the latter until it floated him, after which all his care was to keep him there. The dawn came slowly. He watched its growing hopefully, yet sometimes afraid. Would it bring the Romans or the pirates? If the pirates, his charge was lost.

At last morning broke in full, the air without a breath. Off to the left he saw the land, too far to think of attempting to make it. Here and there men were adrift like himself. In spots the sea was blackened by charred and sometimes smoking fragments. A galley up a long way was lying to with a torn sail hanging from the tilted yard, and the oars all idle. Still farther away he could discern moving specks, which he thought might be ships in flight or pursuit, or they might be white birds awing.

An hour passed thus. His anxiety increased. If relief came not speedily, Arrius would die. Sometimes he seemed already dead, he lay so still. He took the helmet off, and then, with greater difficulty, the cuirass; the heart he found fluttering. He took hope at the sign, and held on. There was nothing to do but wait, and, after the manner of his people, pray.

Chapter VI

THE throes of recovery from drowning are more painful than the drowning. These Arrius passed through, and, at length, to Ben-Hur's delight, reached the point of speech.

Gradually, from incoherent questions as to where he was, and by whom and how he had been saved, he reverted to the battle. The doubt of the victory stimulated his faculties to full return, a result aided not a little by a long rest—such as could be had on their frail support. After a while he became talkative.

"Our rescue, I see, depends upon the result of the fight. I see also what thou hast done for me. To speak fairly, thou hast saved my life at the risk of thy own. I make the acknowledgment broadly; and, whatever cometh, thou hast my thanks. More than that, if fortune doth but serve me kindly, and we get well out of this peril, I will do thee such favor as becometh a Roman who hath power and opportunity to prove his gratitude. Yet, yet it is to be seen if, with thy good intent, thou hast really done me a kindness; or, rather, speaking to thy good-will"—he hesitated—"I would exact of thee a promise to do me, in a certain event, the greatest favor one man can do another—and of that let me have thy pledge now."

"If the thing be not forbidden, I will do it," Ben-Hur replied.

Arrius rested again.

"Art thou, indeed, a son of Hur, the Jew?" he next asked.

"It is as I have said."

"I knew thy father—"

Judah drew himself nearer, for the tribune's voice was weak—he drew nearer, and listened eagerly—at last he thought to hear of home.

"I knew him, and loved him," Arrius continued.

There was another pause, during which something diverted the speaker's thought.

"It cannot be," he proceeded, "that thou, a son of his, hast not heard of Cato and Brutus.[67] They were very great men, and never as great as in death. In their dying, they left this law—A Roman may not survive his good-fortune. Art thou listening?"

"I hear."

"It is a custom of gentlemen in Rome to wear a ring. There is one on my hand. Take it now."

He held the hand to Judah, who did as he asked.

"Now put it on thine own hand."

Ben-Hur did so.

"The trinket hath its uses," said Arrius next. "I have property and money. I am accounted rich even in Rome. I have no family. Show the ring to my freedman, who hath control in my absence; you will find him in a villa near Misenum. Tell him how it came to thee, and ask anything, or all he may have; he will not refuse the demand. If I live, I will do better by thee. I will make thee free, and restore thee to thy home and people; or thou mayst give thyself to the pursuit that pleaseth thee most. Dost thou hear?"

"I could not choose but hear."

"Then pledge me. By the gods—"

"Nay, good tribune, I am a Jew."

"By thy God, then, or in the form most sacred to those of thy faith—pledge me to do what I tell thee now, and as I tell thee; I am waiting, let me have thy promise."

"Noble Arrius, I am warned by thy manner to expect something of gravest concern. Tell me thy wish first."

"Wilt thou promise then?"

"That were to give the pledge, and—Blessed be the God of my fathers! yonder cometh a ship!"

"In what direction?"

"From the north."

"Canst thou tell her nationality by outward signs?"

"No. My service hath been at the oars."

"Hath she a flag?"

"I cannot see one."

Arrius remained quiet some time, apparently in deep reflection.

"Does the ship hold this way yet?" he at length asked.

"Still this way."

"Look for the flag now."

"She hath none."

"Nor any other sign?"

---

67 Cato the Younger (95–46 BCE) and Brutus (85–42 BCE) were both members of the Roman Senate and opponents of Julius Caesar. Both men distinguished themselves by their devotion to the ideals of the Roman Republic. Both Cato and Brutus committed suicide, deeming it the most honorable way to die.

"She hath a sail set, and is of three banks, and cometh swiftly—that is all I can say of her."

"A Roman in triumph would have out many flags. She must be an enemy. Hear now," said Arrius, becoming grave again, "hear, while yet I may speak. If the galley be a pirate, thy life is safe; they may not give thee freedom; they may put thee to the oar again; but they will not kill thee. On the other hand, I—"

The tribune faltered.

"Perpol!" he continued, resolutely. "I am too old to submit to dishonor. In Rome, let them tell how Quintus Arrius, as became a Roman tribune, went down with his ship in the midst of the foe. This is what I would have thee do. If the galley prove a pirate, push me from the plank and drown me. Dost thou hear? Swear thou wilt do it."

"I will not swear," said Ben-Hur, firmly; "neither will I do the deed. The Law, which is to me most binding, O tribune, would make me answerable for thy life. Take back the ring"— he took the seal from his finger—"take it back, and all thy promises of favor in the event of delivery from this peril. The judgment which sent me to the oar for life made me a slave, yet I am not a slave; no more am I thy freedman. I am a son of Israel, and this moment, at least, my own master. Take back the ring."

Arrius remained passive.

"Thou wilt not?" Judah continued. "Not in anger, then, nor in any despite, but to free myself from a hateful obligation, I will give thy gift to the sea. See, O tribune!"

He tossed the ring away. Arrius heard the splash where it struck and sank, though he did not look.

"Thou hast done a foolish thing," he said; "foolish for one placed as thou art. I am not dependent upon thee for death. Life is a thread I can break without thy help; and, if I do, what will become of thee? Men determined on death prefer it at the hands of others, for the reason that the soul which Plato giveth us is rebellious at the thought of self-destruction; that is all. If the ship be a pirate, I will escape from the world. My mind is fixed. I am a Roman. Success and honor are all in all. Yet I would have served thee; thou wouldst not. The ring was the only witness of my will available in this situation. We are both lost. I will die regretting the victory and glory wrested from me; thou wilt live to die a little later, mourning the pious duties undone because of this folly. I pity thee."

Ben-Hur saw the consequences of his act more distinctly than before, yet he did not falter.

"In the three years of my servitude, O tribune, thou wert the first to look upon me kindly. No, no! There was another." The voice dropped, the eyes became humid, and he saw plainly as if it were then before him the face of the boy who helped him to a drink by the old well at Nazareth. "At least," he proceeded, "thou wert the first to ask me who I was; and if, when I reached out and caught thee, blind and sinking the last time, I, too, had thought of the many ways in which thou couldst be useful to me in my wretchedness, still the act was not all selfish; this I pray you to believe. Moreover, seeing as God giveth me to now, the ends I dream of are to be wrought by fair means alone. As a thing of conscience, I would rather die with thee than be thy slayer. My mind is firmly set as thine; though thou wert to offer me all Rome, O tribune, and it belonged to thee to make the gift good, I would not kill thee. Thy Cato and Brutus were as little children compared to the Hebrew whose law a Jew must obey."

"But my request. Hast—"

"Thy command would be of more weight, and that would not move me. I have said."

Both became silent, waiting.

Ben-Hur looked often at the coming ship. Arrius rested with closed eyes, indifferent.

"Art thou sure she is an enemy?" Ben-Hur asked.

"I think so," was the reply.

"She stops, and puts a boat over the side."

"Dost thou see her flag?"

"Is there no other sign by which she may be known if Roman?"

"If Roman, she hath a helmet over the mast's top."

"Then be of cheer, I see the helmet."

Still Arrius was not assured.

"The men in the small boat are taking in the people afloat. Pirates are not humane."

"They may need rowers," Arrius replied, recurring, possibly, to times when he had made rescues for the purpose.

Ben-Hur was very watchful of the actions of the strangers.

"The ship moves off," he said.

"Whither?"

"Over on our right there is a galley which I take to be deserted. The new-comer heads towards it. Now she is alongside. Now she is sending men aboard."

Then Arrius opened his eyes and threw off his calm.

"Thank thou thy God," he said to Ben-Hur, after a look at the galleys, "thank thou thy God, as I do my many gods. A pirate would sink, not save, yon ship. By the act and the helmet on the mast I know a Roman. The victory is mine. Fortune hath not deserted me. We are saved. Wave thy hand—call to them—bring them quickly. I shall be duumvir, and thou! I knew thy father, and loved him. He was a prince indeed. He taught me a Jew was not a barbarian. I will take thee with me. I will make thee my son. Give thy God thanks, and call the sailors. Haste! The pursuit must be kept. Not a robber shall escape. Hasten them!"

Judah raised himself upon the plank, and waved his hand, and called with all his might; at last he drew the attention of the sailors in the small boat, and they were speedily taken up.

Arrius was received on the galley with all the honors due a hero so the favorite of Fortune. Upon a couch on the deck he heard the particulars of the conclusion of the fight. When the survivors afloat upon the water were all saved and the prize secured, he spread his flag of commandant anew, and hurried northward to rejoin the fleet and perfect the victory. In due time the fifty vessels coming down the channel closed in upon the fugitive pirates, and crushed them utterly; not one escaped. To swell the tribune's glory, twenty galleys of the enemy were captured.

Upon his return from the cruise, Arrius had warm welcome on the mole at Misenum. The young man attending him very early attracted the attention of his friends there; and to their questions as to who he was the tribune proceeded in the most affectionate manner to tell the story of his rescue and introduce the stranger, omitting carefully all that pertained to the latter's previous history. At the end of the narrative, he called Ben-Hur to him, and said, with a hand resting affectionately upon his shoulder,

"Good friends, this is my son and heir, who, as he is to take my property—if it be the will of the gods that I leave any—shall be known to you by my name. I pray you all to love him as you love me."

Speedily as opportunity permitted, the adoption was formally perfected. And in such manner the brave Roman kept his faith with Ben-Hur, giving him happy introduction into the imperial world. The month succeeding Arrius's return, the *armilustrium*[68] was celebrated with the utmost magnificence in the theatre of Scaurus. One side of the structure was taken up with military trophies; among which by far the most conspicuous and most admired were twenty prows, complemented by their corresponding aplustra, cut bodily from as many galleys; and over them, so as to be legible to the eighty thousand spectators in the seats, was this inscription:

TAKEN FROM THE PIRATES IN THE GULF OF EURIPUS,

BY

QUINTUS ARRIUS,

DUUMVIR

Book Fifth[69]

"Only the actions of the just
Smell sweet and blossom in the dust."

SHIRLEY.[70]

"And, through the heat of conflict, keeps the law,
In calmness made, and sees what he foresaw."

WORDSWORTH.[71]

Chapter I

The morning after the bacchanalia in the saloon of the palace, the divan was covered with young patricians. Maxentius might come, and the city throng to receive him; the legion might descend from Mount Sulpius in glory of arms and armor; from Nymphæum to Omphalus there might be ceremonial splendors to shame the most notable ever before seen or heard of in the gorgeous East; yet would the many continue to sleep ignominiously on the divan where they had fallen or been carelessly tumbled by the indifferent slaves; that they would be able to take part in the reception that day was about as possible as for the lay-figures in the studio of a modern artist to rise and go bonneted and plumed through the one, two, three of a waltz.

Not all, however, who participated in the orgy were in the shameful condition. When dawn began to peer through the skylights of the saloon, Messala arose, and took the chaplet from his head, in sign that the revel was at end; then he gathered his robe about him, gave a last look at the scene, and, without a word, departed for his quarters. Cicero could not have retired with more gravity from a night-long senatorial debate.

---

68 Ancient Roman religious rite held in October honoring Mars, the god of war.
69 Judah Ben-Hur is adopted by Quintus Arrius. Eventually Ben-Hur returns to Judea, where Messala still holds a position of Roman authority. The fifth book begins with events leading up to the grand chariot race between Ben-Hur (driving a chariot harnessed to the great Arabian horses of Sheik Ilderim) and Messala.
70 From the poem, "The Contention of Ajax and Ulysses," by English poet and playwright James Shirley (1596–1666).
71 From "Character of the Happy Warrior," by the English poet William Wordsworth (1770–1850).

Three hours afterwards two couriers entered his room, and from his own hand received each a despatch, sealed and in duplicate, and consisting chiefly of a letter to Valerius Gratus, the procurator, still resident in Cæsarea. The importance attached to the speedy and certain delivery of the paper may be inferred. One courier was to proceed overland, the other by sea; both were to make the utmost haste.

It is of great concern now that the reader should be fully informed of the contents of the letter thus forwarded, and it is accordingly given:

"ANTIOCH, *XII. Kal. Jul.*

"Messala to Gratus.

"O my Midas!

"I pray thou take no offence at the address, seeing it is one of love and gratitude, and an admission that thou art most fortunate among men; seeing, also, that thy ears are as they were derived from thy mother, only proportionate to thy matured condition.

"O my Midas!

"I have to relate to thee an astonishing event, which, though as yet somewhat in the field of conjecture, will, I doubt not, justify thy instant consideration.

"Allow me first to revive thy recollection. Remember, a good many years ago, a family of a prince of Jerusalem, incredibly ancient and vastly rich—by name Ben-Hur. If thy memory have a limp or ailment of any kind, there is, if I mistake not, a wound on thy head which may help thee to a revival of the circumstance.

"Next, to arouse thy interest. In punishment of the attempt upon thy life—for dear repose of conscience, may all the gods forbid it should ever prove to have been an accident!—the family were seized and summarily disposed of, and their property confiscated. And inasmuch, O my Midas! as the action had the approval of our Cæsar, who was as just as he was wise—be there flowers upon his altar forever!—there should be no shame in referring to the sums which were realized to us respectively from that source, for which it is not possible I can ever cease to be grateful to thee, certainly not while I continue, as at present, in the uninterrupted enjoyment of the part which fell to me.

"In vindication of thy wisdom—a quality for which, as I am now advised, the son of Gordius, to whom I have boldly likened thee, was never distinguished among men or gods—I recall further that thou didst make disposition of the family of Hur, both of us at the time supposing the plan hit upon to be the most effective possible for the purposes in view, which were silence and delivery over to inevitable but natural death. Thou wilt remember what thou didst with the mother and sister of the malefactor; yet, if now I yield to a desire to learn whether they be living or dead, I know, from knowing the amiability of thy nature, O my Gratus, that thou wilt pardon me as one scarcely less amiable than thyself.

"As more immediately essential to the present business, however, I take the liberty of inviting to thy remembrance that the actual criminal was sent to the galleys a slave for life—so the precept ran; and it may serve to make the event which I am about to relate the more astonishing by saying here that I saw and read the receipt for his body delivered in course to the tribune commanding a galley.

"Thou mayst begin now to give me more especial heed, O my most excellent Phrygian![72]

---

72 A reference likening Gratus to one of the heroic kings of the ancient land of Phrygia.

"Referring to the limit of life at the oar, the outlaw thus justly disposed of should be dead, or, better speaking, some one of the three thousand Oceanides[73] should have taken him to husband at least five years ago. And if thou wilt excuse a momentary weakness, O most virtuous and tender of men! inasmuch as I loved him in childhood, and also because he was very handsome—I used in much admiration to call him my Ganymede—he ought in right to have fallen into the arms of the most beautiful daughter of the family. Of opinion, however, that he was certainly dead, I have lived quite five years in calm and innocent enjoyment of the fortune for which I am in a degree indebted to him. I make the admission of indebtedness without intending it to diminish my obligation to thee.

"Now I am at the very point of interest.

"Last night, while acting as master of the feast for a party just from Rome—their extreme youth and inexperience appealed to my compassion—I heard a singular story. Maxentius, the consul, as you know, comes to-day to conduct a campaign against the Parthians. Of the ambitious who are to accompany him there is one, a son of the late duumvir Quintus Arrius. I had occasion to inquire about him particularly. When Arrius set out in pursuit of the pirates, whose defeat gained him his final honors, he had no family; when he returned from the expedition, he brought back with him an heir. Now be thou composed as becomes the owner of so many talents in ready sestertia! The son and heir of whom I speak is he whom thou didst send to the galleys—the very Ben-Hur who should have died at his oar five years ago—returned now with fortune and rank, and possibly as a Roman citizen, to— Well, thou art too firmly seated to be alarmed, but I, O my Midas! I am in danger—no need to tell thee of what. Who should know, if thou dost not?

"Sayest thou to all this, tut-tut?

"When Arrius, the father, by adoption, of this apparition from the arms of the most beautiful of the Oceanides (see above my opinion of what she should be), joined battle with the pirates, his vessel was sunk, and but two of all her crew escaped drowning—Arrius himself and this one, his heir.

"The officers who took them from the plank on which they were floating say the associate of the fortunate tribune was a young man who, when lifted to the deck, was in the dress of a galley slave.

"This should be convincing, to say least; but lest thou say tut-tut again, I tell thee, O my Midas! that yesterday, by good chance—I have a vow to Fortune in consequence—I met the mysterious son of Arrius face to face; and I declare now that, though I did not then recognize him, he is the very Ben-Hur who was for years my playmate; the very Ben-Hur who, if he be a man, though of the commonest grade, must this very moment of my writing be thinking of vengeance—for so would I were I he—vengeance not to be satisfied short of life; vengeance for country, mother, sister, self, and—I say it last, though thou mayst think it would be first—for fortune lost.

"By this time, O good my benefactor and friend! my Gratus! in consideration of thy sestertia in peril, their loss being the worst which could befall one of thy high estate—I quit calling thee after the foolish old King of Phrygia—by this time, I say (meaning after having read me so far), I have faith to believe thou hast ceased saying tut-tut, and art ready to think what ought to be done in such emergency.

---

73 In ancient Greek mythology three thousand nymphs also known as the Oceanides presided over all sources of fresh water.

"It were vulgar to ask thee now what shall be done. Rather let me say I am thy client; or, better yet, thou art my Ulysses[74] whose part it is to give me sound direction.

"And I please myself thinking I see thee when this letter is put into thy hand. I see thee read it once, thy countenance all gravity, and then again with a smile; then, hesitation ended, and thy judgment formed, it is this, or it is that; wisdom like Mercury's, promptitude like Cæsar's.

"The sun is now fairly risen. An hour hence two messengers will depart from my door, each with a sealed copy hereof; one of them will go by land, the other by sea, so important do I regard it that thou shouldst be early and particularly informed of the appearance of our enemy in this part of our Roman world.

"I will await thy answer here.

"Ben-Hur's going and coming will of course be regulated by his master, the consul, who, though he exert himself without rest day and night, cannot get away under a month. Thou knowest what work it is to assemble and provide for an army destined to operate in a desolate, townless country.

"I saw the Jew yesterday in the Grove of Daphne; and if he be not there now, he is certainly in the neighborhood, making it easy for me to keep him in eye. Indeed, wert thou to ask me where he is now, I should say, with the most positive assurance, he is to be found at the old Orchard of Palms, under the tent of the traitor Sheik Ilderim, who cannot long escape our strong hand. Be not surprised if Maxentius, as his first measure, places the Arab on the ship for forwarding to Rome.

"I am so particular about the whereabouts of the Jew because it will be important to thee, O illustrious! when thou comest to consider what is to be done; for already I know, and by the knowledge I flatter myself I am growing in wisdom, that in every scheme involving human action there are three elements always to be taken in account—time, place, and agency.

"If thou sayest this is the place, have thou then no hesitancy in trusting the business to thy most loving friend, who would be thy aptest scholar as well.

MESSALA."

Chapter II

About the time the couriers departed from Messala's door with the despatches (it being yet the early morning hour), Ben-Hur entered Ilderim's tent. He had taken a plunge into the lake, and breakfasted, and appeared now in an under-tunic, sleeveless, and with skirt scarcely reaching to the knee.

The sheik saluted him from the divan.

"I give thee peace, son of Arrius," he said, with admiration, for, in truth, he had never seen a more perfect illustration of glowing, powerful, confident manhood. "I give thee peace and good-will. The horses are ready, I am ready. And thou?"

"The peace thou givest me, good sheik, I give thee in return. I thank thee for so much good-will. I am ready."

Ilderim clapped his hands.

---

74 King of ancient Ithaca who fought at Troy and was renowned throughout all of the ancient Greek world for his wisdom and cunning.

"I will have the horses brought. Be seated."

"Are they yoked?"

"No."

"Then suffer me to serve myself," said Ben-Hur. "It is needful that I make the acquaint-ance of thy Arabs. I must know them by name, O sheik, that I may speak to them singly; nor less must I know their temper, for they are like men: if bold, the better of scolding; if timid, the better of praise and flattery. Let the servants bring me the harness."

"And the chariot?" asked the shiek.

"I will let the chariot alone to-day. In its place, let them bring me a fifth horse, if thou hast it; he should be barebacked, and fleet as the others."

Ilderim's wonder was aroused, and he summoned a servant immediately.

"Bid them bring the harness for the four," he said; "the harness for the four, and the bridle for Sirius."

Ilderim then arose.

"Sirius is my love, and I am his, O son of Arrius. We have been comrades for twenty years—in tent, in battle, in all stages of the desert we have been comrades. I will show him to you."

Going to the division curtain, he held it, while Ben-Hur passed under. The horses came to him in a body. One with a small head, luminous eyes, neck like the segment of a bended bow, and mighty chest, curtained thickly by a profusion of mane soft and wavy as a damsel's locks, nickered low and gladly at sight of him.

"Good horse," said the sheik, patting the dark-brown cheek. "Good horse, good-morning." Turning then to Ben-Hur, he added, "This is Sirius, father of the four here. Mira, the mother, awaits our return, being too precious to be hazarded in a region where there is a stronger hand than mine. And much I doubt," he laughed as he spoke—"much I doubt, O son of Arrius, if the tribe could endure her absence. She is their glory; they wor-ship her; did she gallop over them, they would laugh. Ten thousand horsemen, sons of the desert, will ask to-day, 'Have you heard of Mira?' And to the answer, 'She is well,' they will say, 'God is good! blessed be God!'"

"Mira—Sirius—names of stars, are they not, O sheik?" asked Ben-Hur, going to each of the four, and to the sire, offering his hand.

"And why not?" replied Ilderim. "Wert thou ever abroad on the desert at night?"

"No."

"Then thou canst not know how much we Arabs depend upon the stars. We bor-row their names in gratitude, and give them in love. My fathers all had their Miras, as I have mine; and these children are stars no less. There, see thou, is Rigel, and there Antares; that one is Atair, and he whom thou goest to now is Aldebaran, the young-est of the brood, but none the worse of that—no, not he! Against the wind he will carry thee till it roar in thy ears like Akaba; and he will go where thou sayest, son of Arrius—ay, by the glory of Solomon! he will take thee to the lion's jaws, if thou darest so much."

The harness was brought. With his own hands Ben-Hur equipped the horses; with his own hands he led them out of the tent, and there attached the reins.

"Bring me Sirius," he said.

An Arab could not have better sprung to seat on the courser's back.

"And now the reins."

They were given him, and carefully separated.

"Good sheik," he said, "I am ready. Let a guide go before me to the field, and send some of thy men with water."

There was no trouble at starting. The horses were not afraid. Already there seemed a tacit understanding between them and the new driver, who had performed his part calmly, and with the confidence which always begets confidence. The order of going was precisely that of driving, except that Ben-Hur sat upon Sirius instead of standing in the chariot. Ilderim's spirit arose. He combed his beard, and smiled with satisfaction as he muttered, "He is not a Roman, no, by the splendor of God!" He followed on foot, the entire tenantry of the *dowar*—men, women, and children—pouring after him, participants all in his solicitude, if not in his confidence.

The field, when reached, proved ample and well fitted for the training, which Ben-Hur began immediately by driving the four at first slowly, and in perpendicular lines, and then in wide circles. Advancing a step in the course, he put them next into a trot; again progressing, he pushed into a gallop; at length he contracted the circles, and yet later drove eccentrically here and there, right, left, forward, and without a break. An hour was thus occupied. Slowing the gait to a walk, he drove up to Ilderim.

"The work is done, nothing now but practice," he said. "I give you joy, Sheik Ilderim, that you have such servants as these. See," he continued, dismounting and going to the horses, "see, the gloss of their red coats is without spot; they breathe lightly as when I began. I give thee great joy, and it will go hard if"—he turned his flashing eyes upon the old man's face—"if we have not the victory and our—"

He stopped, colored, bowed. At the sheik's side he observed, for the first time, Balthasar, leaning upon his staff, and two women closely veiled. At one of the latter he looked a second time, saying to himself, with a flutter about his heart, "'Tis she—'tis the Egyptian!" Ilderim picked up his broken sentence—

"The victory, and our revenge!" Then he said aloud, "I am not afraid; I am glad. Son of Arrius, thou art the man. Be the end like the beginning, and thou shalt see of what stuff is the lining of the hand of an Arab who is able to give."

"I thank thee, good sheik," Ben-Hur returned, modestly, "Let the servants bring drink for the horses."

With his own hands he gave the water.

Remounting Sirius, he renewed the training, going as before from walk to trot, from trot to gallop; finally, he pushed the steady racers into the run, gradually quickening it to full speed. The performance then became exciting; and there were applause for the dainty handling of the reins, and admiration for the four, which were the same, whether they flew forward or wheeled in varying curvature. In their action there were unity, power, grace, pleasure, all without effort or sign of labor. The admiration was unmixed with pity or reproach, which would have been as well bestowed upon swallows in their evening flight.

In the midst of the exercises, and the attention they received from all the bystanders, Malluch came upon the ground, seeking the sheik.

"I have a message for you, O sheik," he said, availing himself of a moment he supposed favorable for the speech —"a message from Simonides, the merchant."

"Simonides!" ejaculated the Arab. "Ah! 'tis well. May Abaddon take all his enemies!"

"He bade me give thee first the holy peace of God," Malluch continued; "and then this despatch, with prayer that thou read it the instant of receipt."

Ilderim, standing in his place, broke the sealing of the package delivered to him, and from a wrapping of fine linen took two letters, which he proceeded to read.

[No. 1.]

"Simonides to Sheik Ilderim.

"O friend!
"Assure thyself first of a place in my inner heart.
"Then—
"There is in thy dowar a youth of fair presence, calling himself the son of Arrius; and such he is by adoption.
"He is very dear to me.
"He hath a wonderful history, which I will tell thee; come thou to-day or to-morrow, that I may tell thee the history, and have thy counsel.
"Meantime, favor all his requests, so they be not against honor. Should there be need of reparation, I am bound to thee for it.
"That I have interest in this youth, keep thou private.
"Remember me to thy other guest. He, his daughter, thyself, and all whom thou mayst choose to be of thy company, must depend upon me at the Circus the day of the games. I have seats already engaged.
"To thee and all thine, peace.
"What should I be, O my friend, but thy friend?

"SIMONIDES."

[No. 2.]

"Simonides to Sheik Ilderim.

"O friend!
"Out of the abundance of my experience, I send you a word.
"There is a sign which all persons not Romans, and who have moneys or goods subject to despoilment, accept as warning—that is, the arrival at a seat of power of some high Roman official charged with authority.
"To-day comes the Consul Maxentius.
"Be thou warned!
"Another word of advice.
"A conspiracy, to be of effect against thee, O friend, must include the Herods as parties; thou hast great properties in their dominions.
"Wherefore keep thou watch.
"Send this morning to thy trusty keepers of the roads leading south from Antioch, and bid them search every courier going and coming; if they find private despatches relating to thee or thy affairs, *thou shouldst see them.*
"You should have received this yesterday, though it is not too late, if you act promptly.
"If couriers left Antioch this morning, your messengers know the byways, and can get before them with your orders.
"Do not hesitate

"Burn this after reading.

"O my friend! thy friend,

SIMONIDES"

Ilderim read the letters a second time, and refolded them in the linen wrap, and put the package under his girdle.

The exercises in the field continued but a little longer—in all about two hours. At their conclusion, Ben-Hur brought the four to a walk, and drove to Ilderim.

"With leave, O sheik," he said, "I will return thy Arabs to the tent, and bring them out again this afternoon."

Ilderim walked to him as he sat on Sirius, and said, "I give them to you, son of Arrius, to do with as you will until after the games. You have done with them in two hours what the Roman—may jackals gnaw his bones fleshless!—could not in as many weeks. We will win—by the splendor of God, we will win!"

At the tent Ben-Hur remained with the horses while they were being cared for; then, after a plunge in the lake and a cup of arrack with the sheik, whose flow of spirits was royally exuberant, he dressed himself in his Jewish garb again, and walked with Malluch on into the Orchard.

There was much conversation between the two, not all of it important. One part, however, must not be overlooked. Ben-Hur was speaking.

"I will give you," he said, "an order for my property stored in the khan this side the river by the Seleucian Bridge. Bring it to me to-day, if you can. And, good Malluch—if I do not overtask you—"

Malluch protested heartily his willingness to be of service.

"Thank you, Malluch, thank you," said Ben-Hur. "I will take you at your word, remembering that we are brethren of the old tribe, and that the enemy is a Roman. First, then—as you are a man of business, which I much fear Sheik Ilderim is not—"

"Arabs seldom are," said Malluch, gravely.

"Nay, I do not impeach their shrewdness, Malluch. It is well, however, to look after them. To save all forfeit or hindrance in connection with the race, you would put me perfectly at rest by going to the office of the Circus, and seeing that he has complied with every preliminary rule; and if you can get a copy of the rules, the service may be of great avail to me. I would like to know the colors I am to wear, and particularly the number of the crypt I am to occupy at the starting; if it be next Messala's on the right or left, it is well; if not, and you can have it changed so as to bring me next the Roman, do so. Have you good memory, Malluch?"

"It has failed me, but never, son of Arrius, where the heart helped it as now."

"I will venture, then, to charge you with one further service. I saw yesterday that Messala was proud of his chariot, as he might be, for the best of Cæsar's scarcely surpass it. Can you not make its display an excuse which will enable you to find if it be light or heavy? I would like to have its exact weight and measurements—and, Malluch, though you fail in all else, bring me exactly the height his axle stands above the ground. You understand, Malluch? I do not wish him to have any actual advantage of me. I do not care for his splendor; if I beat him, it will make his fall the harder, and my triumph the more complete. If there are advantages really important, I want them."

"I see, I see!" said Malluch. "A line dropped from the centre of the axle is what you want."

"Thou hast it; and be glad, Malluch—it is the last of my commissions. Let us return to the dowar."

At the door of the tent they found a servant replenishing the smoke-stained bottles of leben freshly made, and stopped to refresh themselves. Shortly afterwards Malluch returned to the city.

During their absence, a messenger well mounted had been despatched with orders as suggested by Simonides. He was an Arab, and carried nothing written.

Chapter IV

ILDERIM returned to the dowar next day about the third hour. As he dismounted, a man whom he recognized as of his own tribe came to him and said, "O sheik, I was bidden give thee this package, with request that thou read it at once. If there be answer, I was to wait thy pleasure."

Ilderim gave the package immediate attention. The seal was already broken. The address ran, *To Valerius Gratus at Cæsarea.*

"Abaddon take him!" growled the sheik, at discovering a letter in Latin.

Had the missive been in Greek or Arabic, he could have read it; as it was, the utmost he could make out was the signature in bold Roman letters—MESSALA—whereat his eyes twinkled.

"Where is the young Jew?" he asked.

"In the field with the horses," a servant replied.

The sheik replaced the papyrus in its envelopes, and, tucking the package under his girdle, remounted the horse. That moment a stranger made his appearance, coming, apparently, from the city.

"I am looking for Sheik Ilderim, surnamed the Generous," the stranger said.

His language and attire bespoke him a Roman.

What he could not read, he yet could speak; so the old Arab answered, with dignity, "I am Sheik Ilderim."

The man's eyes fell; he raised them again, and said, with forced composure, "I heard you had need of a driver for the games."

Ilderim's lip under the white mustache curled contemptuously.

"Go thy way," he said. "I have a driver."

He turned to ride away, but the man, lingering, spoke again.

"Sheik, I am a lover of horses, and they say you have the most beautiful in the world."

The old man was touched; he drew rein, as if on the point of yielding to the flattery, but finally replied, "Not to-day, not to-day; some other time I will show them to you. I am too busy just now."

He rode to the field, while the stranger betook himself to town again with a smiling countenance. He had accomplished his mission.

And every day thereafter, down to the great day of the games, a man—sometimes two or three men—came to the sheik at the Orchard, pretending to seek an engagement as driver.

In such manner Messala kept watch over Ben-Hur.

Chapter V

THE sheik waited, well satisfied, until Ben-Hur drew his horses off the field for the forenoon—well satisfied, for he had seen them, after being put through all the other paces, run full speed in such manner that it did not seem there were one the slowest and another the fastest—run, in other words, as if the four were one.

"This afternoon, O sheik, I will give Sirius back to you." Ben-Hur patted the neck of the old horse as he spoke. "I will give him back, and take to the chariot."

"So soon?" Ilderim asked.

"With such as these, good sheik, one day suffices. They are not afraid; they have a man's intelligence, and they love the exercise. This one," he shook a rein over the back of the youngest of the four—"you called him Aldebaran, I believe—is the swiftest; in once round a stadium he would lead the others thrice his length."

Ilderim pulled his beard, and said, with twinkling eyes, "Aldebaran is the swiftest; but what of the slowest?"

"This is he." Ben-Hur shook the rein over Antares. "This is he: but he will win, for, look you, sheik, he will run his utmost all day—all day; and, as the sun goes down, he will reach his swiftest."

"Right again," said Ilderim.

"I have but one fear, O sheik."

The sheik became doubly serious.

"In his greed of triumph, a Roman cannot keep honor pure. In the games—all of them, mark you—their tricks are infinite; in chariot-racing their knavery extends to everything—from horse to driver, from driver to master. Wherefore, good sheik, look well to all thou hast; from this till the trial is over, let no stranger so much as see the horses. Would you be perfectly safe, do more—keep watch over them with armed hand as well as sleepless eye; then I will have no fear of the end."

At the door of the tent they dismounted.

"What you say shall be attended to. By the splendor of God, no hand shall come near them except it belong to one of the faithful. To-night I will set watches. But, son of Arrius"—Ilderim drew forth the package, and opened it slowly, while they walked to the divan and seated themselves—"son of Arrius, see thou here, and help me with thy Latin."

He passed the despatch to Ben-Hur.

"There; read—and read aloud, rendering what thou findest into the tongue of thy fathers. Latin is an abomination."

Ben-Hur was in good spirits, and began the reading carelessly. "*Messala to Gratus!*" He paused. A premonition drove the blood to his heart. Ilderim observed his agitation.

"Well; I am waiting."

Ben-Hur prayed pardon, and recommenced the paper, which, it is sufficient to say, was one of the duplicates of the letter despatched so carefully to Gratus by Messala the morning after the revel in the palace.

The paragraphs in the beginning were remarkable only as proof that the writer had not outgrown his habit of mockery; when they were passed, and the reader came to the parts intended to refresh the memory of Gratus, his voice trembled, and twice he stopped to regain his self-control. By a strong effort he continued. " 'I recall further,' " he read, " 'that thou didst make disposition of the family of Hur' "—there the reader again paused and drew a long breath—" 'both of us at the time supposing the plan hit upon to be the most effective possible for the purposes in view, which were silence and delivery over to inevitable but natural death.' "

Here Ben-Hur broke down utterly. The paper fell from his hands, and he covered his face.

"They are dead—dead. I alone am left."

The sheik had been a silent, but not unsympathetic, witness of the young man's suffering; now he arose and said, "Son of Arrius, it is for me to beg thy pardon. Read the paper by thyself. When thou art strong enough to give the rest of it to me, send word, and I will return."

He went out of the tent, and nothing in all his life became him better.

Ben-Hur flung himself on the divan and gave way to his feelings. When somewhat recovered, he recollected that a portion of the letter remained unread, and, taking it up, he resumed the reading. "Thou wilt remember," the missive ran, "what thou didst with the mother and sister of the malefactor; yet, if now I yield to a desire to learn if they be living or dead"—Ben-Hur started, and read again, and then again, and at last broke into exclamation. "He does not know they are dead; he does not know it! Blessed be the name of the Lord! there is yet hope." He finished the sentence, and was strengthened by it, and went on bravely to the end of the letter.

"They are not dead," he said, after reflection; "they are not dead, or he would have heard of it."

A second reading, more careful than the first, confirmed him in the opinion. Then he sent for the sheik.

"In coming to your hospitable tent, O sheik," he said, calmly, when the Arab was seated and they were alone, "it was not in my mind to speak of myself further than to assure you I had sufficient training to be intrusted with your horses. I declined to tell you my history. But the chances which have sent this paper to my hand and given it to me to be read are so strange that I feel bidden to trust you with everything. And I am the more inclined to do so by knowledge here conveyed that we are both of us threatened by the same enemy, against whom it is needful that we make common cause. I will read the letter and give you explanation; after which you will not wonder I was so moved. If you thought me weak or childish, you will then excuse me."

The sheik held his peace, listening closely, until Ben-Hur came to the paragraph in which he was particularly mentioned: "'I saw the Jew yesterday in the Grove of Daphne;'" so ran the part, "'and if he be not there now, he is certainly in the neighborhood, making it easy for me to keep him in eye. Indeed, wert thou to ask me where he is now, I should say, with the most positive assurance, he is to be found at the old Orchard of Palms.'"

"A—h!" exclaimed Ilderim, in such a tone one might hardly say he was more surprised than angry; at the same time, he clutched his beard.

"'At the old Orchard of Palms,'" Ben-Hur repeated, "'under the tent of the traitor sheik Ilderim.'"

"Traitor!—I?" the old man cried, in his shrillest tone, while lip and beard curled with ire, and on his forehead and neck the veins swelled and beat as they would burst.

"Yet a moment, sheik," said Ben-Hur, with a deprecatory gesture. "Such is Messala's opinion of you. Hear his threat." And he read on—"'under the tent of the traitor sheik Ilderim, who cannot long escape our strong hand. Be not surprised if Maxentius, as his first measure, places the Arab on ship for forwarding to Rome.'"

"To Rome! Me—Ilderim—sheik of ten thousand horsemen with spears—me to Rome!"

He leaped rather than rose to his feet, his arms outstretched, his fingers spread and curved like claws, his eyes glittering like a serpent's.

"O God!—nay, by all the gods except of Rome!—when shall this insolence end? A freeman am I; free are my people. Must we die slaves? Or, worse, must I live a dog, crawling to a master's feet? Must I lick his hand lest he lash me? What is mine is not mine; I am not my own; for breath of body I must be beholden to a Roman. Oh, if I were young again! Oh, could I shake off twenty years—or ten—or five!"

He ground his teeth and shook his hands overhead; then, under the impulse of another idea, he walked away and back again to Ben-Hur swiftly, and caught his shoulder with a strong grasp.

"If I were as thou, son of Arrius—as young, as strong, as practised in arms; if I had a motive hissing me to revenge—a motive, like thine, great enough to make hate holy—Away with disguise on thy part and on mine! Son of Hur, son of Hur, I say—"

At that name all the currents of Ben-Hur's blood stopped; surprised, bewildered, he gazed into the Arab's eyes, now close to his, and fiercely bright.

"Son of Hur, I say, were I as thou, with half thy wrongs, bearing about with me memories like thine, I would not, I could not, rest." Never pausing, his words following each other torrent-like, the old man swept on. "To all my grievances, I would add those of the world, and devote myself to vengeance. From land to land I would go firing all mankind. No war for freedom but should find me engaged; no battle against Rome in which I would not bear a part. I would turn Parthian,[75] if I could not better. If men failed me, still I would not give over the effort—ha, ha, ha! By the splendor of God! I would herd with wolves, and make friends of lions and tigers, in hope of marshalling them against the common enemy. I would use every weapon. So my victims were Romans, I would rejoice in slaughter. Quarter I would not ask; quarter I would not give. To the flames everything Roman; to the sword every Roman born. Of nights I would pray the gods, the good and the bad alike, to lend me their special terrors—tempests, drought, heat, cold, and all the nameless poisons they let loose in air, all the thousand things of which men die on sea and on land. Oh, I could not sleep. I—I—"

The sheik stopped for want of breath, panting, wringing his hands. And, sooth to say, of all the passionate burst Ben-Hur retained but a vague impression wrought by fiery eyes, a piercing voice, and a rage too intense for coherent expression.

For the first time in years, the desolate youth heard himself addressed by his proper name. One man at least knew him, and acknowledged it without demand of identity; and he an Arab fresh from the desert!

How came the man by his knowledge? The letter? No. It told the cruelties from which his family had suffered; it told the story of his own misfortunes, but it did not say he was the very victim whose escape from doom was the theme of the heartless narrative. That was the point of explanation he had notified the sheik would follow the reading of the letter. He was pleased, and thrilled with hope restored, yet kept an air of calmness.

"Good sheik, tell me how you came by this letter."

"My people keep the roads between cities," Ilderim answered, bluntly. "They took it from a courier."

"Are they known to be thy people?"

"No. To the world they are robbers, whom it is mine to catch and slay."

"Again, sheik. You call me son of Hur—my father's name. I did not think myself known to a person on earth. How came you by the knowledge?"

Ilderim hesitated; but, rallying, he answered, "I know you, yet I am not free to tell you more."

---

75 Parthia was a kingdom located in present-day Iraq and frequently at war with Rome.

"Some one holds you in restraint?"

The sheik closed his mouth, and walked away; but, observing Ben-Hur's disappointment, he came back, and said, "Let us say no more about the matter now. I will go to town; when I return, I may talk to you fully. Give me the letter."

Ilderim rolled the papyrus carefully, restored it to its envelopes, and became once more all energy.

"What sayest thou?" he asked, while waiting for his horse and retinue. "I told what I would do, were I thou, and thou hast made no answer."

"I intended to answer, sheik, and I will." Ben-Hur's countenance and voice changed with the feeling invoked. "All thou hast said, I will do—all at least in the power of a man. I devoted myself to vengeance long ago. Every hour of the five years passed, I have lived with no other thought. I have taken no respite. I have had no pleasures of youth. The blandishments of Rome were not for me. I wanted her to educate me for revenge. I resorted to her most famous masters and professors—not those of rhetoric or philosophy: alas! I had no time for them. The arts essential to a fighting-man were my desire. I associated with gladiators, and with winners of prizes in the circus; and they were my teachers. The drill-masters in the great camp accepted me as a scholar, and were proud of my attainments in their line. O sheik, I am a soldier; but the things of which I dream require me to be a captain. With that thought, I have taken part in the campaign against the Parthians; when it is over, then, if the Lord spare my life and strength—then"—he raised his clenched hands, and spoke vehemently—"then I will be an enemy Roman-taught in all things; then Rome shall account to me in Roman lives for her ills. You have my answer, sheik."

Ilderim put an arm over his shoulder, and kissed him, saying, passionately, "If thy God favor thee not, son of Hur, it is because he is dead. Take thou this from me—sworn to, if so thy preference run: thou shalt have my hands, and their fulness—men, horses, camels, and the desert for preparation. I swear it! For the present, enough. Thou shalt see or hear from me before night."

Turning abruptly off, the sheik was speedily on the road to the city.

Chapter VI

THE intercepted letter was conclusive upon a number of points of great interest to Ben-Hur. It had all the effect of a confession that the writer was a party to the putting-away of the family with murderous intent; that he had sanctioned the plan adopted for the purpose; that he had received a portion of the proceeds of the confiscation, and was yet in enjoyment of his part; that he dreaded the unexpected appearance of what he was pleased to call the chief malefactor, and accepted it as a menace; that he contemplated such further action as would secure him in the future, and was ready to do whatever his accomplice in Cæsarea might advise.

And, now that the letter had reached the hand of him really its subject, it was notice of danger to come, as well as a confession of guilt. So when Ilderim left the tent, Ben-Hur had much to think about, requiring immediate action. His enemies were as adroit and powerful as any in the East. If they were afraid of him, he had greater reason to be afraid of them. He strove earnestly to reflect upon the situation, but could not; his feelings constantly overwhelmed him. There was a certain qualified pleasure in the assurance that his mother and sister were alive; and it mattered little that the foundation of the assurance was a mere inference. That there was one person who could tell him where they were seemed to his hope so long deferred as if discovery were now close at hand. These were mere causes of feeling; underlying them, it must be confessed he had a superstitious fancy that God was about to make ordination in his behalf, in which event faith whispered him to stand still.

Occasionally, referring to the words of Ilderim, he wondered whence the Arab derived his information about him; not from Malluch certainly; nor from Simonides, whose interests, all adverse, would hold him dumb. Could Messala have been the informant? No, no: disclosure might be dangerous in that quarter. Conjecture was vain; at the same time, often as Ben-Hur was beaten back from the solution, he was consoled with the thought that whoever the person with the knowledge might be, he was a friend, and, being such, would reveal himself in good time. A little more waiting—a little more patience. Possibly the errand of the sheik was to see the worthy; possibly the letter might precipitate a full disclosure.

And patient he would have been if only he could have believed Tirzah and his mother were waiting for him under circumstances permitting hope on their part strong as his; if, in other words, conscience had not stung him with accusations respecting them.

To escape such accusations, he wandered far through the Orchard, pausing now where the date-gatherers were busy, yet not too busy to offer him of their fruit and talk with him; then, under the great trees, to watch the nesting birds, or hear the bees swarming about the berries bursting with honeyed sweetness, and filling all the green and golden spaces with the music of their beating wings.

By the lake, however, he lingered longest. He might not look upon the water and its sparkling ripples, so like sensuous life, without thinking of the Egyptian[76] and her marvellous beauty, and of floating with her here and there through the night, made brilliant by her songs and stories; he might not forget the charm of her manner, the lightness of her laugh, the flattery of her attention, the warmth of her little hand under his upon the tiller of the boat. From her it was for his thought but a short way to Balthasar, and the strange things of which he had been witness, unaccountable by any law of nature; and from him, again, to the King of the Jews, whom the good man, with such pathos of patience, was holding in holy promise, the distance was even nearer. And there his mind stayed, finding in the mysteries of that personage a satisfaction answering well for the rest he was seeking. Because, it may have been, nothing is so easy as denial of an idea not agreeable to our wishes, he rejected the definition given by Balthasar of the kingdom the king was coming to establish. A kingdom of souls, if not intolerable to his Sadducean faith, seemed to him but an abstraction drawn from the depths of a devotion too fond and dreamy. A kingdom of Judea, on the other hand, was more than comprehensible: such had been, and, if only for that reason, might be again. And it suited his pride to think of a new kingdom broader of domain, richer in power, and of a more unapproachable splendor than the old one; of a new king wiser and mightier than Solomon—a new king under whom, especially, he could find both service and revenge. In that mood he returned to the dowar.

---

76 Earlier, Ben-Hur had met the beautiful Egyptian temptress, Iras. In the story, Iras is the daughter of Balthasar, one of the Three Wise Men from the East who visited Christ at his birth in Bethlehem.

The mid-day meal disposed of, still further to occupy himself, Ben-Hur had the char-iot rolled out into the sunlight for inspection. The word but poorly conveys the careful study the vehicle underwent. No point or part of it escaped him. With a pleasure which will be better understood hereafter, he saw the pattern was Greek, in his judgment preferable to the Roman in many respects; it was wider between the wheels, and lower and stronger, and the disadvantage of greater weight would be more than compen-sated by the greater endurance of his Arabs. Speaking generally, the carriage-makers of Rome built for the games almost solely, sacrificing safety to beauty, and durability to grace; while the chariots of Achilles and "the king of men,"[77] designed for war and all its extreme tests, still ruled the tastes of those who met and struggled for the crowns Isthmian and Olympic.

Next he brought the horses, and, hitching them to the chariot, drove to the field of exercise, where, hour after hour, he practised them in movement under the yoke. When he came away in the evening, it was with restored spirit, and a fixed purpose to defer action in the matter of Messala until the race was won or lost. He could not forego the pleasure of meeting his adversary under the eyes of the East; that there might be other competitors seemed not to enter his thought. His confidence in the result was absolute; no doubt of his own skill; and as to the four, they were his full partners in the glorious game.

"Let him look to it, let him look to it! Ha, Antares—Aldebaran! Shall he not, O hon-est Rigel? And thou, Atair, king among coursers, shall he not beware of us? Ha, ha! good hearts!"

So in rests he passed from horse to horse, speaking, not as a master, but the senior of as many brethren.

After nightfall, Ben-Hur sat by the door of the tent waiting for Ilderim, not yet returned from the city. He was not impatient, or vexed, or doubtful. The sheik would be heard from, at least. Indeed, whether it was from satisfaction with the performance of the four, or the refreshment there is in cold water succeeding bodily exercise, or supper partaken with royal appetite, or the reaction which, as a kindly provision of nature, always follows depression, the young man was in good-humor verging upon elation. He felt himself in the hands of Providence no longer his enemy. At last there was a sound of horse's feet coming rapidly, and Malluch rode up.

"Son of Arrius," he said, cheerily, after salutation, "I salute you for Sheik Ilderim, who requests you to mount and go to the city. He is waiting for you."

Ben-Hur asked no questions, but went in where the horses were feeding. Aldebaran came to him, as if offering his service. He played with him lovingly, but passed on, and chose another, not of the four—they were sacred to the race. Very shortly the two were on the road, going swiftly and in silence.

Some distance below the Seleucian Bridge, they crossed the river by a ferry, and, riding far round on the right bank, and recrossing by another ferry, entered the city from the west. The detour was long, but Ben-Hur accepted it as a precaution for which there was good reason.

Down to Simonides' landing they rode, and in front of the great warehouse, under the bridge, Malluch drew rein.

---

77 A reference to Agamemnon, the Achaean king who set off to Troy to wage war alongside fellow Achaean, Achilles. He commanded the united Greek forces during the Trojan War.

"We are come," he said. "Dismount."

Ben-Hur recognized the place.

"Where is the sheik?" he asked.

"Come with me. I will show you."

A watchman took the horses, and almost before he realized it Ben-Hur stood once more at the door of the house up on the greater one, listening to the response from within —"In God's name, enter."

Chapter VII

MALLUCH stopped at the door; Ben-Hur entered alone.

The room was the same in which he had formerly interviewed Simonides,[78] and it had been in nowise changed, except now, close by the arm-chair, a polished brazen rod, set on a broad wooden pedestal, arose higher than a tall man, holding lamps of silver on sliding arms, half a dozen or more in number, and all burning. The light was clear, bringing into view the panelling on the walls, the cornice with its row of gilded balls, and the dome dully tinted with violet mica.

Within, a few steps, Ben-Hur stopped.

Three persons were present, looking at him—Simonides, Ilderim, and Esther.

He glanced hurriedly from one to another, as if to find answer to the question half formed in his mind, What business can these have with me? He became calm, with every sense on the alert, for the question was succeeded by another, Are they friends or enemies?

At length, his eyes rested upon Esther.

The men returned his look kindly; in her face there was something more than kindness— something too *spirituel* for definition, which yet went to his inner consciousness without definition.

Shall it be said, good reader? Back of his gaze there was a comparison in which the Egyptian arose and set herself over against the gentle Jewess; but it lived an instant, and, as is the habit of such comparisons, passed away without a conclusion.

"Son of Hur—"

The guest turned to the speaker.

"Son of Hur," said Simonides, repeating the address slowly, and with distinct emphasis, as if to impress all its meaning upon him most interested in understanding it, "take thou the peace of the Lord God of our fathers—take it from me." He paused, then added, "From me and mine."

The speaker sat in his chair; there were the royal head, the bloodless face, the masterful air, under the influence of which visitors forgot the broken limbs and distorted body of the man. The full black eyes gazed out under the white brows steadily, but not sternly. A moment thus, then he crossed his hands upon his breast.

The action, taken with the salutation, could not be misunderstood, and was not.

"Simonides," Ben-Hur answered, much moved, "the holy peace you tender is accepted. As son to father, I return it to you. Only let there be perfect understanding between us."

---

78 Simonides has acted as chief steward of the House of Hur after fleeing to Antioch. From that distance, he was able to keep some of the Hur family's fortune from the hands of Messala and Gratus.

Thus delicately he sought to put aside the submission of the merchant, and, in place of the relation of master and servant, substitute one higher and holier.

Simonides let fall his hands, and, turning to Esther, said, "A seat for the master, daughter."

She hastened, and brought a stool, and stood, with suffused face, looking from one to the other—from Ben-Hur to Simonides, from Simonides to Ben-Hur; and they waited, each declining the superiority direction would imply. When at length the pause began to be embarrassing, Ben-Hur advanced, and gently took the stool from her, and, going to the chair, placed it at the merchant's feet.

"I will sit here," he said.

His eyes met hers—an instant only; but both were better of the look. He recognized her gratitude, she his generosity and forbearance.

Simonides bowed his acknowledgment.

"Esther, child, bring me the paper," he said, with a breath of relief.

She went to a panel in the wall, opened it, took out a roll of papyri, and brought and gave it to him.

"Thou saidst well, son of Hur," Simonides began, while unrolling the sheets. "Let us understand each other. In anticipation of the demand—which I would have made hadst thou waived it—I have here a statement covering everything necessary to the understanding required. I could see but two points involved—the property first, and then our relation. The statement is explicit as to both. Will it please thee to read it now?"

Ben-Hur received the papers, but glanced at Ilderim.

"Nay," said Simonides, "the sheik shall not deter thee from reading. The account—such thou wilt find it—is of a nature requiring a witness. In the attesting place at the end thou wilt find, when thou comest to it, the name—Ilderim, Sheik. He knows all. He is thy friend. All he has been to me, that will he be to thee also."

Simonides looked at the Arab, nodding pleasantly, and the latter gravely returned the nod, saying, "Thou hast said."

Ben-Hur replied, "I know already the excellence of his friendship, and have yet to prove myself worthy of it." Immediately he continued, "Later, O Simonides, I will read the papers carefully; for the present, do thou take them, and if thou be not too weary, give me their substance."

Simonides took back the roll.

"Here, Esther, stand by me and receive the sheets, lest they fall into confusion."

She took place by his chair, letting her right arm fall lightly across his shoulder, so, when he spoke, the account seemed to have rendition from both of them jointly.

"This," said Simonides, drawing out the first leaf, "shows the money I had of thy father's, being the amount saved from the Romans; there was no property saved, only money, and that the robbers would have secured but for our Jewish custom of bills of exchange. The amount saved, being sums I drew from Rome, Alexandria, Damascus, Carthage, Valentia, and elsewhere within the circle of trade, was one hundred and twenty talents Jewish money."

He gave the sheet to Esther, and took the next one.

"With that amount—one hundred and twenty talents— I charged myself. Hear now my credits. I use the word, as thou wilt see, with reference rather to the proceeds gained from the use of the money."

From separate sheets he then read footings, which, fractions omitted, were as follows: "CR.

"By ships	....	60	talents.
"goods in store	....	110	"
"cargoes in transit	....	75	"
"camels, horses, etc.	....	20	"
"warehouses	....	10	"
"bills due	....	54	"
"money on hand and subject to draft	....	<u>224</u>	"
Total	....	553	" "

"To these now, to the five hundred and fifty-three talents gained, add the original capital I had from thy father, and thou hast SIX HUNDRED AND SEVENTY-THREE TALENTS!—and all thine—making thee, O son of Hur, the richest subject in the world."

He took the papyri from Esther, and, reserving one, rolled them and offered them to Ben-Hur. The pride perceptible in his manner was not offensive; it might have been from a sense of duty well done; it might have been for Ben-Hur without reference to himself.

"And there is nothing," he added, dropping his voice, but not his eyes—"there is nothing now thou mayst not do."

The moment was one of absorbing interest to all present. Simonides crossed his hands upon his breast again; Esther was anxious; Ilderim nervous. A man is never so on trial as in the moment of excessive good-fortune.

Taking the roll, Ben-Hur arose, struggling with emotion.

"All this is to me as a light from heaven, sent to drive away a night which has been so long I feared it would never end, and so dark I had lost the hope of seeing," he said, with a husky voice. "I give first thanks to the Lord, who has not abandoned me, and my next to thee, O Simonides. Thy faithfulness outweighs the cruelty of others, and redeems our human nature. 'There is nothing I cannot do:' be it so. Shall any man in this my hour of such mighty privilege be more generous than I? Serve me as a witness now, Sheik Ilderim. Hear thou my words as I shall speak them—hear and remember. And thou, Esther, good angel of this good man! hear thou also."

He stretched his hand with the roll to Simonides.

"The things these papers take into account—all of them: ships, houses, goods, camels, horses, money; the least as well as the greatest—give I back to thee, O Simonides, making them all thine, and sealing them to thee and thine forever."

Esther smiled through her tears; Ilderim pulled his beard with rapid motion, his eyes glistening like beads of jet. Simonides alone was calm.

"Sealing them to thee and thine forever," Ben-Hur continued, with better control of himself, "with one exception, and upon one condition."

The breath of the listeners waited upon his words.

"The hundred and twenty talents which were my father's thou shalt return to me." Ilderim's countenance brightened.

"And thou shalt join me in search of my mother and sister, holding all thine subject to the expense of discovery, even as I will hold mine."

Simonides was much affected. Stretching out his hand, he said, "I see thy spirit, son of Hur, and I am grateful to the Lord that he hath sent thee to me such as thou art. If I served well thy father in life, and his memory afterwards, be not afraid of default to thee; yet must I say the exception cannot stand."

Exhibiting, then, the reserved sheet, he continued,

"Thou hast not all the account. Take this and read—read aloud."

Ben-Hur took the supplement, and read it.

"Statement of the servants of Hur, rendered by Simonides, steward of the estate.

1. Amrah, Egyptian, keeping the palace in Jerusalem.
2. Simonides, the steward, in Antioch.
3. Esther, daughter of Simonides."

Now, in all his thoughts of Simonides, not once had it entered Ben-Hur's mind that, by the law, a daughter followed the parent's condition. In all his visions of her, the sweet-faced Esther had figured as the rival of the Egyptian, and an object of possible love. He shrank from the revelation so suddenly brought him, and looked at her blushing; and, blushing, she dropped her eyes before him. Then he said, while the papyrus rolled itself together,

"A man with six hundred talents is indeed rich, and may do what he pleases; but, rarer than the money, more priceless than the property, is the mind which amassed the wealth, and the heart it could not corrupt when amassed. O Simonides—and thou, fair Esther— fear not. Sheik Ilderim here shall be witness that in the same moment ye were declared my servants, that moment I declared ye free; and what I declare, that will I put in writing. Is it not enough? Can I do more?"

"Son of Hur," said Simonides, "verily thou dost make servitude lightsome. I was wrong; there are some things thou canst not do: thou canst not make us free in law. I am thy servant forever, because I went to the door with thy father one day, and in my ear the awl-marks[79] yet abide."

"Did my father that?"

"Judge him not," cried Simonides, quickly. "He accepted me a servant of that class because I prayed him to do so. I never repented the step. It was the price I paid for Rachel, the mother of my child here; for Rachel, who would not be my wife unless I became what she was."

"Was she a servant forever?"

"Even so."

Ben-Hur walked the floor in pain of impotent wish.

"I was rich before," he said, stopping suddenly. "I was rich with the gifts of the generous Arrius; now comes this greater fortune, and the mind which achieved it. Is there not a purpose of God in it all? Counsel me, O Simonides! Help me to see the right and do it. Help

---

79 Many cultures in the time of the Roman Empire pierced the ears of their slaves with an awl and then made them wear an earring that denoted their slave status.

me to be worthy my name, and what thou art in law to me, that will I be to thee in fact and deed. I will be thy servant forever."

Simonides' face actually glowed.

"O son of my dead master! I will do better than help; I will serve thee with all my might of mind and heart. Body, I have not; it perished in thy cause; but with mind and heart I will serve thee. I swear it, by the altar of our God, and the gifts upon the altar! Only make me formally what I have assumed to be."

"Name it," said Ben-Hur, eagerly.

"As steward the care of the property will be mine."

"Count thyself steward now; or wilt thou have it in writing?"

"Thy word simply is enough; it was so with the father, and I will not more from the son. And now, if the understanding be perfect"—Simonides paused.

"It is with me," said Ben-Hur.

"And thou, daughter of Rachel, speak!" said Simonides, lifting her arm from his shoulder.

Esther, left thus alone, stood a moment abashed, her color coming and going; then she went to Ben-Hur, and said, with a womanliness singularly sweet, "I am not better than my mother was; and, as she is gone, I pray you, O my master, let me care for my father."

Ben-Hur took her hand, and led her back to the chair, saying, "Thou art a good child. Have thy will."

Simonides replaced her arm upon his neck, and there was silence for a time in the room.

Chapter VIII

SIMONIDES looked up, none the less a master.

"Esther," he said, quietly, "the night is going fast; and, lest we become too weary for that which is before us, let the refreshments be brought."

She rang a bell. A servant answered with wine and bread, which she bore round.

"The understanding, good my master," continued Simonides, when all were served, "is not perfect in my sight. Henceforth our lives will run on together like rivers which have met and joined their waters. I think their flowing will be better if every cloud is blown from the sky above them. You left my door the other day with what seemed a denial of the claims which I have just allowed in the broadest terms; but it was not so, indeed it was not. Esther is witness that I recognized you; and that I did not abandon you, let Malluch say."

"Malluch!" exclaimed Ben-Hur.

"One bound to a chair, like me, must have many hands far-reaching, if he would move the world from which he is so cruelly barred. I have many such, and Malluch is one of the best of them. And, sometimes"—he cast a grateful glance at the sheik—"sometimes I borrow from others good of heart, like Ilderim the Generous—good and brave. Let him say if I either denied or forgot you."

Ben-Hur looked at the Arab.

"This is he, good Ilderim, this is he who told you of me?"

Ilderim's eyes twinkled as he nodded his answer.

"How, O my master," said Simonides, "may we without trial tell what a man is? I knew you; I saw your father in you; but the kind of man you were I did not know. There are people to whom fortune is a curse in disguise. Were you of them? I sent Malluch to find out for me, and in the service he was my eyes and ears. Do not blame him. He brought me report of you which was all good."

"I do not," said Ben-Hur, heartily. "There was wisdom in your goodness."

"The words are very pleasant to me," said the merchant, with feeling, "very pleasant. My fear of misunderstanding is laid. Let the rivers run on now as God may give them direction."

After an interval he continued:

"I am compelled now by truth. The weaver sits weaving, and, as the shuttle flies, the cloth increases, and the figures grow, and he dreams dreams meanwhile; so to my hands the fortune grew, and I wondered at the increase, and asked myself about it many times. I could see a care not my own went with the enterprises I set going. The simooms which smote others on the desert jumped over the things which were mine. The storms which heaped the seashore with wrecks did but blow my ships the sooner into port. Strangest of all, I, so dependent upon others, fixed to a place like a dead thing, had never a loss by an agent—never. The elements stooped to serve me, and all my servants, in fact, were faithful."

"It is very strange," said Ben-Hur.

"So I said, and kept saying. Finally, O my master, finally I came to be of your opinion— God was in it—and, like you, I asked, What can his purpose be? Intelligence is never wasted; intelligence like God's never stirs except with design. I have held the question in heart, lo! these many years, watching for an answer. I felt sure, if God were in it, some day, in his own good time, in his own way, he would show me his purpose, making it clear as a whited house upon a hill. And I believe he has done so."

Ben-Hur listened with every faculty intent.

"Many years ago, with my people—thy mother was with me, Esther, beautiful as morning over old Olivet—I sat by the wayside out north of Jerusalem, near the Tombs of the Kings, when three men passed[80] by riding great white camels, such as had never been seen in the Holy City. The men were strangers, and from far countries. The first one stopped and asked me a question. 'Where is he that is born King of the Jews?' As if to allay my wonder, he went on to say, 'We have seen his star in the east, and have come to worship him.' I could not understand, but followed them to the Damascus Gate; and of every person they met on the way—of the guard at the Gate, even—they asked the question. All who heard it were amazed like me. In time I forgot the circumstance, though there was much talk of it as a presage of the Messiah. Alas, alas! What children we are, even the wisest! When God walks the earth, his steps are often centuries apart. You have seen Balthasar?"

"And heard him tell his story," said Ben-Hur.

"A miracle!—a very miracle!" cried Simonides. "As he told it to me, good my master, I seemed to hear the answer I had so long waited; God's purpose burst upon me. Poor will the King be when he comes—poor and friendless; without following, without armies, without cities or castles; a kingdom to be set up, and Rome reduced and blotted out. See, see, O my master! thou flushed with strength, thou trained to arms, thou burdened with riches; behold the opportunity the Lord hath sent thee! Shall not his purpose be thine? Could a man be born to a more perfect glory?"

Simonides put his whole force in the appeal.

---

80 The Three Wise Men made famous in the story of Christ's nativity. Matt. 2:1–2.

"But the kingdom, the kingdom!" Ben-Hur answered, eagerly. "Balthasar says it is to be of souls."

The pride of the Jew was strong in Simonides, and therefore the slightly contemptuous curl of the lip with which he began his reply:

"Balthasar has been a witness of wonderful things—of miracles, O my master; and when he speaks of them, I bow with belief, for they are of sight and sound personal to him. But he is a son of Mizraim, and not even a proselyte. Hardly may he be supposed to have special knowledge by virtue of which we must bow to him in a matter of God's dealing with our Israel. The prophets had their light from Heaven directly, even as he had his—many to one, and Jehovah the same forever. I must believe the prophets.—Bring me the Torah, Esther."

He proceeded without waiting for her.

"May the testimony of a whole people be slighted, my master? Though you travel from Tyre, which is by the sea in the north, to the capital of Edom, which is in the desert south, you will not find a lisper of the Shema,[81] an alms-giver in the Temple, or any one who has ever eaten of the lamb of the Passover, to tell you the kingdom the King is coming to build for us, the children of the covenant, is other than of this world, like our father David's. Now where got they the faith, ask you? We will see presently."

Esther here returned, bringing a number of rolls carefully enveloped in dark-brown linen lettered quaintly in gold.

"Keep them, daughter, to give to me as I call for them," the father said, in the tender voice he always used in speaking to her, and continued his argument:

"It were long, good my master—too long, indeed—for me to repeat to you the names of the holy men who, in the providence of God, succeeded the prophets, only a little less favored than they—the seers who have written and the preachers who have taught since the Captivity; the very wise who borrowed their lights from the lamp of Malachi, the last of his line, and whose great names Hillel and Shammai never tired of repeating in the colleges. Will you ask them of the kingdom? Thus, the Lord of the sheep in the Book of Enoch[82]—who is he? Who but the King of whom we are speaking? A throne is set up for him; he smites the earth, and the other kings are shaken from their thrones, and the scourges of Israel flung into a cavern of fire flaming with pillars of fire. So also the singer of the Psalms of Solomon[83]—'Behold, O Lord, and raise up to Israel their king, the son of David, at the time thou knowest, O God, to rule Israel, thy children… And he will bring the peoples of the heathen under his yoke to serve him… And he shall be a righteous king taught of God, … for he shall rule all the earth by the word of his mouth forever.' And last, though not least, hear Ezra, the second Moses, in his visions of the night, and ask him who is the lion with human voice that says to the eagle—which is Rome—'Thou hast loved liars, and overthrown the cities of the industrious, and razed their walls, though they did thee no harm. Therefore, begone, that the earth may be refreshed, and recover itself, and hope in the justice and piety of him who made her.' Whereat the eagle was seen no more. Surely, O

---

81 Daily Jewish prayers.
82 Ancient Jewish text ascribed to Noah's great grandfather, Enoch. It includes parables, prophecies, and angelic visions.
83 Eighteen psalms traditionally attributed to David's son, Solomon, are not included in the standard canonized scriptures of the Christian Church.

my master, the testimony of these should be enough! But the way to the fountain's head is open. Let us go up to it at once.—Some wine, Esther, and then the Torah."

"Dost thou believe the prophets, master?" he asked, after drinking. "I know thou dost, for of such was the faith of all thy kindred.—Give me, Esther, the book which hath in it the visions of Isaiah."

He took one of the rolls which she had unwrapped for him, and read, "'The people that walked in darkness have seen a great light: they that dwell in the land of the shadow of death, upon them hath the light shined[84]... For unto us a child is born, unto us a son is given: and the government shall be upon his shoulder. ... Of the increase of his government and peace there shall be no end, upon the throne of David, and upon his kingdom, to order it, and to establish it with judgment and with justice from henceforth even forever.'—Believest thou the prophets, O my master?—Now, Esther, the word of the Lord that came to Micah."

She gave him the roll he asked.

"'But thou,'" he began reading—"'but thou, Bethlehem Ephrath, though thou be little among the thousands of Judah, yet out of thee shall he come forth unto me that is to be ruler in Israel.'—This was he, the very child Balthasar saw and worshipped in the cave. Believest thou the prophets, O my master?—Give me, Esther, the words of Jeremiah."

Receiving that roll, he read as before, "'Behold, the days come, saith the Lord, that I will raise unto David a righteous branch, and a king shall reign and prosper, and shall execute judgment and justice in the earth. In his days Judah shall be saved, and Israel shall dwell safely.'[85] As a king he shall reign—as a king, O my master! Believest thou the prophets?—Now, daughter, the roll of the sayings of that son of Judah in whom there was no blemish."

She gave him the Book of Daniel.

"Hear, my master," he said: "'I saw in the night visions, and behold, one like the Son of man came with the clouds of heaven... And there was given him dominion, and glory, and a kingdom, that all people, nations, and languages should serve him; his dominion is an everlasting dominion, which shall not pass away, and his kingdom that which shall not be destroyed.'[86]—Believest thou the prophets, O my master?"

"It is enough. I believe," cried Ben-Hur.

"What then?" asked Simonides. "If the King come poor, will not my master, of his abundance, give him help?"

"Help him? To the last shekel and the last breath. But why speak of his coming poor?"

"Give me, Esther, the word of the Lord as it came to Zechariah," said Simonides.

She gave him one of the rolls.

"Hear how the King will enter Jerusalem." Then he read, "'Rejoice greatly, O daughter of Zion... Behold, thy King cometh unto thee with justice and salvation; lowly, and riding upon an ass, and upon a colt, the foal of an ass.'"[87]

Ben-Hur looked away.

"What see you, O my master?"

"Rome!" he answered, gloomily—"Rome, and her legions. I have dwelt with them in their camps. I know them."

---

84 Is. 9:2.
85 Jer. 23:5–6.
86 Dan. 7:13–14.
87 Zech. 9:9.

"Ah!" said Simonides. "Thou shalt be a master of legions for the King, with millions to choose from."

"Millions!" cried Ben-Hur.

Simonides sat a moment thinking.

"The question of power should not trouble you," he next said.

Ben-Hur looked at him inquiringly.

"You were seeing the lowly King in the act of coming to his own," Simonides answered— "seeing him on the right hand, as it were, and on the left the brassy legions of Cæsar, and you were asking, What can he do?"

"It was my very thought."

"O my master!" Simonides continued. "You do not know how strong our Israel is. You think of him as a sorrowful old man weeping by the rivers of Babylon.[88] But go up to Jerusalem next Passover, and stand on the Xystus or in the Street of Barter, and see him as he is. The promise of the Lord to father Jacob coming out of Padan-Aram was a law under which our people have not ceased multiplying—not even in captivity; they grew under foot of the Egyptian; the clench of the Roman has been but wholesome nurture to them; now they are indeed 'a nation, and a company of nations.' Nor that only, my master; in fact, to measure the strength of Israel—which is, in fact, measuring what the King can do—you shall not bide solely by the rule of natural increase, but add thereto the other—I mean the spread of the faith, which will carry you to the far and near of the whole known earth. Further, the habit is, I know, to think and speak of Jerusalem as Israel, which may be likened to our finding an embroidered shred, and holding it up as a magisterial robe of Cæsar's. Jerusalem is but a stone of the Temple, or the heart in the body. Turn from beholding the legions, strong though they be, and count the hosts of the faithful waiting the old alarm, 'To your tents, O Israel!'[89]—count the many in Persia, children of those who chose not to return with the returning; count the brethren who swarm the marts of Egypt and Farther Africa; count the Hebrew colonists eking profit in the West—in Lodinum and the trade-courts of Spain; count the pure of blood and the proselytes in Greece and in the isles of the sea, and over in Pontus, and here in Antioch, and, for that matter, those of that city lying accursed in the shadow of the unclean walls of Rome herself; count the worshippers of the Lord dwelling in tents along the deserts next us, as well as in the deserts beyond the Nile: and in the regions across the Caspian, and up in the old lands of Gog and Magog even, separate those who annually send gifts to the Holy Temple in acknowledgment of God—separate them, that they may be counted also. And when you have done counting, lo! my master, a census of the sword hands that await you; lo! a kingdom ready fashioned for him who is to do 'judgment and justice in the whole earth'—in Rome not less than in Zion. Have then the answer, What Israel can do, that can the King."

The picture was fervently given.

Upon Ilderim it operated like the blowing of a trumpet. "Oh that I had back my youth!" he cried, starting to his feet.

Ben-Hur sat still. The speech, he saw, was an invitation to devote his life and fortune to the mysterious Being who was palpably as much the centre of a great hope with Simonides as with the devout Egyptian. The idea, as we have seen, was not a new one, but had come to

---

88 Psalm 137:1.
89 1 Kings 12:16.

him repeatedly; once while listening to Malluch in the Grove of Daphne; afterwards more distinctly while Balthasar was giving his conception of what the kingdom was to be; still later, in the walk through the old Orchard, it had risen almost, if not quite, into a resolve. At such times it had come and gone only an idea, attended with feelings more or less acute. Not so now. A master had it in charge, a master was working it up; already he had exalted it into a *cause* brilliant with possibilities and infinitely holy. The effect was as if a door theretofore unseen had suddenly opened flooding Ben-Hur with light, and admitting him to a service which had been his one perfect dream—a service reaching far into the future, and rich with the rewards of duty done, and prizes to sweeten and soothe his ambition. One touch more was needed.

"Let us concede all you say, O Simonides," said Ben-Hur—"that the King will come, and his kingdom be as Solomon's; say also I am ready to give myself and all I have to him and his cause; yet more, say that I should do as was God's purpose in the ordering of my life and in your quick amassment of astonishing fortune; then what? Shall we proceed like blind men building? Shall we wait till the King comes? Or until he sends for me? You have age and experience on your side. Answer."

Simonides answered at once.

"We have no choice; none. This letter"—he produced Messala's despatch as he spoke—"this letter is the signal for action. The alliance proposed between Messala and Gratus we are not strong enough to resist; we have not the influence at Rome nor the force here. They will kill you if we wait. How merciful they are, look at me and judge."

He shuddered at the terrible recollection.

"O good my master," he continued, recovering himself; "how strong are you—in purpose, I mean?"

Ben-Hur did not understand him.

"I remember how pleasant the world was to me in my youth," Simonides proceeded.

"Yet," said Ben-Hur, "you were capable of a great sacrifice."

"Yes; for love."

"Has not life other motives as strong?" Simonides shook his head.

"There is ambition."

"Ambition is forbidden a son of Israel."

"What, then, of revenge?"

The spark dropped upon the inflammable passion; the man's eyes gleamed; his hands shook; he answered, quickly, "Revenge is a Jew's of right; it is the law."

"A camel, even a dog, will remember a wrong," cried Ilderim.

Directly Simonides picked up the broken thread of his thought.

"There is a work, a work for the King, which should be done in advance of his coming. We may not doubt that Israel is to be his right hand; but, alas! it is a hand of peace, without cunning in war. Of the millions, there is not one trained band, not a captain. The mercenaries of the Herods I do not count, for they are kept to crush us. The condition is as the Roman would have it; his policy has fruited well for his tyranny; but the time of change is at hand, when the shepherd shall put on armor, and take to spear and sword, and the feeding flocks be turned to fighting lions. Some one, my son, must have place next the King at his right hand. Who shall it be if not he who does this work well?"

Ben-Hur's face flushed at the prospect, though he said, "I see; but speak plainly. A deed to be done is one thing; how to do it is another."

Simonides sipped the wine Esther brought him, and replied,

"The sheik, and thou, my master, shall be principals, each with a part. I will remain here, carrying on as now, and watchful that the spring go not dry. Thou shalt betake thee to Jerusalem, and thence to the wilderness, and begin numbering the fighting-men of Israel, and telling them into tens and hundreds, and choosing captains and training them, and in secret places hoarding arms, for which I shall keep thee supplied. Commencing over in Perea, thou shalt go then to Galilee, whence it is but a step to Jerusalem. In Perea, the desert will be at thy back, and Ilderim in reach of thy hand. He will keep the roads, so that nothing shall pass without thy knowledge. He will help thee in many ways. Until the ripening time no one shall know what is here contracted. Mine is but a servant's part. I have spoken to Ilderim. What sayest thou?"

Ben-Hur looked at the sheik.

"It is as he says, son of Hur," the Arab responded. "I have given my word, and he is content with it; but thou shalt have my oath, binding me, and the ready hands of my tribe, and whatever serviceable thing I have."

The three—Simonides, Ilderim, Esther—gazed at Ben-Hur fixedly.

"Every man," he answered, at first sadly, "has a cup of pleasure poured for him, and soon or late it comes to his hand, and he tastes and drinks—every man but me. I see, Simonides, and thou, O generous sheik!—I see whither the proposal tends. If I accept, and enter upon the course, farewell peace, and the hopes which cluster around it. The doors I might enter and the gates of quiet life will shut behind me, never to open again, for Rome keeps them all; and her outlawry will follow me, and her hunters; and in the tombs near cities and the dismal caverns of remotest hills, I must eat my crust and take my rest."

The speech was broken by a sob. All turned to Esther, who hid her face upon her father's shoulder.

"I did not think of you, Esther," said Simonides, gently, for he was himself deeply moved.

"It is well enough, Simonides," said Ben-Hur. "A man bears a hard doom better, knowing there is pity for him. Let me go on."

They gave him ear again.

"I was about to say," he continued, "I have no choice, but take the part you assign me; and as remaining here is to meet an ignoble death, I will to the work at once."

"Shall we have writings?" asked Simonides, moved by his habit of business.

"I rest upon your word," said Ben-Hur.

"And I," Ilderim answered.

Thus simply was effected the treaty which was to alter Ben-Hur's life. And almost immediately the latter added,

"It is done, then."

"May the God of Abraham help us!" Simonides exclaimed.

"One word now, my friends," Ben-Hur said, more cheerfully. "By your leave, I will be my own until after the games. It is not probable Messala will set peril on foot for me until he has given the procurator time to answer him; and that cannot be in less than seven days from the despatch of his letter. The meeting him in the Circus is a pleasure I would buy at whatever risk."

Ilderim, well pleased, assented readily, and Simonides, intent on business, added, "It is well; for look you, my master, the delay will give me time to do you a good part. I understood you to speak of an inheritance derived from Arrius. Is it in property?"

"A villa near Misenum, and houses in Rome."

"I suggest, then, the sale of the property, and safe deposit of the proceeds. Give me an account of it, and I will have authorities drawn, and despatch an agent on the mission forthwith. We will forestall the imperial robbers at least this once."

"You shall have the account to-morrow."

"Then, if there be nothing more, the work of the night is done," said Simonides.

Ilderim combed his beard complacently, saying, "And well done."

"The bread and wine again, Esther. Sheik Ilderim will make us happy by staying with us till to-morrow, or at his pleasure; and thou, my master—"

"Let the horses be brought," said Ben-Hur. "I will return to the Orchard. The enemy will not discover me if I go now, and"—he glanced at Ilderim—"the four will be glad to see me."

As the day dawned, he and Malluch dismounted at the door of the tent.

Chapter IX

NEXT night, about the fourth hour, Ben-Hur stood on the terrace of the great warehouse with Esther. Below them, on the landing, there was much running about, and shifting of packages and boxes, and shouting of men, whose figures, stooping, heaving, hauling, looked, in the light of the crackling torches kindled in their aid, like the laboring genii of the fantastic Eastern tales. A galley was being laden for instant departure. Simonides had not yet come from his office, in which, at the last moment, he would deliver to the captain of the vessel instructions to proceed without stop to Ostia, the seaport of Rome, and, after landing a passenger there, continue more leisurely to Valentia, on the coast of Spain.

The passenger is the agent going to dispose of the estate derived from Arrius the duumvir. When the lines of the vessel are cast off, and she is put about, and her voyage begun, Ben-Hur will be committed irrevocably to the work undertaken the night before. If he is disposed to repent the agreement with Ilderim, a little time is allowed him to give notice and break it off. He is master, and has only to say the word.

Such may have been the thought at the moment in his mind. He was standing with folded arms, looking upon the scene in the manner of a man debating with himself. Young, handsome, rich, but recently from the patrician circles of Roman society, it is easy to think of the world besetting him with appeals not to give more to onerous duty or ambition attended with outlawry and danger. We can even imagine the arguments with which he was pressed; the hopelessness of contention with Cæsar; the uncertainty veiling everything connected with the King and his coming; the ease, honors, state, purchasable like goods in market; and, strongest of all, the sense newly acquired of home, with friends to make it delightful. Only those who have been wanderers long desolate can know the power there was in the latter appeal.

Let us add now, the world—always cunning enough of itself; always whispering to the weak, Stay, take thine ease; always presenting the sunny side of life—the world was in this instance helped by Ben-Hur's companion.

"Were you ever at Rome?" he asked.

"No," Esther replied.

"Would you like to go?"

"I think not."

"Why?"

"I am afraid of Rome," she answered, with a perceptible tremor of the voice.

He looked at her then—or rather down upon her, for at his side she appeared little more than a child. In the dim light he could not see her face distinctly; even the form was shadowy. But again he was reminded of Tirzah, and a sudden tenderness fell upon him—just so the lost sister stood with him on the house-top the calamitous morning of the accident to Gratus. Poor Tirzah! Where was she now? Esther had the benefit of the feeling evoked. If not his sister, he could never look upon her as his servant, and that she was his servant in fact would make him always the more considerate and gentle towards her.

"I cannot think of Rome," she continued, recovering her voice, and speaking in her quiet, womanly way—"I cannot think of Rome as a city of palaces and temples, and crowded with people; she is to me a monster which has possession of one of the beautiful lands, and lies there luring men to ruin and death—a monster which it is not possible to resist—a ravenous beast gorging with blood. Why—"

She faltered, looked down, stopped.

"Go on," said Ben-Hur, reassuringly.

She drew closer to him, looked up again, and said, "Why must you make her your enemy? Why not rather make peace with her, and be at rest? You have had many ills, and borne them; you have survived the snares laid for you by foes. Sorrow has consumed your youth; is it well to give it the remainder of your days?"

The girlish face under his eyes seemed to come nearer and get whiter as the pleading went on; he stooped towards it, and asked, softly, "What would you have me do, Esther?"

She hesitated a moment, then asked, in return, "Is the property near Rome a residence?"

"Yes."

"And pretty?"

"It is beautiful—a palace in the midst of gardens and shell-strewn walks; fountains without and within; statuary in the shady nooks; hills around covered with vines, and so high that Neapolis and Vesuvius are in sight, and the sea an expanse of purpling blue dotted with restless sails. Cæsar has a country-seat near by, but in Rome they say the old Arrian villa is the prettiest."

"And the life there, is it quiet?"

"There was never a summer day, never a moonlit night, more quiet, save when visitors come. Now that the old owner is gone, and I am here, there is nothing to break its silence—nothing, unless it be the whispering of servants, or the whistling of happy birds, or the noise of fountains at play; it is changeless, except as day by day old flowers fade and fall, and new ones bud and bloom, and the sunlight gives place to the shadow of a passing cloud. The life, Esther, was all too quiet for me. It made me restless by keeping always present a feeling that I, who have so much to do, was dropping into idle habits, and tying myself with silken chains, and after a while—and not a long while either—would end with nothing done."

She looked off over the river.

"Why did you ask?" he said.

"Good my master—"

"No, no, Esther—not that. Call me friend—brother, if you will; I am not your master, and will not be. Call me brother."

He could not see the flush of pleasure which reddened her face, and the glow of the eyes that went out lost in the void above the river.

"I cannot understand," she said, "the nature which prefers the life you are going to—a life of—"

"Of violence, and it may be of blood," he said, completing the sentence.

"Yes," she added, "the nature which could prefer that life to such as might be in the beautiful villa."

"Esther, you mistake. There is no preference. Alas! the Roman is not so kind. I am going of necessity. To stay here is to die; and if I go there, the end will be the same—a poisoned cup, a bravo's blow, or a judge's sentence obtained by perjury. Messala and the procurator Gratus are rich with plunder of my father's estate, and it is more important to them to keep their gains now than was their getting in the first instance. A peaceable settlement is out of reach, because of the confession it would imply. And then—then— Ah, Esther, if I could buy them, I do not know that I would. I do not believe peace possible to me; no, not even in the sleepy shade and sweet air of the marble porches of the old villa—no matter who might be there to help me bear the burden of the days, nor by what patience of love she made the effort. Peace is not possible to me while my people are lost, for I must be watchful to find them. If I find them, and they have suffered wrong, shall not the guilty suffer for it? If they are dead by violence, shall the murderers escape? Oh, I could not sleep for dreams! Nor could the holiest love, by any stratagem, lull me to a rest which conscience would not strangle."

"Is it so bad then?" she asked, her voice tremulous with feeling. "Can nothing, nothing, be done?"

Ben-Hur took her hand.

"Do you care so much for me?"

"Yes," she answered, simply.

The hand was warm, and in the palm of his it was lost. He felt it tremble. Then the Egyptian came, so the opposite of this little one; so tall, so audacious, with a flattery so cunning, a wit so ready, a beauty so wonderful, a manner so bewitching. He carried the hand to his lips, and gave it back.

"You shall be another Tirzah to me, Esther."

"Who is Tirzah?"

"The little sister the Roman stole from me, and whom I must find before I can rest or be happy."

Just then a gleam of light flashed athwart the terrace and fell upon the two; and, looking round, they saw a servant roll Simonides in his chair out of the door. They went to the merchant, and in the after-talk he was principal.

Immediately the lines of the galley were cast off, and she swung round, and, midst the flashing of torches and the shouting of joyous sailors, hurried off to the sea—leaving Ben-Hur committed to the cause of the KING WHO WAS TO COME.

Chapter X

THE day before the games, in the afternoon, all Ilderim's racing property was taken to the city, and put in quarters adjoining the Circus. Along with it the good man carried a great deal of property not of that class; so with servants, retainers mounted and armed, horses in leading, cattle driven, camels laden with baggage, his outgoing from the Orchard was not unlike a tribal migration. The people along the road failed not to laugh at his motley procession; on the other side, it was observed that, with all his irascibility, he was not in the least offended by their rudeness. If he was under surveillance, as he had reason to believe, the informer would describe the semi-barbarous show with which he came up to the races. The Romans would laugh; the city would be amused; but what cared he? Next morning the pageant would be far on the road to the desert, and going with it would be every movable thing of value belonging to the Orchard—everything save such as were essential to the success of his four. He was, in fact, started home; his tents were all folded; the dowar was no more; in twelve hours all would be out of reach, pursue who might. A man is never safer than when he is under the laugh; and the shrewd old Arab knew it.

Neither he nor Ben-Hur overestimated the influence of Messala; it was their opinion, however, that he would not begin active measures against them until after the meeting in the Circus; if defeated there, especially if defeated by Ben-Hur, they might instantly look for the worst he could do; he might not even wait for advices from Gratus. With this view, they shaped their course, and were prepared to betake themselves out of harm's way. They rode together now in good spirits, calmly confident of success on the morrow.

On the way, they came upon Malluch in waiting for them. The faithful fellow gave no sign by which it was possible to infer any knowledge on his part of the relationship so recently admitted between Ben-Hur and Simonides, or of the treaty between them and Ilderim. He exchanged salutations as usual, and produced a paper, saying to the sheik, "I have here the notice of the editor of the games, just issued, in which you will find your horses published for the race. You will find in it also the order of exercises. Without waiting, good sheik, I congratulate you upon your victory."

He gave the paper over, and, leaving the worthy to master it, turned to Ben-Hur.

"To you, also, son of Arrius, my congratulations. There is nothing now to prevent your meeting Messala. Every condition preliminary to the race is complied with. I have the assurance from the editor himself."

"I thank you, Malluch," said Ben-Hur.

Malluch proceeded:

"Your color is white, and Messala's mixed scarlet and gold. The good effects of the choice are visible already. Boys are now hawking white ribbons along the streets; to-morrow every Arab and Jew in the city will wear them. In the Circus you will see the white fairly divide the galleries with the red."

"The galleries—but not the tribunal over the Porta Pompæ."

"No; the scarlet and gold will rule there. But if we win"—Malluch chuckled with the pleasure of the thought —"if we win, how the dignitaries will tremble! They will bet, of course, according to their scorn of everything not Roman—two, three, five to one on Messala, because he is Roman." Dropping his voice yet lower, he added, "It ill becomes a Jew of good standing in the Temple to put his money at such a hazard; yet, in confidence, I will have a friend next behind the consul's seat to accept offers of three to one, or five, or ten—the madness may go to such height. I have put to his order six thousand shekels for the purpose."

"Nay, Malluch," said Ben-Hur, "a Roman will wager only in his Roman coin. Suppose you find your friend to-night, and place to his order sestertii in such amount as you choose. And look you, Malluch—let him be instructed to seek wagers with Messala and his supporters; Ilderim's four against Messala's."

Malluch reflected a moment.

"The effect will be to centre interest upon your contest."

"The very thing I seek, Malluch."

"I see, I see."

"Ay, Malluch; would you serve me perfectly, help me to fix the public eye upon our race—Messala's and mine."

Malluch spoke quickly—"It can be done."

"Then let it be done," said Ben-Hur.

"Enormous wagers offered will answer; if the offers are accepted, all the better."

Malluch turned his eyes watchfully upon Ben-Hur.

"Shall I not have back the equivalent of his robbery?" said Ben-Hur, partly to himself. "Another opportunity may not come. And if I could break him in fortune as well as in pride! Our father Jacob could take no offence."

A look of determined will knit his handsome face, giving emphasis to his further speech.

"Yes, it shall be. Hark, Malluch! Stop not in thy offer of sestertii. Advance them to talents, if any there be who dare so high. Five, ten, twenty talents; ay, fifty, so the wager be with Messala himself."

"It is a mighty sum," said Malluch. "I must have security."

"So thou shalt. Go to Simonides, and tell him I wish the matter arranged. Tell him my heart is set on the ruin of my enemy, and that the opportunity hath such excellent promise that I choose such hazards. On our side be the God of our fathers. Go, good Malluch. Let this not slip."

And Malluch, greatly delighted, gave him parting salutation, and started to ride away, but returned presently.

"Your pardon," he said to Ben-Hur. "There was another matter. I could not get near Messala's chariot myself, but I had another measure it; and, from his report, its hub stands quite a palm higher from the ground than yours."

"A palm! So much?" cried Ben-Hur, joyfully.

Then he leaned over to Malluch.

"As thou art a son of Judah, Malluch, and faithful to thy kin, get thee a seat in the gallery over the Gate of Triumph, down close to the balcony in front of the pillars, and watch well when we make the turns there; watch well, for if I have favor at all, I will—Nay, Malluch, let it go unsaid! Only get thee there, and watch well."

At that moment a cry burst from Ilderim.

"Ha! By the splendor of God! what is this?"

He drew near Ben-Hur with a finger pointing on the face of the notice.

"Read," said Ben-Hur.

"No; better thou."

Ben-Hur took the paper, which, signed by the prefect of the province as editor, performed the office of a modern programme, giving particularly the several divertisements provided for the occasion. It informed the public that there would be first a procession of extraordinary splendor; that the procession would be succeeded by the customary honors to the god Consus, whereupon the games would begin; running, leaping, wrestling, boxing, each in the order stated. The names of the competitors were given, with their several nationalities and schools of training, the trials in which they had been engaged, the prizes won, and the prizes now offered; under the latter head the sums of money were stated in illuminated letters, telling of the departure of the day when the simple chaplet of pine or laurel was fully enough for the victor, hungering for glory as something better than riches, and content with it.

Over these parts of the programme Ben-Hur sped with rapid eyes. At last he came to the announcement of the race. He read it slowly. Attending lovers of the heroic sports were assured they would certainly be gratified by an Orestean struggle unparalleled in Antioch. The city offered the spectacle in honor of the consul. One hundred thousand sestertii and a crown of laurel were the prizes. Then followed the particulars. The entries were six in all— fours only permitted; and, to further interest in the performance, the competitors would be turned into the course together. Each four then received description.

"I. A four of Lysippus the Corinthian—two grays, a bay, and a black; entered at Alexandria last year, and again at Corinth, where they were winners. Lysippus, driver. Color, yellow.

"II. A four of Messala of Rome—two white, two black; victors of the Circensian as exhibited in the Circus Maximus[90] last year. Messala, driver. Colors, scarlet and gold.

"III. A four of Cleanthes the Athenian—three gray, one bay; winners at the Isthmian last year. Cleanthes, driver. Color, green.

"IV. A four of Dicæus the Byzantine—two black, one gray, one bay; winners this year at Byzantium. Dicæus, driver. Color, black.

"V. A four of Admetus the Sidonian—all grays. Thrice entered at Cæsarea, and thrice victors. Admetus, driver. Color, blue.

"VI. A four of Ilderim, sheik of the Desert. All bays; first race. Ben-Hur, a Jew, driver. Color, white."

Ben-Hur, a Jew, driver!

Why that name instead of Arrius?

Ben-Hur raised his eyes to Ilderim. He had found the cause of the Arab's outcry. Both rushed to the same conclusion.

The hand was the hand of Messala!

Chapter XI

EVENING was hardly come upon Antioch, when the Omphalus, nearly in the centre of the city, became a troubled fountain from which in every direction, but chiefly down to the Nymphæum and east and west along the Colonnade of Herod, flowed currents of people, for the time given up to Bacchus and Apollo.

For such indulgence anything more fitting cannot be imagined than the great roofed streets, which were literally miles on miles of porticos wrought of marble, polished to the last degree of finish, and all gifts to the voluptuous city by princes careless of expenditure where, as in this instance, they thought they were eternizing themselves. Darkness was not permitted anywhere; and the singing, the laughter, the shouting, were incessant, and in compound like the roar of waters dashing through hollow grots, confused by a multitude of echoes.

The many nationalities represented, though they might have amazed a stranger, were not peculiar to Antioch. Of the various missions of the great empire, one seems to have been the fusion of men and the introduction of strangers to each other; accordingly, whole peoples rose up and went at pleasure, taking with them their costumes, customs, speech, and gods; and where they chose, they stopped, engaged in business, built houses, erected altars, and were what they had been at home.

---

90 The main venue of chariot racing in the ancient city of Rome.

There was a peculiarity, however, which could not have failed the notice of a looker-on this night in Antioch. Nearly everybody wore the colors of one or other of the chari-oteers announced for the morrow's race. Sometimes it was in form of a scarf, sometimes a badge; often a ribbon or a feather. Whatever the form, it signified merely the wearer's partiality; thus, green published a friend of Cleanthes the Athenian, and black an adher-ent of the Byzantine. This was according to a custom, old probably as the day of the race of Orestes—a custom, by the way, worthy of study as a marvel of history, illustra-tive of the absurd yet appalling extremities to which men frequently suffer their follies to drag them.

The observer abroad on this occasion, once attracted to the wearing of colors, would have very shortly decided that there were three in predominance—green, white, and the mixed scarlet and gold.

But let us from the streets to the palace on the island.

The five great chandeliers in the saloon are freshly lighted. The assemblage is much the same as that already noticed in connection with the place. The divan has its corps of sleep-ers and burden of garments, and the tables yet resound with the rattle and clash of dice. Yet the greater part of the company are not doing anything. They walk about, or yawn tre-mendously, or pause as they pass each other to exchange idle nothings. Will the weather be fair to-morrow? Are the preparations for the games complete? Do the laws of the Circus in Antioch differ from the laws of the Circus in Rome? Truth is, the young fellows are suffer-ing from *ennui*. Their heavy work is done; that is, we would find their tablets, could we look at them, covered with memoranda of wagers—wagers on every contest; on the running, the wrestling, the boxing; on everything but the chariot-race.

And why not on that?

Good reader, they cannot find anybody who will hazard so much as a denarius with them against Messala.

There are no colors in the saloon but his.

No one thinks of his defeat.

Why, they say, is he not perfect in his training? Did he not graduate from an imperial *lanista*?[91] Were not his horses winners at the Circensian in the Circus Maximus? And then—ah, yes! he is a Roman!

In a corner, at ease on the divan, Messala himself may be seen. Around him, sitting or standing, are his courtierly admirers, plying him with questions. There is, of course, but one topic.

Enter Drusus and Cecilius.

"Ah!" cries the young prince, throwing himself on the divan at Messala's feet, "Ah, by Bacchus, I am tired!"

"Whither away?" asks Messala.

"Up the street; up to the Omphalus, and beyond—who shall say how far? Rivers of people; never so many in the city before. They say we will see the whole world at the Circus to-morrow."

Messala laughed scornfully.

"The idiots! *Perpol!* They never beheld a Circensian with Cæsar for editor. But, my Drusus, what found you?"

"Nothing."

---

91 A Roman professional trainer of gladiators.

"O—ah! You forget," said Cecilius.

"What?" asked Drusus.

"The procession of whites."

"*Mirabile!*"[92] cried Drusus, half rising. "We met a faction of whites, and they had a banner. But—ha, ha, ha!"

He fell back indolently.

"Cruel Drusus—not to go on," said Messala.

"Scum of the desert were they, my Messala, and garbage-eaters from the Jacob's Temple in Jerusalem. What had I to do with them?"

"Nay," said Cecilius, "Drusus is afraid of a laugh, but I am not, my Messala."

"Speak thou, then."

"Well, we stopped the faction, and—"

"Offered them a wager," said Drusus, relenting, and taking the word from the shadow's mouth. "And—ha, ha, ha!—one fellow with not enough skin on his face to make a worm for a carp stepped forth, and—ha, ha, ha!—said yes. I drew my tablets. 'Who is your man?' I asked. 'Ben-Hur, the Jew,' said he. Then I: 'What shall it be? How much?' He answered, 'A—a—' Excuse me, Messala. By Jove's thunder, I cannot go on for laughter! Ha, ha, ha!"

The listeners leaned forward.

Messala looked to Cecilius.

"A shekel," said the latter.

"A shekel! A shekel!"

A burst of scornful laughter ran fast upon the repetition.

"And what did Drusus?" asked Messala.

An outcry over about the door just then occasioned a rush to that quarter; and, as the noise there continued, and grew louder, even Cecilius betook himself off, pausing only to say, "The noble Drusus, my Messala, put up his tablets and—lost the shekel."

"A white! A white!"

"Let him come!"

"This way, this way!"

These and like exclamations filled the saloon, to the stoppage of other speech. The dice-players quit their games; the sleepers awoke, rubbed their eyes, drew their tablets, and hurried to the common centre.

"I offer you—"

"And I—"

"I—"

The person so warmly received was the respectable Jew, Ben-Hur's fellow-voyager from Cyprus. He entered grave, quiet, observant. His robe was spotlessly white; so was the cloth of his turban. Bowing and smiling at the welcome, he moved slowly towards the central table. Arrived there, he drew his robe about him in a stately manner, took seat, and waved his hand. The gleam of a jewel on a finger helped him not a little to the silence which ensued.

"Romans—most noble Romans—I salute you!" he said.

"Easy, by Jupiter! Who is he?" asked Drusus.

"A dog of Israel—Sanballat by name—purveyor for the army; residence, Rome; vastly rich; grown so as a contractor of furnishments which he never furnishes. He spins

---

92 Latin for "wonderful."

mischiefs, nevertheless, finer than spiders spin their webs. Come—by the girdle of Venus! let us catch him!"

Messala arose as he spoke, and, with Drusus, joined the mass crowded about the purveyor.

"It came to me on the street," said that person, producing his tablets, and opening them on the table with an impressive air of business, "that there was great discomfort in the palace because offers on Messala were going without takers. The gods, you know, must have sacrifices; and here am I. You see my color; let us to the matter. Odds first, amounts next. What will you give me?"

The audacity seemed to stun his hearers.

"Haste!" he said. "I have an engagement with the consul."

The spur was effective.

"Two to one," cried half a dozen in a voice.

"What!" exclaimed the purveyor, astonished. "Only two to one, and yours a Roman!"

"Take three, then."

"Three say you—only three—and mine but a dog of a Jew! Give me four."

"Four it is," said a boy, stung by the taunt.

"Five—give me five," cried the purveyor, instantly.

A profound stillness fell on the assemblage.

"The consul—your master and mine—is waiting for me."

The inaction became awkward to the many.

"Give me five—for the honor of Rome, five."

"Five let it be," said one in answer.

There was a sharp cheer—a commotion—and Messala himself appeared.

"Five let it be," he said.

And Sanballat smiled, and made ready to write.

"If Cæsar die to-morrow," he said, "Rome will not be all bereft. There is at least one other with spirit to take his place. Give me six."

"Six be it," answered Messala.

There was another shout louder than the first.

"Six be it," repeated Messala. "Six to one—the difference between a Roman and a Jew. And, having found it, now, O redemptor of the flesh of swine, let us on. The amount—and quickly. The consul may send for thee, and I will then be bereft."

Sanballat took the laugh against him coolly, and wrote, and offered the writing to Messala.

"Read, read!" everybody demanded.

And Messala read:

"*Mem.*—Chariot-race. Messala of Rome, in wager with Sanballat, also of Rome, says he will beat Ben-Hur, the Jew. Amount of wager, twenty talents. Odds to Sanballat, six to one.

"Witnesses: SANBALLAT."

There was no noise, no motion. Each person seemed held in the pose the reading found him. Messala stared at the memorandum, while the eyes which had him in view opened wide, and stared at him. He felt the gaze, and thought rapidly. So lately he stood in the same place, and in the same way hectored the countrymen around him. They would remember it. If he refused to sign, his hero-ship was lost. And sign he could not; he was not worth one hundred talents, nor the fifth part of the sum. Suddenly his mind became a blank; he stood speechless; the color fled his face. An idea at last came to his relief.

"Thou Jew!" he said, "where hast thou twenty talents? Show me."

Sanballat's provoking smile deepened.

"There," he replied, offering Messala a paper.

"Read, read!" arose all around.

Again Messala read:

"AT ANTIOCH, *Tammuz* 16*th day.*

"The bearer, Sanballat of Rome, hath now to his order with me fifty talents, coin of Cæsar.

SIMONIDES."

"Fifty talents, fifty talents!" echoed the throng, in amazement.

Then Drusus came to the rescue.

"By Hercules!" he shouted, "the paper lies, and the Jew is a liar. Who but Cæsar hath fifty talents at order? Down with the insolent white!"

The cry was angry, and it was angrily repeated; yet Sanballat kept his seat, and his smile grew more exasperating the longer he waited. At length Messala spoke.

"Hush! One to one, my countrymen—one to one, for love of our ancient Roman name."

The timely action recovered him his ascendency.

"O thou circumcised dog!" he continued, to Sanballat, "I gave thee six to one, did I not?"

"Yes," said the Jew, quietly.

"Well, give me now the fixing of the amount."

"With reserve, if the amount be trifling, have thy will," answered Sanballat.

"Write, then, five in place of twenty."

"Hast thou so much?"

"By the mother of the gods, I will show you receipts."

"Nay, the word of so brave a Roman must pass. Only make the sum even—six make it, and I will write."

"Write it so."

And forthwith they exchanged writings.

Sanballat immediately arose and looked around him, a sneer in place of his smile. No man better than he knew those with whom he was dealing.

"Romans," he said, "another wager, if you dare! Five talents against five talents that the white will win. I challenge you collectively."

They were again surprised.

"What!" he cried, louder. "Shall it be said in the Circus to-morrow that a dog of Israel went into the saloon of the palace full of Roman nobles—among them the scion of a Cæsar—and laid five talents before them in challenge, and they had not the courage to take it up?"

The sting was unendurable.

"Have done, O insolent!" said Drusus, "write the challenge, and leave it on the table; and to-morrow, if we find thou hast indeed so much money to put at such hopeless hazard, I, Drusus, promise it shall be taken."

Sanballat wrote again, and, rising, said, unmoved as ever, "See, Drusus, I leave the offer with you. When it is signed, send it to me any time before the race begins. I will be found with the consul in a seat over the Porta Pompæ. Peace to you; peace to all."

He bowed, and departed, careless of the shout of derision with which they pursued him out of the door.

In the night the story of the prodigious wager flew along the streets and over the city; and Ben-Hur, lying with his four, was told of it, and also that Messala's whole fortune was on the hazard.

And he slept never so soundly.

Chapter XII

THE Circus at Antioch stood on the south bank of the river, nearly opposite the island, differing in no respect from the plan of such buildings in general.

In the purest sense, the games were a gift to the public; consequently, everybody was free to attend; and, vast as the holding capacity of the structure was, so fearful were the people, on this occasion, lest there should not be room for them, that, early the day before the opening of the exhibition, they took up all the vacant spaces in the vicinity, where their temporary shelter suggested an army in waiting.

At midnight the entrances were thrown wide, and the rabble, surging in, occupied the quarters assigned to them, from which nothing less than an earthquake or an army with spears could have dislodged them. They dozed the night away on the benches, and breakfasted there; and there the close of the exercises found them, patient and sight-hungry as in the beginning.

The better people, their seats secured, began moving towards the Circus about the first hour of the morning, the noble and very rich among them distinguished by litters and retinues of liveried servants.

By the second hour, the efflux from the city was a stream unbroken and innumerable.

Exactly as the gnomon of the official dial up in the citadel pointed the second hour half gone, the legion, in full panoply, and with all its standards on exhibit, descended from Mount Sulpius; and when the rear of the last cohort disappeared in the bridge, Antioch was literally abandoned—not that the Circus could hold the multitude, but that the multitude was gone out to it, nevertheless.

A great concourse on the river shore witnessed the consul come over from the island in a barge of state. As the great man landed, and was received by the legion, the martial show for one brief moment transcended the attraction of the Circus.

At the third hour, the audience, if such it may be termed, was assembled; at last, a flourish of trumpets called for silence, and instantly the gaze of over a hundred thousand persons was directed towards a pile forming the eastern section of the building.

There was a basement first, broken in the middle by a broad arched passage, called the Porta Pompæ, over which, on an elevated tribunal magnificently decorated with insignia and legionary standards, the consul sat in the place of honor. On both sides of the passage the basement was divided into stalls termed *carceres*, each protected in front by massive gates swung to statuesque pilasters. Over the stalls next was a cornice crowned by a low balustrade; back of which the seats arose in theatre arrangement, all occupied by a throng of dignitaries superbly attired. The pile extended the width of the Circus, and was flanked on both sides by towers which, besides helping the architects give grace to their work, served the *velaria*, or purple awnings, stretched between them so as to throw the whole quarter in a shade that became exceedingly grateful as the day advanced.

This structure, it is now thought, can be made useful in helping the reader to a sufficient understanding of the arrangement of the rest of the interior of the Circus. He has only to fancy himself seated on the tribunal with the consul, facing to the west, where everything is under his eye.

On the right and left, if he will look, he will see the main entrances, very ample, and guarded by gates hinged to the towers.

Directly below him is the arena—a level plane of considerable extent, covered with fine white sand. There all the trials will take place except the running.

Looking across this sanded arena westwardly still, there is a pedestal of marble supporting three low conical pillars of gray stone, much carven. Many an eye will hunt for those pillars before the day is done, for they are the first goal, and mark the beginning and end of the race-course. Behind the pedestal, leaving a passage-way and space for an altar, commences a wall ten or twelve feet in breadth and five or six in height, extending thence exactly two hundred yards, or one Olympic stadium. At the farther, or westward, extremity of the wall there is another pedestal, surmounted with pillars which mark the second goal.

The racers will enter the course on the right of the first goal, and keep the wall all the time to their left. The beginning and ending points of the contest lie, consequently, directly in front of the consul across the arena; and for that reason his seat was admittedly the most desirable in the Circus.

Now if the reader, who is still supposed to be seated on the consular tribunal over the Porta Pompæ, will look up from the ground arrangement of the interior, the first point to attract his notice will be the marking of the outer boundary-line of the course—that is, a plain-faced, solid wall, fifteen or twenty feet in height, with a balustrade on its cope, like that over the *carceres*, or stalls, in the east. This balcony, if followed round the course, will be found broken in three places to allow passages of exit and entrance, two in the north and one in the west; the latter very ornate, and called the Gate of Triumph, because, when all is over, the victors will pass out that way, crowned, and with triumphal escort and ceremonies.

At the west end the balcony encloses the course in the form of a half-circle, and is made to uphold two great galleries.

Directly behind the balustrade on the coping of the balcony is the first seat, from which ascend the succeeding benches, each higher than the one in front of it; giving to view a spectacle of surpassing interest—the spectacle of a vast space ruddy and glistening with human faces, and rich with vari-colored costumes.

The commonalty occupy quarters over in the west, beginning at the point of termination of an awning, stretched, it would seem, for the accommodation of the better classes exclusively.

Having thus the whole interior of the Circus under view at the moment of the sounding of the trumpets, let the reader next imagine the multitude seated and sunk to sudden silence, and motionless in its intensity of interest.

Out of the Porta Pompæ over in the east rises a sound mixed of voices and instruments harmonized. Presently, forth issues the chorus of the procession with which the celebration begins; the editor and civic authorities of the city, givers of the games, follow in robes and garlands; then the gods, some on platforms borne by men, others in great four-wheel carriages gorgeously decorated; next them, again, the contestants of the day, each in costume exactly as he will run, wrestle, leap, box, or drive.

Slowly crossing the arena, the procession proceeds to make circuit of the course. The display is beautiful and imposing. Approval runs before it in a shout, as the water rises and swells in front of a boat in motion. If the dumb, figured gods make no sign of appreciation of the welcome, the editor and his associates are not so backward.

The reception of the athletes is even more demonstrative, for there is not a man in the assemblage who has not something in wager upon them, though but a mite or farthing. And it is noticeable, as the classes move by, that the favorites among them are speedily singled out: either their names are loudest in the uproar, or they are more profusely showered with wreaths and garlands tossed to them from the balcony.

If there is a question as to the popularity with the public of the several games, it is now put to rest. To the splendor of the chariots and the superexcellent beauty of the horses, the charioteers add the personality necessary to perfect the charm of their display. Their tunics, short, sleeveless, and of the finest woollen texture, are of the assigned colors. A horseman accompanies each one of them except Ben-Hur, who, for some reason—possibly distrust—has chosen to go alone; so, too, they are all helmeted but him. As they approach, the spectators stand upon the benches, and there is a sensible deepening of the clamor, in which a sharp listener may detect the shrill piping of women and children; at the same time, the things roseate flying from the balcony thicken into a storm, and, striking the men, drop into the chariot-beds, which are threatened with filling to the tops. Even the horses have a share in the ovation; nor may it be said they are less conscious than their masters of the honors they receive.

Very soon, as with the other contestants, it is made apparent that some of the drivers are more in favor than others; and then the discovery follows that nearly every individual on the benches, women and children as well as men, wears a color, most frequently a ribbon upon the breast or in the hair: now it is green, now yellow, now blue; but, searching the great body carefully, it is manifest that there is a preponderance of white, and scarlet and gold.

In a modern assemblage called together as this one is, particularly where there are sums at hazard upon the race, a preference would be decided by the qualities or performance of the horses; here, however, nationality was the rule. If the Byzantine and Sidonian found small support, it was because their cities were scarcely represented on the benches. On their side, the Greeks, though very numerous, were divided between the Corinthian and the Athenian, leaving but a scant showing of green and yellow. Messala's scarlet and gold would have been but little better had not the citizens of Antioch, proverbially a race of courtiers, joined the Romans by adopting the color of their favorite. There were left then the country people, or Syrians, the Jews, and the Arabs; and they, from faith in the blood of the sheik's four, blent largely with hate of the Romans, whom they desired, above all things, to see beaten and humbled, mounted the white, making the most noisy, and probably the most numerous, faction of all.

As the charioteers move on in the circuit, the excitement increases; at the second goal, where, especially in the galleries, the white is the ruling color, the people exhaust their flowers and rive the air with screams.

"Messala! Messala!"

"Ben-Hur! Ben-Hur!"

Such are the cries.

Upon the passage of the procession, the factionists take their seats and resume conversation.

"Ah, by Bacchus! was he not handsome?" exclaims a woman, whose Romanism is betrayed by the colors flying in her hair.

"And how splendid his chariot!" replies a neighbor, of the same proclivities. "It is all ivory and gold. Jupiter grant he wins!"

The notes on the bench behind them were entirely different.

"A hundred shekels on the Jew!"

The voice is high and shrill.

"Nay, be thou not rash," whispers a moderating friend to the speaker. "The children of Jacob are not much given to Gentile sports, which are too often accursed in the sight of the Lord."

"True, but saw you ever one more cool and assured? And what an arm he has!"

"And what horses!" says a third.

"And for that," a fourth one adds, "they say he has all the tricks of the Romans."

A woman completes the eulogium:

"Yes, and he is even handsomer than the Roman."

Thus encouraged, the enthusiast shrieks again, "A hundred shekels on the Jew!"

"Thou fool!" answers an Antiochian, from a bench well forward on the balcony. "Knowest thou not there are fifty talents laid against him, six to one, on Messala? Put up thy shekels, lest Abraham rise and smite thee."

"Ha, ha! thou ass of Antioch! Cease thy bray. Knowest thou not it was Messala betting on himself?"

Such the reply.

And so ran the controversy, not always good-natured.

"When at length the march was ended and the Porta Pompæ received back the procession, Ben-Hur knew he had his prayer.

The eyes of the East were upon his contest with Messala.

Chapter XIII

ABOUT three o'clock, speaking in modern style, the programme was concluded except the chariot-race. The editor, wisely considerate of the comfort of the people, chose that time for a recess. At once the *vomitoria* were thrown open, and all who could hastened to the portico outside where the restaurateurs had their quarters. Those who remained yawned, talked, gossiped, consulted their tablets, and, all distinctions else forgotten, merged into but two classes—the winners, who were happy, and the losers, who were grum and captious.

Now, however, a third class of spectators, composed of citizens who desired only to witness the chariot-race, availed themselves of the recess to come in and take their reserved seats; by so doing they thought to attract the least attention and give the least offence. Among these were Simonides and his party, whose places were in the vicinity of the main entrance on the north side, opposite the consul.

As the four stout servants carried the merchant in his chair up the aisle, curiosity was much excited. Presently some one called his name. Those about caught it and passed it on along the benches to the west; and there was hurried climbing on seats to get sight of the man about whom common report had coined and put in circulation a romance so mixed of good fortune and bad that the like had never been known or heard of before.

Ilderim was also recognized and warmly greeted; but nobody knew Balthasar or the two women who followed him closely veiled.

The people made way for the party respectfully, and the ushers seated them in easy speaking distance of each other down by the balustrade overlooking the arena. In providence of comfort, they sat upon cushions and had stools for foot-rests.

The women were Iras and Esther.

Upon being seated, the latter cast a frightened look over the Circus, and drew the veil closer about her face; while the Egyptian, letting her veil fall upon her shoulders, gave herself to view, and gazed at the scene with the seeming unconsciousness of being stared at, which, in a woman, is usually the result of long social habitude.

The new-comers generally were yet making their first examination of the great spectacle, beginning with the consul and his attendants, when some workmen ran in and commenced to stretch a chalked rope across the arena from balcony to balcony in front of the pillars of the first goal.

About the same time, also, six men came in through the Porta Pompæ and took post, one in front of each occupied stall; whereat there was a prolonged hum of voices in every quarter.

"See, see! The green goes to number four on the right; the Athenian is there."

"And Messala—yes, he is in number two."

"The Corinthian—"

"Watch the white! See, he crosses over, he stops; number one it is—number one on the left."

"No, the black stops there, and the white at number two."

"So it is."

These gate-keepers, it should be understood, were dressed in tunics colored like those of the competing charioteers; so, when they took their stations, everybody knew the particular stall in which his favorite was that moment waiting.

"Did you ever see Messala?" the Egyptian asked Esther.

The Jewess shuddered as she answered no. If not her father's enemy, the Roman was Ben-Hur's.

"He is beautiful as Apollo."

As Iras spoke, her large eyes brightened and she shook her jewelled fan. Esther looked at her with the thought, "Is he, then, so much handsomer than Ben-Hur?" Next moment she heard Ilderim say to her father, "Yes, his stall is number two on the left of the Porta Pompæ;" and, thinking it was of Ben-Hur he spoke, her eyes turned that way. Taking but the briefest glance at the wattled face of the gate, she drew the veil close and muttered a little prayer.

Presently Sanballat came to the party.

"I am just from the stalls, O sheik," he said, bowing gravely to Ilderim, who began combing his beard, while his eyes glittered with eager inquiry. "The horses are in perfect condition."

Ilderim replied simply, "If they are beaten, I pray it be by some other than Messala."

Turning then to Simonides, Sanballat drew out a tablet, saying, "I bring you also something of interest. I reported, you will remember, the wager concluded with Messala last night, and stated that I left another which, if taken, was to be delivered to me in writing to-day before the race began. Here it is."

Simonides took the tablet and read the memorandum carefully.

"Yes," he said, "their emissary came to ask me if you had so much money with me. Keep the tablet close. If you lose, you know where to come; if you win"—his face knit hard— "if you win—ah, friend, see to it! See the signers escape not; hold them to the last shekel. That is what they would with us."

"Trust me," replied the purveyor.

"Will you not sit with us?" asked Simonides.

"You are very good," the other returned; "but if I leave the consul, young Rome yonder will boil over. Peace to you; peace to all."

At length the recess came to an end.

The trumpeters blew a call at which the absentees rushed back to their places. At the same time, some attendants appeared in the arena, and, climbing upon the division wall, went to an entablature near the second goal at the west end, and placed upon it seven wooden balls; then returning to the first goal, upon an entablature there they set up seven other pieces of wood hewn to represent dolphins.

"What shall they do with the balls and fishes, O sheik?" asked Balthasar.

"Hast thou never attended a race?"

"Never before; and hardly know I why I am here."

"Well, they are to keep the count. At the end of each round run thou shalt see one ball and one fish taken down."

The preparations were now complete, and presently a trumpeter in gaudy uniform arose by the editor, ready to blow the signal of commencement promptly at his order. Straightway the stir of the people and the hum of their conversation died away. Every face near-by, and every face in the lessening perspective, turned to the east, as all eyes settled upon the gates of the six stalls which shut in the competitors.

The unusual flush upon his face gave proof that even Simonides had caught the universal excitement. Ilderim pulled his beard fast and furious.

"Look now for the Roman," said the fair Egyptian to Esther, who did not hear her, for, with close-drawn veil and beating heart, she sat watching for Ben-Hur.

The structure containing the stalls, it should be observed, was in form of the segment of a circle, retired on the right so that its central point was projected forward, and midway the course, on the starting side of the first goal. Every stall, consequently, was equally distant from the starting-line or chalked rope above mentioned.

The trumpet sounded short and sharp; whereupon the starters, one for each chariot, leaped down from behind the pillars of the goal, ready to give assistance if any of the fours proved unmanageable.

Again the trumpet blew, and simultaneously the gatekeepers threw the stalls open.

First appeared the mounted attendants of the charioteers, five in all, Ben-Hur having rejected the service. The chalked line was lowered to let them pass, then raised again. They were beautifully mounted, yet scarcely observed as they rode forward; for all the time the trampling of eager horses, and the voices of drivers scarcely less eager, were heard behind in the stalls, so that one might not look away an instant from the gaping doors.

The chalked line up again, the gate-keepers called their men; instantly the ushers on the balcony waved their hands, and shouted with all their strength, "Down! down!"

As well have whistled to stay a storm.

Forth from each stall, like missiles in a volley from so many great guns, rushed the six fours; and up the vast assemblage arose, electrified and irrepressible, and, leaping upon the benches, filled the Circus and the air above it with yells and screams. This was the time for which they had so patiently waited!—this the moment of supreme interest treasured up in talk and dreams since the proclamation of the games!"

"He is come—there—look!" cried Iras, pointing to Messala.

"I see him," answered Esther, looking at Ben-Hur.

The veil was withdrawn. For an instant the little Jewess was brave. An idea of the joy there is in doing an heroic deed under the eyes of a multitude came to her, and she understood ever after how, at such times, the souls of men, in the frenzy of performance, laugh at death or forget it utterly.

The competitors were now under view from nearly every part of the Circus, yet the race was not begun; they had first to make the chalked line successfully.

The line was stretched for the purpose of equalizing the start. If it were dashed upon, discomfiture of man and horses might be apprehended; on the other hand, to approach it timidly was to incur the hazard of being thrown behind in the beginning of the race; and that was certain forfeit of the great advantage always striven for—the position next the division wall on the inner line of the course.

This trial, its perils and consequences, the spectators knew thoroughly; and if the opinion of old Nestor, uttered what time he handed the reins to his son, were true—

"It is not strength, but art, obtained the prize,
And to be swift is less than to be wise"—[93]

all on the benches might well look for warning of the winner to be now given, justifying the interest with which they breathlessly watched for the result.

The arena swam in a dazzle of light; yet each driver looked first thing for the rope, then for the coveted inner line. So, all six aiming at the same point and speeding furiously, a collision seemed inevitable; nor that merely. What if the editor, at the last moment, dissatisfied with the start, should withhold the signal to drop the rope? Or if he should not give it in time?

The crossing was about two hundred and fifty feet in width. Quick the eye, steady the hand, unerring the judgment required. If now one look away! or his mind wander! or a rein slip! And what attraction in the *ensemble* of the thousands over the spreading balcony! Calculating upon the natural impulse to give one glance—just one—in sooth of curiosity or vanity, malice might be there with an artifice; while friendship and love, did they serve the same result, might be as deadly as malice.

The divine last touch in perfecting the beautiful is animation. Can we accept the saying, then these latter days, so tame in pastime and dull in sports, have scarcely anything to compare to the spectacle offered by the six contestants. Let the reader try to fancy it; let him first look down upon the arena, and see it glistening in its frame of dull-gray granite walls; let him then, in this perfect field, see the chariots, light of wheel, very graceful, and ornate as paint and burnishing can make them—Messala's rich with ivory and gold; let him see the drivers, erect and statuesque, undisturbed by the motion of the cars, their limbs naked, and fresh and ruddy with the healthful polish of the baths—in their right hands goads, suggestive of torture dreadful to the thought—in their left hands, held in careful separation, and high, that they may not interfere with view of the steeds, the reins passing taut from the fore ends of the carriage-poles; let him see the fours, chosen for beauty as well as speed; let him see them in magnificent action, their masters not more conscious of the situation and all that is asked and hoped from them—their heads tossing, nostrils in play, now distent, now contracted—limbs too dainty for the sand which they

---

93 Famous aphorism of Homer.

touch but to spurn—limbs slender, yet with impact crushing as hammers—every muscle of the rounded bodies instinct with glorious life, swelling, diminishing, justifying the world in taking from them its ultimate measure of force; finally, along with chariots, drivers, horses, let the reader see the accompanying shadows fly; and, with such distinctness as the picture comes, he may share the satisfaction and deeper pleasure of those to whom it was a thrilling fact, not a feeble fancy. Every age has its plenty of sorrows; heaven help where there are no pleasures!

The competitors having started each on the shortest line for the position next the wall, yielding would be like giving up the race; and who dared yield? It is not in common nature to change a purpose in mid-career; and the cries of encouragement from the balcony were indistinguishable and indescribable: a roar which had the same effect upon all the drivers.

The fours neared the rope together. Then the trumpeter by the editor's side blew a signal vigorously. Twenty feet away it was not heard. Seeing the action, however, the judges dropped the rope, and not an instant too soon, for the hoof of one of Messala's horses struck it as it fell. Nothing daunted, the Roman shook out his long lash, loosed the reins, leaned forward, and, with a triumphant shout, took the wall.

"Jove with us! Jove with us!" yelled all the Roman faction, in a frenzy of delight.

As Messala turned in, the bronze lion's head at the end of his axle caught the fore-leg of the Athenian's right-hand trace-mate, flinging the brute over against its yoke-fellow. Both staggered, struggled, and lost their headway. The ushers had their will at least in part. The thousands held their breath with horror; only up where the consul sat was there shouting.

"Jove with us!" screamed Drusus, frantically.

"He wins! Jove with us!" answered his associates, seeing Messala speed on.

Tablet in hand, Sanballat turned to them; a crash from the course below stopped his speech, and he could not but look that way.

Messala having passed, the Corinthian was the only contestant on the Athenian's right, and to that side the latter tried to turn his broken four; and then, as ill-fortune would have it, the wheel of the Byzantine, who was next on the left, struck the tail-piece of his chariot, knocking his feet from under him. There was a crash, a scream of rage and fear, and the unfortunate Cleanthes fell under the hoofs of his own steeds: a terrible sight, against which Esther covered her eyes.

On swept the Corinthian, on the Byzantine, on the Sidonian.

Sanballat looked for Ben-Hur, and turned again to Drusus and his coterie.

"A hundred sestertii on the Jew!" he cried.

"Taken!" answered Drusus.

"Another hundred on the Jew!" shouted Sanballat.

Nobody appeared to hear him. He called again; the situation below was too absorbing, and they were too busy shouting, "Messala! Messala! Jove with us!"

When the Jewess ventured to look again, a party of workmen were removing the horses and broken car; another party were taking off the man himself; and every bench upon which there was a Greek was vocal with execrations and prayers for vengeance. Suddenly she dropped her hands; Ben-Hur, unhurt, was to the front, coursing freely forward along with the Roman! Behind them, in a group, followed the Sidonian, the Corinthian, and the Byzantine.

The race was on; the souls of the racers were in it; over them bent the myriads.

Chapter XIV

WHEN the dash for position began, Ben-Hur, as we have seen, was on the extreme left of the six. For a moment, like the others, he was half blinded by the light in the arena; yet he managed to catch sight of his antagonists and divine their purpose. At Messala, who was more than an antagonist to him, he gave one searching look. The air of passionless hauteur characteristic of the fine patrician face was there as of old, and so was the Italian beauty, which the helmet rather increased; but more—it may have been a jealous fancy, or the effect of the brassy shadow in which the features were at the moment cast, still the Israelite thought he saw the soul of the man as through a glass, darkly: cruel, cunning, desperate; not so excited as determined—a soul in a tension of watchfulness and fierce resolve.

In a time not longer than was required to turn to his four again, Ben-Hur felt his own resolution harden to a like temper. At whatever cost, at all hazards, he would humble this enemy! Prize, friends, wagers, honor—everything that can be thought of as a possible interest in the race was lost in the one deliberate purpose. Regard for life even should not hold him back. Yet there was no passion, on his part; no blinding rush of heated blood from heart to brain, and back again; no impulse to fling himself upon Fortune: he did not believe in Fortune; far otherwise. He had his plan, and, confiding in himself, he settled to the task never more observant, never more capable. The air about him seemed aglow with a renewed and perfect transparency.

When not half-way across the arena, he saw that Messala's rush would, if there was no collision, and the rope fell, give him the wall; that the rope would fall, he ceased as soon to doubt; and, further, it came to him, a sudden flash-like insight, that Messala knew it was to be let drop at the last moment (prearrangement with the editor could safely reach that point in the contest); and it suggested, what more Roman-like than for the official to lend himself to a countryman who, besides being so popular, had also so much at stake? There could be no other accounting for the confidence with which Messala pushed his four forward the instant his competitors were prudentially checking their fours in front of the obstruction—no other except madness.

It is one thing to see a necessity and another to act upon it. Ben-Hur yielded the wall for the time.

The rope fell, and all the fours but his sprang into the course under urgency of voice and lash. He drew head to the right, and, with all the speed of his Arabs, darted across the trails of his opponents, the angle of movement being such as to lose the least time and gain the greatest possible advance. So, while the spectators were shivering at the Athenian's mishap, and the Sidonian, Byzantine, and Corinthian were striving, with such skill as they possessed, to avoid involvement in the ruin, Ben-Hur swept around and took the course neck and neck with Messala, though on the outside. The marvellous skill shown in making the change thus from the extreme left across to the right without appreciable loss did not fail the sharp eyes upon the benches: the Circus seemed to rock and rock again with prolonged applause. Then Esther clasped her hands in glad surprise; then Sanballat, smiling, offered his hundred sestertii a second time without a taker; and then the Romans began to doubt, thinking Messala might have found an equal, if not a master, and that in an Israelite!

And now, racing together side by side, a narrow interval between them, the two neared the second goal.

The pedestal of the three pillars there, viewed from the west, was a stone wall in the form of a half-circle, around which the course and opposite balcony were bent in exact parallelism. Making this turn was considered in all respects the most telling test of a charioteer; it was, in fact, the very feat in which Orestes failed. As an involuntary admission of interest on the part of the spectators, a hush fell over all the Circus, so that for the first time in the race the rattle and clang of the cars plunging after the tugging steeds were distinctly heard. Then, it would seem, Messala observed Ben-Hur, and recognized him; and at once the audacity of the man flamed out in an astonishing manner.

"Down Eros, up Mars!" he shouted, whirling his lash with practised hand—"Down Eros, up Mars!" he repeated, and caught the well-doing Arabs of Ben-Hur a cut the like of which they had never known.

The blow was seen in every quarter, and the amazement was universal. The silence deepened; up on the benches behind the consul the boldest held his breath, waiting for the outcome. Only a moment thus: then, involuntarily, down from the balcony, as thunder falls, burst the indignant cry of the people.

The four sprang forward affrighted. No hand had ever been laid upon them except in love; they had been nurtured ever so tenderly; and as they grew, their confidence in man became a lesson to men beautiful to see. What should such dainty natures do under such indignity but leap as from death?

Forward they sprang as with one impulse, and forward leaped the car. Past question, every experience is serviceable to us. Where got Ben-Hur the large hand and mighty grip which helped him now so well? Where but from the oar with which so long he fought the sea? And what was this spring of the floor under his feet to the dizzy eccentric lurch with which in the old time the trembling ship yielded to the beat of staggering billows, drunk with their power? So he kept his place, and gave the four free rein, and called to them in soothing voice, trying merely to guide them round the dangerous turn; and before the fever of the people began to abate, he had back the mastery. Nor that only: on approaching the first goal, he was again side by side with Messala, bearing with him the sympathy and admiration of every one not a Roman. So clearly was the feeling shown, so vigorous its manifestation, that Messala, with all his boldness, felt it unsafe to trifle further.

As the cars whirled round the goal, Esther caught sight of Ben-Hur's face—a little pale, a little higher raised, otherwise calm, even placid.

Immediately a man climbed on the entablature at the west end of the division wall, and took down one of the conical wooden balls. A dolphin on the east entablature was taken down at the same time.

In like manner, the second ball and second dolphin disappeared.

And then the third ball and third dolphin.

Three rounds concluded: still Messala held the inside position; still Ben-Hur moved with him side by side; still the other competitors followed as before. The contest began to have the appearance of one of the double races which became so popular in Rome during the later Cæsarean period—Messala and Ben-Hur in the first, the Corinthian, Sidonian, and Byzantine in the second. Meantime the ushers succeeded in returning the multitude to their seats, though the clamor continued to run the rounds, keeping, as it were, even pace with the rivals in the course below.

In the fifth round the Sidonian succeeded in getting a place outside Ben-Hur, but lost it directly.

The sixth round was entered upon without change of relative position.

Gradually the speed had been quickened—gradually the blood of the competitors warmed with the work. Men and beasts seemed to know alike that the final crisis was near, bringing the time for the winner to assert himself.

The interest which from the beginning had centred chiefly in the struggle between the Roman and the Jew, with an intense and general sympathy for the latter, was fast changing to anxiety on his account. On all the benches the spectators bent forward motionless, except as their faces turned following the contestants. Ilderim quitted combing his beard, and Esther forgot her fears.

"A hundred sestertii on the Jew!" cried Sanballat to the Romans under the consul's awning.

There was no reply.

"A talent—or five talents, or ten; choose ye!"

He shook his tablets at them defiantly.

"I will take thy sestertii," answered a Roman youth, preparing to write.

"Do not so," interposed a friend.

"Why?"

"Messala hath reached his utmost speed. See him lean over his chariot-rim, the reins loose as flying ribbons. Look then at the Jew."

The first one looked.

"By Hercules!" he replied, his countenance falling. "The dog throws all his weight on the bits. I see, I see! If the gods help not our friend, he will be run away with by the Israelite. No, not yet. Look! Jove with us, Jove with us!"

The cry, swelled by every Latin tongue, shook the *velaria* over the consul's head.

If it were true that Messala had attained his utmost speed, the effort was with effect; slowly but certainly he was beginning to forge ahead. His horses were running with their heads low down; from the balcony their bodies appeared actually to skim the earth; their nostrils showed blood-red in expansion; their eyes seemed straining in their sockets. Certainly the good steeds were doing their best! How long could they keep the pace? It was but the commencement of the sixth round. On they dashed. As they neared the second goal, Ben-Hur turned in behind the Roman's car.

The joy of the Messala faction reached its bound: they screamed and howled, and tossed their colors; and Sanballat filled his tablets with wagers of their tendering.

Malluch, in the lower gallery over the Gate of Triumph, found it hard to keep his cheer. He had cherished the vague hint dropped to him by Ben-Hur of something to happen in the turning of the western pillars. It was the fifth round, yet the something had not come; and he had said to himself, the sixth will bring it; but, lo! Ben-Hur was hardly holding a place at the tail of his enemy's car.

Over in the east end, Simonides' party held their peace. The merchant's head was bent low. Ilderim tugged at his beard, and dropped his brows till there was nothing of his eyes but an occasional sparkle of light. Esther scarcely breathed. Iras alone appeared glad.

Along the home-stretch—sixth round—Messala leading, next him Ben-Hur, and so close it was the old story:

"First flew Eumelus on Pheretian steeds;
With those of Tros bold Diomed succeeds;
Close on Eumelus' back they puff the wind,
And seem just mounting on his car behind;

Full on his neck he feels the sultry breeze,
And, hovering o'er, their stretching shadow sees."[94]

Thus to the first goal, and round it. Messala, fearful of losing his place, hugged the stony wall with perilous clasp; a foot to the left, and he had been dashed to pieces; yet, when the turn was finished, no man, looking at the wheel-tracks of the two cars, could have said, here went Messala, there the Jew. They left but one trace behind them.

As they whirled by, Esther saw Ben-Hur's face again, and it was whiter than before.

Simonides, shrewder than Esther, said to Ilderim, the moment the rivals turned into the course, "I am no judge, good sheik, if Ben-Hur be not about to execute some design. His face hath that look."

To which Ilderim answered, "Saw you how clean they were and fresh? By the splendor of God, friend, they have not been running! But now watch!"

One ball and one dolphin remained on the entablatures; and all the people drew a long breath, for the beginning of the end was at hand.

First, the Sidonian gave the scourge to his four, and, smarting with fear and pain, they dashed desperately forward, promising for a brief time to go to the front. The effort ended in promise. Next, the Byzantine and Corinthian each made the trial with like result, after which they were practically out of the race. Thereupon, with a readiness perfectly explicable, all the factions except the Romans joined hope in Ben-Hur, and openly indulged their feeling.

"Ben-Hur! Ben-Hur!" they shouted, and the blent voices of the many rolled overwhelmingly against the consular stand.

From the benches above him as he passed, the favor descended in fierce injunctions.

"Speed thee, Jew!"

"Take the wall now!"

"On! loose the Arabs! Give them rein and scourge!"

"Let him not have the turn on thee again. Now or never!"

Over the balustrade they stooped low, stretching their hands imploringly to him.

Either he did not hear, or could not do better, for halfway round the course and he was still following; at the second goal even still no change!

And now, to make the turn, Messala began to draw in his left-hand steeds, an act which necessarily slackened their speed. His spirit was high; more than one altar was richer of his vows; the Roman genius was still president. On the three pillars only six hundred feet away were fame, increase of fortune, promotions, and a triumph ineffably sweetened by hate, all in store for him! That moment Malluch, in the gallery, saw Ben-Hur lean forward over his Arabs, and give them the reins. Out flew the many-folded lash in his hand; over the backs of the startled steeds it writhed and hissed, and hissed and writhed again and again; and though it fell not, there were both sting and menace in its quick report; and as the man passed thus from quiet to resistless action, his face suffused, his eyes gleaming, along the reins he seemed to flash his will; and instantly not one, but the four as one, answered with a leap that landed them alongside the Roman's car. Messala, on the perilous edge of the goal, heard, but dared not look to see what the awakening portended. From the people he received no sign. Above the noises of the race

---

94 Alexander Pope's (1688–1744) translation of Homer's *Iliad*, XXIII, 455–61.

there was but one voice, and that was Ben-Hur's. In the old Aramaic, as the sheik himself, he called to the Arabs,

"On, Atair! On, Rigel! What, Antares! dost thou linger now? Good horse—oho, Aldebaran! I hear them singing in the tents. I hear the children singing and the women— singing of the stars, of Atair, Antares, Rigel, Aldebaran, victory!—and the song will never end. Well done! Home to-morrow, under the black tent—home! On, Antares! The tribe is waiting for us, and the master is waiting! 'Tis done! 'tis done! Ha, ha! We have overthrown the proud. The hand that smote us is in the dust. Ours the glory! Ha, ha!—steady! The work is done—soho! Rest!"

There had never been anything of the kind more simple; seldom anything so instantaneous.

At the moment chosen for the dash, Messala was moving in a circle round the goal. To pass him, Ben-Hur had to cross the track, and good strategy required the movement to be in a forward direction; that is, on a like circle limited to the least possible increase. The thousands on the benches understood it all: they saw the signal given—the magnificent response; the four close outside Messala's outer wheel, Ben-Hur's inner wheel behind the other's car—all this they saw. Then they heard a crash loud enough to send a thrill through the Circus, and, quicker than thought, out over the course a spray of shining white and yellow flinders flew. Down on its right side toppled the bed of the Roman's chariot. There was a rebound as of the axle hitting the hard earth; another and another; then the car went to pieces; and Messala, entangled in the reins, pitched forward headlong.

To increase the horror of the sight by making death certain, the Sidonian, who had the wall next behind, could not stop or turn out. Into the wreck full speed he drove; then over the Roman, and into the latter's four, all mad with fear. Presently, out of the turmoil, the fighting of horses, the resound of blows, the murky cloud of dust and sand, he crawled, in time to see the Corinthian and Byzantine go on down the course after Ben-Hur, who had not been an instant delayed.

The people arose, and leaped upon the benches, and shouted and screamed. Those who looked that way caught glimpses of Messala, now under the trampling of the fours, now under the abandoned cars. He was still; they thought him dead; but far the greater number followed Ben-Hur in his career. They had not seen the cunning touch of the reins by which, turning a little to the left, he caught Messala's wheel with the iron-shod point of his axle, and crushed it; but they had seen the transformation of the man, and themselves felt the heat and glow of his spirit, the heroic resolution, the maddening energy of action with which, by look, word, and gesture, he so suddenly inspired his Arabs. And such running! It was rather the long leaping of lions in harness; but for the lumbering chariot, it seemed the four were flying. When the Byzantine and Corinthian were half-way down the course, Ben-Hur turned the first goal.

And the race was WON!

The consul arose; the people shouted themselves hoarse; the editor came down from his seat, and crowned the victors.

The fortunate man among the boxers was a low-browed, yellow-haired Saxon, of such brutalized face as to attract a second look from Ben-Hur, who recognized a teacher with whom he himself had been a favorite at Rome. From him the young Jew looked up and beheld Simonides and his party on the balcony. They waved their hands to him. Esther kept her seat; but Iras arose, and gave him a smile and a wave of her fan—favors not the less intoxicating to him because we know, O reader, they would have fallen to Messala had he been the victor.

The procession was then formed, and, midst the shouting of the multitude which had had its will, passed out of the Gate of Triumph.

And the day was over.

Book Eighth[95]

Chapter VIII

THE streets were full of people going and coming, or grouped about the fires roasting meat, and feasting and singing, and happy. The odor of scorching flesh mixed with the odor of cedar-wood aflame and smoking loaded the air; and as this was the occasion when every son of Israel was full brother to every other son of Israel, and hospitality was without bounds, Ben-Hur was saluted at every step, while the groups by the fires insisted, "Stay and partake with us. We are brethren in the love of the Lord." But with thanks to them he hurried on, intending to take horse at the khan and return to the tents on the Cedron.

To make the place, it was necessary for him to cross the thoroughfare so soon to receive sorrowful Christian perpetuation. There also the pious celebration was at its height. Looking up the street, he noticed the flames of torches in motion streaming out like pennons; then he observed that the singing ceased where the torches came. His wonder rose to its highest, however, when he became certain that amidst the smoke and dancing sparks he saw the keener sparkling of burnished spear-tips, arguing the presence of Roman soldiers. What were they, the scoffing legionaries, doing in a Jewish religious procession? The circumstance was unheard of, and he stayed to see the meaning of it.

The moon was shining its best; yet, as if the moon and the torches, and the fires in the street, and the rays streaming from windows and open doors were not enough to make the way clear, some of the processionists carried lighted lanterns; and fancying he discovered a special purpose in the use of such equipments, Ben-Hur stepped into the street so close to the line of march as to bring every one of the company under view while passing. The torches and the lanterns were being borne by servants, each of whom was armed with a bludgeon or a sharpened stave. Their present duty seemed to be to pick out the smoothest paths among the rocks in the street for certain dignitaries among them—elders and priests; rabbis with long beards, heavy brows, and beaked noses; men of the class potential in the councils of Caiaphas and Hannas.[96] Where could they be going? Not to the Temple, certainly, for the route to the sacred house from Zion, whence these appeared to be coming, was by the Xystus. And their business—if peaceful, why the soldiers?

As the procession began to go by Ben-Hur, his attention was particularly called to three persons walking together. They were well towards the front, and the servants who went

95 The story picks up here in the last chapters of Book Eight, the novel's final sections. After Ben-Hur defeats and humiliates Messala in the chariot race, he is able to locate his mother and sister, who have been imprisoned since his arrest years before. They have both contracted leprosy, a condition thought to be hopeless, yet they are both cured when they meet Jesus of Nazareth. Ben-Hur becomes increasingly interested in Jesus and the importance he may have as the Jews' long-awaited Messiah.

96 The two high priests who presided over the Jewish Temple at the time of Jesus's death.

before them with lanterns appeared unusually careful in the service. In the person moving on the left of this group he recognized a chief policeman of the Temple; the one on the right was a priest; the middle man was not at first so easily placed, as he walked leaning heavily upon the arms of the others, and carried his head so low upon his breast as to hide his face. His appearance was that of a prisoner not yet recovered from the fright of arrest, or being taken to something dreadful—to torture or death. The dignitaries helping him on the right and left, and the attention they gave him, made it clear that if he were not himself the object moving the party, he was at least in some way connected with the object—a witness or a guide, possibly an informer. So if it could be found who he was the business in hand might be shrewdly guessed. With great assurance, Ben-Hur fell in on the right of the priest, and walked along with him. Now if the man would lift his head! And presently he did so, letting the light of the lanterns strike full in his face, pale, dazed, pinched with dread; the beard roughed; the eyes filmy, sunken, and despairing. In much going about following the Nazarene, Ben-Hur had come to know his disciples as well as the Master; and now, at sight of the dismal countenance, he cried out,

"The 'Scariot!"

Slowly the head of the man turned until his eyes settled upon Ben-Hur, and his lips moved as if he were about to speak; but the priest interfered.

"Who art thou? Begone! he said to Ben-Hur, pushing him away.

The young man took the push good-naturedly, and, waiting an opportunity, fell into the procession again. Thus he was carried passively along down the street, through the crowded lowlands between the hill Bezetha and the Castle of Antonia, and on by the Bethesda reservoir to the Sheep Gate. There were people everywhere, and everywhere the people were engaged in sacred observances.

It being Passover night, the valves of the Gate stood open. The keepers were off somewhere feasting. In front of the procession as it passed out unchallenged was the deep gorge of the Cedron, with Olivet beyond, its dressing of cedar and olive trees darker of the moonlight silvering all the heavens. Two roads met and merged into the street at the gate—one from the northeast, the other from Bethany. Ere Ben-Hur could finish wondering whether he were to go farther, and if so, which road was to be taken, he was led off down into the gorge. And still no hint of the purpose of the midnight march.

Down the gorge and over the bridge at the bottom of it. There was a great clatter on the floor as the crowd, now a straggling rabble, passed over beating and pounding with their clubs and staves. A little farther, and they turned off to the left in the direction of an olive orchard enclosed by a stone wall in view from the road. Ben-Hur knew there was nothing in the place but old gnarled trees, the grass, and a trough hewn out of a rock for the treading of oil after the fashion of the country. While, yet more wonder-struck, he was thinking what could bring such a company at such an hour to a quarter so lonesome, they were all brought to a standstill. Voices called out excitedly in front; a chill sensation ran from man to man; there was a rapid falling-back, and a blind stumbling over each other. The soldiers alone kept their order.

It took Ben-Hur but a moment to disengage himself from the mob and run forward. There he found a gateway without a gate admitting to the orchard, and he halted to take in the scene.

A man in white clothes, and bareheaded, was standing outside the entrance, his hands crossed before him—a slender, stooping figure, with long hair and thin face—in an attitude of resignation and waiting.

It was the Nazarene!

Behind him, next the gateway, were the disciples in a group; they were excited, but no man was ever calmer than he. The torchlight beat redly upon him, giving his hair a tint ruddier than was natural to it; yet the expression of the countenance was as usual all gentleness and pity.

Opposite this most unmartial figure stood the rabble, gaping, silent, awed, cowering—ready at a sign of anger from him to break and run. And from him to them—then at Judas, conspicuous in their midst—Ben-Hur looked—one quick glance, and the object of the visit lay open to his understanding. Here was the betrayer, there the betrayed; and these with clubs and staves, and the legionaries, were brought to take him.

A man may not always tell what he will do until the trial is upon him. This was the emergency for which Ben-Hur had been for years preparing. The man to whose security he had devoted himself, and upon whose life he had been building so largely, was in personal peril; yet he stood still. Such contradictions are there in human nature! To say truth, O reader, he was not entirely recovered from the picture of the Christ before the Gate Beautiful as it had been given by the Egyptian; and, besides that, the very calmness with which the mysterious person confronted the mob held him in restraint by suggesting the possession of a power in reserve more than sufficient for the peril. Peace and good-will, and love and non-resistance, had been the burden of the Nazarene's teaching; would he put his preaching into practice? He was master of life; he could restore it when lost; he could take it at pleasure. What use would he make of the power now? Defend himself? And how? A word—a breath—a thought were sufficient. That there would be some signal exhibition of astonishing force beyond the natural Ben-Hur believed, and in that faith waited. And in all this he was still measuring the Nazarene by himself—by the human standard.

Presently the clear voice of the Christ arose.

"Whom seek ye?"

"Jesus of Nazareth," the priest replied.

"I am he."

At these simplest of words, spoken without passion or alarm, the assailants fell back several steps, the timid among them cowering to the ground; and they might have let him alone and gone away had not Judas walked over to him.

"Hail, master!"

With this friendly speech, he kissed him.

"Judas," said the Nazarene, mildly, "betrayest thou the Son of man with a kiss?[97] Wherefore art thou come?"

Receiving no reply, the Master spoke to the crowd again.

"Whom seek ye?"

"Jesus of Nazareth."

"I have told you that I am he. If, therefore, you seek me, let these go their way."

At these words of entreaty the rabbis advanced upon him; and, seeing their intent, some of the disciples for whom he interceded drew nearer; one of them cut off a man's ear, but without saving the Master from being taken. And yet Ben-Hur stood still! Nay, while the officers were making ready with their ropes the Nazarene was doing his greatest

---

97 Luke 22:48.

charity—not the greatest in deed, but the very greatest in illustration of his forbearance, so far surpassing that of men.

"Suffer ye thus far," he said to the wounded man, and healed him with a touch.

Both friends and enemies were confounded—one side that he could do such a thing, the other that he would do it under the circumstances.

"Surely he will not allow them to bind him!"

Thus thought Ben-Hur.

"Put up thy sword into the sheath; the cup which my Father hath given me, shall I not drink it?"[98] From the offending follower, the Nazarene turned to his captors. "Are you come out as against a thief, with swords and staves to take me? I was daily with you in the Temple, and you took me not; but this is your hour, and the power of darkness."[99]

The posse plucked up courage and closed about him; and when Ben-Hur looked for the faithful they were gone—not one of them remained.

The crowd about the deserted man seemed very busy, with tongue, hand, and foot. Over their heads, between the torch-sticks, through the smoke, sometimes in openings between the restless men, Ben-Hur caught momentary glimpses of the prisoner. Never had anything struck him as so piteous, so unfriended, so forsaken! Yet, he thought, the man could have defended himself—he could have slain his enemies with a breath, but he would not. What was the cup his father had given him to drink? And who was the father to be so obeyed? Mystery upon mystery—not one, but many.

Directly the mob started in return to the city, the soldiers in the lead. Ben-Hur became anxious; he was not satisfied with himself. Where the torches were in the midst of the rabble he knew the Nazarene was to be found. Suddenly he resolved to see him again. He would ask him one question.

Taking off his long outer garment and the handkerchief from his head, he threw them upon the orchard wall, and started after the posse, which he boldly joined. Through the stragglers he made way, and by littles at length reached the man who carried the ends of the rope with which the prisoner was bound.

The Nazarene was walking slowly, his head down, his hands bound behind him; the hair fell thickly over his face, and he stooped more than usual; apparently he was oblivious to all going on around him. In advance a few steps were priests and elders talking and occasionally looking back. When, at length, they were all near the bridge in the gorge, Ben-Hur took the rope from the servant who had it, and stepped past him.

"Master, master!" he said, hurriedly, speaking close to the Nazarene's ear. "Dost thou hear, master? A word—one word. Tell me—"

The fellow from whom he had taken the rope now claimed it.

"Tell me" Ben-Hur continued, "goest thou with these of thine own accord?"

The people were come up now, and in his own ears asking angrily, "Who art thou, man?"

"O master," Ben-Hur made haste to say, his voice sharp with anxiety, "I am thy friend and lover. Tell me, I pray thee, if I bring rescue, wilt thou accept it?"

The Nazarene never so much as looked up or allowed the slightest sign of recognition; yet the something which when we are suffering is always telling it to such as look at us, though they be strangers, failed not now. "Let him alone," it seemed to say; "he has been

---

98 John 18:11.
99 Luke 22:53.

abandoned by his friends; the world has denied him; in bitterness of spirit, he has taken farewell of men; he is going he knows not where, and he cares not. Let him alone."

And to that Ben-Hur was now driven. A dozen hands were upon him, and from all sides there was shouting, "He is one of them. Bring him along; club him—kill him!"

With a gust of passion which gave him many times his ordinary force, Ben-Hur raised himself, turned once about with his arms outstretched, shook the hands off, and rushed through the circle which was fast hemming him in. The hands snatching at him as he passed tore his garments from his back, so he ran off the road naked[100]; and the gorge, in keeping of the friendly darkness, darker there than elsewhere, received him safe.

Reclaiming his handkerchief and outer garments from the orchard wall, he followed back to the city gate; thence he went to the khan, and on the good horse rode to the tents of his people out by the Tombs of the Kings.

As he rode, he promised himself to see the Nazarene on the morrow—promised it, not knowing that the unfriended man was taken straightway to the house of Hannas to be tried that night.

The heart the young man carried to his couch beat so heavily he could not sleep; for now clearly his renewed Judean kingdom resolved itself into what it was—only a dream. It is bad enough to see our castles overthrown one after another with an interval between in which to recover from the shock, or at least let the echoes of the fall die away; but when they go altogether—go as ships sink, as houses tumble in earthquakes—the spirits which endure it calmly are made of stuffs sterner than common, and Ben-Hur's was not of them. Through vistas in the future, he began to catch glimpses of a life serenely beautiful, with a home instead of a palace of state, and Esther its mistress. Again and again through the leaden-footed hours of the night he saw the villa by Misenum, and with his little countrywoman strolled through the garden, and rested in the panelled atrium; overhead the Neapolitan sky, at their feet the sunniest of sun-lands and the bluest of bays.

In plainest speech, he was entering upon a crisis with which to-morrow and the Nazarene will have everything to do.

Chapter IX

NEXT morning, about the second hour, two men rode full speed to the doors of Ben-Hur's tents, and dismounting, asked to see him. He was not yet risen, but gave directions for their admission.

"Peace to you, brethren," he said, for they were of his Galileans, and trusted officers. "Will you be seated?"

"Nay," the senior replied, bluntly, "to sit and be at ease is to let the Nazarene die. Rise, son of Judah, and go with us. The judgment has been given. The tree of the cross is already at Golgotha."

Ben-Hur stared at them.

"The cross!" was all he could for the moment say.

"They took him last night, and tried him," the man continued. "At dawn they led him before Pilate. Twice the Roman denied his guilt; twice he refused to give him over. At last he washed his hands, and said, 'Be it upon you then;' and they answered—"

---

100 Wallace is identifying Ben-Hur with an unidentified man who ran away naked from the scene of Jesus's arrest. Mark 14:52.

"Who answered?"

"They—the priests and people—'His blood be upon us and our children.'"

"Holy father Abraham!" cried Ben-Hur; "a Roman kinder to an Israelite than his own kin! And if—ah, if he should indeed be the son of God, what shall ever wash his blood from their children? It must not be—'tis time to fight!"

His face brightened with resolution, and he clapped his hands.

"The horses—and quickly!" he said to the Arab who answered the signal. "And bid Amrah send me fresh garments, and bring my sword! It is time to die for Israel, my friends. Tarry without till I come."

He ate a crust, drank a cup of wine, and was soon upon the road.

"Whither would you go first?" asked the Galilean.

"To collect the legions."

"Alas!" the man replied, throwing up his hands.

"Why alas?"

"Master"—the man spoke with shame—"master, I and my friend here are all that are faithful. The rest do follow the priests."

"Seeking what?" and Ben-Hur drew rein.

"To kill him."

"Not the Nazarene?"

"You have said it."

Ben-Hur looked slowly from one man to the other. He was hearing again the question of the night before: "The cup my Father hath given me, shall I not drink it?" In the ear of the Nazarene he was putting his own question, "If I bring thee rescue, wilt thou accept it?" He was saying to himself, "This death may not be averted. The man has been travelling towards it with full knowledge from the day he began his mission: it is imposed by a will higher than his; whose but the Lord's! If he is consenting, if he goes to it voluntarily, what shall another do?" Nor less did Ben-Hur see the failure of the scheme he had built upon the fidelity of the Galileans; their desertion, in fact, left nothing more of it. But how singular it should happen that morning of all others! A dread seized him. It was possible his scheming, and labor, and expenditure of treasure might have been but blasphemous contention with God. When he picked up the reins and said, "Let us go, brethren," all before him was uncertainty. The faculty of resolving quickly, without which one cannot be a hero in the midst of stirring scenes, was numb within him.

"Let us go, brethren; let us to Golgotha."

They passed through excited crowds of people going south, like themselves. All the country north of the city seemed aroused and in motion.

Hearing that the procession with the condemned might be met with somewhere near the great white towers left by Herod, the three friends rode thither, passing round southeast of Akra. In the valley below the Pool of Hezekiah, passage-way against the multitude became impossible, and they were compelled to dismount, and take shelter behind the corner of a house and wait.

The waiting was as if they were on a river bank, watching a flood go by, for such the people seemed.

There are certain chapters in the First Book of this story which were written to give the reader an idea of the composition of the Jewish nationality as it was in the time of Christ. They were also written in anticipation of this hour and scene; so that he who has read them with attention can now see all Ben-Hur saw of the going to the crucifixion—a rare and wonderful sight!

Half an hour—an hour—the flood surged by Ben-Hur and his companions, within arm's reach, incessant, undiminished. At the end of that time he could have said, "I have seen all the castes of Jerusalem, all the sects of Judea, all the tribes of Israel, and all the nationalities of earth represented by them." The Libyan Jew went by, and the Jew of Egypt, and the Jew from the Rhine; in short, Jews from all East countries and all West countries, and all islands within commercial connection; they went by on foot, on horseback, on camels, in litters and chariots, and with an infinite variety of costumes, yet with the same marvellous similitude of features which to-day particularizes the children of Israel, tried as they have been by climates and modes of life; they went by speaking all known tongues, for by that means only were they distinguishable group from group; they went by in haste—eager, anxious, crowding—all to behold one poor Nazarene die, a felon between felons.

These were the many, but they were not all.

Borne along with the stream were thousands not Jews—thousands hating and despising them—Greeks, Romans, Arabs, Syrians, Africans, Egyptians, Easterns. So that, studying the mass, it seemed the whole world was to be represented, and, in that sense, present at the crucifixion.

The going was singularly quiet. A hoof-stroke upon a rock, the glide and rattle of revolving wheels, voices in conversation, and now and then a calling voice, were all the sounds heard above the rustle of the mighty movement. Yet was there upon every countenance the look with which men make haste to see some dreadful sight, some sudden wreck, or ruin, or calamity of war. And by such signs Ben-Hur judged that these were the strangers in the city come up to the Passover, who had had no part in the trial of the Nazarene, and might be his friends.

At length, from the direction of the great towers, Ben-Hur heard, at first faint in the distance, a shouting of many men.

"Hark! they are coming now," said one of his friends.

The people in the street halted to hear; but as the cry rang on over their heads, they looked at each other, and in shuddering silence moved along.

The shouting drew nearer each moment; and the air was already full of it and trembling, when Ben-Hur saw the servants of Simonides coming with their master in his chair, and Esther walking by his side; a covered litter was next behind them.

"Peace to you, O Simonides—and to you, Esther," said Ben-Hur, meeting them. "If you are for Golgotha, stay until the procession passes; I will then go with you. There is room to turn in by the house here."

The merchant's large head rested heavily upon his breast; rousing himself, he answered, "Speak to Balthasar; his pleasure will be mine. He is in the litter."

Ben-Hur hastened to draw aside the curtain. The Egyptian was lying within, his wan face so pinched as to appear like a dead man's. The proposal was submitted to him.

"Can we see him?" he inquired, faintly.

"The Nazarene? yes; he must pass within a few feet of us."

"Dear Lord!" the old man cried, fervently. "Once more, once more! Oh, it is a dreadful day for the world!"

Shortly the whole party were in waiting under shelter of the house. They said but little, afraid, probably, to trust their thoughts to each other; everything was uncertain, and nothing so much so as opinions. Balthasar drew himself feebly from the litter, and stood supported by a servant; Esther and Ben-Hur kept Simonides company.

Meantime the flood poured along, if anything, more densely than before; and the shouting came nearer, shrill up in the air, hoarse along the earth, and cruel. At last the procession was up.

"See!" said Ben-Hur, bitterly; "that which cometh now is Jerusalem."

The advance was in possession of an army of boys, hooting and screaming, "The King of the Jews! Room, room for the King of the Jews!"

Simonides watched them as they whirled and danced along, like a cloud of summer insects, and said, gravely, "When these come to their inheritance, son of Hur, alas for the city of Solomon!"[101]

A band of legionaries fully armed followed next, marching in sturdy indifference, the glory of burnished brass about them the while.

Then came the NAZARENE!

He was nearly dead. Every few steps he staggered as if he would fall. A stained gown badly torn hung from his shoulders over a seamless undertunic. His bare feet left red splotches upon the stones. An inscription on a board was tied to his neck. A crown of thorns had been crushed hard down upon his head, making cruel wounds from which streams of blood, now dry and blackened, had run over his face and neck. The long hair, tangled in the thorns, was clotted thick. The skin, where it could be seen, was ghastly white. His hands were tied before him. Back somewhere in the city he had fallen exhausted under the transverse beam of his cross, which, as a condemned person, custom required him to bear to the place of execution: now a countryman carried the burden in his stead. Four soldiers went with him as a guard against the mob, who sometimes, nevertheless, broke through, and struck him with sticks, and spit upon him. Yet no sound escaped him, neither remonstrance nor groan; nor did he look up until he was nearly in front of the house sheltering Ben-Hur and his friends, all of whom were moved with quick compassion. Esther clung to her father; and he, strong of will as he was, trembled. Balthasar fell down speechless. Even Ben-Hur cried out, "O my God! my God!" Then, as if he divined their feelings or heard the exclamation, the Nazarene turned his wan face towards the party, and looked at them each one, so they carried the look in memory through life. They could see he was thinking of them, not himself, and the dying eyes gave them the blessing he was not permitted to speak.

"Where are thy legions, son of Hur?" asked Simonides, aroused.

"Hannas can tell thee better than I."

"What, faithless?"

"All but these two."

"Then all is lost, and this good man must die!"

The face of the merchant knit convulsively as he spoke, and his head sank upon his breast. He had borne his part in Ben-Hur's labors well, and he had been inspired by the same hopes, now blown out never to be rekindled.

Two other men succeeded the Nazarene bearing crossbeams.

"Who are these?" Ben-Hur asked of the Galileans.

"Thieves appointed to die with the Nazarene," they replied.

---

101 Jerusalem.

Next in the procession stalked a mitred figure clad all in the golden vestments of the high-priest. Policemen from the Temple curtained him round about; and after him, in order, strode the sanhedrim, and a long array of priests, the latter in their plain white garments overwrapped by abnets of many folds and gorgeous colors.

"The son-in-law of Hannas," said Ben-Hur, in a low voice.

"Caiaphas! I have seen him," Simonides replied, adding, after a pause during which he thoughtfully watched the haughty pontiff, "And now I am convinced. With such assurance as proceeds from clear enlightenment of the spirit—with absolute assurance—now know I that he who first goes yonder with the inscription about his neck is what the inscription proclaims him—KING OF THE JEWS. A common man, an impostor, a felon, was never thus waited upon. For look! Here are the nations—Jerusalem, Israel. Here is the ephod,[102] here the blue robe with its fringe, and purple pomegranates, and golden bells, not seen in the street since the day Jaddua went out to meet the Macedonian[103]—proofs all that this Nazarene is King. Would I could rise and go after him!"

Ben-Hur listened surprised; and directly, as if himself awakening to his unusual display of feeling, Simonides said, impatiently,

"Speak to Balthasar, I pray you, and let us begone. The vomit of Jerusalem is coming." Then Esther spoke.

"I see some women there, and they are weeping. Who are they?"

Following the point of her hand, the party beheld four women in tears; one of them leaned upon the arm of a man of aspect not unlike the Nazarene's. Presently Ben-Hur answered,

"The man is the disciple whom the Nazarene loves the best of all;[104] she who leans upon his arm is Mary, the Master's mother; the others are friendly women of Galilee."

Esther pursued the mourners with glistening eyes until the multitude received them out of sight.

It may be the reader will fancy the foregoing snatches of conversation were had in quiet; but it was not so. The talking was, for the most part, like that indulged by people at the seaside under the sound of the surf; for to nothing else can the clamor of this division of the mob be so well likened.

The demonstration was the forerunner of those in which, scarce thirty years later, under rule of the factions, the Holy City was torn to pieces; it was quite as great in numbers, as fanatical and bloodthirsty; boiled and raved, and had in it exactly the same elements— servants, camel-drivers, marketmen, gate-keepers, gardeners, dealers in fruits and wines, proselytes, and foreigners not proselytes, watchmen and menials from the Temple, thieves, robbers, and the myriad not assignable to any class, but who, on such occasions as this, appeared no one could say whence, hungry and smelling of caves and old tombs— bareheaded wretches with naked arms and legs, hair and beard in uncombed mats, and each with one garment the color of clay; beasts with abysmal mouths, in outcry effective as lions calling each other across desert spaces. Some of them had swords; a greater number flourished spears and javelins; though the weapons of the many were staves and knotted

---

102 A priestly garment made of linen cloth.
103 Jaddua served as the high priest in Jerusalem in the time of Alexander the Great's conquest of the region.
104 Reference to the Apostle and Gospel writer, John.

clubs, and slings, for which latter selected stones were stored in scrips, and sometimes in sacks improvised from the foreskirts of their dirty tunics. Among the mass here and there appeared persons of high degree—scribes, elders, rabbis, Pharisees with broad fringing, Sadducees in fine cloaks—serving for the time as prompters and directors. If a throat tired of one cry, they invented another for it; if brassy lungs showed signs of collapse, they set them going again; and yet the clamor, loud and continuous as it was, could have been reduced to a few syllables—King of the Jews!—Room for the King of the Jews!—Defiler of the Temple!—Blasphemer of God!—Crucify him, crucify him! And of these cries the last one seemed in greatest favor, because, doubtless, it was more directly expressive of the wish of the mob, and helped to better articulate its hatred of the Nazarene.

"Come," said Simonides, when Balthasar was ready to proceed—"come, let us forward."

Ben-Hur did not hear the call. The appearance of the part of the procession then passing, its brutality and hunger for life, were reminding him of the Nazarene—his gentleness, and the many charities he had seen him do for suffering men. Suggestions beget suggestions; so he remembered suddenly his own great indebtedness to the man; the time he himself was in the hands of a Roman guard going, as was supposed, to a death as certain and almost as terrible as this one of the cross; the cooling drink he had at the well by Nazareth, and the divine expression of the face of him who gave it; the later goodness, the miracle of Palm-Sunday; and with these recollections, the thought of his present powerlessness to give back help for help or make return in kind stung him keenly, and he accused himself. He had not done all he might; he could have watched with the Galileans, and kept them true and ready; and this—ah! this was the moment to strike! A blow well given now would not merely disperse the mob and set the Nazarene free; it would be a trumpet-call to Israel, and precipitate the long-dreamt-of war for freedom. The opportunity was going; the minutes were bearing it away; and if lost! God of Abraham! Was there nothing to be done—nothing?

That instant a party of Galileans caught his eye. He rushed through the press and overtook them.

"Follow me," he said. "I would have speech with you."

The men obeyed him, and when they were under shelter of the house, he spoke again:

"You are of those who took my swords, and agreed with me to strike for freedom and the King who was coming. You have the swords now, and now is the time to strike with them. Go, look everywhere, and find our brethren, and tell them to meet me at the tree of the cross making ready for the Nazarene. Haste all of you! Nay, stand not so! The Nazarene is the King, and freedom dies with him."

They looked at him respectfully, but did not move.

"Hear you?" he asked.

Then one of them replied,

"Son of Judah"—by that name they knew him—"son of Judah, it is you who are deceived, not we or our brethren who have your swords. The Nazarene is not the King; neither has he the spirit of a king. We were with him when he came into Jerusalem; we saw him in the Temple; he failed himself, and us, and Israel; at the Gate Beautiful he turned his back upon God and refused the throne of David. He is not King, and Galilee is not with him. He shall die the death. But hear you, son of Judah. We have your swords, and we are ready now to draw them and strike for freedom; and so is Galilee. Be it for freedom, O son of Judah, for freedom! and we will meet you at the tree of the cross."

The sovereign moment of his life was upon Ben-Hur. Could he have taken the offer and said the word, history might have been other than it is; but then it would have been history ordered by men, not God—something that never was, and never will be. A confusion fell upon him; he knew not how, though afterwards he attributed it to the Nazarene; for when the Nazarene was risen, he understood the death was necessary to faith in the resurrection, without which Christianity would be an empty husk. The confusion, as has been said, left him without the faculty of decision; he stood helpless—wordless even. Covering his face with his hand, he shook with the conflict between his wish, which was what he would have ordered, and the power that was upon him.

"Come; we are waiting for you," said Simonides, the fourth time.

Thereupon he walked mechanically after the chair and the litter. Esther walked with him. Like Balthasar and his friends, the Wise Men, the day they went to the meeting in the desert, he was being led along the way.

Chapter X

WHEN the party—Balthasar, Simonides, Ben-Hur, Esther, and the two faithful Galileans—reached the place of crucifixion, Ben-Hur was in advance leading them. How they had been able to make way through the great press of excited people, he never knew; no more did he know the road by which they came or the time it took them to come. He had walked in total unconsciousness, neither hearing nor seeing anybody or anything, and without a thought of where he was going, or the ghostliest semblance of a purpose in his mind. In such condition a little child could have done as much as he to prevent the awful crime he was about to witness. The intentions of God are always strange to us; but not more so than the means by which they are wrought out, and at last made plain to our belief.

Ben-Hur came to a stop; those following him also stopped. As a curtain rises before an audience, the spell holding him in its sleep-awake rose, and he saw with a clear understanding.

There was a space upon the top of a low knoll rounded like a skull, and dry, dusty, and without vegetation, except, some scrubby hyssop. The boundary of the space was a living wall of men, with men behind struggling, some to look over, others to look through it. An inner wall of Roman soldiery held the dense outer wall rigidly to its place. A centurion kept eye upon the soldiers. Up to the very line so vigilantly guarded Ben-Hur had been led; at the line he now stood, his face to the northwest. The knoll was the old Aramaic Golgotha—in Latin, Calvaria; anglicized, Calvary; translated, The Skull.[105]

On its slopes, in the low places, on the swells and higher hills, the earth sparkled with a strange enamelling. Look where he would outside the walled space, he saw no patch of brown soil, no rock, no green thing; he saw only thousands of eyes in ruddy faces; off a little way in the perspective only ruddy faces without eyes; off a little farther only a broad, broad circle, which the nearer view instructed him was also of faces. And this was the ensemble of three millions of people; under it three millions of hearts throbbing with passionate interest in what was taking place upon the knoll; indifferent as to the thieves, caring only for the Nazarene, and for him only as he was an object of hate or fear or curiosity—he who loved them all, and was about to die for them.

---

105 Matt. 27:33.

In the spectacle of a great assemblage of people there are always the bewilderment and fascination one feels while looking over a stretch of sea in agitation, and never had this one been exceeded; yet Ben-Hur gave it but a passing glance, for that which was going on in the space described would permit no division of his interest.

Up on the knoll so high as to be above the living wall, and visible over the heads of an attending company of notables, conspicuous because of his mitre and vestments and his haughty air, stood the high-priest. Up the knoll still higher, up quite to the round summit, so as to be seen far and near, was the Nazarene, stooped and suffering, but silent. The wit among the guard had complemented the crown upon his head by putting a reed in his hand for a sceptre. Clamors blew upon him like blasts—laughter—execrations—sometimes both together indistinguishably. A man—*only* a man, O reader, would have charged the blasts with the remainder of his love for the race, and let it go forever.

All the eyes then looking were fixed upon the Nazarene. It may have been pity with which he was moved; whatever the cause, Ben-Hur was conscious of a change in his feelings. A conception of something better than the best of this life—something so much better that it could serve a weak man with strength to endure agonies of spirit as well as of body; something to make death welcome—perhaps another life purer than this one—perhaps the spirit-life which Balthasar held to so fast, began to dawn upon his mind clearer and clearer, bringing to him a certain sense that, after all, the mission of the Nazarene was that of guide across the boundary for such as loved him; across the boundary to where his kingdom was set up and waiting for him. Then, as something borne through the air out of the almost forgotten, he heard again, or seemed to hear, the saying of the Nazarene,

"I AM THE RESURRECTION AND THE LIFE."[106]

And the words repeated themselves over and over, and took form, and the dawn touched them with its light, and filled them with a new meaning. And as men repeat a question to grasp and fix the meaning, he asked, gazing at the figure on the hill fainting under its crown, Who the Resurrection? and who the Life?

"I AM,"

the figure seemed to say—and say it for him; for instantly he was sensible of a peace such as he had never known—the peace which is the end of doubt and mystery, and the beginning of faith and love and clear understanding.

From this dreamy state Ben-Hur was aroused by the sound of hammering. On the summit of the knoll he observed then what had escaped him before—some soldiers and workmen preparing the crosses. The holes for planting the trees were ready, and now the transverse beams were being fitted to their places.

"Bid the men make haste," said the high-priest to the centurion. "These"—and he pointed to the Nazarene—"must be dead by the going-down of the sun, and buried that the land may not be defiled. Such is the Law."

With a better mind, a soldier went to the Nazarene and offered him something to drink, but he refused the cup. Then another went to him and took from his neck the board with

---

106 John 11:25.

the inscription upon it, which he nailed to the tree of the cross—and the preparation was complete.

"The crosses are ready," said the centurion to the pontiff, who received the report with a wave of the hand and the reply,

"Let the blasphemer go first. The Son of God should be able to save himself. We will see."

The people to whom the preparation in its several stages was visible, and who to this time had assailed the hill with incessant cries of impatience, permitted a lull which directly became a universal hush. The part of the infliction most shocking, at least to the thought, was reached—the men were to be nailed to their crosses. When for that purpose the soldiers laid their hands upon the Nazarene first, a shudder passed through the great concourse; the most brutalized shrank with dread. Afterwards there were those who said the air suddenly chilled and made them shiver.

"How very still it is!" Esther said, as she put her arm about her father's neck.

And remembering the torture he himself had suffered, he drew her face down upon his breast, and sat trembling.

"Avoid it, Esther, avoid it!" he said. "I know not but all who stand and see it—the innocent as well as the guilty—may be cursed from this hour."

Balthasar sank upon his knees.

"Son of Hur," said Simonides, with increasing excitement—"son of Hur, if Jehovah stretch not forth his hand, and quickly, Israel is lost—and we are lost."

Ben-Hur answered, calmly, "I have been in a dream, Simonides, and heard in it why all this should be, and why it should go on. It is the will of the Nazarene—it is God's will. Let us do as the Egyptian here—let us hold our peace and pray."

As he looked up on the knoll again, the words were wafted to him through the awful stillness—

"I AM THE RESURRECTION AND THE LIFE."

He bowed reverently as to a person speaking.

Up on the summit meantime the work went on. The guard took the Nazarene's clothes from him; so that he stood before the millions naked. The stripes of the scourging he had received in the early morning were still bloody upon his back; yet he was laid pitilessly down, and stretched upon the cross—first, the arms upon the transverse beam; the spikes were sharp—a few blows, and they were driven through the tender palms; next, they drew his knees up until the soles of the feet rested flat upon the tree; then they placed one foot upon the other, and one spike fixed both of them fast. The dulled sound of the hammering was heard outside the guarded space; and such as could not hear, yet saw the hammer as it fell, shivered with fear. And withal not a groan, or cry, or word of remonstrance from the sufferer: nothing at which an enemy could laugh; nothing a lover could regret.

"Which way wilt thou have him faced?" asked a soldier, bluntly.

"Towards the Temple," the pontiff replied. "In dying I would have him see the holy house hath not suffered by him."

The workmen put their hands to the cross, and carried it, burden and all, to the place of planting. At a word, they dropped the tree into the hole; and the body of the Nazarene also dropped heavily, and hung by the bleeding hands. Still no cry of pain—only the exclamation divinest of all recorded exclamations,

"Father, forgive them, for they know not what they do."[107]

The cross, reared now above all other objects, and standing singly out against the sky, was greeted with a burst of delight; and all who could see and read the writing upon the board over the Nazarene's head made haste to decipher it. Soon as read, the legend was adopted by them and communicated, and presently the whole mighty concourse was ringing the salutation from side to side, and repeating it with laughter and groans,

"King of the Jews! Hail, King of the Jews!"[108]

The pontiff, with a clearer idea of the import of the inscription, protested against it, but in vain; so the titled King, looking from the knoll with dying eyes, must have had the city of his fathers at rest below him—she who had so ignominiously cast him out.

The sun was rising rapidly to noon; the hills bared their brown breasts lovingly to it; the more distant mountains rejoiced in the purple with which it so regally dressed them. In the city, the temples, palaces, towers, pinnacles, and all points of beauty and prominence seemed to lift themselves into the unrivalled brilliance, as if they knew the pride they were giving the many who from time to time turned to look at them. Suddenly a dimness began to fill the sky and cover the earth—at first no more than a scarce perceptible fading of the day; a twilight out of time; an evening gliding in upon the splendors of noon. But it deepened, and directly drew attention; whereat the noise of the shouting and laughter fell off, and men, doubting their senses, gazed at each other curiously: then they looked to the sun again; then at the mountains, getting farther away; at the sky and the near landscape, sinking in shadow; at the hill upon which the tragedy was enacting; and from all these they gazed at each other again, and turned pale, and held their peace.

"It is only a mist or passing cloud," Simonides said soothingly to Esther, who was alarmed. "It will brighten presently."

Ben-Hur did not think so.

"It is not a mist or a cloud," he said. "The spirits who live in the air—the prophets and saints—are at work in mercy to themselves and nature. I say to you, O Simonides, truly as God lives, he who hangs yonder is the Son of God."

And leaving Simonides lost in wonder at such a speech from him, he went where Balthasar was kneeling near by, and laid his hand upon the good man's shoulder.

"O wise Egyptian, hearken! Thou alone wert right— he Nazarene is indeed the Son of God."

Balthasar drew him down to him, and replied, feebly, "I saw him a child in the manger where he was first laid; it is not strange that I knew him sooner than thou; but oh that I should live to see this day! Would I had died with my brethren! Happy Melchior! Happy, happy Gaspar!"[109]

"Comfort thee!" said Ben-Hur. "Doubtless they too are here."

The dimness went on deepening into obscurity, and that into positive darkness, but without deterring the bolder spirits upon the knoll. One after the other the thieves were raised on their crosses, and the crosses planted. The guard was then withdrawn, and the people set free closed in upon the height, and surged up it, like a converging wave. A man

---

107 Luke 23:34.

108 Mark 15:18.

109 Balthasar, Melchior and Gaspar are the traditional names given the Three Wise Men who came from the East bearing gifts to the Christ child when he lay in a manger in Bethlehem.

might take a look, when a new-comer would push him on, and take his place, to be in turn pushed on—and there were laughter and ribaldry and revilements, all for the Nazarene.

"Ha, ha! If thou be King of the Jews, save thyself," a soldier shouted.[110]

"Ay," said a priest, "if he will come down to us now, we will believe in him."[111]

Others wagged their heads wisely, saying, "He would destroy the Temple, and rebuild it in three days, but cannot save himself."[112]

Others still: "He called himself the Son of God; let us see if God will have him."[113]

What all there is in prejudice no one has ever said. The Nazarene had never harmed the people; far the greater part of them had never seen him except in this his hour of calamity; yet—singular contrariety!—they loaded him with their curses, and gave their sympathy to the thieves.

The supernatural night, dropped thus from the heavens, affected Esther as it began to affect thousands of others braver and stronger.

"Let us go home," she prayed—twice, three times—saying, "It is the frown of God, father. What other dreadful things may happen, who can tell? I am afraid."

Simonides was obstinate. He said little, but was plainly under great excitement. Observing, about the end of the first hour, that the violence of the crowding up on the knoll was somewhat abated, at his suggestion the party advanced to take position nearer the crosses. Ben-Hur gave his arm to Balthasar; yet the Egyptian made the ascent with difficulty. From their new stand, the Nazarene was imperfectly visible, appearing to them not more than a dark suspended figure. They could hear him, however—hear his sighing, which showed an endurance or exhaustion greater than that of his fellow-sufferers; for they filled every lull in the noises with their groans and entreaties.

The second hour after the suspension passed like the first one. To the Nazarene they were hours of insult, provocation, and slow dying. He spoke but once in the time. Some women came and knelt at the foot of his cross. Among them he recognized his mother with the beloved disciple.

"Woman," he said, raising his voice, "behold thy son!" And to the disciple, "Behold thy mother!"[114]

The third hour came, and still the people surged round the hill, held to it by some strange attraction, with which, in probability, the night in mid-day had much to do. They were quieter than in the preceding hour; yet at intervals they could be heard off in the darkness shouting to each other, multitude calling unto multitude. It was noticeable, also, that coming now to the Nazarene, they approached his cross in silence, took the look in silence, and so departed. This change extended even to the guard, who so shortly before had cast lots for the clothes of the crucified; they stood with their officers a little apart, more watchful of the one convict than of the throngs coming and going. If he but breathed heavily, or tossed his head in a paroxysm of pain, they were instantly on the alert. Most marvellous of all, however, was the altered behavior of the high-priest and his following, the wise men who had assisted him in the trial in the night, and, in the victim's face, kept place by him with zealous approval. When the darkness began to fall, they began to lose their confidence.

---

110 Luke 23:37.
111 Matt. 27:42.
112 Matt. 27:40.
113 Matt. 27:43.
114 John 19:26–27.

There were among them many learned in astronomy and familiar with the apparitions so terrible in those days to the masses; much of the knowledge was descended to them from their fathers far back; some of it had been brought away at the end of the Captivity; and the necessities of the Temple service kept it all bright. These closed together when the sun commenced to fade before their eyes,[115] and the mountains and hills to recede; they drew together in a group around their pontiff, and debated what they saw. "The moon is at its full," they said, with truth, "and this cannot be an eclipse." Then, as no one could answer the question common with them all—as no one could account for the darkness, or for its occurrence at that particular time, in their secret hearts they associated it with the Nazarene, and yielded to an alarm which the long continuance of the phenomenon steadily increased. In their place behind the soldiers, they noted every word and motion of the Nazarene, and hung with fear upon his sighs, and talked in whispers. The man might be the Messiah, and then— But they would wait and see!

In the meantime Ben-Hur was not once visited by the old spirit. The perfect peace abode with him. He prayed simply that the end might be hastened. He knew the condition of Simonides' mind—that he was hesitating on the verge of belief. He could see the massive face weighed down by solemn reflection. He noticed him casting inquiring glances at the sun, as seeking the cause of the darkness. Nor did he fail to notice the solicitude with which Esther clung to him, smothering her fears to accommodate his wishes.

"Be not afraid," he heard him say to her; "but stay and watch with me. Thou mayst live twice the span of my life, and see nothing of human interest equal to this; and there may be revelations more. Let us stay to the close."

When the third hour was about half gone, some men of the rudest class—wretches from the tombs about the city—came and stopped in front of the centre cross.

"This is he, the new King of the Jews," said one of them.

The others cried, with laughter, "Hail, all hail, King of the Jews!"

Receiving no reply, they went closer.

"If thou be King of the Jews, or Son of God, come down," they said, loudly.

At this, one of the thieves quit groaning, and called to the Nazarene, "Yes, if thou be Christ, save thyself and us."

The people laughed and applauded; then, while they were listening for a reply, the other felon was heard to say to the first one, "Dost thou not fear God? We receive the due rewards of our deeds; but this man hath done nothing amiss."[116]

The bystanders were astonished; in the midst of the hush which ensued, the second felon spoke again, but this time to the Nazarene:

"Lord," he said, "remember me when thou comest into thy kingdom."[117]

Simonides gave a great start. "When thou comest into thy kingdom!" It was the very point of doubt in his mind; the point he had so often debated with Balthasar.

"Didst thou hear?" said Ben-Hur to him. "The kingdom cannot be of this world. Yon witness saith the King is but going to his kingdom; and, in effect, I heard the same in my dream."

"Hush!" said Simonides, more imperiously than ever before in speech to Ben-Hur. "Hush, I pray thee! If the Nazarene should answer—"

---

115 Mark 15:33.
116 Luke 23:40–41.
117 Luke 23:42.

And as he spoke the Nazarene did answer, in a clear voice, full of confidence:
"Verily I say unto thee, To-day shalt thou be with me in Paradise!"[118]
Simonides waited to hear if that were all; then he folded his hands and said, "No more, no more, Lord! The darkness is gone; I see with other eyes—even as Balthasar, I see with eyes of perfect faith."

The faithful servant had at last his fitting reward. His broken body might never be restored; nor was there riddance of the recollection of his sufferings, or recall of the years embittered by them; but suddenly a new life was shown him, with assurance that it was for him—a new life lying just beyond this one—and its name was Paradise. There he would find the Kingdom of which he had been dreaming, and the King. A perfect peace fell upon him.

Over the way, in front of the cross, however, there were surprise and consternation. The cunning casuists there put the assumption underlying the question and the admission underlying the answer together. For saying through the land that he was the Messiah, they had brought the Nazarene to the cross; and, lo! on the cross, more confidently than ever, he had not only reasserted himself, but promised enjoyment of his Paradise to a malefactor. They trembled at what they were doing. The pontiff, with all his pride, was afraid. Where got the man his confidence except from Truth? And what should the Truth be but God? A very little now would put them all to flight.

The breathing of the Nazarene grew harder; his sighs became great gasps. Only three hours upon the cross, and he was dying!

The intelligence was carried from man to man, until every one knew it; and then everything hushed; the breeze faltered and died; a stifling vapor loaded the air; heat was superadded to darkness; nor might any one unknowing the fact have thought that off the hill, out under the overhanging pall, there were three millions of people waiting awe-struck what should happen next—they were so still!

Then there went out through the gloom, over the heads of such as were on the hill within hearing of the dying man, a cry of despair, if not reproach:

"My God! my God! why hast thou forsaken me?"[119]

The voice startled all who heard it. One it touched uncontrollably.

The soldiers in coming had brought with them a vessel of wine and water, and set it down a little way from Ben-Hur. With a sponge dipped into the liquor, and put on the end of a stick, they could moisten the tongue of a sufferer at their pleasure. Ben-Hur thought of the draught he had had at the well near Nazareth; an impulse seized him; catching up the sponge, he dipped it into the vessel, and started for the cross.

"Let him be!" the people in the way shouted, angrily. "Let him be!"

Without minding them, he ran on, and put the sponge to the Nazarene's lips.

Too late, too late!

The face then plainly seen by Ben-Hur, bruised and black with blood and dust as it was, lighted nevertheless with a sudden glow; the eyes opened wide, and fixed upon some one visible to them alone in the far heavens; and there were content and relief, even triumph, in the shout the victim gave.

"It is finished! It is finished!"[120]

---

118 Luke 23:43.
119 Mark 15:34.
120 John 19:30.

So a hero, dying in the doing a great deed, celebrates his success with a last cheer.

The light in the eyes went out; slowly the crowned head sank upon the laboring breast. Ben-Hur thought the struggle over; but the fainting soul recollected itself, so that he and those around him caught the other and last words, spoken in a low voice, as if to one listening close by:

"Father, into thy hands I commend my spirit."[121]

A tremor shook the tortured body; there was a scream of fiercest anguish, and the mission and the earthly life were over at once. The heart, with all its love, was broken; for of that, O reader, the man died!

Ben-Hur went back to his friends, saying, simply, "It is over; he is dead."

In a space incredibly short the multitude was informed of the circumstance. No one repeated it aloud; there was a murmur which spread from the knoll in every direction; a murmur that was little more than a whispering, "He is dead! he is dead!" and that was all. The people had their wish; the Nazarene was dead; yet they stared at each other aghast. His blood was upon them![122] And while they stood staring at each other, the ground commenced to shake; each man took hold of his neighbor to support himself; in a twinkling the darkness disappeared, and the sun came out; and everybody, as with the same glance, beheld the crosses upon the hill all reeling drunken-like in the earthquake. They beheld all three of them; but the one in the centre was arbitrary; it alone would be seen; and for that it seemed to extend itself upwards, and lift its burden, and swing it to and fro higher and higher in the blue of the sky. And every man among them who had jeered at the Nazarene; every one who had struck him; every one who had voted to crucify him; every one who had marched in the procession from the city; every one who had in his heart wished him dead, and they were as ten to one, felt that he was in some way individually singled out from the many, and that if he would live he must get away quickly as possible from that menace in the sky. They started to run; they ran with all their might; on horseback, and camels, and in chariots they ran, as well as on foot; but then, as if it were mad at them for what they had done, and had taken up the cause of the unoffending and friendless dead, the earthquake pursued them, and tossed them about, and flung them down, and terrified them yet more by the horrible noise of great rocks grinding and rending beneath them. They beat their breasts and shrieked with fear. His blood was upon them! The home-bred and the foreign, priest and layman, beggar, Sadducee, Pharisee, were overtaken in the race, and tumbled about indiscriminately. If they called on the Lord, the outraged earth answered for him in fury, and dealt them all alike. It did not even know wherein the high-priest was better than his guilty brethren; overtaking him, it tripped him up also, and smirched the fringing of his robe, and filled the golden bells with sand, and his mouth with dust. He and his people were alike in the one thing at least—the blood of the Nazarene was upon them all!

When the sunlight broke upon the crucifixion, the mother of the Nazarene, the disciple, and the faithful women of Galilee, the centurion and his soldiers, and Ben-Hur and his party, were all who remained upon the hill. These had not time to observe the flight of the multitude; they were too loudly called upon to take care of themselves.

"Seat thyself here," said Ben-Hur to Esther, making a place for her at her father's feet. "Now cover thine eyes, and look not up; but put thy trust in God, and the spirit of yon just man so foully slain."

"Nay," said Simonides, reverently, "let us henceforth speak of him as the Christ."

---

121 Luke 23:46.
122 Matt. 27:54.

"Be it so," said Ben-Hur.

Presently a wave of the earthquake struck the hill. The shrieks of the thieves upon the reeling crosses were terrible to hear. Though giddy with the movements of the ground, Ben-Hur had time to look at Balthasar, and beheld him prostrate and still. He ran to him and called—there was no reply. The good man was dead! Then Ben-Hur remembered to have heard a cry in answer, as it were, to the scream of the Nazarene in his last moment; but he had not looked to see from whom it had proceeded; and ever after he believed the spirit of the Egyptian accompanied that of his Master over the boundary into the kingdom of Paradise. The idea rested not only upon the cry heard, but upon the exceeding fitness of the distinction. If faith were worthy reward in the person of Gaspar, and love in that of Melchior, surely he should have some special meed who through a long life had so excellently illustrated the three virtues in combination—Faith, Love, and Good Works.

The servants of Balthasar had deserted their master; but when all was over, the two Galileans bore the old man in his litter back to the city.

It was a sorrowful procession that entered the south gate of the palace of the Hurs about the set of sun that memorable day. About the same hour the body of the Christ was taken down from the cross.

The remains of Balthasar were carried to the guest-chamber. All the servants hastened weeping to see him; for he had the love of every living thing with which he had in anywise to do; but when they beheld his face, and the smile upon it, they dried their tears, saying, "It is well. He is happier this evening than when he went out in the morning."

Ben-Hur would not trust a servant to inform Iras what had befallen her father. He went himself to see her and bring her to the body. He imagined her grief; she would now be alone in the world; it was a time to forgive and pity her. He remembered he had not asked why she was not of the party in the morning, or where she was; he remembered he had not thought of her; and, from shame, he was ready to make any amends, the more so as he was about to plunge her into such acute grief.

He shook the curtains of her door; and though he heard the ringing of the little bells echoing within, he had no response; he called her name, and again he called—still no answer. He drew the curtain aside and went into the room; she was not there. He ascended hastily to the roof in search of her; nor was she there. He questioned the servants; none of them had seen her during the day. After a long quest everywhere through the house, Ben-Hur returned to the guest-chamber, and took the place by the dead which should have been hers; and he bethought him there how merciful the Christ had been to his aged servant. At the gate of the kingdom of Paradise happily the afflictions of this life, even its desertions, are left behind and forgotten by those who go in and rest.

When the gloom of the burial was nigh gone, on the ninth day after the healing, the law being fulfilled, Ben-Hur brought his mother and Tirzah home; and from that day, in that house the most sacred names possible of utterance by men were always coupled worshipfully together,

God the Father and Christ the Son

About five years after the crucifixion, Esther, the wife of Ben-Hur, sat in her room in the beautiful villa by Misenum. It was noon, with a warm Italian sun making summer for the roses and vines outside. Everything in the apartment was Roman, except that Esther wore the garments of a Jewish matron. Tirzah and two children at play upon a lion's skin on the floor were her companions; and one had only to observe how carefully she watched them to know that the little ones were hers.

Time had treated her generously. She was more than ever beautiful, and in becoming mistress of the villa she had realized one of her cherished dreams.

In the midst of this simple, home-like scene, a servant appeared in the doorway, and spoke to her.

"A woman in the atrium to speak with the mistress."

"Let her come. I will receive her here."

Presently the stranger entered. At sight of her the Jewess arose, and was about to speak; then she hesitated, changed color, and finally drew back, saying, "I have known you, good woman. You are—"

"I was Iras, the daughter of Balthasar."

Esther conquered her surprise, and bade the servant bring the Egyptian a seat.

"No," said Iras, coldly. "I will retire directly."

The two gazed at each other. We know what Esther presented—a beautiful woman, a happy mother, a contented wife. On the other side, it was very plain that fortune had not dealt so gently with her former rival. The tall figure remained with some of its grace; but an evil life had tainted the whole person. The face was coarse; the large eyes were red and pursed beneath the lower lids; there was no color in her cheeks. The lips were cynical and hard, and general neglect was leading rapidly to premature old age. Her attire was ill chosen and draggled. The mud of the road clung to her sandals. Iras broke the painful silence.

"These are thy children?"

Esther looked at them, and smiled.

"Yes. Will you not speak to them?"

"I would scare them," Iras replied. Then she drew closer to Esther, and, seeing her shrink, said, "Be not afraid. Give thy husband a message for me. Tell him his enemy is dead, and that for the much misery he brought me I slew him."

"His enemy!"

"The Messala. Further, tell thy husband that for the harm I sought to do him I have been punished until even he would pity me."

Tears arose in Esther's eyes, and she was about to speak.

"Nay," said Iras, "I do not want pity or tears. Tell him, finally, I have found that to be a Roman is to be a brute. Farewell."

She moved to go. Esther followed her.

"Stay, and see my husband. He has no feeling against you. He sought for you everywhere. He will be your friend. I will be your friend. We are Christians."

The other was firm.

"No; I am what I am of choice. It will be over shortly."

"But"—Esther hesitated—"have we nothing you would wish; nothing to—to—"

The countenance of the Egyptian softened; something like a smile played about her lips. She looked at the children upon the floor.

"There is something," she said.

Esther followed her eyes, and with quick perception answered, "It is yours."

Iras went to them, and knelt on the lion's skin, and kissed them both. Rising slowly, she looked at them; then passed to the door and out of it without a parting word. She walked rapidly, and was gone before Esther could decide what to do.

Ben-Hur, when he was told of the visit, knew certainly what he had long surmised—that on the day of the crucifixion Iras had deserted her father for Messala. Nevertheless, he set out immediately and hunted for her vainly; they never saw her more, or heard of her. The blue bay, with all its laughing under the sun, has yet its dark secrets. Had it a tongue, it might tell us of the Egyptian.

Simonides lived to be a very old man. In the tenth year of Nero's reign,[123] he gave up the business so long centred in the warehouse at Antioch. To the last he kept a clear head and a good heart, and was successful.

One evening, in the year named, he sat in his arm-chair on the terrace of the warehouse. Ben-Hur and Esther, and their three children, were with him. The last of the ships swung at mooring in the current of the river; all the rest had been sold. In the long interval between this and the day of the crucifixion but one sorrow had befallen them: that was when the mother of Ben-Hur died; and then and now their grief would have been greater but for their Christian faith.

The ship spoken of had arrived only the day before, bringing intelligence of the persecution of Christians begun by Nero in Rome, and the party on the terrace were talking of the news when Malluch, who was still in their service, approached and delivered a package to Ben-Hur.

"Who brings this?" the latter asked, after reading.

"An Arab."

"Where is he?"

"He left immediately."

"Listen," said Ben-Hur to Simonides.

He read then the following letter:

"I, Ilderim, the son of Ilderim the Generous, and sheik of the tribe of Ilderim, to Judah, son of Hur.

"Know, O friend of my father's, how my father loved you. Read what is herewith sent, and you will know. His will is my will; therefore what he gave is thine.

"All the Parthians took from him in the great battle in which they slew him I have retaken—this writing, with other things, and vengeance, and all the brood of that Mira who in his time was mother of so many stars.

"Peace be to you and all yours.

"This voice out of the desert is the voice of

"ILDERIM, *Sheik*."

Ben-Hur next unrolled a scrap of papyrus yellow as a withered mulberry leaf. It required the daintiest handling. Proceeding, he read:

"Ilderim, surnamed the Generous, sheik of the tribe of Ilderim, to the son who succeeds me.

---

123 Nero was emperor of Rome from 54–68.

"All I have, O son, shall be thine in the day of thy succession, except that property by Antioch known as the Orchard of Palms; and it shall be to the son of Hur who brought us such glory in the Circus—to him and his forever.

"Dishonor not thy father.

ILDERIM THE GENEROUS, *Sheik.*"

"What say you?" asked Ben-Hur, of Simonides.

Esther took the papers pleased, and read them to herself. Simonides remained silent. His eyes were upon the ship; but he was thinking. At length he spoke.

"Son of Hur," he said, gravely, "the Lord has been good to you in these later years. You have much to be thankful for. Is it not time to decide finally the meaning of the gift of the great fortune now all in your hand, and growing?"

"I decided that long ago. The fortune was meant for the service of the giver; not a part, Simonides, but all of it. The question with me has been, How can I make it most useful in his cause? And of that tell me, I pray you."

Simonides answered,

"The great sums you have given to the Church here in Antioch, I am witness to. Now, instantly almost with this gift of the generous sheik's, comes the news of the persecution of the brethren in Rome. It is the opening of a new field. The light must not go out in the capital."

"Tell me how I can keep it alive."

"I will tell you. The Romans, even this Nero, hold two things sacred—I know of no others they so hold—they are the ashes of the dead and all places of burial. If you cannot build temples for the worship of the Lord above ground, then build them below the ground; and to keep them from profanation, carry to them the bodies of all who die in the faith."

Ben-Hur arose excitedly.

"It is a great idea," he said. "I will not wait to begin it. Time forbids waiting. The ship that brought the news of the suffering of our brethren shall take me to Rome. I will sail to-morrow."

He turned to Malluch.

"Get the ship ready, Malluch, and be thou ready to go with me."

"It is well," said Simonides.

"And thou, Esther, what sayest thou?" asked Ben-Hur.

Esther came to his side, and put her hand on his arm, and answered,

"So wilt thou best serve the Christ. O my husband, let me not hinder, but go with thee and help."

* * *

If any of my readers, visiting Rome, will make the short journey to the Catacomb of San Calixto, which is more ancient than that of San Sebastiano, he will see what became of the fortune of Ben-Hur, and give him thanks. Out of that vast tomb Christianity issued to supersede the Cæsars.

THE END

Chapter Eighteen

EMMA DOROTHY ELIZA NEVITTE SOUTHWORTH
(1819–1899)

E. D. E. N. Southworth began her long writing career in 1845, after her husband had deserted her to seek his fortune in South America. Initially, writing was a way to supplement her salary as a schoolteacher, as she provided for herself and her two children. Southworth's stories gained such widespread popularity that she became one of only a select number of American women writers able to make a comfortable living at their craft. Over the course of her half-century career, she wrote some sixty novels and countless short stories.

Southworth's early stories appear in a number of periodicals, including the *National Era*, the same newspaper that had introduced the world to Harriet Beecher Stowe's *Uncle Tom's Cabin*. In 1857, Southworth signed an exclusive contract to publish her works in Robert Bonner's *New York Ledger*, a weekly periodical that enjoyed a readership of some 380,000 by the 1870s. It was in the *New York Ledger* that a serialized version of *The Hidden Hand: Or, Capitola the Madcap*, first appeared in 1859. It would turn out to be Southworth's most popular work, so popular in fact that she expanded its story and turned it into a stand-alone novel published in 1888. It also appeared in over forty theatrical versions throughout the nineteenth century.

The Hidden Hand is a wonderful example of what Southworth would tell others was her early, wild work. In these early works, Southworth frequently chose to present her heroines as straining against the traditional gender roles of the period. Although she never openly presented her heroines as iconoclastic champions of what today we might call feminism, her extremely adventurous early female protagonists often displayed a pronounced desire and ability to be the equal of any man. In *The Hidden Hand*, Capitola is a young girl—much like Alger's Ragged Dick—who is forced to grow up in the slum of Rag Alley, surviving by her wits alone. At first she even dresses like a boy. As the novel proceeds, she takes part in a series of daring adventures, including rescuing damsels in distress and thwarting bandits and even murderers. In Capitola, Southworth was able to tap into some of the deepest frustrations and hopes of American women when it came to the issue of female empowerment. By creating strong female characters who were never afraid to push against the more conservative societal gender norms of her day, Southworth rose to become one of the most popular American writers of the nineteenth century.

THE HIDDEN HAND:
OR,
CAPITOLA THE MADCAP

CAPITOLA.

Frontispiece illustration of Capitola (*The Hidden Hand*, New York: G. W. Dillingham Co., 1908).

The Hidden Hand originally appeared in serialized form in 1859 in Richard Bonner's immensely successful newspaper, *The New York Ledger*. *The Ledger* reprinted the tale twice more (1868–69 and 1883) before Southworth turned the story into a book in 1888, when she slightly adjusted the text to put greater emphasis on the character of Capitola. The present text is reprinted from the first book edition, published in 1888 by G. W. Dillingham of New York.

Chapter I

The Nocturnal Visit

*** Whence is that knocking?
How is't with me when every sound appals me?
*** I hear a knocking
In the south entry! Hark!—more knocking!
—*Shakespeare*[1]

HURRICANE HALL is a large old family mansion, built of dark, red sandstone, in one of the loneliest and wildest of the mountain regions of Virginia.

The estate is surrounded on three sides by a range of steep, gray rocks, spiked with clumps of dark evergreens, and called, from its horseshoe form, the Devil's Hoof.

On the fourth side the ground gradually descends in broken rock and barren soil to the edge of the wild mountain stream known as the Devil's Run.

When storms and floods were high, the loud roaring of the wild mountain gorges, and the terrific raging of the torrent over its rocky course, gave to this savage locality its ill-omened names of Devil's Hoof, Devil's Run and Hurricane Hall.

Major Ira Warfield, the lonely proprietor of the Hall, was a veteran officer, who, in disgust at what he supposed to be ill-requited services, had retired from public life to spend the evening of his vigorous age on this his patrimonial estate. Here he lived in seclusion, with his old-fashioned housekeeper, Mrs. Condiment, and his old family servants and his favorite dogs and horses. Here his mornings were usually spent in the chase, in which he excelled, and his afternoon and evenings were occupied in small convivial suppers among his few chosen companions of the chase or the bottle.

In person, Major Warfield was tall and strongly built, reminding one of some old iron-limbed Douglas[2] of the olden time. His features were large and harsh; his complexion dark red, as that of one bronzed by long exposure and flushed with strong drink. His fierce, dark gray eyes were surmounted by thick, heavy black brows, that, when gathered into a frown, reminded one of a thunder cloud, as the flashing orbs beneath them did of lightning. His hard, harsh face was surrounded by a thick growth of iron-gray hair and beard that met beneath his chin. His usual habit was a black cloth coat, crimson vest, black leather breeches, long, black yarn stockings, fastened at the knees, and morocco slippers with silver buttons.

In character Major Warfield was arrogant, domineering and violent—equally loved and feared by his faithful old family servants at home—disliked and dreaded by his neighbors and acquaintances abroad, who, partly from his *house* and partly from his character, fixed upon him the appropriate Nickname of Old Hurricane.

There was, however, other ground of dislike besides that of his arrogant mind, violent temper and domineering habits. Old Hurricane was said to be an old bachelor, yet rumor whispered that there was in some obscure part of the world, hidden away from human sight, a deserted wife and child, poor, forlorn, and heartbroken. It was farther whispered that the elder brother of Ira Warfield had mysteriously disappeared, and not without suspicion of foul play on the part of the only person in the world who had a strong interest in his

---

1 William Shakespeare (1564–1616), *Macbeth*, 2.2.
2 Colloquial phrase for a strong and independent Scotsman.

"taking off." However these things might be, it was known for a certainty that Old Hurricane had an only sister, widowed, sick and poor, who with her son dragged on a wretched life of ill-requited toil, severe privation, and painful infirmity, in a distant city, unaided, unsought and uncared for by her cruel brother.

It was the night of the last day of October, eighteen hundred and forty-five. The evening had closed in dark and gloomy. About dusk the wind arose in the northwest, driving up masses of leaden-hued clouds, and in a few minutes the ground was covered deep with snow, and the air was filled with driving sleet.

As this was All Hallow Eve,[3] the dreadful inclemency of the weather did not prevent the negroes of Hurricane Hall from availing themselves of their capricious old master's permission, and going off in a body to a banjo break-down, held in the negro quarters of their next neighbor.

Upon this evening, then, there was left at Hurricane Hall only Major Warfield; Mrs. Condiment, his little old housekeeper; and Wool, his body-servant.

Early in the evening the old hall was shut up closely to keep out as much as possible the sound of the storm that roared through the mountain chasms, and cannonaded the walls of the house as if determined to force an entrance. As soon as she had seen that all was safe, Mrs. Condiment went to bed and went to sleep.

It was about ten o'clock that night that Old Hurricane, well wrapped up in his quilted flannel dressing-gown, sat in his well-padded easy chair before a warm and bright fire, taking his comfort in his own most comfortable bedroom. This was the hour of the coziest enjoyment to the self-indulgent old Sybarite,[4] who dearly loved his own case. And indeed every means and appliance of bodily comfort was at hand. Strong oaken shutters and thick heavy curtains at the windows kept out every draft of air, and so deadened the sound of the wind that its subdued moaning was just sufficient to remind one of the stormy weather without in contrast to the bright warmth within. Old Hurricane, as I said, sat well wrapped up in his wadded dressing-gown, and reclining in his padded easy chair, with his head thrown back and his feet upon the fire irons, toasting his shins and sipping his punch. On his right hand stood a little table with a lighted candle, a stack of clay pipes, a jug of punch, lemons, sugar, Holland gin, etc., while on the hearth sat a kettle of boiling water to help to replenish the jug if needful.

On his left hand stood his cozy bedstead with its warm crimson curtains festooned back, revealing the luxurious swell of the full feather bed, and pillows with their snow-white linen, and lambswool blankets inviting repose. Between this bedstead and the corner of the fireplace stood Old Hurricane's ancient body-servant, Wool, engaged in warming a crimson cloth nightcap.

"Fools!" muttered Old Hurricane over his punch—"jacks! they'll all get the pleurisy except those that get drunk! Did they *all* go, Wool?"

"Ebery man, 'oman and chile, sar!—'cept 'tis me and coachman, sar."

"More fools they! And I shouldn't wonder if *you*, you old scarecrow, didn't want to go too!"

"No, Marse——"

"I know better, sir! don't contradict *me!* Well, as soon as I'm in bed, and that won't be long now, you may go!—so that you can get back in time to wait on me to-morrow morning!"

---

3 Halloween.
4 A person devoted to luxury and pleasure.

"Thanky, Marse."

"Hold your tongue! You are as big a fool as the rest."

"I take this," said Old Hurricane, as he sipped his punch and smacked his lips—"I take this to be the very quintessence of human enjoyment—sitting here in my soft, warm chair before the fire, toasting my legs, sipping my punch, listening on the one hand to the storm without, and glancing on the other hand at my comfortable bed waiting there to receive my sleepy head. If there is anything better than this in this world, I wish somebody would let me know it."

"It's all werry comfortable indeed, Marse," said the obsequious Wool.

"I wonder now if there is anything on the face of the earth that would tempt *me* to leave my cozy fireside and go abroad to-night? I wonder how large a promise of pleasure or profit or glory it would take now?"

"Much as ebber Congress itse'f could give if it give you a penance for all your sarvins," suggested Wool.

"Yes, and more! for I wouldn't leave my home comforts to-night to ensure not only the pension but the thanks of Congress!" said the old man, replenishing his glass with steaming punch, and drinking it off leisurely.

The clock struck eleven. The old man replenished his glass, and while sipping its contents said:

"You may fill the warming-pan and warm my bed, Wool. The fumes of this fragrant punch are beginning to rise to my head and make me sleepy."

The servant filled the warming-pan with glowing embers, shut down the lid, and thrust it between the sheets, to warm the couch of the luxurious Old Hurricane. The old man continued to toast his feet, sip his punch, and smack his lips. He finished his glass, set it down, and was just in the act of drawing on his woolen nightcap, preparatory to stepping into his well-warmed bed, when he was suddenly startled by a loud ringing of the hall door-bell.

"What the foul fiend can that mean at this time of night!" exclaimed Old Hurricane, dropping his nightcap, and turning sharply around towards Wool, who, warming-pan in hand, stood staring with astonishment. "What does that mean, I ask you?"

" 'Deed, I dunno, sar, less it's some benighted traveler in search o' shelter out'n de storm."

"Humph! and in search of supper, too, of course, and everybody gone away or gone to bed but you and me!"

At that moment the ringing was followed by a loud knocking.

"Marse, don't less you and me listen to it, and then we aint 'obliged to sturb ourselves wid answering of it," suggested Wool.

" 'Sdeath, sir! do you think that I am going to turn a deaf ear to a stranger that comes to my house for shelter on such a night as this? Go and answer the bell directly."

"Yes, sar."

"But stop—look here, sirrah—mind, I am not to be disturbed. If it is a traveler, ask him in, set refreshments before him, and show him to bed. I'm not going to leave my warm room to welcome anybody to-night, please the Lord. Do you hear?"

"Yes, sar," said the darkey, retreating.

As Wool took a shaded taper and opened the door leading from his master's chamber, the wind was heard howling through the long passages ready to burst into the cozy bedroom.

"SHUT THE DOOR, you scoundrel!" roared the old man, folding the skirt of his warm dressing-gown across his knees, and hovering closer to the fire.

Wool quickly obeyed, and was heard retreating down the steps.

"Whew!" said the old man, spreading his hands over the blaze with a look of comfortable appreciation. "What would induce *me* to go abroad on such a night as this? Wind blowing great guns from the north-west—snow falling fast from the heavens, and rising just as fast before the wind from the ground!—cold as Lapland, dark as Erebus![5] No telling the earth from the sky. Whew!" and to comfort the cold thought, Old Hurricane poured out another glass of smoking punch, and began to sip it.

"How I thank the Lord that I am not a doctor! If I were a doctor now, the sound of that bell at this hour of night would frighten me; I should think some old woman had been taken with the pleurisy, and wanted me to get up and go out in the storm, to turn out of my warm bed to ride ten miles through the snow to prescribe for her. A doctor never can feel sure, even in the worst of weathers, of a good night's rest. But, thank heaven, I am free from all such annoyances, and if I am sure of anything in this world it is of my comfortable night's sleep," said Old Hurricane, as he sipped his punch, smacked his lips and toasted his feet.

At this moment Wool re-appeared.

"SHUT THE DOOR, you villain! Do you intend to stand there holding it open on me all night?" vociferated the old man.

Wool hastily closed the offending portals, and hurried to his master's side.

"Well, sir, who was it rung the bell?"

"Please, Marster, sir, it wer' de Reverend Mr. Parson Goodwin."

"Goodwin? Been to make a sick-call, I suppose, and got caught in the snow-storm. I declare it is as bad to be a parson as it is to be a doctor. Thank the Lord *I* am not a parson either; if I were now, I might be called away from my cozy arm-chair and fireside to ride twelve miles to comfort some old man dying of quinsy. Wool, here—help me into bed, pile on more comforters, tuck me up warm, put a bottle of hot water to my feet, and then go and attend to the parson," said the old man, getting up and moving towards his inviting couch.

"Sar! sar! stop, sar, if you *please!*" cried Wool, going after him.

"Why, what does the old fool mean," exclaimed Old Hurricane angrily.

"Sar, de Reverend Mr. Parson Goodwin say how he must see you yourse'f, personable, alone!"

"See *me,* you villain! Didn't you tell him that I had retired?"

"Yes, Marse, I tell him how you wer' gone to bed and asleep more'n an hour ago, and he ordered me to come wake you up, and say how it were a matter o' life and death!"

"Life and death? What have I to do with life and death? *I won't stir!* If the parson wants to see *me,* he will have to come up here and see me in bed," exclaimed Old Hurricane, suiting the action to the word, by jumping into bed and drawing all the comforters and blankets up around his head and shoulders.

"Mus' I fetch his reverence up, sar?"

"Yes, *I* wouldn't get up and go down to see—Washington—SHUT THE DOOR, you rascal, or I'll throw the bootjack at your wooden head!"

Wool obeyed with alacrity, and in time to escape the threatened missile.

---

5 In Greek mythology considered to be a place of darkness inhabited by the dead.

After an absence of a few minutes he was heard returning, attending upon the footsteps of another. And the next minute he entered, ushering in the Rev. Mr. Goodwin, the parish minister of Bethlehem, St. Mary's.

"How do you do? How do you do? Glad to see you, sir! glad to see you, though obliged to receive you in bed! Fact is, I caught a cold with this severe change of weather, and took a warm negus[6] and went to bed to sweat it off! You'll excuse me! Wool, draw that easy chair up to my bedside for worthy Mr. Goodwin, and bring him a glass of warm negus! It will do him good after his cold ride!"

"I thank you, Major Warfield! I will take the seat, but not the negus, if you please, to-night."

"Not the negus! Oh, come now, you are joking! Why, it will keep you from catching cold, and be a most comfortable nightcap, disposing you to sleep and sweat like a baby! Of course you spend the night with us?"

"I thank you, no. I must take the road again in a few minutes."

"Take the road again to-night! Why, man alive, it is midnight, and the snow driving like all Lapland!"

"Sir, I am sorry to refuse your proffered hospitality, and leave your comfortable roof to-night, and sorrier still to have to take you with me," said the pastor, gravely.

"Take ME with you! No, no, my good sir—no, no, that is too good a joke—ha! ha!"

"Sir, I fear that you will find it a very serious one!—Your servant told you that my errand was one of imminent urgency?"

"Yes, something like life and death——"

"Exactly—down in the cabin near the Punch Bowl, there is an old woman dying——"

"There—I knew it! I was just saying there might be an old woman dying! But, my dear sir, what's that to me? What can I do?"

"Humanity, sir, would prompt you!"

"But, my dear sir, how can I help her? I am not a physician to prescribe——"

"She is far past a physician's help!"

"Nor am I a priest to hear her confession——"

"Her confession God has already received."

"Well, and I'm not a lawyer to draw up her will!"

"No sir; but you are recently appointed one of the Justices of the Peace for Alleghany?"

"Yes! well, what of that? That does not comprise the duty of getting up out of my warm bed and going through a snow-storm to see an old woman expire."

"I regret to inconvenience you, sir; but in this instance your duty demands your attendance at the bedside of this dying woman——"

"I tell you I can't go and I won't! Anything in reason, I'll do! Anything I can send, she shall have!—Here! Wool, look in my breeches pocket and take out my purse and hand it! And then go and wake Mrs. Condiment, and ask her to fill a large basket full of everything a poor old dying woman might want, and you shall carry it!"

"Spare your pains, sir! The poor woman is already past all earthly, selfish wants! She only asks your presence at her dying bed."

"But I can't go! I! the idea of turning out of my warm bed and exposing myself to a snow-storm this time of night!"

"Excuse me for insisting, sir; but this is an *official* duty," said the parson, mildly but firmly.

---

6 A drink made with port wine, sugar and lemon.

"I'll—I'll throw up my commission to-morrow!" growled the old man.

"To-morrow you may do that! but meanwhile, to-night, being still in the commission of the peace, you are bound to get up and go with me to this woman's bedside."

"And what the demon is wanted of me there?"

"To receive her dying deposition!"

"To receive a dying deposition! Good Heaven! was she murdered, then?" exclaimed the old man, in alarm, as he started out of bed and began to draw on his nether garments.

"Be composed—she was not murdered!" said the pastor.

"Well, then, what is it? Dying deposition! It must concern a crime!" exclaimed the old man, hastily drawing on his coat.

"It *does* concern a crime."

"What crime, for the love of Heaven?"

"I am not at liberty to tell you. She will do that."

"Wool, go down and rouse up Jehu, and tell him to put Parson Goodwin's mule in the stable for the night. And tell him to put the black draught-horses to the close carriage, and light both the front lanterns—for we shall have a dark, stormy road—SHUT THE DOOR, you infernal!—I beg your pardon, parson, but that villain always leaves the door ajar after him."

The good pastor bowed gravely. And the major completed his toilet by the time the servant returned and reported the carriage ready.

It was dark as pitch when they emerged from the hall-door out into the front portico, before which nothing could be seen but two red bull's eyes of the carriage lanterns, and nothing heard but the dissatisfied whinnying and pawing of the horses.

Chapter II

The Masks

"What are these?
So withered and so wild in their attire
That look not like th' inhabitants of earth
And yet are on't?"

—Macbeth[7]

"To *the devil's* Punch Bowl"—was the order given by Old Hurricane as he followed the minister into the carriage. "And now, sir," he continued, addressing his companion, "I think you had better repeat that part of the church litany that prays to be delivered from 'battle, murder, and sudden death;'[8] for if we should be so lucky as to escape Black Donald and his gang, we shall have at least an equal chance of being upset in the darkness of these dreadful mountains."

"A pair of saddle-mules would have been a safer conveyance, certainly," said the minister.

---

7 William Shakespeare, *Macbeth*, 1.3.

8 "Battle, murder, and sudden death" is a phrase from the *American Book of Common Prayer* (1789).

Old Hurricane knew that, but though a great sensualist, he was a brave man, and so he had rather risk his life in a close carriage than suffer cold upon a sure-footed mule's back.

Only by previous knowledge of the route could any one have told the way the carriage went. Old Hurricane and the minister both knew that they drove, lumbering, over the rough road leading by serpentine windings down that rugged fall of ground to the river's bank, and that then turning to the left by a short bend, they passed in behind that range of horse-shoe rocks that sheltered Hurricane Hall—thus, as it were, doubling their own road. Beneath that range of rocks, and between it and another range, there was an awful abyss or chasm of cleft, torn and jagged rocks, opening as it were from the bowels of the earth, in the shape of a mammoth bowl, in the bottom of which, almost invisible from its great depth, seethed and boiled a mass of dark water of what seemed to be a lost river or a subterranean spring. This terrific phenomenon was called the Devil's Punch Bowl.

Not far from the brink of this awful abyss, and close behind the horse-shoe range of rocks, stood an humble log cabin, occupied by an old free negro, who picked up a scanty living by telling fortunes and showing the way to the Punch Bowl. Her cabin went by name of the Witch's Hut—or Old Hat's cabin. A short distance from Hat's cabin the road became impassable, and the travelers got out, and preceded by the coachman bearing the lantern, struggled along on foot through the drifted snow and against the buffeting wind and sleet to where a faint light guided them to the house.

The pastor knocked. The door was immediately opened by a negro, whose sex from the strange anomalous costume it was difficult to guess. The tall form was rigged out first in a long, red, cloth petticoat, above which was buttoned a blue cloth surtout. A man's old black beaver hat sat upon the strange head and completed this odd attire.

"Well, Hat, how is your patient?" inquired the pastor, as he entered, preceding the magistrate.

"You will see, sir," replied the old woman.

The two visitors looked around the dimly-lighted, miserable room, in one corner of which stood a low bed, upon which lay extended the form of an old, feeble, and gray-haired woman.

"How are you, my poor soul, and what can I do for you now I am here?" inquired Old Hurricane, who in the actual presence of suffering, was not utterly without pity.

"You are a magistrate?" inquired the dying woman.

"Yes, my poor soul."

"And qualified to administer an oath and take your deposition," said the minister.

"Will it be legal—will it be evidence in a court of law?" asked the woman, lifting her dim eyes to the major.

"Certainly, my poor soul! certainly," said the latter, who, by the way, would have said anything to soothe her.

"Send everyone but yourself from the room."

"What, my good soul, send the parson out in the storm? That will never do! Won't it be just as well to let him go up in the corner yonder?"

"No! *You* will repent it unless this communication is strictly private."

"But—my good soul, if it is to be used in a court of law?"

"That will be according to your own discretion!"

"My dear parson," said Old Hurricane, going to the minister, "would you be so good as to retire?"

"There is a fire in the woodshed, master," said Hat, leading the way.

"Now, my good soul, now! You want first to be put upon your oath?"

"Yes, sir."

The old man drew from his great coat pocket a miniature copy of the Scriptures, and with the usual formalities administered the oath.

"Now then, my good soul, begin—'the truth, the whole truth, and nothing but the truth' you know. But first, your name?"

"Is it possible you don't know me, master?"

"Not I, in faith!"

"For the love of Heaven, look at me and try to recollect me, sir! It is necessary some one in authority should be able to know me," said the woman, raising her haggard eyes to the face of her visitor.

The old man adjusted his spectacles and gave her a scrutinizing look, exclaiming at intervals:

"Lord bless my soul! it is! it is! it aint! it must! it can't be! Granny Grewell, the—the—the—midwife that disappeared from here some twelve or thirteen years ago!"

"Yes, master, I am Nancy Grewell, the ladies' nurse who vanished from sight so mysteriously some thirteen years ago!" replied the woman.

"Heaven help our hearts! And for what crime was it you ran away? Come—make a clean breast of it, woman. You have nothing to fear in doing so, for you are past the arm of earthly law now!"

"I know it, master."

"And the best way to prepare to meet the Divine Judge is to make all the reparation that you can by a full confession!"

"I know it, sir—if I had committed a crime; but I have commited no crime, neither did I run away!"

"What? what? what?—What was it then? Remember, witness, you are on your oath?"

"I know that, sir, and I will tell the truth; but it must be in my own way."

At this moment a violent blast of wind and hail roared down the mountain side and rattled against the walls, shaking the witch's hut, as if it would have shaken it about their ears.

It was a proper overture to the tale that was about to be told. Conversation was impossible until the storm raved past and was heard dying in deep, reverberating echoes from the depths of the Devil's Punch Bowl.

"It was some thirteen years ago," began Granny Grewell, "upon just such a night of storm as this, that I was mounted on my old mule Molly, with my saddle-bags full of dried yarbs, and stilled waters and sich, as I allus carried when I was out 'tendin' on the sick. I was on my way a-going to see a lady as I was sent for to tend.

"Well, master! I'm not 'shamed to say, as I never was afraid of man, beast, *nor* sperrit! and never stopped at going out at all hours of the night, through the most lonesome roads, if so be I was called upon so to do! Still I must say that jest as me and Molly my mule got into that deep, thick, lonesome woods as stands round the old Hidden House in the hollow I did feel queerish; 'case it was the dead hour of the night, and it was said how strange things were seen and hearn, yes, and done too, in that dark, deep, lonesome place! I seen how even my mule Molly felt queer too, by the way she stuck up her ears, stiff as quills. So, partly to keep up my own spirits, and partly to 'courage her, says I, 'Molly,' says I, 'what are ye afeard on? Be a man Molly!' But Molly stepped out cautious, and pricked up her long ears all the same.

"Well, master, it was so dark I couldn't see a yard past Molly's ears, and the path was so narrow and the bushes so thick we could hardly get along! but just as we came to that little creek as they calls the Spout, cause the water jumps and jets along till it empties into the Punch Bowl, and just as Molly was cautiously putting her forefoot into the water, out starts two men from the bushes and seizes poor Molly's bridle!"

"Good heaven!" exclaimed Major Warfield.

"Well, master, before I could cry out one of them willians seized me by the scruff of my neck, and with his other hand upon my mouth, he says:

"'Be silent, you old fool, or I'll blow your brains out!'"

"And then, master, I saw for the first time that *their faces were covered over with black crape.* I couldn't a-screamed if they'd let me! for my breath was gone and my senses were going along with 'em from the fear that was on me.

"'Don't struggle; come along quietly and you shall not be hurt,' says the man as had spoke before.

"Struggle! I couldn't a-struggled to a-saved my soul! I couldn't speak! I couldn't breathe! I liked to have a-dropped right offen Molly's back. One on 'em says, says he:

"'Give her some brandy!' And 'tother takes out a flask and puts it to my lips and says, says he:

"'Here drink this.'

"Well, master, as he had me still by the scruff o' the neck I couldn't do no other ways but open my mouth and drink it. And as soon as I took a swallow my breath come back and my speech.

"'And oh, gentlemen,' says I, ef it's *"your money or your life,"* you mean, I haint it about me! 'Deed 'clare to the Lord-a-mighty I haint! It's wrapped up in an old cotton glove in a hole in the plastering in the chimney-corner at home, and ef you'll spare my life, you can go there and get it,' says I.

"'You old blockhead,' says they, 'we want neither one nor 'tother! Come along quietly and you shall receive no harm. But at the first cry, or attempt to escape—*this* shall stop you!' And with that the willain held the muzzle of a pistol so nigh to my nose that I smelt brimstone, while 'tother one bound a silk hankercher 'round my eyes, and then took poor Molly's bridle and led her along. I couldn't see, in course, and I dassint breathe for fear 'o the pistol. But I said my prayers to myself all the time.

"Well, master, they led the mule on down the path until we comed to a place wide enough to turn, when they turned us 'round and led us back outen the wood, and then round and round, and up and down, and cross ways and length ways, as if they didn't want me to find where they were taking me.

"Well, sir, when they'd walked about in this 'fused way, leadin' of the mule about a mile, I knew we was in the woods again—*the very same woods and the very same path*—I knowed by the feel of the place and the sound of the bushes, as we hit up against them each side, and also by the rumbling of the Spout as it tumbled along toward the Punch Bowl. We went down and down and down, and lower and lower and lower, until we got right down in the bottom of that hollow.

"Then we stopped. A gate was opened. I put up my hand to raise the handkercher and see where I was; but just at that minute I felt the muzzle o' the pistol like a ring of ice right ag'in' my right temple, and the willain growling into my ear:

"'*If you do*——!'

"But I didn't—I dropped my hand down as if I had been shot, and afore I had seen anything, either. So we went through the gate and up a gravelly walk—I knew it by the crackling of the gravel under Molly's feet—and stopped at a horse-block, where one o' them willains lifted me off. I put up my hand again.

"'Do *if you dare*,' says t'other one, with the muzzle of the pistol at my head.

"I dropped my hand like lead. So they lead me on a little way, and then up some steps. I counted them to myself as I went along. They were six. You see, master, I took all this pains to know the house again. Then they opened a door that opened in the middle. Then they went along a passage and up more stairs—there was ten and a turn, and then ten more. Then along another passage, and up another flight of stairs just like the first. Then along another passage and up a third flight of stairs. They was alike.

"Well, sir, here we was at the top o' the house. One o' them willains opened a door on the left side, and t'other said:

"'There—go in and do your duty!' and pushed me through the door, and shut and locked it on me. Good gracious, sir, how scared I was! I slipped off the silk handkercher, and 'feared as I was, I didn't forget to put it in my bosom.

"Then I looked about me. Right afore me on the hearth was a little weeny taper burning, that showed I was in a great big garret with sloping walls. At one end two deep dormer windows, and a black walnut bureau standing between them. At t'other end a great tester bedstead with dark curtains. There was a dark carpet on the floor. And with all there were so many dark objects and so many shadows, and the little taper burned so dimly that I could hardly tell t'other from which, or keep from breaking my nose against things as I groped about.

"And what was in this room for to do? I couldn't even form an idee. But presently my blood ran cold to hear a groan from behind the curtains! then another! and another! then a cry as if some child in mortal agony, saying:

"'*For the love of Heaven, save me!*'

"I ran to the bed and dropped the curtains, and liked to have fainted at what I saw!"

"And what did you see?" asked the magistrate.

"Master, behind those dark curtains I saw a young creature tossing about on the bed, flinging her fair and beautiful arms about, and tearing wildly at the fine lace that trimed her night-dress. But, master, that wasn't what almost made me faint—it was that *her right hand was sewed up in black crape, and her whole face and head completely covered with black crape, drawn down and fastened securely around her throat, leaving only a small slit at the lips and nose to breathe through!*"

"What! take care, woman! remember that you are upon your oath!" said the magistrate.

"I know it, master! And as I hope to be forgiven, I am telling you the truth."

"Go on, then."

"Well, sir, she was a young creature, scarcely past childhood, if one might judge by her small size and soft, rosy skin. I asked her to let me take that black crape from her face and head, but she threw up her hands and exclaimed:

"'*Oh, no, no, no! for my life, no!*'

"Well, master, I hardly know how to tell you what followed—" said the old woman, hesitating in embarrassment.

"Go right straight on like a car of Juggernaut, woman! Remember— the whole truth!"

"Well, master, in the next two hours there were twins born in that room—a boy and a girl; the boy was dead, the girl living. And all the time I heard the measured tramping of one of them willians up and down the passage outside of that room. Presently the steps stopped, and there was a rap at the door. I went and listened, but did not open it.

"Is it all over?' the voice asked.

"Before I could answer, a cry from the bed caused me to look round. There was the poor masked mother stretching out her white arms towards me in the most imploring way. I hastened back to her.

"'Tell *him—no—no.*' she said.

"'Have you got through?' asked the man at the door, rapping impatiently.

"'No, no,' said I, as directed.

"He resumed his tramping up and down, and I went back to my patient. She beckoned me to come close, and whispered:

"'*Save my child! the living one I mean! hide her! oh, hide her from him!* When he demands the babe, give him the poor little dead one—he cannot hurt that! And he will not know there was another. Oh! hide and save my child!'

"Master, I was used to queer doings, but this was a little the queerest. But if I was to conceal that second child in order to save it, it was necessary to stop its mouth, for it was squalling like a wild cat. So I took a vial of paregoric[9] from my pocket and gave it a drop, and it went off to sleep like an angel. I wrapped it up warm and lay it along with my shawl and bonnet in a dark corner. Just then the man rapped again.

"'Come in, master,' said I.

"'No, bring me the babe,' he said.

"I took up the dead infant. Its mother kissed its brow, and dropped tears upon its little cold face. And I carried it to the man outside.

"'Is it asleep?' the villain asked me.

"'Yes, master'—said I, as I put it, well wrapped up, in his arms—'very sound asleep.'

"'So much the better,' said the knave, walking away.

"I bolted the door and went back to my patient. With her free hand she seized mine and pressed it to her lips, then held up her left hand and pointed to the wedding ring upon her third finger.

"'Draw it off and keep it,' she said, 'conceal the child under your shawl, and take her with you when you go! save her, and your fortune shall be made.'

"I declare, master, I hadn't time to think, before I heard one of them wretches rap at the door.

"'Come! get ready to go,' he said.

"*She* also beckoned me. I hastened to her. With eager whispers and imploring gestures she prayed me to take her ring and save her child.

"'But *you,*' said I—'who is to attend to you?'

"'I do not know or care! Save *her!*'"

"The rapping continued. I ran to the corner where I had left my things. I put on my bonnet, made a sort of sling around my neck of the silk handkercher, opened the large part of it like a hammock, and laid the little sleeping babe there. I folded my big shawl around my breast, and nobody any the wiser. The rapping was very impatient.

"I am coming,' said I.

"'*Remember!*' whispered the poor girl.

---

9 An opium-based medicine used to calm children.

"*'I will,'* said I, and went and opened the door. There stood t'other willain, with his head covered with black crape. I dreamt of nothing but black-headed demons for six months afterwards.

"'Are you ready?' says he.

"'Yes, your worship,' says I.

"'Come along, then.'

"And binding another silk handkercher round my eyes, he led me along.

"Instead of my mule, a carriage stood near the horse block.

"'Get in,' says he, holding the pistol to my ears by way of argument.

"I got in. He jumped up upon the driver's seat and we drove like the wind. In another direction from that in which we come, in course, for there was no carriage road *there.* The carriage whirled along at such a rate it made me quite giddy. At last it stopped again. The man in the mask got down and opened the door.

"'Where are you taking me?' says I.

'"Be quiet,' says he, 'or——' And with that he put the pistol to my cheek, ordered me to get out, take the bandage from my eyes, and walk before him. I did so, and saw dimly that we were in a part of the country that I was never at before. We were in a dark road through a thick forest. On the left side of the road, in a clearing, stood an old house; a dim light was burning in a lower window.

"'Go on in there,' said the willain, putting the pistol to the back of my head. As the door stood ajar, I went in, to a narrow dark passage, the man all the time at my back. He opened a door on the left side, and made me go into a dark room. Just then the unfortunate child that had been moving restlessly began to wail. Well it might, poor starved thing.

"'What's that?' says the miscreant, under his breath, and stopping short.

"It ain't nothing, sir,' says I, and 'hush-h-h' to the baby. But the poor little wretch raised a squall.

"'What is the meaning of this?' says he. 'Where did that child come from? Why the demon don't you speak?' And with that he seized me again by the scruff of the neck, and shook me.

'"Oh, master! for the love of heaven, don't,' says I, 'this is only a poor unfortunet infant as its parents wanted to get outen the way, and hired me to take care on. And I have had it wrapped up under my shawl all the time 'cept when I was in your house, when I put it to sleep in the corner.'

"'Humph—and you had that child concealed under your shawl' when I first stopped you in the woods?'

"In course, master,' says I.

"'Whose is it?'

"'Master,' says I, 'it's—it's a dead secret!' for I hadn't another lie ready.

"He broke out into a rude, scornful laugh, and seemed not half to believe me, and yet not to care about questioning me too closely. He made me sit down then in the dark, and went out and turned the key on me. I wet my finger with the paragoric and put it to the baby's lips to quiet its pains of hunger. Then I heard a whispering in the next room. Now, my eyesight never was good, but to make up for it I believe I had the sharpest ears that ever was, and I don't think anybody could have heard that whispering but me. I saw a little glimmer of light through the chinks that showed me where the door was, and so I creeped up to it, and put my ear to the keyhole. Still they whispered so low that no ears could o' heard them but my sharp ones. The first words I heard good, was a grumbling voice asking:

"'How old?'

"'Fifty—more or less, but strong, active, a good nurse, and a very light mulatto,' says *my* willian's voice.

"'Hum—too old,' says the other.

"'But I will throw the child in.'

"A low, crackling laugh the only answer.

"'You mean *that* would be only a bother. Well, I want to get rid of the pair of them,' said *my* willian, 'so name the price you are willing to give.'

'"Cap'n, you and me have had too many transactions together to make any flummery about this. *You* want to get shet o' them pair. *I* hain't no objections to turning an honest penny. So jest make out the papers—bill o' sale o' the 'oman Kate, or whatsoever her name may be, and the child, with any price you please, so it is only a make-believe price! and I'll engage to take her away, and make the most I can of them in the South—that won't be much, seeing its only an old 'oman and child—scarcely a fair profit on the expense o' takin' o' her out. Now, as money's no object to *you*, Cap'n——'

'"Very well, have your own way, only don't let that woman escape and return, *for if you do——*'

"I understand, cap'n; but I reckon you needn't threaten, for if you could blow *me*—why I would return you the same favor,' said the other, raising his voice, and laughing aloud.

'"Be quiet, fool, or come away farther—here.' And the two willians moved out of even my hearing.

"I should o' been uneasy, master, if it hadn't been the 'oman they were talking about was named *Kate*, and that warn't my name, which were well beknown to be Nancy.

"Presently I heard the carriage drive away. And almost immediately after the door was unlocked, and a great, big, black-bearded and black-headed beast of a ruffian came in, and says he:

"'Well, my woman, have you had any supper?'

"'No,' said I, 'I hain't; and ef I'm to stay here any length of time, I'd be obleeged to you to let me have some hot water and milk to make pap for this perishing baby.'

'"Follow me,' says he.

"And he took me into the kitchen at the back of the house, where there was a fire in the fireplace, and a cupboard with all that I needed. Well, sir, not to tire you, I made a nursing bottle for the baby, and fed it. And then I got something for my own supper, or rather, breakfast, for it was now near the dawn of day. Well, sir, I thought I would try to get out and look about myself, to see what the neighborhood looked like by daylight; but when I tried the door I found myself locked up, a close prisoner. I looked out of the window, and saw nothing but a little back yard, closed in by the woods. I tried to raise the sash, but it was nailed down. The black-headed monster came in just about that minute, and seeing what I was a-doing of, says he:

"'Stop that.'

'"What am I stopped here for?' says I; 'a free 'oman,' says I, 'a-'vented of going about her own business?' says I.

"But he only laughed a loud, crackling, scornful laugh, and went out, turning the key after him.

"A little after sunrise, an old, dried-up, spiteful-looking hag of a woman came in, and began to get breakfast.

"'What am I kept here for?' says I to her.

"But she took no notice at all; nor could I get so much as a single word outen her. In fact, master, the little 'oman was deaf an' dumb.

"Well, sir, to be short, I was kept in that place all day long, and when night come I was druv into a shay at the point of the pistol, and rattled along as fast as the horses could gallop over a road as I knew nothing of. We changed horses wunst or twict, and just about the dawn of day we come to a broad river with a vessel laying to, not far from the shore.

"As soon as the shay druv down on the sands, the willain as had run away with me puts a pipe to his willainous mouth and blows like mad. Somebody else blowed back from the vessel. Then a boat was put off and rowed ashore. I was forced to get into it and was follered by the willain. We was rowed to the vessel, and I was druv up the ladder on to the decks. And there, master, right afore my own looking eyes, me and the baby was traded off to the captain! It was no use for me to 'splain or 'spostulate! I wan't b'lieved. The willain as had stole me got back into the boat and went ashore. And I saw him get into the shay and drive away. It was no use for me to howl and cry, though I did both, for I couldn't even hear myself for the swearing of the captain and the noise of the crew, as they was a gettin' of the vessel under way. Well, sir, we sailed down that river and out to sea.

"Now, sir, come a strange providence, which the very thoughts of it might convert a heathen! We had been to sea about five days when a dreadful storm riz. Oh, master! the inky blackness of the sky, the roaring of the wind, the raging of the sea, the leaping of the waves, and the rocking of that vessel—and every once in a while, sea and ship all ablaze with the blinding lightning—was a thing to see, not to hear tell of! I tell you, marster, that looked like the wrath of God! And then the cursing and swearing and bawling of the captain and the crew, as they were a-takin' in of sail, was enough to raise one's hair on their head! I hugged the baby to my breast—and went to praying as hard as ever I could pray.

"Presently I felt an awful shock, as if heaven and earth had come together, and then everybody screaming, 'She's struck! She's struck!' I felt the vessel trembling like a live creetur, and the water a pouring in everywhere. I hugged the babe and scrambled up the companion-way to the deck. It was pitch dark, and I heard every man rushing towards one side of the vessel.

"A flash of lightning, that made everything as bright as day again, showed me that they were all taking to the boat. I rushed after, calling to them to save me and the baby. But no one seemed to hear me; they were all too busy trying to save themselves and keep others out of the boat, and cursing and swearing and hollering that there was no more room, that the boat would be swamped, and so on. The end was, that all who could crowd into the boat did so. And me and the baby and a poor sailor lad and the black cook were left behind to perish.

"But, marster, as it turned out, we as was left to die were the only ones saved. We watched after that boat with longing eyes, though we could only see it when the lightning flashed. And every time we saw it, it was further off. At last, marster, a flash of lightning showed us the boat as far off as ever we could see her, capsized and beaten hither and thither by the wild waves—its crew had perished.

"Marster, as soon as the sea had swallowed up that wicked captain and crew, the wind died away, the waves fell, and the storm lulled—just as if it had done what it was sent to do and was satisfied. The wreck—where we poor forlorn ones stood—the wreck that had shivered and trembled with every wave that struck it—until we had feared it would break up every minute, became still and firm on its sand-bar, as a house on dry land.

"Daylight came at last. And a little after sunrise we saw a sail bearing down upon us. We could not signal the sail, but by the mercy of Providence, she saw us and lay to, and sent off a boat, and picked us up and took us on board—me and the baby, and the cook and the sailor lad.

"It was a foreign wessel, and we could not understand a word they said, nor they us. All we could do was by signs. But they were very good to us, dried our clothes and gave us breakfast, and made us lie down and rest. And then put about and continued their course. The sailor lad—Herbert Greyson—soon found out and told me they were bound for New York. And, in fact, marster, in about ten days we made that port.

"When the ship anchored below the Battery, the officers and passengers made me up a little bundle of clothes and a little purse of money, and put me ashore, and there I was in a strange city, so bewildered I didn't know which way to turn. While I was a-standing there, in danger of being run over by the omnibuses, the sailor boy came to my side and told me that he and the cook was gwine to engage on board of another 'Merican wessel, and axed me what I was gwine to do. I told him how I didn't know what I should do. Then he said he'd show me where I could go and stay all night, and so he took me into a little by-street to a poor-looking house, where the people took lodgers, and there he left me to go aboard his ship. As he went away he advised me to take care of my money, and try to get a serv-ant's place.

"Well, marster, I aint a gwine to bother you with telling you of how I toiled and strug-gled along in that great city—first living out as a servant, and afterwards renting a room and taking in washing and ironing—aye! how I toiled and struggled—for—ten—long—years, hoping for the time to come when I should be able to return to this neighborhood, where I was known, and expose the evil deeds of them willains. And for this cause I lived on toiling and struggling, and laying up money, penny by penny. Sometimes I was fool enough to tell my story in the hopes of getting pity and help—but telling my story always made it worse for me! some thought me crazy and others thought me deceitful, which is not to be wondered at, for I was a stranger, and my adventures were indeed beyond belief.

"No one ever helped me but the lad Herbert Greyson. Whenever he came from sea, he sought me out, and made a little present to me or Cap.

"Cap, marster, was Capitola, the child. The reason I gave her that name was because on that ring I had drawn from the masked mother's hand were the two names—Eugene—Capitola.

"Well, marster, the last time Herbert Greyson came home, he gave me five dollars, and that, with what I had saved, was enough to pay my passage to Norfolk.

"I left my little Cap in the care of the people of the house—she was big enough to pay for her keep in work—and I took passage for Norfolk. When I got there I fell ill, spent all my money, and was at last taken to the poorhouse. Six months passed away before I was discharged. And then six more before I had earned and saved money enough to pay my way on here.

"I reached here three days ago, and found a wheatfield growing where my cottage-fire used to burn, and all my old cronies dead, all except Old Hat, who has received and given me shelter. Sir, my story is done— make what you can of it!" said the invalid, sinking down in her bed as if utterly exhausted.

Old Hurricane, whose countenance had expressed emotions as powerful as they were various while listening to this tale, now arose, stepped cautiously to the door, drew the bolt, and coming back bent his head and asked:

"What more of the child?"

"Cap, sir. I have not heard a word of Cap since I left her to try to find out her friends. But any one interested in her might inquire for her at Mrs. Simmons's, laundress, No. 8 Rag Alley."

"You say the names upon that ring were—Eugene—Capitola?"

"Yes, sir, they were."

"Have you that ring about you?"

"No, master. I thought it was best in case of accidents to leave it with the child."

"Have you told *her* any part of this strange history?"

"No, master, nor hinted it; she was too young for such a confidence."

"You were right! Had she any mark about her person by which she could be identified?"

"Yes, master, a very strange one. In the middle of her left palm was the perfect image of a crimson hand, about half an inch in length. There was also another. Herbert Greyson, to please me, marked upon her forearm in Indian ink her name and birthday—'Capitola, Oct. 31st, 1832.'"

"Right! Now tell me, my good soul, do you know, from what you were enabled to observe, what house that was where Capitola was born?"

"I am on my oath! No, sir, I do not *know*—but—"

"You suspect?"

The woman nodded.

"It was—" said Old Hurricane, stooping and whispering a name that was heard by no one but the sick woman.

She nodded again, with a look of intense meaning.

"Does your old hostess here, Hat, know or suspect anything of this story?" inquired Major Warfield.

"Not a word! No soul but yourself has heard it!"

"That is right! Still be discreet! If you would have the wicked punished and the innocent protected, be silent and wary. Have no anxiety about the girl! What man can do for her, will I do, and quickly! And now good creature, day is actually dawning. You must seek repose. And I must call the parson in and return home. I will send Mrs. Condiment over with food, wine, medicine, clothing, and every comfort that your condition requires," said Old Hurricane, rising, and calling in the clergyman, with whom he soon after left the hut for home.

They reached Hurricane Hall in time for an early breakfast, which the astonished housekeeper had prepared, and for which their night's adventures had certainly given them a good appetite.

Major Warfield kept his word, and as soon as breakfast was over he dispatched Mrs. Condiment with a carriage filled with provisions for the sick woman. But they were not needed. In a couple of hours the housekeeper returned with the intelligence that the old nurse was dead. The false strength of mental excitement that had enabled her to tell so long and dreadful a tale, had been the last flaring up of the flame of life, that almost immediately went out.

"I am not sorry, upon the whole, for now I shall have the game in my own hands!" muttered Old Hurricane to himself—"Ah! Gabriel Le Noir! better you had cast yourself down from the highest rock of this range and been dashed to pieces below, than have thus fallen into my power!"

Chapter III

The Quest

"Then did Sir Knight abandon dwelling,
And out he rode."
                                        —*Hudibras*[10]

PURSUANT TO THE orders of Major Warfield, the corpse of the old midwife was the next day after her decease brought over and quietly interred in the family graveyard of Hurricane Hall.

And then Major Warfield astounded his household by giving orders to his housekeeper and his body-servant to prepare his wardrobe and pack his trunks for a long journey to the north.

"What can the major be thinking of, to be setting out for the north at this time of the year?" exclaimed good little Mrs. Condiment, as she picked over her employer's shirts, selecting the newest and warmest to be done up for the occasion.

"Lord A'mighty only knows; but 'pears to me marster's never been right in his head-piece since Hallow-eve night, when he took that ride to the Witch's Hut," replied Wool, who, with brush and sponge, was engaged in rejuvenating his master's outer-garments.

But let his family wonder as they would, Old Hurricane kept his own counsel—only just as he was going away, lest mystery should lead to investigation, and that to discovery, the old man gave out that he was going north to invest capital in bank-stock, and so, quite unattended, he departed.

His servant, Wool, indeed, accompanied him as far as Tip-Top, the little hamlet on the mountain at which he was to meet the eastern stage; but there, having seen his master comfortably deposited in the inside of the coach, and the luggage safely stowed in the boot, Wool was ordered to return with the carriage. And Major Warfield proceeded on his journey alone. This also caused much speculation in the family.

"Who's gwine to make his punch and warm his bed and put his slippers on the hearth and hang his gown to de fire—that's what I want to know!" cried the grieved and indignant Wool.

"Oh, the waiters at the taverns where he stops can do that for him," said Mrs. Condiment.

"No, they can't, nuther! they don't know his ways! they don't know nuffin' 'bout him! I 'clare, I think our old marse done gone clean crazy! I shouldn't be s'prised he'd gone off to de norf to get married, and was to bring home a young wife we-dem!"

"Tut! tut! tut! such talk!—that will never do!" exclaimed the deeply-shocked Mrs. Condiment.

"Werry well! all I say is, 'Dem as libs longest will see most!' said Wool, shaking his white head. After which undeniable apothegm[11] the conversation came to a stand.

---

10 "Hudibras" is the most famous poem of the English poet and satirist Samuel Butler (1613–1680).
11 A short, clever, and instructive saying.

Meanwhile, Old Hurricane pursued his journey—a lumbering, old-fashioned stage-coach ride—across the mountains, creeping a snail's crawl up one side of the precipice and clattering thunderously down the other at a headlong speed that pitched the back-seat passengers into the bosoms of the front ones, and threatened even to cast the coach over the heads of the horses. Three days and nights of such rugged riding brought the traveler to Washington City, where he rested one night, and then took the cars for New York. He rested another night in Philadelphia, resumed his journey by the first train in the morning, and reached New York about noon.

The crowd, the noise, the hurry and confusion at the wharf almost drove this irascible old gentleman mad! "No, confound you!"

"I'll see your neck stretched first, you villain!"

"Out of my way or I'll break your head, sirrah!" were some of his responses to the solicitous attentions of cabmen and porters. At length, taking up his heavy carpet-bag in both hands, Old Hurricane began to lay about him, with such effect that he speedily cleared a passage for himself through the crowd. Then addressing a coachman who had not offended, by speaking first, he said:

"Here, sir! Here are my checks! Go get my luggage and take it to the Astor House.[12] Hand the clerk this card, and tell him I want a good room, well warmed. I shall take a walk around the city before going. And hark ye! If one of my trunks is missing, I'll have you hanged, you rogue!"

"Breach of trust isn't a hanging matter in New York, your honor," laughed the hack-man, as he touched his hat and hurried off towards the crowd collected around the bag-gage car.

Old Hurricane made a step or two, as if he would have pursued and punished the flip-pancy of the man; but finally thought better of it, picked up his portmanteau and walked up the street slowly, with frequent pauses and bewildered looks, as though he had forgotten his directions, or lost his way, and yet hesitated to inquire of any one for the obscure little alley in which he had been told to look for his treasure.

Chapter IV

Capitola

"Her sex a page's dress belied,
Obscured her charms, but could not hide."
—*Scott*[13]

"PLEASE, SIR, do you want your carpet-bag carried?" asked a voice near.

Old Hurricane looked around him with a puzzled air, for he thought that a young *girl* had made this offer, so soft and clear were the notes of the voice that spoke.

"It was I, sir! here I am, at your's and everybody's service, sir!" said the same voice.

And turning, Old Hurricane saw sitting astride a pile of boxes at the corner store, a very ragged lad, some thirteen years of age.

---

12 The first grand luxury hotel in New York City.
13 Sir Walter Scott (1771–1832), "Marmion."

"Good gracious!" thought Old Hurricane, as he gazed upon the boy, "this must be crown-prince and heir-apparent to the 'king of shreds and patches.'"[14]

"Well, old gent., you'll know me next time, that's certain!" said the lad, returning the look with interest.

It is probable Old Hurricane did not hear this irreverent speech, for he continued to gaze with pity and dismay upon the ragamuffin before him. He was a handsome boy, too, notwithstanding the deplorable state of his wardrobe. Thick, clustering curls of jet black hair fell in tangled disorder around a forehead broad, white, and smooth as that of a girl; slender and quaintly-arched black eyebrows played above a pair of mischievous, dark gray eyes, that sparkled beneath the shade of long, thick, black lashes; a little turned-up nose, and red, pouting lips, completed the character of a countenance full of fun, frolic, spirit, and courage.

"Well, governor, if you've looked long enough, maybe you'll take me into service!" said the lad, winking to a group of his fellow newsboys that had gathered at the corner.

"Dear! dear! dear! he looks as if he had never in his life seen soap and water or a suit of whole clothes!" ejaculated the old gentleman; adding, kindly,—"Yes, I reckon I will give you the job, my son!"

"*His son!* Oh, crickey, do you hear *that*, fellows? *His son!* Oh, Lor'! my governor's turned up at last. I'm his son! oh, gemini! But what did I tell you? I always had a sort of impression that I *must* have had a father in some former period of my life; and, behold, here he is! Who knows but I might have had a *mother* also? But that isn't likely. Still, I'll ask him:—How's the old woman, sir?" said the newsboy, jumping off the boxes and taking the carpet-bag in his hand.

"What are you talking about, you infatuated tatterdemalion?[15] Come along! If it weren't for pity, I'd have you put in the pillory!" exclaimed Old Hurricane, shaking his cane at the offender.

"Thanky, sir! I have not had a pillow under my head for a long time!"

"Silence, ragamuffin!"

"Just so, sir! 'a dumb devil is better than a talking one!'" answered the lad, demurely, following his employer.

They went on some distance, Old Hurricane diligently reading the names of the streets at the corners. Presently, he stopped again, bewildered, and after gazing around himself for a few minutes, said:

"Boy!"

"Yes, sir!"

"Do you know such a place as Rag Alley, in Manillo Street?"

"Rag Alley, sir?"

"Yes; a sort of narrow, dark, musty place, with a row of old, tumbledown tenements each side, where poor wretches live all huddled up together, fifty in a house, eh!—I was told I couldn't drive up it in a carriage, so I had to walk! Do you know such a place?"

"Do *I* know such a place! Do *I* know Rag Alley?—oh, my eye! Oh, he! he! he!"

"What are you laughing at *now*, you miscellaneous assortment of variegated pieces?"

"Oh! oh, dear! I was laughing to think how well I knew Rag Alley."

"Humph! you *do* look as if you were born and bred there."

---

14 Shakespeare, *Hamlet*, 3.4.
15 A person in tattered, shabby clothing.

"But, sir, I wasn't."

"Humph! how did you get into life, then?"

"I don't know, governor, unless I was raked up from a gutter by some old woman in the rag-picking line," said the newsboy, demurely.

"Humph! I think that quite likely. But now, do you say that you know where that alley is?"

"Oh, don't set me off again! Oh, he, he, he!—yes, sir, I know."

"Well, then, show me the way, and don't be a fool."

"I'd scorn to be it, sir. This is the way," said the lad, taking the lead.

They walked on several squares, and then the boy stopped, and pointing down a cross-street, said:

"There, governor, there you are!"

"There! Where? Why, that's a handsome street!" said Old Hurricane, gazing up in admiration at the opposite blocks of stately brown stone mansions.

"That's it, hows'ever. That's Rag Alley. 'Taint called Rag Alley *now*, though! It's called Hifalutin Terrace! Them *tenements* you talk of were pulled down more'n a year ago, and these houses put up in their place," said the newsboy.

"Dear! dear! dear! what changes! And what became of the poor tenants?" asked Old Hurricane, gazing in dismay at the inroads of improvements.

"The tenants?—poor wretches! How do I know? Carted away, blown away, thrown away—with the other rubbish—What became of the *tenants?*

'Ask of the winds that far around
With fragments strewed the sea'-ty!

I heard that spouted at a school exhibition once, governor," said the boy, demurely.

"Humph! well, well, the trace is lost! What shall I do?—put advertisements in all the daily papers,—apply at the chief police office. Yes, I'll do *both,*" muttered Old Hurricane, to himself. Then, speaking out, he called:

"Boy!"

"Yes, sir."

"Call me a coach."

"Yes, sir." And the lad was off like an arrow to do his bidding.

In a few moments the coach drove up. The newsboy, that was sitting beside the driver, jumped down, and said:

"Here it is, sir."

"Thank you, my son. Here is your fee," said Old Hurricane, putting a silver dollar into the lad's hand.

"What! Lor'! It an't *be*! but it *is*! He must have made a *mistake*! What if he *did*, I don't care. Yes, I do, *too.* 'Honor bright,'" exclaimed the newsboy, looking in wonder and desire and sore temptation upon the largest piece of money he had ever touched in his life.

"Governor!"

"Well, boy," said the old gentleman, with his feet upon the steps of the coach.

"You've been and done and gone and give me a whole dollar by mistake!"

"And why should you think it a mistake, you impertinent monkey?"

"Your honor didn't *mean* it!"

"Why not, you young rascal?—of course I did. Take it and be off with you!" said Old Hurricane, beginning to ascend the steps.

"I'm a great mind to!" said the newsboy, still gazing on the coin with satisfaction and desire; "I'm a *great* mind to! but I *won't*! 'Taint fair.— Governor, I say!"

"What now, you troublesome fellow?"

"Do stop a minute! *Don't* tempt me too hard! 'cause, you see, I aint sure I could keep honest, if I was tempted *too* hard."

"What do you mean now, you ridiculous little ape?"

"I mean I know you're from the country, and don't know no better, and I mustn't impose upon your ignorance."

"*My ignorance,* you impudent villain!" exclaimed the old man, with rising wrath.

"Yes, governor; you haint cut your eye teeth yet! you aint up to snuff! you don't know nothing! Why, *this* is too much for toting a carpet-bag a half a dozen squares! and it's very well you fell in with a honest lad like *me*, that wouldn't impose on your innocence! Bless you, the usual price isn't more'n a dime, or if you're rich and generous, a shilling, but——"

"What the deuce do I care for the usual price, you—you—you perfect prodigy of patches!—there, for the Lord's sake, go get yourself a decent suit of clothes. Drive on, coachman!" roared Old Hurricane, flinging an eagle[16] upon the sidewalk, and rolling off in his cab.

"Poor, dear, old gentleman! I wonder where his *keeper* is? How could he have got *loose?* Maybe I'd better go and tell the police! But then I don't know who he is, or where he's gone. But he is *very* crazy, and I'm afraid he'll fling away every cent of his money before his friends can catch him! I know what I'll do! I'll go to the stand and watch for the coach to come back, and ask the driver what he has done with the poor, dear old fellow!" said the newsboy, picking up the gold coin, and putting it into his pocket. And then he started, but with an eye to business, singing out:

"Herald! *Tribune! Express!* last account of the orful accident— steamer!" etc., etc., etc., selling his papers as he went on to the coach stand. He found the coachman already there. And to his anxious inquiries as to the sanity of the old gentleman, that Jehu replied:

"Oh, bless your soul, crazy? no! no more'n you or I. He's a real nob! a real Virginian, F. F. V.,[17] with money like the sands on the seashore. Keep the tin, lad—he knowed what he was a-doin' on."

"Oh! it—it a'most scares me to have so much money!" exclaimed the boy, half in delight, half in dismay; "but to-night I'll have a warm supper, and sleep in a bed once more! And to-morrow a new suit of clothes! So here goes——

"Herald!—*Express*—full account—the horrible murder—Bell street," etc., etc., etc., crying his papers until he was out of hearing.

Never in his life had the newsboy felt so prosperous and happy.

Chapter V

The Discovery

"And at the magistrate's command
They next undid the leathern band
That bound her tresses there,
And raised her felt hat from her head,
And down her slender form there spread
Black ringlets rich and rare."[18]

---

16 An old coin worth ten dollars.
17 First family of Virginia.
18 A variation on a passage from Sir Walter Scott's poem "Marmion."

OLD HURRICANE meanwhile dined at the public table at the Astor, and afterwards went to his room, to rest, smoke and ruminate. And he finished the evening by supping and retiring to bed.

In the morning, after an early breakfast, he wrote a dozen advertisements, and called a coach and rode around to leave them with the various daily papers for immediate publication. Then, to lose no time, he rode up to the Recorder's office to set the police upon the search.

As he was about to enter the front portal, he observed the doorway and passage blocked up with even a larger crowd than usual.

And seeing the coachman who had waited upon him the previous day, he inquired of him—

"What is the matter here?"

"Nothing, your honor, 'cept a boy tuk up for wearing girl's clothes, or a girl took up for wearing boy's, I dunno which," said the man touching his hat.

"Let me pass, then, I must speak to the chief of police," said Old Hurricane, shoving his way into the Recorder's room.

"This is not the office of the chief, sir; you will find him on the other side of the hall," said a bystander.

But before Old Hurricane had gathered the sense of these words, a sight within the office drew his steps thither. Up before the Recorder stood a lad of about thirteen years, who, despite his smart new suit of gray casinet,[19] his long rolling black ringlets, and his downcast and blushing face, Old Hurricane immediately recognized as his acquaintance of the preceding day, the saucy young tatterdemalion.

Feeling sorry for the friendless boy, the old man impulsively went up to him and patted him on the shoulder, saying:

"What! in trouble, my lad? never mind—never look down! I'll warrant ye an honest lad from what I've seen myself! Come, come! pluck up a spirit! I'll see you through, my lad!"

"'*Lad!*' Lord bless your soul, sir, *he's* no more a lad than you or I. The young rascal is a girl in boy's clothes, sir!" said the officer who had the culprit in custody.

"What—what—what!" exclaimed Old Hurricane, gazing in consternation from the young prisoner to the accuser; "what—what! my newsboy, my saucy little prince of patches, a girl in boy's clothes!!!"

"Yes, sir—a young scoundrel! I actually twigged him selling papers at the Fulton Ferry this morning! A little rascal!"

"A girl in boy's clothes! A *girl!*" exclaimed Old Hurricane, with his eyes nearly starting out of his head.

Just then the young culprit looked up in his face with an expression half melancholy, half mischievous, that appealed to the rugged heart of the old man. Turning around to the policeman, he startled the whole office by roaring out:

"*Girl* is she, sir?—then, demmy, sir! whether a girl in *boy's* clothes, or *men's* clothes, or *soldier's* clothes, or *sailor's* clothes, or, *any* clothes, or NO clothes, sir! treat her with the delicacy due to womanhood, sir! aye, and the tenderness owed to *child*hood! for she is but a bit of a poor, friendless, motherless, fatherless *child*, lost and wandering in your great Babylon! No more hard words to *her*, sir—or by the everlasting——"

"Order," put in the calm and dignified Recorder.

---

19 A lightweight twill cloth usually used to make trousers.

Old Hurricane, though his face was still purple, his veins swollen and his eyeballs glaring with anger, immediately recovered himself, turned and bowed to the Recorder and said:

"Yes, sir, I will keep order, if you'll make that brute of a policeman reform his language."

And so saying, Old Hurricane subsided into a seat, immediately behind the child, to watch the examination.

"What'll they do with her, do you think?" he inquired of a bystander.

"Send her *up*, in course."

"*Up?*—where?"

"To Blackwell's Island[20]—to the work'us, in course."

"To the *work*-house—*her*, that *child?*—the wretches! Um-m-m-me! Oh-h-h-h!" groaned Old Hurricane, stooping and burying his shaggy, gray head in his great hands.

He felt his shoulder touched, and looking up saw that the little prisoner had turned around, and was about to speak to him.

"Governor," said the same clear voice that he had even at first supposed to belong to a girl—"Governor, don't you keep on letting out that way! You don't know nothing! You're in the Recorder's Court! If you don't mind your eye, they'll commit you for contempt!"

"Will they? Then they'll do *well*, lad! *lass*, I mean, I plead guilty to contempt. Send a child like *you* to the——! They *shan't do it!* Simply, they *shan't do it!* I—Major Warfield, of Virginia—tell you so, my boy—*girl*, I mean!"

"But, you innocent old lion, instead of freeing *me*, you'll find *yourself* shut up between four walls, and very narrow ones at that, *I* tell you! You'll think yourself in a coffin! Governor, they call it—*The Tombs!*"[21] whispered the child.

"Attention!" said the clerk.

The little prisoner turned and faced the court. And the "old lion" buried his shaggy, gray head and beard in his hands, and groaned aloud.

"Now, then, what is your name, my lad—my *girl*, I should say?" inquired the clerk.

"Capitola, sir."

Old Hurricane pricked up his ears and raised his head, muttering to himself—"*Cap-it-o-la!* That's a very odd name. Can't surely be *two* in the world of the same. *Cap-it-o-la!*—if it should be *my* Capitola, after all? I shouldn't wonder at all! I'll listen, and say nothing." And with this wise resolution Old Hurricane again dropped his head upon his hands.

"You say your name is Capitola—Capitola what?" inquired the clerk, continuing the examination.

"Nothing, sir."

"Nothing! What do you mean?"

"I have no name but Capitola, sir!"

"Who is your father?"

"Never had any that I know, sir."

"Your mother?"

"Never had a mother either, sir, as ever I heard."

"Where do you live?"

"About in spots, in the city, sir."

---

20 A narrow island in New York City's East River, Blackwell's Island contained a number of buildings, including a prison, as well as an insane asylum and a hospital.

21 Reference to the New York City's prison located in lower Manhattan.

"Oh—oh—oh!" groaned Old Hurricane within his hands.

"What is your calling?" inquired the clerk.

"Selling newspapers, carrying portmanteaus and packages, sweeping before doors, clearing off snow, blacking boots, and so on."

"Little odd jobs in general, eh?"

"Yes, sir, anything that I can turn my hand to, and get to do."

"Boy—*girl* I should say—what tempted you to put yourself into male attire?"

"Sir?"

"In boy's clothes, then?"

"Oh, yes—*want*, sir—and—and *danger*, sir," cried the little prisoner, putting her hands to a face crimson with blushes, and for the first time since her arrest upon the eve of sobbing.

"Oh—oh—oh!" groaned Old Hurricane from his chair.

"Want? Danger! How is that?" continued the clerk.

"Your honor mightn't like to know."

"By all means. It is, in fact, necessary that you should give an account of yourself," said the clerk.

Old Hurricane once more raised his head, opened his ears, and gave close attention.

One circumstance he had particularly remarked—the language used by the poor child during her examination was much superior to the slang she had previously affected, to support her assumed character of newsboy.

"Well, well—why do you pause? Go on—go on my good boy—*girl* I mean," said the Recorder, in a tone of kind encouragement.

Chapter VI

A Short, Sad Story

"Ah! poverty is a weary thing,
It burdeneth the brain.
It maketh even the little child
To murmur and complain."

"IT IS NOT much I have to tell," began Capitola. "I was brought up in Rag Alley and its neighborhood, by an old woman named Nancy Grewell."

"Ah!" ejaculated Old Hurricane.

"She was a washerwoman, and rented one scantily-furnished room from a poor family named Simmons."

"Oh!" cried Old Hurricane.

"Granny, as I called her, was very good to me, and I never suffered cold, nor hunger, until about eighteen months ago, when Granny took it into her head to go down to Virginia."

"Humph!" exclaimed Old Hurricane.

"When Granny went away, she left me a little money and some good clothes, and told me to be sure to stay with the people where she left me, for that she would be back in about a month. But, your honor, that was the very last I ever saw or heard of poor Granny. She never came back again; and by that I know she must have died."

"Ah-h-h!" breathed the old man, puffing fast.

"The first month or two after Granny left, I did well enough. And then, when the little money was all gone, I eat with the Simmons's, and did little odd jobs for my food. But by and by Mr. Simmons got out of work, and the family fell into want, and they wished me to go out and beg for them. *I just couldn't do that;* and so they told me I should look out for myself."

"Were there no customers of your grandmother that you could have applied to for employment?" asked the Recorder.

"No, sir. My Granny's customers were mostly boarders at the small taverns, and they were always changing. I did apply to two or three houses where the landladies knew Granny; but they didn't want me."

"*Oh-h-h!*" groaned Major Warfield, in the tone of one in great pain.

"I wouldn't have that old fellow's conscience for a good deal," whispered a spectator, "for, as sure as shooting, that gal's his unlawful child."

"Well—go on. What next?" asked the clerk.

"Well, sir, though the Simmons's had nothing to give me except a crust now and then, they still let me sleep in the house, for the little jobs I could do for them. But at last Simmons got work on the railroad a way off somewhere, and they all moved away from the city."

"And you were left alone?"

"Yes, sir, I was left alone in the empty, unfurnished house. Still it was a *shelter*, and I was glad of it, and I dreaded the time when it would be rented by another tenant, and I should be turned into the street."

"Oh! oh! oh, Lord!" groaned the major.

"But it was never rented again; for the word went around that the whole row was to be pulled down; and so I thought I had leave to stay, at least as long as the *rats* did," continued Capitola, with somewhat of her natural roguish humor twinkling in her dark, gray eyes.

"But how did you get your bread?" inquired the Recorder.

"Did not get it at all, sir. *Bread* was too dear! I sold my clothes, piece by piece, to the old man, over the way, and bought corn meal, and picked up trash to make a fire, and cooked a little mush every day in an old tin can that had been left behind. And so I lived on for two or three weeks. And then when my clothes were all gone—except the suit I had upon my back—and my meal was almost out, instead of making *mush* every day I economized, and made *gruel*."

"But my boy—*my good girl*, I mean—before you became so destitute, you should have found *some*thing or other to do," said the Recorder.

"Sir, I was trying to get jobs every hour in the day. I'd have done *any*thing honest. I went around to all the houses Granny knew, but they didn't want a girl. Some of the good-natured landlords said, if I was a *boy* now, they could keep me opening oysters, but as I was a *girl*, they had no work for me. I even went to the offices to get papers to sell, but they told me that crying papers was not proper work for a girl. I even went down to the ferry-boats and watched for the passengers coming ashore, and ran and offered to carry their carpet-bags or portmanteaus; but some growled at me, and others laughed at me, and one old gentleman asked me if I thought *he* was a North American Indian, to strut up Broadway with a female behind him carrying his pack. And so, sir, while all the ragged boys I knew could get little jobs to earn bread, I, because I was a girl, was not allowed to carry a gentleman's parcel, or black his boots, or shovel the snow off a shopkeeper's pavement, or put in coal, or do *any*thing that *I* could do just as well as *they*. And so because I was a girl, there seemed to be nothing but starvation or beggary before me."

"Oh, Lord! oh, Lord! that such things should be!" cried Old Hurricane.

"That was *bad*, sir! but there was *worse* behind! There came a day when my meal—even the last dust of it, was gone! Then I kept life in me by drinking water, and by sleeping all I could. At first I could not sleep for the gnawing—gnawing—in my stomach; but afterwards I slept deeply, from exhaustion, and then I'd dream of feasts and the richest sort of food, and of eating such quantities! and really, sir, I seemed to taste it and enjoy it and get the good of it—almost as much as if it was all true! One morning after such a dream I was waked up by a great noise, outside. I staggered upon my feet and crept to the window! and there, sir, were the workmen all outside, a pulling down the house over my head!"

"Good Heaven!" ejaculated Old Hurricane, who seemed to constitute himself the chorus of this drama.

"Sir, they didn't know that I or any one was in the empty house! Fright gave me strength to run down stairs and run out. Then I stopped. Oh! I stopped and looked up and down the street! What should I do? The last shelter was gone away from me!—the house where I had lived so many years and that seemed like a friend to me, was falling before my eyes! I thought I'd just go and pitch myself into the river, and end it all!"

"That was a very wicked thought," said the Recorder.

"Yes, sir, I know it was; and besides, I was dreadfully afraid of being suffocated in the dirty water around the wharf!!!" said Capitola, with a sparkle of that irrepressible humor that effervesced even through all her trouble. "Well, sir, the hand that feeds young ravens kept me from dying that day. I found a five-cent piece in the street, and resolved not to smother myself in the river mud as long as it lasted. So I bought a muffin, ate it, and went down to the wharf to look for a job. I looked all day, but found none, and when night came I went into a lumber-yard and hid myself behind a pile of planks that kept the wind off me, and I went to sleep and dreamed a beautiful dream of living in a handsome house, with friends all around me, and everything good to eat, and drink, and wear!"

"Poor, poor child; but your dream may come true yet!" muttered Old Hurricane to himself.

"Well, your Honor, next day I spent another penny out of my half-dime, and looked in vain for work all day, and slept at night in a broken-down omnibus that had happened to be left on the stand. And so, not to tire your patience, a whole week passed away. I lived on my half-dime, spending a penny a day for a muffin, until the last penny was gone, and sleeping at night wherever I could—sometimes under the front stoop of a house, sometimes in an old broken carriage, and sometimes behind a pile of boxes on the sidewalk!"

"That was a dreadful exposure for a young girl," said the Recorder.

A burning blush flamed up over the young creature's cheek, as she answered:

"Yes, sir, that was the worst of all; that finally drove me to putting on boy's clothes."

"Let us hear all about it."

"Oh, sir—I can't—I—how can I? Well, being always exposed, sleeping out-doors, I was often in danger from bad boys and bad men," said Capitola, and dropping her head upon her breast, and covering her crimson cheeks with her hands, for the first time she burst into tears and sobbed aloud.

"Come, come, my little man!—my good little *woman*, I mean— don't take it so to heart! You couldn't help it!" said Old Hurricane, with raindrops glittering even in his own stormy eyes.

Capitola looked up with her whole countenance flashing with spirit, and exclaimed, "Oh! but I took care of myself, sir! I did, indeed, your Honor! You mustn't, either you or the old gentleman, dare to think but what I did."

"Oh, of course! of course!" said a bystander, laughing.

Old Hurricane sprung up, bringing his feet down upon the floor with a resound that made the great hall ring again, exclaiming:

"What do you mean by 'of course,' 'of course,' you villain? Demmy! *I'll swear* she took care of herself, you varlet; and if any man dares to hint otherwise, I'll ram his falsehood down his throat with the point of my walking-stick, and make him swallow both!"

"Order, order!" said the clerk.

Old Hurricane immediately wheeled to the right-about, faced and saluted the bench in military fashion, and then said:

"Yes, sir! I'll regard order! but, in the meanwhile, if the court does not protect this child from insult, I must, order or no order!" and with that the old gentleman once more subsided into his seat.

"Governor, don't you be so noisy! You'll get yourself stopped up into a jug next! Why, you remind me of an uproarious old fellow poor Granny used to talk about, that they called Old Hurricane, because he was so stormy!" whispered Capitola, turning towards him.

"Humph! *she's heard of me*, then!" muttered the old gentleman, to himself.

"Well, sir—I mean Miss—go on!" said the clerk, addressing Capitola.

"Yes, sir. Well, your Honor, at the end of five days, being a certain Thursday morning, when I couldn't get a job of work for love nor money, when my last penny was spent for my last roll—and my last roll was eaten up—and I was dreading the gnawing hunger by day, and the horrid perils of the night, I thought to myself *if I were only a boy*, I might carry packages, and shovel in coal, and do lots of jobs by day, and sleep without terror by night! And then I felt bitter against fate for not making me a boy! And so thinking and thinking and thinking, I wandered on until I found myself in Rag Alley, where I used to live, standing right between the pile of broken bricks, plaster, and lumber, that used to be my home, and the old pawnbroker's shop where I sold my clothes for meal. And then, all of a sudden, a bright thought struck me: *and I made up my mind to be a boy!*"

"Made up your mind to be a boy!"

"Yes, sir! for it was so easy! I wondered how I came to be so stupid as not to have thought of it before! I just ran across to the old shop, and offered to swap my suit of girl's clothes, that was good, though dirty, for *any*, even the raggedest suit of boy's clothes he had, whether they'd fit me or not, so they would only stay on me. The old fellow put his finger to his nose, as if he thought I'd been stealing and wanted to dodge the police. So he took down an old, not very ragged, suit that he said would fit me, and opened a door, and told me to go in his daughter's room and put 'em on.

"Well! not to tire your honors, I went into that little back parlor *a girl*, and I came out *a boy*, with a suit of pants and jacket, with my hair cut short and a cap on my head! The pawnbroker gave me a penny roll and a six-pence for my black ringlets."

"All seemed grist that came to his mill!" said Old Hurricane.

"Yes, Governor, he was a dealer in general. Well, the first thing I did was to hire myself to him, at a sixpence a day, and find myself, to shovel in his coal. That didn't take me but a day. So at night he paid me, and I slept in peace behind a stack of boxes. Next morning I was up before the sun, and down to the office of the little penny paper, the 'Morning Star.' I bought two dozen of 'em, and ran as fast as I could to the ferry-boats to sell to the early passengers. Well, sir, in an hour's time I had sold out, and pocketed just two shillings, and felt myself on the high road to fortune!"

"And so that was the way by which you came to put yourself in male attire?"

"Yes, sir! and the only thing that made me feel sorry, was to see what a fool I had been, not to turn to a boy before, when it was so easy! And from that day forth I was happy and prosperous! I found plenty to do! I carried carpet-bags, held horses, put in coal, cleaned sidewalks, blacked gentlemen's boots, and did everything an honest lad could turn his hand to! And so for more'n a year I was as happy as a king, and should have kept on so, only I forgot and let my hair grow, and instead of cutting it off, just tucked it up under my cap; and so this morning, on the ferry-boat, in a high breeze, the *wind blowed off my cap* and the *policeman blowed on me!*"

"Twasn't altogether her long hair, your honor; for I had seen her before, having known her when she lived with old Mrs. Grewell, in Rag Alley," interrupted the officer.

"You may sit down my child," said the Recorder, in a tone of encouragement.

Chapter VII

Metamorphosis of the Newsboy

With caution judge of probability.
Things deemed unlikely, e'en impossible,
Experience oft hath proved to be true.
                                    —*Shakespeare*[22]

"WHAT SHALL WE do with her?" inquired the Recorder, *sotto voce*, of a brother magistrate who appeared to be associated with him on the bench.

"Send her to the Refuge," replied the other, in the same tone.

"What are they consulting about?" asked Old Hurricane, whose ears were not of the best.

"They are talking of sending her to the Refuge," answered a bystander.

"Refuge? Is there a Refuge for destitute children in New York? Then Babylon is not so bad as I thought it. What is this Refuge?"

"It is a prison where juvenile delinquents are trained to habits of—"

"A prison! send *her* to a prison! never!" burst forth Old Hurricane, rising and marching up to the Recorder.

He stood hat in hand before him, and said:

"Your Honor, if a proper legal guardian appears to claim this young person, and holds himself in all respects responsible for her, may she not be at once delivered into his hands?"

"Assuredly," answered the magistrate, with the manner of one glad to be rid of the charge.

"Then, sir, I, Ira Warfield, of Hurricane Hall, in Virginia, present myself as the guardian of this girl, Capitola Black, whom I claim as my ward. And I will enter into a recognizance for any sum to appear and prove my right, if it should be disputed. For my personal responsibility, sir, I refer you to the proprietors of the Astor, who have known me many years."

"It is not necessary, Major Warfield: we assume the fact of your responsibility and deliver up the young girl to your charge."

---

22 Although Southworth attributes this passage to Shakespeare, it does not appear anywhere in his standard works.

"I thank you, sir," said Old Hurricane, bowing low.

Then hurrying across the room where sat the reporters for the press, he said:

"Gentlemen, I have a favor to ask of you—it is that you will altogether drop this case of the boy in girl's clothes—I mean the *girl* in girl's clothes—I declare, I don't know what I mean! nor I shan't, neither, until I see the creature in its proper dress; but this I wish to *request* of you, gentlemen, that you will drop that item from your report, or if you must mention it, treat it with delicacy, as the good name of a young lady is involved."

The reporters, with sidelong glances, winks, and smiles, gave him the required promise, and Old Hurricane returned to the side of his *protégée*.

"Capitola, are you willing to go with me?"

"Jolly willing, governor."

"Then come along, my coach is waiting," said Old Hurricane.

And, bowing to the Court, he took the hand of his charge, and led her forth amid the ill-suppressed jibes of the crowd.

"There's a hoary-headed old sinner!" said one.

"She's as like him as two peas," quoth another.

"Wonder if there's any more belonging to him of the same sort," inquired a third.

Leaving all this sarcasm behind him, Old Hurricane handed his *protégée* into the coach, took the seat beside her, and gave orders to be driven out towards Harlem.

As soon as they were seated in the coach, the old man turned to his charge and said:

"Capitola, I shall have to trust to your girl's wit, to get yourself into your proper clothes again without exciting farther notice."

"Yes, governor."

"My boy, girl, I mean! I am not the governor of Virginia, though if every one had his rights I don't know but I should be! However, I am only Major Warfield," said the old man, naively, for he had not the most distant idea that the title bestowed on him by Capitola, was a mere remnant of her newsboys' slang.

"Now, my lad—pshaw! my lass, I mean, how shall we get you metamorphosed again?"

"I know, gov—major, I mean. There is a shop of ready-made clothing at the 'Needle Woman's Aid,' corner of the next square. I can get out there and buy a full suit."

"Very well! stop at the next corner, driver," called Old Hurricane.

The next minute the coach drew up before a warehouse of ready-made garments.

Old Hurricane jumped out, and leading his charge, entered the shop.

Luckily, there was behind the counter only one person—a staid, elderly, kind-looking woman.

"Here, madam," said Old Hurricane, stooping confidentially to her ear—"I am in a little embarrassment that I hope you will be willing to help me out of for a consideration. I came to New York in pursuit of my ward—this young girl here, whom I found in boy's clothes. I now wish to restore her to her proper dress, before presenting her to my friends, of course. Therefore, I wish you to furnish her with a half a dozen complete suits of female attire, of the very best you have that will fit her. And also to give her the use of a room and of your own aid in changing her dress. I will pay you liberally."

Half suspicious and half scandalized, the worthy woman gazed with scrutiny first into the face of the guardian, and then into that of the ward; but finding in the extreme youth of the one and the advanced age of the other, and in the honest expression of both, something to allay her fears, if not to inspire her confidence, she said:

"Very well, sir. Come after me, young gentleman—young lady, I should say." And calling in a boy to mind the shop, she conducted Capitola to an inner apartment.

Old Hurricane went out and dismissed his coach. When it was entirely out of sight, he hailed another that was passing by empty, and engaged it to take himself and a young lady to the Washington House.[23]

When he re-entered the shop he found the shopwoman and Capitola returned and waiting for him.

Capitola was indeed transfigured. Her bright black hair, parted in the middle, fell in ringlets each side her blushing cheeks; her dark gray eyes were cast down in modesty at the very same instant that her ripe red lips were puckered up with mischief. She was well and properly attired in a gray silk dress, crimson merino[24] shawl, and a black velvet bonnet.

The other clothing that had been purchased was done up in packages and put into the coach.

And after paying the shopwoman handsomely, Old Hurricane took the hand of his ward, handed her into the coach, and gave the order:

"To the Washington House."

The ride was performed in silence.

Capitola sat deeply blushing at the recollection of her male attire, and profoundly cogitating as to what could be the relationship between herself and the gray old man whose claim the Recorder had so promptly admitted. There seemed but one way of accounting for the great interest he took in her fate. Capitola came to the conclusion that the grim old lion before her was no more nor less than—her own father! poor Cap had been too long tossed about New York not to know more of life than at her age she should have known. She had indeed the *innocence* of youth, but not its *simplicity*.

Old Hurricane, on his part, sat with his thick cane grasped in his two knobby hands, standing between his knees, his grizzled chin resting upon it, and his eyes cast down as in deep thought.

And so in silence they reached the Washington House.

Major Warfield then conducted his ward into the ladies' parlor, and went and entered his own and her name upon the books as "Major Warfield and his ward Miss Black," for whom he engaged two bedrooms and a private parlor.

Then leaving Capitola to be shown to her apartment by a chambermaid, he went out and ordered her luggage up to her room, and dismissed the coach.

Next he walked to the Astor House, paid his bill, collected his baggage, took another carriage and drove back to the Washington Hotel.

All this trouble Old Hurricane took to break the links of his action and prevent scandal. This filled up a long forenoon.

He dined alone with his ward in their private parlor.

Such a dinner poor Cap had never even *smelt* before! How intensely she enjoyed it with all its surroundings!—the comfortable room, the glowing fire, the clean table, the rich food, the obsequious attendance, her own genteel and becoming dress, the company of a highly respectable guardian—all, all, so different from anything she had ever been accustomed to, and so highly appreciated.

How happy she felt! how much happier from the contrast of her previous wretchedness! to be suddenly freed from want, toil, fear, and all the evils of destitute orphanage, and to

---

23 Another prominent luxury hotel in New York City.
24 A highly prized wool.

find herself blest with wealth, leisure, and safety, under the care of a rich, good, and kind father! (for such Capitola continued to believe her guardian to be.) It was an incredible thing! It was like a fairy tale!

Something of what was passing in her mind was perceived by Old Hurricane, who frequently burst into uproarious fits of laughter, as he watched her.

At last, when the dinner and dessert were removed, and the nuts, raisins, and wine placed upon the table, and the waiters had retired from the room and left them alone, sitting one on each side of the fire, with the table and its luxuries between them, Major Warfield suddenly looked up and asked:

"Capitola, whom do you think that I am?"

"Old Hurricane, to be sure! I knew you from Granny's description, the moment you broke out so in the police office," answered Cap.

"Humph! yes, you're right; and it was your granny that bequeathed you to me, Capitola."

"Then she is really dead?"

"Yes. There—don't cry about her. She was very old, and she died happy. Now, Capitola, if you please me, I mean to adopt you as my own daughter."

"Yes, father."

"No, no,—you needn't call me father, you know, because it isn't true. Call me *uncle! uncle! uncle!*"

"Is *that* true, sir?" asked Cap, demurely.

"No, no, no; but it will *do!* it will do! Now, Cap, how much do you know? anything? Ignorant as a horse, I am afraid."

"Yes, sir, even as a *colt.*"

"Can you read at all?"

"Yes, sir. I learned at the Sunday school."

"Cast accounts and write?"

"I can keep your books at a pinch, sir."

"Humph! who taught you these accomplishments?"

"Herbert Greyson, sir."

"Herbert Greyson! I've heard that name before! here it is again. Who *is* that Herbert Greyson?"

"He's second mate on the *Susan*, sir, that is expected in every day."

"Umph! Umph!—take a glass of wine, Capitola?"

"No, sir; I never touch a single drop."

"Why? why? good wine after dinner, my child, is a good thing, let me tell you."

"Ah, sir, my life has shown me too much misery that has come of drinking wine."

"Well, well, as you please. Why, where has the girl run off to?" exclaimed the old man, breaking off, and looking with amazement at Capitola, who had suddenly started up and rushed out of the room.

In an instant she rushed in again exclaiming:

"*Oh, he's come! he's come!* I heard his voice!"

"Who's come, you madcap?" inquired the old man.

"Oh, Herbert Greyson! Herbert Greyson! His ship is in, and he has come here! he *always* comes here—most of the sea-officers do!" exclaimed Cap, dancing around until all her black ringlets flew up and down. Then suddenly pausing, she came quietly to his side, and said, solemnly:

"Uncle! Herbert has been at sea three years! he knows nothing of my past misery and destitution, nor of my ever wearing boy's clothes. Uncle, *please* don't tell him, especially of the boy's clothes!" And in the earnestness of her appeal, Capitola clasped her hands and raised her eyes to the old man's face. How soft those gray eyes looked when praying! but for all that, the very spirit of mischief still lurked about the corners of the plump, arch lips.

"Of course I shall tell no one. I am not so proud of your masquerading as to publish it. And as for this young fellow, I shall probably never see him!" exclaimed Old Hurricane.

Chapter VIII

Herbert Greyson

> "A kind, true heart, a spirit high,
> That cannot fear and will not bow,
> Is flashing in his manly eye
> And stamped upon his brow."
> —*Halleck*[25]

IN A FEW MINUTES Capitola came bounding up the stairs again, exclaiming, joyously—

"Here he is, uncle! here is Herbert Greyson! Come along Herbert! You must come in and see my new uncle!" And she broke into the room, dragging before her astonished guardian a handsome, dark-eyed young sailor, who bowed, and then stood blushing at his enforced intrusion.

"I beg your pardon, sir," he said, "for bursting in upon you in this way; but——"

"I dragged him here willy-nilly," said Capitola.

"Still, if I had had time to think, I should not have intruded."

"Oh, say no more, sir! You are heartily welcome!" exclaimed the old man, thrusting out his rugged hand and seizing the bronzed one of the youth. "Sit down, sir,—sit down! *Good Lord, how like!*" he added, mentally.

Then, seeing the young sailor still standing blushing and hesitating, he struck his cane upon the floor and roared out:

"DEMMY, SIT DOWN, SIR! When Ira Warfield *says* sit down, he MEANS sit down!"

"Ira Warfield!" exclaimed the young man, starting back in astonishment—one might almost say in consternation.

"Aye sir! Ira Warfield! that's my name! Never heard any ill of it, did you?"

The young man did not answer, but continued gazing in amazement upon the speaker.

"Nor any good of it either, perhaps,—eh, uncle?" archly put in Capitola.

"Silence, you monkey! Well, young man! well, what is the meaning of all this?" exclaimed Old Hurricane, impatiently.

"Oh, your pardon, sir! this was sudden. But you must know I had once a relative of that name—an uncle."

"*And have still, Herbert!* and have still, lad! Come, come, boy! I am not sentimental, nor romantic, nor melo-dramatic, nor anything of that sort. I don't know how to strike an attitude and exclaim—'Come to my bosom, sole remaining offspring of a dear, departed sister,' or any of the like stage-playing. But I tell you, lad, that I like your looks; and I like what I have heard of you from this girl and *another* old woman, now dead; and so—but sit down, *sit down*

---

25 Fitz-Greene Halleck (1790–1867), American poet.

demmy, sir, SIT DOWN, and we'll talk over the walnuts and the wine! Capitola, take *your* seat, too!" ordered the old man, throwing himself into his chair. Herbert also drew his chair up.

Capitola resumed her seat, saying to herself,

"Well, well, I am determined not to be surprised at anything that happens, being perfectly clear in my own mind that this is all nothing but a dream. But how pleasant it is to dream that I have found a rich uncle and he has found a nephew, and that nephew is Herbert Greyson! I do believe that I had rather *die* in my sleep than wake from *this* dream!"

"Herbert!" said Old Hurricane, as soon as they had gathered around the table, "Herbert, this is my ward, Miss Black, the daughter of a deceased friend. Capitola, this is the only son of my departed sister."

"*Hem-m-m!* we have had the pleasure of being acquainted with each other before!" said Cap, pinching up her lip, and looking demure.

"But not of really knowing who 'each other' *was*, you monkey! Herbert, fill your glass! Here's to our better acquaintance!"

"I thank you, sir. I never touch wine," said the young man.

"'Never touch wine!' here's *another*! here's a young prig! I don't believe you! yes, I do too! Demmy, sir,—if you never touch *wine* it's because you prefer *brandy!*—Waiter!"

"I thank you, sir. Order no brandy for me. If I never use intoxicating liquors, it is because I gave a promise to that effect to my dying mother!"

"Say no more—say no more, lad! Drink water, if you like. *It won't hurt you!*" exclaimed the old man, filling and quaffing a glass of champagne. Then he said:

"I quarreled with your mother, Herbert, for marrying a man that I *hated*—yes, *hated*, Herbert! for he differed with me about the tariff and—the Trinity! Oh, how I hated him, boy, until he died! and then I wondered in my soul, as I wonder even now, how I ever *could* have been so infuriated against a poor fellow now cold in his grave—as I shall be in time! I wrote to my sister, and expressed my feelings; but somehow or other, Herbert, we never came to a right understanding again. She answered my letter affectionately enough, but she refused to accept a home for herself and child under my roof, saying that she thanked me for my offer, but that the house which had been closed against her husband ought never to become the refuge of his widow. After that we never corresponded, and I have no doubt, Herbert, that she, naturally enough, taught you to dislike me."

"Not so, sir! Indeed, you wrong her! She might have been loyal to my father's memory without being resentful towards you. She said that you had a noble nature, but it was often obscured by violent passions. On her deathbed she bade me, should I ever meet you, to say that she repented her refusal of your offered kindness."

"And *consented* that it should be transferred to her orphan boy?" added Old Hurricane, with the tears like raindrops in his stormy eyes.

"No, sir, she said not so."

"But yet she would not have disapproved a service offered to her son."

"Uncle—since you permit me to call you so—I want nothing. I have a good berth in the *Susan* and a kind friend in her captain."

"You have all your dear mother's pride, Herbert."

"And all his uncle's," put in Cap.

"Hush, magpie! But is the merchant service agreeable to you, Herbert?"

"Not perfectly, sir; but one must be content."

"Demmy, sir, my sister's son *need* not be content unless he has a mind to! And if you prefer the navy—"

"No, sir. I like the navy even less than the merchant service."

"Then *what would* suit you, lad? Come, you have betrayed the fact that you are not alto-gether satisfied."

"On the contrary, sir, I told you distinctly that I really wanted nothing, and that I must be satisfied."

"And I say demmy, sir, you *shan't* be satisfied, unless you like to! Come, if you don't like the navy, what do you say to the army, eh?"

"It is a proud, aspiring profession, sir," said the young man, as his face lighted up with enthusiasm.

"Then, demmy, if you like the army, sir, you shall enter it. Yes, sir. Demmy, the adminis-tration, confound them, has not done me justice, but they'll scarcely dare to refuse to send my nephew to West Point, when I demand it."

"To West Point!" exclaimed Herbert, in delight.

"Aye, youngster, to West Point. I shall see to it, when I pass through Washington on our way to Virginia. We start on the early train to-morrow morning. In the meantime, young man, you take leave of your captain, pack up your traps and join us. You must go with me, and make Hurricane Hall your home until you go to West Point."

"Oh, what a capital old governor our uncle is!" exclaimed Cap, jumping up and clap-ping her hands.

"Sir, indeed you overwhelm me with this most unexpected kindness. I do not know as yet how much of it I ought to accept. But accident will make me, whether or no, your travelling companion for a great part of the way, as I also start for Virginia to-morrow, to visit dear friends there whose house was always my mother's home and mine, and who, since my bereavement, have been to me like a dear mother and brother. I have not seen them for *years* and before I go anywhere else, even to your kind roof, I must go *there*," said Herbert gravely.

"And who are those dear friends of yours, Herbert, and where do they live? If I can serve them, they shall be rewarded for their kindness unto you, my boy."

"Oh, sir, yes, yes! you can indeed serve them! They are a poor widow and her only son! She has seen better days; but now takes in sewing to support herself and boy. When my mother was living, during the last years of her life, when she also was a poor widow with an only son, they joined their slender means, and took a house and lived together. When my mother died leaving me a boy of ten years old, this poor woman still sheltered and worked for me as for her own son, until ashamed of being a burden to her, I ran away and went to sea!"

"Noble woman! I will make her fortune!" exclaimed Old Hurricane, jumping up and walking up and down the floor.

"Oh, *do*, sir! Oh, *do!* dear uncle. I don't wish you to expend either money or influence upon *my* fortunes; but oh! do educate Traverse! he is such a gifted lad—so intellectual! even his Sunday school teacher says that he is sure to work his way to distinction, although now he is altogether dependent on his Sunday school for his learning. Oh, sir, if you would only educate the son *he'd* make a fortune for his mother!"

"Generous boy, to plead for your friends rather than for yourself! But I am strong enough, thank God, to help you all! You shall go to West Point. Your young friend shall go to school, and then to college," said Old Hurricane, with a burst of honest enthusiasm.

"And where shall I go, sir?" inquired Cap.

"To the lunatic asylum, you imp!" exclaimed the old man; then turning to Herbert, he continued: "Yes, lad, I will do as I say; as for the poor but noble-hearted widow——"

"You'll marry her yourself, as a reward, won't you, uncle?" asked the incorrigible Cap.

"Perhaps I will, you monkey, if it is only to bring somebody home to keep you in order!" said Old Hurricane; then turning again to Herbert, he resumed: "As to the widow, Herbert, I will place her above want."

"Over my head," cried Cap.

"And now, Herbert, I will trouble you to ring for coffee, and after we have had that, I think that we had better separate, and prepare for our journey to-morrow."

Herbert obeyed, and after the required refreshment had been served and partaken of, the little circle broke up for the evening, and soon after retired to rest.

Early the next morning, after a hasty breakfast, the three took their seats in the express train for Washington, where they arrived upon the evening of the same day. They put up for the night at Brown's,[26] and the next day Major Warfield, leaving his party at their hotel, called upon the President, the Secretary of War, and other high official dignitaries, and put affairs in such a train that he had little doubt of the ultimate appointment of his nephew to a cadetship at West Point.

The same evening, wishing to avoid the stage route over the mountains, he took with his party the night boat for Richmond, where in due time they arrived, and whence they took the valley line of coaches that passed through Tip-Top, which they reached upon the morning of the fourth day of their long journey. Here they found Major Warfield's carriage waiting for him, and here they were to separate—Major Warfield and Capitola to turn off to Hurricane Hall, and Herbert Greyson to keep on the route to the town of Staunton.

It was as the three sat in the parlor of the little hotel, where the stage stopped to change horses, their adieus were made.

"Remember, Herbert, that I am willing to go to the utmost extent of my power to benefit the good widow and her son, who were so kind to my nephew in his need. Remember that I hold it a sacred debt that I owe them. Tell them so. And mind, Herbert, I shall expect you back in a week at farthest."

"I shall be punctual, sir! God bless you my dear uncle! you have made me very happy in being the bearer of such glad tidings to the widow and the fatherless. And now I hear the horn blowing—Good-bye, uncle! Good-bye, Capitola. I am going to carry them great joy, such great joy, uncle, as *you* who have everything you want, can scarcely imagine." And, shaking hands heartily with his companions, Herbert ran through the door, and jumped aboard the coach just as the impatient driver was about to leave him behind.

As soon as the coach had rolled out of sight Major Warfield handed Capitola into his carriage that had long been waiting, and took the seat by her side—much to the scandalization of Wool, who muttered to his horses:

"There, I told you so! I said how he'd go and bring home a young wife, and behold he's gone and done it!"

"Uncle!" said Capitola, as the carriage rolled lazily along—"Uncle! do you know you never once asked Herbert the *name* of the widow you are going to befriend, and that he never told you!"

"By George! that is true! how strange! yet I did not seem to *miss* the name. How did it ever happen, Capitola? did he omit it on purpose, do you think?"

---

26 Luxury hotel located in Washington, DC.

"Why, *no,* uncle! *he,* boy-like, always spoke of them as 'Traverse' and 'Traverse's mother'; and you, like yourself, called her nothing but the 'poor widow,' and the 'struggling mother,' and the 'noble woman,' and so on; and her son, as the 'boy,' the 'youth,' 'young Traverse,' Herbert's 'friend,' etc. I, for my part, had *some* curiosity to see whether you and Herbert would go on talking of them forever, without having to use their surnames. And behold he even went off without naming them!"

"By George! and so he did. It was the strangest oversight. But I'll write as soon as I get home and ask him."

"No, uncle, just for the fun of the thing, wait until he comes back and see how long it will be and how much he will talk of them without mentioning their names."

"Ha! ha! ha! so I will, Cap! so I will. Besides, whatever their names are, it's nothing to me. 'A rose by any other name would smell as sweet,' you know. And if she is 'Mrs. Tagfoot Waddle,' I shall still think so good a woman exalted as a Montmorencie[27]!—Mind there, Wool! This road is getting rough!"

"Over it now, Marster!" said Wool, after a few heavy jolts—"Over it now, Missus! and de rest of de way is perfectly delightful."

Cap looked out of the window, and saw before her a beautiful piece of scenery—first, just below them, the wild mountain stream of the Demon's Run, and beyond it the wild dell dented into the side of the mountain, like the deep print of an enormous horse's hoof, in the midst of which gleaming redly among its richly tinted autumn woods, stood Hurricane Hall.

Chapter IX

Marah Rocke

"There sits upon her matron face
A tender and a thoughtful grace,
Though very still,—for great distress
Hath left this patient mournfulness."[28]

BESIDE AN OLD, rocky road, leading from the town of Staunton, out to the forest-crowned hills beyond, stood alone, a little, gray stone cottage, in the midst of a garden enclosed by a low, moldering stone wall. A few gnarled and twisted fruit trees, long past bearing, stood around the house, that their leafless branches could not be said to shade. A little wooden gate, led up an old paved walk to the front door, on each side of which were large windows.

In this poor cottage, remote from other neighbors, dwelt the friends of Herbert Greyson, the widow Rocke and her son Traverse.

No one knew who she was, or whence, or why she came. Some fifteen years before she had appeared in the town, clothed in rusty mourning and accompanied by a boy of about two years of age. She had rented that cottage, furnished it poorly, and had settled there, supporting herself and child by needlework.

At the time that Doctor Greyson died and his widow and son were left perfectly destitute, and it became necessary for Mrs. Greyson to look out for an humble lodging where

27 French title of nobility referring to a family holding a barony.
28 Shakespeare, *Romeo and Juliet,* 2.2.

she could find the united advantages of cheapness, cleanliness, and pure air, she was providentially led to inquire at the cottage of the widow Rocke, whom she found only too glad to increase her meagre income by letting half her little house to such unexceptionable tenants as the widow Greyson and her son.

And thus commenced between the two poor young women and the two boys an acquaintance that ripened into friendship, and thence into that devoted love so seldom seen in this world.

Their households became united. One fire, one candle and one table served the little family, and thus considerable expense was saved as well as much social comfort gained. And when the lads grew too old to sleep with their mothers, one bed held the two boys and the other accommodated the two women. And despite toil, want, care—the sorrow for the dead and the neglect of the living, this was a loving, contented and cheerful little household. How much of their private history these women might have confided to each other, was not known, but it was certain that they continued fast friends up to the time of the death of Mrs. Greyson. After which the widow Rocke assumed a double burthen, and became a second mother to the orphan boy, until Herbert himself, ashamed of taxing her small means, ran away, as he had said, and went to sea.

Every year had Herbert written to his kind foster-mother, and his dear brother, as he called Traverse. And at the end of every prosperous voyage, when he had a little money he had sent them funds; but not always did these letters or remittances reach the widow's cottage, and long seasons of intense anxiety would be suffered by her for the fate of her sailor boy, as she always called Herbert. Only three times in all these years had Herbert found time and means to come down and see them—and that was long ago. It was many months over two years since they had even received a letter from him. And now the poor widow and her son were almost tempted to think that their sailor boy had quite forsaken them.

It is near the close of a late autumnal evening, that I shall introduce you, reader, into the interior of the widow's cottage.

You enter by the little wooden gate, pass up the moldering, paved walk between the old, leafless lilac bushes, and pass through the front door, right into a large, clean, but poor-looking, sitting-room and kitchen.

Everything was old, though neatly and comfortably arranged about the room: a faded home-made carpet covered the floor, a threadbare crimson curtain hung before the window, a ricketty walnut table, dark with age, sat under the window against the wall; old walnut chairs were placed each side of it; old plated candlesticks, with the silver all worn off, graced the mantel-piece; a good fire—a cheap comfort in that well-wooded country—blazed upon the hearth; on the right side of the fireplace a few shelves contained some well-worn books, a flute, a few minerals and other little treasures belonging to Traverse; on the left hand there was a dresser containing the little delft-ware, tea-service and plates and dishes of the small family.

Before the fire, with her knitting in her hand, sat Marah Rocke, watching the kettle as it hung singing over the blaze, and the oven of biscuits that sat baking upon the hearth.

Marah Rocke was at this time about thirty-five years of age, and of a singularly refined and delicate aspect for one of her supposed rank; her little form, slight and flexible as that of a young girl, was clothed in a poor, but neat, black dress, relieved by a pure white collar around her throat; her jet black hair was parted plainly over her "low, sweet brow," brought down each side her thin cheeks, and gathered into a bunch at the back of her shapely little head; her face was oval, with regular features and pale olive complexion; serious lips, closed in pensive thought, and soft, dark-brown eyes, full of tender affections and sorrowful memories, and too often cast down in meditation beneath the heavy shadows of their long, thick eyelashes, completed the melancholy beauty of a countenance not often seen among the hard-working children of toil.

Marah Rocke was a very hard-working woman, sewing all day long and knitting through the twilight, and then again resuming her needle by candle-light, and sewing until midnight, and yet Marah Rocke made but a poor and precarious living for herself and son—needlework, so ill-paid in large cities, is even worse paid in the country towns, and though the cottage hearth was never cold, the widow's meals were often scant. Lately her son, Traverse, who occasionally earned a trifle of money by doing, "with all his might, whatever his hand could find to do," has been engaged by a grocer in the town to deliver his goods to his customers during the illness of the regular porter; for which, as he was only a substitute, he received the very moderate sum of twenty-five cents a day.

This occupation took Traverse from home at daybreak in the morning, and kept him absent until eight o'clock at night. Nevertheless, the widow always gave him a hot breakfast before he went out in the morning, and kept a comfortable supper waiting for him at night.

It was during the last social meal that the youth would tell his mother all that had occurred in his world outside the home that day, and all that he expected to come to pass the next, for Traverse was wonderfully hopeful and sanguine.

And after supper the evening was generally spent by Traverse in hard study, beside his mother's sewing-stand.

Upon this evening, when the widow sat waiting for her son, he seemed to be detained longer than usual. She almost feared that the biscuits would be burned, or, if taken from the oven, be cold, before he would come to enjoy them; but just as she had looked for the twentieth time at the little black walnut clock that stood between those old plated candlesticks on the mantel-piece, the sound of quick, light, joyous footsteps was heard resounding along the stony street, the gate was opened, a hand laid upon the door-latch, and the next instant entered a youth some seventeen years of age, clad in a homespun suit, whose coarse material and clumsy make could not disguise his noble form or graceful air.

He was like his mother, with the same oval face, regular features, and pale olive complexion, with the same full, serious lips, the same dark tender brown eyes, shaded by long black lashes, and the same wavy, jet black hair—but there was a difference in the character of their faces; where hers showed refinement and melancholy, his exhibited strength and cheerfulness—his loving brown eyes, instead of drooping sadly under the shadow of their lashes, looked you brightly and confidently full in the face—and lastly, his black hair curled crisply around a broad, high forehead, royal with intellect. Such was the boy that entered the room and came joyously forward to his mother, clasping his arm around her neck, saluting her on both cheeks, and then, laughingly claiming his childish privilege of kissing "the pretty little black mole on her throat."

"Will you never have outgrown your babyhood, Traverse?" asked his mother, smiling at his affectionate ardor.

"Yes, dear little mother! in everything but the privilege of fondling you! that feature of babyhood I never *shall* outgrow!" exclaimed the youth, kissing her again with all the ardor of his true and affectionate heart, and starting up to help her set the table.

He dragged the table out from under the window, spread the cloth, and placed the cups and saucers upon it, while his mother took the biscuits from the oven and made the tea; so that in ten minutes from the moment in which he entered the room, mother and son were seated at their frugal supper.

"I suppose, to-morrow being Saturday, you will have to get up earlier than usual to go to the store?" said his mother.

"No, ma'am!" replied the boy, looking up brightly, as if he were telling a piece of good news. "I am not wanted any longer! Mr. Spicer's own man has got well again and returned to work."

"So you are discharged?" said Mrs. Rocke, sadly.

"Yes, ma'am! but just think how fortunate that is! for I shall have a chance to-morrow of mending the fence, and nailing up the gate, and sawing wood enough to last you a week, besides doing all the other little odd jobs that have been waiting for me so long; and then on Monday I shall get more work!"

"I wish I were sure of it!" said the widow, whose hopes had long since been too deeply crushed to permit her ever to be sanguine.

When their supper was over, and the humble service cleared away, the youth took his books and applied himself to study on the opposite side of the table at which his mother sat busied with her needlework. And there fell a perfect silence between them.

The widow's mind was anxious and her heart heavy; many cares never communicated to cloud the bright sunshine of her boy's soul, oppressed hers. The rent had fallen fearfully behind hand, and the landlord threatened, unless the money could be raised to pay him, to seize their furniture and eject them from the premises. And how this money was to be raised, she could not see at all! True, this meek Christian had often in her sad experience proved God's special providence at her utmost need, and now she believed in His ultimate interference, but in what manner He would now interpose she could not imagine, and her faith grew dim, and her hope dark, and her love cold.

While she was revolving these sad thoughts in her mind, Traverse suddenly thrust aside his books, and with a deep sigh, turned to his mother, and said:

"Mother, what *do* you think has ever become of Herbert?"

"I do not know. I dread to conjecture. It has now been nearly three years since we heard from him!" exclaimed the widow, with the tears welling up to her brown eyes.

"You think he has been lost at sea, mother, but I don't! I simply think his *letters* have been lost! And somehow to-night I can't fix my mind on my lessons, or keep it *off* Herbert! He is running in my head all the time! If I were fanciful now, I *should* believe that Herbert was dead and his spirit was about me!—Good heavens mother! whose step is that?" suddenly exclaimed the youth, starting up and assuming an attitude of intense listening, as a firm and ringing step, attended by a peculiar whistling approached up the street and entered the gate.

"It is Herbert! it is Herbert!" cried Traverse, starting across the room and tearing open the door with a suddenness that threw the entering guest forward upon his own bosom, but his arms were soon around the newcomer, clasping him closely there, while he breathlessly exclaimed:

"Oh, Herbert! I am so glad to see you! Oh, Herbert! why didn't you come or write all this long time? Oh, Herbert! how long have you been ashore? I was just talking about you!"

"Dear fellow!—dear fellow! I have come to make you glad at last, and repay all your great kindness; but now let me speak to my second mother," said Herbert, returning

Traverse's embrace, and then gently extricating himself and going to where Mrs. Rocke stood up, pale, trembling and incredulous; she had not yet recovered from the great shock of his unexpected appearance.

"Dear mother, won't you welcome me?" asked Herbert, going up to her. His words dissolved the spell that bound her; throwing her arms around his neck and bursting into tears, she exclaimed:

"Oh, my son! my son! my sailor boy! my other child! how glad I am to have you back once more! Welcome?—to be sure you are welcome!—is my own circulating blood welcome back to my heart?—but sit you down and rest by the fire! I will get your supper directly!"

"Sweet mother, do not take the trouble! I supped twenty miles back where the stage stopped."

"And will you take nothing at all?"

"Nothing, dear mother, but your kind hand to kiss again and again!" said the youth, pressing that hand to his lips, and then allowing the widow to put him into a chair right in front of the fire.

Traverse sat on one side of him and his mother on the other, each holding a hand of his, and gazing on him with mingled incredulity, surprise and delight, as if, indeed, they could not realize his presence except by devouring him with their eyes.

And for the next half-hour all their talk was as wild and incoherent as the conversation of long-parted friends suddenly brought together, is apt to be.

It was all made up of hasty questions, hurried one upon another, so as to leave but little chance to have any of them answered, and wild exclamations and disjointed sketches of travel, interrupted by frequent ejaculations; yet through all the widow and her son, perhaps through the quickness of their *love* as well as of their intellect, managed to get some knowledge of the past three years of their "sailor boy's" life and adventures, and they entirely vindicated his constancy when they learned how frequently and regularly he had written, though they had never received his letters.

"And now," said Herbert, looking from side to side, from mother to son, "I have told you all *my* adventures, I am dying to tell you something that concerns *yourselves.*"

"That concerns *us?*" exclaimed mother and son in a breath.

"Yes, ma'am! yes, sir! that concerns you both eminently; but first of all, let me ask how you are getting on at this present time?"

"Oh, as usual," said the widow, smiling, for she did not wish to damp the spirits of her sailor boy; "as usual, of course. Traverse has not been able to accomplish his darling purpose of entering the Seminary yet; but——"

"But I'm getting on quite well with my education for all that," interrupted Traverse; "for I belong to Dr. Day's Bible class in the Sabbath school, which is a class of *young men,* you know! and the doctor is so good as to think that I have some mental gifts worth cultivating, so he does not confine his instructions to me to the Bible class alone, but permits me to come to him in his library at Willow Heights for an hour, twice a week, when he examines me in Latin and Algebra, and sets me new exercises, which I study and write out at night; so that you see I am doing very well."

"Indeed, the doctor, who is a great scholar, and one of the trustees and examiners of the Seminary, says that he does not know any young man *there,* with all the advantages of the institution around him, who is getting along so fast as Traverse is, with all the difficulties he has to encounter. The doctor says it is all because Traverse is profoundly in earnest, and that one of these days he will be——"

"There, mother! don't repeat all the doctor's kind speeches! He only says such things to encourage a poor boy in the pursuit of knowledge under difficulties," said Traverse, blushing and laughing.

—"Will be an honor to his kindred, country and race," said Herbert, finishing the widow's incomplete quotation.

"It was something like that, indeed," she said, nodding and smiling.

"You do me proud!" said Traverse, touching his forelock with comic gravity. "But," inquired he, suddenly changing his tone and becoming serious, "was it not—*is* it not—noble in the doctor to give up an hour of his precious time twice a week, for no other cause than to help a poor, struggling fellow like me up the ladder of learning?"

"I should think it was; but he is not the first noble heart I ever heard of," said Herbert, with an affectionate glance that directed the compliment, "nor is his the last that *you* will meet with. I *must* tell you the good news now."

"Oh, tell it! tell it! have you got a ship of your own, Herbert?"

"No, nor is it about myself that I am anxious to tell you. Mrs. Rocke, you may have heard that I had a rich uncle, whom I had never seen, because, from the time of my dear mother's marriage to that of her death, she and her brother, this very uncle, had been estranged?"

"Yes," said the widow, speaking in a very low tone, and bending her head over her work; "yes, I have heard so; but your mother and myself seldom alluded to the subject."

"Exactly! mother never was fond of talking of him! Well, when I came on shore, and went, as usual, up to the old Washington House, who should I meet with, all of a sudden, but this rich uncle. He had come to New York to claim a little girl whom I happened to know, and who happened to recognize me, and name me to him. Well, I knew him *only* by his name; but he knew me both by my name and by my likeness to his sister, and received me with wonderful kindness, offered me a home under his roof, and promised to get for me an appointment to West Point. Are you not glad?—say, are you not glad?" he exclaimed, jocosely clapping his hand upon Traverse's knee, and then turning around and looking at his mother.

"Oh, yes, indeed I am *very* glad, Herbert!" exclaimed Traverse, heartily grasping and squeezing his friend's hand.

"Yes, yes, I am indeed sincerely glad of your good fortune, dear boy," said the widow; but her voice was very faint, and her head bent still lower over her work.

"Ha! ha! ha! I *knew* you'd be glad for *me*; but now I require you to be glad for *yourselves.* Now listen: When I told my honest old uncle—for he *is* honest, with all his eccentricities—when I told him of what friends you had been to me——"

"Oh *no! you did not! You did not mention* US TO HIM!" cried the widow, suddenly starting up and clasping her hands together, while she gazed in an agony of entreaty into the face of the speaker.

"Why not?—why in the world not? Was there anything improper in doing so?" inquired Herbert, in astonishment, while Traverse himself gazed in amazement at the excessive and unaccountable agitation of his mother.

"Why, mother? Why shouldn't he have mentioned us? Was there anything strange or wrong in that?" inquired Traverse.

"No, oh, no; certainly not!—I forgot, it was so sudden," said the widow sinking back in her chair and struggling for self-control.

"Why, mother, what in the world is the meaning of this?" asked her son.

"Nothing, nothing, boy; only we are poor folks, and should not be forced upon the attention of a wealthy gentleman," she said, with a cold, unnatural smile, putting her hand to her brow and striving to gain composure. Then, as Herbert continued silent and amazed, she said to him:

"Go on—go on—you were saying something about my—about Major Warfield's kindness to you—go on." And she took up her work and tried to sew, but she was as pale as death, and trembling all over at the same time, while every nerve was acute with attention to catch every word that might fall from the lips of Herbert.

"Well," recommenced the young sailor, "I was just saying that when I mentioned you and Traverse to my uncle, and told him how kind and disinterested you had been to me—you being like a mother, and Traverse like a brother,—he was really moved almost to tears! Yes, I declare I saw the raindrops glittering in his tempestuous old orbs, as he walked the floor muttering to himself, 'Poor woman—good, excellent woman.'"

While Herbert spoke, the widow dropped her work without seeming to know that she had done so; her fingers twitched so nervously that she had to hold both hands clasped together, and her eyes were fixed in intense anxiety upon the face of the youth, as she repeated:

"Go on—oh, go on! What more did he say when you talked of us?"

"He said everything that was kind and good. He said that he could not do too much to compensate you for the past."

"Oh! did he say that?" exclaimed the widow, breathlessly.

"Yes—and a great deal more!—that all that he could do for you or your son was but a sacred debt he owed you."

"Oh, he acknowledged it! he acknowledged it! thank heaven! oh, thank heaven! Go on, Herbert! Go on!"

"He said that he would in future take the whole charge of the boy's advancement in life, and that he would place you above want forever; that he would, in fact, compensate for the past by doing you and yours full justice."

"Thank heaven! Oh, thank heaven!" exclaimed the widow, no longer concealing her agitation, but throwing down her work, and starting up and pacing the floor in excess of joy.

"Mother," said Traverse, uneasily, going to her and taking her hand, "mother, what is the meaning of all this? Do come and sit down!"

She immediately turned and walked back to the fire, and resting her hands upon the back of the chair, bent upon them a face radiant with youthful beauty. Her cheeks were brightly flushed, her eyes were sparkling with light, her whole countenance resplendent with joy—she scarcely seemed twenty years of age.

"Mother, tell us what it is," pleaded Traverse, who feared for her sanity.

"Oh, boys, I am so happy! at last! at last! after eighteen years of patient 'hoping against hope!' I shall go mad with joy!"

"Mother," said Herbert, softly.

"Children, I am not crazy! I know what I am saying, though I did not intend to say it! And you shall know, too! But first I must ask Herbert another question: Herbert, are you very sure that he—Major Warfield,—knew who we were?"

"Yes, indeed. Didn't I tell him all about you? Your troubles, your struggles, your disinterestedness, and all your history since ever I knew you?" answered Herbert, who was totally unconscious that he had left Major Warfield in ignorance of one very important fact—her *surname*.

"Then you are sure he knew who *he* was talking about?"

"Of course, he did!"

"He could not have failed to do so, indeed! But, Herbert, did he mention any other important fact, that you have not yet communicated to us?"

"No, ma'am."

"Did he allude to any previous acquaintance with us?"

"No, ma'am, unless it might have been in the words I repeated to you—there was nothing else!—except that he bade me hurry to you and make you glad with his message, and return as soon as possible to let him know whether you accept his offers."

"Accept them! accept them! of course I do! I have waited for them for years!—oh! children! you gaze on me as if you thought me mad! I am not so! nor can I now explain myself! for since *he* has not chosen to be confidential with Herbert, I can not be so prematurely! but you will know all, when Herbert shall have borne back my message to Major Warfield."

It was, indeed, a mad evening in the cottage. And even when the little family had separated and retired to bed the two youths lying together, as formerly, could not sleep for talking; while the widow, on her lonely couch, lay awake for joy.

Chapter X

The Room of the Trap-Door

"If you have hitherto concealed this sight,
Let it be tenable, in your silence still;
And whatsoever else doth hap to-night,
Give it an understanding, but no tongue."
—*Shakespeare*[29]

CAPITOLA MEANWHILE, in the care of the major, arrived at Hurricane Hall, much to the discomfiture of good Mrs. Condiment, who was quite unprepared to expect the new inmate; and when Major Warfield said:

"Mrs. Condiment, this is your young lady, take her up to the best bedroom, where she can take off her bonnet and shawl," the worthy dame, thinking secretly: "The old fool has gone and married a young wife, sure enough; a mere chit of a child"—made a very deep courtesy, and a very queer cough, and said:

"I'm mortified, Madam, at the fire not being made in the best bedroom; but then I was not warned of *your* coming, Madam!"

"Madam! Is the old woman crazed? This child is no 'madam'! She is Miss Black, my ward, the daughter of a deceased friend!" sharply exclaimed Old Hurricane.

"Excuse me, Miss, I did not know; I was unprepared to receive a young lady. Shall I attend you, Miss Black?" said the old lady in a mollified tone.

"If you please," said Capitola, and arose to follow her.

"Not expecting you, Miss, I have no proper room prepared—most of them are not furnished, and in some, the chimneys are foul; indeed, the only tolerable room I can put you in is the room with the trap-door—if you would not object to it?" said Mrs. Condiment, as with a candle in her hand, she preceded Capitola along the gloomy hall, and then opened a door that led into a narrow passage.

"A room with a trap-door?—that's a curious thing; but why should I object to it! I don't at all. I think I should rather like it," said Capitola.

---

29 *Hamlet*, 1.2.

"I will show it to you and tell you about it, and then if you like it, well and good! If not, I shall have to put you in a room that leaks, and has swallows' nests in the chimney," answered Mrs. Condiment, as she led the way along the narrow passages, and up and down dark, black stairs, and through bare and deserted rooms, and along other passages until she reached a remote chamber, opened the door, and invited her guest to enter.

It was a large shadowy room, through which the single candle shed such a faint, uncertain light, that at first Capitola could see nothing but black masses looming up through the darkness.

But when Mrs. Condiment advanced and set the candle upon the chimney-piece, and Capitola's sight accommodated itself to the scene, she saw that upon the right of the chimney-piece stood a tall tester bedstead,[30] curtained with very dark crimson serge; on the left hand, thick curtains of the same color draped the windows. Between these windows, directly opposite the bed, stood a dark mahogany dressing-bureau, with a large looking-glass; a wash-stand in the left-hand corner of the chimney-place; and a rocking-chair and two plain chairs completed the furniture of this room, that I am particular in describing, as upon the simple accident of its arrangement, depended, upon two occasions, the life and honor of its occupant. There was no carpet on the floor, with the exception of a large old Turkey rug which was laid before the fireplace.

"Here, my dear, this room is perfectly dry and comfortable, and we always keep kindlings built up in the fireplace ready to light in case a guest should come," said Mrs. Condiment, applying a match to the wastepaper under the pineknots and logs that filled the chimney. Soon there arose a cheerful blaze that lighted up all the room, glowing on the crimson serge bed-curtains and window-curtains, and flashing upon the large looking-glass between them.

"There, my dear; sit down, and make yourself comfortable," said Mrs. Condiment, drawing up the rocking-chair.

Capitola threw herself into it, and looked around and around the room, and then into the face of the old lady, saying:

"But what about the trap-door?—I see no trap-door!"

"Ah, yes—look!" said Mrs. Condiment, lifting up the rug and revealing a large *drop* some four feet square, that was kept up in its place by a short iron bolt. "Now, my dear, take care of yourself, for this bolt slides very easily, and if, while you happened to be walking across this place, you were to push the bolt back, the trap-door would drop and you fall down— heaven knows where!"

"Is there a cellar under there?" inquired Capitola, gazing with interest upon the door.

"Lord knows, child; I don't! I did once make one of the nigger men let it down, so I could look in it; but, Lord, child, I saw nothing but a great, black, deep vacuity, without bottom or sides! It put such a horror over me, that I never looked down there since, and never want to, I'm sure."

"Ugh! for goodness sake what was the horrid thing made for!" ejaculated Capitola, gazing as if fascinated by the trap.

"The Lord only knows, my dear; for it was made long before ever the house came into the major's family. *But they do say——*" whispered Mrs. Condiment, mysteriously.

"Ah! what do they say?" asked Capitola, eagerly throwing off her bonnet and shawl, and settling herself to hear some thrilling explanation.

---

30 A bed frame crowned with canopy held up by four posts.

Mrs. Condiment slowly replaced the rug, drew another chair to the side of the young girl, and said:

"They do say it was—*a trap for Indians.*"

"A trap for Indians?"

"Yes, my dear. You must know that this room belongs to the *oldest part of the house*. It was all built as far back as the old French and Indian war;[31] but this room belonged to the part that dates back to the first settlement of the country."

"Then I shall like it better than any room in the house, for I doat on old places with stories to them. Go on, please."

"Yes, my dear. Well, first of all, this place was a part of the grant of land given to the *Le Noirs.* And the first owner, old Henri Le Noir, was said to be one of the grandest villains that ever was heard of. Well, you see, he lived out here in his hunting-lodge, which is this part of the house."

"Oh, my! then this very room was a part of the old pioneer hunter's lodge?"

"Yes, my dear, and they do say that he had this place made as a trap for the Indians. You see, they say he was on terms of friendship with the Succapoos, a little tribe of Indians that was nearly wasted away, though among the few that was left there were several braves! Well, he wanted to buy a certain large tract of land from this tribe, and they were all willing to sell it, except these half a dozen warriors, who wanted it for camping-ground. So what does this awful villain do, but lay a snare for them. He makes a great feast in his lodge and invites his red brothers to come to it; and they come. Then he proposes that they stand upon his blanket and all swear eternal brotherhood, which he made the poor souls believe was the right way to do it. Then when they all six stood close together as they could stand, with hands held up touching above their heads, all of a sudden the black villain sprung the bolt, the trap fell, and the six men went down—down, the Lord knows where."

"Oh, that is horrible! horrible!" cried Capitola, "but where do you think they fell to?"

"I tell you the Lord only knows. They say that it is a bottomless abyss, with no outlet but one crooked one miles long that reaches to the Demon's Punch Bowl. But if there *is* a bottom to that abyss, that bottom is strewn with human bones."

"Oh, horrible! most horrible!" exclaimed Capitola.

"Perhaps you are afraid to sleep here by yourself; if so, there's the damp room—"

"Oh, no! oh, no! I am not afraid. I have been in too much deadly peril from the *living* ever to fear the *dead*. No, I like the room, with its strange legend; but tell me, did that human devil escape without punishment from the tribe of the murdered victims?"

"Lord, child, how were they to know of what was done? There wasn't a man left to tell the tale. Besides, the tribe was now brought down to a few old men, women, and children. So, when he showed a bill of sale for the land he wanted, signed by the six braves–'their marks' in six blood-red arrows, there was none to contradict him."

"How was his villainy found out?"

"Well, it was said he married, had a family, and prospered for a long while; but that the poor Succapoos always suspected him, and bore a long grudge, and that when the sons of the murdered warriors grew up to be powerful braves, one night they set upon the house and massacred the whole family except the eldest son, a lad of ten, who escaped and ran away and gave the alarm to the blockhouse, where there were soldiers stationed. It is said

---

31 The American theater (1754–63) of the world-wide Seven Years' War. In America, it was primarily a struggle between the forces allied with either England or France.

that after killing and scalping father, mother, and children, the savages threw the dead bodies down that trap-door. And they had just set fire to the house, and were dancing their wild
dance around it, when the soldiers arrived and dispersed the party, and put out the fire."

"Oh, what bloody, bloody days!"

"Yes, my dear, and as I told you before, if that horrible pit *has* any bottom, that bottom
is strewn with human skeletons!"

"It is an awful thought——"

"As I said, my dear, if you feel at all afraid you can have another room."

"Afraid—what of? Those skeletons, supposing them to be there, cannot hurt me.
I am not afraid of the dead—I only dread the living, and not them much either," said
Capitola.

"Well, my dear, you will want a waiting-woman, anyhow, and I think I will send Pitapat
to wait on you; she can sleep on a pallet in your room, and be some company."

"And who is Pitapat, Mrs. Condiment?"

"Pitapat? Lord, child, she is the youngest of the housemaids. I've called her Pitapat ever
since she was a little one beginning to walk, when she used to steal away from her mother,
Dorcas, the cook, and I would hear her little feet coming pit-a-pat, pit-a-pat up the dark
stairs up to my room. As it was often the only sound to be heard in the still house, I grew to
call my little visitor Pitapat."

"Then let me have Pitapat by all means. I like company, especially company that I can
send away when I choose."

"Very well, my dear, and now I think you'd better smooth your hair and come down
with me to tea, for it is full time, and the major, as you may know, is not the most patient
of men."

Capitola took a brush from her traveling bag, hastily arranged her black ringlets, and
announced herself ready.

They left the room, and traversed the same labyrinth of passages, stairs, empty rooms
and halls, back to the dining-room, where a comfortable fire burned and a substantial supper was spread.

Old Hurricane took Capitola's hand with a hearty grasp, and placed her in a chair at
the side, and then took his own seat at the foot of the table.

Mrs. Condiment sat at the head and poured out the tea.

"Uncle," said Capitola, suddenly, "what is under the trap-door in my room?"

"What! have they put you in *that* room?" exclaimed the old man, hastily looking up.

"There was no other one prepared, sir," said the housekeeper.

"Besides, I like it very well, uncle," said Capitola.

"Humph! humph! humph!" grunted the old man, only half satisfied.

"But uncle, what is under the trap-door?" persisted Capitola, "what's under it?"

"Oh, I don't know—an old cave that was once used as a dry cellar, until an underground
stream broke through and made it too damp—so it is said. I never explored it."

"But, uncle, what about the——"

Here Mrs. Condiment stretched out her foot, and trod upon the toes of Capitola so
sharply as to make her stop short, while she dexterously changed the conversation by asking the major if he would not send Wool to Tip-Top in the morning for another bag of
coffee.

Soon after supper was over, Capitola, saying that she was tired, bade her uncle good-
night, and, attended by her little black maid Pitapat, whom Mrs. Condiment had called

up for the purpose, retired to her distant chamber. There were already collected her three trunks, which the liberality of her uncle had filled.

As soon as she had got in and locked the door, she detached one of the strongest straps from her largest trunk, and then turned up the rug and secured the end of the strap to the ring in the trap-door. Then she withdrew the bolt, and holding on to one end of the strap, gently lowered the trap, and kneeling, gazed down into an awful black void—without boundaries, without sight, without sounds, except a deep, faint, subterranean roaring as of water.

"Bring the light, Pitapat, and hold it over this place, and take care you don't fall in," said Capitola. "Come, as I've got a 'pit' in my name and you've got a 'pit' in yours, we'll see if we two can't make something of this third 'pit'!"

'"Deed, I'se 'fraid, Miss," said the poor little darkey.

"Afraid! what of?"

"Ghoses."

"Nonsense. I'll agree to lay every ghost you see!"

The little maid approached, candle in hand, but in such a gingerly sort of way, that Capitola seized the light from her hand, and stooping, held it down as far as she could reach, and gazed once more into the abyss. But this only made the horrible darkness "visible";[32] no object caught or reflected a single ray of light—all was black, hollow, void and silent, except the faint, deep, distant roaring as of subterraneous water!

Capitola pushed the light as far down as she could possibly reach, and then yielding to a strange fascination, dropt it into the abyss! It went down, down, down into the darkness, until far below it glimmered out of sight! Then with an awful shudder Capitola pulled up and fastened the trapdoor, laid down the rug and said her prayers, and went to bed by the fire-light,—with little Pitapat sleeping on a pallet. The last thought of Cap, before falling to sleep, was:

"It is awful to go to bed over such a horrible mystery; but I *will* be a hero!"

Chapter XI

A Mystery and a Storm at Hurricane Hall

"Bid her address her prayers to Heaven!
Learn if she *there* may be forgiven;
Its mercy may absolve her yet!
But *here* upon this earth beneath,
There is *no spot* where she and I
Together for an *hour* could breathe!"
                                        —*Byron*[33]

EARLY THE NEXT morning Capitola arose, made her toilet, and went out to explore the outer walls of her part of the old house, to discover, if possible, some external entrance into the unknown cavity under her room. It was a bright, cheerful, healthy, autumnal morning, well adapted to dispel all clouds of mystery and superstition. Heaps of crimson and golden-hued leaves, glimmering with hoar frost, lay drifted against the old walls, and when these

---

32 John Milton (1608–1674), *Paradise Lost*, bk. 1, line 71.
33 George Gordon, Lord Byron (1788–1824), "Parisina."

were brushed away by the busy feet and hands of the young girl, they revealed nothing but the old moldering foundation; not a vestige of a cellar-door or window was visible.

Capitola abandoned the fruitless search, and turned to go into the house. And saying to herself:

"I'll think no more of it! I dare say, after all, it is nothing but a very dark cellar without window and with a well, and the story of the murders and of the skeletons, is all moonshine!" She ran into the dining-room, and took her seat at the breakfast table.

Old Hurricane was just then storming away at his factotum Wool for some misdemeanor, the nature of which Capitola did not hear, for upon her appearance, he suffered his wrath to subside in a few reverberating low thunders, gave his ward a grumphy "Good-morning," and sat down to his breakfast.

After breakfast Old Hurricane took his great coat and cocked hat, and stormed forth upon the plantation to blow up his lazy overseer, Mr. Will Ezy, and his idle negroes, who had loitered or frolicked away all the days of their master's absence.

Mrs. Condiment went away to mix a plum pudding for dinner and Cap was left alone.

After wandering through the lower rooms of the house, the stately old-fashioned drawing-room, the family parlor, the dining-room, etc., Cap found her way through all the narrow back passages and steep little staircases back to her own chamber.

The chamber looked quite different by daylight—the cheerful wood fire burning in the chimney right before her, opposite the door by which she entered; the crimson curtained bedstead on her right hand; the crimson draped windows, with the rich old mahogany bureau and dressing-glass standing between them, on her left; the polished, dark oak floor; the rich Turkey rug, concealing the trap-door; the comfortable rocking-chair; the new work-stand; placed there for her use that morning, and her own well-filled trunks standing in the corners, looked altogether too cheerful to associate with dark thoughts.

Besides, Capitola had not the least particle of gloom, superstition or marvelousness in her disposition. She loved old houses and old legends well enough to enjoy them; but was not sufficiently credulous to believe, or cowardly to fear, them.

She had, besides, a pleasant morning's occupation before her, in unpacking her three trunks and arranging her wardrobe and her possessions, which were all upon the most liberal scale, for Major Warfield at every city where they had stopped had given his poor little *protégée* a virtual *carte blanche* for purchases, having said to her:

"Capitola, I'm an old bachelor; I've not the least idea what a young girl requires; all I know is, that you have nothing but your clothes, and must want sewing and knitting needles, and brushes and scissors, and combs and boxes and smelling-bottles and tooth-powder; and *such*. So come along with me to one of those Vanity Fairs[34] they call fancy stores, and get what you want; I'll foot the bill."

And Capitola, who firmly believed that she had the most sacred of claims upon Major Warfield, whose resources she also supposed to be unlimited, did not fail to indulge her taste for rich and costly toys, and supplied herself with a large ivory dressing-case, lined with velvet, and furnished with ivory-handled combs and brushes, silver boxes and crystal bottles; a papier mâché work-box, with gold thimble, needle-case and perforator and gold-mounted scissors and winders; and an ebony writing-desk, with silver-mounted crystal standishes; each of these—boxes and desk—were filled with all things requisite in the

---

34 Place in John Bunyan's (1628–1688) allegorical *Pilgrim's Progress* (1678) where pilgrims are tempted by the pleasures and goods of the world.

several departments. And now as Capitola unpacked them and arranged them upon the top of the bureau, it was with no small degree of appreciation. The rest of the forenoon was spent in arranging the best articles of her wardrobe in her bureau drawers.

Having locked the remainder in her trunks, and carefully smoothed her hair, and dressed herself in a brown merino, she went down stairs and sought out Mrs. Condiment, whom she found in the housekeeper's little room, and to whom she said:

"Now, Mrs. Condiment, if uncle has any needlework wanted to be done, any buttons to be sewed on, or anything of the kind, just let me have it; I'm just dying to use it!"

"My dear Miss Black——"

"Please to call me Capitola, or even Cap. I never was called Miss Black in my life, until I came here, and I don't like it at all!"

"Well then, my dear Miss Cap, I wish you would wait till to-morrow, for I just came in here in a great hurry to get a glass of brandy out of the cupboard to put in the sauce for the plum pudding, as dinner will be on the table in ten minutes."

With a shrug of her little shoulders, Capitola left the housekeeper's room, and hurried through the central front hall and out at the front door, to look about and breathe the fresh air for a while.

As she stepped upon the front piazza she saw Major Warfield walking up the steep lawn, followed by Wool, leading a pretty, mottled, iron-gray pony, with a side-saddle on his back.

"Ah, I'm glad you're down, Cap! Come! look at this pretty pony! he is good for nothing as a working horse, and is too light to carry *my* weight, and so I intend to give him to you! You must learn to ride," said the old man, coming up the steps.

"Give him to me! I learn to ride! Oh, uncle! Oh, uncle! I shall go perfectly crazy with joy!" exclaimed Cap, dancing and clapping her hands with delight.

"Oh, well, a tumble or two in learning will bring you back to your senses, I reckon!"

"Oh, uncle! oh, uncle! when shall I begin!"

"You shall take your first tumble immediately after dinner, when, being well-filled, you will not be so brittle and apt to break in falling!"

"Oh, uncle! I shall not fall! I feel I sha'n't! I feel I've a natural gift for holding on!"

"Come, come, get in! get in! I want my dinner!" said Old Hurricane, driving his ward in before him to the dining-room, where the dinner was smoking upon the table.

After dinner Cap, with Wool for a riding-master, took her first lesson in equestrianism. She had the four great requisites for forming a good rider—a well-adapted figure, a fondness for the exercise, perfect fearlessness and presence of mind. She was not once in danger of losing her seat, and during that single afternoon's exercises, she made considerable progress in learning to manage her steed.

Old Hurricane, whom the genial autumn afternoon had tempted out to smoke his pipe in his arm-chair on the porch, was a pleased spectator of her performances, and expressed his opinion that *in time* she would become the best rider in the neighborhood, and that she should have the best riding-dress and cap that could be made at Tip-Top.

Just now, in lack of an equestrian dress, poor Cap was parading around and around the lawn with her head bare and her hair flying, and her merino skirt exhibiting more ankles than grace.

It was while Old Hurricane still sat smoking his pipe and making his comments, and Capitola still ambled around and around the lawn, that a horseman suddenly appeared galloping as fast as the steep nature of the ground would admit, up towards the house, and before they could form an idea of who he was, the horse was at the block, and the rider dismounted and standing before Major Warfield.

"Why, Herbert, my boy! back so soon! We didn't expect you for a week to come! This is sudden, indeed! So much the better! so much the better! Glad to see you, lad!" exclaimed Old Hurricane, getting up and heartily shaking the hand of his nephew.

Capitola came ambling up, and in the effort to spring nimbly from her saddle, tumbled off, much to the delight of Wool, who grinned from ear to ear, and of Old Hurricane, who, with an "I said so," burst into a roar of laughter.

Herbert Greyson sprang to assist her; but before he reached the spot, Cap had picked herself up, straightened her disordered dress, and now she ran to meet and shake hands with him.

There was such a sparkle of joy and glow of affection in the meeting between these two, that Old Hurricane, who saw it, suddenly hushed his laugh, and grunted to himself:

"Humph, humph, humph! I like that; that's better than I could have planned it myself; let *that* go on, and then, Gabe Le Noir, we'll see under what name and head the old divided manor will be held!"

Before his mental soliloquy was concluded, Herbert and Capitola came up to him. He welcomed Herbert again with great cordiality, and then called to his man to put up the horses, and bade the young people follow him into the house, as the air was getting chilly.

"And how did you find your good friends, lad?" inquired Old Hurricane, when they had reached the sitting parlor.

"Oh, very well, sir; and very grateful for your offered kindness; and, indeed, so anxious to express their gratitude, that—that I shortened my visit, and came away immediately to tell you."

"Right, lad, right! You come by the down coach?"

"Yes, sir; and got off at Tip-Top, where I hired a horse to bring me here. I must ask you to let one of your men take him back to Mr. Merry, at the Antlers' Inn, to-morrow."

"Surely, surely, lad! Wool shall do it!"

"And so, Herbert, the poor woman was delighted with the prospect of better times?" said Old Hurricane, with a little glow of benevolent self-satisfaction.

"Oh, yes, sir! delighted beyond all measure!"

"Poor thing! poor thing! See, young folks, how easy it is for the wealthy, by sparing a little of their superfluous means, to make the poor and virtuous happy. And the boy, Herbert, the boy?"

"Oh, sir! delighted for himself, but still more delighted for his mother; for her joy was such as to astonish and even alarm me! Before that, I had thought Marah Rocke a proud woman, but——"

"WHAT—*say that again!*" exclaimed Major Warfield.

"I say that I thought she was a proud woman, but——"

"Thought WHO was a proud woman, sir?" roared Old Hurricane.

"Marah Rocke!" replied the young man, with wonder.

Major Warfield started up, seized the chair upon which he had sat, and struck it upon the ground with such force as to shatter it to pieces; then turning, he strode up and down the floor with such violence that the two young people gazed after him in consternation and fearful expectancy. Presently he turned suddenly, strode up to Herbert Greyson, and stood before him.

His face was purple, his veins swollen until they stood out upon his forehead like cords, his eyes were protruded and glaring, his mouth clenched until the grizzly gray moustache and beard were drawn in, his whole huge frame was quivering from head to foot! It was impossible to tell what passion—whether rage, grief, or shame, the most possessed him, for all three seemed tearing his giant frame to pieces.

For an instant he stood speechless, and Herbert feared he would fall into a fit; but the old giant was too strong for that! For one short moment he stood thus, and in a terrible voice he asked:

"Young man! did you—*did* you know—the SHAME that you dashed into my face, with the name of that woman?"

"Sir, I know nothing but that she is the best and dearest of her sex!" exclaimed Herbert, beyond all measure amazed at what he heard and saw.

"Best and dearest!" thundered the old man—"oh, idiot! is she still a siren, and are you a dupe? But that cannot be! No, sir! it is I whom you *both* would dupe! Ah, I see it all now! *This* is why you artfully concealed her name from me until you had won my promise! It shall not serve either you or her, sir! I break my promise—thus!"—bending and snapping his own cane, and flinging the fragments behind his back—"there, sir! when you can make those ends of dry cedar grow together again, and bear green leaves, you may hope to reconcile Ira Warfield and Marah Rocke! I break my promise sir, as *she* broke——"

The old man suddenly sunk back into the nearest chair, dropped his shaggy head and face into his hands, and remained trembling from head to foot, while the convulsive heaving of his chest, and the rising and falling of his huge shoulders, betrayed that his heart was nearly bursting with such suppressed sobs as only can be forced from manhood by the fiercest anguish.

The young people looked on in wonder, awe and pity; and then their eyes met—those of Herbert silently inquired:

"What can all this mean?"—Those of Capitola as mutely answered:

"Heaven only knows."

In his deep pity for the old man's terrible anguish, Herbert could feel no shame nor resentment for the false accusation made upon himself. Indeed, his noble and candid nature easily explained all as the ravings of some heart-rending remembrance. Waiting, therefore, until the violent convulsions of the old man's frame had somewhat subsided, Herbert went to him, and with a low and respectful intonation of voice, said:

"Uncle, if you think that there was any collusion between myself and Mrs. Rocke, you wrong us both. You will remember that when I met you in New York, I had not seen or heard from *her* for years, nor had I then any expectation of ever seeing you. The subject of the poor widow came up between us accidentally, and if it is true that I omitted to call her by *name*, it must have been because we both then felt too tenderly by her to call her anything else but 'the poor widow, the poor mother, the good woman,' and so on—and all this she is still."

The old man without raising his head, held out one hand to his nephew, saying in a voice still trembling with emotion:

"Herbert, I wronged you; forgive me."

Herbert took and pressed that rugged and hairy old hand to his lips, and said:

"Uncle, I do not in the least know what is the cause of your present emotion, but——"

"Emotion! demmy, sir! what do you mean by emotion? Am *I* a man to give way to emotion? Demmy, sir, mind what you say!" roared the old lion, getting up and shaking himself free of all weaknesses.

"I merely meant to say, sir, that if I could possibly be of any service to you, I am entirely at your orders."

"Then go back to that woman and tell her never to dare to utter, or even to *think* my name again, if she values her life!"

"Sir, you do not mean it! and as for Mrs. Rocke, she is a good woman I feel it my duty to uphold!"

"Good! ugh! ugh! ugh! I'll command myself! I'll not give way again. Good! ah, lad, it is quite plain to me now, that you are an innocent dupe. Tell me, now, for instance, do you know anything of that woman's life, before she came to reside at Staunton?"

"Nothing; but from what I've seen of her since, I'm *sure* she always *was* good."

"Did she never mention her former life at all?"

"Never; but, mind! I hold to my faith in her and would stake my salvation on her integrity," said Herbert, warmly.

"Then you'd lose it, lad, that's all; but I have an explanation to make to you, Herbert. You must give me a minute or two of your company alone, in the library, before tea."

And so saying, Major Warfield arose and led the way across the hall to the library, that was immediately back of the drawing-room.

Throwing himself into a leathern chair beside the writing table, he motioned for his companion to take the one on the opposite side. A low fire smoldering on the hearth before them, so dimly lighted the room, that the young man arose again to pull the bell rope; but the other interrupted with:

"No, you need not ring for lights, Herbert: my story is one that should be told in the dark! listen, lad; but drop your eyes, the while!"

"I am all attention, sir!"

"Herbert! the poet says, that:

'At thirty man suspects himself a fool,
Knows it at forty and reforms his rule.'[35]

But boy, at the ripe age of forty-five, I succeeded in achieving the most sublime folly of my life! I should have taken a degree in madness, and been raised to a professor's chair in some College of Lunacy! Herbert, at the age of forty-five I fell in love with and married a girl of sixteen, out of a log cabin! merely forsooth, because she had a pretty skin like the leaf of the white japonica,[36] soft, gray eyes like a timid fawn's and a voice like a cooing turtle dove's! because those delicate cheeks flushed, and those soft eyes fell when I spoke to her, and the cooing voice trembled when she replied! because the delicate face brightened when I came, and faded when I turned away! because

'She wept with delight when I gave her a smile,
And trembled with fear at my frown,' etc.

Because she adored me as a sort of god, I loved her as an angel, and married her! married her secretly! for fear of the ridicule of my brother officers, put her in a pastoral log cabin in the woods below the block-house, and visited her there by stealth, like Numa did his nymph in the cave![37] But I was watched, my hidden treasure was discovered—and coveted by a younger and prettier fellow than myself—Perdition!

---

35 Edward Young (1683–1765), *Night Thoughts*, "Night I."
36 Beautiful flowering plant sometimes called the "Rose of Winter."
37 Numa Pomplius was the second king of Rome. He was tutored by the nymph Egeria, who taught him the wisdom that allowed him to make Rome a great city.

I cannot tell this story in detail! One night I came home very late and quite unexpectedly, and found—this man in my wife's cabin! I broke the man's head and ribs and left him for dead. I tore the woman out of my heart and cauterized its bleeding wounds!—This man was Gabriel Le Noir! Satan burn him forever!—This woman was Marah Rocke, God forgive her! I could have divorced the woman, but as I did not dream of ever marrying again, I did not care to drag my shame before a public tribunal. There! you know all! let the subject sink forever!" said Old Hurricane, wiping great drops of sweat from his laboring brows.

"Uncle! I have heard your story and believe you, of course! But I am bound to tell you, that without even having heard your poor wife's defence, I *believe, and uphold her to be innocent!* I think *you* have been as grossly deceived as she has been fearfully wronged! and that time and providence will prove this!" exclaimed Herbert, fervently.

A horrible laugh of scorn was his only answer, as Old Hurricane arose, shook himself and led the way back to the parlor.

Chapter XII

Marah's Dreams

"And now her narrow kitchen walls
Stretched away into stately halls;
The weary wheel to a spinnet turned,
The tallow candle an astral burned;
A manly form at her side she saw,
And joy was duty and love was law."
—*Whittier*[38]

ON THE SAME Saturday morning that Herbert Greyson hurried away from his friend's cottage, to travel post to Hurricane Hall, for the sole purpose of accelerating the coming of her good fortune, Marah Rocke walked about the house with a step so light, with eyes so bright, and cheeks so blooming, that one might have thought that years had rolled backward in their course and made her a young girl again!

Traverse gazed upon her in delight. Reversing the words of the text, he said:

"We must call you no longer Marah (which is bitter), but we must call you Naomi (which is beautiful), mother!"

"Young flatterer!" she answered, smiling and slightly flushing. "But tell me truly, Traverse, am I very much faded? have care, and toil, and grief made me look old?"

"You! old!" exclaimed the boy, running his eyes over her beaming face and graceful form with a look of non-comprehension that might have satisfied her, but did not, for she immediately repeated:

"Yes, do I look old? Indeed, I do not ask from vanity, child! Ah, it little becomes me to be vain; but I do wish to look well in some one's eyes!"

"I wish there was a looking-glass in the house, mother, that it might tell you, you should be called Naomi, instead of Marah!"

---

38 From the poem, "Maud Muller" by American poet John Greenleaf Whittier (1807–1892).

"Ah! that is just what *he* used to say to me in the old happy time,—the time in Paradise, before the serpent entered!"

"What 'he,' mother?"

"Your father, boy, of course!"

That was the first time she had ever mentioned his father to her son, and now she spoke of him with such a flush of joy and hope, that even while her words referred darkly to the past, her eyes looked brightly to the future! All this, taken with the events of the preceding evening, greatly bewildered the mind of Traverse, and agitated him with the wildest conjectures.

"Mother, will you tell me about my father, and also what it is beyond this promised kindness of Major Warfield that has made you so happy!" he asked.

"Not now, my boy! dear boy, not now! I must not, I cannot, I dare not yet! Wait a few days and you shall know all! Oh, it is hard to keep a secret from my boy! but then it is not only *my* secret, but another's! You do not think hard of me for withholding it now, do you Traverse?" she asked, affectionately.

"No, dear mother, of course I don't. I know you must be right, and I am glad to see you happy."

"Happy! Oh, boy, you don't know how happy I am! I did not think any human being could ever feel so joyful in this erring world, much less I! One cause of this excess of joyful feeling must be from the contrast! else it were dreadful to be so happy!"

"Mother, I don't know what you mean," said Traverse, uneasily, for he was too young to understand these paradoxes of feeling and thought, and there were moments when he feared for his mother's reason.

"Oh, Traverse, think of it! eighteen long, long years of estrangement, sorrow, and dreadful suspense! eighteen long, long, weary years of patience against anger, and loving against hatred, and hoping against despair! your young mind cannot grasp it—your very life is not so long. I was seventeen then; I am thirty-five now. And after wasting all my young years of womanhood in loving, hoping, longing—lo! the light of life has dawned at last."

"God save you, mother!" said the boy, fervently, for her wild, unnatural joy continued to augment his anxiety.

"Ah, Traverse, I dare not tell you the secret now, and yet I am always letting it out; because my heart overflows from its fulness. Ah, boy, many, many weary nights have I lain awake from grief; but last night I lay awake from joy. Think of it."

The boy's only reply to this was a deep sigh. He was becoming seriously alarmed.

"I never saw her so excited. I wish she would get calm," was his secret thought.

Then, with the design of changing the current of her ideas, he took off his coat, and said:

"Mother, my pocket is half torn out, and though there's no danger of my losing a great deal out of it, still I'll get you, please, to sew it in while I mend the fence."

"Sew the pocket! mend the fence! Well," smiled Mrs. Rocke, "we'll do so, if it will amuse you. The mended fence will be a convenience to the next tenant, and the patched coat will do for some poor boy. Ah, Traverse, we must be very good to the poor, in more ways than in giving them what we do not ourselves need, for we shall know what it is to have been poor," she concluded, in more serious tones than she had yet used.

Traverse was glad of this, and went out to his work feeling somewhat better satisfied.

This delirium of happiness lasted intermittently a whole week, during the last three days of which Mrs. Rocke was constantly going to the door and looking up the road, as if expecting some one. The mail came from Tip-Top to Staunton only once a week, on Saturday mornings. Therefore, when Saturday came again, she sent her son to the post office, saying:

"If they do not come to-day, they will surely write."

Traverse hastened with all his speed, and got there so soon that he had to wait for the mail to be opened.

Meanwhile, at home, the widow walked the floor in restless, joyous anticipation, or went to the door and strained her eyes up the road to watch for Traverse, and perhaps for some one else's coming. At last she discerned her son, who came down the road, walking rapidly, smiling triumphantly, and holding a letter up to view.

She ran out of the gate to meet him, seized and kissed the letter, and then, with her face burning, her heart palpitating, and her fingers trembling, she hastened into the house, threw herself into the little low chair by the fire, and opened the letter. It was from Herbert, and read thus:

HURRICANE HALL, Nov. 30th, 1845.

MY DEAREST AND BEST MRS. ROCKE:—May God strengthen you to read the few bitter lines I have to write. Most unhappily, Major Warfield did *not* know exactly who you were, when he promised so much. Upon learning your name he withdrew all his promises. At night, in his library, he told me all your early history. Having heard all, the very worst, I believe you as pure as an angel. So I told him. So I would uphold with my life, and seal with my death. Trust yet in God, and believe in the earnest respect and affection of your grateful and attached son.

HERBERT GREYSON.

P.S.—For henceforth I shall call you mother.

Quietly she finished reading, pressed the letter again to her lips, reached it to the fire, saw it, like her hopes, shrivel up to ashes, and then she arose, and with her trembling fingers clinging together, walked up and down the floor.

There were no tears in her eyes, but oh, such a look of unutterable woe on her pale, blank, despairing face.

Traverse watched her, and saw that something had gone frightfully wrong; that some awful revolution of fate or revulsion of feeling had passed over her in this dread hour.

Cautiously he approached her, gently he laid his hand upon her shoulder, tenderly he whispered:

"Mother!"

She turned and looked strangely at him, then exclaiming:

"Oh, Traverse, how happy I was this day week!" She burst into a flood of tears.

Traverse threw his arm around his mother's waist, and half-coaxed and half-bore her to her low chair, and sat her in it, and knelt by her side; and embracing her fondly, whispered:

"Mother, don't weep so bitterly. You have *me*, am *I* nothing? Mother, *I* love you more than son ever loved his mother, or suitor his sweetheart, or husband his wife. Oh, is *my* love nothing, mother?"

Only sobs answered him.

"Mother," he pleaded, "you are all the world to *me*—let me be all the world to *you*. I *can* be it, mother,—I can be it; try me. I will make every effort for my mother, and the Lord will bless us."

Still no answer but convulsive sobs.

"Oh, mother, mother, I will try to do for you more than ever son did for mother, or man for woman before, dear mother, if you will not break my heart by weeping so."

The sobbing abated a little, partly from exhaustion and partly from the soothing influences of the boy's loving words.

"Listen, dear mother, what I will do. In the olden times of chivalry, young knights bound themselves by sacred vows to the service of some lady, and labored long and perilously in her honor; for her, blood was spilt—for her, fields were won; but, mother, never yet toiled knight in the battlefield for his lady-love as I will, in the battle of life, for my dearest lady— my own mother."

She reached out her hand, and silently pressed his.

"Come, come," said Traverse—"lift up your head and smile! We are young yet, both you and I! for after all you are not much older than your son! and we two will journey up and down the hills of life together—all in all to each other; and when at last we are old, as we shall be when you are seventy-seven and I am sixty—we will leave all our fortune that we shall have made to found a home for widows and orphans,—as *we were*, and we will pass out and go to Heaven together."

Now indeed this poor, modern Hagar looked—and smiled at the oddity of her Ishmael's far-reaching thought.[39]

In that poor household grief might not be indulged. Marah Rocke took down her work-basket and sat down to finish a lot of shirts, and Traverse went out with his horse and saw, to look for a job at cutting wood for twenty-five cents a cord. Small beginnings of the fortune that was to found and endow asylums! but many a fortune has been commenced upon less!

Marah Rocke had managed to dismiss her boy with a smile—but that was the last effort of nature; as soon as he was gone and she found herself alone, tear after tear welled up in her eyes and rolled down her pale cheeks; sigh after sigh heaved her bosom!

Ah! the transitory joy of the past week had been but the lightning's arrowy course *scathing* where it illumined!

She felt as if this last blow, that had struck her down from the height of hope to the depth of despair, had broken her heart—as if the power of reaction was gone, and she mourned as one who would not be comforted.

While she sat thus the door opened, and before she was aware of his presence, Herbert Greyson entered the room and came softly to her side. Ere she could speak to him, he dropped upon one knee at her feet, bowed his young head lowly over the hand that he took and pressed to his lips. Then he arose and stood before her. This was not unnatural or exaggerated—it was his way of expressing the reverential sympathy and compassion he felt for her strange, life-long martyrdom.

"Herbert, you here? why we only got your letter this morning," she said, in tones of gentle inquiry, as she arose and placed a chair for him.

"Yes, I could not bear to stay away from you, at such a time; I came up in the same mail-coach that brought my letter; but I kept myself out of Traverse's sight, for I could not bear to intrude upon you in the first hour of your disappointment," said Herbert, in a broken voice.

"Oh! that need not have kept you away, dear boy; I did not cry much; I am used to trouble, you know; I shall get over this also—after a little while—and things will go in the old

---

39 Genesis 21. Hagar was a servant of Abraham who bore him a son named Ishmael. Because of his wife, Sarah, Abraham expelled both Hagar and Ishmael into the wilderness. They were eventually saved by an angel.

way," said Marah Rocke, struggling to repress the rising emotion that however overcame her, for dropping her head upon her "sailor boy's" shoulder, she burst into a flood of tears and wept plenteously.

"Dear mother, be comforted," he said; "dear mother, be comforted."

Chapter XIII

Marah's Memories

"In the shade of the apple tree again
She saw a rider draw his rein.
And gazing down with a timid grace,
She felt his pleased eyes read her face."
—*Whittier*[40]

"DEAR MARAH, I cannot understand your strong attachment to that bronzed and grizzled old man, who has besides treated you so barbarously," said Herbert.

"Is he bronzed and gray?" asked Marah, looking up with gentle pity in her eyes and tone.

"Why of course he is. He is sixty-three."

"He was forty-five when I first knew him, and he was very handsome then—at least I thought him the very perfection of manly strength, and beauty, and goodness. True, it was the mature, warm beauty of the Indian summer—for he was more than middle-aged; but it was very genial to the chilly, loveless morning of my early life," said Marah, dropping her head upon her hand, and sliding into reminiscences of the past.

"Dear Marah, I wish you would tell me all about your marriage and misfortunes," said Herbert, in a tone of the deepest sympathy and respect.

"Yes, he was very handsome," continued Mrs. Rocke, speaking more to herself than to her companion; "his form was tall, full and stately; his complexion warm, rich and glowing; his fine face was lighted up by a pair of strong, dark gray eyes, full of fire and tenderness, and was surrounded by waving masses of jet black hair and whiskers—they are gray now, you say, Herbert?"

"Gray and grizzled, and bristling up around his hard face, like thorn-bushes around a rock in winter!" said Herbert, bluntly, for it enraged his honest but inexperienced boyish heart to hear this wronged woman speak so enthusiastically.

"Ah! it is winter with him *now*, but *then* it was glorious Indian summer. *He* was a handsome, strong and ardent man. *I* was a young, slight, pale girl, with no beauty but the cold and colorless beauty of a statue; with no learning, but such as I had picked up from a country school; with no love to bless my lonely life—for I was a friendless orphan, without either parents or relatives, and living by sufferance in a cold and loveless home."

"Poor girl!" murmured Herbert, in almost inaudible tones.

"Our log cabin stood beside the military road leading through the wilderness to the Fort where he was stationed. And oh, when he came riding by each day, upon his noble, coal black steed, and in his martial uniform, looking so vigorous, handsome and kingly, he seemed to me almost a god to worship. Sometimes he drew rein in front of the old oak tree that stood in front of our cabin, to breathe his horse, or to ask for a draught of water. I used to bring it to him. Oh! then, when he looked at me, his eyes seemed to send new warmth to

---

40 Whittier, "Maud Muller."

my chilled heart; when he spoke, too, his tones seemed to strengthen me; while he stayed, his presence seemed to protect me."

"'Ay, *such* protection as vultures give to doves—covering and devouring them,'" muttered Herbert to himself. Mrs. Rocke, too absorbed in her reminiscences to heed his interruptions, continued:

"One day he asked me to be his wife. I do not know what I answered, or if I answered anything. I only know that when I understood what he meant my heart trembled with instinctive terror at its own excessive joy! We were privately married by the chaplain at the Fort. There were no accommodations for the wives of officers there. And besides, my husband did not wish to announce our marriage, until he was ready to take me to his princely mansion in Virginia."

"Humph!" grunted Herbert, inwardly, for comment.

"But he built for me a pretty cabin in the woods below the Fort, furnished it simply, and hired a half-breed Indian woman to wait on me. Oh, I was too happy! To my wintry spring of life summer had come, warm, rich and beautiful! There is a clause in the marriage service which enjoins the husband to *cherish* his wife. I do not believe many people ever stop to think how much is in that word. He *did;* he cherished my little thin, chill, feeble life, until I became strong, warm and healthful. Oh! even as the blessed sun warms and animates, and glorifies the earth, causing it to brighten with life, and blossom with flowers, and bloom with fruit, so did my husband enrich, and cherish, and bless my life. Such happiness could not and it did not last."

"Of course not," muttered Herbert to himself.

"At first the fault was in myself. Yes, Herbert, it was! you need not look incredulous, or hope to cast all the blame on him! Listen: happy, grateful, adoring as I was, I was also shy, timid, and bashful—never proving the deep love I bore my husband except by the most perfect self-abandonment to his will. All this deep though quiet devotion he understood as mere passive obedience void of love. As this continued he grew uneasy, and often asked me if I cared for him at all, or if it were possible for a young girl like me to love an old man like himself."

"A very natural question," thought Herbert.

"Well, I used to whisper in answer, 'Yes,' and still 'Yes.' But this never satisfied Major Warfield. One day, when he asked me if I cared for him the least in the world, I suddenly answered, that if he were to die I should throw myself across his grave, and lie there until death should release me! whereupon he broke into a loud laugh, saying, 'Methinks the lady doth protest too much.'[41] I was already blushing deeply at the unwonted vehemence of my own words, although I had spoken only as I felt—the very, very truth; but his laugh and his jest so increased my confusion—that—in fine that was the first and last time I ever *did* protest! Like Lear's Cordelia, I was tongue-tied[42]—I had no words to assure him. Sometimes I wept to think how poor I was in resources to make him happy. Then came another annoyance—my name and fame were freely discussed at the Fort."

"A natural consequence," sighed Herbert.

"The younger officers discovered my woodland home, and often stole out to reconnoitre my cabin. Among them was Captain Le Noir, who, after he had discovered my retreat, picked acquaintance with Lura, my attendant. Making the woodland sports his pretext, he

41 Shakespeare, *Hamlet*, 3.2.
42 Shakespeare, *King Lear*, 1.1.

haunted the vicinity of my cabin, often stopping at the door to beg a cup of water, which of course was never denied, or else to offer a bunch of partridges, or a brace of rabbits, or some other game, the sports of his gun, which equally of course was never accepted. One beautiful morning in June, finding my cabin door open and myself alone, he ventured unbidden across my threshold, and by his free conversation, and bold admiration, offended and alarmed me. Some days afterwards, in the mess-room at the Fort, being elevated by wine, he boasted among his mess-mates of the intimate terms of friendly acquaintance upon which he falsely asserted that he had the pleasure of standing with 'Warfield's pretty little favorite,' as he insolently called me. When my husband heard of this, I learned for the first time of the terrific violence of his temper. It was awful! It frightened me almost to death. There was a duel, of course. Le Noir was very dangerously wounded—scarred across the face for life, and was confined many weeks to his bed. Major Warfield was also slightly hurt, and laid up at the Fort for a few days, during which I was not permitted to see him."

"Is it possible that even *then* he did not see your danger, and acknowledge your marriage, and call you to his bedside?" inquired Herbert impatiently.

"No! no! if he *had,* all after suffering had been spared! No! at the end of four days he came back to me; but we met only for bitter reproaches on his part, and sorrowful tears on mine. He charged me with coldness, upon account of the disparity in our years, and of preference for Captain Le Noir, because he was 'a pretty fellow.' I knew this was not true of me. I knew that I loved my husband's very footprints better than I did the whole human race besides; but I could not tell him so then. Oh, in those days, though my heart was so full, I had so little power of utterance. There he stood before me! he that had been so ruddy and buoyant, now so pale from loss of blood, and so miserable, that I could have fallen and groveled at his feet in sorrow and remorse at not being able to make him happy!"

"There are some persons whom we can never make happy! It is not in them to be so." commented Herbert.

"He made me promise never to see or to speak to Le Noir again—a promise eagerly given but nearly impossible to keep. My husband spent as much time with me as he possibly could spare from his military duties, and looked forward with impatience to the autumn, when it was thought that he would be at liberty to take me home. He often used to tell me that we should spend our Christmas at his house, Hurricane Hall, and that I should play Lady Bountiful, and distribute Christmas gifts to the negroes, and that they would love me. And oh! with what joy I anticipated that time of honor and safety and careless ease, as an acknowledged wife, in the home of my husband! There, too, I fondly believed our child would be born. All his old tenderness returned for me, and I was as happy if not as wildly joyful, as at first."

"'Twas but a lull in the storm," said Herbert.

"Aye! 'twas but a lull in the storm, or rather *before* the storm! I do think that from the time of that duel, Le Noir had resolved upon our ruin. As soon as he was able to go out, he haunted the woods around my cabin, and continually lay in wait for me. I could not go out even in the company of my maid Lura to pick blackberries and wild plums, or gather forest roses, or to get fresh water at the spring, without being intercepted by Le Noir and his offensive admiration. He seemed to be ubiquitous! He met me everywhere—except in the presence of Major Warfield. I did not tell my husband, because I feared that if I did he would have killed Le Noir, and died for the deed."

"Humph! it would have been 'good riddance of bad rubbish' in *both* cases!" muttered Herbert, under his teeth.

"But instead of telling him, I confined myself strictly to my cabin. One fatal day my husband, on leaving me in the morning, said that I need not wait up for him at night, for that it would be very late when he came, even if he came at all. He kissed me very fondly when he went away. Alas! alas! it was the last—last time! At night I went to bed disappointed, yet still so expectant that I could not sleep. I know not how long I had waited thus, or how late it was when I heard a tap at the outer door, and heard the bolt undraw, and a footstep enter, and a low voice asking:

"'*Is she asleep?*' and Lura's reply in the affirmative. Never doubting it was my husband, I lay there in pleased expectation of his entrance. He came in, and began to take off his coat in the dark. I spoke, telling him that there were matches on the bureau. He did not reply, at which I was surprised; but before I could even repeat my words, the outer door was burst violently open, hurried footsteps crossed the entry, a light flashed into my room, my husband stood in the door in full military uniform, with a light in his hand and the aspect of an avenging demon on his brow and——

"HORROR OF HORRORS! the half-undressed man in my chamber was Captain Le Noir! I saw, and swooned away!"

"But you were saved! you were saved!" gasped Herbert, white with emotion.

"Oh, I was saved, but not from sorrow—not from shame! I awoke from that deadly swoon to find myself alone, deserted, cast away! Oh! torn out from the warmth and light and safety of my home in my husband's heart, and hurled forth shivering, faint and helpless upon the bleak world! and all this in twenty-four hours! Ah! I did not lack the power of expression then! happiness had never given it to me—anguish conferred it upon me! that one fell stroke of fate cleft the rock of silence in my soul, and the fountain of utterance gushed freely forth. I wrote to him—but my letters might as well have been dropped into a well. I went to him, but was spurned away. I prayed him with tears to have pity on our unborn babe; but he laughed aloud in scorn, and called it by an opprobrious name! Letters, prayers, tears, were all in vain. He never *had* acknowledged our marriage, he now declared that he never *would* do so; he discarded me, disowned my child, and forbade us ever to take his name!"

"Oh, Marah! and you but seventeen years of age! without a father or a brother or a friend in the world to take your part! without even means to employ an advocate!" exclaimed Herbert, covering his face with his hands and sinking back.

"Nor would I have used any of these agencies, had I possessed them! If my wifehood and motherhood, my affection and my helplessness, were not advocates strong enough to win my cause, I could not have borne to employ others."

"Oh, Marah, with none to pity or to help! it was monstrous to have abandoned you so!"

"No! hush; consider the overwhelming evidence against me! I considered it even in the tempest and whirlwind of my anguish, and never once blamed and never once was angry with my husband. For I knew— not *he*, but the terrible circumstantial evidence had ruined me!"

"Ay, but did you not explain it to him?"

"How could I, alas! when I did not understand it myself? How Le Noir knew that Major Warfield was not expected home that fatal night—how he got into my house, whether by conspiring with my little maid, or by deceiving her—or lastly, how Major Warfield came to burst in upon him so suddenly, I did not know, and do not to this day!"

"But you told Major Warfield all that you have told me?"

"Oh, yes! again and again, calling Heaven to witness my truth! In vain! *'he had seen with his own eyes,'* he said. Against all I could say or do, there was built up a wall of scornful incredulity, on which I might have dashed my brains out to no purpose!"

"Oh, Marah! Marah! with none to pity or to save!" again exclaimed Herbert.

"Yes," said the meek creature, bowing her head; "God pitied and helped me! First he sent me a son that grew strong and handsome in body, good and wise in soul. Then he kept alive in my heart faith and hope and charity. He enabled me, through long years of unremitting and ill-requited toil, to live on, loving against anger, waiting against time, and hoping against despair!"

"Why did you leave your western home and come to Staunton, Marah?" asked Herbert.

"To be where I could sometimes hear of my husband, without intruding on him. I took your widowed mother in because she was *his* sister, though I never told her who I was, lest *she* should wrong and scorn me, as *he* had done. When she died I cherished you, Herbert, first because you were *his* nephew, but now, dear boy, for your own sake, also."

"And I, while I live, will be a son to you, Madam! I will be your constant friend at Hurricane Hall. He talks of making me his heir. Should he persist in such blind injustice, the day I come into the property, I shall turn it all over to his widow and son. But I do not believe that he *will* persist; I, for my part, still hope for the best."

"I also hope for the best, for whatever God wills is sure to happen, and his will is surely the best! Yes, Herbert, I also hope—*beyond the grave!*" said Marah Rocke, with a wan smile.

The little clock that stood between the tall plated candlesticks on the mantel-piece struck twelve, and Marah rose from her seat, saying:

"Traverse, poor fellow, will be home to his dinner. Not a word to him, Herbert, please! I do not wish the poor lad to know how much he has lost, and above all, I do not wish him to be prejudiced against his father."

"You are right, Marah," said Herbert, "for if he were told, the natural indignation that your wrongs would arouse in his heart, would totally unfit him to meet his father, in a proper spirit, in that event for which I still hope—a future and a perfect family union!"

HERBERT GREYSON remained a week with his friends, during which time he paid the quarter's rent, and relieved his adopted mother of that cause of anxiety. Then he took leave and departed for Hurricane Hall, on his way to Washington City, whence he was immediately going to pass his examination and await his appointment.

Chapter XIV

The Wasting Heart

"Then she took up the burden of life again,
Saying only, 'It might have been.'
Alas for them both, and alas for us all,
Who vainly the dreams of youth recall,
For of all sad words of lips, or pen,
The saddest are these—'It might have been.'"
—*Whittier*[43]

---

43 Whittier, "Maud Muller."

By THE TACIT consent of all parties, the meteor hope that had crossed and vanished from Marah Rocke's path of life was never mentioned again. Mother and son went about their separate tasks. Traverse worked at jobs all day, studied at night, and went twice a week to recite his lessons to his patron, Doctor Day, at Willow Hill. Marah sewed as usual all day, and prepared her boy's meals at the proper times. But day by day her cheeks grew paler, her form thinner, her step fainter. Her son saw this decline with great alarm. Sometimes he found her in a deep, troubled reverie, from which she would awaken with heavy sighs. Sometimes he surprised her in tears. At such times he did not trouble her with questions that he instinctively felt she could not or would not answer; but he came gently to her side, put his arms about her neck, stooped and laid her face against his breast, and whispered assurances of his "true love," and his boyish hopes of "getting on," of "making a fortune," and bringing "brighter days" for her!

And she would return his caresses, and with a faint smile reply that he "must not mind" her, that she was only "a little low-spirited," that she would "get over it soon."

But as day followed day, she grew visibly thinner and weaker, dark shadows settled under her hollow eyes and in her sunken cheeks. One evening, while standing at the table washing up their little tea-service, she suddenly dropped into her chair and fainted. Nothing could exceed the alarm and distress of poor Traverse. He hastened to fix her in an easy position, bathed her face and hands in vinegar and water—the only restoratives in their meagre stock—and called upon her by every loving epithet to live and speak to him. The fit yielded to his efforts, and presently, with a few fluttering inspirations, her breath returned and her eyes opened. Her very first words were attempts to re-assure her dismayed boy. But Traverse could no more be flattered. He entreated his mother to go at once to bed. And though the next morning, when she arose, she looked not worse than usual, Traverse left home with a heart full of trouble. But instead of turning down the street to go to his work in the town, he turned up the street towards the wooded hills beyond, now glowing in their gorgeous autumn foliage, and burning in the brilliant morning sun.

A half hour's walk brought him to a high and thickly-wooded hill, up which a private road led through a thicket of trees to a handsome gray stone country seat, situated in the midst of beautifully ornamented grounds, and known as Willow Heights, the residence of Doctor William Day, a retired physician of great repute, and a man of earnest piety. He was a widower with one fair daughter, Clara, a girl of fourteen, then absent at boarding-school. Traverse had never seen this girl, but his one great admiration was the beautiful Willow Heights, and its worthy proprietor. He opened the highly ornate iron gate, and entered upon an avenue of willows that led up to the house, a two-storied edifice of gray stone, with full-length front piazzas above and below.

Arrived at the door, he rang the bell, which was answered promptly by a good-humored-looking negro boy, who at once showed Traverse to the library up stairs, where the good doctor sat at his books. Doctor Day was at this time about fifty years of age, tall and stoutly built, with a fine head and face, shaded by soft, bright flaxen hair and beard; thoughtful and kindly dark blue eyes; and an earnest, penetrating smile, that reached like sunshine the heart of any one upon whom it shone. He wore a cheerful-looking flowered chintz dressing-gown corded around his waist; his feet were thrust into embroidered slippers; and he sat in his elbow-chair at his reading table, poring over a huge folio volume. The whole aspect of the man, and of his surroundings, was kindly cheerfulness. The room opened upon the upper front piazza, and the windows were all up to admit the bright morning sun and genial air, at the same time that there was a glowing fire in the grate to temper its chilliness. Traverse's soft step across the carpeted floor was not heard by the doctor, who was only made aware of his presence by his stepping between the sunshine and his table. Then the doctor arose, and with his intense smile extended his hands, and greeted the boy with:

"Well, Traverse, lad, you are always welcome! I did not expect you until night, as usual, but as you are here, so much the better! Got your exercise all ready, eh?—Heaven bless you, lad! what is the matter?" inquired the good man suddenly, on first observing the boy's deeply troubled looks.

"My mother, sir! my mother!" was all that Traverse could at first utter.

"Your mother! My dear lad, what about her—is she ill?" inquired the doctor, with interest.

"Oh, sir, I am afraid she is going to die!" exclaimed the boy in a choking voice, struggling hard to keep from betraying his manhood by bursting into tears.

"Going to die—oh! pooh, pooh, pooh, she is not going to die, lad! tell me all about it," said the doctor, in an encouraging tone.

"She has had so much grief, and care, and anxiety, sir—Doctor, is there any such malady as a broken heart?"

"Broken heart?—pooh, pooh! no, my child, no! never heard of such a thing in thirty years' medical experience! Even that story of a porter who broke his heart trying to lift a ton of stone is all a fiction. No such disease as a broken heart. But tell me about your mother!"

"It is of her that I am talking; she has had so much trouble in her life, and now I think she is sinking under it; she has been failing for weeks, and last night, while washing the teacups, she fainted away from the table!"

"Heaven help us, that looks bad," said the doctor.

"Oh, does it? does it, sir? *She* said it was 'nothing much.' Oh, Doctor, don't say she will die! don't! if she were to die—if mother were to die, I'd give right up! I never should do a bit of good in the world, for *she* is all the motive I have in this life! To study hard—to work hard, and make her comfortable and happy, so as to make up to her for all she has suffered, is my greatest wish and endeavor! Oh, don't say mother will die, it would ruin me!" cried Traverse.

"My dear boy, I don't say anything of the sort! I say, judging from your account, that her health must be attended to immediately. And— true I have retired from practice; but I will go and see your mother, Traverse!"

"Oh, sir, if you only would! I came to ask you to do that very thing! I should not have presumed to ask such a favor for any cause but this of my dear mother's life and health, and you will go to see her?"

"Willingly and without delay, Traverse," said the good man, rising immediately and hurrying into an adjoining chamber.

"Order the gig while I dress, Traverse, and I will take you back with me," he added, as he closed the chamber door behind him.

By the time Traverse had gone down, given the necessary orders and returned to the library, the doctor emerged from his chamber, buttoned up in his gray frock coat, and booted, gloved and capped for the ride.

They went down together, entered the gig, and drove rapidly down the willow avenue, slowly through the iron gate and through the dark thicket, and down the wooded hill to the high road, and then as fast as the sorrel mare could trot towards town. In fifteen minutes, the doctor pulled up his gig, at the right-hand side of the road before the cottage gate.

They entered the cottage, Traverse going first in order to announce the doctor. They found Mrs. Rocke, as usual, seated in her low chair by the little fire, bending over her needlework. She looked up with surprise as they came in.

"Mother, this is Doctor Day, come to see you," said Traverse.

She arose from her chair, and raised those soft and timid dark gray eyes to the stranger's face, where they met that sweet, intense smile that seemed to encourage while it shone upon her.

"We have never met before, Mrs. Rocke, but we both feel too much interest in this good lad here to meet as strangers now," said the doctor, extending his hand.

"Traverse gives me every day fresh cause to be grateful to you, sir, for kindness that we can never, never repay," said Marah Rocke, pressing that bountiful hand, and then placing a chair, which the doctor took.

Traverse seated himself at a little distance, and as the doctor conversed with and covertly examined his mother's face, *he* watched the doctor's countenance, as if life and death hung upon the character of its expression. But while they talked, not one word was said upon the subject of sickness or medicine. They talked of Traverse. The doctor assured his mother that her son was a boy of such fine talent, character and promise, that he had already made such rapid progress in his classical and mathematical studies, that he ought immediately to enter upon a course of reading for one of the learned professions.

The mother turned a smile full of love, pride and sorrow upon the fine, intellectual face of her boy, and said:

"You are like the angel in Cole's picture of life.[44] You point the youth to the far-up temple of fame——"

"And leave him to get there as he can. Not at all madam! Let us see. Traverse, you are now going on eighteen years of age; if you had your choice, which of the learned professions would you prefer for yourself— law, physic, or divinity?"

The boy looked up and smiled, then dropped his head and seemed to reflect.

"Perhaps you have never thought upon the subject. Well, you must take time—you must take time! so as to be firm in your decision when you have once decided," said the doctor.

"Oh, sir, I have thought of it long! and my choice has been long and firmly decided, were I only free to follow it!"

"Speak, lad! What is your choice?"

"Why, don't you *know*, sir? Can't you guess? Why, your *own* profession, *of course*, sir! Certainly sir, I could not think of any other!" exclaimed the boy, with sparkling eyes and flushed cheeks.

"*That's* my own lad!" exclaimed the doctor, enthusiastically seizing the boy's hand with one of his, and clapping the other down upon his palm; for if the doctor had an admiration in the world it was for his own profession. "*That's* my own lad! *My* profession! the *healing* art! why, it is the *only* profession worthy the study of an immortal being. *Law* sets people by

---

44 The famous American landscape painter, Thomas Cole (1801–1848), created an allegorical sequence consisting of four paintings in 1842 called "The Voyage of Life." In these paintings an angel serves as a guide.

the ears together! *Divinity* should never be considered as a profession—it is a divine *mission!* Physic! physic, my boy! The *healing* art! *that's* the profession for you! And I am very glad to hear you declare for it, too; for *now* the way is perfectly clear!"

Both mother and son looked up in surprise.

"Yes, the way is perfectly clear. Nothing is easier! Traverse shall come and read medicine in my office. I shall be glad to have the lad there. It will amuse me to give him instruction occasionally! I have a positive mania for teaching."

"And for doing good! Oh, sir, how have we deserved this kindness at your hands? and how shall we ever, ever repay it?" cried Mrs. Rocke, in a broken voice, while the tears filled her gentle eyes.

"Oh, pooh, pooh! a mere nothing, ma'am! a mere nothing for me to do, whatever it may prove to him. It is very hard, indeed, if I am to be crushed under a cart load of thanks for doing something for a boy I like, when it does not cost me a cent of money, or a breath of effort."

"Oh, sir, your generous refusal of our thanks does but deepen our obligation," said Marah, still weeping.

"Now, my dear madam, will you persist in making me confess that it is all selfishness on my part? I *like* the boy, I tell you! I shall like his bright, cheerful face in my office. I can make him very useful to me, also——"

"Oh, sir! if you can and *will* only make him useful to you——"

"Why, to be sure I can, and will! He can act as my clerk, keep my accounts, write my letters, drive out with me, and sit in the gig while I go in to visit my patients, for though I have pretty much retired from practice, still——"

"Still you visit and prescribe for the sick poor, gratis!" added Marah, feelingly.

"Pooh, pooh! habit, madam, habit! 'ruling passion strong in death,' etc. I can't, for the life of me, keep from giving people bread pills! And now, by the way, I must be off to see some of my patients in Staunton! Traverse, my lad—my young medical assistant, I mean—are you willing to go with me?"

"Oh, sir," said the boy, and here his voice broke down with emotion.

"Come along, then!" laughed the doctor; "you shall drive with me into the village as a commencement."

Traverse got his hat, while the doctor held out his hand to Mrs. Rocke, who, with her eyes full of tears, and her voice faltering with emotion, began again to thank him, when he good-humoredly interrupted her by saying:

"Now, my good little woman, *do—pray—hush!* I'm a selfish fellow, as you'll see! I do nothing but what pleases my own self, and makes me happy! Good-bye! God bless you, madam!" he cried, cordially shaking her hand. "Come, Traverse," he added, hurriedly striding out of the door and through the yard, to the gate before which the old green gig and sorrel mare were still waiting.

"Traverse, I brought you out again to-day, more especially to speak of your mother and her state of health," said Doctor Day, very seriously, as they both took their seats in the gig and drove on towards the town. "Traverse, your mother is in no immediate danger of death; in fact, she has no disease whatever!"

"Oh, sir, you do not think her ill, then! I thought you did not, from the fact that you never felt her pulse, or gave her a prescription!" exclaimed Traverse, delightedly, for in one thing the lad resembled his mother—he was sensitive and excitable—easily depressed and easily exhilarated.

"Traverse, I said your mother is in no immediate danger of death, for that in fact she has no disease; but yet, Traverse, brace yourself up, for I am about to strike you a heavy blow! Traverse! Marah Rocke is—*starving!*"

"STARVING! Heaven of Heavens! no! that is not so! it cannot be! My mother starving! oh, horrible! horrible! But, Doctor, it cannot—cannot be! Why, we have two meals a day at our house!" cried the boy, almost beside himself with agitation.

"Lad, there are other starvations beside the total lack of food! there are slow starvations and divers ones! Marah Rocke is starving slowly and in every way! mind, soul and body! her body is slowly wasting from the want of proper nutriment, her heart from the want of human sympathy, her mind from the need of social intercourse. Her whole manner of life must be changed if she is to live at all!"

"Oh, sir, I understand you now! I feel, I feel that you speak the very truth! Something must be done! I must do something. What shall it be? Oh, advise me, sir!"

"I must reflect a little, Traverse," said the doctor, thoughtfully, as he drove along with very slack reins.

"And so, how thoughtless of me! I forgot, indeed I did, sir, when I so gladly accepted your offer for me to read with you, I forgot that if I spent every day reading in your office, my mother would sadly miss the dollar and a half a week I made by doing little odd jobs in town."

"But *I* did not forget it, boy; rest easy upon that score; and now let me reflect how we can best serve your good little mother!" said the doctor, and he drove slowly and thoughtfully along for about twenty minutes before he spoke again, when he said:

"Traverse, Monday is the first of the month. You shall set in with me then. Come to me, therefore, on Monday, and I think by that time, I shall have thought upon some plan for your mother. In the meantime, you may make as much money at jobs as you can, and also you must accept from me for her a bottle or so of port wine and a turkey or two! Tell her, if she demurs, that it is the doctor's prescription, and that for fear of accidents he always prefers to send his own physic!"

"Oh, Doctor Day, if I could only thank you aright!" cried Traverse.

"Pooh, pooh! nonsense! there is no time for it. Here we are at Spicer's grocery store, where I suppose you are again employed. Yes? Well, jump out then. You can still make half a day. Mind, remember on Monday next December 1st, you enter my office as my medical student, and by that time I shall have some plan arranged for your mother Good-bye! God bless you lad!" said the good doctor, as he drove off and left Traverse standing in the genial autumn sunshine, with his heart swelling and his eyes overflowing with excess of gratitude and happiness.

Chapter XV

Cap's Country Capers

"A willful elf—an uncle's child.
That half a pet and half a pest,
Was still reproved, endured, caressed
Yet never tamed, though never spoiled."

CAPITOLA AT FIRST was delighted and half incredulous at the great change in her fortunes. The spacious and comfortable mansion of which she found herself the little mistress; the high rank of the veteran officer who claimed her as his ward and niece; the abundance, regularity, and respectability of her new life; the leisure, the privacy, the attendance of servants, were all so entirely different from anything to which she had previously been accustomed, that there were times when she doubted its reality, and distrusted her own identity or her sanity.

Sometimes, of a morning, after a very vivid dream of the alleys, cellars, and gutters, rag-pickers, newsboys, and beggars of New York, she would open her eyes upon her own comfortable chamber, with its glowing fire and crimson curtains, its bright mirror crowning the walnut bureau between them, and would jump up and gaze wildly around, not remembering where she was, or how she came thither.

Sometimes, suddenly started by an intense realization of the contrast between her past and her present life, she would mentally inquire:

"Can this be really *I* myself, and not another? *I*, the little houseless wanderer through the streets and alleys of New York? *I*, the little newsgirl in boy's clothes? *I*, the wretched little vagrant that was brought up before the Recorder, and was about to be sent to the House of Refuge for juvenile delinquents? Can this be *I*, Capitola, the little outcast of the city, now changed into Miss Black, the young lady, perhaps the heiress of a fine old country seat! calling a fine old military officer uncle! having a handsome income of pocket-money settled upon me! having carriages, and horses, and servants to attend me? No; it can't be! it's just impossible. No—I see how it is. I'm crazy, that's what *I* am—crazy! For now I think of it, the last thing I remember of my former life was being brought before the Recorder for wearing boy's clothes. Now I'm sure that it was upon that occasion that I went suddenly mad with trouble, and all the rest is a lunatic's fancy. This fine old country seat, of which I vainly think myself the mistress, is just the pauper mad-house to which the magistrates have sent me. This fine old military officer whom I call my uncle is the head-doctor. The servants who come at my call are the keepers.

"There is no figure out of my past life in my present one, except Herbert Greyson. But, pshaw! *he* is not 'the nephew of his uncle!' he is only my old comrade Herbert Greyson, the sailor lad, who comes here to the mad-house to see me, and out of compassion humors all my fancies.

"I wonder how long they'll keep me here? Forever I hope. Until I get cured I'm sure! I hope they *won't* cure me. I vow I won't *be* cured. It's a great deal too pleasant to be mad, and I'll *stay* so. I'll keep on calling myself Miss Black, and this mad-house my country seat, and the head-doctor my uncle, and the keepers servants until the end of time—so I will. Catch me coming to my senses when it's so delightful to be mad. I'm too sharp for *that*. I didn't grow up in Rag Alley, New York, for nothing."

So, half in jest and half in earnest, Capitola soliloquized upon her change of fortune.

Her education was commenced, but progressed rather irregularly. Old Hurricane bought her books and maps, slates and copy-books, set her lessons in grammar, geography and history, and made her write copies, do sums, and read and recite lessons to him. Mrs. Condiment taught her the mysteries of cutting and basting, back-stitching and felling, hemming and seaming. A pupil as sharp as Capitola soon mastered her tasks, and found herself each day with many hours of leisure, with which she did not know what to do.

These hours were at first occupied with exploring the old house, with all its attics, cuddies, cock-lofts and cellars; then in wandering through the old ornamental grounds, that were, even in winter and in total neglect, beautiful with their wild growth of evergreens; thence she extended her researches into the wild and picturesque country around.

She was never weary of admiring the great forest that climbed the heights of the mountains behind their house; the great bleak precipices of gray rocks seen through the leafless branches of the trees; the rugged falling ground that lay before the house, and between it and the river; and the river itself, with its rushing stream and raging rapids.

Capitola had become as skilful as she had first been a fearless rider. But her rides were confined to the domain between the mountain range and the river; she was forbidden to ford the one or to climb the other. Perhaps if such a prohibition had never been made, Cap would never thought of doing the one or the other; but we all know the diabolical fascination there is in forbidden pleasures for young human nature. And no sooner had Cap been commanded, if she valued her safety, not to cross the water or climb the precipice, than, as a natural consequence, she began to wonder what was in the valley behind the mountain, and what might be in the woods across the river! and she longed, above all things, to explore and find out for herself. She would eagerly have done so, notwithstanding the prohibition; but Wool, who always attended her rides, was sadly in the way; if she could only get rid of Wool, she resolved to go upon a limited exploring expedition.

One day a golden opportunity occurred. It was a day of unusual beauty, when autumn seemed to be smiling upon the earth with her brightest smiles before passing away. In a word, it was Indian summer. The beauty of the weather had tempted Old Hurricane to ride to the county seat on particular business connected with his ward herself.

Capitola, left alone, amused herself with her tasks until the afternoon; then calling a boy, she ordered him to saddle her horse and bring him around.

"My dear, what do you want with your horse? There is no one to attend you; Wool has gone with his master," said Mrs. Condiment, as she met Capitola in the hall, habited for her ride.

"I know that; but I cannot be mewed up here in the old house and deprived of my afternoon ride!" exclaimed Capitola, decidedly.

"But, my dear, you must never think of riding out alone!" exclaimed the dismayed Mrs. Condiment.

"Indeed I shall though!—and glad of the opportunity!" added Cap, mentally.

"But, my dear love, it is improper, imprudent, dangerous."

"Why so?" asked Cap.

"Good gracious, upon every account. Suppose you were to meet with ruffians; suppose— oh, heaven!—suppose you were to meet with— BLACK DONALD!"

"Mrs. Condiment, once for all do tell me who this terrible Black Donald *is?* Is he the Evil One himself, or the Man in the Iron Mask,[45] or the individual that struck Billy Patterson, or—who is he?"

"Who is Black Donald? Good gracious, child, you ask me who is Black Donald?"

"Yes—*who* is he? *where* is he? WHAT is he, that every cheek turns pale at the mention of his name?" asked Capitola.

"Black Donald! Oh, my child, may you never know more of Black Donald than I can tell you. Black Donald is the chief of a band of ruthless desperadoes that infest these mountain roads, robbing mail-coaches, stealing negroes, breaking into houses, and committing every sort of depredation. Their hands are red with murder, and their souls black with darker crimes."

---

45 The "Man in the Iron Mask" was made famous by the French novelist Alexander Dumas. The man in the mask was a mysterious prisoner held captive for over forty years by King Louis XIV.

"Darker crimes than murder!" ejaculated Capitola.

"Yes, child, yes—there *are* darker crimes! Only last winter he and three of his gang broke into a solitary house where there was a lone woman and her daughter, and—it is not a story for you to hear, but if the people had caught Black Donald then, they would have burnt him at a stake. His life is forfeit by a hundred crimes. He is an outlaw, and a heavy price is set upon his head."

"And can no one take him?"

"No, my dear; at least, no one has been able to do so yet. His very haunts are unknown, but are supposed to be in concealed mountain caverns."

"How I would like the glory of capturing Black Donald!" said Capitola.

"*You*, child—*you* capture Black Donald! You are crazy."

"Oh, by stratagem I mean, not by force! Oh, how I should like to capture Black Donald!—There's my horse. Good-bye!"

And, before Mrs. Condiment could raise another objection, Capitola ran out, sprang into her saddle, and was seen careering down the hill towards the river as fast as her horse could fly.

"My lord, but the major will be hopping if he finds it out," was good Mrs. Condiment's dismayed exclamation.

Rejoicing in her freedom, Cap galloped down to the water's edge, and then walked her horse up and down along the course of the stream until she found a good fording place. Then gathering up her riding-skirt and throwing it over the neck of her horse, she plunged boldly into the stream, and with the water splashing and foaming all around her, urged him onward until they crossed the river and climbed up the opposite bank. A bridle-path lay before her, leading from the fording place through a deep wood. That path attracted her; she followed it, charmed alike by the solitude of the wood, the novelty of the scene, and her own sense of freedom. But one thought was given to the story of Black Donald, and that was a reassuring one.

"If Black Donald is a mail-robber, then this little bridle-path is far enough off *his* beat."

And so saying, she gaily galloped along, singing as she went, following the narrow path up hill and down dale through the wintry woods. Drawn on by the attraction of the *unknown*, and deceiving herself by the continued repetition of one resolve, namely:

"When I get to the top of the *next* hill, and see what lies beyond, *then* I will turn back," she galloped on and on—on and on—on and on! until she had put several miles between herself and her home, until her horse began to exhibit signs of weariness, and the level rays of the setting sun were striking redly through the leafless branches of the trees.

Cap drew rein on the top of a high, wooded hill, and looked about her. On her left hand the sun was sinking like a ball of fire below the horizon; all around her everywhere were the wintry woods; far away, in the direction whence she had come, she saw the tops of the mountains behind Hurricane Hall, looking like blue clouds against the southern horizon; the Hall itself and the river below were out of sight.

"I wonder how far I am from home?" said Capitola, uneasily; "somewhere between six and seven miles, I reckon. Dear me, I didn't mean to ride so far. I've got over a great deal of ground in these two hours. I shall not get back so soon; my horse is tired to death; it will take me three hours to reach Hurricane Hall. Good gracious, it will be pitch dark before I get there. No, thank heaven, there'll be a moon. But won't there be a row, though! Whew! Well, I must turn about and lose no time. Come, Gyp! get up, Gyp! good horse! we're going home!"

And so saying, Capitola turned her horse's head and urged him into a gallop.

She had gone on for about a mile, and it was growing dark, and her horse was again slackening his pace, when she *thought* she heard the sound of another horse's hoofs behind her. She drew rein and listened, and was sure of it.

Now, without being the least of a coward, Capitola thought of the loneliness of the woods, and the lateness of the hour, her own helplessness, and—Black Donald! And thinking "discretion the better part of valor," she urged her horse once more into a gallop, for a few hundred yards; but the jaded beast soon broke into a trot, and subsided into a walk that threatened soon to come to a stand still. The invisible pursuer gained on her.

In vain she urged her steed with whip and voice; the poor beast would obey and trot for a few yards, and then fall into a walk.

The thundering footfalls of the pursuing horse were close in the rear.

"Oh, Gyp! is it possible that, instead of my capturing Black Donald, you are going to let Black Donald or somebody else catch *me?*" exclaimed Capitola, in mock despair, as she urged her wearied steed.

In vain! The pursuing horseman was beside her! a strong hand was laid upon her bridle! a mocking voice was whispering in her ear:

"Whither away so fast, pretty one?"

Chapter XVI

Cap's Fearful Adventure

"Who passes by this road so late?
Companion of the Marjolaine!
Who passes by this road so late?
Say! oh, say!"
    —Old French Song[46]

OF A NATURALLY STRONG constitution and adventurous disposition, and inured from infancy to danger, Capitola possessed a high degree of courage, self-control, and presence of mind.

At the touch of that ruthless hand, at the sound of that gibing voice, all her faculties instantly collected and concentrated themselves upon the emergency. As by a flash of lightning she saw every feature of her imminent danger—the loneliness of the woods, the lateness of the hour, the recklessness of her fearful companion, and her own weakness. In another instant her resolution was taken and her course determined. So, when the stranger repeated his mocking question:

"Whither away so fast, pretty one?" she answered with animation:

"Oh, I am going home, and so glad to have company; for indeed I was dreadfully afraid of riding alone through these woods to-night!"

"Afraid, pretty one—what of?"

"Oh, of ghosts and witches, wild beasts, runaway negroes and—Black Donald!"

"Then you are not afraid of *me?*"

---

46 From the traditional French folk song, "Compaganon de la marjolaine."

"Lors! no, indeed! I guess I ain't! why should I be afraid of a respectable-looking gentleman like you, sir?"

"And so you are going home—where *is* your home, pretty one?"

"On the other side of the river; but you need not keep on calling me 'pretty one,' it must be as tiresome to you to repeat it as it is to me to hear it."

"What shall I call you, then, my dear?"

"You may call me Miss Black, or if you are friendly, you may call me Capitola."

"CAPITOLA!" exclaimed the man, in a deep and changed voice, as he dropped her bridle.

"Yes, Capitola! what objection have you got to that? It is a pretty name, isn't it? but if you think it is too long, and if you feel *very* friendly, you may call me Cap."

"Well, then, my pretty Cap, where do you live across the river?" asked the stranger, recovering his self-possession.

"Oh, at a rum old place they call Hurricane Hall, with a rum old military officer they call Old Hurricane," said Capitola, for the first time stealing a sidelong glance at her fearful companion.

It was not Black Donald—that was the first conclusion to which she rashly jumped. He appeared to be a gentlemanly ruffian about forty years of age, well dressed in a black riding suit; black beaver hat drawn down close over his eyes; black hair and whiskers; heavy black eyebrows that met across his nose; drooping eyelashes, and eyes that looked out under the corners of the lids; altogether a sly, sinister, cruel face, a cross between fox and tiger! it warned Capitola to expect no mercy there! After the girl's last words he seemed to have fallen into thought for a moment, and then again he spoke:

"Well, my pretty Cap, how long have you been living at Hurricane Hall?"

"Ever since my guardian, Major Warfield, brought me from the city of New York, where I received my education—*(in the streets)*" she mentally added.

"Humph! why did you ride so fast, my pretty Cap?" he asked, eyeing her from the corner of her eyes.

"Oh, sir, because I was *afraid*, as I told you before; afraid of runaway negroes and wild beasts, and so on—but now with a good gentleman like *you* I don't feel afraid at all; and I'm very glad to be able to walk poor Gyp; because he's tired, poor fellow!"

"Yes, poor fellow!" said the traveler, in a mocking tone, "he *is* tired; suppose you *dismount* and let him rest. Come, I'll get off, too, and we will sit down here by the roadside and have a friendly conversation."

Capitola stole a glance at his face. Yes, notwithstanding his light tone, he was grimly in earnest; there was no mercy to be expected from that sly, sinister, cruel face.

"Come, my pretty Cap, what say you?"

"I don't care if I *do*," she said, riding to the edge of the path, drawing rein, and looking down as if to examine the ground.

"Come, little beauty, must I help you off?" asked the stranger.

"N-n-no," answered Capitola, with deliberate hesitation, "no, this is not a good place to sit down and talk; it's all full of brambles."

"Very well; shall we go on a little further?"

"Oh, yes; but I don't want to ride fast, because it will tire my horse."

"You shall go just as you please, my angel," said the traveler.

"I wonder whether this wretch thinks me very simple or very depraved—he must have come to one or the other conclusion," thought Capitola.

They rode on very slowly for a mile further, and then having arrived at an open glade, the stranger drew rein, and said:

"Come, pretty lark, hop down! here's a nice place to sit and rest."

"Very well, come help me off!" said Capitola, pulling up her horse— then, as by a sudden impulse, she exclaimed, "I don't like *this* place either! it's right on the top of the hill! so windy! and just see how rocky the ground is! No! I'll not sit and rest *here,* and that I tell you!"

"I am afraid you are trifling with me, my pretty bird! take care! I'll not be trifled with!" said the man.

"I don't know what you mean by *trifling* with you, any more than the dead. But I'll not sit down there on those sharp rocks, and so I tell you. If you will be civil and ride along with me until we get to the foot of the hill, I know a *nice* place, where we can sit down and have a *good* talk, and I will tell you all my travels, and you shall tell me all yours."

"Ex-actly—and where is that nice place?"

"Why, in the valley at the foot of the hill."

"Come! come on, then."

"Slowly, slowly!" said Capitola—"I won't tire my horse." They rode over the hill, down the gradual descent, and on towards the centre of the valley.

They were now within a quarter of a mile of the river, on the opposite side of which was Hurricane Hall and—*safety!* The stranger drew rein, saying:

"Come, my cuckoo! here we are at the bottom of the valley! now or never!"

"Oh! now, of course! you see I keep my promise," answered Capitola, pulling up her horse. The man sprang from his saddle and came to her side.

"Please to be careful, now, don't let my riding-skirt get hung in the stirrup," said Capitola, cautiously disengaging her drapery, rising in the saddle and giving the stranger her hand. In the act of jumping, she suddenly stopped and looked down, exclaiming:

"Good gracious! how very damp the ground is here in the bottom of the valley!"

"More objections, I suppose, my pretty one! but they won't serve you any longer. I am bent upon having a cozy chat with you, upon that very turf!" said the stranger, pointing to a little cleared space among the trees beside the path.

"Now, don't be cross; just see how damp it is there; it would spoil my riding-dress, and give me my death of cold."

"*Humph,*" said the stranger, looking at her with a sly, grim, cruel resolve.

"I'll tell you what it is," said Cap, "I'm not witty nor amusing, nor will it *pay* to sit out in the night air to hear *me* talk; but since you wish it, and since you were so good as to guard me through these woods, and since I *promised,* why, damp as it is, I will even get off and talk with you!"

"That's my birdling."

"But hold on one minute. Is there nothing you can get to put there for me to sit on—no stump, nor dry stone?"

"No, my dear, I don't see any."

"Could you not turn your hat down and let me sit on that?"

"Ha, ha, ha! why, your weight would crush it as flat as a flounder!"

"Oh! I know now!" exclaimed Capitola, with sudden delight. "You just spread your saddle-cloth down there, and that will make a beautiful seat, and I'll sit and talk with you so nicely—only you must not want me to stay long, because if I don't get home soon I shall catch a scolding."

"You shall neither catch a scolding nor a cold on my account, pretty one!" said the man, going to his horse to get the saddle-cloth.

"Oh, don't take off the saddle; it will detain you too long," said Cap, impatiently.

"My pretty Cap, I cannot get the cloth without taking it off," said the man, beginning to unbuckle the girth.

"Oh, yes you can! you can draw it from under!" persisted Cap.

"Impossible, my angel!" said the man, lifting off the saddle from his horse and laying it carefully by the roadside.

Then he took off the gay, crimson saddle-cloth, and carried it into the little clearing and began carefully to spread it down.

Now was Cap's time. *Her* horse had recovered from his fatigue. The stranger's horse was in the path before her. While the man's back was turned, she raised her riding-whip, and with a shout, gave the front horse a sharp lash that sent him galloping furiously ahead. Then instantaneously putting whip to her own horse, she started into a run.

Hearing the shout, the lash, and the starting of the horses, the baffled villain turned and saw that his game was lost! He had been outwitted by a child! He gnashed his teeth and shook his fist in rage.

Turning, as she wheeled out of sight, Capitola—I'm sorry to say— put her thumb to the side of her nose, and whirled her lingers into a semicircle, in a gesture more expressive than elegant.

Chapter XVII

Another Storm at Hurricane Hall

"At this, Sir Knight grew high in wroth,
And lifting hands and eyes up both,
Three times he smote on stomach stout,
From whence, at length, fierce words broke out."
—*Hudibras*[47]

THE MOON was shining full upon the river and household beyond, when Capitola dashed into the water, and amid the sparkling and leaping of the foam, made her way to the other bank, and rode up the rugged ascent. On the outer side of the lawn wall, the moonbeams fell full upon the little figure of Pitapat, waiting there.

"Why, Patty, what takes *you* out so late as this?" asked Capitola, as she rode up to the gate.

"Oh, Miss Caterpillar, I'se waitin' for you! Ole Marse is dreadful, *he* is! jes fit to burst the shingles offen the roof with swearing! So I come out to warn you, so you can steal in the back way and go to your rooms so he won't see you, and I'll go and send Wool to put your horse away, and then I'll bring you up some supper, and tell Ole Marse how you've been home ever so long, and gone to bed with a werry bad head-ache."

"Thank you, Patty. It is perfectly astonishing, how easy lying is to you. You really deserve to have been born in Rag Alley. But I won't trouble the Recording Angel to make another entry against you on my account."

"Yes, Miss," said Pitapat, who thought that her mistress was complimenting her.

---

47 Samuel Butler, "Hudibras."

"And now, Patty, stand out of my way. I'm going to ride straight up to the horse-block, dismount, and walk right into the presence of Major Warfield!" said Capitola, passing through the gate.

"Oh, Miss Caterpillar, don't! don't! he'll kill you, so he will!"

"Who's afeared?" muttered Cap to herself, as she put her horse to his mettle, and rode gaily through the evergreens, up to the horse-block where she sprang down lightly from her saddle.

Gathering up her train with one hand and tossing back her head, she swept along toward the house with the air of a young princess.

There was a vision calculated to test her firmness. Reader! did you ever see a raging lion tearing to and fro the narrow limits of his cage, and occasionally shaking the amphitheatre with his tremendous roar? or a furious bull tossing his head and tail, and ploughing up the earth with his hoofs as he careered back and forth between the boundaries of his pen? If you have seen and noted these mad brutes, you may form some faint idea of the frenzy of Old Hurricane, as he stormed up and down the floor of the front piazza.

Cap had just escaped an actual danger of too terrible a character to be frightened now by sound and fury. Composedly she walked up into the porch, and said:

"Good evening, uncle."

The old man stopped short in his furious strides, and glared upon her with his terrible eyes.

Cap stood fire without blenching, merely remarking:

"Now I have no doubt that in the days when you went battling, that look used to strike terror into the heart of the enemy, but it doesn't into mine, somehow!"

"Miss!" roared the old man, bringing down his cane with a resounding thump upon the floor; "Miss!! how *dare* you have the impudence to face me, much less the—the—the assurance!—the effrontery!—the audacity! the *brass* to speak to me!"

"Well, I declare," said Cap, calmly untying her hat, "this is the first time I ever heard it was impudent in a little girl to give her uncle good evening."

The old man trotted up and down the piazza two or three turns, then stopping short before the delinquent, he struck his cane down upon the floor with a ringing stroke, and thundered:

"Young woman! tell me instantly, and without prevarication, where you have been?"

"Certainly, sir; 'going to and fro in the earth, and walking up and down in it!'" said Cap, quietly.

"Flames and furies, that is no answer at all! Where have you been?" roared Old Hurricane, shaking with excitement.

"Look here, uncle, if you go on that way you'll have a fit presently!" said Cap, calmly.

"Where have you been!" thundered Old Hurricane.

"Well, since you will know—just across the river, and through the woods and back again!"

"And didn't I *forbid* you to do that, minion? and how *dare* you disobey me? *You*, the creature of my bounty! *you*, the miserable little vagrant that I picked up in the alleys of New York, and tried to make a young lady of; but an old proverb says—'You can't make a silken purse out of a pig's ear!' How dare *you*, you little beggar, disobey your benefactor!—a man of my age, character and position?—I—I—" Old Hurricane turned abruptly, and raged up and down the piazza.

All this time Capitola had been standing quietly, holding up her train with one hand and her riding hat in the other. At this last insult she raised her dark gray eyes to his face with one long, indignant, sorrowful gaze, then turning silently away, and entering the house, she left Old Hurricane to storm up and down the piazza until he had raged himself to rest.

Reader! I do not defend, far less approve, poor Cap! I only tell her story and describe her as I have seen her, leaving her to your charitable interpretation.

Next morning Capitola came down into the breakfast-room with one idea prominent in her hard little head—to which she mentally gave expression:

"Well as I like that old man, he must not permit himself to talk to me in *that* indecent strain, and so he must be made to know."

When she entered the breakfast-room, she found Mrs. Condiment already at the head of the table, and Old Hurricane at the foot. He had quite got over his rage, and turned around blandly to welcome his ward, saying:

"Good-morning, Cap."

Without taking the slightest notice of the salutation, Cap sailed on to her seat.

"Humph! did you hear me say, '*Good-morning*,' Cap?"

Without paying the least attention, Capitola reached out her hand and took a cup of coffee from Mrs. Condiment.

"Humph! Humph! GOOD-MORNING, Capitola!" said Old Hurricane, with marked emphasis. Apparently without hearing him, Cap helped herself to a buckwheat cake, and daintily buttered it.

"Humph! humph! humph! well, as you said yourself, 'a dumb devil is better than a speaking one!'" ejaculated Old Hurricane, as he sat down and subsided into silence.

Doubtless the old man would have flown into another passion, had that been possible; but, in truth, he had spent so much vitality in rage number *one*, that he had none left to sustain rage number *two*. Besides, he knew it would be necessary to blow up Bill Ezy, his lazy overseer, before night, and perhaps saved himself for that performance. He finished his meal in silence, and went out.

Cap finished hers; and, 'tempering justice with mercy,' went up stairs to his room, and looked over all his appointments and belongings to find what she could do for his extra comfort; and found a job in newly lining his warm slippers, and the sleeves of his dressing-gown.

They met again at the dinner-table.

"How do you do, Cap?" said Old Hurricane, as he took his seat.

Capitola poured out a glass of water and drank it in silence, and without looking at him.

"Oh! very well! 'a dumb devil, etc.,'" exclaimed Old Hurricane, addressing himself to his dinner. When the meal was over they again separated. The old man went to his study to examine his farm books, and Capitola back to her chamber to finish lining his warm slippers.

Again at tea they met.

"Well, Cap, is 'the dumb devil' cast out yet?" he said, sitting down.

Capitola took a cup of tea from Mrs. Condiment and passed it on to him in silence.

"Humph, not gone yet, eh?—poor girl! how it must try you!" said Old Hurricane.

After supper the old man found his dressing-gown and slippers before the fire all ready for his use.

"Cap, you monkey! you did this," he said, turning around. But Capitola had already left the room.

Next morning at breakfast there was a repetition of the same scene. Early in the forenoon Major Warfield ordered his horses, and, attended by Wool, rode up to Tip-Top. He did not return either to dinner or tea, but as that circumstance was not unusual it gave no one uneasiness. Mrs. Condiment kept his supper warm, and Capitola had his dressing-gown and slippers ready.

She was turning them before the fire when the old man arrived. He came in quite gayly, saying:

"Now, Cap, I think I have found a *talisman* at last to cast out that 'dump devil.' I heard you wishing for a watch the other day. Now, as devils belong to eternity, and have no business with *time*, of course the sight of this little time-keeper must put yours to flight!" and so saying he laid upon the table, before the eyes of Capitola, a beautiful little gold watch and chain. She glanced at it, as it lay glittering and sparkling in the lamp-light, and then turned abruptly and walked away.

"Humph! that's always the way the devils do! fly when they can't stand shot!"

Capitola deliberately walked back, laid a paper over the little watch and chain, as if to cover its fascinating sparkle and glitter, and said:

"Uncle, your bounty is large, and your present is beautiful; but there is something that poor Capitola values more than that——"

She paused, dropped her head upon her bosom, a sudden blush flamed up over her face, and teardrops glistened in her downcast eyes; she put both hands before her burning face for a moment, and then dropping them, resumed:

"Uncle! you rescued me from misery, and perhaps, *perhaps* early death! you have heaped benefits and bounties upon me without measure! you have placed me in a home of abundance, honor and security! for all this, if I were not grateful, I should deserve no less than death! But, uncle, there is a sin that is worse, or at least more *ungenerous*, than ingratitude! it is to put a helpless fellow creature under heavy obligations, and then treat that grateful creature with undeserved contempt and cruel unkindness!" Once more her voice was choked with feeling.

For some reason or other, Capitola's tears, perhaps because they were so rare, always moved Old Hurricane to his heart's centre; going towards her softly he said:

"Now, my dear, now my child, now my little Cap, you *know* it was all for your own good! Why, my clear, I never for one instant regretted bringing you to the house, and I wouldn't part with you for a kingdom! Come now, my child, come to the heart of your old uncle."

Now the soul of Capitola naturally abhorred sentiment! If ever she gave way to serious emotion, she was sure to avenge herself by being more capricious than before. Consequently flinging herself out of the caressing arms of Old Hurricane, she exclaimed:

"Uncle! I won't be treated with both kicks and half-pennies by the same person—and so I tell you. I'm not a cur to be fed with roast-beef and beaten with a stick! nor, nor, nor a Turk's slave to be caressed and oppressed as her master likes!—Such abuse as you heaped upon me, I never heard—no, not even in Rag Alley."

"Oh, my dear, my dear, for Heaven's sake forget Rag Alley."

"I won't! I vow I'll go back to Rag Alley, for a very little more! Freedom and peace are even sweeter than wealth and honors!"

"Ah, but I wouldn't let you, my little Cap."

"Then I'd have you up before the nearest magistrate, to show by what right you detained me! Ah, ha! I wasn't brought up in New York for nothing!"

"Whee-ew! and all this because, for her own good, I gave my own niece and ward a little gentle admonition."

"Gentle admonition! Do you call *that* gentle admonition? Why, uncle, you are enough to frighten most people to death with your fury! You are a perfect dragon! a griffin! a Russian bear! a Bengal tiger! a Numidian lion! I declare if I don't write and ask some menagerie man to send a party down here to catch you for his show. You'd *draw*, I tell you!"

"Yes! especially with *you* for a keeper to stir me up once in a while with a long pole!"

"And that I'd engage to do—*cheap!*"

The entrance of Mrs. Condiment with the tea-tray put an end to the controversy. It was, as yet, a drawn battle.

"And what about the watch, my little Cap?"

"Take it back, uncle, if you please."

"But they won't have it back! it has got your initials engraved upon it—look here," said the old man, holding the watch to her eyes.

"C. L.N. Those are not my initials," said Capitola, looking up with surprise.

"Why, so they are not! the blamed fools have made a mistake!—but you'll have to take it, Cap."

"No, uncle, keep it for the present," said Capitola, who was too honest to take a gift that she felt she did not deserve, and yet too proud to confess as much.

Peace was proclaimed—for the present.

Alas! 'twas but of short continuance. During these two days of coolness and enforced quietude Old Hurricane had gathered a store of bad humors that required expenditure.

So the very next day something went wrong upon the farm, and Old Hurricane came storming home, driving his overseer, poor, old, meek Billy Ezy and his man Wool, before him.

Billy Ezy was whimpering; Wool was sobbing aloud; Old Hurricane was roaring at them both as he drove them on before him—swearing that Ezy should go and find himself a new home, and Wool should go and seek another master.

And for this cause Old Hurricane was driving them on to his study, that he might pay the overseer his last quarter's salary, and give the servant a written order to find a master.

He raged past Capitola in the hall, and meeting Mrs. Condiment at the study door, ordered her to bring in her account book directly, for that he would not be imposed upon any longer, but meant to drive all the lazy, idle, dishonest eye-servants[48] and time-servers[49] from the house and land!

"What's the matter now?" said Capitola meeting her.

"Oh, child, he's in his terrible tantrums again! He gets into these ways every once in a while, when a young calf perishes, or a sheep is stolen, or anything goes amiss, and then he abuses us all for a pack of loiterers, sluggards and thieves, and *pays* us off and *orders* us off. We don't go, of course, because we know he doesn't mean it; still it is very trying to be talked to so. Oh! I should go, but, Lord, child! he's a bear, but we love him."

Just as she spoke the study door opened, and Bill Ezy came out sobbing, and Wool lifting up his voice and fairly roaring.

Mrs. Condiment stepped out of the parlor door.

---

48 A phrase denoting servants who only work when they are watched.
49 A person who shapes his or her behavior or ideas to please superiors.

"What's the matter, you blockhead?" she asked of Wool.

"Oh! Boo-hoo-woo! Ole Marse been and done and gone and guv me a line to find an— an—another—Boo-hoo-woo!" sobbed Wool, ready to break his heart.

"Give you a line to find another Boo-hoo-woo! I wouldn't do it if I were you, Wool!" said Capitola.

"Give me the paper, Wool," said Mrs. Condiment, taking the "permit" and tearing it up, and adding:

"There! now you go home to your quarter, and keep out of your old master's sight until he gets over his anger, and then you know very well that it will be all right. There! go along with you."

Wool quickly got out of the way, and made room for the overseer, who was snivelling like a whipped school-boy, and to whom the housekeeper said:

"I thought *you* were wiser than to take this so to heart, Mr. Ezy!"

"Oh, mum! what could you expect?—an old sarvint as has sarved the major faithful these forty years, to be discharged at sixty-five! *Oh! hoo-ooo-oo!*" whimpered the overseer.

"But then you have been discharged so often, you ought to be used to it by this time! you get discharged just as Wool gets sold—about once a month! but do you ever go?"

"Oh, mum! but he's in airnest this time! 'deed he is, mum! *terrible* in airnest! and all about that misfortnet bob-tail colt getting stole! I know how it wur some of Black Donald's gang as done it! As if I could always be on my guard against *they* devils! And he *means* it this time, mum! He's *terrible* in airnest!"

"Tut! he's *always* in earnest for as long as it lasts! Go home to your family and to-morrow go about your business, as usual."

Here the study bell rang violently and Old Hurricane's voice was heard calling—"Mrs. Condiment! Mrs. Condiment!"

"Oh, lor! he's coming!" cried Bill Ezy, running off as fast as age and grief would let him.

"Mrs. Condiment! Mrs. Condiment!" called the voice.

"Yes, sir! yes!" answered the housekeeper, hurrying to obey the call.

Capitola walked up and down the hall for half an hour, at the end of which Mrs. Condiment came out "with a smile on her lip and a tear in her eye," and saying:

"Well, Miss Capitola, I'm paid off and discharged also!"

"What for?"

"For aiding and abetting the rebels! in a word, for trying to comfort poor Ezy and Wool."

"And are you going?"

"Certainly not! I sha'n't budge! I would not treat the old man so badly as to take him at his word!" and, with a strange smile, Mrs. Condiment hurried away just in time to escape Old Hurricane, who came raving out of the study.

"Get out of my way, you beggar!" he cried, pushing past Capitola, and hurrying from the house.

"Well, I declare, that *was* pleasant!" thought Cap, as she entered the parlor.

"Mrs. Condiment, what will he say when he comes back and finds you all here still?" she asked.

"Say?—nothing. After this passion is over, he will be so exhausted that he will not be able to get up another rage in two or three days."

"Where has he gone?"

"To Tip-Top; and alone, too; he was so mad with poor Wool that he wouldn't even permit him to attend."

"Alone? has he gone alone! *Oh, won't I give him a dose when he comes back?*" thought Capitola.

Meanwhile Old Hurricane stormed along towards Tip-Top, lashing off the poor dogs that wished to follow him, and cutting at every living thing that crossed his path. His business at the village was to get bills printed and posted, offering an additional reward for the apprehension of "the marauding outlaw Black Donald." That day, he dined at the village tavern—"The Antlers," by Mr. Merry—and differed, disputed, or quarrelled, as the case might be, with every man whom he happened to come in contact with.

Towards evening he set off for home. It was much later than his usual hour of returning; but he felt weary, exhausted, and indisposed to come into his own dwelling where his furious temper had created so much unhappiness. Thus, though it was very late, he did not hurry; he almost hoped that every one might be in bed when he should return. The moon was shining brightly when he passed the gate and rode up the evergreen avenue to the horse-block in front of the house. There he dismounted and walked up into the piazza, where a novel vision met his surprised gaze.

It was Capitola, walking up and down the floor, with rapid, almost masculine strides, and apparently in a state of great excitement.

"Oh, is it you, my little Cap? Good-evening, my dear," he said, very kindly.

Capitola "pulled up" in her striding walk, wheeled around, faced him, drew up her form, folded her arms, threw back her head, set her teeth, and glared at him.

"What the demon do you mean by *that?*" cried Old Hurricane.

"SIR!" she exclaimed, bringing down one foot with a sharp stamp— "SIR, how *dare* you the impudence to *face* me, much less the—the— the—the brass! the *bronze!* the COPPER! to speak to me?"

"Why, what in the name of all the lunatics in Bedlam does the girl mean? Is she crazy?" exclaimed the old man, gazing upon her in astonishment.

Capitola turned and strode furiously up and down the piazza, and then, stopping suddenly and facing him, with a sharp stamp of her foot, exclaimed:

"OLD GENTLEMAN, tell me instantly, and without prevarication, where have you been?"

"To the demon with you! what do you mean? Have you taken leave of your senses?" demanded Old Hurricane.

Capitola strode up and down the floor a few times, and stopping short and shaking her fist, exclaimed:

'DIDN'T you know, you headstrong, reckless, desperate, frantic veteran! *didn't* you know the jeopardy in which you placed yourself by riding out alone at this hour? Suppose three or four great runaway negresses had sprung out of the bushes—and—and—"

She broke off, apparently for want of breath, and strode up and down the floor; then, pausing suddenly before him, with a stern stamp of her foot and a fierce glare of her eye, she continued:

"You shouldn't have come back *here* any more! No dishonored old man should have entered the house of which *I* call myself the mistress!"

"Oh, I take! I take! ha! ha! ha! Good, Cap, good! You are holding up the glass before me; but your mirror is not quite large enough to reflect 'Old Hurricane,' my dear—'*I owe you* one,'" said the old man, as he passed into the house, followed by his capricious favorite.

Chapter XVIII

The Doctor's Daughter

"Oh, her smile, it seemed half holy,
As if drawn from thoughts more far,
Than our common jestings are.
And if any painter drew her,
he would paint her unaware
With a halo round her hair."
                    —*E. B. Browning*[50]

ON THE APPOINTED day, Traverse took his way to Willow Heights, to keep his tryst and enter upon the medical studies in the good doctor's office. He was anxious also to know if his patron had as yet thought of any plan by which his mother might better her condition. He was met at the door by little Mattie, the parlor maid, who told him to walk right up stairs into the study, where his master was expecting him.

Traverse went up quietly and opened the door of that pleasant study-room, to which the reader has already been introduced, and the windows of which opened upon the upper front piazza.

Now, however, as it was quite cold, the windows were down, though the blinds were open, and through them streamed the golden rays of the morning sun that fell glistening upon the fairy hair and white raiment of a young girl, who sat reading before the fire.

The doctor was not in the room, and Traverse in his native modesty was just about to retreat, when the young creature looked up from her book, and seeing him, arose with a smile, and came forward, saying:

"You are the young man whom my father was expecting, I presume. Sit down, he has stepped out, but will be in again very soon."

Now, Traverse being unaccustomed to the society of young ladies felt excessively bashful when suddenly coming into the presence of this refined and lovely girl. With a low bow and a deep blush he took the chair she placed for him.

With natural politeness, she closed her book and addressed herself to entertaining him.

"I have heard that your mother is an invalid, I hope she is better?"

"I thank you—yes, ma'am—Miss," stammered Traverse, in painful embarrassment. Understanding the timidity of the bashful boy, and seeing that her efforts to entertain only troubled him, she placed the newspapers on the table before him, saying:

"Here are the morning journals if you would like to look over them, Mr. Rocke," and then she resumed her book.

"I thank you, Miss," replied the youth, taking up a paper, more for the purpose of covering his embarrassment, than for any other.

Mr. Rocke! Traverse was seventeen years of age, and had never been called Mr. Rocke before! This young girl was the very first to compliment him with the manly title, and he felt a boyish gratitude to her and a harmless wish that his well-brushed Sunday suit of black was not *quite* so rusty and threadbare, tempered by an innocent exultation in the thought that no gentleman in the land could exhibit fresher linen, brighter shoes or cleaner hands than himself.

---

50 From "A Portrait" by English poet Elizabeth Barrett Browning (1806–1861).

But not many seconds were spent in such egotism. He stole a glance at his lovely companion sitting on the opposite side of the fireside—he was glad to see that she was already deeply engaged in reading, for it enabled him to observe her, without embarrassment or offence. He had scarcely dared to look at her before, and had no distinct idea of her beauty.

There had been for him only a vague, dazzling vision of a golden-haired girl in floating white raiment, wafting the fragrance of violets as she moved, and with a voice sweeter than the notes of the cushat dove as she spoke.

Now he saw that the golden hair flowed in ringlets around a fair, roseate face, soft and bright with feeling and intelligence. As her dark blue eyes followed the page, a smile intense with meaning deepened the expression of her countenance. That intense smile!—it was like her father's, only lovelier—more heavenly. That intense smile! It had, even on the old doctor's face, an inexpressible charm for Traverse—but on the lovely young face of his daughter it exercised an ineffable fascination. So earnest and so unconscious became the gaze of poor Traverse that he was only brought to a sense of propriety by the opening of the door, and the entrance of the doctor, who exclaimed:

"Ah! here already, Traverse! that is punctual!—This is my daughter Clara, Traverse! Clara, this is Traverse, you've heard me speak about!— But, I dare say, you've already become acquainted," concluded the doctor, drawing his chair up to the reading-table, sitting down and folding his dressing-gown around his limbs.

"Well, Traverse, how is the little mother?" he presently inquired.

"I was just telling Miss Day that she was much better, sir," said Traverse.

"Ah, ha! ah, ha!" muttered the doctor to himself—"that's kitchen physic—roast turkey and port wine! and moral medicine, hope! and mental medicine, sympathy."

"Well, Traverse," he said aloud, "I have been racking my brain for a plan for your mother—and to no purpose! Traverse, your mother should be in a home of peace, plenty and cheerfulness!—I can speak before my little Clara here! I never have any secrets from *her*—Your mother wants good living, cheerful company, and freedom from toil and care! The situation of gentleman's or lady's housekeeper in some home of abundance, where she would be esteemed as a member of the family, would suit her; but where to find such a place! I have been inquiring—without mentioning her name, of course—among all my friends, but not one of them wants a housekeeper, or knows a soul who does want one, and so I am 'at sea on the subject.' I'm ashamed of myself for not succeeding better!"

"Oh, sir, do not do yourself so great injustice," said Traverse.

"Well, the fact is after boasting so confidently that I would find a good situation for Mrs. Rocke, lo and behold! I have proved myself as yet *only* a boaster!"

"Father," said Clara, turning upon him her sweet eyes.

"Well, my love?"

"Perhaps Mrs. Rocke would do us the favor to come *here* and take charge *of our* household."

"Eh! what! I never thought of that! I never had a housekeeper in my life!" exclaimed the doctor.

"No, sir, because you never *needed* one before, but now we really *do*. Aunt Moggy has been a very faithful and efficient manager, although she is a colored woman; but she is getting very old."

"Yes, and deaf, and blind, and careless! I know she is! I have no doubt in the world she scours the coppers with the table napkins, and washes her face and hands in the soup tureen."

"Oh *father!*" said Clara.

"Well, Clara, at least she wants looking after."

"Father, she wants rest in her old age."

"No doubt of it! no doubt of it!"

"And, father, I intend, of course, in time, to be your housekeeper; but having spent all my life at a boarding-school, I know very little about domestic affairs, and I require a great deal of instruction; so I really do think that there is no one needs Mrs. Rocke's assistance more than we do, and if she will do us the favor to come, we cannot do better than engage her."

"To be sure! to be sure! Lord bless my soul! to think it should never have entered my stupid old head, until it was put there by Clare! Here was I searching blindly all over the country for a situation for Mrs. Rocke, and wanting her all the time more than any one else! That's the way, Traverse, that's the way with us all, my boy! While we are looking away off yonder for the solution of our difficulties, the remedy is all the time lying just under our noses!"

"But so close to our eyes, father, that we cannot see it!" said Clara.

"Just so, Clare! just so! You are always ahead of me in ideas! Now, Traverse, when you go home this evening you shall take a note to your mother, setting forth our wishes—mine and Clara's; if she accedes to them she will make us very happy."

With a good deal of manly strength of mind Traverse had all his mother's tenderness of heart. It was with difficulty that he could keep back his tears or control his voice, while he answered:

"I remember reading, sir, that the young queen of England[51] when she came to her throne wished to provide handsomely for an orphan companion of her childhood; and seeing that no office in her household suited the young person, she created one for her benefit. Sir, I believe you have made one for my mother."

"Not at all! not at all! If she doesn't come to look after our housekeeping, old Moggy will be greasing our griddles with tallow candle ends next! If you don't believe *me*, ask Clara! ask Clara!"

Not "believe" him! If the doctor had affirmed that the moon was made of moldy cheese, Traverse would have deemed it his duty to stoutly maintain that astronomical theory. He felt hurt that the doctor should use such a phrase.

"Yes, indeed, we really *do* need her, Traverse," said the doctor's daughter.

"*Traverse!*" It had made him proud to hear her call him, for the first time in his life, "Mr. Rocke," but it made him deeply happy to hear her call him "Traverse." It had such a *sisterly* sound coming from this sweet creature. How he wished that she really *were* his sister! but then the idea of that fair, golden-haired, blue-eyed, white-robed angel being the sister of such a robust, rugged, sun-burned boy as himself! The thought was so absurd, extravagant, impossible, that the poor boy heaved an unconscious sigh.

"Why, what's the matter, Traverse? What are you thinking of so intently?"

"Of your great goodness, sir, among other things."

"Tut! let's hear no more of that. I please myself," said the doctor; "and now, Traverse, let's go to work decently and in order; but first let me settle *this* point: if your good little mother determines in our favor, Traverse, then of course *you* will live with us also, so I shall

---

51 Victoria became Queen of England in 1837 at the age of 18.

have my young medical assistant always at hand. That will be very convenient; and then we shall have no more long, lonesome evenings, Clara, shall we, dear? And now, Traverse, I will mark out your course of study, and set you to work at once."

"Shall I leave the room, father?" inquired Clara.

"No, no, my dear; certainly not. I have not had you home so long as to get tired of the sight of you yet. No, Clare, no; you are not in our way—is she, Traverse?"

"Oh, sir, the idea——" stammered Traverse, blushing deeply to be so appealed to.

In his way! why a pang had shot through his bosom at the very mention of her going.

"Very well, then; here, Traverse—here are your books; you are to begin with this one; keep this Medical Dictionary at hand for reference. Bless me! it will bring back my own student days to go over the ground with you, my boy."

Clara took her work-box and sat down to stitch a pair of dainty wristbands for her father's shirts.

The doctor took up the morning papers.

Traverse opened his book and commenced his readings. It was a quiet but by no means a dull circle. Occasionally Clara and her father exchanged words, and once in a while the doctor looked over his pupil's shoulder, or gave him a direction.

Traverse studied *con amore*[52] and with intelligent appreciation. The presence of the doctor's lovely daughter, far from disturbing him, calmed and steadied his soul into a state of infinite content. If the presence of the beautiful girl was ever to become an agitating element, the hour had not yet come.

So passed the time until the dinner-bell rang.

By the express stipulation of the doctor himself, it was arranged that Traverse should always dine with his family. After dinner an hour, which the doctor called a digestive hour, was spent in loitering about, and then the studies were resumed.

At six o'clock in the evening Traverse took leave of the doctor and his fair daughter and started for home.

"Be sure to persuade your mother to come, Traverse," said Clara.

"She will not need persuasion; she will be only too glad to come, Miss," said Traverse, with a deep bow, turning and hurrying away towards home. With "winged feet" he ran down the wooded hill and got into the highway and hastened on with such speed that in half an hour he reached his mother's little cottage. He was all agog with joy and eagerness to tell her the good news.

Chapter XIX

The Resigned Soul

"This day be bread and peace my lot;
All else beneath the sun
Thou knowest if best bestowed or not,
And let thy will be done."
—*Pope*[53]

---

52 Italian for "with devotion."
53 From "Universal Prayer" by English poet and translator Alexander Pope (1688–1744).

Poor Marah Rocke had schooled her soul to resignation; had taught herself just to do the duty of each day as it came, and leave the future—where indeed it must always remain—in the hands of God. Since the doctor's delicate and judicious kindness had cherished her life, some little health and cheerfulness had returned to her.

Upon this particular evening of the day upon which Traverse entered upon his medical studies, she felt very hopeful.

The little cottage fire burned brightly; the hearth was swept clean; the tea-kettle was singing over the blaze; the tiny tea-table, with its two cups and saucers, and two plates and knives, was set; everything was neat, comfortable and cheerful for Traverse's return. Marah sat in her little low chair, putting the finishing touches to a set of fine shirts.

She was not anxiously looking for her son; for he had told her that he should stay at the doctor's until six o'clock; therefore she did not expect him until seven.

But so fast had Traverse walked that just as the minute hand pointed to half-past six, the latch was raised and Traverse ran in—his face flushed with joy.

The first thing he did was to run to his mother, fling his arms around her neck, and kiss her. Then he threw himself into his chair to take breath.

"Now then, what's the matter, Traverse? You look as if somebody had left you a fortune."

"And so they have, or as good as done so!" exclaimed Traverse, panting for breath.

"What in the world do you mean?" exclaimed Marah, her thoughts naturally flying to Old Hurricane, and suggesting his possible repentance or relenting.

"Read that, mother, read that!" said Traverse, eagerly putting a note in her hand.

She opened it, and read:

WILLOW HEIGHTS—Monday.

Dear Madam:—My little daughter Clara, fourteen years of age, has just returned from boarding-school to pursue her studies at home. Among other things, she must learn domestic affairs, of which she knows nothing. If you will accept the position of housekeeper and matronly companion of my daughter, I will make the terms such as shall reconcile you to the change. We shall also do all that we can to make you happy. Traverse will explain to you the details. Take time to think of it, but if possible let us have your answer by Traverse, when he comes to-morrow. If you accede to this proposition you will give my daughter and myself sincere satisfaction. Yours truly,

William Day

Marah finished reading, and raised her eyes, full of amazement, to the face of her son.

"Mother!" said Traverse, speaking fast and eagerly, "they say they really cannot do without you. They have troops of servants, but the old cook is in her dotage and does all sorts of strange things—such as frying buckwheat cakes in lamp-oil and the like."

"Oh, hush! what exaggeration!"

"Well, I don't *say* she does *that* exactly, but she isn't equal to her situation, without a housekeeper to look after her; and they want you very much indeed."

"And what is to become of *your* home, if I break up?" suggested the mother.

"Oh, that is the very best of it! The doctor says if you consent to come, that I must also live there, and that then he can have his medical assistant always at hand, which will be very convenient."

Marah smiled dubiously.

"I do not understand it; but one thing I do know, Traverse: there is not such a man as the doctor appears in this world more than once in a hundred years."

"Not in a thousand years, mother! and as for his daughter—oh, you should see Miss Clara, mother! Her father calls her Clare—Clare Day— how the name suits her! She is so fair and bright! with such a warm, thoughtful, sunny smile that goes right to your heart! Her face is indeed like a clear day, and her beautiful smile is the sunshine that lights it up!" said the enthusiastic youth, whose admiration was as yet too simple and single-hearted and unselfish to tie his tongue.

The mother smiled at his earnestness—smiled without the least misgiving; for to her apprehension the youth was still a boy, to wonder at and admire beauty without being in the least danger of having his peace of mind disturbed by love. And as yet her idea of him was just.

"And mother, of course you will go," said Traverse.

"Oh, I do not know. The proposition was so sudden and unexpected, and is so serious and important that I must take time to reflect," said Mrs. Rocke, thoughtfully.

"How much time, mother? Will until to-morrow morning do? It must, little mother, because I promised to carry your consent back with me. Indeed I did mother!" exclaimed the impatient boy.

Mrs. Rocke dropped her head upon her hand, as was her custom when in deep thought. Presently she said:

"Travy, I'm afraid this is not a genuine offer of a situation of housekeeper. I'm afraid that it is only a ruse to cover a scheme of benevolence, and that they don't really want me, and I should only be in their way."

"Now, mother, I do assure you, they *do* want you! Think of that young girl and elderly gentleman—can either of *them* take charge of a large establishment like that of Willow Heights?"

"Well argued, Traverse; but granting that they need a housekeeper, how do I know I would suit them?"

"Why you may take their own words for that, mother."

"But how can *they* know? I am afraid they would be disappointed."

"Wait until they complain, mother."

"I don't believe they ever *would.*"

"I don't believe they ever would have *cause.*"

"Well, granting also that I should suit them——"

The mother paused and sighed. Traverse filled up the blank by saying:

"I suppose you mean if you *should* suit them, they might not suit you."

"No, I do not mean that! I am *sure* they would suit me! but there is *one* in the world, who may one day come to reason and take bitter umbrage at the fact that *I* should accept a subordinate situation in any household, murmured Mrs. Rocke, almost unconsciously.

"Then that 'one in the world,' whoever he, she, or *it* may be, had better place you above the necessity, or else hold his, her, or its tongue!— Mother, *I* think that goods thrown in our way by Providence had better be accepted, leaving the consequences to Him!"

"Traverse, dear, I shall pray over this matter to-night, and sleep on it; and He to whom even the fall of a sparrow[54] is not indifferent will guide me," said Mrs. Rocke; and here the debate ended.

---

54 Matthew 10:29; Shakespeare, *Hamlet*, 5.2.

The remainder of the evening was spent in laudation of Clara Day, and in writing a letter to Herbert Greyson, at West Point, in which all these laudations were reiterated, and in the course of which Traverse wrote these innocent words—"I have known Clara Day scarcely twelve hours, and I admire her as much as I love you! and oh, Herbert! if you could only rise to be a major-general and marry Clara Day, I should be the happiest fellow alive!" Would Traverse as willingly dispose of Clara's hand a year or two after this time? I trow not!

The next morning after breakfast Mrs. Rocke gave in her decision.

"Tell the doctor, Traverse," she said, "that I understand and appreciate his kindness; that I will not break up my humble home as yet; but I will lock up my house and come a month on trial; if I can perform the duties of the situation satisfactorily, well and good! I will remain; if not, why then, having my home still in possession, I can return to it."

"Wise little mother! she will not cut down the bridge behind her!" exclaimed Traverse, joyfully, as he bade his mother good-bye for the day, and hastened up to Willow Heights with her answer. This answer was received by the good doctor and his lovely daughter with delight as unfeigned as it was unselfish. They were pleased to have a good housekeeper; but they were far better pleased to offer a poor struggling mother a comfortable and even luxurious home.

On the next Monday morning, Mrs. Rocke having completed all her arrangements, and closed up her house, entered upon the duties of her new situation.

Clara gave her a large and airy bed-chamber for her own use, communicating with a smaller one for the use of her son; besides this, as housekeeper, she had of course the freedom of the whole house.

Traverse watched with anxious vigilance to find out whether the efforts of his mother really improved the condition of the housekeeping, and was delighted to find that the coffee was clearer and finer flavored; the bread whiter and lighter; the cream richer, the butter fresher, and the beefsteak juicier than he had ever known them to be on the doctor's table; that on the dinner-table, from day to day, dishes succeeded each other in a well-ordered variety and well-dressed style—in a word, that in every particular, the comfort of the family was greatly enhanced by the presence of the housekeeper, and that the doctor and his daughter knew it.

While the doctor and the student were engaged in the library, Clara spent many hours of the morning in Mrs. Rocke's company learning the arts of domestic economy and considerably assisting her in the preparation of delicate dishes.

In the evening the doctor, Clara, Mrs. Rocke, and Traverse gathered around the fire as one family—Mrs. Rocke and Clara engaged in needlework, and the doctor or Traverse in reading aloud, for their amusement, some agreeable book. Sometimes Clara would richly entertain them with music—singing and accompanying herself upon the piano.

An hour before bedtime the servants were always called in, and general family prayer offered up.

Thus passed the quiet, pleasant, profitable days. Traverse was fast falling into a delicious dream, from which, as yet, no rude shock threatened to wake him. Willow Heights seemed to him Paradise, its inmates angels, and his own life—beatitude!

Chapter XX

The Outlaw's Rendezvous

"Our plots fall short like darts which rash hands throw
With an ill aim, and have too far to go;

Nor can we long discoveries prevent;
God is too much about the innocent!"
—*Sir Robert Howard*[55]

"THE OLD ROAD Inn," described in the dying deposition of poor Nancy Grewell, was situated some miles from Hurricane Hall, by the side of a forsaken turnpike in the midst of a thickly wooded, long and narrow valley, shut in by two lofty ranges of mountains.

Once this turnpike was lively with travel, and this inn gay with custom; but, for the last twenty-five years, since the highway had been turned off in another direction, both road and tavern had been abandoned, and suffered to fall to ruin. The road was washed and furrowed into deep and dangerous gullies, and obstructed by fallen timber; the house was disfigured by mouldering walls, broken chimneys and patched windows.

Had any traveler lost himself, and chanced to have passed that way, he might have seen a little, old, dried-up woman, sitting knitting at one of the windows. She was known by those who were old enough to remember her and her home as Granny Raven, the daughter of the last proprietor of the inn. She was reputed to be dumb, but none could speak with certainty of the fact. In truth, for as far back as the memory of the "oldest inhabitant" could reach, she had been feared, disliked and avoided, as one of malign reputation; indeed, the ignorant and superstitious believed her to possess the "evil eye," and to be gifted with "second sight."

But of late years as the old road and the old inn were quite forsaken, so the old beldame was quite forgotten.

It was one evening, a few weeks after Capitola's fearful adventure in the forest, that this old woman carefully closed up every door and window in the front of the house, stopping every crevice through which a ray of light might gleam and warn that impossible phenomenon—a chance traveler, on the old road, of life within the habitation.

Having, so to speak, hermetically sealed the front of the house, she betook herself to a large back kitchen.

This kitchen was strangely and rudely furnished—having an extra broad fireplace with the recesses on each side of the chimney filled with oaken shelves, laden with strong pewter plates, dishes and mugs; all along the walls were arranged rude, oaken benches; down the length of the room, was left, always standing, a long deal table, capable of accommodating from fifteen to twenty guests.

On entering this kitchen Granny Raven struck a light, kindled a fire, and began to prepare a large supper.

Nor did this old beldame look unlike the ill-omened bird whose name she bore, in her close clinging black gown, and flapping black cape and hood, and with her sharp eyes, hooked nose and protruding chin.

Having put a large sirloin of beef before the fire, she took down a pile of pewter plates and arranged them along on the sides of the table; then to every plate she placed a pewter mug. A huge wheaten loaf of bread, a great roll of butter and several plates of pickles were next put upon the board, and when all was ready the old woman sat down to the patient turning of the spit.

She had not been thus occupied more than twenty minutes when a hasty, scuffling step was heard at the back of the house, accompanied by a peculiar whistle, immediately under the window.

---

55 Robert Howard (1626–1698) was an English poet and playwright.

"That's 'Headlong Hal,' for a penny! He never can learn the cat's tread!" thought the crone, as she arose and withdrew the bolt of the back door.

A little, dark-skinned, black-eyed, black-haired, thin and wiry man came hurrying in, exclaiming:

"How now, old girl—supper ready?"

She shook her head, pointed to the roasting beef, lifted up both hands with the ten fingers spread out twice, and then made a rotary motion with one arm.

"Oh—you mean it will be done in twenty turns; but hang me if I understand your dumb show half the time.—Have none of the men come yet?"

She put her fingers together, flung her hands wildly apart in all directions, brought them slowly together again, and pointed to the supper table.

"Um!—that is to say they are dispersed about their business, but will all be here to-night?"

She nodded.

"Where's the cap'n?"

She pointed over her left shoulder upwards—placed her two hands out broad from her temples—then made a motion as of lifting and carrying a basket, and displaying goods.

"Humph! humph! gone to Tip-Top to sell goods disguised as a peddler!"

She nodded. And before he could put another question, a low, soft *mew* was heard at the door.

"There's 'Stealthy Steve!'—he might walk with hobnailed high-lows over a gravelly road, and you would never hear his footfall," said the man, as the door noiselessly opened and shut, and a soft-footed, low-voiced, subtile-looking mulatto entered the kitchen, and gave good evening to its occupants.

"Ha! I'm devilish glad you've come, Steve, for hang me if I'm not tired to death trying to talk to this crone, who, to the charms of old age and ugliness, adds that of dumbness. Seen the cap'n?"

"No, he's gone out to hear the people talk, and find out what they think of him."

Hal burst into a loud and scornful laugh, saying—"I should think it would not require much seeking to discover that!"

Here the old woman came forward, and, by signs, managed to inquire whether he had brought her "the tea."

Steve drew a packet from his pocket, saying, softly,

"Yes, mother, when I was in Spicer's store I saw this lying with other things on the counter, and remembering you, quietly put it into my pocket."

The old crone's eyes danced; she seized the packet, patted the excellent thief on the shoulder, wagged her head deridingly at the delinquent one, and hobbled off to prepare her favorite beverage.

While she was thus occupied the whistle was once more heard at the door, followed by the entrance of a man decidedly the most repulsive-looking of the whole party—a man one having a full pocket would scarcely like to meet on a lonely road in a dark night. In form he was of Dutch proportions, short but stout; with a large, round head covered with stiff, sandy hair; broad, flat face; coarse features; pale, half-closed eyes, and an expression of countenance strangely made up of elements as opposite as they were forbidding—a mixture of stupidity and subtilty, cowardice and ferocity, caution and cruelty. His name in the gang was Demon Dick, a sobriquet of which he was eminently deserving and characteristically proud.

He came in sulkily, neither saluting the company nor returning their salutations. He pulled a chair to the fire, threw himself into it, and ordered the old woman to draw him a mug of ale.

"Dick's in a bad humor to-night," murmured Steve, softly.

"When was he ever in a good one?" roughly broke forth Hal.

"H-sh!" said Steve, glancing at Dick, who, with a hideous expression, was listening to the conversation.

"There's the cap'n!" exclaimed Hal, as a ringing footstep sounded outside, followed by the abrupt opening of the door and entrance of the leader.

Setting down a large basket, and throwing off a broad-brimmed Quaker hat and broad-skirted overcoat, Black Donald stood roaring with laughter.

Black Donald, from his great stature, might have been a giant walked out of the age of fable into the middle of the nineteenth century. From his stature alone he might have been chosen leader of this band of desperadoes. He stood six feet eight inches in his boots, and was stout and muscular in proportion. He had a well-formed, stately head, fine aquiline features, dark complexion, strong, steady, dark eyes, and an abundance of long, curling black hair and beard that would have driven to despair a Broadway beau, broken the heart of a Washington belle, or made his own fortune in any city of America as a French count or a German baron! He had decidedly "the air noble and distinguished."

While he threw his broad brim in one direction and his broad coat in another and gave way to peals of laughter, Headlong Hal said:

"Cap'n, I don't know what *you* think of it; but *I* think it just as churlish to laugh alone as to get drunk in solitude."

"Oh, you shall laugh! Wait until I tell you! But first, answer me: Does not my broad-skirted gray coat and broad-brimmed gray hat make me look about twelve inches shorter and broader?"

"That's so, Cap'n!"

"And when I bury my black beard and chin deep down in this drab neckcloth, and pull the broad brim low over my black hair and eyes, I look as mild and respectable as William Penn."[56]

"Yes, verily, friend Donald," said Hal.

"Well, in this meek guise I went peddling to-day."

"Aye, Cap'n we knew it; and you'll go once too often."

"I *have* gone just once too often."

"I knew it."

"We said so."

"D——n!" were some of the ejaculations as the members of the band sprang to their feet and handled secret arms.

"Pshaw! put up your knives and pistols! There is no danger; I was not traced; our rendezvous is still a secret for which the government would pay a thousand dollars!"

"How, then, do you say that you went once too often, Cap'n?"

"It *was* accurate. I *should* have said that I had gone for the last time, for that it would not be safe to venture again. Come—I must tell you the whole story;—but in the meantime let

---

56 The Quaker William Penn (1644–1718) founded Pennsylvania and was renowned for his pacifism and honesty.

us have supper. Mother Raven, dish the beef. Dick, draw the ale. Hal, cut the bread. Steve, carve. Bestir yourselves, burn you! or you shall have no story!" exclaimed the captain, flinging himself into a chair at the head of the table.

When his orders had been obeyed, and the men were gathered around the table, and the first draught of ale had been quaffed by all, Black Donald asked:

"Where do you think I went peddling to-day?"

"Devil knows," said Hal.

"That's a secret between the Demon and Black Donald," said Dick.

"Hush! he's about to tell us," murmured Steve.

"Wooden heads! you'd never guess, I went—I went to—Do you give it up? I went right straight into the lion's jaws—not only into the very clutches, but into the very teeth, and down the very throat of the lion! and have come out as safe as Jonas from the whale's belly!—in a word, I have been up to the county seat where the court is now in session, and sold cigar-cases, snuff-boxes and smoking caps to the grand and petit jury, and a pair of gold spectacles to the learned judge himself!"

"No!"

"No!!"

"No!!!" exclaimed Hal, Steve and Dick in a breath.

"Yes! and moreover, I offered a pair of patent steel spring handcuffs to the sheriff, John Keepe, in person, and pressed him to purchase them, assuring him that he would have occasion for their use if ever he caught that grand rascal, Black Donald!"

" 'Ah! the atrocious villain, if I thought I should ever have the satisfaction of springing them upon *his* wrists, I'd buy them at my own proper cost!' said the sheriff, taking them in his hands, and examining them curiously.

" 'Ah! he's a man of Belial,[57] that same Black Donald!—thee'd better buy the handcuffs, John,' said I.

" 'Nay, friend, I don't know; and as for Black Donald, we have some hopes of taking the wretch at last!' said the simple gentleman.

" 'Ah, verily, John, that's a good hearing for peaceful travelers like myself,' said I.

" 'Excellent! excellent! for when that fell marauder once swings from a gallows——'

" 'His neck will be broken, John!'

" 'Yes, friend; yes, probably; after which honest men may travel in safety! Ah! never have I adjusted a hempen cravat about the throat of any aspirant for such an honor with less pain than I shall officiate at the last toilet of Black Donald!'

" 'If thee catch him?'

" 'Exactly friend, if I catch him; but the additional reward offered by Major Warfield, together with the report that he often frequents our towns and villages in disguise, will stimulate people to renewed efforts to discover and capture him,' said the sheriff.

" 'Ah! that will be a great day for Alleghany. And when Black Donald is hanged, I shall make an effort to be present at the solemnity *myself!*'

" 'Do friend,' said the sheriff, 'and I will see to getting you a good place for witnessing the proceedings.'

" 'I have no doubt thee will, John—a very good place! and I assure thee, that there will not be one present more interested in those proceedings than *myself*,' said I.

---

57 A man in league with the devil.

"'Of course that is very natural; for there is no one more in danger from these marauders than men of your itinerant calling. Good heavens! it was but three years ago a peddler was robbed and murdered in the woods around the Hidden House.'

"'Just so, John,' said I; 'and it's my opinion that often when I've been traveling along the road at night Black Donald hasn't been *far off!* But tell me, John, so that I may have a chance of earning that thousand dollars—what disguises does this son of Moloch[58] take?'

"'Why, friend, it is said that he appears as a Methodist missionary, going about selling tracts; and sometimes as a knife-grinder, and sometimes simulates your calling as a peddler!' said the unsuspicious sheriff.

"I thought, however, it was time to be off, so I said, 'thee had better let me sell thee those handcuffs, John. Allow me! I will show thee their beautiful machinery! Hold out thy wrists, if thee pleases, John.'

"The unsuspicious officer, with a face brimful of interest, held out his wrists for experiment.

"I snapped the ornaments on them in a little less than no time, and took up my pack and disappeared before the sheriff had collected his faculties and found out his position."

"Ha, ha, ha! haw, haw, haw! ho, ho, ho!" laughed the outlaws, in every key of laughter— "and so our captain, instead of being pinioned by the sheriff, turned the tables and actually manacled his honor! Hip, hip, hurrah! three times three for the merry captain, that manacled the sheriff!"

"Hush, burn you! there's some one coming!" exclaimed the captain, rising and listening. "It is Le Noir, who was to meet me here to-night on important business."

Chapter XXI

Gabriel Le Noir

"Naught's had! all's spent!
When our desires are gained without content."
—*Shakespeare*[59]

"THE COLONEL!" exclaimed the three men in a breath, as the door opened and a tall, handsome and distinguished-looking gentleman, wrapped in a black military coat, and having his black beaver pulled low over his brow, strode into the room.

All arose upon their feet to greet him as though he had been a prince.

With a haughty wave of his hand, he bade them resume their seats, and beckoning their leader, said:

"Donald, I would have a word with you."

"At your command, Colonel," said the outlaw, rising and taking a candle and leading the way into the adjoining room, the same in which fourteen years before old Granny Grewell and the child had been detained.

---

58 Ancient Canaanite god associated with human sacrifice.
59 Shakespeare, *Macbeth*, 3.2.

Setting the candle upon the mantel-piece, Black Donald stood waiting for the visitor to open the conversation; a thing that the latter seemed in no hurry to do, for he began walking up and down the room in stern silence.

"You seem disturbed, Colonel," at length said the outlaw.

"I *am* disturbed—*more* than disturbed! I am suffering!"

"Suffering, Colonel!"

"Aye!—suffering!—from what, think you?—the pangs of remorse!"

"Remorse! ha-ha-ha-ha-ha!" laughed the outlaw till all the rafters rang.

"Aye, man, you may laugh! but I repeat that I am tortured with remorse!—and for what do you suppose?—for those acts of self-preservation that fanatics and fools would stigmatize as crimes? No, my good fellow; but for one 'unacted crime!'"

"I told your honor so!" cried the outlaw, triumphantly.

"Donald, when I go to church, as I do constantly, I hear the preacher prating of repentance; but, man, I never knew the meaning of the word until recently!"

"And I can almost guess what it is that has enlightened your honor!" said the outlaw.

"Yes! it is that miserable old woman and babe! Donald, in every vein of my soul, I repent not having silenced them both forever while they were yet in my power!"

"Just so, Colonel; the dead never come back; or, if they do, are not recognized as property-holders in this world! I wish your honor had taken my advice, and sent that woman and child on a longer journey."

"Donald—I was younger then than now. I—*shrank from bloodshed,*" said the man, in a husky voice.

"Bah! superstition. Bloodshed!—blood is shed every day! 'We kill to live,' say the butchers. *So do we!* Every creature preys upon some other creature weaker than himself—the big beasts eat up the little ones; artful men live on the simple; so be it! the world was made for the strong and cunning; let the weak and foolish look to themselves!" said the outlaw, with a loud laugh.

While he spoke, the visitor resumed his rapid, restless striding up and down the room. Presently he came again to the side of the robber, and whispered:

"Donald, that girl has returned to the neighborhood, brought back by old Warfield. My son met her in the woods a month ago, fell into conversation with her—heard her history, or as much of it as she herself knows. Her name is Capitola! she is the living image of her mother. How she came under the notice of old Warfield—to what extent he is acquainted with her birth and rights—what proofs may be in his possession, I know not. All that I have discovered, after the strictest inquiry that I was enabled to make, is this: that the old beggar-woman that died and was buried at Major Warfield's expense, was no other than Nancy Grewell, returned—that the night before she died she sent for Major Warfield, and had a long talk with him, and that shortly afterwards the old scoundrel traveled to the North and brought home this girl."

"Humph! it is an ugly business, your honor, especially with your honor's little prejudice against–"

"Donald! this is no time for weakness! I have gone too far to stop—*Capitola must die.*"

"That's so, Colonel; the pity is that it wasn't found out fourteen years ago. It is so much easier to pinch a baby's nose until it falls asleep, than to stifle a young girl's shrieks and cries! Then the baby would not have been missed; but the young girl will be sure to be inquired after."

"I know that there will be additional risk; but there shall be the larger compensation, larger than your most sanguine hopes would suggest. Donald, listen!" said the colonel, stooping and whispering low—"the day that you bring me undeniable proof that Capitola Le Noir is dead you finger one thousand dollars!"

"Ha-ha-ha!" laughed the outlaw, in angry scorn—"Capitola Le Noir is the sole heiress of a fortune—in land, negroes, coal-mines, iron-foundries, railway shares and bank-stock, of half a million of dollars—and you ask me to get her out of your way for a thousand dollars! I'll do it! you know I will! ha-ha-ha!"

"Why, the government doesn't value your whole carcass at more than I offer you for the temporary use of your hands, you villain!" frowned the colonel.

"No ill names, your honor! Between *us* they are like kicking guns—apt to recoil!"

"You forget that you are in my power."

"I remember that your honor is in mine! Ha-ha-ha! The day Black Donald stands at the bar, the honorable Colonel Le Noir will probably be beside him."

"Enough of this! Confound you, do you take me for one of your pals?"

"No, your worship! my pals are too poor to hire their work done; but then they are brave enough to do it themselves."

"Enough of this, I say! Name the price of this new service!"

"Ten thousand dollars—five thousand in advance—the remainder when the deed is accomplished."

"Extortioner!—shameless, ruthless extortioner!"

"Your honor *will* fall into that vulgar habit of calling ill names!—it isn't worth while; it doesn't pay. If your honor doesn't like my terms you needn't employ me; what is certain is that I cannot work for less."

"You take advantage of my necessities."

"Not at all; but the truth is, Colonel, that I am tired of this sort of life, and wish to retire from active business. Besides, every man has his ambition, and I have mine. I wish to emigrate to the glorious West, settle, marry, turn my attention to politics, be elected to Congress, then to the Senate, then to the Cabinet, then to the White House; for success in which career, I flatter myself nature and education have especially fitted me. Ten thousand dollars will give me a fair start. Many a successful politician, your honor *knows*, has started on less character and less capital!"

To this impudent slander the colonel made no answer; with his arms folded, and his head bowed upon his chest, he walked moodily up and down the length of the apartment; then muttering, "Why should I hesitate?" he came to the side of the outlaw, and said:

"I agree to your terms; accomplish the work, and the sum shall be yours. Meet me here on to-morrow evening to receive the earnest money. In the meantime, in order to make sure of the girl's identity, it will be necessary for you to get sight of her beforehand at her home, if possible; find out her habits and her haunts—where she walks, or rides—when she is most likely to be alone, and so on. Be very careful! A mistake might be fatal."

"Your honor may trust me."

"And now good-bye; remember, to-morrow evening," said the colonel, as, wrapping himself closely in his dark cloak, and pulling his hat low over his eyes, he passed out by the back passage-door, and left the house.

"Ha! ha-ha! Why does that man think it needful to *look* so villainous! If I were to go about in such a bandit-like dress as *that*, every child I met would take me for—what I am," laughed Black Donald, returning to his comrades.

During the next hour other members of the band dropped in, until some twenty men were collected together in the large kitchen around the long table, where the remainder of the night was spent in revelry.

Chapter XXII

The Smuggler and Capitola

"Come buy of me! come buy! come buy!
Buy, lads, or else the lasses cry;
I have lawns as white as snow;
Silk as black as e'er was crow;
Gloves as sweet as damask roses;
Veils for faces; musk for noses;
Pins and needles made of steel;
All you need from head to heel."
            —*Shakespeare*[60]

"IF I AM not allowed to walk or ride out alone I shall 'gang daft.' I know I shall. Was ever such a dull, lonesome, hum-drum place as this same Hurricane Hall?" complained Cap, as she sat sewing with Mrs. Condiment in the housekeeper's room.

"You don't like this quiet country life?" inquired Mrs. Condiment.

"No; no better than I do a quiet country grave-yard. I don't want to return to dust before my time, I tell you," said Cap, yawning dismally over her work.

"I HEAR YOU, VIXEN!" roared the voice of Old Hurricane, who presently came storming in and saying:

"If you want a ride go and get ready quickly and come with me; I am going down to the water-mill, please the Lord, to warn Hopkins off the premises, worthless villain! had my grain there since yesterday morning, and hasn't sent it home yet! shan't stay in my mill another month. Come, Cap, be off with you and get ready!"

The girl did not need a second bidding, but flew to prepare herself, while the old man ordered the horses.

In ten minutes more Capitola and Major Warfield cantered away.

They had been gone about two hours, and it was almost time to expect their return, and Mrs. Condiment had just given orders for the tea-table to be set, when Wool came into her room and said there was a sailor at the hall-door with some beautiful foreign goods which he wished to show to the ladies of the house.

"A sailor, Wool, a sailor with foreign goods for sale? I am *very* much afraid he's one of these smugglers I've heard tell of; and I'm not sure about the right of buying from smugglers! However, I suppose there's no harm in looking at his goods. You may call him in, Wool," said the old lady, tampering with temptation.

"He *do* look like a smudgeler, dat's a fact," said Wool, whose ideas of the said craft were purely imaginary.

"I don't know him to be a smuggler, and it's wrong to judge, particularly beforehand," said the old lady, nursing ideas of rich silks and satins, imported free of duty and sold at half price, and trying to deceive herself.

While she was thus thinking, the door opened, and Wool ushered in a stout, jolly-looking tar, dressed in a wide pea-jacket, duck trowsers and tarpaulin hat, and carrying in his hand a large pack. He took off his hat and scraped his foot behind him, and remained standing

---

60 Shakespeare, *The Winter's Tale*, 4.4.

before the housekeeper, with his head tied up in a red bandanna handkerchief, and his chin sunken in a red comforter that was wound around his throat.

"Sit down, my good man, and rest while you show me the goods," said Mrs. Condiment, who, whether he were smuggler or not, was inclined to show the traveler all lawful kindness.

The sailor scraped his foot again, sat down on a low chair, put his hat on one side, drew the pack before him, untied it, and first displayed a rich, golden-hued fabric, saying:

"Now here, ma'am, is a rich China silk I bought in the streets of Shanghai, where the long-legged chickens come from; come, now, I'll ship it off cheap——"

"Oh, that is a great deal too gay and handsome for an old woman like me," said Mrs. Condiment.

"Well, ma'am, perhaps there's young ladies in the fleet? Now this would rig out a smart young craft as gay as a clipper! Better take it, ma'am. I'll ship it off cheap."

"Wool," said Mrs. Condiment, turning to the servant, "go down to the kitchen and call up the house-servants; perhaps they would like to buy something."

As soon as Wool had gone, and the good woman was left alone with the sailor, she stooped and said:

"I did not wish to inquire before the servantman, but, my good sir, I do not know whether it is right to buy from you."

"Why so, ma'am?" asked the sailor, with an injured look.

"Why, I am afraid—I am *very* much afraid you risk your life and liberty in an unlawful trade."

"Oh, ma'am, on my soul these things are honestly come by, and you have no right to accuse me!" said the sailor, with a look of subdued indignation.

"I know I haven't, and meant no harm; but did these goods pass through the custom-house?"

"Oh, ma'am, now, that's not a fair question!"

"It is as I suspected, I cannot buy from you, my good friend; I do not judge you; I don't know whether smuggling is right or wrong; but I know that it is unlawful, and I cannot feel free to encourage any man in a traffic in which he risks his life and liberty, poor fellow!"

"Oh, ma'am," said the sailor, evidently on the brink of bursting into laughter—"if we risk our lives, sure it's our own business, and if you've no scruples on your *own* account you needn't have any on *ours!*"

While he was speaking the sound of many shuffling feet was heard along the passage, and the room was soon half filled with colored people come in to deal with the sailor.

"You may *look* at these goods; but you must not buy anything."

"Lor', missus, why?" asked Little Pitapat.

"Because I want you to lay out all your money with my friend Mr. Crash, at Tip-Top."

"But after de good gemman has had de trouble?" said Pitapat.

"He shall have his supper and a mug of ale and go on his journey," said Mrs. Condiment.

The sailor arose and scraped his foot behind him in acknowledgment of this kindness, and began to unpack his wares and display them all over the floor.

And while the servants in wonder and delight examined these treasures and inquired their prices, a fresh, young voice was heard carolling along the hall, and the next moment Capitola, in her green riding-habit and hat, entered the room.

She turned her mischievous gray eyes about, pursed up her lips, and asked Mrs. Condiment if she were about to open a fancy bazaar.

"No, my dear Miss Capitola. It is a sailor with foreign goods for sale," answered the old lady.

"A sailor with foreign goods for sale! umph! yes! I know. Isn't he a smuggler?" whispered Capitola.

"Indeed, I'm afraid so, my dear! In fact he don't deny it!" whispered back the matron.

"Well, *I* think it's strange a man that smuggles can't lie!"

"Well, I don't know, my dear; maybe he thinks it's no harm to smuggle, and he *knows* it would be a sin to lie. But where is your uncle, Miss Capitola?"

"Gone around to the stable to blow Jem up for mounting him on a lame horse; he swears Jem shall find another master before to-morrow's sun sets. But now I want to talk to that bold buccaneer. Say you, sir! Show me your foreign goods; I'm very fond of smugglers myself!"

"You are right, my dear young lady! *You* would give poor sailors some little chance to turn an honest penny."

"Certainly! brave fellows! Show me that splendid fabric that shines like cloth of gold."

"This, my young lady, is a real, genuine China silk; I bought it myself in my last cruise in the streets of Shanghai, where the long-legged chickens——"

"And fast young men come from! I know the place. I've been all along there!" interrupted Capitola, her gray eyes glittering with mischief.

"This, you will perceive, young lady, is an article that cannot be purchased anywhere except——"

"From the manufactory of foreign goods in the city of New York, or from their traveling agents."

"Oh, my dear young lady, how you wrong me! This article came from——"

"The factory of Messrs. Hocus & Pocus, corner of Cant and Come-it street, city of Gotham!"

"Oh, my dear young lady——"

"Look here, my brave buccaneer, I know all about it. I told you I'd been along there!" said the girl; and turning to Mrs. Condiment, she said: "See here, my dear, good soul if you want to buy that 'India' silk that you are looking at so longingly, you may do it with a safe conscience. True, it never passed through the custom-house—because it was made in New York. I know all about it! *All* these 'foreign goods' are manufactured at the north and sent by agents all over the country. These agents dress and talk like sailors, and assume a mysterious manner on purpose to be suspected of smuggling—because they know well enough fine ladies will buy much quicker and pay much more, if they only fancy they are cheating Uncle Sam, in buying foreign goods from a smuggler at half price!"

"So, then, you are not a smuggler, after all!" said Mrs. Condiment, looking almost regretfully at the sailor.

"Why, ma'am, you know I told you you were accusing me wrongfully."

"Well, but really, now, there was something about you that looked sort of suspicious."

"What did I tell you! a look put on on purpose," said Cap.

"Well—he knows that if he wanted to pass for a smuggler, it didn't take *here,*" said Mrs. Condiment.

"No—*that* it didn't!" muttered the object of these commentaries.

"Well, my good man, since you are, after all, an honest peddler, just hand me that silk, and don't ask me an unreasonable price for it, because I'm a judge of silks, and I won't pay more than it is worth," said the old lady.

"Madam, I leave it to your own conscience. You shall give me just what you think it's worth."

"Humph! that's too fair by half. I begin to think this fellow is worse than he seems!" said Capitola to herself.

After a little hesitation a price was agreed upon, and the dress bought.

Then the servants received permission to invest their little change in ribbons, handkerchiefs, tobacco, snuff, or whatever they thought they needed. When the purchases were all made, and the peddler had done up his diminished pack and replaced his hat upon his head and was preparing to leave, Mrs. Condiment said:

"My good man, it is getting very late, and we do not like to see a traveler leave our house at this hour; pray remain until morning, and then, after an early breakfast, you can pursue your way in safety."

"Thank you, kindly, ma'am, but I must be far on my road to-night," said the peddler.

"But, my good man, you are a stranger in this part of the country, and don't know the danger you run," said the housekeeper.

"Danger, ma'am, in this quiet country!"

"Oh, dear, yes, my good man, particularly with your valuable pack—oh, my good gracious!" cried the old lady, with an appalled look.

"Indeed, ma'am, you—you make me sort of uneasy! What danger can there be for a poor, peaceful peddler pursuing his path?"

"Oh, my good soul, may Heaven keep you from—BLACK DONALD!"

"Black Donald—who's he?"

"Oh, my good man, he's the awfulest villain that ever went unhung!"

"Black Donald! Black Donald! never heard that name before in my life! Why is the fellow called *Black* Donald?"

"Oh, sir, he's called Black Donald for his black soul, black deeds, and—and—also, I believe, for his jet black hair and beard."

"Oh, my countrymen, what a falling *up* was there!" exclaimed Capitola, at this anti-climax.

"And how shall I keep from meeting this villain?" asked the peddler.

"Oh, sir, how can I tell you? You never can form an idea where he is or where he isn't! Only think, he may be in our very midst any time, and we not know it. Why, only yesterday the desperate villain handcuffed the very sheriff in the very courtyard! Yet I wonder the sheriff did not know him at once! For my own part, I'm sure *I* should know Black Donald the minute I clapped my two looking eyes on him!"

"Should you, ma'am?"

"Yes, indeed, by his long, black hair and beard! They say it is half a yard long. Now a man of such a singular appearance as *that* must be easily recognized!"

"Of course! Then you never met this wretch face to face?"

"Me! *me!* am I standing here alive? Do you suppose I should be standing here if ever I had met that demon? Why, man, I never leave this house, even in the day-time, except with two bull-dogs and a servant, for fear I should meet Black Donald! I know if ever I should meet that demon, I should drop dead with terror. I feel I should!"

"But maybe now, ma'am, the man may not be so bad, after all. Even the devil is not so black as he is painted."

"The devil may *not* be, but Black Donald *is.*"

"What do *you* think of this outlaw, young lady?" asked the peddler, turning to Capitola.

"Why, I *like* him!" said Cap.

"You do?"

"Yes, I *do!* I like men whose very names strike terror into the hearts of commonplace people!"

"Oh, Miss Black!" exclaimed Mrs. Condiment.

"Yes, I *do,* ma'am. And if Black Donald were only as honest as he is brave, I should quite *adore* him! so there! And if there is one person in the world I long to see, it is Black Donald."

"Do you *really* wish to see him?" asked the peddler, looking intently into the half earnest, half satirical face of the girl.

"Yes, I *do* wish to see him above all things."

"And do you know what happened to the rash girl who wished to see the devil?"

"No—what did?"

"She saw him!"

"Oh, if that's all, I dare it! and if wishing will bring me the sight of this notorious outlaw, lo! I wish it. I wish it. I wish to see Black Donald," said Capitola.

The peddler deliberately arose and put down his pack and his hat; then he suddenly tore off the scarf from his neck and the handkerchief from his head, lifted his chin and shook loose a great, rolling mass of black hair and beard; drew himself up, struck an attitude, called up a look, and exclaimed:

"Behold Black Donald!"

With a piercing shriek, Mrs. Condiment swooned and fell to the floor; the poor negroes, men and maids, were struck dumb and motionless with consternation; Capitola gazed for one lost moment in admiration and curiosity; in the meantime Black Donald quickly resumed his disguises, took up his pack and walked out of the room.

Capitola was the first to recover her presence of mind; the instinct of the huntress possessed her; starting forward, she exclaimed:

"Pursue him! catch him! come with me! Cowards! will you let a robber and murderer escape!" and she ran out and overtook the outlaw in the middle of the hall. With the agile leap of a little terrier she sprang up behind him, seized the thick collar of his pea-jacket with both hands, and drawing up her feet, hung there with all her weight, crying:

"Help! murder! murder! help! Come to my aid! I've caught Black Donald!"

He could have killed her instantly in any one of a dozen ways! He could have driven in her temples with a blow of his sledge-hammer fist; he could have broken her neck with the grip of his iron fingers; he only wished to shake her off without hurting her—a difficult task, for there she hung, a dead weight, at the collar of his coat at the back of his neck.

"Oh, very well!" he cried, laughing aloud. "Such adhesiveness I never saw! You stick to me like a wife to her husband. So, if you won't let go, I shall have to take you along, that's all! So here I go, like Christian with his bundle of sin on his back."[61]

And loosing the upper button of his pea-jacket so as to give him more breath, and putting down his peddler's pack to relieve himself as much as possible, the outlaw strode through the hall-door, down the steps, and down the evergreen avenue leading to the woods.

---

61 Reference to Christian, the protagonist in John Bunyan's *Pilgrim's Progress* (1678), who must make his journey to the Celestial City weighed down by his sin, which he carries bundled on his back.

Capitola, still clinging to the back of his coat-collar, with her feet drawn up, a dead weight, and still crying:

"Help! murder! I've caught Black Donald, and I'll *die* before I'll let him go."

"You're determined to be an outlaw's bride, that's certain. Well I've no particular objection," cried Black Donald, roaring with laughter as he strode on.

It was "a thing to see, not hear"—that brave, rash, resolute imp clinging like a terrier, or a crab, or a briar, on to the back of that gigantic ruffian, whom, if she had no strength to stop, she was determined not to release.

They had nearly reached the foot of the descent when a great noise and hallooing was heard behind them. It was the negroes, who, having recovered from their panic, and armed themselves with guns, pistols, swords, pokers, tongs, and pitch-forks, were now in hot pursuit.

And cries of "Black Donald!" "Black Donald!" "Black Donald!" filled the air.

"I've got him! I've got him! help! help! quick! quick!" screamed Capitola, clinging closer than ever.

Though still roaring with laughter at the absurdity of his position, Black Donald strode on faster than before and was in a fair way of escape, when lo! suddenly coming up the path in front of him, he met—

OLD HURRICANE!!!

As the troop of miscellaneously-armed negroes running down the hill were still making eve "hideous" with yells of "Black Donald!" "Black Donald!" and Capitola still clinging and hanging on at the back of his neck continued to cry: "I've caught him! I've caught him! help! help!" something like the truth flashed in a blinding way upon Old Hurricane's perceptions.

Roaring forth something between a recognition and defiance, the old man threw up his fat arms, and as fast as age and obesity would permit, ran up the hill to intercept the outlaw.

There was no time for trifling now! The army of negroes was at his heels; the old veteran in his path; the girl clinging a dead weight to his jacket behind. An idea suddenly struck him which he wondered had not done so before—quickly unbuttoning and throwing off his garment he dropped both captor and jacket behind him on the ground.

And before Capitola had picked herself up, Black Donald, bending his huge head and shoulders forward and making a battering-ram of himself, ran with all his force and butted Old Hurricane in the stomach, pitched him into the horse-pond, leaped over the park fence and disappeared in the forest.

What a scene! what a row followed the escape and flight of the famous outlaw!

Who could imagine, far less describe it!—a general tempest in which every individual was a particular storm.

There stood the baffled Capitola, extricating her head from the pea-jacket, and with her eyes fairly flashing out *sparks* of anger, exclaiming:

"Oh, wretches! wretches that you are! if you'd been worth *salt* you could have caught him while I clung to him so!"

There wallowed Old Hurricane, spluttering, floundering, half-drowning, in the horse-pond, making the most frantic efforts to curse and swear as he struggled to get out.

There stood the crowd of negroes brought to a sudden stand by a panic of horror at seeing the dignity of their master so outraged.

And most frenzied of all, there ran Wool around and around the margin of the pond, in a state of violent perplexity how to get his master out without half-drowning himself.

"Blurr-urr-rr! flitch! filch! Blurr-ur! spluttered and sneezed and strangled Old Hurricane, as he floundered to the edge of the pond. *Blurr-urr-rr!* Help me out, you scoundrel! I'll break every bone in your—*flitch!*—body! Do you hear me—*ca-snish!*—villain you! *flitch! flitch! ca-snish! oh-h!"*

Wool, with his eyes starting from his head, and his hair standing up with horrors of all sorts, plunged at last into the water and pulled his old master up upon his feet.

"Ca-snish! ca-snish! blurr-rr! flitch!—what are you gaping there for as if you'd raised the devil, you crowd of born fools!" howled Old Hurricane, as soon as he could get the water out of his mouth and nose—"what are you standing there for?—after him! after him, I say! Scour the woods in every direction! His freedom to any man who brings me Black Donald, dead or alive!—Wool!"

"Yes, sir," said that functionary who was busying himself with squeezing the water out of his master's garments.

"Wool, let me alone! take the fleetest horse in the stable! ride for your life to the Court House! Tell Keepe to have new bills posted everywhere, offering an additional five hundred dollars for the apprehension of that—that—that"—for the want of a word strong enough to express himself, Old Hurricane suddenly stopped, and for lack of his stick to make silence emphatic, he seized his gray hair with both hands and groaned aloud.

Wool waited no second bidding, but flew to do his errand.

Capitola came to the old man's side, saying:

"Uncle, hadn't you better hurry home—you'll take cold."

"Cold?—*Cold!* demmy! I never was so hot in my life!" cried the old man; "but demmy! you're right! run to the house, Capitola, and tell Mrs. Condiment to have me a full suit of dry clothes before the fire in my chamber. Go, child! every man-jack is off after Black Donald, and there is nobody but you, and Condiment, and the housemaids to take care of me. Stop, look for my stick first; where did that black demon throw it?— demmy! I'd as well be without my legs!"

Capitola picked up the old man's cane and hat, and put the one on his head and the other in his hand, and then hastened to find Mrs. Condiment, and tell her to prepare to receive her half-drowned patron. She found the old lady scarcely recovered from the effects of her recent fright, but ready on the instant to make every effort on behalf of Old Hurricane, who presently after arrived dripping wet at the house.

Leaving the old gentleman to the care of his housekeeper, we must follow Black Donald.

Hatless and coatless, with his long black hair and beard blown by the wind, the outlaw made tracks for his retreat—occasionally stopping to turn and get breath, and send a shout of laughter at his baffled pursuers.

That same night, at the usual hour, the gang met at their rendezvous, the deserted inn, beside the old road through the forest. They were in the midst of their orgies around the supper-table, when the well-known ringing step of the leader sounded under the back windows without, the door was burst open, and the captain, hatless, coatless, with his dark elf locks flying, and every sign of haste and disorder, rushed into the room.

He was met by a general rising and outcry:—"Hi! hillo! what's up?" exclaimed every man, starting to his feet and laying hands upon secret arms, prepared for instant resistance.

For a moment Black Donald stood with his leonine head turned and looking back over his stalwart shoulders, as if in expectation of pursuit, and then, with a loud laugh, turned to his men, exclaiming:

"Ho! you thought me followed! So I have been! but not as close as hound to heel!"

"In fact, Captain, you look as if you'd but escaped with your skin this time!" said Hal.

"Faith! the captain looks well peeled!" said Stephen.

"Worse than that, boys! worse than that! Your chief has not only lost his pack, his hat and his coat, but—his *heart!* Not only are the outworks battered, but the citadel itself is taken! Not only has he been captured, but *captivated!* and all by a little minx of a girl!—Boys, your chief is in love!" exclaimed Black Donald, throwing himself into his seat at the head of the table, and quaffing off a large draught of ale.

"Hip! hip! hurraw! three times three for the Captain's love!" cried Hal, rising to propose the toast, which was honored with enthusiasm.

"Now tell us all about it, Captain. Who is she? where did you see her? is she fair or dark? tall or short? thin or plump? what's her name? and is she kind?" asked Hal.

"First guess where I have been to-day."

"You and your demon only know!"

"I guess they also know at Hurricane Hall, for it is there I have been!"

"Well, then, why didn't you go to perdition at once?" exclaimed Hal, in a consternation that was reflected in every countenance present.

"Why, because when I go *there* I intend to take you all with me and remain!" answered Black Donald.

"Tell us about the visit to Hurricane Hall," said Hal.

Whereupon Black Donald commenced, and concealing only the motive of his visit, gave his comrades a very graphic, spicy and highly colored narrative of his adventure at Hurricane Hall, and particularly of his "passages at arms" with the little witch, Capitola, whom he described as:

"*Such a girl!* slender, petite, lithe, with bright, black ringlets dancing around a little face full of fun, frolic, mischief and spirit, and eyes quick and vivacious as those of a monkey, darting hither and thither from object to object."

"The Captain *is* in love, sure enough," said Steve.

"Bravo! here's success to the Captain's love!—*She's* a brick!" shouted the men.

"Oh, she *is,*" assented their chief, with enthusiasm.

"Long life to her! three times three for the pretty witch of Hurricane Hall!" roared the men, rising to their feet and raising their full mugs high in the air, before pledging the toast.

"*That* is all very well, boys; but I want more substantial compliments than words—*Boys! I must have that girl!*"

"Who doubts it, Captain?—of course you will take her at once if you want her," said Hal, confidently.

"But, I must have *help* in taking her."

"Captain, I volunteer for one!" exclaimed Hal.

"And I, for another," added Steve.

"And *you,* Dick?" inquired the leader, turning towards the sullen man, whose greater atrocity had gained for him the name of Demon Dick.

"What is the use of volunteering when the captain has only to *command,*" said this individual, sulkily.

"Ah! when the enterprise is simply the robbing of a mail-coach, in which you all have equal interest, then, indeed, your captain has only to command, and you to obey; but *this* is a more delicate matter of entering a lady's chamber and carrying her off for the captain's arms, and so should only be entrusted to those whose feelings of devotion to the captain's person prompt them to volunteer for the service," said Black Donald.

"How elegantly our captain speaks! he ought to be a lawyer," said Steve.

"The captain knows I'm with him for everything," said Dick, sulkily.

"Very well, then! for a personal service like this, a delicate service requiring devotion, I should scorn to give *commands!* I thank you for your offered assistance, my friends, and shall count on you three, Hal, Stephen and Richard, for the enterprise," said the captain.

"Ay! ay! ay!" said the three men in a breath.

"For the time and place and manner of the seizure of the girl, we must reflect. Let us see! there is to be a fair in the village next week, during the session of the court. Old Hurricane will be at court as usual. And for one day, at least, his servants will have a holiday to go to the fair. They will not get home until the next morning. The house will be ill-guarded. We must find out the particular day and night when this shall be so. Then you three shall watch your opportunity, enter the house by stealth, conceal yourselves in the chamber of the girl, and at midnight, when all is quiet, gag her and bring her away."

"Excellent!" said Hal.

"And mind, no liberty except the simple act of carrying her off is to be taken with your captain's prize," said the leader, with a threatening glare of his lion-like eye.

"Oh, no! no! not for the world! She shall be as sacred from insult as though she were an angel and we saints," said Hal, both the others assenting.

"And now not a word more. We will arrange the further details of this business hereafter," said the captain, as a peculiar signal was given at the door.

Waving his hand for the men to keep their places, Black Donald went out and opened the back passage-door, admitting Colonel Le Noir.

"Well," said the latter, anxiously.

"Well, sir, I have contrived to see her; come into the front room and I will tell you all about it," said the outlaw, leading the way into the old parlor that had been the scene of so many of their conspiracies.

"Does Capitola Le Noir still live?" hoarsely demanded the colonel, as the two conspirators reached the parlor.

"Still live? yes; 'twas but yesterday we agreed upon her death. Give a man time. Sit down, Colonel; take this seat! we will talk the matter over again."

With something very like a sigh of relief, Colonel Le Noir threw himself into the offered chair.

Black Donald drew another chair up and sat down beside his patron.

"Well, Colonel, I have contrived to see the girl as I told you," he began.

"But you have not done the deed; when will it be done?"

"Colonel, my patron, be patient. Within twelve days I shall claim the last instalment of the ten thousand dollars agreed upon between us for this job."

"But why so long? since it is to be done, why not have it over at once?" said Colonel Le Noir, starting up and pacing the floor impatiently.

"Patience, my Colonel. The cat may play with the mouse most delightfully before devouring it."

"What do you mean?"

"My Colonel, I have seen the girl under circumstances that have fired my heart with an uncontrollable desire for her——"

"Ha-ha-ha!" scornfully laughed the colonel. "Black Donald, the mail-robber, burglar, outlaw, the subject of the grand passion!"

"Why not, my Colonel. Listen, you shall hear, and then you shall judge whether or not you yourself might not have been fired by the fascination of such a witch!" said the outlaw, who straightway commenced and gave his patron the same account of his visit to Hurricane Hall that he had already related to his comrades.

The colonel heard the story with many a "pish," "tush" and "pshaw," and when the man had concluded the tale, he exclaimed:

"Is that all? Then we may continue our negotiations—*I* care not. Carry her off! marry her! do as you please with her! only at the end of all— *kill her!*" hoarsely whispered Le Noir.

"That is just what I intend, Colonel."

"That will do if the event be certain; but it must be certain. I cannot breathe freely while *my brother's heiress lives!*" whispered Le Noir.

"Well, Colonel, be content; here is my hand upon it. In six days Capitola will be in my power. In twelve days *you* shall be out of *hers.*"

"It is a bargain," said each of the conspirators in a breath, as they shook hands and parted—Le Noir to his home and Black Donald to join his comrades' revelry.

* * *

Editor's Note

The Hidden Hand: The End of the Story

Southworth excelled in writing tales that begin with a series of disparate storylines that she would then carefully weave together. These slowly revealed and highly complex storylines proved to be immensely popular with her readers, and Southworth employed this formula to great effect in the long and complicated story of Capitola in *The Hidden Hand*. We learn by the novel's end that Clara is a rich heiress, and that Capitola is a member of the Le Noir family. In fact, Capitola's mother has been kept prisoner by Gabriel Le Noir for nearly 18 years, first in his house and then in a mental institution. By the story's end, Capitola has married Herbert Greyson, Clara has married Traverse and Old Hurricane has reconciled with his child-bride Marah Rocke. As one last act of rebellious adventure, Capitola enacts a plan to free Black Donald from prison, where he is set to be executed on her wedding day. He escapes and reforms. The women, although married, continue to exercise considerable control over their men, guiding their lives and keeping them in line when necessary.

Chapter Nineteen

CHARLES MONROE SHELDON

(1857–1946)

Charles Sheldon was born the son of a Congregational pastor and farmer. He followed his father's footsteps into the Congregational ministry in 1886 and eventually took a church in Topeka, Kansas, where he lived the rest of his life. Sheldon was an early crusader for race relations and class equality. In 1891, he spent three weeks living in Topeka's black ghetto. In the years to follow, he would tirelessly work to preach, educate and see that material assistance reached the poorer elements of Topeka's population. He personified the social gospel claim that devout, hardworking Christians could indeed establish the Kingdom of God on earth. Along with his concern for the poor, Sheldon also worked hard for various temperance, peace and ecumenical causes.

In 1891, Sheldon began telling what he called "sermon stories" to his congregation during his Sunday evening services. He read 30 such stories before he retired from the pulpit in 1919. He published some of them in the Congregational periodical, *The Advance*. Little notice was taken of Sheldon's writing ability, however, until the appearance of *In His Steps* (1897). Like many of Sheldon's stories, *In His Steps* was part of a larger social gospel literary genre, popular in the late nineteenth century, in which Christian values were focused on meeting specific social needs.

In His Steps is built around a simple narrative concerning a group of citizens who decide to guide their lives for a year by framing their decisions with the question: "What would Jesus do?" When published, the book became an overnight sensation. Hundreds of thousands of copies were sold by its official publisher, but because of a problem with the copyright, no fewer than 16 other publishers began to print their own editions soon after its initial appearance. By 1900, millions of copies were in print, and by 1930, Sheldon proclaimed that more than 20 million copies were circulating in dozens of languages. From its humble beginnings as a sermon series, *In His Steps* became one of the best-known stories of the late nineteenth and early twentieth centuries.

IN HIS STEPS.

"What Would Jesus Do?"

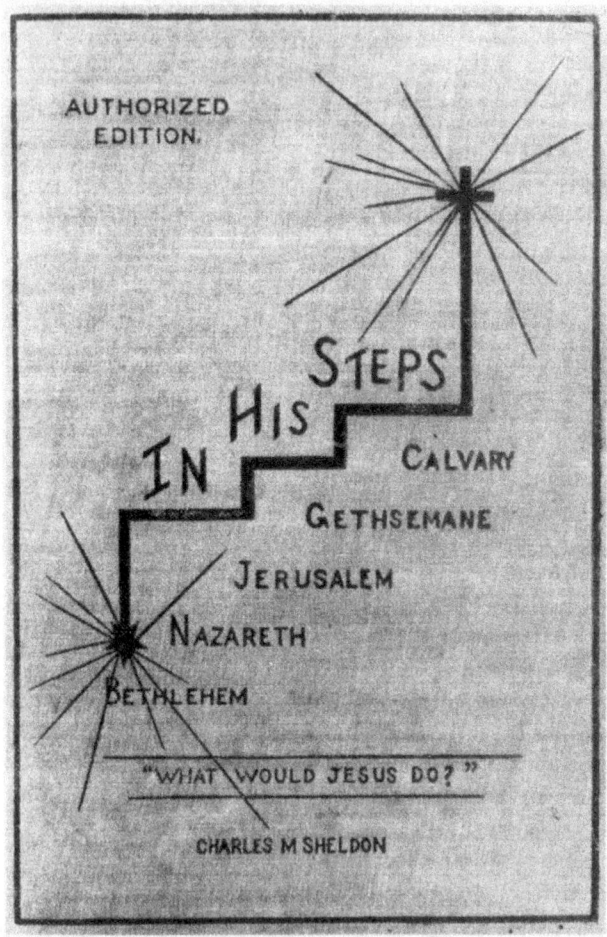

Cover of the first cloth edition of Charles Sheldon's *In His Steps* (Chicago: Advance Publishing, Co., 1898).

Charles Sheldon, *In His Steps: "What Would Jesus Do?"* Chicago: Advance Publishing Co., 1898.

Preface

The sermon story, IN HIS STEPS, or "What Would Jesus Do?" was first written in the winter of 1896, and read by the author, a chapter at a time, to his Sunday evening congregation in the Central Congregational Church, Topeka, Kansas. It was then printed as a serial in THE ADVANCE (Chicago), and its reception by the readers of that paper was such that the publishers of THE ADVANCE made arrangements for its appearance in book form. It was their desire, in which the author heartily joined, that the story might reach as many readers as possible, hence succeeding editions of paper-covered volumes at a price within the reach of nearly all readers.

The story has been warmly and thoughtfully welcomed by Endeavor societies, temperance organizations, and Y. M. C. A.'s. It is the earnest prayer of the author that the book may go its way with a great blessing to the churches for the quickening of Christian discipleship, and the hastening of the Master's kingdom on earth.

CHARLES M. SHELDON.

Topeka, Kansas, November, 1897.

Chapter I

"For hereunto were ye called; because Christ also suffered for
you, leaving you an example, that ye should follow his steps."[1]

IT WAS FRIDAY morning and the Rev. Henry Maxwell was trying to finish his Sunday morning sermon. He had been interrupted several times and was growing nervous as the morning wore away and the sermon grew very slowly towards a satisfactory finish.

"Mary," he called to his wife, as he went up stairs after the last interruption, "if any one comes after this, I wish you would say that I am very busy and cannot come down unless it is something very important."

"Yes, Henry. But I am going over to visit the Kindergarten and you will have the house all to yourself."

The minister went up into his study and shut the door. In a few minutes he heard his wife go out.

He settled himself at his desk with a sigh of relief and began to write. His text was from First Peter, ii: 21.

"For hereunto were ye called; because Christ also suffered for you, leaving you an example, that ye should follow his steps."

He had emphasized in the first part of his sermon the Atonement as a personal sacrifice, calling attention to the fact of Jesus' suffering in various ways, in his life as well as in his death. He had gone on to emphasize the Atonement from the side of example, giving illustrations from the life and teaching of Jesus, to show how faith in the Christ helped to save men because of the pattern or character he displayed for their imitation. He was now on the third and last point, the necessity of following Jesus in his sacrifice and example.

---

1 1 Peter 2:21.

He had just put down, "3: Steps; What are they?" And was about to enumerate them in logical order when the bell rang sharply. It was one of those clock-work bells and always went off as a clock might go if it tried to strike twelve all at once.

Henry Maxwell sat at his desk and frowned a little. He made no movement to answer the bell. Very soon it rang again. Then he rose and walked over to one of his windows which commanded a view of the front door.

A man was standing on the steps. He was a young man very shabbily dressed.

"Looks like a tramp," said the minister. "I suppose I'll have to go down, and—"

He did not finish the sentence, but he went down stairs and opened the front door.

There was a moment's pause as the two men stood facing each other; then the shabby-looking young man said,

"I'm out of a job, sir, and thought maybe you might put me in the way of getting something."

"I don't know of anything. Jobs are scarce," replied the minister beginning to shut the door slowly.

"I didn't know but you might perhaps be able to give me a line to the city railway or superintendent of the shops or something," continued the young man, shifting his faded hat from one hand to the other nervously.

"It would be of no use. You will have to excuse me. I am very busy this morning. I hope you will find something. Sorry I can't give you something to do here. But I keep only a horse and a cow and do the work myself."

The Rev. Henry Maxwell closed the door and heard the man walk down the steps. As he went up into his study he saw from his hall window that the man was going slowly down the street, still holding his hat between his hands. There was something in the figure so dejected, homeless and forsaken, that the minister hesitated a moment as he stood looking at it. Then he turned to his desk, and with a sigh began the writing where he had left off.

He had no more interruptions and when his wife came in two hours later, the sermon was finished, the loose leaves gathered up and neatly tied together and laid on his Bible, all ready for the Sunday morning service.

"A queer thing happened at the Kindergarten this morning, Henry," said his wife while they were eating dinner. "You know I went over with Mrs. Brown to visit the school, and just after the games, while the children were at the tables, the door opened and a young man came in, holding a dirty hat in both hands. He sat down near the door and never said a word. Only looked at the children. He was evidently a tramp, and Miss Wren and her assistant, Miss Kyle, were a little frightened at first, but he sat there very quietly and after a few minutes he went out."

"Perhaps he was tired and wanted to rest somewhere. The same man called here, I think. Did you say he looked like a tramp?"

"Yes, very dusty, shabby and generally tramp-like. Not more than thirty or thirty-three years old, I should say."

"The same man," said the Rev. Henry Maxwell thoughtfully.

"Did you finish your sermon, Henry?" his wife asked after a pause.

"Yes, all done. It has been a very busy week with me. The two sermons cost me a good deal of labor."

"They will be appreciated by a large audience to-morrow, I hope," replied his wife smiling. "What are you going to preach about in the morning?"

"Following Christ. I take up the Atonement under the heads of Sacrifice and Example, and then show the steps needed to follow his sacrifice and example.

"I am sure it is a good sermon. I hope it won't rain Sunday. We have had so many rainy days lately."

"Yes, the audiences have been quite small for some time. People will not come out to church in a storm." The Rev. Henry Maxwell sighed as he said it. He was thinking of the careful, laborious efforts he had made in preparing sermons for large audiences that failed to appear.

But Sunday morning dawned on the town of Raymond one of those perfect days that sometimes come after long periods of wind and rain and mud. The air was clear and bracing, the sky was free from all threatening signs, and every one in Henry Maxwell's parish prepared to go to church. When the service opened at eleven o'clock, the large building was filled with an audience of the best-dressed, most comfortable looking people in Raymond.

The First Church of Raymond believed in having the best music that money could buy and its quartette choir this morning was a great source of pleasure to the congregation. The anthem was inspiring. All the music was in keeping with the subject of the sermon. And the anthem was an elaborate adaptation to the most modern music, of the hymn.

"Jesus, I my cross have taken,
All to leave and follow thee."[2]

Just before the sermon, the soprano sang a solo, the well known hymn,

"Where He leads me I will follow,
I'll go with Him, with Him all the way."[3]

Rachel Winslow looked very beautiful that morning as she stood up behind the screen of carved oak which was significantly marked with the emblems of the cross and the crown. Her voice was even more beautiful than her face, and that meant a great deal. There was a general rustle of expectation over the audience as she rose. Henry Maxwell settled himself contentedly behind the pulpit. Rachel Winslow's singing always helped him. He generally arranged for a song before the sermon. It made possible a certain inspiration of feeling that he knew made his delivery more impressive.

People said to themselves they had never heard such singing even in the First Church. It is certain that if it had not been a church service, her solo would have been vigorously applauded. It even seemed to Henry Maxwell when she sat down that something like an attempted clapping of hands or a striking of feet on the floor swept through the church. He was startled by it. As he rose, however, and laid his sermon on the open Bible, he said to himself he had been deceived. Of course it could not occur. In a few moments he was absorbed in his sermon and everything else was forgotten in the pleasure of the delivery.

No one had ever accused Henry Maxwell of being a dull preacher. On the contrary he had often been charged with being sensational. Not in what he said so much as in his way of saying it. But the First Church people liked that. It gave their preacher and their parish a pleasant distinction that was agreeable.

---

2 From the hymn "Jesus, I My Cross Have Taken," by Henry Francis Lyte (1833).
3 From the popular hymn "Where He Leads Me," by Ernest W. Blandy and John Norris (1890).

It was also true that the pastor of the First Church loved to preach. He seldom exchanged.[4] He was eager to be in his own pulpit when Sunday came. There was an exhilerating half-hour for him as he stood facing a church full of people and knew that he had a hearing. He was peculiarly sensitive to variations in the attendance. He never preached well before a small audience. The weather also affected him decidedly. He was at his best before just such an audience as faced him now, on just such a morning. He felt a glow of satisfaction as he went on. The church was the first in the city. It had the best choir. It had a membership composed of the leading people, representatives of the wealth, society and intelligence of Raymond. He was going abroad on a three months' vacation in the summer, and the circumstances of his pastorate, his influence and his position as pastor of the first church in the city—

It is not certain that the Rev. Henry Maxwell knew just how he could carry on all that thought in connection with his sermon, but as he drew near the end of it he knew that he had at some point in his delivery had all these feelings. They had entered into the very substance of his thought, it might have been all in a few seconds of time; but he had been conscious of defining his position and his emotions as well as if he had held a soliloquy, and his delivery partook of the thrill of deep personal satisfaction.

The sermon was interesting. It was full of striking sentences. They would have commanded attention printed. Spoken with the passion of a dramatic utterance that had the good taste never to offend with a suspicion of ranting or declamation, they were very effective. If the Rev. Henry Maxwell that morning felt satisfied with the conditions of his pastorate, the parish of First Church also had a similar feeling as it congratulated itself on the presence in the pulpit of this scholarly, refined, somewhat striking face and figure, preaching with such animation and freedom from all vulgar, noisy, or disagreeable mannerism.

Suddenly, into the midst of this perfect accord and concord between preacher and audience, there came a very remarkable interruption. It would be difficult to indicate the extent of the shock which this interruption measured. It was so unexpected, so entirely contrary to any thought of any person present that it offered no room for argument, or, for the time being, of resistance.

The sermon had come to a close. The Rev. Henry Maxwell had turned the half of the big Bible over upon his manuscript and was about to sit down, as the quartette prepared to rise and sing the closing selection,

"All for Jesus, All for Jesus,
All my being's ransomed powers,"[5]

when the entire congregation was startled by the sound of a man's voice. It came from the rear of the church, from one of the seats under the gallery. The next moment the figure of a man came out of the shadow there and walked down the middle aisle.

Before the startled congregation realized what was being done, the man had reached the open space in front of the pulpit and had turned about, facing the people.

---

4 An arrangement to "exchange" pulpits, and thus preaching responsibilities, with other pastors in the area.
5 From the hymn "All for Jesus" by Mary James and Asa Hull (1871).

"I've been wondering since I came in here—" they were the words he used under the gallery, and he repeated them, "if it would be just the thing to say a word at the close of this service. I'm not drunk and I'm not crazy, and I'm perfectly harmless; but if I die, as there is every likelihood I shall in a few days, I want the satisfaction of thinking that I said my say in a place like this, before just this sort of a crowd."

Henry Maxwell had not taken his seat and he now remained standing, leaning on his pulpit, looking down at the stranger. It was the man who had come to his house Friday morning, the same dusty, worn, shabby-looking young man. He held his faded hat in his two hands. It seemed to be a favorite gesture. He had not been shaved and his hair was rough and tangled. It was doubtful if any one like this had ever confronted the First Church within the sanctuary. It was tolerably familiar with this sort of humanity out on the street, around the Railroad shops, wandering up and down the avenue, but it had never dreamed of such an incident as this so near.

There was nothing offensive in the man's manner or tone. He was not excited and he spoke in a low but distinct voice. Henry Maxwell was conscious, even as he stood there smitten into dumb astonishment at the event, that somehow the man's action reminded him of a person he had once seen walking and talking in his sleep.

No one in the church made any motion to stop the stranger or in any way interrupt him. Perhaps the first shock of his sudden appearance deepened into genuine perplexity concerning what was best to do. However that may be, he went on as if he had no thought of interruption and no thought of the unusual element he had introduced into the decorum of the First Church service. And all the while he was speaking, Henry Maxwell leaned over the pulpit, his face growing more white and sad every moment. But he made no movement to stop him and the people sat smitten into breathless silence. One other face, that of Rachel Winslow, from the choir seats, stared white and intent down at the shabby figure with the faded hat. Her face was striking at any time. Under the pressure of the present unheard-of incident, it was as personally distinct as if it had been framed in fire.

"I'm not an ordinary tramp, though I don't know of any teaching of Jesus that makes one kind of a tramp less worth saving than another. Do you?" He put the question as naturally as if the whole congregation had been a small private Bible class. He paused just a moment and coughed painfully. Then he went on.

"I lost my job ten months ago. I am a printer by trade. The new linotype machines are beautiful specimens of invention, but I know six men who have killed themselves inside of the year just on account of those machines. Of course I don't blame the newspapers for getting the machines. Meanwhile, what can a man do? I know I never learned but the one trade and that's all I can do. I've tramped all over the country trying to find something. There are a good many others like me. I'm not complaining, am I? Just stating facts. But I was wondering, as I sat there under the gallery, if what you call following Jesus is the same thing as what he taught. What did he mean when he said, 'Follow me?' The minister said," here the man turned about and looked up at the pulpit, "that it was necessary for the disciple of Jesus to follow his steps, and he said the steps were, obedience, faith, love, and imitation. But I did not hear him tell just what he meant that to mean, especially the last step. What do Christians mean by following the steps of Jesus? I've tramped through this city for three days trying to find a job and in all that time I've not had a word of sympathy or comfort except from your minister here, who said he was sorry for me and hoped I would find a job somewhere. I suppose it is because you get so imposed on by the professional tramp that you have lost your interest in the other sort. I'm not blaming anybody, am I? Just stating facts? Of course I understand you can't all go out of your way to hunt up jobs for people like me. I'm not asking you to, but what I feel puzzled about is, what is meant by following Jesus? Do you mean that you are suffering and denying yourselves and trying to save lost suffering humanity just as I understand Jesus did? What do you mean by it? I see the ragged edge of things a good deal. I understand there are more than five hundred men in this city in my case. Most of them have families. My wife died four months ago. I'm glad she is out of trouble. My little girl is staying with a printer's family until I find a job. Somehow I get puzzled when I see so many Christians living in luxury and singing, 'Jesus, I my cross have taken, all to leave and follow thee,' and remember how my wife died in a tenement in New York city, gasping for air and asking God to take the little girl too. Of course I don't expect you people can prevent every one from dying of starvation, lack of proper nourishment and tenement air, but what does following Jesus mean? I understand that Christian people own a good many of the tenements. A member of a church was the owner of the one where my wife died, and I have wondered if following Jesus all the way was true in his case. I heard some people singing at a church prayer meeting the other night,

'All for Jesus, all for Jesus;
All my being's ransomed powers;
All my thoughts and all my doings,
All my days and all my hours;'

and I kept wondering as I sat on the steps outside just what they meant by it. It seems to me there's an awful lot of trouble in the world that somehow wouldn't exist if all the people who sing such songs went and lived them out. I suppose I don't understand. But what would Jesus do? Is that what you mean by following his steps? It seems to me sometimes as if the people in the city churches had good clothes and nice houses to live in, and money to spend for luxuries, and could go away on summer vacations and all that, while the people outside of the churches, thousands of them, I mean, die in tenements and walk the streets for jobs, and never have a piano or a picture in the house, and grow up in misery and drunkenness and sin—" the man gave a queer lurch over in the direction of the communion table and laid one grimy hand on it. His hat fell upon the carpet at his feet. A stir went through the congregation. Dr. West half rose from his feet, but as yet the silence was unbroken by any voice or movement worth mentioning in the audience. The man passed his other hand across his eyes, and then, without any warning, fell heavily forward on his face, full length, up the aisle.

Henry Maxwell spoke, "We will consider the service dismissed." He was down the pulpit stairs and kneeling by the prostrate form before any one else. The audience instantly rose and the aisle was crowded. Dr. West pronounced the man alive. He had fainted away. "Some heart trouble," the doctor also muttered as he helped carry him into the pastor's study.

Henry Maxwell and a group of his church members remained some time in the study. The man lay on the couch there and breathed heavily. When the question of what to do with him came up, the minister insisted upon taking him to his house. He lived near by and had an extra room. Rachel Winslow said, "Mother has no company at present. I am sure we would be glad to give him a place with us." She looked strangely agitated. No one noticed it particularly. They were all excited over the strange event, the strangest that First Church people could remember. But the minister insisted on taking charge of the man and when a carriage came, the unconscious but living form was carried to his house and with the entrance of that humanity into the minister's spare room a new chapter in Henry Maxwell's life began, and yet no one, himself least of all, dreamed of the remarkable change it was destined to make in all his after definition of Christian discipleship.

The event created a great sensation in the First Church parish. People talked of nothing else for a week. It was the general impression that the man had wandered into the church in a condition of mental disturbance caused by his troubles, and that all the time he was talking he was in a strange delirium of fever and really ignorant of his surroundings. That was the most charitable construction to put upon his action; it was the general agreement also that there was a singular absence of anything bitter or complaining in what the man had said. He had throughout spoken in a mild apologetic tone, almost as if he were one of the congregation seeking for light on a very difficult subject.

The third day after his removal to the minister's house there was a marked change in his condition. The doctor spoke of it and offered no hope. Saturday morning he still lingered, although he had rapidly failed as the week drew near to its close. Sunday morning just before the clock struck one, he rallied and asked if his child had come. The minister had sent for her at once as soon as he had been able to secure her address from some letters found in the man's pocket. He had been conscious and able to talk coherently only a few moments since his attack. "The child is coming. She will be here," Henry Maxwell said as he sat there, his face showing marks of the strain of the week's vigil. For he had insisted on sitting up nearly every night.

"I shall never see her in this world," the man whispered. Then he uttered with great difficulty the words, "You have been good to me. Somehow I feel as if it was what Jesus would do." After a few moments he turned his head slightly, and before Henry Maxwell could realize the fact, the doctor said, "He is gone."

The Sunday morning that dawned on the city of Raymond was exactly like the Sunday of the week before. Henry Maxwell entered his pulpit to face one of the largest congregations that had ever crowded First Church. He was haggard and looked as if he had just risen from a long illness. His wife was at home with the little girl who had come on the morning train an hour after her father died. He lay in that spare room, his troubles over, and Henry Maxwell could see the face as he opened the Bible and arranged his different notices on the side of the desk as he had been in the habit of doing for ten years.

The service that morning contained a new element. No one could remember when the minister had preached in the morning without notes. As a matter of fact he had done so occasionally when he first entered the ministry, but for a long time he had carefully written out every word of his morning sermon, and nearly always his evening discourse as well. It cannot be said that his sermon this morning was very striking or impressive. He talked with considerable hesitation. It was evident that some great idea struggled in his thought for utterance but it was not expressed in the theme he had chosen for his preaching. It was near the close of his sermon that he began to gather a certain strength that had been painfully lacking at the beginning. He closed the Bible and stepping out at the side of the desk, he faced his people, and began to talk to them about the remarkable scene of the week before.

"Our brother," somehow the words sounded a little strange coming from Henry Maxwell's lips, "passed away this morning. I have not yet had time to learn all his history. He had one sister living in Chicago. I have written her and have not yet received an answer. His little girl is with us and will remain for the time."

He paused and looked over the house. He thought he had never seen so many earnest faces during the entire pastorate. He was not able yet to tell his people his experiences, the crisis through which he was even now moving. But something of his feeling passed from him to them, and it did not seem to him that he was acting under a careless impulse at all to go on and break to them, this morning, something of the message he bore in his heart. So he went on.

"The appearance and words of this stranger in the church last Sunday made a very powerful impression on me. I am not able to conceal from you or myself the fact that what he said, followed as it has been by his death in my house, has compelled me to ask as I never asked before, 'What does following Jesus mean?' I am not in a position yet to utter any condemnation of this people, or, to a certain extent, of myself, either in our Christlike relations to this man or the number he represents in the world. But all that does not prevent me from feeling that much that the man said was so vitally true that we must face it in an attempt to answer it or else stand condemned as Christian disciples. A good deal that was said here last Sunday was in the nature of a challenge to Christianity as it is seen and felt in our churches. I have felt this with increasing emphasis every day since. And I do not know that any time is more appropriate than the present for me to propose a plan or a purpose which has been forming in my mind as a satisfactory reply to much that was said here last Sunday."

Again Henry Maxwell paused and looked into the faces of his people. There were some strong, earnest men and women in the First Church. The minister could see Edward Norman, Editor of the Raymond "Daily News." He had been a member of First Church for ten years. No man was more honored in the community. There was Alexander Powers, Superintendent of the Railroad shops. There was Donald Marsh, President of Lincoln College, situated in the suburbs of Raymond. There was Milton Wright, one of the great merchants of Raymond, having in his employ at least one hundred men in various shops. There was Dr. West who, although still comparatively young, was quoted as authority in special surgical cases. There was young Jasper Chase, the author, who had written one successful book and was said to be at work on a new novel. There was Miss Virginia Page, the heiress, who through the recent death of her father had inherited a million at least, and was gifted with unusual attractions of person and intellect. And not least of all, Rachel Winslow from her seat in the choir glowed with her peculiar beauty of light this morning because she was so intensely interested in the whole scene.

There was some reason perhaps, in view of such material in the First Church, for Henry Maxwell's feeling of satisfaction whenever he considered his parish as he had the previous Sunday. There was a large number of strong individual characters who claimed membership there. But as he noted their faces this morning, Henry Maxwell was simply wondering how many of them would respond to the strange proposition he was about to make. He continued slowly, taking time to choose his words carefully and giving the people an impression they had never felt before, even when he was at his best, with his most dramatic delivery.

"What I am going to propose now is something which ought not to appear unusual or at all impossible of execution. Yet I am aware that it will be so regarded by a large number, perhaps, of the members of the church. But in order that we may have a thorough understanding of what we are considering, I will put my proposition very plainly, perhaps bluntly. I want volunteers from the First Church who will pledge themselves earnestly and honestly for an entire year not to do anything without first asking the question, 'What would Jesus do?' And after asking that question, each one will follow Jesus as exactly as he knows how, no matter what the results may be. I will of course include myself in this company of volunteers, and shall take for granted that my church here will not be surprised at my future conduct as based upon this standard of action, and will not oppose whatever is done if they think Christ would do it. Have I made my meaning clear? At the close of the service here I want all those members of the church who are willing to join such a company to remain, and we will talk over the details of the plan. Our motto will be, 'What would Jesus do?' Our aim will be to act just as he would if he were in our places, regardless of immediate results. In other words, we propose to follow Jesus' steps as closely and as literally as we believe he taught his disciples to do. And those who volunteer to do this will pledge themselves for an entire year, beginning with to-day, so to act."

Henry Maxwell paused again and looked over his church. It is not easy to describe the sensation that such a simple proposition apparently made. Men glanced at one another in astonishment. It was not like Henry Maxwell to define Christian discipleship in this way. There was evident confusion of thought over his proposition. It was understood well enough, but there was apparently a great difference of opinion as to the application of Jesus' teaching and example.

Henry Maxwell calmly closed the service with a brief prayer. The organist began his postlude immediately after the benediction and the people began to go out. There was a great deal of conversation. Animated groups stood all over the church discussing the minister's proposition. It was evidently provoking great discussion. After several minutes Henry Maxwell asked all who expected to remain, to pass into the lecture room on the side. He himself was detained at the front of the church talking with several persons there, and when he finally turned around, the church was empty. He walked over to the lecture room entrance and went in. He was almost startled to see the people who were there. He had not made up his mind about any of his members, but he had hardly expected that so many were ready to enter into such a literal testing of their discipleship as now awaited them. There were perhaps fifty members present. Among them were Rachel Winslow and Virginia Page, Mr. Norman, President Marsh, Alexander Powers the Railroad Superintendent, Milton Wright, Dr. West, and Jasper Chase.

The pastor closed the door of the lecture room and stood before the little group. His face was pale and his lips trembled with emotion. It was to him a genuine crisis in his own life and that of his parish. No man can tell until he is moved by the Divine Spirit what he may do, or how he may change the current of a lifetime of fixed habits of thought and speech and action. Henry Maxwell did not, as we have said, yet know himself all that he was passing through, but he was conscious of a great upheaval in his definitions of Christian discipleship and he was moved with a depth of feeling he could not measure, as he looked into the faces of these men and women on this occasion.

It seemed to him that the most fitting word to be spoken first was that of prayer. He asked them all to pray with him. And almost with the first syllable he uttered there was a distinct presence of the Spirit felt by them all. As the prayer went on, this presence grew in power. They all felt it. The room was filled with it as plainly as if it had been visible. When the prayer closed there was a silence that lasted several moments. All the heads were bowed. Henry Maxwell's face was wet with tears. If an audible voice from heaven had sanctioned their pledge to follow the Master's steps, not one person present could have felt more certain of the divine blessing. And so the most serious movement ever started in the First Church of Raymond was begun.

"We all understand," said Henry Maxwell speaking very quietly, "what we have undertaken to do. We pledge ourselves to do everything in our daily lives after asking the question, 'What would Jesus do?' regardless of what may be the result to us. Some time I shall be able to tell you what a marvelous change has come over my life within a week's time. I cannot now. But the experience I have been through since last Sunday has left me so dissatisfied with my previous definition of discipleship that I have been compelled to take this action. I did not dare begin it alone. I know that I am being led by the hand of divine love in all this. The same divine impulse must have led you also. Do we understand fully what we have undertaken?"

"I want to ask a question," said Rachel Winslow.

Every one turned towards her. Her faced glowed with a beauty that no loveliness could ever create.

"I am a little in doubt as to the source of our knowledge concerning what Jesus would do. Who is to decide for me just what he would do in my case? It is a different age. There are many perplexing questions in our civilization that are not mentioned in the teaching of Jesus. How am I going to tell what he would do?"

"There is no way that I know of," replied Mr. Maxwell, "except as we study Jesus through the medium of the Holy Spirit. You remember what Christ said speaking to his disciples about the Holy Spirit:

"'Howbeit, when He, the Spirit of Truth is come, He shall guide you into all the truth: for He shall not speak from Himself; but what things soever He shall hear, these shall He speak: and He shall declare unto you the things that are to come. He shall glorify me: for He shall take of mine and shall declare it unto you. All things whatsoever the Father hath are mine: therefore said I that He taketh of mine and shall declare it unto you.'[6]

"There is no other test that I know of. We shall all have to decide what Jesus would do after going to that source of knowledge."

"What if others say of us when we do certain things, that Jesus would not do so?" asked the Superintendent of railroads.

"We cannot prevent that. But we must be absolutely honest with ourselves. The standard of Christian action cannot vary in most of our acts."

"And yet what one church member thinks Jesus would do, another refuses to accept as his possible course of action. What is to render our conduct uniformly Christlike? Will it be possible to reach the same conclusions always in all cases?" asked President Marsh.

Henry Maxwell was silent some time. Then he answered:

"No. I don't know that we can expect that. But when it comes to a genuine, honest, enlightened following of Jesus' steps, I cannot believe there will be any confusion either in our own minds or in the judgment of others. We must be free from fanaticism on one hand and too much caution on the other. If Jesus' example is the example for the world, it certainly must be feasible to follow it. But we need to remember this great fact. After we have asked the Spirit to tell us what Jesus would do and have received an answer to it, we are to act regardless of the results to ourselves. Is that understood?"

All the faces in the room were raised toward the minister in solemn assent. There was no misunderstanding the proposition. Henry Maxwell's face quivered again as he noted the

---

6 John 16:13–15.

President of the Endeavor Society,[7] with several members, seated back of the older men and women.

They remained a little longer talking over details and asking questions, and agreed to report to one another every week at a regular meeting the result of their experiences in following Jesus in this way. Henry Maxwell prayed again. And again, as before, the Spirit made Himself manifest. Every head remained bowed a long time. They went away finally in silence. There was a feeling that prevented speech. Henry Maxwell shook hands with them all as they went out. Then he went to his own study room back of the pulpit and kneeled down. He remained there alone nearly half an hour. When he went home, he went into the room where the dead body lay. As he looked at the face, he cried in his heart again for strength and wisdom. But not even yet did he realize that a movement had been begun which would lead to the most remarkable series of events that the city of Raymond had ever known.

Chapter II

"He that saith he abideth in Him ought himself also to walk even as He walked."[8]

EDWARD NORMAN, editor of the Raymond "Daily News," sat in his office room Monday morning and faced a new world of action. He had made his pledge in good faith to do everything after asking, "What would Jesus do?" and as he supposed with his eyes open to all the possible results. But as the regular life of the paper started on another week's rush and whirl of activity he confronted it with a degree of hesitation and a feeling nearly akin to fear. He had come down to the office very early and for a few minutes was by himself. He sat at his desk in a growing thoughtfulness that finally became a desire which he knew was as great as it was unusual. He had yet to learn, with all the others in that little company pledged to do the Christlike thing, that the Spirit of Life was moving in power through his own life as never before. He rose and shut his door and then did what he had not done for years. He kneeled down by his desk and prayed for the divine presence and wisdom to direct him.

He rose with the day before him and his promise distinct and clear in his mind. "Now for action," he seemed to say. But he would be led by events as fast as they came on.

He opened his door and began the routine of the office work. The managing editor had just come in and was at his desk in the adjoining room. One of the reporters there was pounding out something on a type writer.

Edward Norman began an editorial. The "Daily News" was an evening paper and Norman usually completed his leading editorial before eight o'clock.

He had been writing about fifteen minutes when the managing editor called out, "Here's this press report of yesterday's prize fight at the Resort. It will make up three columns and a half. I suppose it all goes in?"

Edward Norman was one of those newspaper men who keep an eye on every detail of the paper. The managing editor always consulted his chief in matters of both small and large importance. Sometimes as in this case it was merely a nominal inquiry.

---

7 Christian Endeavor Societies were organized youth groups that functioned on both a local and national level.

8 1 John 2:6.

"Yes—No. Let me see it."

He took the type-written matter just as it came from the telegraph editor, and ran over it carefully. Then he laid the sheets down on his desk and did some very hard thinking.

"We won't run this in to-day," he said finally.

The managing editor was standing in the doorway between the two rooms. He was astonished at the editor's remark and thought he had perhaps misunderstood him.

"What did you say?"

"Leave it out. We won't use it."

"But—" The managing editor was simply dumfounded. He stared at Norman as if the editor were out of his mind.

"I think, Clark, that it ought not to be printed, and that's the end of it," said Edward Norman, looking up from his desk.

Clark seldom had any words with the chief. Norman's word had always been law in the office and he had seldom been known to change his mind. The circumstances now, however, seemed to be so extraordinary that Clark could not help expressing himself.

"Do you mean that the paper is to go to press without a word of the prize fight in it?"

"Yes, that's just what I mean."

"But it's unheard of. All the other papers will print it. What will our subscribers say? Why, it's simply—" Clark paused, unable to find words to say what he thought.

Edward Norman looked at Clark thoughtfully. The managing editor was a member of a church of a different denomination from that of Norman's. The two men had never talked together on religious matters although they had been associated on the paper for several years.

"Come in here a minute, Clark, and shut the door," said Norman.

Clark came in and the two men faced each other alone. Norman did not speak for a minute. Then he said abruptly,

"Clark, if Christ were editing a daily paper do you honestly think he would print three columns and a half of prize fight in it?"

Clark gasped in astonishment. Finally he replied—"No, I don't suppose he would."

"Well, that's my only reason for shutting this account out of the "News." I have decided not to do a thing in connection with the paper for a whole year that I honestly believe Jesus would not do."

Clark could not have looked more amazed if the chief had suddenly gone crazy. In fact, he did think something was wrong, though Mr. Norman was one of the last men in the world, in his judgment, to lose his mind.

"What effect will that have on the paper?" he finally managed to ask in a faint voice.

"What do you think?" asked Edward Norman, with a keen glance.

"I think it will simply ruin the paper," replied Clark promptly. He was gathering up his bewildered senses and began to remonstrate. "Why, it isn't feasible to run a paper now-a-days on any such basis. It's too ideal. The world isn't ready for it. You can't make it pay. Just as sure as you live, if you shut out this prize fight report you will lose hundreds of subscribers. It doesn't take a prophet to say that. The very best people in town are eager to read it. They know it has taken place and when they get the paper this evening they will expect half a page at least. Surely, you can't afford to disregard the wishes of the public to such an extent. It will be a great mistake if you do, in my opinion."

Edward Norman sat silent a minute. Then he spoke gently, but firmly.

"Clark, what in your honest opinion is the right standard for determining conduct? Is the only right standard for every one the probable action of Jesus? Would you say that the highest best law for a man to live by was contained in asking the question, 'What would Jesus do?' and then doing it regardless of results? In other words do you think men everywhere ought to follow Jesus' example as close as they can in their daily lives?"

Clark turned red, and moved uneasily in his chair before he answered the editor's question.

"Why,—yes,—. I suppose if you put it on the ground of what they ought to do there is no other standard of conduct. But the question is, what is feasible? Is it possible to make it pay? To succeed in the newspaper business we have got to conform to the customs and the recognized methods of society. We can't do as we would do in an ideal world."

"Do you mean that we can't run the paper strictly on Christian principles and make it succeed?"

"Yes, that's just what I mean. It can't be done. We'll go bankrupt in thirty days."

Edward Norman did not reply at once. He was very thoughtful.

"We shall have occasion to talk this over again, Clark. Meanwhile, I think we ought to understand each other frankly. I have pledged myself for a year to do everything connected with the paper after answering the question, 'What would Jesus do?' as honestly as possible. I shall continue to do this in the belief that not only can we succeed but that we can succeed better than we ever did."

Clark rose. "Then the report does not go in?"

"It does not. There is plenty of good material to take its place, and you know what it is."

Clark hesitated.

"Are you going to say anything about the absence of the report?"

"No, let the paper go to press as if there had been no such thing as a prize fight yesterday."

Clark walked out of the room to his own desk feeling as if the bottom had dropped out of everything. He was astonished, bewildered, excited and considerably enraged. His great respect for Norman checked his rising indignation and disgust, but with it all was a feeling of growing wonder at the sudden change of motive which had entered the office of the "Daily News" and threatened as he firmly believed, to destroy it.

Before noon every reporter, pressman and employee on the "Daily News" was informed of the remarkable fact that the paper was going to press without a word in it about the famous prize fight of Sunday. The reporters were simply astonished beyond measure at the announcement of the fact. Every one in the stereotyping and composing rooms had something to say about the unheard of omission. Two or three times during the day when Mr. Norman had occasion to visit the composing rooms, the men stopped their work or glanced around their cases looking at him curiously. He knew that he was being observed strangely and said nothing, and did not appear to note it.

There had been several changes in the paper suggested by the editor, but nothing marked. He was waiting, and thinking deeply. He felt as if he needed time and considerable opportunity for the exercise of his best judgment in several matters before he answered his ever present question in the right way. It was not because there were not a great many things in the life of the paper that were contrary to the spirit of Christ that he did not act at once, but because he was yet greatly in doubt concerning what action Jesus would take.

When the "Daily News" came out that evening it carried to its subscribers a distinct sensation. The presence of the report of the prize fight could not have produced anything equal to the effect of its omission. Hundreds of men in the hotels and stores down town, as well as regular subscribers, eagerly opened the paper and searched it through for the account of the great fight. Not finding it, they rushed to the news stand and bought other papers. Even the newsboys had not all understood the fact of the omission. One of them was calling out, "Daily News! Full 'count great prize fight 't Resort. News, Sir!"

A man on the corner of the Avenue close by the "News" office bought the paper, looked over its front page hurriedly and then angrily called the boy back.

"Here boy! What's the matter with your paper! There is no prize fight here! What do you mean by selling old papers?"

"Old papers, nuthin!" replied the boy indignantly. "Dat's to-day's paper. What's de matter wid you?"

"But there's no account of any prize fight here! Look!"

The man handed back the paper and the boy glanced at it hurriedly. Then he whistled, while a bewildering look crept over his face. Seeing another boy running by with papers he called out, "Say, Sam, lemme see your pile!" A hasty examination revealed the remarkable fact that all the copies of the "News" were silent on the prize fight.

"Here, give me another paper! One with the prize fight account!" shouted the customer. He received it and walked off, while the two boys remained comparing notes and lost in wonder at the event. "Somp'n slipped a cog in the Newsy sure," said first boy. But he couldn't tell why and rushed over to the "News" office to find out.

There were several other boys at the delivery room and they were all excited and disgusted. The amount of slangy remonstrances hurled at the clerk back of the long counter would have driven any one else to despair. He was used to more or less of it all the time and consequently hardened to it.

Mr. Norman was just coming down stairs on his way home and he paused as he went by the door of the delivery room and looked in.

"What's the matter here, George?" he asked the clerk as he noted the unusual confusion.

"The boys say they can't sell any copies of the 'News' to-night because the prize fight is not in it," replied George looking curiously at the editor as so many of the employees had done during the day.

Mr. Norman hesitated a moment, then walked into the room and confronted the boys.

"How many papers are there here, boys? Count them out and I'll buy them to-night."

There was a wild stare and a wild counting of papers on the part of the boys.

"Give them their money, George, and if any of the other boys come in with the same complaint buy their unsold copies. Is that fair?" he asked the boys who were smitten into unusual silence by the unheard-of action on the part of the editor.

"Fair! Well, I should—But will you keep dis up? Will dis be a continual performance for de benefit of de fraternity?"

Mr. Norman smiled slightly but he did not think it was necessary to answer the question. He walked out of the office and went home. On the way he could not avoid that constant query, "Would Jesus have done it?" It was not so much with reference to this last transaction as to the entire motive that had urged him on since he had made the promise. The news boys were necessarily sufferers through the action he had taken. Why should they lose money by it? They were not to blame. He was a rich man and could afford to put a little brightness into their lives if he chose to do it. He believed as he went on his way home that Jesus would have done either what he did or something similar in order to be free from any possible feeling of injustice. He was not deciding these questions for any one else but for his own conduct. He was not in a position to dogmatize and he felt that he could answer only with his own judgment and conscience as to his interpretation of Jesus' probable action. The falling off in sales of the paper he had in a certain measure foreseen. But he was yet to realize the full extent of the loss to the paper if such a policy should be continued.

During the week he was in receipt of numerous letters commenting on the absence from the "News" of the account of the prize fight. Two or three of these letters may be of interest.

Editor of the "News."
Dear Sir:
I have been deciding for some time to change my paper. I want a journal that is up to the times, progressive and enterprising, supplying the public demand at all points. The recent freak of your paper in refusing to print the account of the famous contest at the Resort has decided me finally to change my paper. Please discontinue it.

Very truly yours,

——————. ——————.

(Here followed the name of a business man who had been a subscriber for many years.)

Edward Norman.
Editor of the "Daily News": Raymond.

Dear Ed.
What is this sensation you have given the people of your burg? Hope you don't intend to try the "Reform Business," through the avenue of the Press. It's dangerous to experiment much along that line. Take my advice and stick to the enterprising modern methods you have made so successful for the "News." The public wants prize fights and such. Give it what it wants and let some one else do the Reforming business.

Yours,

——————. ——————.

(Here followed the name of one of Norman's old friends, the editor of a daily in an adjoining town.)

My dear Mr. Norman:
I hasten to write you a note of appreciation for the evident carrying out of your promise. It is a splendid beginning and no one feels the value of it better than I do. I know something of what it will cost you, but not all.

Your Pastor,
Henry Maxwell.

One letter which he opened immediately after reading this from Maxwell revealed to him something of the loss to his business that possibly awaited him.

Mr. Edward Norman;
Editor of the "Daily News":
Dear Sir.
At the expiration of my advertising limit you will do me the favor not to continue as you have done heretofore. I enclose check for payment in full and shall consider my account with your paper closed after date.

Very truly yours,

——————. ——————.

(Here followed the name of one of the largest dealers in Tobacco in the city. He had been in the habit of inserting a column of conspicuous advertising and paying for it a very large price.)

Edward Norman laid this letter down very thoughtfully, and then after a moment he took up a copy of his paper and looked through the advertising columns. There was no connection implied in the tobacco merchant's letter between the omission of the prize fight and the withdrawal of the advertisement. But he could not avoid putting the two together. In point of fact, he afterwards learned that the tobacco dealer withdrew his advertisement because he had heard that the editor of the "News" was about to enter upon some queer reform policy that would be certain to reduce its subscription list.

But the letter directed Norman's attention to the advertising phase of his paper. He had not considered this before. As he glanced over the columns he could not escape the conviction that Jesus could not permit some of them in his paper. What would Jesus do with that other long advertisement of liquor? Raymond enjoyed a system of high license,[9] and the saloon and the billiard hall and the beer garden were a part of the city's Christian civilization. He was simply doing what every other business man in Raymond did. And it was one of the best paying sources of revenue. What would the paper do if it cut these out? Could it live? That was the question. But—was that the question after all? "What would Jesus do?" That was the question he was answering, or trying to answer, this week. Would Jesus advertise whisky and tobacco in his paper?

Edward Norman asked it honestly, and after a prayer for help and wisdom he asked Clark to come into the office.

Clark came in feeling that the paper was at a crisis and prepared for almost anything after his Monday morning experience. This was Thursday.

"Clark," said Norman, speaking slowly and carefully, "I have been looking at our advertising columns and have decided to dispense with some of the matter as soon as the contracts run out. I wish you would notify the advertising agent not to solicit or renew the ads. I have marked here."

He handed the paper with the marked places over to Clark, who took it and looked over the columns with a very serious air.

"This will mean a great loss to the 'News.' How long do you think you can keep this sort of thing up?" Clark was astonished at the editor's action and could not understand it.

"Clark, do you think if Jesus were the editor and proprietor of a daily paper in Raymond he would print advertisements of whisky and tobacco in it?"

Clark looked at his chief with that same look of astonishment which had greeted the question before.

"Well—no—I don't suppose he would. But what has that to do with us? We can't do as he would. Newspapers can't be run on any such basis."

"Why not?" asked Edward Norman quietly.

"Why not! Because they will lose more money than they make, that's all." Clark spoke out with an irritation that he really felt. "We shall certainly bankrupt the paper with this sort of business policy."

"Do you think so?" Norman asked the question not as if he expected an answer but simply as if he were talking with himself. After a pause he said,

---

9 The sale and consumption of alcohol are allowed within city limits.

"You may direct Marks to do as I said. I believe it is what Jesus would do, and as I told you, Clark, that is what I have promised to try to do for a year, regardless of what the results may be to me. I cannot believe that by any kind of reasoning we could reach a conclusion justifying Jesus in the advertisement, in this age, of whisky and tobacco in a newspaper. There are some other advertisements of a doubtful character I shall study into. Meanwhile I feel a conviction in regard to these that cannot be silenced."

Clark went back to his desk feeling as if he had been in the presence of a very peculiar person. He could not grasp the meaning of it all. He felt enraged and alarmed. He was sure any such policy would ruin the paper as soon as it became generally known that the editor was trying to do everything by such an absurd moral standard. What would become of business if this standard were adopted? It would upset every custom and introduce endless confusion. It was simply foolishness. It was downright idiocy. So Clark said to himself, and when Marks was informed of the action, he seconded the managing editor with some very forcible ejaculations. What was the matter with the chief? Was he insane? Was he going to bankrupt the whole business?

But Edward Norman had not faced his most serious problem.

When he came down to the office Friday morning he was confronted with the usual program for the Sunday morning edition. The "News" was one of the few evening papers to issue a Sunday edition, and it had always been remarkably successful financially. There was an average of one page of literary and religious items to thirty or forty pages of sport, theater, gossip, fashion, society and political material. This made a very interesting magazine of all sorts of reading matter and had always been welcomed by all the subscribers, church members and all, as a Sunday necessity.

Edward Norman now faced this fact and put to himself the question, "What would Jesus do?" If he were editor of a paper would he deliberately plan to put into the homes of all the church people and Christians of Raymond such a collection of reading matter on the one day of the week which ought to be given up to something better and holier? He was of course familiar with the regular argument for the Sunday paper that the public needed something of the sort and the working man, especially, who would not go to church any way, ought to have something entertaining and instructive on Sunday, his only day of rest. But suppose the Sunday morning paper did not pay? Suppose there was no money in it? How eager would the editor or the proprietor be then to supply this crying need of the working man? Edward Norman communed honestly with himself over the subject. Taking everything into account, would Jesus probably edit a Sunday morning paper? No matter whether it paid. That was not the question. As a matter of fact the Sunday "News" paid so well that it would be a direct loss of thousands of dollars to discontinue it. Besides, the regular subscribers had paid for a seven-day paper. Had he any right now to give them anything less than they had supposed they had paid for?

He was honestly perplexed by the question. So much was involved in the discontinuance of the Sunday edition that for the first time he almost declined to be guided by the standard of Jesus' probable action. He was sole proprietor of the paper. It was his to shape as he chose. He had no board of directors to consult as to policy. But as he sat there surrounded by the usual quantity of material for the Sunday edition, he reached some definite conclusions. And among them was the determination to call in the force of the paper and frankly state his motive and purpose.

He sent word for Clark and the other men in the office, including the few reporters who were in the building and the foreman, with what men were in the composing room (it was early in the morning and they were not all in) to come into the mailing room. This was a large room, and the men came in, wondering, and perched around on the tables and counters. It was a very unusual proceeding, but they all agreed that the paper was being run on new principles any how, and they all watched Mr. Norman curiously as he spoke.

"I called you in here to let you know my plans for the future of the "News." I propose certain changes which I believe are necessary. I understand that some things I have already done are regarded by the men as very strange. I wish to state my motive in doing what I have done." Here he told the men what he had already told Clark and they stared, as he had done, and looked as painfully conscious.

"Now in acting on this standard of conduct I have reached a conclusion which will, no doubt, cause some surprise. I have decided that the Sunday morning edition of the "News" shall be discontinued after next Sunday's issue. I shall state in that issue my reasons for discontinuing. In order to make up to the subscribers the amount of reading matter they may suppose themselves entitled to, we can issue a double number on Saturday, as is done by very many evening papers that make no attempt at a Sunday edition. I am convinced that, from a Christian point of view, more harm than good has been done by our Sunday morning paper. I do not believe that Jesus would be responsible for it if He were in my place to-day. It will occasion some trouble to arrange the details caused by this change with the advertisers and subscribers. That is for me to look after. The change itself is one that will take place. So far as I can see, the loss will fall on myself. Neither the reporters nor the press men need make any particular changes in their plans."

Edward Norman looked around the room and no one spoke. He was struck for the first time in his life with the fact that in all the years of his newspaper life he had never had the force of the paper together in this way. "Would Jesus do that? That is, would He probably run a newspaper on some loving family plan where editors, reporters, pressmen and all, met to discuss and devise and plan for the making of a paper that should have in view—"

He caught himself drawing almost away from the facts of typographical unions and office rules and reporters' enterprise, and all the cold business-like methods that make a great daily successful. But still, the vague picture that came up in the mailing room would not fade away, even when he had gone into his office and the men had gone back to their places with wonder in their looks and questions of all sorts on their tongues as they talked over the editor's remarkable actions.

Clark came in and had a long serious talk with the chief. He was thoroughly roused and his protest almost reached the point of resigning his place. Norman guarded himself carefully. Every minute of the interview was painful to him but he felt more than ever the necessity of doing the Christlike thing. Clark was a very valuable man. It would be difficult to fill his place. But he was not able to give any reasons for continuing the Sunday paper that answered the question, "What would Jesus do?" by letting Jesus print that edition.

"It comes to this, then," said Clark finally. "You will bankrupt the paper in thirty days. We might as well face that future fact."

"I don't think we shall. Will you stay by the "News" until it is bankrupt?" asked Edward Norman with a strange smile.

"Mr. Norman, I don't understand you. You are not the same man this week that I ever knew."

"I don't know myself, either, Clark. Something remarkable has caught me up and borne me on. But I was never more convinced of final success and power for the paper. You have not answered my question. Will you stay with me?"

Clark hesitated a moment and finally said, yes. Norman shook hands with him and turned to his desk. Clark went back into his room stirred by a number of conflicting emotions. He had never before known such an exciting and mentally disturbing week, and he felt now as if he were connected with an enterprise that might at any moment collapse and ruin him and all connected with it.

Sunday morning dawned again on Raymond, and Henry Maxwell's church was again crowded. Before the service began, Edward Norman attracted general attention. He sat quietly in his usual place about three seats from the pulpit. The Sunday morning issue of the "News" containing the statement of its discontinuance had been read by nearly every man in the house. The announcement had been expressed in such remarkable language that every reader was struck by it. No such series of distinct sensations had ever disturbed the usual business custom of Raymond. The events connected with the "News" were not all. People were eagerly talking about the strange things done during the week by Alexander Powers at the Railroad shops, and by Milton Wright in his stores on the avenue. The service progressed upon a distinct wave of excitement in the pews. Henry Maxwell faced it all with a calmness which indicated a strength and purpose more than usual. His prayers were very helpful. His sermon was not so easy to describe. How would a minister be apt to preach to his people if he came before them after an entire week of eager asking, "How would Jesus preach? What would He probably say?" It is very certain that Henry Maxwell did not preach as he had done two Sundays before. Tuesday of the past week he had stood by the grave of the dead stranger and said the words, "Earth to earth, ashes to ashes, dust to dust," and still he was moved by the spirit of a deeper impulse than he could measure as he thought of his people and yearned for the Christ message when he should be in his pulpit again.

Now that Sunday had come and the people were there to hear, what would the Master tell them? He agonized over his preparation for them and yet he knew he had not been able to fit his message into his ideal of the Christ. Nevertheless no one in the First Church could remember hearing such a sermon before. There was in it rebuke for sin, especially hypocrisy. There was definite rebuke of the greed of wealth and the selfishness of fashion, two things that First Church never heard rebuked this way before, and there was a love of his people that gathered new force as the sermon went on. When it was finished there were those who were saying in their hearts, "The Spirit moved that sermon." And they were right.

Then Rachel Winslow rose to sing. This time, after the sermon, by Henry Maxwell's request. Rachel's singing did not provoke applause this time. What deeper feeling carried people's hearts into a reverent silence and tenderness of thought? Rachel was beautiful. But the consciousness of her remarkable loveliness had always marred her singing with those who had the deepest spiritual feeling. It had also marred her rendering of certain kinds of music with herself. To-day this was all gone. There was no lack of power in her grand voice. But there was an actual added element of humility and purity which the audience strictly felt and bowed to.

Before the service closed, Henry Maxwell asked those who had remained the week before to stay again for a few moments for consultation, and any others who were willing to make the pledge taken at that time. When he was at liberty he went into the lecture room.

To his astonishment it was almost filled. This time a large proportion of young people had come. But among them were a few business men and officers of the church.

As before, Henry Maxwell asked them to pray with him. And as before a distinct answer came in the presence of the Divine Spirit. There was no doubt in the minds of any one present that what they proposed to do was so clearly in line with the divine will, that a blessing rested on it in a very special manner.

They remained some time to ask questions and consult together. There was a feeling of fellowship such as they had never known in their church membership. Edward Norman's action was well understood by them all, and he answered several questions.

"What will be the probable result of your discontinuance of the Sunday paper?" asked Alexander Powers who sat next to him.

"I don't know yet. I presume it will result in a falling off of subscriptions and advertisements. I anticipate that."

"Do you have any doubts about your action? I mean do you regret it or fear it is not what Jesus would do?" asked Henry Maxwell.

"Not in the least. But I would like to ask for my own satisfaction, if any one of you here thinks Jesus would issue a Sunday morning paper?"

No one spoke for a minute. Then Jasper Chase said, "We seem to think alike on that, but I have been puzzled several times during the week to know just what He would do. It is not always an easy question to answer."

"I find that trouble," said Virginia Page. She sat by Rachel Winslow. Every one who knew Virginia Page was wondering how she would succeed in keeping her promise

"I think perhaps I find it specially difficult to answer the question on account of my money. Jesus never owned any property, and there is nothing in his example to guide me in the use of mine. I am studying and praying. I think I see clearly a part of what He would do, but not all. 'What would Jesus do with a million dollars?' is my question really. I confess that I am not yet able to answer it to my satisfaction."

"I could tell you what to do with a part of it," said Rachel, turning her face towards Virginia.

"That does not trouble me," replied Virginia with a slight smile. "What I am trying to discover is a principle of Jesus that will enable me to come the nearest possible to His action as it ought to influence the entire course of my life so far as my wealth and its use are concerned."

"That will take time," said Henry Maxwell slowly. All the rest in the room were thinking hard of the same thing. Milton Wright told something of his experience. He was gradually working out a plan for his business relations with his employees and it was opening up a new world to him and them. A few of the younger men told of special attempts to answer the question. There was almost general consent over the fact that the application of the Jesus spirit and practice to every day life was the serious thing. It required a knowledge of Him and an insight into His motives that most of them did not yet possess.

When they finally adjourned after a silent prayer that marked with growing power the Divine Presence, they went away discussing earnestly their difficulties and seeking light from one another.

Rachel Winslow and Virginia Page went out together. Edward Norman and Milton Wright became so interested in their mutual conference that they walked on past Norman's home and came back together. Jasper Chase and the President of the Endeavor Society stood talking earnestly in one corner of the room. Alexander Powers and Henry Maxwell remained even after all the others had gone.

"I want you to come down to the shops to-morrow and see my plan and talk to the men. Somehow I feel as if you could get nearer to them than any one else just now."

"I don't know about that, but I will come," replied Henry Maxwell a little sadly. How was he fitted to stand before two or three hundred working men and give them a message? Yet in the moment of his weakness, as he asked the question, he rebuked himself for it. What would Jesus do? That was an end to the discussion.

He went down the next day and found Alexander Powers in his office. It lacked a few minutes of twelve and the Superintendent said, "Come up stairs, and I'll show you what I've been trying to do."

They went through the machine shops, climbed a long flight of stairs and entered a very large empty room. It had once been used by the company for a store room.

"Since making that promise a week ago I have had a good many things to think of," said the Superintendent, "and among them is this: Our company gives me the use of this room and I am going to fit it up with tables and a coffee plant in the corner there where those steam pipes are. My plan is to provide a good place where the men can come up and eat their noon lunch and give them, two or three times a week, the privilege of a fifteen minutes' talk on some subject that will be a real help to them in their lives."

Maxwell looked surprised and asked if the men would come for any such purpose.

"Yes, they'll come. After all, I know the men pretty well. They are among the most intelligent working men in the country to-day. But they are as a whole, entirely removed from all church influence. I asked, 'What would Jesus do?' And among other things it seemed to me He would begin to act in some way to add to the lives of these men more physical and spiritual comfort. It is a very little thing, this room and what it represents, but I acted on the first impulse to do the first thing that appealed to my good sense and I want to work out this idea. I want you to speak to the men when they come up at noon. I have asked them to come up and see the place and I'll tell them something about it."

Henry Maxwell was ashamed to say how uneasy he felt at being asked to speak a few words to a company of working men. How could he speak without notes, or to such a crowd? He was honestly in a condition of genuine fright over the prospect. He actually felt afraid of facing these men. He shrank from the ordeal of confronting such a crowd, so different from the Sunday audiences he was familiar with.

There were half a dozen long rude tables and benches in the great room, and when the noon whistle sounded the men poured up stairs from the machine shop below and seating themselves at the tables began to eat their lunch. There were perhaps three hundred of them. They had read the Superintendent's notice which he had posted up in various places, and came largely out of curiosity.

They were favorably impressed. The room was large and airy, free from smoke and dust and well warmed from the steam pipes.

About twenty minutes of one, Alexander Powers told the men what he had in mind. He spoke very simply, like one who understands thoroughly the character of his audience, and then introduced the Rev. Henry Maxwell of the First Church, his pastor, who had consented to speak a few minutes.

Henry Maxwell will never forget the feelings with which for the first time he confronted that grimy-faced audience of working men. Like hundreds of other ministers he had never spoken to any gathering except those made up of people of his own class in the sense that they were familiar, in their dress and education and habits, to him. This was a new world to him, and nothing but his new rule of conduct could have made possible his message and its effect. He spoke on the subject of satisfaction with life; what caused it; what its real sources were. He had the great good sense on this first appearance not to recognize the men as a class distinct from himself. He did not use the term "working men," and did not say a word to suggest any difference between their lives and his own.

The men were pleased. A good many of them shook hands with him before going down to their work, and Henry Maxwell telling it all to his wife when he reached home, said that never in all his life had he known the delight he then felt in having a hand-shake from a man of physical labor. The day marked an important one in his Christian experience, more important than he knew. It was the beginning of a fellowship between him and the working world. It was the first plank laid down to help bridge the chasm between the church and labor in Raymond.

Alexander Powers went back to his desk that afternoon much pleased with his plan and seeing much help in it for the men. He knew where he could get some good tables from an abandoned eating house at one of the stations down the road, and he saw how the coffee arrangement could be made a very attractive feature. The men had responded even better than he anticipated and the whole thing could not help being a great benefit to them.

He took up the routine of his work with a glow of satisfaction. After all, he wanted to do as Jesus would, he said to himself.

It was nearly four o'clock when he opened one of the company's long envelopes which he supposed contained orders for the purchasing of stores. He ran over the first page of type-written matter in his usual quick, businesslike manner before he saw that he was reading what was not intended for his office but for the Superintendent of the Freight Department.

He turned over a page mechanically, not meaning to read what was not addressed to him, but, before he knew it, he was in possession of evidence which conclusively proved that the company was engaged in a systematic violation of the Interstate Commerce Laws of the United States. It was as distinct and unequivocal breaking of law as if a private citizen should enter a house and rob the inmates. The discrimination shown in rebates was in total contempt of all the statute. Under the laws of the state it was also a distinct violation of certain provisions recently passed by the legislature to prevent railroad trusts. There was no question that he held in his hand evidence sufficient to convict the company of willful, intelligent violation of the law of the Commission and the law of the state also.

He dropped the papers on his desk as if they were poison, and instantly the question flashed across his mind, "What would Jesus do?" He tried to shut the question out. He tried to reason with himself by saying it was none of his business. He had supposed in a more or less indefinite way as did nearly all of the officers of the Company, that this had been going on right along in nearly all the roads. He was not in a position, owing to his place in the shops, to prove anything direct, and he had regarded it all as a matter which did not concern him at all. The papers now before him revealed the entire affair. They had through some carelessness in the address come into his hands. What business of his was it? If he saw a man entering his neighbor's house to steal would it not be his duty to inform the officers of the law? Was a railroad company such a different thing, was it under a different rule of conduct so that it could rob the public and defy law and be undisturbed because it was such a great organization? What would Jesus do? Then there was his family. Of course if he took any steps to inform the Commission it would mean the loss of his position. His wife and daughters had always enjoyed luxury and a good place in society. If he came out against this lawlessness as a witness it would drag him into courts, his motives would be misunderstood, and the whole thing would end in his disgrace and the loss of his position. Surely, it was none of his business. He could easily get the papers back to the Freight Department and no one be the wiser. Let the iniquity go on. Let the law be defied. What was it to him? He would work out his plans for bettering the conditions just about him. What more could a man do in this railroad business where there was so much going on any way that made it impossible to live by the Christian standard? But what would Jesus do if He knew the facts? That was the question that confronted Alexander Powers as the day wore into evening.

The lights in the office had been turned on. The whir of the great engine and the crash of the planer in the big shop continued until six o'clock.

Then the whistle blew, the engines slowed down, the men dropped their tools and ran for the block house.

Alexander Powers heard the familiar click, click, of the blocks as the men filed passed the window of the block house just outside. He said to his clerks, "I'm not going just yet. I have something extra to-night." He waited until he heard the last man deposit his block. The men behind the block case went out. The engineer and his assistants had work for half an hour, but they went out at another door.

At seven o'clock that evening any one who had looked into the Superintendent's office would have seen an unusual sight. He was kneeling down and his face was buried in his hands as he bowed his head upon the papers on his desk.

Chapter III

"If any man cometh unto me and hateth not his own father and mother and wife and children and brethren and sisters, yea, and his own life also, he cannot be my disciple." * * * "And whosoever forsaketh not all that he hath, he cannot be my disciple."[10]

WHEN RACHEL WINSLOW and Virginia Page separated after the meeting at the First Church on Sunday, they agreed to continue their conversation the next day. Virginia asked Rachel to come and lunch with her at noon, and Rachel accordingly rang the bell at the Page mansion about half past eleven, Virginia herself met her and the two were soon talking earnestly.

"The fact is," Rachel was saying, after they had been talking a few minutes, "I cannot reconcile it with my judgment of what He would do. I cannot tell another person what to do, but I feel that I ought not to accept this offer."

"What will you do, then?" asked Virginia with great interest.

"I don't know yet. But I have decided to refuse this offer."

Rachel picked up a letter that had been lying in her lap and ran over its contents again. It was a letter from the manager of a comic opera offering her a place with a large traveling company for the season. The salary was a very large figure, and the prospect held out by the manager was flattering. He had heard Rachel sing that Sunday morning when the stranger had interrupted the service. He had been much impressed. There was money in that voice and it ought to be used in comic opera, so said the letter, and the manager wanted a reply as soon as possible.

---

10 Luke 14:26 and 33.

"There's no virtue in saying No to this offer when I have the other one," Rachel went on thoughtfully. "That's harder to decide. But I've about made up my mind. To tell the truth, Virginia, I'm completely convinced in the first case that Jesus would never use any talent like a good voice just to make money. But now take this concert offer. Here is a reputable company to travel with an impersonator and a violinist and a male quartette. All people of good reputation. I'm asked to go as one of the company and sing leading soprano. The salary—I mentioned it, didn't I?—is to be guaranteed two hundred dollars a month for the season. But I don't feel satisfied that Jesus would go. What do you think?"

"You mustn't ask me to decide for you," replied Virginia with a sad smile. "I believe Mr. Maxwell was right when he said we must each one of us decide according to the judgment we felt for ourselves to be Christlike. I am having a harder time than you are, dear, to decide what He would do."

"Are you?" Rachel asked. She rose and walked over to the window and looked out. Virginia came and stood by her. The street was crowded with life and the two young women looked at it silently for a moment. Suddenly Virginia broke out as Rachel had never heard her before.

"Rachel, what does all this contrast in conditions mean to you as you ask this question of what Jesus would do? It maddens me to think that the society in which I have been brought up, the same to which we are both said to belong, is satisfied year after year to go on dressing and eating and having a good time, giving and receiving entertainments, spending its money on houses and luxuries and, occasionally, to ease its conscience, donating, without any personal sacrifice, a little money to charity. I have been educated, as you have, in one of the most expensive schools of America. Launched into society as an heiress. Supposed to be in a very enviable position. I'm perfectly well, I can travel or stay at home. I can do as I please. I can gratify almost any want or desire and yet, when I honestly try to imagine Jesus living the life I have lived and am expected to live, and doing for the rest of my life what thousands of other rich people do, I am under condemnation for being one of the most wicked, selfish, useless creatures in the world. I have not looked out of this window for weeks without a feeling of horror towards myself as I see the humanity that pours by this house."

Virginia turned away and walked up and down the room. Rachel watched her and could not repress the rising tide of her own growing definition of discipleship. Of what Christian use was her own talent of song? Was the best she could do to sell her talent for so much a month, go on a concert company's tour, dress beautifully, enjoy the excitement of public applause and gain a reputation as a great singer? Was that what Jesus would do?

She was not morbid. She was in sound health, was conscious of great powers as a singer, and knew that if she went out into public life she could make a great deal of money and become well known. It is doubtful if she overestimated her ability to accomplish all she thought herself capable of. And Virginia—what she had just said smote Rachel with great force because of the similar position in which the two friends found themselves.

Lunch was announced and they went out and were joined by Virginia's grandmother, Madam Page, a handsome, stately woman of sixty-five, and Virginia's brother, Rollin, a young man who spent most of his time at one of the clubs and had no particular ambition for anything, but a growing admiration for Rachel Winslow, and whenever she dined or lunched at the Page mansion, if he knew of it, he always planned to be at home.

These three made up the Page family. Virginia's father had been a banker and grain speculator. Her mother had died ten years before. Her father within the past year. The grandmother, a Southern woman in birth and training, had all the traditions and feelings that accompany the possession of wealth and social standing that have never been disturbed. She was a shrewd, careful, business woman of more than average ability. The family property and wealth were invested, in large measure, under her personal care. Virginia's portion was, without any restriction, her own. She had been trained by her father to understand the ways of the business world, and even the grandmother had been compelled to acknowledge the girl's capacity for taking care of her own money.

Perhaps two persons could not be found anywhere less capable of understanding a girl like Virginia than Madam Page and Rollin. Rachel, who had known the family since she was a girl playmate of Virginia's, could not help thinking of what confronted Virginia in her own home when she once decided on the course which she honestly believed Jesus would take. To-day at lunch, as she recalled Virginia's outbreak in the front room, she tried to picture the scene that would at some time occur between Madam Page and her granddaughter.

"I understand that you are going on the stage, Miss Winslow. We shall all be delighted, I'm sure," said Rollin, during one of the pauses in the conversation which had not been animated.

Rachel colored and felt annoyed.

"Who told you?" she asked, while Virginia, who had been very silent and reserved suddenly roused herself and appeared ready to join in the talk.

"Oh! we hear a thing or two on the street. Besides, every one saw Crandall the manager at church two weeks ago. He doesn't go to church to hear the preaching. In fact I know other people who don't either, not when there's something better to hear."

Rachel did not color this time, but she answered quietly,

"You're mistaken. I'm not going on the stage."

"It's a great pity. You'd make a hit. Everybody is talking about your singing."

This time Rachel flushed with genuine anger.

Before she could say anything, Virginia broke in.

"Whom do you mean by 'everybody?'"

"Whom? I mean all the people who hear Miss Winslow on Sunday. What other time do they hear her? It's a great pity, I say, that the general public outside of Raymond cannot hear her voice."

"Let us talk about something else," said Rachel a little sharply. Madam Page glanced at her and spoke with a gentle courtesy.

"My dear, Rollin never could pay an indirect compliment. He is like his father in that. But we are all curious to know something of your plans. We claim the right from old acquaintance, you know. And Virginia had already told us of your concert company offer."

"I supposed of course that was public property," said Virginia, smiling across the table. "It was in the "News" yesterday."

"Yes, yes," replied Rachel hastily. "I understand that, Madam Page. Well, Virginia and I have been talking about it. I have decided not to accept, and that is as far as I have gone yet."

Rachel was conscious of the fact that the conversation had, up to this point, been narrowing her hesitation concerning the company's offer down to a decision that would absolutely satisfy her own judgment of Jesus' probable action. It had been the last thing in the world, however, that she had desired to have her decision made in any way so public as this. Somehow what Rollin Page had said and his manner in saying it had hastened her judgment in the matter.

"Would you mind telling us, Rachel, your reasons for refusing the offer? It looks like a good opportunity for a young girl like you. Don't you think the general public ought to hear you? I feel like Rollin about that. A voice like yours belongs to a larger audience than Raymond and the First Church."

Rachel Winslow was naturally a girl of great reserve. She shrank from making her plans or her thoughts public. But with all her repression there was possible in her an occasional sudden breaking out that was simply an impulsive, thoughtful, frank, truthful expression of her most inner personal feeling. She spoke now in reply to Madam Page in one of those rare moments of unreserve that added to the attractiveness of her whole character.

"I have no other reason than a conviction that Jesus would do the same thing," she said looking in Madam Page's eyes with a clear earnest gaze.

Madam Page turned red and Rollin stared. Before her grandmother could say anything, Virginia spoke. Her rising color showed how she was stirred. Virginia's pale, clear complexion was that of health, but it was generally in marked contrast to Rachel's tropical type of beauty.

"Grandmother, you know we promised to make that the standard of our conduct for a year. Mr. Maxwell's proposition was plain to all who heard it. We have not been able to arrive at our decisions very rapidly. The difficulty in knowing what Jesus would do has perplexed Rachel and me a good deal."

Madam Page looked sharply at Virginia before she said anything.

"Of course, I understand Mr. Maxwell's statement. It is perfectly impracticable to put it into practice. I felt confident at the time that those who promised would find it out after a trial and abandon it as visionary and absurd. I have nothing to say about Miss Winslow's affairs, but—" (she paused and continued with a sharpness that was new to Rachel,) "I hope you have no foolish notions in this matter, Virginia."

"I have a great many notions," replied Virginia quietly. "Whether they are foolish or not depends upon my right understanding of what He would do. As soon as I find out, I shall do it."

"Excuse me, ladies," said Rollin rising from the table. "The conversation is getting beyond my depth. I shall retire to the library for a cigar."

He went out of the dining room and there was silence for a moment. Madam Page waited until the servant had brought in something and then asked her to go out. She was angry and her anger was formidable, although checked in some measure by the presence of Rachel.

"I am older by several years than you, young ladies," she said, and her traditional type of bearing seemed to Rachel to rise up like a great frozen wall between her and every conception of Jesus as a sacrifice. "What you have promised in a spirit of false emotion, I presume, is impossible of performance."

"Do you mean, grandmother, that we cannot possibly act as Jesus would, or do you mean that if we try to, we shall offend the customs and prejudices of society?" asked Virginia.

"It is not required! It is not necessary! Besides how can you act with any—"

Madam Page paused, broke off her sentence, and then turned to Rachel.

"What will your mother say to your decision? My dear, is it not foolish? What do you expect to do with your voice, any way?"

"I don't know what mother will say yet," Rachel answered, with a great shrinking from trying to give her mother's probable answer. If there was a woman in all Raymond with great ambitions for her daughter's success as a singer, Mrs. Winslow was that woman.

"O you will see it in a different light after wise thought of it. My dear," continued Madam Page rising from the table, "you will live to regret it if you do not accept the concert company's offer or something like it."

Rachel said something that contained a hint of the struggle she was still having. And after a little she went away, feeling that her departure was to be followed by a painful conversation between Virginia and her grandmother. As she afterward learned Virginia passed through a crisis of feeling during that scene with her grandmother that hastened her final decision as to the use of her money and her social position.

Rachel was glad to escape and be by herself. A plan was slowly forming in her mind and she wanted to be alone to think it out carefully. But before she had walked two blocks she was annoyed to find Rollin Page walking beside her.

"Sorry to disturb your thought, Miss Winslow, but I happened to be going your way and had an idea you might not object. In fact I've been walking here for a whole block and you haven't objected."

"I did not see you," replied Rachel.

"I wouldn't mind that if you only thought of me once in a while," said Rollin suddenly. He took one last nervous puff of his cigar, tossed it into the street and walked along with a pale face.

Rachel was surprised but not startled. She had known Rollin as a boy, and there had been a time when they had used each other's first names familiarly. Lately, however, something in Rachel's manner had put an end to that. She was used to his direct attempts at compliment and was sometimes amused by them. To-day she honestly wished him anywhere else.

"Do you ever think of me, Miss Winslow?" asked Rollin after a pause.

"Oh, yes, quite often!" said Rachel with a smile.

"Are you thinking of me now?"

"Yes, that is—yes, I am.

"What?"

"Do you want me to be absolutely truthful?'

"Of course."

"Then I was thinking that I wished you were not here."

Rollin bit his lip and looked gloomy. Rachel had not spoken anything as he wished.

"Now look here, Rachel—Oh, I know that's forbidden, but I've got to speak sometime; you know how I feel. What makes you treat me so hard? You used to like me a little, you know."

"Did I? Of course we used to get on very well as boy and girl. But we are older now."

Rachel still spoke in the light, easy way she had used since her first annoyance at seeing him. She was still somewhat preoccupied with her plan which had been disturbed by Rollin's appearance.

They walked along in silence a little way. The avenue was full of people. Among the persons passing was Jasper Chase. He saw Rachel and Rollin and bowed as he went by. Rollin was watching Rachel closely.

"I wish I were Jasper Chase; maybe I'd stand some show then,'" he said moodily.

Rachel colored in spite of herself. She did not say anything, and quickened her pace a little. Rollin seemed determined to say something and Rachel seemed helpless to prevent him. After all, she thought, he might as well know the truth one time as another.

"You know well enough, Rachel, how I feel towards you. Isn't there any hope? I could make you happy. I've loved you a good many years—"

"Why, how old do you think I am?" broke in Rachel with a nervous laugh. She was shaken out of her usual poise of manner.

"You know what I mean," went on Rollin doggedly. "And you have no right to laugh at me just because I want you to marry me."

"I'm not! But it is useless for you to speak,—Rollin," said Rachel after a little hesitation, and then using his name in such a frank, simple way that he could attach no meaning to it beyond the familiarity of the family acquaintance. "It is impossible." She was still a little agitated by the fact of receiving a proposal of marriage on the avenue. But the noise on the street and sidewalk made the conversation as private as if they were in the house.

"Would you—that is—do you think—if you gave me time I would—"

"No!" said Rachel. She spoke firmly; perhaps, she thought afterwards, although she did not mean to, she spoke harshly.

They walked on for some time without a word. They were nearing Rachel's home and she was anxious to end the scene.

As they turned off the avenue into one of the quiet streets, Rollin spoke suddenly and with more manliness than he had yet shown. There was a distinct note of dignity in his voice that was new to Rachel.

"Miss Winslow, I ask you to be my wife. Is there any hope for me that you will ever consent?"

"None in the least." Rachel spoke decidedly.

"Will you tell me why?" He asked the question as if he had a right to a truthful answer.

"I do not feel towards you as a woman ought to feel towards the man she ought to marry."

"In other words you do not love me?"

"I do not. And I cannot."

"Why?" That was another question and Rachel was a little surprised that he should ask it.

"Because—" she hesitated for fear she might say too much in an attempt to speak the exact truth.

"Tell me just why. You can't hurt me more than you have already."

"Well, I don't and can't love you because you have no purpose in life. What do you ever do to make the world better? You spend your time in club life, in amusements, in travel, in luxury. What is there in such a life to attract a woman?"

"Not much, I guess," said Rollin with a little laugh. "Still, I don't know as I am any worse than the rest of the men around me. I'm not so bad as some. Glad to know your reason."

He suddenly stopped, took off his hat, bowed gravely and turned back. Rachel went on home and hurried into her room, disturbed in many ways by the event which had so unexpectedly thrust itself into her experience.

When she had time to think it all over, she found herself condemned by the very judgment she had passed on Rollin Page. What purpose had she in life? She had been abroad and studied music with one of the famous teachers of Europe. She had come home to

Raymond and had been singing in the First Church choir now for a year. She was well paid. Up to that Sunday two weeks ago, she had been quite satisfied with herself and her position. She had shared her mother's ambition, and anticipated growing triumphs in the musical world. What possible career was before her except the regular career of every singer?

She asked the question again and, in the light of her recent reply to Rollin, asked again if she had any very great purpose in life herself? What would Jesus do? There was a fortune in her voice. She knew it, not necessarily as a matter of personal pride or professional egotism but simply as a fact. And she was obliged to acknowledge that until two weeks ago she had purposed to use her voice to make money and win admiration and applause. Was that a much higher purpose after all, than Rollin Page lived for?

She sat in her room a long time and finally went down stairs, resolved to have a frank talk with her mother about the concert company's offer and her new plan which was gradually shaping in her mind. She had already had one talk with her mother and knew that she expected Rachel to accept the offer and enter on a successful career as a public singer.

"Mother," Rachel said, coming at once to the point, as much as she dreaded the interview, "I have decided not to go out with the company. I have a good reason for it."

Mrs. Winslow was a large, handsome woman, fond of much company, ambitious for a distinct place in society, and devoted, according to her definitions of success, to the success of her children. Her youngest boy, Lewis, ten years younger than Rachel, was ready to graduate from a military academy in the summer. Meanwhile she and Rachel were at home together. Rachel's father, like Virginia's had died while the family were abroad. Like Virginia she found herself, under her present rule of conduct, in complete antagonism with her own immediate home circle.

Mrs. Winslow waited for Rachel to go on.

"You know the promise I made two weeks ago, mother?"

"Mr. Maxwell's promise?"

"No, mine. You know what it was, mother?"

"I suppose I do. Of course all the church members mean to imitate Christ and follow him as far as is consistent with our present day surroundings. But what has that to do with your decision in the concert company's matter?"

"It has everything to do with it. After asking, 'What would Jesus do?' and going to the source of authority for wisdom, I have been obliged to say that I do not believe He would, in my case, make that use of any voice."

"Why? Is there anything wrong about such a career?"

"No, I don't know that I can say there is."

"Do you presume to sit in judgment on other people who go out to sing in this way? Do you presume to say that they are doing what Christ would not do?"

"Mother, I wish you to understand me. I judge no one else. I condemn no other professional singers. I simply decide my own course. As I look at it, I have a conviction that Jesus would do something else."

"What else?" Mrs. Winslow had not yet lost her temper. She did not understand the situation, nor Rachel in the midst of it, but she was anxious that her daughter's career should be as distinguished as her natural gifts promised. And she felt confident that, when the present unusual religious excitement in the First Church had passed away, Rachel would go on with her public life according to the wishes of the family. She was totally unprepared for Rachel's next remark.

"What? Something that will serve mankind where it most needs the service of song. Mother, I have made up my mind to use my voice in some way so as to satisfy my own soul that I am doing something better than please fashionable audiences or make money, or even gratify my own love of singing. I am going to do something that will satisfy me when I ask, 'What would Jesus do?' And I am not satisfied, and cannot be, when I think of myself as singing myself into the career of a concert company performer."

Rachel spoke with a vigor and earnestness that surprised her mother. Mrs. Winslow was angry now. And she never tried to conceal her feelings.

"It is simply absurd! Rachel, you are a fanatic. What can you do?"

"The world has been served by men and women who have given it other things that were gifts. Why should I, because I am blessed with a natural gift at once proceed to put a market price on it and make all the money I can out of it? You know, mother, that you have taught me to think of a musical career always in the light of a financial and social success. I have been unable, since I made my promise, two weeks ago, to imagine Jesus joining a concert company to do what I would do and live the life I would have to live if I joined it."

Mrs. Winslow rose and then sat down again. With a great effort she composed herself.

"What do you intend to do then? You have not answered my question."

"I shall continue to sing for the time being in the church. I am pledged to sing there through spring. During the week, I am going to sing at the White Cross meetings down in the Rectangle."

"What! Rachel Winslow! Do you know what you are saying? Do you know what sort of people those are down there?"

Rachel almost quailed before her mother. For a moment she shrank back and was silent.

"I know very well. That is the reason I am going. Mr. and Mrs. Gray have been working there several weeks. I learned only this morning that they wanted singers from the churches to help them in their meetings. They use a tent. It is in a part of the city where Christian work is most needed. I shall offer them my help. Mother!" Rachel cried out with the first passionate utterance she had yet used, "I want to do something that will cost me something in the way of sacrifice. I know you will not understand me. But I am hungry to suffer something. What have we done all our lives for the suffering, sinning side of Raymond? How much have we denied ourselves or given of our personal ease and pleasure to bless the place in which we live or imitate the life of the Savior of the world? Are we always to go on doing as society selfishly dictates, moving on its narrow little round of pleasures and entertainments and never knowing the pain of things that cost?"

"Are you preaching at me?" asked Mrs. Winslow slowly. Rachel understood her mother's words.

"No, I am preaching at myself," she replied gently. She paused a moment as if she thought her mother would say something more and then went out of the room. When she reached her own room she felt that, so far as her mother was concerned, she could expect no sympathy or even a fair understanding from her.

She kneeled down. It is safe to say that within the two weeks since Henry Maxwell's church had faced that shabby figure with the faded hat, more members of his parish had been driven to their knees in prayer than during all the previous term of his pastorate.

When she rose, her beautiful face was wet with tears. She sat thoughtfully a little while and then wrote a note to Virginia Page. She sent it to her by a messenger, and then went down stairs again and told her mother that she and Virginia were going down to the Rectangle that evening to see Mr. and Mrs. Gray, the evangelists.

"Virginia's uncle, Dr. West, will go with us if she goes. I have asked her to call him up by telephone and go with us. The Doctor is a friend of the Grays, and attended some of the meetings last winter."

Mrs. Winslow did not say anything. Her manner showed her complete disapproval of Rachel's course and Rachel felt her unspoken bitterness.

About seven o'clock the Doctor and Virginia appeared, and together the three started for the scene of the White Cross meetings.

The Rectangle was the most notorious district in all Raymond. It was in the territory close by the great Railroad Shops and the packing houses. The slum and tenement district of Raymond congested its most wretched elements about the Rectangle. This was a barren field used in the summer by circus companies and wandering showmen. It was shut in by rows of saloons, gambling hells, and cheap, dirty boarding and lodging houses.

The First Church of Raymond had never touched the Rectangle problem. It was too dirty, too coarse, too sinful, too awful for close contact. Let us be honest. There had been an attempt to cleanse this sore spot by sending down an occasional committee of singers, of Sunday-school teachers, or gospel visitors from various churches. But the church of Raymond as an institution had never really done anything to make the Rectangle any less a stronghold of the devil as the years went by.

Into this heart of the coarse part of the sin of Raymond, the traveling evangelist and his brave little wife had pitched a good sized tent and begun meetings. It was the spring of the year and the evenings were beginning to be pleasant. The evangelists had asked for the help of Christian people and had received more than the usual amount of encouragement. But they felt a great need of more and better music. During the meetings on the Sunday just gone, the assistant at the organ had been taken ill. The volunteers from the city were few and the voices of ordinary quality.

"There will be a small meeting to-night, John," said his wife, as they entered the tent a little after seven o'clock and began to arrange the chairs and light up.

"Yes, I think so." Mr. Gray was a small energetic man with a pleasant voice and the courage of a high-born fighter. He had already made friends in the neighborhood and one of his converts, a heavy faced man who had just come in, began to help in the arrangement of the seats.

It was after eight o'clock when Alexander Powers opened the door of his office and started to go home. He was going to take a car at the corner of the Rectangle. But as he neared it he was roused by a voice coming from the tent.

It was the voice of Rachel Winslow. It struck through his consciousness of struggle over his own question that had sent him into the Divine presence for an answer. He had not yet reached a conclusion. He was troubled with uncertainty. His whole previous course of action as a railroad man was the poorest possible preparation for anything sacrificial. And he could not yet say what he would do in the matter.

Hark! What was she singing? How did Rachel Winslow happen to be down here? Several windows near by went up. Some men quarreling in a saloon stopped and listened. Other figures were walking rapidly in the direction of the Rectangle and the tent.

Surely Rachel Winslow never was happier in her life. She never had sung like that in the First Church. It was a marvelous voice. What was it she was singing? Again Alexander Powers, Superintendent of the Machine Shops, paused and listened.

"Where He leads me I will follow,
Where He leads me I will follow,
Where He leads me I will follow,
I'll go with Him, with Him,
All the way."

The brutal, stolid, coarse, impure life of the Rectangle stirred itself into new life, as the song, as pure as the surroundings were vile, floated out into saloon and den and foul lodging. Some one stumbling hastily by Alexander Powers said in answer to a question,

"The tent's beginning to run over to-night. That's what the talent calls music, eh?"

The Superintendent turned towards the tent. Then he stopped. And after a moment of indecision be went on to the corner and took the car for his home. But before he was out of the sound of Rachel's voice he knew that he had settled for himself the question of what Jesus would do.

Chapter IV

"If any man would come after me, let him deny himself and take up his cross daily and follow me."[11]

Henry Maxwell paced his study back and forth. It was Wednesday and he had started to think out the subject of his evening service which fell upon that night.

Out of one of his study windows he could see the tall chimneys of the railroad shops. The top of the evangelist's tent just showed over the buildings around the Rectangle.

The pastor of the First Church looked out of this window every time he turned in his walk. After a while he sat down at his desk and drew a large piece of paper towards him.

After thinking several moments he wrote in large letters the following:

A NUMBER OF THINGS THAT JESUS WOULD PROBABLY DO IN THIS PARISH

1. Live in a simple, plain manner, without needless luxury on the one hand or undue asceticism on the other.
2. Preach fearlessly to the hypocrites in the church no matter what their social importance or wealth.
3. Show in some practical form sympathy and love for the common people as well as for the well to do, educated, refined people who make up the majority of the church and parish.
4. Identify himself with the great causes of Humanity in some personal way that would call for self denial and suffering.
5. Preach against the saloon in Raymond.
6. Become known as a friend and companion of the sinful people in the Rectangle.

---

11 Luke 9:23.

7. Give up the summer trip to Europe this year. (I have been abroad twice and cannot claim any special need of rest. I am well, and could forego this pleasure, using the money for some one who needs a vacation more than I do. There are probably plenty of such people in the city.)

8. What else would Jesus do as Henry Maxwell?

He was conscious, with a humility that once was a stranger to him, that his outline of Jesus' probable action was painfully lacking in depth and power, but he was seeking carefully for concrete shapes into which he might cast his thought of Jesus' conduct. Nearly every point he had put down, meant, for him, a complete overturning of the custom and habit of years in the ministry. In spite of that, he still searched deeper for sources of the Christlike spirit. He did not attempt to write any more, but sat at his desk absorbed in his attempt to catch more and more of the spirit of Jesus in his own life. He had forgotten the particular subject for his prayer meeting with which he had begun his morning study.

He was so absorbed over his thought that he did not hear the bell ring and he was roused by the servant who announced a caller. He had sent up his name, Mr. Gray.

Maxwell stepped to the head of the stairs and asked Gray to come up.

"We can talk better up here."

So Gray came up and stated the reason for his call.

"I want you, Mr. Maxwell, to help me. Of course you have heard what a wonderful meeting we had Monday night and last night. Miss Winslow has done more with her voice than I could, and the tent won't hold the people."

"I've heard of that. It's the first time the people there have heard her. It's no wonder they are attracted."

"It has been a wonderful revelation to us, and a most encouraging event in our work. But I came to ask if you could not come down to-night and preach. I am suffering with a severe cold. I do not dare to trust my voice again. I know it is asking a good deal for such a busy man. But if you can't come, say so freely and I'll try somewhere else."

"I'm sorry, but it's my regular prayer meeting night," said Henry Maxwell. Then he flushed and added, "I shall be able to arrange it in some way so as to come down. You can count on me."

Gray thanked him earnestly and rose to go.

"Won't you stay a minute, Gray, and let us have a prayer together?"

"Yes," said Gray, simply.

So the two men kneeled together in the study. Mr. Maxwell prayed like a child. Gray was touched to tears as he kneeled there. There was something almost pitiful in the way this man who had lived his ministerial life in such a narrow limit of exercise now begged for wisdom and strength to speak a message to the people in the Rectangle.

Gray rose and held out his hand.

"God bless you, Mr. Maxwell. I'm sure the Spirit will give you power to-night."

Henry Maxwell made no answer. He did not even trust himself to say that he hoped so. But he thought of his promise and it brought a certain peace that was refreshing to his heart and mind alike.

So that is how it came about that when the First Church audience came into the lecture room that evening it was met with another surprise.

There was an unusually large number present. The prayer meetings ever since that remarkable Sunday morning, had been attended as never before in the history of the First Church.

Henry Maxwell came at once to the point. He spoke of Gray's work and of his request.

"I feel as if I were called to go down there to-night, and I will leave it with you to say whether you will go on with the meeting here. I think perhaps the best plan would be for a few volunteers to go down to the Rectangle with me prepared to help in the after-meeting, and the rest remain here and pray that the Spirit's power may go with us."

So half a dozen of the men went with Henry Maxwell, and the rest of the audience stayed in the lecture room. Maxwell could not escape the thought as he left the room that probably in his entire church membership there might not be found a score of disciples who were capable of doing work that would successfully lead needy, sinful men into the knowledge of Christ. The thought did not linger in his mind to vex him as he went on his way, but it was simply a part of his whole new conception of the meaning of Christian discipleship.

When he and his little company of volunteers reached the Rectangle, the tent was already crowded. They had difficulty in getting to the little platform. Rachel was there with Virginia and Jasper Chase who had come instead of the Doctor to-night.

When the meeting began with a song in which Rachel sang the solo and the people were asked to join in the chorus, not a foot of standing room was left in the tent. The night was mild and the sides of the tent were up and a great border of faces stretched around, looking in and forming part of the audience.

After the singing, and a prayer by one of the city pastors who was present, Gray stated the reasons for his inability to speak, and in his simple manner turned the service over to "Brother Maxwell of the First Church."

"Who's de bloke?" asked a hoarse voice near the outside of the tent.

"De Fust Church parson. We've got de whole high tone swell outfit to-night."

"Did you say Fust Church? I know him. My landlord has got a front pew up there," said another voice and there was a laugh, for the speaker was a saloon keeper.

"Trow out de life line cross de dark wave!" began a drunken man near by, singing in such an unconscious imitation of a local traveling singer's nasal tone that roars of laughter and jeers of approval rose around him. The people in the tent turned in the direction of the disturbance. There were shouts of "Put him out!" "Give the Fust Church a chance!" "Song! Song! Give us another song!"

Henry Maxwell stood up, and a great wave of actual terror went over him. This was not like preaching to the well-dressed, respectable, good-mannered people on the boulevard. He began to speak, but the confusion increased. Gray went down into the crowd but did not seem able to quiet it. Henry Maxwell raised his arm and his voice. The crowd in the tent began to pay some attention, but the noise on the outside increased. In a few minutes the audience was beyond Maxwell's control. He turned to Rachel with a sad smile.

"Sing something, Miss Winslow. They will listen to you," he said, and then sat down and put his face in his hands.

It was Rachel's opportunity and she was fully equal to it. Virginia was at the organ and Rachel asked her to play a few notes of the hymn,

"Savior, I follow on,
Guided by Thee,
Seeing not yet the hand
That leadeth me;
Hushed be my heart and still,

Fear I no farther ill,
Only to meet thy will,
My will shall be."

Rachel had not sung the first line before the people in the tent were all turned towards her, hushed and reverent. Before she had finished the verse the Rectangle was subdued and tamed. It lay like some wild beast at her feet and she sang it into harmlessness. Ah! What were the flippant, perfumed, critical audiences in concert halls compared with this dirty, drunken, impure, degraded, besotted humanity that trembled and wept and grew strangely, sadly thoughtful, under the touch of the divine ministry of this beautiful young woman. Henry Maxwell, as he raised his head and saw the transformed mob, had a glimpse of something that Jesus would probably do with a voice like Rachel Winslow's. Jasper Chase sat with his eyes on the singer, and his greatest longing as an ambitious author was swallowed up in the thought of what Rachel Winslow's love might sometime mean to him. And over in the shadow, outside, stood the last person any one might have expected to see at a gospel tent service—Rollin Page, who, jostled on every side by rough men and women who stared at the swell in the fine clothes, seemed careless of his surroundings and at the same time evidently swayed by the power that Rachel possessed. He had just come over from the club. Neither Rachel nor Virginia saw him that night.

The song was over. Henry Maxwell rose again. This time he felt calm. What would Jesus do? He spoke as he thought once he never could. Who were these people? They were immortal souls. What was Christianity? A calling of sinners, not the righteous, to repentance. How would Jesus speak? What would He say? He could not tell all that his message would include, but he felt sure of a part of it. And in that certainty he spoke on. Never before had he felt "compassion for the multitude." What had the multitude been to him during his ten years in the First Church, but a vague, dangerous, dirty, troublesome factor in society, outside of the church and his reach, an element that caused him, occasionally, an unpleasant feeling of conscience; a factor in Raymond that was talked about at associations as the "masses," in papers written by the brethren in attempts to show why the "masses" were not being reached. But to-night, as he faced the "masses," he asked himself whether, after all, this was not just about such a multitude as Jesus faced oftenest, and he felt the genuine emotion of love for a crowd which is one of the best indications a preacher ever has that he is living close to the heart of the world's eternal Life. It is easy to love an individual sinner, especially if he is personally picturesque, or interesting. To love a multitude of sinners, is distinctly a Christlike quality.

When the meeting closed, there was no special interest shown. The people rapidly melted away from the tent, and the saloons, which had been experiencing a dull season while the meetings progressed, again drove a thriving trade. The Rectangle, as if to make up for lost time, started in with vigor on its usual night-life of debauch. Henry Maxwell and his little party, including Virginia, Rachel, and Jasper Chase, walked down past the row of saloons and dens, until they reached the corner where the cars passed.

"This is a terrible spot," said Henry Maxwell, as they stood waiting for their car. "I never realized that Raymond had such a festering sore. It does not seem possible that this is a city full of Christian disciples."

He paused and then continued:

"Do you think any one can ever remove this great curse of the saloon? Why don't we all act together against the traffic? What would Jesus do? Would He keep silent? Would He vote to license these causes of crime and death?"

Henry Maxwell was talking to himself more than to the others. He remembered that he had always voted for license, and so had nearly all of his church members. What would Jesus do? Could he answer that question? Would Jesus preach and act against the saloon, if he lived to-day? How would he preach and act? Suppose it was not popular to preach against license? Suppose the Christian people thought it was all that could be done, to license the evil, and so get revenue from a necessary sin? Or suppose the church members owned property where the saloons stood—what then? He knew that these were the facts in Raymond. What would Jesus do?

He went up into his study, the next morning, with that question only partly answered. He thought of it all day. He was still thinking of it, and reaching certain real conclusions, when the evening "News" came. His wife brought it up, and sat down a few minutes while he read it to her.

The "Evening News" was at present the most sensational paper in Raymond. That is to say, it was being edited in such a remarkable fashion, that its subscribers had never been so excited over a newspaper before.

First, they had noticed the absence of the prize fight, and gradually it began to dawn upon them, that the "News" no longer printed accounts of crime with detailed descriptions, or scandals in private life. Then they noticed that the advertisements of liquor and tobacco were being dropped, together with certain other advertisements of a questionable character. The discontinuance of the Sunday paper caused the greatest comment of all, and now the character of the editorials was creating the greatest excitement. A quotation from the Monday paper of this week will show what Edward Norman was doing to keep his promise. The editorial was headed,

THE MORAL SIDE OF POLITICAL QUESTIONS

The editor of the 'News' has always advocated the principles of the great political party at present in power, and has, therefore, discussed all political questions from a standpoint of expediency, or of belief in the party, as opposed to other organizations. Hereafter, to be perfectly honest with all our readers, the editor will present and discuss political questions from the standpoint of right and wrong. In other words, the first question will not be, 'Is it in the interest of our party?' or 'Is it according to the principles laid down by the party?' but the question first asked will be, 'Is this measure in accordance with the spirit and teachings of Jesus, as the author of the greatest standard of life known to men?' That is, to be perfectly plain, the moral side of every political question will be considered its most important side, and the ground will be distinctly taken, that nations, as well as individuals, are under the same law, to do all things to the glory of God, as the first rule of action.

The same principle will be observed in this office towards candidates for places of responsibility and trust in the Republic. Regardless of party politics, the editor of the 'News' will do all in his power to bring the best men into power, and will not, knowingly, help to support for office any candidate who is unworthy, however much he may be endorsed by the party. The first question asked about the man, as about the measure, will be, 'Is he the right man for the place? Is he a good man with ability?'

There had been more of this; but we have quoted enough to show the character of the editorials. Hundreds of men in Raymond had read it, and rubbed their eyes in amazement. A good many of them had promptly written to the "News," telling the editor to stop their paper. The paper still came out, however, and was eagerly read all over the city. At the end of the week, Edward Norman knew very well that he had actually lost already a large number of valuable subscribers. He faced the conditions calmly, although Clark, the managing editor, grimly anticipated ultimate bankruptcy, especially since Monday's editorial.

To-night, as Henry Maxwell read to his wife, he could see on almost every column evidences of Norman's conscientious obedience to his promise. There was an absence of slangy, sensational scare-heads. The reading matter under the head lines was in perfect keeping with them. He noticed in two columns that the reporters names appeared, signed, at the bottom. And there was a distinct advance in the dignity and style of their contributions.

"So Norman is beginning to get his reporters to sign their work. He has talked with me about that. It is a good thing. It fixes responsibility for items where it belongs, and raises the standard of work done. A good thing all around, for public and writers."

Henry Maxwell suddenly paused. His wife looked up from some work she was doing. He was reading something with the utmost interest.

"Listen to this, Mary," he said after a moment, while his voice trembled:

This morning Alexander Powers, Superintendent of the L. and T. R. R. shops in this city, handed his resignation to the road, and gave as the reason the fact that certain proof had fallen into his hands of the violation of the Interstate Commerce Law, and also of the State law which has recently been framed to prevent and punish railroad pooling for the benefit of certain favored shippers. Mr. Powers states in his resignation that he can no longer consistently withhold the information he possesses against the road. He has placed his evidence against the company in the hands of the Commission, and it is now for them to take action upon it.

The "News" wishes to express itself on this action of Mr. Powers. In the first place, he has nothing to gain by it. He has lost a valuable place, voluntarily, when, by keeping silent, he might have retained it. In the second place, we believe his action ought to receive the approval of all thoughtful, honest citizens, who believe in seeing law obeyed and law-breakers brought to justice. In a case like this, where evidence against a railroad company is generally understood to be almost impossible to obtain, it is the general belief that the officers of the road are often in possession of criminating facts, but do not consider it to be any of their business to inform the authorities that the law is being defied. The entire result of this evasion of responsibility on the part of those who are responsible, is demoralizing to every young man connected with the road. The editor of the "News" recalls the statement made by a prominent railroad official in this city a little while ago, that nearly every clerk in a certain department of the road who understood how large sums of money were made by shrewd violations of the Interstate Commerce Law, was ready to admire the shrewdness with which it was done, and declared that they would all do the same thing, if they were high enough in railroad circles to attempt it.[12]

It is not necessary to say that such a condition of business is destructive to all the nobler and higher standards of conduct; and no young man can live in such an atmosphere of unpunished dishonesty and lawlessness, without wrecking his character.

In our judgment, Mr. Powers did the only thing that a Christian man can do. He has rendered brave and useful service to the state and the general public. It is not always an easy

---

12 [Author's Original Note] This was actually said in one of the General Offices of a great western railroad, to the author's knowledge.

matter to determine the relations that exist between the individual citizen and his fixed duty to the public. In this case, there is no doubt in our minds that the step which Mr. Powers has taken commends itself to every man who believes in law and its enforcement. There are times when the individual must act for the people, in ways that will mean sacrifice and loss to him of the gravest character. Mr. Powers will be misunderstood and misrepresented; but there is no question that his course will he approved by every citizen who wishes to see the greatest corporations, as well as the weakest individual, subject to the same law. Mr. Powers has done all that a loyal, patriotic citizen could do. It now remains for the Commission to act upon his evidence, which, we understand, is overwhelming proof of the lawlessness of the L. and T. Let the law be enforced, no matter who the persons may be who have been guilty.'"

Henry Maxwell finished reading and dropped the paper.

"I must go and see Powers. This is the result of his promise."

He rose, and as he was going out, his wife said,

"Do you think, Henry, that Jesus would have done that?"

Henry Maxwell paused a moment. Then be answered slowly,

"Yes, I think He would. At any rate, Powers has decided so, and each one of us who made the promise understands that he is not deciding Jesus' conduct for any one else, only for himself."

"How about his family? How will Mrs. Powers and Celia be likely to take it?"

"Very hard, I have no doubt. That will be Powers's cross in this matter. They will not understand his motive."

Henry Maxwell went out and walked over to the next block, where the Superintendent lived. To his relief, Powers himself came to the door.

The two men shook hands silently. They instantly understood each other, without words. There had never been such a bond of union between the minister and his parishioner.

"What are you going to do?" Henry Maxwell asked, after they had talked over the facts in the case.

"You mean another position? I have no plans yet. I can go back to my old work as a telegraph operator. My family will not suffer except in a social way."

Alexander Powers spoke calmly, if sadly. Henry Maxwell did not need to ask him how his wife and daughter felt. He knew well enough that the Superintendent had suffered deepest at that point.

"There is one matter I wish you would see to," said Powers after a while, "and that is the work begun at the Shops. So far as I know, the Company will not object to that going right on. It is one of the contradictions of the railroad world that the Y. M. C. A.'s, and other Christian influences, are encouraged by the roads, while all the time the most un-Christian and lawless acts are being committed in the official management of the roads themselves. Of course it is understood that it pays a railroad to have in its employ men who are temperate, and honest, and Christian. So I have no doubt the Master Mechanic will have the same courtesy extended to him that I had, in the matter of the room and its uses. But what I want you to do, Mr. Maxwell, is to see that my plan is carried out. Will you? You understand what the idea was in general. You made a very favorable impression on the men. Go down there as often as you can. Get Milton Wright interested to provide something for the furnishing and expense of the coffee plant and reading tables. Will you do it?"

"Yes," replied Henry Maxwell. He stayed a little longer. Before he went away, he and the Superintendent had a prayer together, and they parted with that silent hand-grasp that seemed to them like a new token of their Christian discipleship and fellowship.

The pastor of the First Church went home stirred deeply by the events of the week. Gradually the truth was growing upon him that the pledge to do as Jesus would was working out a revolution in his parish and throughout the city. Every day added to the serious results of obedience to that pledge. Henry Maxwell did not pretend to see the end. He was, in fact, only now at the very beginning of events that were destined to change the history of hundreds of families, not only in Raymond but throughout the entire country. As he thought of Edward Norman and Rachel and Mr. Powers, and of the results that had already come from their actions, he could not help a feeling of intense interest in the probable effect, if all the persons in the First Church who had made the pledge, faithfully kept it. Would they all keep it, or would some of them turn back when the cross became too heavy?

He was asking this question the next morning, as he sat in his study, when the President of the Endeavor Society called to see him.

"I suppose I ought not to trouble you with my case, said young Morris, coming at once to his errand, "but I thought, Mr. Maxwell, that you might advise me a little."

"I'm" glad you came. Go on, Fred." Henry Maxwell had known the young man ever since his first year in the pastorate, and loved and honored him for his consistent, faithful service in the church.

"Well, the fact is, I'm out of a job. You know I've been doing reporter work on the morning 'Sentinel' since I graduated last year. Well, last Saturday Mr. Burr asked me to go down the road Sunday morning and get the details of that train robbery at the Junction, and write the thing up for the extra edition that came out Monday morning, just to get the start of the 'News.' I refused to go, and Burr gave me my dismissal. He was in a bad temper, or I think perhaps he would not have done it. He has always treated me well before. Now, don't you think Jesus would have done as I did? I ask because the other fellows say I was a fool not to do the work. I want to feel that a Christian acts from motives that may seem strange to others, sometimes, but not foolish. What do you think?"

"I think you kept your promise, Fred. I cannot believe Jesus would do newspaper work on Sunday as you were asked to do it."

"Thank you, Mr. Maxwell. I felt a little troubled over it, but the longer I think it over the better I feel."

Morris rose to go, and Henry Maxwell rose and laid a loving hand on the young man's shoulder.

"What are you going to do, Fred?"

"I don't know yet. I have thought some of going to Chicago, or some large city."

"Why don't you try the 'News'?"

"They are all supplied. I have not thought of applying there."

Henry Maxwell thought a moment.

"Come down to the 'News' office with me, and let us see Norman about it."

So, a few minutes later, Edward Norman received into his room the minister and young Morris, and Henry Maxwell briefly told the cause of their errand.

"I can give you a place on the 'News'," said Edward Norman, with his keen look softened by a smile that made it winsome. "I want reporters who won't work Sundays. And what is more, I am making plans for a special kind of reporting which I believe young Morris here can develop because he is in sympathy with what Jesus would do."

He assigned Morris a definite task, and Henry Maxwell started back to his study, feeling that kind of satisfaction (and it is a very deep kind) which a man feels when he has been even partly instrumental in finding an unemployed person a situation.

He had intended to go back to his study, but on his way home he passed by one of Milton Wright's stores. He thought he would simply step in and shake hands with his parishioner and bid him God-speed in what he had heard he was doing to put Christ into his business. But when he went into the office, Milton Wright insisted on detaining him to talk over some of his new plans. Henry Maxwell asked himself if this was the Milton Wright he used to know, eminently practical, business-like, according to the regular code of the business world, and viewing everything first and foremost from the standpoint of "Will it pay?"

"There is no use to disguise the fact, Mr. Maxwell that I have been compelled to revolutionize the whole method of my business since I made that promise. I have been doing a great many things, during the last twenty years in this store, that I know Jesus would not do. But that is a small item compared with the number of things I begin to believe Jesus would do. My sins of commission have not been as many as those of omission in business relations."

"What was the first change you made?" asked Henry Maxwell. He felt as if his sermon could wait for him in his study. As the interview with Milton Wright continued, he was not so sure but that he had found material for a sermon without going back to his study.

"I think the first change I had to make was in my thought of my employees. I came down here Monday morning after that Sunday and asked myself, 'What would Jesus do in His relation to these clerks, book-keepers, office boys, draymen, salesmen? Would He try to establish some sort of personal relation to them different from that which I have sustained all these years?' I soon answered the question by saying, Yes. Then came the question of what it would lead me to do. I did not see how I could answer it to my satisfaction without getting all my employees together and having a talk with them. So I sent invitations to all of them, and we had a meeting out there in the warehouse Tuesday night.

"A good many things came out of that meeting. I can't tell you all. I tried to talk with the men as I imagined Jesus might. It was hard work, for I have not been in the habit of it, and I must have made mistakes. But I can hardly make you believe, Mr. Maxwell, the effect of that meeting on some of the men. Before it closed, I saw more than a dozen of them with tears on their faces. I kept asking, 'What would Jesus do?' and the more I asked it, the farther along it pushed me into the most intimate and loving relations with the men who have worked for me all these years. Every day something new is coming up, and I am right now in the midst of a reconstructing of the entire business, so far as its motive for being conducted is concerned. I am so practically ignorant of all plans for co-operation and its application to business that I am trying to get information from every possible source. I have lately made a special study of the life of Titus Salt, the great mill owner of Bradford, England, who afterwards built that model town on the banks of the Aire. There is a good deal in his plans that will help. But I have not yet reached definite conclusions in regard to all the details. I am not enough used to Jesus' methods. But see here."

Milton eagerly reached up into one of the pigeon holes of his desk and took out a paper.

"I have sketched out what seems to me a program such as Jesus might go by in a business like mine. I want you to tell me what you think about it."

WHAT JESUS WOULD PROBABLY DO IN MILTON WRIGHT'S PLACE AS A BUSINESS MAN

1. He would engage in business for the purpose of glorifying God, and not for the primary purpose of making money.

2. All money that might be made he would never regard as his own, but as trust funds to be used for the good of humanity.
3. His relations with all the persons in his employ would be the most loving and helpful. He could not help thinking of them all in the light of souls to be saved. This thought would always be greater than his thought of making money in business.
4. He would never do a single dishonest or questionable thing or try in any remotest way to get the advantage of any one else in the same business.
5. The principle of unselfishness and helpfulness in all the details of the business would direct its details.
6. Upon this principle he would shape the entire plan of his relations to his employees, to the people who were his customers, and to the general business world with which he was connected.

Henry Maxwell read this over slowly. It reminded him of his own attempts, the day before, to put into a concrete form his thought of Jesus' probable action. He was very thoughtful, as he looked up and met Milton Wright's eager gaze.

"Do you believe you can continue to make your business pay on those lines?"

"I do. Intelligent unselfishness ought to be wiser than intelligent selfishness, don't you think? If the men who work as employees begin to feel a personal share in the profits of the business and, more than that, a personal love for themselves on the part of the firm, won't the result be more care, less waste, more diligence, more faithfulness?"

"Yes, I think so. A good many other business men don't, do they? I mean as a general thing. How about your relations to the selfish world that is not trying to make money on Christian principles?"

"That complicates my action of course."

"Does your plan contemplate what is coming to be known as co-operation?"

"Yes, as far as I have gone, it does. As I told you, I am studying out my details carefully. I am absolutely convinced that Jesus in my place would be absolutely unselfish. He would love all these men in his employ. He would consider the main purpose of all the business to be a mutual helpfulness, and would conduct it all so that God's kingdom would be evidently the first object sought. On those general principles, as I say, I am working. I must have time to complete the details."

When Henry Maxwell finally left Milton Wright, he was profoundly impressed with the revolution that was being wrought already in the business. As he passed out of the store he caught something of the new spirit of the place. There was no mistaking the fact that Milton Wright's new relations to his employees were beginning, even so soon, after less than two weeks, to transform the entire business. This was apparent in the conduct and faces of the clerks.

"If Milton Wright keeps on, he will be one of the most influential preachers in Raymond," said Henry Maxwell to himself, when he reached his study. The question rose as to his continuance in this course when he began to lose money by it, as was possible. Henry Maxwell prayed that the Holy Spirit, who had shown Himself with growing power in the company of the First Church disciples, might abide long with them all. And with that prayer on his lips and in his heart, he began the preparation of a sermon in which he was going to present to his people on Sunday the subject of the saloon in Raymond, as he now believed Jesus would do. He had never preached against the saloon in this way before. He knew that the things he should say would lead to serious results. Nevertheless he went on with his work, and every sentence he wrote or shaped was preceded with the question, "Would Jesus say that?" Once in the course of his study, he went down on his knees. No one except himself could know what that meant to him. When had he done that in the preparation of sermons, before the change that had come into his thought of discipleship? As he viewed his ministry now, he did not dare to preach without praying for wisdom. He no longer thought of his dramatic delivery and its effect on his audience. The great question with him now was, "What would Jesus do?"

Saturday night at the Rectangle witnessed some of the most remarkable scenes that Mr. Gray and his wife had ever known. The meetings had intensified with each night of Rachel's singing. A stranger passing through the Rectangle in the daytime might have heard a good deal about the meetings, in one way and another. It cannot be said that, up to that Saturday night, there was any appreciable lack of oaths and impurity and heavy drinking. The Rectangle would not have acknowledged that it was growing any better, or that even the singing had softened its conversation, or its outward manner. It had too much local pride in being "tough." But in spite of itself, there was a yielding to a power it had never measured and did not know well enough to resist beforehand.

Gray had recovered his voice, so that Saturday he was able to speak. The fact that he was obliged to use his voice carefully made it necessary for the people to be very quiet if they wanted to hear. Gradually they had come to understand that this man was talking these many weeks, and using his time and strength, to give them a knowledge of a Savior, all out of a perfectly unselfish love for them. To-night the great crowd was as quiet as Henry Maxwell's decorous audience ever was. The fringe around the tent was deeper, and the saloons were practically empty. The Holy Spirit had come at last, and Gray knew that one of the great prayers of his life was going to be answered.

And Rachel—her singing was the best, most wonderful, Virginia or Jasper Chase had ever known. They had come together again to-night with Dr. West, who had spent all his spare time that week in the Rectangle with some charity cases. Virginia was at the organ, Jasper sat on a front seat looking up at Rachel, and the Rectangle swayed as one man towards the platform as she sang:

"Just as I am, without one plea,
But that thy blood was shed for me,
And that thou bidst me come to thee,
O Lamb of God, I come, I come."

Gray hardly said a word. He stretched out his hand with a gesture of invitation. And down the two aisles of the tent, broken, sinful creatures, men and women, stumbled towards the platform. One woman out of the street was near the organ. Virginia caught the look of her face, and, for the first time in the life of the rich girl, the thought of what Jesus was to a sinful woman came with a suddenness and power that was like nothing but a new birth. Virginia left the organ, went to her, looked into her face and caught her hands in her own. The other girl trembled, then fell on her knees, sobbing, with her head down upon the back of the bench in front of her, still clinging to Virginia. And Virginia, after a moment's hesitation, kneeled down by her and the two heads were bowed close together.

But when the people had crowded in a double row all about the platform, most of them kneeling and crying, a man in evening dress, different from the others, pushed through the seats and came and kneeled down by the side of the drunken man who had disturbed the meeting when Henry Maxwell spoke. He kneeled within a few feet of Rachel Winslow, who was still singing softly. And as she turned for a moment and looked in his direction, she was amazed to see the face of Rollin Page! For a moment her voice faltered. Then she went on:

"Just as I am, thou wilt receive,
Wilt welcome, pardon, cleanse, relieve;
Because thy promise I believe,
O Lamb of God, I come, I come."

The voice was as the voice of divine longing, and the Rectangle, for the time being, was swept into the harbor of redemptive grace.

Chapter V

"If any man serve me, let him follow me."[13]

It was nearly midnight before the service at the Rectangle closed. Gray stayed up long into Sunday morning, praying and talking with a little group of converts that in the great experience of their new life, clung to the evangelist with a personal helplessness that made it as impossible for him to leave them as if they had been depending upon him to save them from physical death. Among these converts was Rollin Page.

Virginia and her uncle had gone home about eleven o'clock, and Rachel and Jasper Chase had gone with them as far as the avenue where Virginia lived. Dr. West had walked on a little way with them to his own house, and Rachel and Jasper had then gone on together to her mother's.

That was a little after eleven. It was now striking midnight, and Jasper Chase sat in his room staring at the papers on his desk and going over the last half-hour with painful persistence.

He had told Rachel Winslow of his love for her, and she had not given her love in return.

It would be difficult to know what was most powerful in the impulse that had moved him to speak to her to-night. He had yielded to his feelings without any special thought of results to himself, because he had felt so certain that Rachel would respond to his love for her. He tried to recall, now, just the impression she made on him when he first spoke to her.

Never had her beauty and her strength influenced him as to-night. While she was singing he saw and heard no one else. The tent swarmed with a confused crowd of faces, and he knew he was sitting there hemmed in by a mob of people; but they had no meaning to him. He felt powerless to avoid speaking to her. He knew he should speak when they were once alone.

Now that he had spoken, he felt that he had misjudged either Rachel or the opportunity. He knew, or thought he did, that she had begun to care for him. It was no secret between them that the heroine of Jasper's first novel had been his own ideal of Rachel, and the hero of the story was himself, and they had loved each other in the book, and Rachel had not objected. No one else knew. The names and characters had been drawn with a subtle skill

---

13 John 12:26.

that revealed to Rachel, when she received a copy of the book from Jasper, the fact of his love for her, and she had not been offended. That was nearly a year ago.

To-night, Jasper Chase recalled the scene between them, with every inflection and movement unerased from his memory. He even recalled the fact that he began to speak just at that point on the avenue where, a few days before, he had met Rachel walking with Rollin Page. He had wondered at the time, what Rollin was saying.

"Rachel," Jasper had said, and it was the first time he had ever spoken her first name, "I never knew until to-night how much I love you. Why should I try to conceal any longer what you have seen me look? You know I love you as my life. I can no longer hide it from you if I would."

The first intimation he had of a refusal was the trembling of Rachel's arm in his own. She had allowed him to speak and had neither turned her face towards him nor away from him. She had looked straight on, and her voice was sad but firm and quiet when she spoke.

"Why do you speak to me now? I cannot bear it—after what we have seen to-night."

"Why—what—" he had stammered, and then was silent.

Rachel withdrew her arm from his, but still walked near him.

Then he cried out, with the anguish of one who begins to see a great loss facing him where he expected a great joy.

"Rachel! Do you not love me? Is not my love for you as sacred as anything in all of life itself?"

She had walked on silent for a few steps, after that. They had passed a street lamp. Her face was pale and beautiful. He had made a movement to clutch her arm. And she had moved a little farther from him.

"No," she had replied. "There was a time—I cannot answer for that—you should not have spoken to me to-night."

He had seen in these words his answer. He was extremely sensitive. Nothing short of a joyous response to his own love would have satisfied him. He could not think of pleading with her.

"Some time—when I am more worthy?" he had asked in a low voice; but she did not seem to hear, and they had parted at her home, and he recalled vividly the fact that no good-night had been said.

Now as he went over the brief but significant scene, he lashed himself for his foolish precipitancy. He had not reckoned on Rachel's tense, passionate absorption of all her feeling in the scenes at the tent which were so new in her mind. But he did not know her well enough, even yet, to understand the meaning of her refusal. When the clock in the First Church steeple struck one, he was still sitting at his desk, staring at the last page of manuscript of his unfinished novel.

Rachel Winslow went up to her room and faced her evening's experience with conflicting emotions. Had she ever loved Jasper Chase? Yes. No. One moment she felt that her life's happiness was at stake over the result of her action. Another, she had a strange feeling of relief that she had spoken as she did. There was one great overmastering feeling in her. The response of the wretched creatures in the tent to her singing, the swift, awesome presence of the Holy Spirit, had affected her as never in all her life before. The moment Jasper had spoken her name and she realized that he was telling her of his love, she had felt a sudden revulsion for him, as if he should have respected the supernatural events they had just witnessed. She felt as if it were not the time to be absorbed in anything less than the divine glory of those conversions. The thought that all the time she was singing with the one passion of her soul to touch the conscience of that tent full of sin, Jasper Chase had been moved by it simply to love her for himself, gave her a shock as of irreverence on her part as well as on his. She could not tell why she felt as she did, only she knew that if he had not told her to-night she would still have felt the same towards him as she always had. What was that feeling? What had he been to her? Had she made a mistake? She went to her book-case and took out the novel which Jasper had given her. Her face deepened in color as she turned to certain passages which she had read often and which she knew Jasper had written for her. She read them again. Somehow they failed to touch her strongly. She closed the book and let it lie on the table. She gradually felt that her thought was busy with the sight she had witnessed in that tent. Those faces, men and women, touched for the first time with the Spirit's glory—what a wonderful thing life was after all! The complete regeneration revealed in the sight of drunken vile, debauched humanity kneeling down to give itself to a life of purity and Christlikeness—oh, it was surely a witness to the superhuman in the world! And the face of Rollin Page by the side of that miserable wreck out of the gutter—she could recall as if she now saw it, Virginia crying with her arms about her brother just before she left the tent, and Mr. Gray kneeling close by, and the girl Virginia had taken into her heart bending her head while Virginia whispered something to her. All these pictures drawn by the Holy Spirit in the human tragedies brought to a climax there in the most abandoned spot in all Raymond, stood out in Rachel's memory now, a memory so recent that her room seemed for the time being to contain all the actors and their movements.

"No! No!" She had said aloud. "He had no right to speak to me after all that! He should have respected the place where our thoughts should have been! I am sure I do not love him. Not enough to give him my life!"

And after she had thus spoken, the evening's experience at the tent came crowding in again, thrusting out all other things. It is perhaps the most striking evidence of the tremendous spiritual factor which had now entered the Rectangle that Rachel felt, even when the great love of a strong man had come very near to her, that the spiritual manifestation moved her with an agitation far greater than anything Jasper had felt for her personally, or she for him.

The people of Raymond awoke Sunday morning to a growing knowledge of events which were beginning to revolutionize many of the regular, customary habits of the town. Alexander Powers's action in the matter of the railroad frauds had created a sensation, not only in Raymond but throughout the country. Edward Norman's daily changes of policy in the conduct of his paper had startled the community and caused more comment than any recent political event. Rachel Winslow's singing at the Rectangle meetings had made a stir in society and excited the wonder of all her friends. Virginia Page's conduct, her presence every night with Rachel, her absence from the usual circle of her wealthy fashionable acquaintances, had furnished a great deal of material for gossip and question. In addition to these events which centered about these persons who were so well known, there had been all through the city, in very many homes and in business and social circles, strange happenings. Nearly one hundred persons in Henry Maxwell's church had made the pledge to do everything after asking, "What would Jesus do?" and the result had been, in many cases, unheard-of actions. The city was stirred as it had never been. As a climax to the week's events had come the spiritual manifestation at the Rectangle, and the announcement which came to most people before church time of the actual conversion at the tent of nearly fifty of the worst characters in the neighborhood, together with the conversion of Rollin Page, the well-known society and club man.

It is no wonder that, under the pressure of all this, the First Church of Raymond came to the morning service in a condition that made it quickly sensitive to any large truth.

Perhaps nothing had astonished the people more than the great change that had come over the minister since he had proposed to them the imitation of Jesus in conduct. The dramatic delivery of his sermons no longer impressed them. The self-satisfied, contented, easy attitude of the fine figure and the refined face in the pulpit, had been displaced by a manner that could not be compared with the old style of his delivery. The sermon had become a message. It was no longer delivered. It was brought to them with a love an earnestness, a passion, a desire, a humility, that poured its enthusiasm about the truth and made the speaker no more prominent than he had to be as the living voice of God. His prayers were unlike any the people had ever heard before. They were often broken, even once or twice they had been actually ungrammatical in a phrase or two. When had Henry Maxwell so far forgotten himself in a prayer as to make a mistake of that sort? He knew that he had often taken as much pride in the diction and the delivery of his prayers as of his sermons. Was it possible he now so abhorred the elegant refinement of a formal public petition that he purposely chose to rebuke himself for his previous precise manner of prayer? It is more likely that he had no thought of all that. His great longing to voice the needs and wants of his people made him unmindful of an occasional mistake. It is certain he had never prayed so effectively as he did now.

There are times when a sermon has a value and power due to conditions in the audience rather than to anything new or startling or eloquent in the words or the arguments presented. Such conditions faced Henry Maxwell this morning as he preached against the saloon, according to his purpose determined on the week before. He had no new statements to make about the evil influence of the saloon in Raymond. What new facts were there? He had no startling illustrations of the power of the saloon in business or politics. What could he say that had not been said by temperance orators a great many times? The effect of his message this morning owed its power to the unusual fact of his preaching about the saloon at all, together with the events that had stirred the people. He had never in the course of his ten years' pastorate mentioned the saloon as something to be regarded in the light of an enemy, not only to the poor and the tempted, but to the business life of the place and the church itself. He spoke now with a freedom that seemed to measure his complete sense of the conviction that Jesus would speak so. At the close he pleaded with the people to remember the new life that had begun at the Rectangle. The regular election of city officers was near at hand. The question of license would be an issue in that election. What of the poor creatures surrounded by the hell of drink while just beginning to feel the joy of deliverance from sin? Who could tell what depended on their environment? Was there one word to be said by the Christian disciple, business man, professional man, citizen, in favor of continuing to license these crime and shame-producing institutions? Was not the most Christian thing they could do to act as citizens in the matter, fight the saloon at the polls, elect good men to the city offices, and clean the municipality? How much had prayers helped to make Raymond better while votes and actions had really been on the side of the enemies of Jesus? Would not Jesus do this? What disciple could imagine Him refusing to suffer or take up His cross in the matter? How much had the members of the First Church ever suffered in an attempt to imitate Jesus? Was Christian discipleship a thing of convenience, of custom, of tradition? Where did the suffering come in? Was it necessary in order to follow Jesus' steps to go up Calvary as well as the Mount of Transfiguration?

His appeal was stronger at this point than he knew. It is not too much to say that the spiritual tension of the First Church reached its highest point right there. The imitation of Jesus which had begun with the volunteers in the church was working like leaven in the organization, and Henry Maxwell would, even this early in his new life, have been amazed if he could have measured the extent of desire on the part of his people to take up the cross. While he was speaking this morning, before he closed with a loving appeal to the discipleship of two thousand years' knowledge of the Master, many a man and woman in the church was saying, as Rachel had said so passionately to her mother, "I want to do something that will cost me something in the way of sacrifice;" "I am hungry to suffer something." Truly Mazzini[14] was right when he said, "No appeal is quite so powerful in the end as the call, 'Come and suffer.' "

The service was over, the great audience had gone, and Henry Maxwell again faced the company gathered in the lecture-room as on the two previous Sundays. He had asked all to remain who had made the pledge of discipleship, and any others who wished to be included. The after-service seemed now to be a necessity. As be went in and faced the people there, his heart trembled. There were at least two hundred present. The Holy Spirit was never so manifest. He missed Jasper Chase. But all the others were present. He asked Milton Wright to pray. The very air was charged with divine possibilities. What could resist such a baptism of power? How had they lived all these years without it?

They counseled together, and there were many prayers. Henry Maxwell dated from that meeting some of the serious events that afterwards became a part of the history of the First Church of Raymond. When finally they went home, all of them were impressed with the joy of the Spirit's power.

Donald Marsh, President of Lincoln College, walked home with Henry Maxwell.

"I have reached one conclusion, Maxwell," said Marsh speaking slowly. "I have found my cross, and it is a heavy one; but I shall never be satisfied until I take it up and carry it."

Maxwell was silent and the President went on.

"Your sermon to-day made clear to me what I have long been feeling I ought to do. What would Jesus do in my place? I have asked the question repeatedly since I made my promise. I have tried to satisfy myself that he would simply go on as I have done, tending to the duties of my college, teaching the classes in Ethics and Philosophy. But I have not been able to avoid the feeling that he would do something more. That something is what I do not want to do. It will cause me genuine suffering to do it. I dread it with all my soul. You may be able to guess what it is?"

"Yes, I think I know," Henry Maxwell replied. "It is my cross, too, I would almost rather do any thing else."

Donald Marsh looked surprised, then relieved. Then he spoke sadly, but with great conviction.

"Maxwell, you and I belong to a class of professional men who have always avoided the duties of citizenship. We have lived in a little world of scholarly seclusion, doing work we have enjoyed, and shrinking from the disagreeable duties that belong to the life of the citizen. I confess with shame that I have purposely avoided the responsibility that I owe to this city personally. I understand that our city officials are a corrupt, unprincipled set of men, controlled in large part by the whisky element, and thoroughly selfish so far as the affairs of city government are concerned. Yet all these years I, with nearly every teacher in

---

14 Giuseppe Mazzini (1805–1872) was an uncompromising Italian revolutionary who fought for a republican government that would represent the interests of all Italians.

the college, have been satisfied to let other men run the municipality, and have lived in a little world of my own, out of touch and sympathy with the real world of the people. 'What would Jesus do?' I have tried even to avoid an honest answer. I can no longer do so. My plain duty is to take a personal part in this coming election, go to the primaries, throw the weight of my influence, whatever it is, towards the nomination and election of good men, and plunge into the very depths of this entire horrible whirlpool of deceit, bribery, political trickery and saloonism as it exists in Raymond to-day. I would sooner walk up to the mouth of a cannon any time than do this. I dread it because I hate the touch of the whole matter. I would give almost anything to be able to say, 'I do not believe Jesus would do anything of the sort.' But I am more and more persuaded that He would. This is where the suffering comes to me. It would not hurt me half so much to lose my position or my home, I loathe the contact with this municipal problem. I would much prefer to remain quietly in my scho-lastic life with my classes in Ethics and Philosophy. But the call has come to me so plainly that I cannot escape: 'Donald Marsh, follow me. Do your duty as a citizen of Raymond at the point where your citizenship will cost you something. Help to cleanse this great munici-pal stable, even if you do have to soil your aristocratic feelings a little.' Maxwell, this is my cross. I must take it up or deny my Lord."

"You have spoken for me also," replied Maxwell, with a sad smile. "Why should I, sim-ply because I am a clergyman, shelter myself behind my refined, sensitive feelings and, like a coward, refuse to touch, except in a sermon possibly, the duty of citizenship? I am unused to the ways of the political life of the city. I have never taken an active part in any nomina-tion of good men. There are hundreds of ministers like me. As a class, we do not practice, in the municipal life, the duties and privileges we preach from the pulpit. What would Jesus do? I am now at a point where, like you, I am driven to answer the question one way. My duty is plain. I must suffer. All my parish work, all my little trials or self-sacrifices, are as nothing to me compared with the breaking into my scholarly, intellectual, self-contained habits of this open, coarse, public fight for a clean city life. I could go and live at the Rectangle the rest of my days and work in the slums for a bare living and I could enjoy it more than the thought of plunging into a fight for the reform of this whisky-ridden city. It would cost me less. But with you I have been unable to shake off my responsibility. The answer to the question, 'What would Jesus do?' in this case leaves me no peace, except when I say, 'Jesus would have me act the part of a Christian citizen.' Marsh, as you say, we pro-fessional men, ministers, professors, artists, literary men, scholars, have almost invariably been political cowards. We have avoided the sacred duties of citizenship, either ignorantly or selfishly. Certainly Jesus, in our age, would not do that. We can do no less than take up this cross and follow Him."

These two men walked on in silence for a while. Finally President Marsh said,

"We do not need to act alone in this matter. With all the men who have made the prom-ise, we certainly can have companionship and strength, even of numbers. Let us organize the Christian forces of Raymond for the battle against rum and corruption. We certainly ought to enter the primaries with a force that will be able to do more than utter a protest. It is a fact that the saloon element is cowardly and easily frightened, in spite of its lawlessness and corruption. Let us plan a campaign that will mean something, because it is organized righteousness. Jesus would use great wisdom in this matter. He would employ means. He would make large plans. Let us do so. If we bear this cross, let us do it bravely, like men."

They talked over the matter a long time, and met again the next day in Henry Maxwell's study to develop plans. The city primaries were called for Friday. Rumors of strange and unheard-of events to the average citizen were current in political circles throughout Raymond. The Crawford system of balloting for nominations was not in use in the state, and the primary was called for a public meeting at the court-house. The citizens of Raymond will never forget that meeting. It was so unlike any political meeting ever held in Raymond before, that there was no attempt at comparison. The special officers to be nominated were Mayor, City Council, Chief of Police, City Clerk, and City Treasurer.

The "Evening News," in its Saturday edition, gave a full account of the primaries, and in the editorial column Edward Norman spoke with a directness and conviction that the Christian people of Raymond were learning to respect deeply, because it was so evidently sincere and unselfish. A part of that editorial is also a part of this history:

"It is safe to say that never before in the history of Raymond was there a primary like the one in the court-house last night. It was, first of all, a complete surprise to the city politicians, who have been in the habit of carrying on the affairs of the city as if they owned them and every one else was simply a tool or a cipher. The over-whelming sur-prise of the wire-puller last night consisted in the fact that a large number of the citizens of Raymond who have heretofore taken no part in the city affairs, entered the primary and controlled it, nominating some of the best men for all the offices to be filled at the coming election.

It was a tremendous lesson in good citizenship. President Marsh of Lincoln College, who never before entered a city primary, and whose face even was not known to many of the ward politicians, made one of the best speeches ever heard in Raymond. It was almost ludicrous to see the faces of the men who for years have done as they pleased, when President Marsh rose to speak. Many of them asked, 'Who is he?' The consterna-tion deepened as the primary proceeded, and it became evident that the old-time ring of city rulers was outnumbered. Henry Maxwell, Pastor of the First Church, Milton Wright, Alexander Powers, Professors Brown, Willard and Park of Lincoln College, Rev. John West, Dr. George Maine of the Pilgrim Church, Dean Ward of the Holy Trinity, and scores of well-known business and professional men, most of them church members, were present, and it did not take long to see that they had all come with the direct and definite purpose of nominating the best men possible. Most of these men had never been seen in a primary. They were complete strangers to the politicians. But they had evidently profited by the politician's methods and were able, by organized and united effort, to nominate the entire ticket.

"As soon as it became plain that the primary was out of their control, the regular ring withdrew in disgust and nominated another ticket. The 'News' simply calls the attention of all decent citizens to the fact that this last ticket contains the names of whisky men, and the line is distinctly and sharply drawn between the machine and corrupt city govern-ment, such as we have known for years, and a clean, honest, capable, business-like city administration, such as every good citizen ought to want. It is not necessary to remind the people of Raymond that the question of local option comes up at the election. That will be the most important question on the ticket. The crisis of our city affairs has been reached. The issue is squarely before us. Shall we continue the rule of rum and boodle and shameless incompetency, or shall we, as President Marsh said in his noble speech, rise as good citizens and begin a new order of things, cleansing our city of the worst enemy known to municipal honesty, and doing what lies in our power to do with the ballot, to purify our civic life?

The 'News' is, positively and without reservation, on the side of the new movement. We shall henceforth do all in our power to drive out the saloon and destroy its political strength. We shall advocate the election of men nominated by the majority of citizens met in the first primary, and we call upon all Christians, church members and lovers of right, purity, temperance, and home, to stand by President Marsh and the rest of the citizens who have thus begun a long-needed reform in our city."

President Marsh read this editorial and thanked God for Edward Norman. At the same time he understood well enough that every other paper in Raymond was on the other side. He did not misunderstand the importance and seriousness of the fight which was only just begun. It was no secret that the "News" had lost enormously since it had been governed by the standard of, "What would Jesus do?" The question now was, "Would the Christian people of Raymond stand by it?" Would they make it possible for Norman to conduct a daily Christian paper? Or would their desire for what is called "news," in the way of crime, scandal, political partisanship of the regular sort, and a dislike to champion so remarkable a reform in journalism, influence them to drop the paper and refuse to give it their financial support? That was, in fact, the question Edward Norman was asking, even while he wrote the Saturday editorial. He knew well enough that his action expressed in that editorial would cost him very dearly from the hands of many business men of Raymond. And still, as he drove his pen over the paper, he asked another question, "What would Jesus do?" That question had become a part of his whole life now. It was greater than any other.

But, for the first time in its history, Raymond had seen the professional men, the teachers, the college professors, the doctors, the ministers, take political action and put themselves definitely and sharply in antagonism to the evil forces that had so long controlled the machine of the municipal government. The fact itself was astonishing. President Marsh acknowledged to himself with a feeling of humiliation, that never before had he known what civic righteousness could accomplish. From that Friday night's work he dated for himself and his college a new definition of the worn phrase, "the Scholar in Politics." Education for him and those who were under his influence, ever after meant some element of suffering. Sacrifice must now enter into the factor of development.

At the Rectangle that week, the tide of spiritual life rose high, and as yet showed no signs of flowing back. Rachel and Virginia went every night. Virginia was rapidly reaching a conclusion with respect to a large part of her money. She had talked it over with Rachel, and they had been able to agree that if Jesus had a vast amount of money at his disposal he might do with some of it as Virginia planned. At any rate, they felt that whatever Jesus might do in such a case would have as large an element of variety in it as the difference in persons and circumstances. There could be no one, fixed, Christian way of using money. The rule that regulated its use was unselfish utility.

But meanwhile the glory of the Spirit's power possessed all their best thought. Night after night that week witnessed miracles as great as walking on the sea, or feeding the multitude with a few loaves and fishes. For what greater miracle than a regenerated humanity? The transformation of these coarse, brutal, sottish lives, into praying rapturous lovers of Jesus, struck Rachel and Virginia every time with the feelings that people may have had when they saw Lazarus walk out of the tomb. It was an experience full of profound excitement to them.

Rollin Page came to all the meetings. There was no doubt of the change that had come over him. He was wonderfully quiet. It seemed as if he were thinking all the time. Certainly he was not the same person. He talked more with Gray than with any one else. He did not avoid Rachel, but he seemed to shrink from any appearance of seeming to wish to renew the old acquaintance with her. Rachel found it even difficult to express to him her pleasure at the new life he had begun to know. He seemed to be waiting to adjust himself to his previous relations before this new life began. He had not forgotten those relations. But he was not yet able to fit his consciousness into new ones.

The end of the week found the Rectangle struggling hard between two mighty opposing forces. The Holy Spirit was battling with all his supernatural strength against the saloon devil which had so long held a jealous grasp on its slaves. If the Christian people of Raymond once could realize what the contest meant to the souls newly awakened to a new life, it did not seem possible that the election could result in the old system of license. But that remained yet to be seen. The horror of the daily surroundings of many of the converts was slowly burning its way into the knowledge of Virginia and Rachel, and every night as they went up town to their luxurious homes they carried heavier hearts.

"A good many of those poor creatures will go back again," Gray would say with a sadness too deep for tears. "The environment does have a good deal to do with the character. It does not stand to reason that these people can always resist the sight and smell of the devilish drink all about them. O Lord! how long shall Christian people continue to support, by their silence and their ballots, the greatest form of slavery now known in America?"

He asked the question, and did not have much hopes of an immediate answer. There was a ray of hope in the action of Friday night's primary; but what the result would be, he did not dare to anticipate. The whisky forces were organized, alert, aggressive, roused into unusual hatred by the events of the last week at the tent and in the city. Would the Christian force act as a unit against the saloon? Or would it be divided on account of its business interests, or because it was not in the habit of acting altogether, as the whisky powers always did? That remained to be seen. Meanwhile the saloon reared itself about the Rectangle like some deadly viper, hissing and coiling, ready to strike its poison into any unguarded part.

Saturday afternoon, as Virginia was just stepping out of her house to go and see Rachel to talk over her new plans, a carriage drove up containing three of her fashionable friends. Virginia went out to the driveway and stood there talking with them. They had not come to make a formal call, but wanted Virginia to go riding with them up on the boulevard. There was a band concert in the Park. The day was too pleasant to be spent in doors.

"Where have you been all this time, Virginia?" asked one of the girls, tapping her playfully on the shoulder with a red silk parasol. "We hear that you have gone into the show business. Tell us about it."

Virginia colored, but after a moment's hesitation she frankly told something of her experience at the Rectangle. The girls in the carriage began to be really interested.

"Tell you what, girls, let's go slumming with Virginia this afternoon instead of going to the band concert! I've never been down to the Rectangle. I've heard it's an awful wicked place and lots to see. Virginia will act as a guide, and it would be real,"—"fun," she was going to say, but Virginia's look made her substitute the word, "interesting."

Virginia was angry. At first thought she said to herself she would never go under any such circumstances. The other girls seemed to be of the same mind as the speaker. They chimed in with earnestness and asked Virginia to take them down there.

Suddenly she saw in the idle curiosity of the girls an opportunity. They had never seen the sin and misery of Raymond. Why should they not see it, even if their motives in going down there were simply to pass away an afternoon.

"Very well, I'll go with you. You must obey my orders, and let me take you where you can see the most," she said, as she entered the carriage and took the seat beside the girl who had first suggested the trip to the Rectangle.

"Hadn't we better take a policeman along," said one of the girls with a nervous laugh. "It really isn't safe down there, you know."

"There's no danger," said Virginia briefly.

"Is it true that Rollin has been converted?" asked the first speaker looking at Virginia curiously. It impressed her during the drive to the Rectangle that all three of her friends were regarding her with close attention as if she were very peculiar.

"Yes, he certainly is. I saw him myself on the night of the first interest shown, a week ago Saturday," replied Virginia who did not know just how to tell that scene.

"I understand he is going around to the clubs talking with his old friends there, trying to preach to them. Doesn't that seem funny?" said the girl with the red silk parasol.

Virginia did not answer, and the other girls were beginning to feel sober as the carriage turned into the street leading to the Rectangle. As they neared the district, they grew more and more nervous. The sights and smells and sounds which had become familiar to Virginia, struck the senses of these refined, delicate, society girls as something horrible. As they entered farther into the district, the Rectangle seemed to stare as with one great, bleary, beer-soaked countenance at this fine carriage with its load of fashionably dressed young ladies. "Slumming" had never been a fad with Raymond society, and this was perhaps the first time that the two had come together in this way. The girls felt that, instead of seeing the Rectangle, they were being the objects of curiosity. They were frightened and disgusted.

Let's go back. I've seen enough," said the girl who was sitting with Virginia.

They were at that moment just opposite a notorious saloon and gambling house. The street was narrow and the sidewalk crowded. Suddenly, out of the door of the saloon a young woman reeled. She was singing, in a broken, drunken sob that seemed to indicate that she partly realized her awful condition, "Just as I am, without one plea;" and as the carriage rolled past she leered at it, raising her face so that Virginia saw it very close to her own. It was the face of the girl who had kneeled sobbing that night, with Virginia kneeling beside her and praying for her.

"Stop!" cried Virginia motioning to the driver, who was looking around. The carriage stopped, and in a moment she was out and had gone up to the girl and taken her by the arm.

"Loreen," she said, and that was all. The girl looked into her face, and her own changed into a look of utter horror. The girls in the carriage were smitten into helpless astonishment. The saloon-keeper had come to the door of the saloon and was standing there looking on, with his hands on his hips. And the Rectangle from its windows, its saloon steps, its filthy sidewalk, gutter and roadway, paused, and with undisguised wonder stared at the two girls. Over the scene the warm sun of spring poured its mellow light. A faint breath of music from the band stand in the park floated into the Rectangle. The concert had begun, and the fashion and wealth of Raymond were displaying themselves up town on the boulevards.

Chapter VI

"For I came to set a man at variance against his father, and the daughter against her mother, and the daughter-in-law against her mother-in-law; and a man's foes shall be they of his own household."
"Be ye therefore imitators of God, as beloved children; and walk in love even as Christ also loved you."[15]

When Virginia left the carriage and went to Loreen, she had no definite idea as to what she would do or what the result of her action would be. She simply saw a soul that had tasted of the joy of a better life slipping back again into its old hell of shame and death. And before she had touched the drunken girl's arm, she had asked only one question, "What would Jesus do?" That question was becoming with her, as with many others, a habit of life.

She looked around now, as she stood close by Loreen, and the whole scene was cruelly vivid to her. She thought first of the girls in the carriage.

"Drive on; don't wait for me! I am going to see my friend here home," she said, calmly enough.

The girl with the red parasol seemed to gasp at the word "friend" when Virginia spoke it. She did not say anything. The other girls seemed speechless.

"Go on! I cannot go back with you," said Virginia.

The driver started the horses slowly. One of the girls leaned a little out of the carriage.

"Can't we—that is—do you want our help? Couldn't we—"

"No, no!" exclaimed Virginia; "you cannot be of any use to me."

The carriage moved on, and Virginia was alone with her charge

She looked up and around. Many faces in the crowd were sympathetic. They were not all cruel or brutal. The Holy Spirit had softened a good deal of the Rectangle.

"Where does she live?" asked Virginia.

No one answered. It occurred to Virginia afterwards, when she had time to think it over, that the Rectangle showed a delicacy in its sad silence that would have done credit to the boulevard.

For the first time it flashed upon her that the immortal being, who was flung like wreckage upon the shore of this earthly hell called the saloon, had no place that could be called home.

The girl suddenly wrenched her arm from Virginia's grasp. In doing it she nearly threw Virginia down.

"You shall not touch me! Leave me! Let me go to hell! That's where I belong! The devil is waiting for me. See him!" she exclaimed hoarsely. She turned and pointed with a shaking finger at the saloon-keeper. The crowd laughed.

Virginia stepped up to her and put her arm about her.

"Loreen," she said firmly, "come with me. You do not belong to hell. You belong to Jesus, and He will save you. Come."

The girl suddenly burst into tears. She was only partly sobered by the shock of meeting Virginia.

Virginia looked around again. "Where does Mr. Gray live?" she asked. She knew the evangelist boarded somewhere near that tent.

A number of voices gave her the direction.

---

15 Matt. 10:35–36 and Eph. 5:1–2.

Virginia and Loreen (*In His* Steps, London: Ward, Locke and Co., 1899).

"Come, Loreen, I want you to go with me to Mrs. Gray's," she said, still keeping her hold of the swaying, trembling creature, who still moaned and sobbed, and now clung to Virginia as before she had repulsed her.

So the two moved on through the Rectangle towards the evangelist's lodging place. The sight seemed to impress the Rectangle seriously. It never took itself seriously when it was drunk; but this was different. The fact that one of the most beautifully-dressed girls in Raymond was taking care of one of the Rectangle's most notorious characters, who reeled along under the influence of liquor, was a fact astonishing enough to throw more or less dignity and importance about Loreen herself. The event of Loreen stumbling through the gutter dead drunk always made the Rectangle laugh and jest. But Loreen staggering along with a young lady from the society circles up town supporting her, was another thing. The Rectangle viewed it with soberness and more or less wondering admiration.

When they reached Mr. Gray's boarding place, the woman who answered Virginia's knock said that both Mr. and Mrs. Gray were out somewhere, and would not be back until six o'clock.

Virginia had not planned anything farther than a possible appeal to the Grays, either to take charge of Loreen for awhile, or find some safe place for her until she was sober again. She stood now at the lodging after the woman had spoken, and she was really at a loss to know what to do. Loreen sank down stupidly on the steps and buried her face in her arms. Virginia eyed the miserable figure with a feeling that she was fearful would grow into disgust.

Finally a thought possessed Virginia that she could not resist. What was to hinder Loreen from going home with her? Why should not this homeless, wretched creature, reeking with the fumes of liquor, be cared for in Virginia's own home, instead of being consigned to strangers in some hospital or house of charity? Virginia really knew very little about any such places of refuge. As a matter of fact, there were two or three such institutions in Raymond; but it is doubtful if any of them would have taken a person like Loreen in her present condition. But that was not the question with Virginia just now. "What would Jesus do with Loreen?" was what Virginia faced, and she finally answered it by touching Loreen again.

"Loreen, come. You are going home with me. We will take the car here at the corner."

Loreen staggered to her feet, and to Virginia's relief, made no trouble. She had expected resistance, or a stubborn refusal to move. When they reached the corner and took the car, it was nearly full of people going up town. Virginia was painfully conscious of the stare that greeted her and her companion as they entered. But her thought was directed more and more to the approaching scene with her grandmother. What would Madam Page say when she saw Loreen?

Loreen was nearly sober now. But she was lapsing into a state of stupor. Virginia was obliged to hold fast to her arm. Several times she lurched heavily against Virginia, and as the two went up the avenue a curious crowd of people turned and gazed at them. When she mounted the steps of the handsome house, Virginia breathed a sigh of relief, even in the face of the interview with her grandmother; and when the door shut and she was in the wide hall with her homeless outcast, she felt equal to anything that might now come.

Madam Page was in the library. Hearing Virginia come in, she came into the hall. Virginia stood there supporting Loreen, who stared stupidly at the rich magnificence of the furnishings around her.

"Grandmother—" Virginia spoke without hesitation and very clearly—"I have brought one of my friends from the Rectangle. She is in trouble and has no home. I am going to care for her a little while."

Madam Page glanced from her granddaughter to Loreen in astonishment.

"Did you say she was one of your friends?" She asked in a cold, sneering voice that hurt Virginia more than anything she had yet felt.

"Yes, I said so." Virginia's face flushed but she seemed to recall the verse that Mr. Gray had used for one of his recent sermons, "A friend of publicans and sinners." Surely Jesus would do this that she was doing.

"Do you know what this girl is?" asked Madam Page in an angry whisper, stepping near Virginia.

"I know very well. She is an outcast. You need not tell me, Grandmother. I know it even better than you do. She is drunk at this minute. But she is also a child of God. I have seen her on her knees repentant. And I have seen Hell reach out its horrible fingers after her again. And by the grace of Christ, I feel that the least I can do is to rescue her from such peril. Grandmother, we call ourselves Christians. Here is a poor, lost human creature, without a home slipping into a possible eternal loss, and we have more than enough. I have brought her here and shall keep her."

Madam Page glared at Virginia and clenched her hands. All this was contrary to her social code of conduct. How could society excuse such familiarity with the scum of the streets? What would Virginia's actions cost the family, in the way of criticism and the loss of standing, and all that long list of necessary relations which people of wealth and position must sustain to the leaders of society? To Madam Page, society represented more than the church or any other institution. It was a power to be feared and obeyed. The loss of its good will was a loss more to be dreaded than anything, except the loss of wealth itself.

She stood erect and stern, and confronted Virginia, fully roused and determined. Virginia placed her arm about Loreen and calmly looked her grandmother in the face.

"You shall not do this, Virginia. You can send her to the asylum for helpless women. We can pay all the expenses. We cannot afford, for the sake of our reputations, to shelter such a person."

"Grandmother, I do not wish to do anything that is displeasing to you; but I am going to keep Loreen here to-night, and longer if I think it is best."

"Then you can answer for the consequences! I do not stay in the same house with a miserable—" Madam Page lost her self-control. Virginia stopped her before she could speak the next word.

"Grandmother, this house is mine. It is your home with me as long as you choose to remain. But in this matter I shall act as I fully believe Jesus would in my place. I am willing to bear all that society may say or do. Society is not my God. By the side of this poor, lost soul, I do not count the verdict of society as of any value."

"I shall not remain here, then," said Madam Page. She turned suddenly and walked to the end of the hall. She then came back, and said, with an emphasis that revealed her intense excitement and passion,

"You can always remember that you have driven your grandmother out of your house in favor of a drunken woman." Then, without waiting for Virginia to reply, she turned again and went up stairs.

Virginia called for a servant, and soon had Loreen cared for. She was fast lapsing into a wretched condition. During the brief scene in the hall, she had clung to Virginia so hard that Virginia's arm was sore from the clutch of the girl's fingers.

Virginia did not know whether her grandmother would leave the house or not. She had abundant means of her own; was perfectly well and vigorous, and capable of caring for herself. She had sisters and brothers living in the South, and was in the habit of spending several weeks in the year with them. Virginia was not anxious about her welfare, so far as that went; but the interview had been a painful one to her. Going over it, as she did in her room before she went down to tea, she found little cause for regret, however. "What would Jesus do?" There was no question in Virginia's mind that she had done the right thing. If she had made a mistake, it was one of the judgment and not of the heart. When the bell rang for tea, she went down, and her grandmother did not appear. She sent a servant to her room, and the servant brought back word that Madam Page was not there. A few minutes later Rollin came in. He brought word that his grandmother had taken the evening train for the South. He had been at the station to see some friends off, and had by chance met his grandmother as he was coming out. She told him her reason for going.

Virginia and Rollin confronted each other at the table with earnest, sad faces.

"Rollin," said Virginia, and, for the first time almost since his conversion, she realized what a wonderful thing her brother's change of life meant to her. "Do you blame me? Am I wrong?"

"No, dear, I cannot believe you are. This is very painful for us. But if you think this poor creature owes her safety and salvation to your personal care, it was the only thing for you to do. O Virginia! to think that we have all these years enjoyed our beautiful home and all these luxuries selfishly, forgetful of the multitude like this woman! Surely Jesus in our places would do what you have done."

And so Rollin comforted Virginia and counselled with her that evening. And of all the wonderful changes that Virginia was henceforth to know on account of her great pledge, nothing affected her so powerfully as the thought of Rollin's change in life. Truly, this man in Christ was a new creature. Old things were passed away. Behold, all things in him had become new.

Dr. West came that evening at Virginia's summons, and did everything necessary for the outcast. She had drunk herself almost into delirium. The best that could be done for her now was quiet nursing, and careful watching, and personal love. So in a beautiful room, with a picture of Christ walking by the sea hanging on the wall, where her bewildered eyes caught daily something more of its hidden meaning, Loreen lay, tossed she hardly knew how into this haven; and Virginia crept nearer the Master than she had ever been, as her heart went out towards this wreck which had thus been flung torn and beaten at her feet.

Meanwhile the Rectangle waited the issue of the election with more than usual interest. And Gray and his wife wept over the pitiable creatures who, after a struggle with surroundings that daily tempted them, too often wearied of the struggle and, like Loreen, threw up their arms and went whirling into the boiling abyss of their previous condition.

The after-meeting at the First Church was now regularly established. Henry Maxwell went into the lecture-room on the Sunday succeeding the week of the primary, and was greeted with an enthusiasm that made him tremble, at first, for its reality. He noted again the absence of Jasper Chase, but all the others were present and they seemed drawn very close together by a bond of common fellowship that demanded and enjoyed mutual confidences. It was the general feeling that the spirit of Jesus was a spirit of very open, frank confession of experience. It seemed the most natural thing in the world for Edward Norman to be telling all the rest of the company about the details of his newspaper.

"The fact is. I have lost a good deal of money during the last three weeks. I cannot tell how much. I am losing a great many subscribers every day."

"What do the subscribers give as their reason for dropping the paper?" asked Henry Maxwell. All the rest were listening eagerly.

"There are a good many different reasons. Some say they want a paper that prints all the news; meaning by that, the crime details, sensations like prize fights, scandals, and horrors of various kinds. Others object to the discontinuance of the Sunday edition. I have lost hundreds of subscribers by that action, although I have made satisfactory arrangements with many of the old subscribers by giving them even more in the extra Saturday edition than they formerly had in the Sunday issue. My greatest loss has come from a falling off in advertisements, and from the attitude I have felt obliged to take on political questions. This last action has really cost me more than any other. The bulk of my subscribers are intensely partisan. I may as well tell you all frankly that, if I continue to pursue the plan which I honestly believe Jesus would in the matter of political issues and their treatment from a non-partisan and moral standpoint, the 'News' will not be able to pay its operating expenses, unless one factor in Raymond can be depended on."

He paused a moment, and the room was very quiet. Virginia seemed specially interested. Her face glowed with interest. It was like the interest of a person who had been thinking hard of the same thing Norman went on now to mention.

"That one factor is the Christian element in Raymond. Say the 'News' has lost heavily from the dropping off of people who do not care for a Christian daily, and from others who simply look upon a newspaper as a purveyor of all sorts of material to amuse and interest them—are there enough genuine Christian people in Raymond who will rally to the support of a paper such as Jesus would probably edit, or are the habits of the people so firmly established in their demands for the regular type of journalism that they will not take a paper unless it is stripped largely of the Christian and moral purpose? I may also say, in this fellowship gathering, that owing to recent complications in my business affairs outside of my paper, I have been obliged to lose a large part of my fortune. I have had to apply the same rule of Jesus' probable conduct to certain transactions with other men who did not apply it to their conduct, and the result has been the loss of a great deal of money. As I understand the promise we made, we were not to ask any questions about, "Will it pay?" but all our action was to be based on the one question, 'What would Jesus do?' Acting on that rule of conduct, I have been obliged to lose nearly all the money I have accumulated in my paper. It is not necessary for me to go into details. There is no question with me now, after the three weeks' experience I have had, that a great many men would lose vast sums of money under the present system of business, if this rule of Jesus were honestly obeyed. I mention my loss here because I have the fullest faith in the final success of a daily paper conducted on the lines I have recently laid down, and I had planned to put into it my entire fortune in order to win final success. As it is now, unless, as I said, the Christian people of Raymond, the church members and professing disciples, will support the paper with subscriptions and advertisements, I cannot continue its publication on the present basis."

Virginia asked a question. She had followed Mr. Norman's confession with the most intense eagerness.

"Do you mean that a Christian daily ought to be endowed with a large sum like a Christian college in order to make it pay?"

"That is exactly what I mean. I have laid out plans for putting into the 'News' such a variety of material, in such a strong and truly interesting way, that it would more than make up for whatever was absent from its columns in the way of un-Christian matter. But my plans called for a very large outlay of money. I am very confident that a Christian daily such as Jesus would approve, containing only what He would print, can be made to succeed financially if it is planned on the right lines. But it will take a large sum of money to work out the plans."

"How much do you think?" asked Virginia quietly.

Edward Norman looked at her keenly, and his face flushed a moment, as an idea of Virginia's purpose crossed his mind. He had known her when she was a little girl in the Sunday-school, and he had been on intimate relations in business with her father.

"I should say a half million dollars, in a town like Raymond, could be well spent in the establishment of a paper such as we have in mind," he answered. And his voice trembled a little. The keen look on Edward Norman's grizzled face flashed out with a stern but thoroughly Christian anticipation of great achievements in the world of newspaper life, as it had opened up to him within the last few seconds.

"Then," said Virginia, speaking as if the thought were fully considered, "I am ready to put that amount of money into the paper on the one condition, of course, that it be carried on as it has been begun."

"Thank God!" exclaimed Henry Maxwell softly. Edward Norman was pale. The rest were looking at Virginia. She had more to say.

"Dear friends," she went on—and there was a sadness in her voice that made an impression on the rest that deepened when they thought it over afterwards—"I do not want any of you to credit me with an act of great generosity or philanthropy. I have come to know lately that the money which I have called my own is not my own, but God's. If I, as a steward of His, see some wise way to invest His money, it is not an occasion of vain glory or thanks from any one simply because I have proved honest in my administration of the funds He has asked me to use for His glory. I have been thinking of this very plan for some time. The fact is, dear friends, that in our coming fight with the whisky power in Raymond—and it has only just begun—we shall need the 'News' to champion the Christian side. You all know that all the other papers are for the saloon. As long as the saloon exists, the work of rescuing dying souls at the Rectangle is carried on at a terrible disadvantage. What can Mr. Gray do with his gospel meetings when half his converts are drinking people, daily tempted and enticed by the saloon on every corner? The Christian daily we must have. It would be giving up to the enemy to have the 'News' fail. I have great confidence in Mr. Norman's ability. I have not seen his plans; but I have the confidence that he has in making the paper succeed if it is carried forward on a large enough scale. I cannot believe that Christian intelligence in journalism will be inferior to un-Christian intelligence, even when it comes to making the paper pay financially. So that is my reason for putting this money—God's, not mine—into this powerful agent for doing as Jesus would. If we can keep such a paper going for one year, I shall be willing to see that amount of money used in the experiment. Do not thank me. Do not consider my promise a wonderful thing. What have I done with God's money all these years but gratify my own selfish, physical, personal desires? What can I do with the rest of it but try to make some reparation for what I have stolen from God? That is the way I look at it now. I believe it is what Jesus would do."

Over the lecture-room swept that unseen yet distinctly felt wave of divine presence. No one spoke for a while. Henry Maxwell standing there, where the faces lifted their intense gaze into his, felt what he had already felt before—a strange setting back out of the nineteenth century into the first, when the disciples had all things in common, and a spirit of fellowship must have flowed freely between them such as the First Church of Raymond had never known. How much had his church membership known of this fellowship in daily interests, before this little company had begun to do as Jesus would do? It was with difficulty that he thought of his present age and its surroundings. The same thought was present with all the rest also. There was an unspoken comradeship such as they had never known. It was present with them while Virginia was speaking, and during the silence that followed. If it had been defined by any one of them, it would, perhaps, have taken some such shape as this: "If I shall, in the course of my obedience to my promise, meet with loss or trouble in the world, I can depend upon the genuine, practical sympathy and fellowship of any other

Christian in this room who has with me made the pledge to do all things by the rule, 'What would Jesus do?'"

All this the distinct wave of spiritual power expressed. It had the effect that a physical miracle may have had on the early disciples in giving them a feeling of confidence in their Lord that helped them to face loss and martyrdom with courage and even joy.

Before they went away this time, there were several confidences like those of Edward Norman. Some of the young men told of the loss of places owing to their honest obedience to their promise. Alexander Powers spoke briefly of the fact that the Commission had promised to take action at the earliest date possible. He was already at his old work of telegraphy. It was a significant fact that since his action in resigning his position, neither his wife nor daughter had appeared in public. No one but himself knew the bitterness of that family estrangement and misunderstanding of the higher motive. Yet many of the disciples present in the meeting carried similar burdens. These were things which they could not talk about. Henry Maxwell, from his knowledge of his church people, could almost certainly know that obedience to this pledge had produced in the heart of families separation of sympathy and even the introduction of enmity and hatred. Truly "a man's foes are they of his own household," when the rule of Jesus is obeyed by some and disobeyed by others. Jesus is a great divider of life. One must walk either parallel with Him or directly across His path.

But more than any other feeling at this meeting, rose the tide of fellowship for one another. Henry Maxwell watched it, trembling for its climax, which he knew was not yet reached. When it was, where would it lead them? He did not know, but he was not unduly alarmed about it. Only, he watched with growing wonder the results of that simple promise as it was being obeyed in these various lives. Those results were already being felt all over the city. Who could measure their influence at the end of the year?

One practical form of this fellowship showed itself in the assurances which Edward Norman received in support of his paper. There was a general flocking towards him when the meeting closed, and the response to his appeal for help from the Christian disciples in Raymond was fully understood by this little company. The value of such a paper in the homes and in behalf of good citizenship, especially at the present crisis in the city, could not be measured. It remained to be seen what could be done now that the paper was endowed so liberally. But it still was true, as Edward Norman insisted, that money alone could not make the paper a power. It must receive the support and sympathy of the Christians in Raymond, before it could be counted as one of the great Christian forces of the city.

The week that followed this Sunday meeting was one of great excitement in Raymond. It was the week of the election. Donald Marsh, true to his promise, took up his cross and bore it manfully, but with shuddering, with groans and even tears, for his deepest conviction was touched, and he tore himself out of the scholarly seclusion of years with a pain and anguish that cost him more than anything he had ever done as a follower of Christ. With him were a few of the college professors who had made the pledge in the First Church. Their experience and suffering were the same as the President's; for their isolation from all the duties of citizenship had been the same. The same was also true of Henry Maxwell, who plunged into the horror of this fight against whisky and its allies, with a sickening dread of each day's encounter with it. For never had he borne such a cross. He staggered under it, and in the brief intervals when he came in from the work and sought the quiet of his study for rest, the sweat broke out on his forehead, and he felt the actual terror of one who marches into unseen, unknown horrors. Looking back on it, afterwards, he was amazed at his experience. He was not a coward; but he felt a dread that any man of his habits feels, when confronted suddenly with a duty which carries with it the doing of certain things so unfamiliar that the actual details connected with it betray his ignorance and fill him with the shame of humiliation.

When Saturday, the election day, came, the excitement rose to its height. An attempt was made to close all the saloons. It was partly successful. But there was a great deal of drinking going on all day. The Rectangle boiled and heaved and cursed and turned its worst side out to the gaze of the city. Gray had continued his meetings during the week and the results had been even greater than he had dared to hope. When Saturday came, it seemed to him that the crisis in his work had been reached. The Holy Spirit and the Satan of rum seemed to rouse up to a desperate conflict. The more interest in the meetings, the more ferocity and vileness outside. The saloon men no longer concealed their feelings. Open threats of violence were made. Once during the week Gray and his little company of helpers were assailed with missiles of various kinds, as they left the tent late at night. The police sent down special protection, and Virginia and Rachel were always under the protection of Rollin or Dr. West. Rachel's power in song had not diminished. Rather, with each night it seemed to add to the intensity and reality of the Spirit's presence.

Gray had, at first, hesitated about having a meeting that night. But he had a simple rule of action, and was always guided by it. The Spirit seemed to lead them to continue the meeting, and so Saturday night he went on as usual.

The excitement all over the city had reached its climax when the polls closed at six o'clock. Never had there been such a contest in Raymond. The issue of license or no license had never been an issue under such circumstances. Never before had such elements in the city been arrayed against each other. It was an unheard-of thing that the president of Lincoln College, the pastor of the First Church, the dean of the Cathedral, the professional men living in the fine houses on the boulevard, should come personally into the wards and, by their presence and their example, represent the Christian conscience of the place. The ward politicians were astonished at the sight. However, their astonishment did not prevent their activity. The fight grew hotter every hour; and when six o'clock came neither side could have guessed at the result with any certainty. Every one agreed that never had there been such an election in Raymond, and both sides awaited the announcement of the result with the greatest interest.

It was after ten o'clock when the meeting at the tent was closed. It had been a strange and, in some respects, a remarkable meeting. Henry Maxwell had come down again, at Gray's request. He was completely worn out by the day's work, but the appeal from Gray came to him in such a form that he did not feel able to resist it. Donald Marsh was also present. He had never been to the Rectangle, and his curiosity was aroused from what he had noticed of the influence of the evangelist in the worst part of the city. Dr. West and Rollin had come with Rachel and Virginia; and Loreen, who had stayed with Virginia, was present near the organ, in her right mind, sober, with a humility and dread of herself that kept her as close to Virginia as a faithful dog. All through the service Loreen sat with bowed head, weeping a part of the time, sobbing when Rachel sang the song, "I was a wandering sheep," clinging with almost visible, tangible yearning to the one hope she had found, listening to prayer and appeal and confession all about her like one who was a part of a new creation, yet fearful of her right to share in it fully.

The tent had been crowded. As on some other occasions there was more or less disturbance on the outside of the tent. This had increased as the night advanced, and Gray thought it wise not to prolong the service. Once in a while a shout as from a large crowd swept into the tent. The returns from the election were beginning to come in, and the Rectangle had emptied every lodging house, den and hovel into the streets.

In spite of the distractions, Rachel's singing kept the crowd in the tent from dissolving. There were a dozen or more conversions. Finally the crowd became restless, and Gray closed the service, remaining a little while with the converts.

Rachel, Virginia, Loreen, Rollin and the Doctor, President Marsh and Henry Maxwell, went out together, intending to go down to their usual waiting place for their car. As they came out of the tent they at once were aware that the Rectangle was trembling on the edge of a drunken riot, and, as they pushed through the gathering mobs in the narrow streets, they began to realize that they themselves were objects of great attention.

"There he is, the bloke in the tall hat. He's the leader!" shouted a rough voice. President Marsh, with his erect, commanding figure, was conspicuous in the little company.

"How has the election gone? It is too early to know the result yet, isn't it?" He asked the question aloud, and a man answered, "They say second and third wards have gone almost solid for no license. If that is so, the whisky men have been beaten."

"Thank God! I hope it is true," exclaimed Henry Maxwell. "Marsh, we are in danger here. Do you realize our situation? We ought to get the ladies to a place of safety."

"That is true," said Marsh gravely. At that moment a shower of stones and other missiles fell over them. The narrow street and sidewalk in front of them were completely choked with the worst elements of the Rectangle.

"This looks serious," said Maxwell. With Marsh and Rollin and Dr. West he started to go forward through the small opening, Virginia, Rachel and Loreen following close and sheltered by the men, who now realized something of their danger. The Rectangle was drunk and enraged. It saw in Daniel Marsh and Henry Maxwell two of the leaders in the election contest who had perhaps robbed them of their beloved saloon.

"Down with the aristocrats!" shouted a shrill voice more like a woman's than a man's.

A shower of mud and stones followed. Rachel remembered afterwards that Rollin jumped directly in front of her and received on his head and chest a number of blows that would probably have struck her if he had not shielded her from them.

And just then, before the police reached them, Loreen darted forward at the side of Virginia and pushed her aside, looking up and screaming. It was so sudden that no one had time to catch the face of the one who did it. But out of the upper window of a room over the very saloon where Loreen had come out a week before, some one had thrown a heavy bottle. It struck Loreen on the head and she fell to the ground. Virginia turned and instantly kneeled down by her. The police officers by that time had reached the little company.

Donald Marsh raised his arm and shouted over the howl that was beginning to rise from the wild beast in the mob,

"Stop! You've killed a woman!"

The announcement partly sobered the crowd.

"Is it true?" Henry Maxwell asked it, as Dr. West kneeled on the other side of Loreen, supporting her.

"She's dying!" said Dr. West briefly.

Loreen opened her eyes and smiled at Virginia. Virginia wiped the blood from her face, and then bent over and kissed her. Loreen smiled again, and the next moment her soul was in Paradise.

And yet, this is only one woman out of thousands killed by this drink devil. Crowd back, now, ye sinful men and women in this filthy street! Let this august, dead form be borne through your stupified, sobered ranks. She was one of your own children. The Rectangle had stamped the image of the beast on her. Thank Him who died for sinners, that the other image of a new soul now shines out of her pale clay! Crowd back! Give them room! Let her pass reverently, followed and surrounded by the weeping, awestruck company of Christians. Ye killed her, ye drunken murderers! And yet, and yet, O Christian America! who killed this woman? Stand back! Silence there! A woman has been killed. Who? Loreen. Child of the streets. Poor, drunken, vile sinner! O Lord God, how long? Yes. The saloon killed her. That is, the voters in Christian America who license the saloon. And the Judgment Day only shall declare who was the murderer of Loreen.

*   *   *

Editor's Note

In His Steps: **The End of the Story**

Following Loreen's death, we discover that the reports of the city voting against licensing were incorrect. The laws for licensing drinking establishments and alcohol passed by "a very meager majority." In the days and months to follow, we find out the "What Would Jesus Do" movement spreads to Chicago, and that a great deal of good work is done both in the poorer parts of Raymond and Chicago. We also learn that Jasper Chase goes back on his pledge to do what Jesus might do and ends up a successful writer of novels, but changes into a bitter, cynical man. Others who joined Henry Maxwell in making the original pledge fare much better, including Rachel and Rollin, who end up in a happy marriage "fully consecrated to the Master's use."